THREE UNOFFICIAL ADVENTURES
FOR MINECRAFTERS!

THE HUGE BOOK OF GRAPHIC NOVELS FOR MINECRAFTERS

CARA J. STEVENS
ILLUSTRATED BY DAVID NORGREN AND ELIAS NORGREN

SKY PONY PRESS
New York

To Mom and Dad,
for giving me roots and wings

Copyright © 2018 by Hollan Publishing, Inc.

Minecraft® is a registered trademark of Notch Development AB.

The Minecraft game is copyright © Mojang AB.

Sky Pony Press books may be purchased in bulk at special discounts for sales promotion, corporate gifts, fund-raising, or educational purposes. Special editions can also be created to specifications. For details, contact the Special Sales Department, Sky Pony Press, 307 West 36th Street, 11th Floor, New York, NY 10018 or info@skyhorsepublishing.com.

Sky Pony® is a registered trademark of Skyhorse Publishing, Inc.®, a Delaware corporation.

Minecraft® is a registered trademark of Notch Development AB. The Minecraft game is copyright © Mojang AB.

Visit our website at www.skyponypress.com.

10 9 8 7 6 5 4 3 2

Library of Congress Cataloging-in-Publication Data is available on file.

Cover design by Brian Peterson
Cover photo by Megan Miller

Print ISBN: 978-1-5107-3739-6

Ebook ISBN: 978-1-5107-3744-0

Printed in China

AN UNOFFICIAL GRAPHIC NOVEL FOR MINECRAFTERS

The BATTLE for the DRAGON'S TEMPLE

CARA J. STEVENS
ART BY DAVID NORGREN

SKY PONY PRESS
NEW YORK

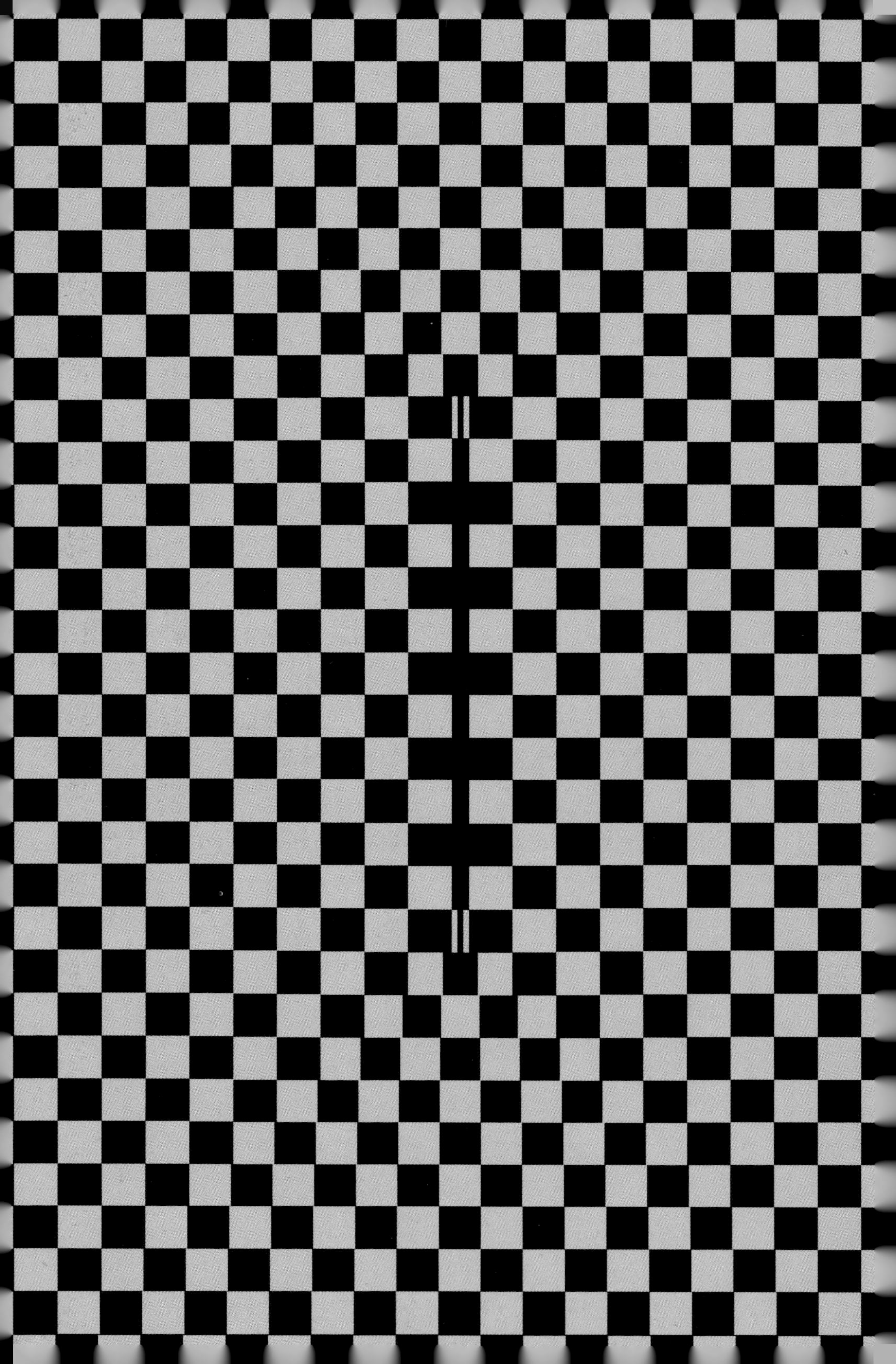

INTRODUCTION

If you have played Minecraft, then you know all about Minecraft worlds. They're made of blocks you can mine: coal, dirt, and sand. In the game, you'll find many different creatures, lands, and villages inhabited by strange villagers with bald heads. The villagers who live there have their own special, magical worlds that are protected by a string of border worlds to stop outsiders from finding them.

When we last left off on the small border world of Xenos, Phoenix had just discovered her true parents were dragon slayers who died in their quest to kill the Ender Dragon.

Our story resumes as Phoenix enjoys quiet time back at home. But her stay is far from peaceful. The elders are not happy about Phoenix's presence in the village, and, unable to stop thinking about her parents' failed quest to kill the dragon, Phoenix wonders whether she should remain at home or set out to finish the deed her parents began long ago.

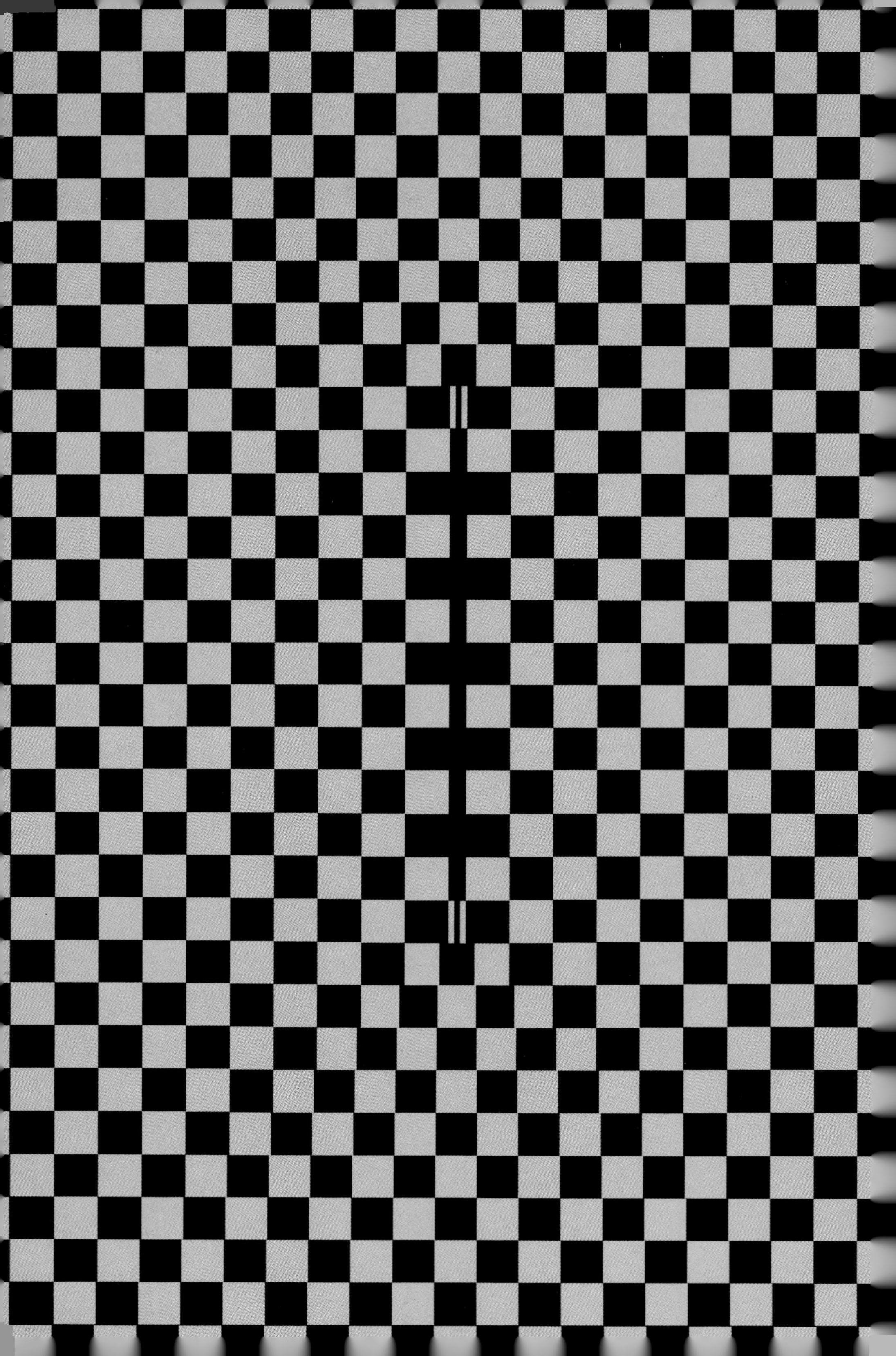

CHAPTER 1

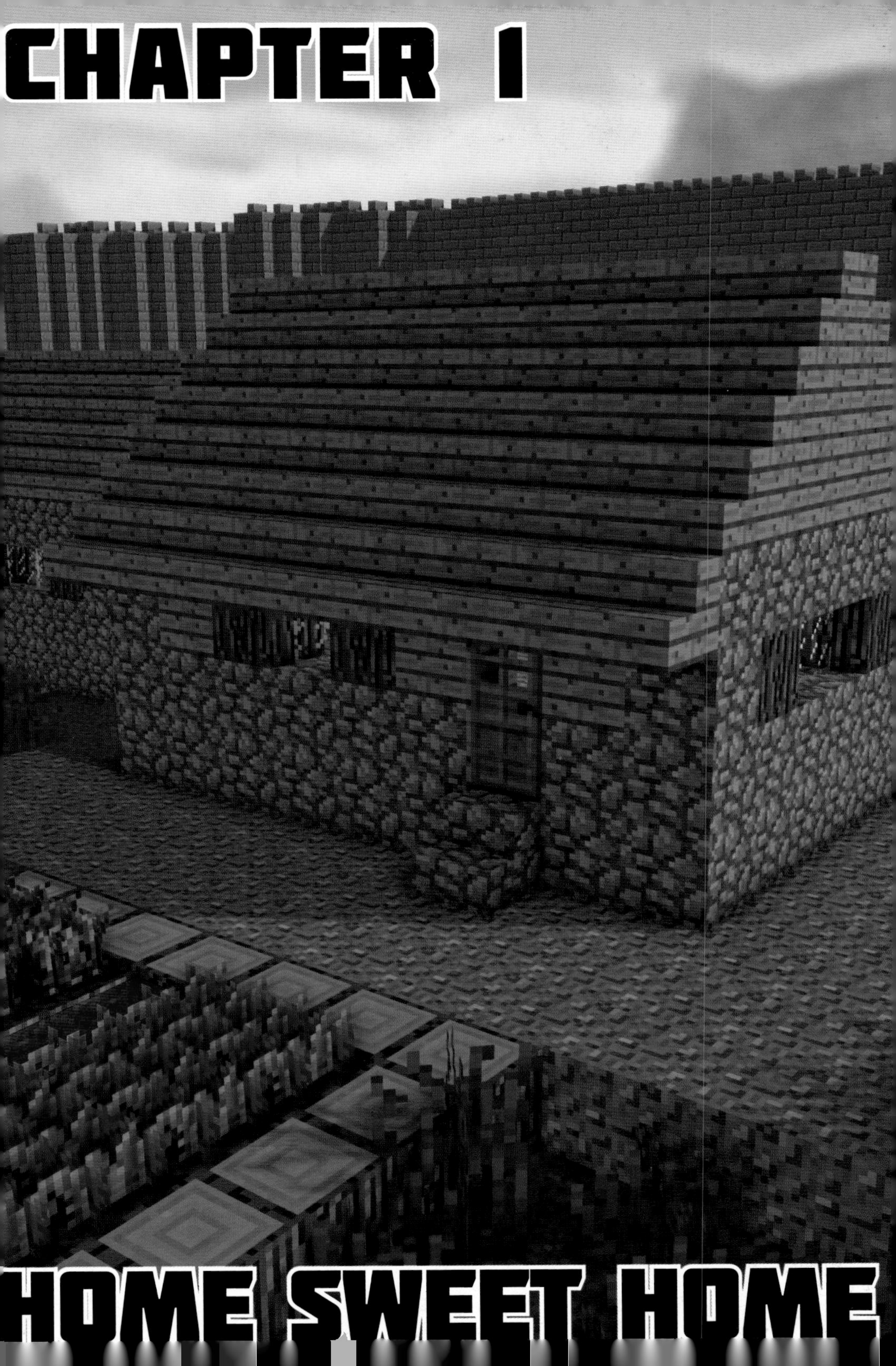

HOME SWEET HOME

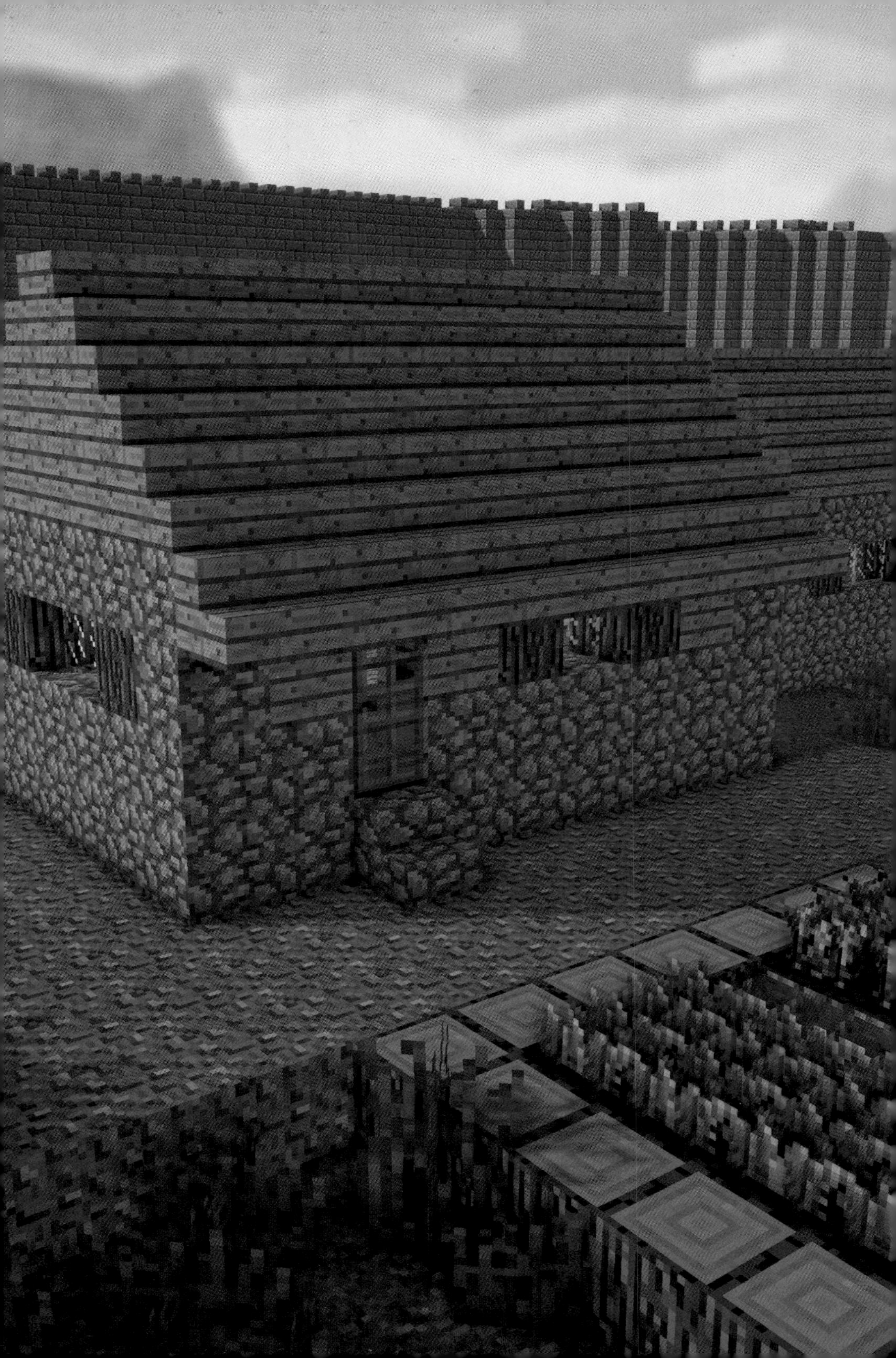

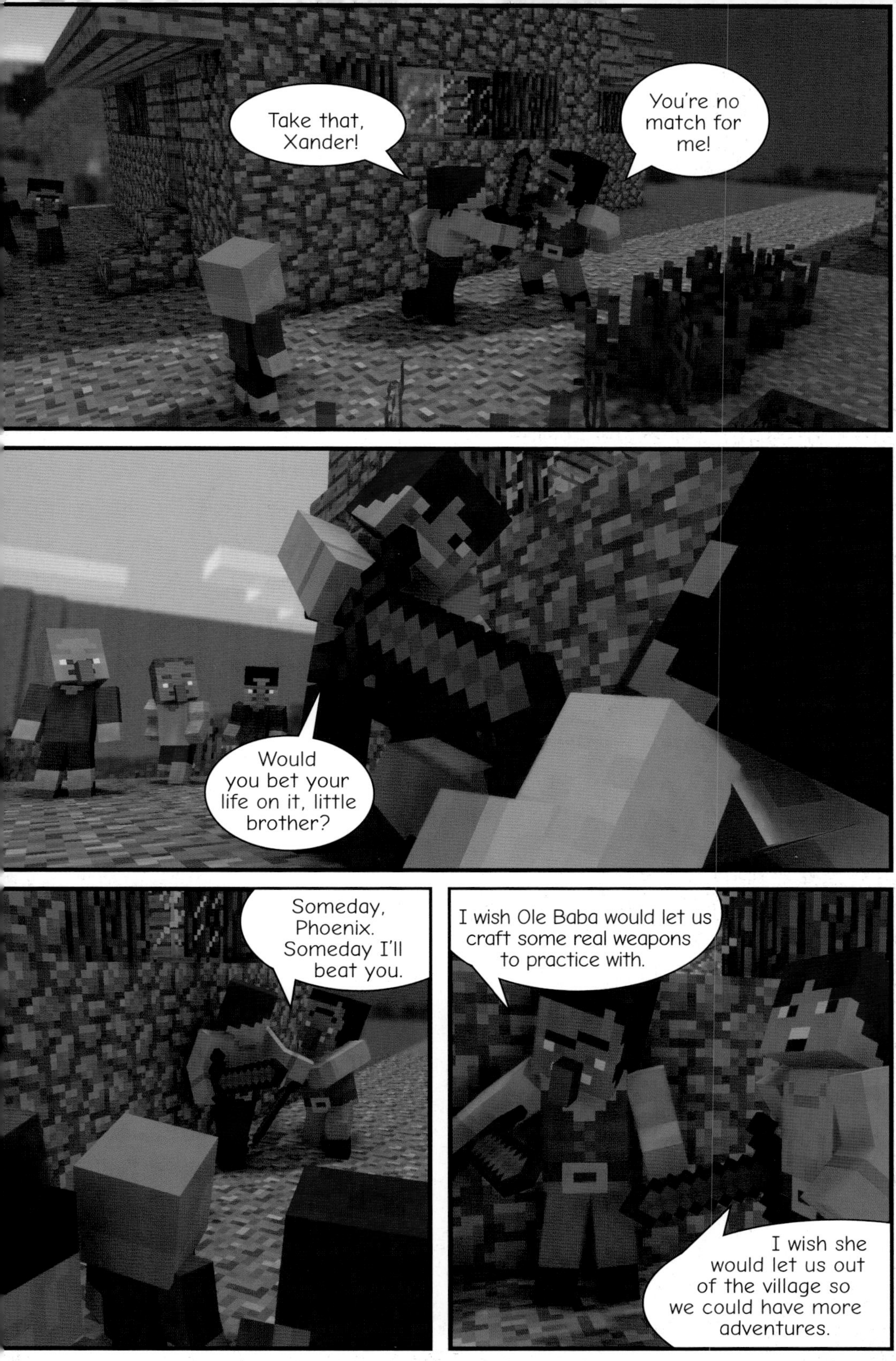
Take that, Xander!
You're no match for me!
Would you bet your life on it, little brother?
Someday, Phoenix. Someday I'll beat you.
I wish Ole Baba would let us craft some real weapons to practice with.
I wish she would let us out of the village so we could have more adventures.

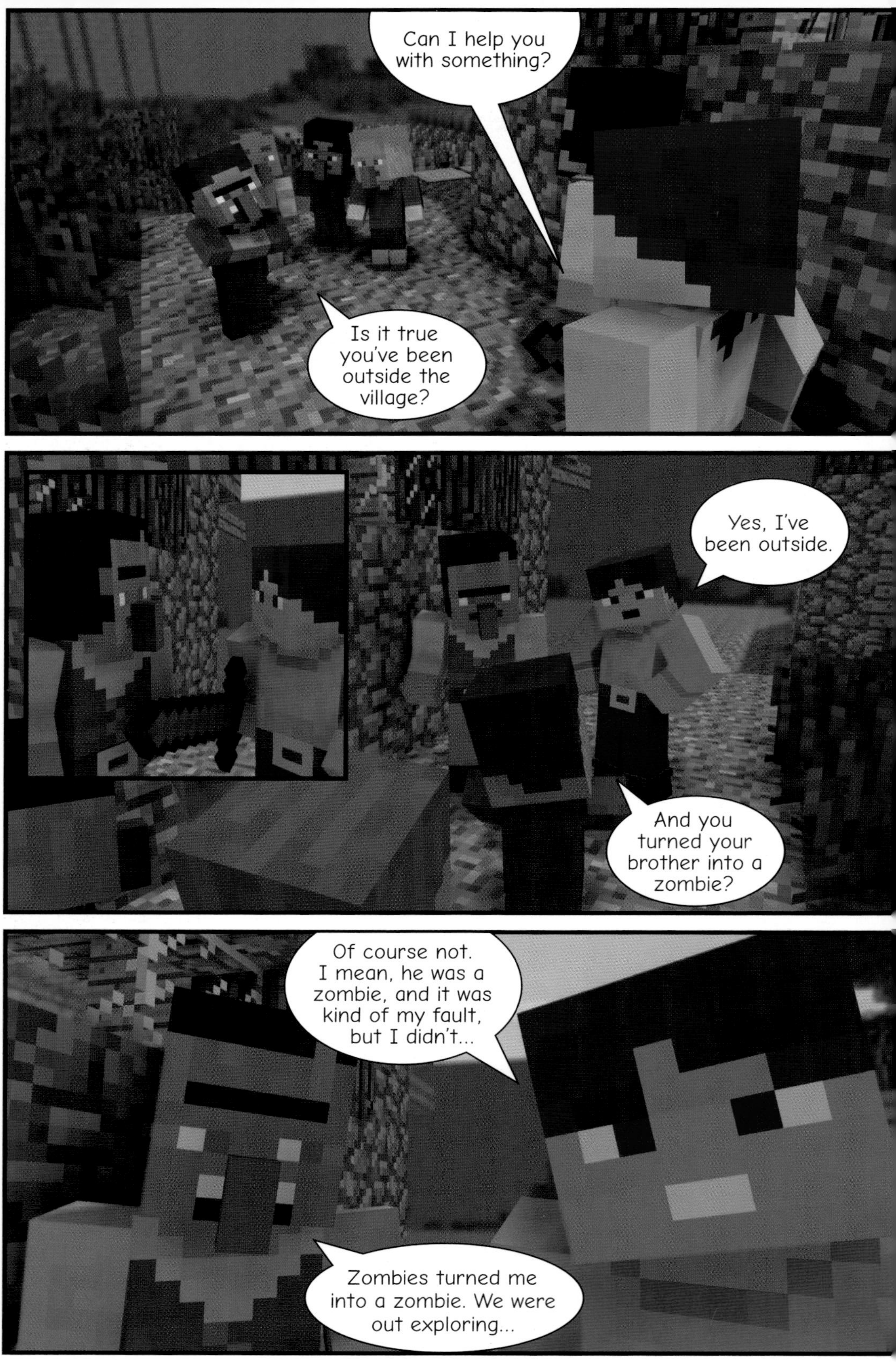
Can I help you with something?
Is it true you've been outside the village?
Yes, I've been outside.
And you turned your brother into a zombie?
Of course not. I mean, he was a zombie, and it was kind of my fault, but I didn't...
Zombies turned me into a zombie. We were out exploring...

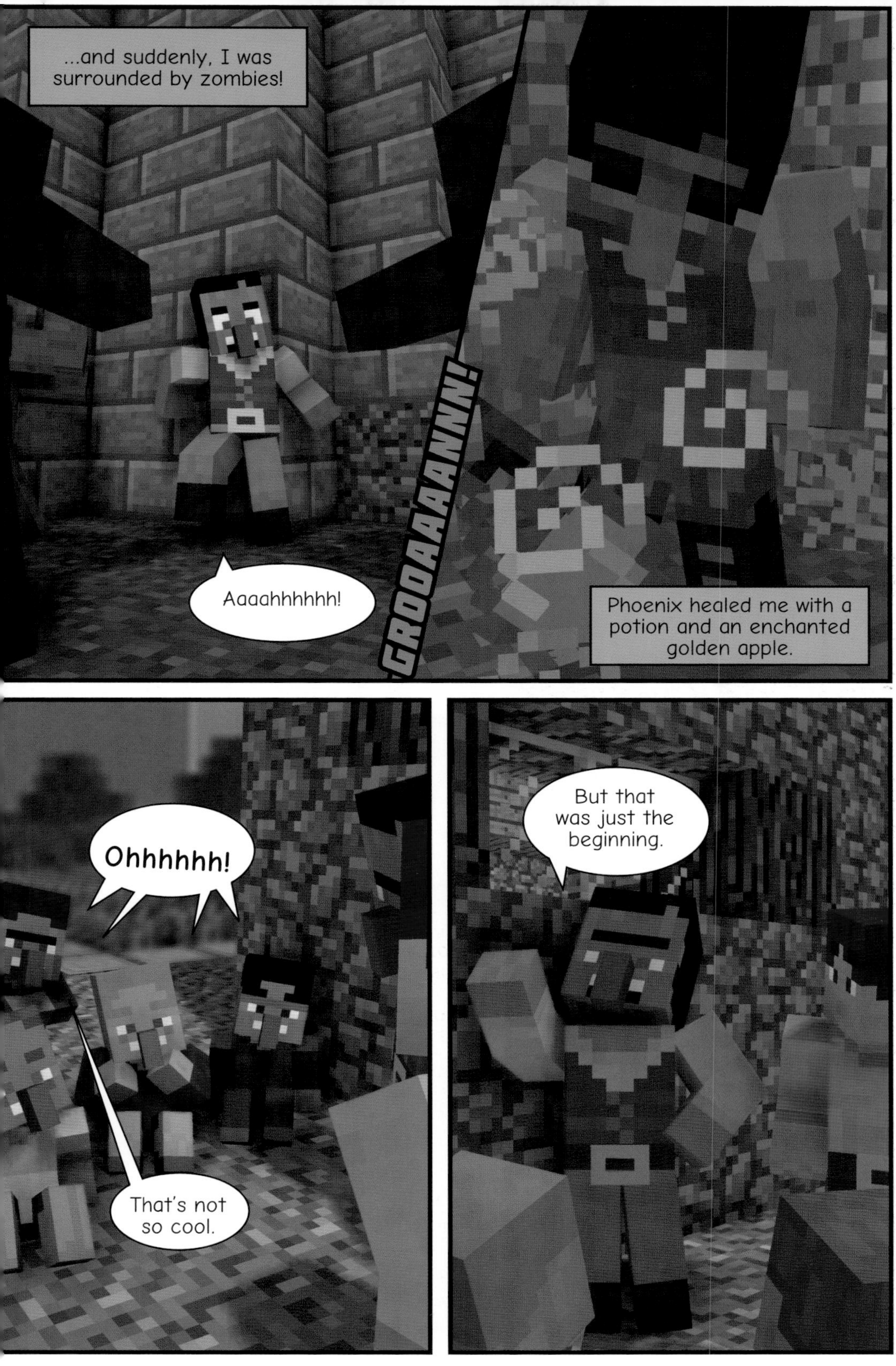
...and suddenly, I was surrounded by zombies!
Aaaahhhhhh!
GROOAAAANN!
Phoenix healed me with a potion and an enchanted golden apple.
Ohhhhhh!
That's not so cool.
But that was just the beginning.

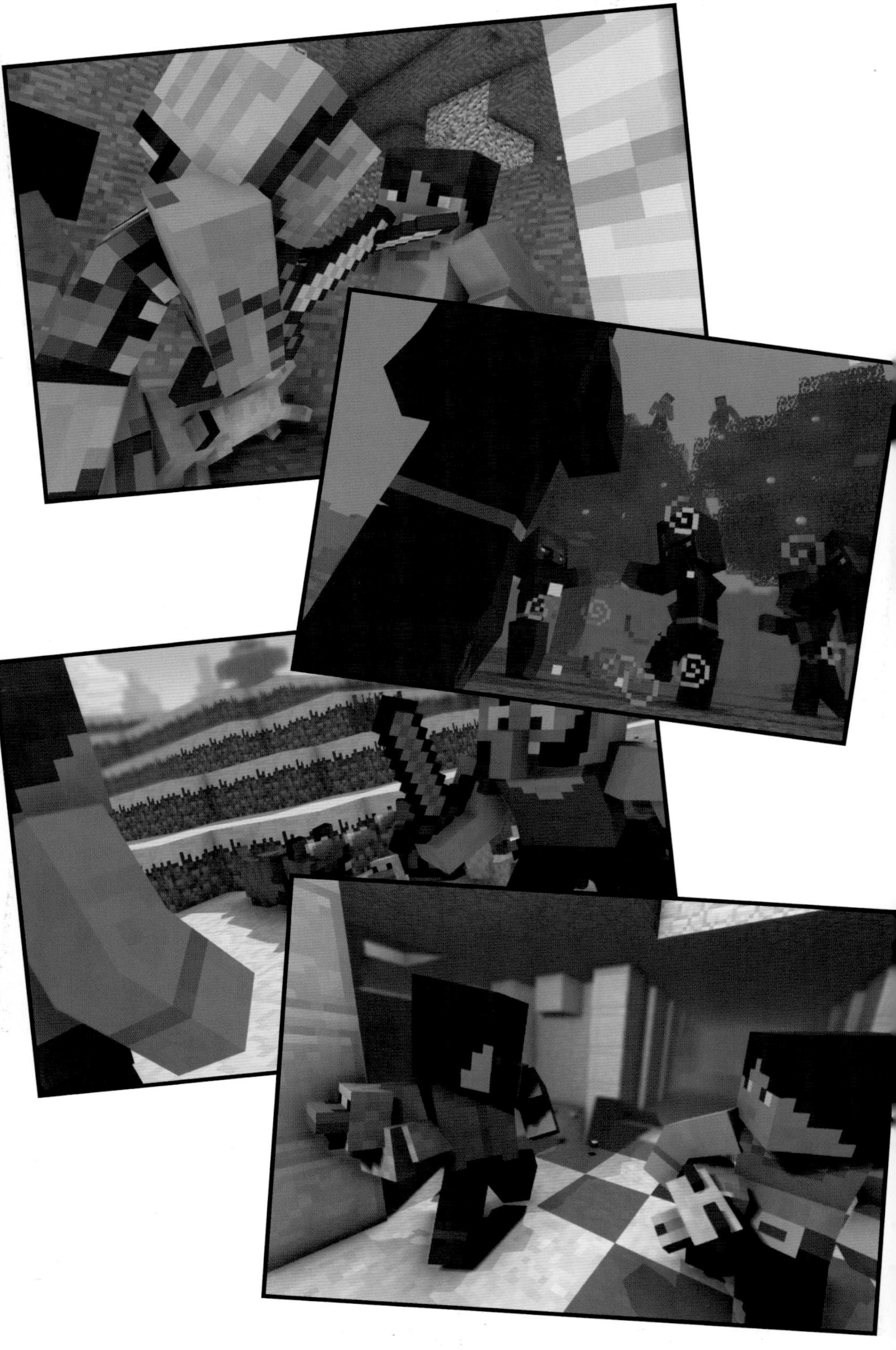

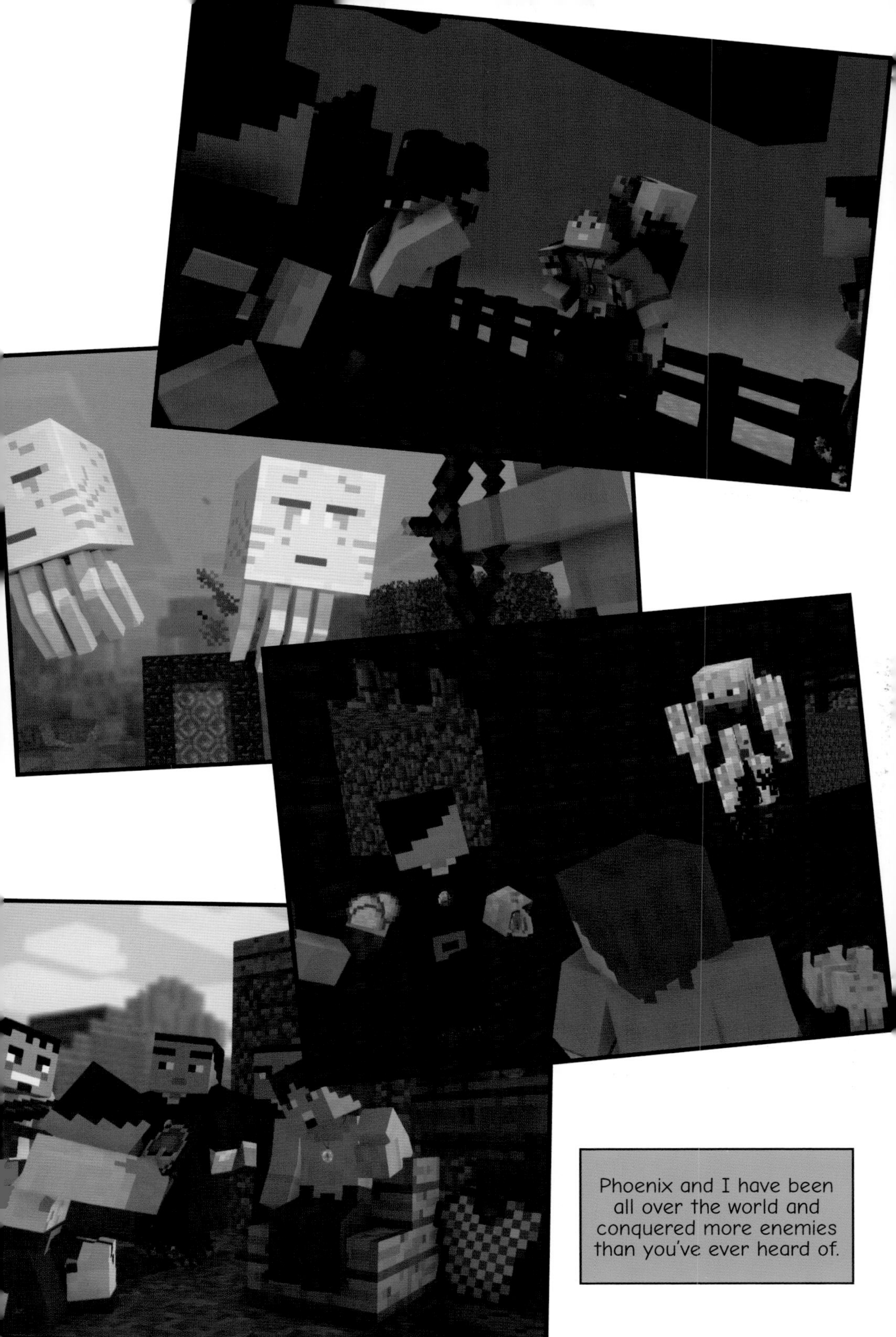
Phoenix and I have been all over the world and conquered more enemies than you've ever heard of.

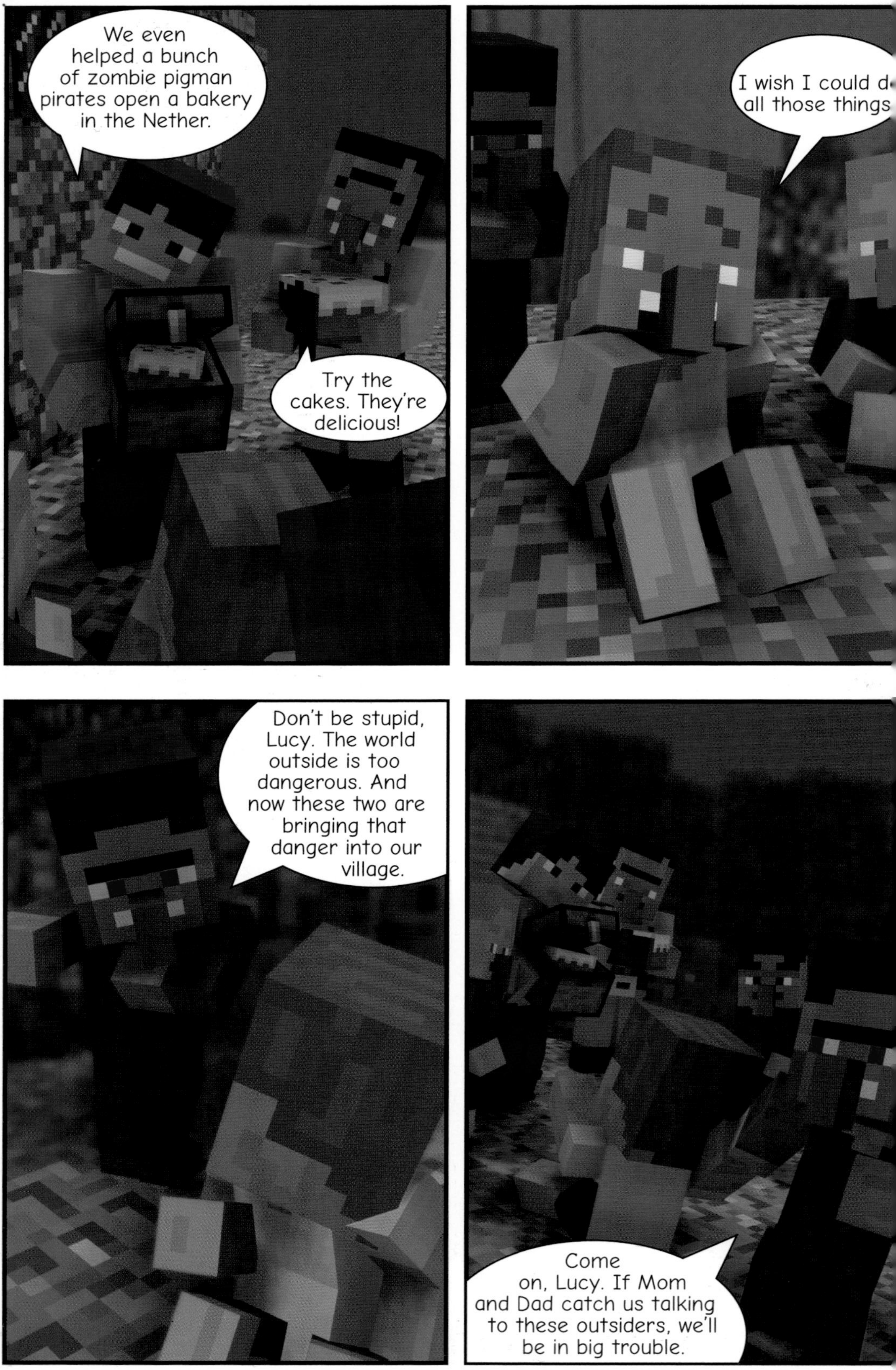
We even helped a bunch of zombie pigman pirates open a bakery in the Nether.
Try the cakes. They're delicious!
I wish I could d all those things
Don't be stupid, Lucy. The world outside is too dangerous. And now these two are bringing that danger into our village.
Come on, Lucy. If Mom and Dad catch us talking to these outsiders, we'll be in big trouble.

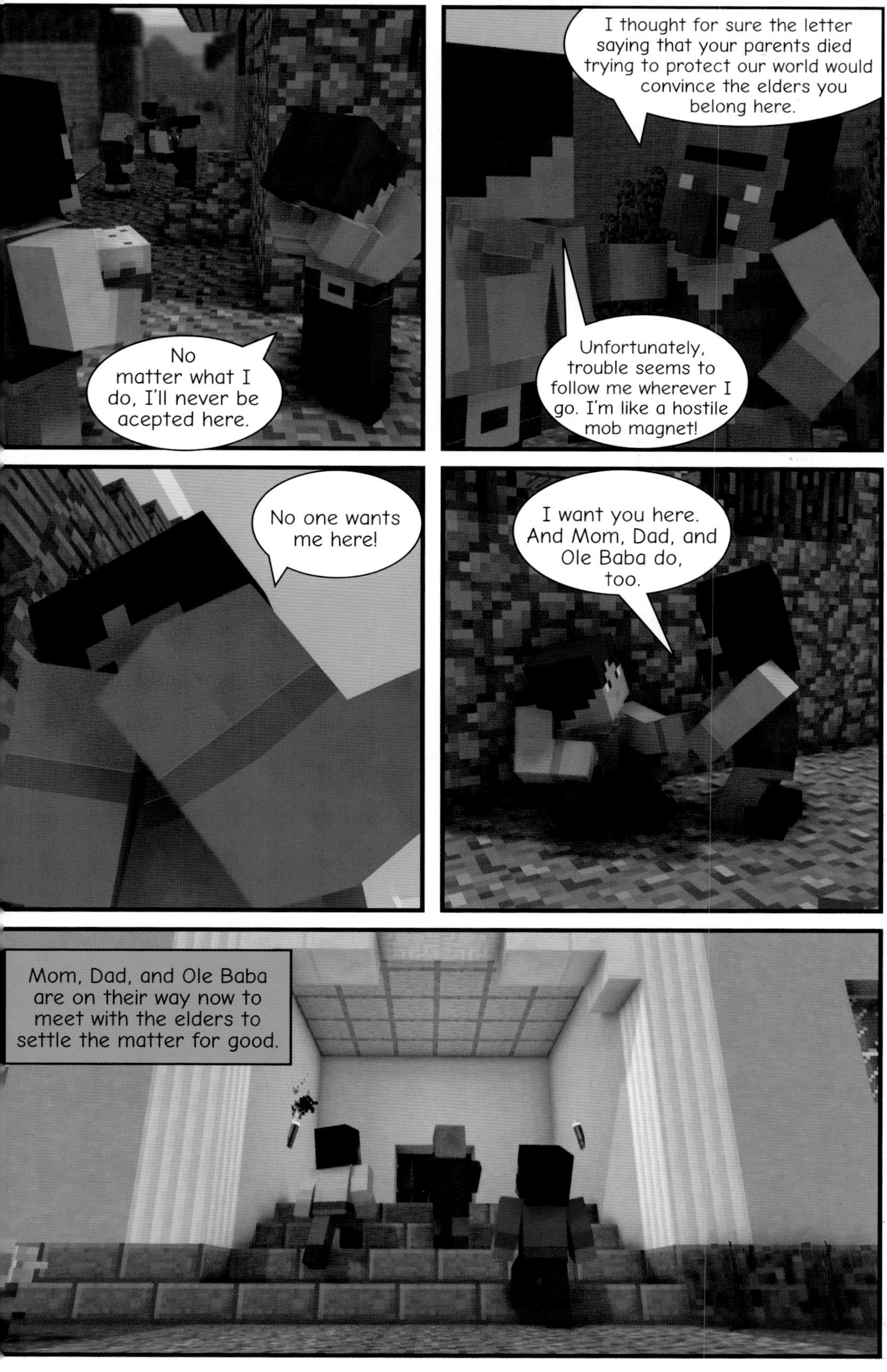
No matter what I do, I'll never be acepted here.
I thought for sure the letter saying that your parents died trying to protect our world would convince the elders you belong here.
Unfortunately, trouble seems to follow me wherever I go. I'm like a hostile mob magnet!
No one wants me here!
I want you here. And Mom, Dad, and Ole Baba do, too.
Mom, Dad, and Ole Baba are on their way now to meet with the elders to settle the matter for good.

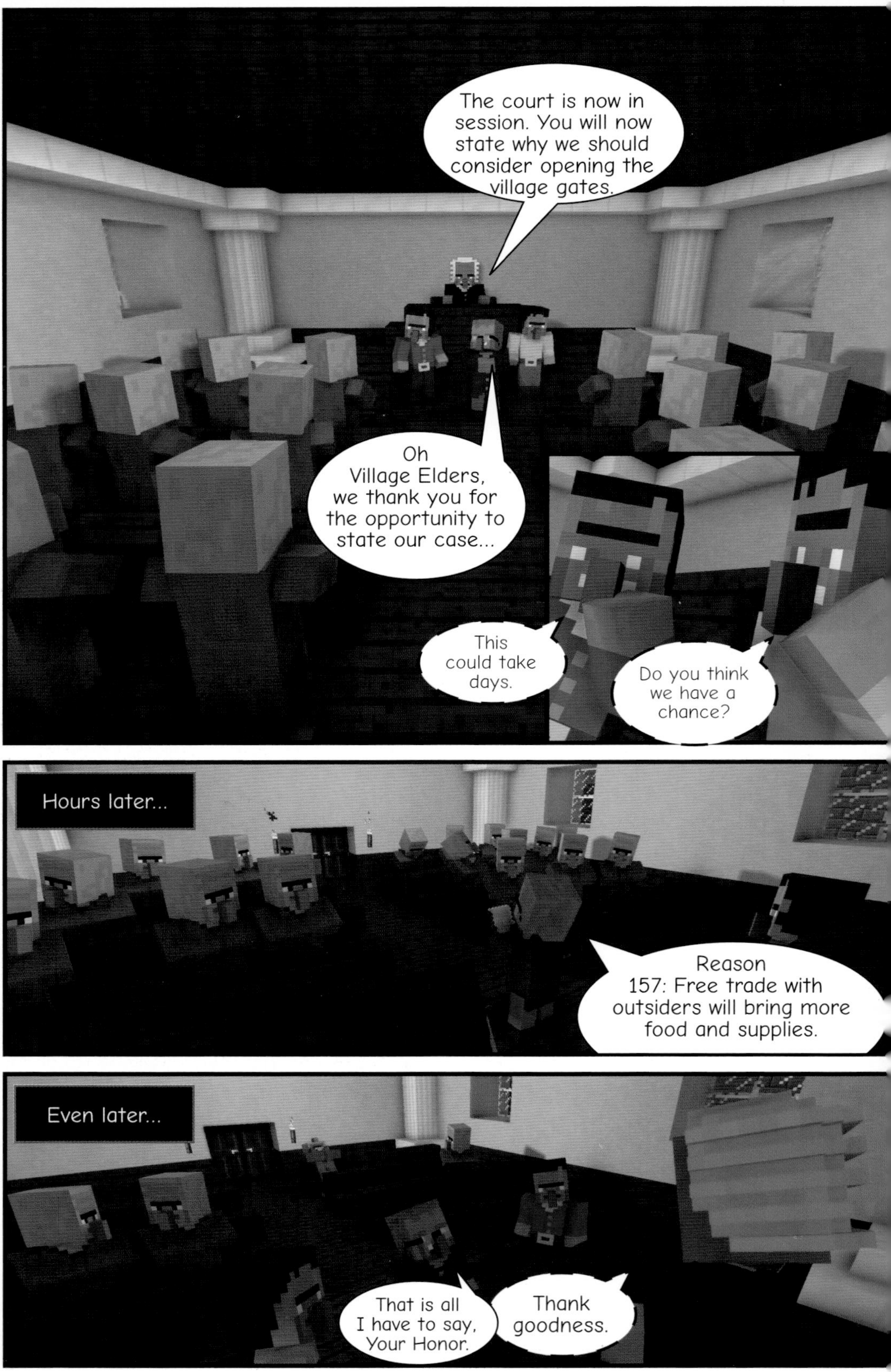
The court is now in session. You will now state why we should consider opening the village gates.
Oh Village Elders, we thank you for the opportunity to state our case...
This could take days.
Do you think we have a chance?
Hours later...
Reason 157: Free trade with outsiders will bring more food and supplies.
Even later...
That is all I have to say, Your Honor.
Thank goodness.

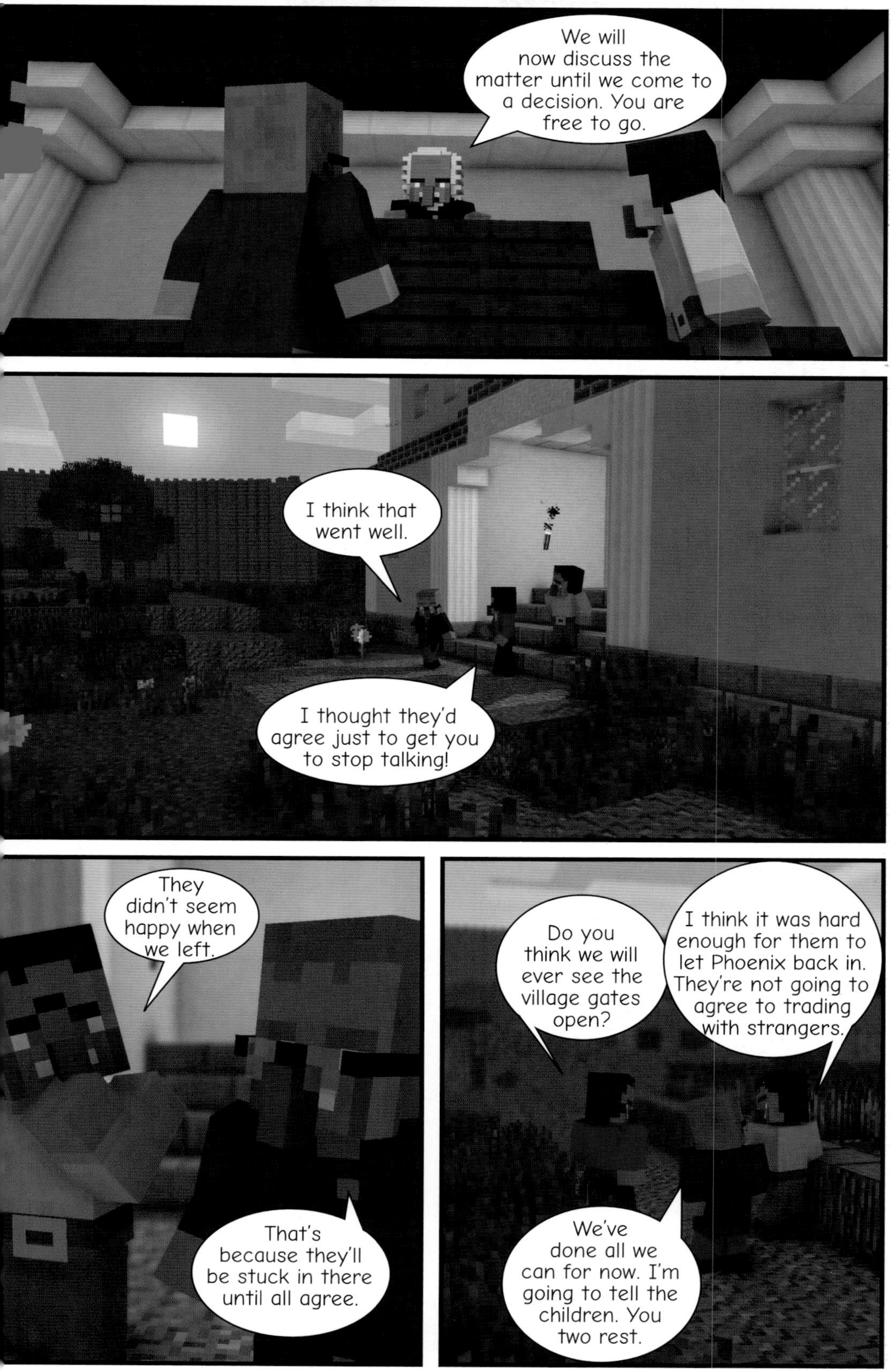
We will now discuss the matter until we come to a decision. You are free to go.
I think that went well.
I thought they'd agree just to get you to stop talking!
They didn't seem happy when we left.
That's because they'll be stuck in there until all agree.
Do you think we will ever see the village gates open?
I think it was hard enough for them to let Phoenix back in. They're not going to agree to trading with strangers.
We've done all we can for now. I'm going to tell the children. You two rest.

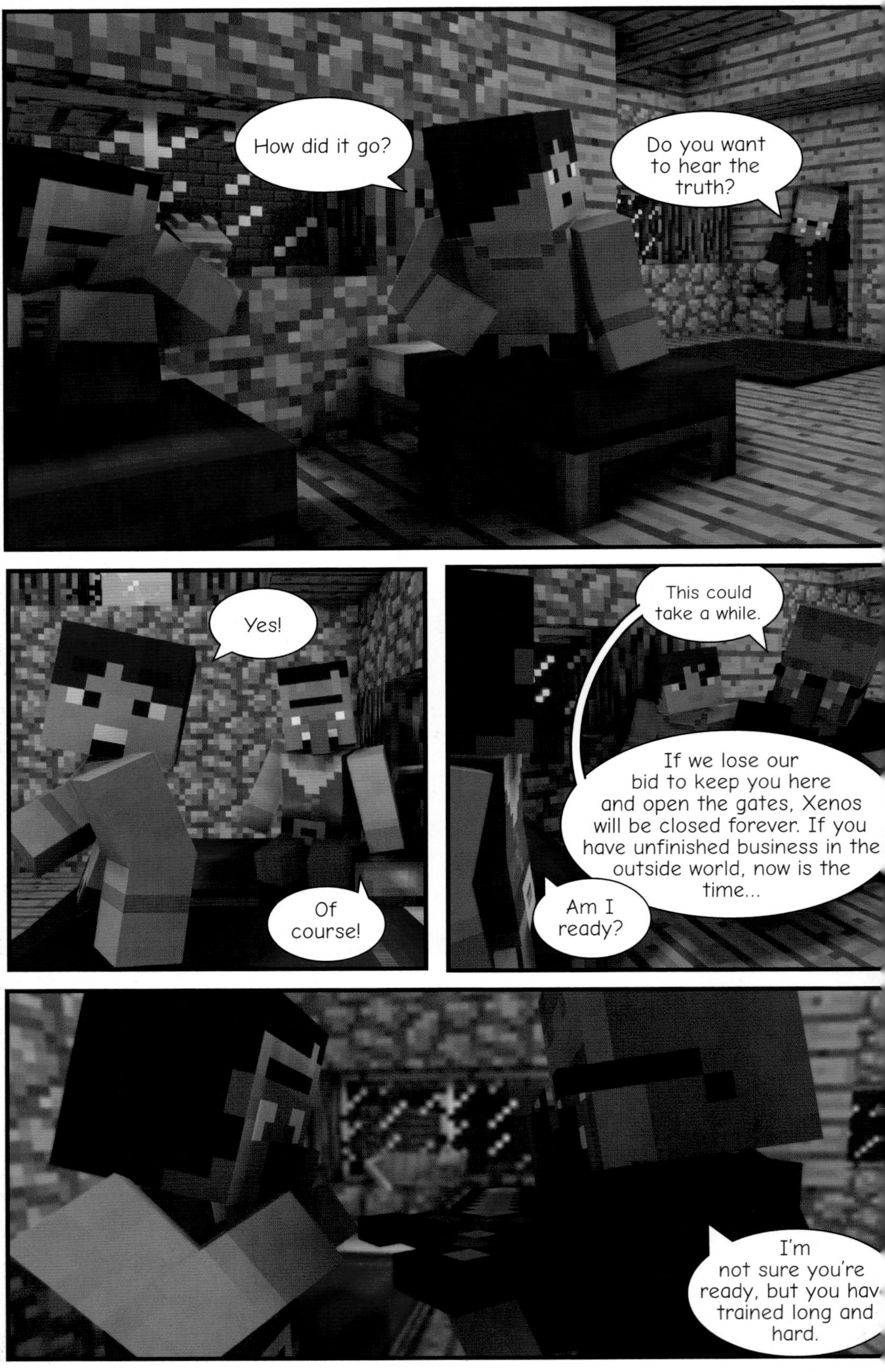
How did it go?
Do you want to hear the truth?
Yes!
Of course!
This could take a while.
If we lose our bid to keep you here and open the gates, Xenos will be closed forever. If you have unfinished business in the outside world, now is the time...
Am I ready?
I'm not sure you're ready, but you hav trained long and hard.

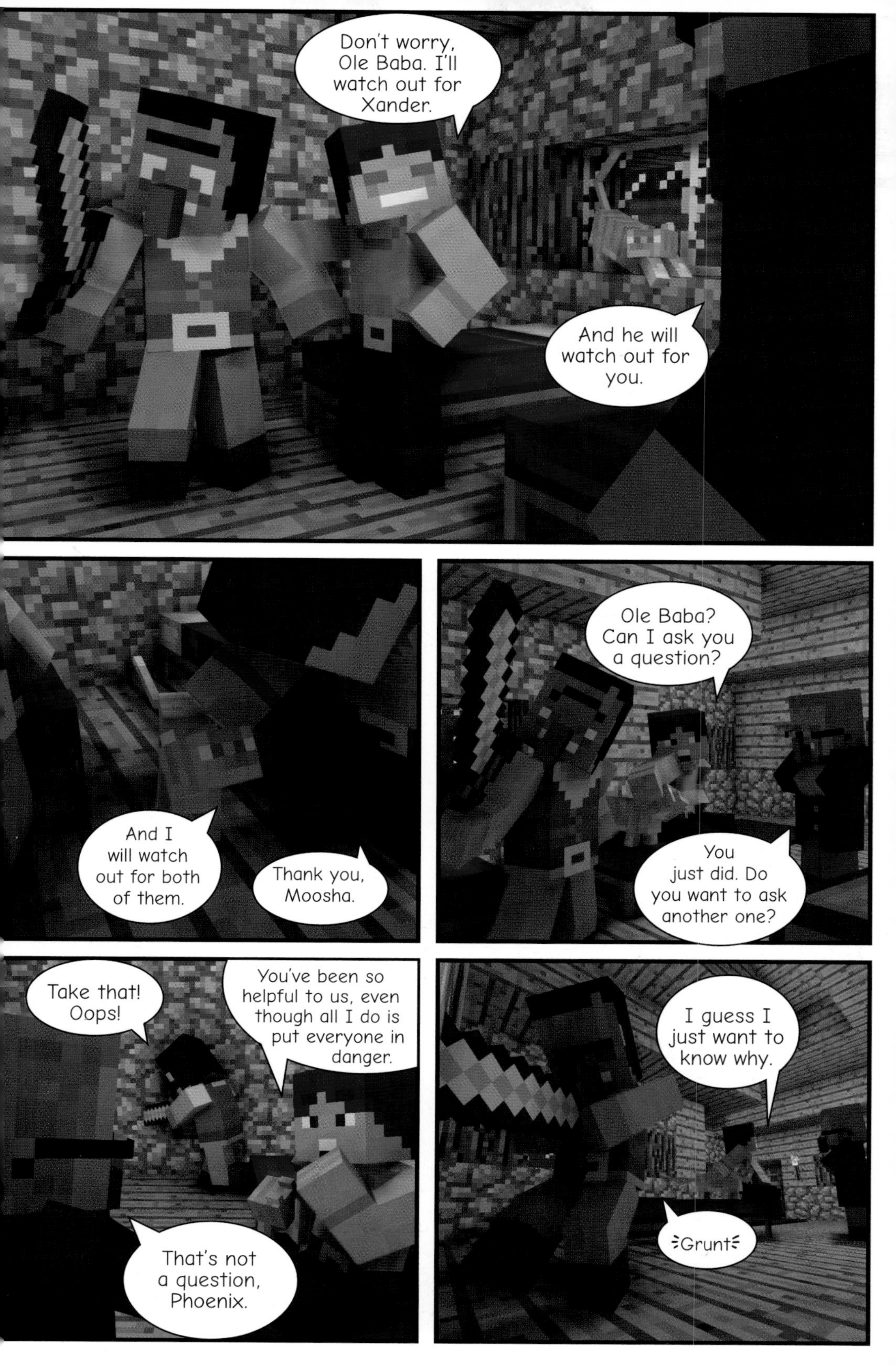
Don't worry, Ole Baba. I'll watch out for Xander.
And he will watch out for you.
And I will watch out for both of them.
Thank you, Moosha.
Ole Baba? Can I ask you a question?
You just did. Do you want to ask another one?
Take that! Oops!
You've been so helpful to us, even though all I do is put everyone in danger.
That's not a question, Phoenix.
I guess I just want to know why.
Grunt

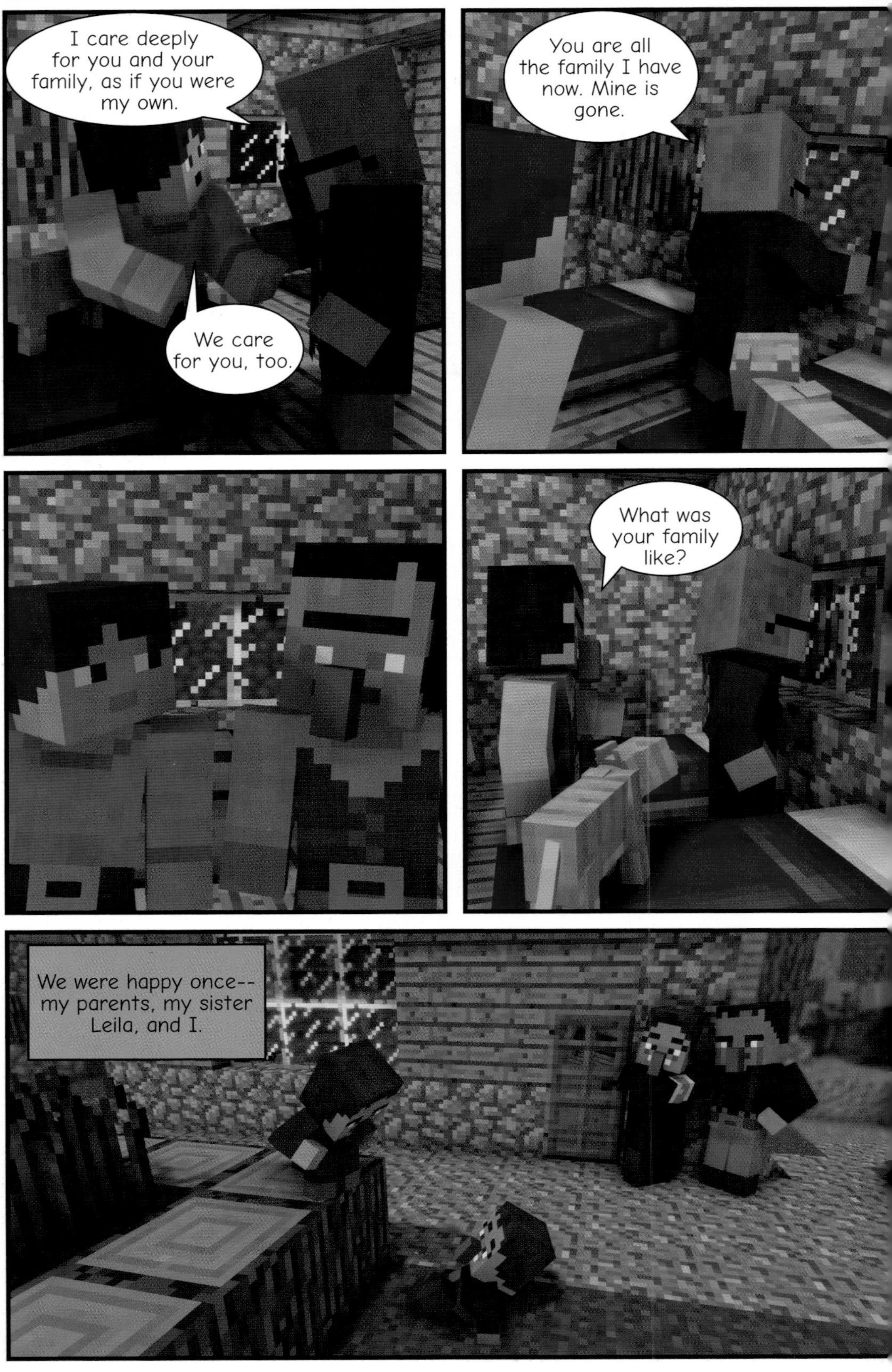
I care deeply for you and your family, as if you were my own.
We care for you, too.
You are all the family I have now. Mine is gone.
What was your family like?
We were happy once-- my parents, my sister Leila, and I.

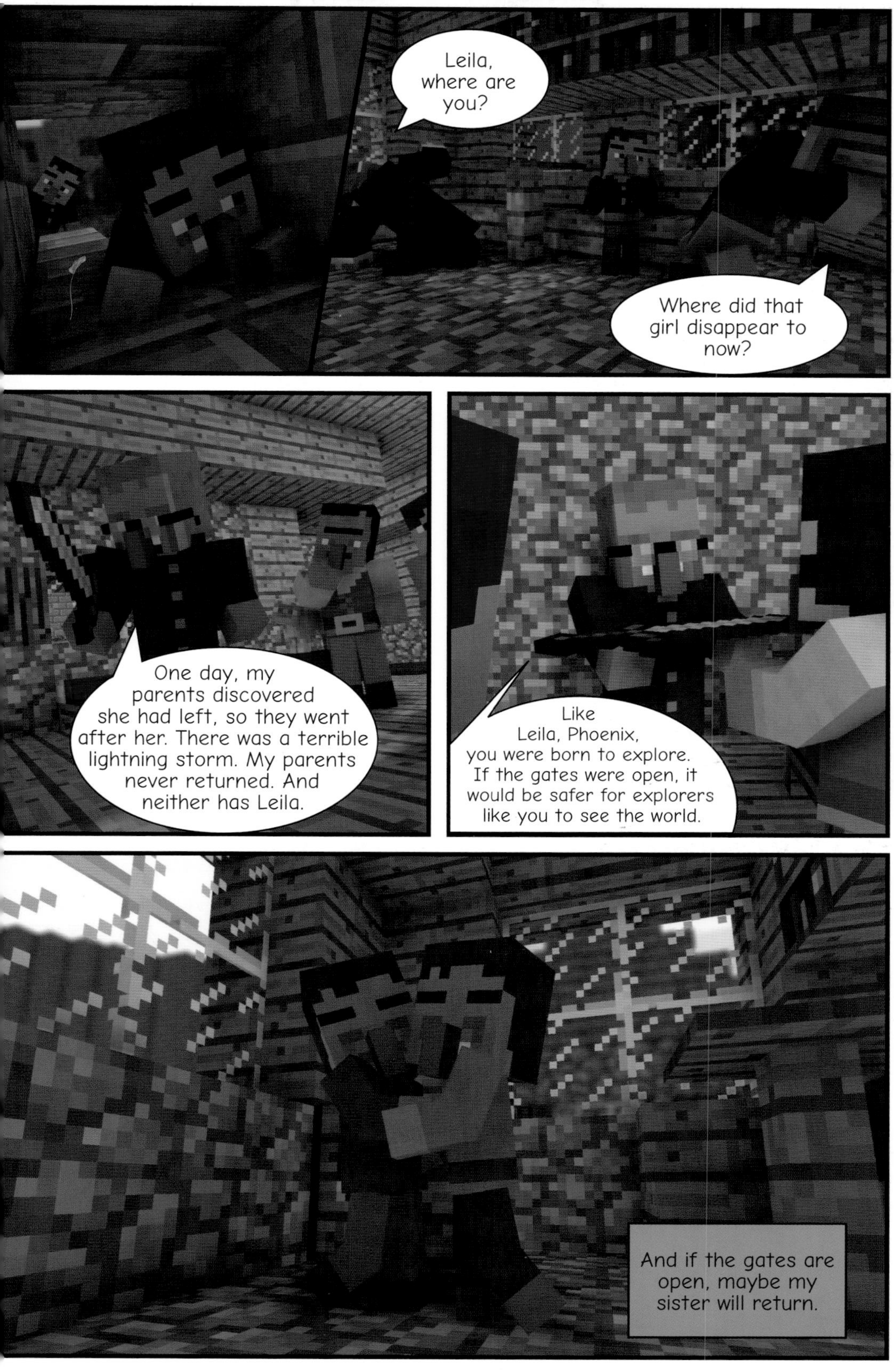
Leila, where are you?
Where did that girl disappear to now?
One day, my parents discovered she had left, so they went after her. There was a terrible lightning storm. My parents never returned. And neither has Leila.
Like Leila, Phoenix, you were born to explore. If the gates were open, it would be safer for explorers like you to see the world.
And if the gates are open, maybe my sister will return.

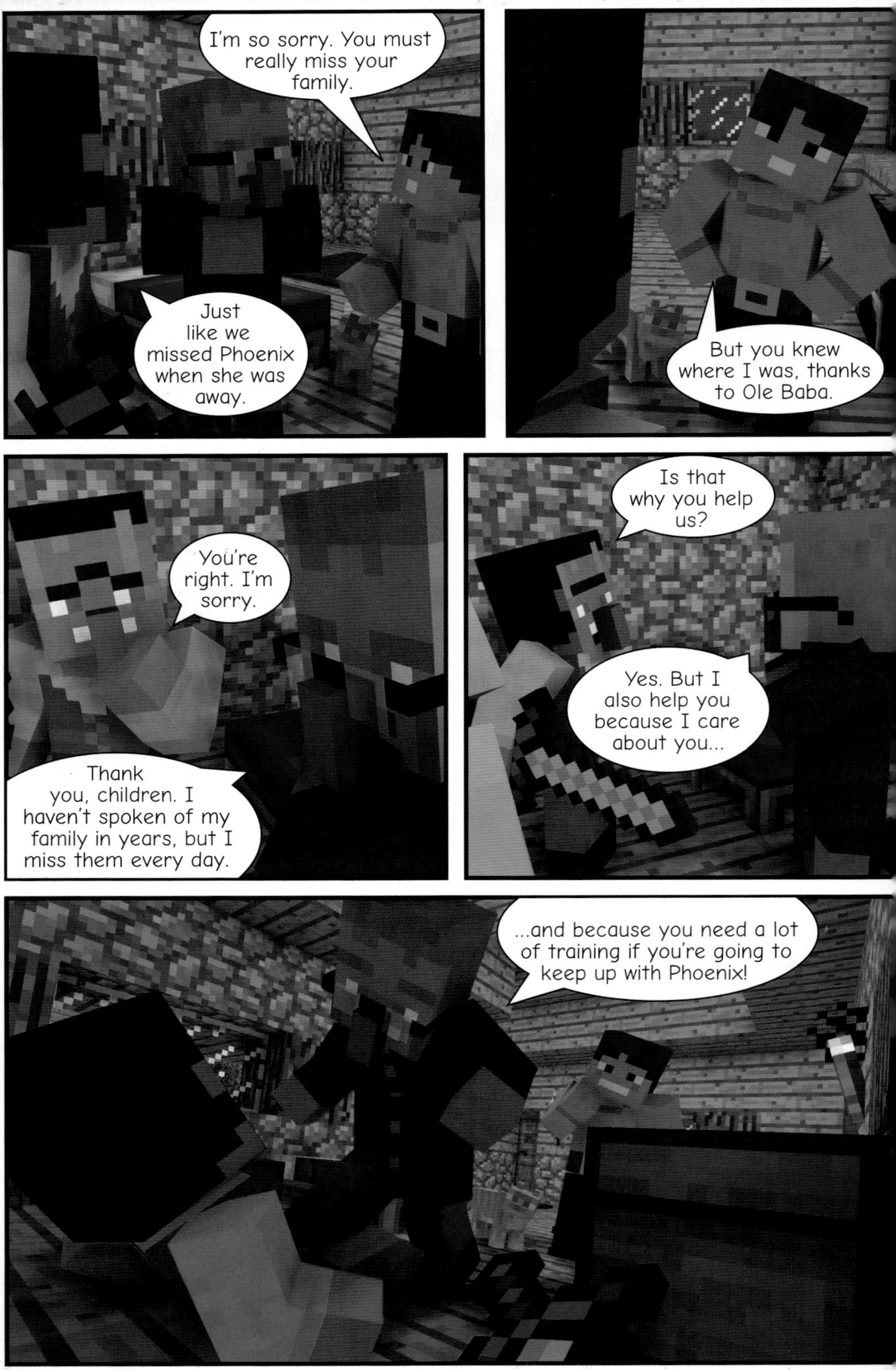
I'm so sorry. You must really miss your family.
Just like we missed Phoenix when she was away.
But you knew where I was, thanks to Ole Baba.
You're right. I'm sorry.
Thank you, children. I haven't spoken of my family in years, but I miss them every day.
Is that why you help us?
Yes. But I also help you because I care about you...
...and because you need a lot of training if you're going to keep up with Phoenix!

CHAPTER 2

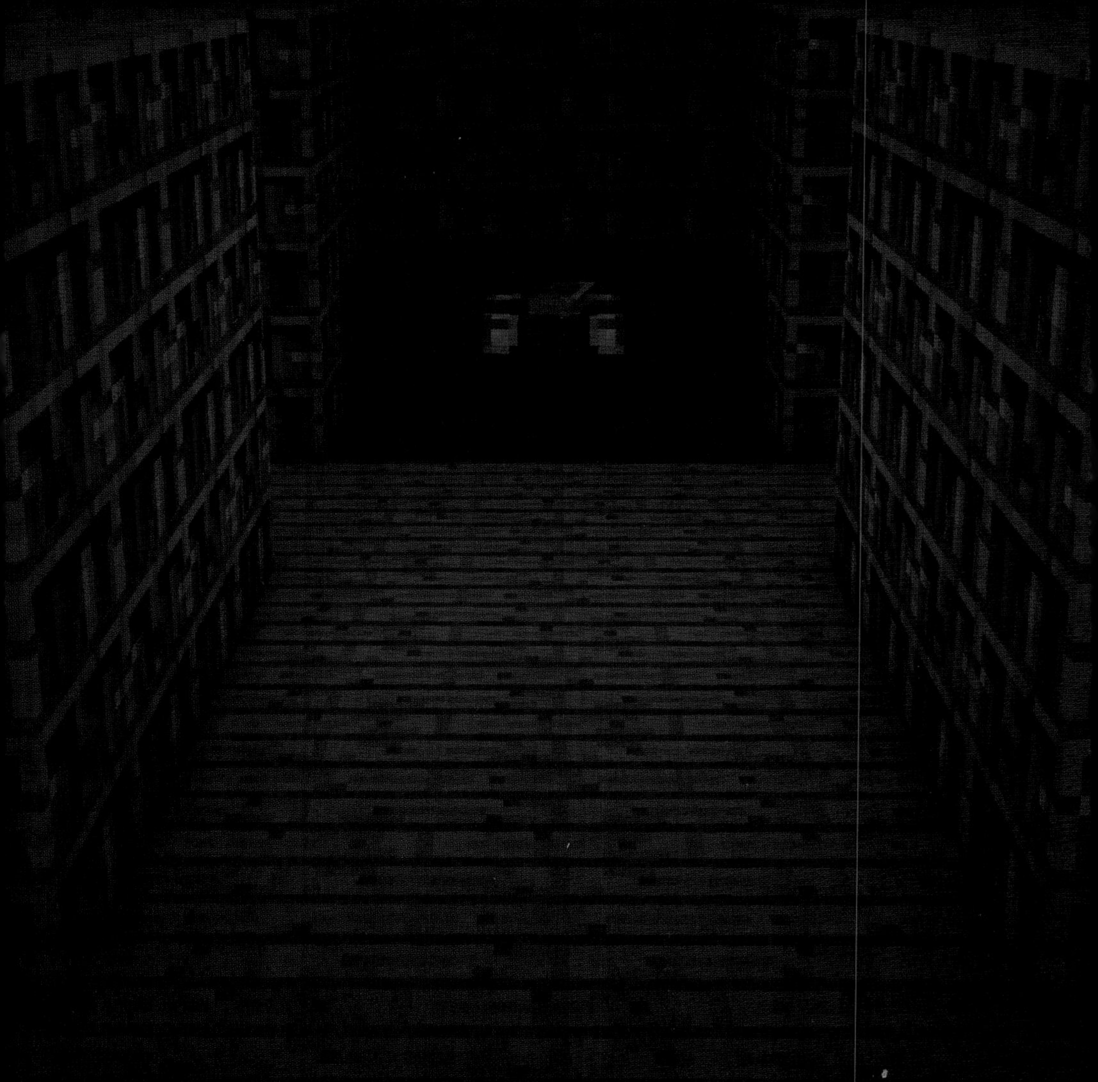

SECRETS

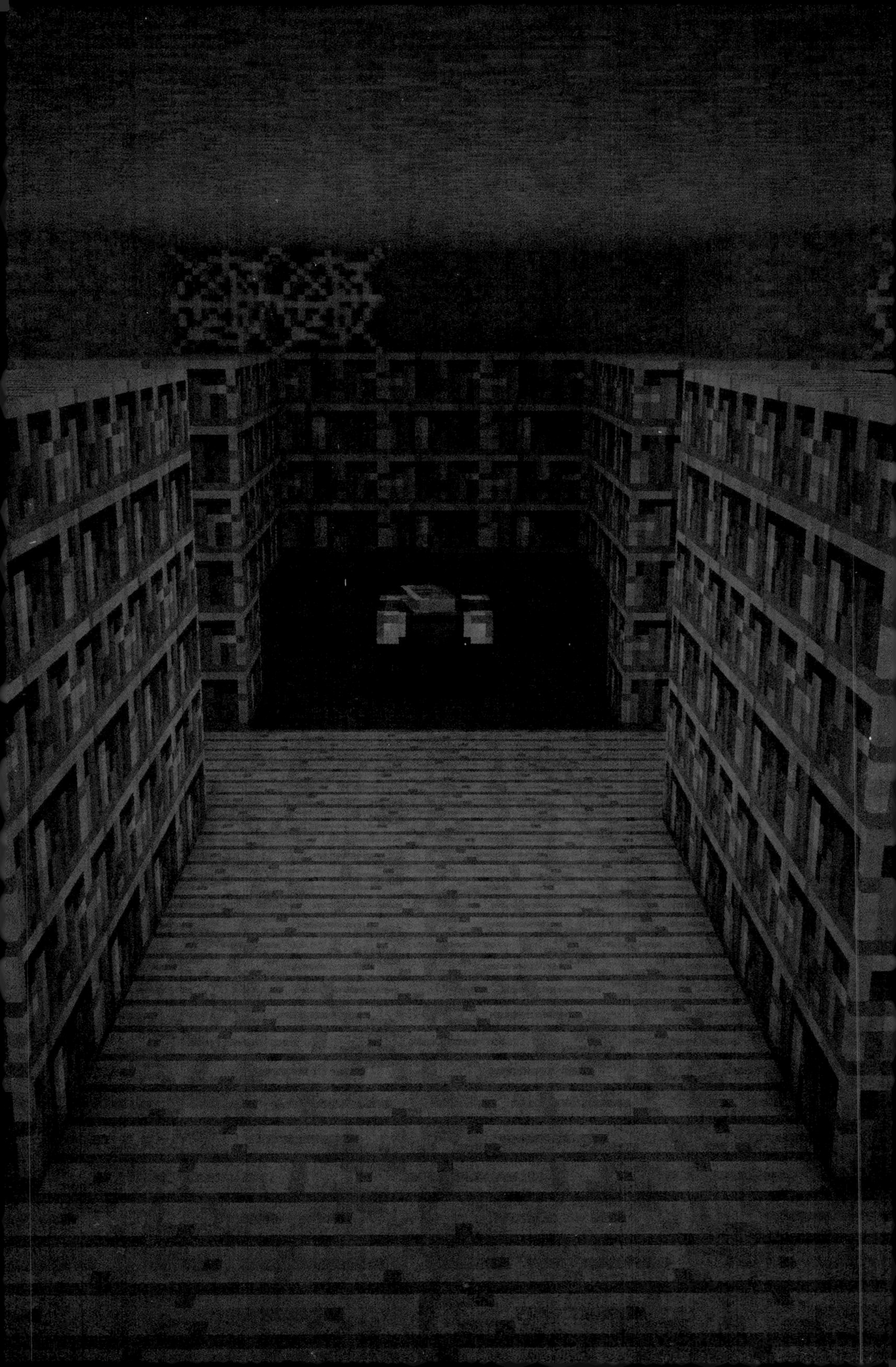

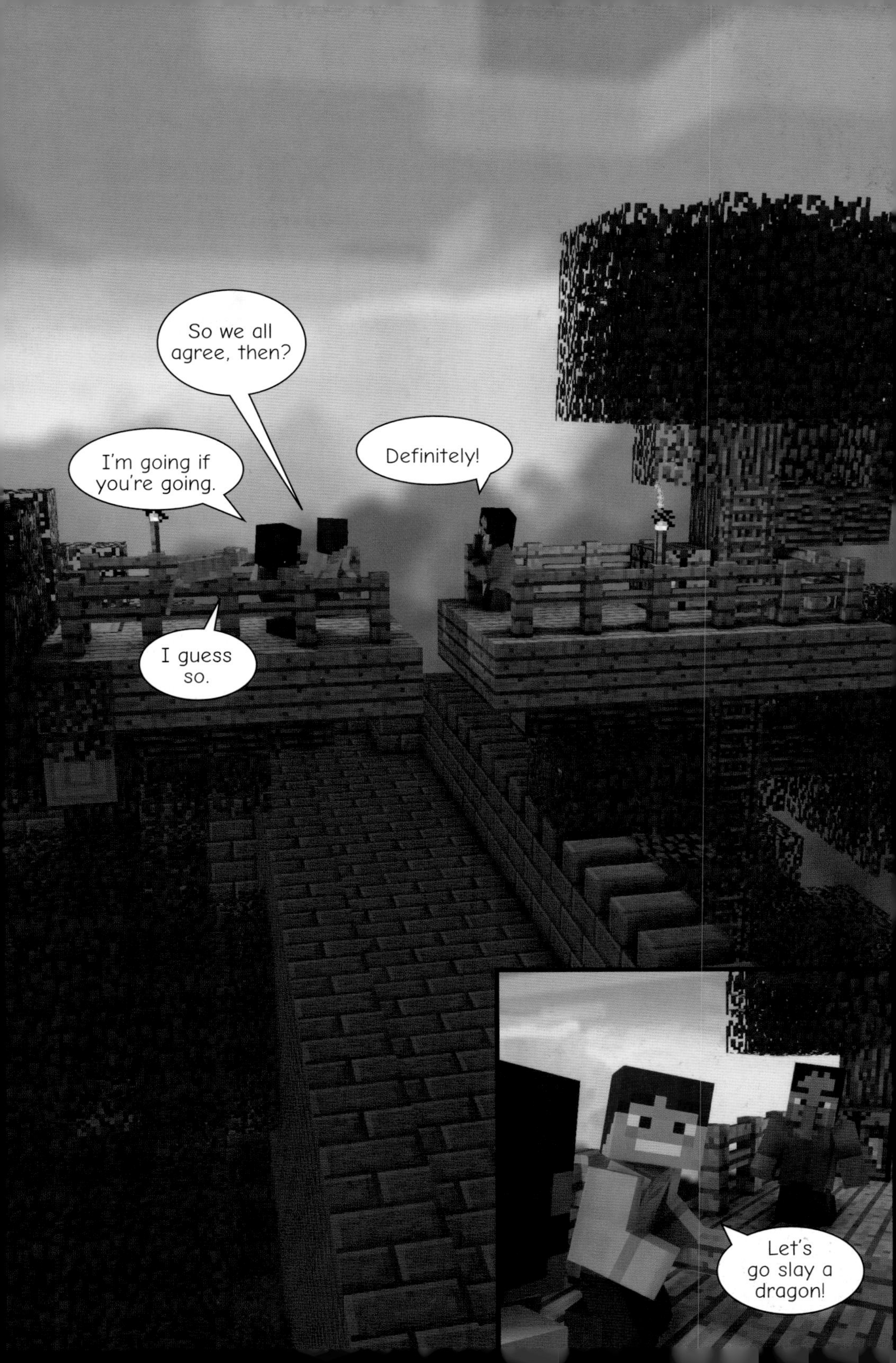
So we all agree, then?
I'm going if you're going.
Definitely!
I guess so.
Let's go slay a dragon!

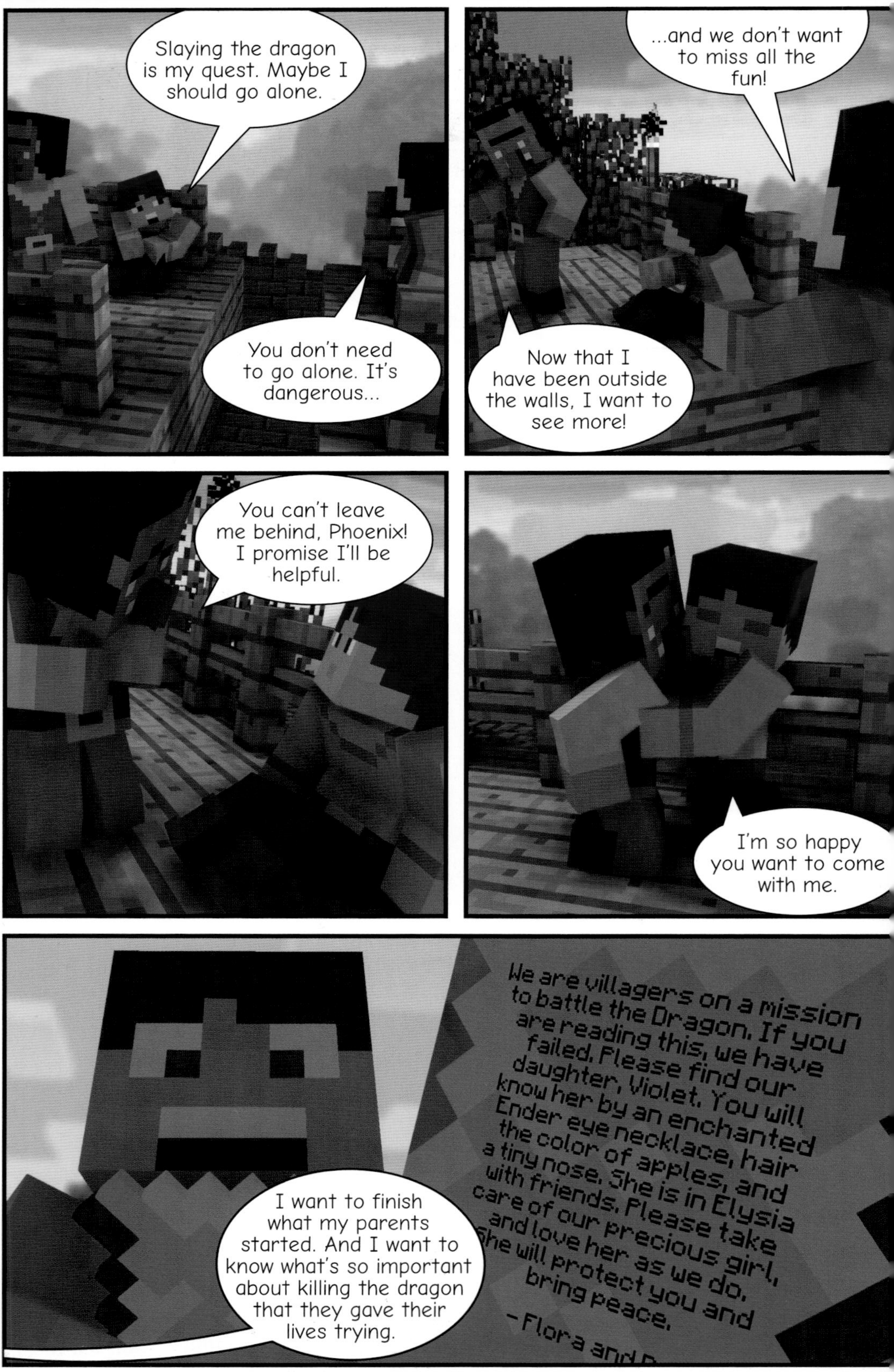

Slaying the dragon is my quest. Maybe I should go alone.
You don't need to go alone. It's dangerous...
...and we don't want to miss all the fun!
Now that I have been outside the walls, I want to see more!
You can't leave me behind, Phoenix! I promise I'll be helpful.
I'm so happy you want to come with me.
We are villagers on a mission to battle the Dragon. If you are reading this, we have failed. Please find our daughter, Violet. You will know her by an enchanted Ender eye necklace, hair the color of apples, and a tiny nose. She is in Elysia with friends. Please take care of our precious girl, and love her as we do. She will protect you and bring peace.
-Flora and
I want to finish what my parents started. And I want to know what's so important about killing the dragon that they gave their lives trying.

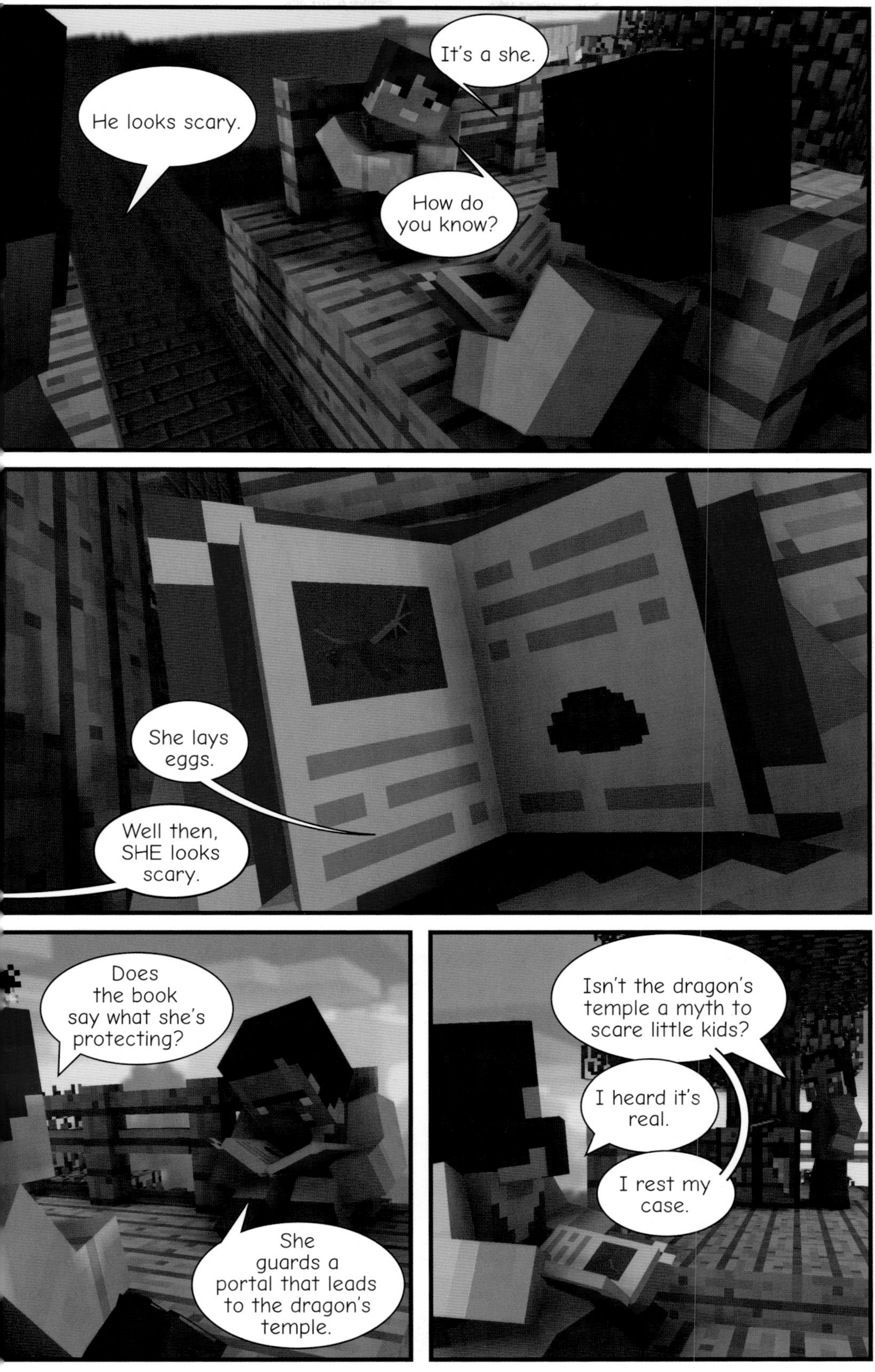
He looks scary.
It's a she.
How do you know?
She lays eggs.
Well then, SHE looks scary.
Does the book say what she's protecting?
She guards a portal that leads to the dragon's temple.
Isn't the dragon's temple a myth to scare little kids?
I heard it's real.
I rest my case.

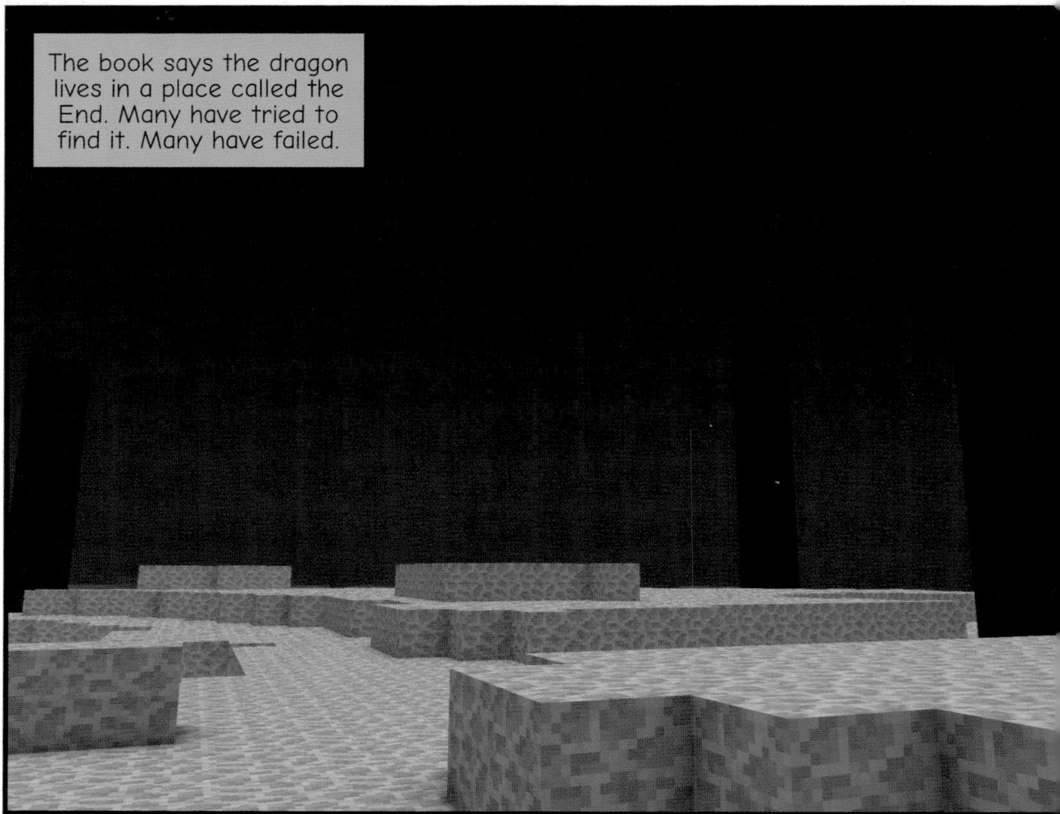
The book says the dragon lives in a place called the End. Many have tried to find it. Many have failed.

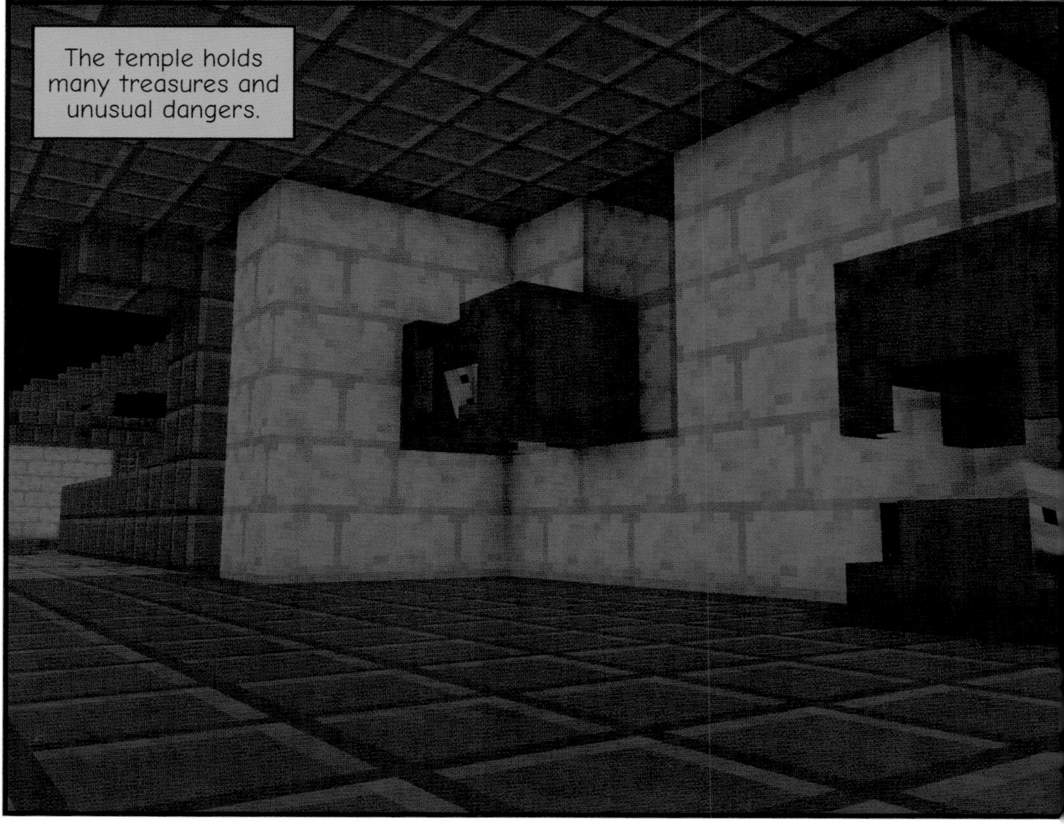
The temple holds many treasures and unusual dangers.

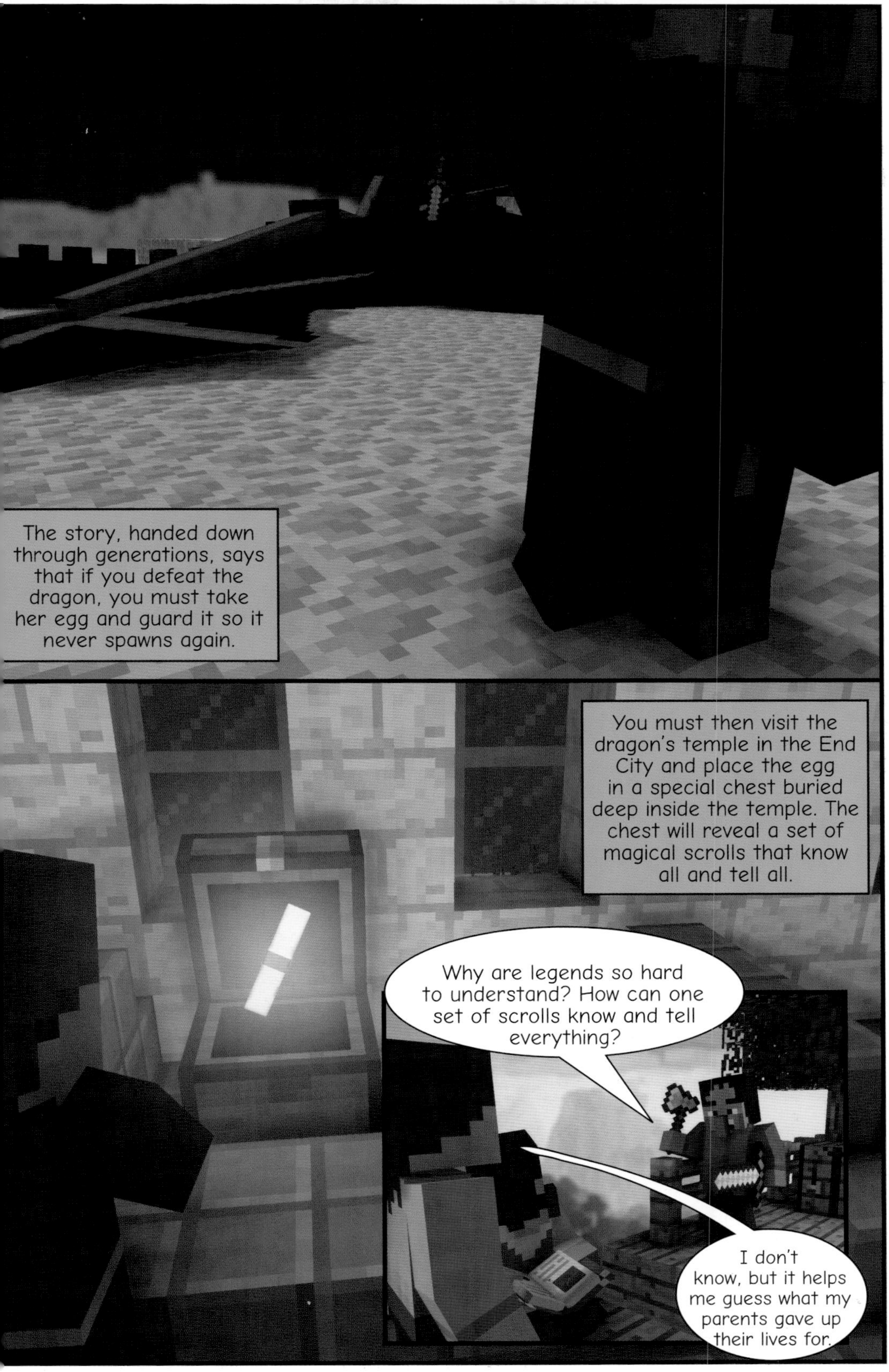
The story, handed down through generations, says that if you defeat the dragon, you must take her egg and guard it so it never spawns again.
You must then visit the dragon's temple in the End City and place the egg in a special chest buried deep inside the temple. The chest will reveal a set of magical scrolls that know all and tell all.
Why are legends so hard to understand? How can one set of scrolls know and tell everything?
I don't know, but it helps me guess what my parents gave up their lives for.

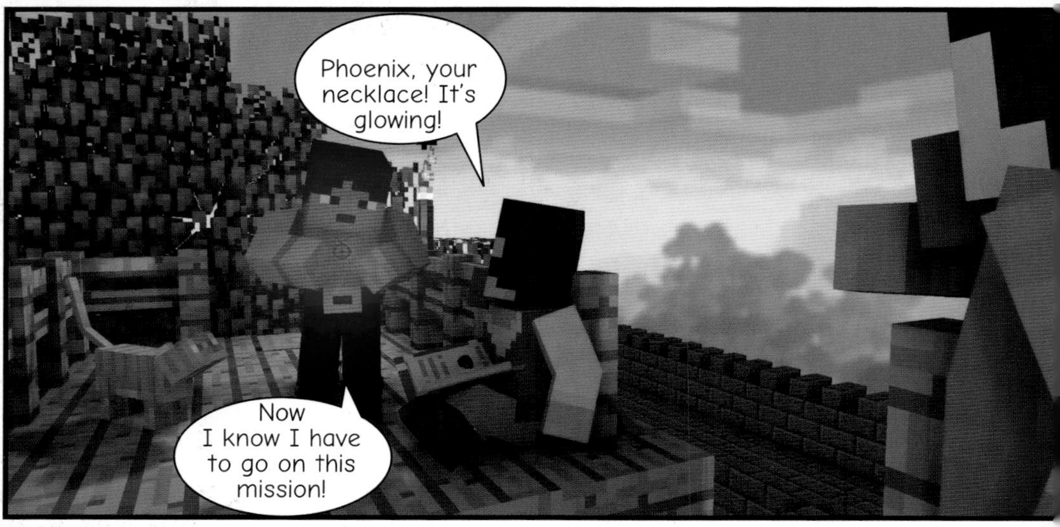
Phoenix, your necklace! It's glowing!
Now I know I have to go on this mission!

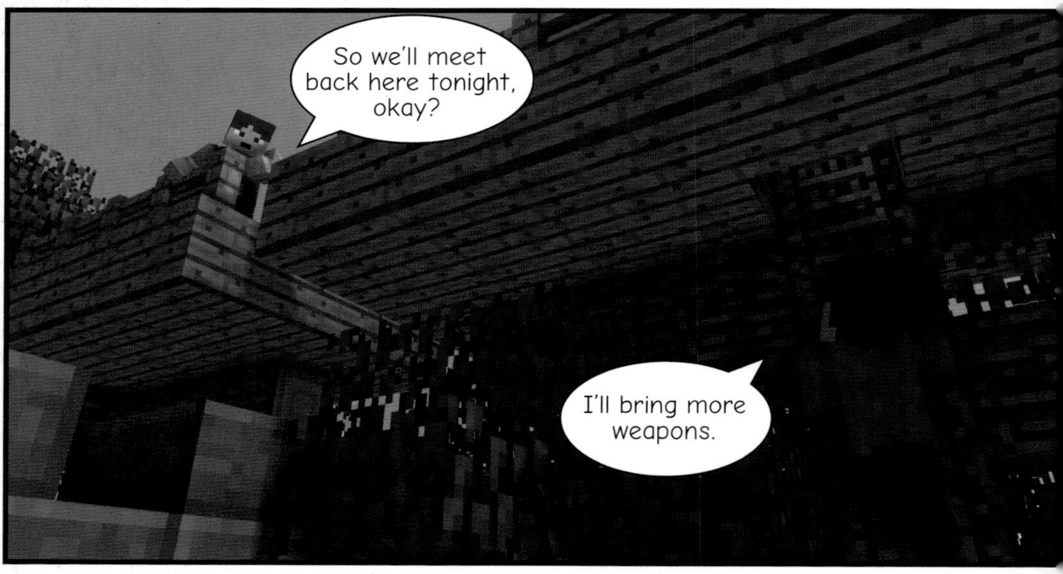
So we'll meet back here tonight, okay?
I'll bring more weapons.

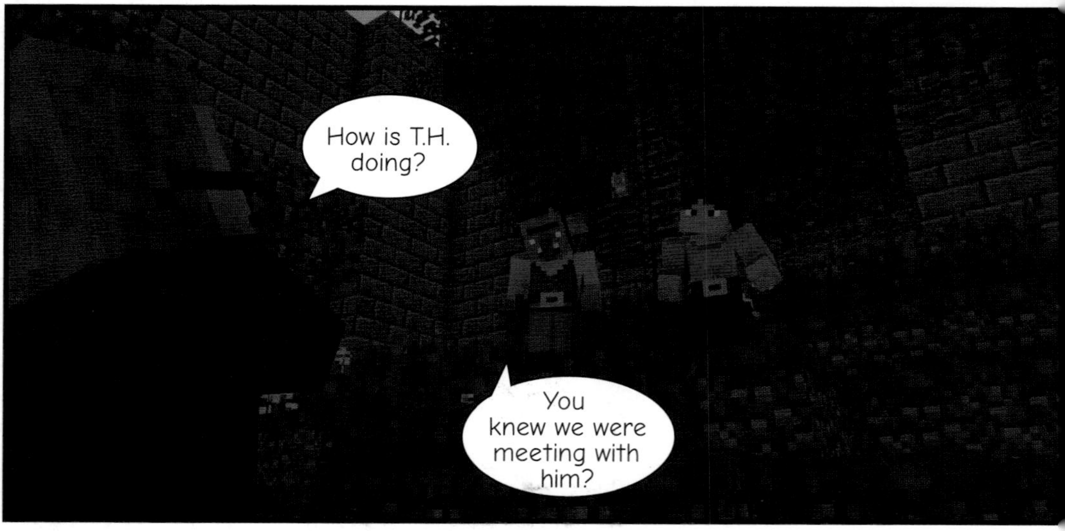
How is T.H. doing?
You knew we were meeting with him?

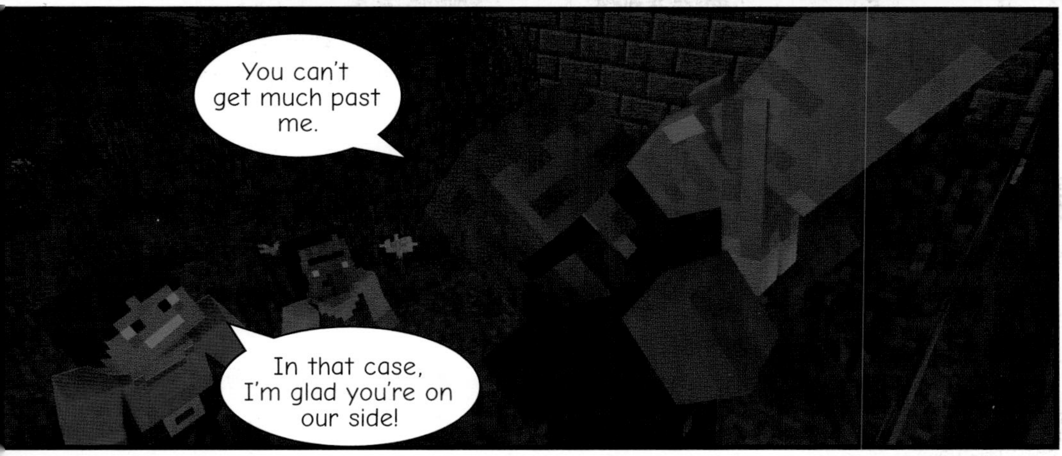
You can't get much past me.
In that case, I'm glad you're on our side!
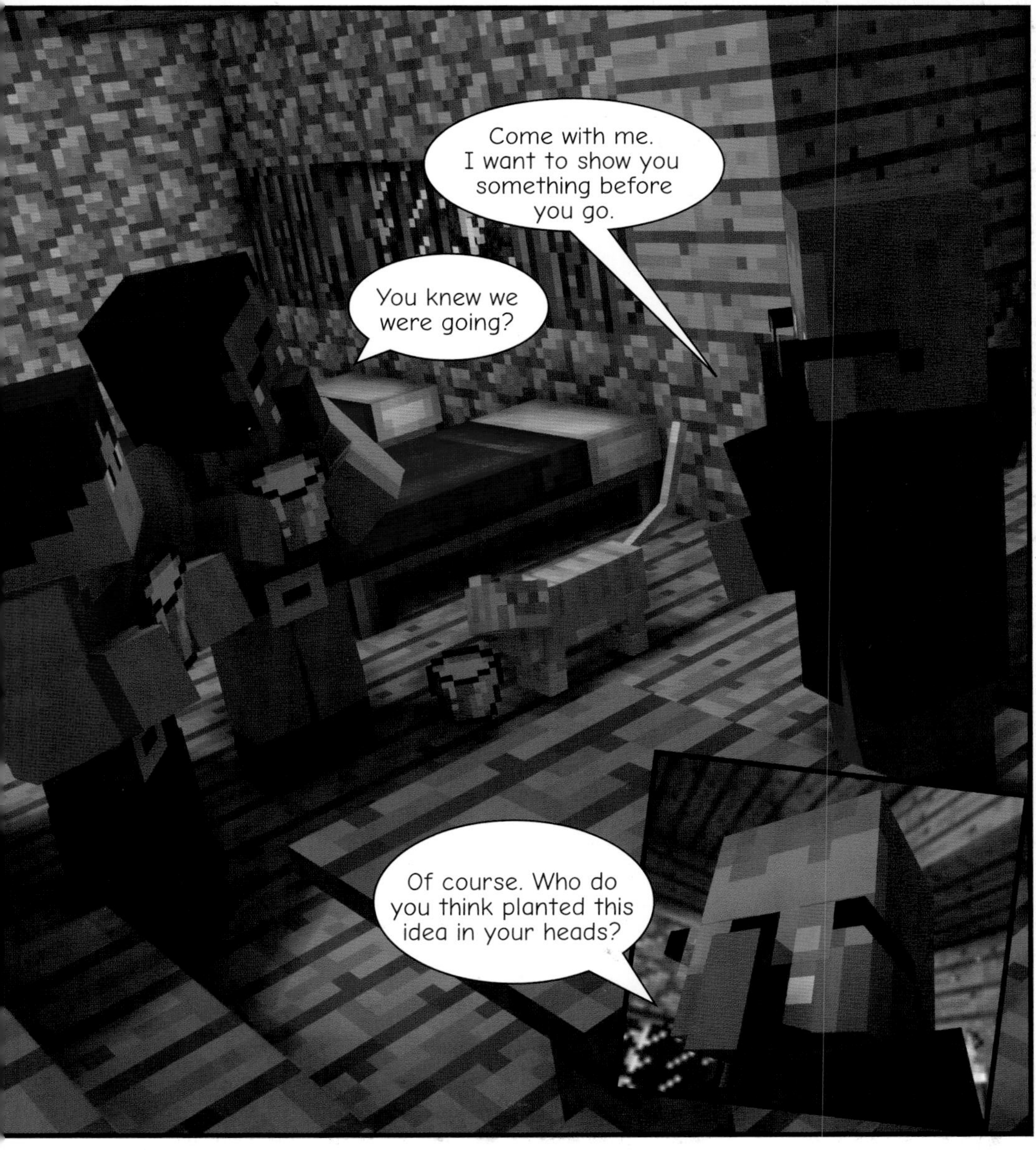
Come with me. I want to show you something before you go.
You knew we were going?
Of course. Who do you think planted this idea in your heads?

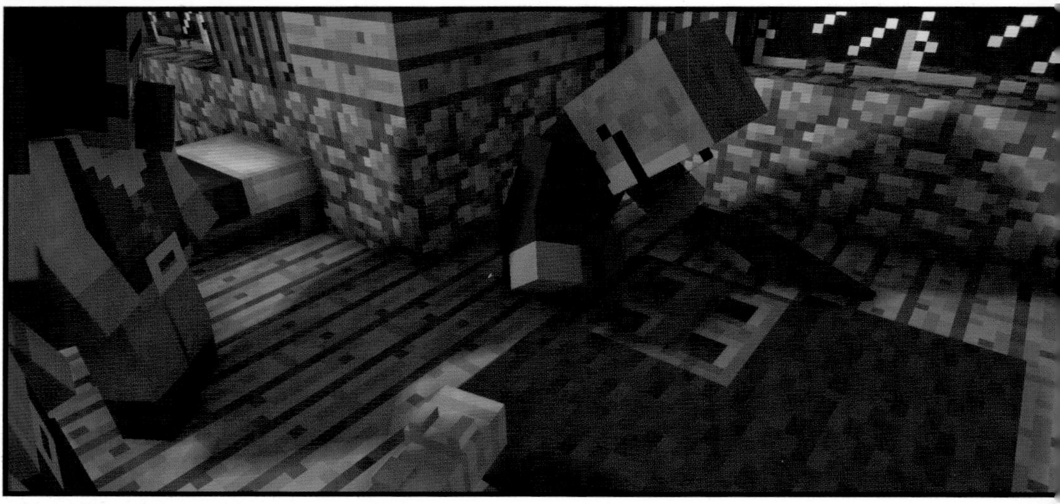

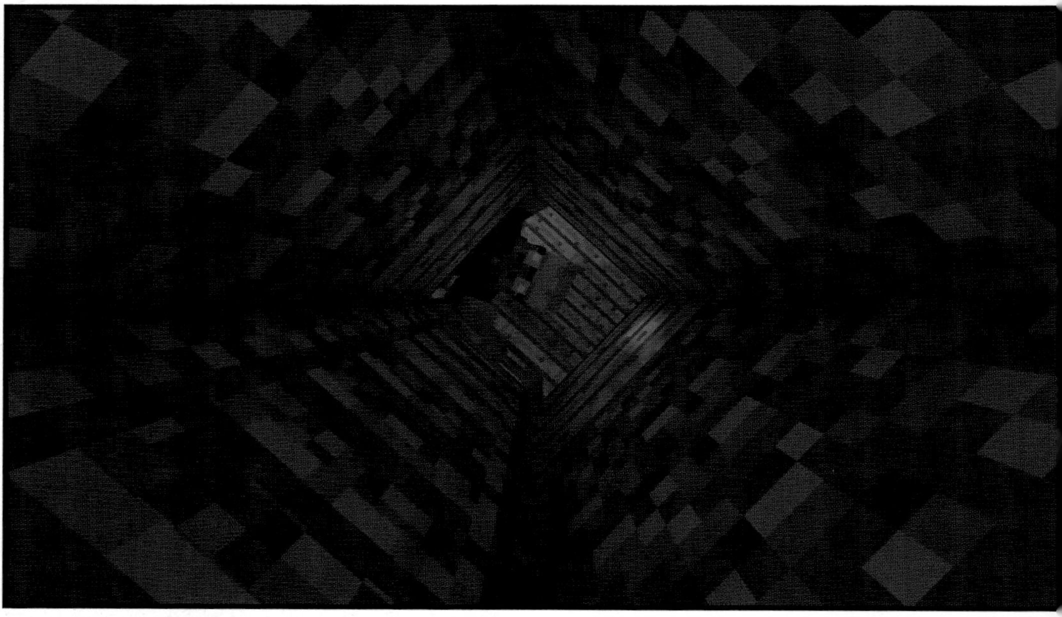

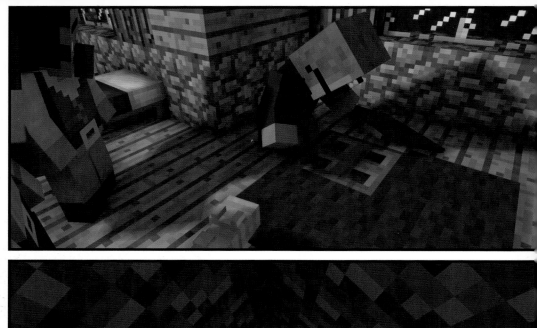

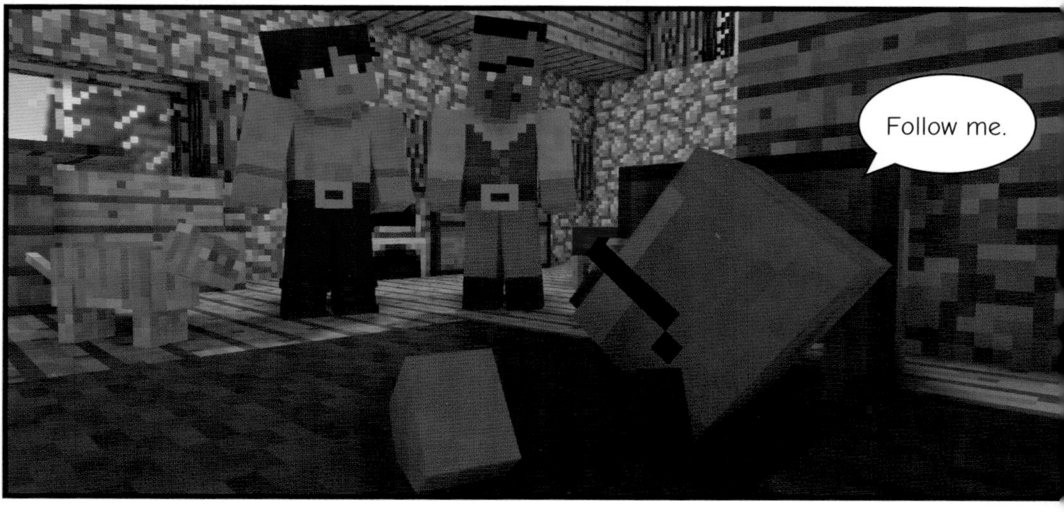
Follow me.

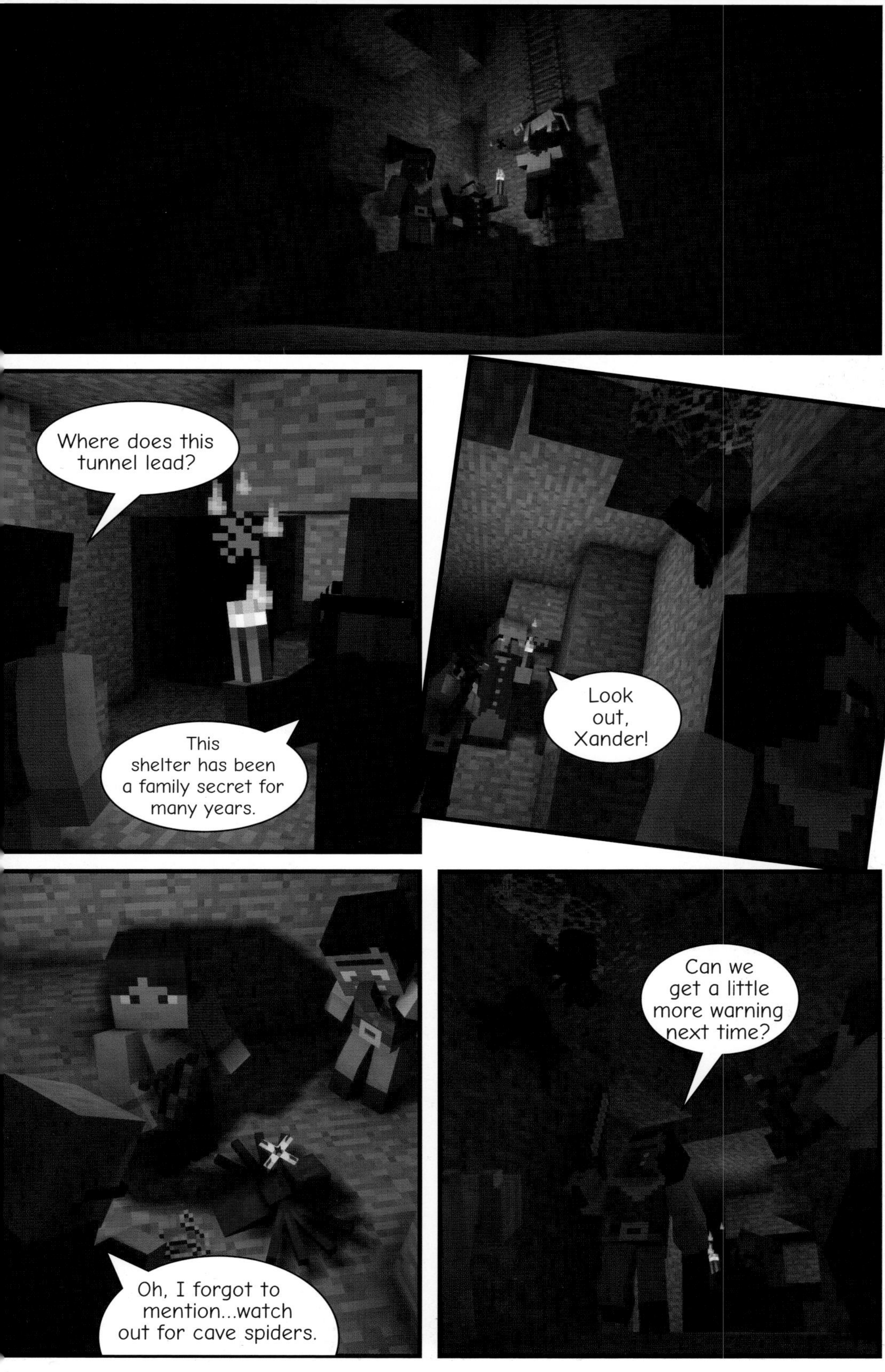
Where does this tunnel lead?
This shelter has been a family secret for many years.
Look out, Xander!
Oh, I forgot to mention...watch out for cave spiders.
Can we get a little more warning next time?

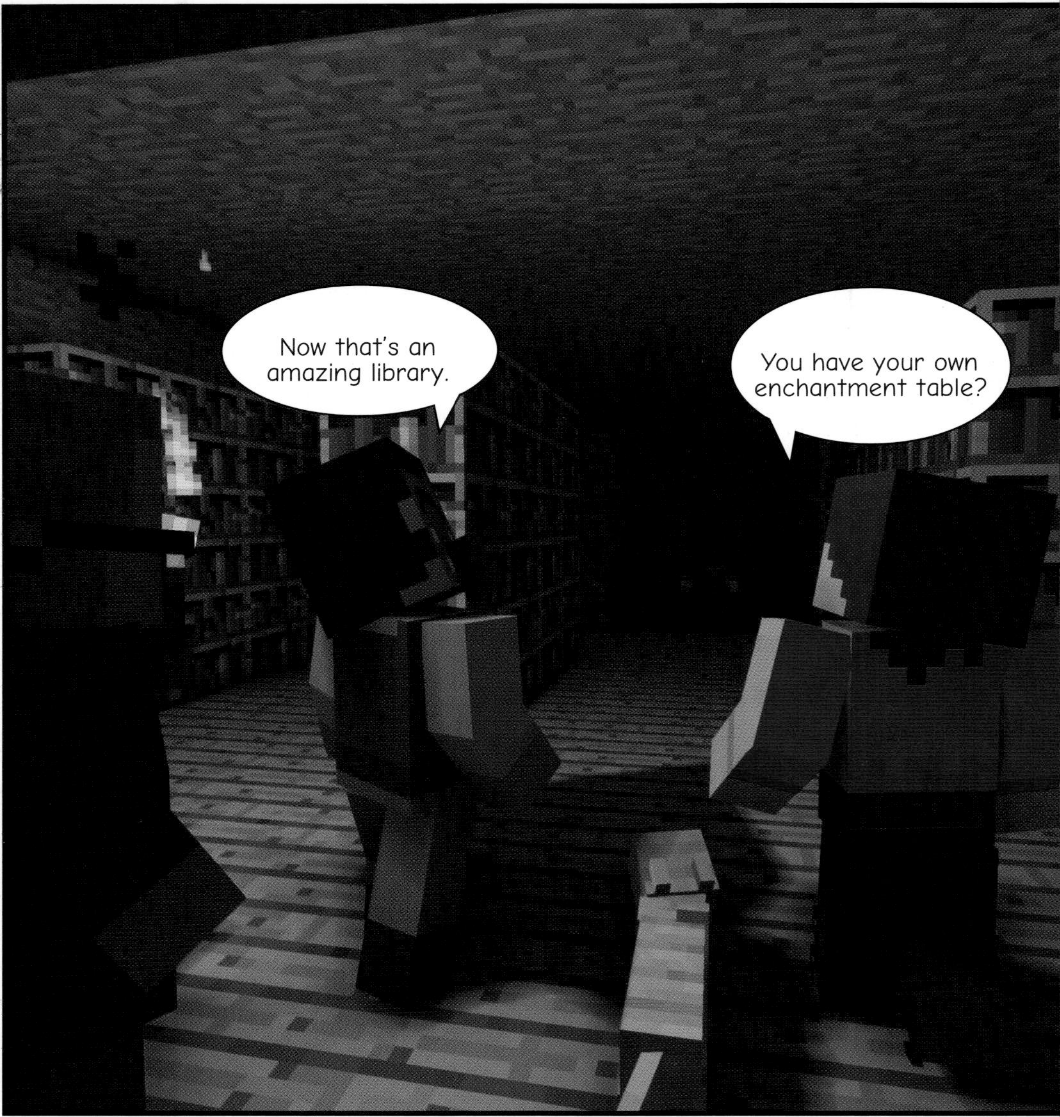
Now that's an amazing library.
You have your own enchantment table?

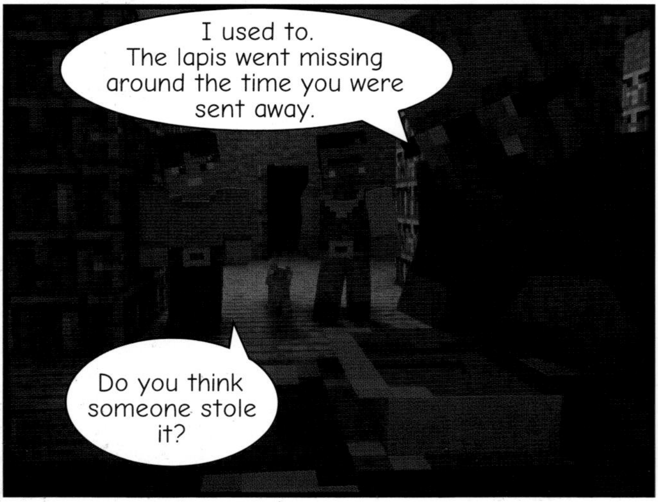
I used to.
The lapis went missing around the time you were sent away.
Do you think someone stole it?

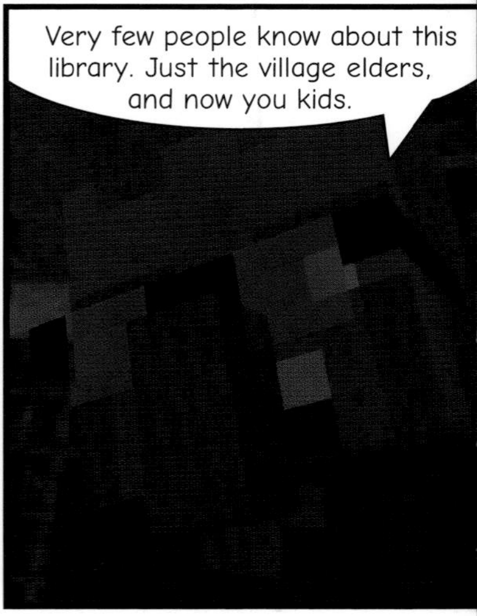
Very few people know about this library. Just the village elders, and now you kids.

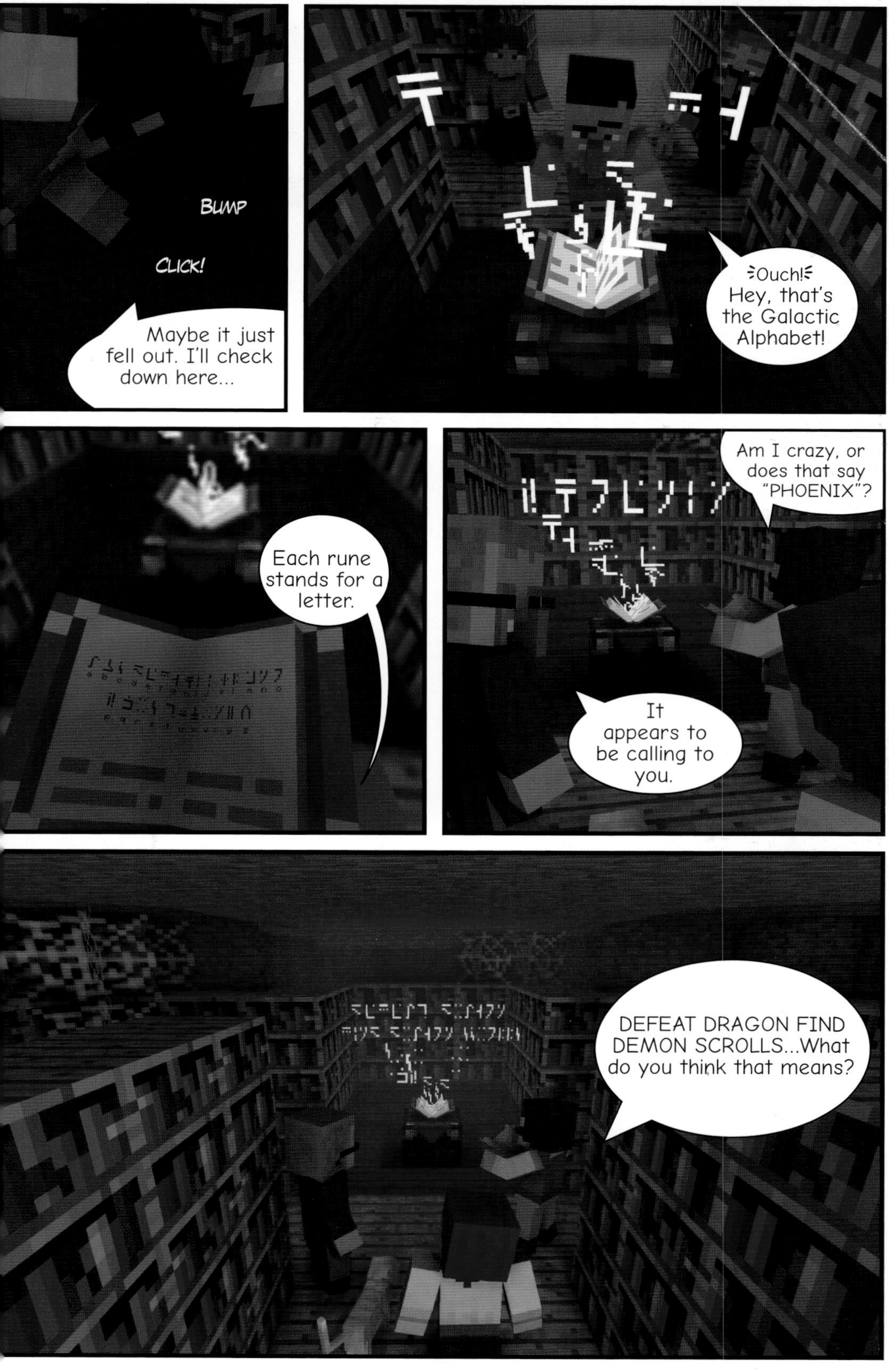
BUMP
CLICK!
Maybe it just fell out. I'll check down here...
Ouch! Hey, that's the Galactic Alphabet!
Each rune stands for a letter.
Am I crazy, or does that say "PHOENIX"?
It appears to be calling to you.
DEFEAT DRAGON FIND DEMON SCROLLS...What do you think that means?

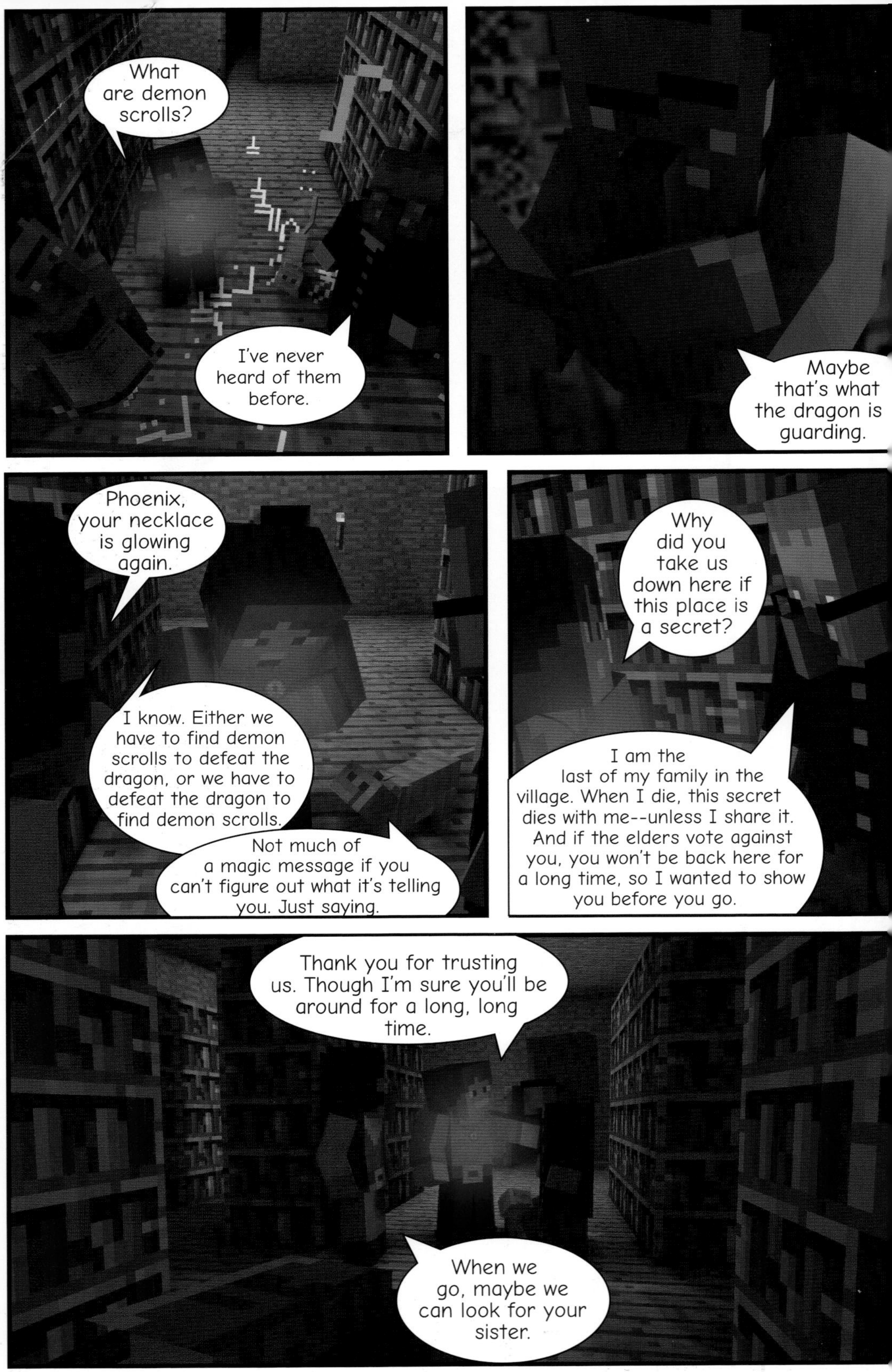
What are demon scrolls?
I've never heard of them before.
Maybe that's what the dragon is guarding.
Phoenix, your necklace is glowing again.
I know. Either we have to find demon scrolls to defeat the dragon, or we have to defeat the dragon to find demon scrolls.
Not much of a magic message if you can't figure out what it's telling you. Just saying.
Why did you take us down here if this place is a secret?
I am the last of my family in the village. When I die, this secret dies with me--unless I share it. And if the elders vote against you, you won't be back here for a long time, so I wanted to show you before you go.
Thank you for trusting us. Though I'm sure you'll be around for a long, long time.
When we go, maybe we can look for your sister.

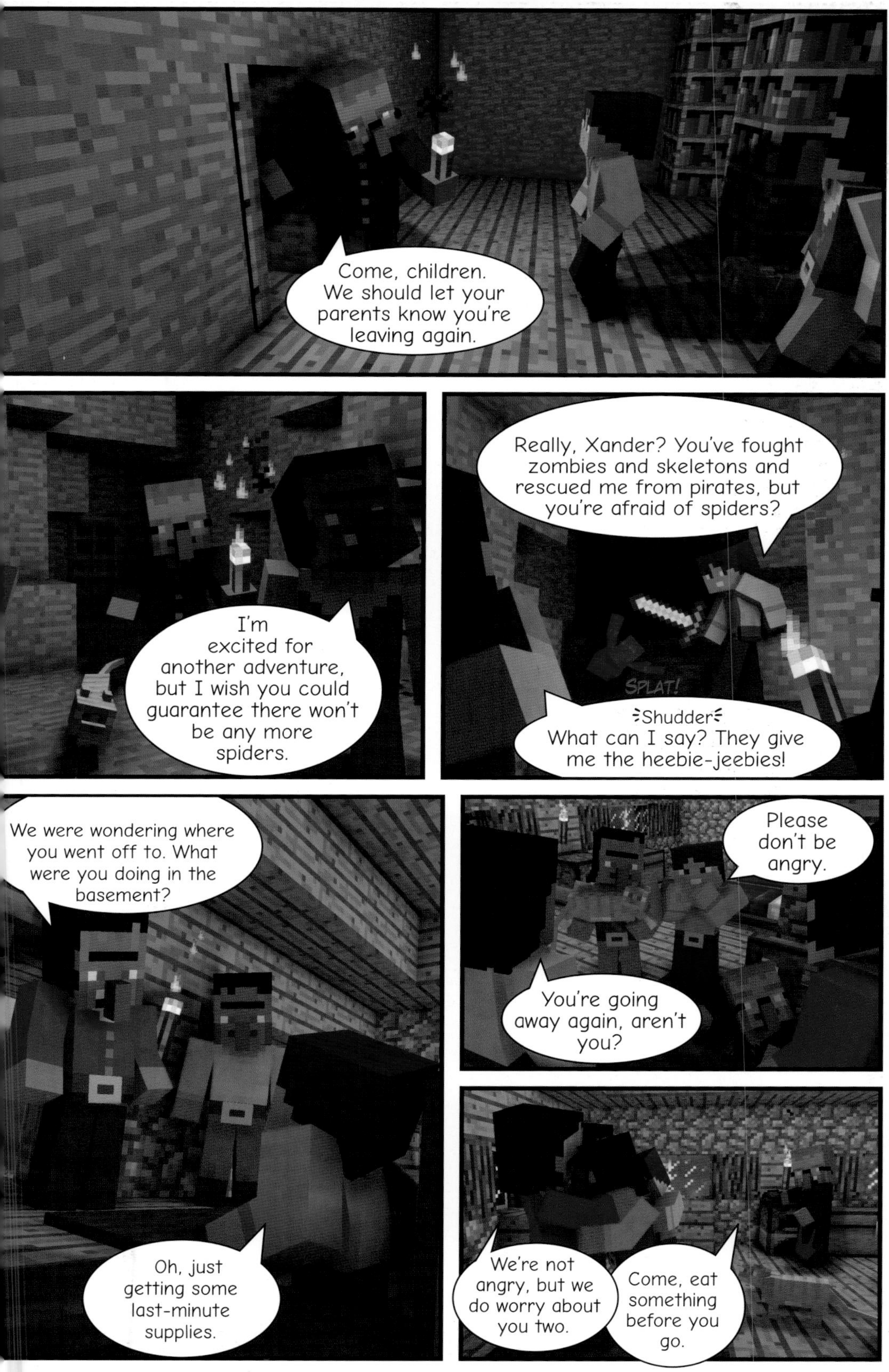
Come, children. We should let your parents know you're leaving again.
I'm excited for another adventure, but I wish you could guarantee there won't be any more spiders.
Really, Xander? You've fought zombies and skeletons and rescued me from pirates, but you're afraid of spiders?
SPLAT!
Shudder
What can I say? They give me the heebie-jeebies!
We were wondering where you went off to. What were you doing in the basement?
Oh, just getting some last-minute supplies.
Please don't be angry.
You're going away again, aren't you?
We're not angry, but we do worry about you two.
Come, eat something before you go.

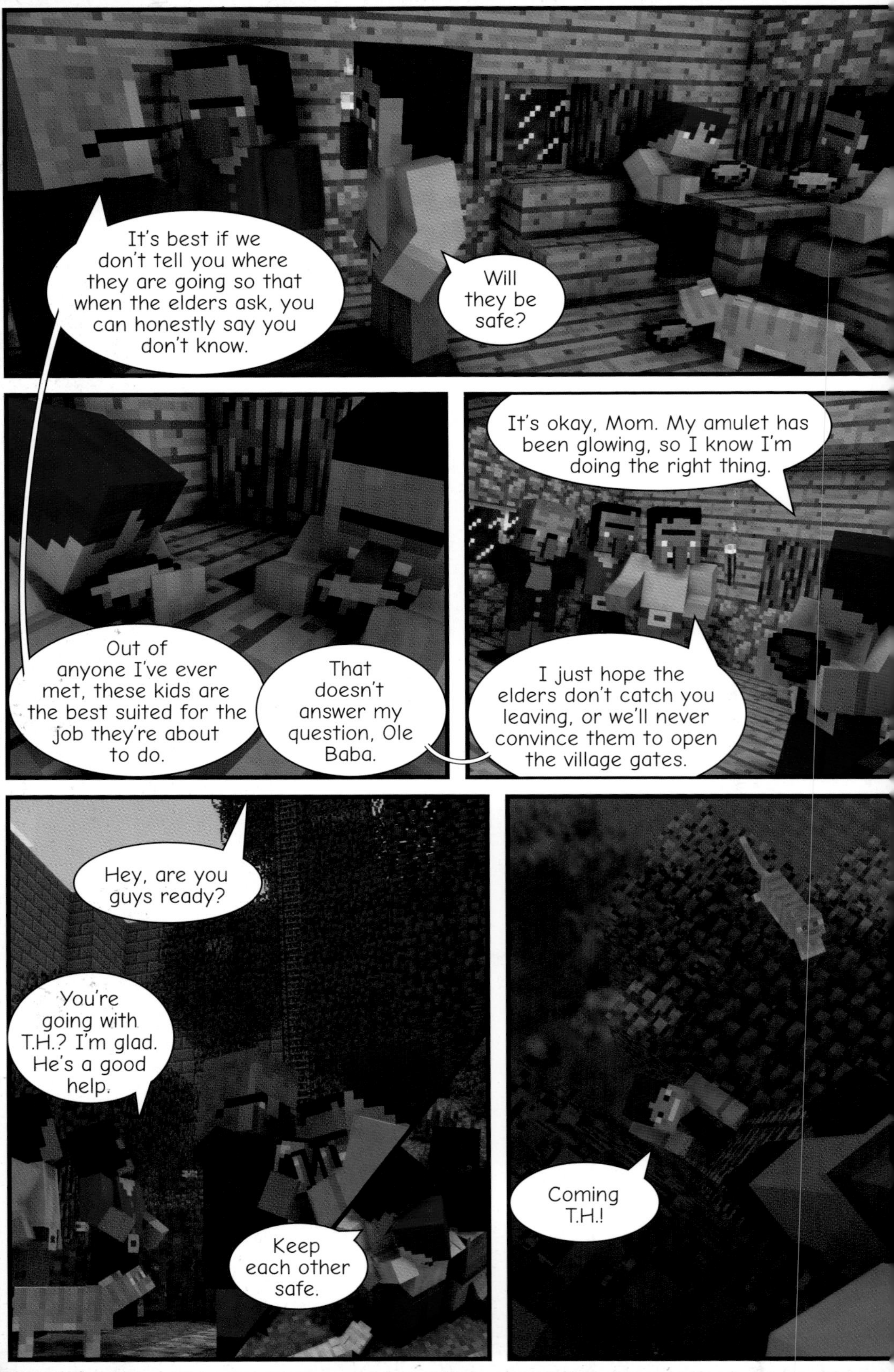

It's best if we don't tell you where they are going so that when the elders ask, you can honestly say you don't know.
Will they be safe?
Out of anyone I've ever met, these kids are the best suited for the job they're about to do.
That doesn't answer my question, Ole Baba.
It's okay, Mom. My amulet has been glowing, so I know I'm doing the right thing.
I just hope the elders don't catch you leaving, or we'll never convince them to open the village gates.
Hey, are you guys ready?
You're going with T.H.? I'm glad. He's a good help.
Keep each other safe.
Coming T.H.!

CHAPTER 3

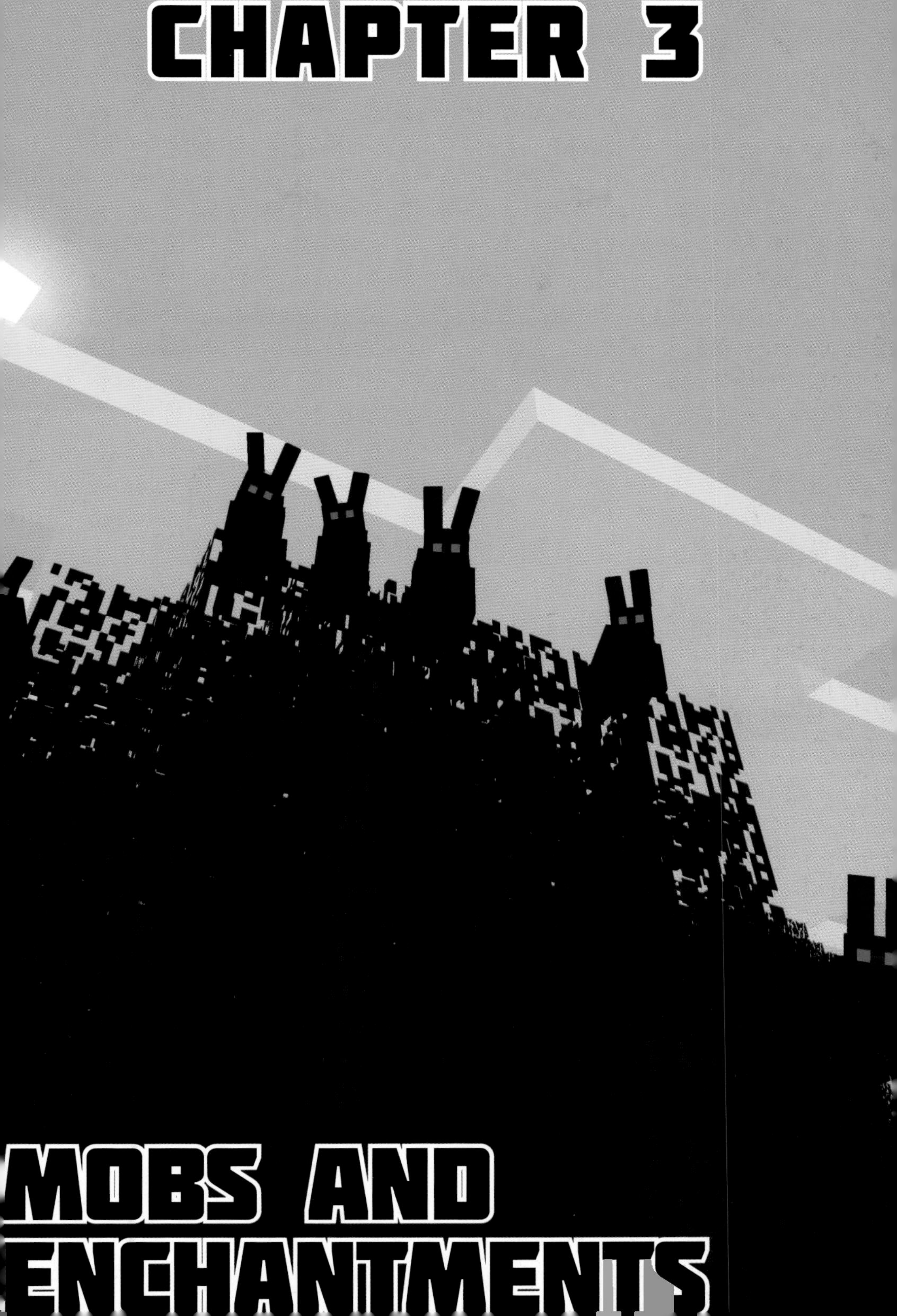

MOBS AND ENCHANTMENTS

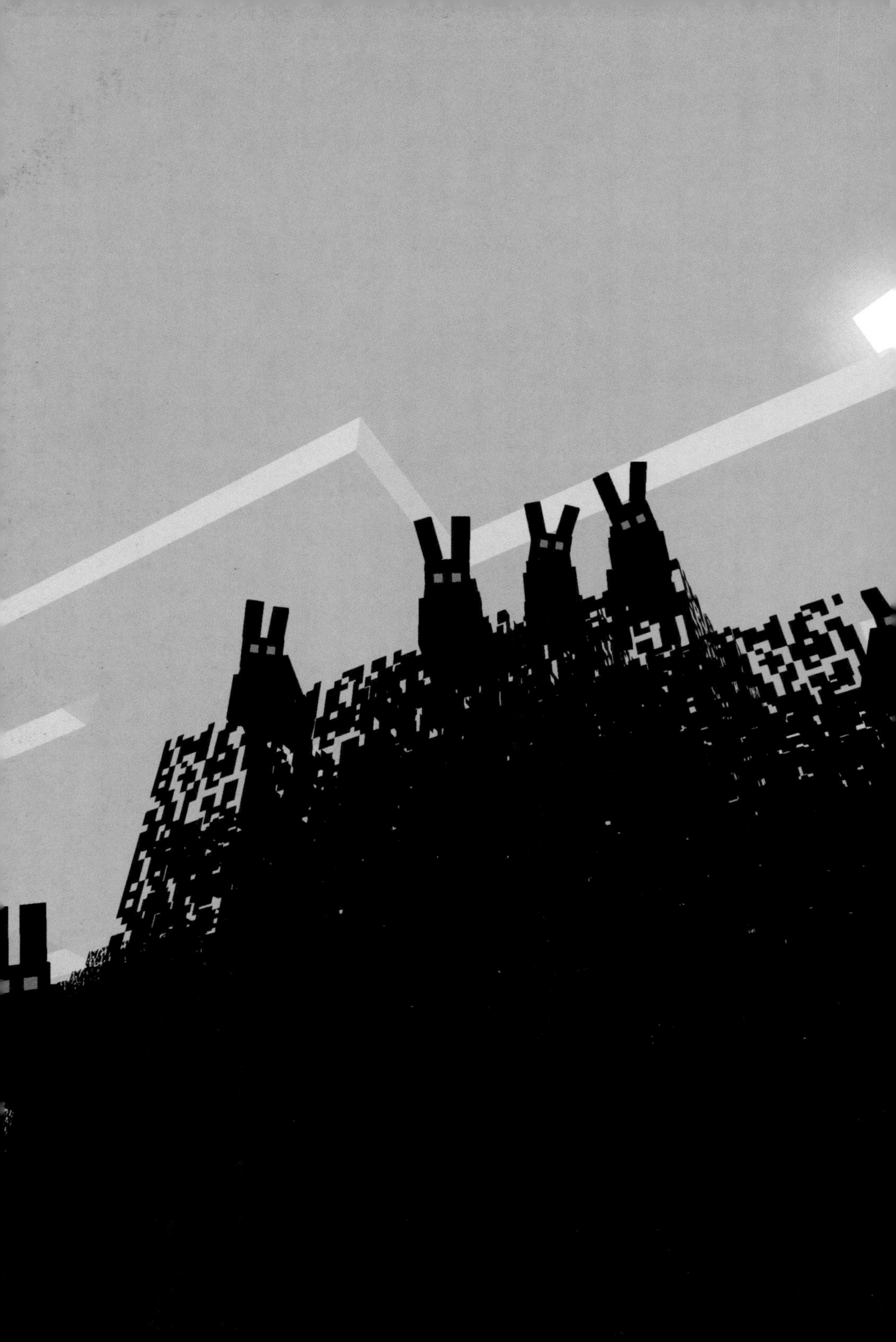

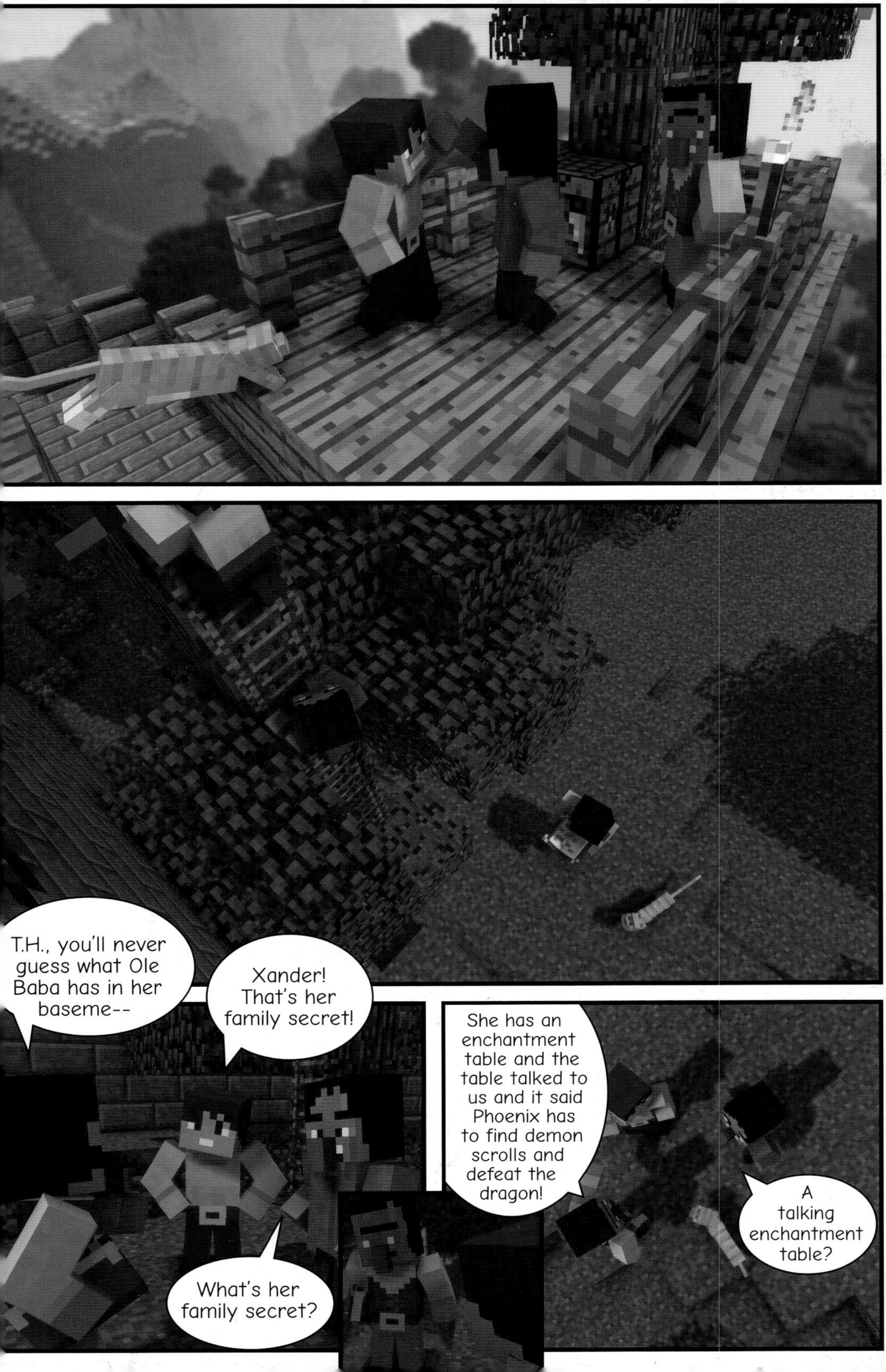
T.H., you'll never guess what Ole Baba has in her baseme--
Xander! That's her family secret!
What's her family secret?
She has an enchantment table and the table talked to us and it said Phoenix has to find demon scrolls and defeat the dragon!
A talking enchantment table?

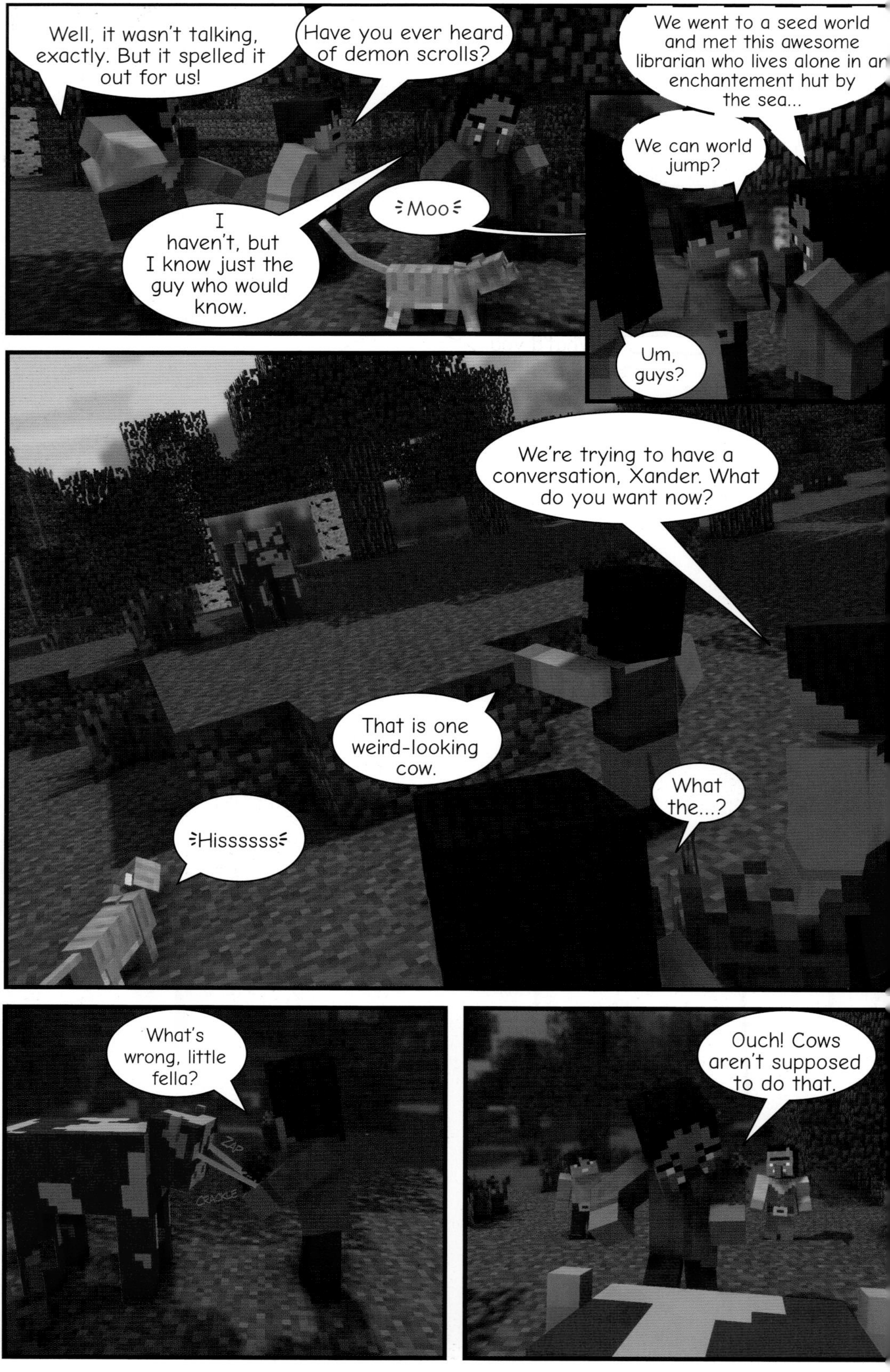
Well, it wasn't talking, exactly. But it spelled it out for us!
Have you ever heard of demon scrolls?
I haven't, but I know just the guy who would know.
Moo
We went to a seed world and met this awesome librarian who lives alone in an enchantement hut by the sea...
We can world jump?
Um, guys?
We're trying to have a conversation, Xander. What do you want now?
That is one weird-looking cow.
What the...?
Hisssssss
What's wrong, little fella?
ZAP
CRACKLE
Ouch! Cows aren't supposed to do that.

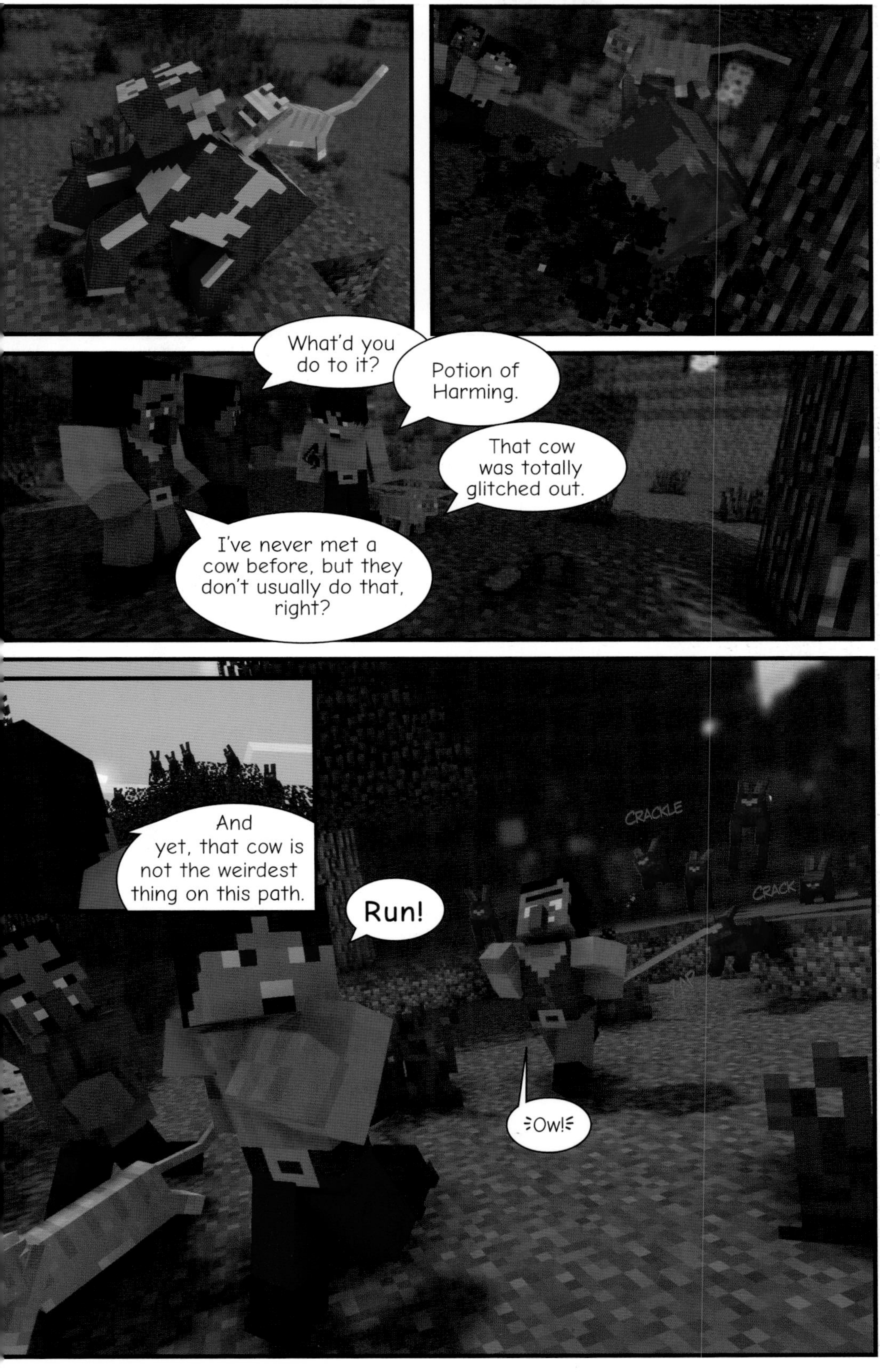
What'd you do to it?
Potion of Harming.
That cow was totally glitched out.
I've never met a cow before, but they don't usually do that, right?
And yet, that cow is not the weirdest thing on this path.
Run!
CRACKLE
CRACK
Ow!

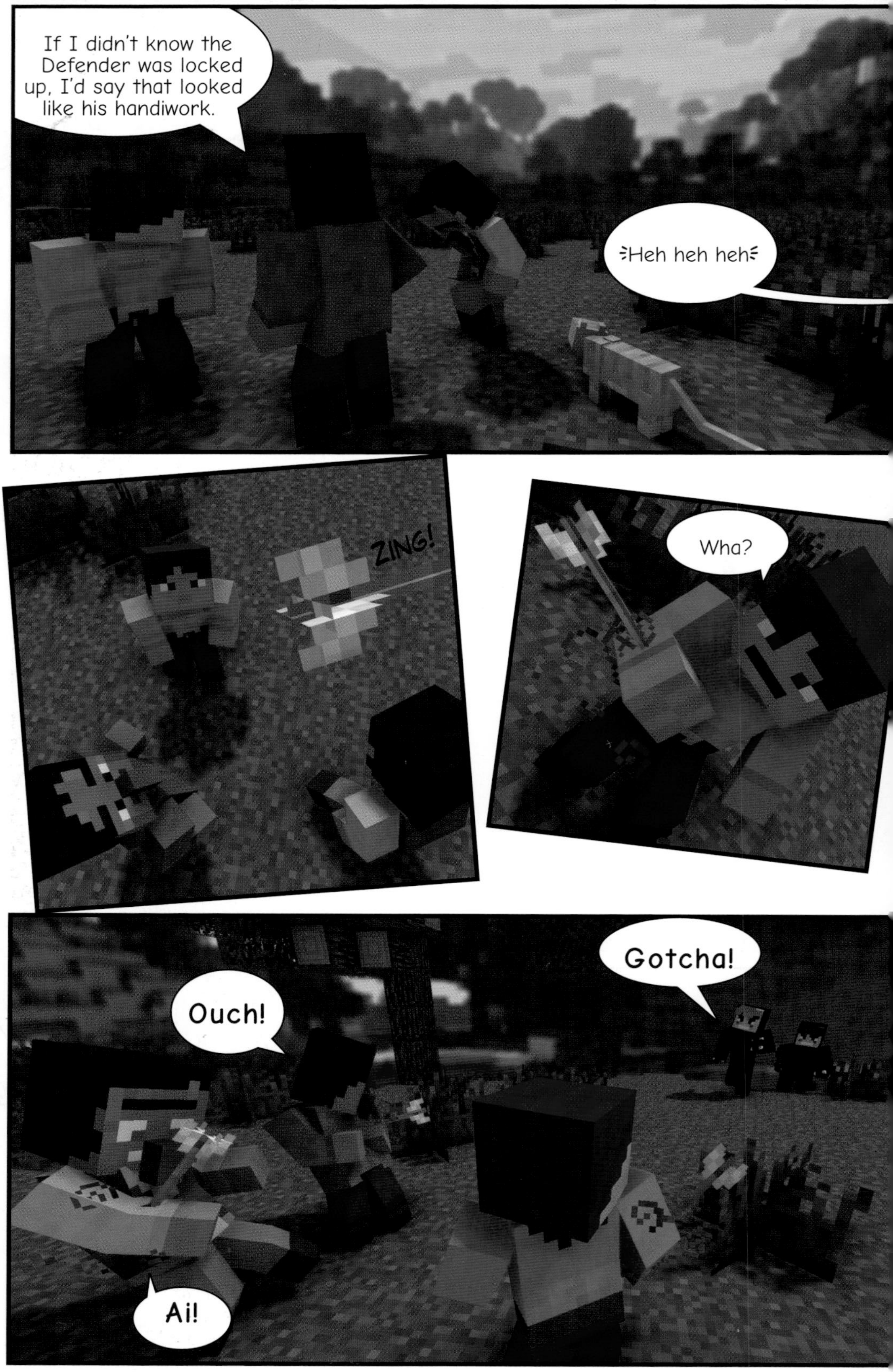
If I didn't know the Defender was locked up, I'd say that looked like his handiwork.
Heh heh heh
ZING!
Wha?
Ouch!
Gotcha!
Ai!

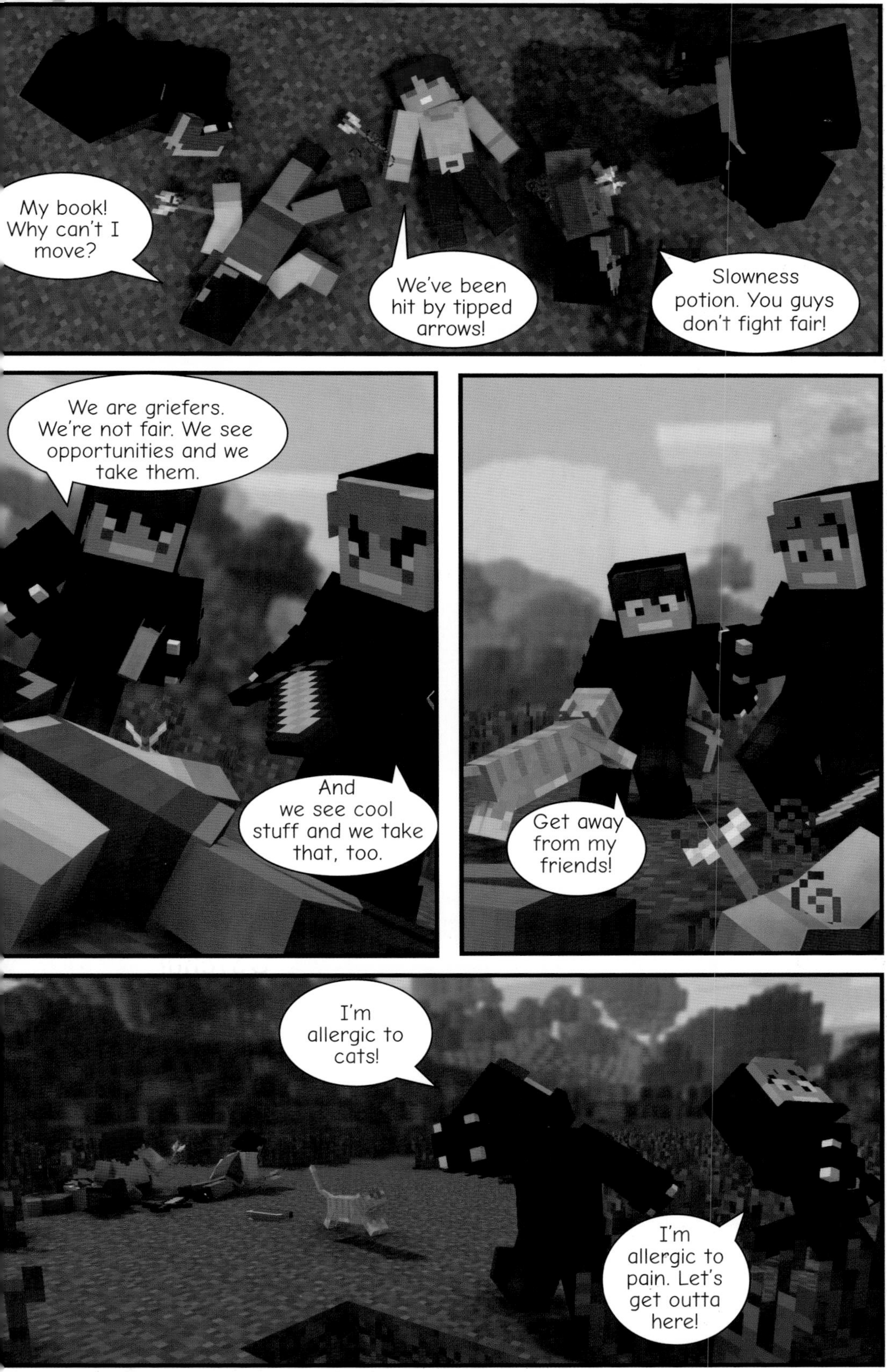
My book! Why can't I move?
We've been hit by tipped arrows!
Slowness potion. You guys don't fight fair!
We are griefers. We're not fair. We see opportunities and we take them.
And we see cool stuff and we take that, too.
Get away from my friends!
I'm allergic to cats!
I'm allergic to pain. Let's get outta here!

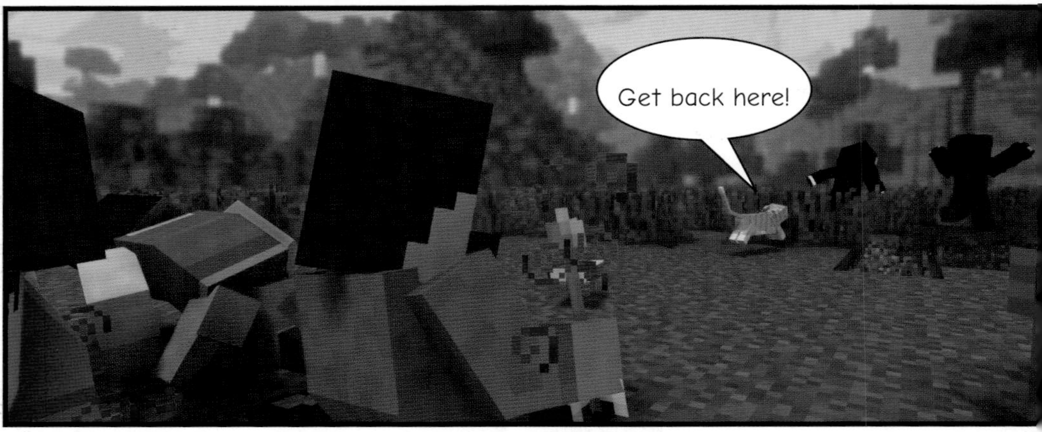
Get back here!

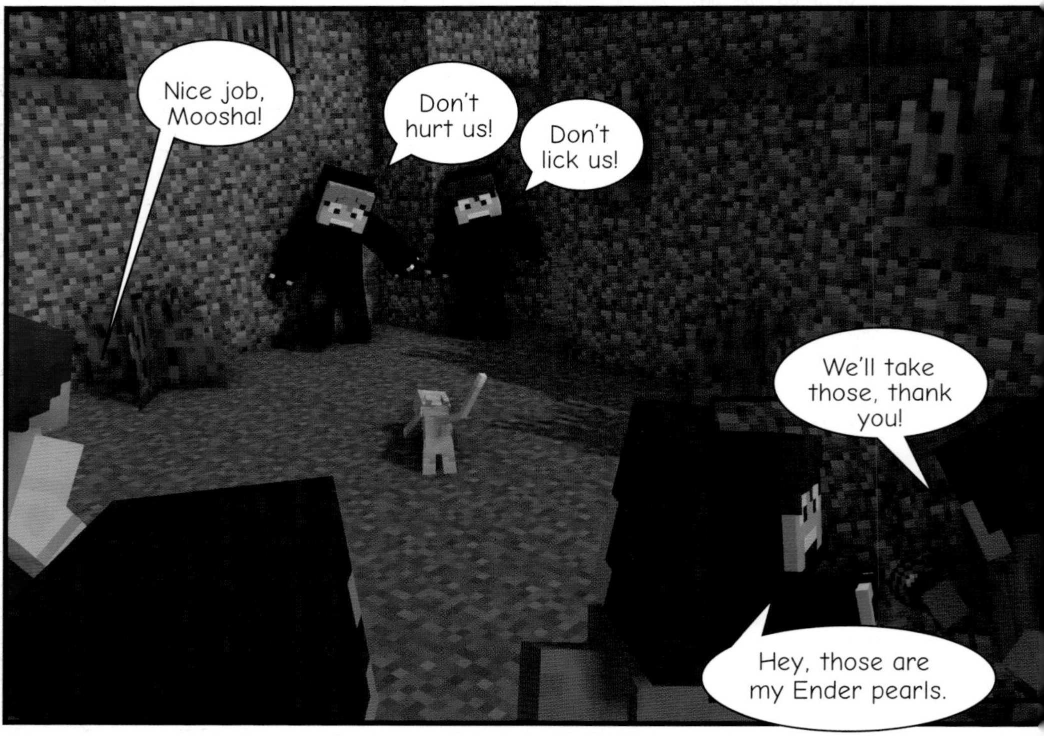
Nice job, Moosha!
Don't hurt us!
Don't lick us!
We'll take those, thank you!
Hey, those are my Ender pearls.

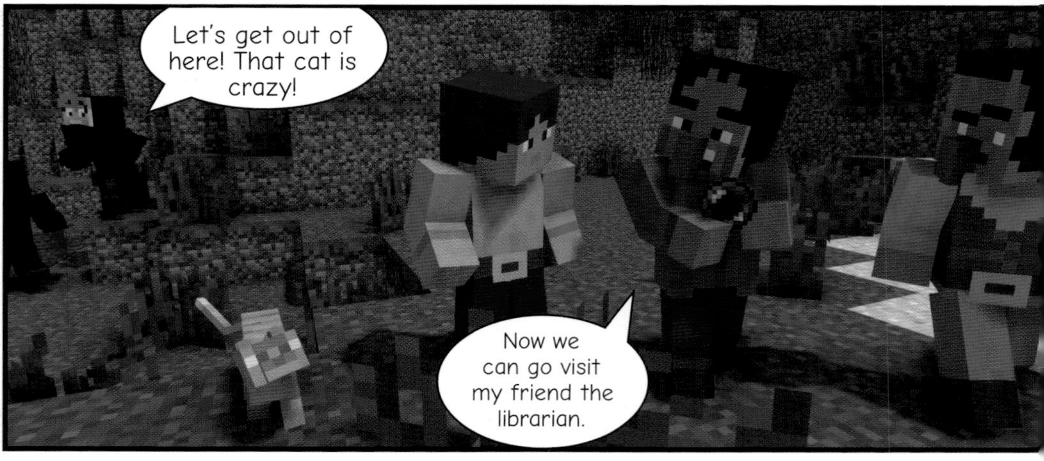
Let's get out of here! That cat is crazy!
Now we can go visit my friend the librarian.

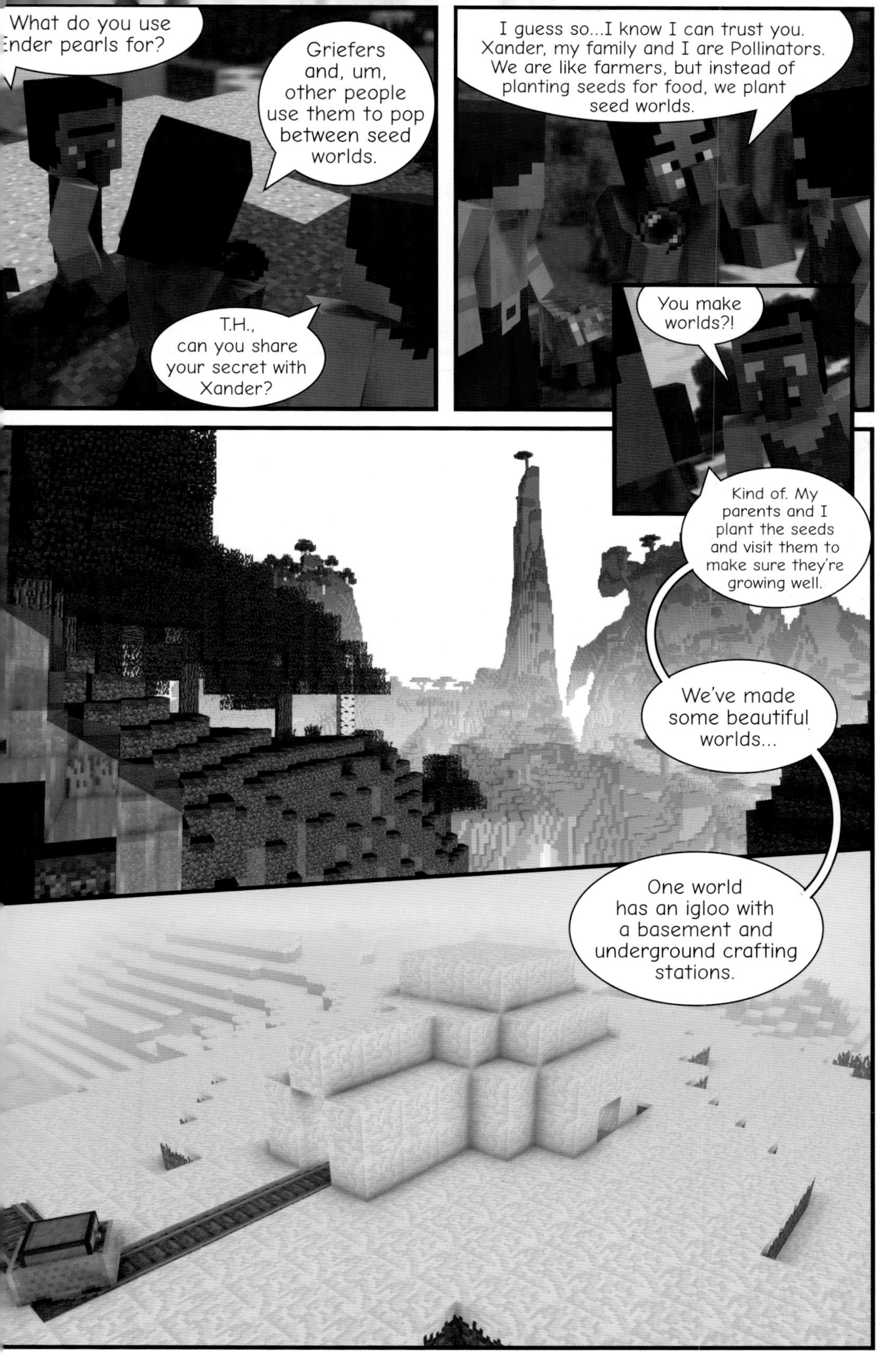
What do you use Ender pearls for?
Griefers and, um, other people use them to pop between seed worlds.
T.H., can you share your secret with Xander?
I guess so...I know I can trust you. Xander, my family and I are Pollinators. We are like farmers, but instead of planting seeds for food, we plant seed worlds.
You make worlds?!
Kind of. My parents and I plant the seeds and visit them to make sure they're growing well.
We've made some beautiful worlds...
One world has an igloo with a basement and underground crafting stations.

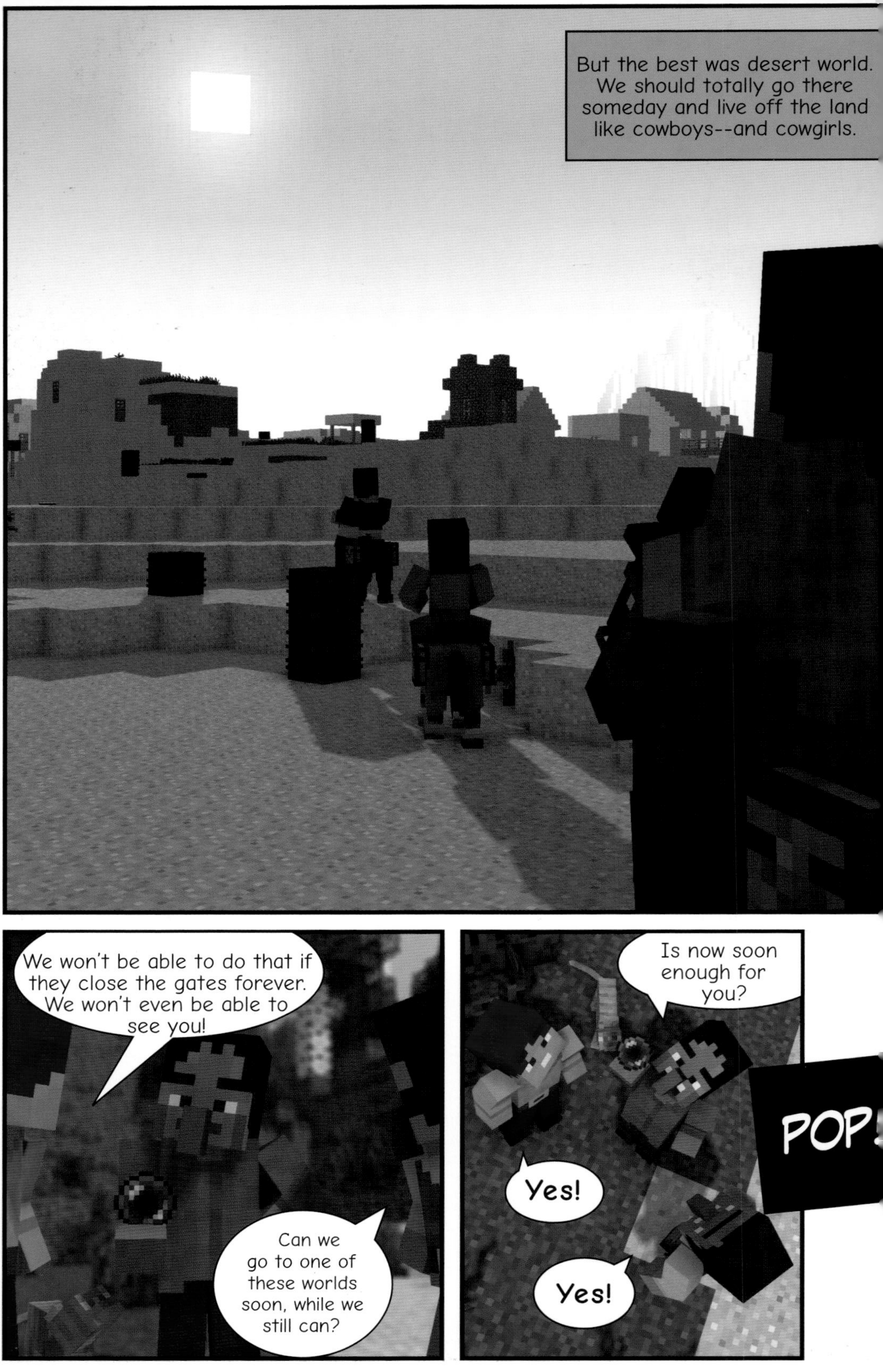
But the best was desert world. We should totally go there someday and live off the land like cowboys--and cowgirls.
We won't be able to do that if they close the gates forever. We won't even be able to see you!
Can we go to one of these worlds soon, while we still can?
Is now soon enough for you?
Yes!
Yes!
POP!

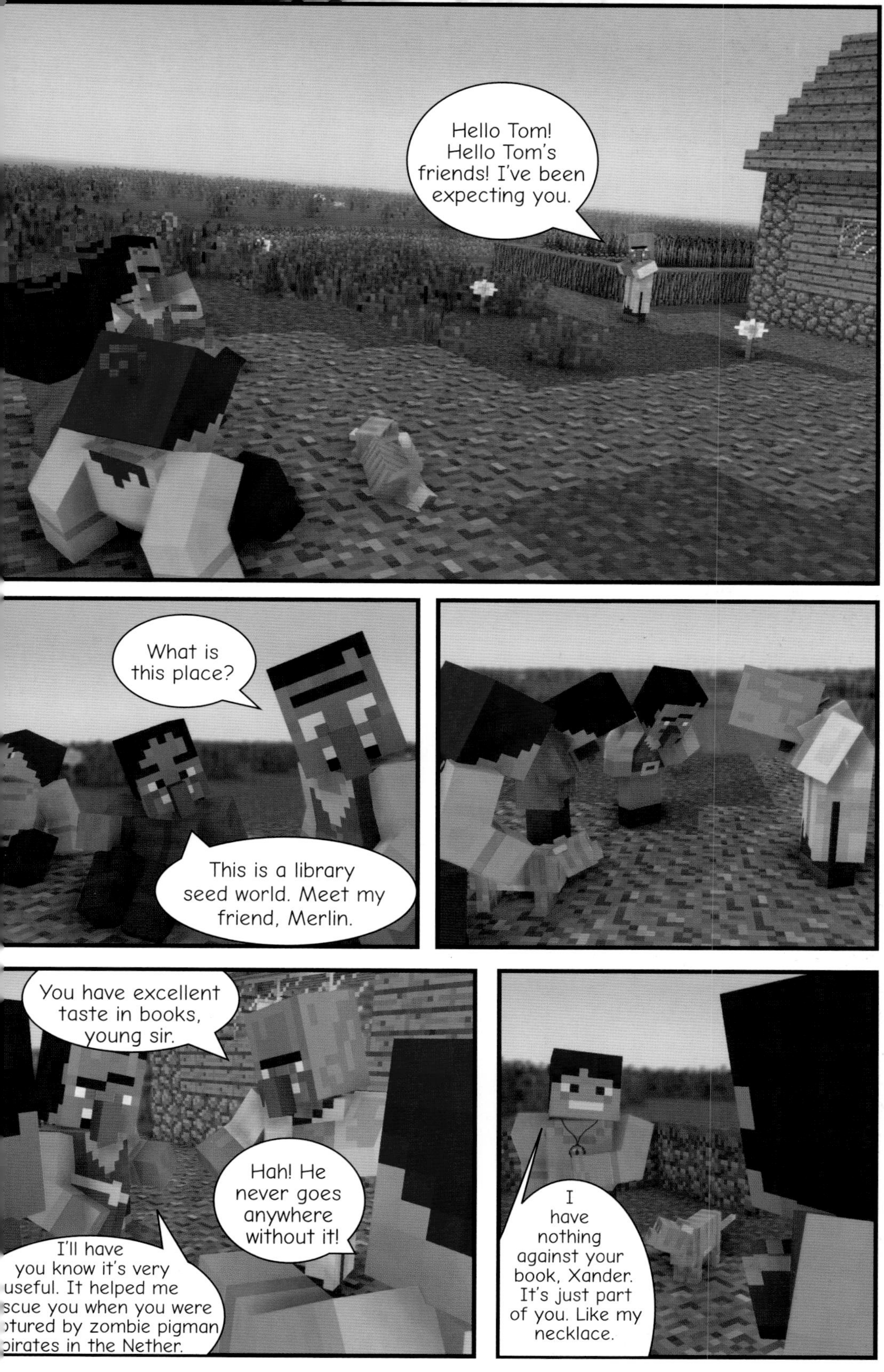
Hello Tom! Hello Tom's friends! I've been expecting you.
What is this place?
This is a library seed world. Meet my friend, Merlin.
You have excellent taste in books, young sir.
Hah! He never goes anywhere without it!
I'll have you know it's very useful. It helped me scue you when you were tured by zombie pigman irates in the Nether.
I have nothing against your book, Xander. It's just part of you. Like my necklace.

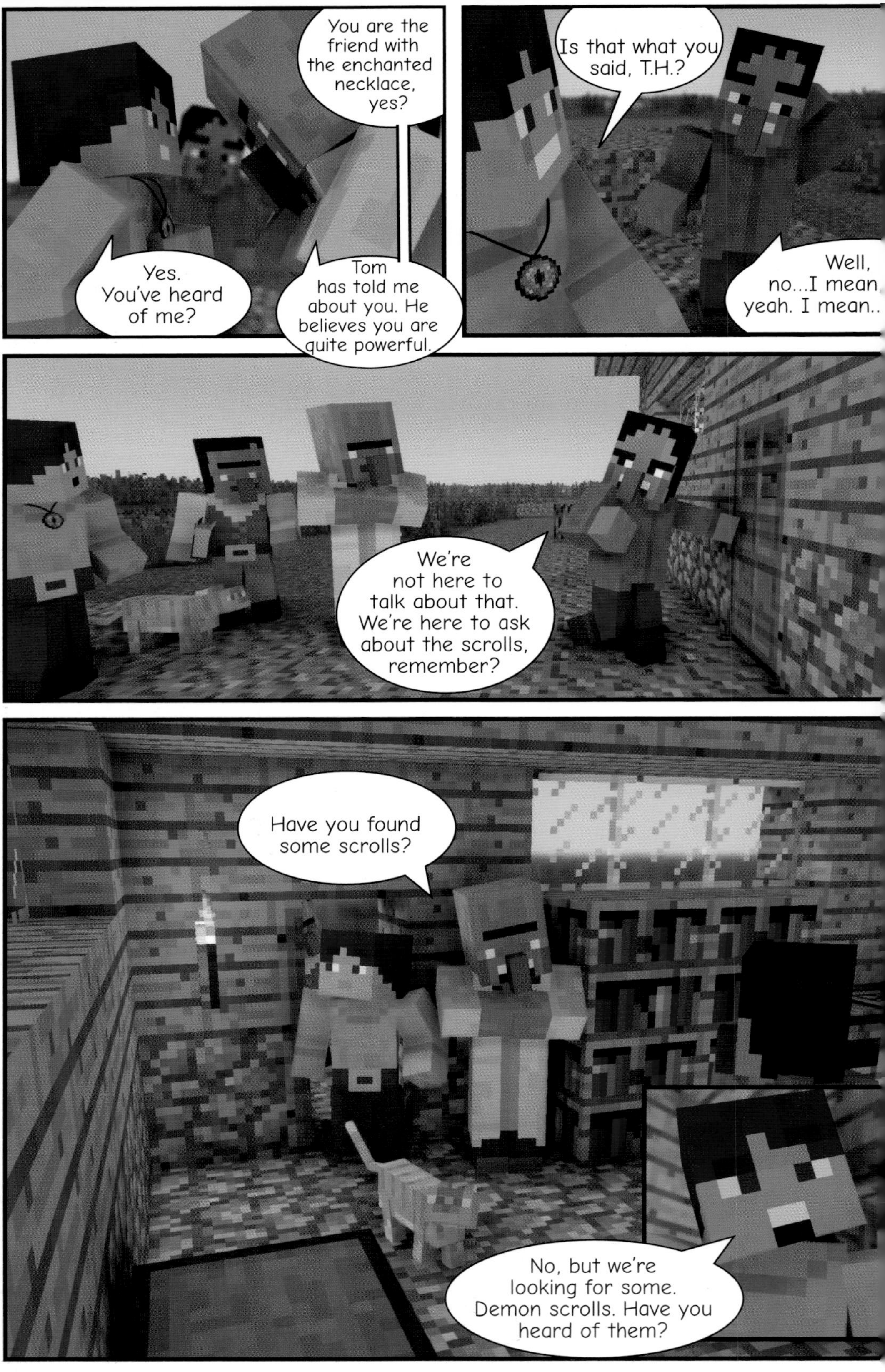
You are the friend with the enchanted necklace, yes?
Yes. You've heard of me?
Tom has told me about you. He believes you are quite powerful.
Is that what you said, T.H.?
Well, no...I mean yeah. I mean..
We're not here to talk about that. We're here to ask about the scrolls, remember?
Have you found some scrolls?
No, but we're looking for some. Demon scrolls. Have you heard of them?

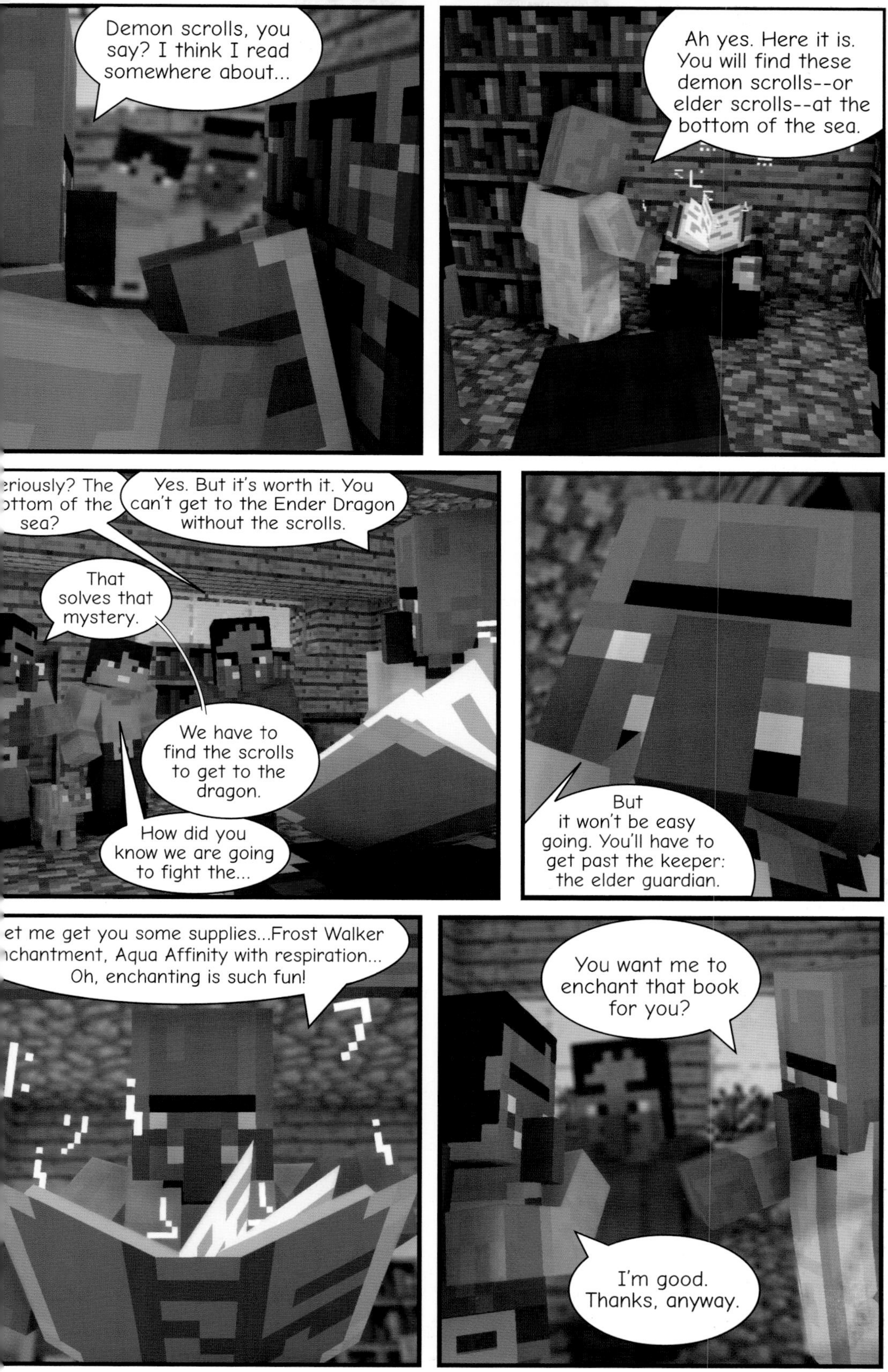
Demon scrolls, you say? I think I read somewhere about...
Ah yes. Here it is. You will find these demon scrolls--or elder scrolls--at the bottom of the sea.
eriously? The ottom of the sea?
Yes. But it's worth it. You can't get to the Ender Dragon without the scrolls.
That solves that mystery.
We have to find the scrolls to get to the dragon.
How did you know we are going to fight the...
But it won't be easy going. You'll have to get past the keeper: the elder guardian.
et me get you some supplies...Frost Walker nchantment, Aqua Affinity with respiration... Oh, enchanting is such fun!
You want me to enchant that book for you?
I'm good. Thanks, anyway.

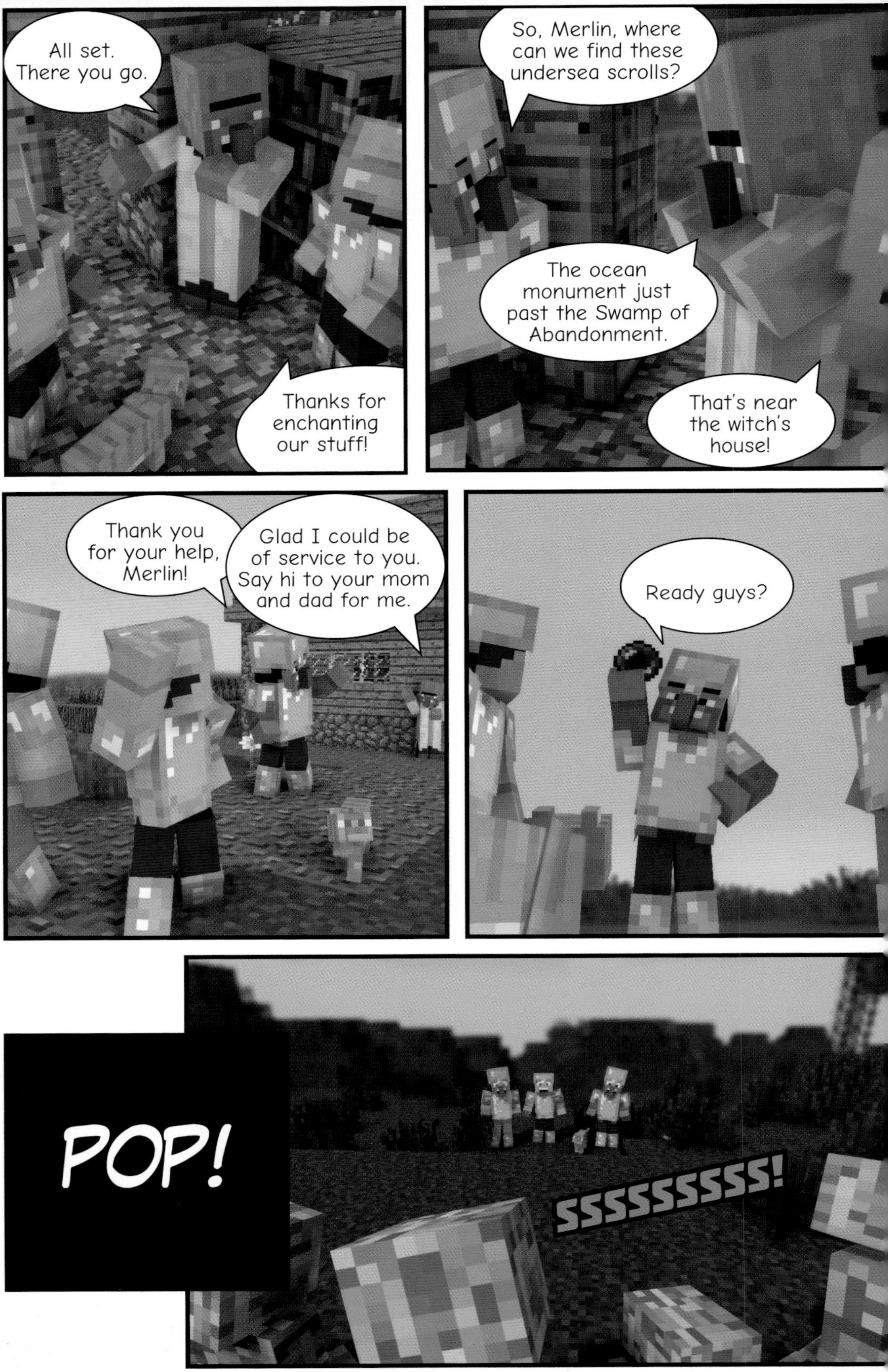
All set. There you go.
Thanks for enchanting our stuff!
So, Merlin, where can we find these undersea scrolls?
The ocean monument just past the Swamp of Abandonment.
That's near the witch's house!
Thank you for your help, Merlin!
Glad I could be of service to you. Say hi to your mom and dad for me.
Ready guys?
POP!
SSSSSSSSS!

CHAPTER 4

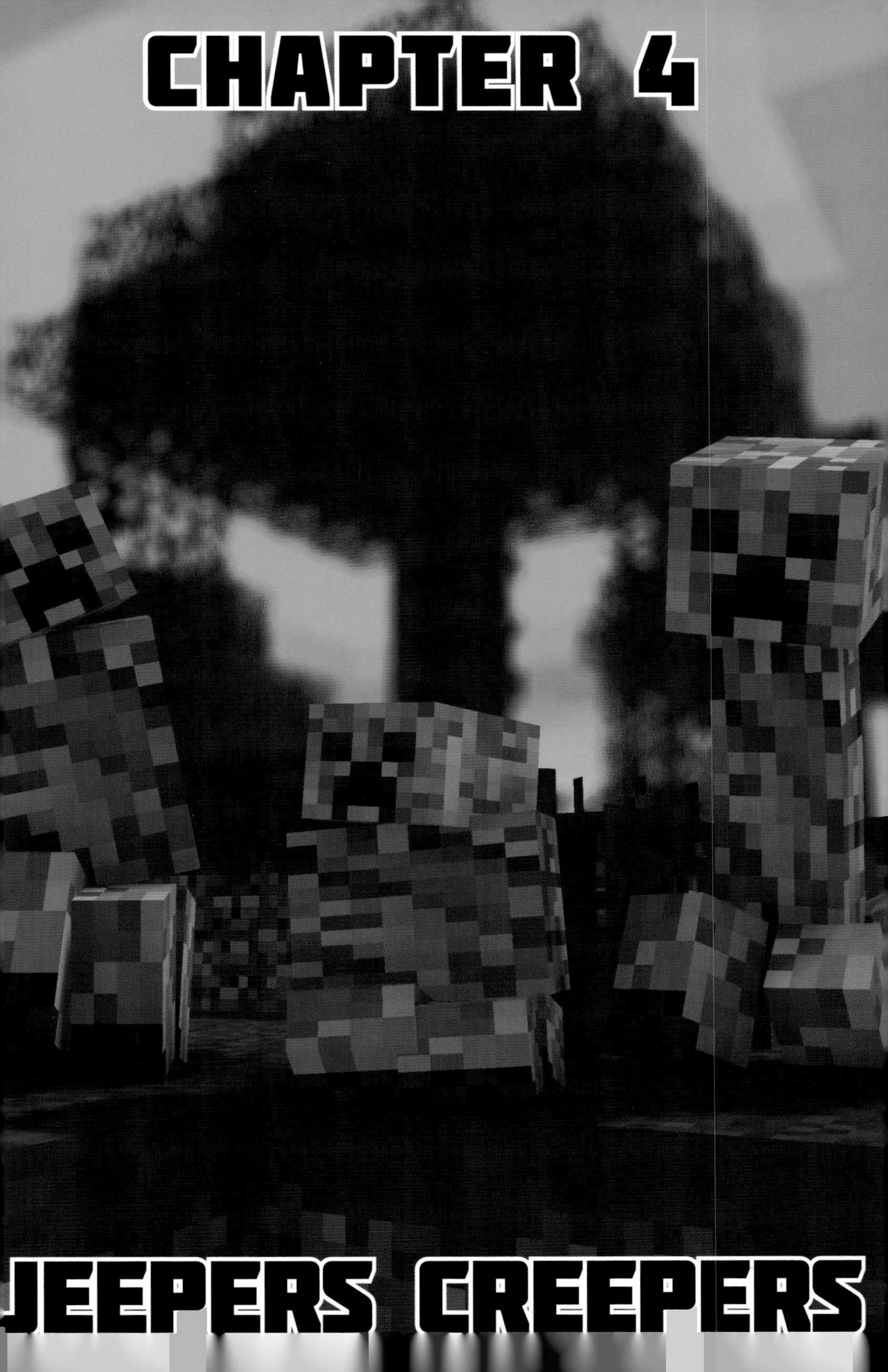

JEEPERS CREEPERS

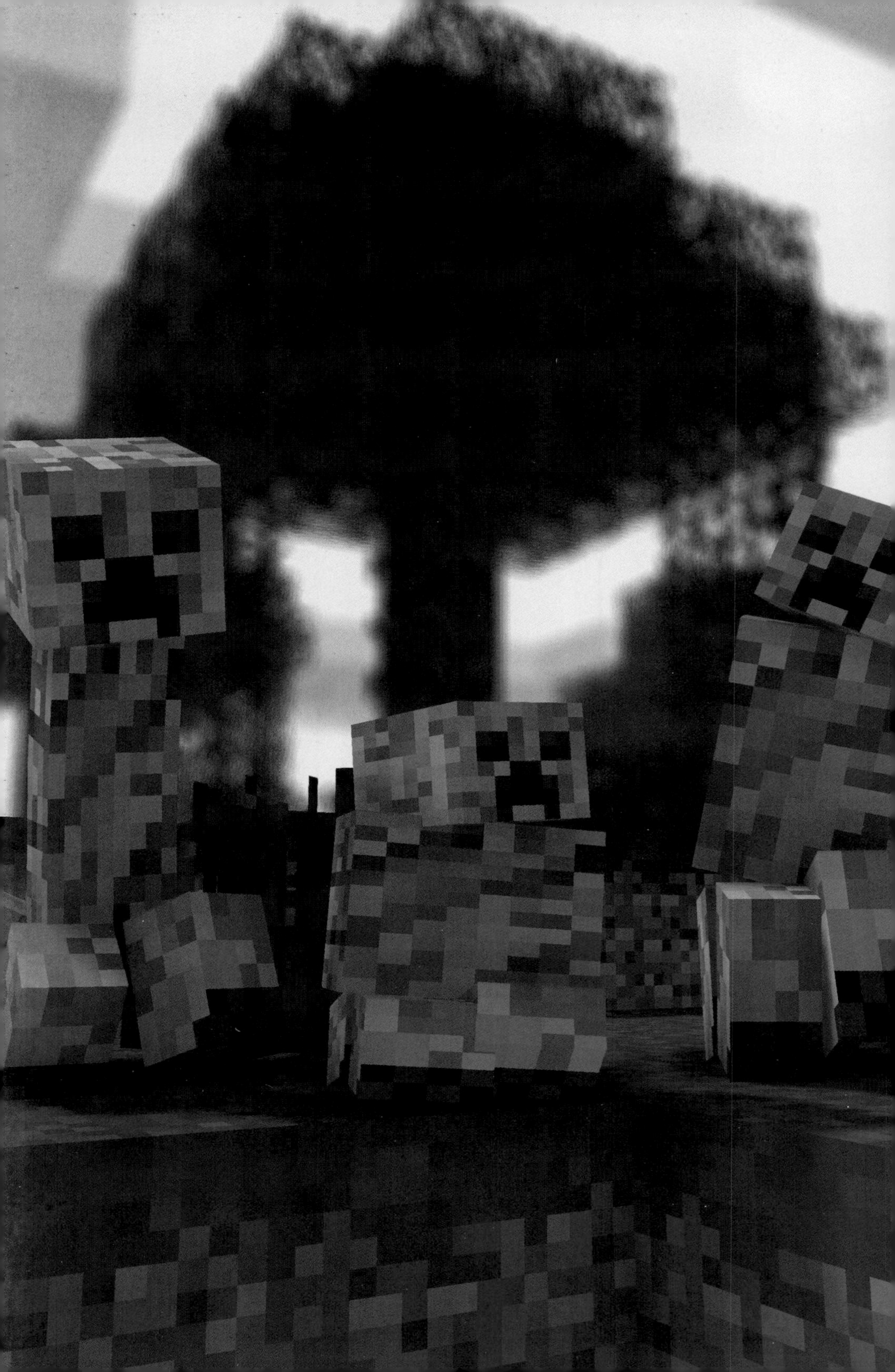

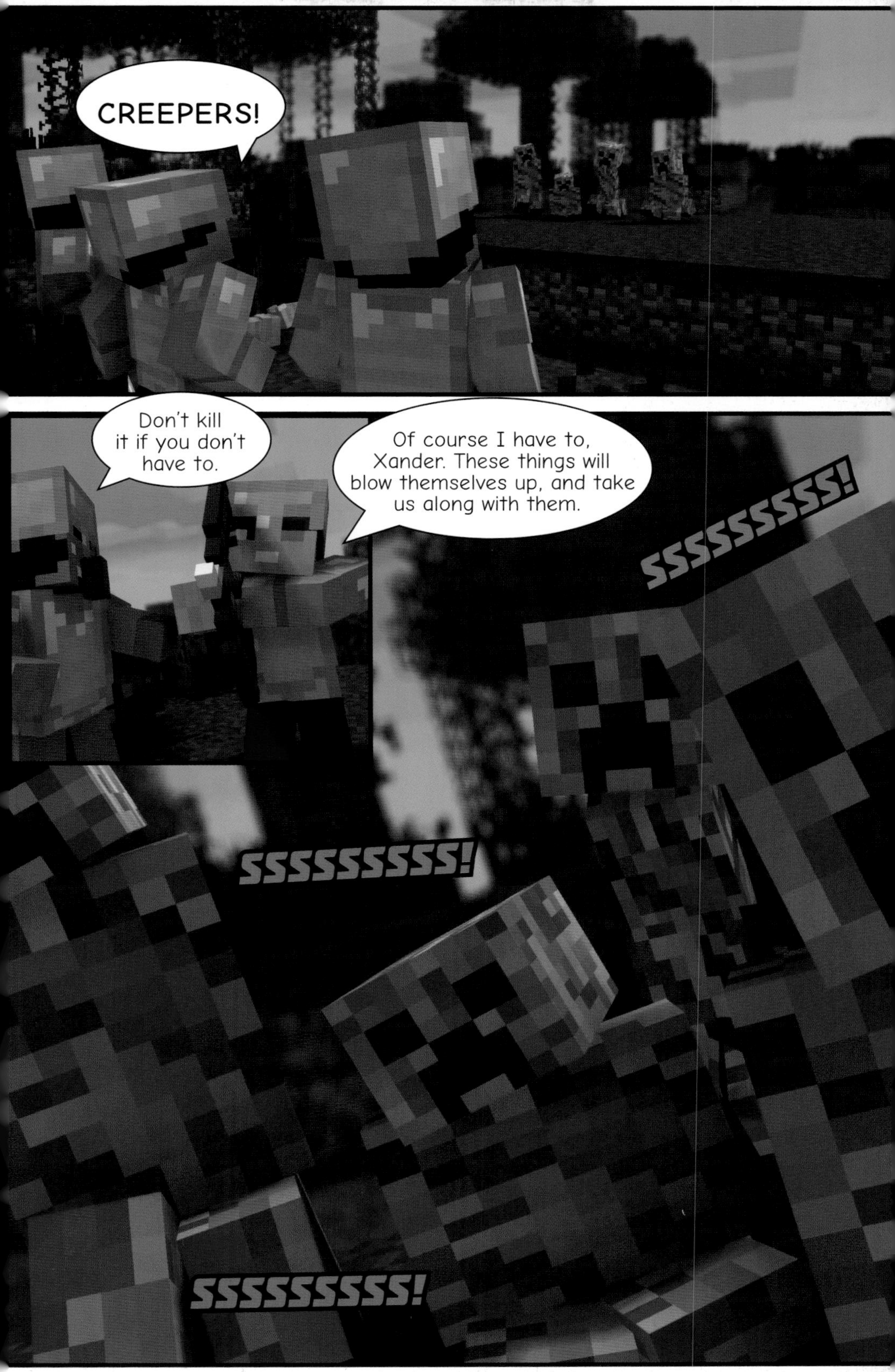
CREEPERS!
Don't kill it if you don't have to.
Of course I have to, Xander. These things will blow themselves up, and take us along with them.
SSSSSSSSS!
SSSSSSSSS!
SSSSSSSSS!

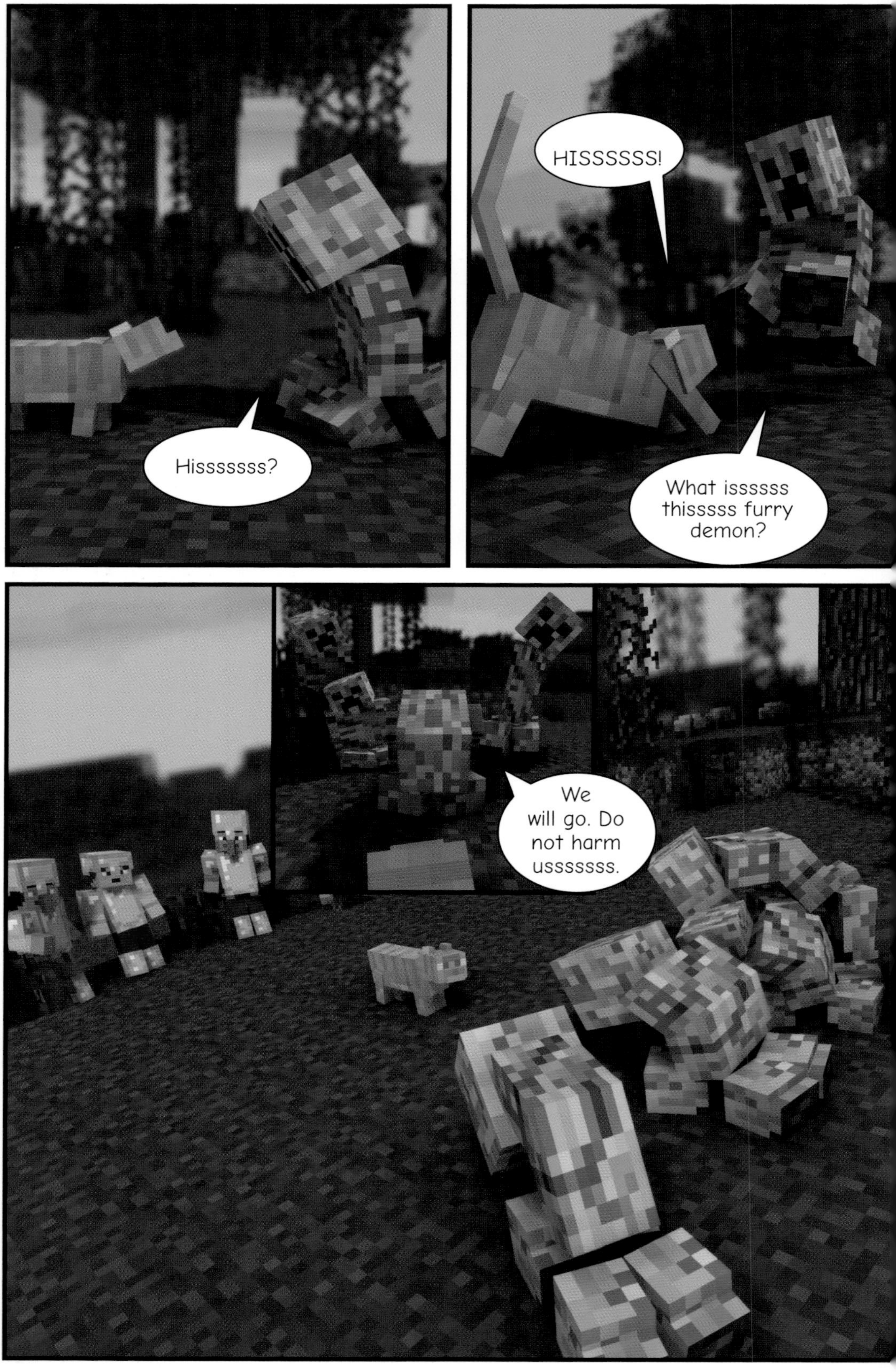
Hisssssss?
HISSSSSS!
What issssss thisssss furry demon?
We will go. Do not harm usssssss.

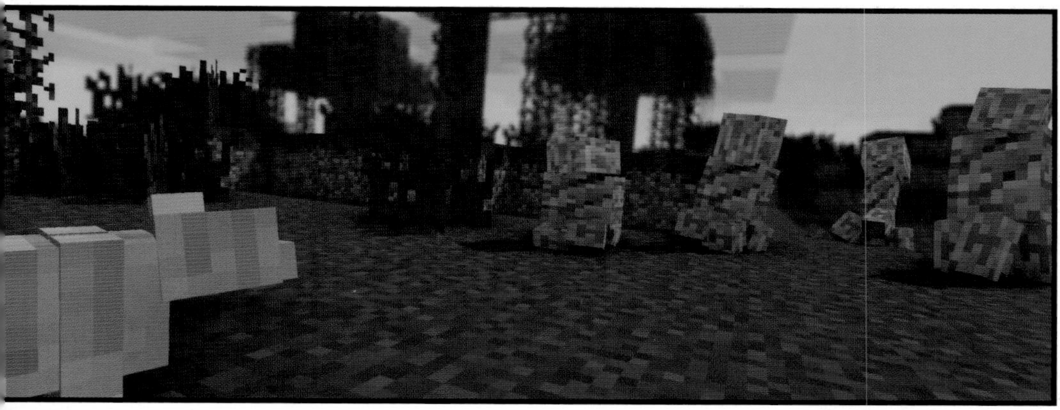

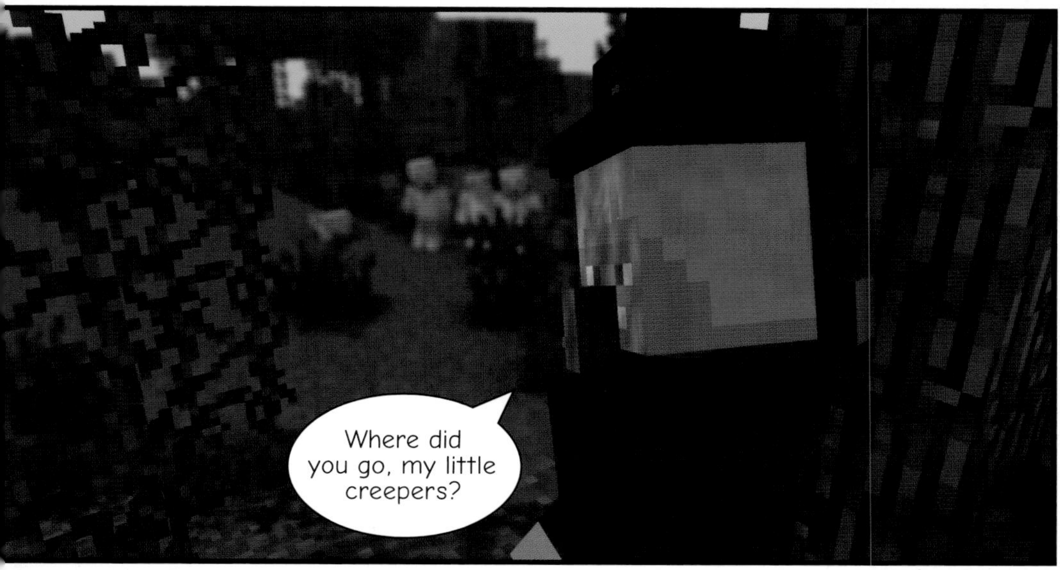
Where did you go, my little creepers?

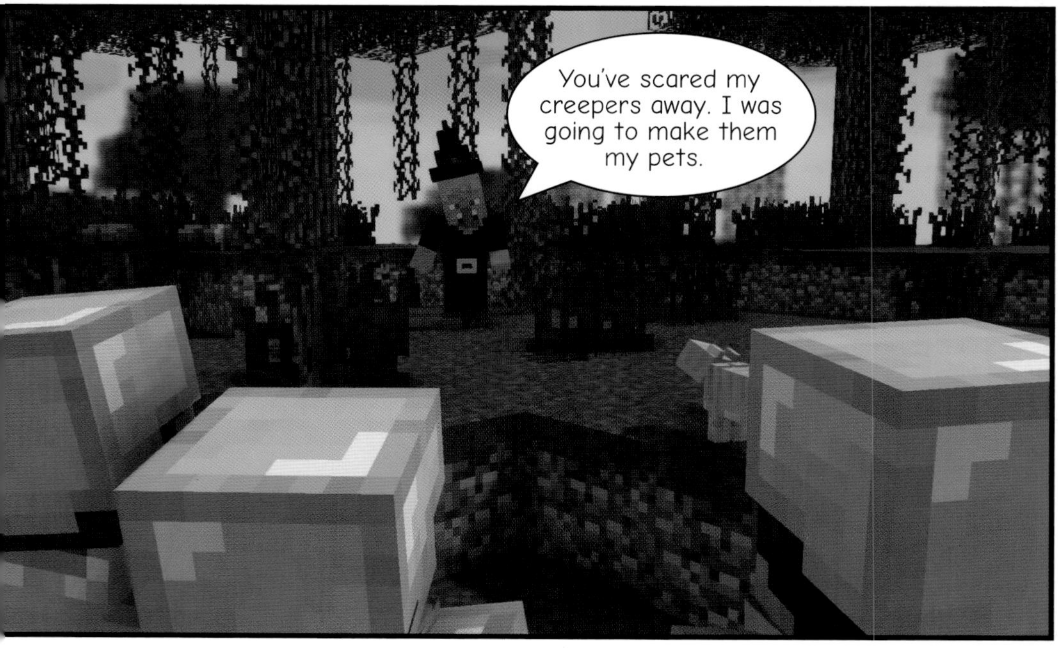
You've scared my creepers away. I was going to make them my pets.

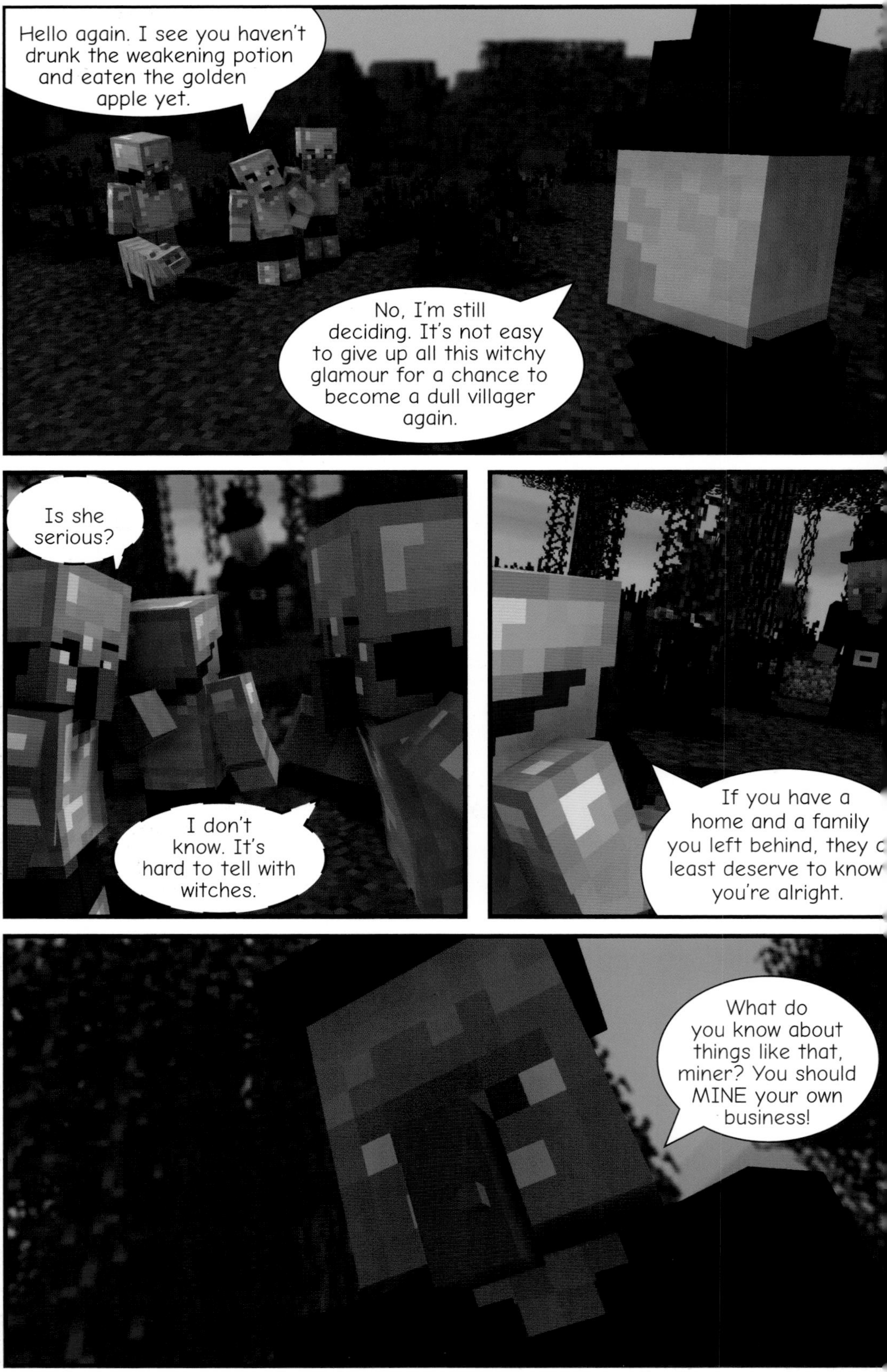
Hello again. I see you haven't drunk the weakening potion and eaten the golden apple yet.
No, I'm still deciding. It's not easy to give up all this witchy glamour for a chance to become a dull villager again.
Is she serious?
I don't know. It's hard to tell with witches.
If you have a home and a family you left behind, they a least deserve to know you're alright.
What do you know about things like that, miner? You should MINE your own business!

s a matter of fact, I know a lot about those things. Don't you remember how we met? You and your creepers kidnapped me!

My family was worried sick, and when I came back, the librarians sent me away. They were afraid I'd bring danger to the village. I stayed away as long as I could.

Now that I'm reunited with my family, I appreciate them more than ever.

That's a very touching story, but what does it have to do with me? My family never understood me when I was there. I left and lived a life of adventure I never would have had in that stuffy village.

I understand that, too. But we're working to open our village so people can come and go as they please. They can go on adventures and return home without getting in trouble.

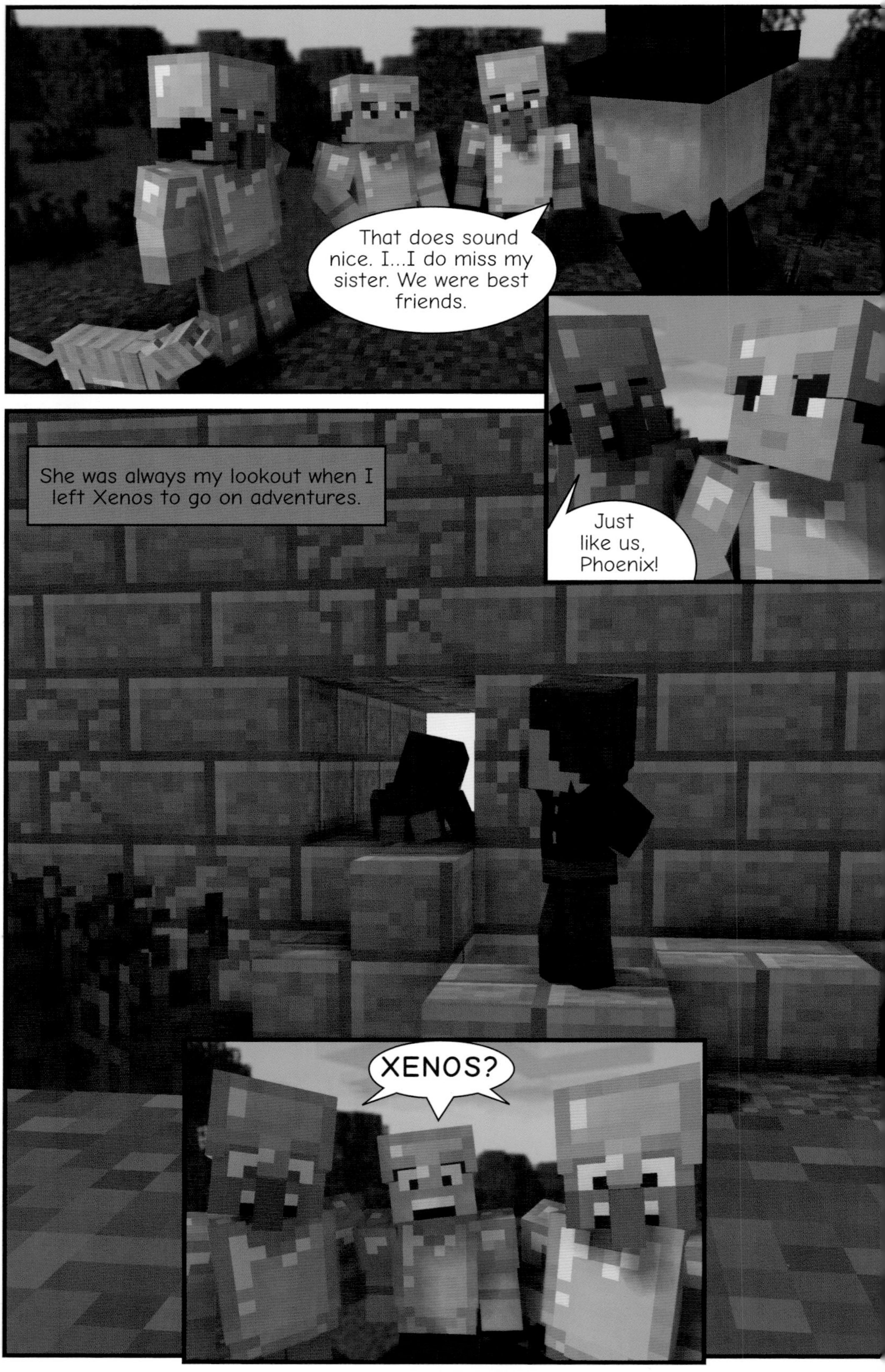
That does sound nice. I...I do miss my sister. We were best friends.
Just like us, Phoenix!
She was always my lookout when I left Xenos to go on adventures.
XENOS?

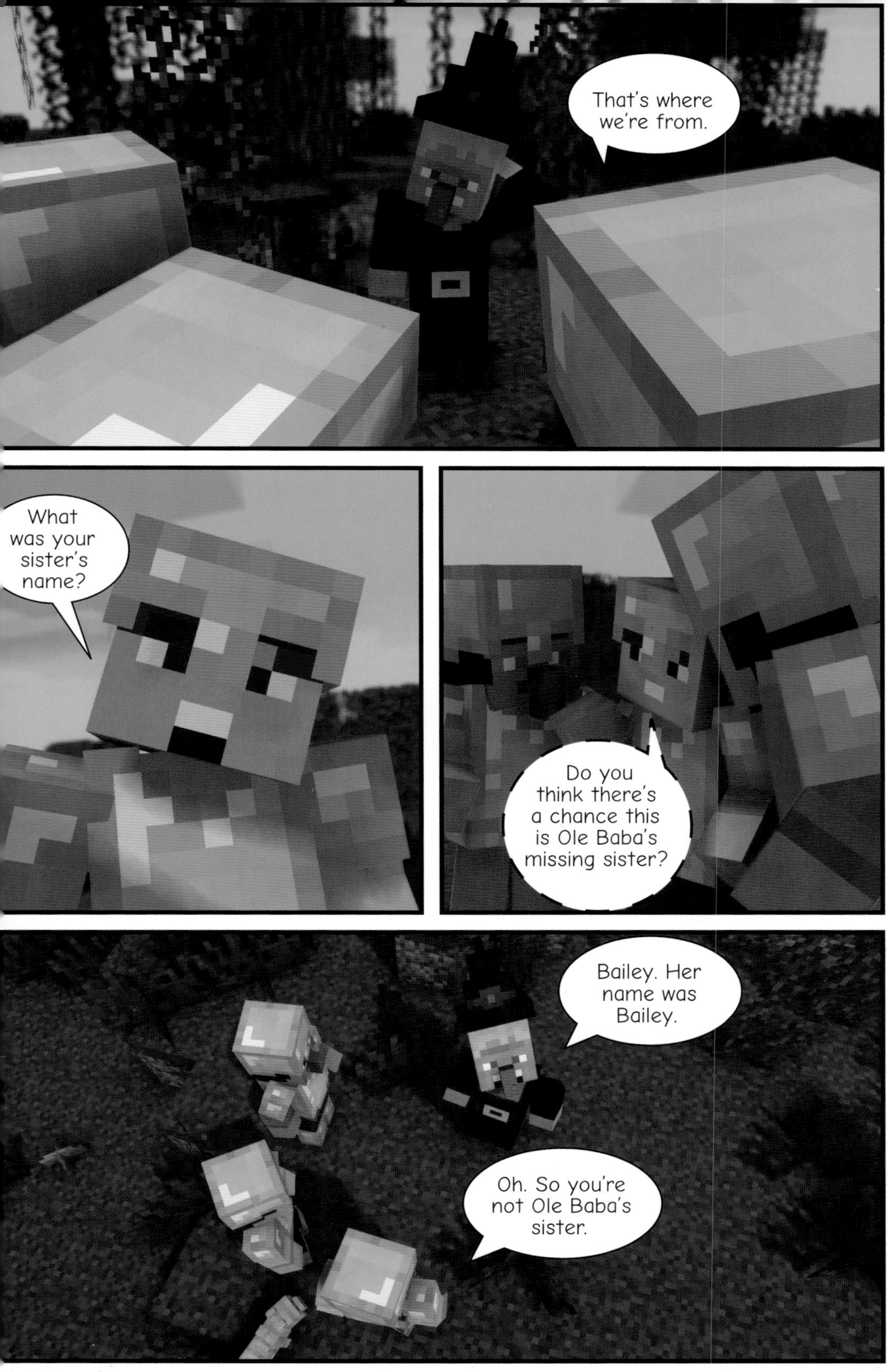
That's where we're from.
What was your sister's name?
Do you think there's a chance this is Ole Baba's missing sister?
Bailey. Her name was Bailey.
Oh. So you're not Ole Baba's sister.

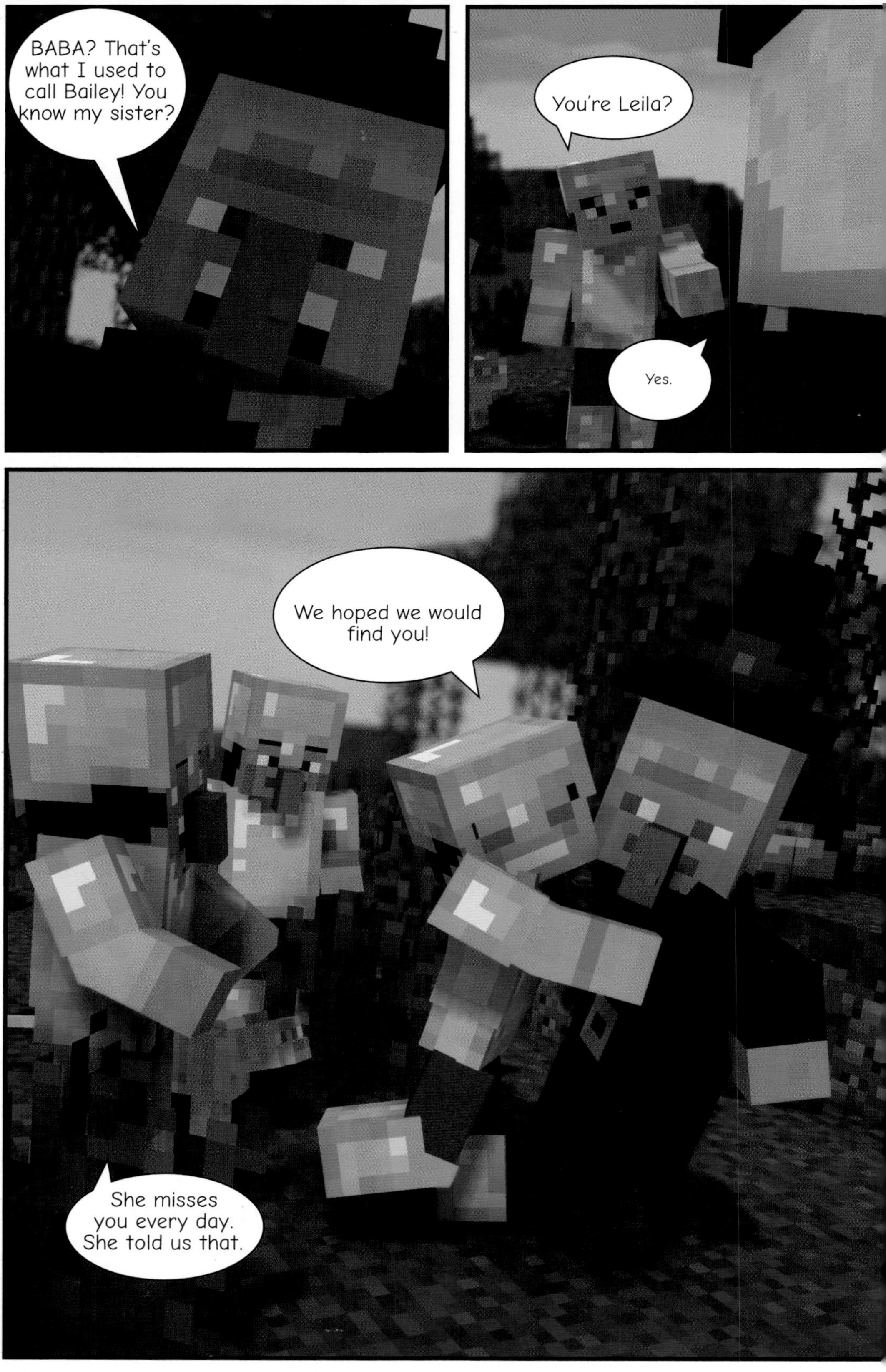

BABA? That's what I used to call Bailey! You know my sister?
You're Leila?
Yes.
We hoped we would find you!
She misses you every day. She told us that.

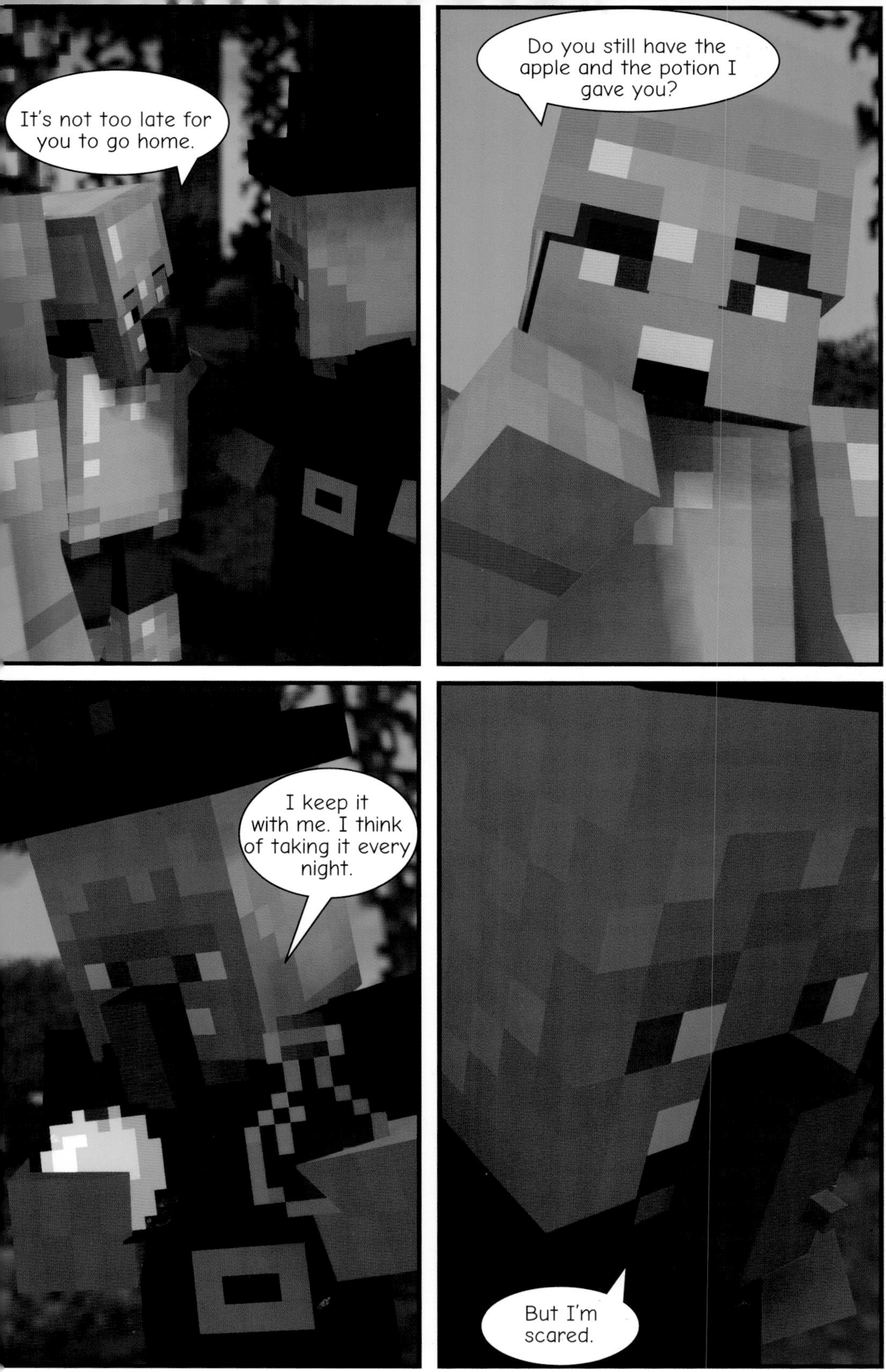
It's not too late for you to go home.
Do you still have the apple and the potion I gave you?
I keep it with me. I think of taking it every night.
But I'm scared.

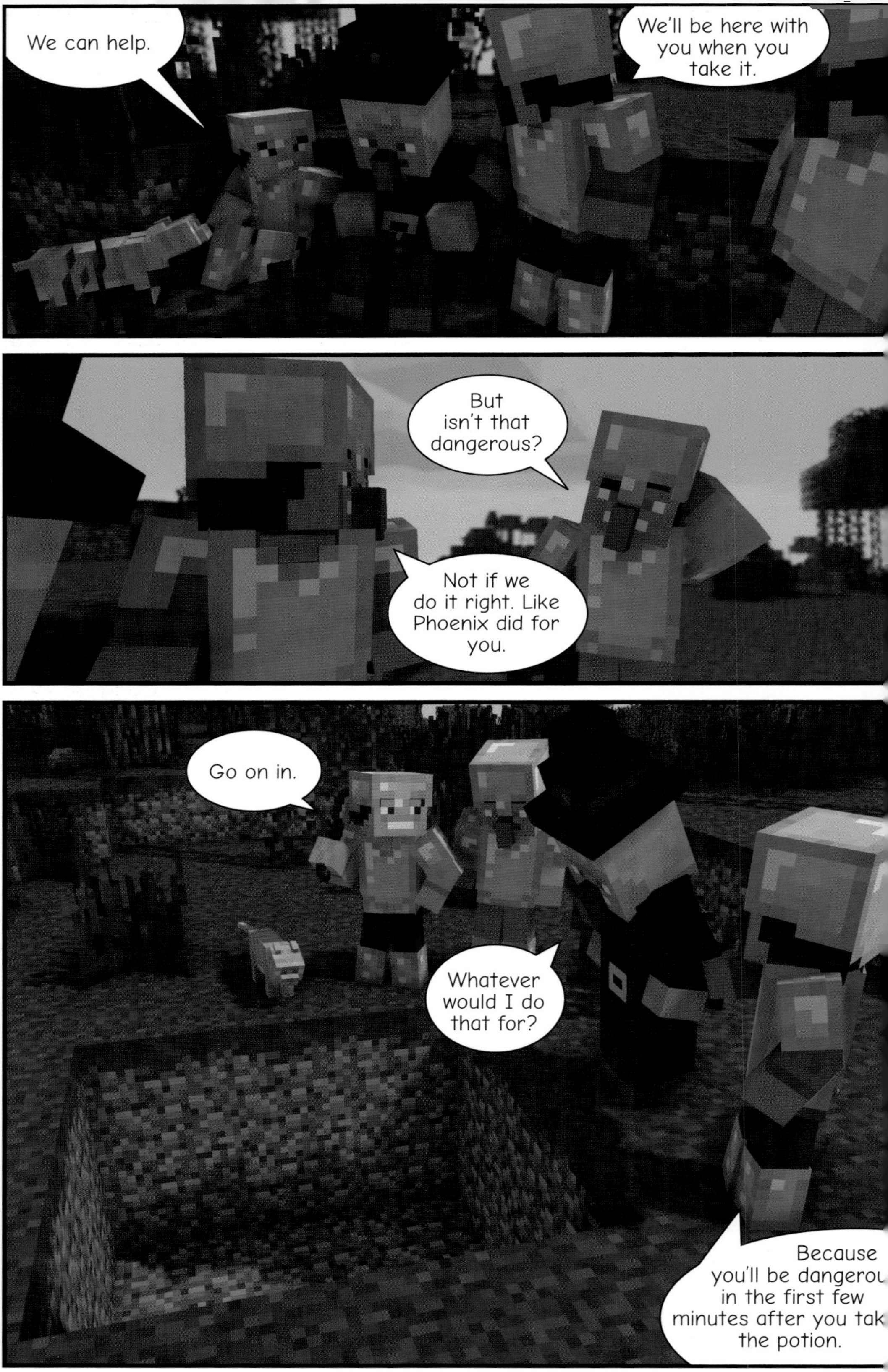
We can help.
We'll be here with you when you take it.
But isn't that dangerous?
Not if we do it right. Like Phoenix did for you.
Go on in.
Whatever would I do that for?
Because you'll be dangerou
in the first few
minutes after you tak
the potion.

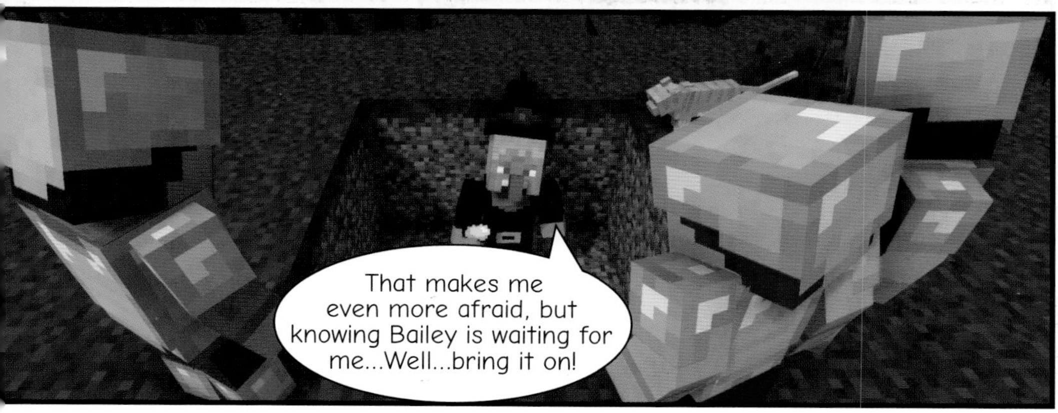
That makes me
even more afraid, but
knowing Bailey is waiting for
me...Well...bring it on!

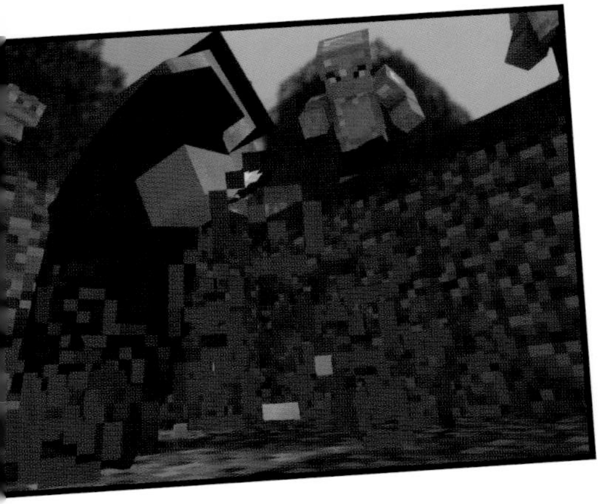

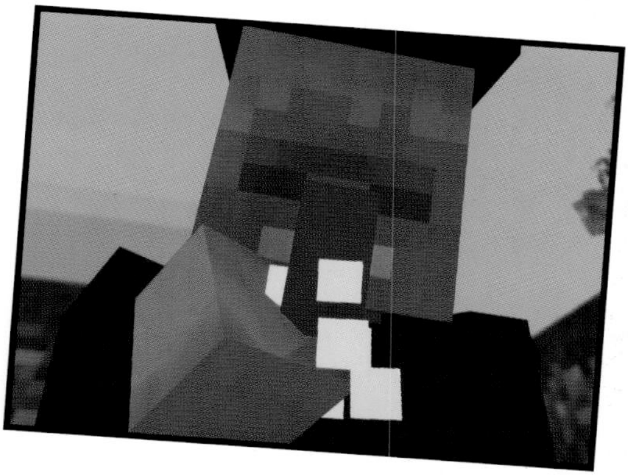

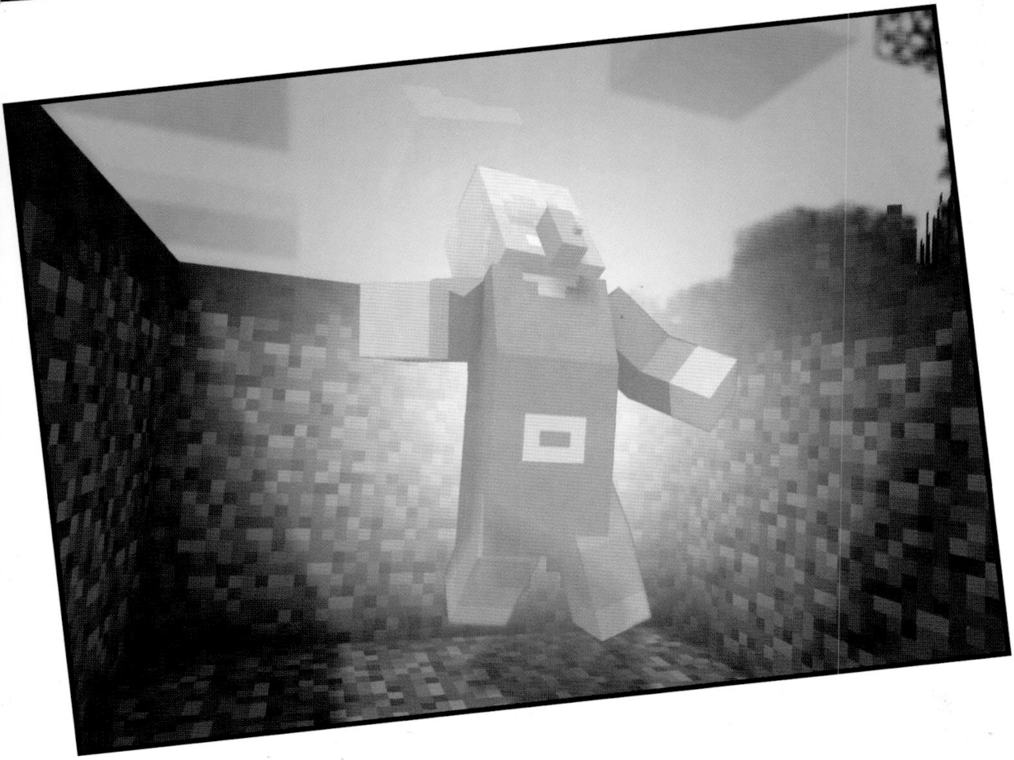

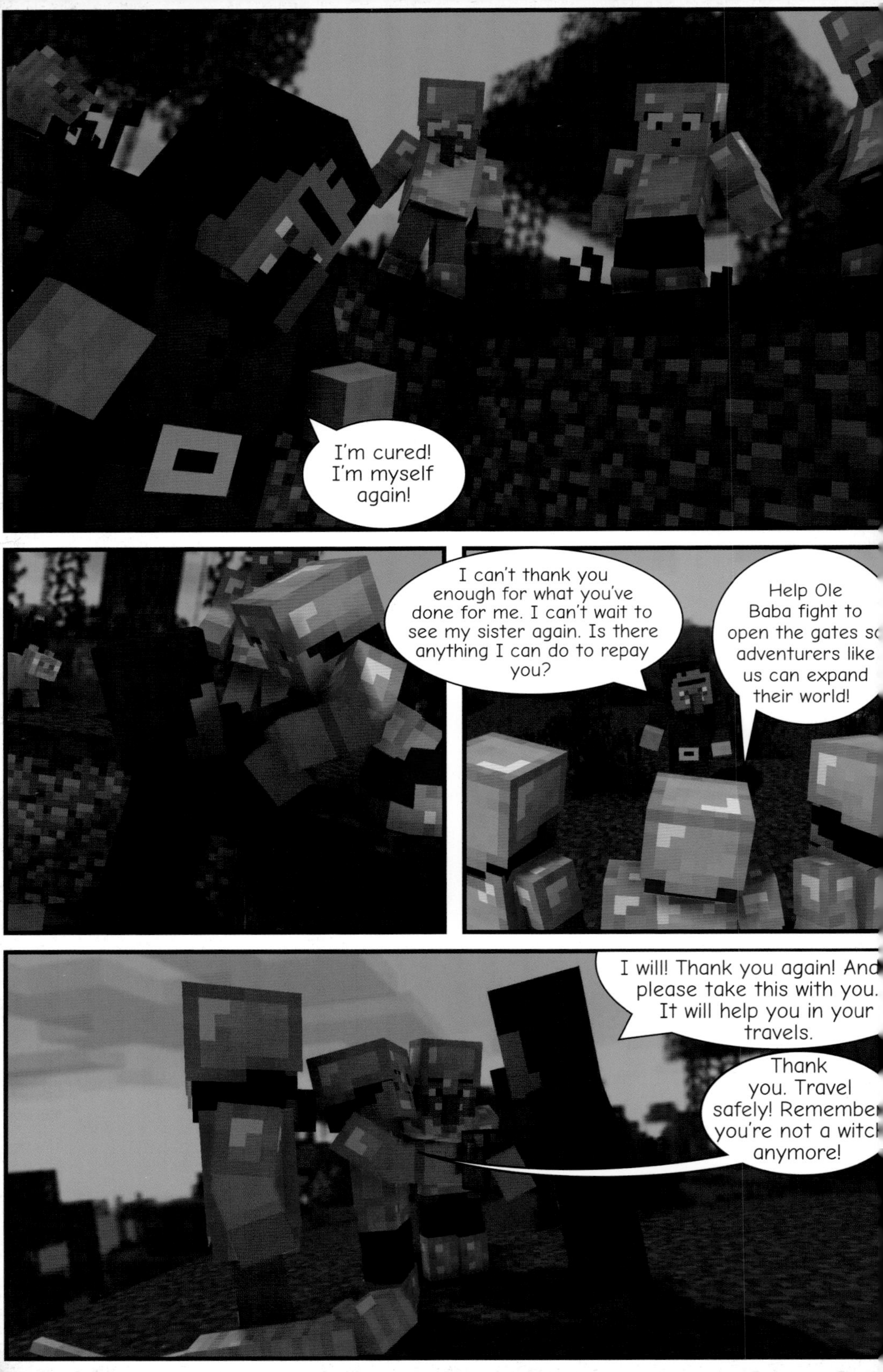
I'm cured! I'm myself again!
I can't thank you enough for what you've done for me. I can't wait to see my sister again. Is there anything I can do to repay you?
Help Ole Baba fight to open the gates so adventurers like us can expand their world!
I will! Thank you again! And please take this with you. It will help you in your travels.
Thank you. Travel safely! Remember you're not a witch anymore!

CHAPTER 5

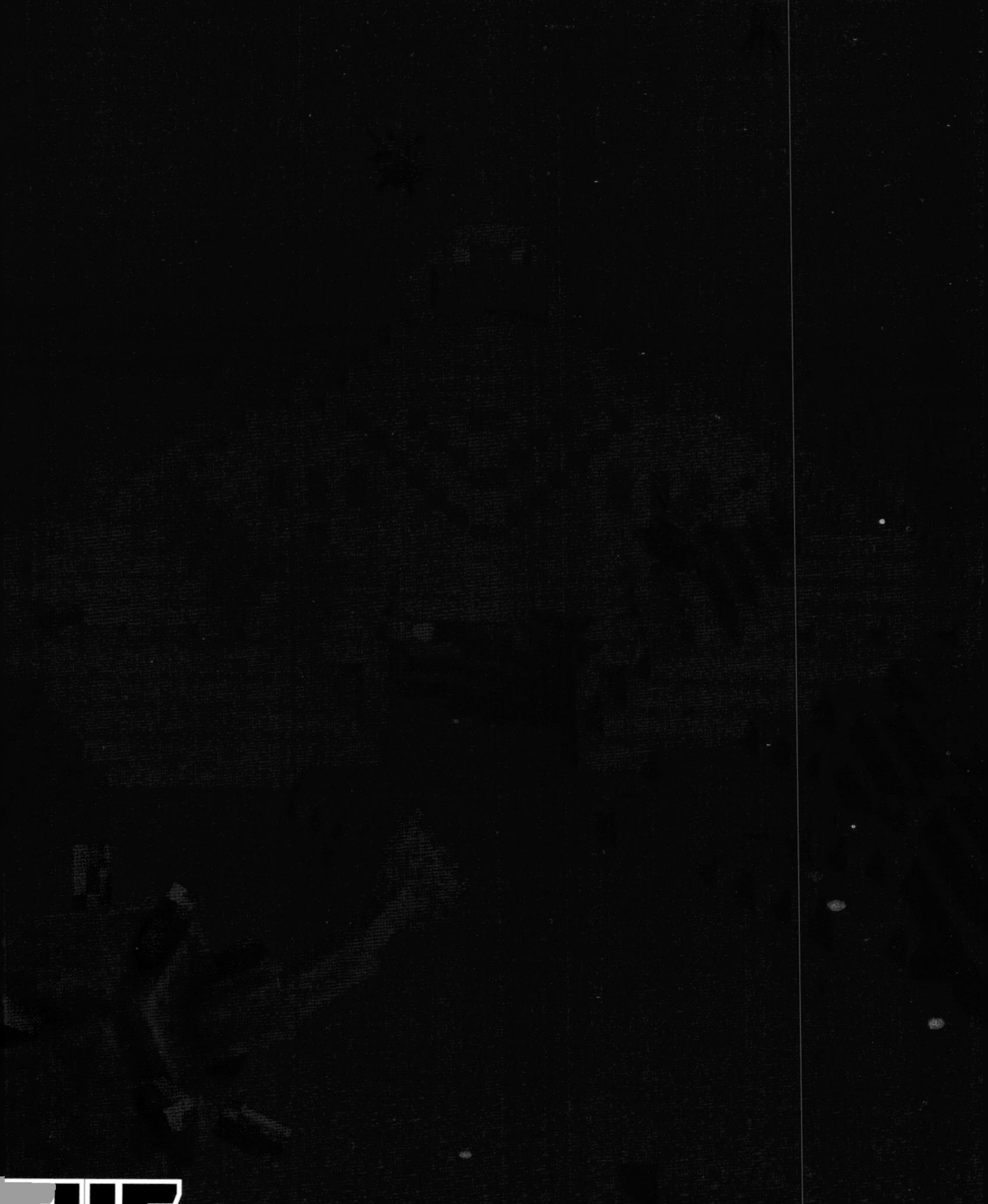

THE GUARDIAN BATTLE

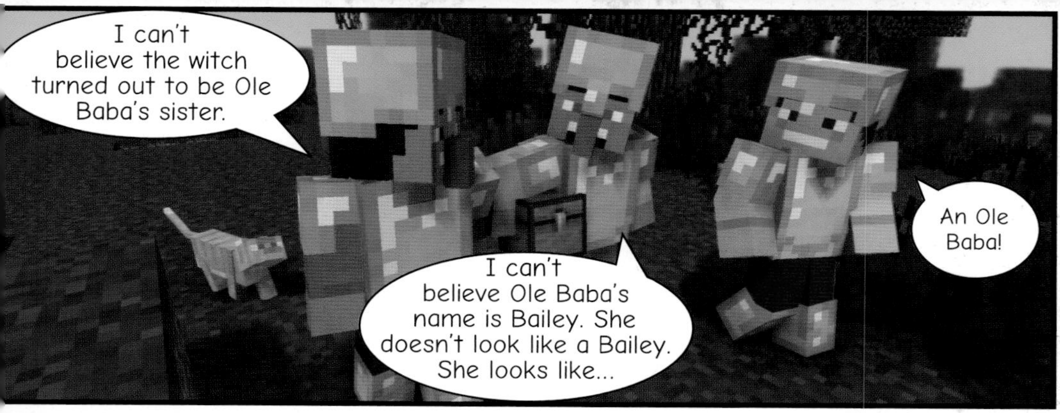
I can't believe the witch turned out to be Ole Baba's sister.
I can't believe Ole Baba's name is Bailey. She doesn't look like a Bailey. She looks like...
An Ole Baba!

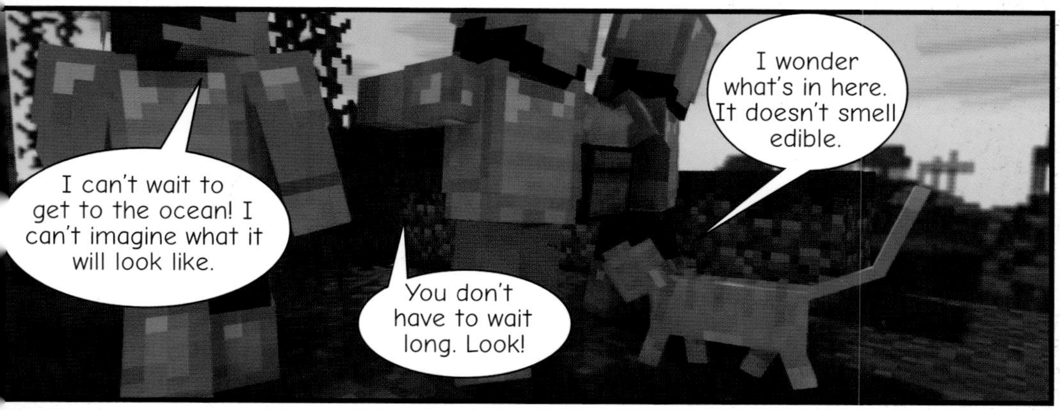
I can't wait to get to the ocean! I can't imagine what it will look like.
You don't have to wait long. Look!
I wonder what's in here. It doesn't smell edible.

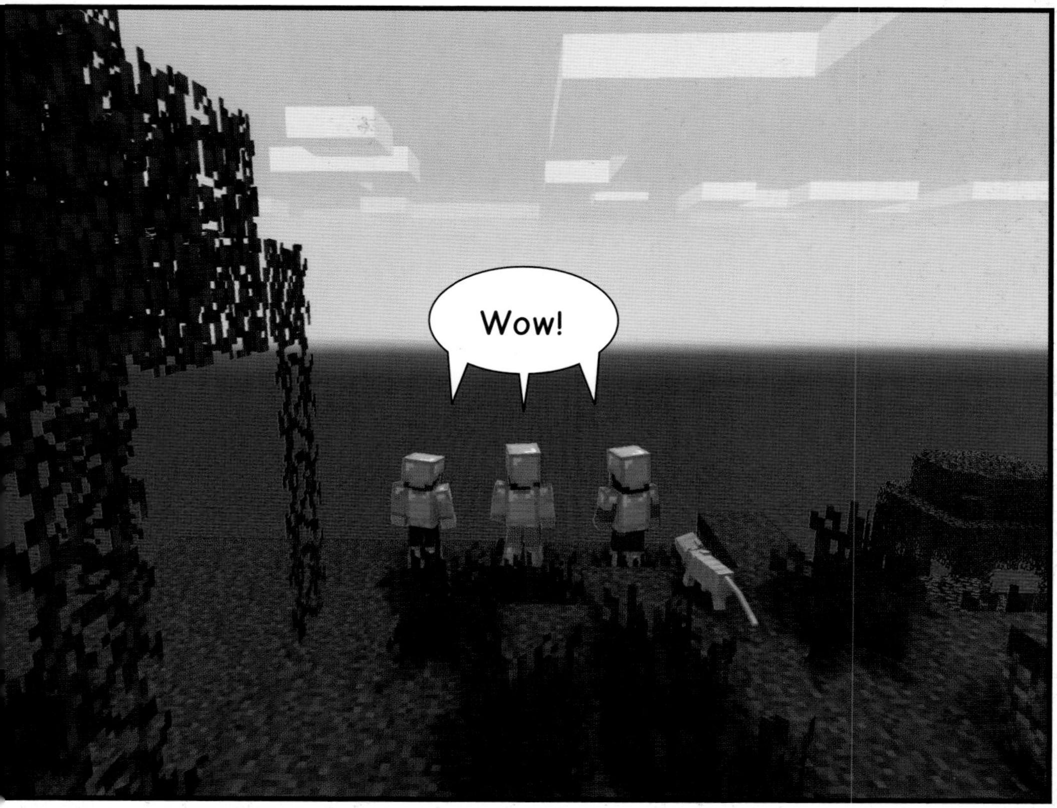
Wow!

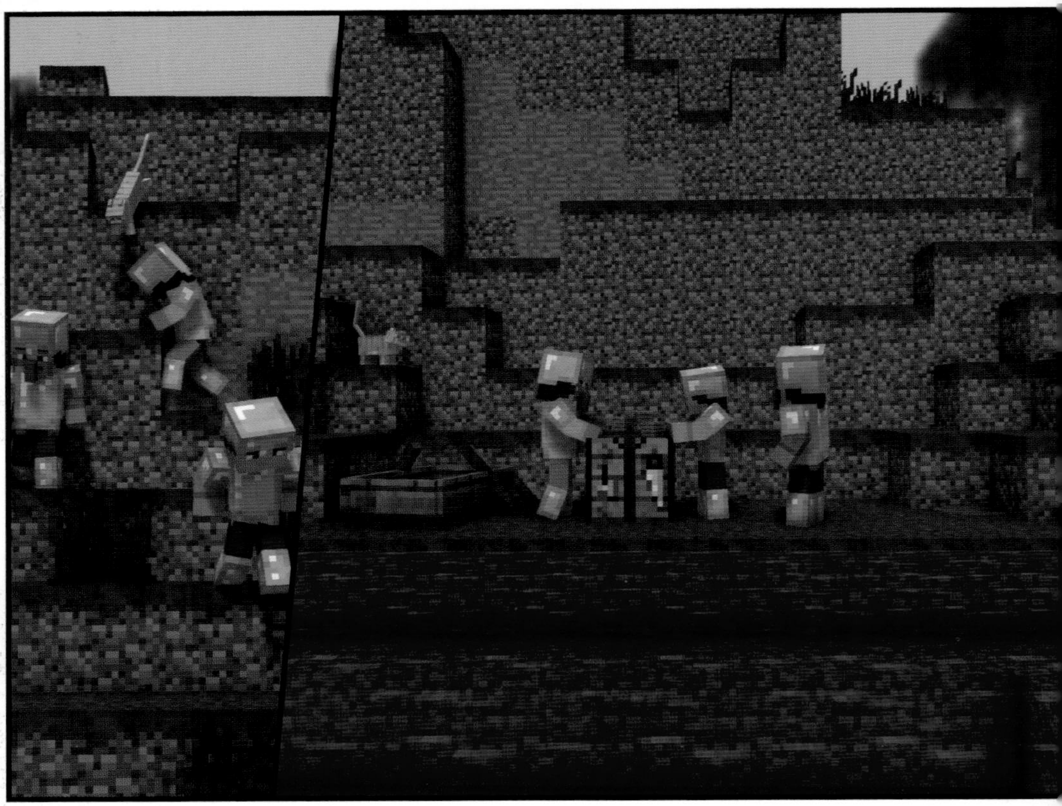

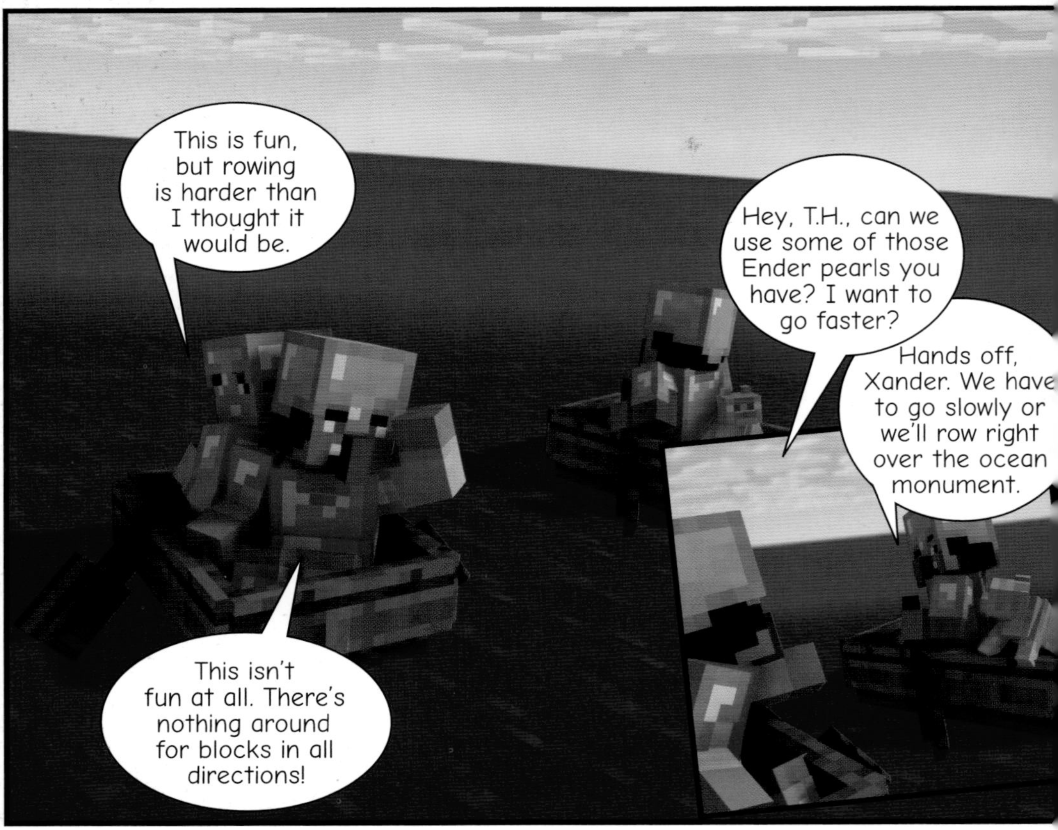

This is fun, but rowing is harder than I thought it would be.
This isn't fun at all. There's nothing around for blocks in all directions!
Hey, T.H., can we use some of those Ender pearls you have? I want to go faster?
Hands off, Xander. We have to go slowly or we'll row right over the ocean monument.

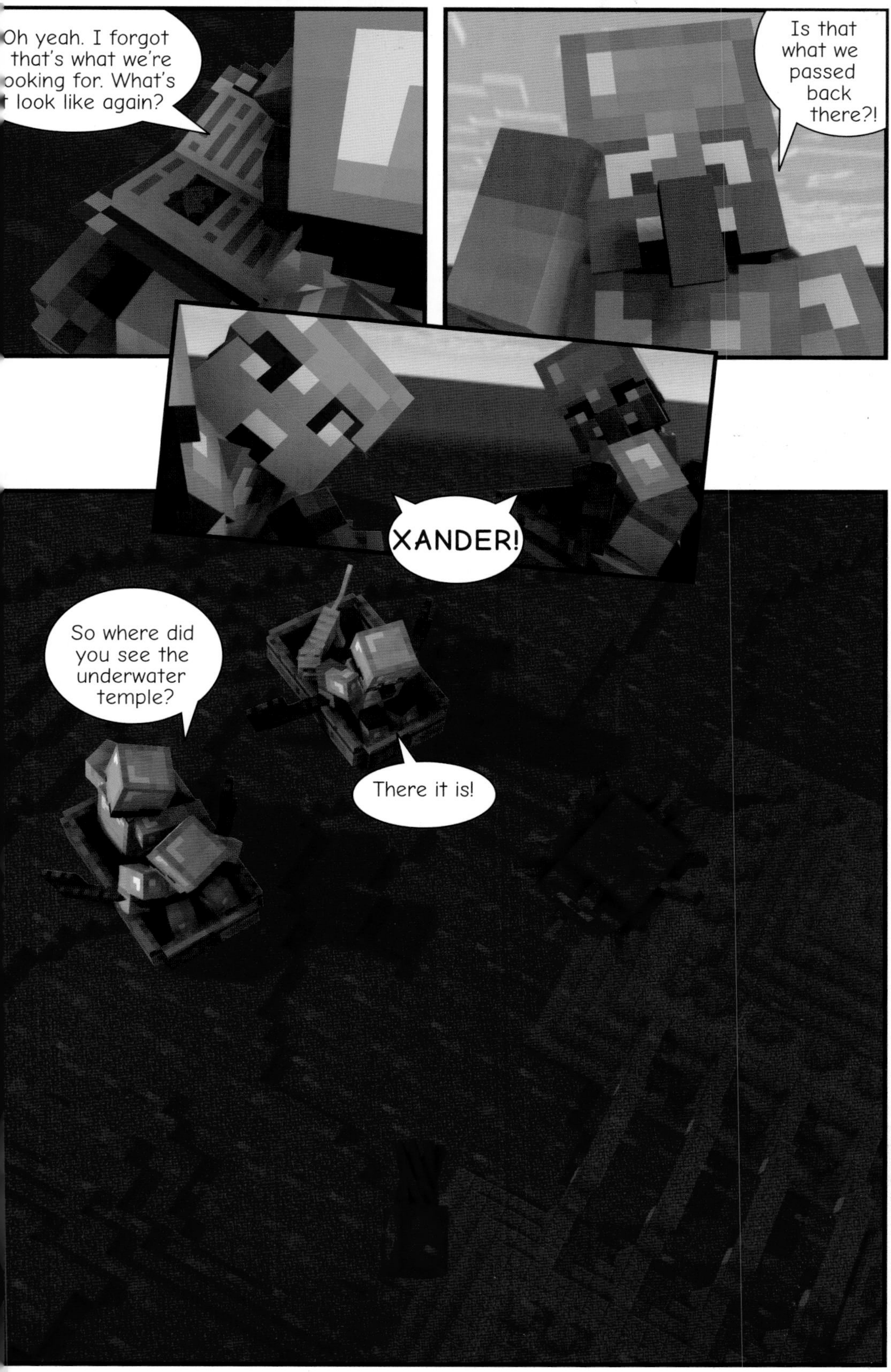
Oh yeah. I forgot that's what we're ooking for. What's t look like again?
Is that what we passed back there?!
XANDER!
So where did you see the underwater temple?
There it is!

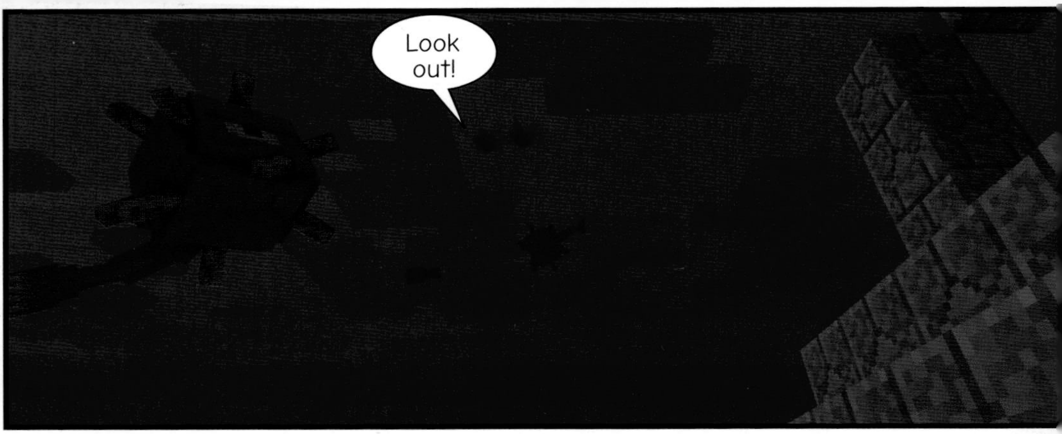
Look out!

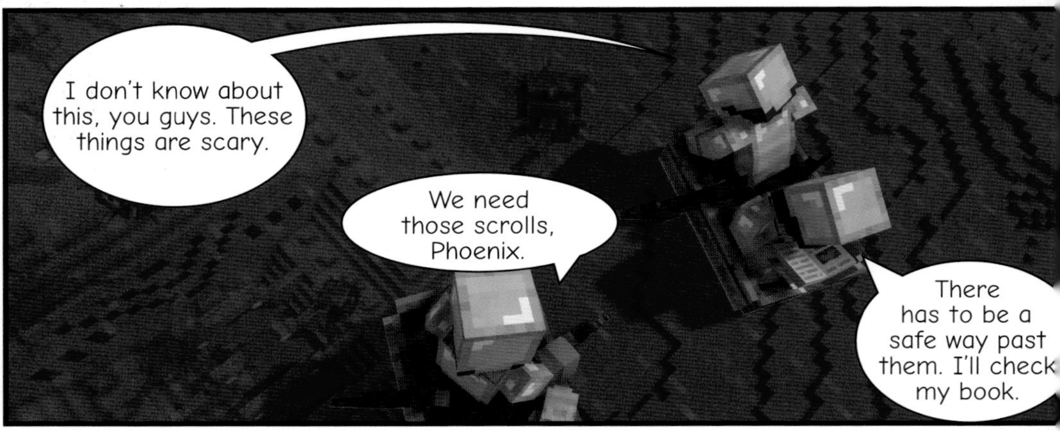
I don't know about this, you guys. These things are scary.
We need those scrolls, Phoenix.
There has to be a safe way past them. I'll check my book.

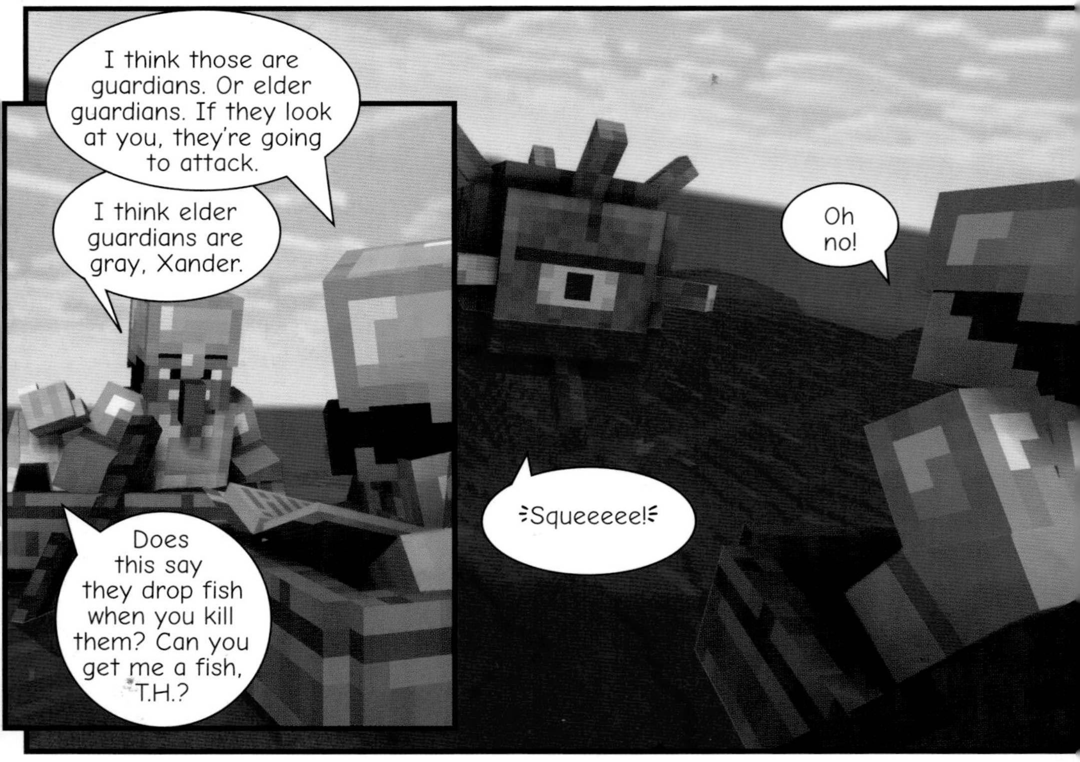
I think those are guardians. Or elder guardians. If they look at you, they're going to attack.
I think elder guardians are gray, Xander.
Does this say they drop fish when you kill them? Can you get me a fish, T.H.?
Oh no!
Squeeeee!

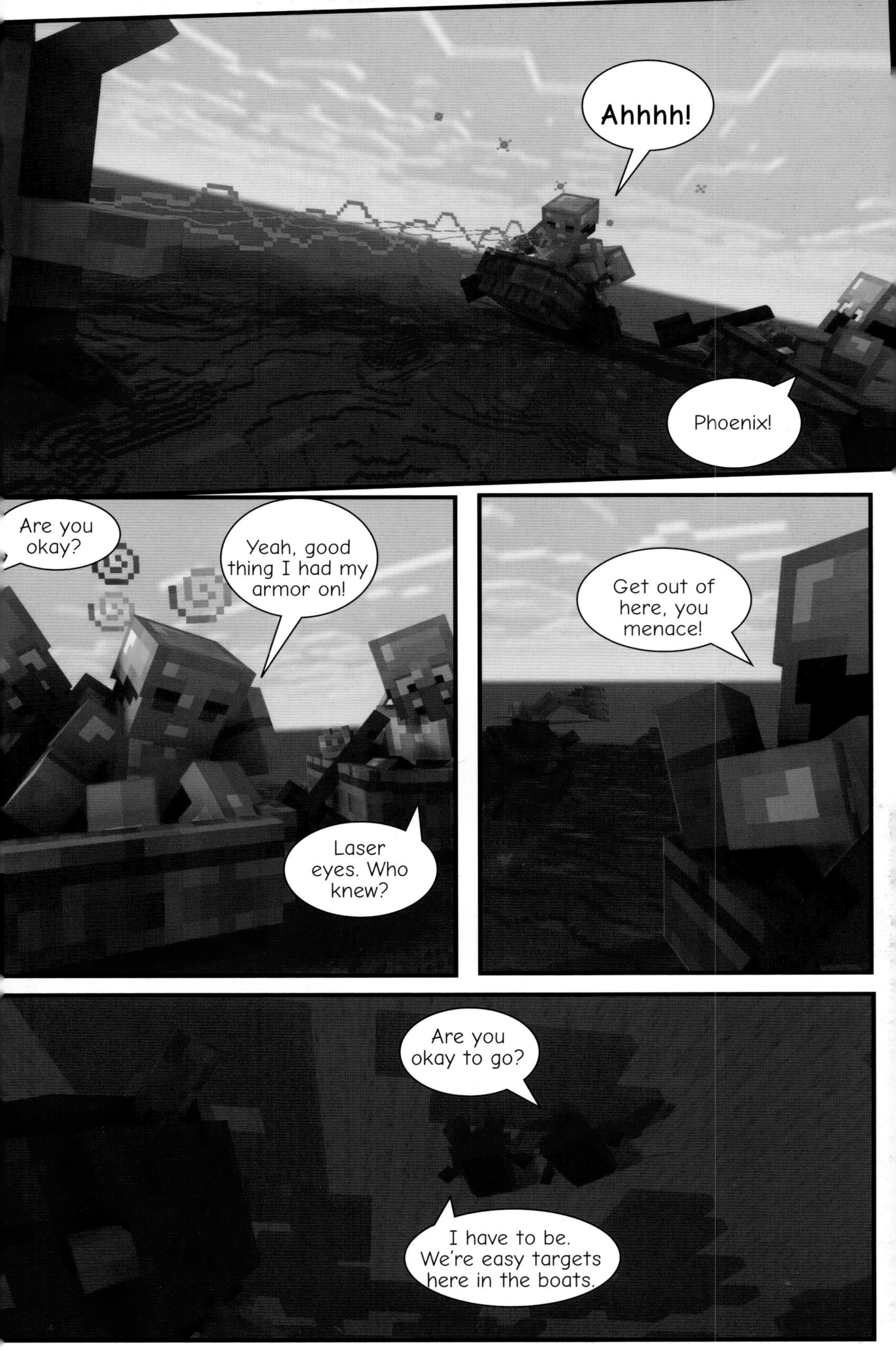
Ahhhh!
Phoenix!
Are you okay?
Yeah, good thing I had my armor on!
Laser eyes. Who knew?
Get out of here, you menace!
Are you okay to go?
I have to be. We're easy targets here in the boats.

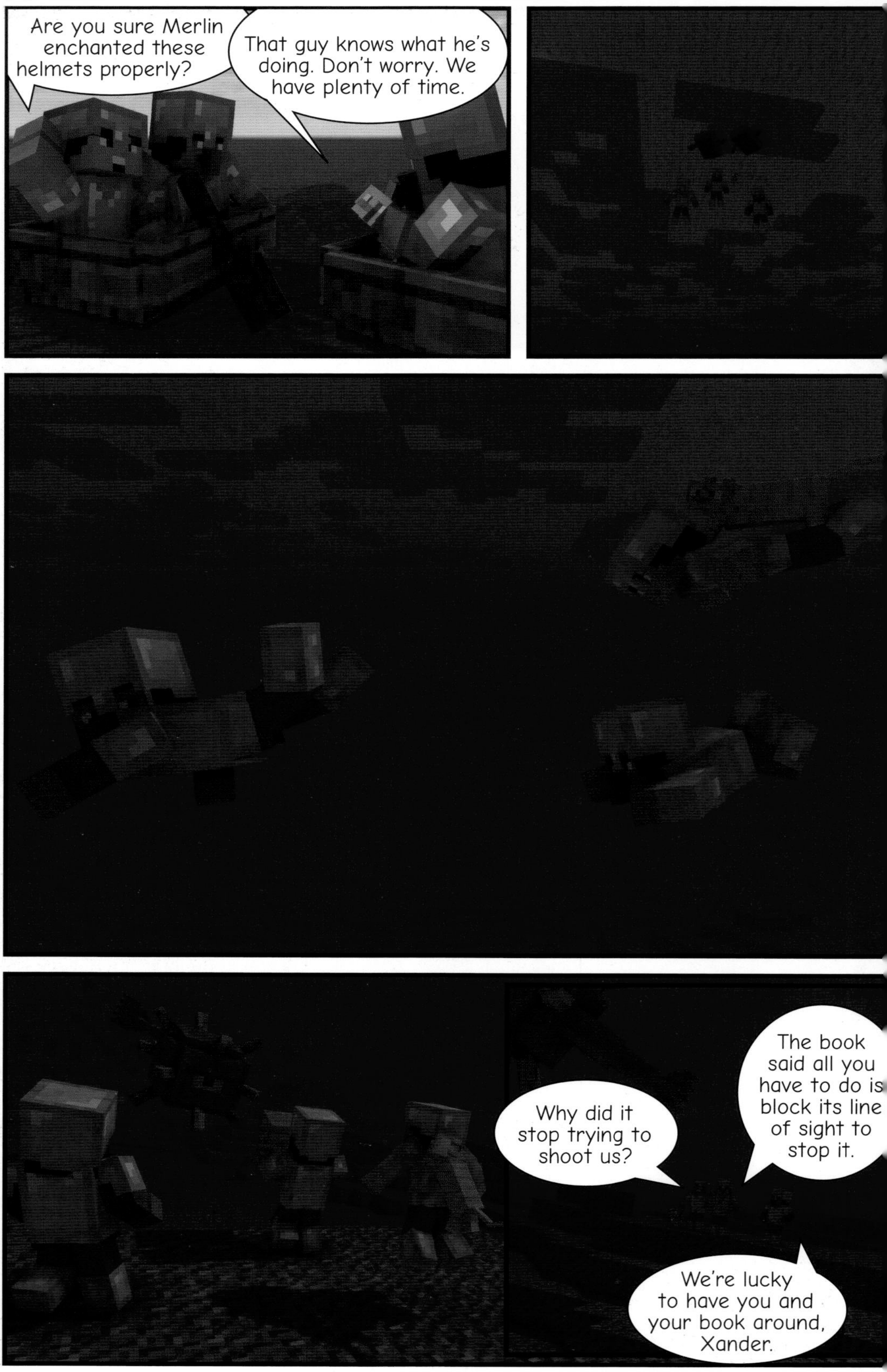

Are you sure Merlin enchanted these helmets properly?
That guy knows what he's doing. Don't worry. We have plenty of time.
Why did it stop trying to shoot us?
The book said all you have to do is block its line of sight to stop it.
We're lucky to have you and your book around, Xander.

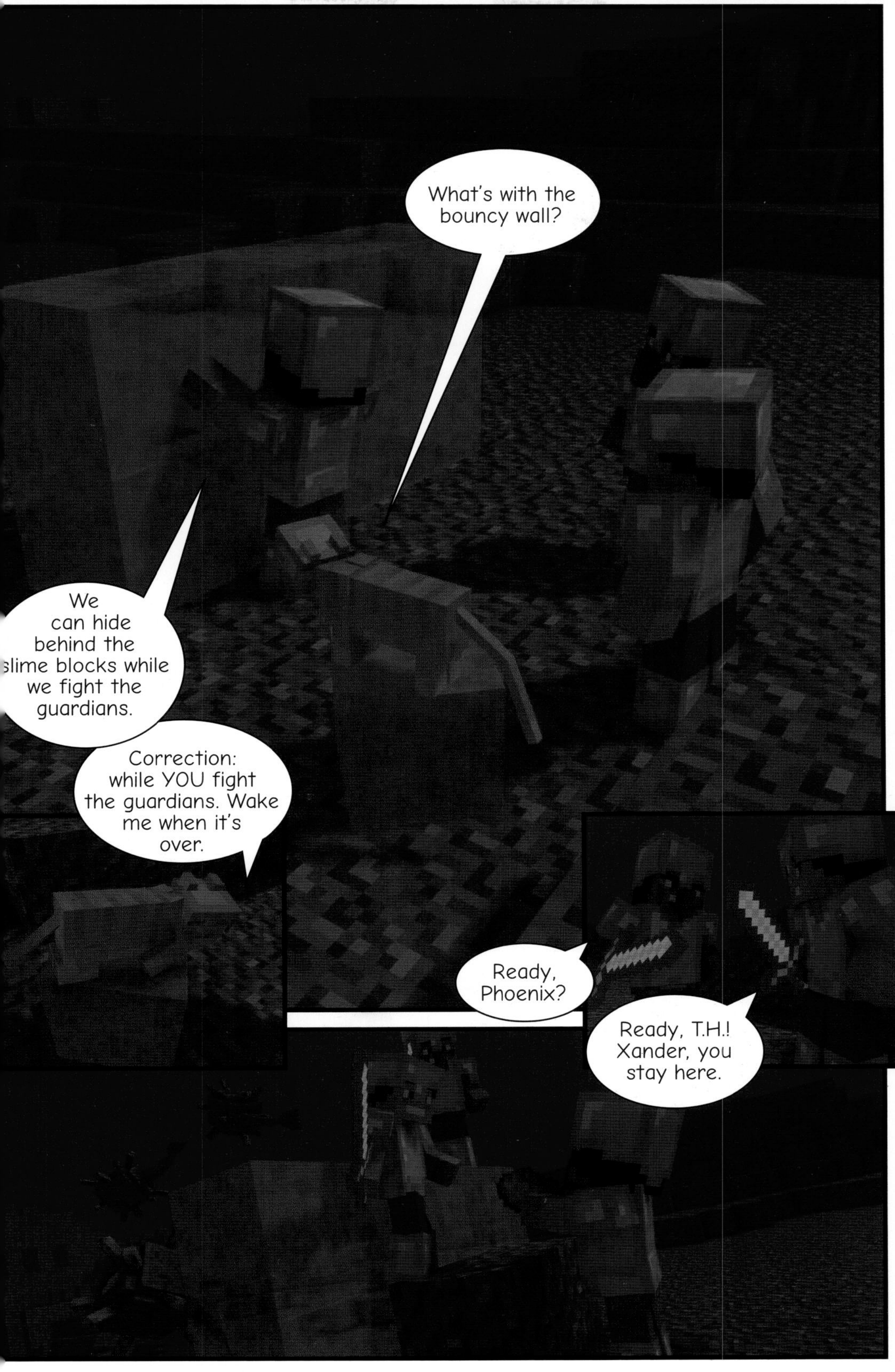
What's with the bouncy wall?
We can hide behind the slime blocks while we fight the guardians.
Correction: while YOU fight the guardians. Wake me when it's over.
Ready, Phoenix?
Ready, T.H.! Xander, you stay here.

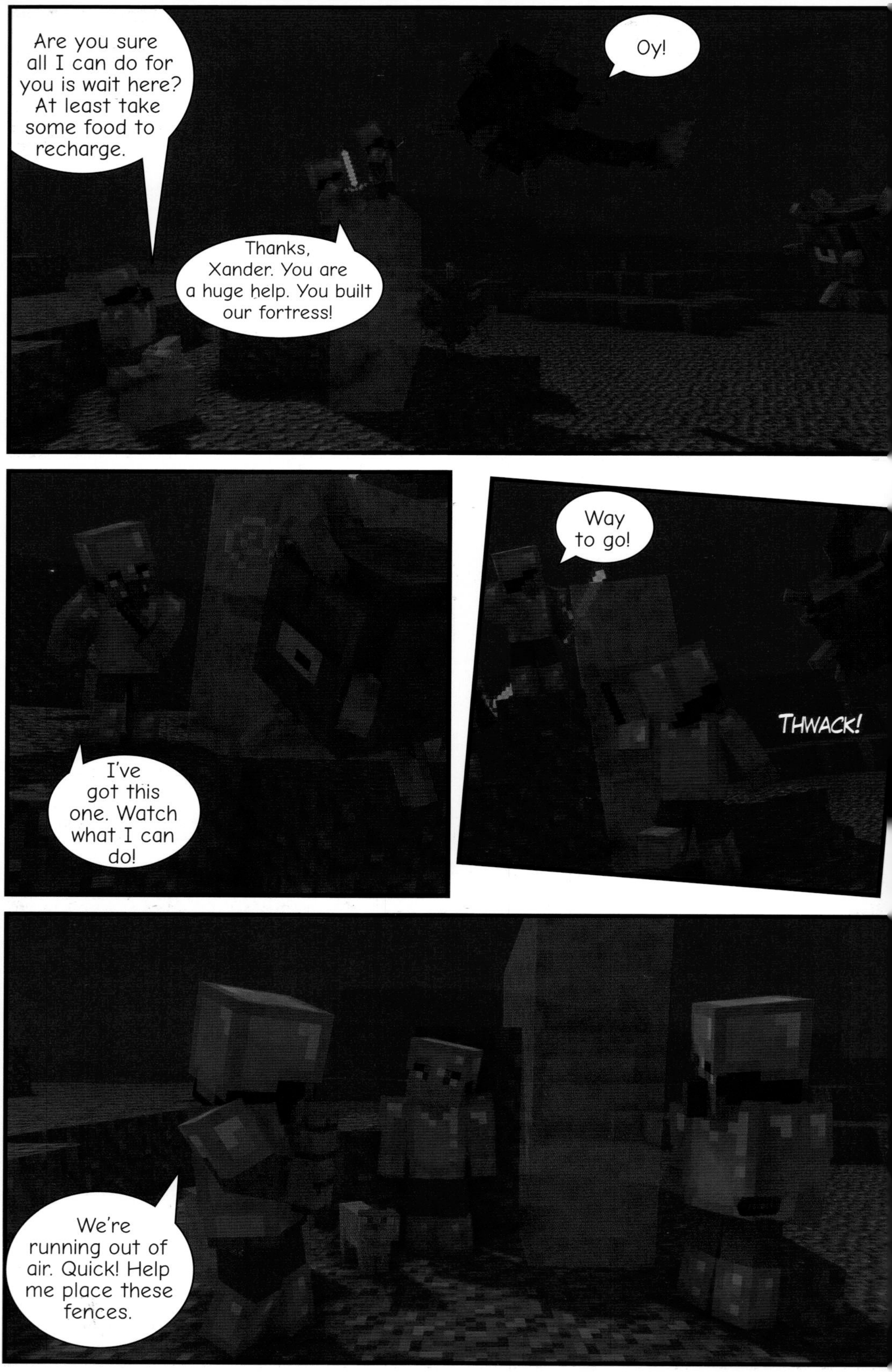
Are you sure all I can do for you is wait here? At least take some food to recharge.
Thanks, Xander. You are a huge help. You built our fortress!
Oy!
I've got this one. Watch what I can do!
Way to go!
THWACK!
We're running out of air. Quick! Help me place these fences.

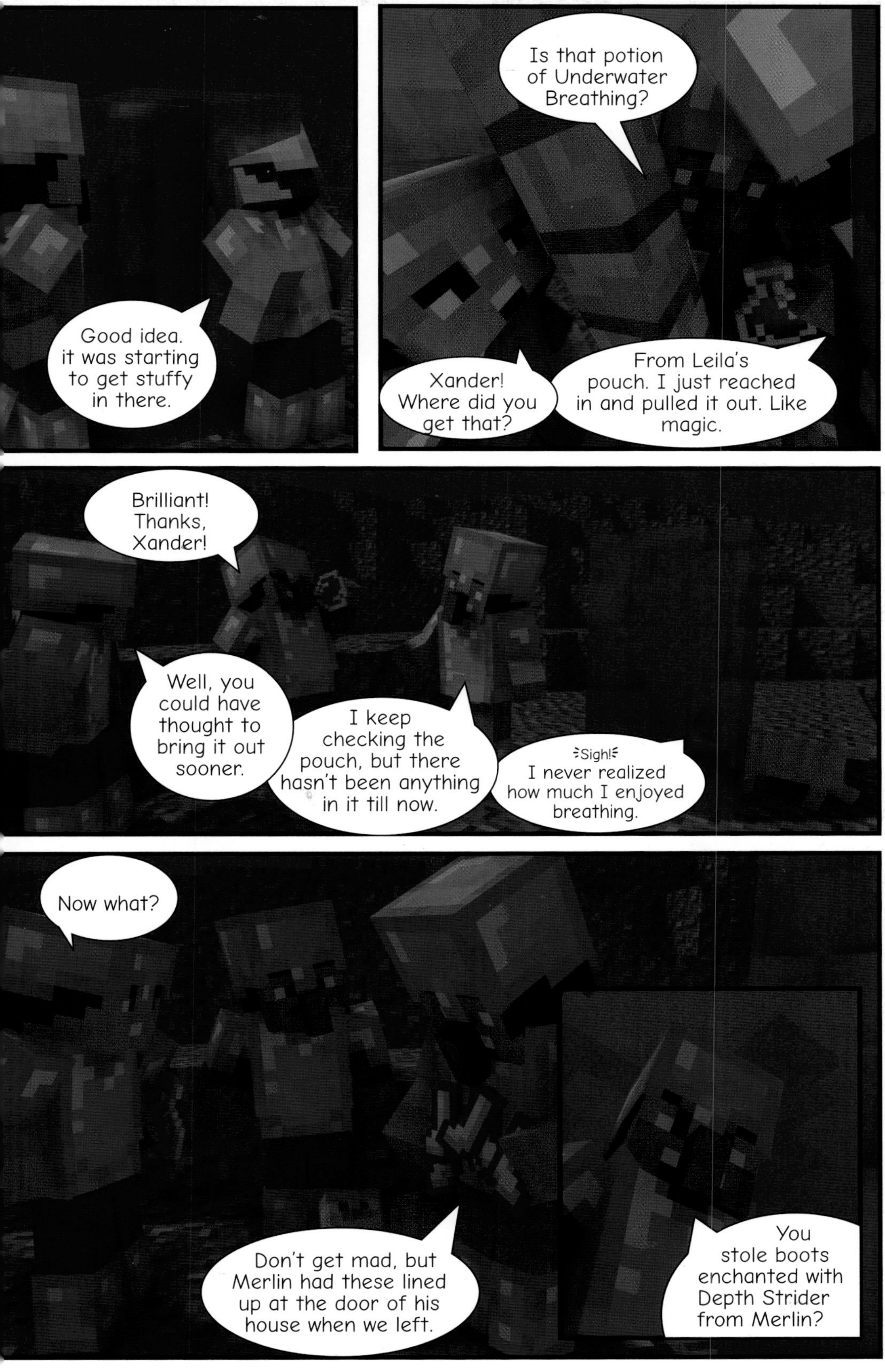
Good idea. it was starting to get stuffy in there.
Is that potion of Underwater Breathing?
Xander! Where did you get that?
From Leila's pouch. I just reached in and pulled it out. Like magic.
Brilliant! Thanks, Xander!
Well, you could have thought to bring it out sooner.
I keep checking the pouch, but there hasn't been anything in it till now.
Sigh!
I never realized how much I enjoyed breathing.
Now what?
Don't get mad, but Merlin had these lined up at the door of his house when we left.
You stole boots enchanted with Depth Strider from Merlin?

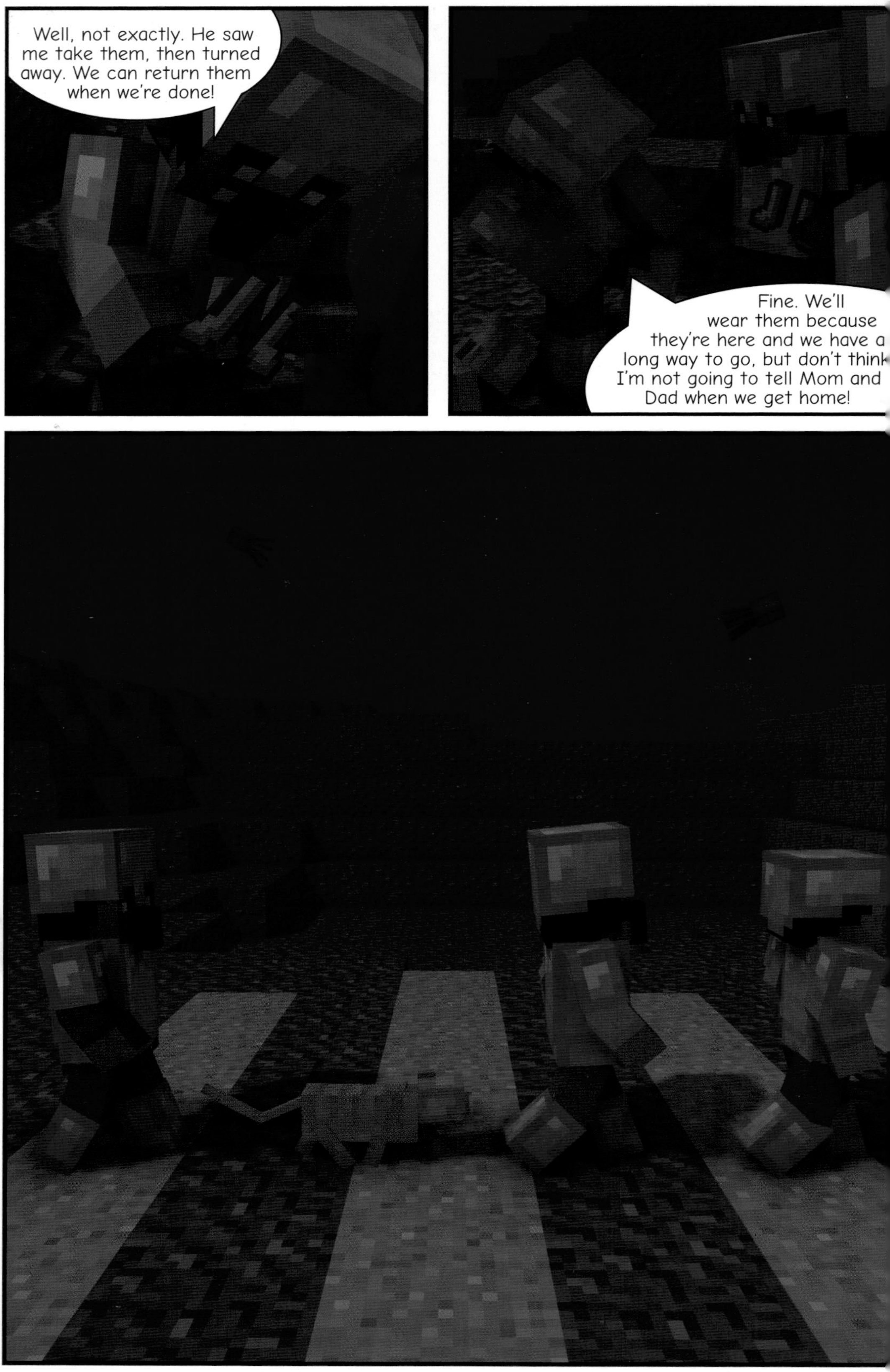
Well, not exactly. He saw me take them, then turned away. We can return them when we're done!
Fine. We'll wear them because they're here and we have a long way to go, but don't think I'm not going to tell Mom and Dad when we get home!

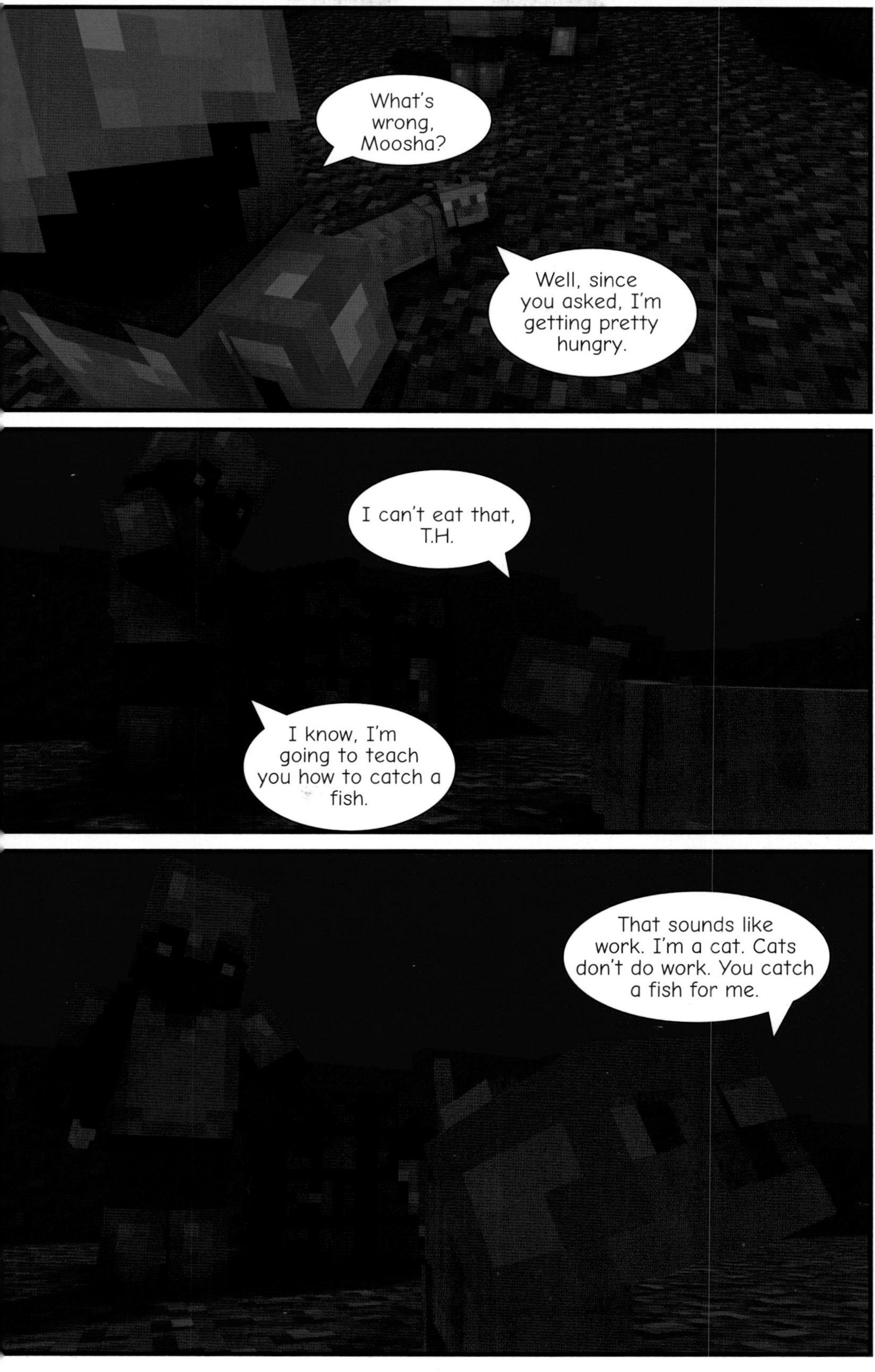
What's wrong, Moosha?
Well, since you asked, I'm getting pretty hungry.
I can't eat that, T.H.
I know, I'm going to teach you how to catch a fish.
That sounds like work. I'm a cat. Cats don't do work. You catch a fish for me.

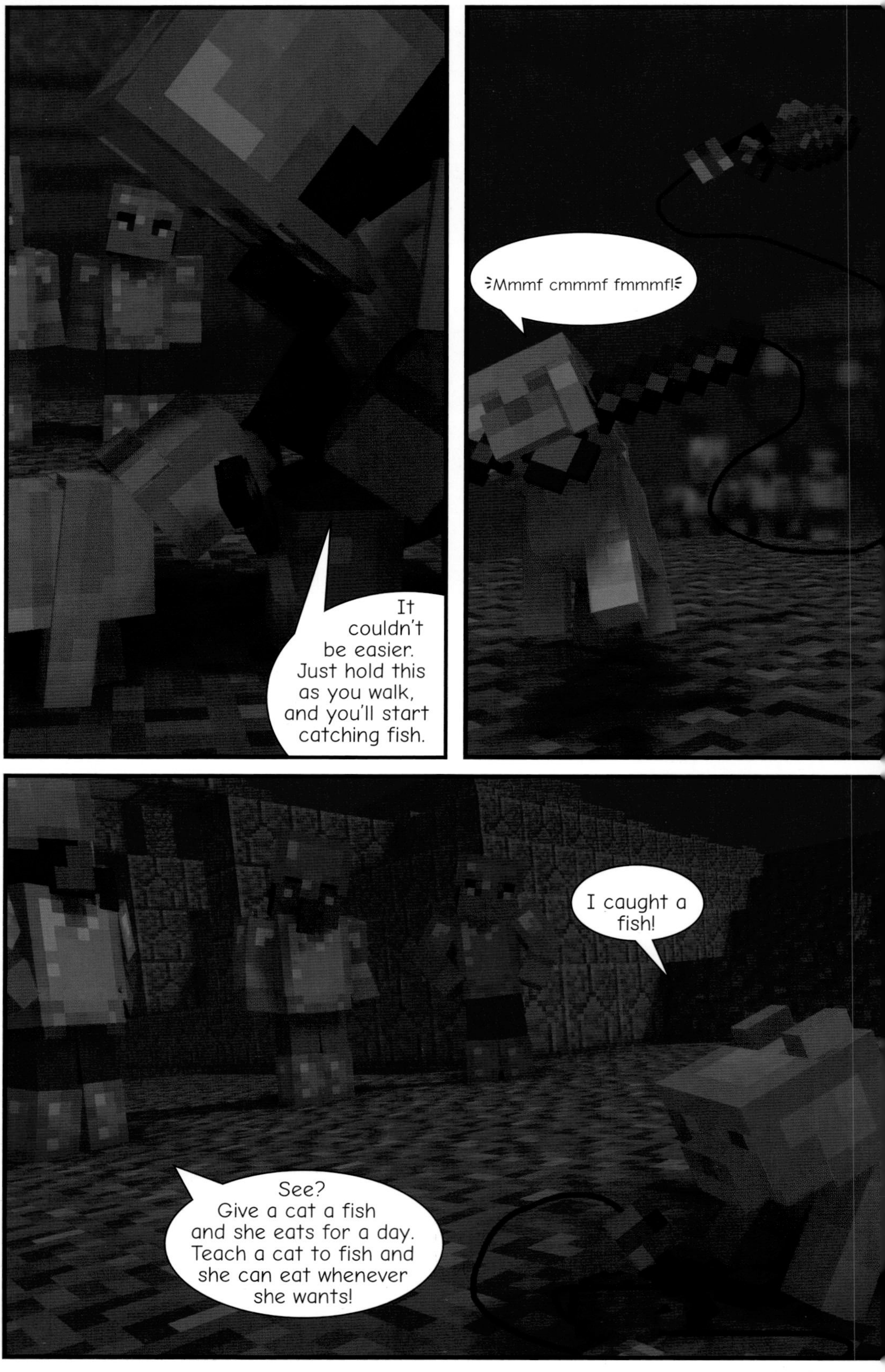
It couldn't be easier. Just hold this as you walk, and you'll start catching fish.
Mmmf cmmmf fmmmf!
I caught a fish!
See? Give a cat a fish and she eats for a day. Teach a cat to fish and she can eat whenever she wants!

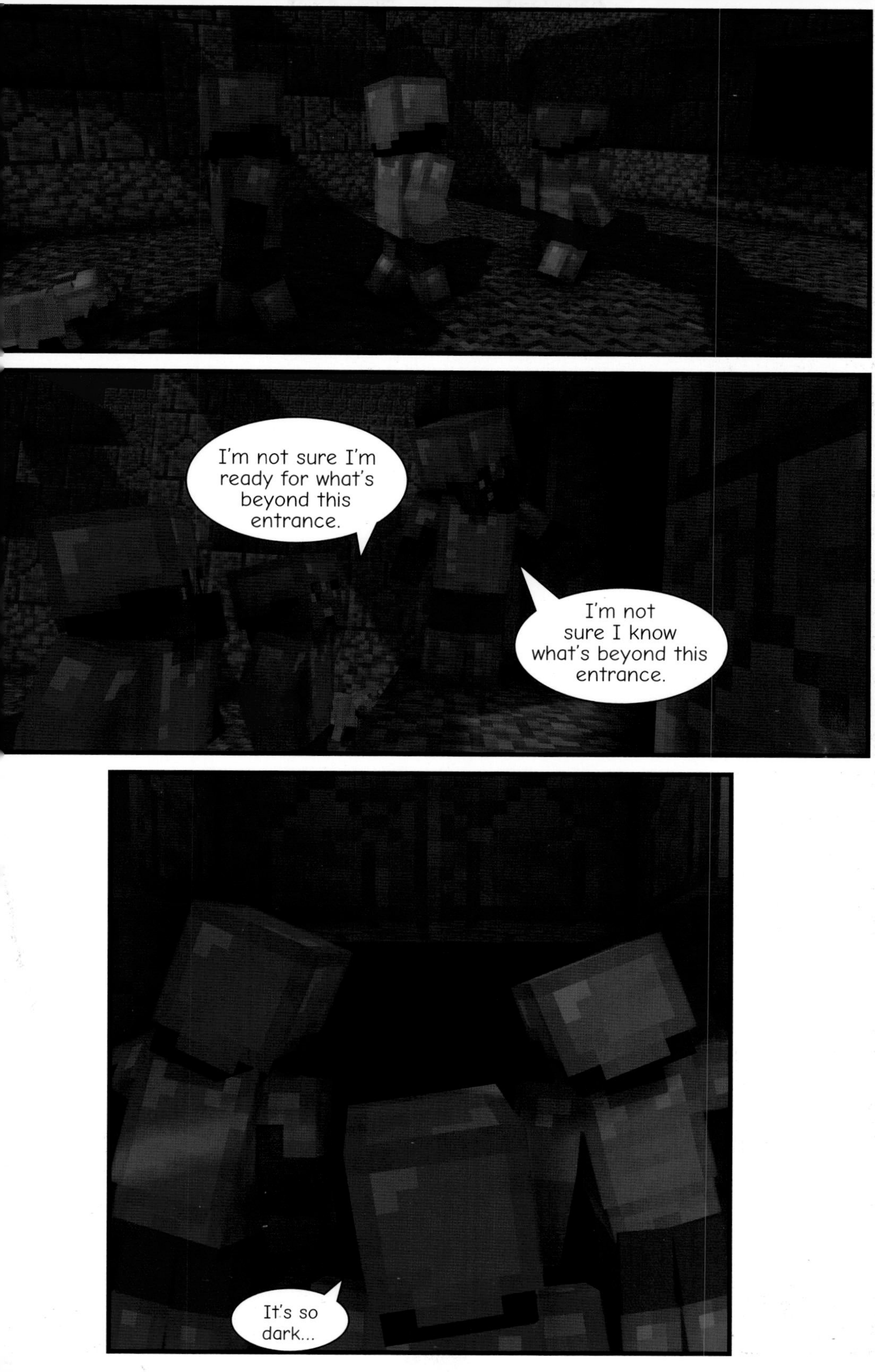
I'm not sure I'm ready for what's beyond this entrance.
I'm not sure I know what's beyond this entrance.
It's so dark...

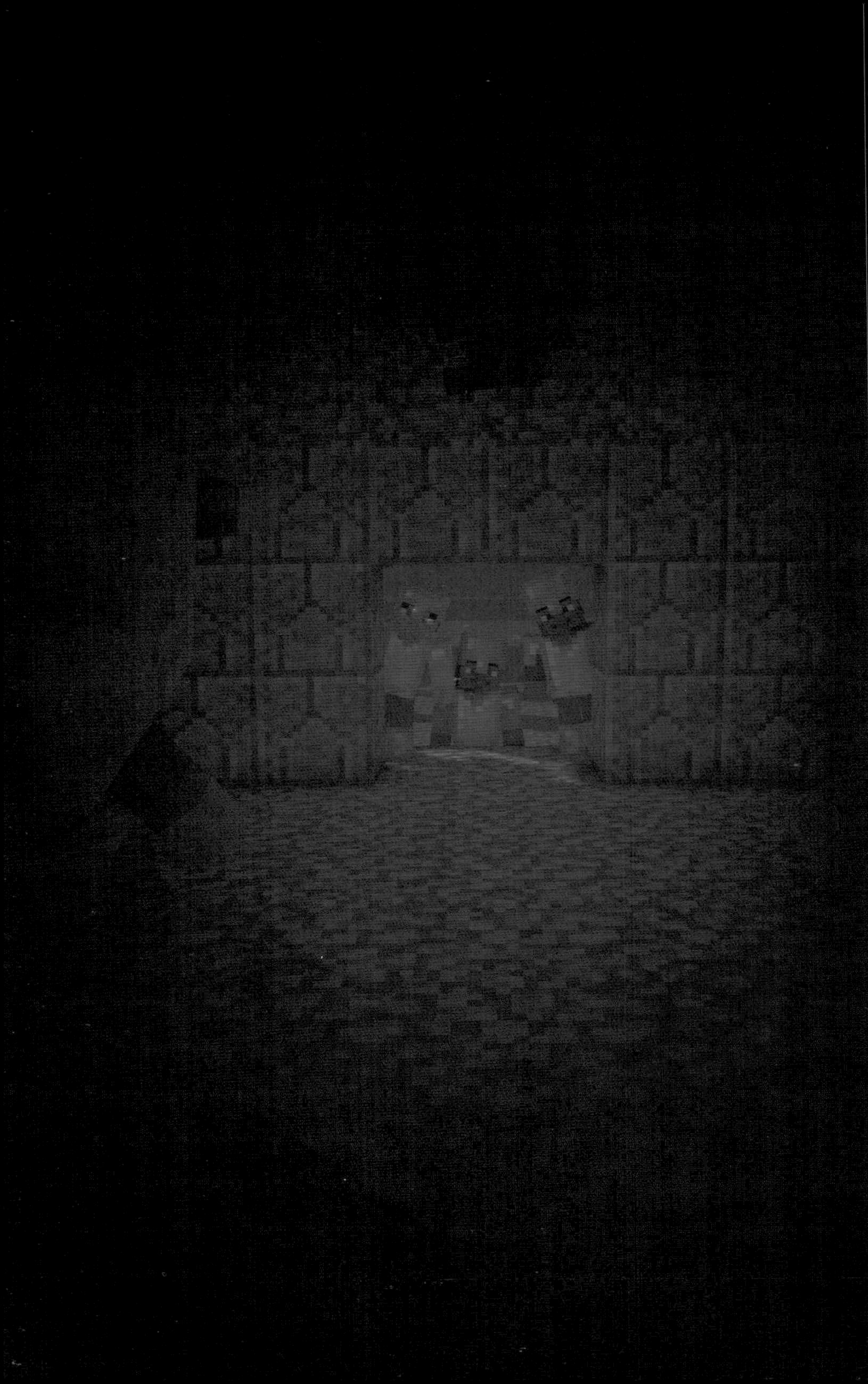

CHAPTER 6

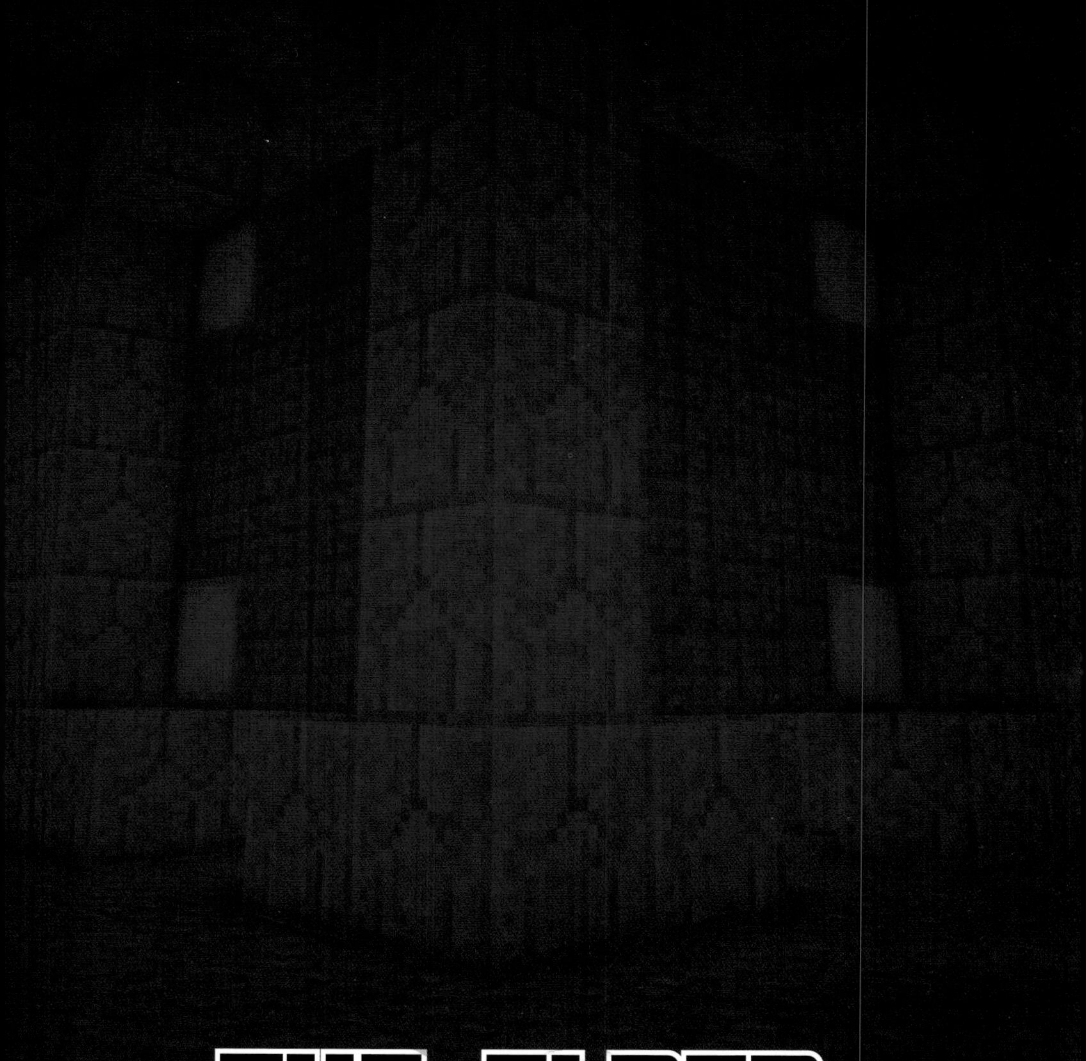

THE ELDER SCROLLS

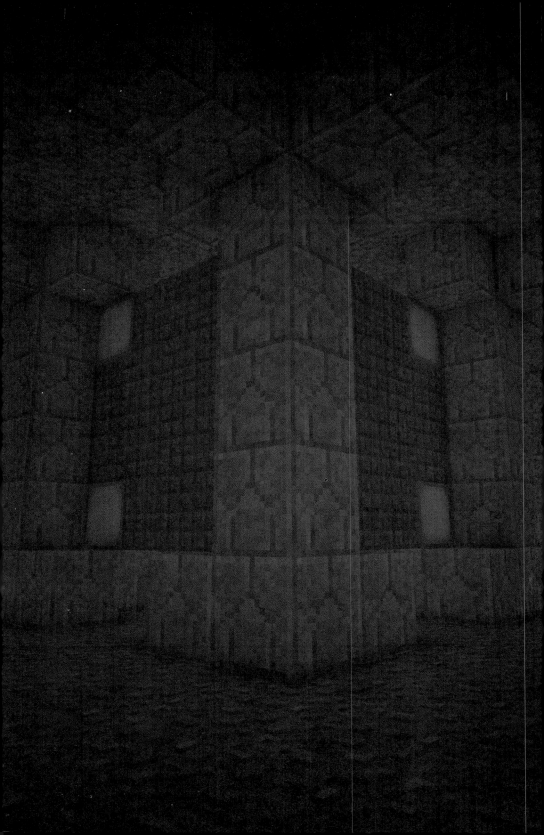

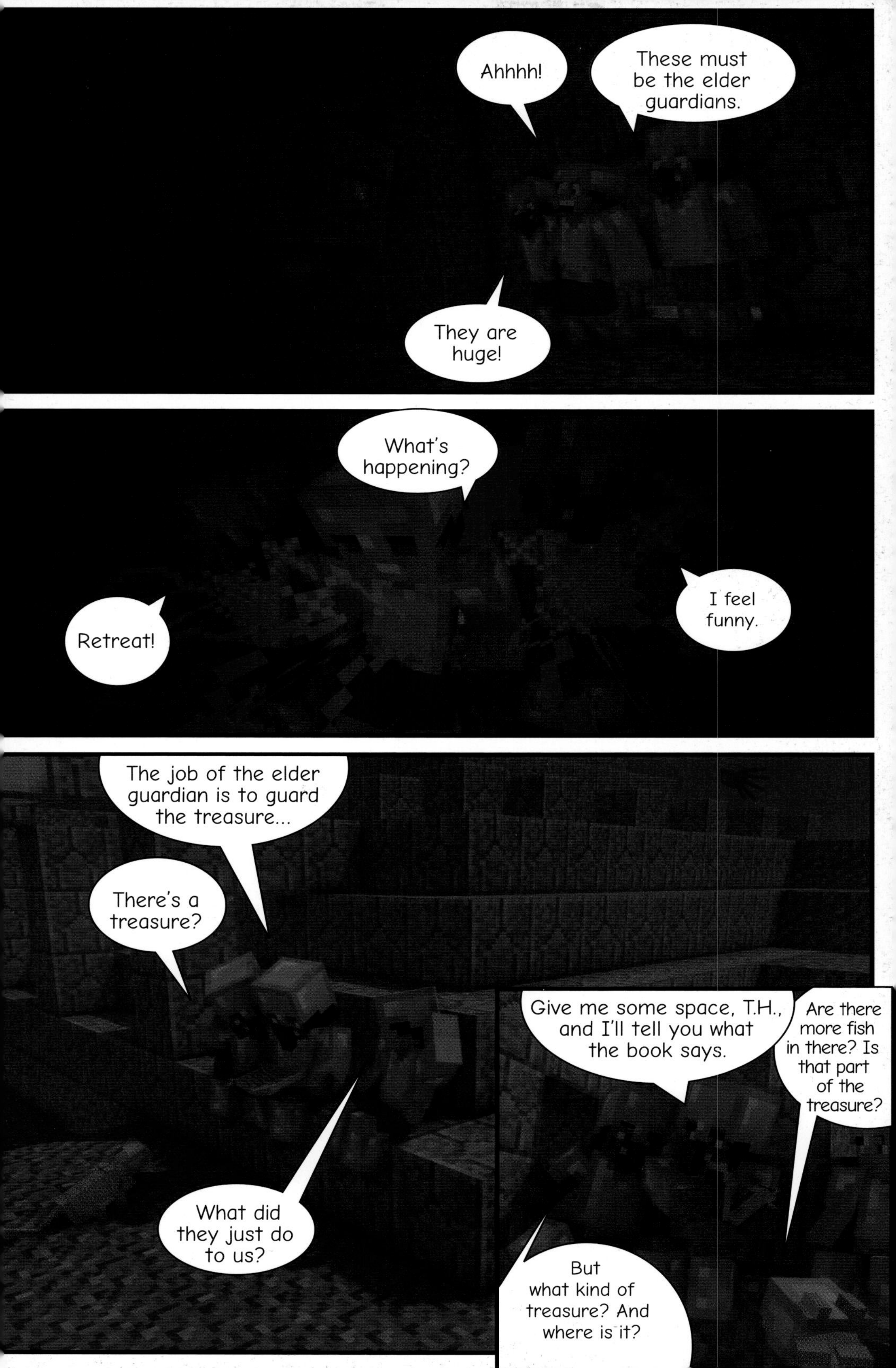
Ahhhh!
These must be the elder guardians.
They are huge!
What's happening?
Retreat!
I feel funny.
The job of the elder guardian is to guard the treasure...
There's a treasure?
What did they just do to us?
Give me some space, T.H., and I'll tell you what the book says.
Are there more fish in there? Is that part of the treasure?
But what kind of treasure? And where is it?

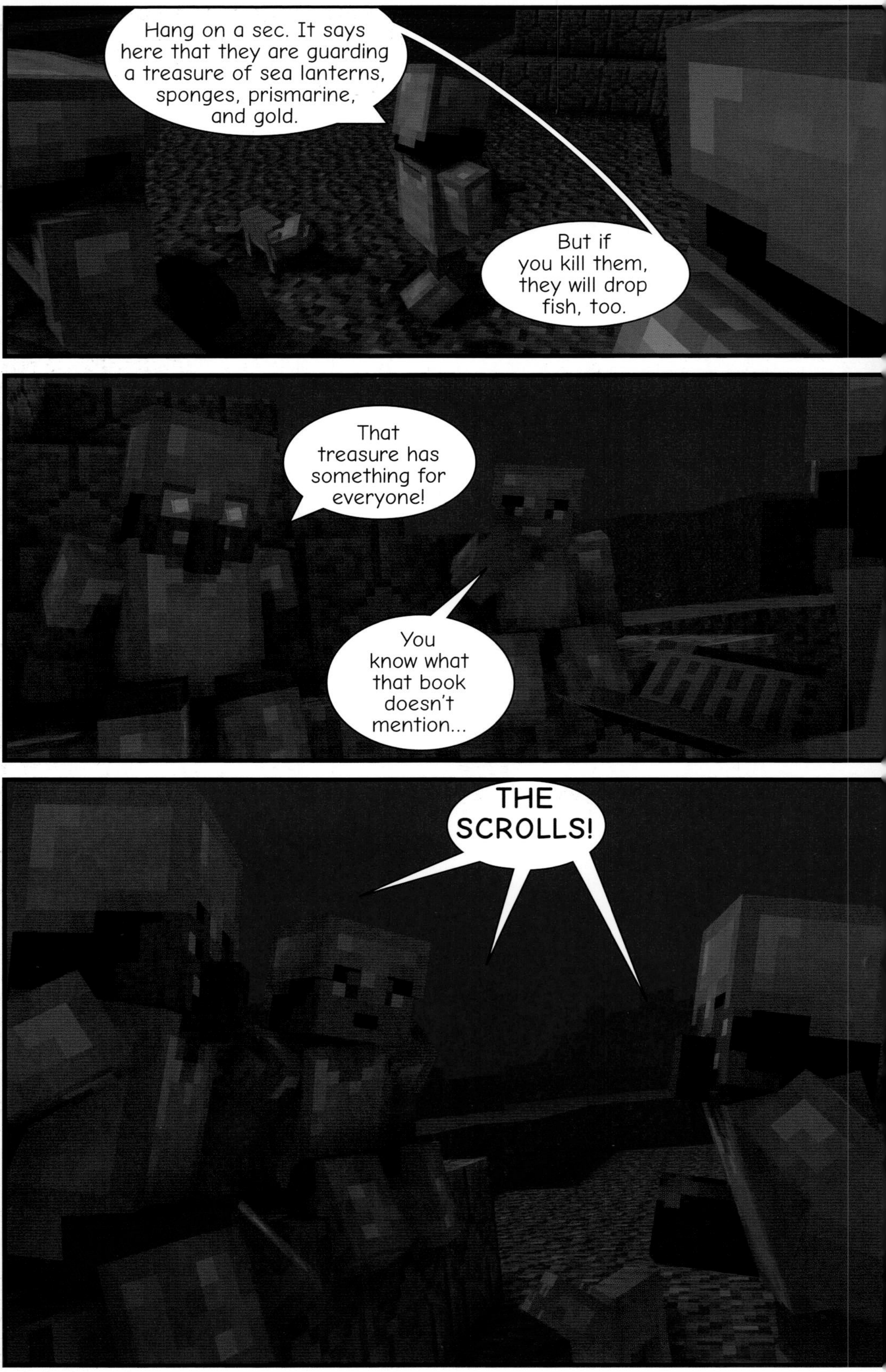
Hang on a sec. It says here that they are guarding a treasure of sea lanterns, sponges, prismarine, and gold.
But if you kill them, they will drop fish, too.
That treasure has something for everyone!
You know what that book doesn't mention...
THE SCROLLS!

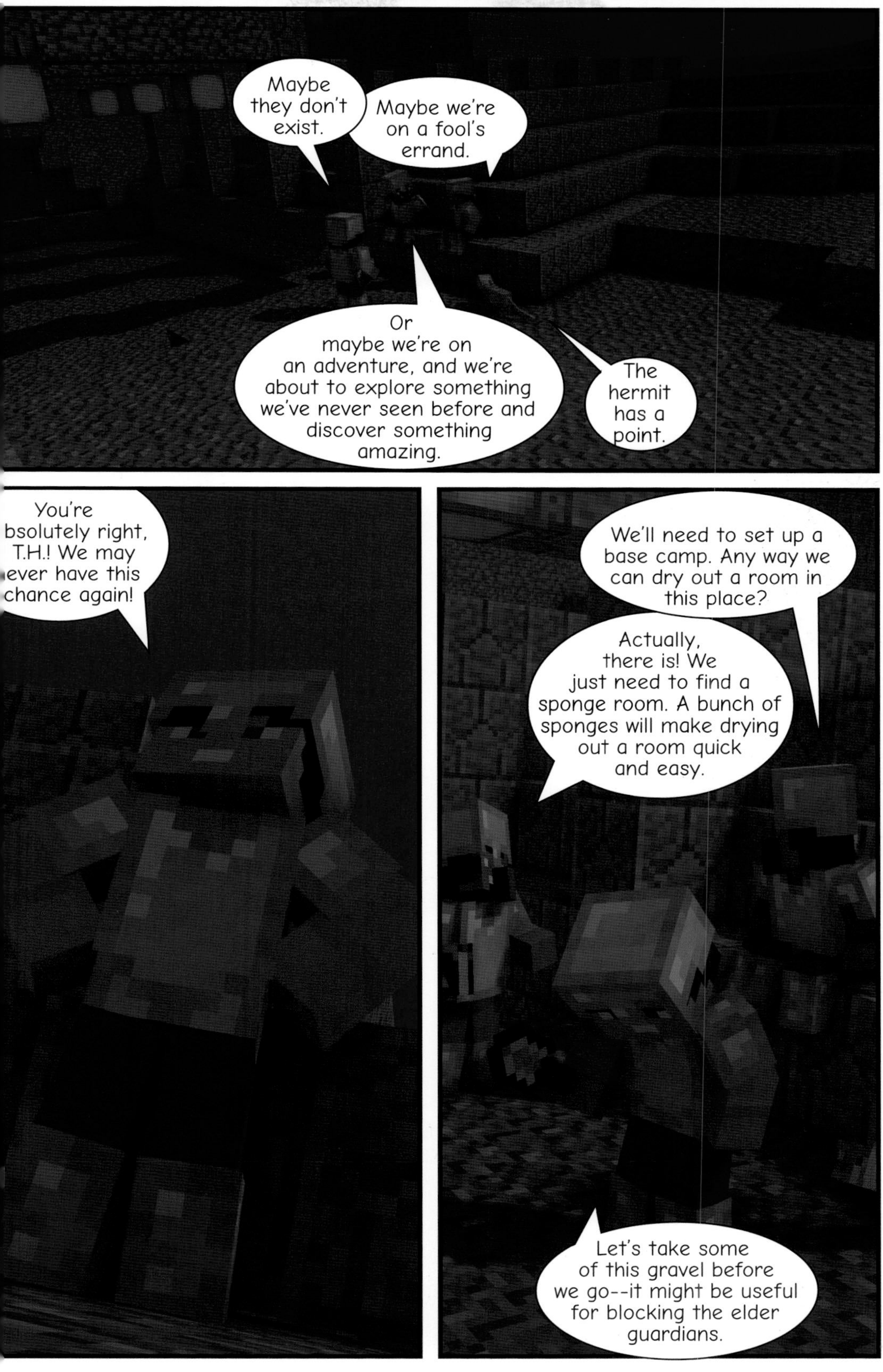
Maybe they don't exist.
Maybe we're on a fool's errand.
Or maybe we're on an adventure, and we're about to explore something we've never seen before and discover something amazing.
The hermit has a point.
You're bsolutely right, T.H.! We may ever have this chance again!
We'll need to set up a base camp. Any way we can dry out a room in this place?
Actually, there is! We just need to find a sponge room. A bunch of sponges will make drying out a room quick and easy.
Let's take some of this gravel before we go--it might be useful for blocking the elder guardians.

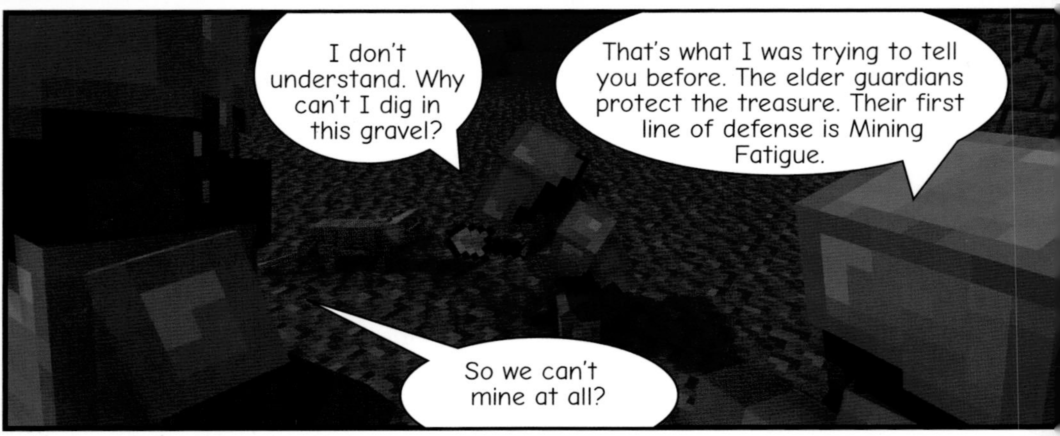
I don't understand. Why can't I dig in this gravel?
That's what I was trying to tell you before. The elder guardians protect the treasure. Their first line of defense is Mining Fatigue.
So we can't mine at all?

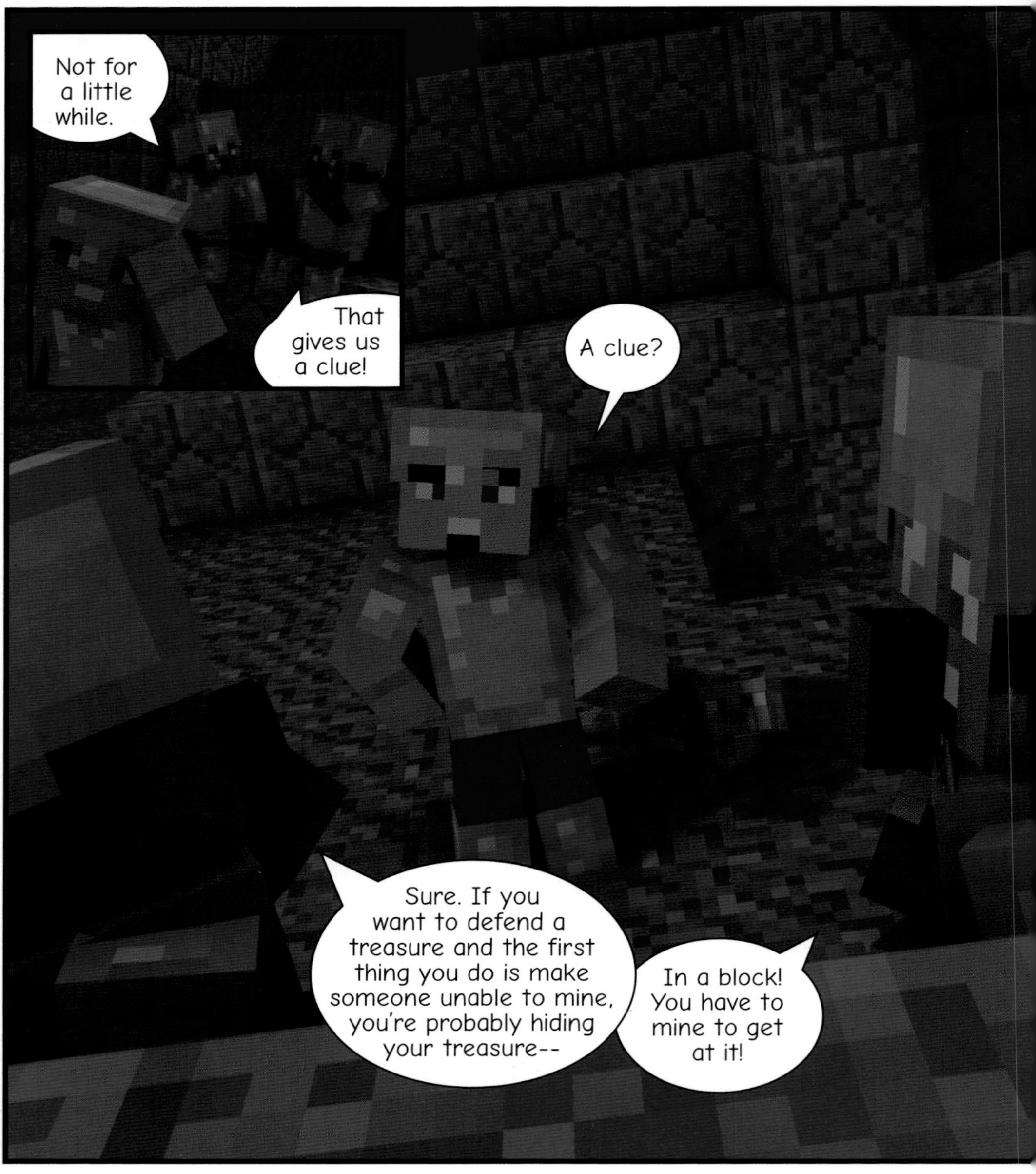
Not for a little while.
That gives us a clue!
A clue?
Sure. If you want to defend a treasure and the first thing you do is make someone unable to mine, you're probably hiding your treasure--
In a block! You have to mine to get at it!

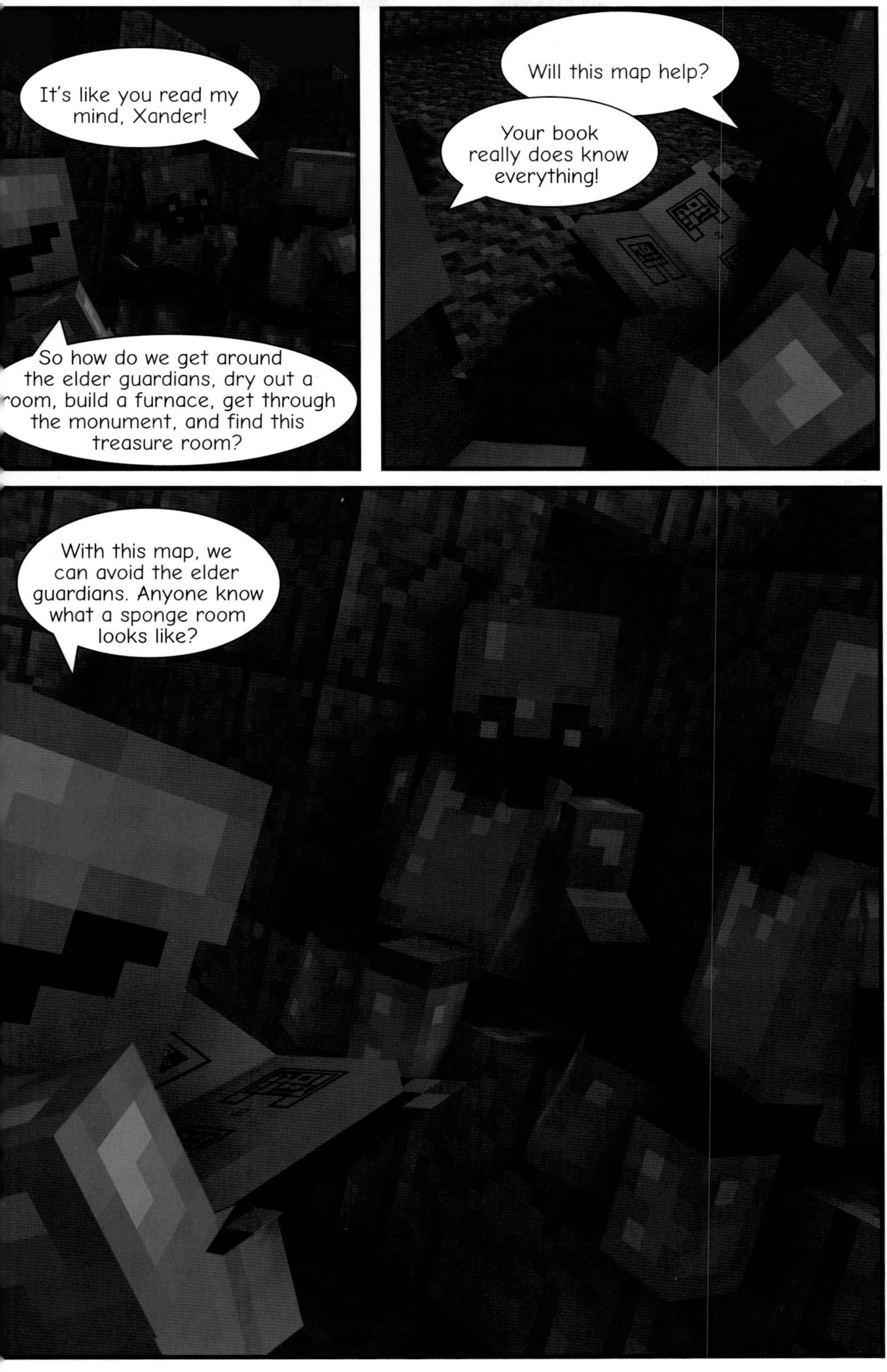
It's like you read my mind, Xander!
So how do we get around the elder guardians, dry out a room, build a furnace, get through the monument, and find this treasure room?
Will this map help?
Your book really does know everything!
With this map, we can avoid the elder guardians. Anyone know what a sponge room looks like?

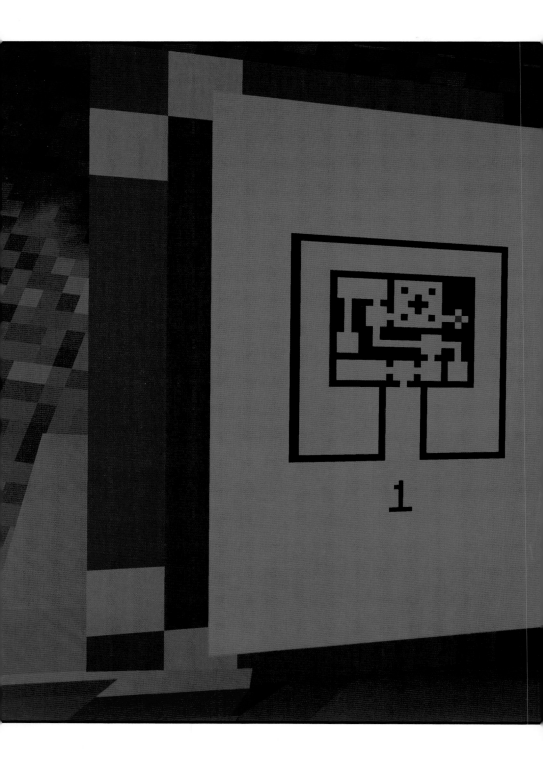

1

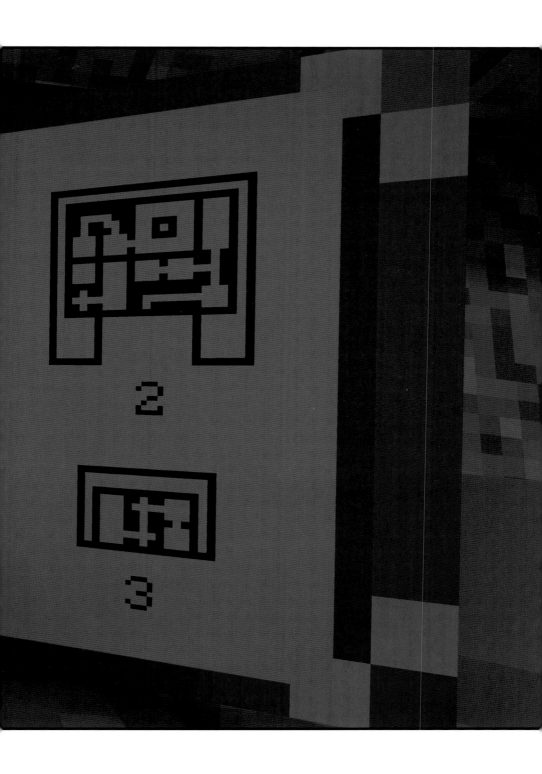

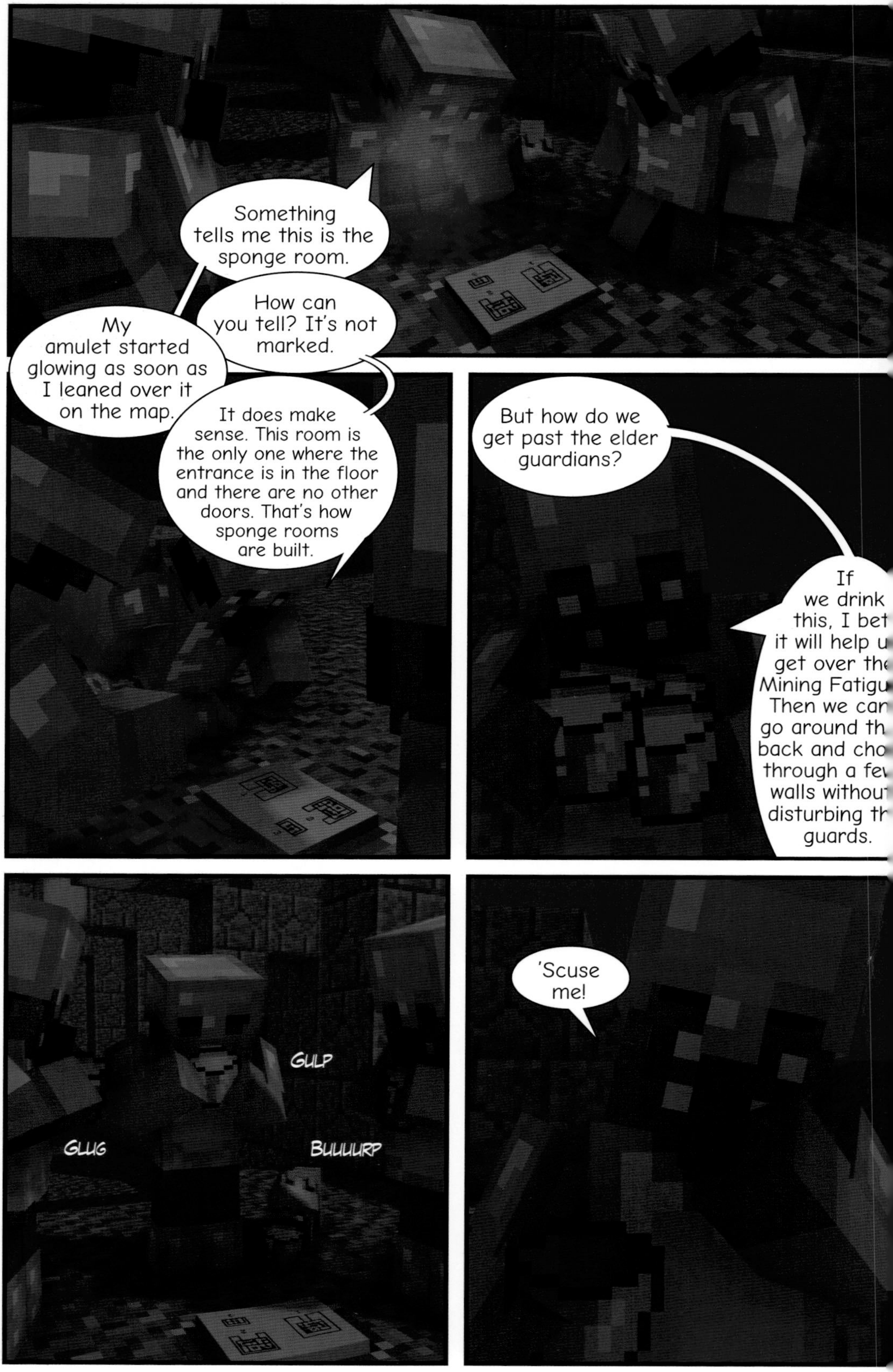
Something tells me this is the sponge room.
How can you tell? It's not marked.
My amulet started glowing as soon as I leaned over it on the map.
It does make sense. This room is the only one where the entrance is in the floor and there are no other doors. That's how sponge rooms are built.
But how do we get past the elder guardians?
If we drink this, I bet it will help u get over the Mining Fatigu Then we car go around th back and cho through a fe walls without disturbing th guards.
GULP
GLUG
BUUUURP
'Scuse me!

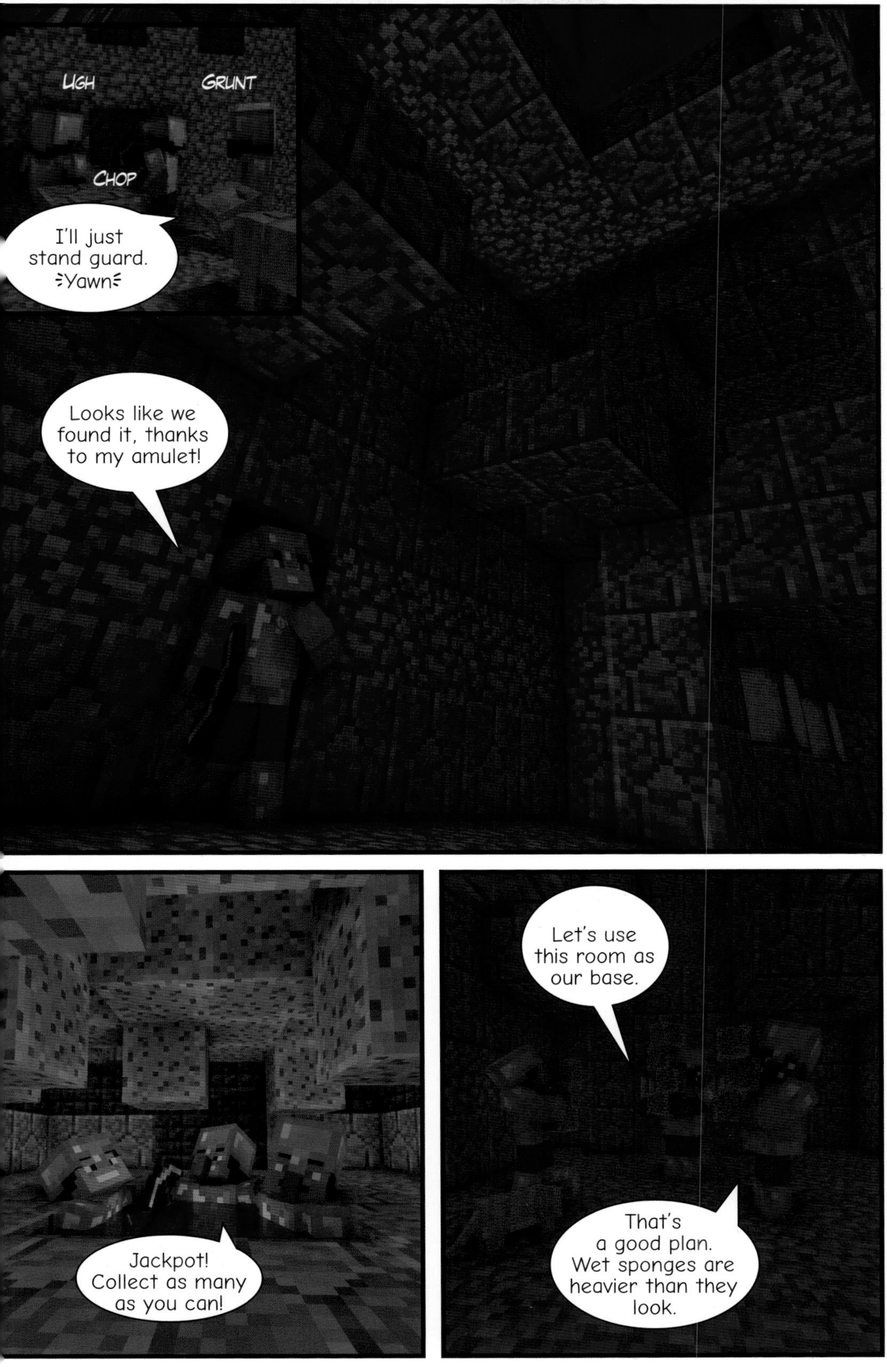
UGH
GRUNT
CHOP
I'll just stand guard. ⁼Yawn⁼
Looks like we found it, thanks to my amulet!
Jackpot! Collect as many as you can!
Let's use this room as our base.
That's a good plan. Wet sponges are heavier than they look.

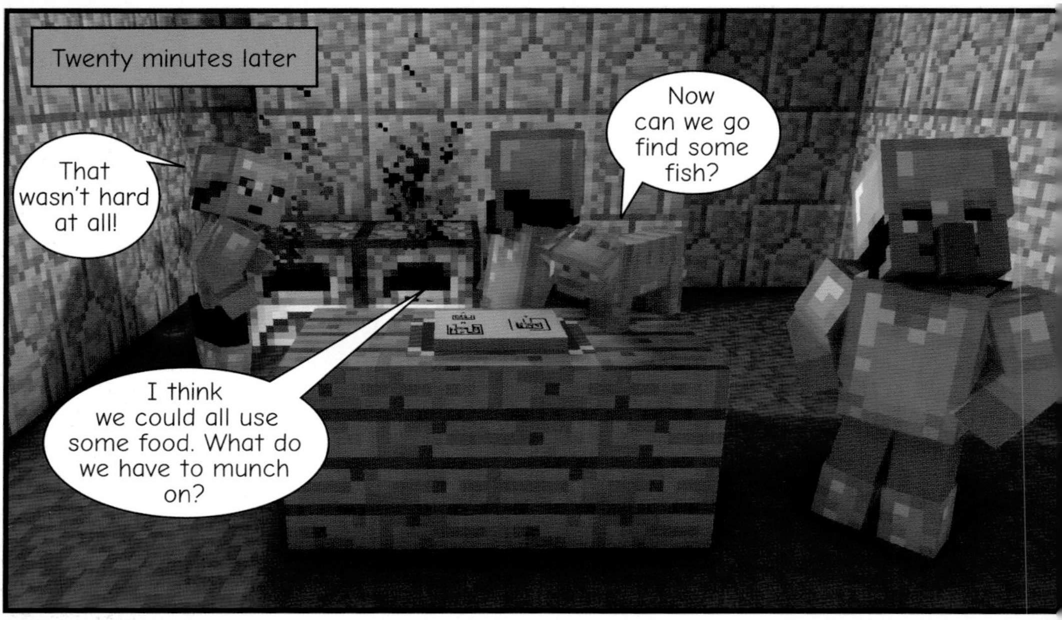
Twenty minutes later
That wasn't hard at all!
Now can we go find some fish?
I think we could all use some food. What do we have to munch on?

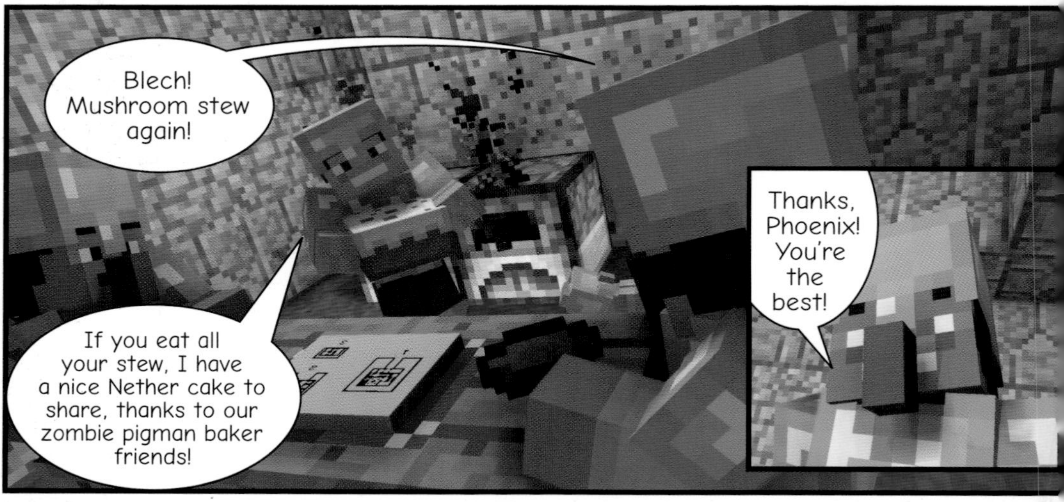
Blech! Mushroom stew again!
If you eat all your stew, I have a nice Nether cake to share, thanks to our zombie pigman baker friends!
Thanks, Phoenix! You're the best!

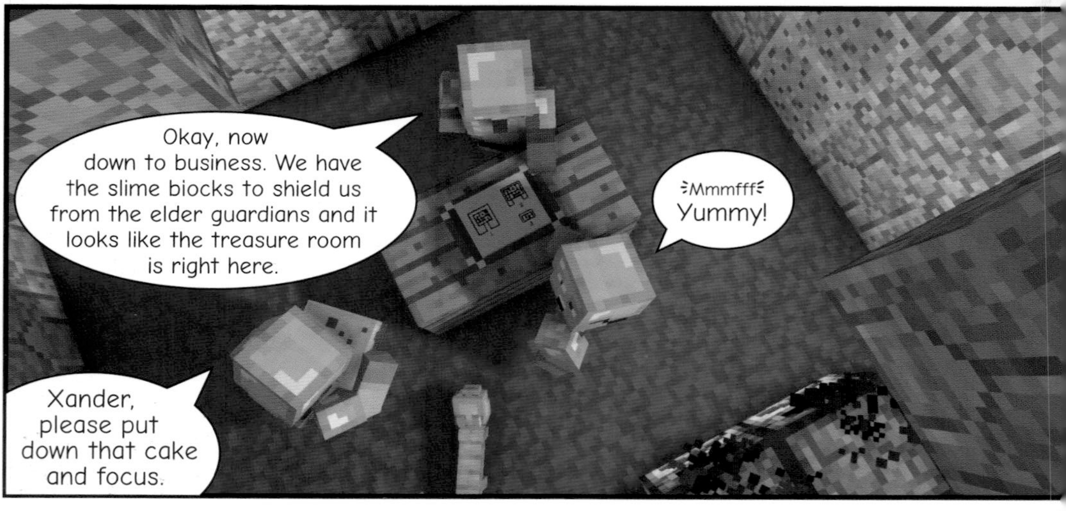
Okay, now down to business. We have the slime biocks to shield us from the elder guardians and it looks like the treasure room is right here.
Mmmfff Yummy!
Xander, please put down that cake and focus.

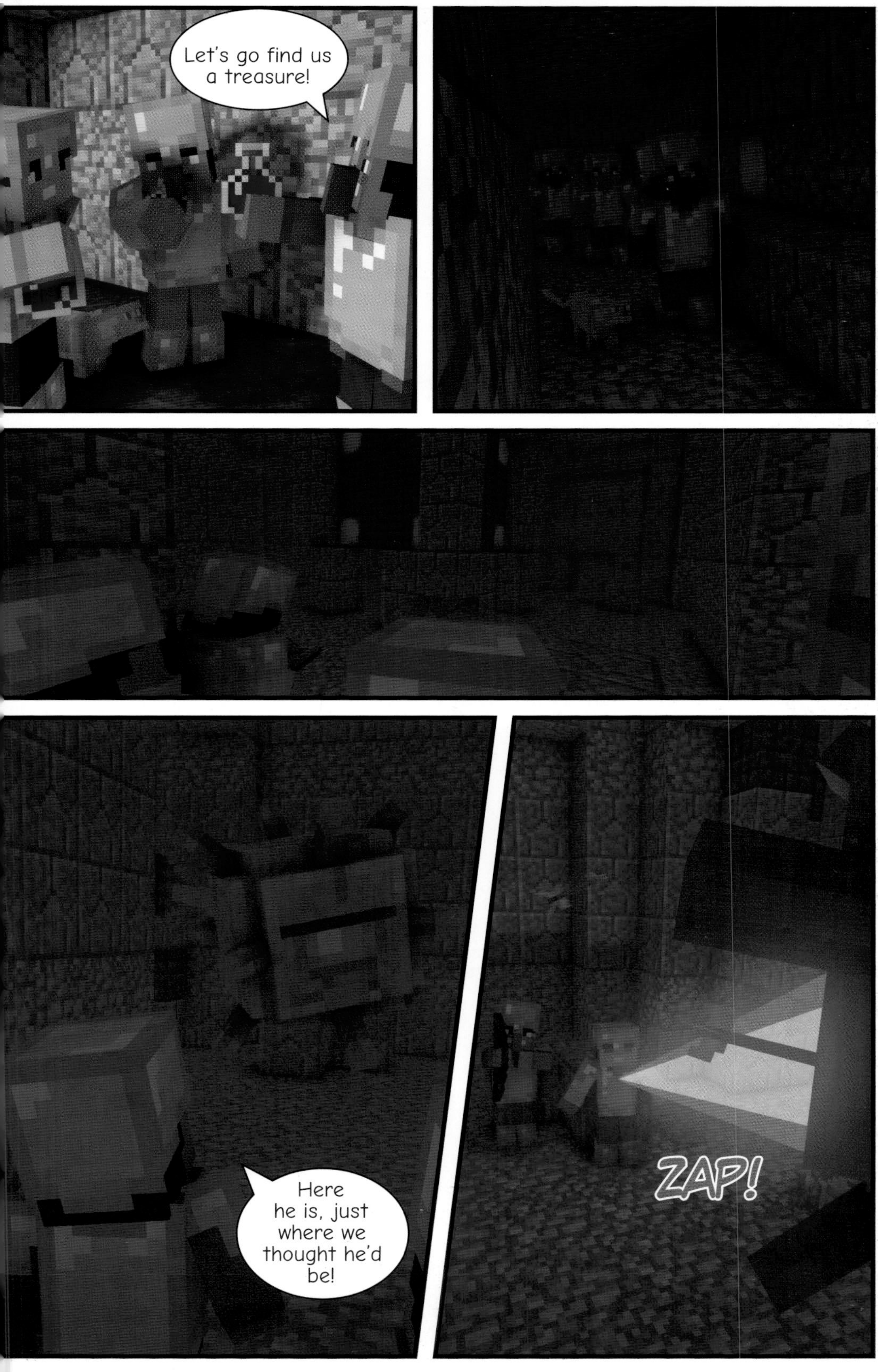

Let's go find us a treasure!
Here he is, just where we thought he'd be!
ZAP!

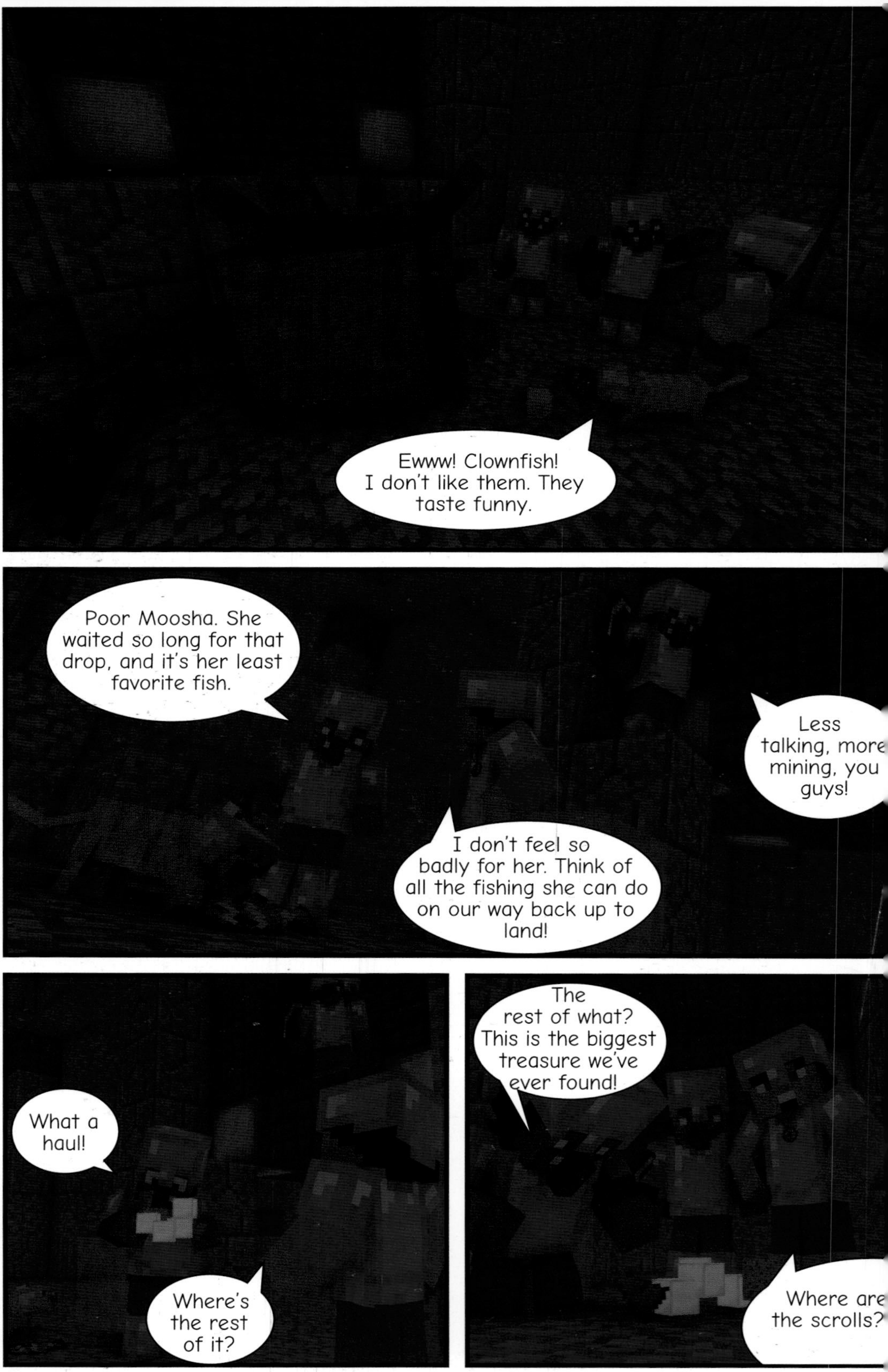
Ewww! Clownfish! I don't like them. They taste funny.
Poor Moosha. She waited so long for that drop, and it's her least favorite fish.
Less talking, more mining, you guys!
I don't feel so badly for her. Think of all the fishing she can do on our way back up to land!
What a haul!
Where's the rest of it?
The rest of what? This is the biggest treasure we've ever found!
Where are the scrolls?

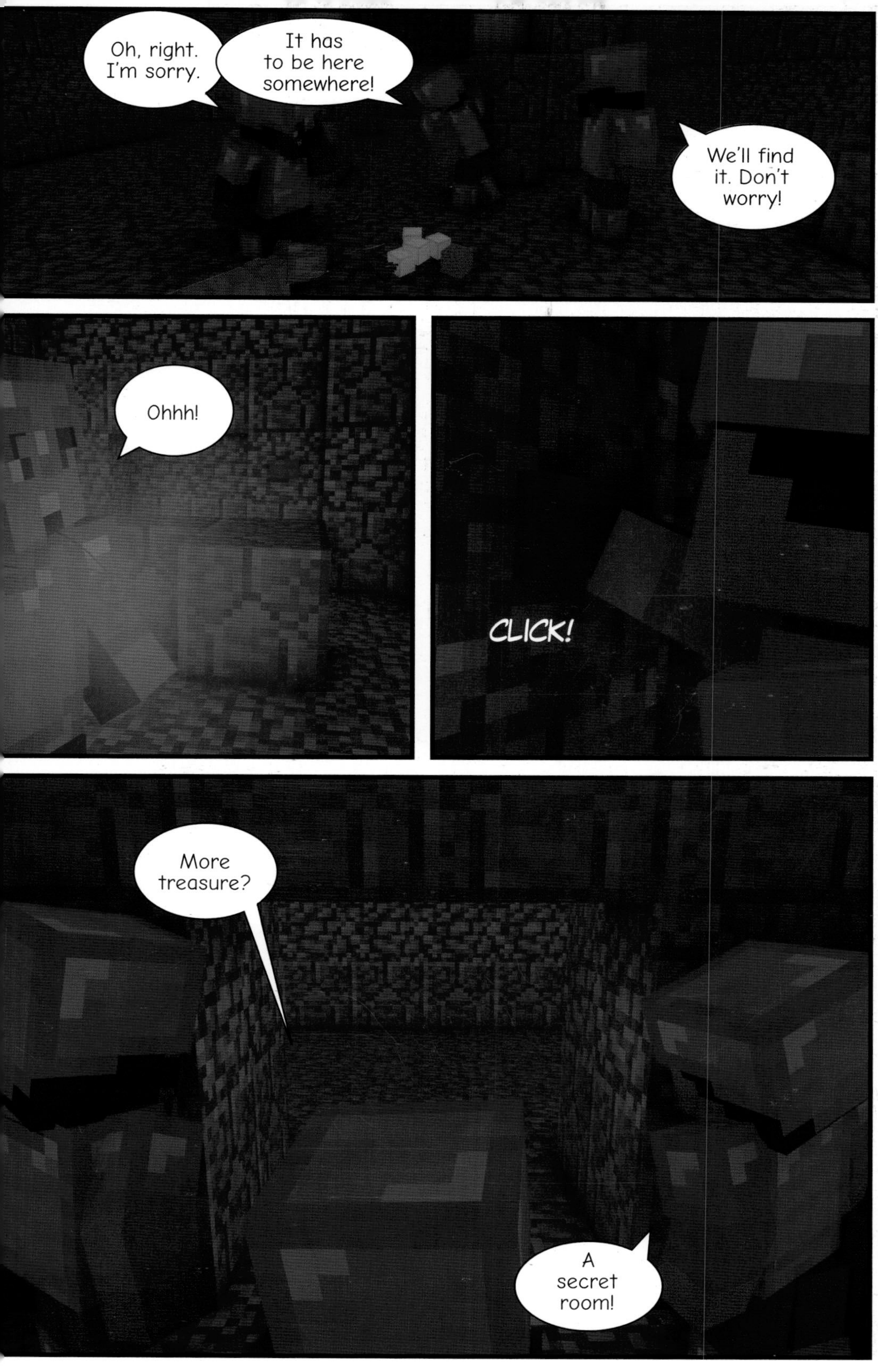
Oh, right. I'm sorry.
It has to be here somewhere!
We'll find it. Don't worry!
Ohhh!
CLICK!
More treasure?
A secret room!

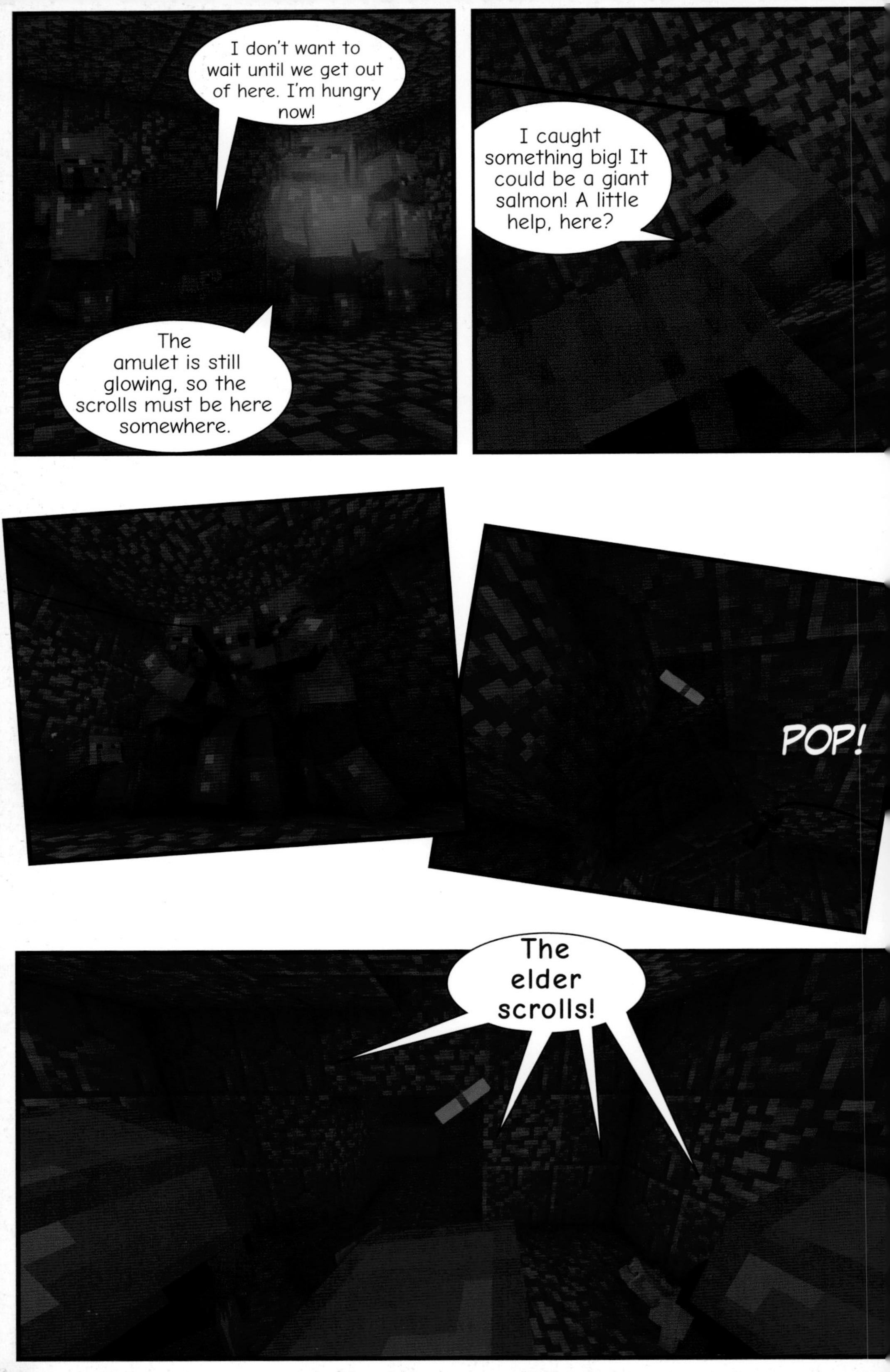
I don't want to wait until we get out of here. I'm hungry now!
The amulet is still glowing, so the scrolls must be here somewhere.
I caught something big! It could be a giant salmon! A little help, here?
POP!
The elder scrolls!

CHAPTER 7

THE RETURN OF THE CREEPERS

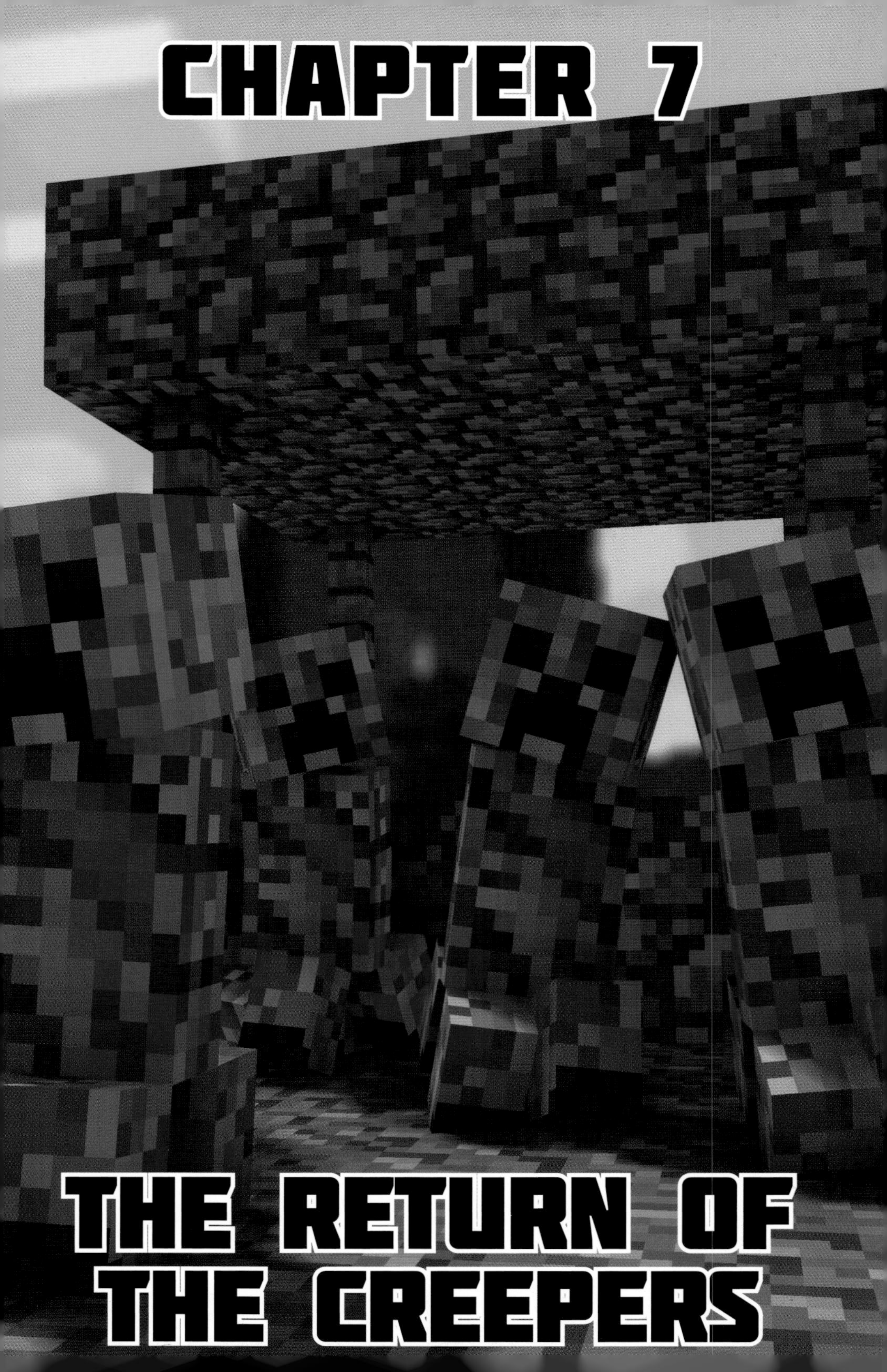

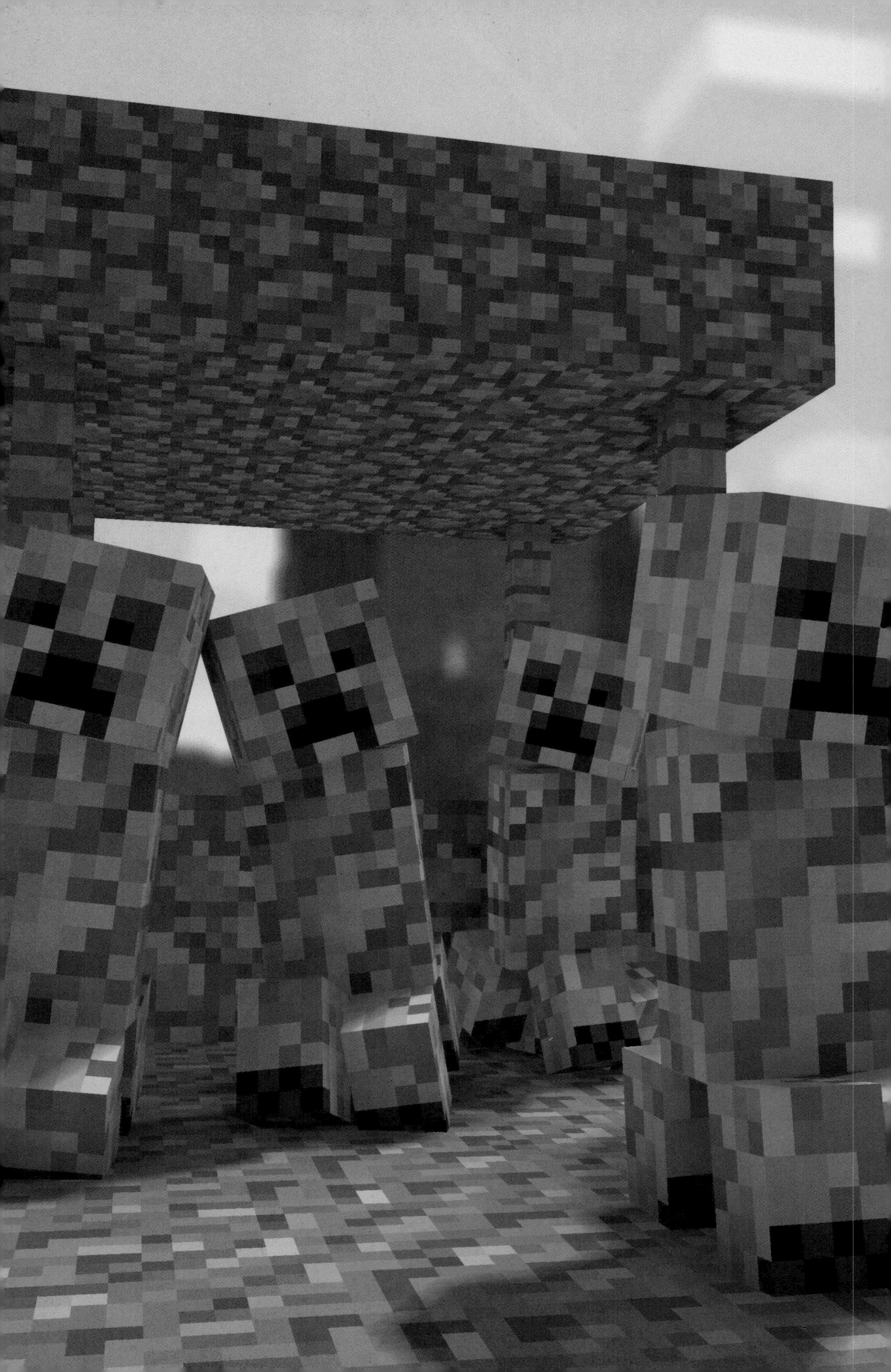

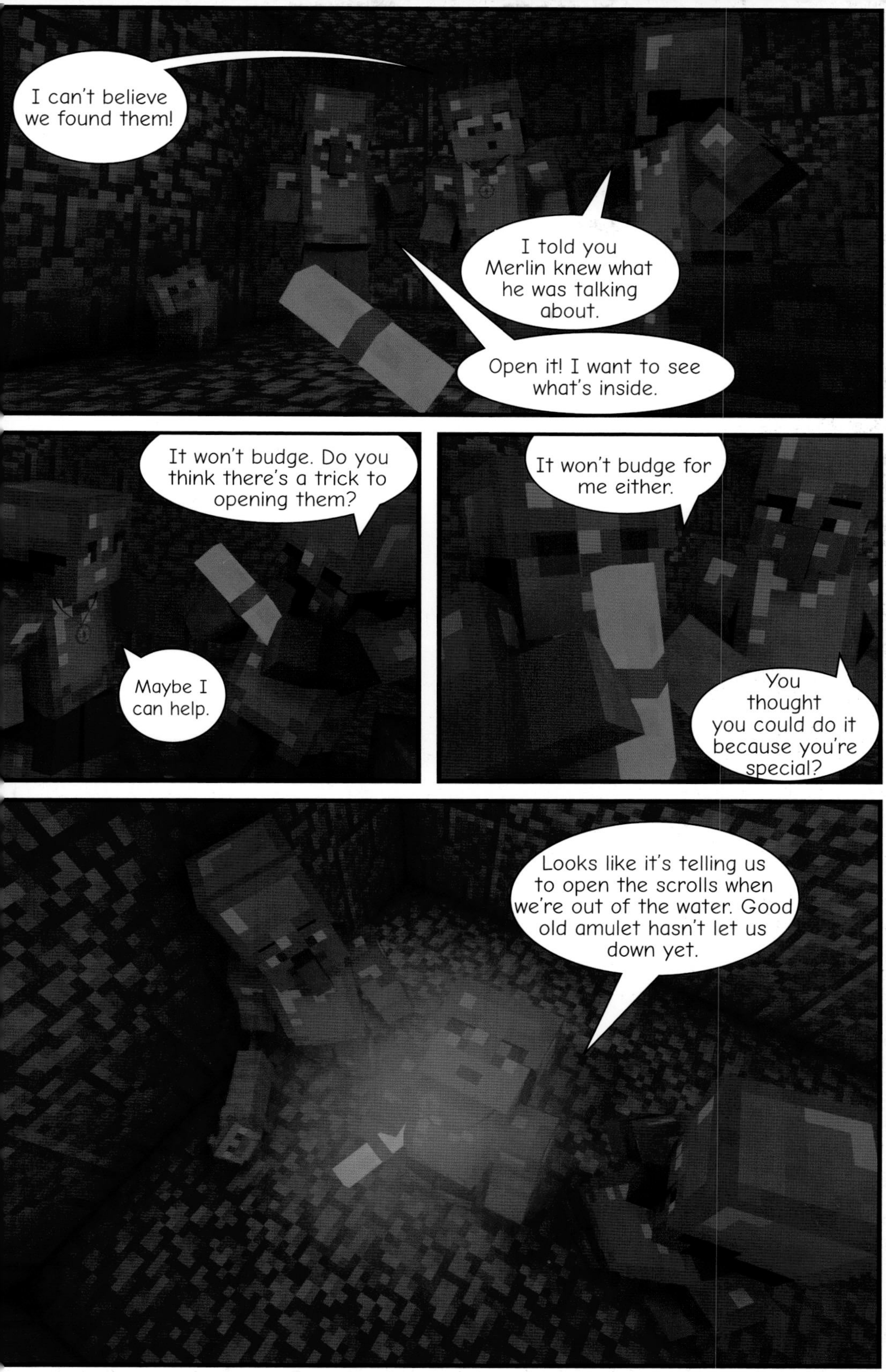
I can't believe we found them!
I told you Merlin knew what he was talking about.
Open it! I want to see what's inside.
It won't budge. Do you think there's a trick to opening them?
Maybe I can help.
It won't budge for me either.
You thought you could do it because you're special?
Looks like it's telling us to open the scrolls when we're out of the water. Good old amulet hasn't let us down yet.

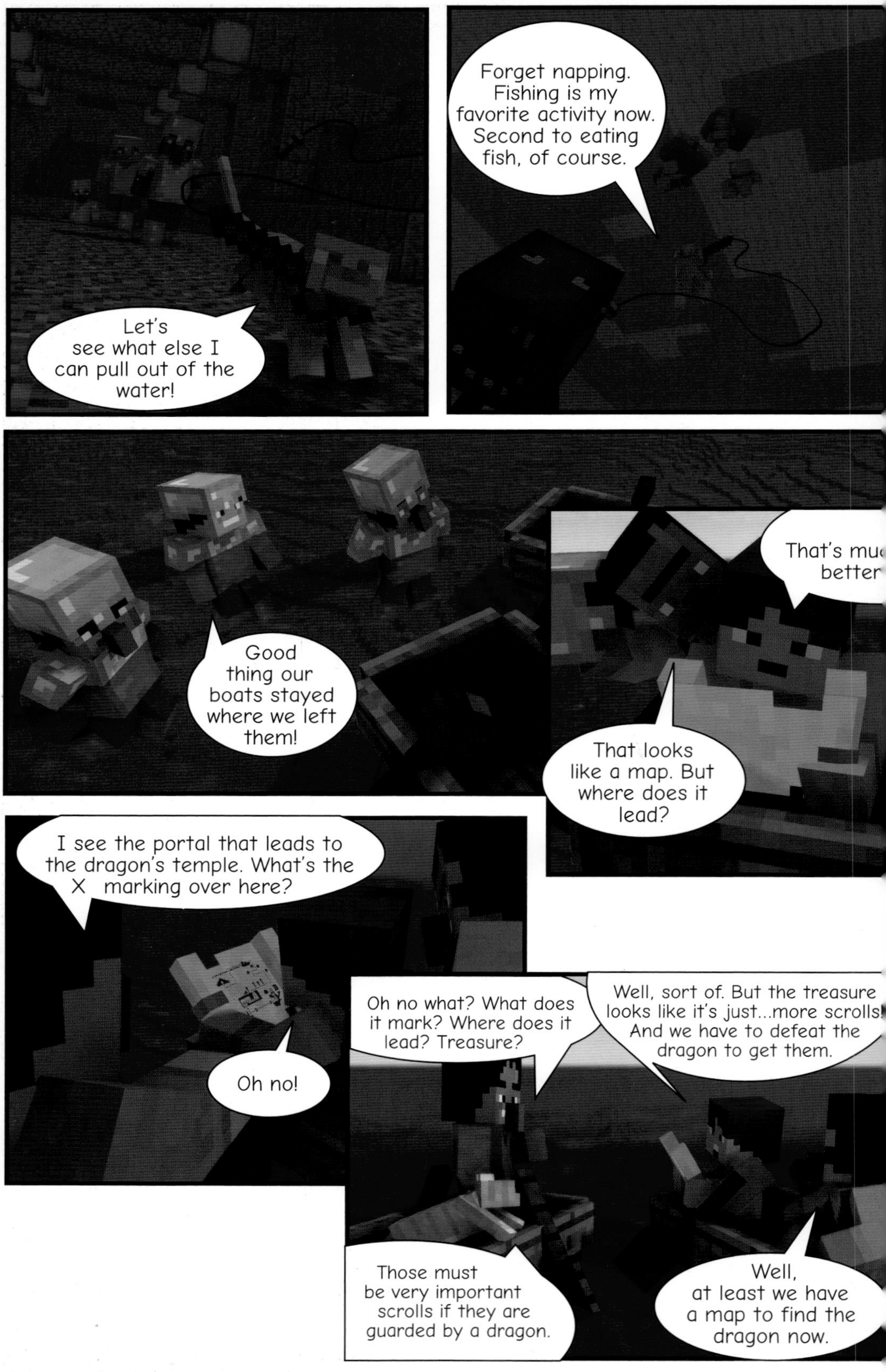
Let's see what else I can pull out of the water!
Forget napping. Fishing is my favorite activity now. Second to eating fish, of course.
Good thing our boats stayed where we left them!
That's mu
better
That looks like a map. But where does it lead?
I see the portal that leads to the dragon's temple. What's the X marking over here?
Oh no!
Oh no what? What does it mark? Where does it lead? Treasure?
Well, sort of. But the treasure looks like it's just...more scrolls! And we have to defeat the dragon to get them.
Those must be very important scrolls if they are guarded by a dragon.
Well, at least we have a map to find the dragon now.

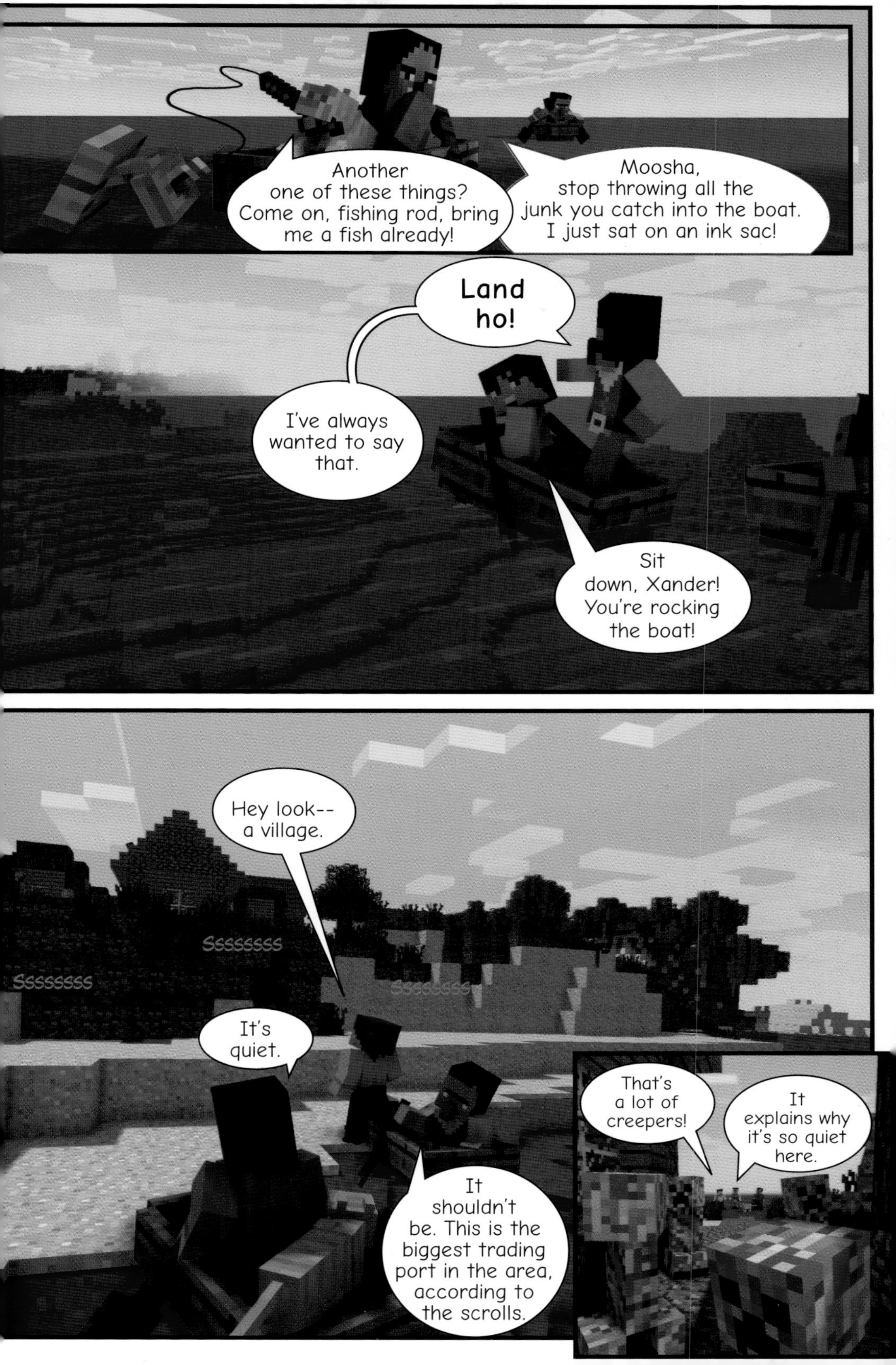
Another one of these things? Come on, fishing rod, bring me a fish already!
Moosha, stop throwing all the junk you catch into the boat. I just sat on an ink sac!
Land ho!
I've always wanted to say that.
Sit down, Xander! You're rocking the boat!
Hey look-- a village.
Ssssssss
Ssssssss
It's quiet.
It shouldn't be. This is the biggest trading port in the area, according to the scrolls.
That's a lot of creepers!
It explains why it's so quiet here.

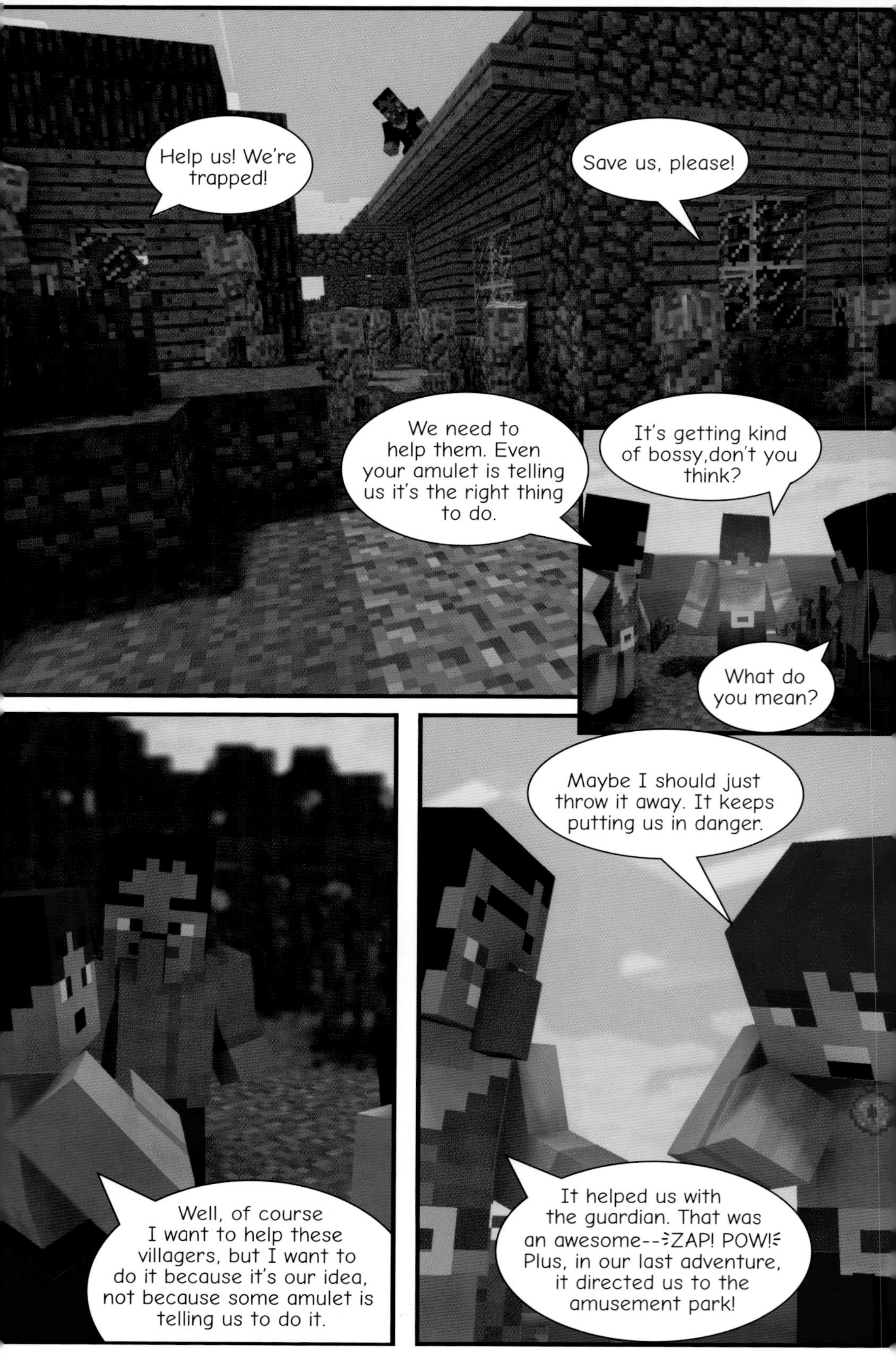
Help us! We're trapped!
Save us, please!
We need to help them. Even your amulet is telling us it's the right thing to do.
It's getting kind of bossy,don't you think?
What do you mean?
Well, of course I want to help these villagers, but I want to do it because it's our idea, not because some amulet is telling us to do it.
Maybe I should just throw it away. It keeps putting us in danger.
It helped us with the guardian. That was an awesome--ZAP! POW!
Plus, in our last adventure, it directed us to the amusement park!

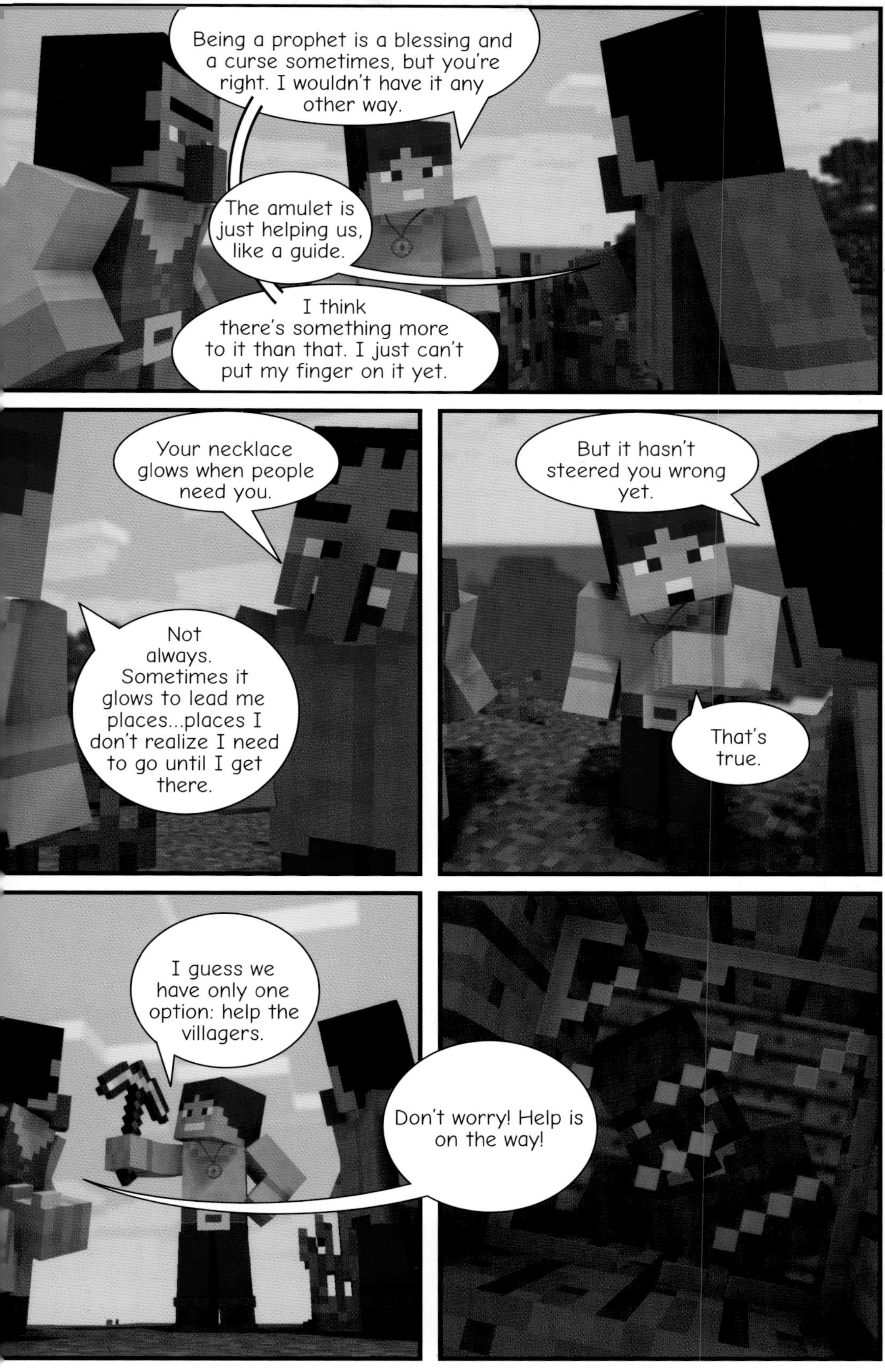

Being a prophet is a blessing and a curse sometimes, but you're right. I wouldn't have it any other way.
The amulet is just helping us, like a guide.
I think there's something more to it than that. I just can't put my finger on it yet.
Your necklace glows when people need you.
Not always. Sometimes it glows to lead me places...places I don't realize I need to go until I get there.
But it hasn't steered you wrong yet.
That's true.
I guess we have only one option: help the villagers.
Don't worry! Help is on the way!

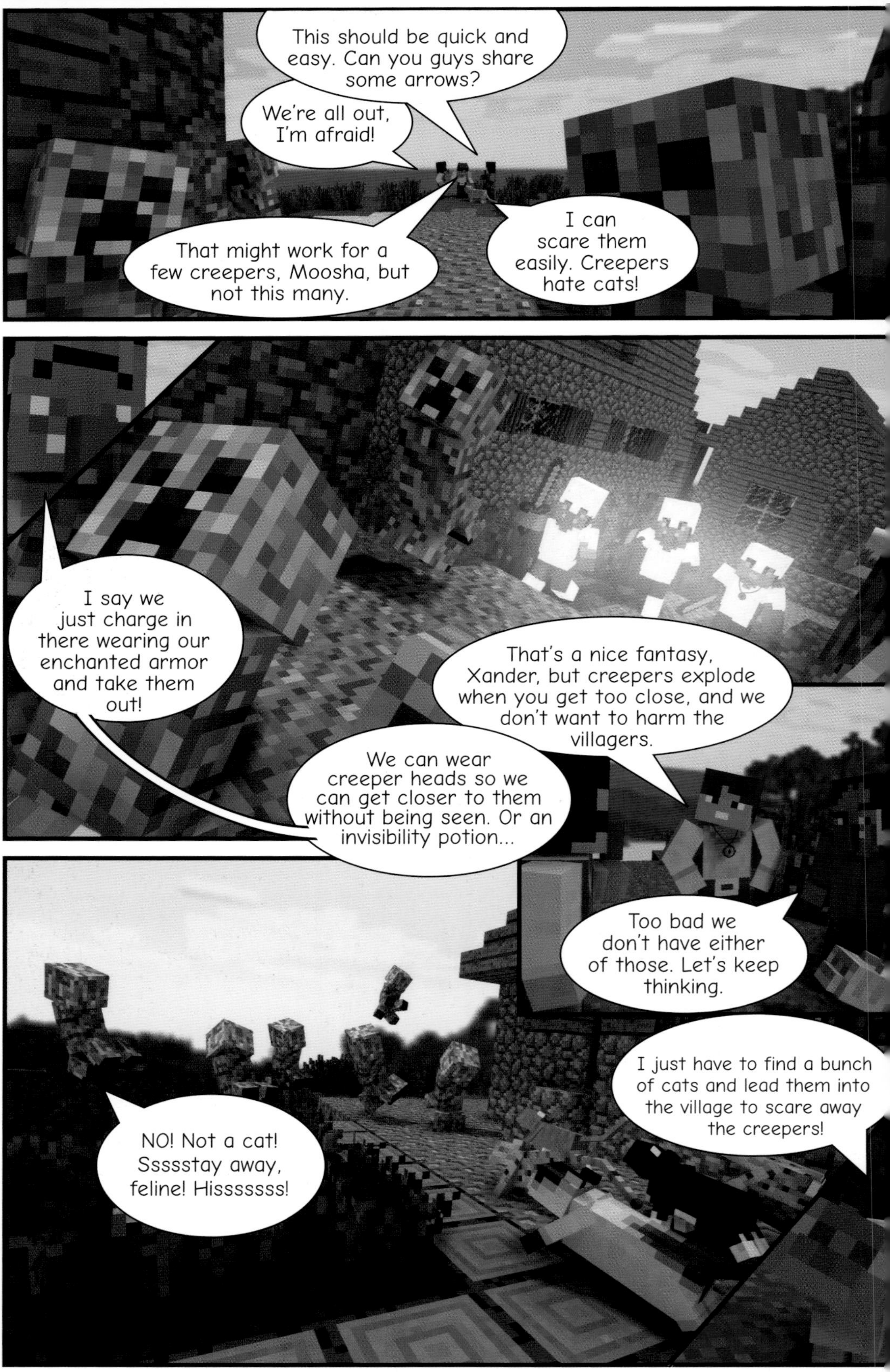
This should be quick and easy. Can you guys share some arrows?
We're all out, I'm afraid!
That might work for a few creepers, Moosha, but not this many.
I can scare them easily. Creepers hate cats!
I say we just charge in there wearing our enchanted armor and take them out!
That's a nice fantasy, Xander, but creepers explode when you get too close, and we don't want to harm the villagers.
We can wear creeper heads so we can get closer to them without being seen. Or an invisibility potion...
Too bad we don't have either of those. Let's keep thinking.
I just have to find a bunch of cats and lead them into the village to scare away the creepers!
NO! Not a cat! Ssssstay away, feline! Hisssssss!

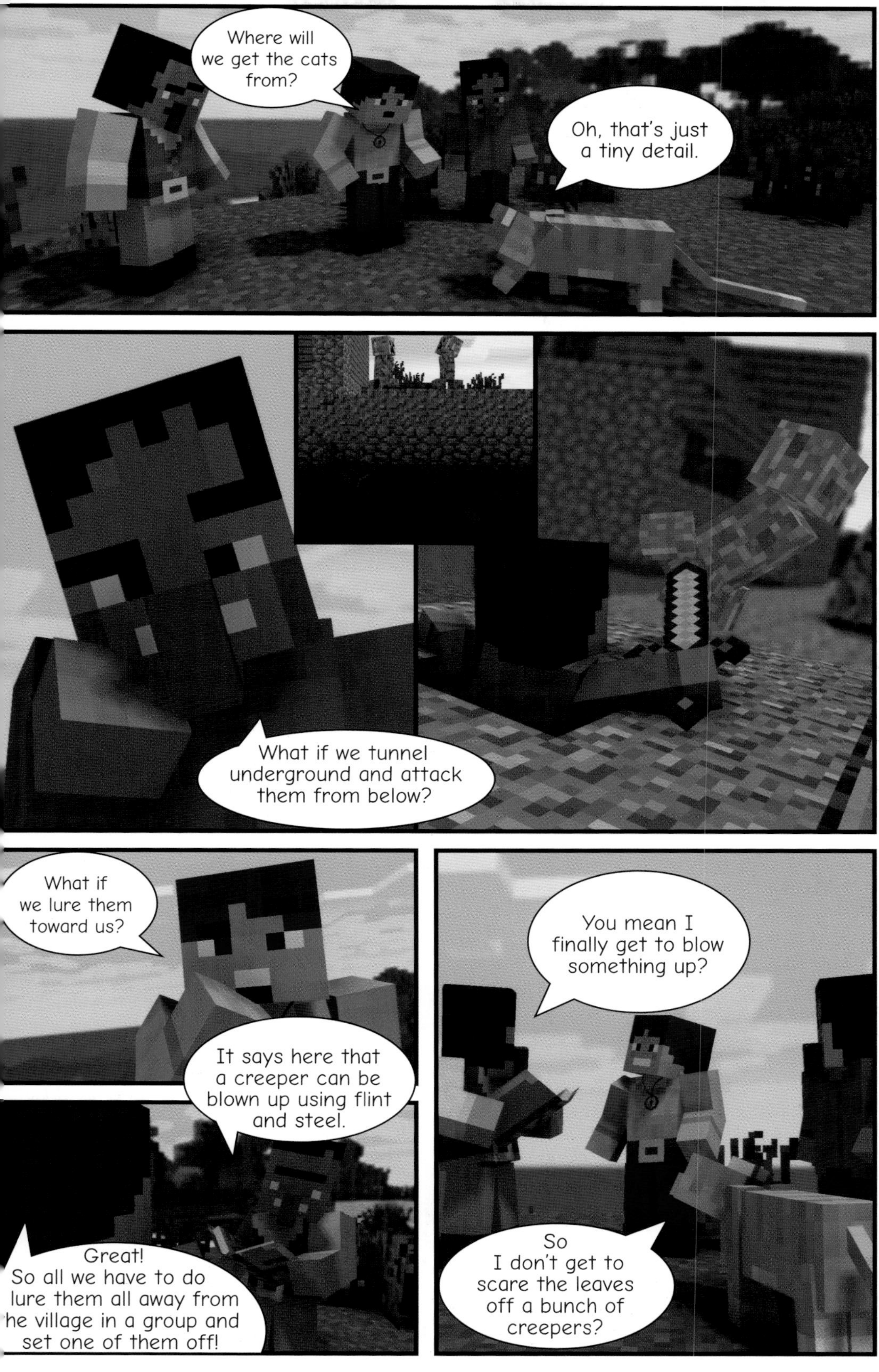
Where will we get the cats from?
Oh, that's just a tiny detail.
What if we tunnel underground and attack them from below?
What if we lure them toward us?
It says here that a creeper can be blown up using flint and steel.
Great! So all we have to do lure them all away from he village in a group and set one of them off!
You mean I finally get to blow something up?
So I don't get to scare the leaves off a bunch of creepers?

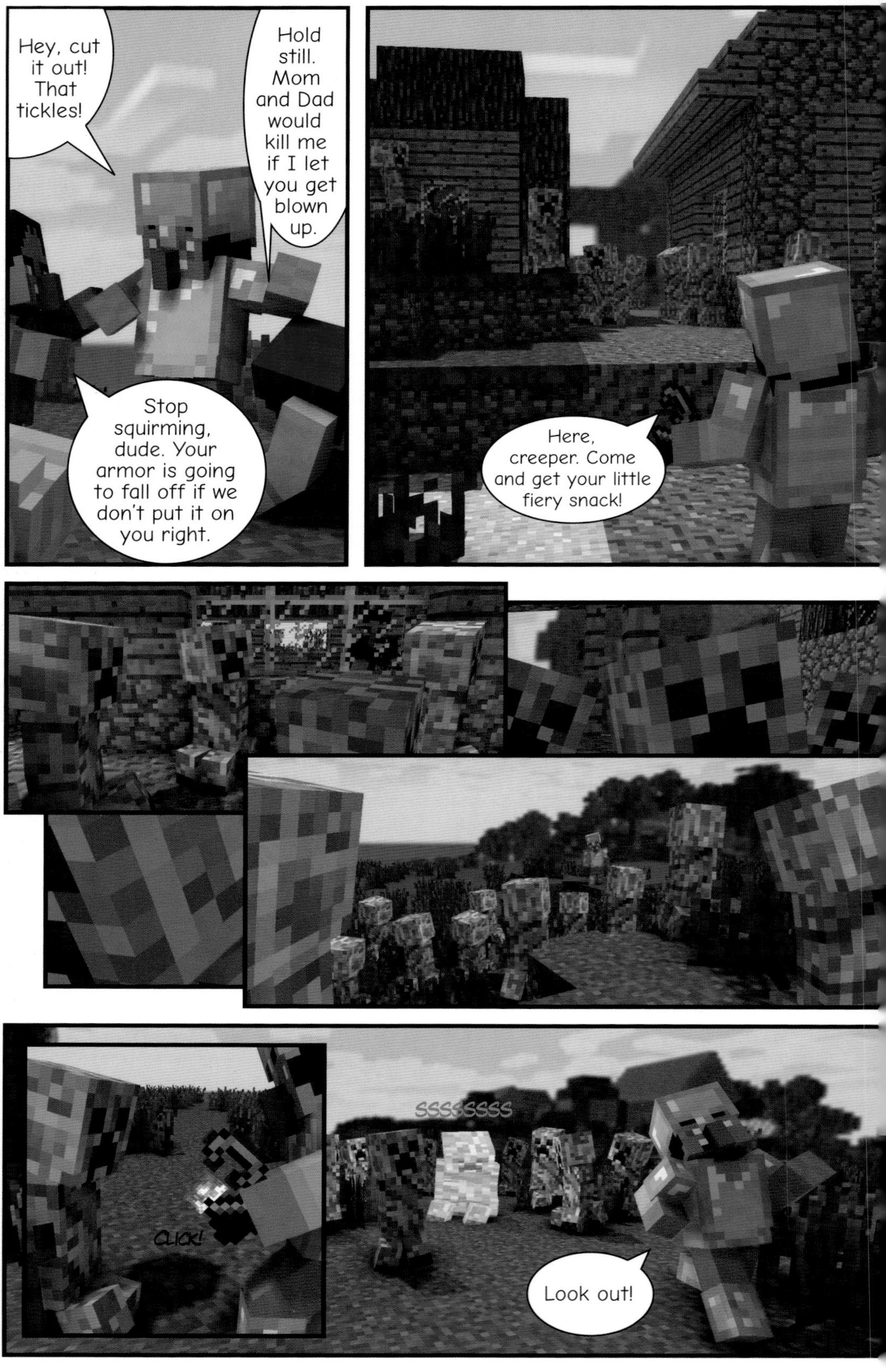

Hey, cut it out! That tickles!
Hold still. Mom and Dad would kill me if I let you get blown up.
Stop squirming, dude. Your armor is going to fall off if we don't put it on you right.
Here, creeper. Come and get your little fiery snack!
CLICK!
SSSSSSSS
Look out!

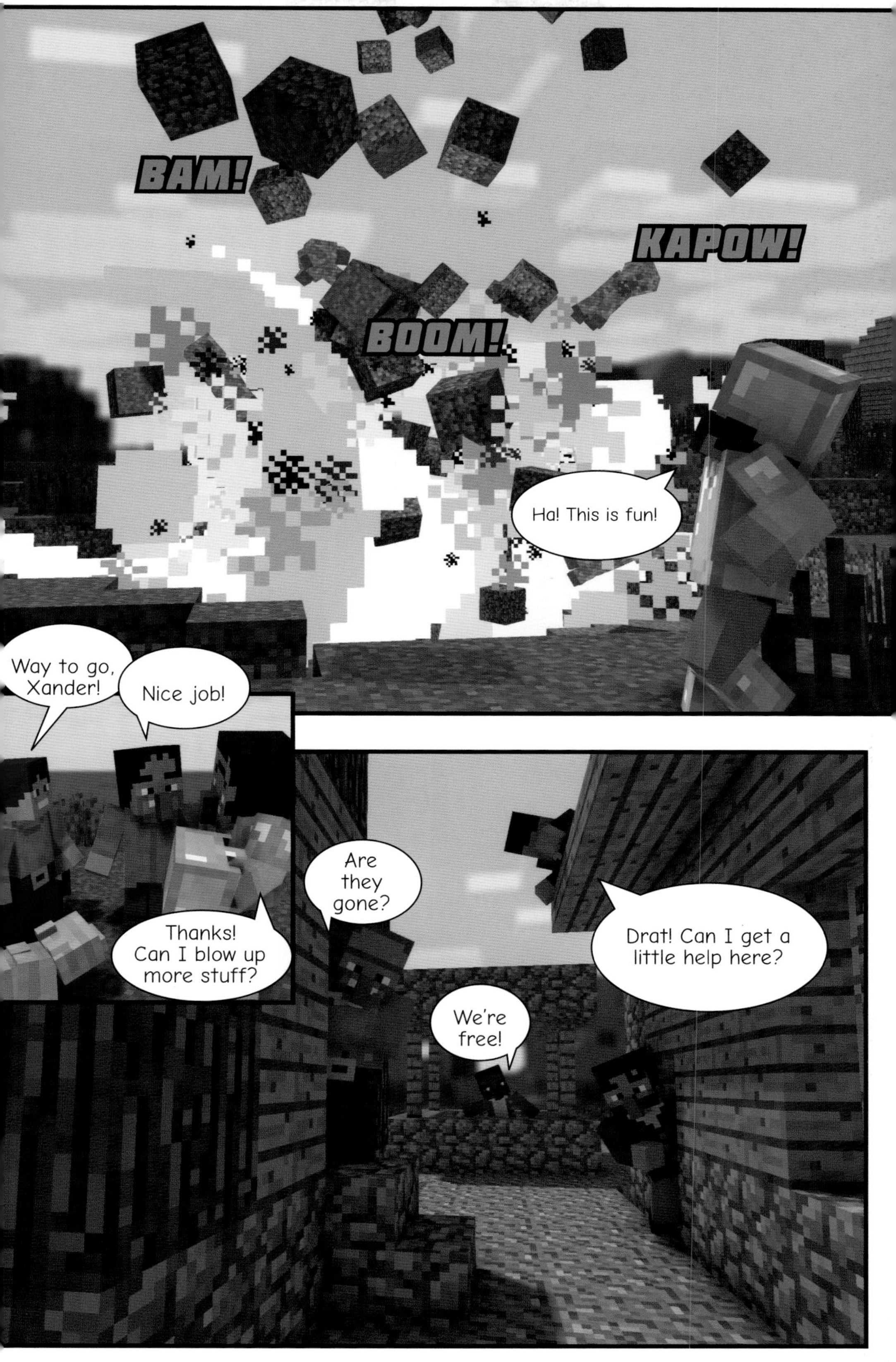
BAM!
KAPOW!
BOOM!
Ha! This is fun!
Way to go, Xander!
Nice job!
Thanks! Can I blow up more stuff?
Are they gone?
Drat! Can I get a little help here?
We're free!

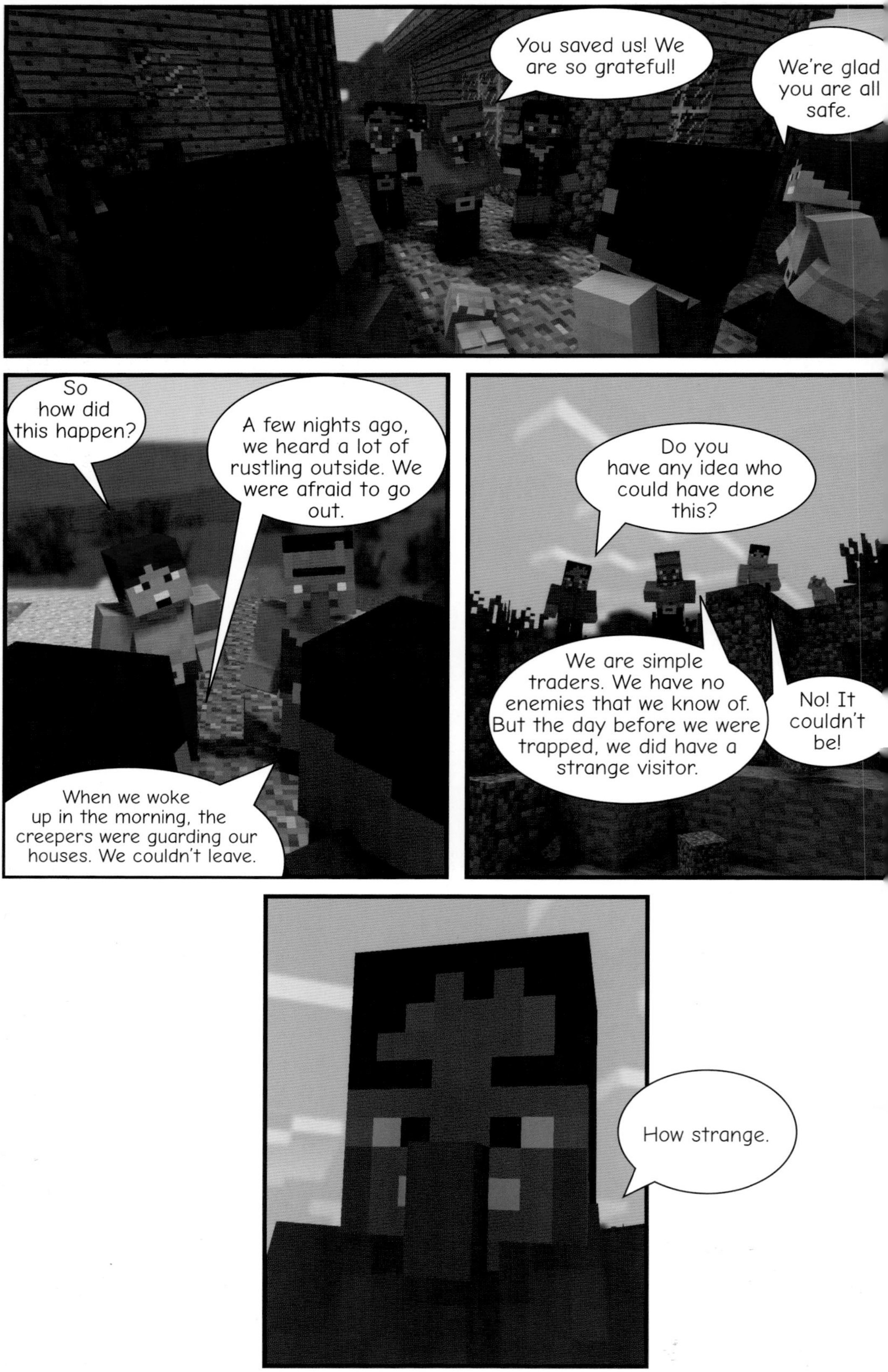
You saved us! We are so grateful!
We're glad you are all safe.
So how did this happen?
A few nights ago, we heard a lot of rustling outside. We were afraid to go out.
When we woke up in the morning, the creepers were guarding our houses. We couldn't leave.
Do you have any idea who could have done this?
We are simple traders. We have no enemies that we know of. But the day before we were trapped, we did have a strange visitor.
No! It couldn't be!
How strange.

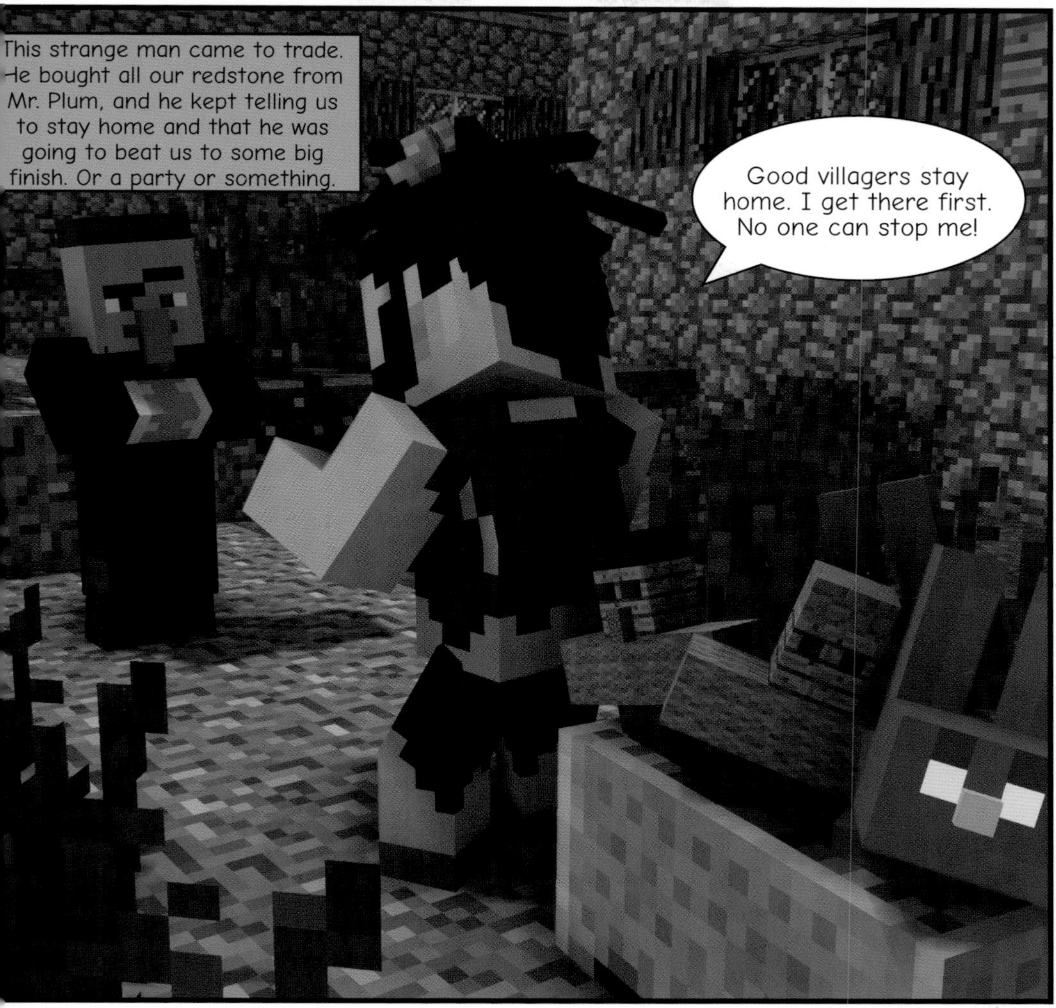

This strange man came to trade. He bought all our redstone from Mr. Plum, and he kept telling us to stay home and that he was going to beat us to some big finish. Or a party or something.
Good villagers stay home. I get there first. No one can stop me!

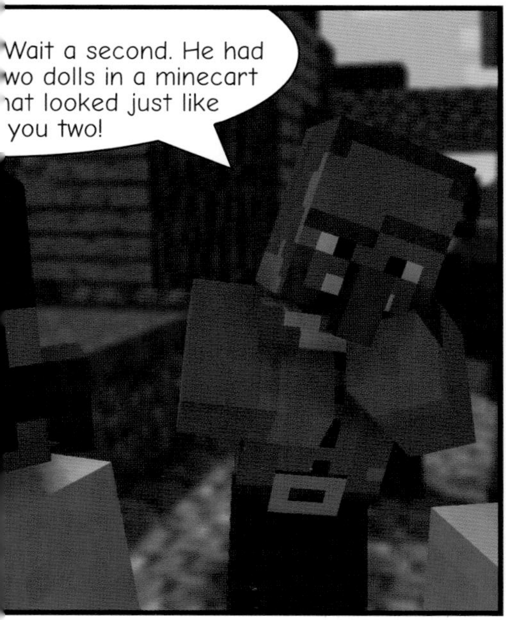

Wait a second. He had wo dolls in a minecart hat looked just like you two!

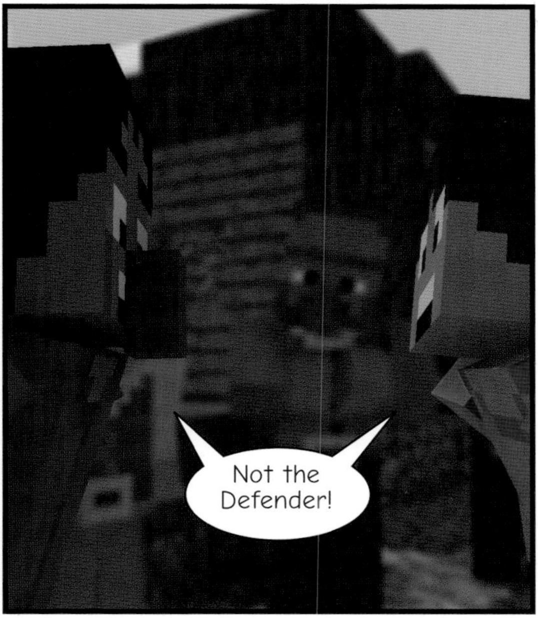

Not the Defender!

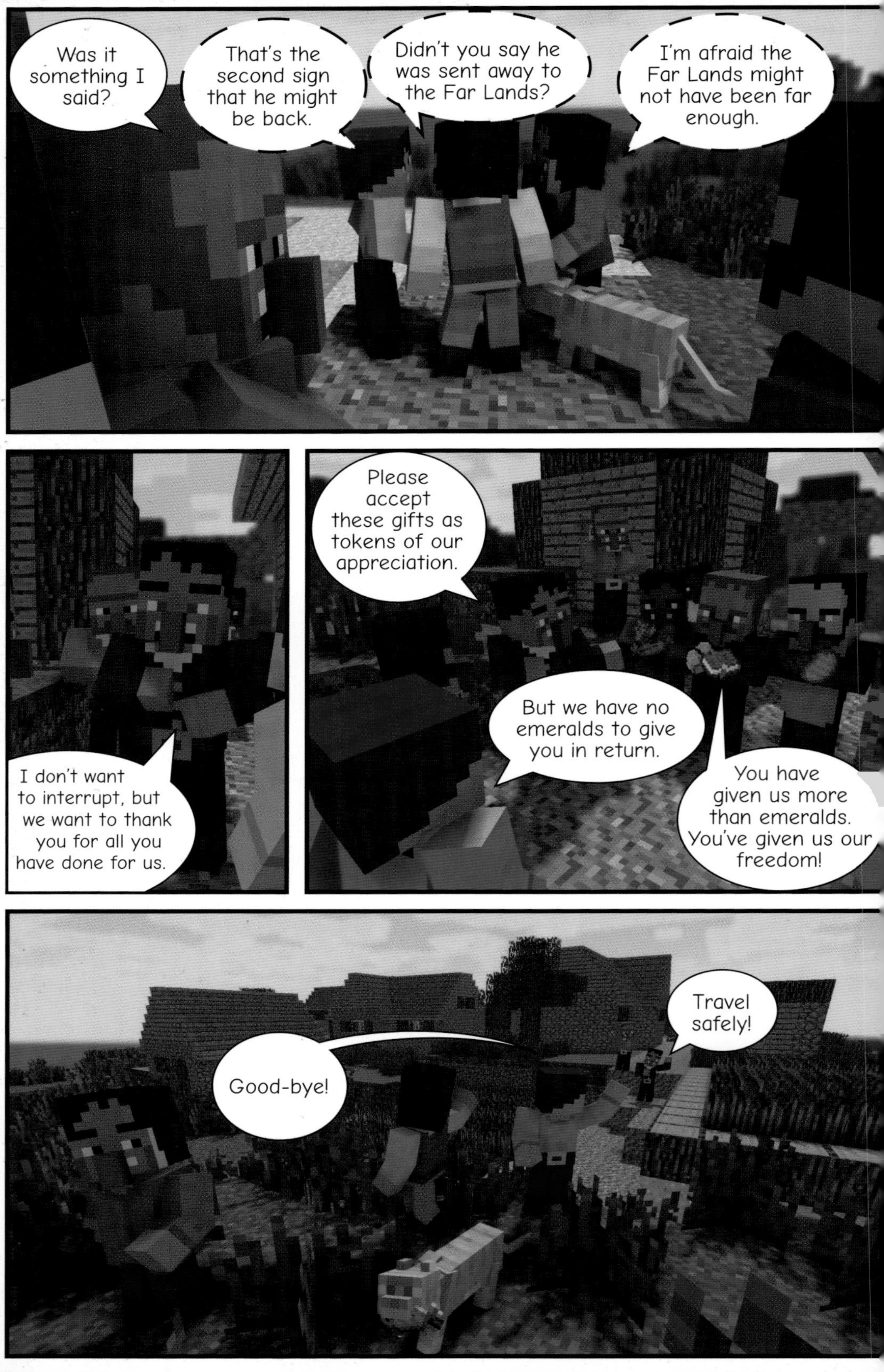
Was it something I said?
That's the second sign that he might be back.
Didn't you say he was sent away to the Far Lands?
I'm afraid the Far Lands might not have been far enough.
I don't want to interrupt, but we want to thank you for all you have done for us.
Please accept these gifts as tokens of our appreciation.
But we have no emeralds to give you in return.
You have given us more than emeralds. You've given us our freedom!
Good-bye!
Travel safely!

CHAPTER 8

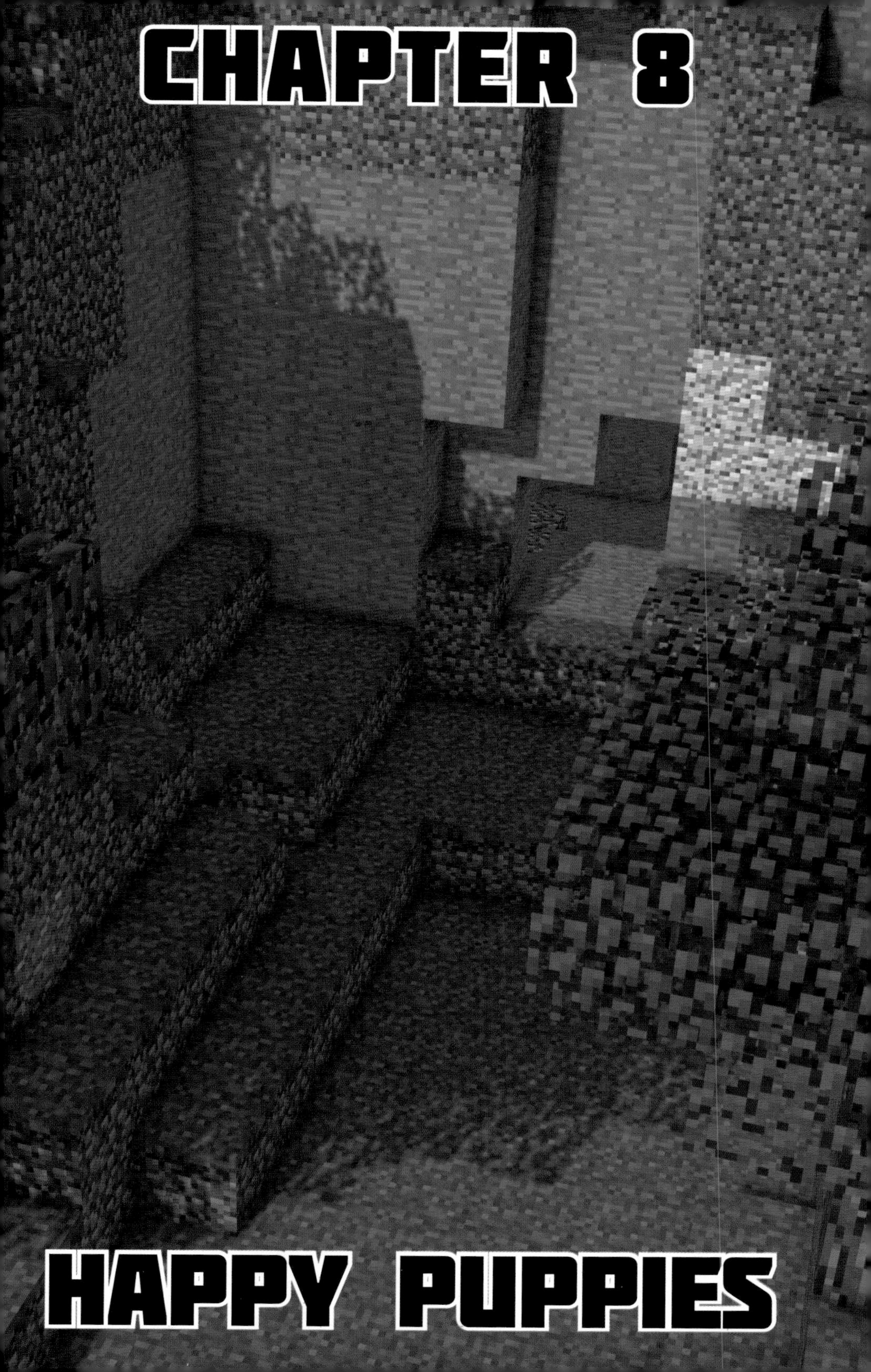

HAPPY PUPPIES

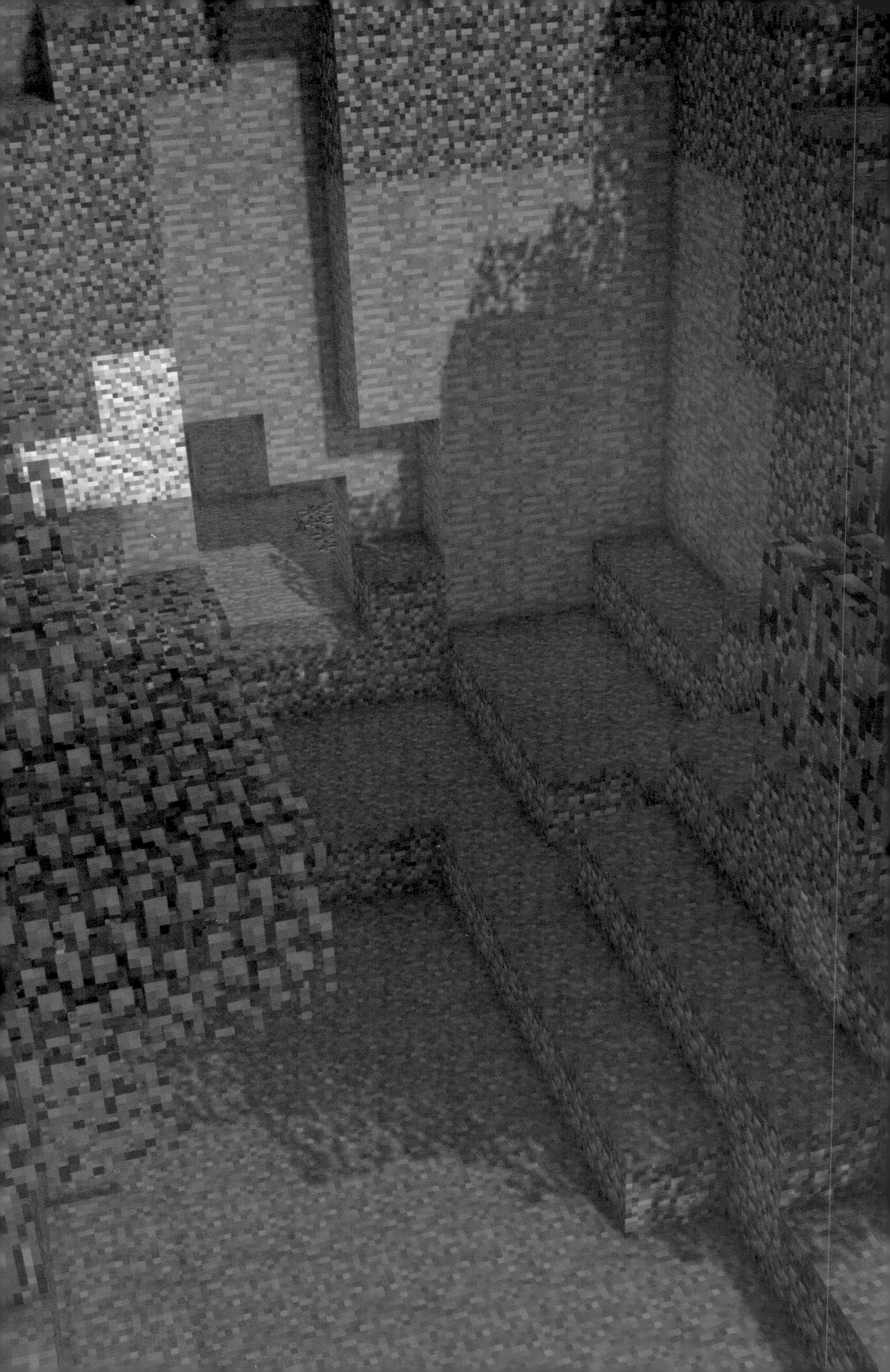

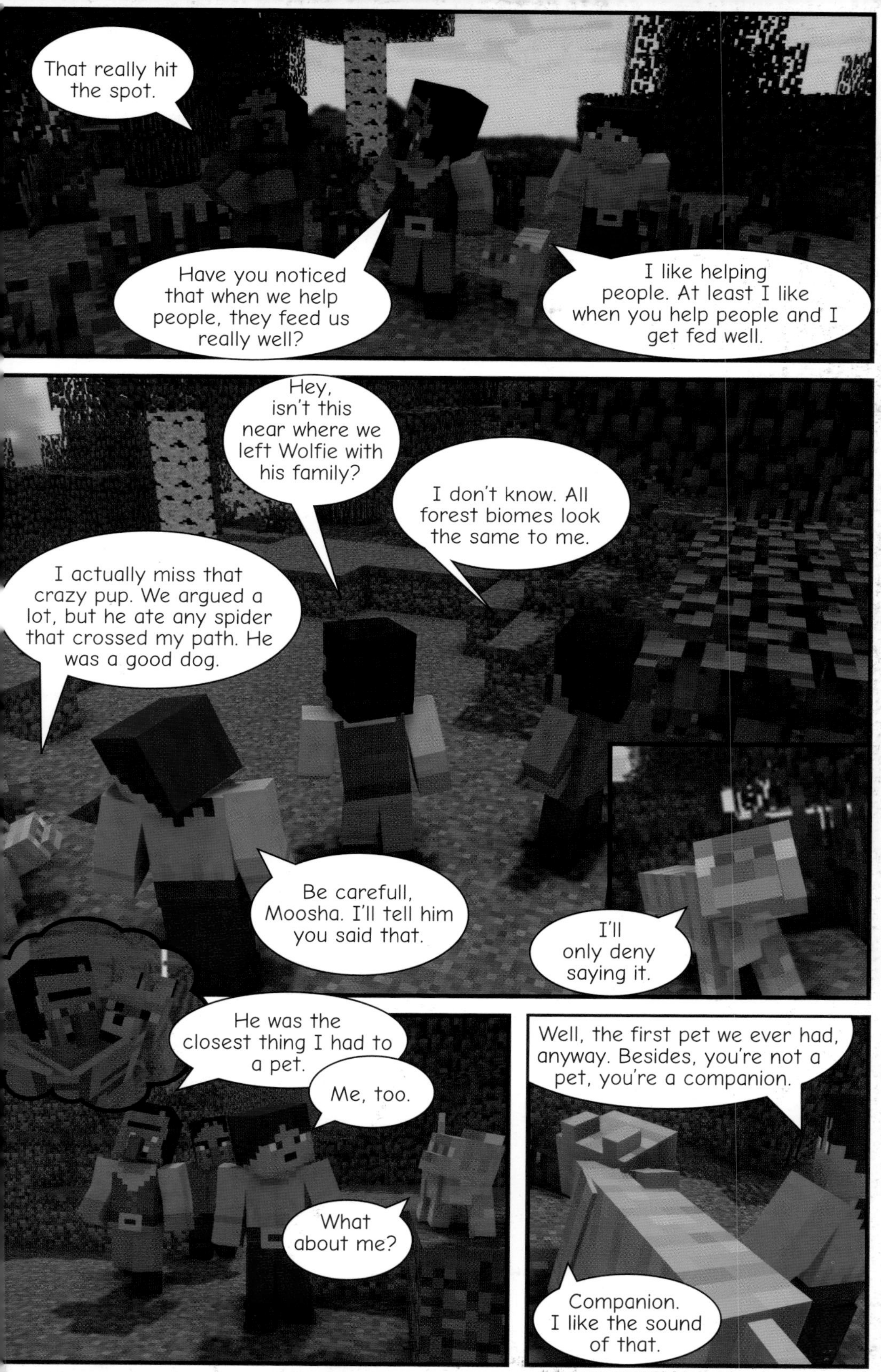

That really hit the spot.
Have you noticed that when we help people, they feed us really well?
I like helping people. At least I like when you help people and I get fed well.
Hey, isn't this near where we left Wolfie with his family?
I don't know. All forest biomes look the same to me.
I actually miss that crazy pup. We argued a lot, but he ate any spider that crossed my path. He was a good dog.
Be carefull, Moosha. I'll tell him you said that.
I'll only deny saying it.
He was the closest thing I had to a pet.
Me, too.
What about me?
Well, the first pet we ever had, anyway. Besides, you're not a pet, you're a companion.
Companion. I like the sound of that.

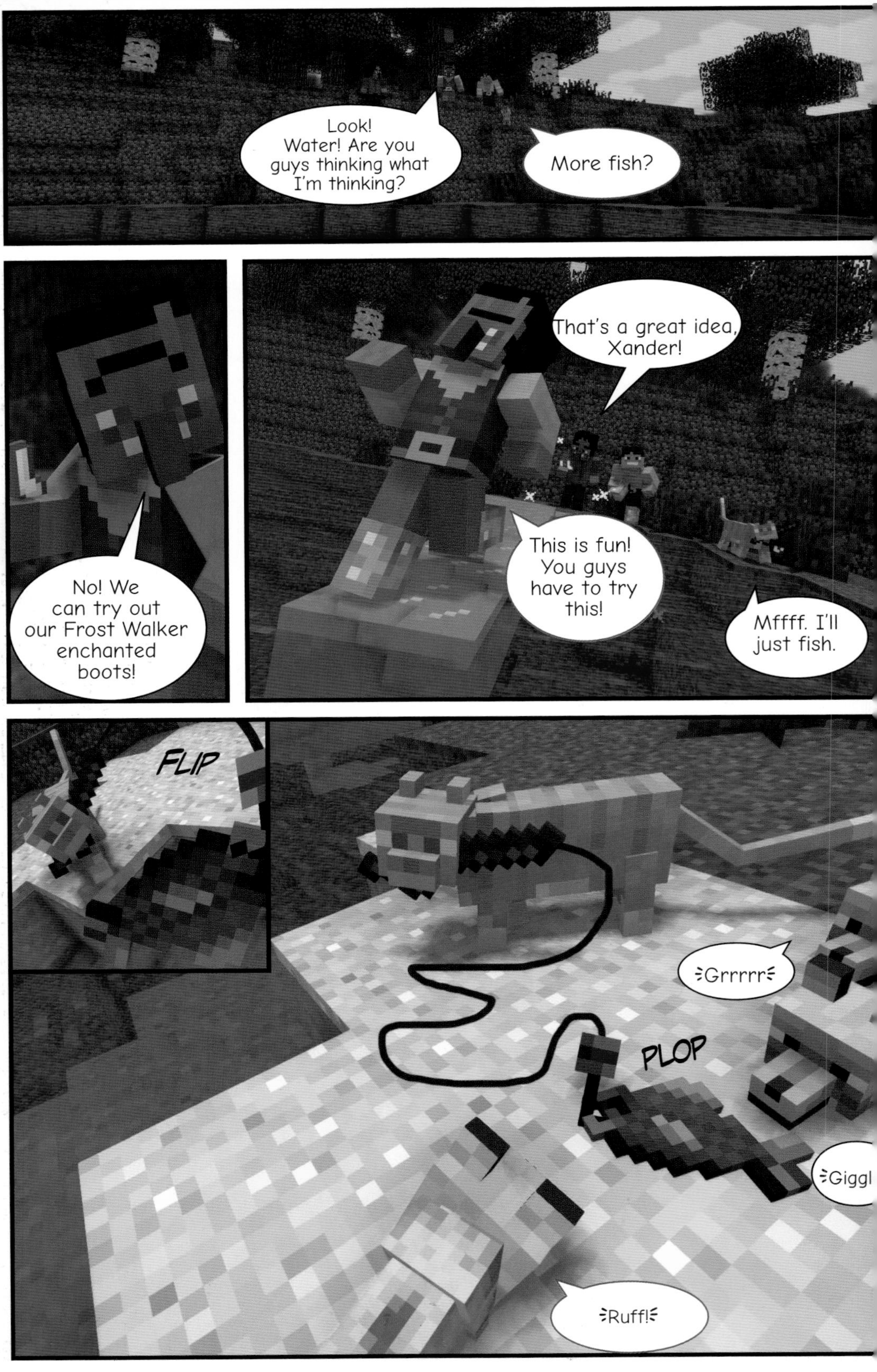
Look! Water! Are you guys thinking what I'm thinking?
More fish?
No! We can try out our Frost Walker enchanted boots!
That's a great idea, Xander!
This is fun! You guys have to try this!
Mffff. I'll just fish.
FLIP
Grrrrr
PLOP
Giggl
Ruff!

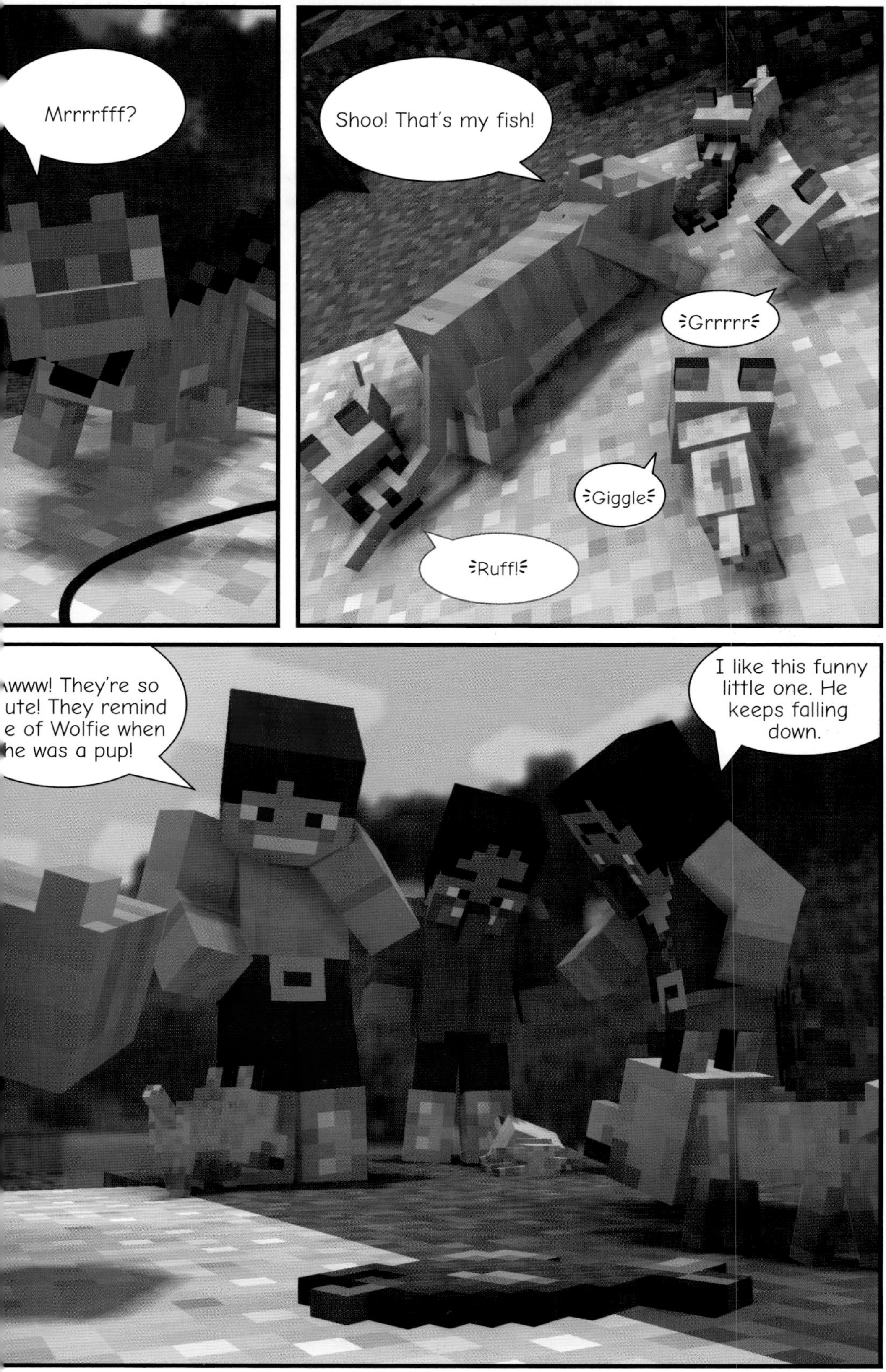
Mrrrrfff?
Shoo! That's my fish!
Grrrrr
Giggle
Ruff!
www! They're so ute! They remind e of Wolfie when he was a pup!
I like this funny little one. He keeps falling down.

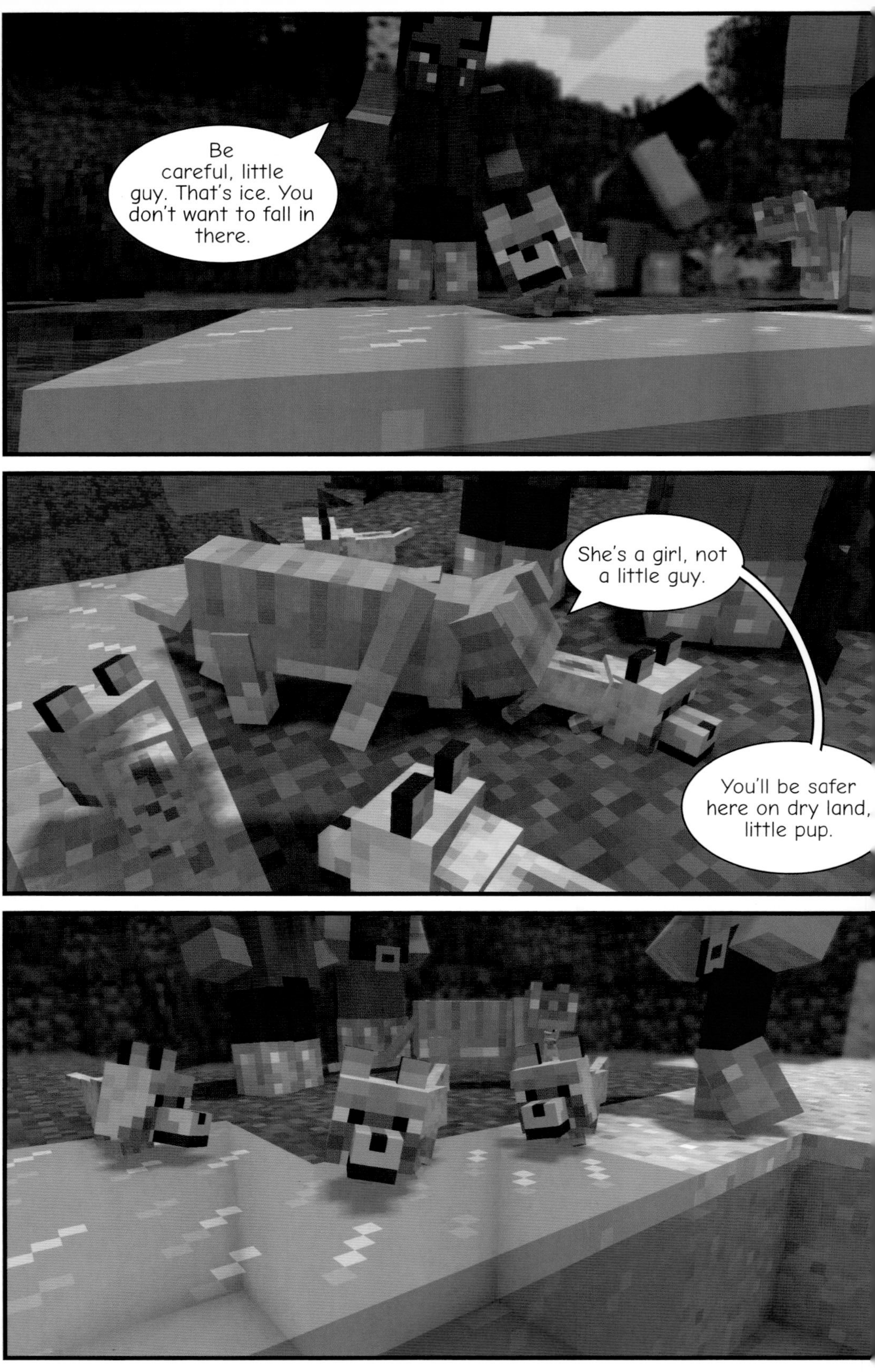
Be careful, little guy. That's ice. You don't want to fall in there.
She's a girl, not a little guy.
You'll be safer here on dry land, little pup.

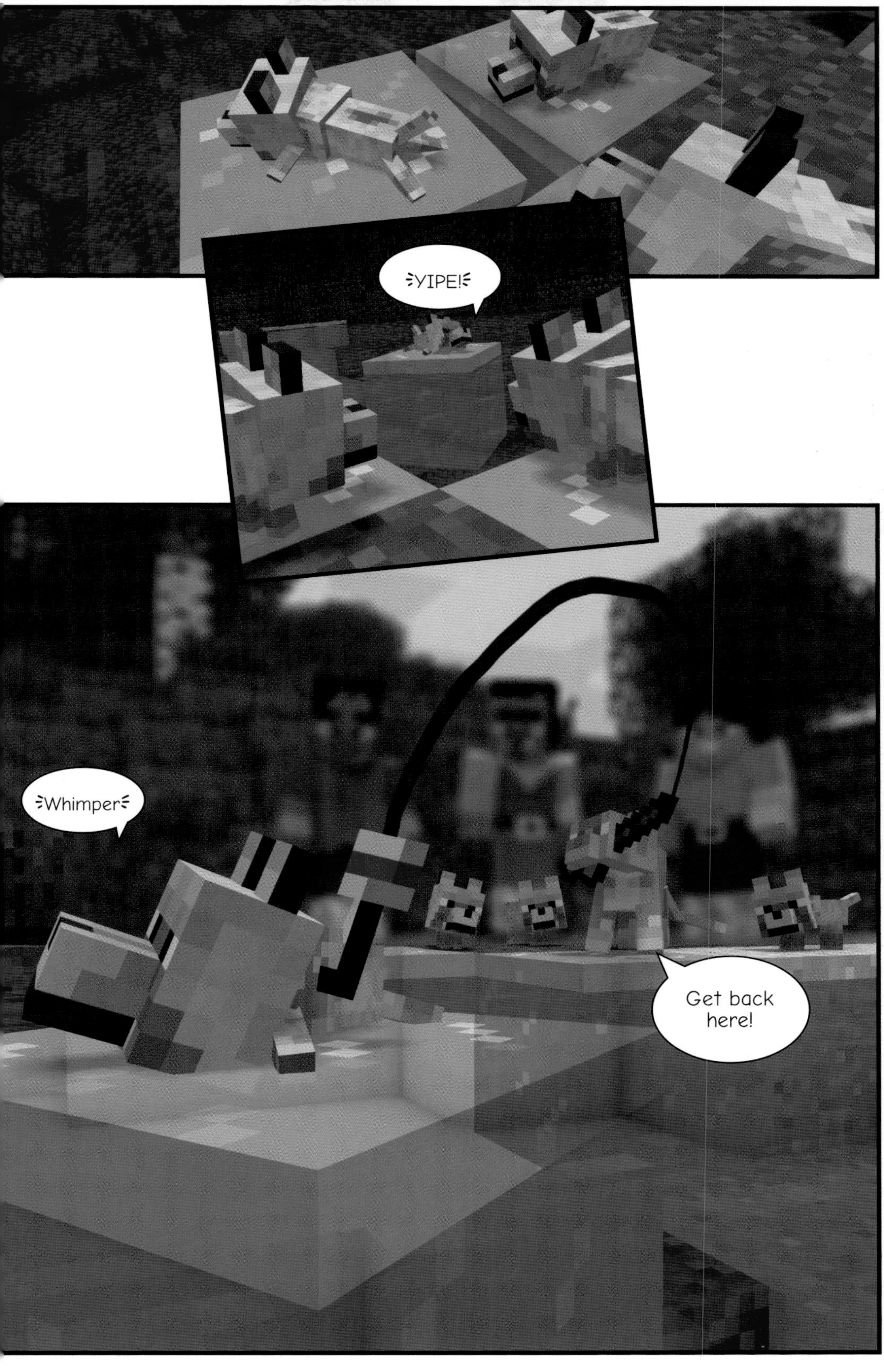
YIPE!
Whimper
Get back here!

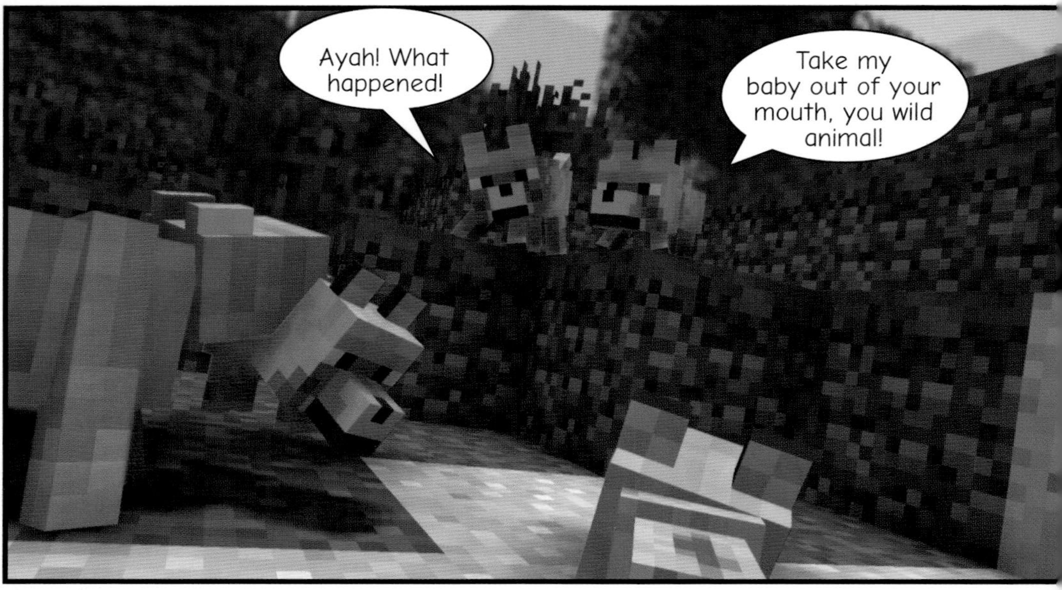
Ayah! What happened!
Take my baby out of your mouth, you wild animal!

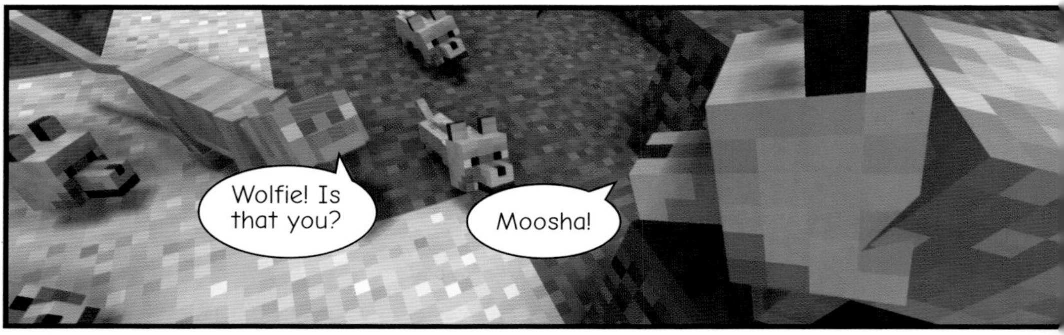
Wolfie! Is that you?
Moosha!

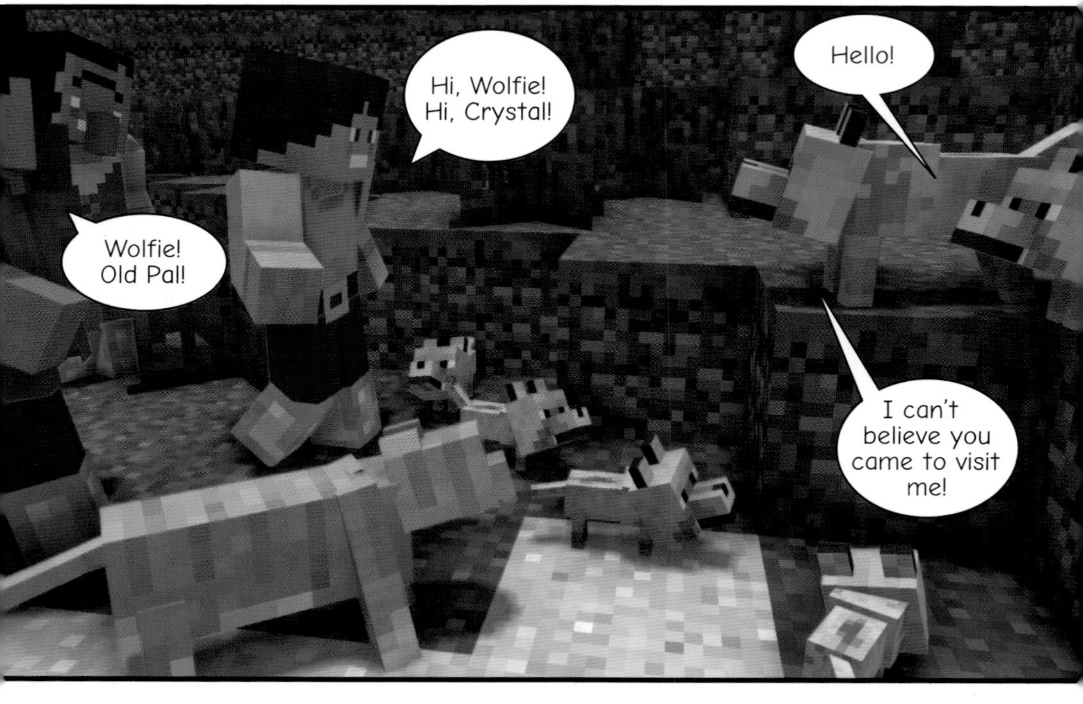
Hi, Wolfie! Hi, Crystal!
Hello!
Wolfie! Old Pal!
I can't believe you came to visit me!

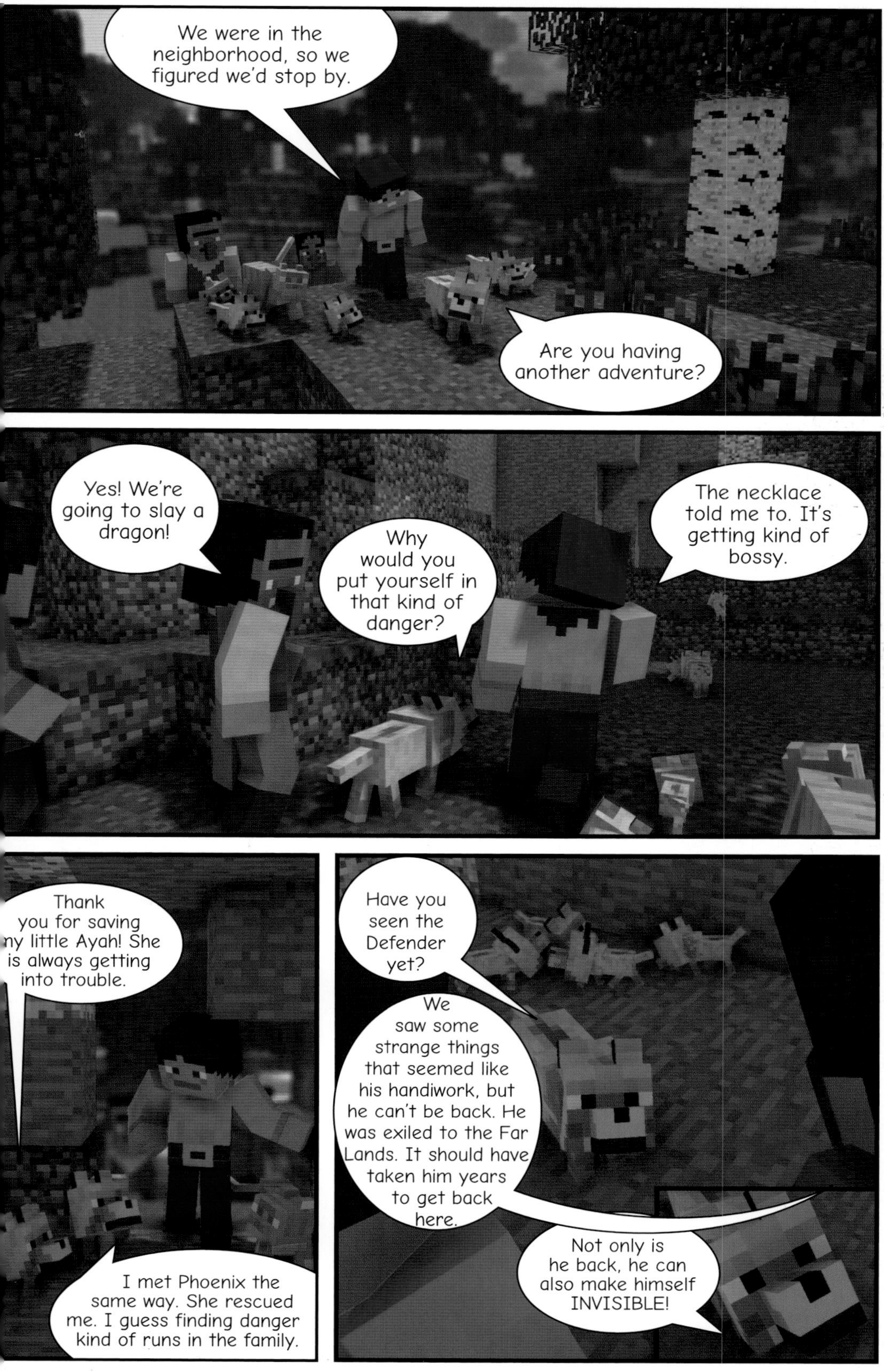
We were in the neighborhood, so we figured we'd stop by.
Are you having another adventure?
Yes! We're going to slay a dragon!
Why would you put yourself in that kind of danger?
The necklace told me to. It's getting kind of bossy.
Thank you for saving ny little Ayah! She is always getting into trouble.
I met Phoenix the same way. She rescued me. I guess finding danger kind of runs in the family.
Have you seen the Defender yet?
We saw some strange things that seemed like his handiwork, but he can't be back. He was exiled to the Far Lands. It should have taken him years to get back here.
Not only is he back, he can also make himself INVISIBLE!

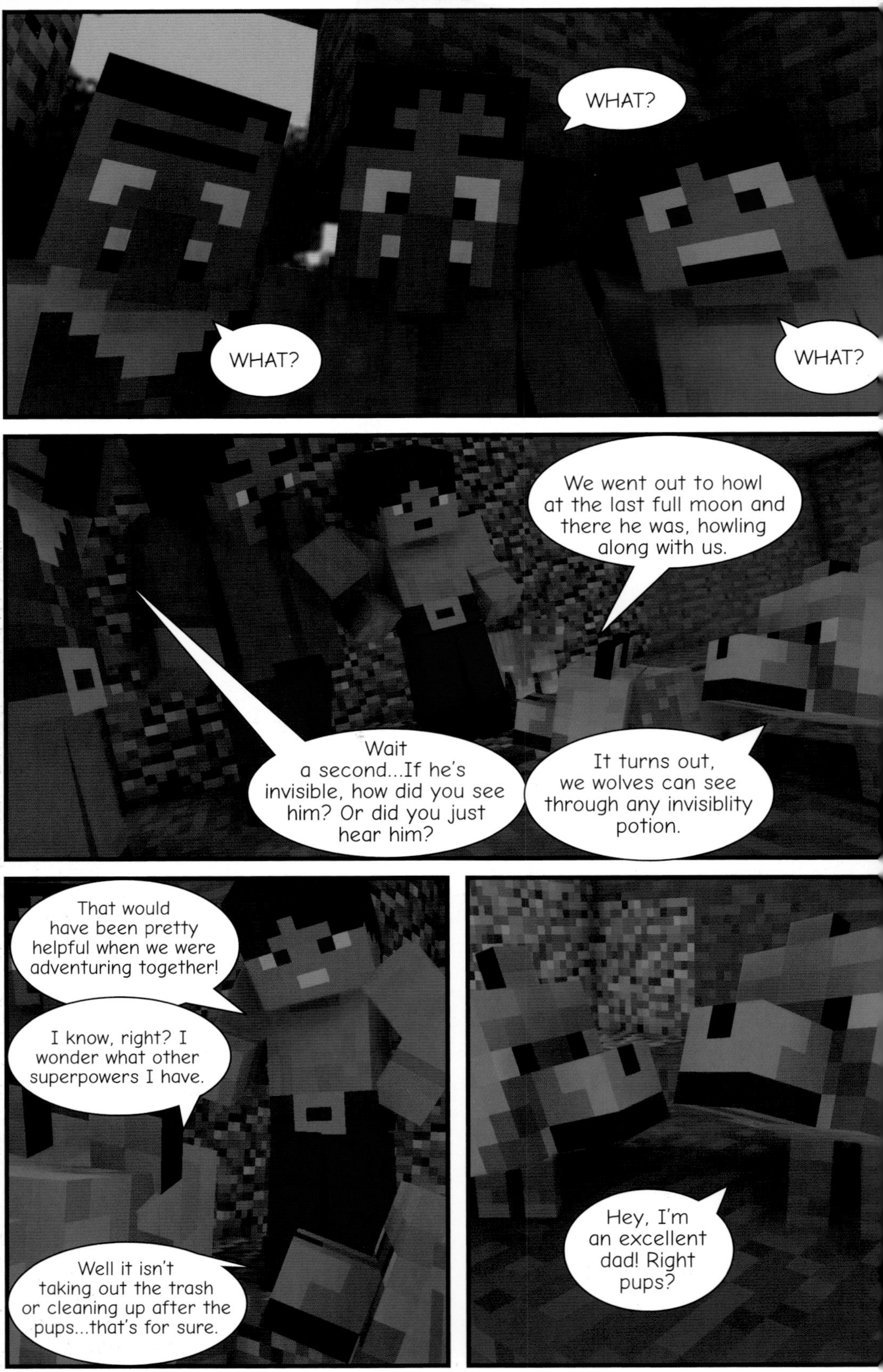
WHAT?
WHAT?
WHAT?
We went out to howl at the last full moon and there he was, howling along with us.
Wait a second...If he's invisible, how did you see him? Or did you just hear him?
It turns out, we wolves can see through any invisiblity potion.
That would have been pretty helpful when we were adventuring together!
I know, right? I wonder what other superpowers I have.
Well it isn't taking out the trash or cleaning up after the pups...that's for sure.
Hey, I'm an excellent dad! Right pups?

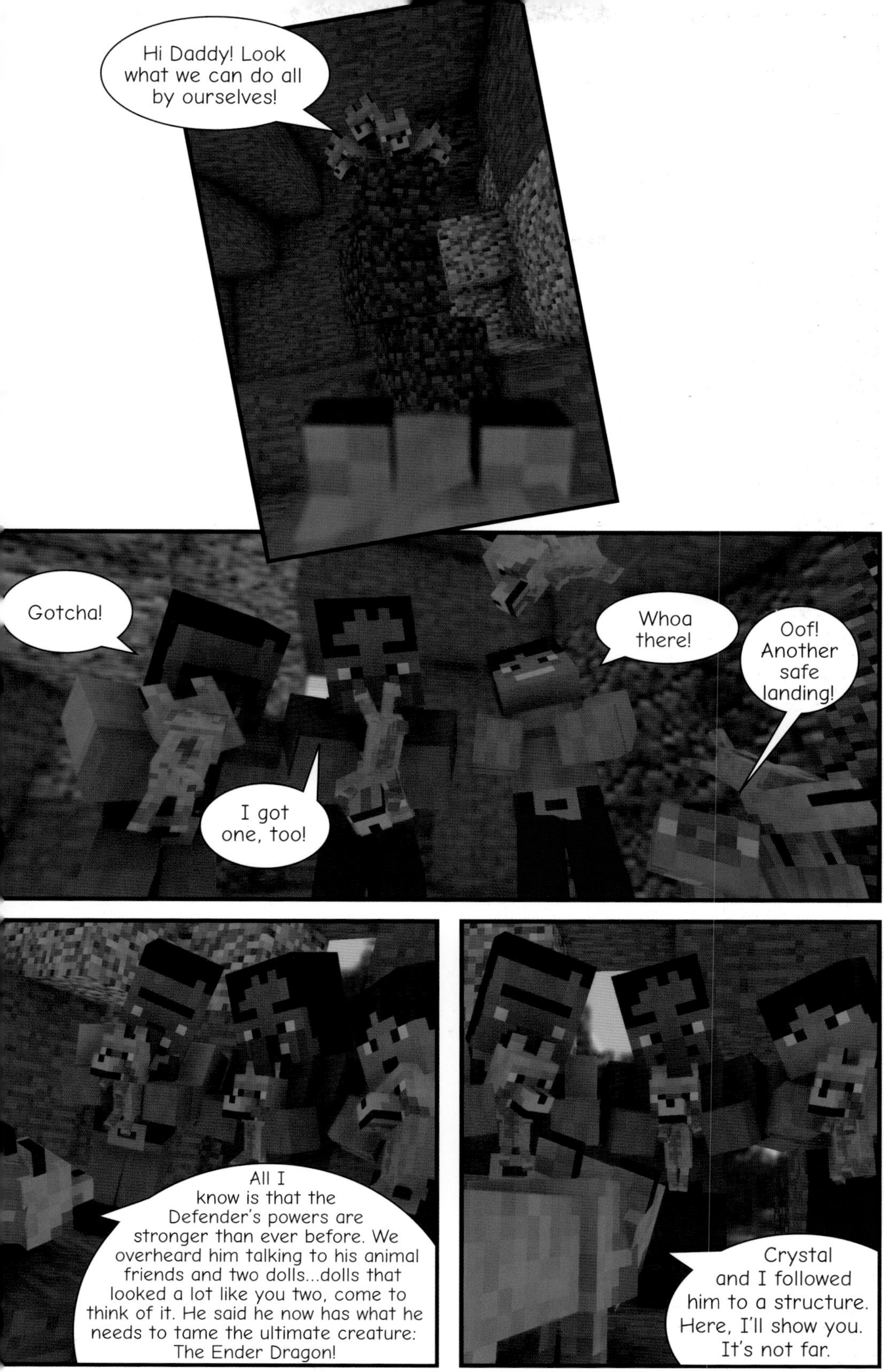
Hi Daddy! Look what we can do all by ourselves!
Gotcha!
Whoa there!
Oof! Another safe landing!
I got one, too!
All I know is that the Defender's powers are stronger than ever before. We overheard him talking to his animal friends and two dolls...dolls that looked a lot like you two, come to think of it. He said he now has what he needs to tame the ultimate creature: The Ender Dragon!
Crystal and I followed him to a structure. Here, I'll show you. It's not far.

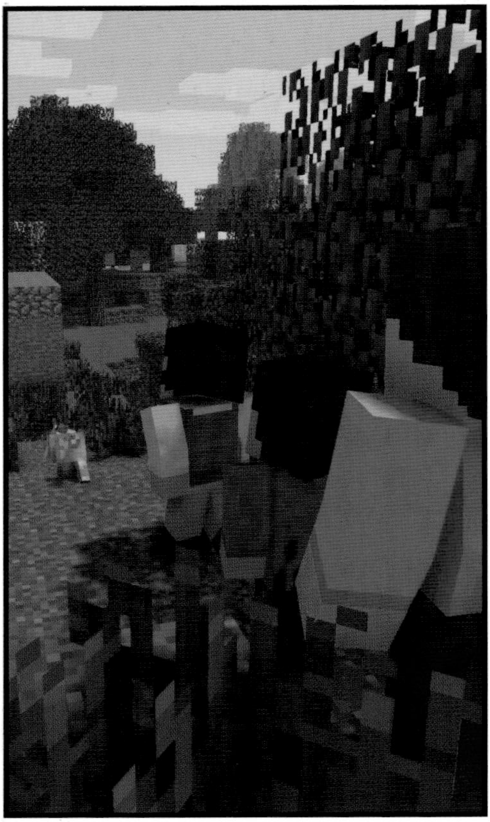

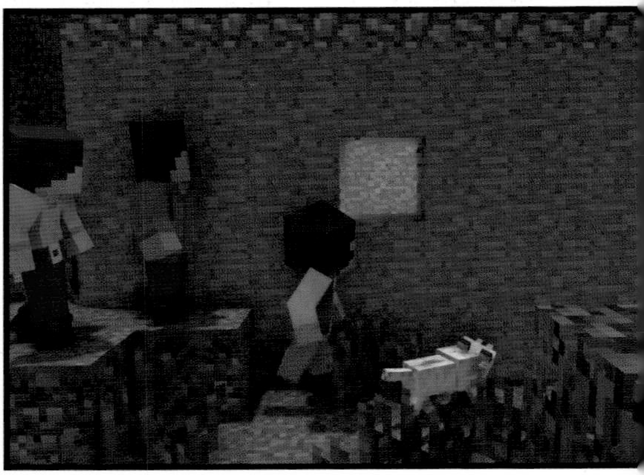

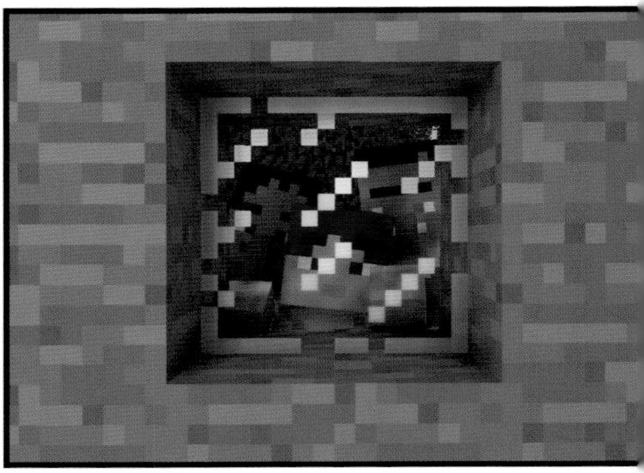

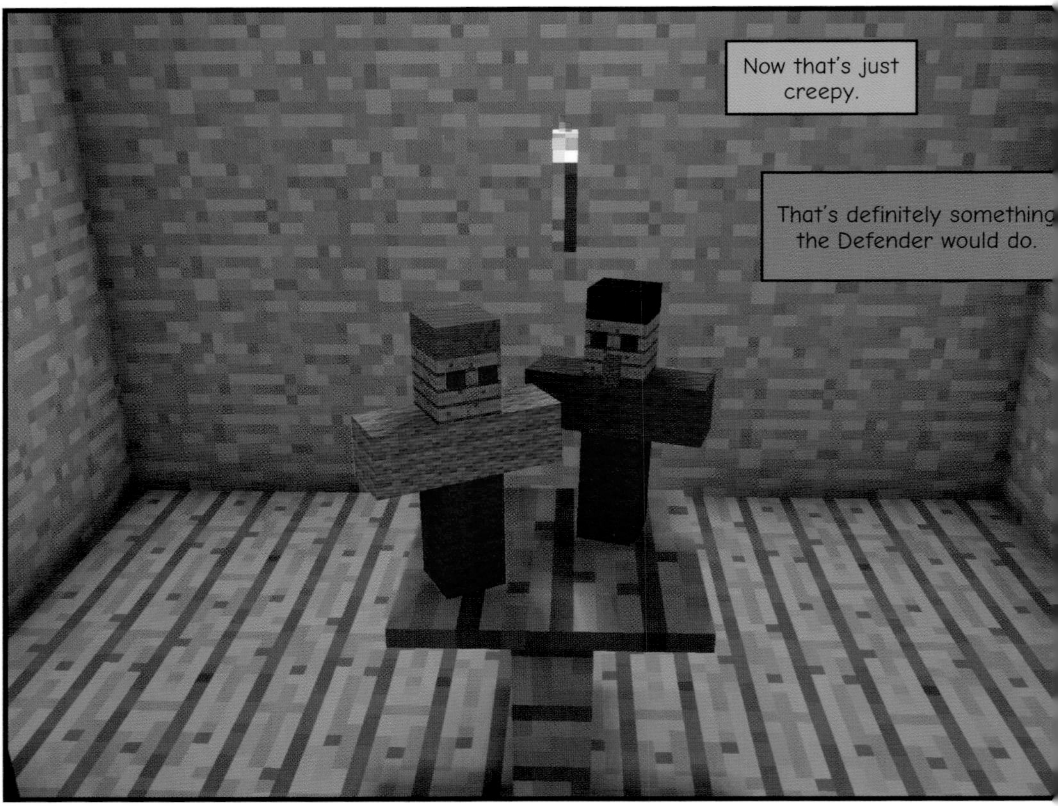
Now that's just creepy.
That's definitely something the Defender would do.

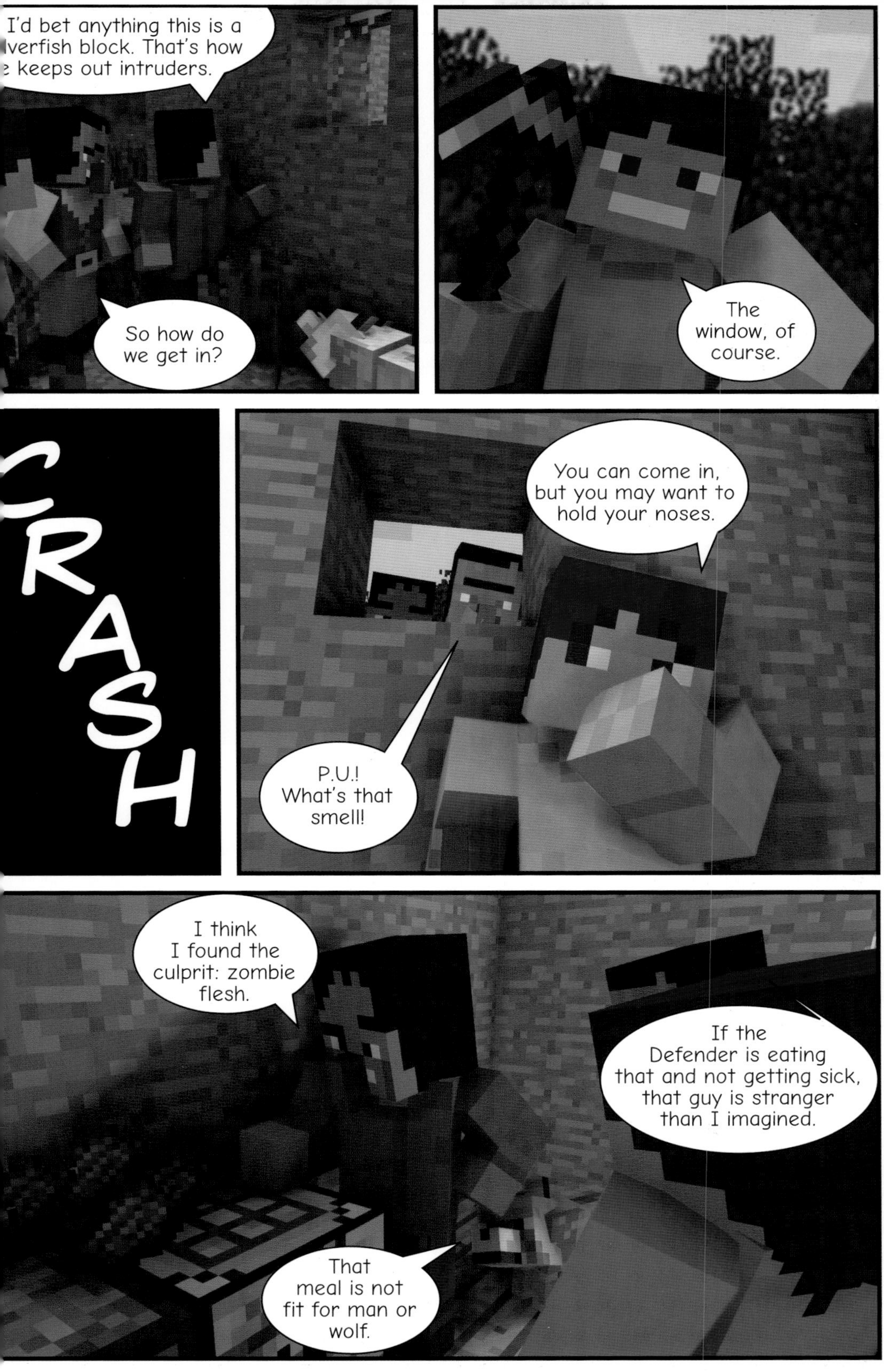
I'd bet anything this is a
lverfish block. That's how
e keeps out intruders.
So how do we get in?
The window, of course.
CRASH
You can come in, but you may want to hold your noses.
P.U.! What's that smell!
I think I found the culprit: zombie flesh.
If the Defender is eating that and not getting sick, that guy is stranger than I imagined.
That meal is not fit for man or wolf.

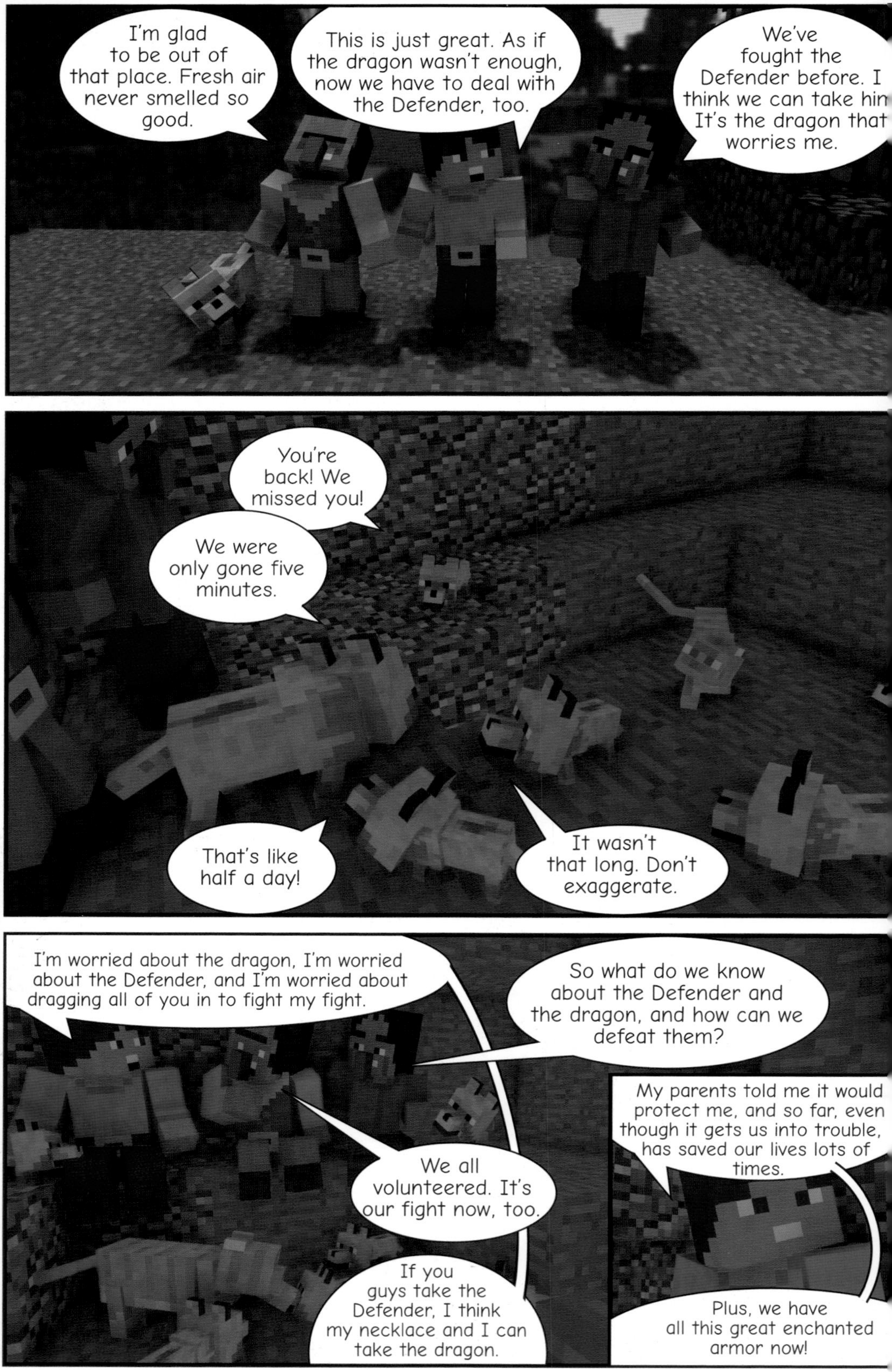

I'm glad to be out of that place. Fresh air never smelled so good.
This is just great. As if the dragon wasn't enough, now we have to deal with the Defender, too.
We've fought the Defender before. I think we can take hin It's the dragon that worries me.
You're back! We missed you!
We were only gone five minutes.
That's like half a day!
It wasn't that long. Don't exaggerate.
I'm worried about the dragon, I'm worried about the Defender, and I'm worried about dragging all of you in to fight my fight.
So what do we know about the Defender and the dragon, and how can we defeat them?
We all volunteered. It's our fight now, too.
If you guys take the Defender, I think my necklace and I can take the dragon.
My parents told me it would protect me, and so far, even though it gets us into trouble, has saved our lives lots of times.
Plus, we have all this great enchanted armor now!

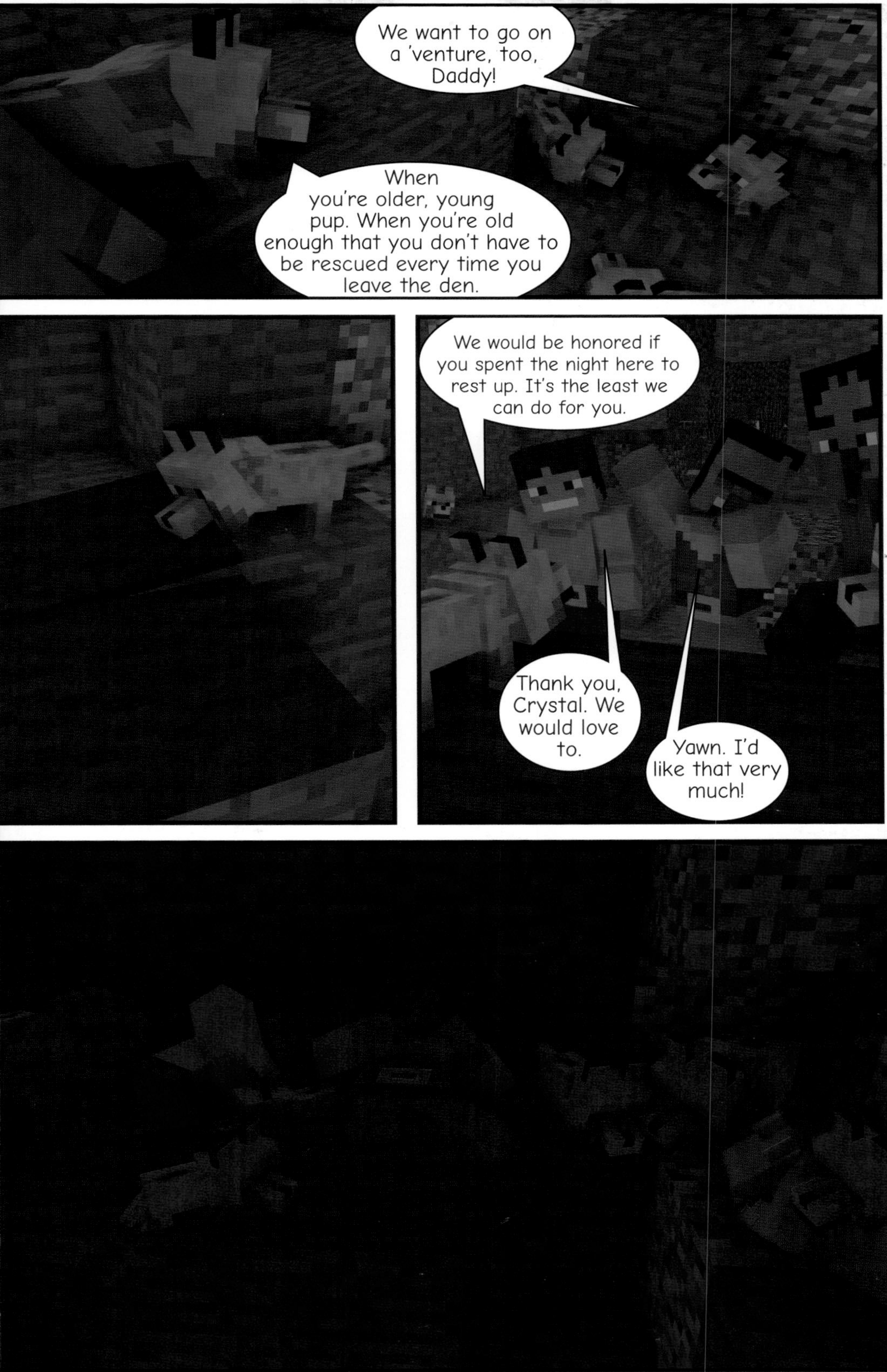
We want to go on a 'venture, too, Daddy!
When you're older, young pup. When you're old enough that you don't have to be rescued every time you leave the den.
We would be honored if you spent the night here to rest up. It's the least we can do for you.
Thank you, Crystal. We would love to.
Yawn. I'd like that very much!

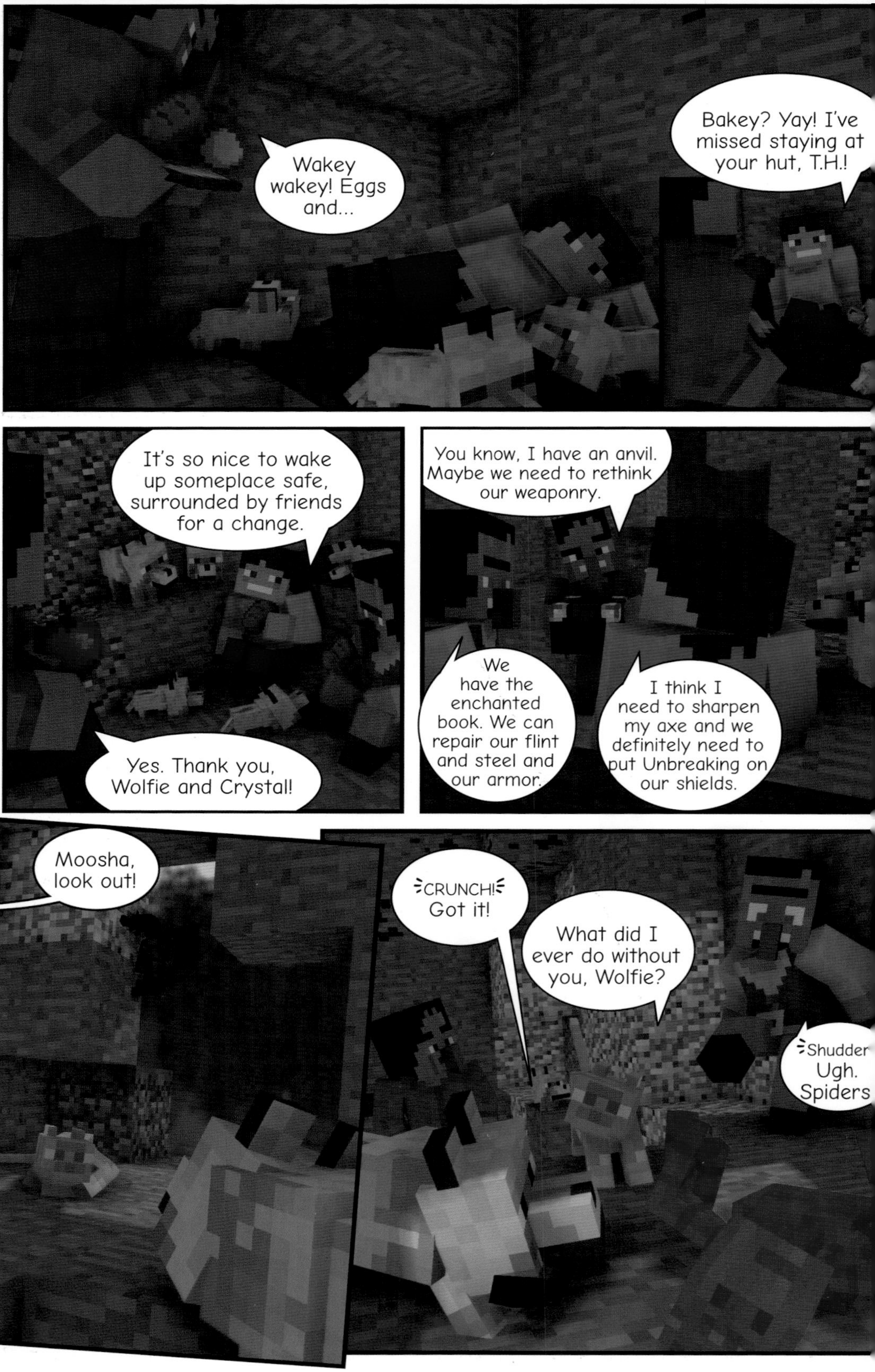
Wakey wakey! Eggs and...
Bakey? Yay! I've missed staying at your hut, T.H.!
It's so nice to wake up someplace safe, surrounded by friends for a change.
Yes. Thank you, Wolfie and Crystal!
You know, I have an anvil. Maybe we need to rethink our weaponry.
We have the enchanted book. We can repair our flint and steel and our armor.
I think I need to sharpen my axe and we definitely need to put Unbreaking on our shields.
Moosha, look out!
CRUNCH!
Got it!
What did I ever do without you, Wolfie?
Shudder
Ugh. Spiders

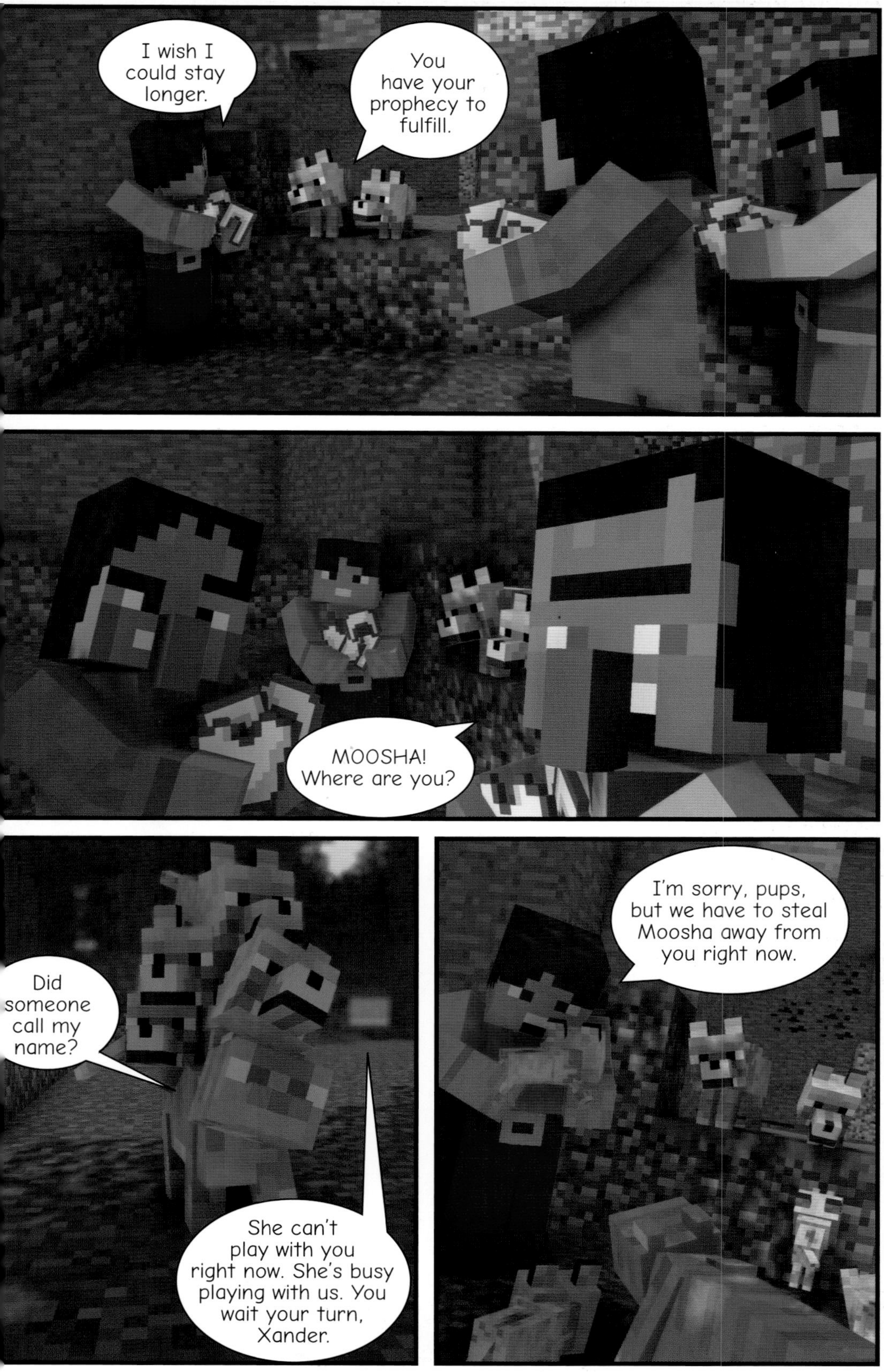
I wish I could stay longer.
You have your prophecy to fulfill.
MOOSHA! Where are you?
Did someone call my name?
She can't play with you right now. She's busy playing with us. You wait your turn, Xander.
I'm sorry, pups, but we have to steal Moosha away from you right now.

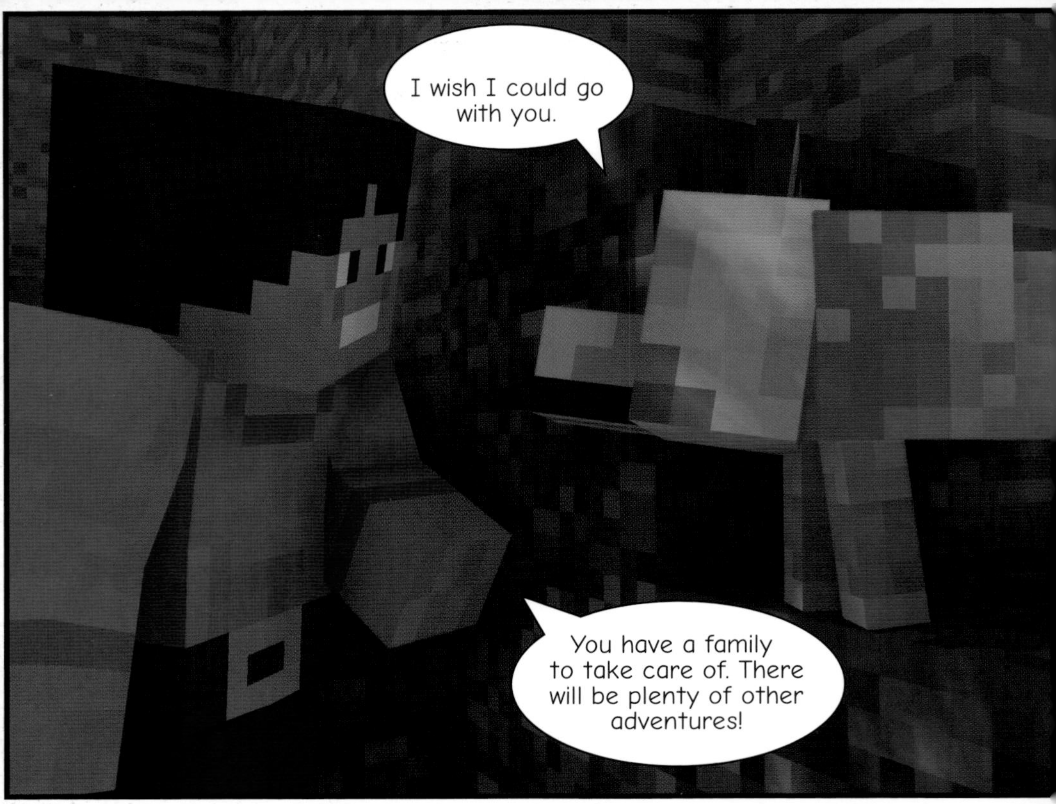
I wish I could go with you.
You have a family to take care of. There will be plenty of other adventures!

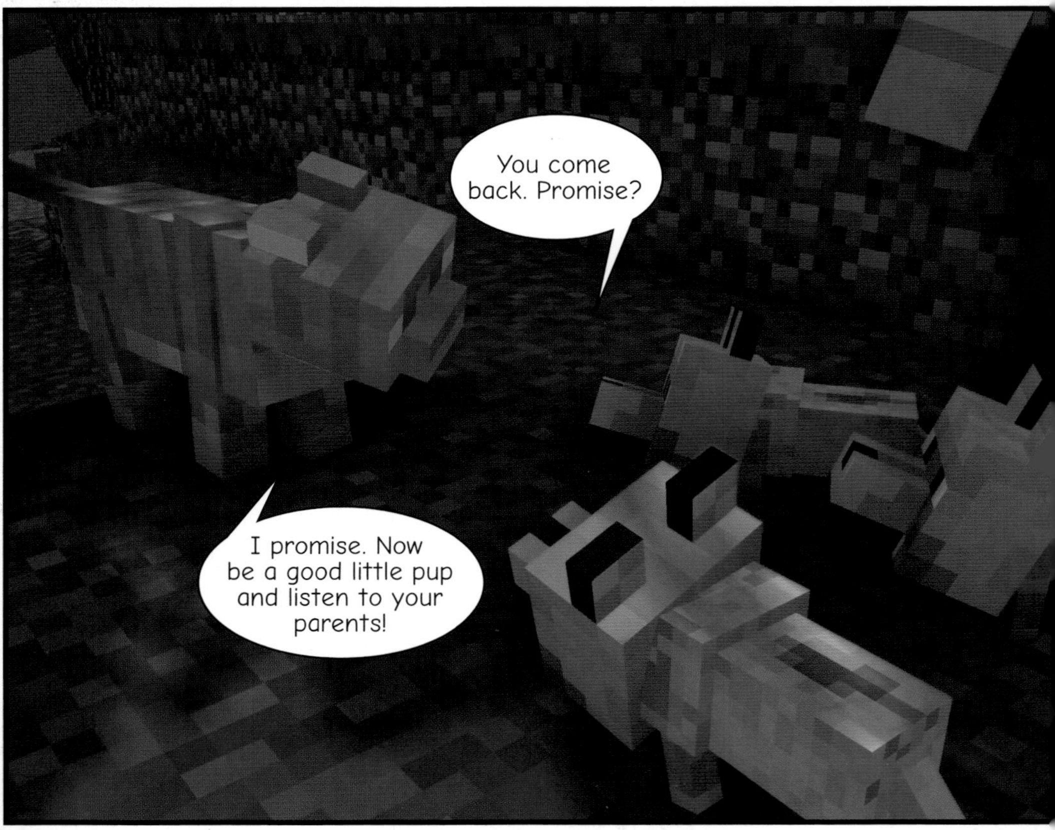
You come back. Promise?
I promise. Now be a good little pup and listen to your parents!

CHAPTER 9

SUMMONING THE DRAGON

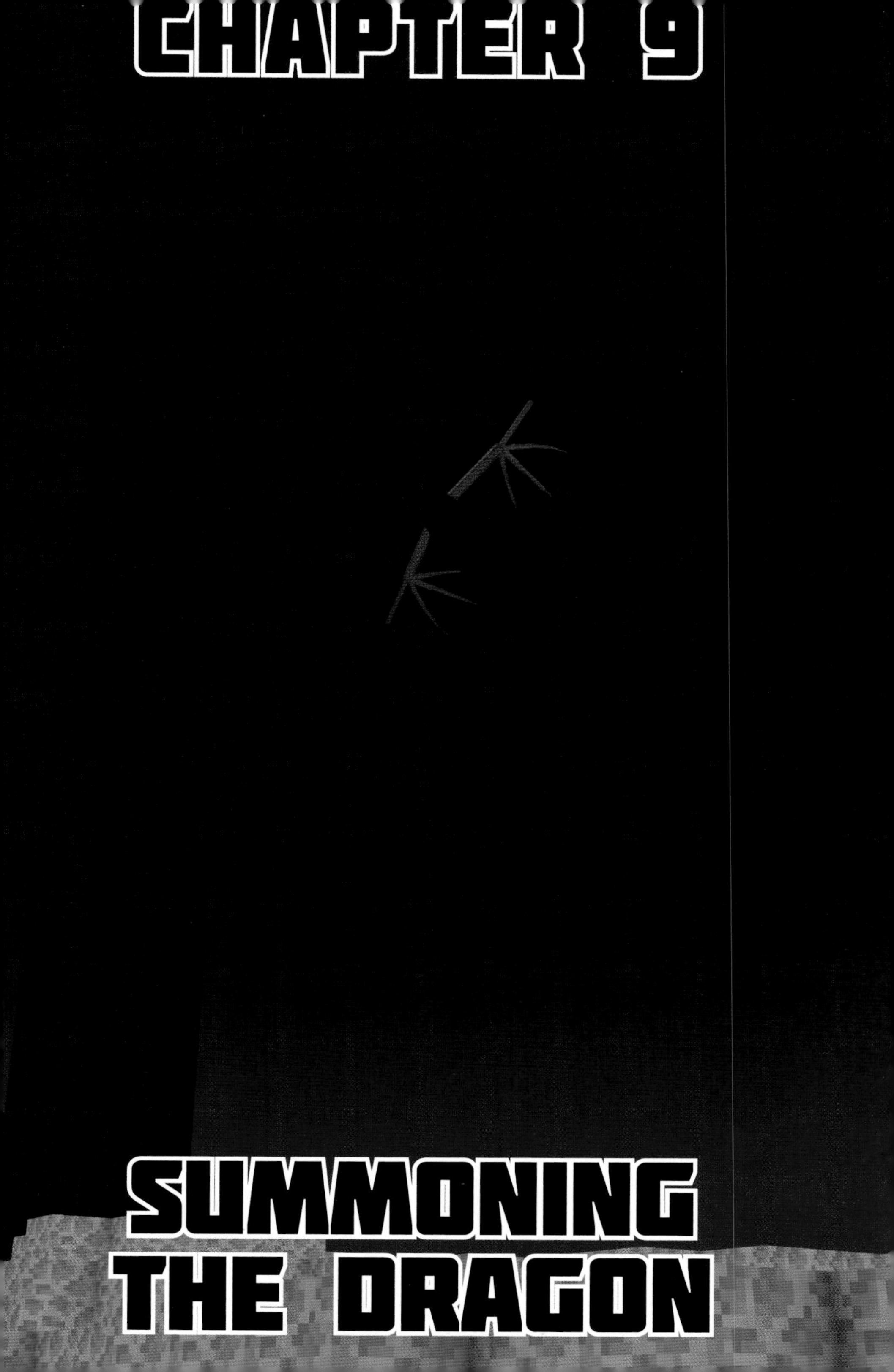

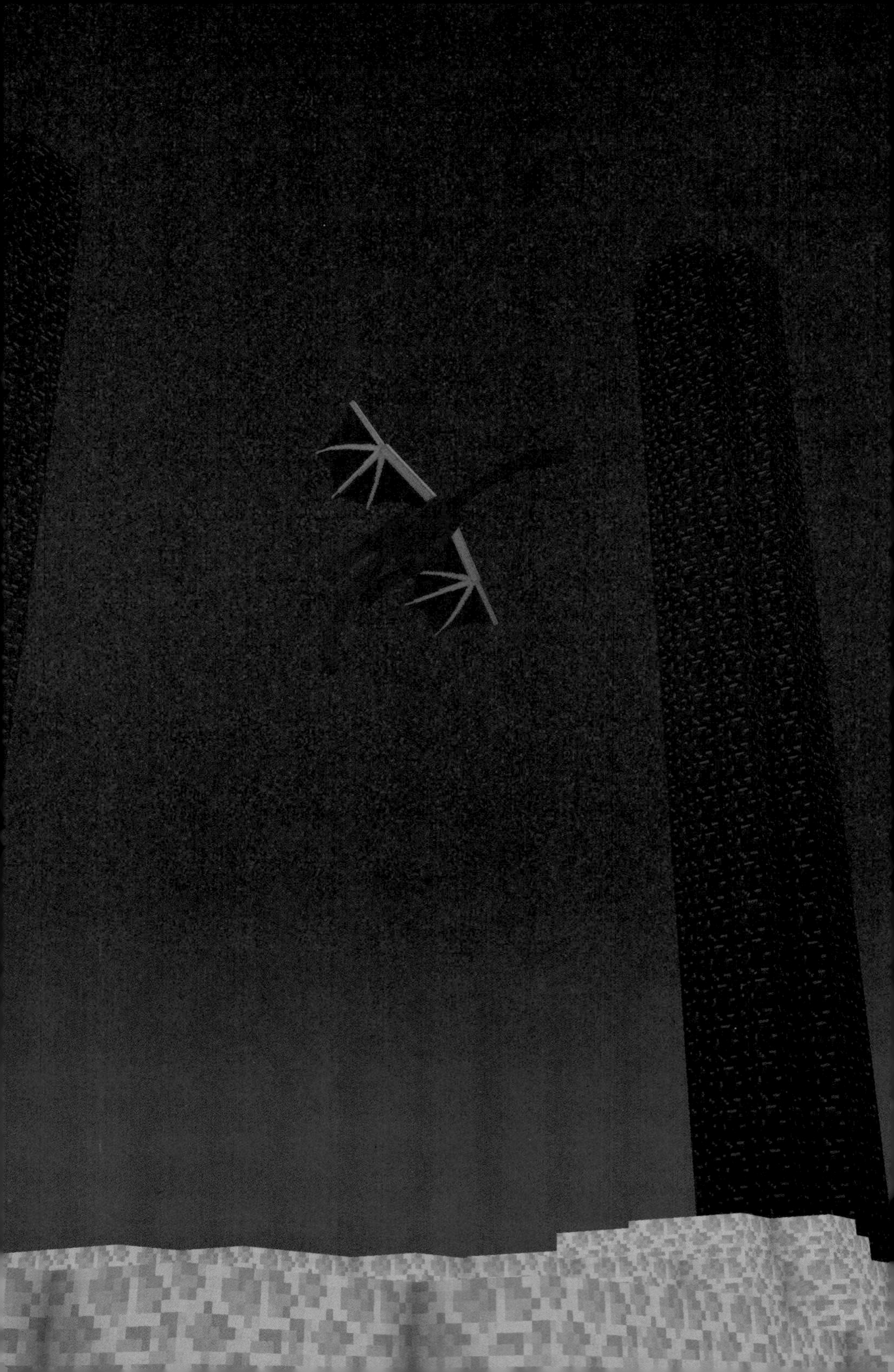

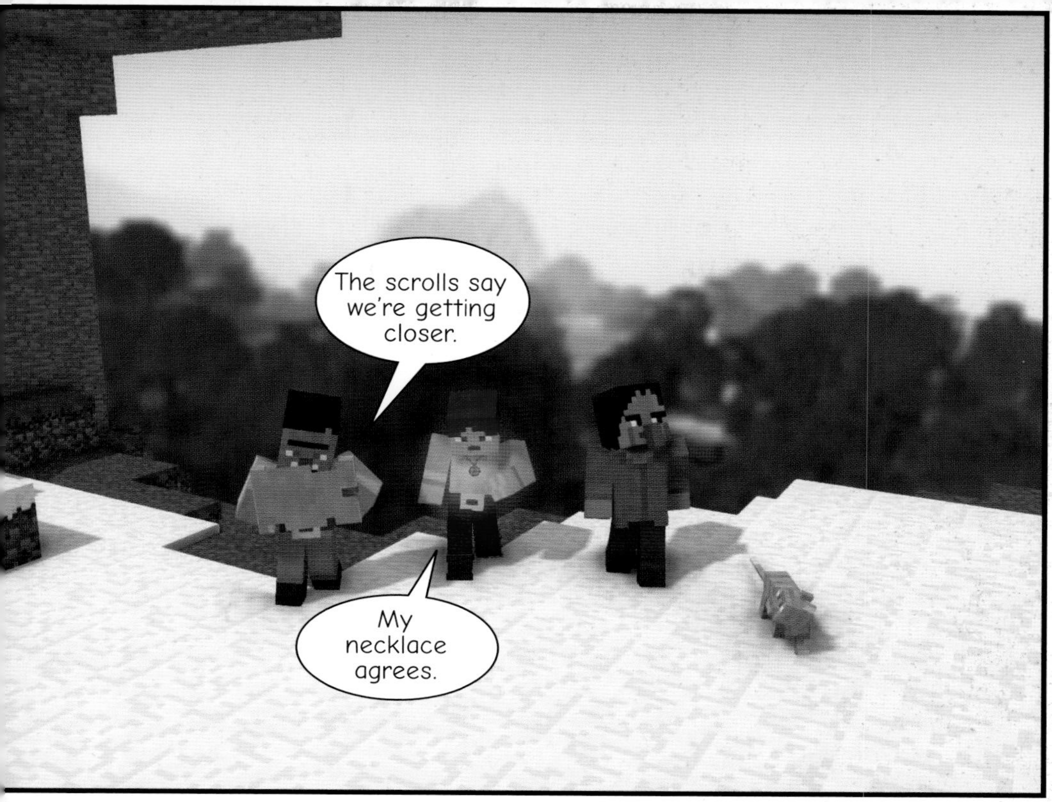
The scrolls say we're getting closer.
My necklace agrees.

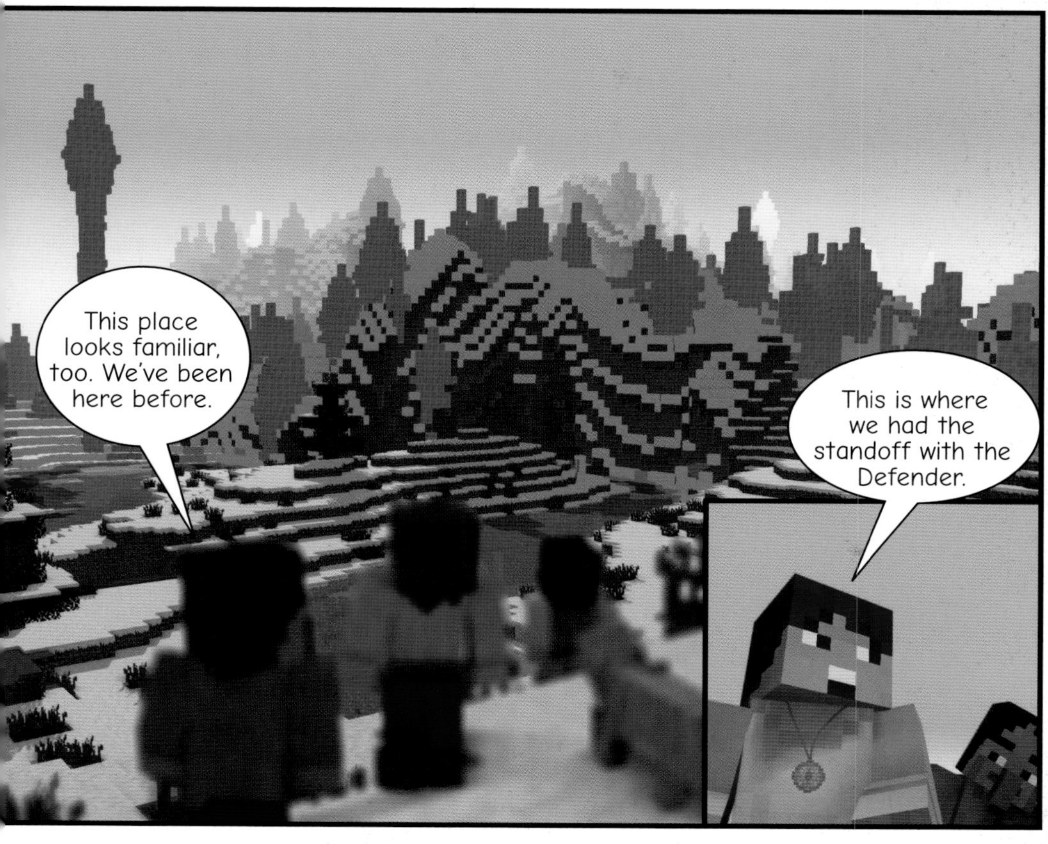
This place looks familiar, too. We've been here before.
This is where we had the standoff with the Defender.

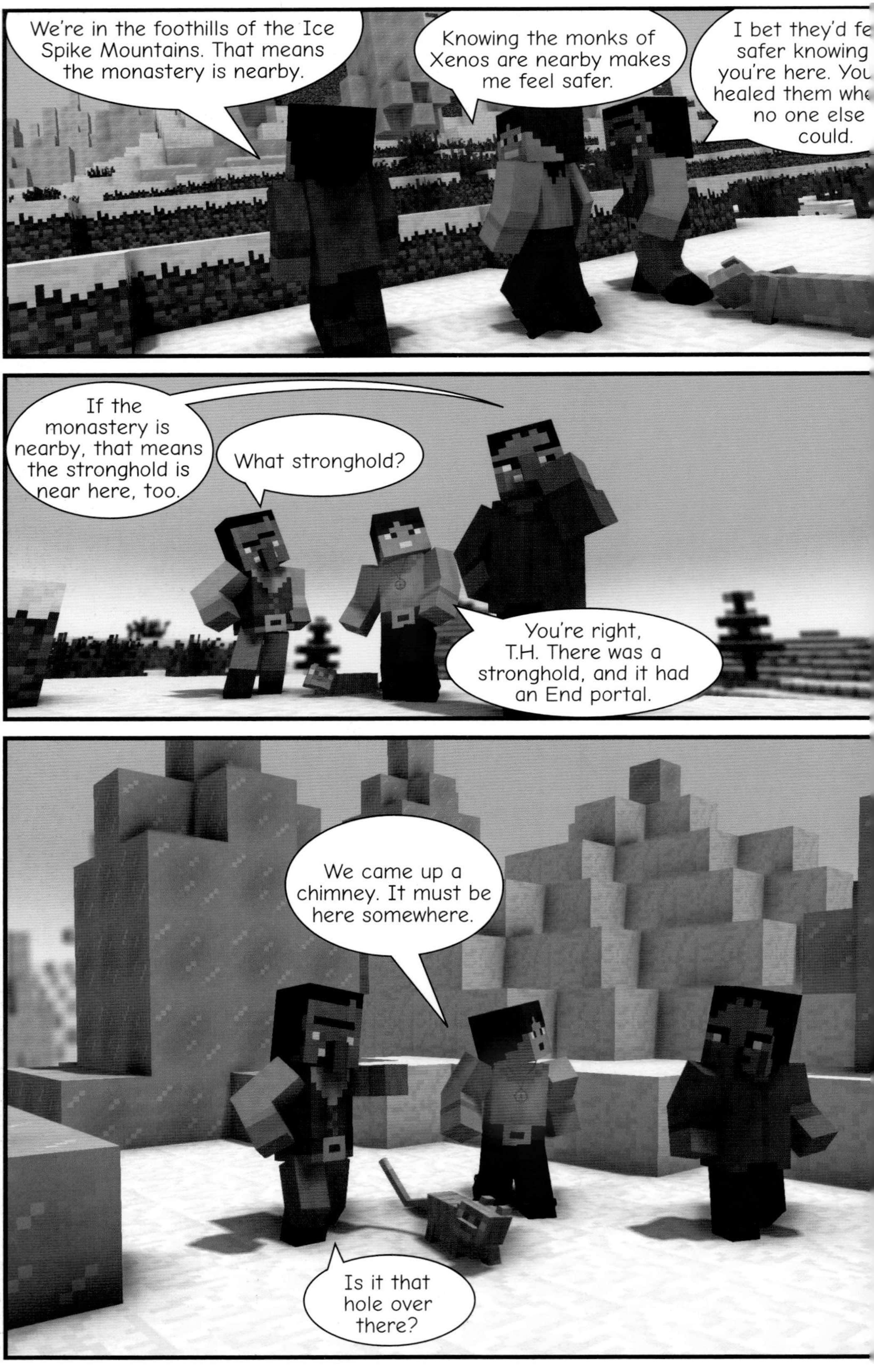
We're in the foothills of the Ice Spike Mountains. That means the monastery is nearby.
Knowing the monks of Xenos are nearby makes me feel safer.
I bet they'd fe safer knowing you're here. You healed them whe no one else could.
If the monastery is nearby, that means the stronghold is near here, too.
What stronghold?
You're right, T.H. There was a stronghold, and it had an End portal.
We came up a chimney. It must be here somewhere.
Is it that hole over there?

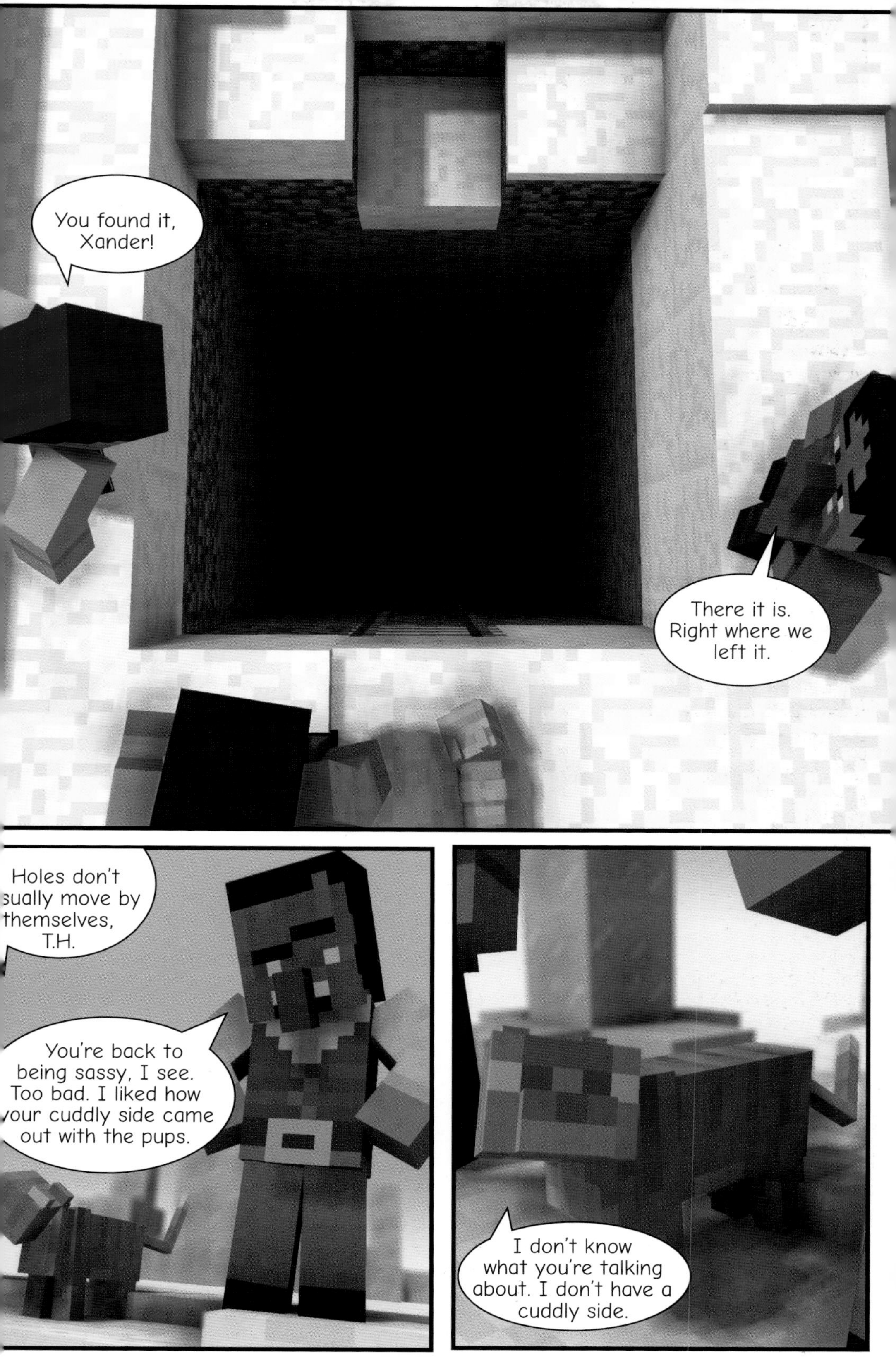
You found it, Xander!
There it is. Right where we left it.
Holes don't usually move by themselves, T.H.
You're back to being sassy, I see. Too bad. I liked how your cuddly side came out with the pups.
I don't know what you're talking about. I don't have a cuddly side.

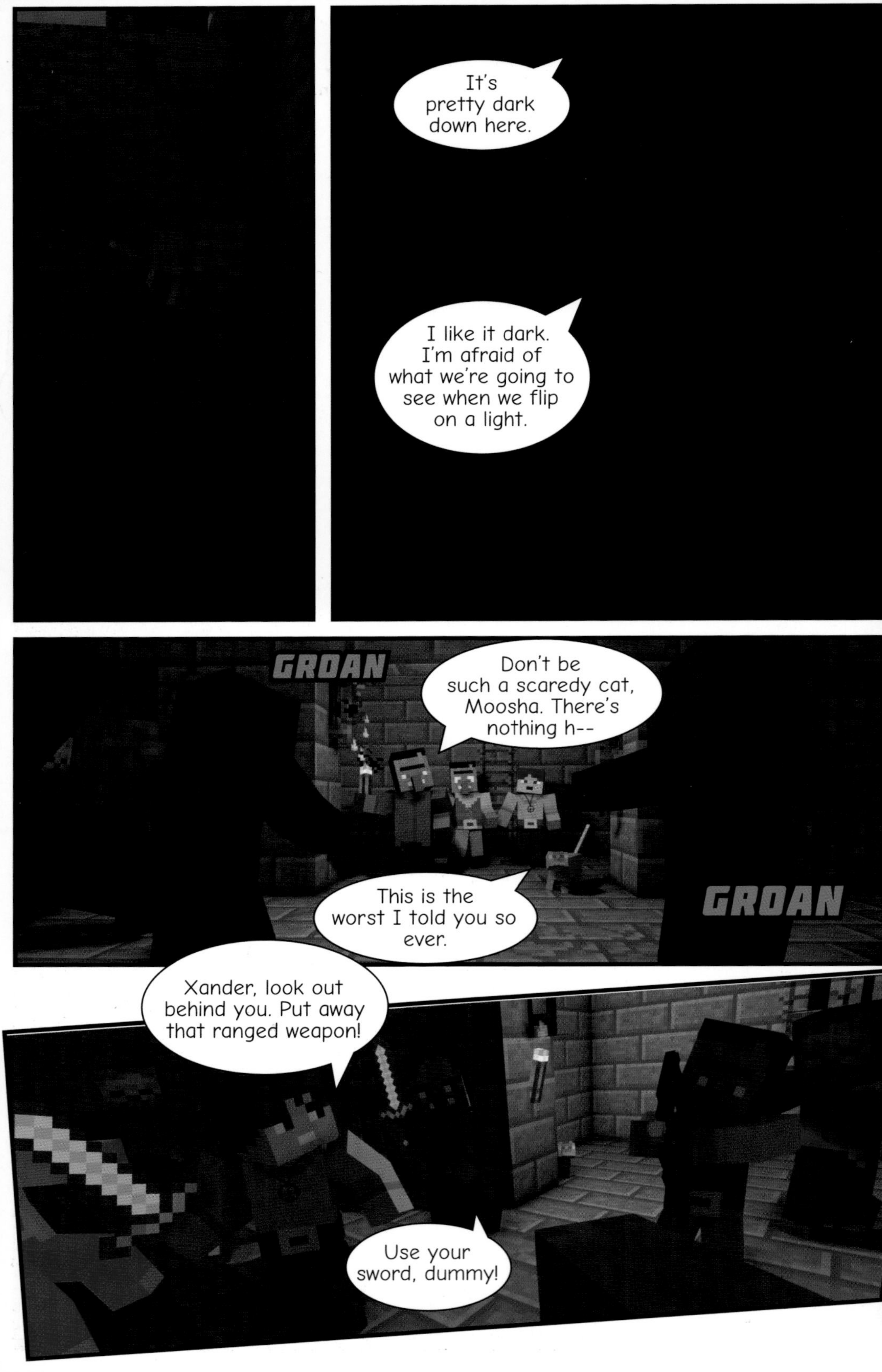
It's pretty dark down here.
I like it dark. I'm afraid of what we're going to see when we flip on a light.
GROAN
Don't be such a scaredy cat, Moosha. There's nothing h--
GROAN
This is the worst I told you so ever.
Xander, look out behind you. Put away that ranged weapon!
Use your sword, dummy!

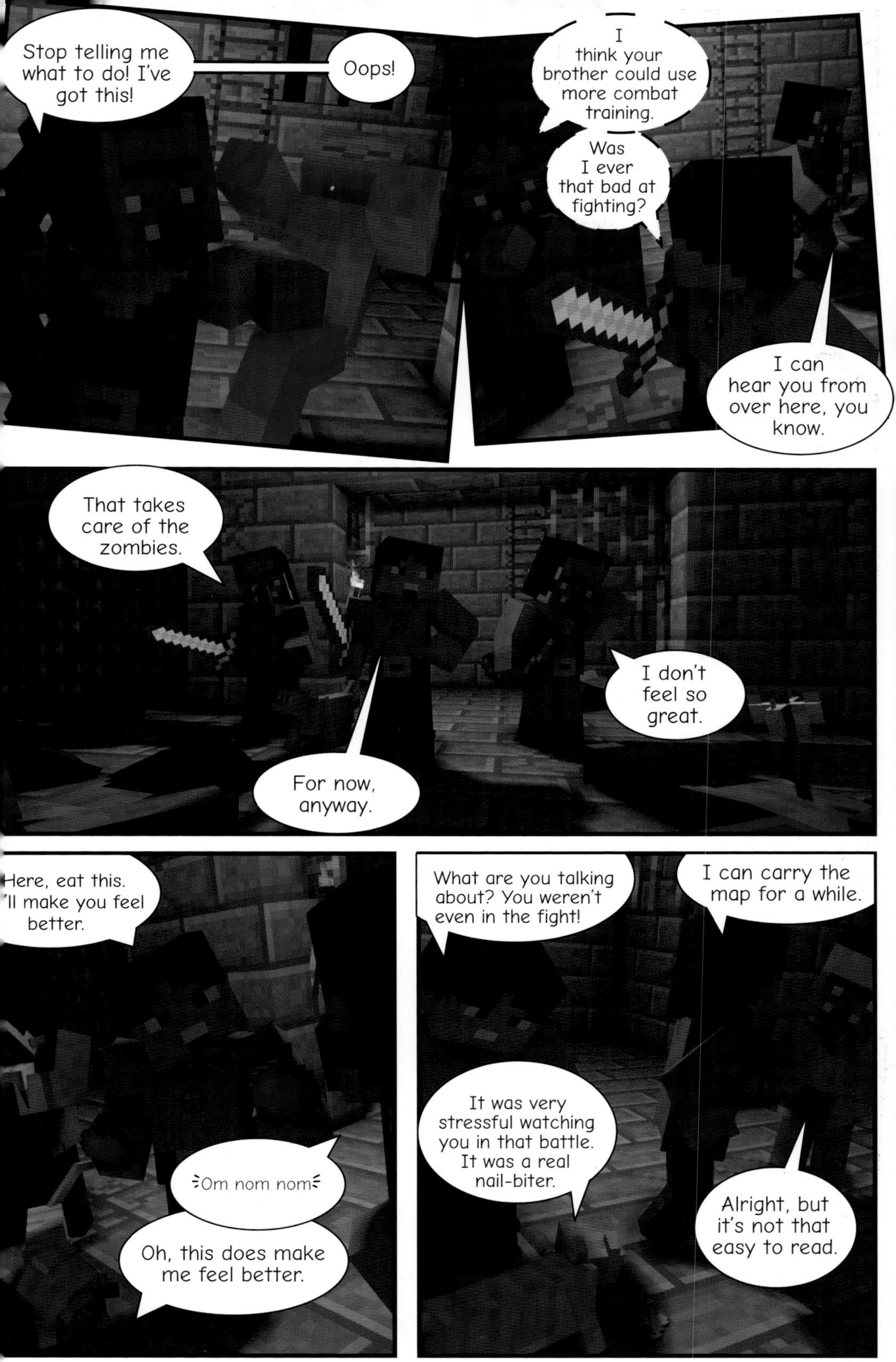
Stop telling me what to do! I've got this!
Oops!
I think your brother could use more combat training.
Was I ever that bad at fighting?
I can hear you from over here, you know.
That takes care of the zombies.
For now, anyway.
I don't feel so great.
Here, eat this. 'll make you feel better.
Om nom nom
Oh, this does make me feel better.
What are you talking about? You weren't even in the fight!
I can carry the map for a while.
It was very stressful watching you in that battle. It was a real nail-biter.
Alright, but it's not that easy to read.

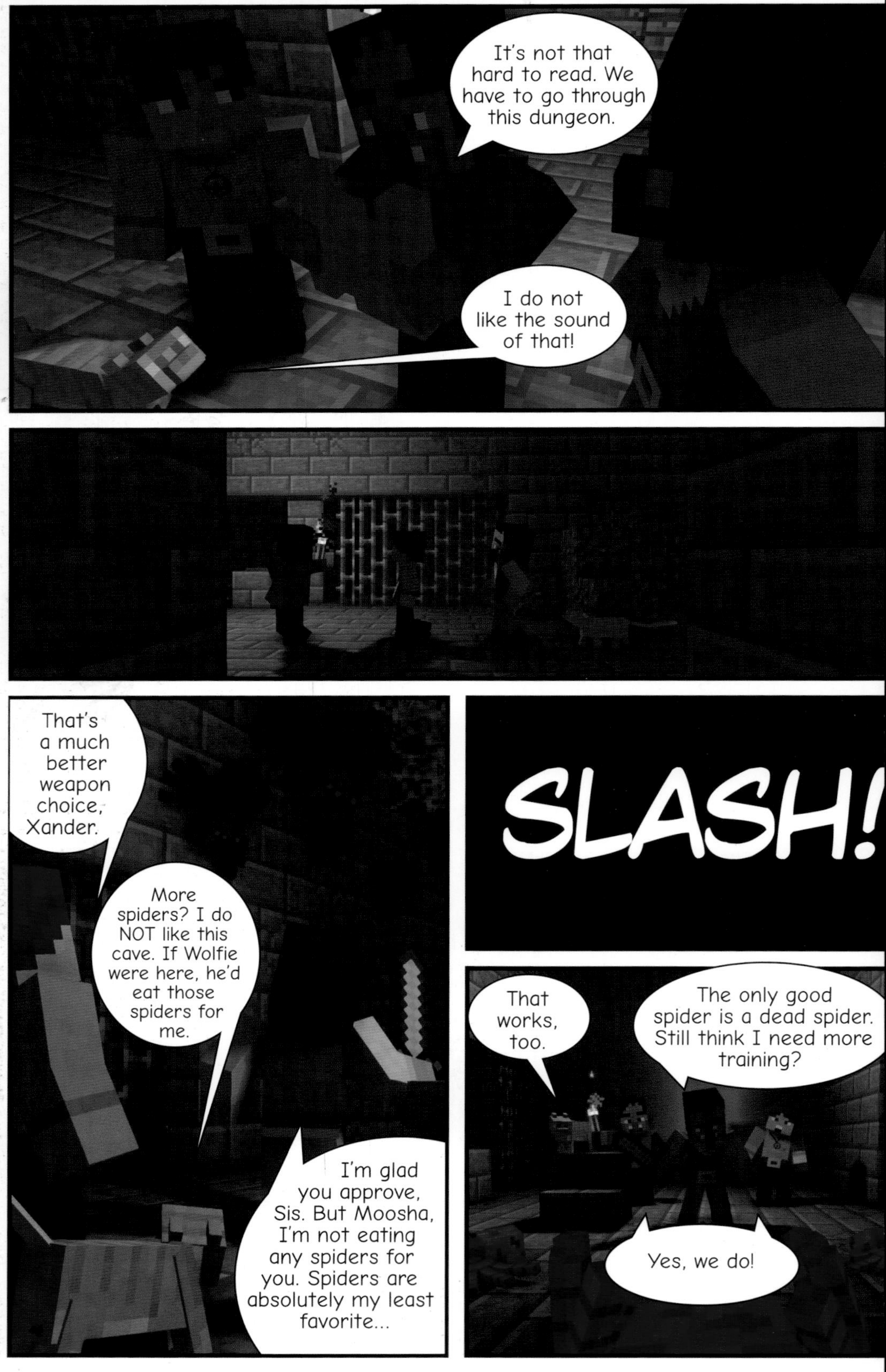
It's not that hard to read. We have to go through this dungeon.
I do not like the sound of that!
That's a much better weapon choice, Xander.
More spiders? I do NOT like this cave. If Wolfie were here, he'd eat those spiders for me.
I'm glad you approve, Sis. But Moosha, I'm not eating any spiders for you. Spiders are absolutely my least favorite...
SLASH!
That works, too.
The only good spider is a dead spider. Still think I need more training?
Yes, we do!

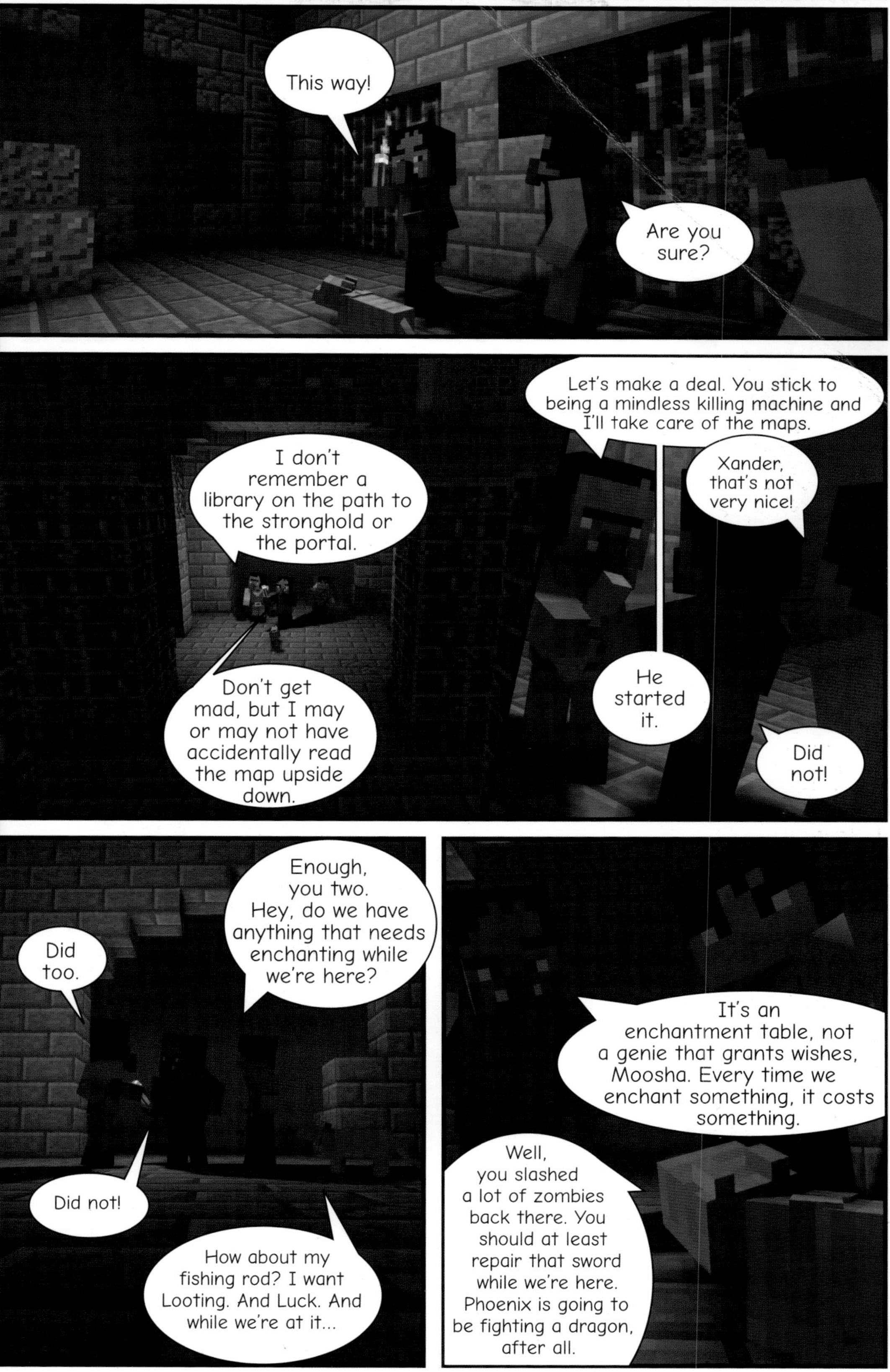
This way!
Are you sure?
I don't remember a library on the path to the stronghold or the portal.
Don't get mad, but I may or may not have accidentally read the map upside down.
Let's make a deal. You stick to being a mindless killing machine and I'll take care of the maps.
Xander, that's not very nice!
He started it.
Did not!
Did too.
Enough, you two. Hey, do we have anything that needs enchanting while we're here?
Did not!
How about my fishing rod? I want Looting. And Luck. And while we're at it...
It's an enchantment table, not a genie that grants wishes, Moosha. Every time we enchant something, it costs something.
Well, you slashed a lot of zombies back there. You should at least repair that sword while we're here. Phoenix is going to be fighting a dragon, after all.

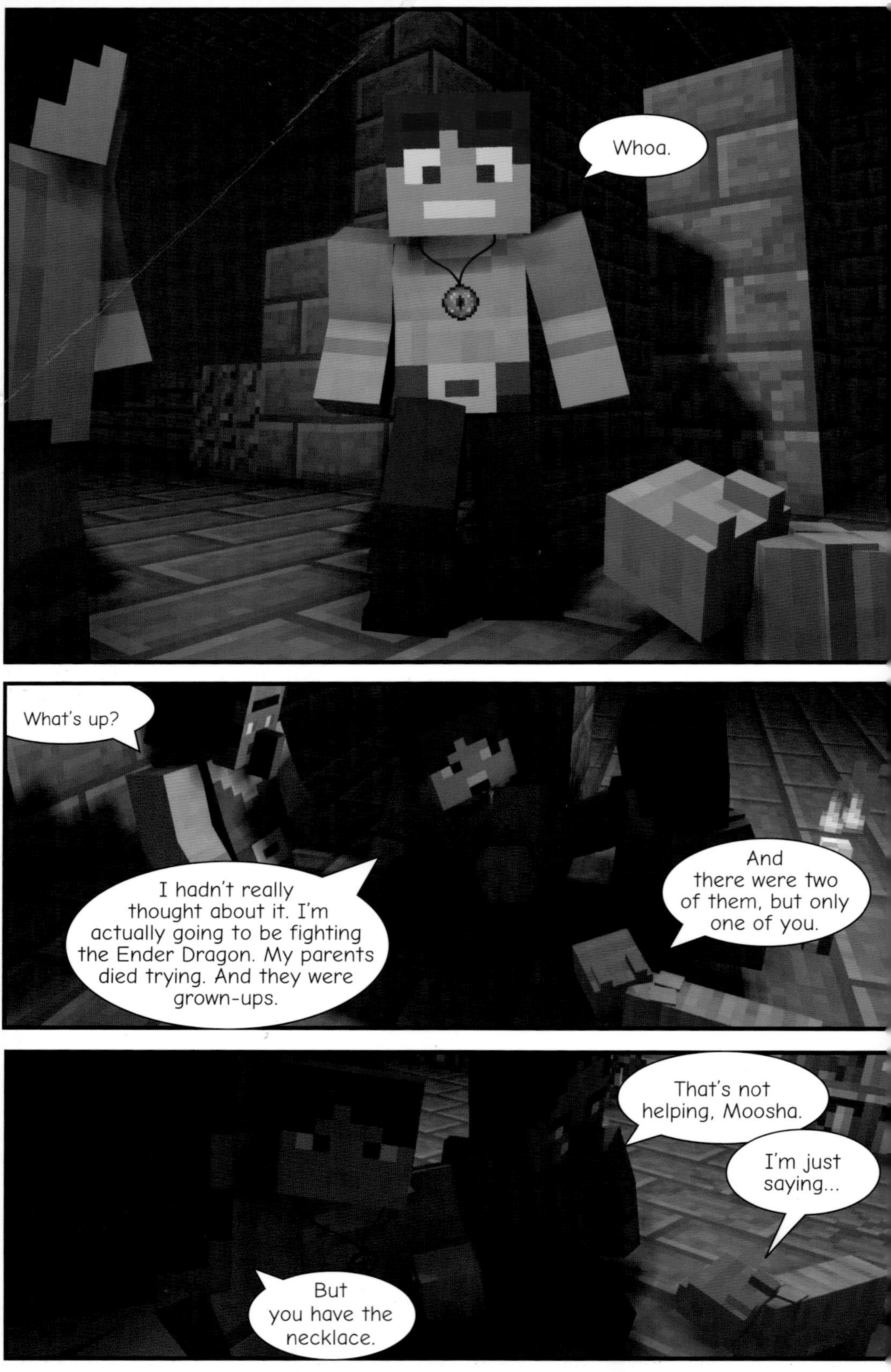
Whoa.
What's up?
I hadn't really thought about it. I'm actually going to be fighting the Ender Dragon. My parents died trying. And they were grown-ups.
And there were two of them, but only one of you.
That's not helping, Moosha.
I'm just saying...
But you have the necklace.

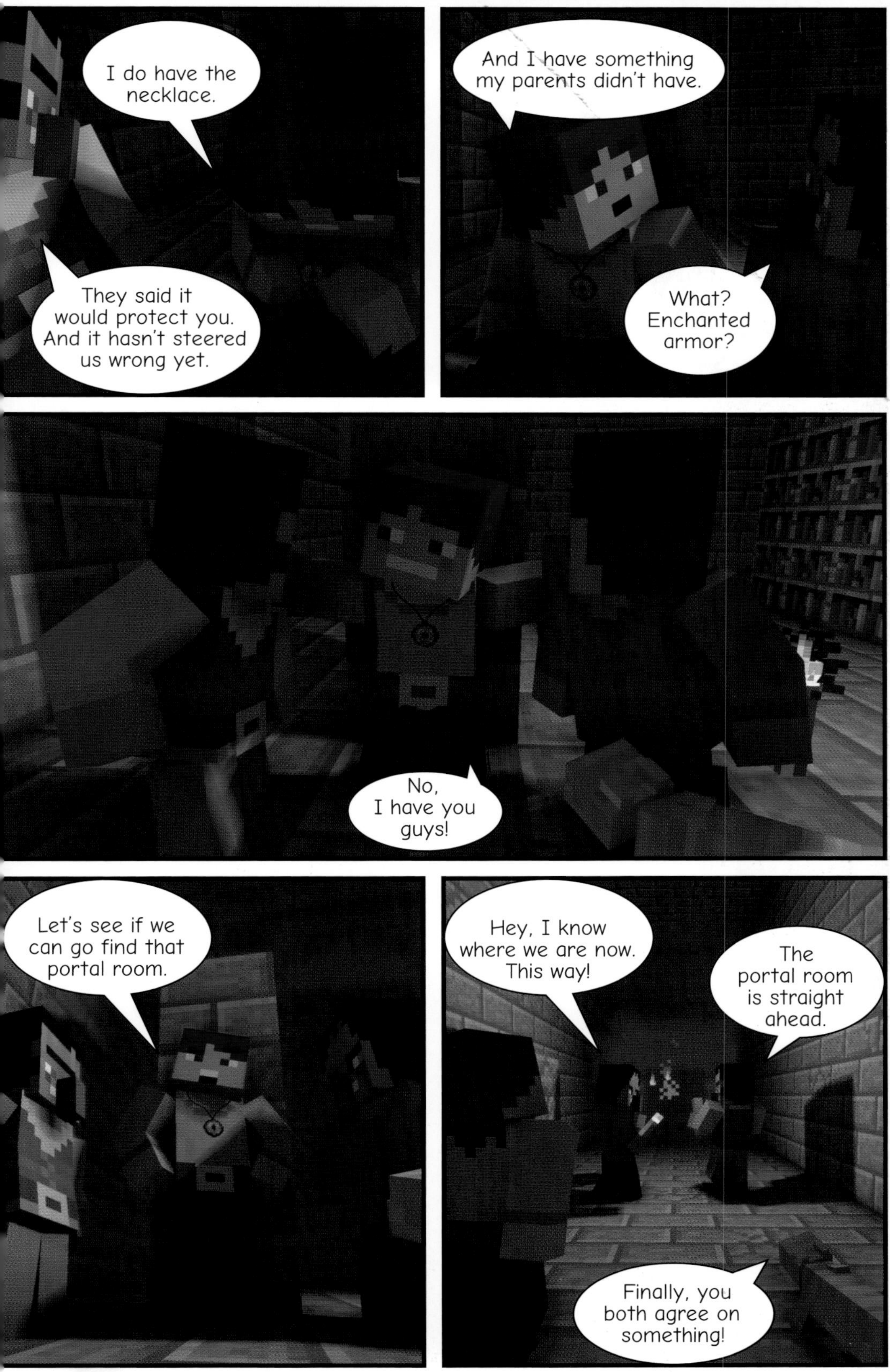
I do have the necklace.
They said it would protect you. And it hasn't steered us wrong yet.
And I have something my parents didn't have.
What? Enchanted armor?
No, I have you guys!
Let's see if we can go find that portal room.
Hey, I know where we are now. This way!
The portal room is straight ahead.
Finally, you both agree on something!

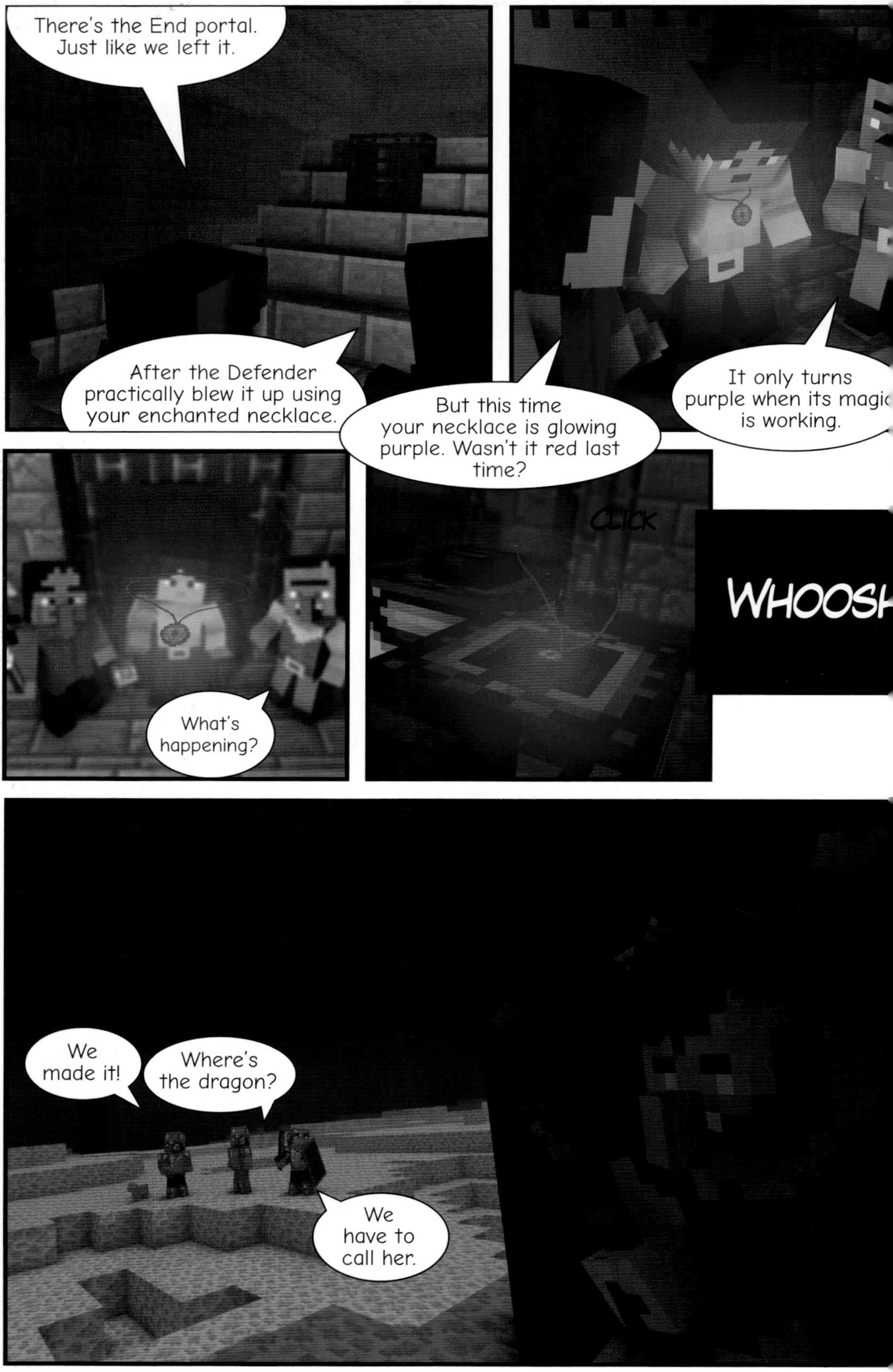
There's the End portal. Just like we left it.
After the Defender practically blew it up using your enchanted necklace.
But this time your necklace is glowing purple. Wasn't it red last time?
It only turns purple when its magic is working.
What's happening?
CLICK
WHOOSH
We made it!
Where's the dragon?
We have to call her.

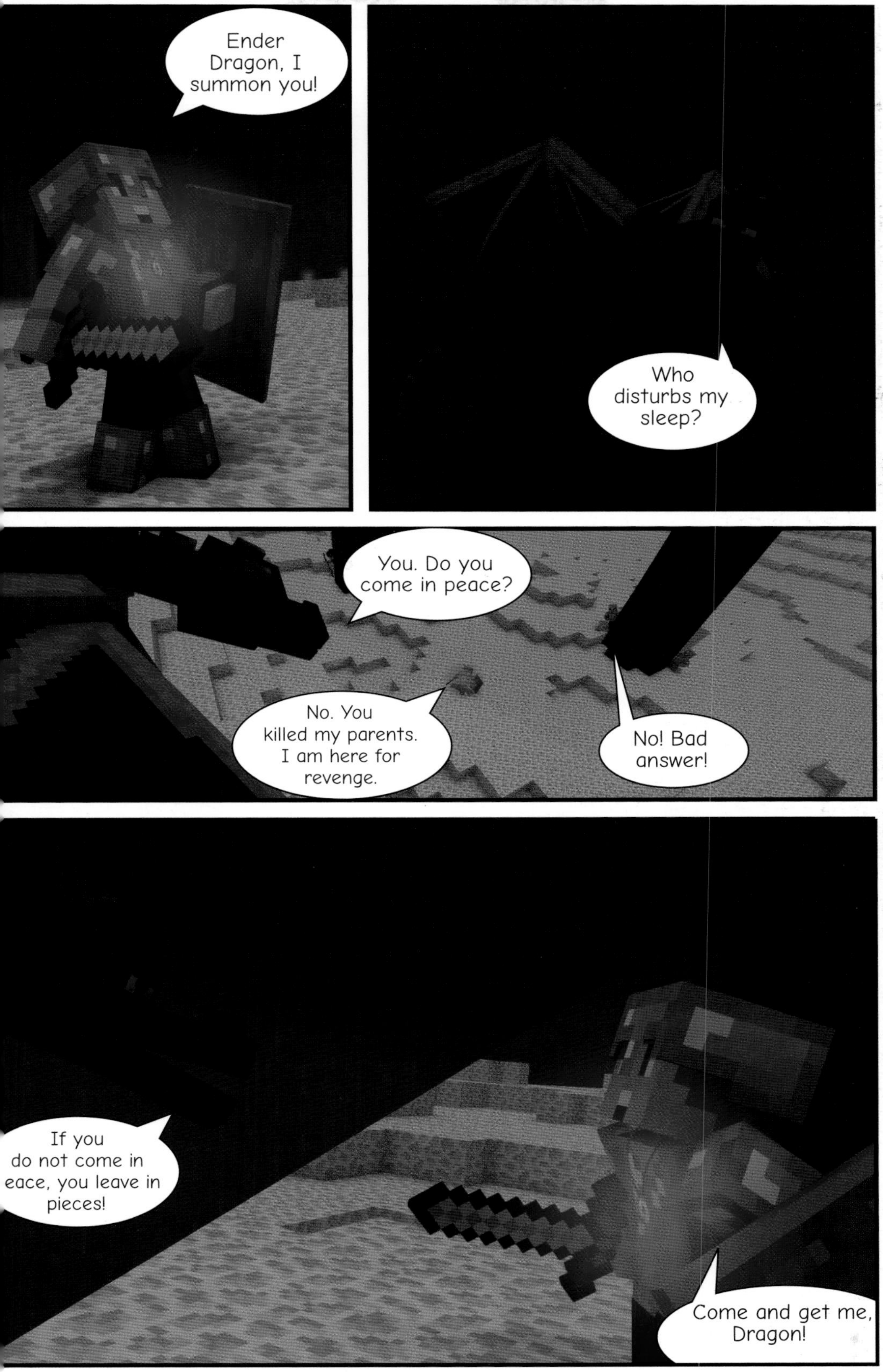
Ender Dragon, I summon you!
Who disturbs my sleep?
You. Do you come in peace?
No. You killed my parents. I am here for revenge.
No! Bad answer!
If you do not come in eace, you leave in pieces!
Come and get me, Dragon!

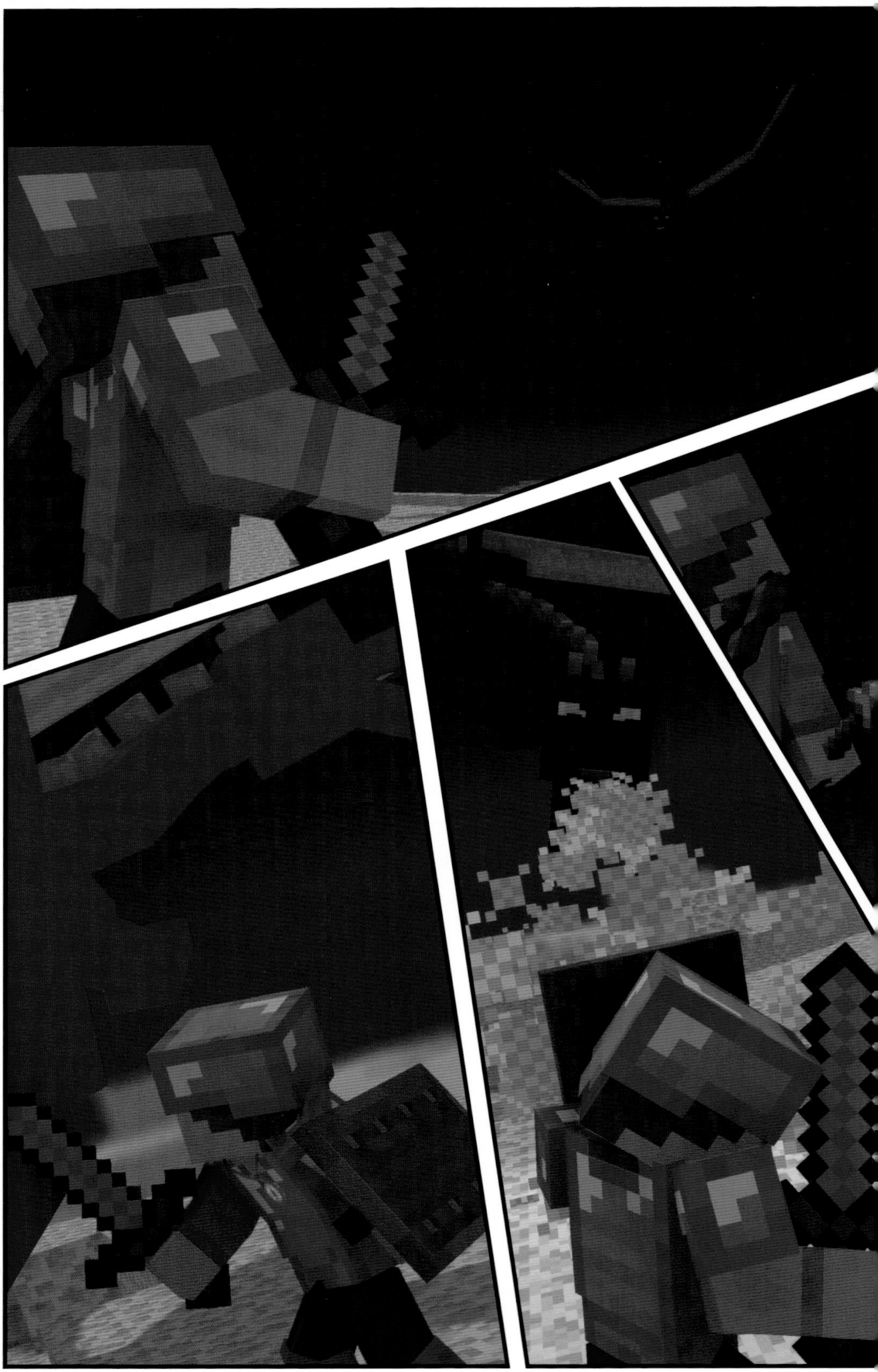

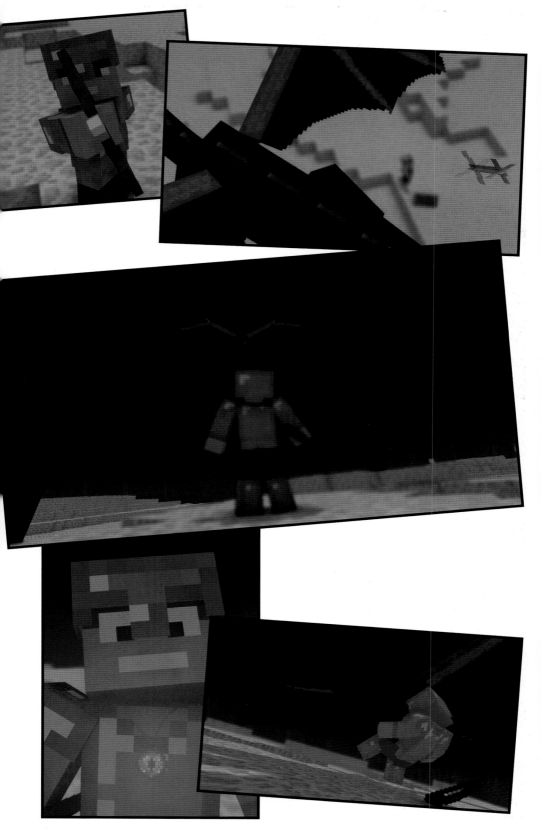

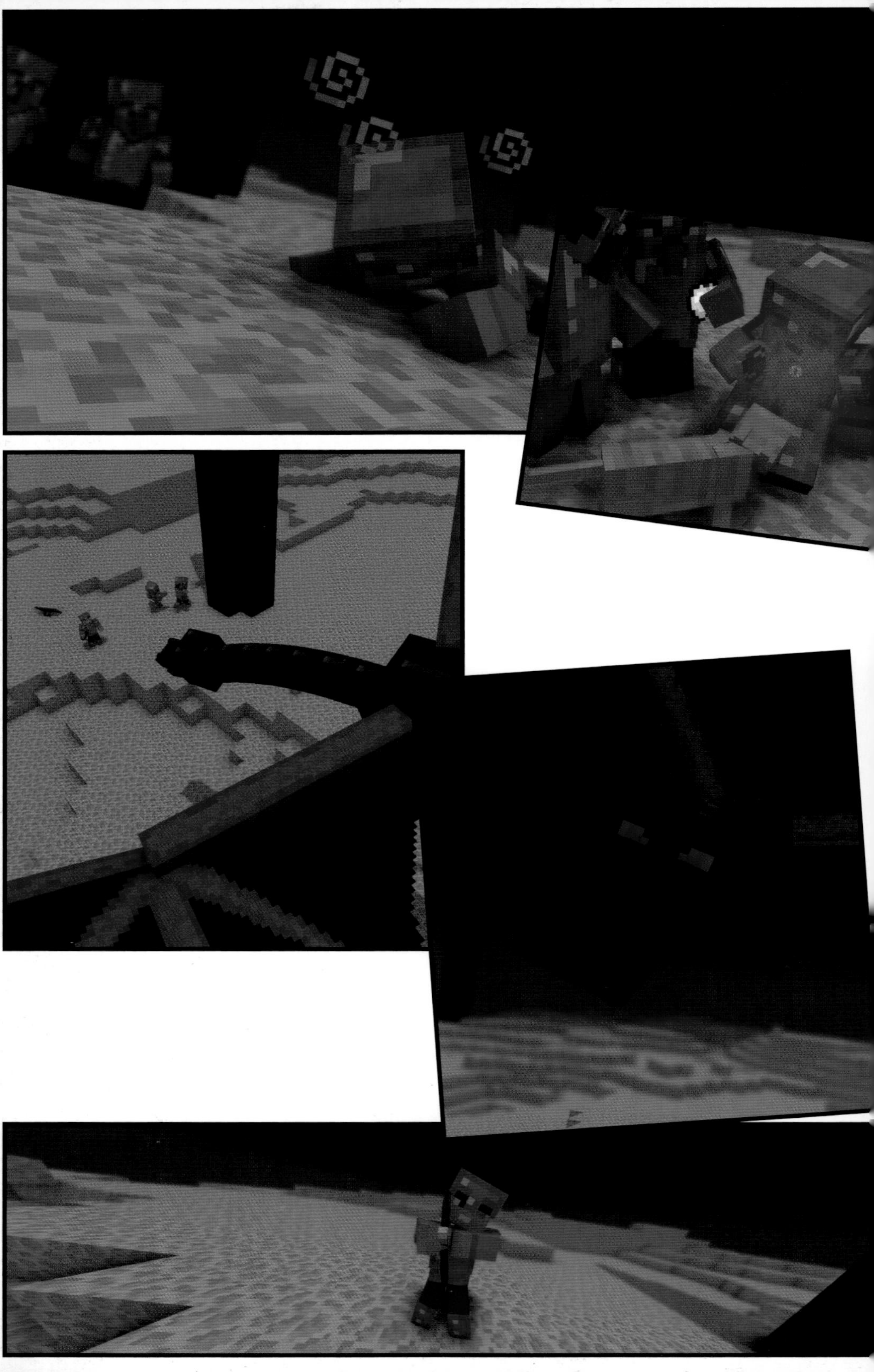

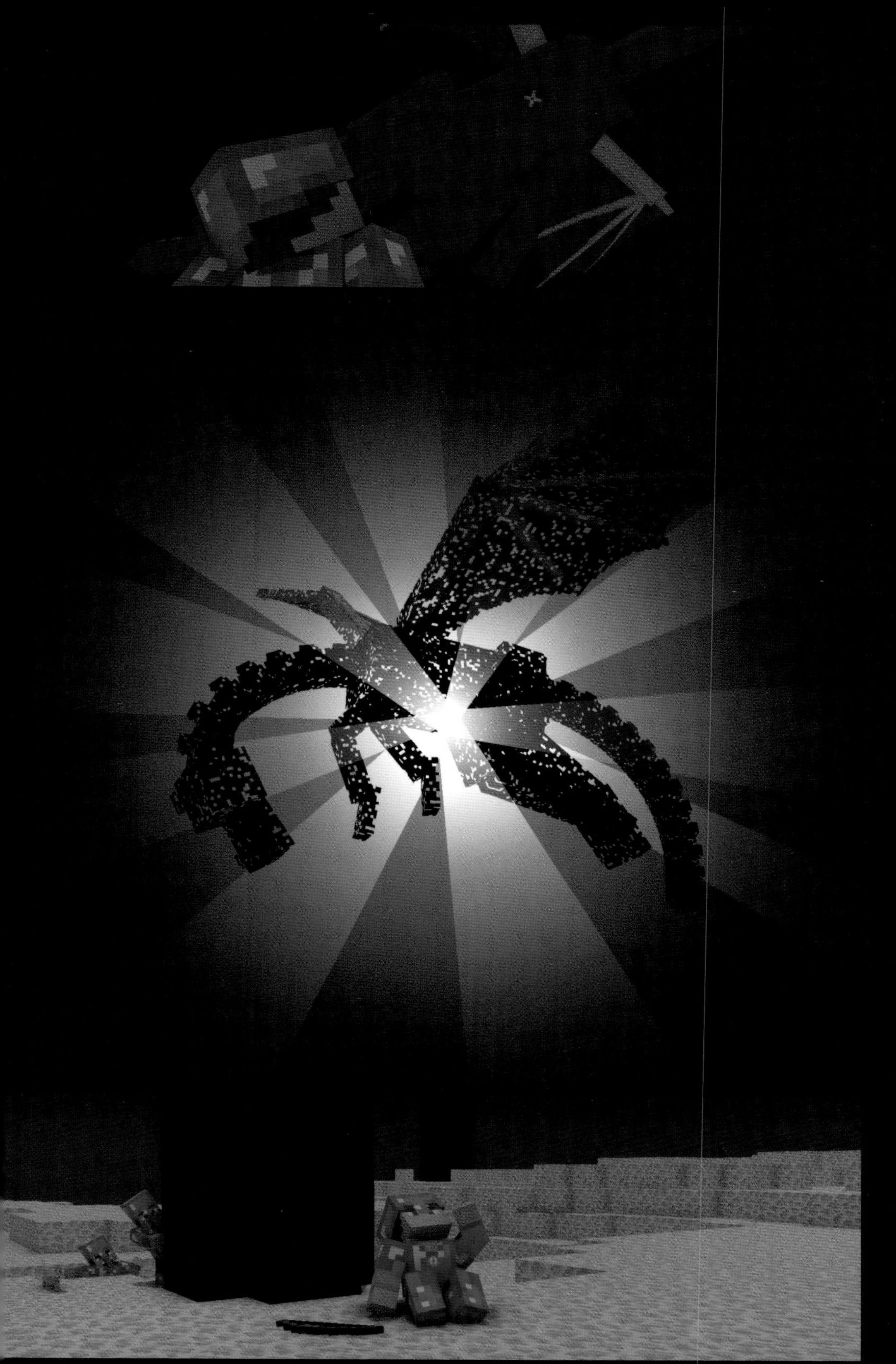

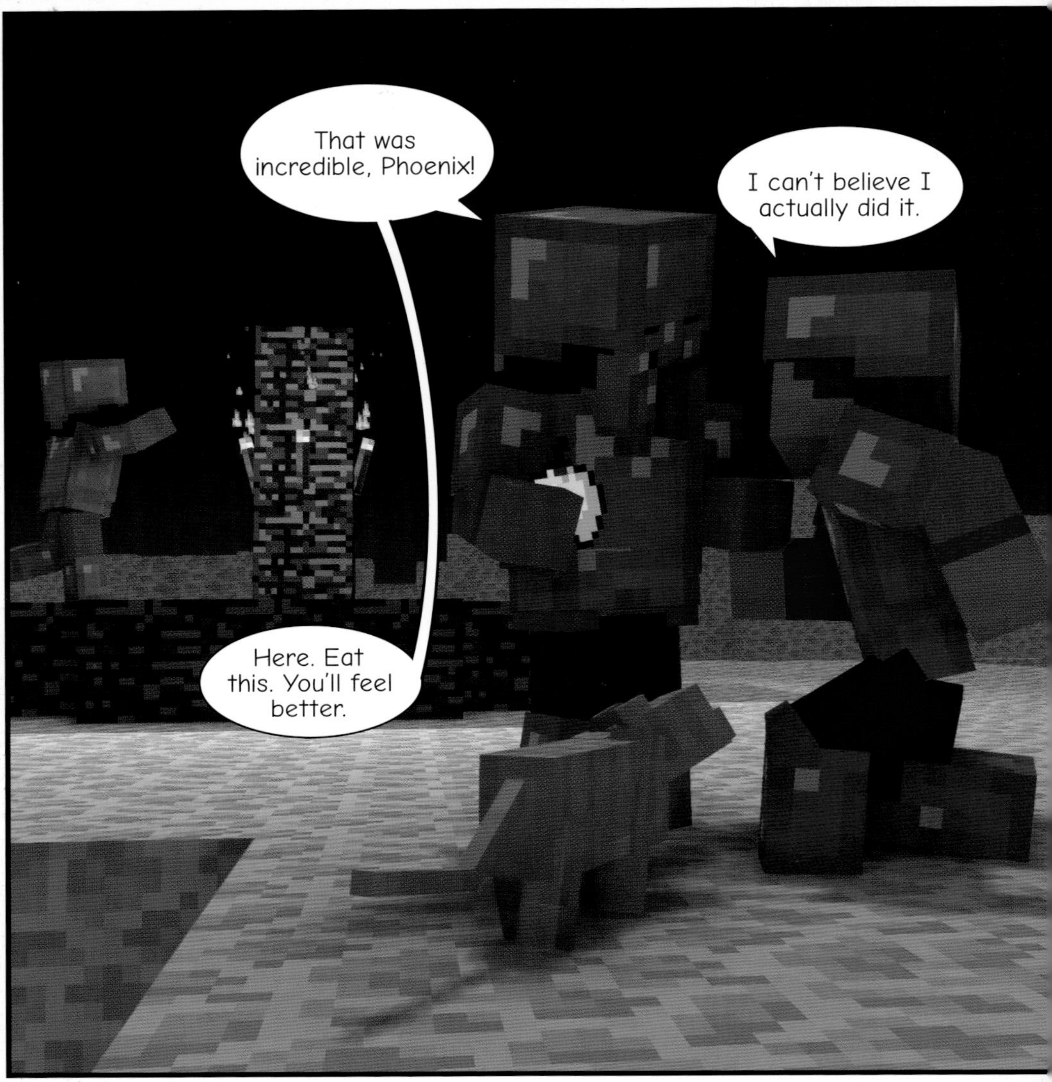
That was incredible, Phoenix!
I can't believe I actually did it.
Here. Eat this. You'll feel better.

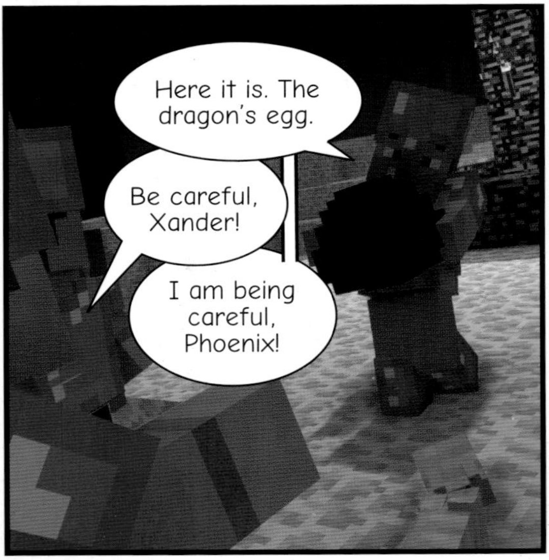
Here it is. The dragon's egg.
Be careful, Xander!
I am being careful, Phoenix!

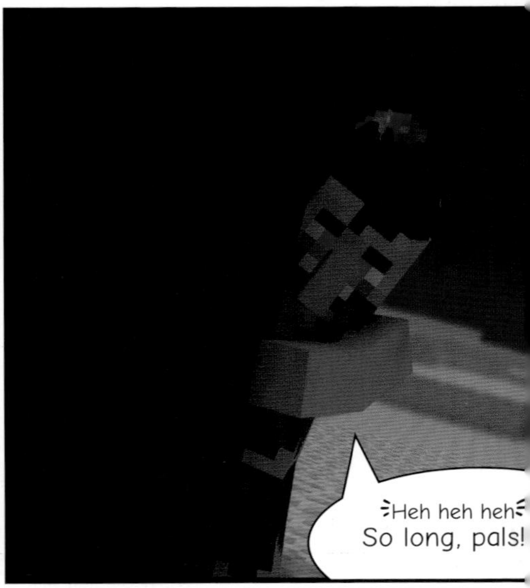
Heh heh heh
So long, pals!

CHAPTER 10

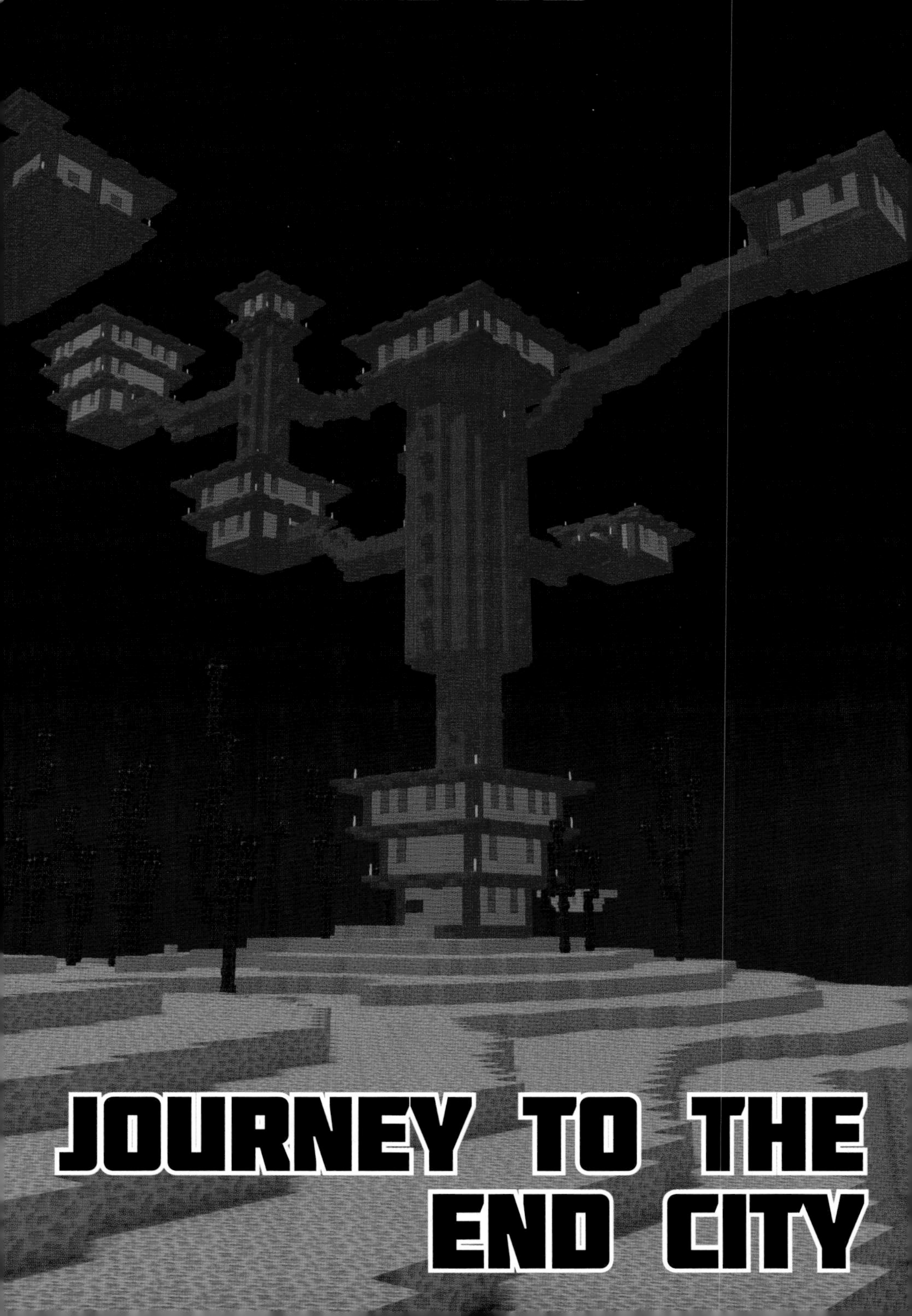

JOURNEY TO THE END CITY

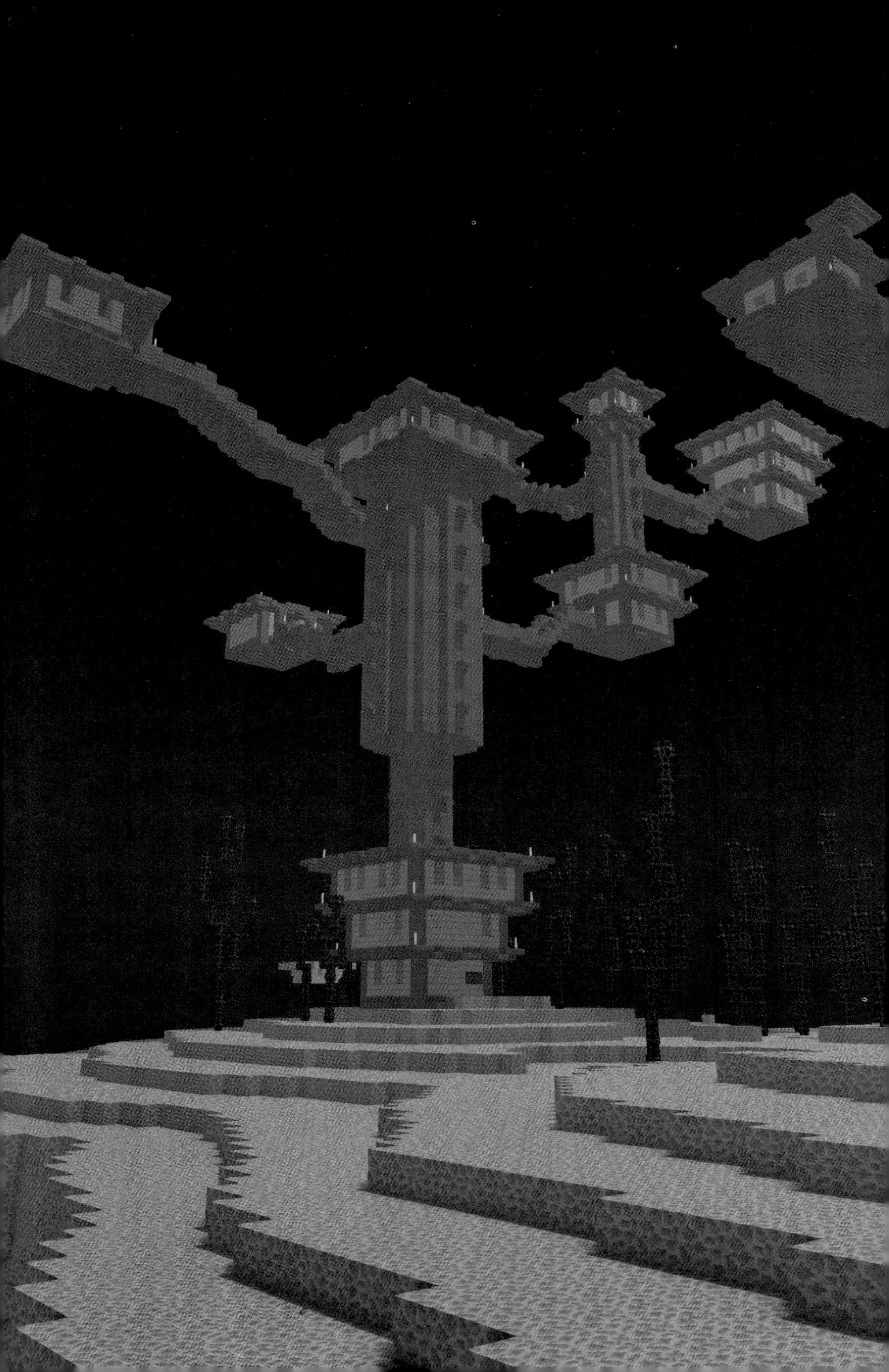

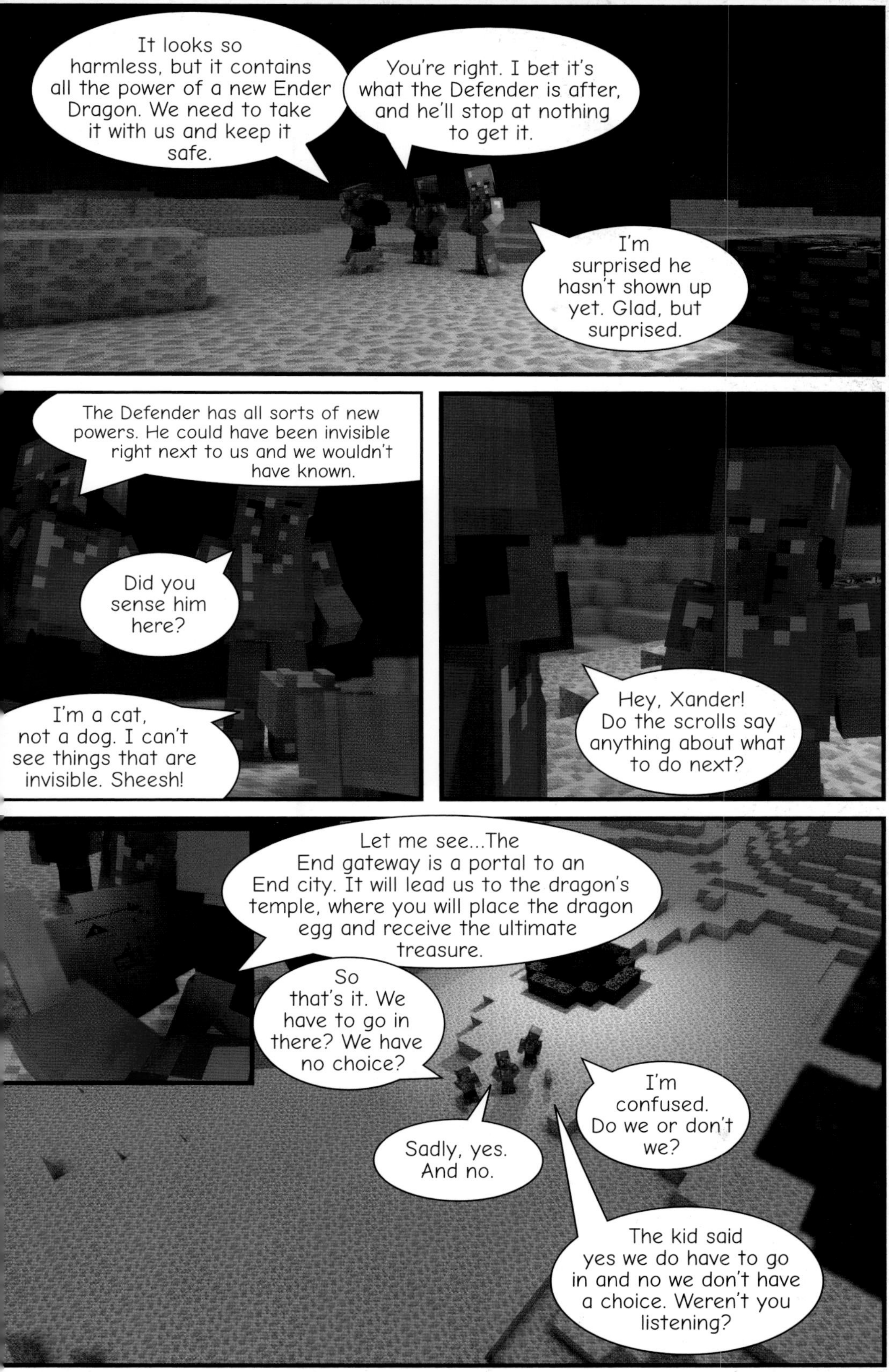

It looks so harmless, but it contains all the power of a new Ender Dragon. We need to take it with us and keep it safe.
You're right. I bet it's what the Defender is after, and he'll stop at nothing to get it.
I'm surprised he hasn't shown up yet. Glad, but surprised.
The Defender has all sorts of new powers. He could have been invisible right next to us and we wouldn't have known.
Did you sense him here?
I'm a cat, not a dog. I can't see things that are invisible. Sheesh!
Hey, Xander! Do the scrolls say anything about what to do next?
Let me see...The End gateway is a portal to an End city. It will lead us to the dragon's temple, where you will place the dragon egg and receive the ultimate treasure.
So that's it. We have to go in there? We have no choice?
Sadly, yes. And no.
I'm confused. Do we or don't we?
The kid said yes we do have to go in and no we don't have a choice. Weren't you listening?

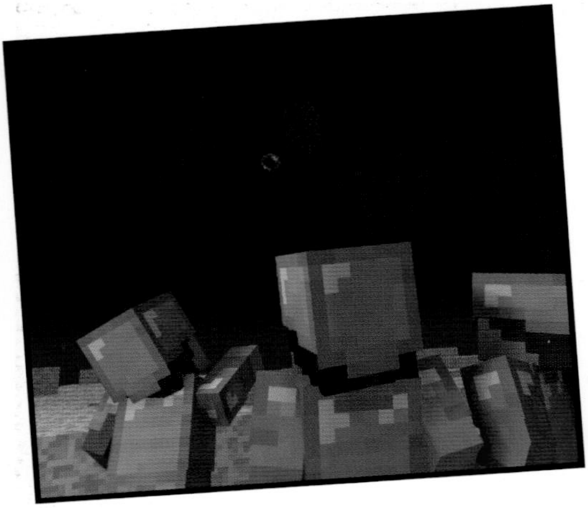

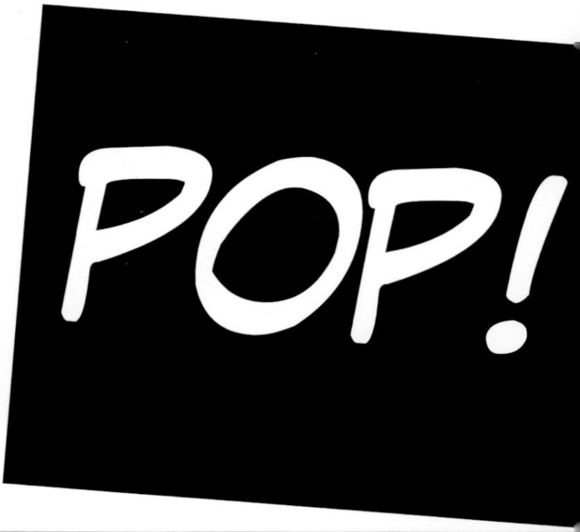
POP!

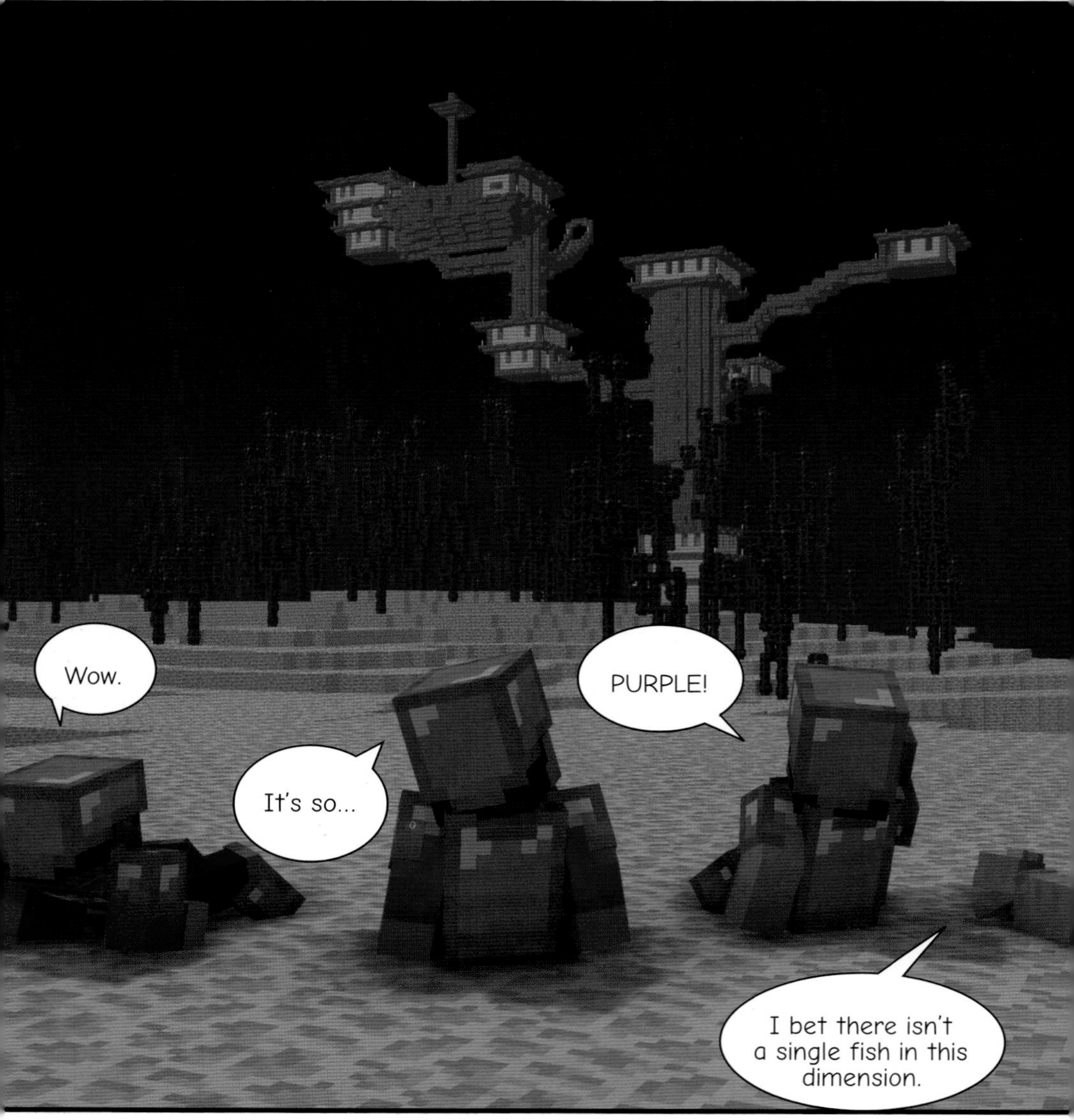
Wow.
It's so...
PURPLE!
I bet there isn't a single fish in this dimension.

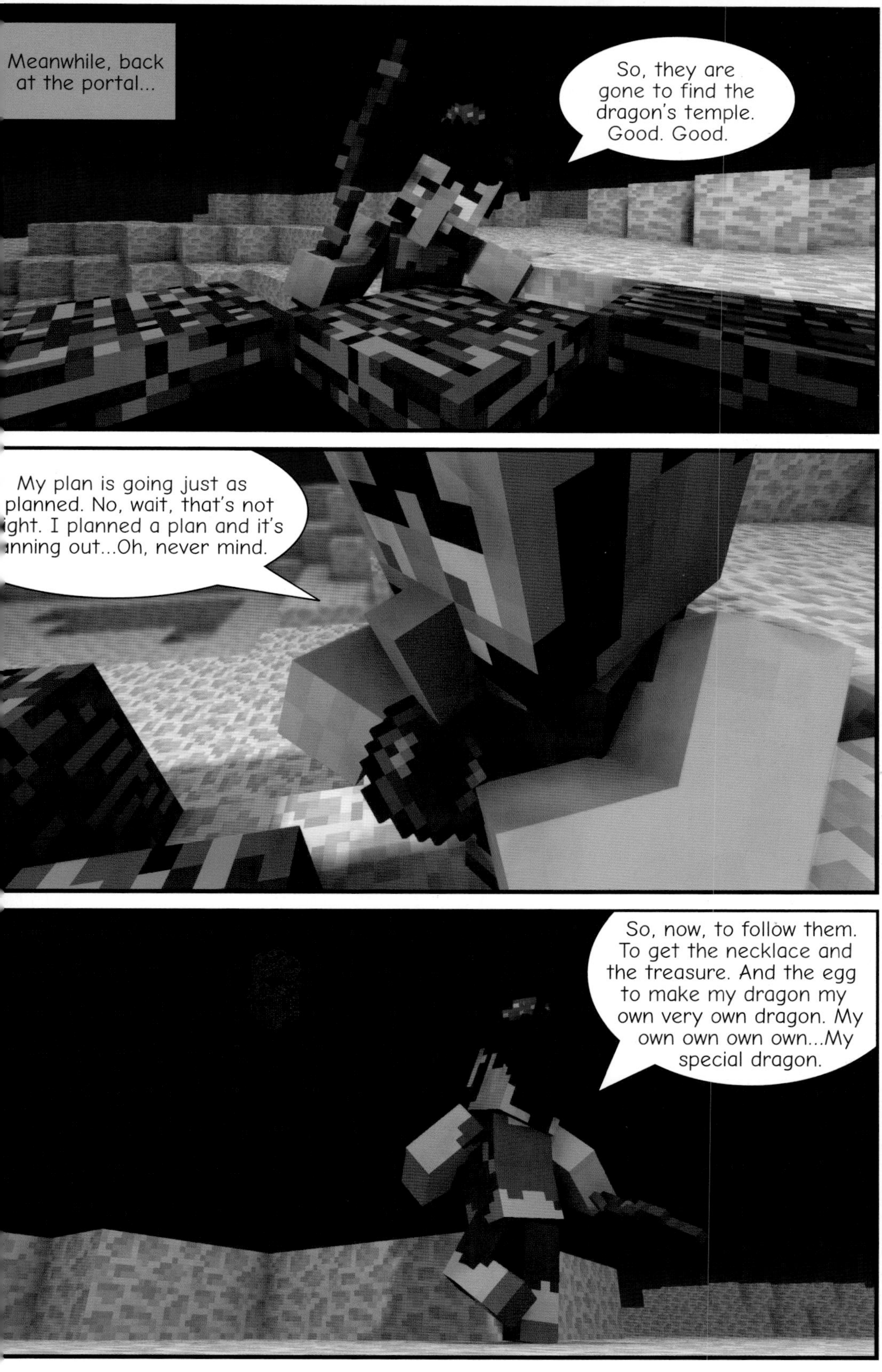
Meanwhile, back at the portal...
So, they are gone to find the dragon's temple. Good. Good.
My plan is going just as planned. No, wait, that's not ight. I planned a plan and it's nning out...Oh, never mind.
So, now, to follow them. To get the necklace and the treasure. And the egg to make my dragon my own very own dragon. My own own own own...My special dragon.

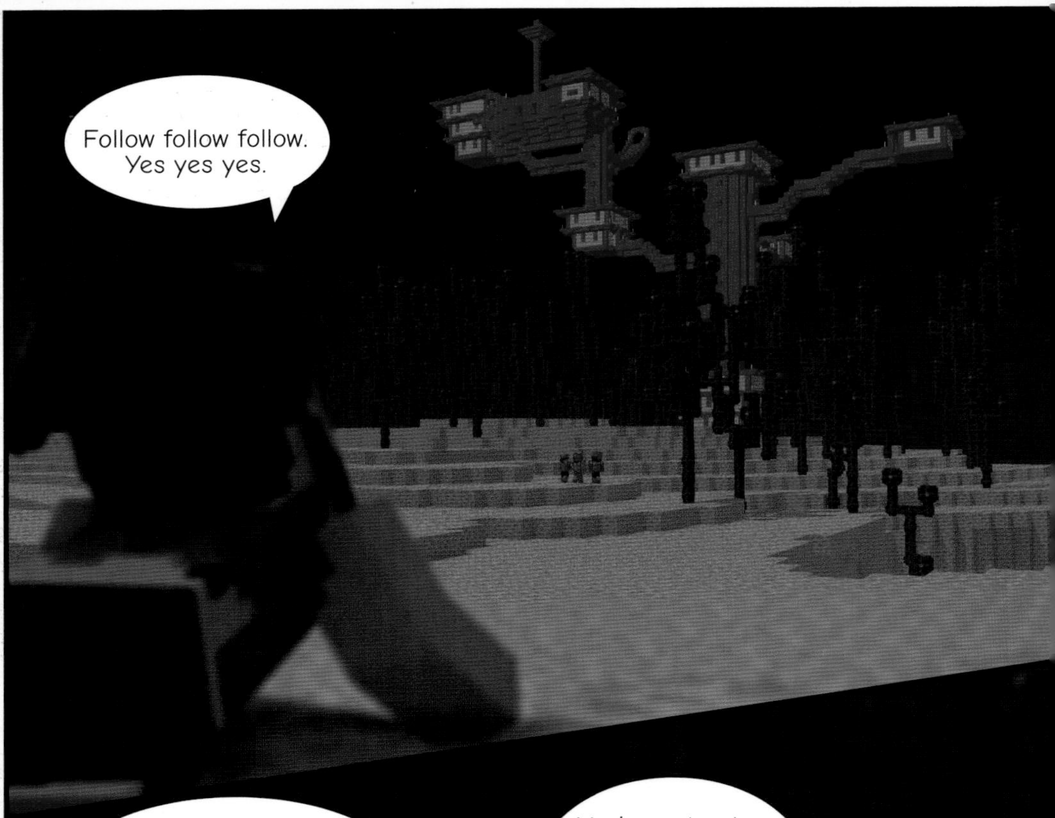
Follow follow follow. Yes yes yes.

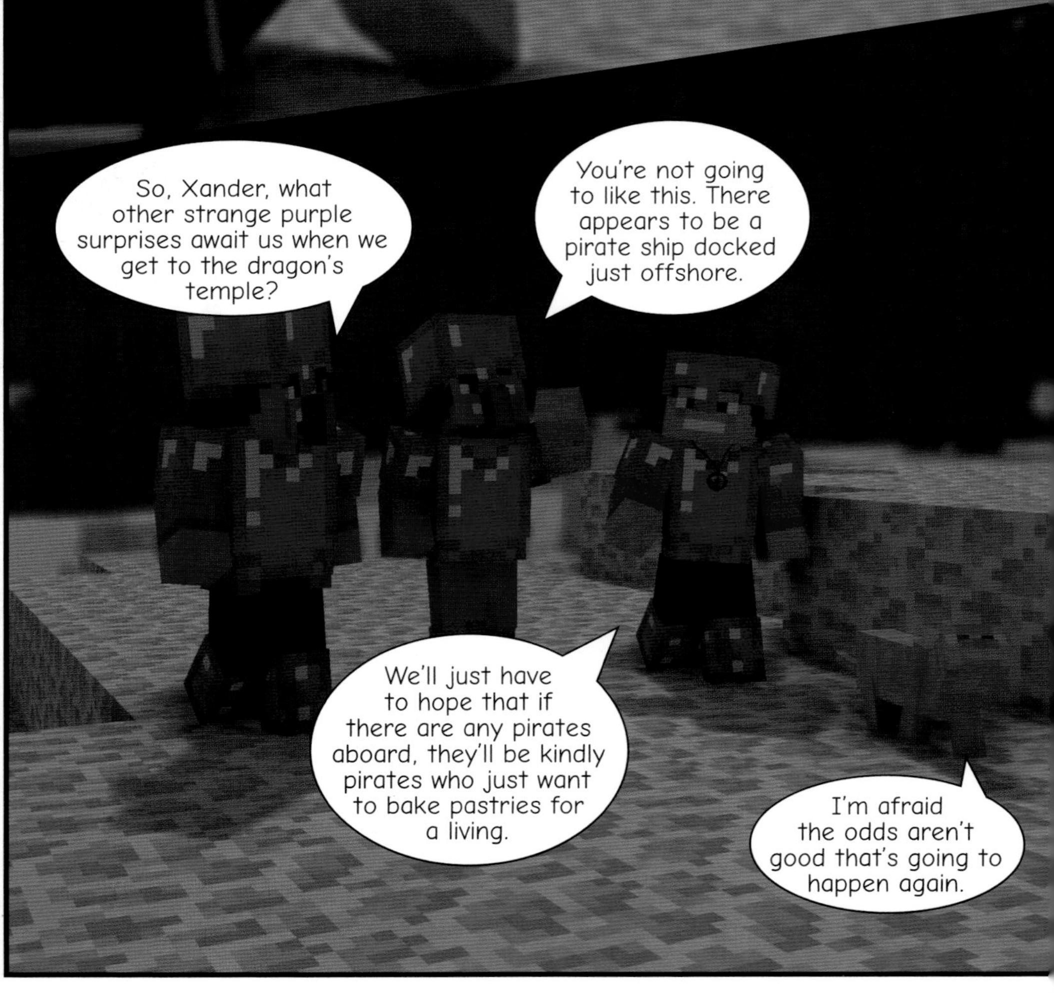
So, Xander, what other strange purple surprises await us when we get to the dragon's temple?
You're not going to like this. There appears to be a pirate ship docked just offshore.
We'll just have to hope that if there are any pirates aboard, they'll be kindly pirates who just want to bake pastries for a living.
I'm afraid the odds aren't good that's going to happen again.

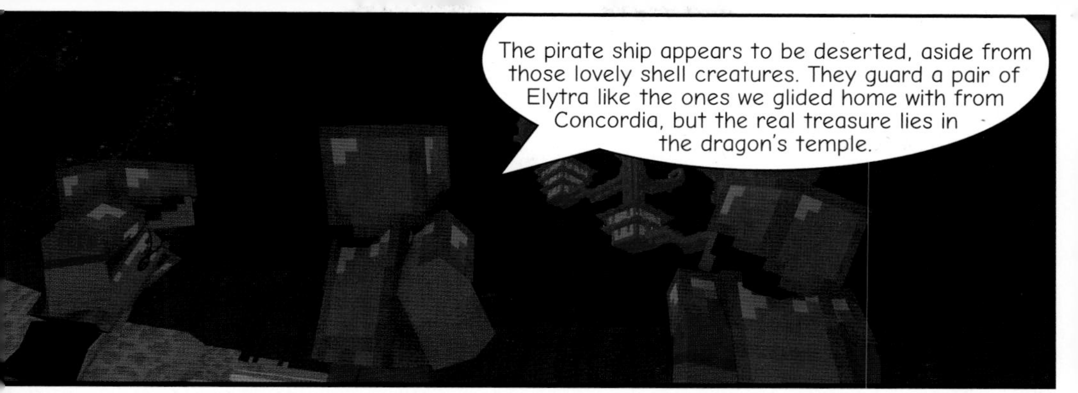
The pirate ship appears to be deserted, aside from those lovely shell creatures. They guard a pair of Elytra like the ones we glided home with from Concordia, but the real treasure lies in the dragon's temple.

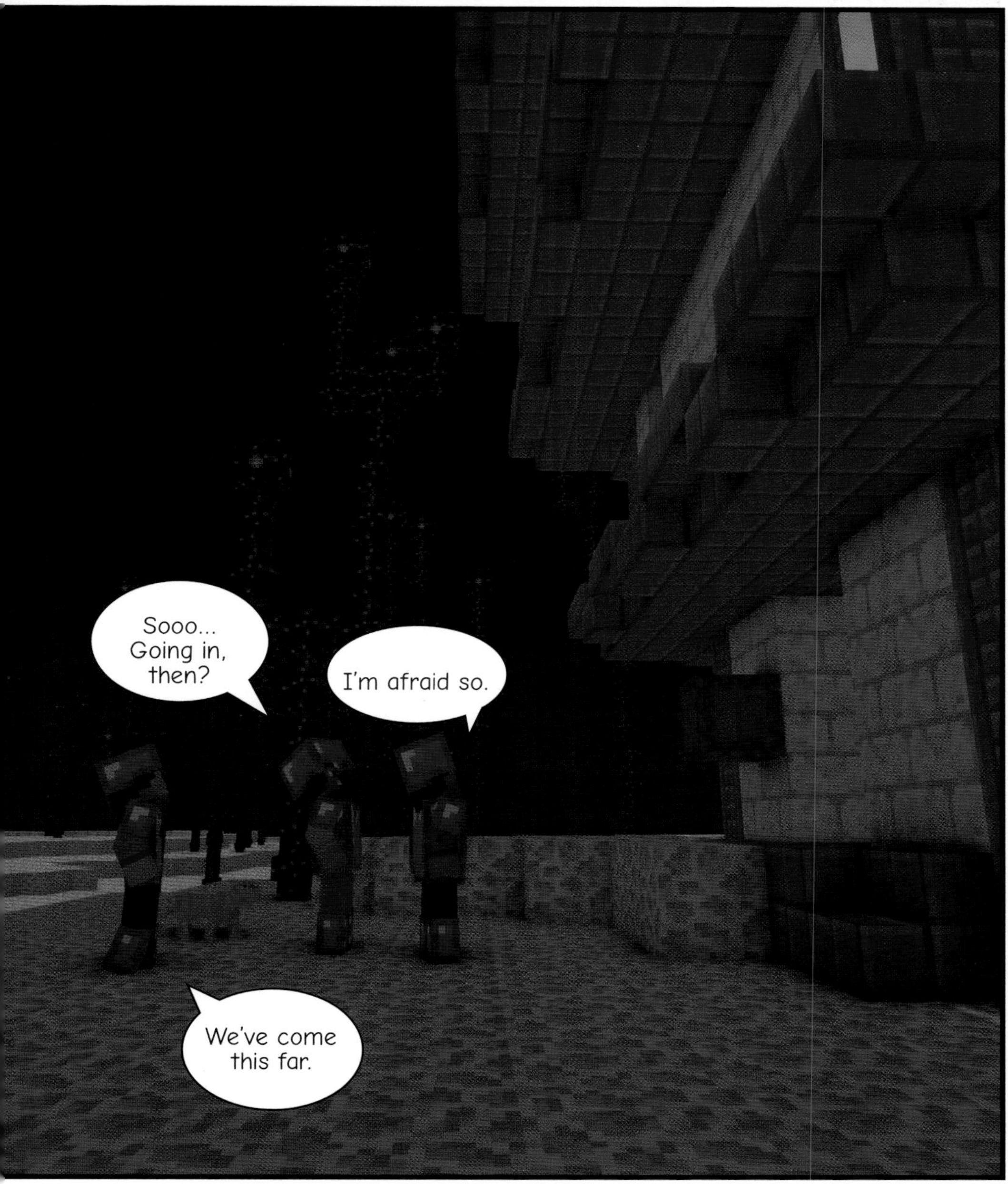
Sooo... Going in, then?
I'm afraid so.
We've come this far.

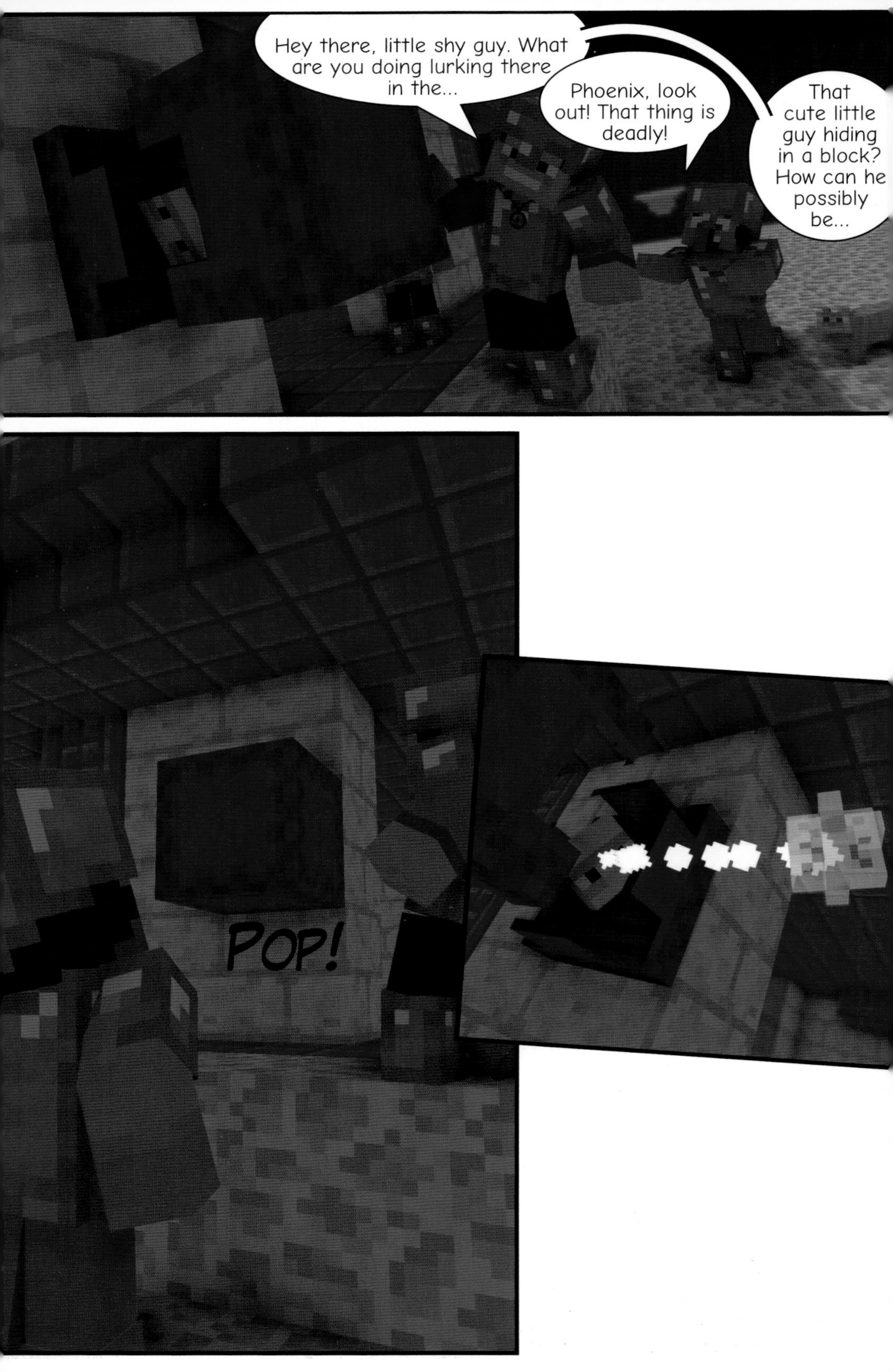
Hey there, little shy guy. What are you doing lurking there in the...
Phoenix, look out! That thing is deadly!
That cute little guy hiding in a block? How can he possibly be...
POP!

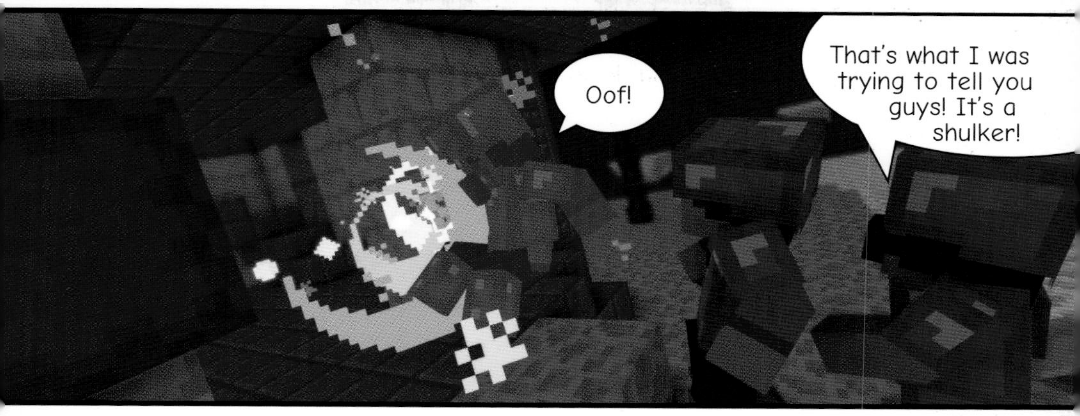
Oof!
That's what I was trying to tell you guys! It's a shulker!

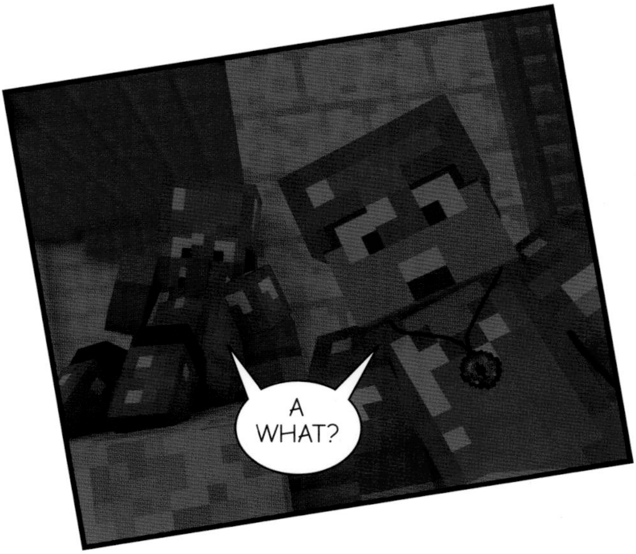
A WHAT?

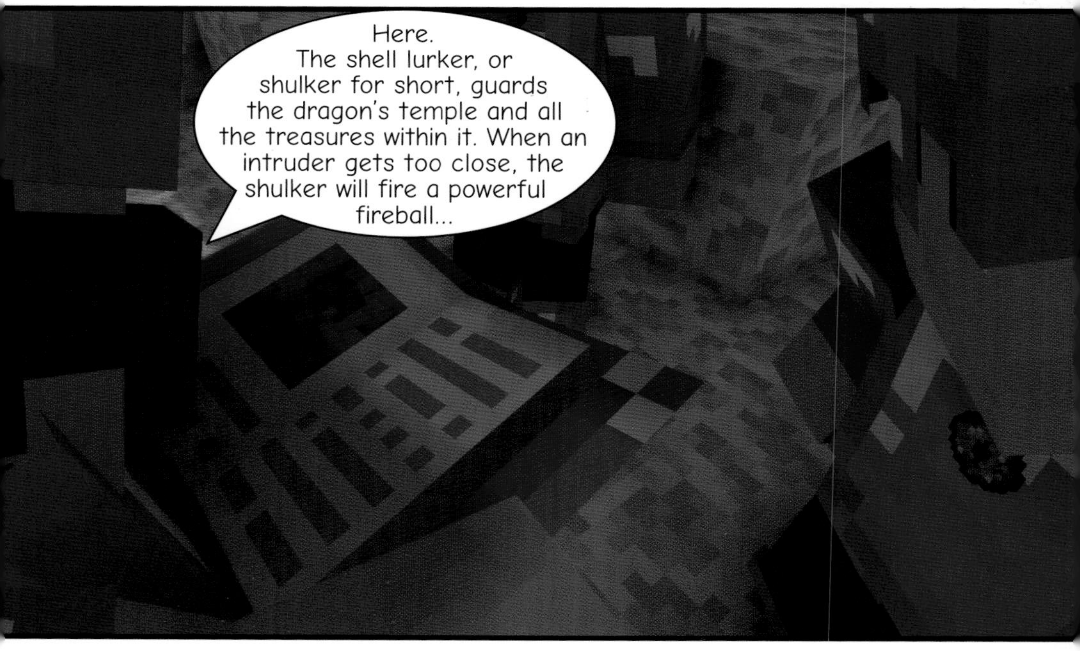
Here. The shell lurker, or shulker for short, guards the dragon's temple and all the treasures within it. When an intruder gets too close, the shulker will fire a powerful fireball...

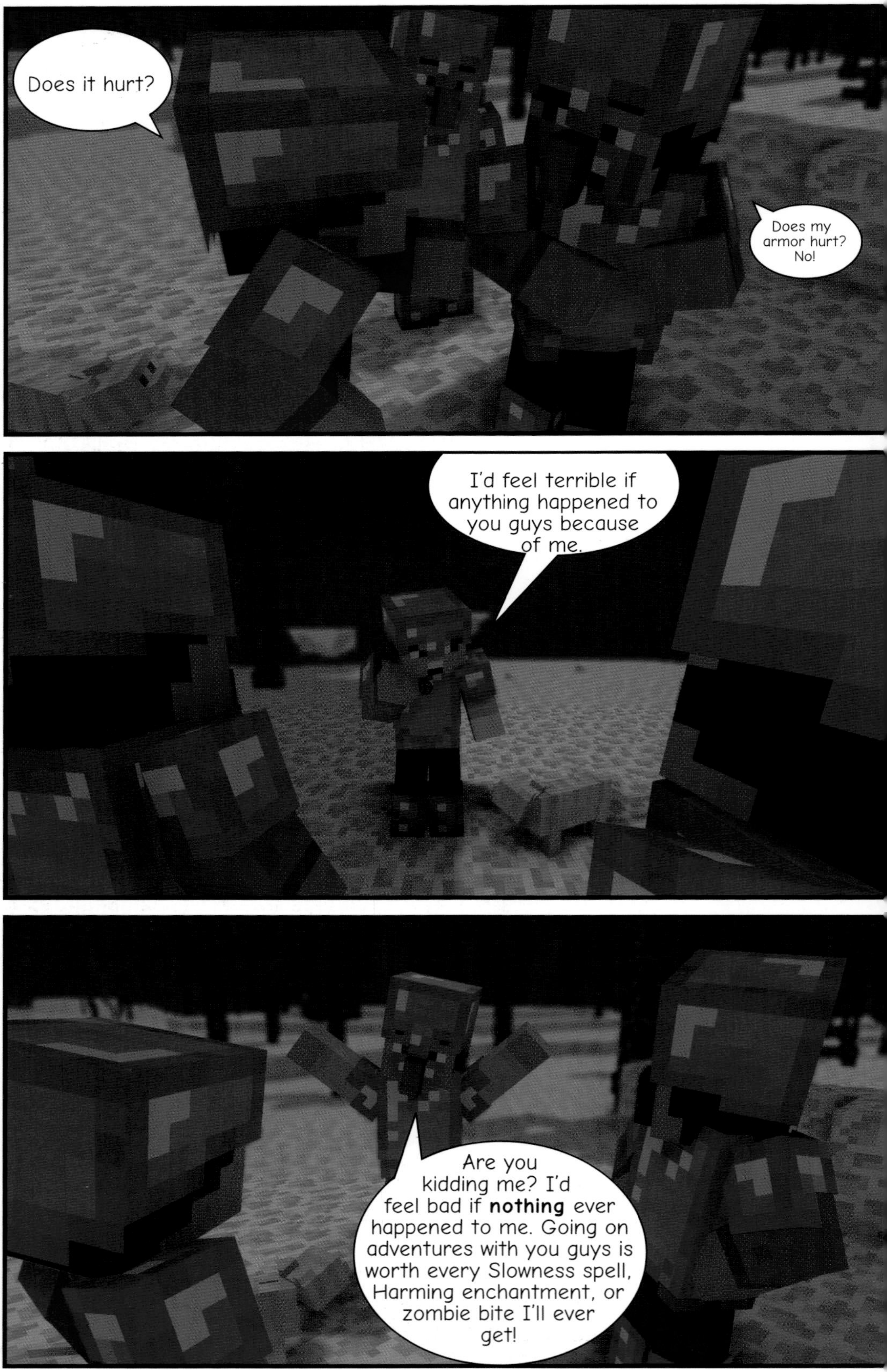
Does it hurt?
Does my armor hurt? No!
I'd feel terrible if anything happened to you guys because of me.
Are you kidding me? I'd feel bad if **nothing** ever happened to me. Going on adventures with you guys is worth every Slowness spell, Harming enchantment, or zombie bite I'll ever get!

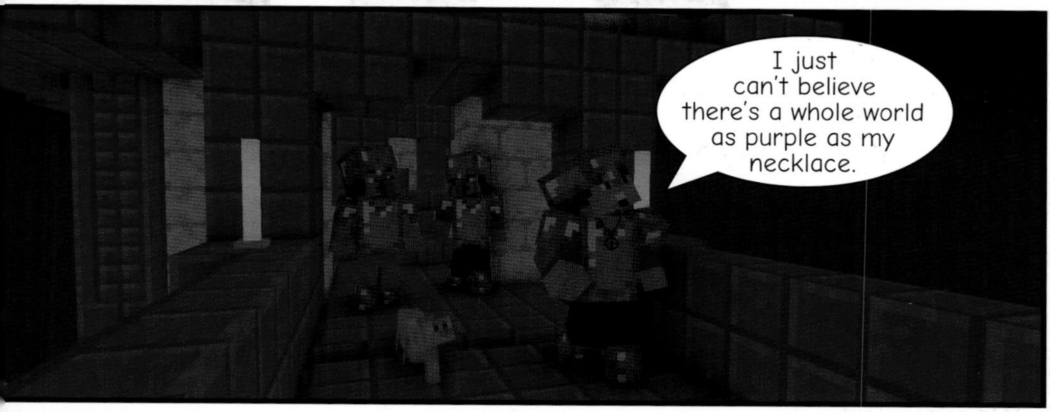
I just can't believe there's a whole world as purple as my necklace.

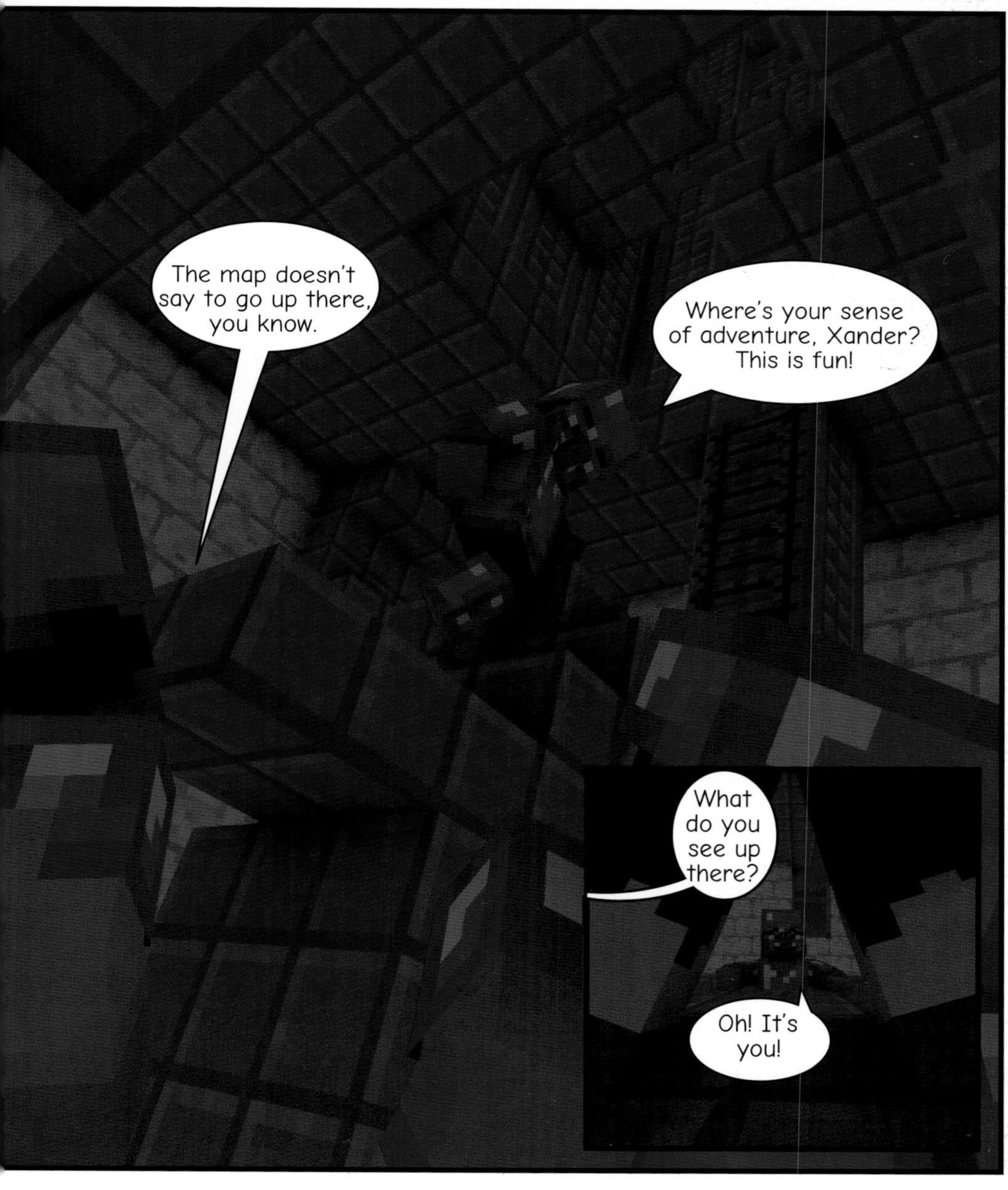
The map doesn't say to go up there, you know.
Where's your sense of adventure, Xander? This is fun!
What do you see up there?
Oh! It's you!

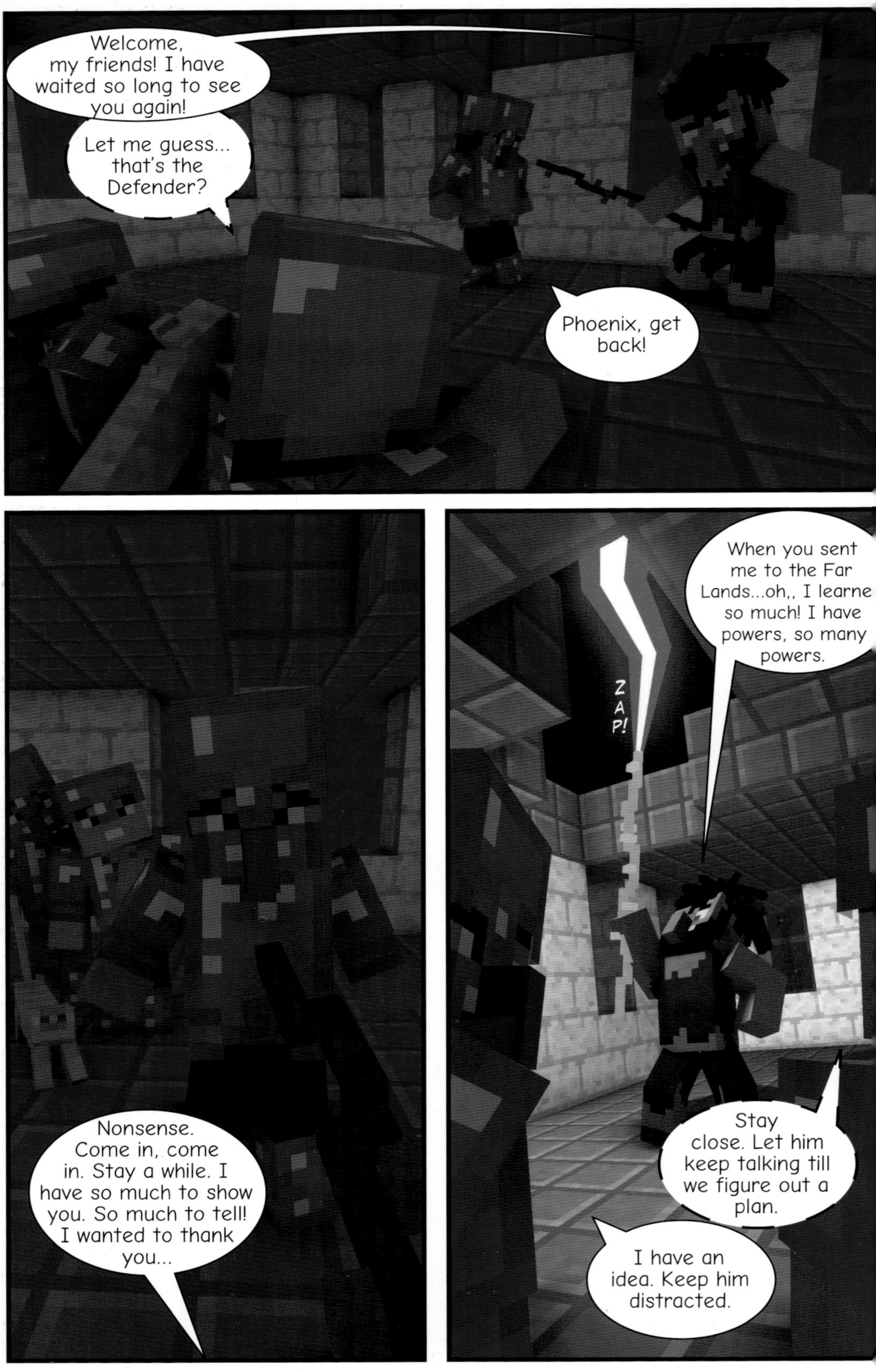
Welcome, my friends! I have waited so long to see you again!
Let me guess... that's the Defender?
Phoenix, get back!
Nonsense. Come in, come in. Stay a while. I have so much to show you. So much to tell! I wanted to thank you...
ZAP!
When you sent me to the Far Lands...oh,, I learne so much! I have powers, so many powers.
Stay close. Let him keep talking till we figure out a plan.
I have an idea. Keep him distracted.

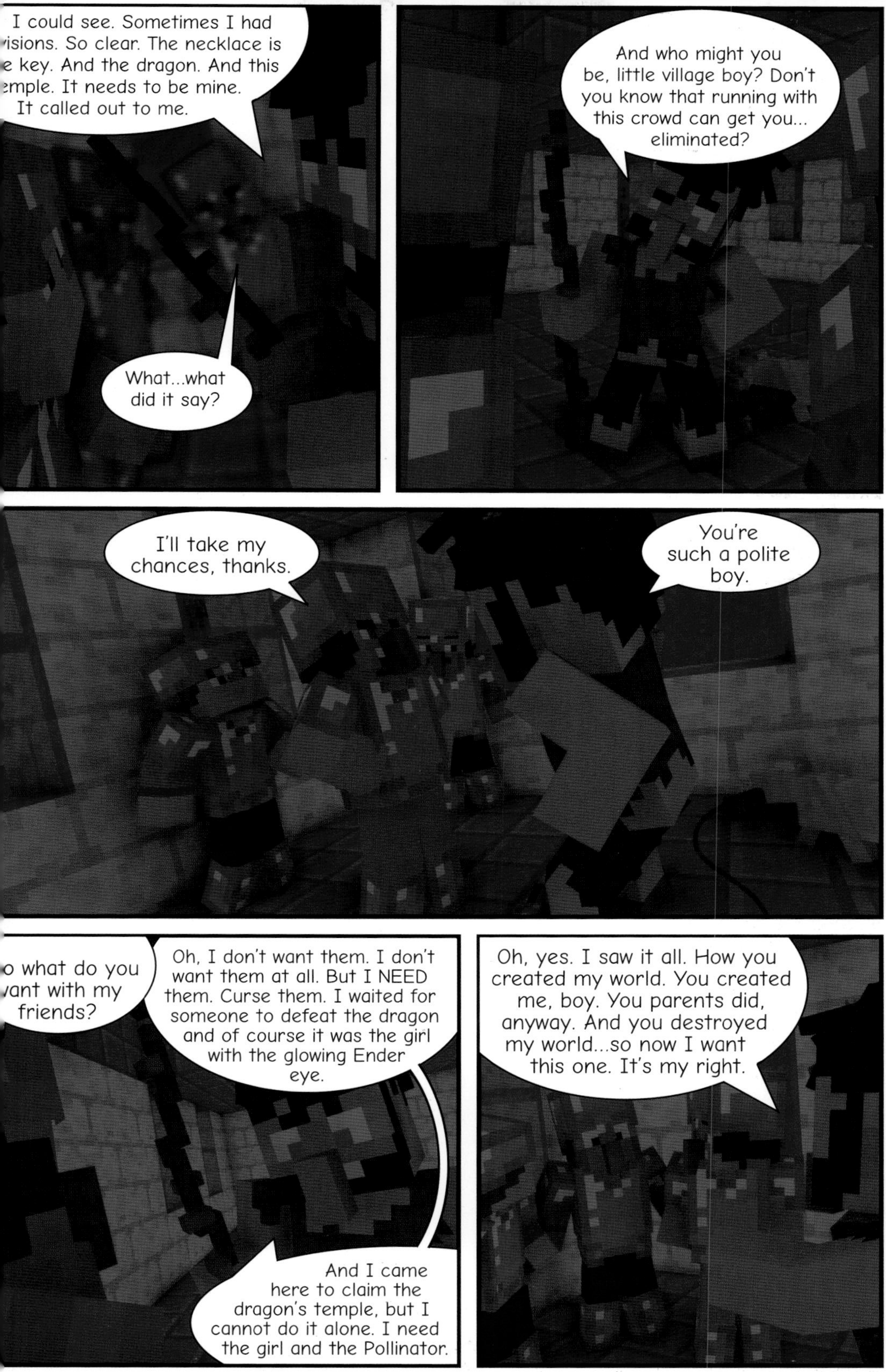
I could see. Sometimes I had visions. So clear. The necklace is the key. And the dragon. And this temple. It needs to be mine. It called out to me.
What...what did it say?
And who might you be, little village boy? Don't you know that running with this crowd can get you... eliminated?
I'll take my chances, thanks.
You're such a polite boy.
So what do you want with my friends?
Oh, I don't want them. I don't want them at all. But I NEED them. Curse them. I waited for someone to defeat the dragon and of course it was the girl with the glowing Ender eye.
And I came here to claim the dragon's temple, but I cannot do it alone. I need the girl and the Pollinator.
Oh, yes. I saw it all. How you created my world. You created me, boy. You parents did, anyway. And you destroyed my world...so now I want this one. It's my right.

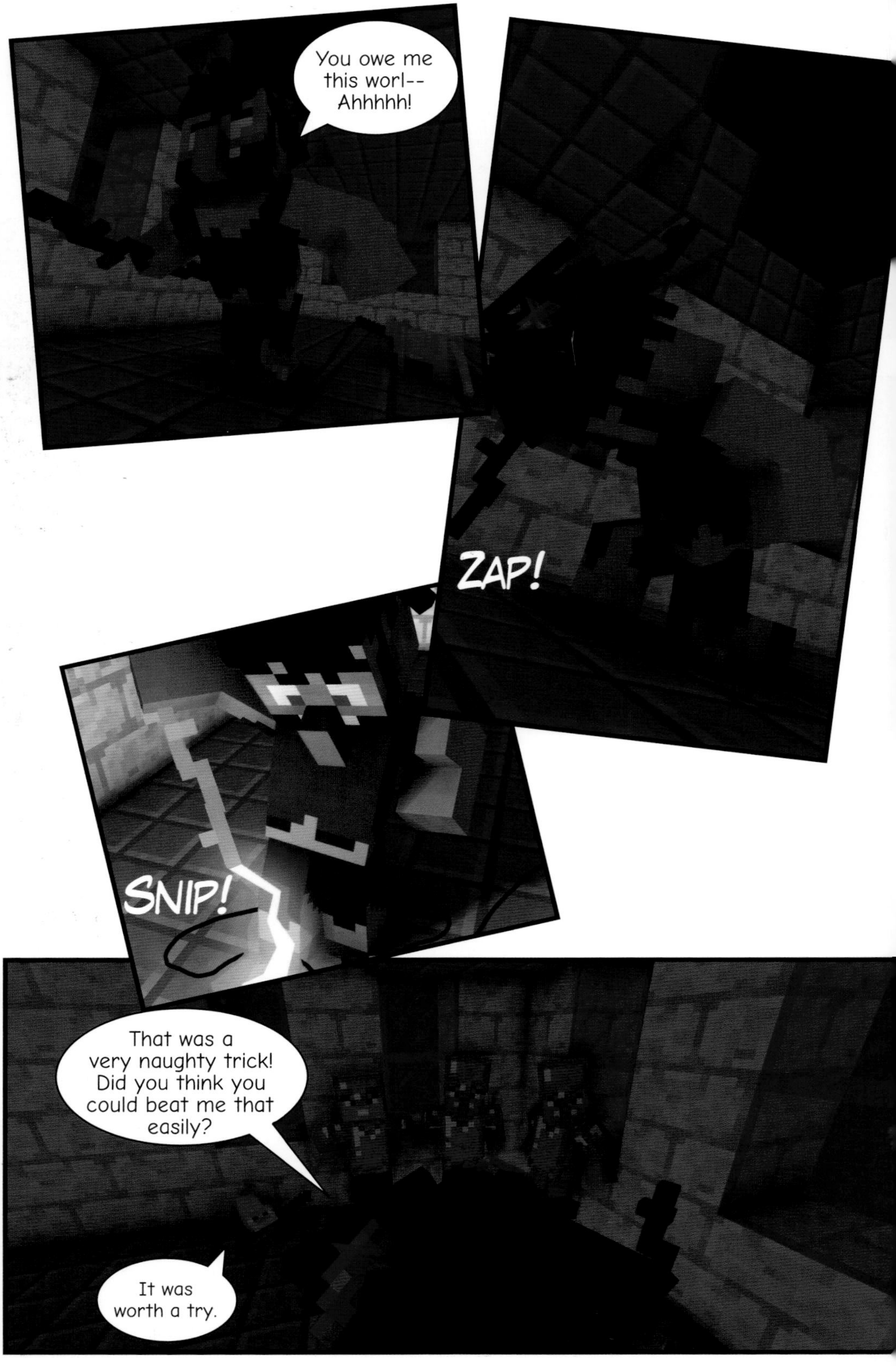
You owe me this worl-- Ahhhhh!
ZAP!
SNIP!
That was a very naughty trick! Did you think you could beat me that easily?
It was worth a try.

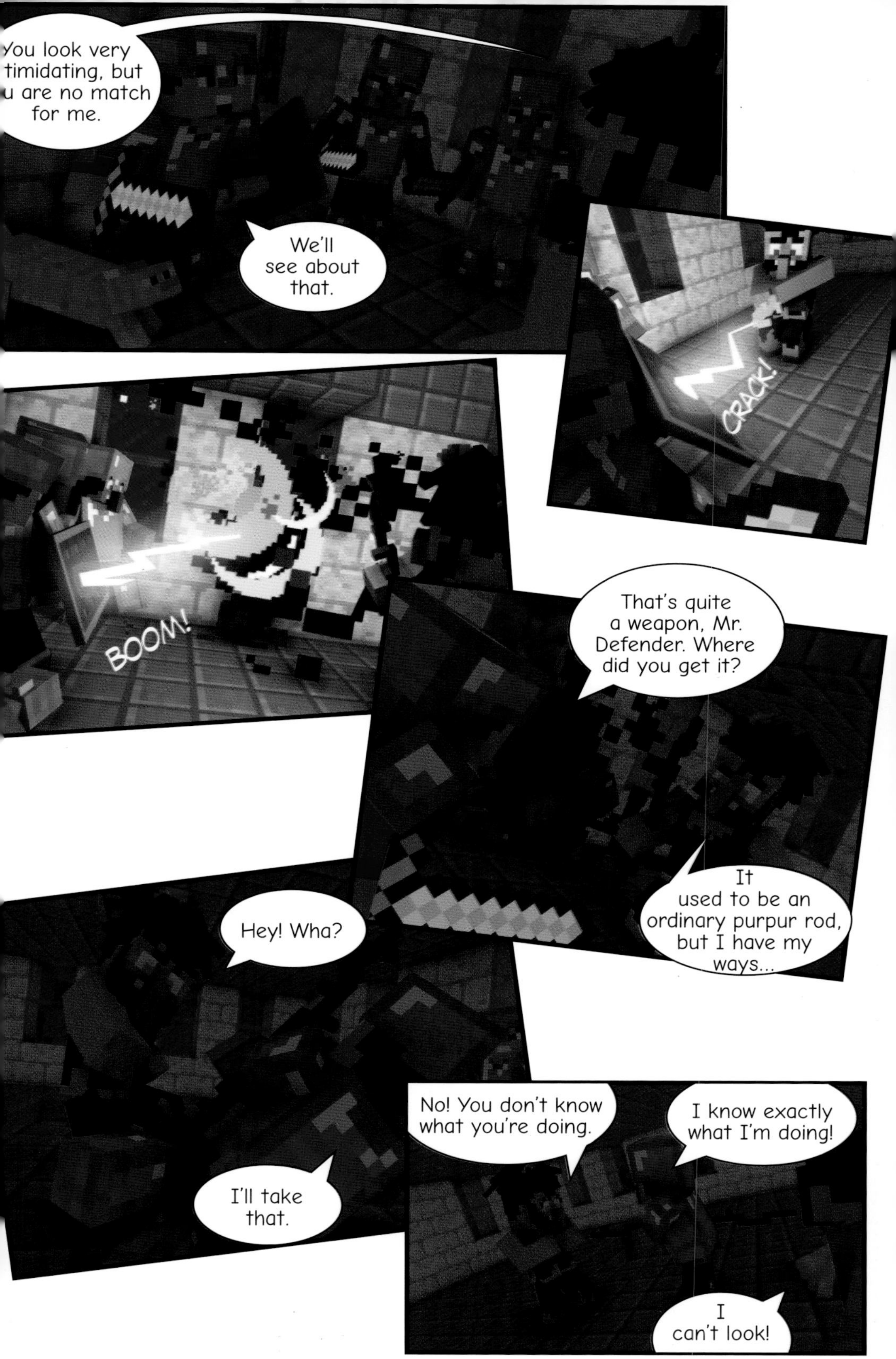
You look very
timidating, but
u are no match
for me.
We'll see about that.
CRACK!
BOOM!
That's quite a weapon, Mr. Defender. Where did you get it?
It used to be an ordinary purpur rod, but I have my ways...
Hey! Wha?
I'll take that.
No! You don't know what you're doing.
I know exactly what I'm doing!
I can't look!

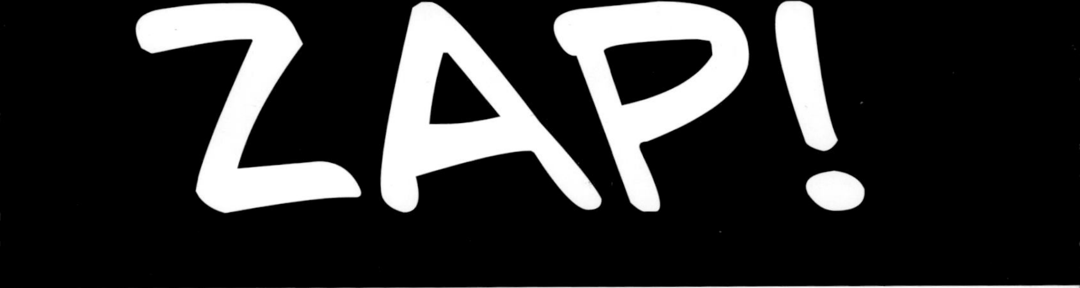
ZAP!

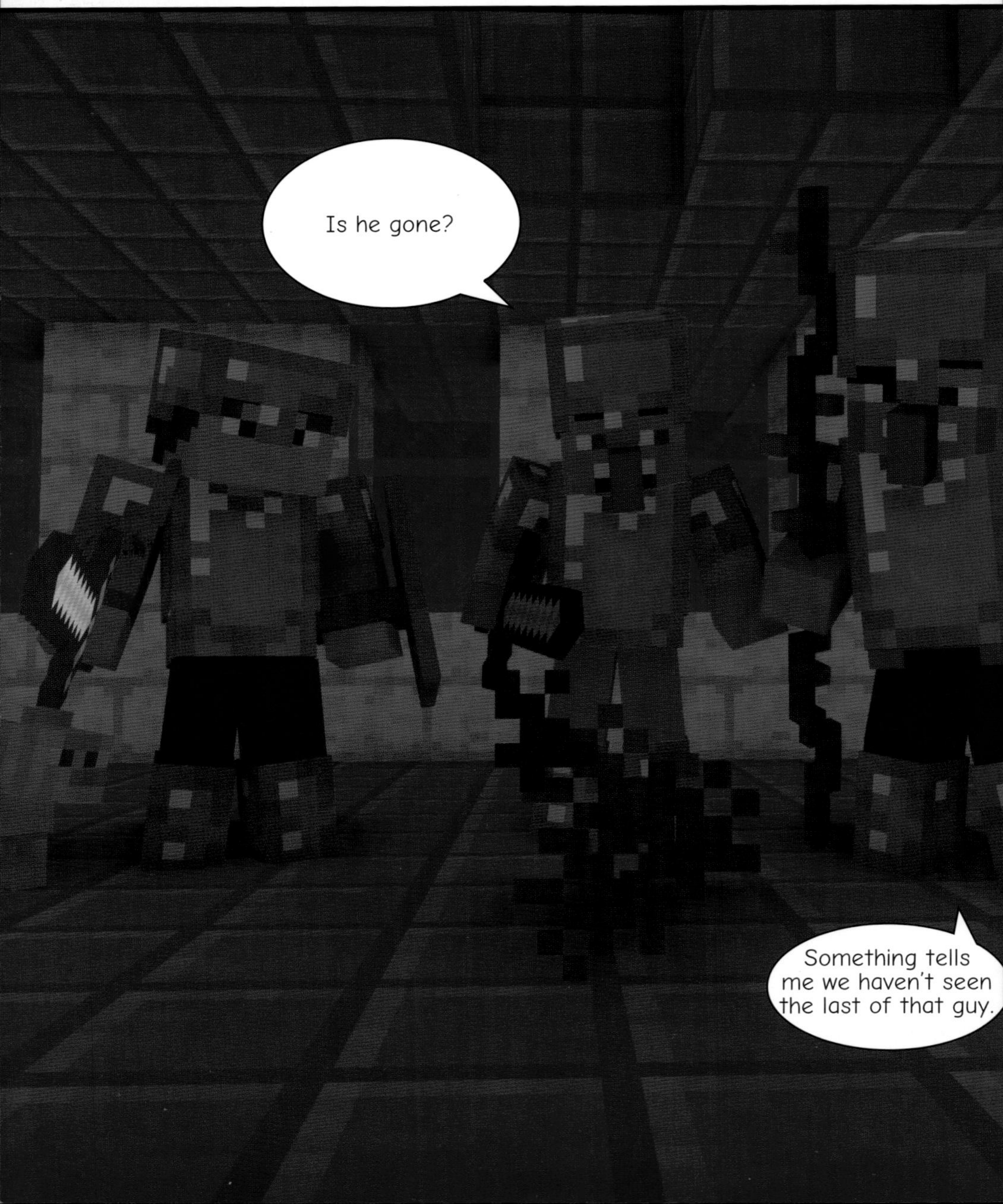
Is he gone?
Something tells me we haven't seen the last of that guy.

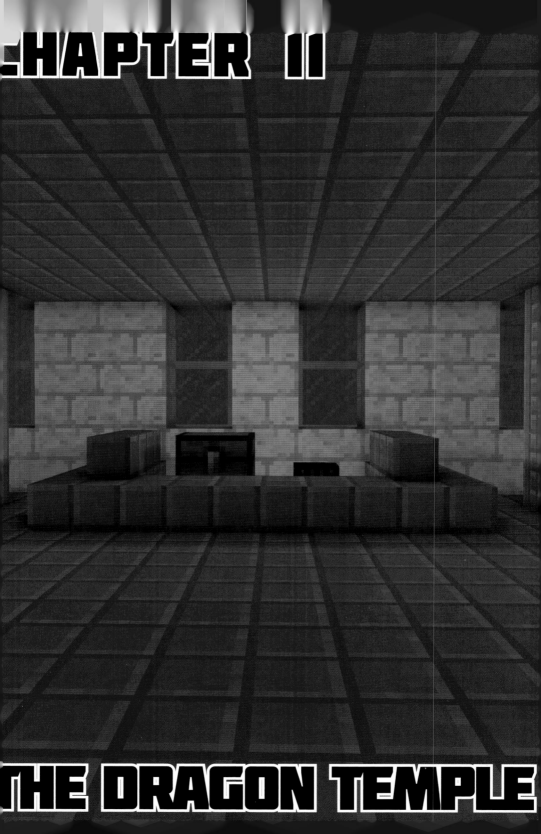

CHAPTER II

THE DRAGON TEMPLE

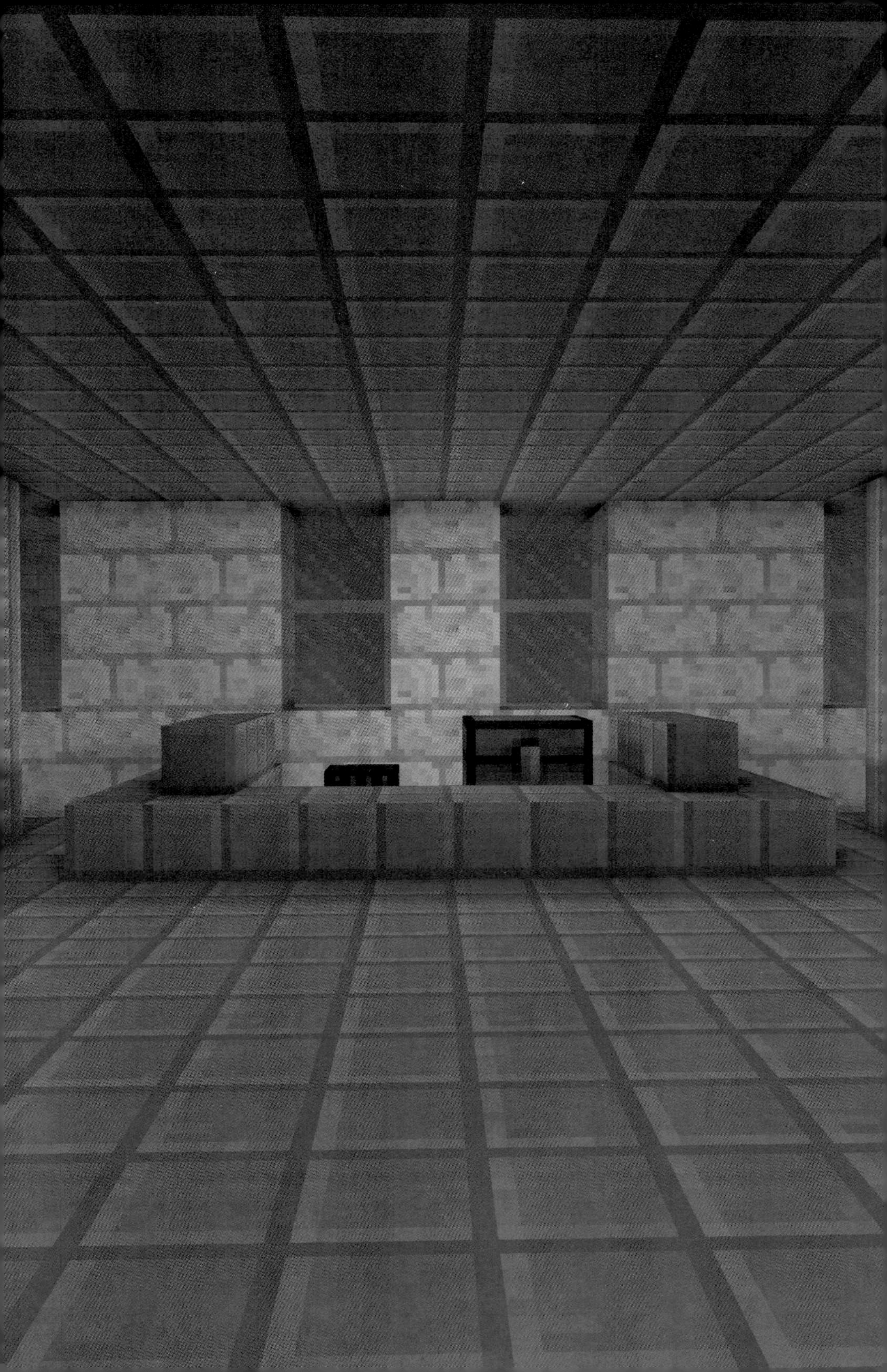

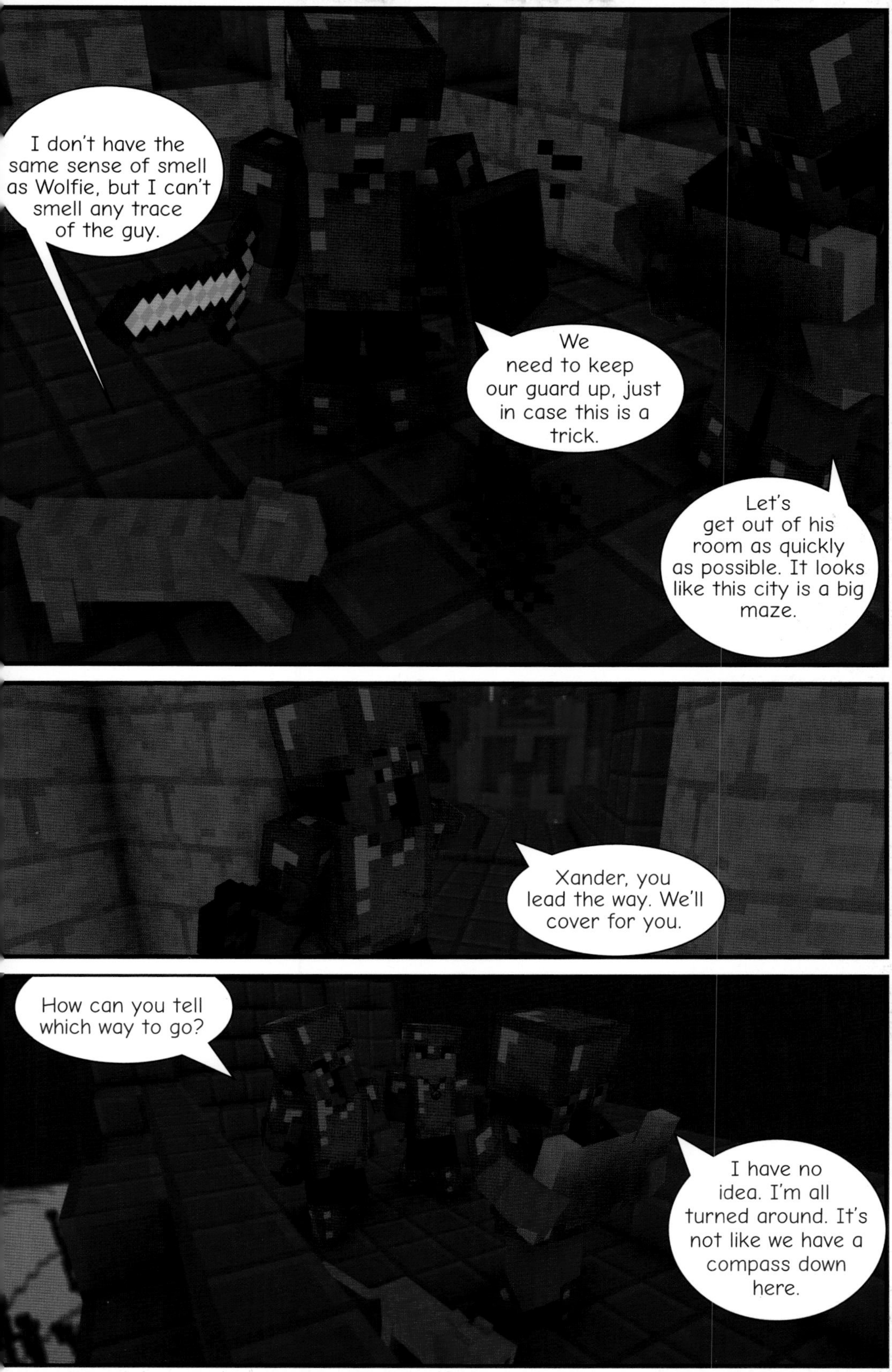
I don't have the same sense of smell as Wolfie, but I can't smell any trace of the guy.
We need to keep our guard up, just in case this is a trick.
Let's get out of his room as quickly as possible. It looks like this city is a big maze.
Xander, you lead the way. We'll cover for you.
How can you tell which way to go?
I have no idea. I'm all turned around. It's not like we have a compass down here.

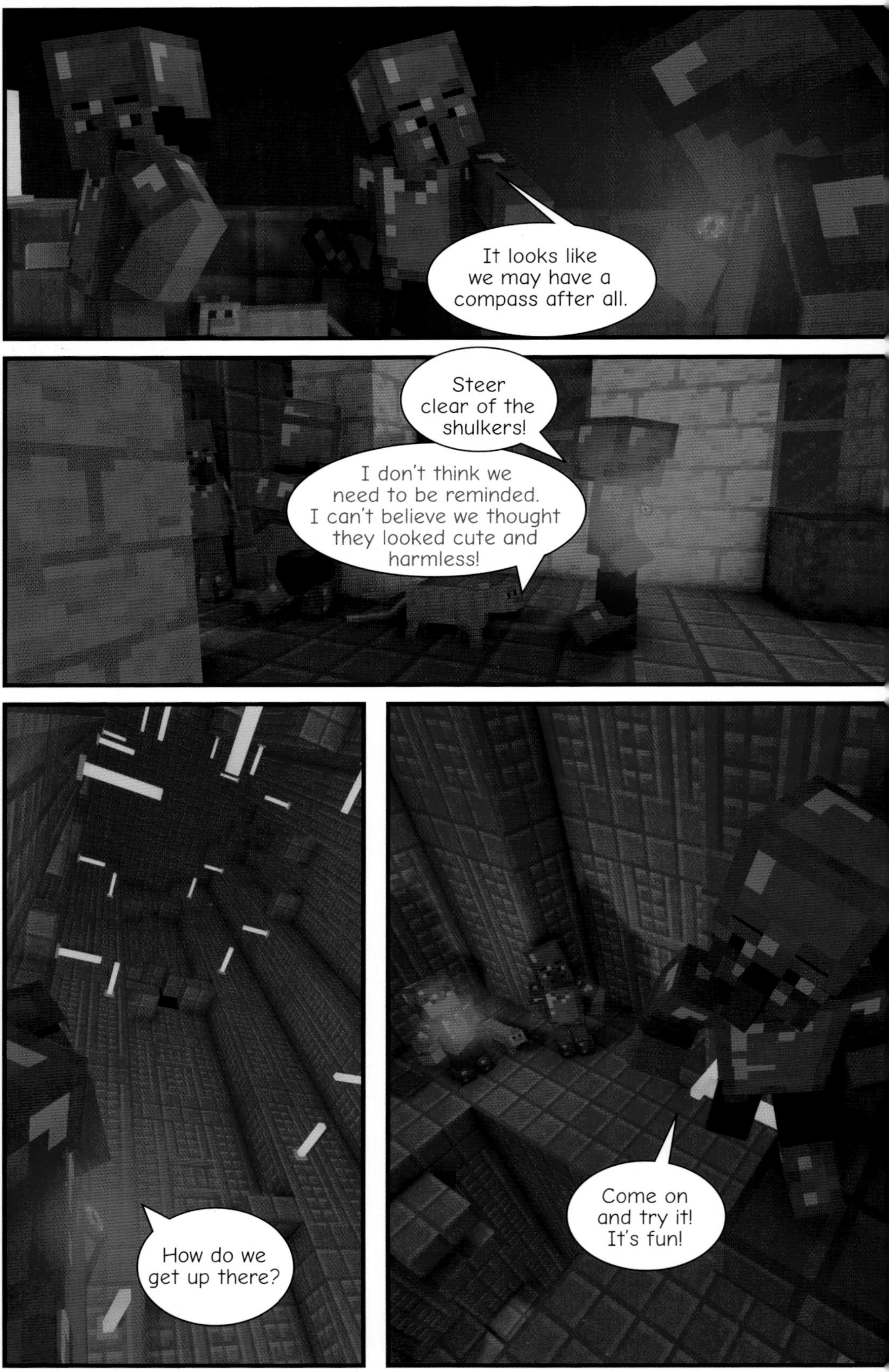
It looks like we may have a compass after all.
Steer clear of the shulkers!
I don't think we need to be reminded. I can't believe we thought they looked cute and harmless!
How do we get up there?
Come on and try it! It's fun!

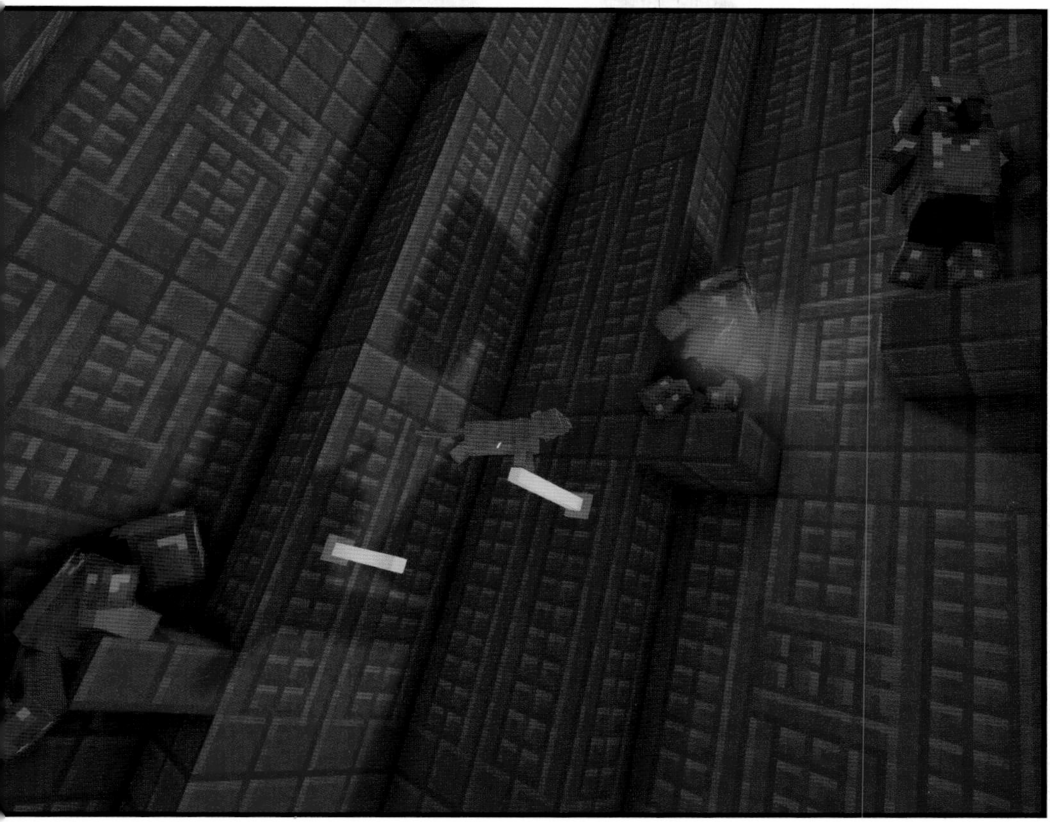

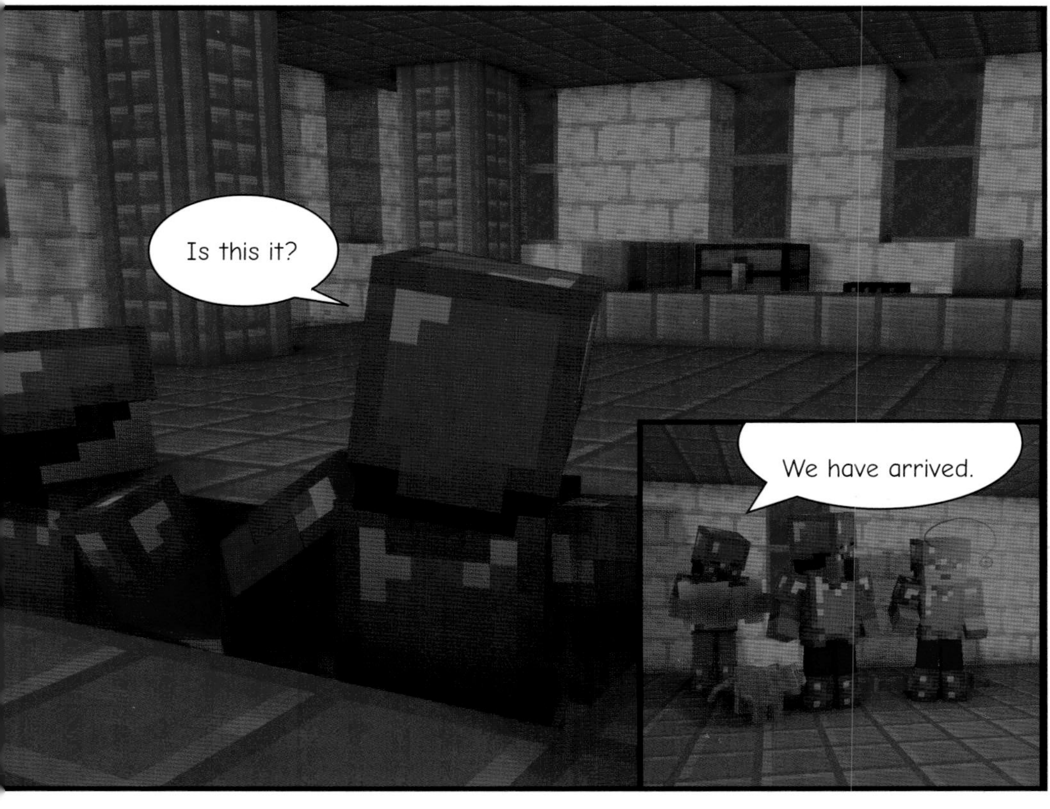
Is this it?
We have arrived.

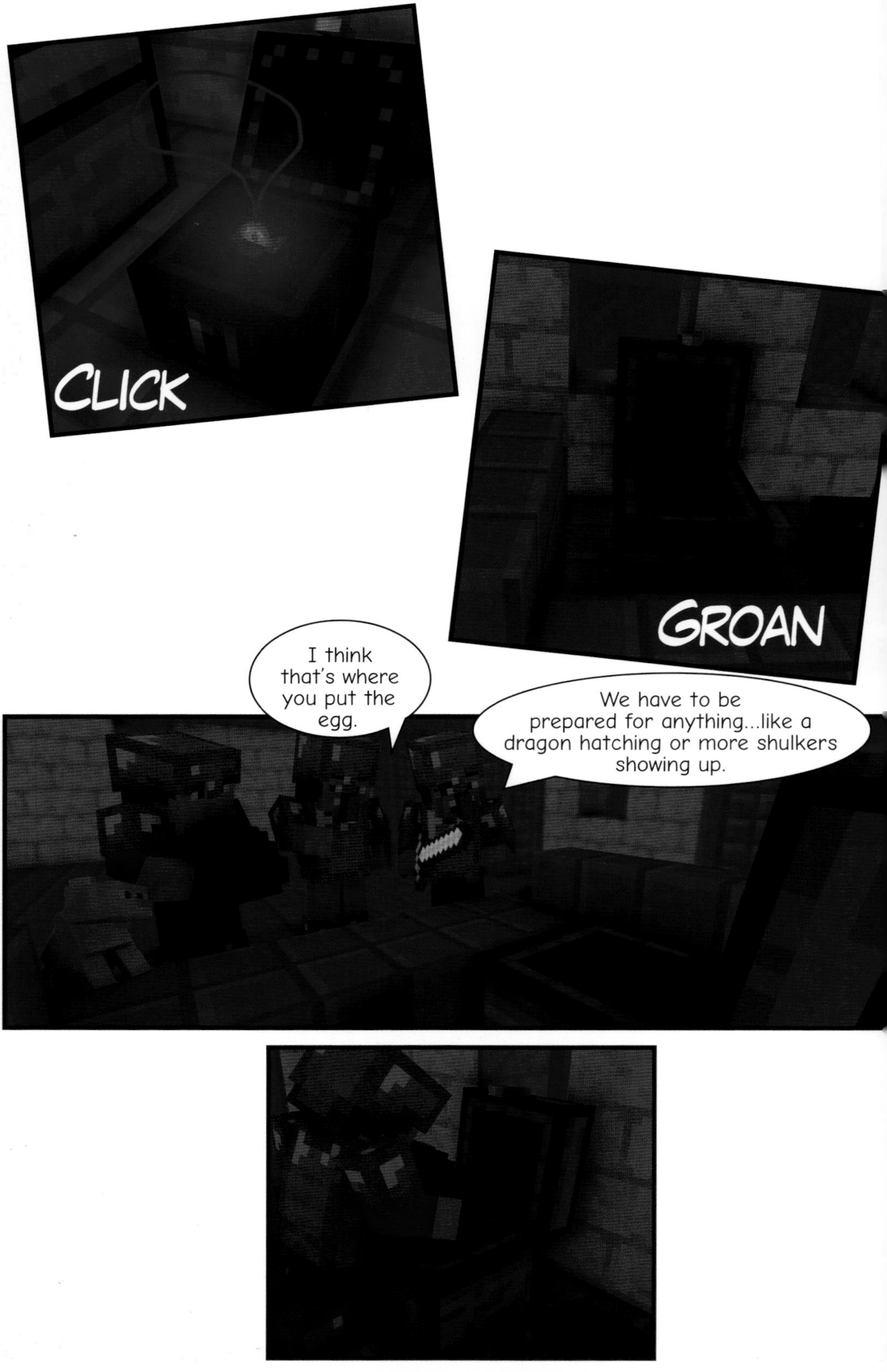
CLICK
GROAN
I think that's where you put the egg.
We have to be prepared for anything...like a dragon hatching or more shulkers showing up.

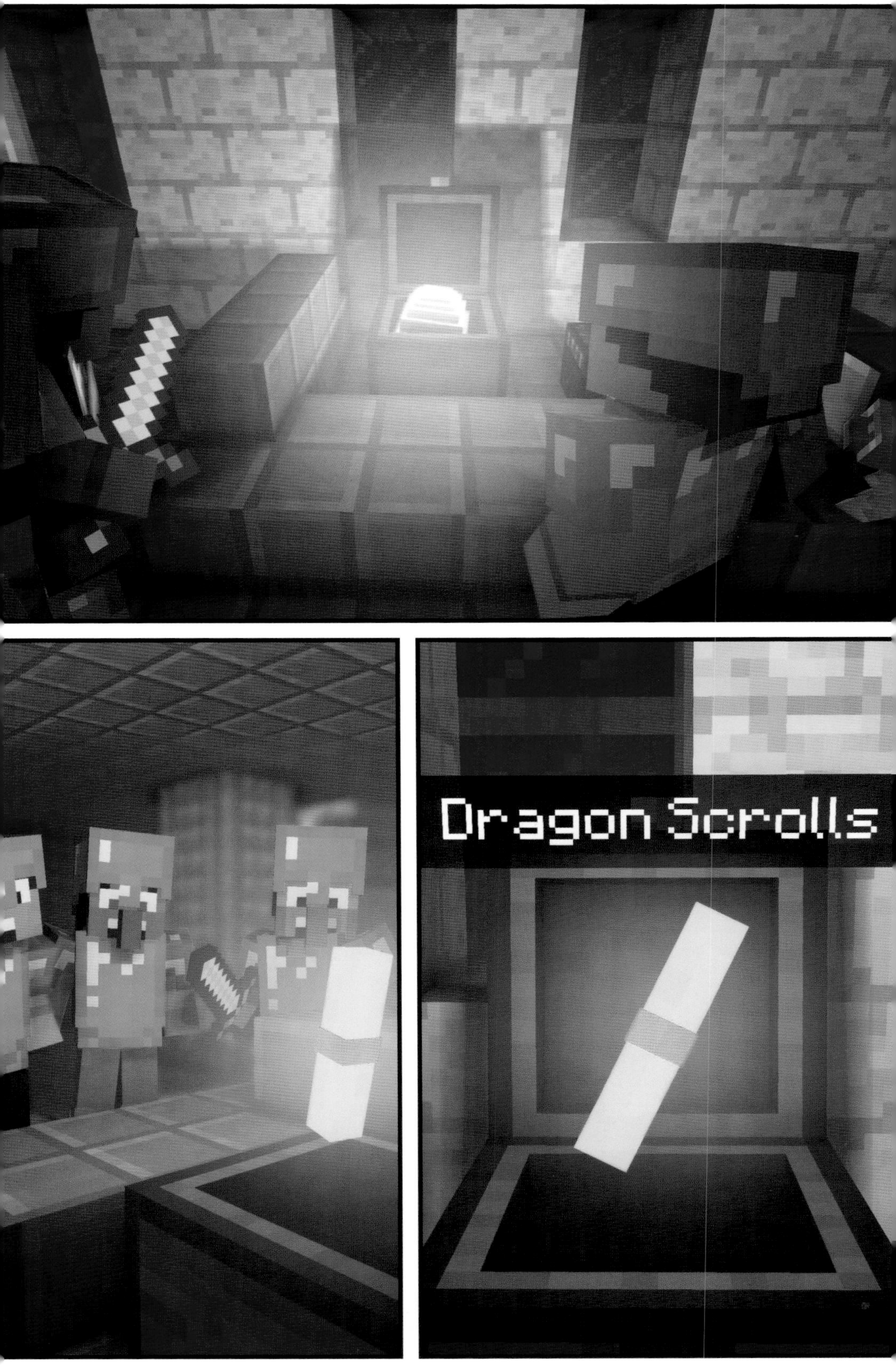
Dragon Scrolls

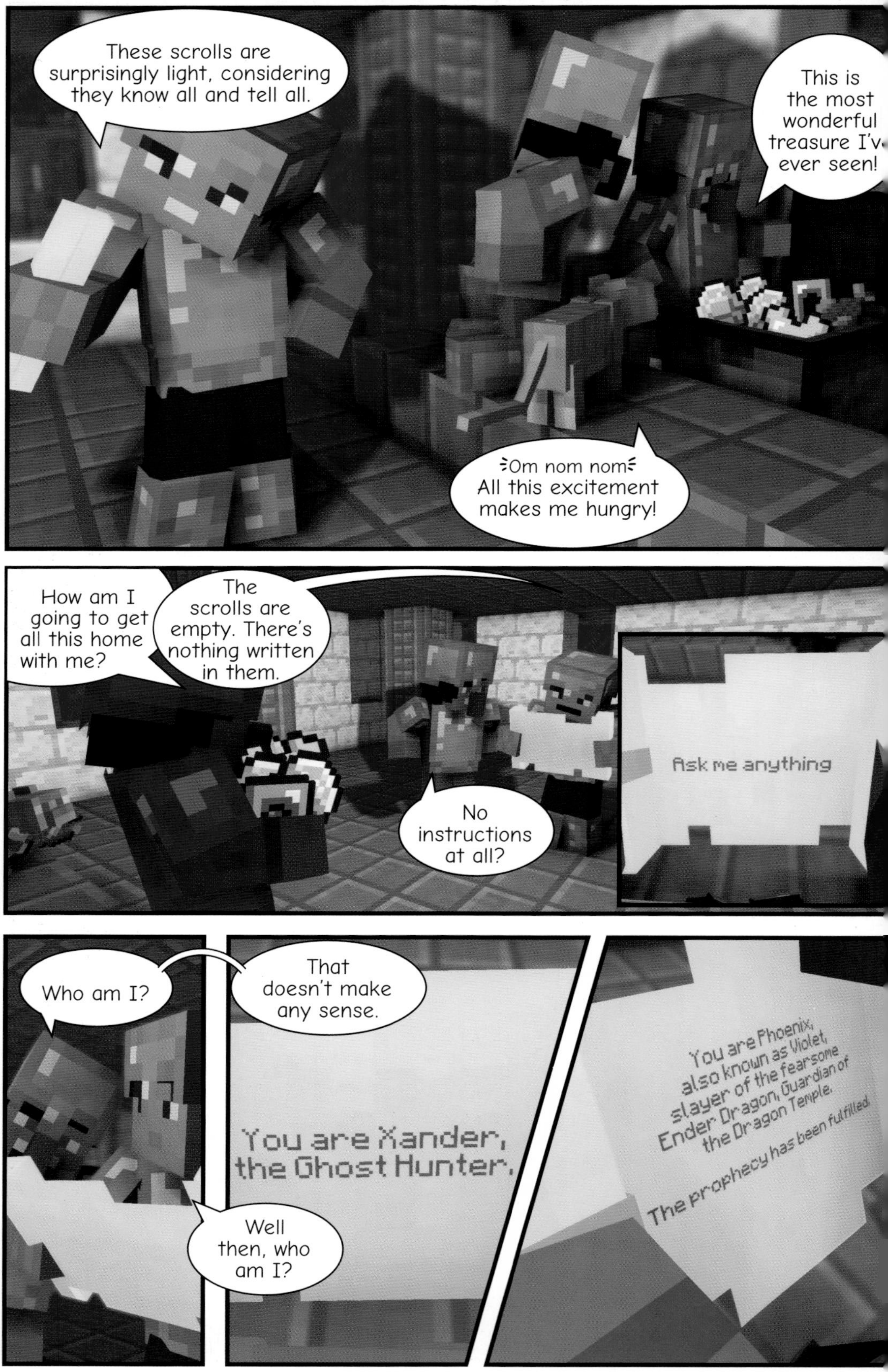
These scrolls are surprisingly light, considering they know all and tell all.
This is the most wonderful treasure I'v ever seen!
Om nom nom
All this excitement makes me hungry!
How am I going to get all this home with me?
The scrolls are empty. There's nothing written in them.
No instructions at all?
Ask me anything
Who am I?
That doesn't make any sense.
You are Xander, the Ghost Hunter.
Well then, who am I?
You are Phoenix, also known as Violet, slayer of the fearsome Ender Dragon, Guardian of the Dragon Temple.
The prophecy has been fulfilled.

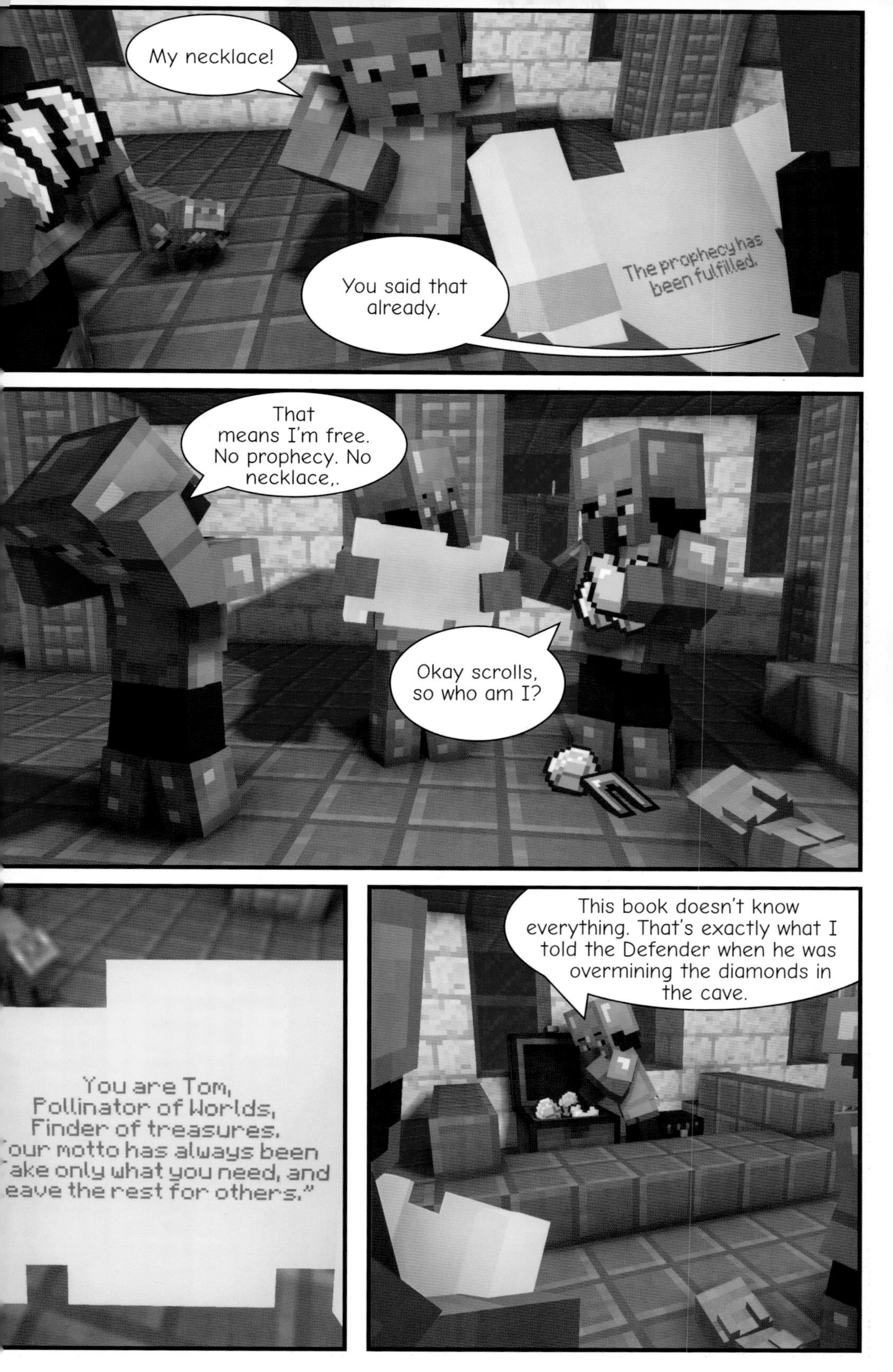
My necklace!
The prophecy has been fulfilled.
You said that already.
That means I'm free. No prophecy. No necklace,.
Okay scrolls, so who am I?
You are Tom, Pollinator of Worlds, Finder of treasures. our motto has always been ake only what you need, and eave the rest for others."
This book doesn't know everything. That's exactly what I told the Defender when he was overmining the diamonds in the cave.

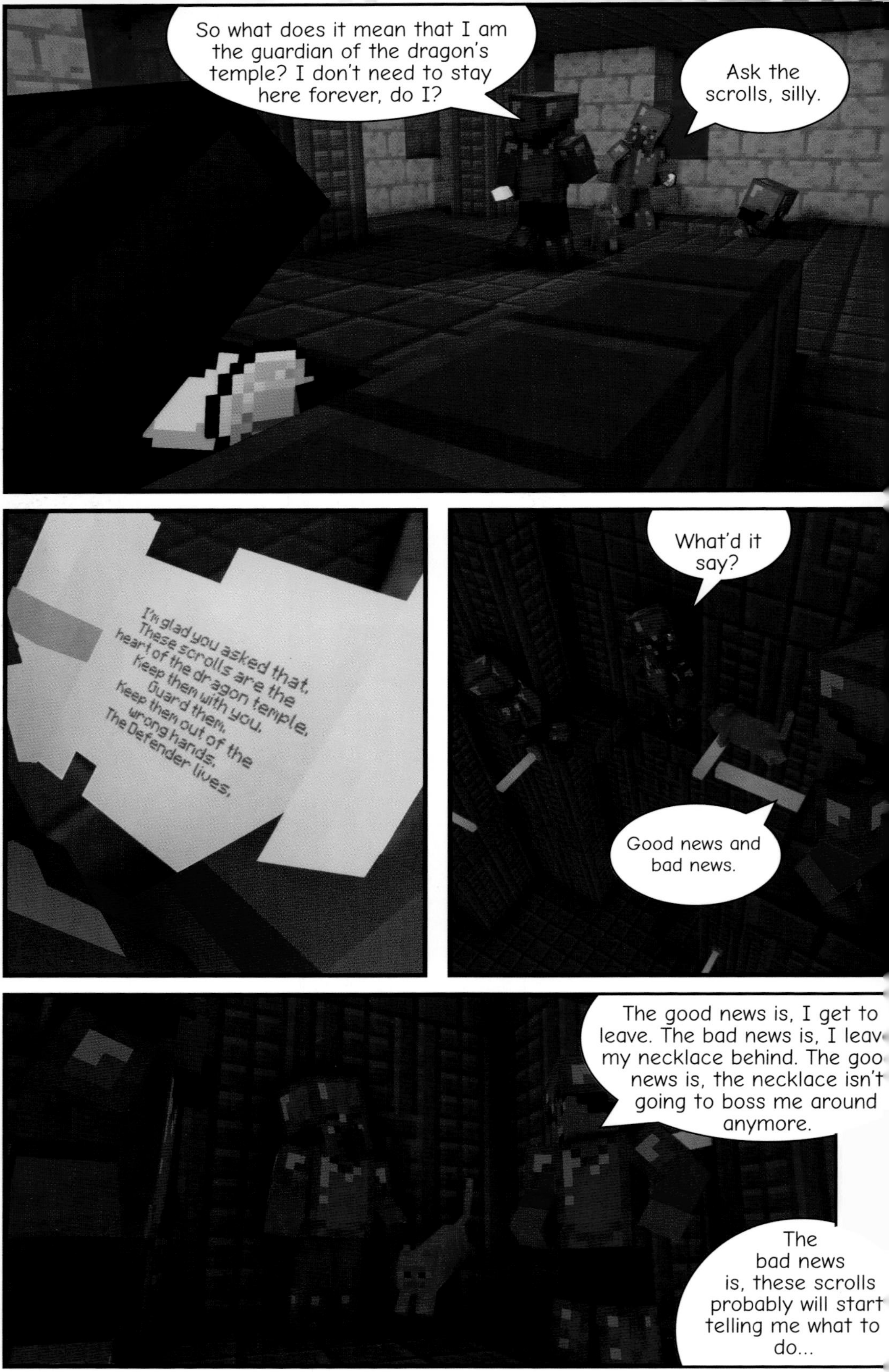

So what does it mean that I am the guardian of the dragon's temple? I don't need to stay here forever, do I?
Ask the scrolls, silly.
I'm glad you asked that. These scrolls are the heart of the dragon temple. Keep them with you. Guard them. Keep them out of the wrong hands. The Defender lives.
What'd it say?
Good news and bad news.
The good news is, I get to leave. The bad news is, I leav my necklace behind. The goo news is, the necklace isn't going to boss me around anymore.
The bad news is, these scrolls probably will start telling me what to do...

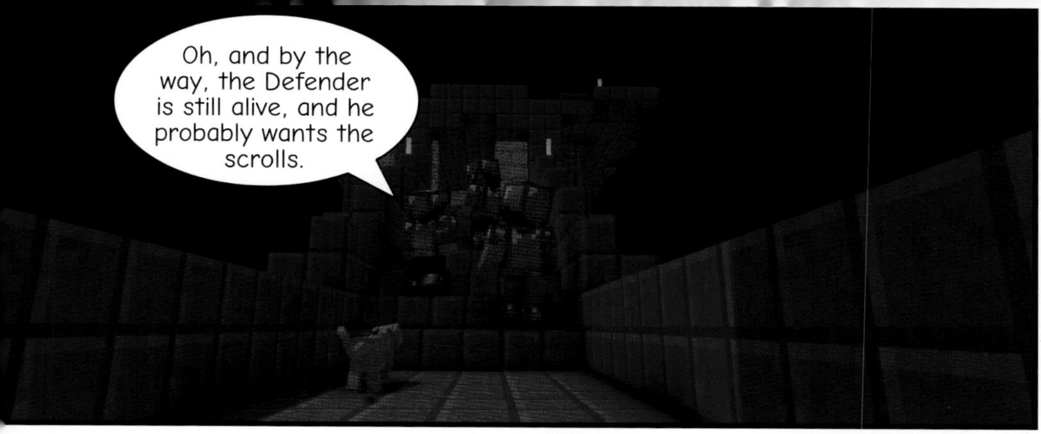

Oh, and by the way, the Defender is still alive, and he probably wants the scrolls.

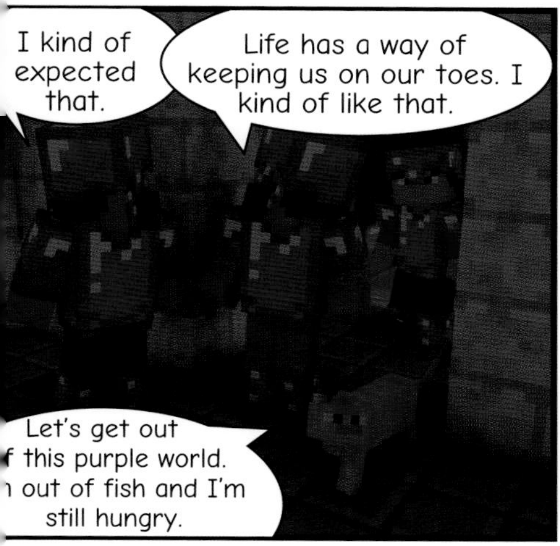

I kind of expected that.
Life has a way of keeping us on our toes. I kind of like that.
Let's get out f this purple world. n out of fish and I'm still hungry.

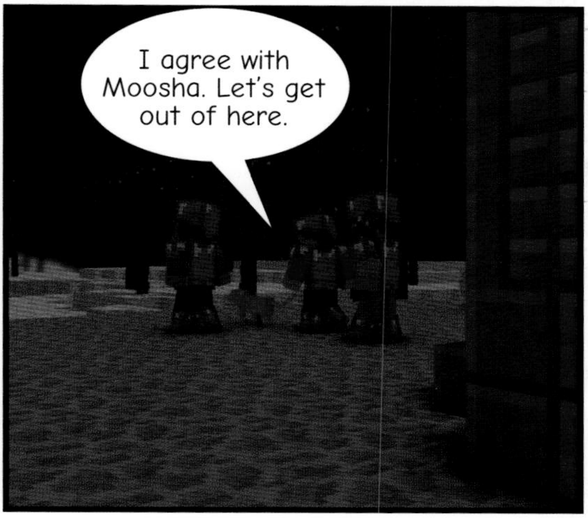

I agree with Moosha. Let's get out of here.

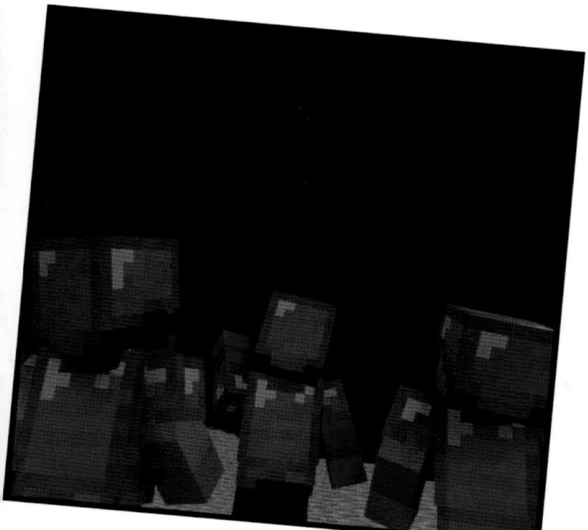

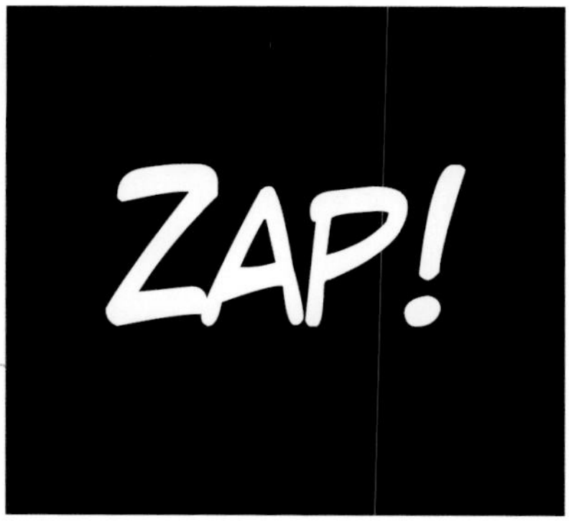

ZAP!

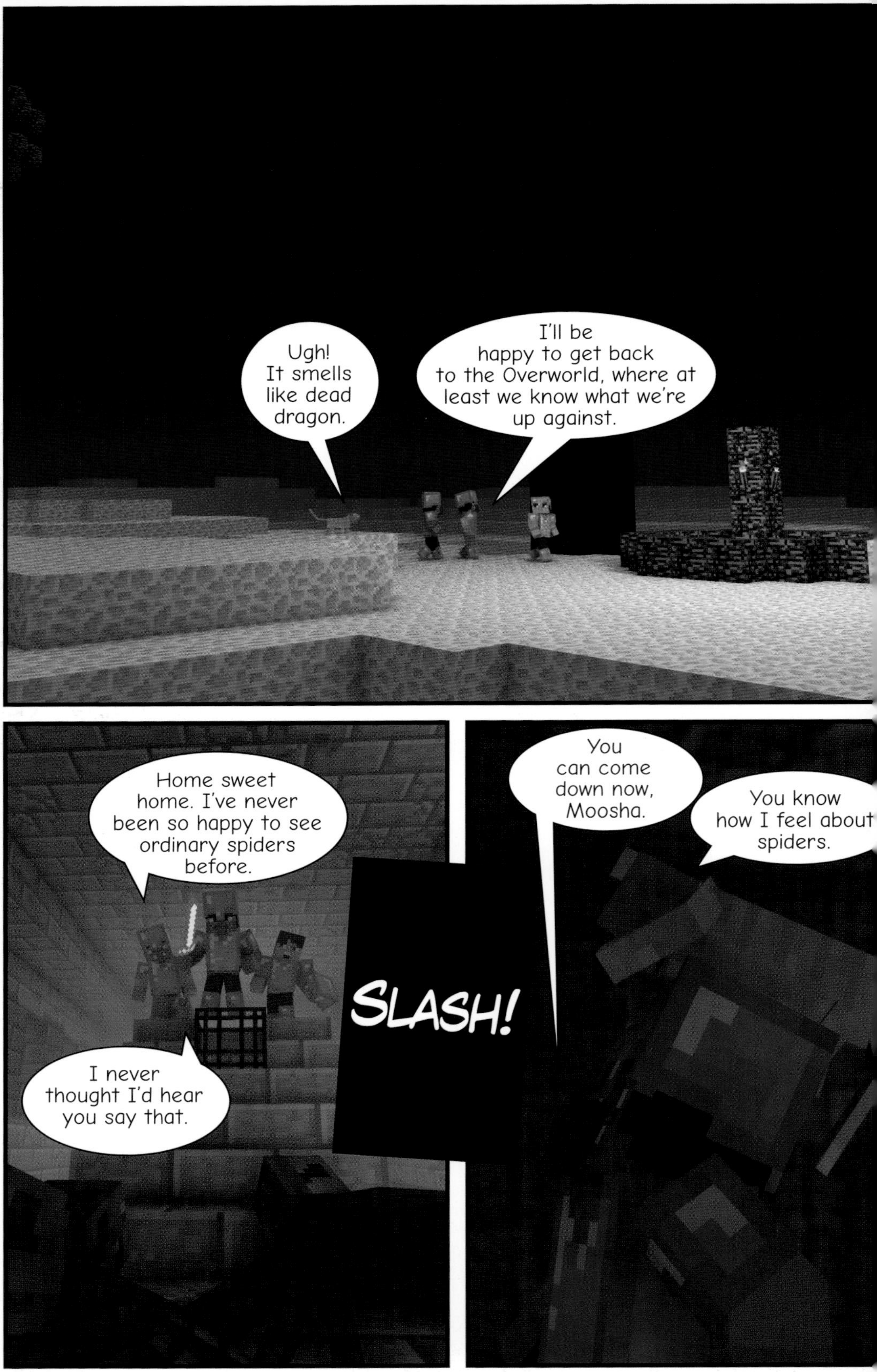
Ugh! It smells like dead dragon.
I'll be happy to get back to the Overworld, where at least we know what we're up against.
Home sweet home. I've never been so happy to see ordinary spiders before.
I never thought I'd hear you say that.
SLASH!
You can come down now, Moosha.
You know how I feel about spiders.

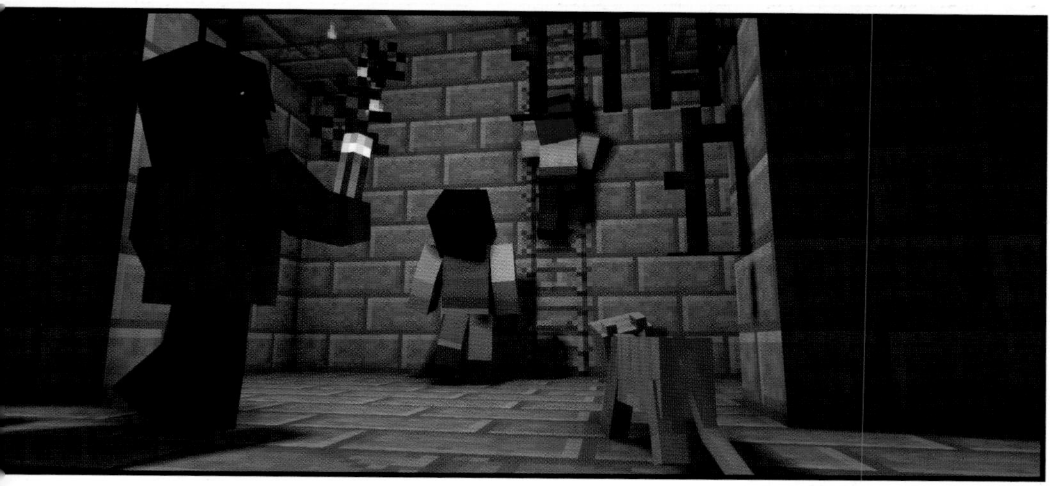

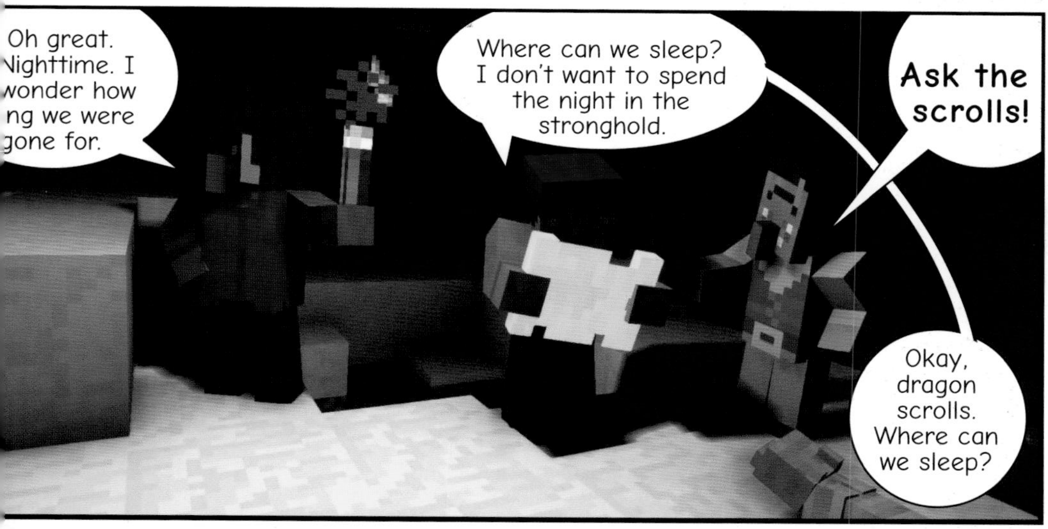
Oh great. Nighttime. I wonder how ng we were gone for.
Where can we sleep? I don't want to spend the night in the stronghold.
Ask the scrolls!
Okay, dragon scrolls. Where can we sleep?

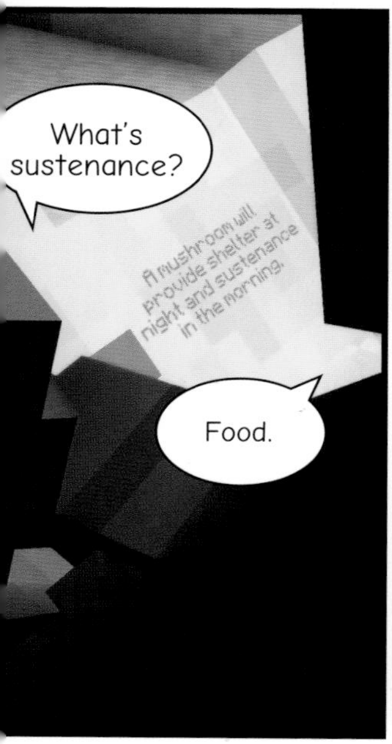
What's sustenance?
A mushroom will provide shelter at night and sustenance in the morning.
Food.

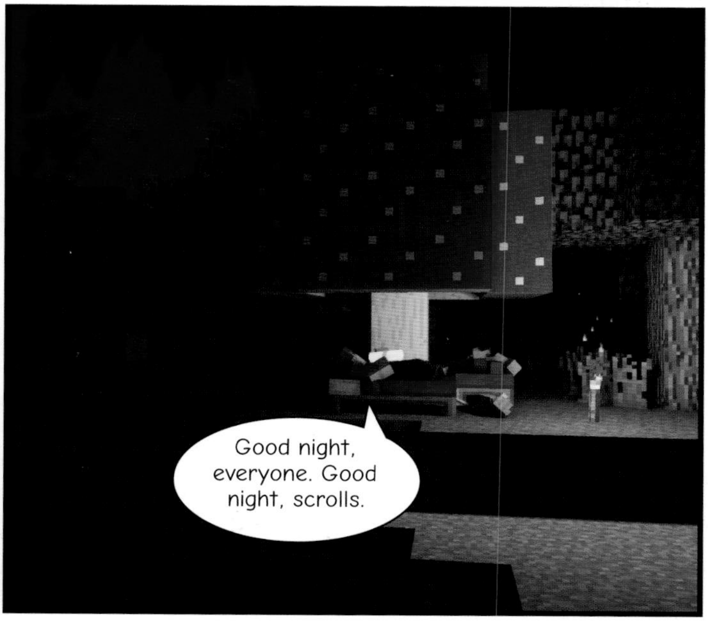
Good night, everyone. Good night, scrolls.

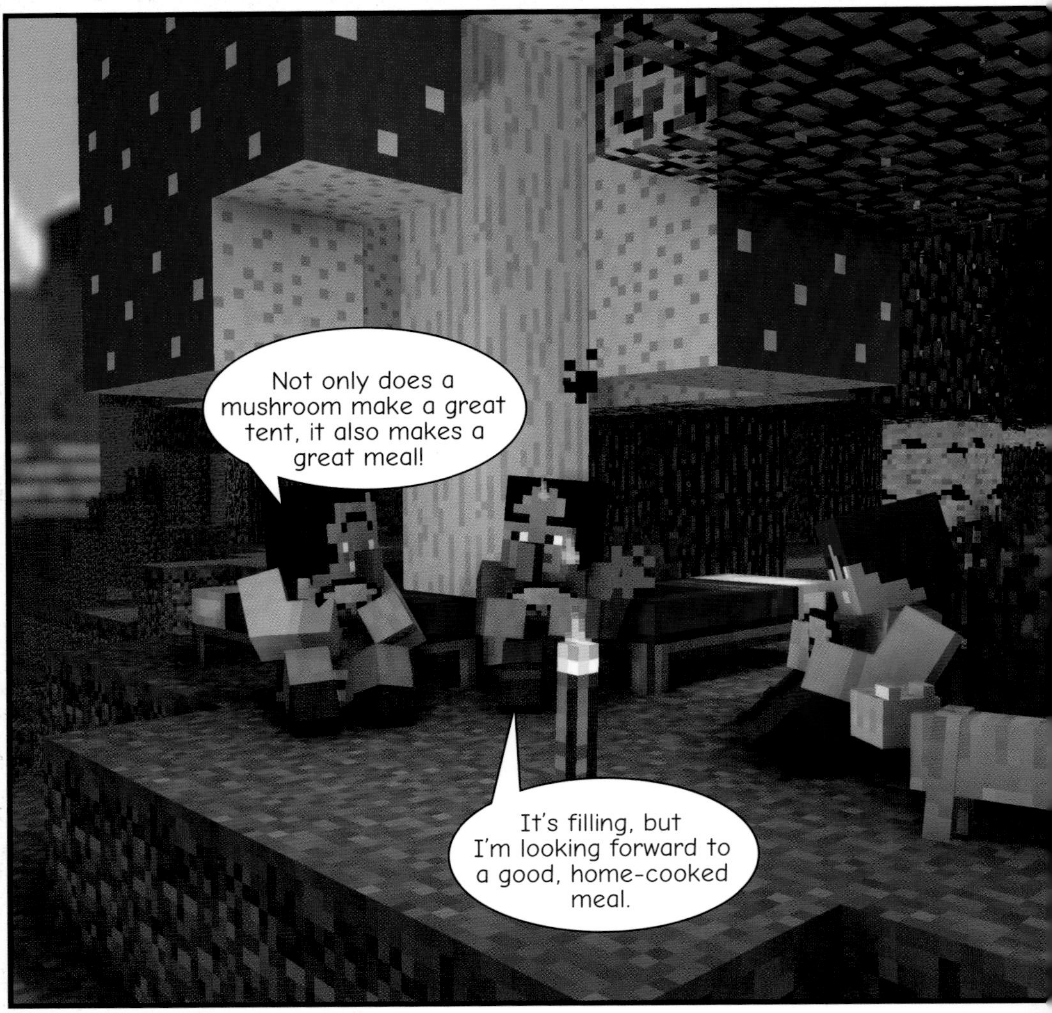
Not only does a mushroom make a great tent, it also makes a great meal!
It's filling, but I'm looking forward to a good, home-cooked meal.

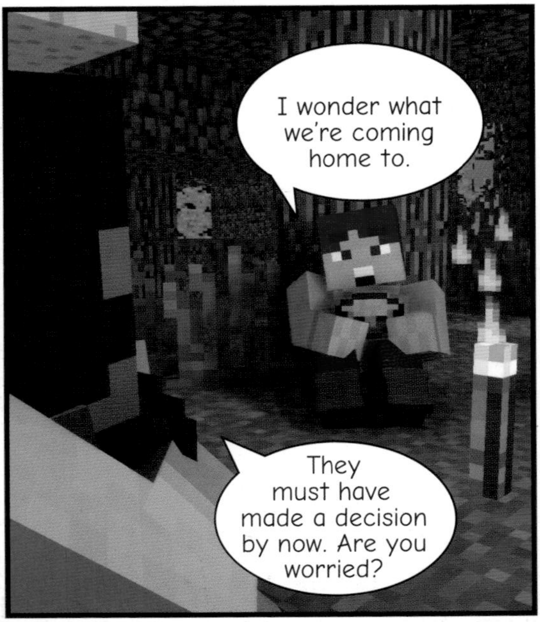
I wonder what we're coming home to.
They must have made a decision by now. Are you worried?

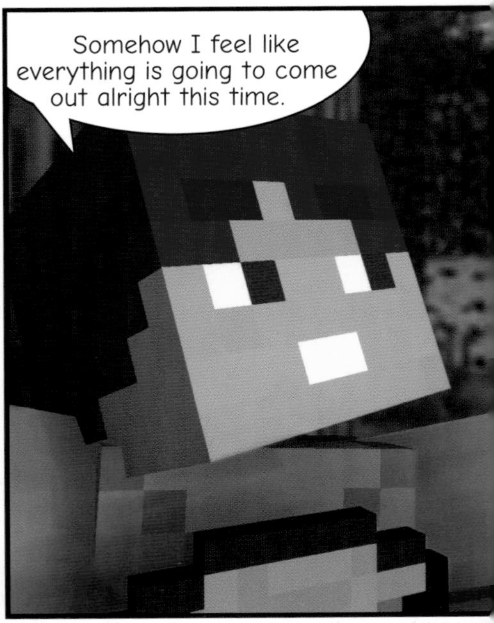
Somehow I feel like everything is going to come out alright this time.

CHAPTER 12

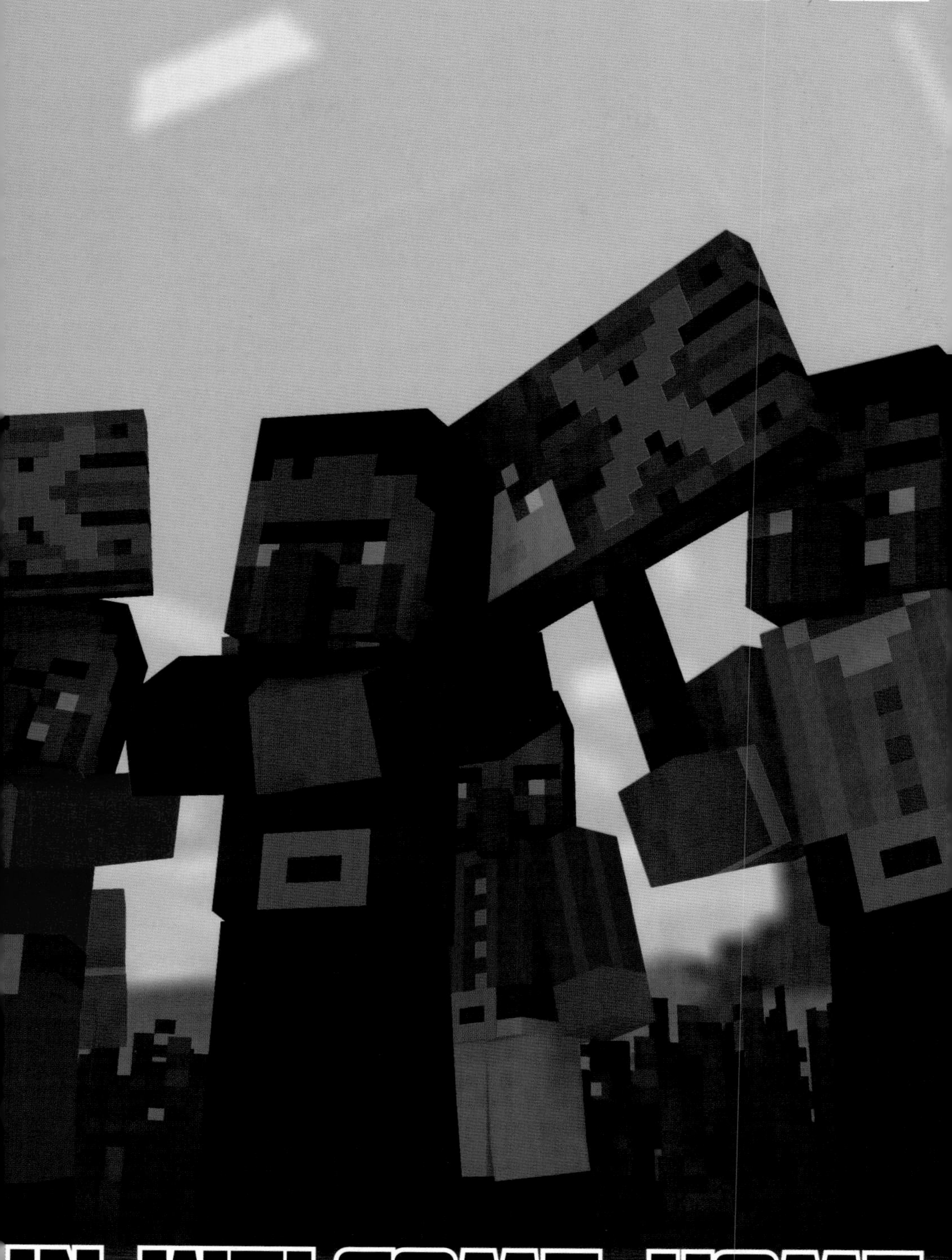

UN-WELCOME HOME

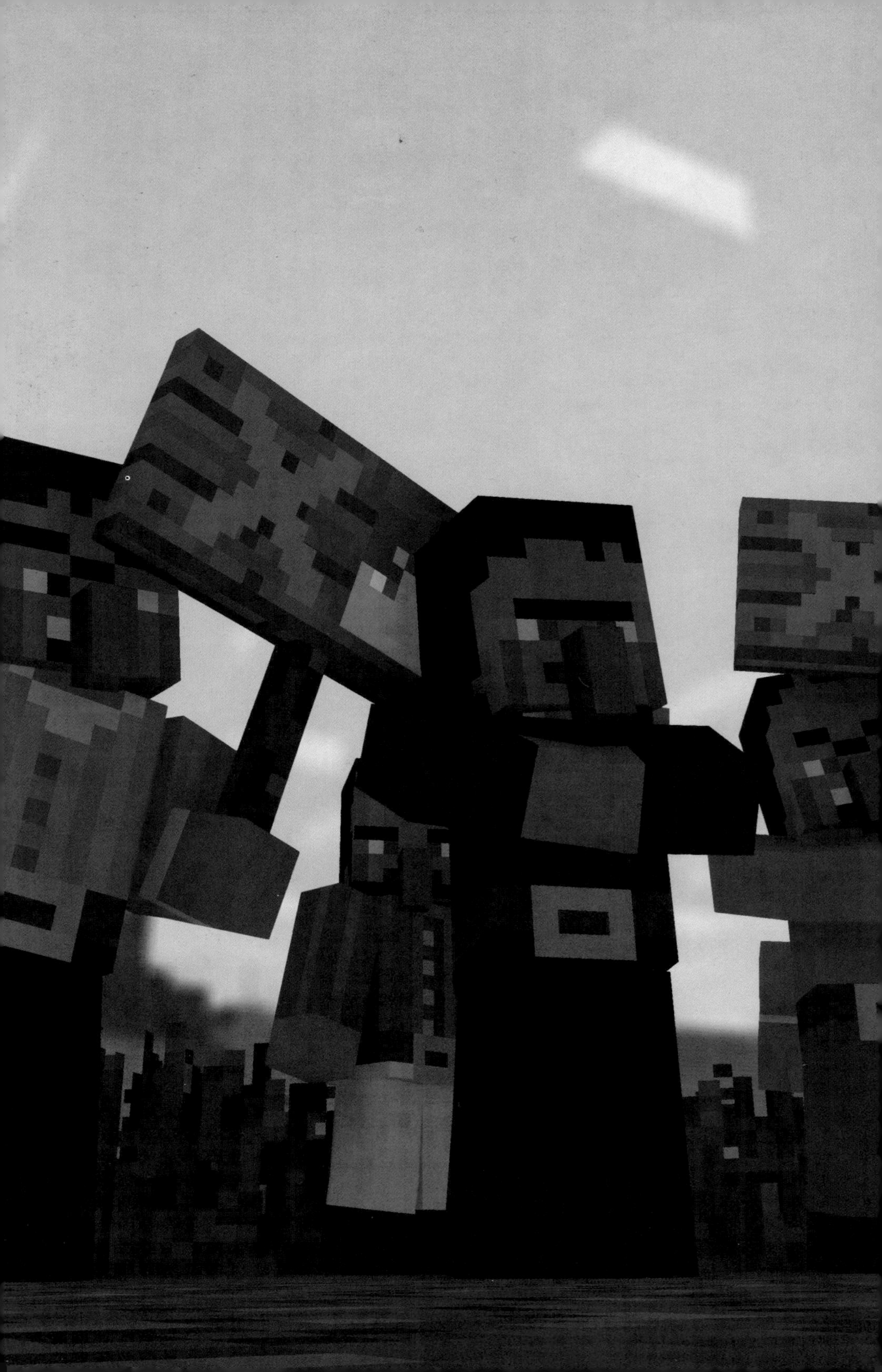

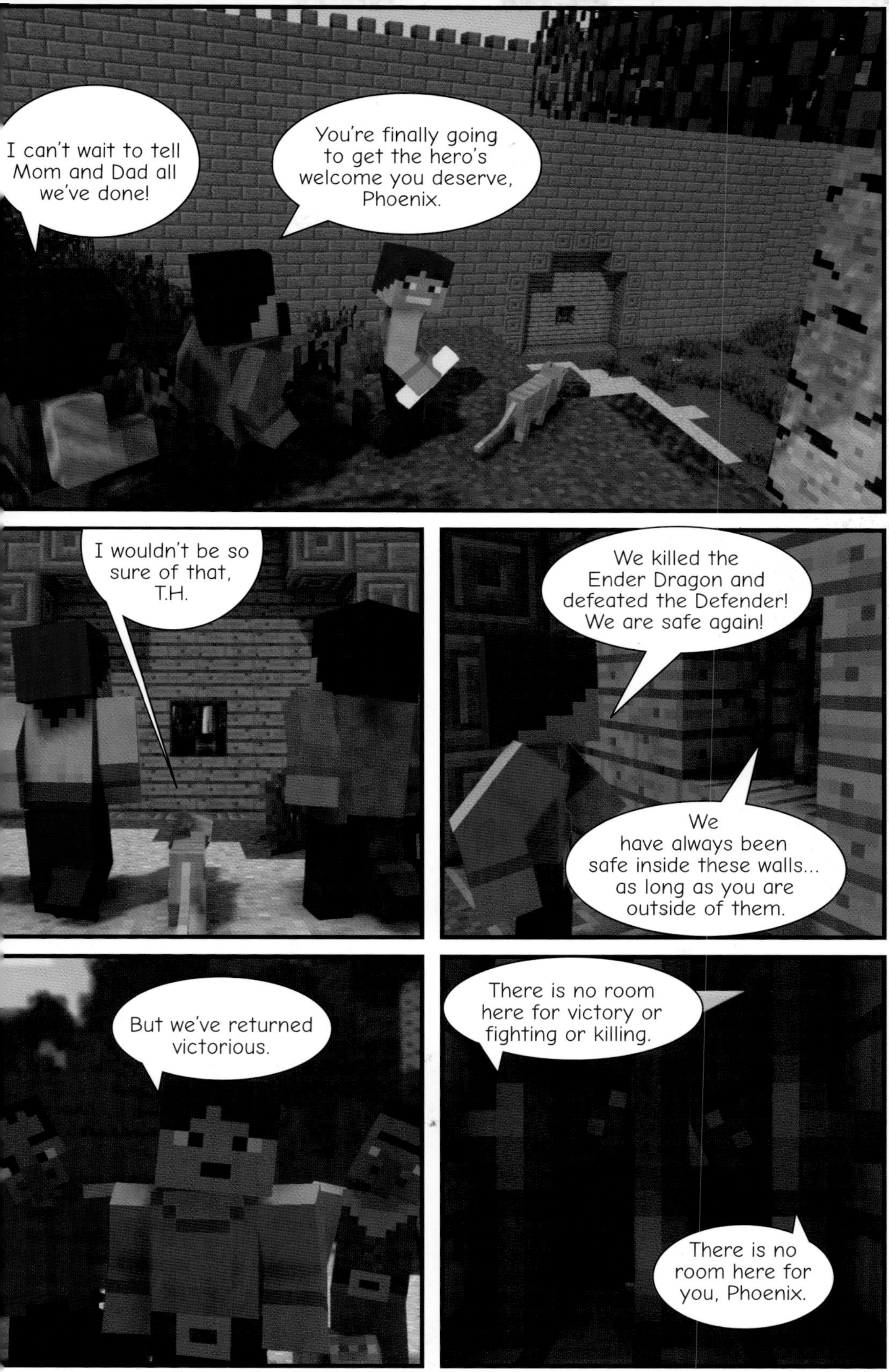
I can't wait to tell Mom and Dad all we've done!
You're finally going to get the hero's welcome you deserve, Phoenix.
I wouldn't be so sure of that, T.H.
We killed the Ender Dragon and defeated the Defender! We are safe again!
We have always been safe inside these walls... as long as you are outside of them.
But we've returned victorious.
There is no room here for victory or fighting or killing.
There is no room here for you, Phoenix.

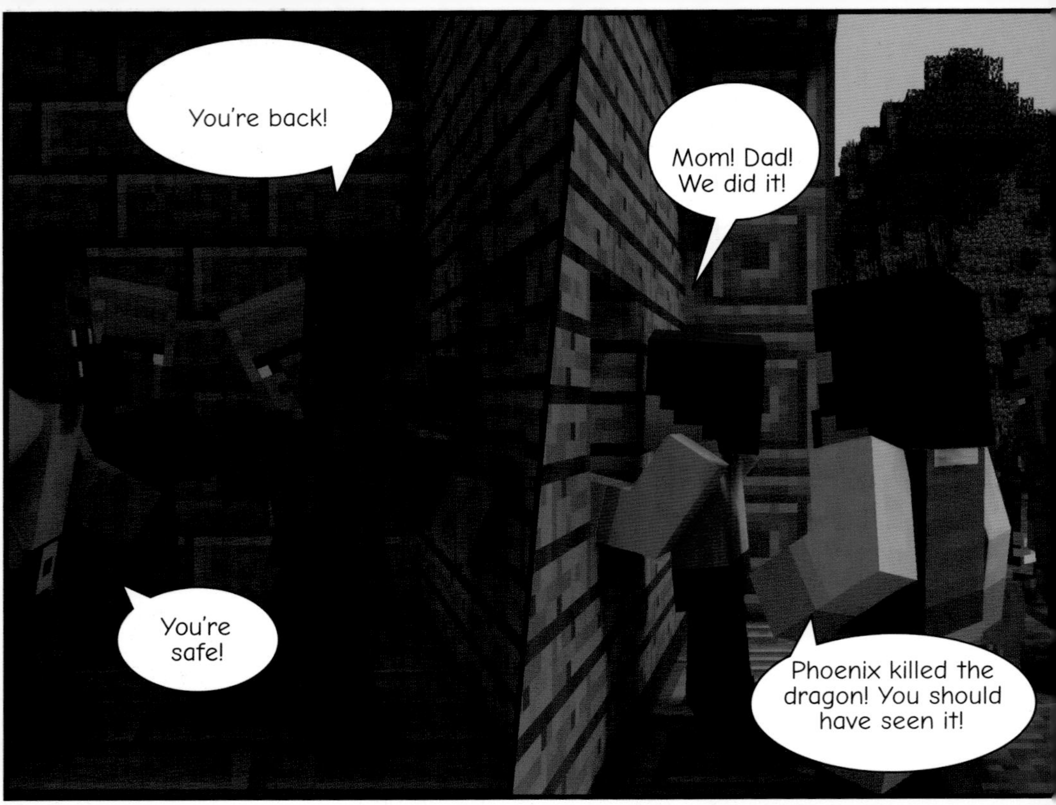
You're back!
Mom! Dad! We did it!
You're safe!
Phoenix killed the dragon! You should have seen it!

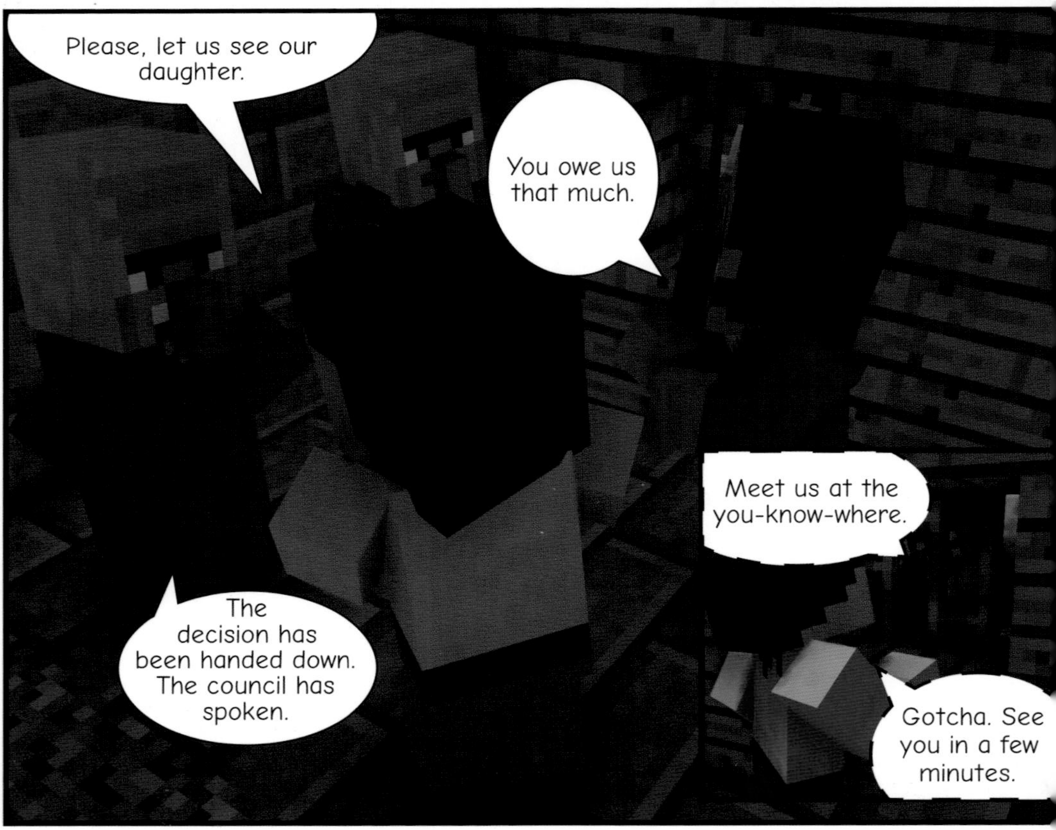
Please, let us see our daughter.
You owe us that much.
Meet us at the you-know-where.
The decision has been handed down. The council has spoken.
Gotcha. See you in a few minutes.

Wait. Those scrolls. What do you have? Where did you get them?
These are nothing. Just the spoils of battle. You wouldn't be interested.
Let Phoenix stay!
Go home outsider!
Booo!
Hooray!
Let's go guys. We should have seen this coming.
We should have asked the scrolls.

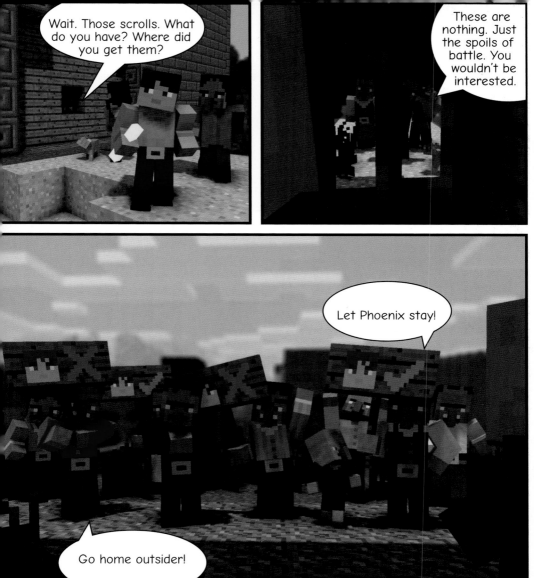

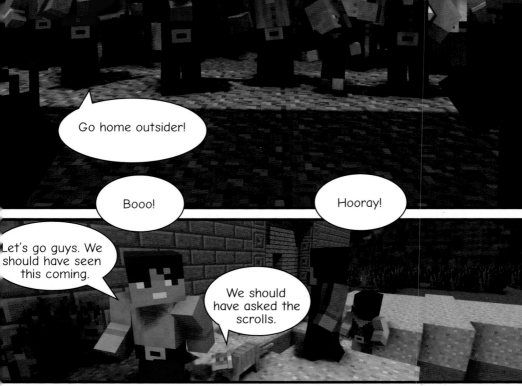

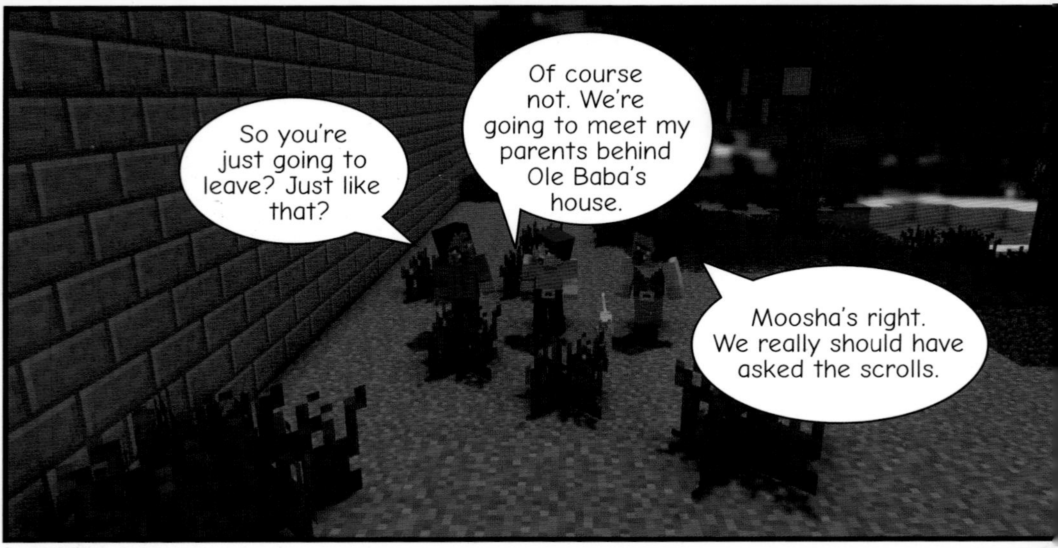
So you're just going to leave? Just like that?
Of course not. We're going to meet my parents behind Ole Baba's house.
Moosha's right. We really should have asked the scrolls.

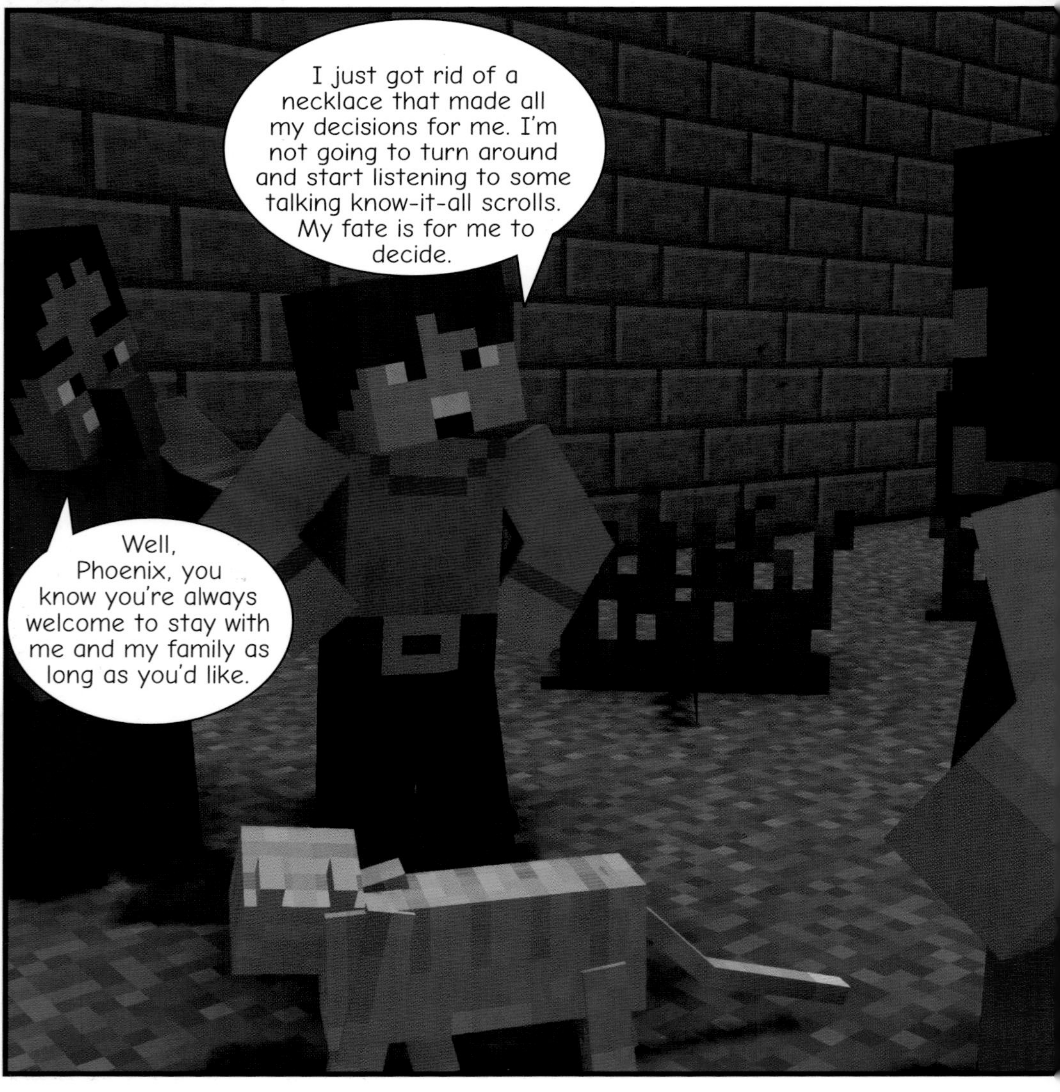
I just got rid of a necklace that made all my decisions for me. I'm not going to turn around and start listening to some talking know-it-all scrolls. My fate is for me to decide.
Well, Phoenix, you know you're always welcome to stay with me and my family as long as you'd like.

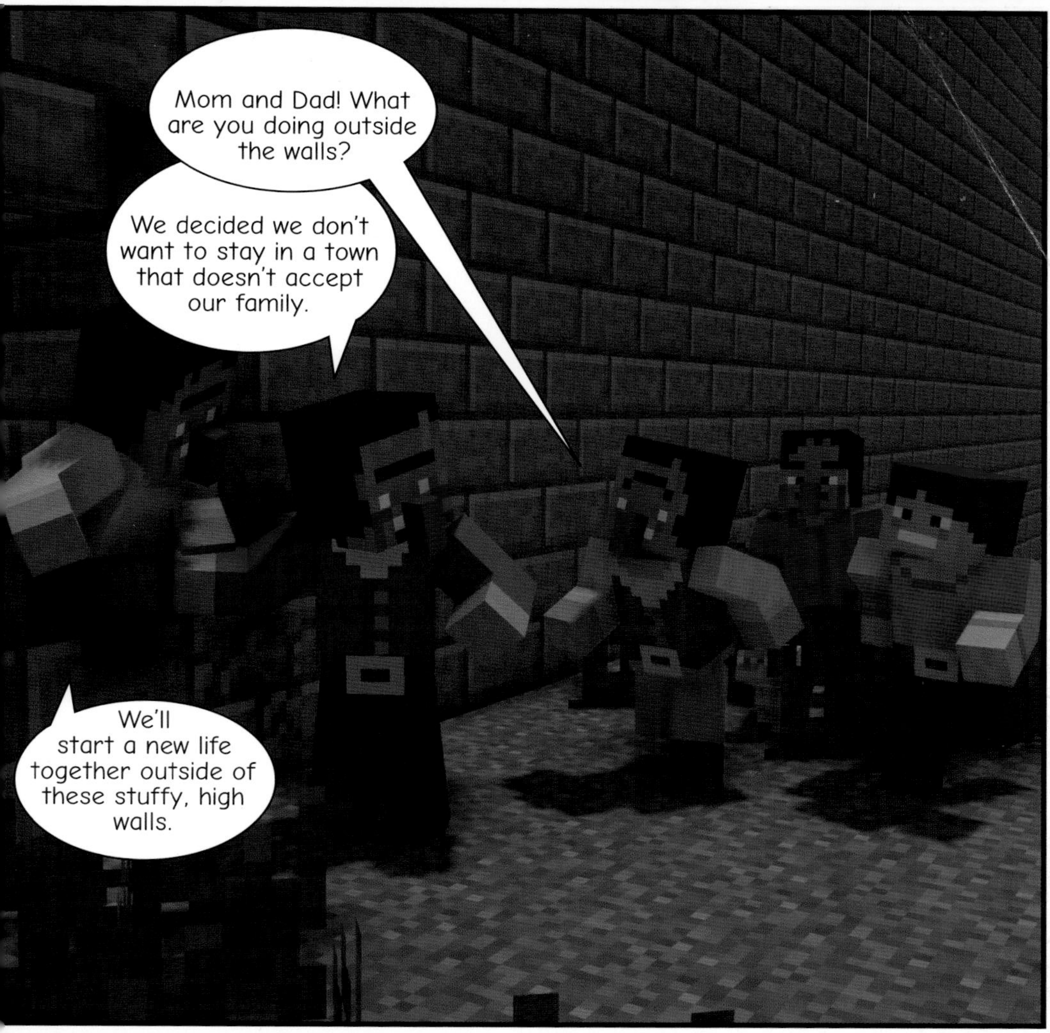
Mom and Dad! What are you doing outside the walls?
We decided we don't want to stay in a town that doesn't accept our family.
We'll start a new life together outside of these stuffy, high walls.

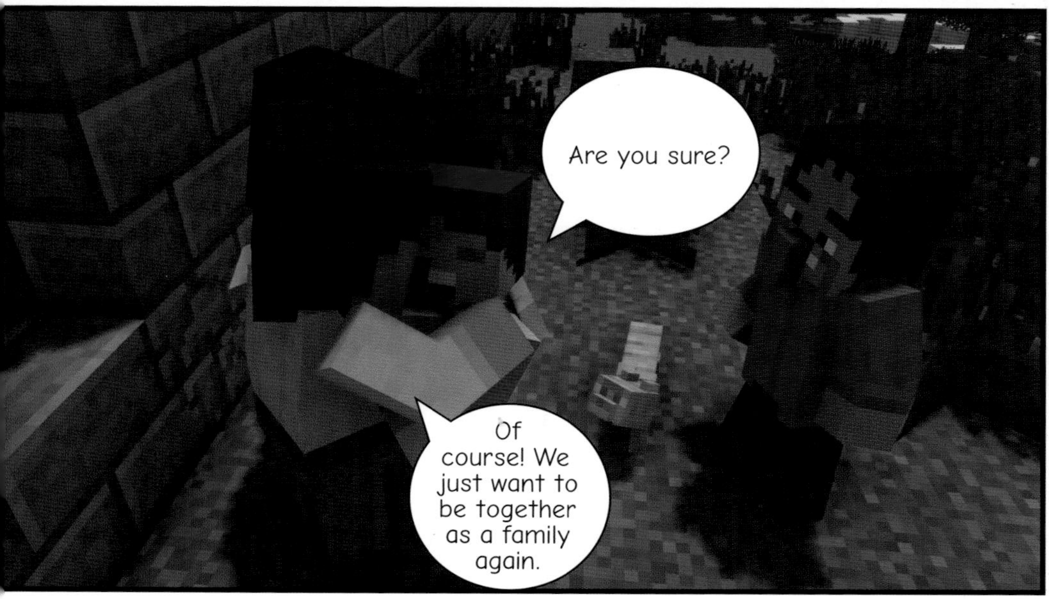
Are you sure?
Of course! We just want to be together as a family again.

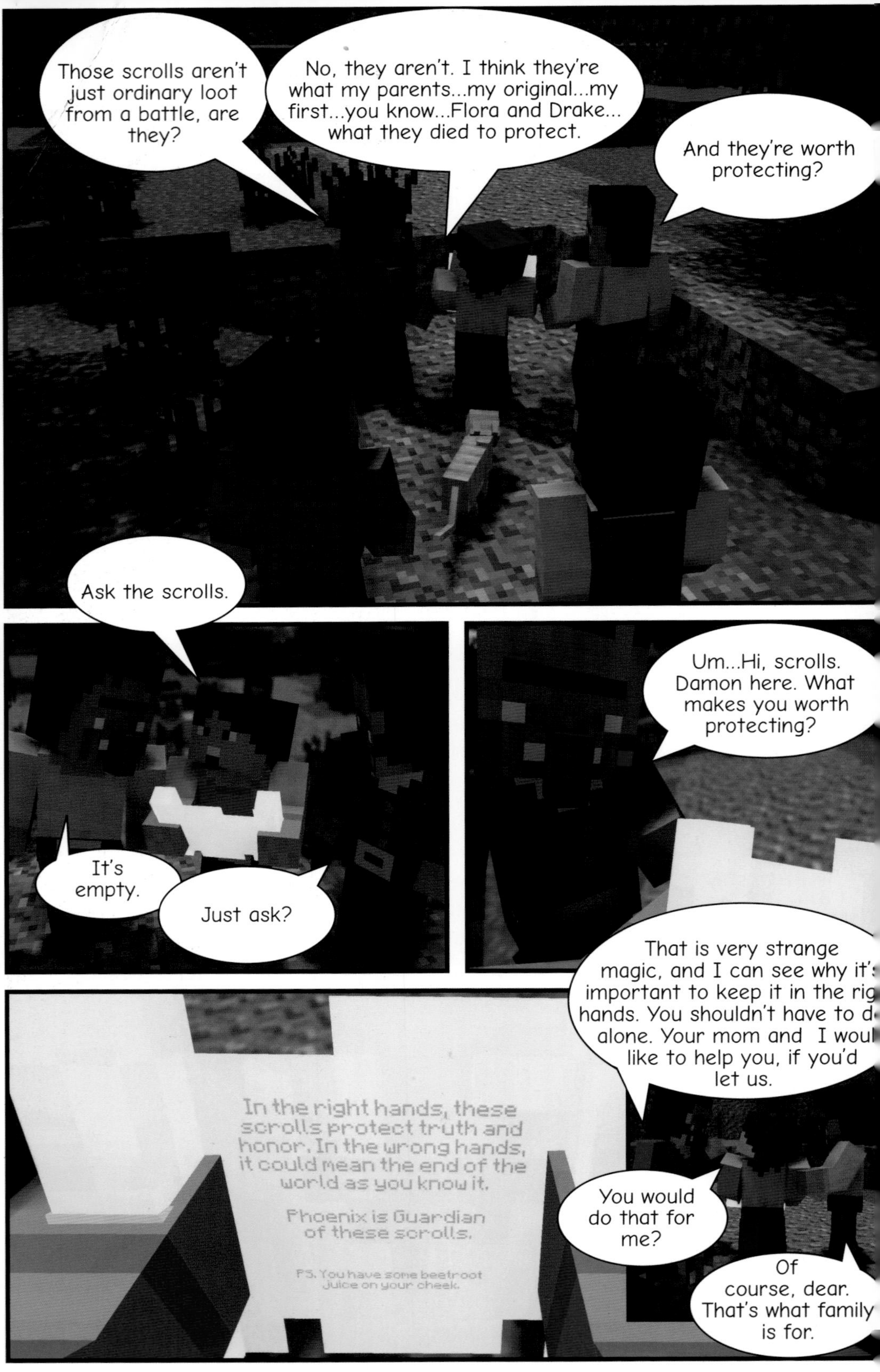
Those scrolls aren't just ordinary loot from a battle, are they?
No, they aren't. I think they're what my parents...my original...my first...you know...Flora and Drake... what they died to protect.
And they're worth protecting?
Ask the scrolls.
It's empty.
Just ask?
Um...Hi, scrolls. Damon here. What makes you worth protecting?
In the right hands, these scrolls protect truth and honor. In the wrong hands, it could mean the end of the world as you know it.
Phoenix is Guardian of these scrolls.
PS. You have some beetroot juice on your cheek.
That is very strange magic, and I can see why it' important to keep it in the rig hands. You shouldn't have to d alone. Your mom and I woul like to help you, if you'd let us.
You would do that for me?
Of course, dear. That's what family is for.

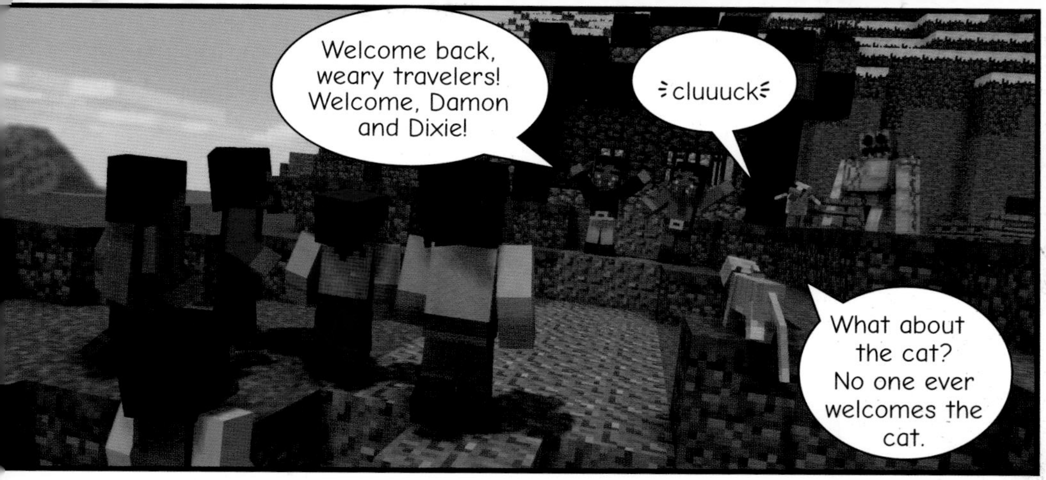
Welcome back, weary travelers! Welcome, Damon and Dixie!
cluuuck
What about the cat? No one ever welcomes the cat.

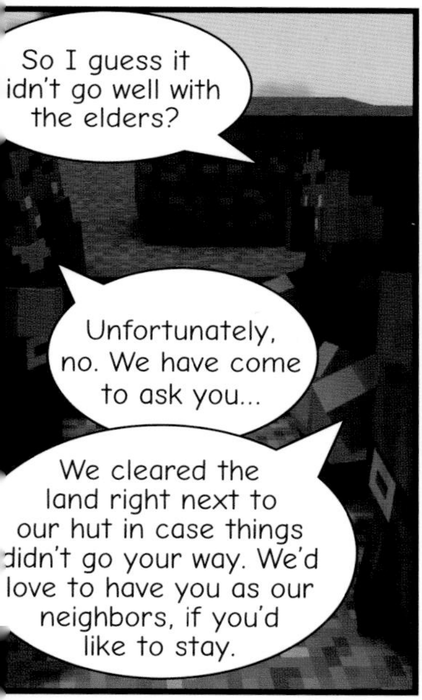
So I guess it idn't go well with the elders?
Unfortunately, no. We have come to ask you...
We cleared the land right next to our hut in case things didn't go your way. We'd love to have you as our neighbors, if you'd like to stay.

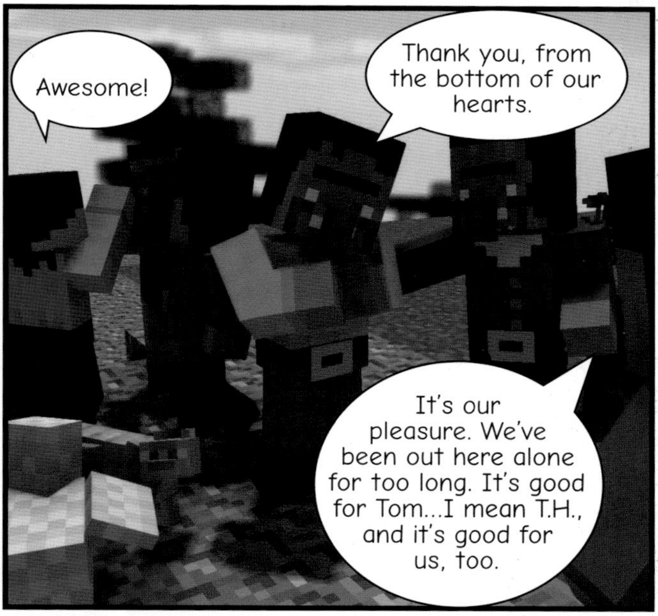
Awesome!
Thank you, from the bottom of our hearts.
It's our pleasure. We've been out here alone for too long. It's good for Tom...I mean T.H., and it's good for us, too.

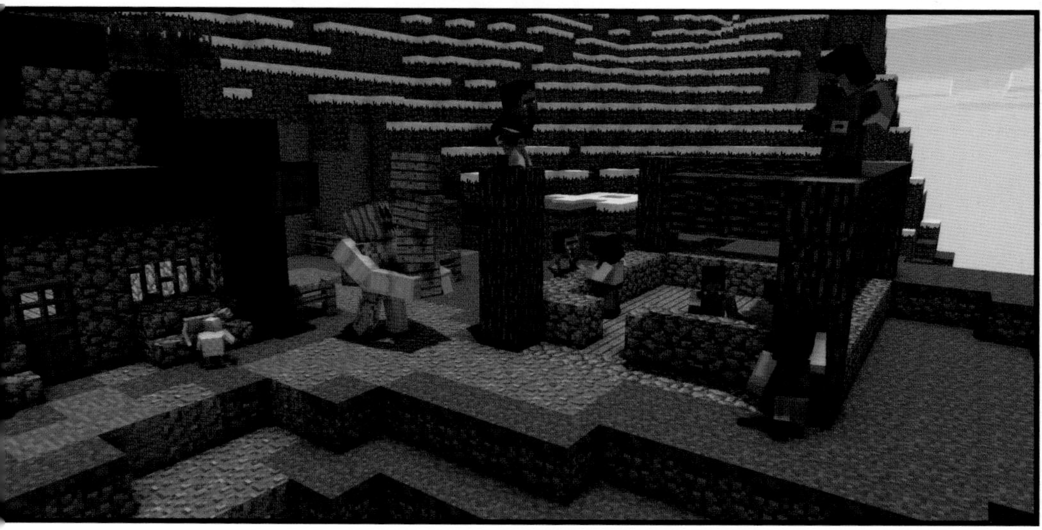

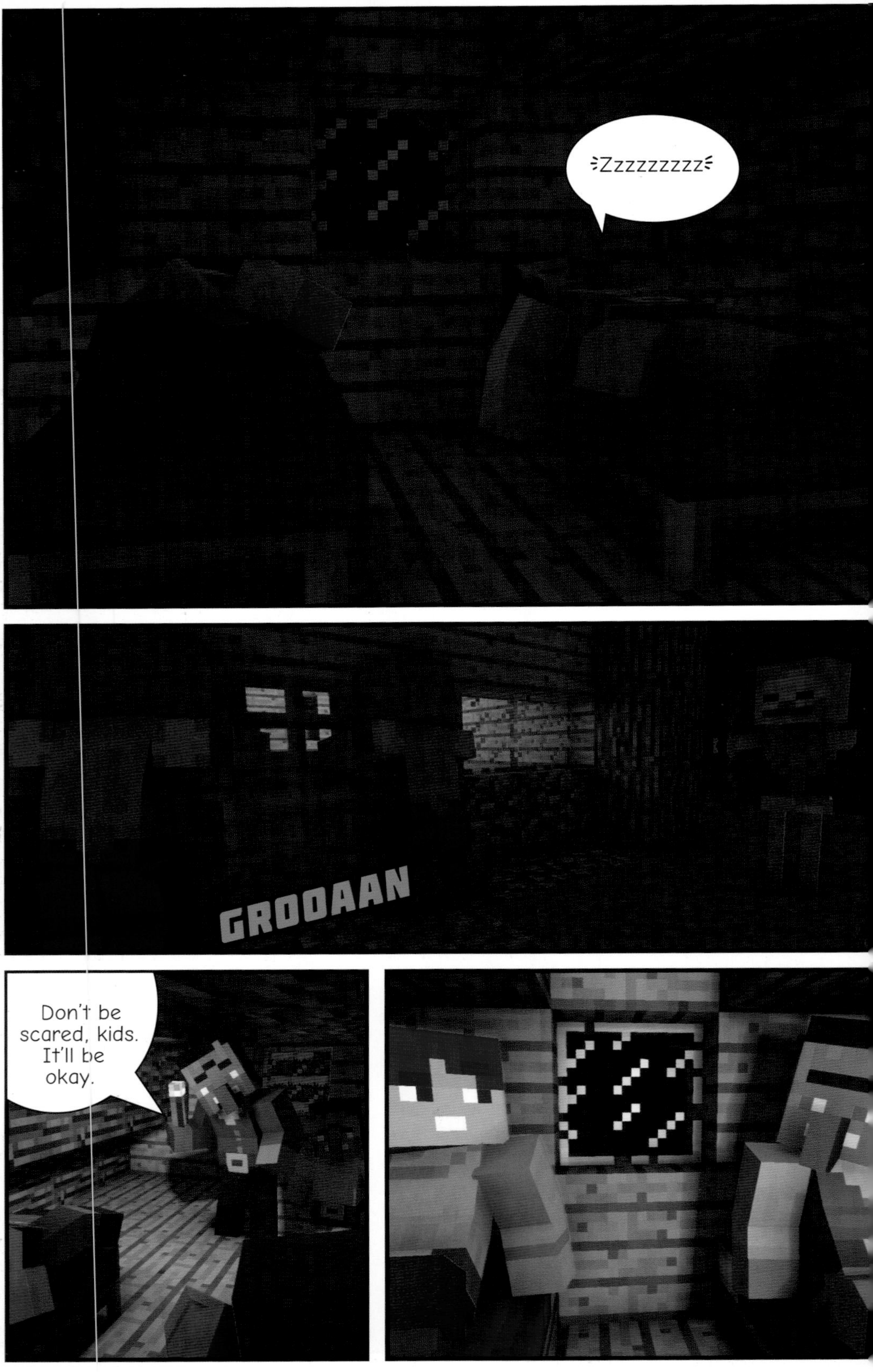
Zzzzzzzzz
GROOAAN
Don't be scared, kids. It'll be okay.

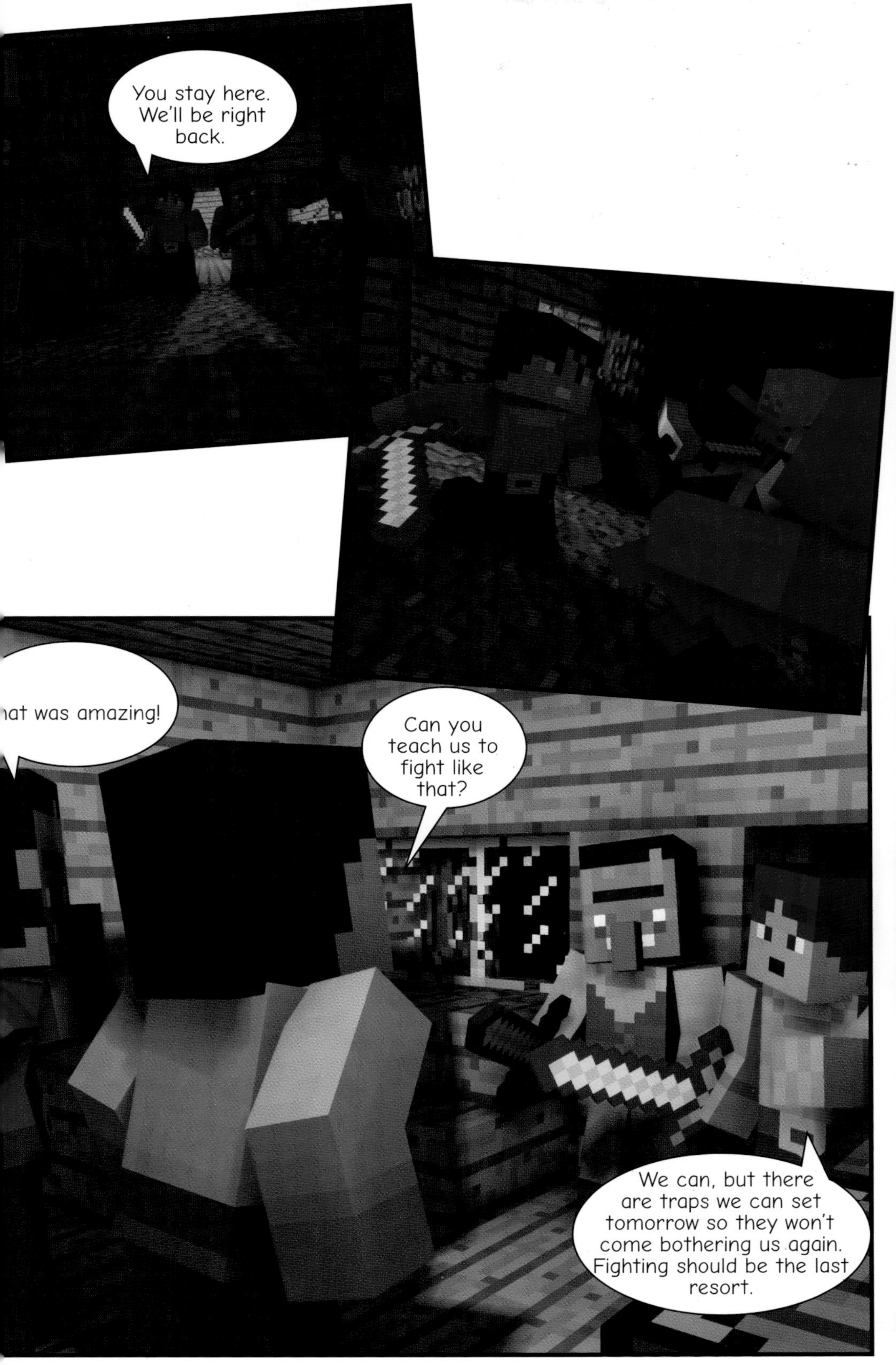
You stay here. We'll be right back.
hat was amazing!
Can you teach us to fight like that?
We can, but there are traps we can set tomorrow so they won't come bothering us again. Fighting should be the last resort.

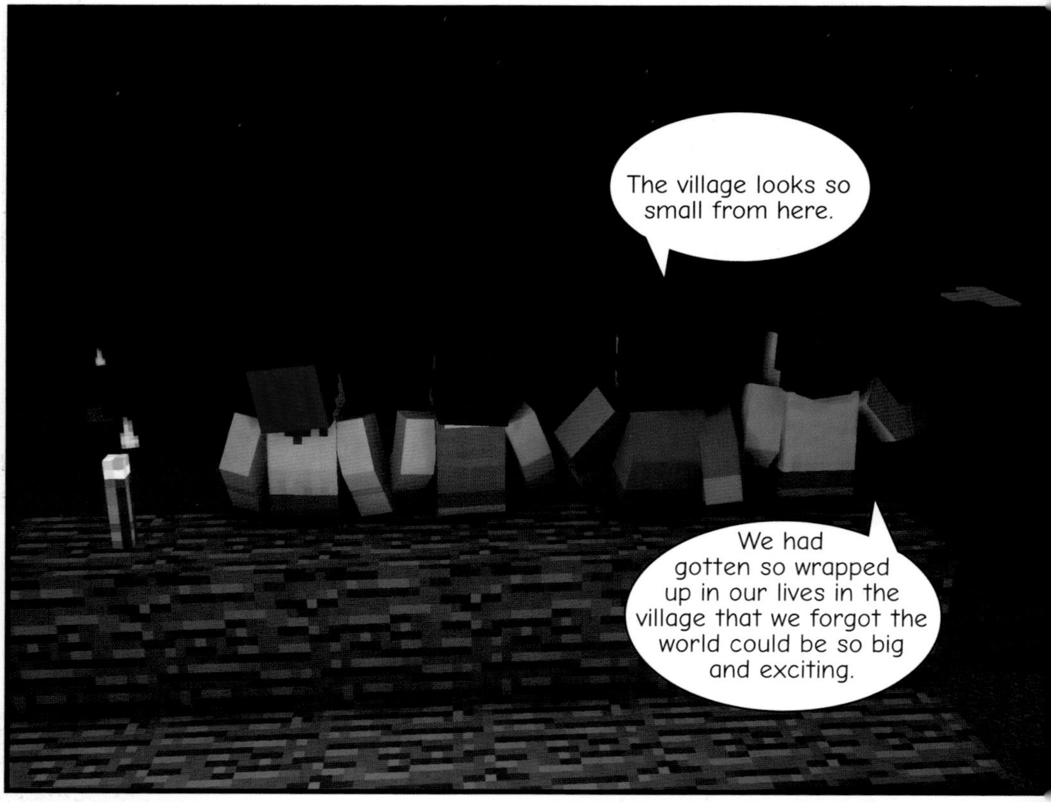
The village looks so small from here.
We had gotten so wrapped up in our lives in the village that we forgot the world could be so big and exciting.

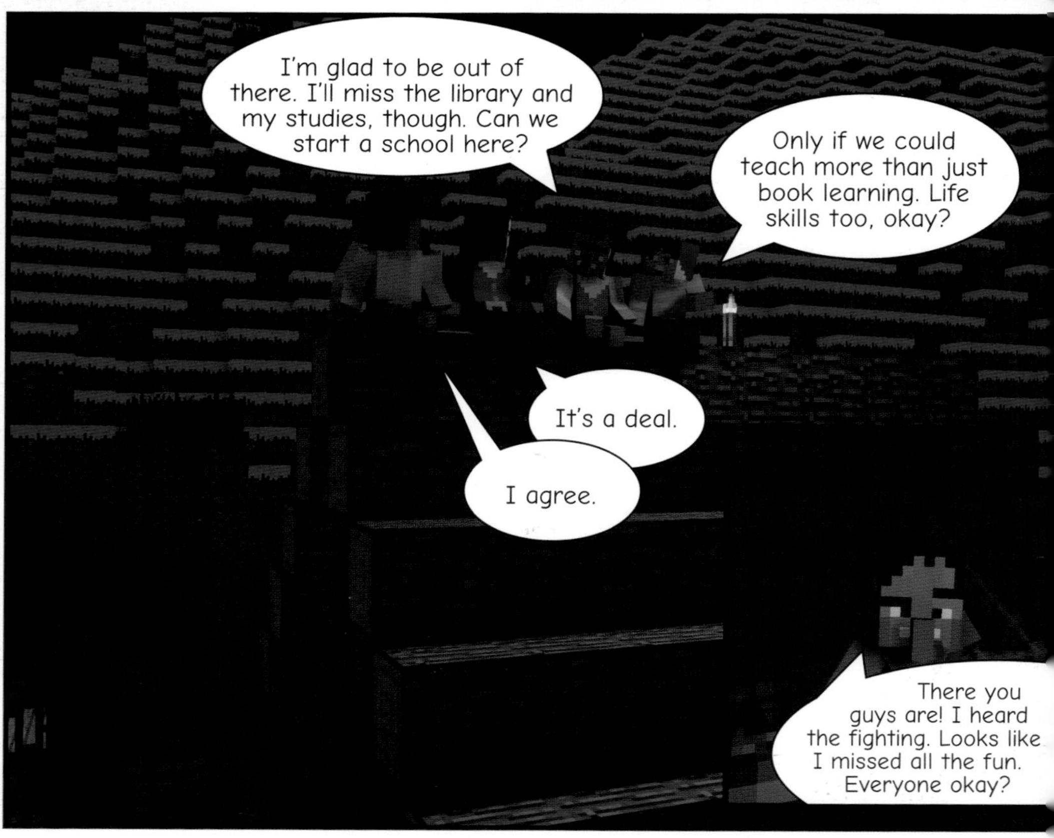
I'm glad to be out of there. I'll miss the library and my studies, though. Can we start a school here?
Only if we could teach more than just book learning. Life skills too, okay?
It's a deal.
I agree.
There you guys are! I heard the fighting. Looks like I missed all the fun. Everyone okay?

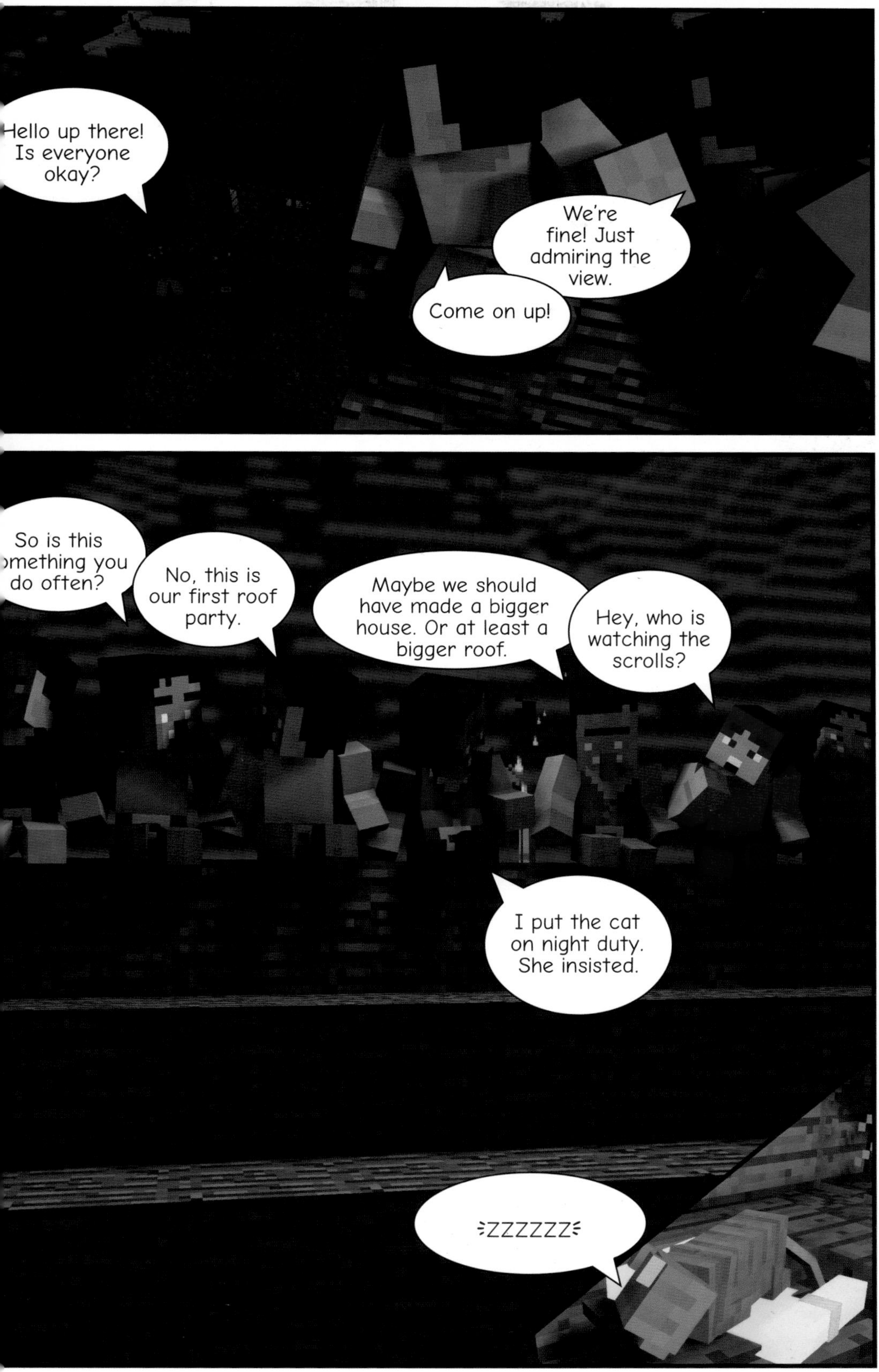
Hello up there! Is everyone okay?
We're fine! Just admiring the view.
Come on up!
So is this mething you do often?
No, this is our first roof party.
Maybe we should have made a bigger house. Or at least a bigger roof.
Hey, who is watching the scrolls?
I put the cat on night duty. She insisted.
ZZZZZZ

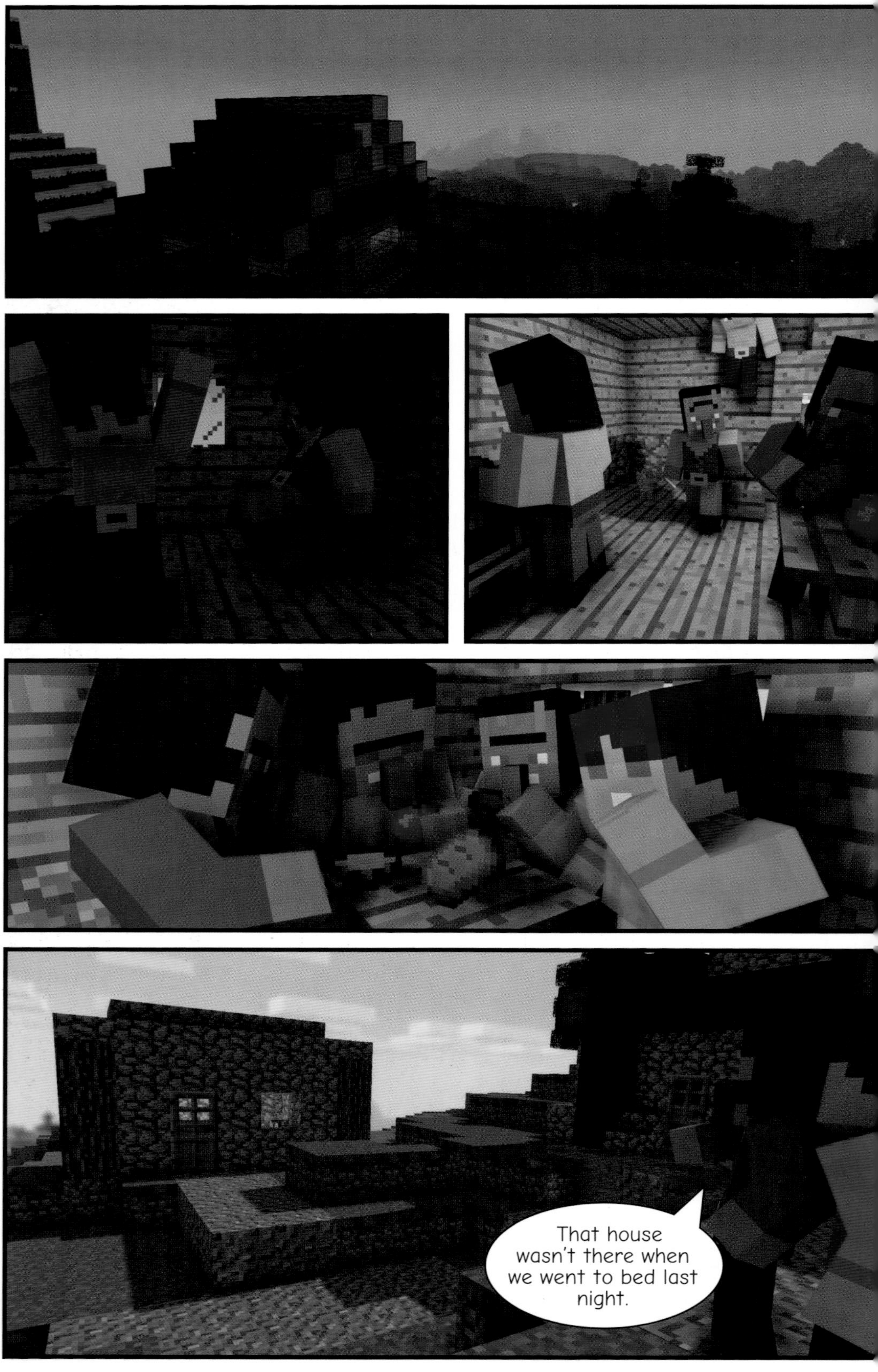
That house wasn't there when we went to bed last night.

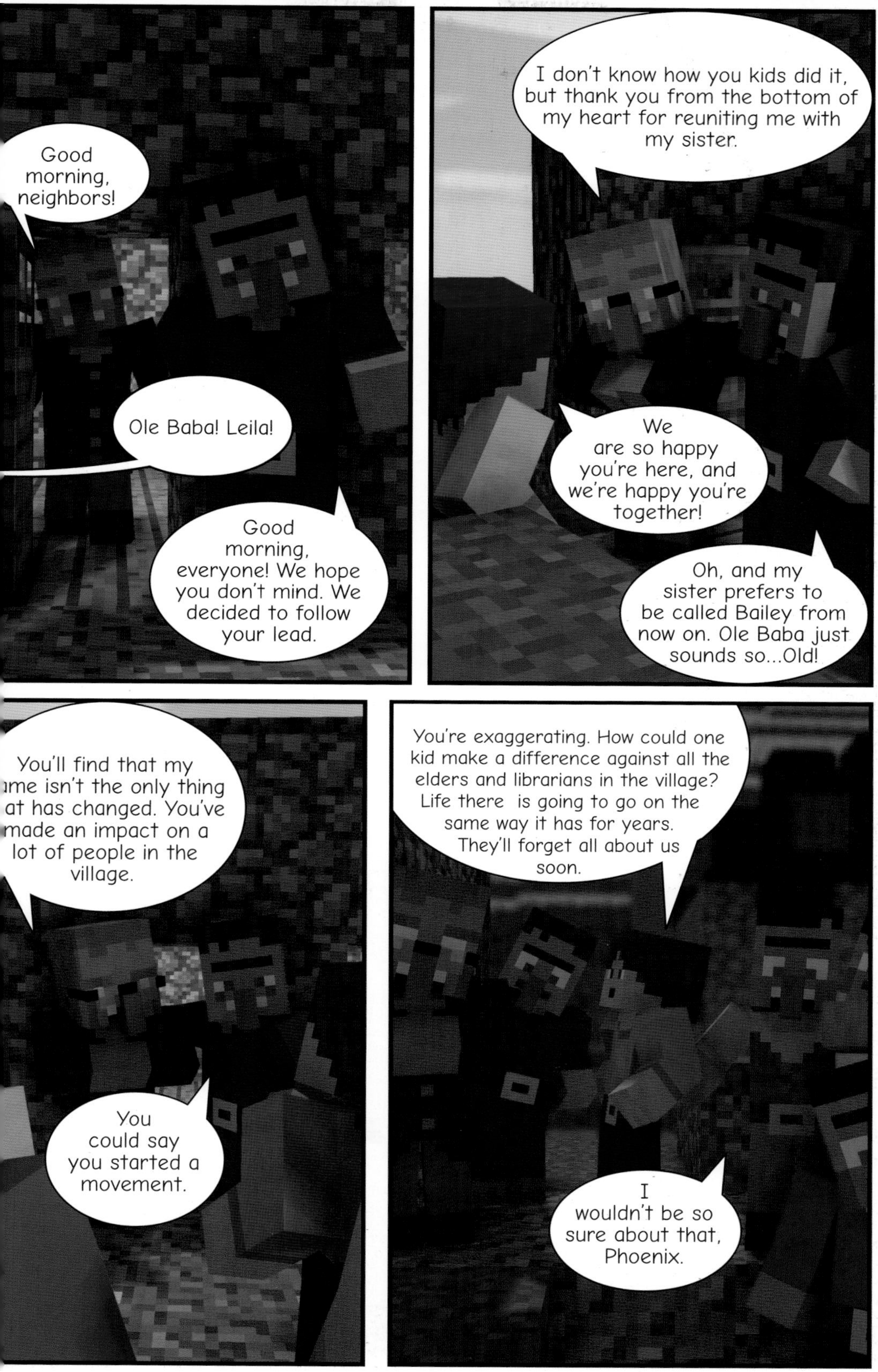
Good morning, neighbors!
Ole Baba! Leila!
Good morning, everyone! We hope you don't mind. We decided to follow your lead.
I don't know how you kids did it, but thank you from the bottom of my heart for reuniting me with my sister.
We are so happy you're here, and we're happy you're together!
Oh, and my sister prefers to be called Bailey from now on. Ole Baba just sounds so...Old!
You'll find that my ame isn't the only thing at has changed. You've made an impact on a lot of people in the village.
You could say you started a movement.
You're exaggerating. How could one kid make a difference against all the elders and librarians in the village? Life there is going to go on the same way it has for years. They'll forget all about us soon.
I wouldn't be so sure about that, Phoenix.

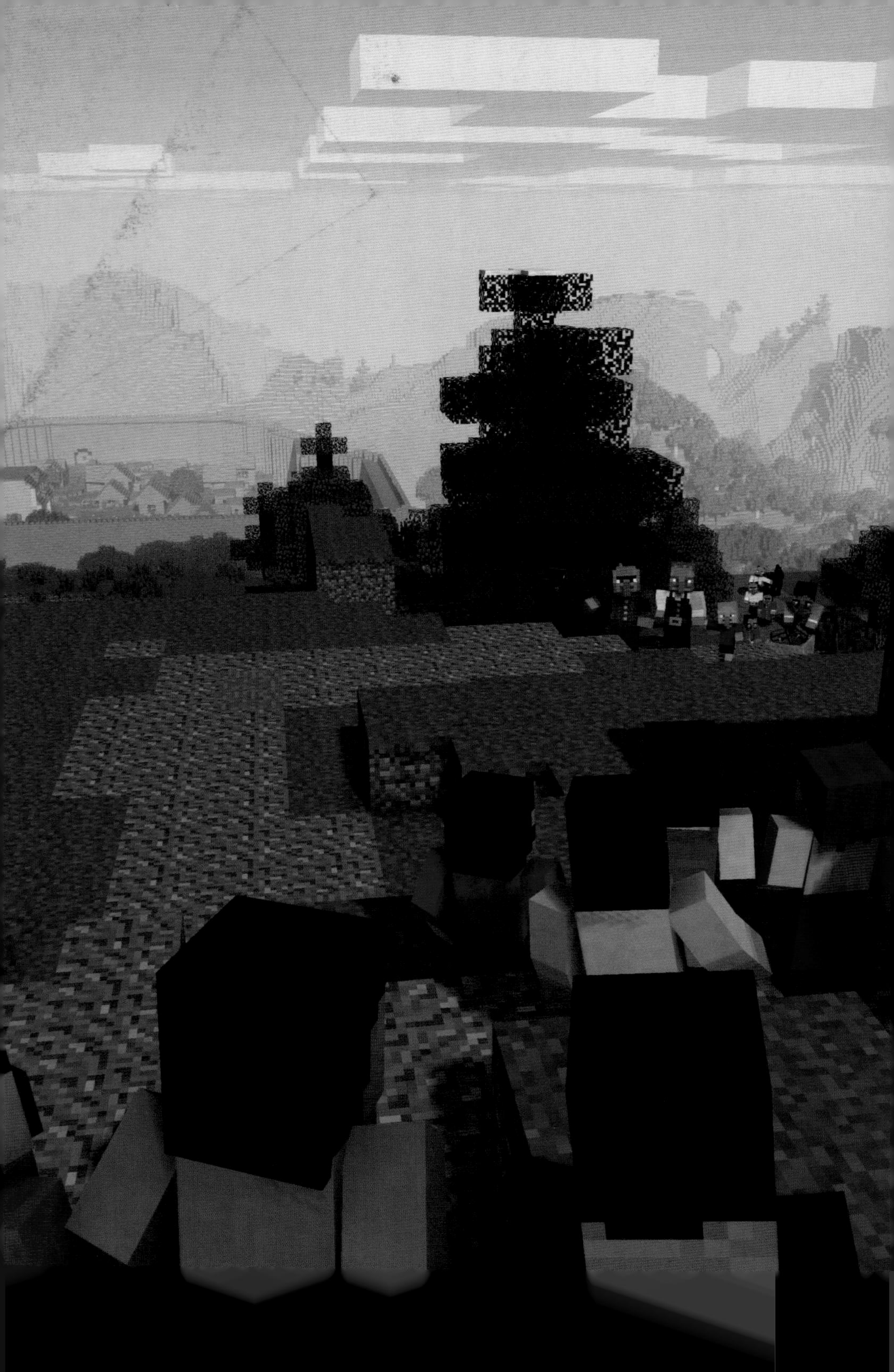

AN UNOFFICIAL GRA
FOR MINECRAFT

CHASING HEROBRINE

CARA J. STEVENS

ART BY **DAVID NORGREN**
AND **ELIAS NORGREN**

SKY PONY PRESS
NEW YORK

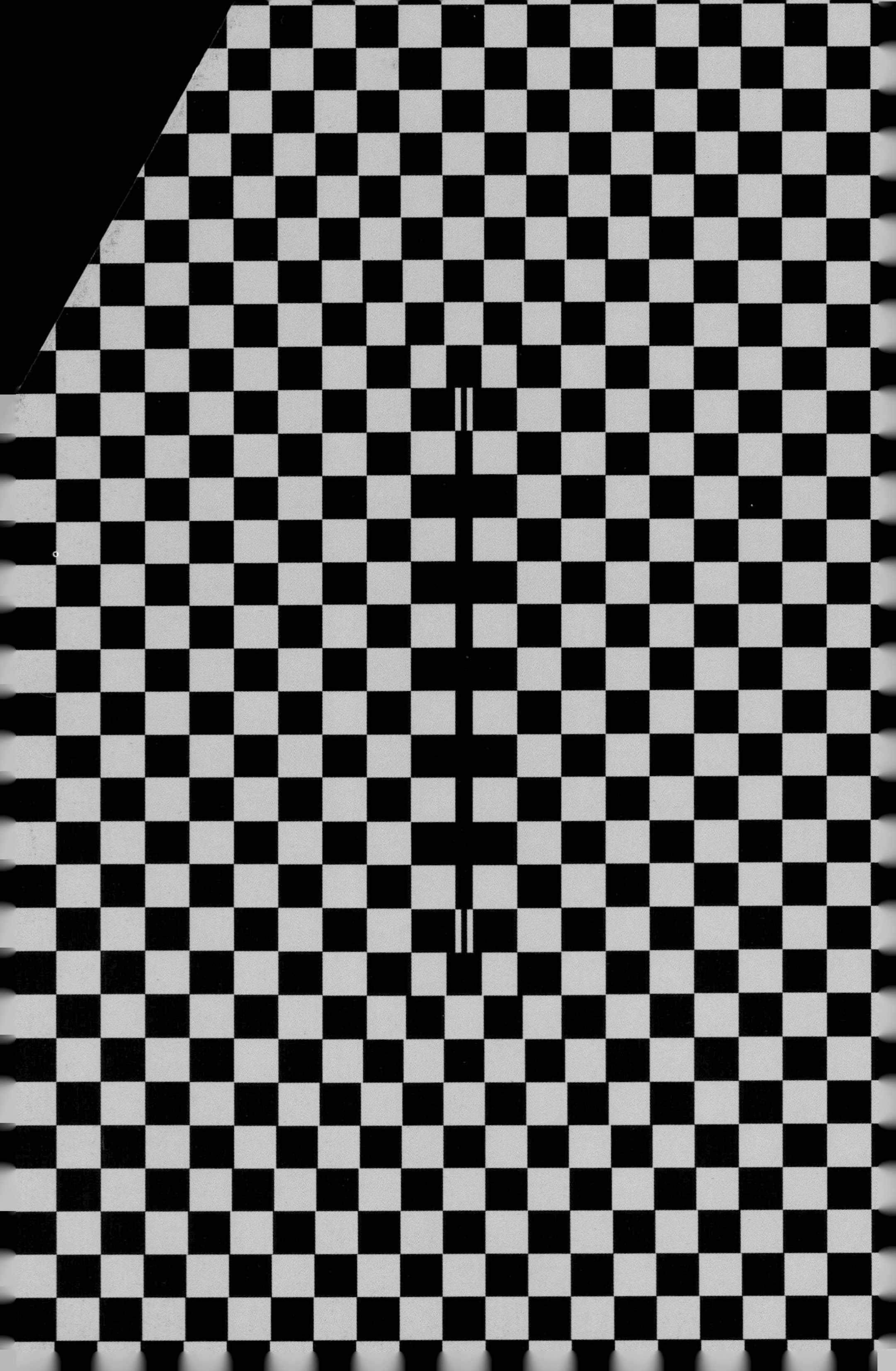

CHAPTER 1

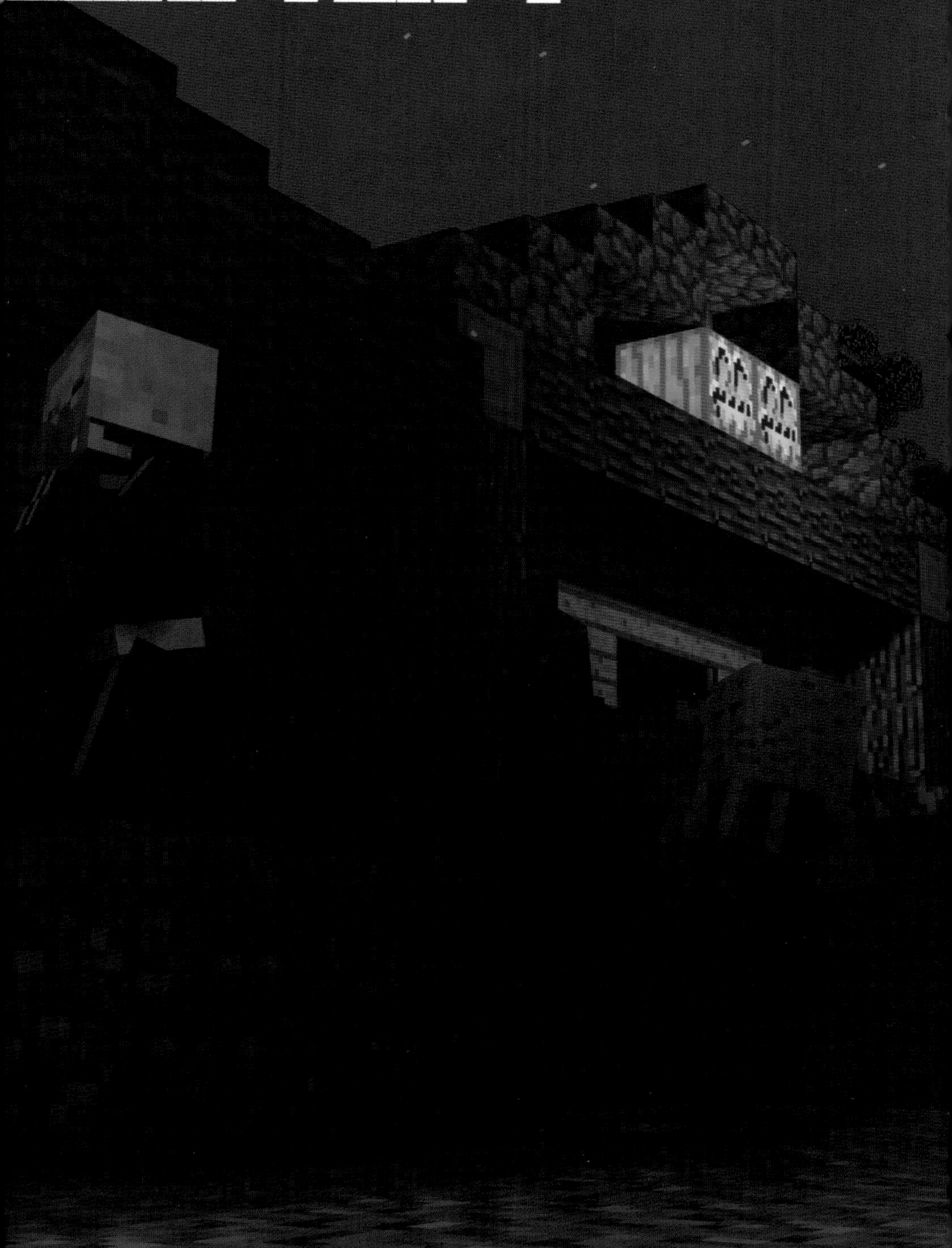

ALL HALLOWS' EVE

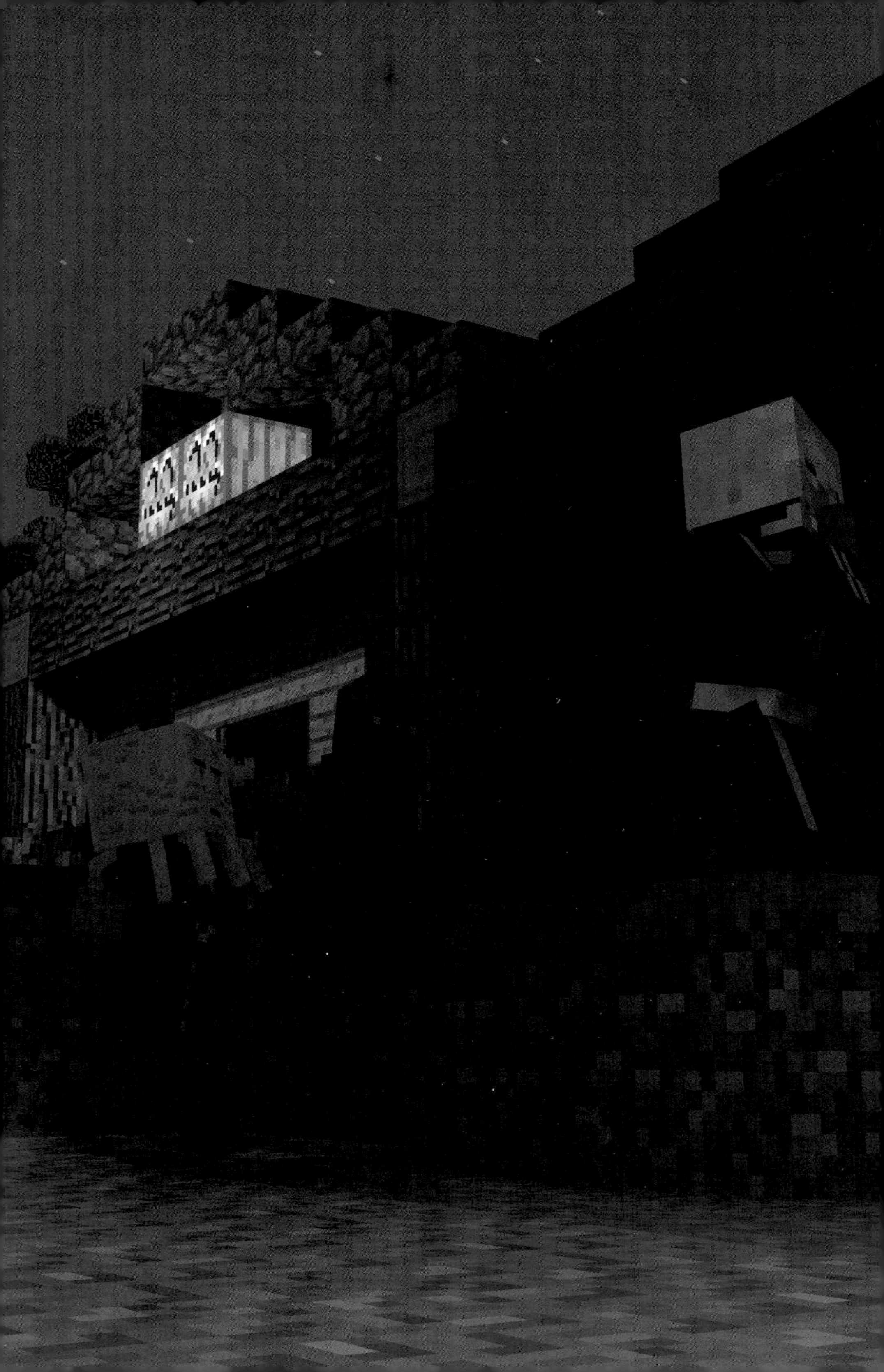

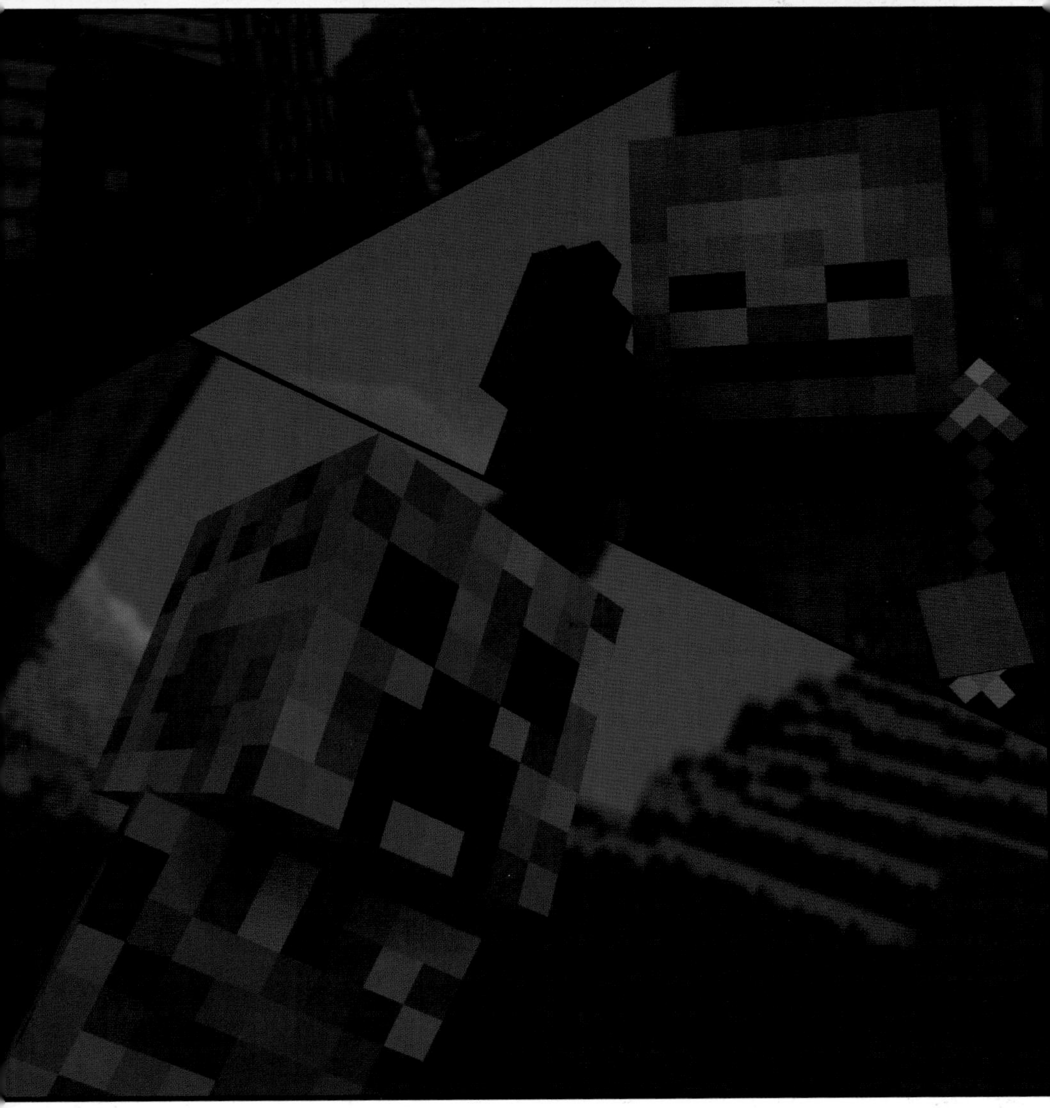

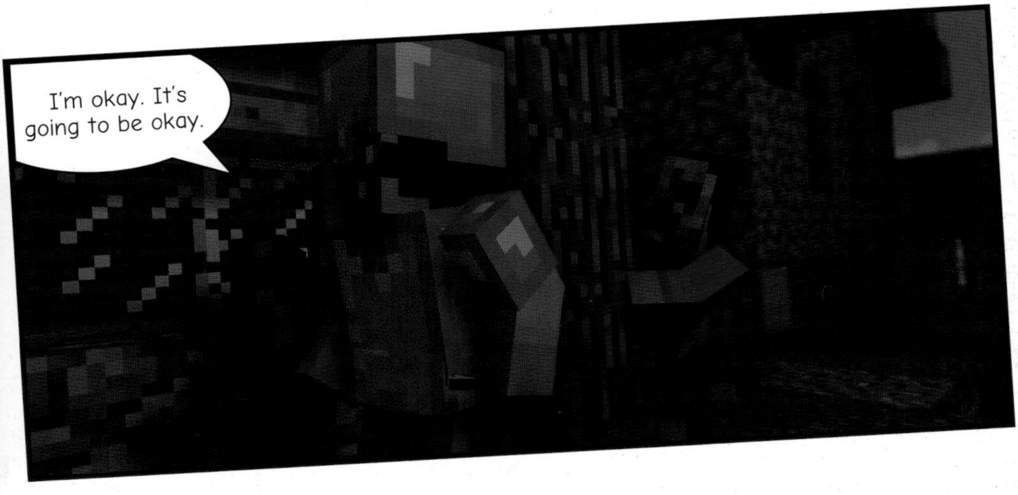
I'm okay. It's going to be okay.

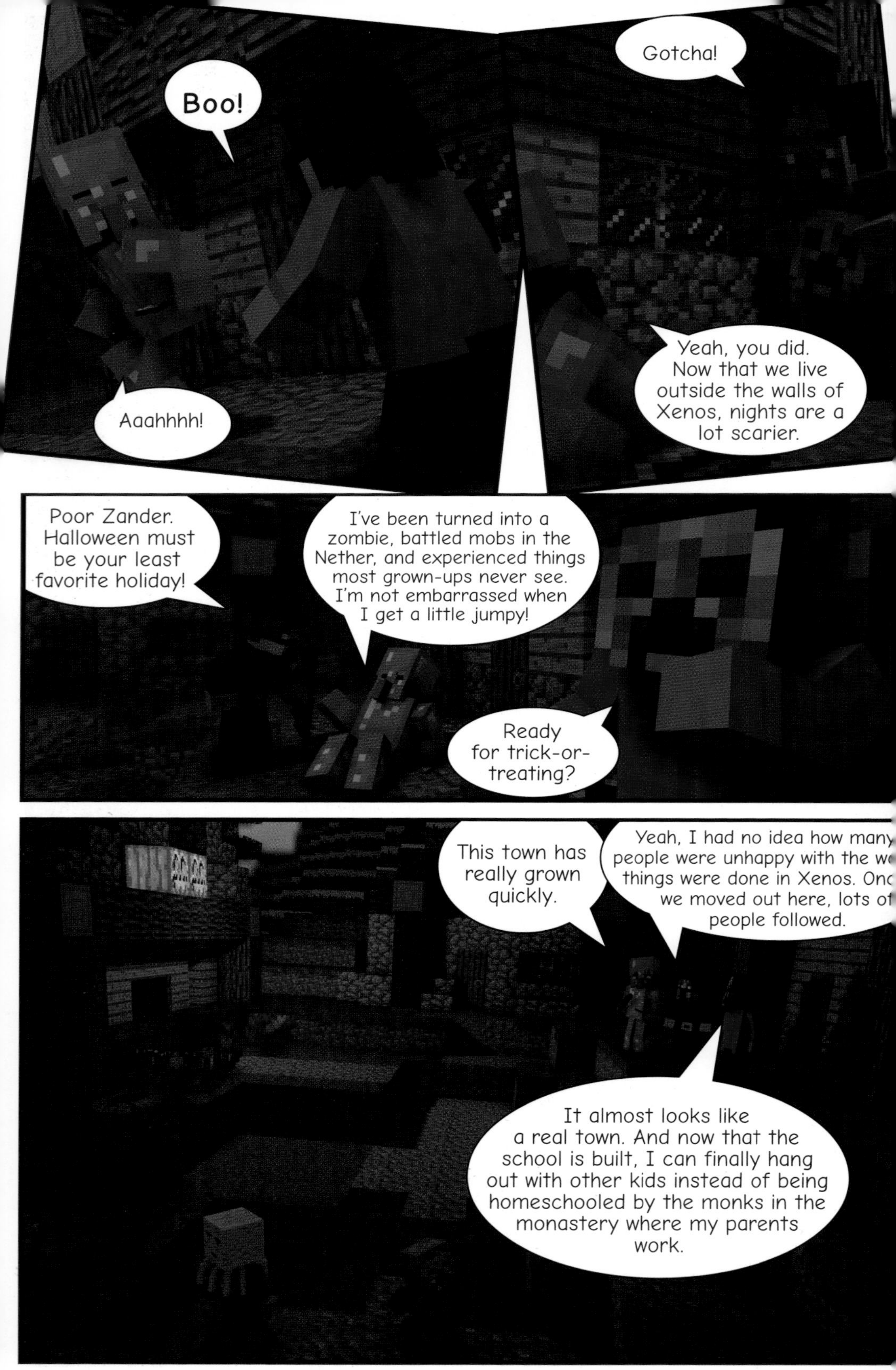

Boo!
Aaahhhh!
Gotcha!
Yeah, you did. Now that we live outside the walls of Xenos, nights are a lot scarier.
Poor Zander. Halloween must be your least favorite holiday!
I've been turned into a zombie, battled mobs in the Nether, and experienced things most grown-ups never see. I'm not embarrassed when I get a little jumpy!
Ready for trick-or-treating?
This town has really grown quickly.
Yeah, I had no idea how many people were unhappy with the w things were done in Xenos. Onc we moved out here, lots of people followed.
It almost looks like a real town. And now that the school is built, I can finally hang out with other kids instead of being homeschooled by the monks in the monastery where my parents work.

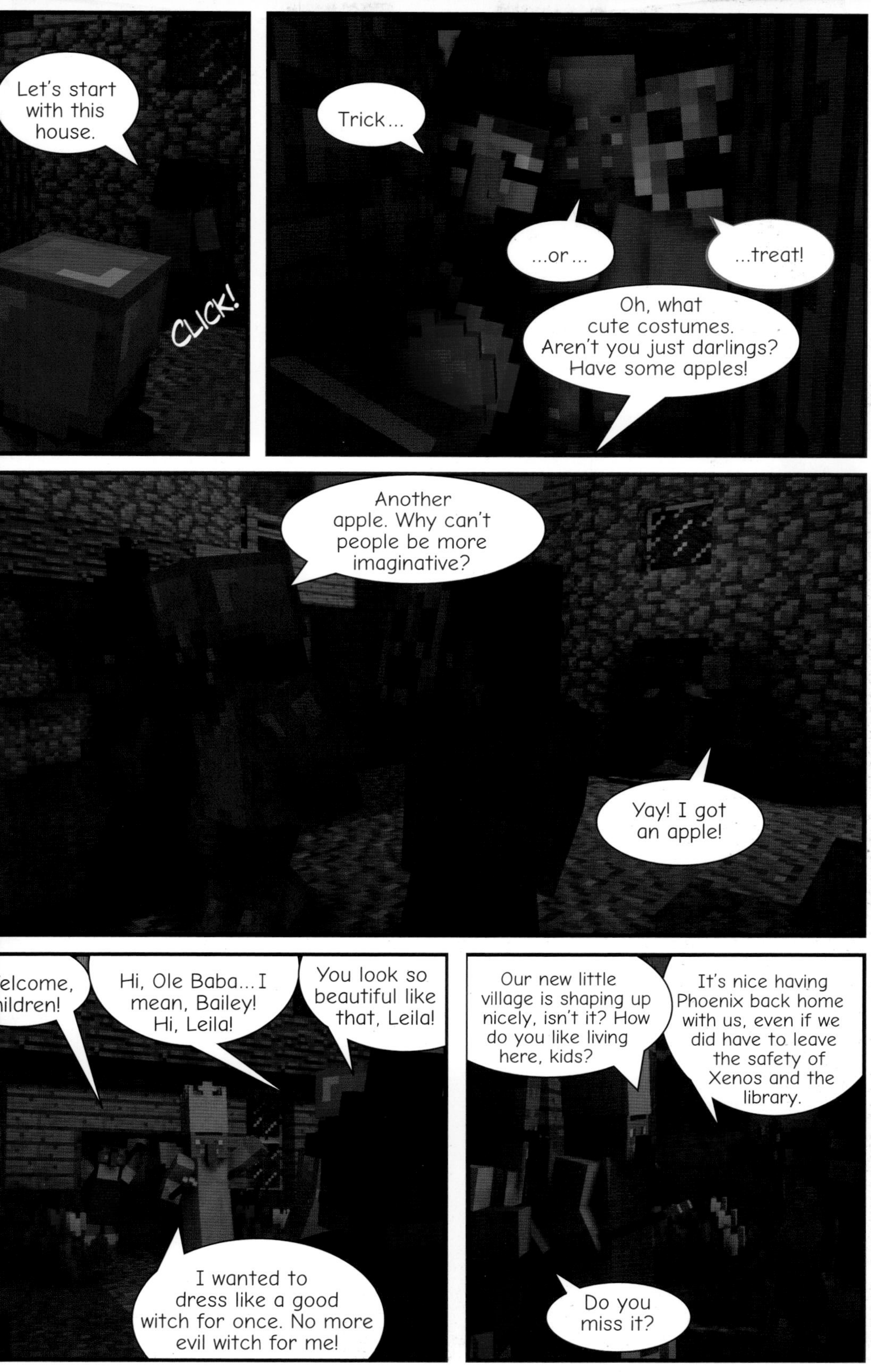
Let's start with this house.
CLICK!
Trick...
...or...
...treat!
Oh, what cute costumes. Aren't you just darlings? Have some apples!
Another apple. Why can't people be more imaginative?
Yay! I got an apple!
elcome, hildren!
Hi, Ole Baba... I mean, Bailey! Hi, Leila!
You look so beautiful like that, Leila!
I wanted to dress like a good witch for once. No more evil witch for me!
Our new little village is shaping up nicely, isn't it? How do you like living here, kids?
It's nice having Phoenix back home with us, even if we did have to leave the safety of Xenos and the library.
Do you miss it?

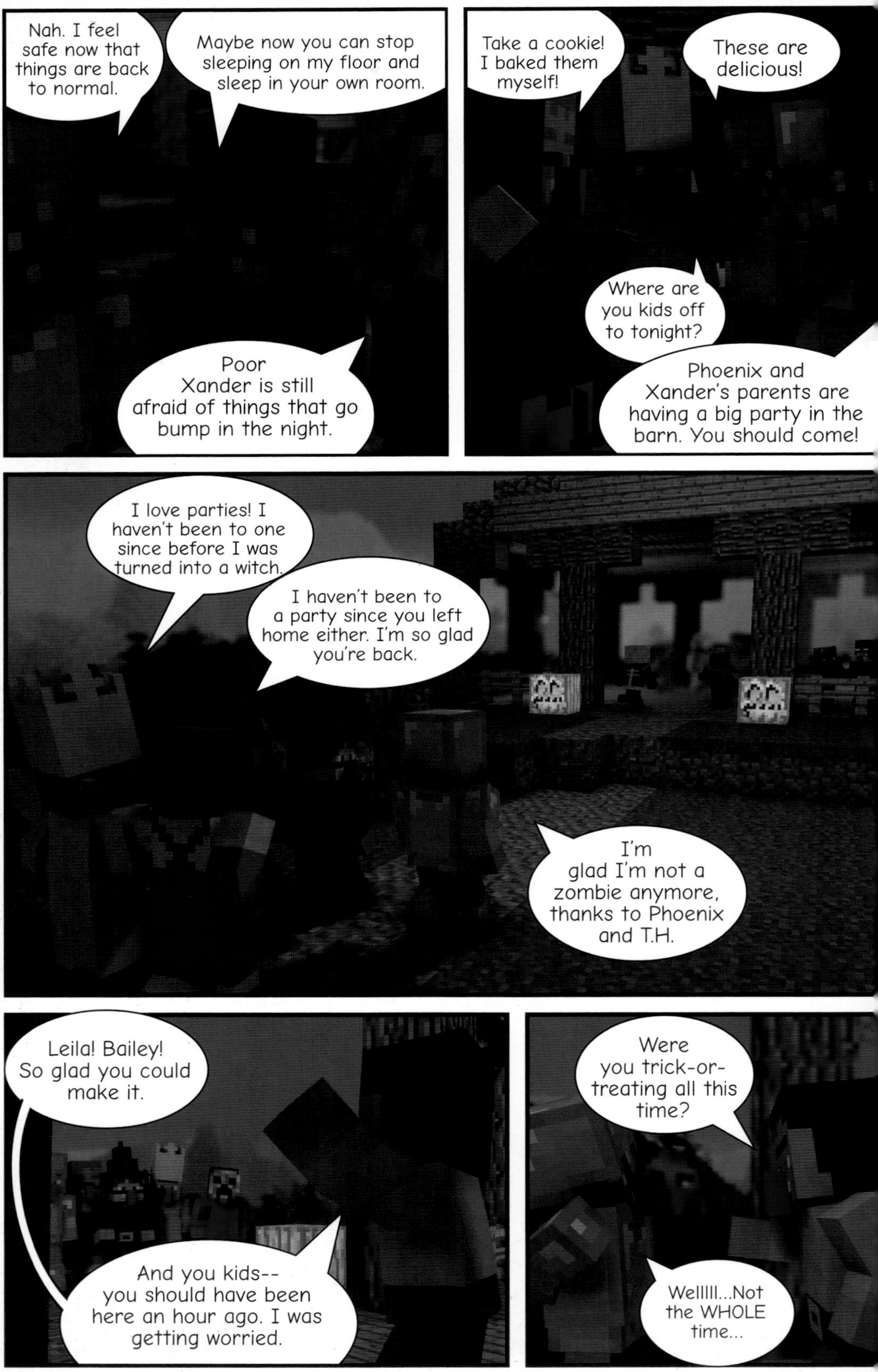
Nah. I feel safe now that things are back to normal.
Maybe now you can stop sleeping on my floor and sleep in your own room.
Poor Xander is still afraid of things that go bump in the night.
Take a cookie! I baked them myself!
These are delicious!
Where are you kids off to tonight?
Phoenix and Xander's parents are having a big party in the barn. You should come!
I love parties! I haven't been to one since before I was turned into a witch.
I haven't been to a party since you left home either. I'm so glad you're back.
I'm glad I'm not a zombie anymore, thanks to Phoenix and T.H.
Leila! Bailey! So glad you could make it.
And you kids--you should have been here an hour ago. I was getting worried.
Were you trick-or-treating all this time?
Wellllll...Not the WHOLE time...

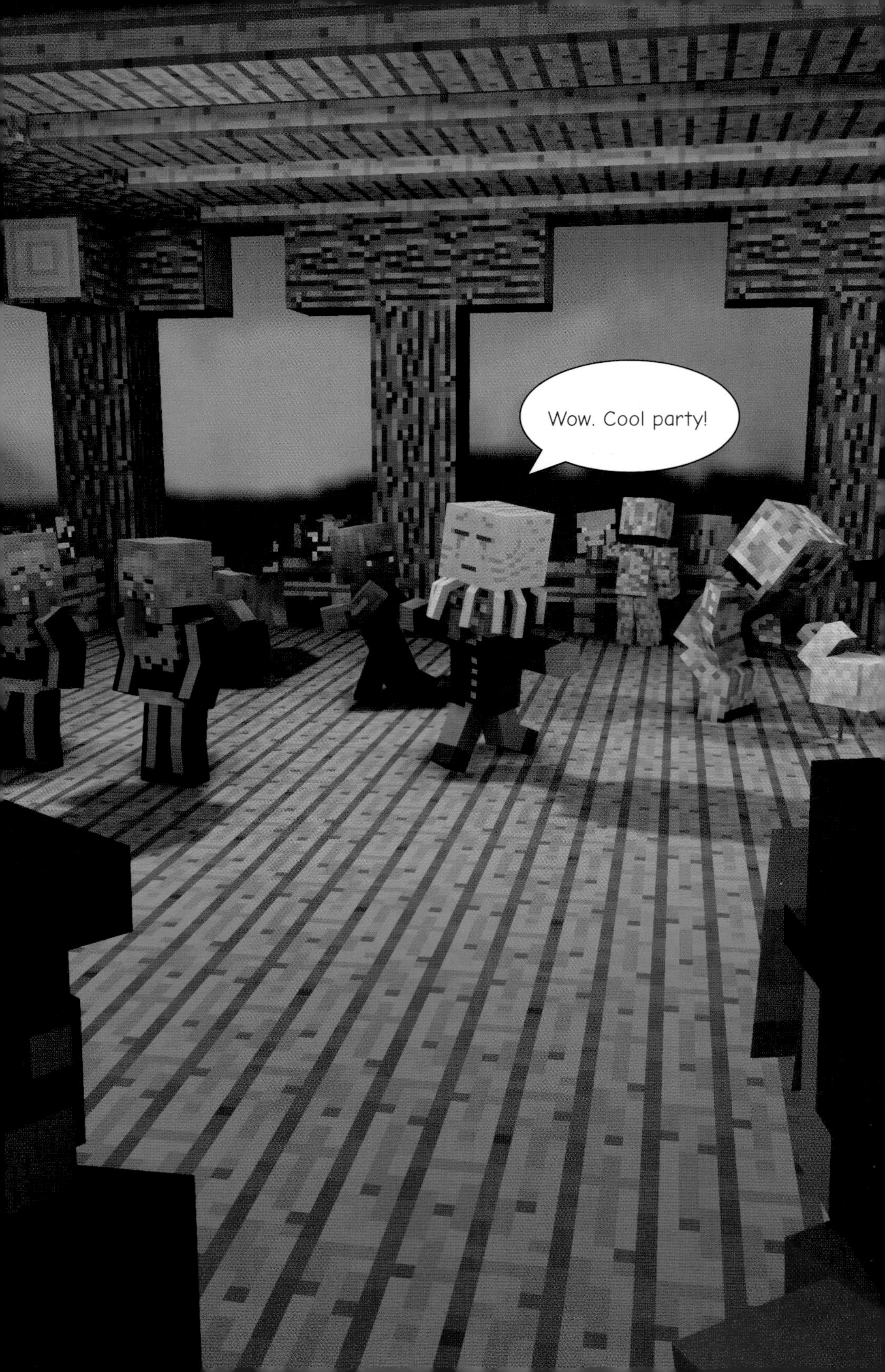
Wow. Cool party!

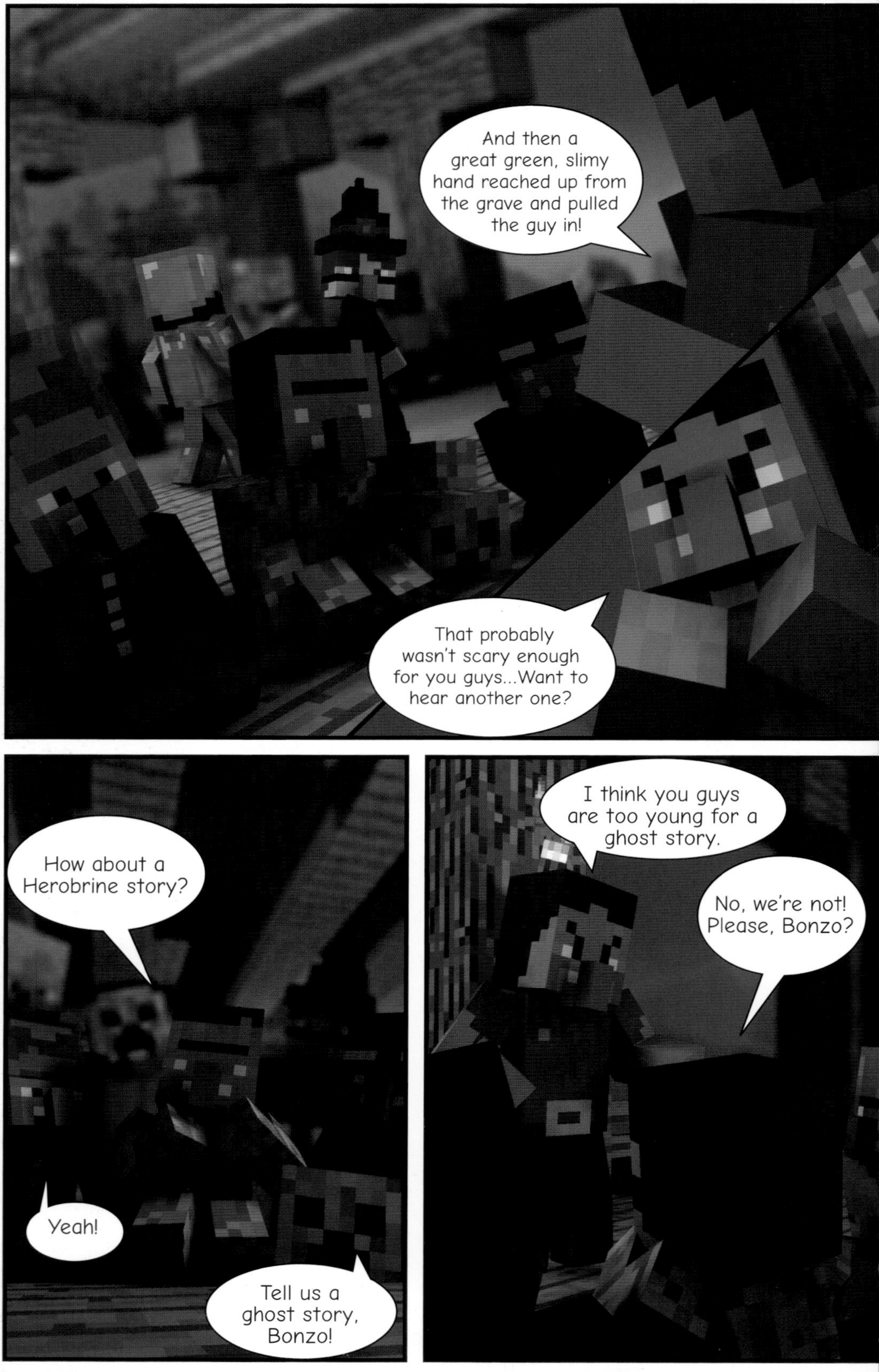
And then a great green, slimy hand reached up from the grave and pulled the guy in!
That probably wasn't scary enough for you guys...Want to hear another one?
How about a Herobrine story?
Yeah!
Tell us a ghost story, Bonzo!
I think you guys are too young for a ghost story.
No, we're not! Please, Bonzo?

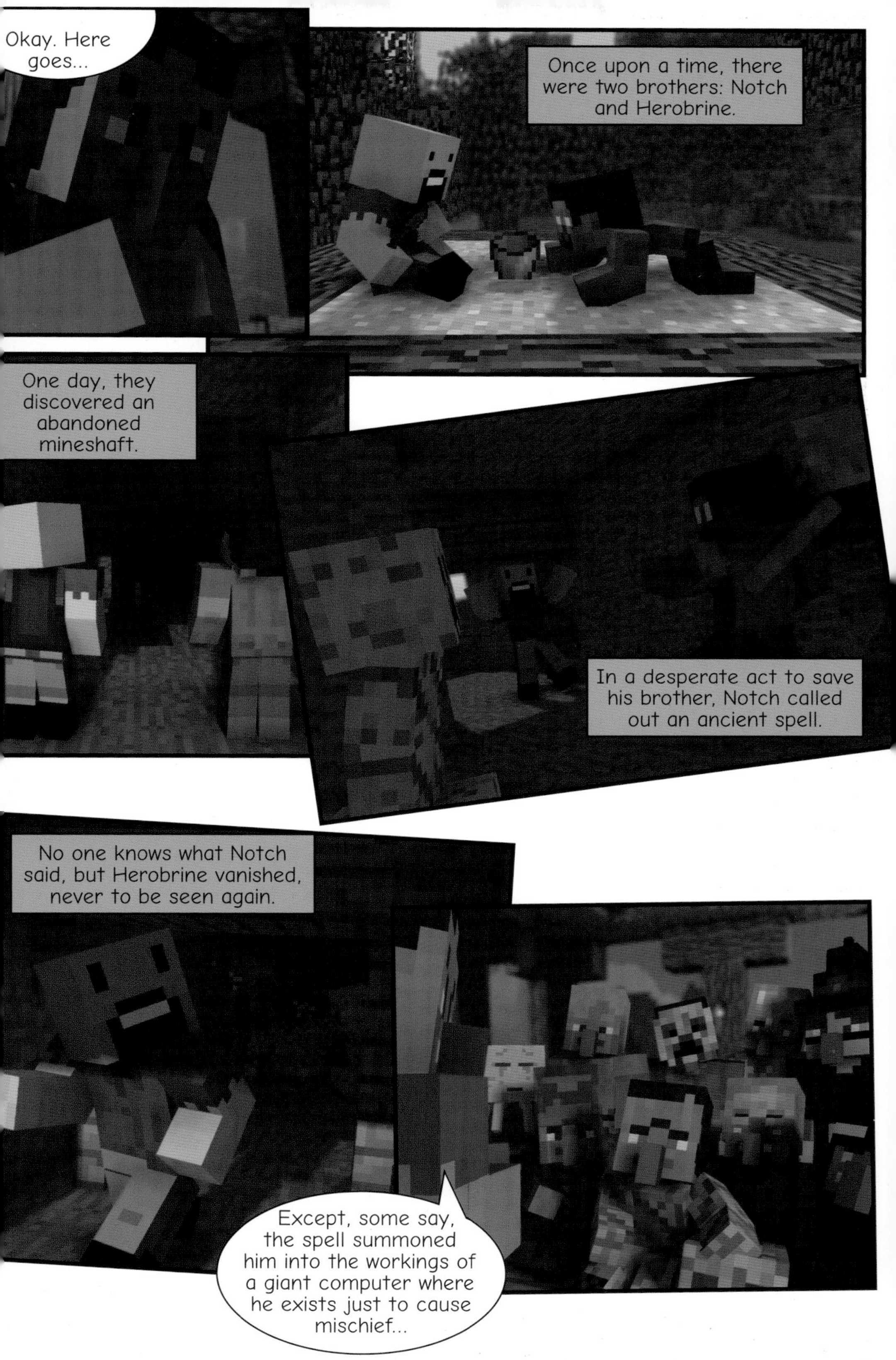
Okay. Here goes...
Once upon a time, there were two brothers: Notch and Herobrine.
One day, they discovered an abandoned mineshaft.
In a desperate act to save his brother, Notch called out an ancient spell.
No one knows what Notch said, but Herobrine vanished, never to be seen again.
Except, some say, the spell summoned him into the workings of a giant computer where he exists just to cause mischief...

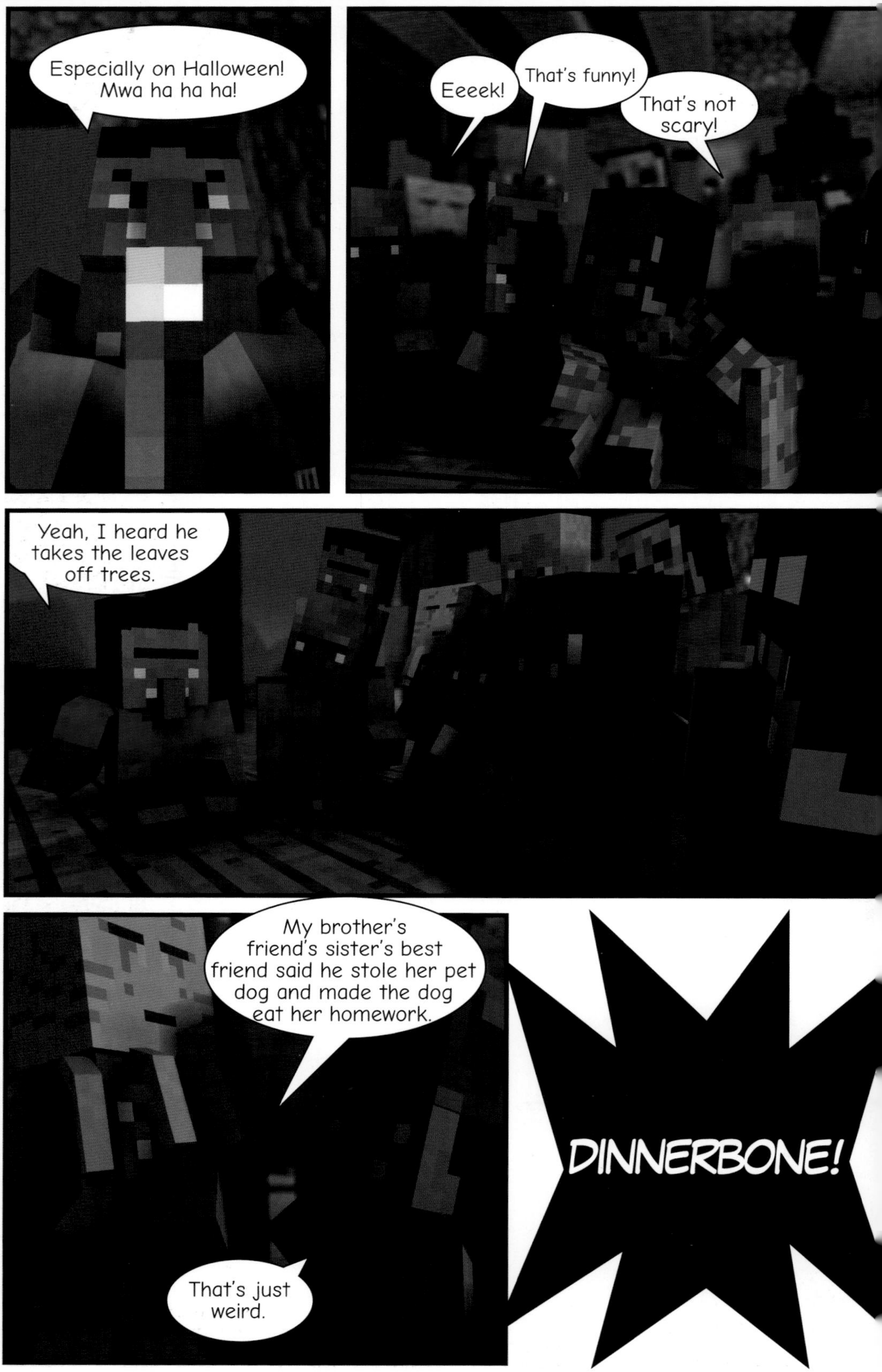

Especially on Halloween! Mwa ha ha ha!
Eeeek!
That's funny!
That's not scary!
Yeah, I heard he takes the leaves off trees.
My brother's friend's sister's best friend said he stole her pet dog and made the dog eat her homework.
That's just weird.
DINNERBONE!

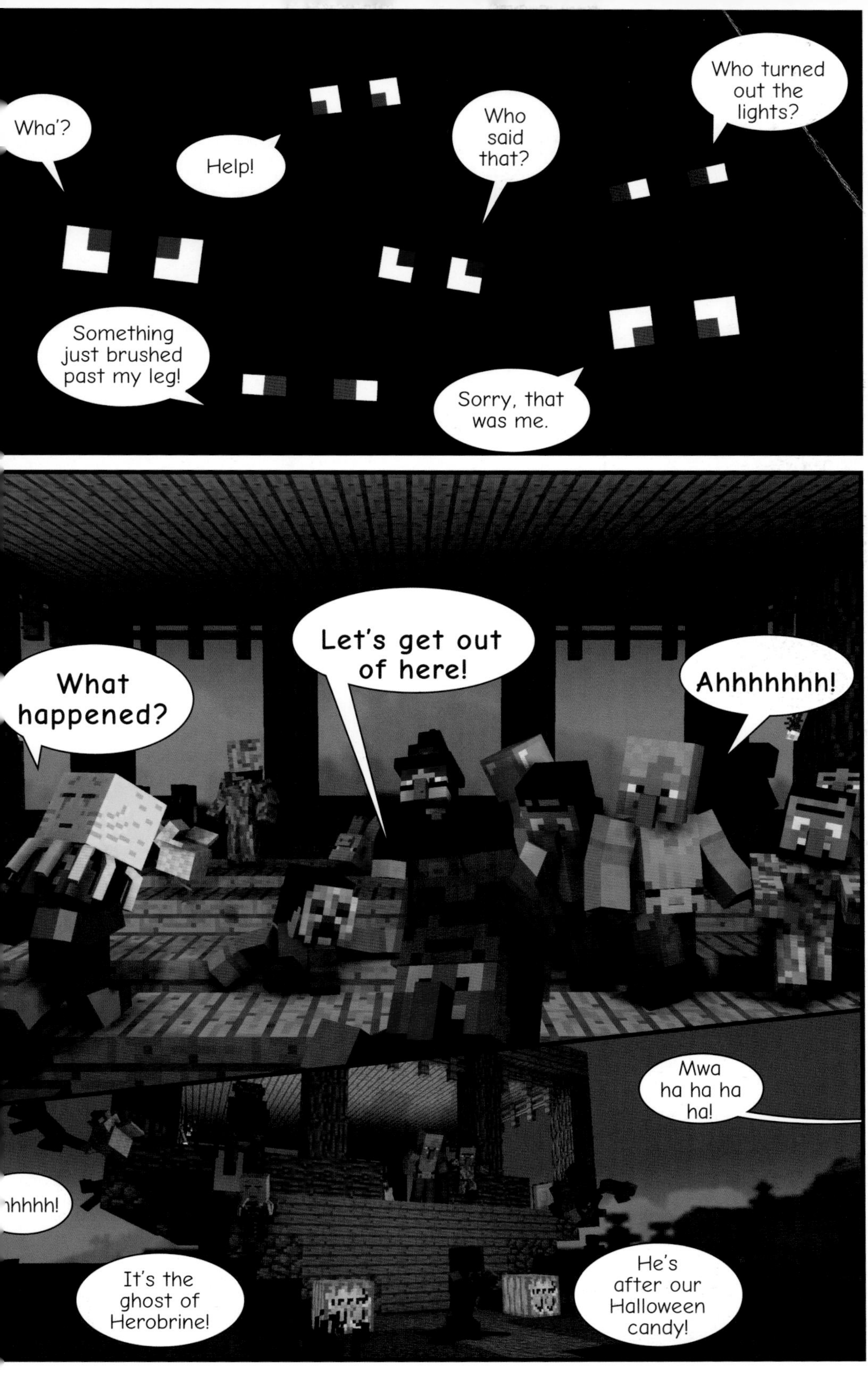
Wha'?
Help!
Who said that?
Who turned out the lights?
Something just brushed past my leg!
Sorry, that was me.
What happened?
Let's get out of here!
Ahhhhhhh!
Mwa ha ha ha ha!
hhhh!
It's the ghost of Herobrine!
He's after our Halloween candy!

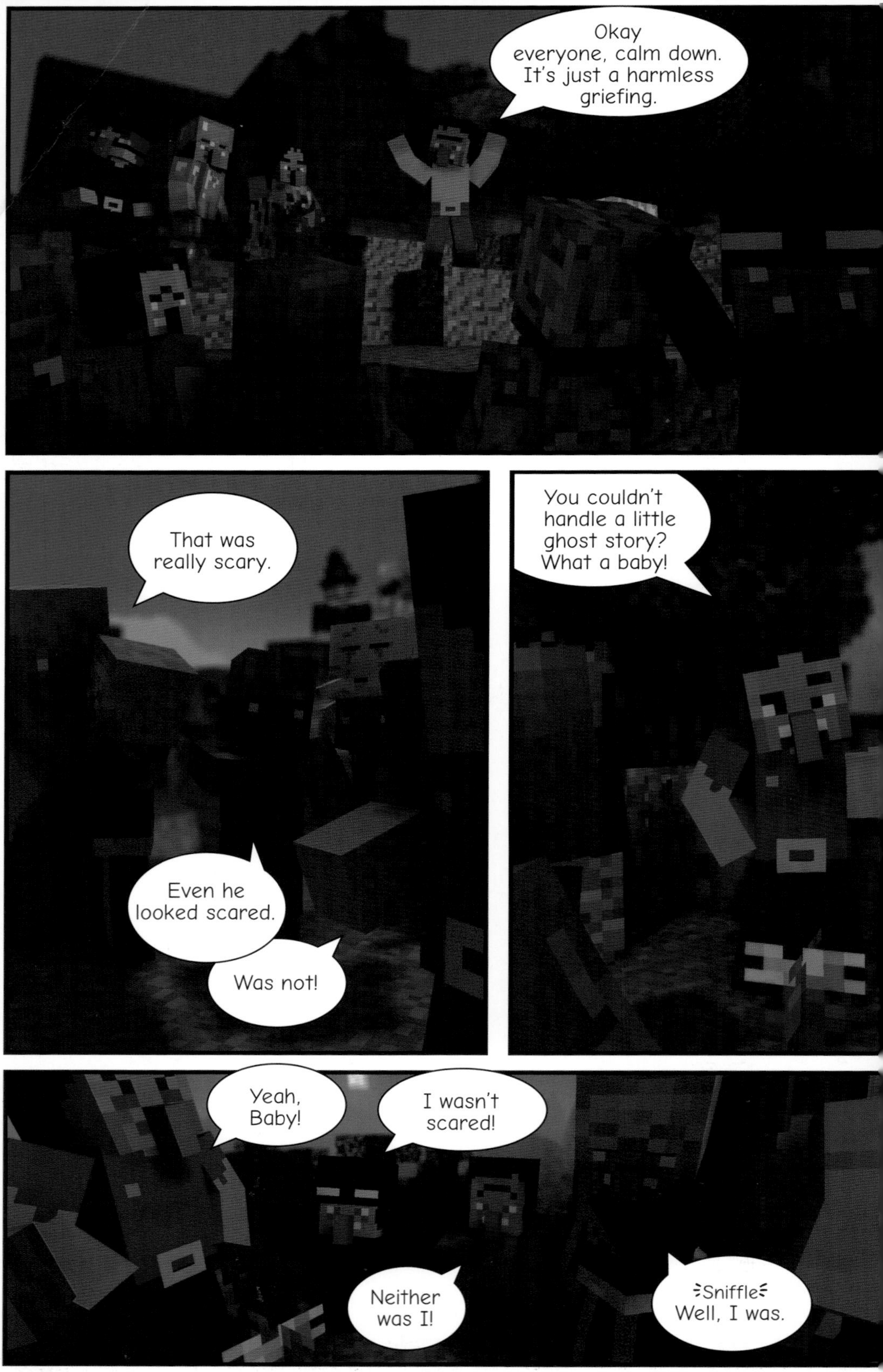
Okay everyone, calm down. It's just a harmless griefing.
That was really scary.
Even he looked scared.
Was not!
You couldn't handle a little ghost story? What a baby!
Yeah, Baby!
I wasn't scared!
Neither was I!
Sniffle
Well, I was.

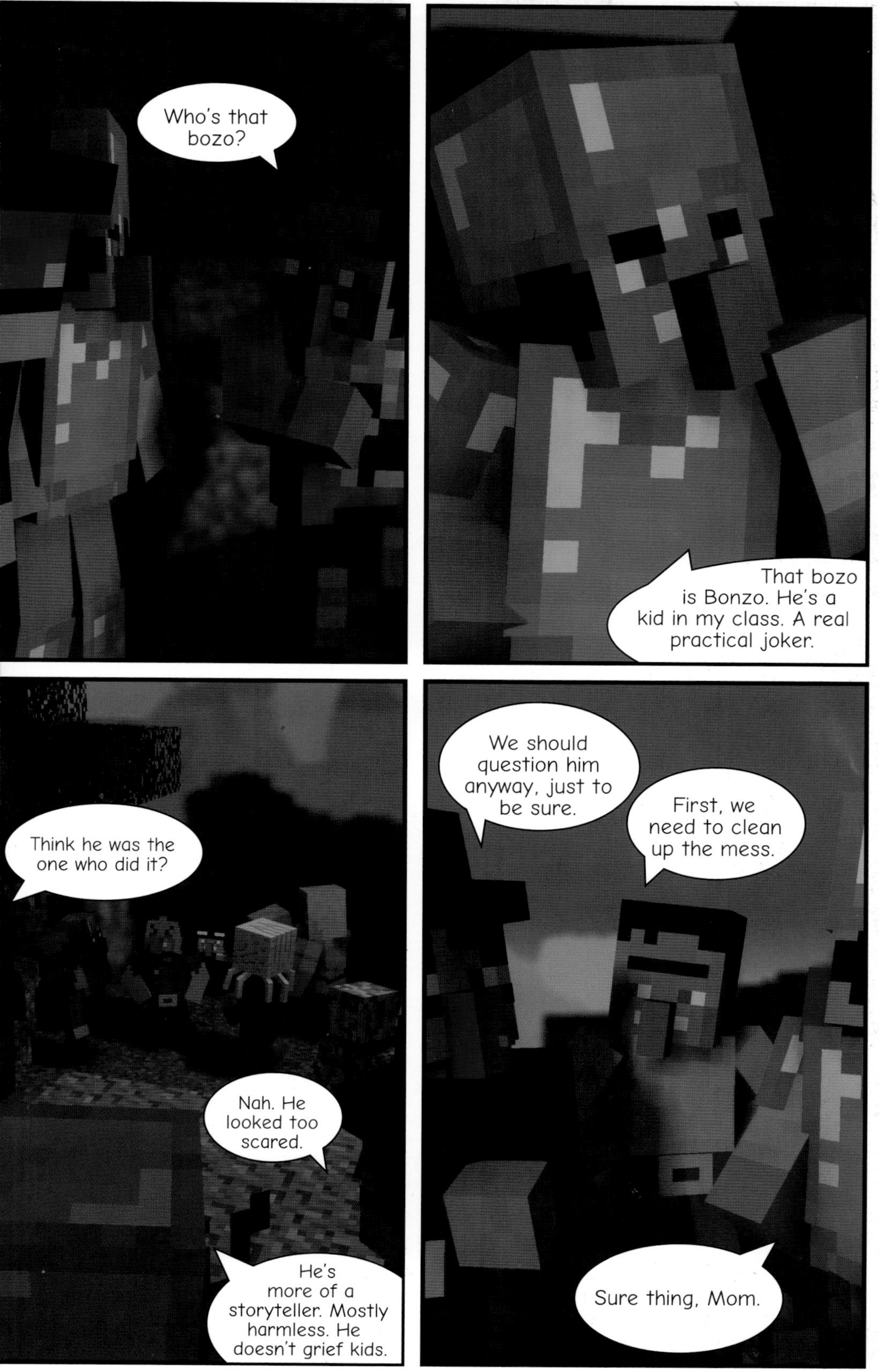
Who's that bozo?
That bozo is Bonzo. He's a kid in my class. A real practical joker.
Think he was the one who did it?
Nah. He looked too scared.
He's more of a storyteller. Mostly harmless. He doesn't grief kids.
We should question him anyway, just to be sure.
First, we need to clean up the mess.
Sure thing, Mom.

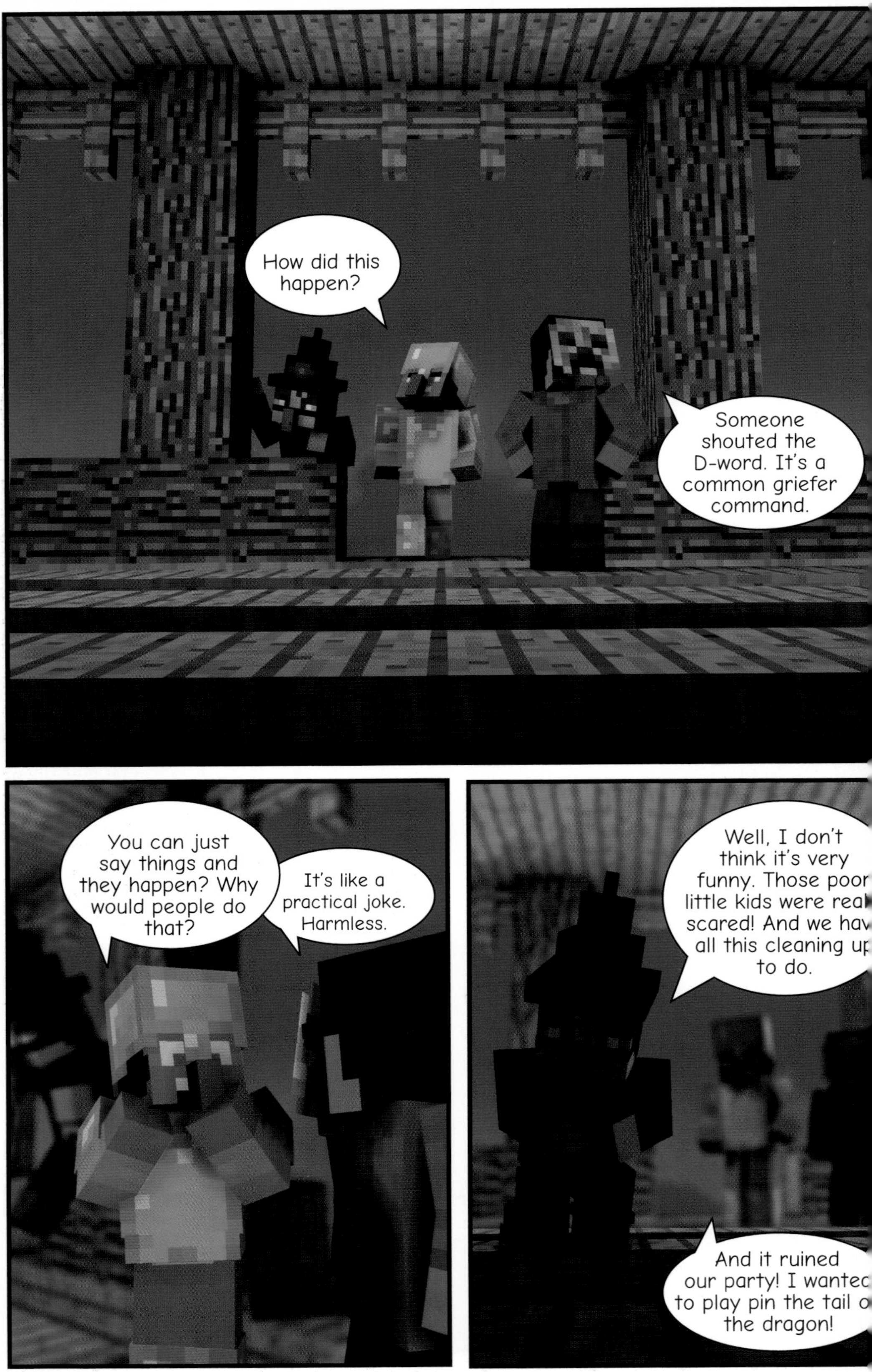
How did this happen?
Someone shouted the D-word. It's a common griefer command.
You can just say things and they happen? Why would people do that?
It's like a practical joke. Harmless.
Well, I don't think it's very funny. Those poor little kids were rea scared! And we hav all this cleaning u to do.
And it ruined our party! I wante to play pin the tail o the dragon!

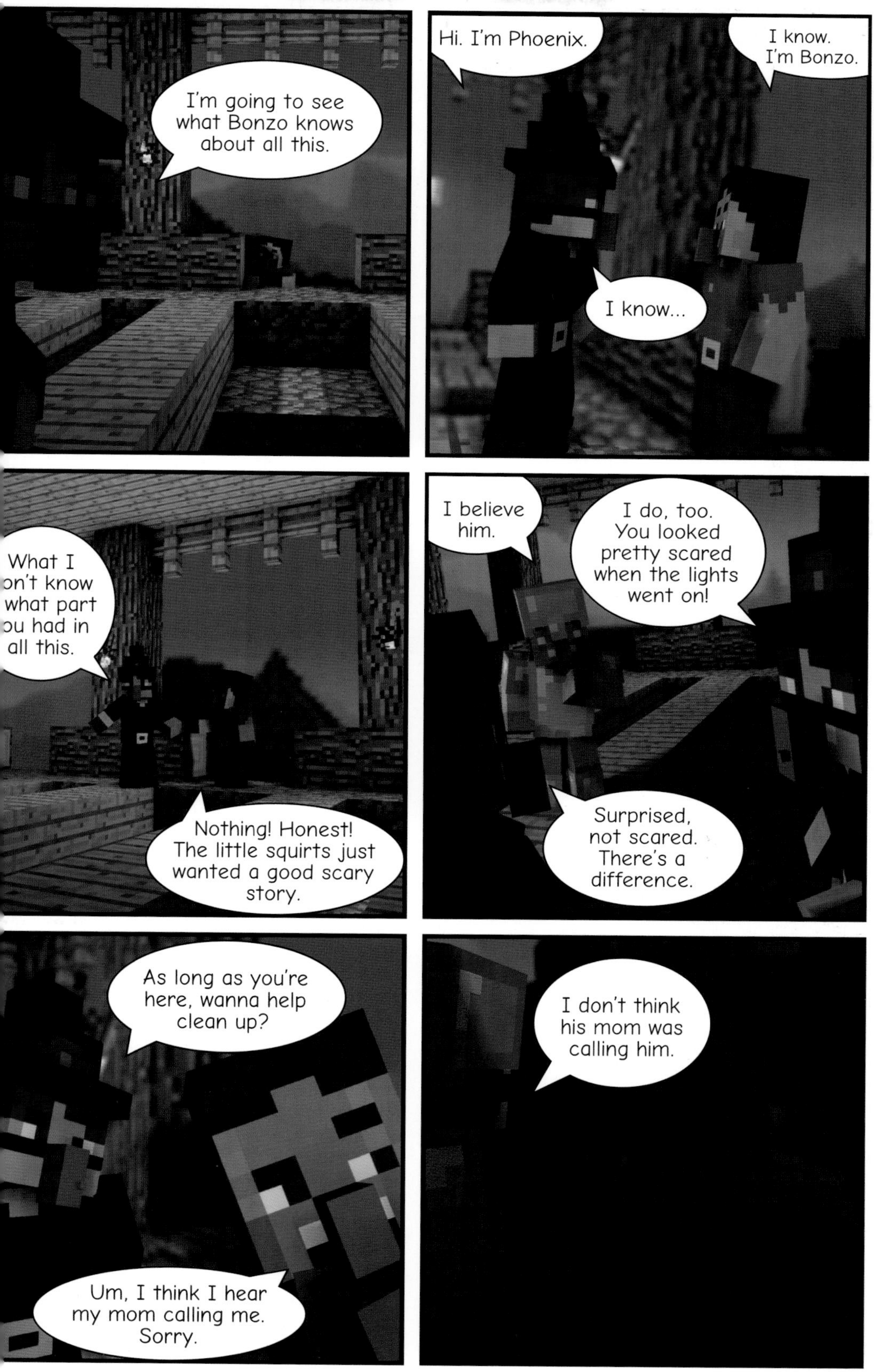
I'm going to see what Bonzo knows about all this.
Hi. I'm Phoenix.
I know. I'm Bonzo.
I know...
What I on't know what part ou had in all this.
Nothing! Honest! The little squirts just wanted a good scary story.
I believe him.
I do, too. You looked pretty scared when the lights went on!
Surprised, not scared. There's a difference.
As long as you're here, wanna help clean up?
Um, I think I hear my mom calling me. Sorry.
I don't think his mom was calling him.

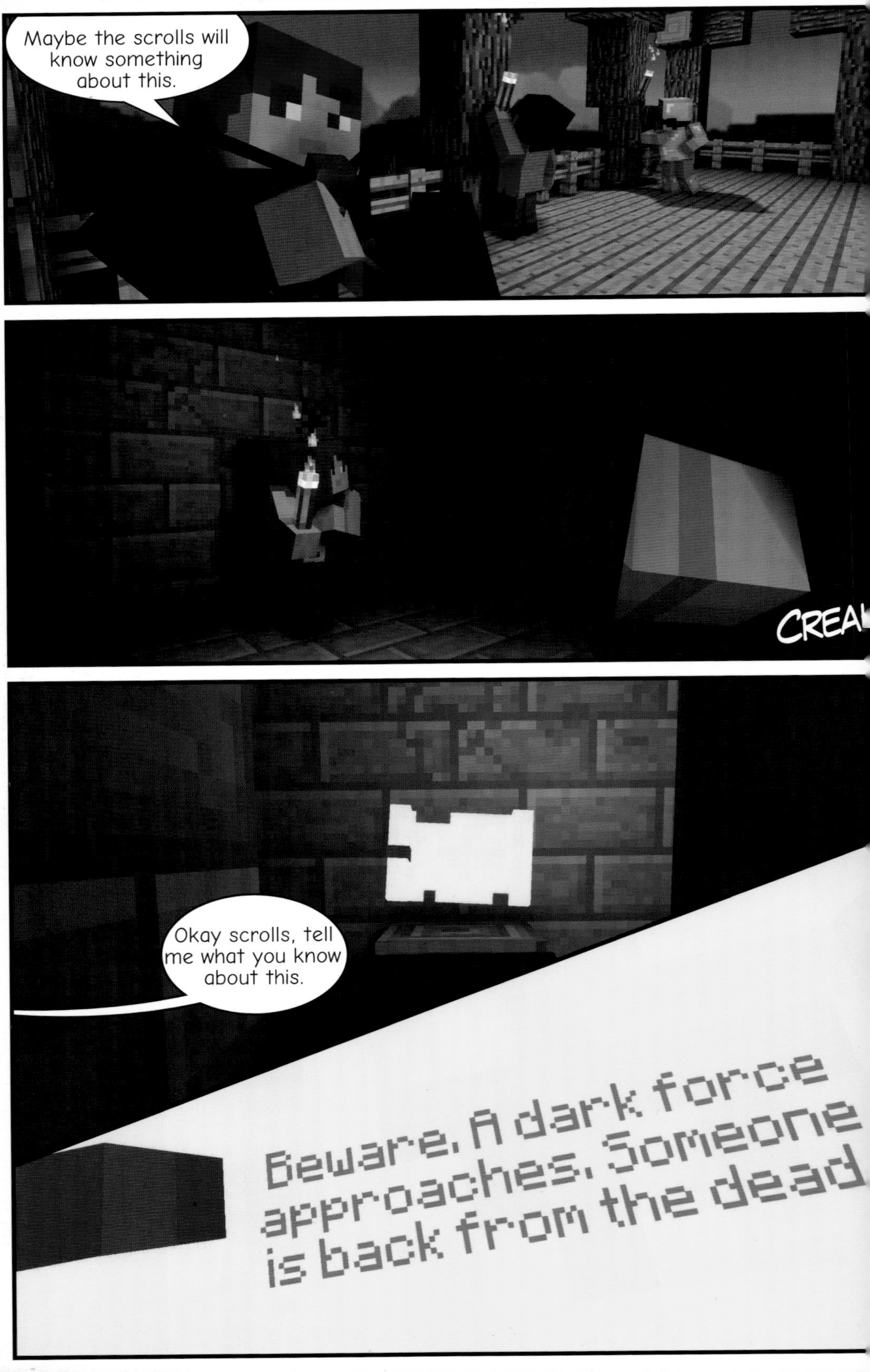

Maybe the scrolls will know something about this.
CREA
Okay scrolls, tell me what you know about this.
Beware. A dark force approaches. Someone is back from the dead

CHAPTER 2

THE MARK OF HEROBRINE

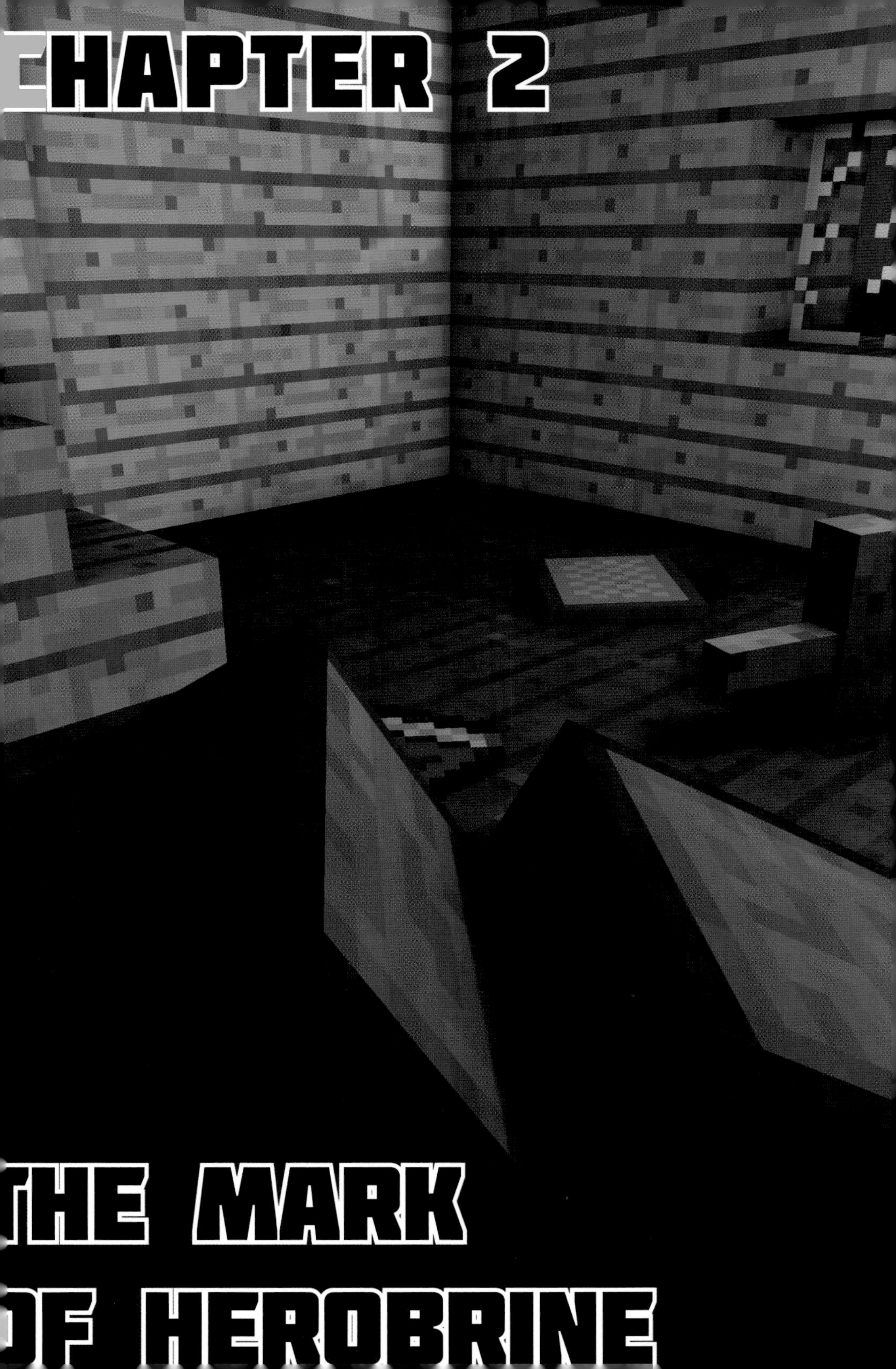

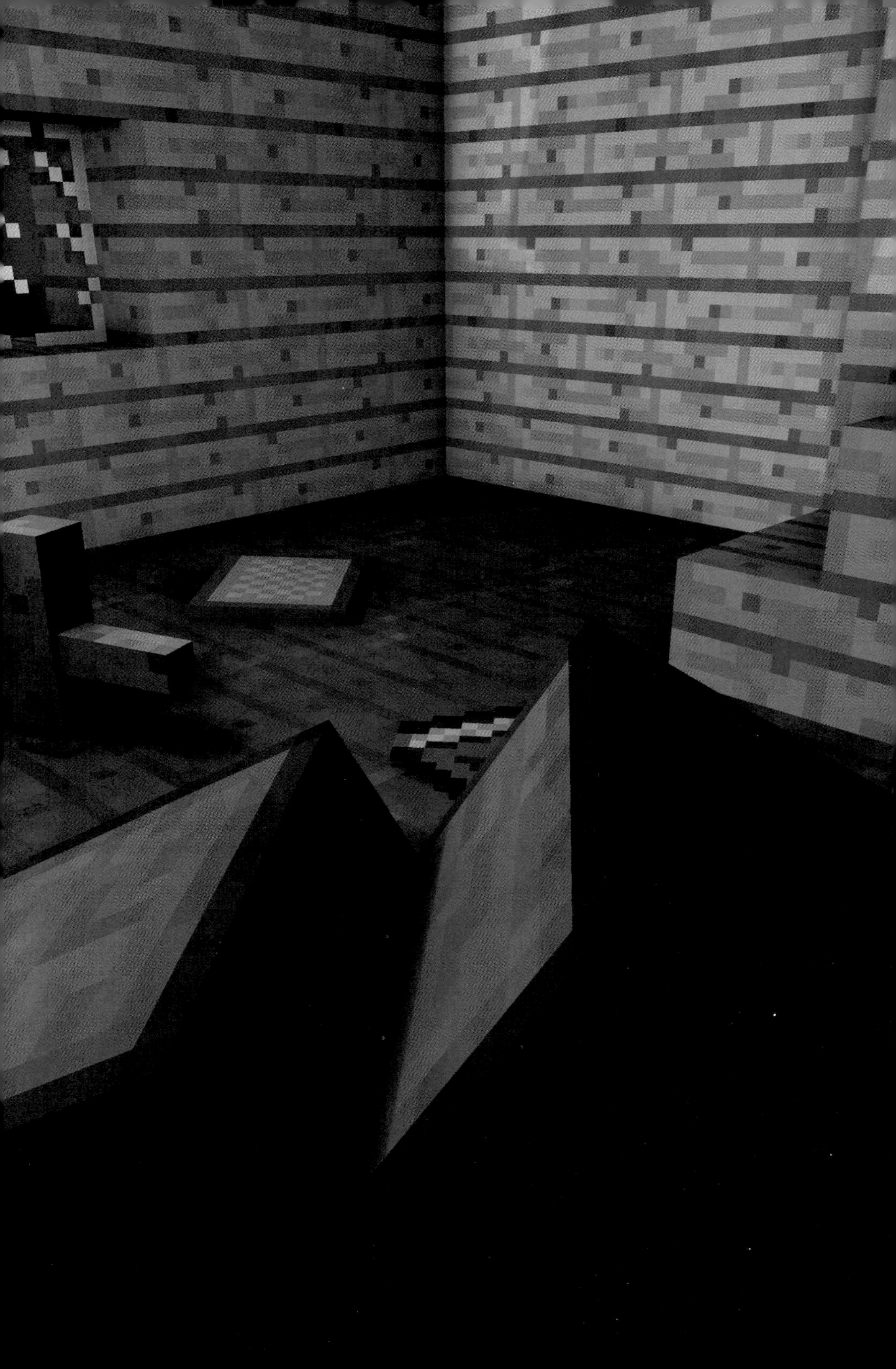

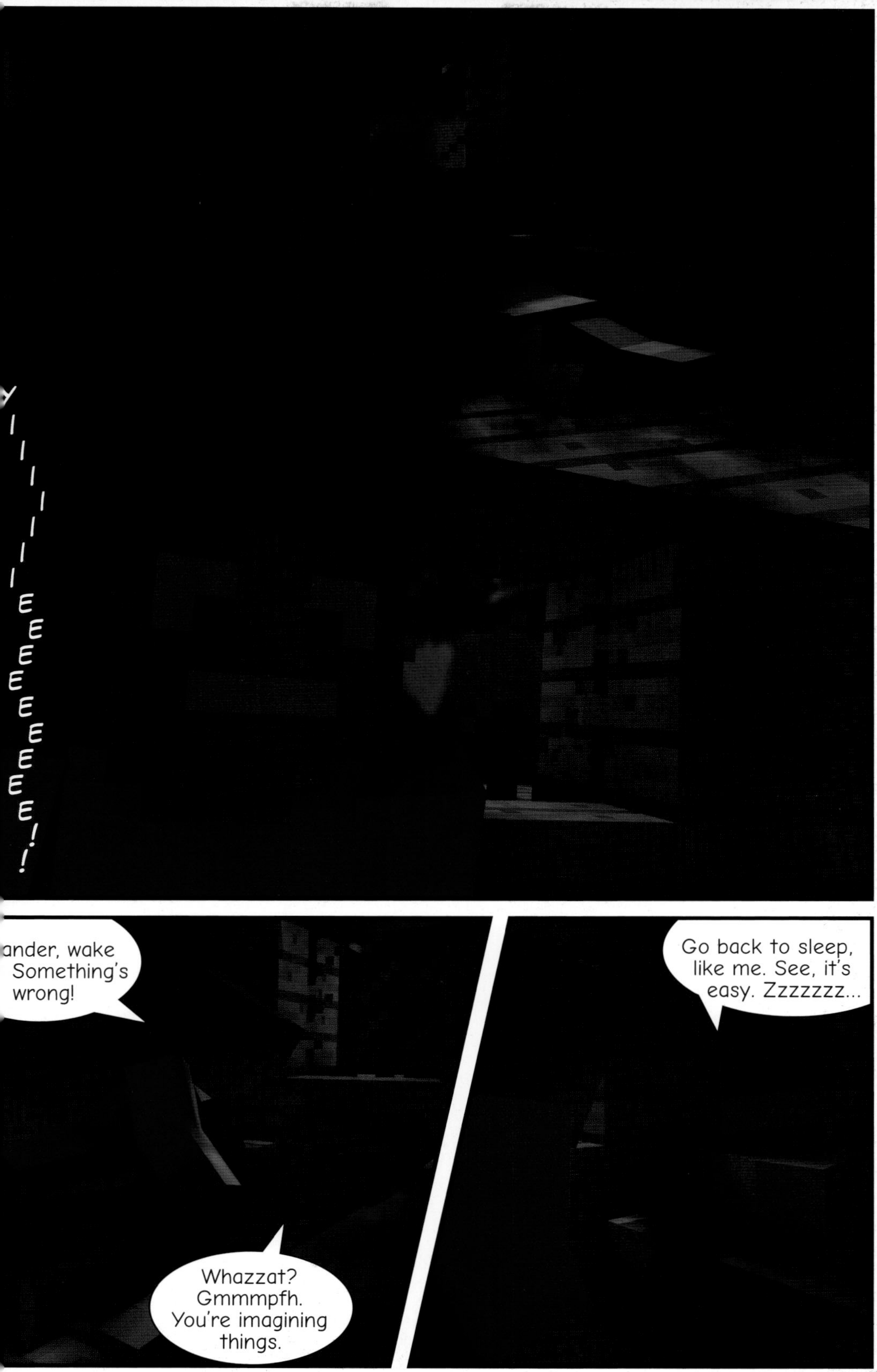
YIIIIIIIEEEEEEEEE!!
ander, wake Something's wrong!
Whazzat? Gmmmpfh. You're imagining things.
Go back to sleep, like me. See, it's easy. Zzzzzzz...

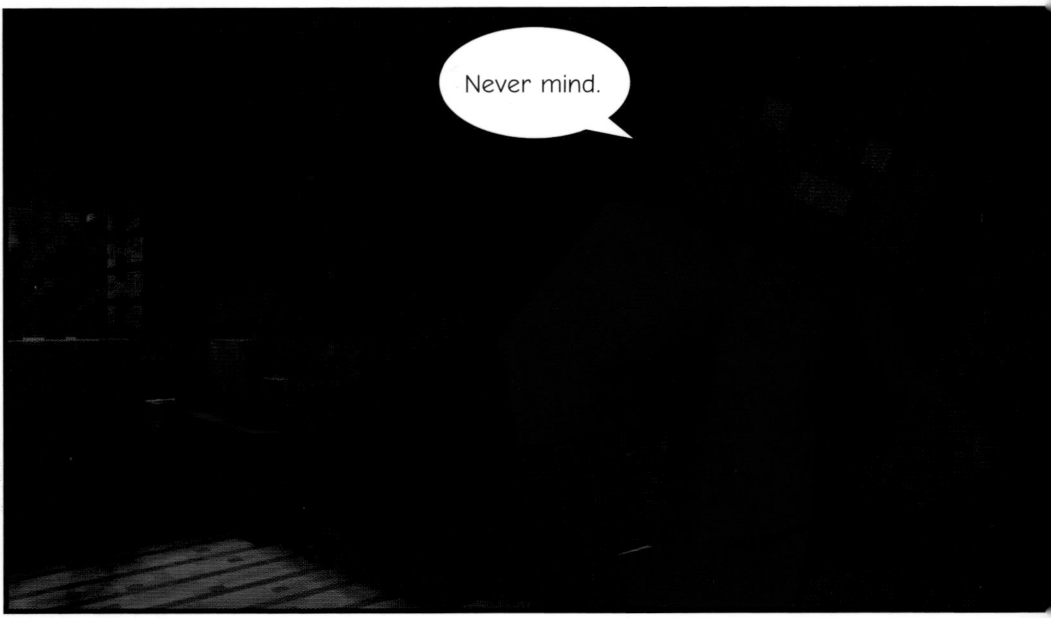
Never mind.

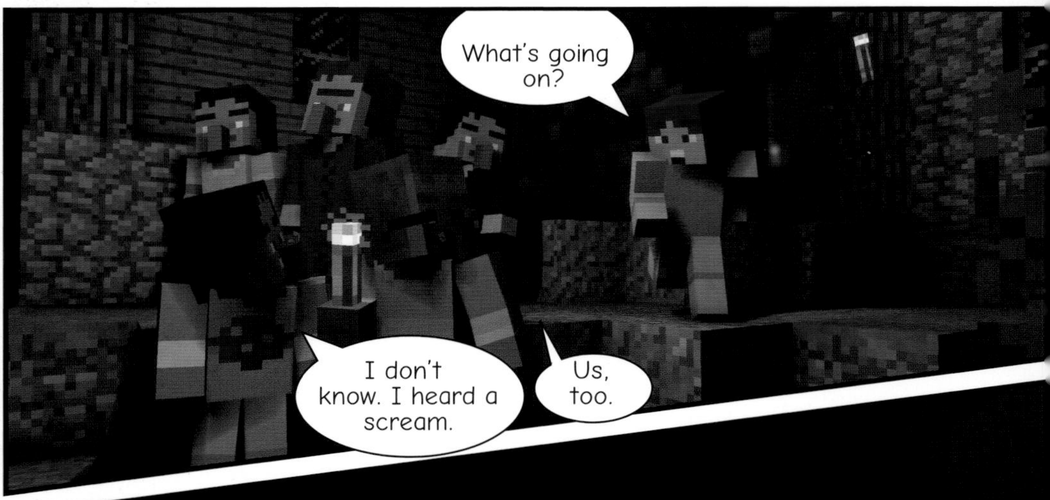
What's going on?
I don't know. I heard a scream.
Us, too.

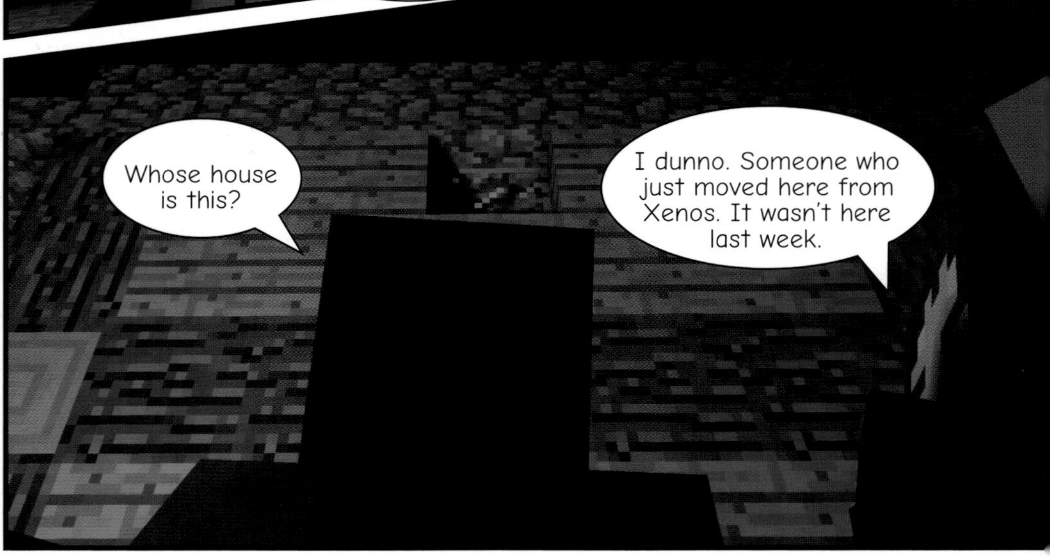
Whose house is this?
I dunno. Someone who just moved here from Xenos. It wasn't here last week.

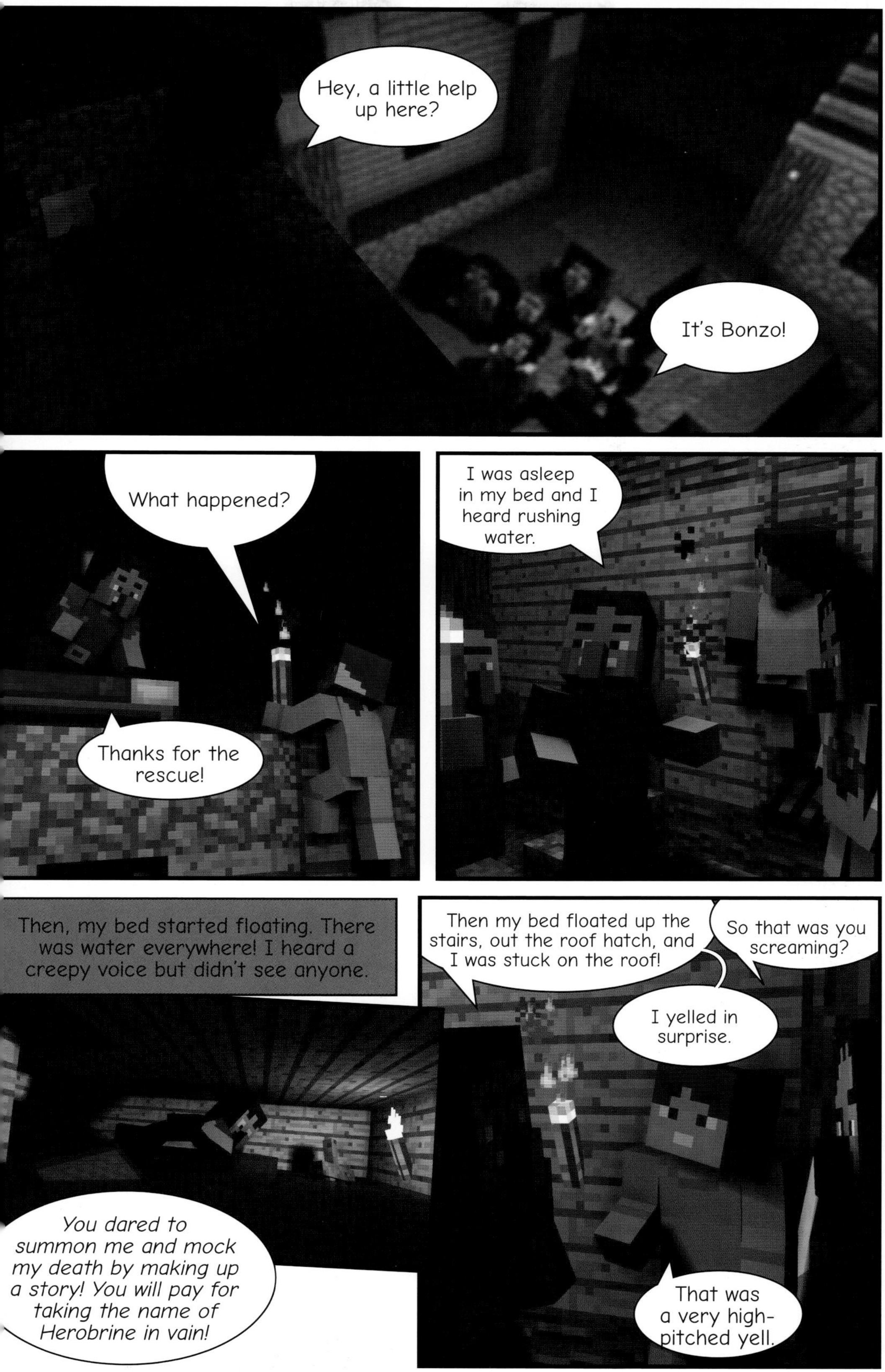
Hey, a little help up here?
It's Bonzo!
What happened?
Thanks for the rescue!
I was asleep in my bed and I heard rushing water.
Then, my bed started floating. There was water everywhere! I heard a creepy voice but didn't see anyone.
You dared to summon me and mock my death by making up a story! You will pay for taking the name of Herobrine in vain!
Then my bed floated up the stairs, out the roof hatch, and I was stuck on the roof!
So that was you screaming?
I yelled in surprise.
That was a very high-pitched yell.

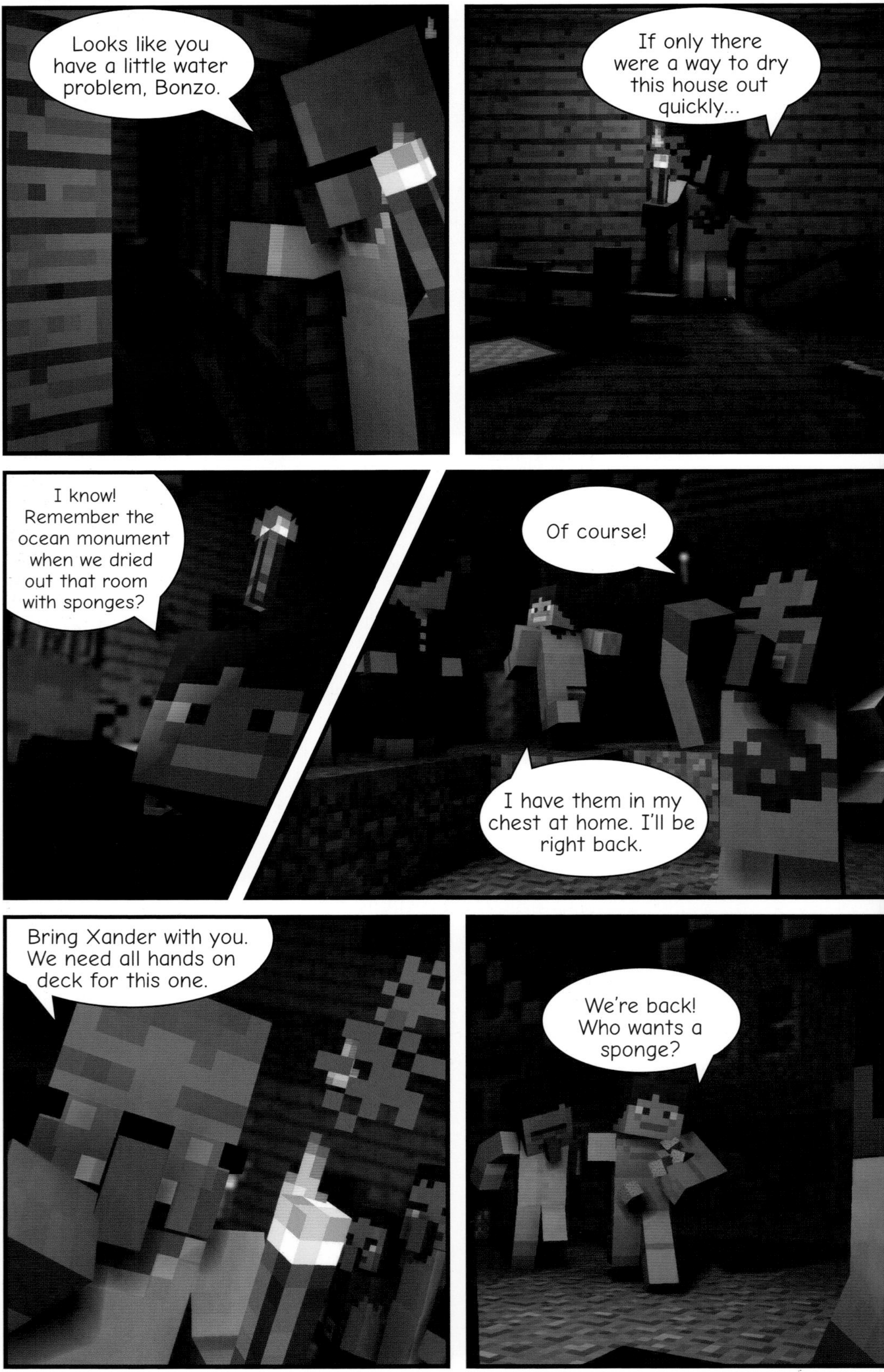
Looks like you have a little water problem, Bonzo.
If only there were a way to dry this house out quickly...
I know! Remember the ocean monument when we dried out that room with sponges?
Of course!
I have them in my chest at home. I'll be right back.
Bring Xander with you. We need all hands on deck for this one.
We're back! Who wants a sponge?

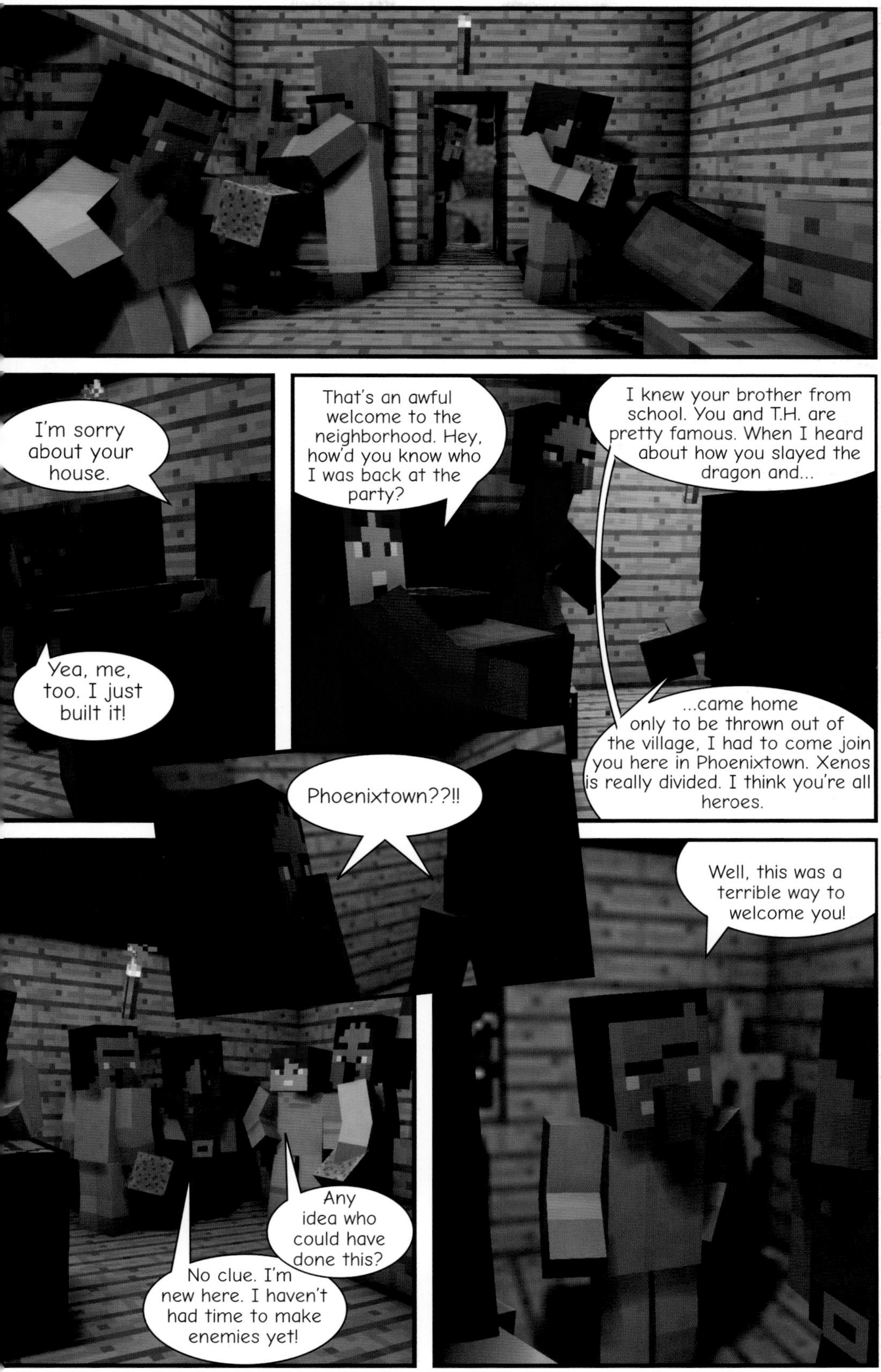
I'm sorry about your house.
Yea, me, too. I just built it!
That's an awful welcome to the neighborhood. Hey, how'd you know who I was back at the party?
I knew your brother from school. You and T.H. are pretty famous. When I heard about how you slayed the dragon and...
...came home only to be thrown out of the village, I had to come join you here in Phoenixtown. Xenos is really divided. I think you're all heroes.
Phoenixtown??!!
Well, this was a terrible way to welcome you!
Any idea who could have done this?
No clue. I'm new here. I haven't had time to make enemies yet!

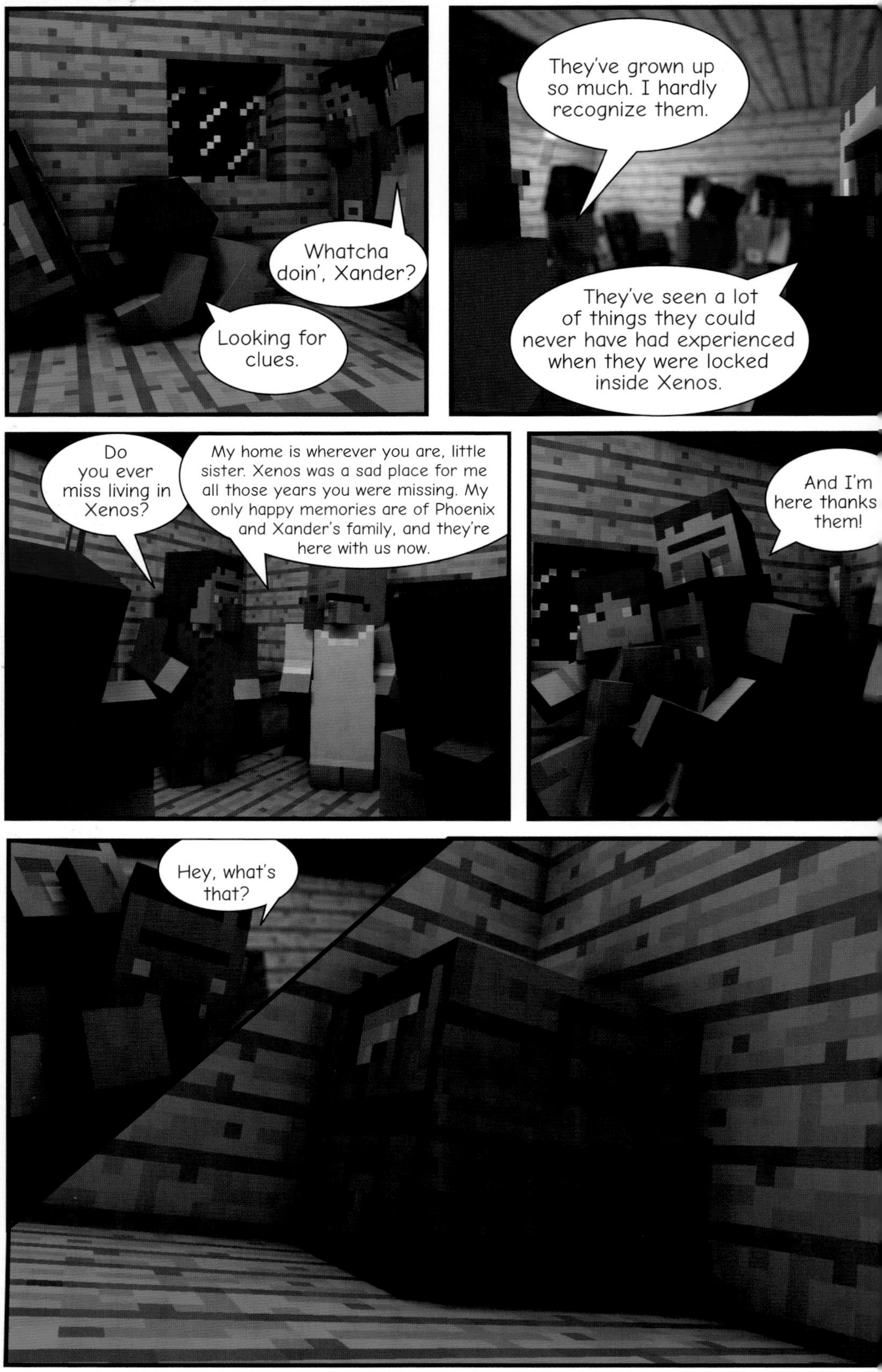
Whatcha doin', Xander?
Looking for clues.
They've grown up so much. I hardly recognize them.
They've seen a lot of things they could never have had experienced when they were locked inside Xenos.
Do you ever miss living in Xenos?
My home is wherever you are, little sister. Xenos was a sad place for me all those years you were missing. My only happy memories are of Phoenix and Xander's family, and they're here with us now.
And I'm here thanks them!
Hey, what's that?

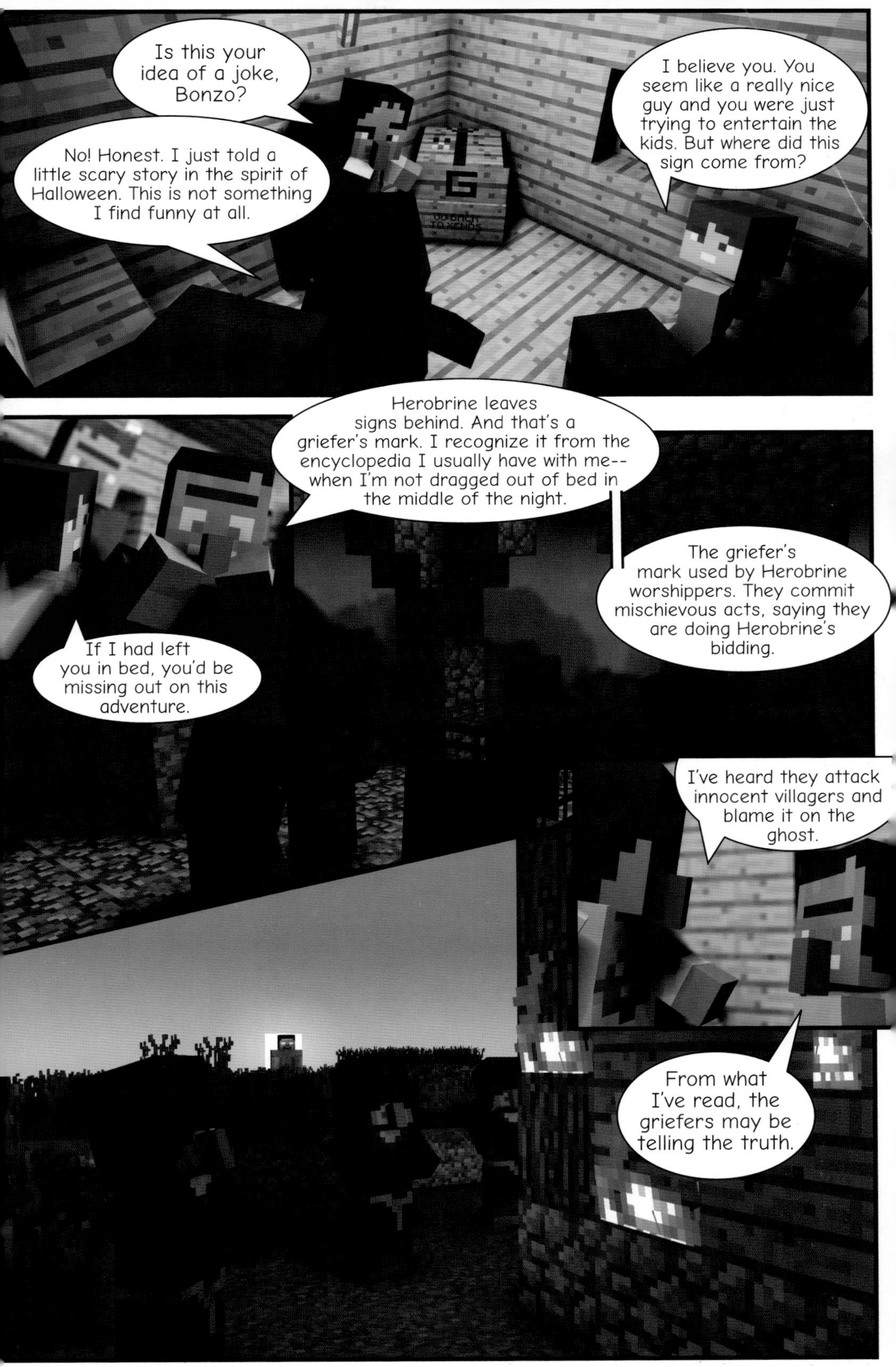

Is this your idea of a joke, Bonzo?
No! Honest. I just told a little scary story in the spirit of Halloween. This is not something I find funny at all.
I believe you. You seem like a really nice guy and you were just trying to entertain the kids. But where did this sign come from?
Herobrine leaves signs behind. And that's a griefer's mark. I recognize it from the encyclopedia I usually have with me--when I'm not dragged out of bed in the middle of the night.
If I had left you in bed, you'd be missing out on this adventure.
The griefer's mark used by Herobrine worshippers. They commit mischievous acts, saying they are doing Herobrine's bidding.
I've heard they attack innocent villagers and blame it on the ghost.
From what I've read, the griefers may be telling the truth.

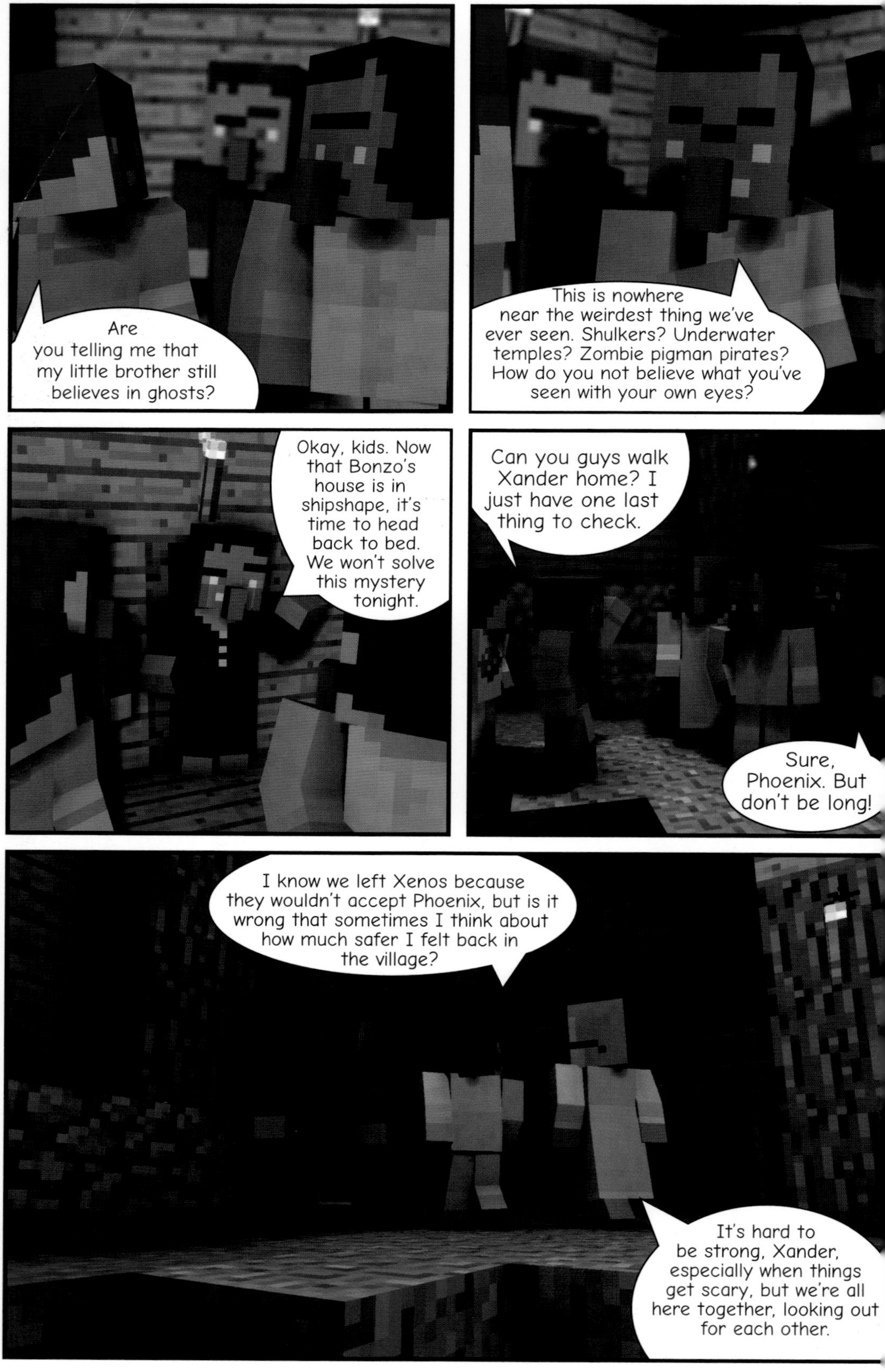
Are you telling me that my little brother still believes in ghosts?
This is nowhere near the weirdest thing we've ever seen. Shulkers? Underwater temples? Zombie pigman pirates? How do you not believe what you've seen with your own eyes?
Okay, kids. Now that Bonzo's house is in shipshape, it's time to head back to bed. We won't solve this mystery tonight.
Can you guys walk Xander home? I just have one last thing to check.
Sure, Phoenix. But don't be long!
I know we left Xenos because they wouldn't accept Phoenix, but is it wrong that sometimes I think about how much safer I felt back in the village?
It's hard to be strong, Xander, especially when things get scary, but we're all here together, looking out for each other.

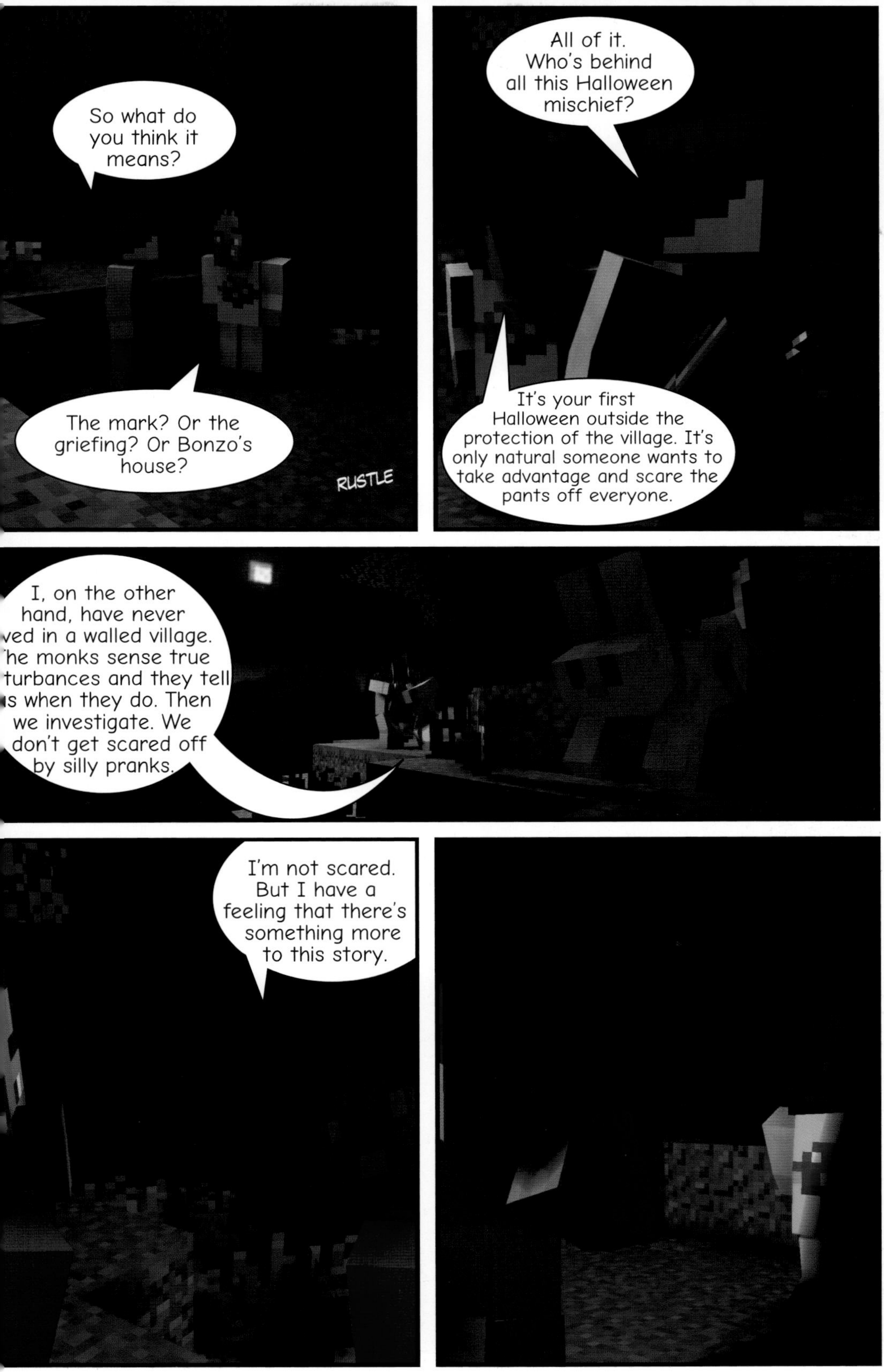
So what do you think it means?
The mark? Or the griefing? Or Bonzo's house?
RUSTLE
All of it. Who's behind all this Halloween mischief?
It's your first Halloween outside the protection of the village. It's only natural someone wants to take advantage and scare the pants off everyone.
I, on the other hand, have never ved in a walled village. he monks sense true turbances and they tell s when they do. Then we investigate. We don't get scared off by silly pranks.
I'm not scared. But I have a feeling that there's something more to this story.

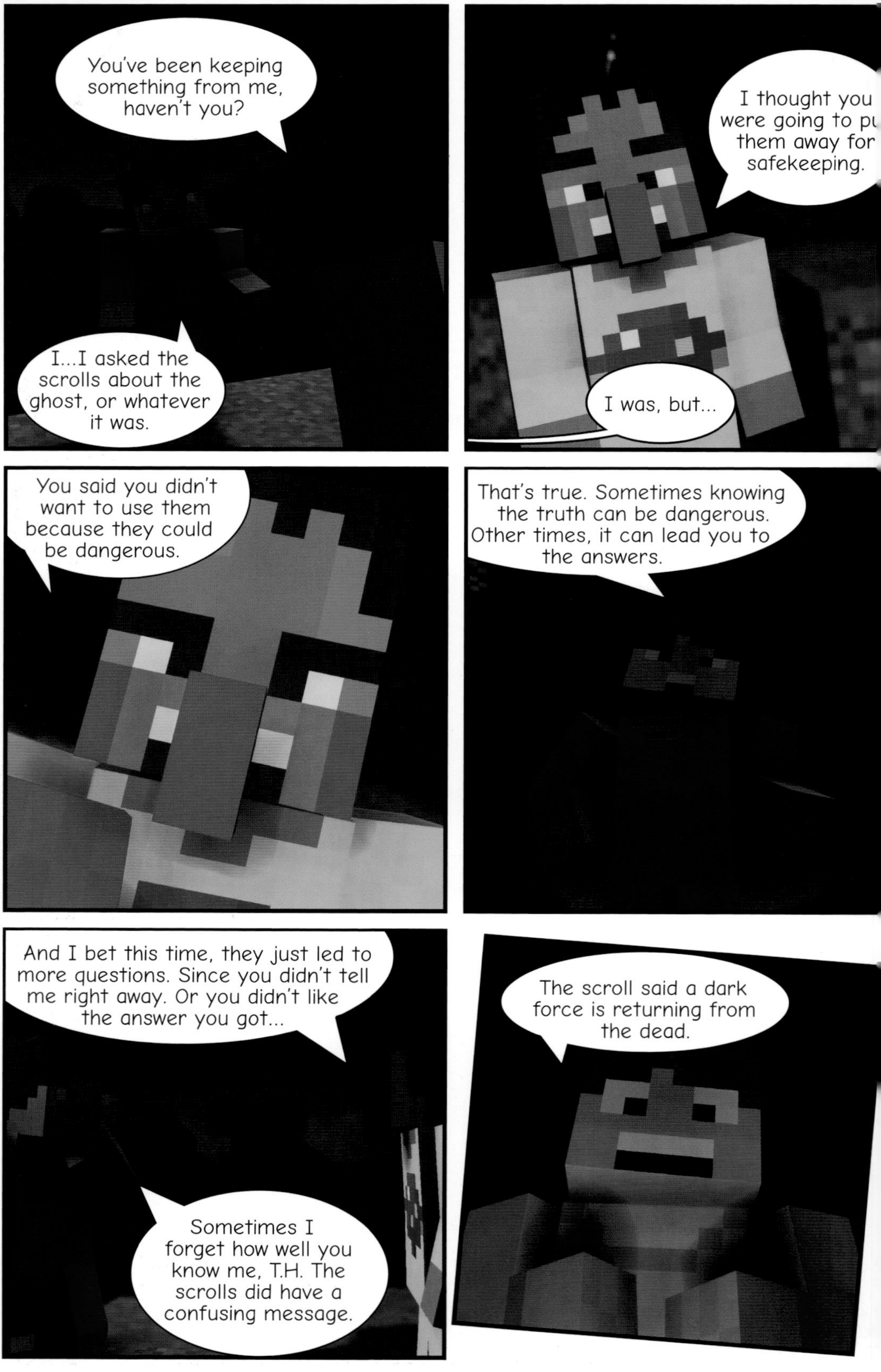
You've been keeping something from me, haven't you?
I...I asked the scrolls about the ghost, or whatever it was.
I thought you were going to pu them away for safekeeping.
I was, but...
You said you didn't want to use them because they could be dangerous.
That's true. Sometimes knowing the truth can be dangerous. Other times, it can lead you to the answers.
And I bet this time, they just led to more questions. Since you didn't tell me right away. Or you didn't like the answer you got...
Sometimes I forget how well you know me, T.H. The scrolls did have a confusing message.
The scroll said a dark force is returning from the dead.

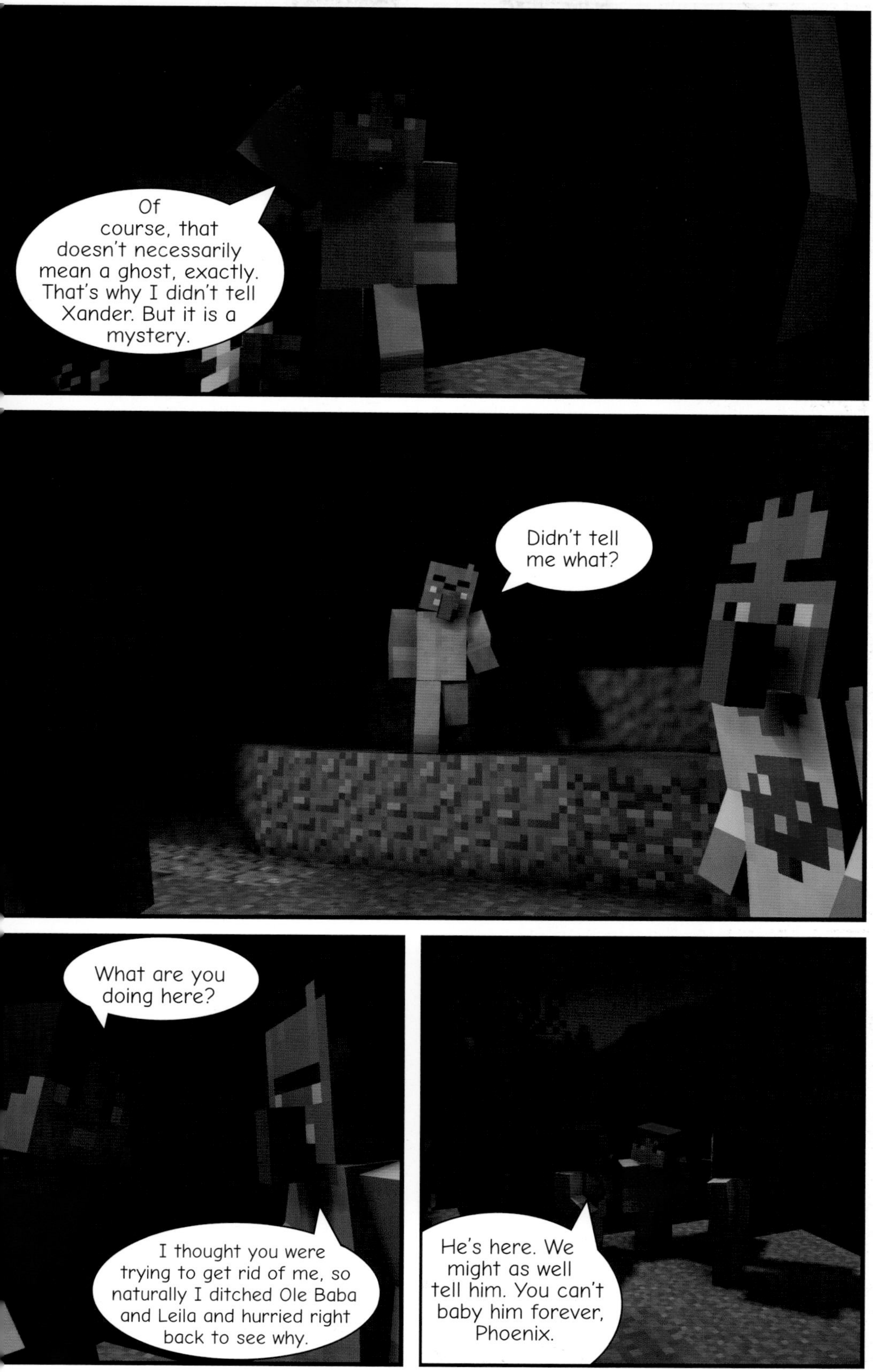
Of course, that doesn't necessarily mean a ghost, exactly. That's why I didn't tell Xander. But it is a mystery.
Didn't tell me what?
What are you doing here?
I thought you were trying to get rid of me, so naturally I ditched Ole Baba and Leila and hurried right back to see why.
He's here. We might as well tell him. You can't baby him forever, Phoenix.

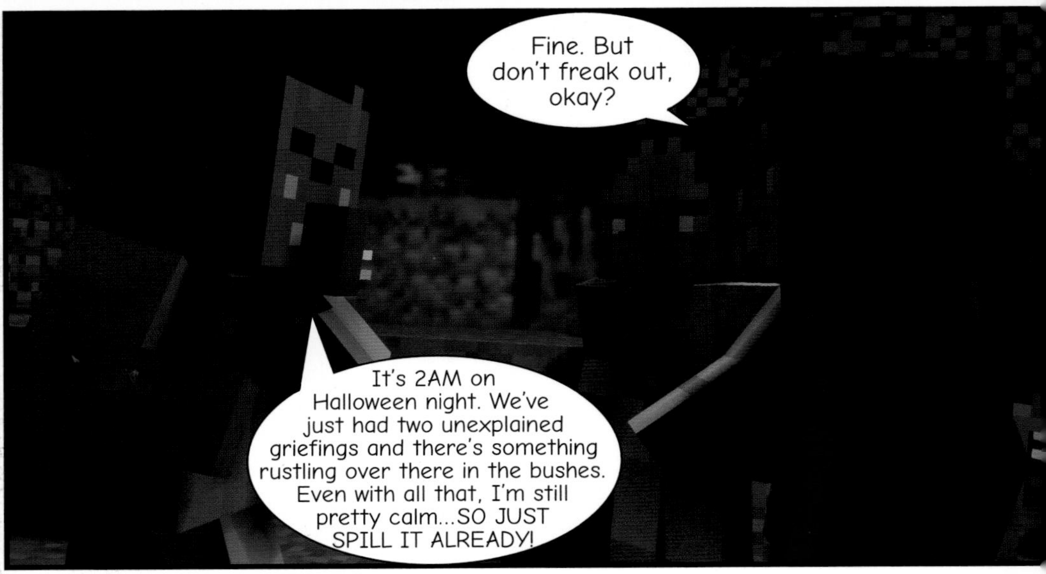
Fine. But don't freak out, okay?
It's 2AM on Halloween night. We've just had two unexplained griefings and there's something rustling over there in the bushes. Even with all that, I'm still pretty calm...SO JUST SPILL IT ALREADY!

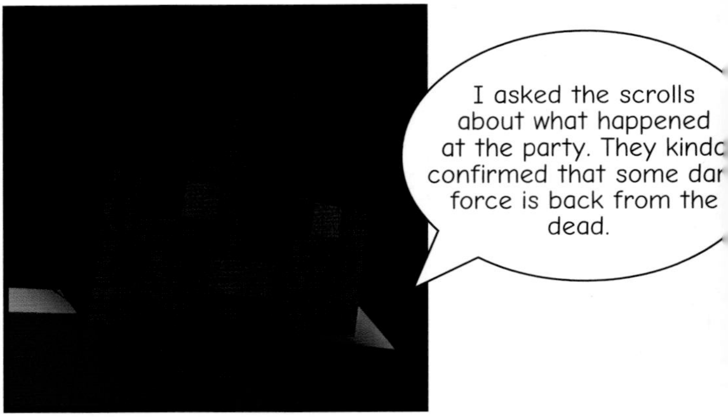
I asked the scrolls about what happened at the party. They kinda confirmed that some dar force is back from the dead.

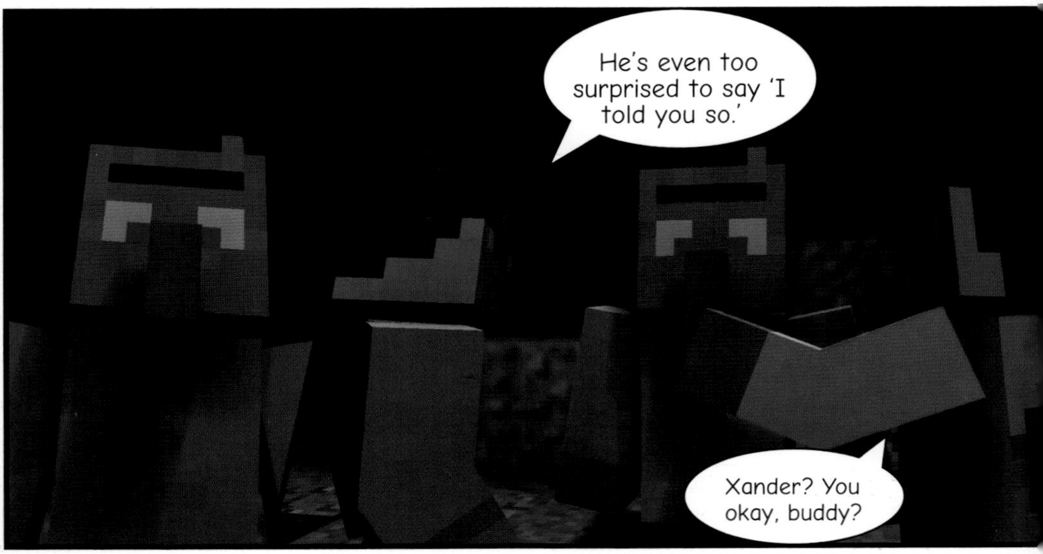
He's even too surprised to say 'I told you so.'
Xander? You okay, buddy?

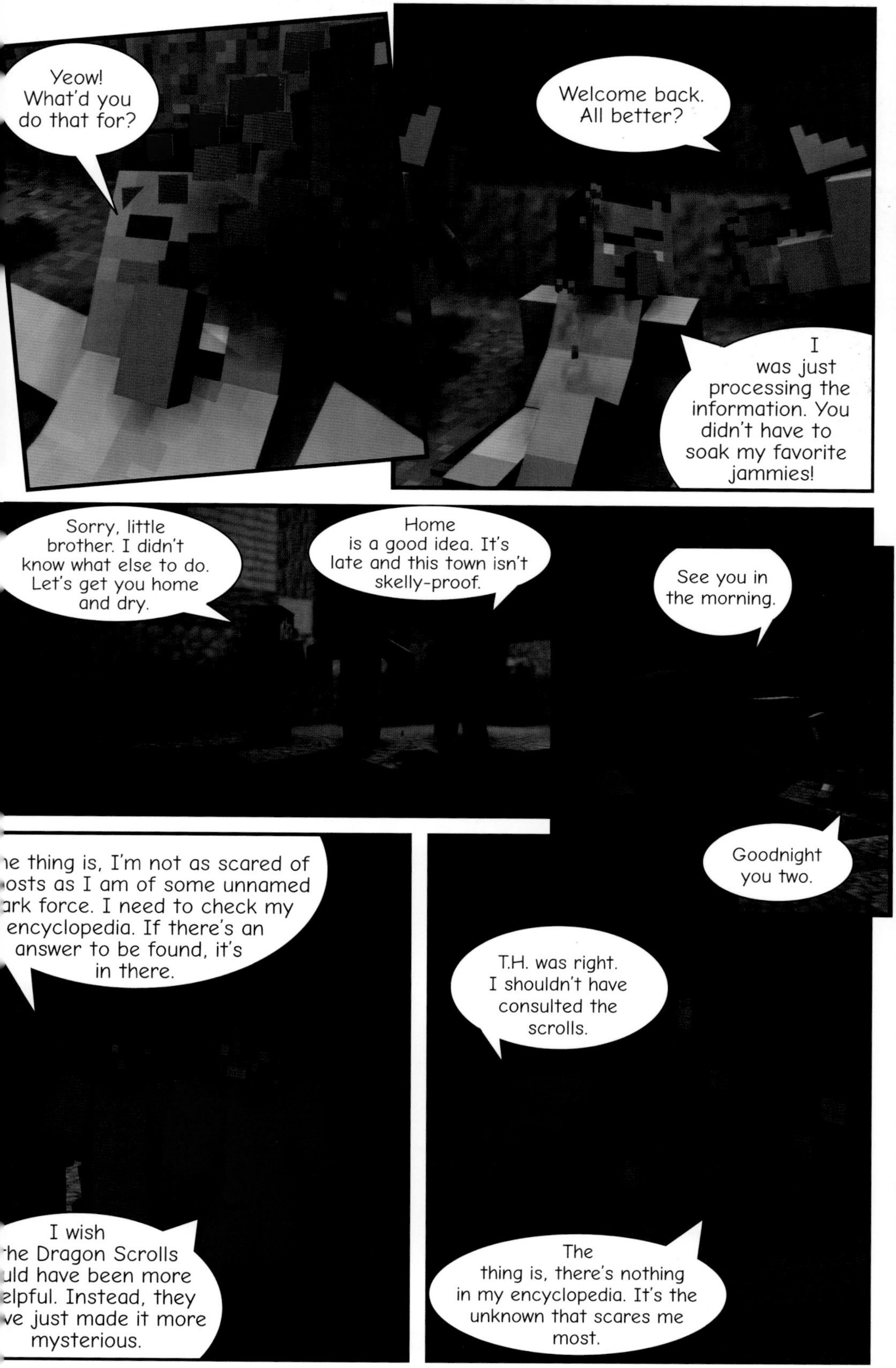
Yeow! What'd you do that for?
Welcome back. All better?
I was just processing the information. You didn't have to soak my favorite jammies!
Sorry, little brother. I didn't know what else to do. Let's get you home and dry.
Home is a good idea. It's late and this town isn't skelly-proof.
See you in the morning.
Goodnight you two.
ne thing is, I'm not as scared of osts as I am of some unnamed ark force. I need to check my encyclopedia. If there's an answer to be found, it's in there.
T.H. was right. I shouldn't have consulted the scrolls.
I wish he Dragon Scrolls uld have been more elpful. Instead, they ve just made it more mysterious.
The thing is, there's nothing in my encyclopedia. It's the unknown that scares me most.

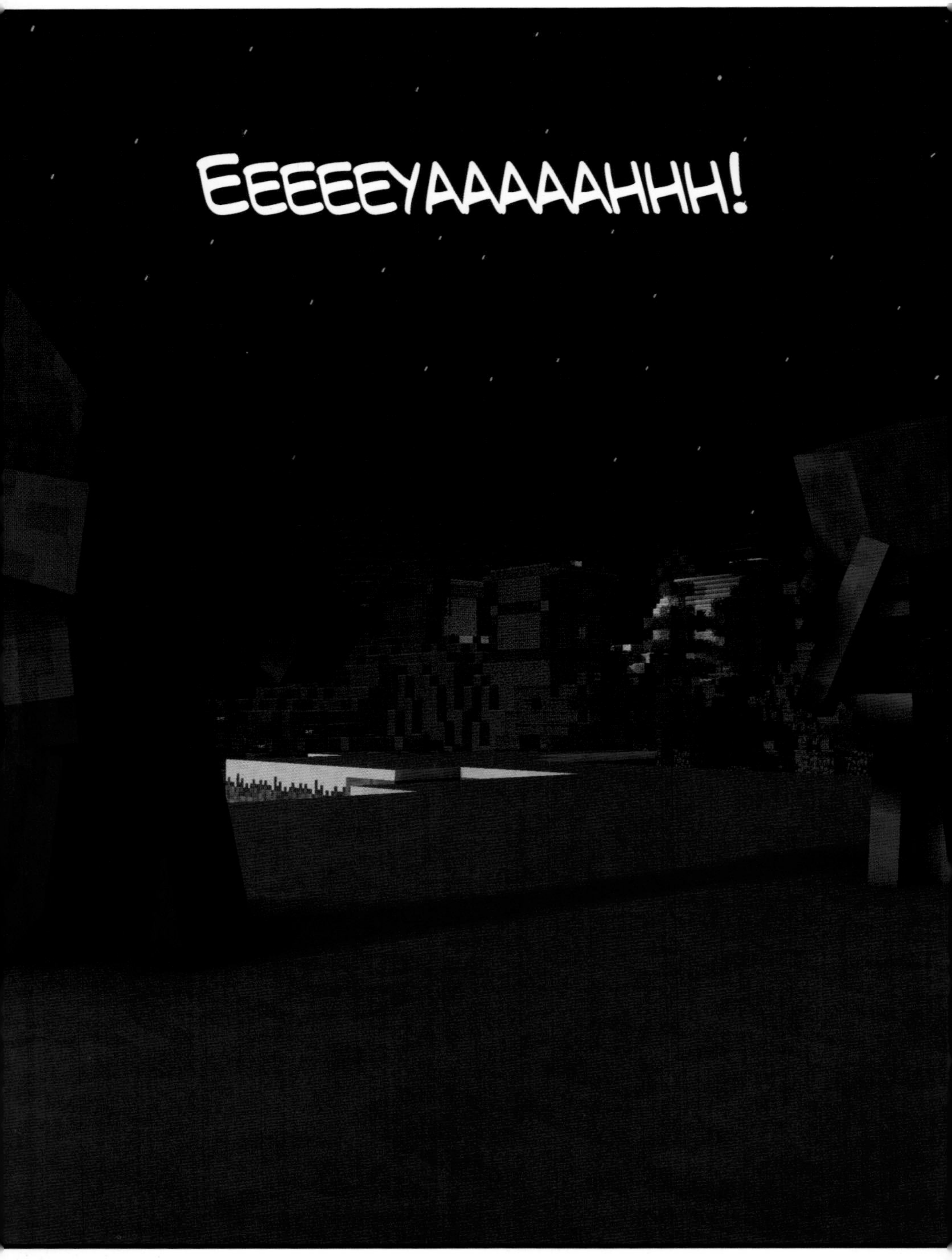
EEEEEEYAAAAAAHHH!

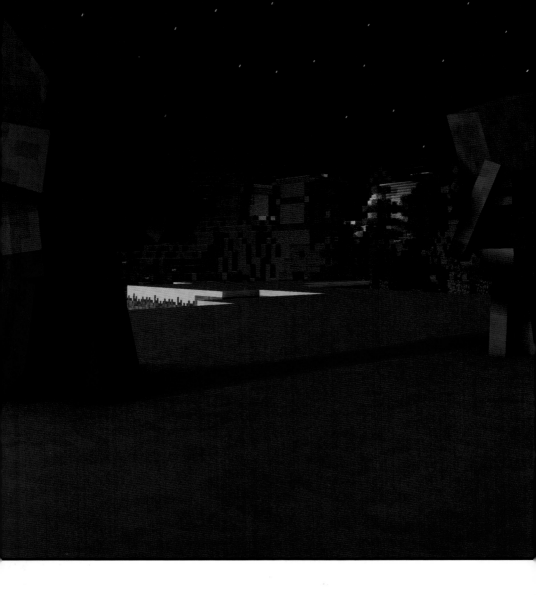

CHAPTER 3

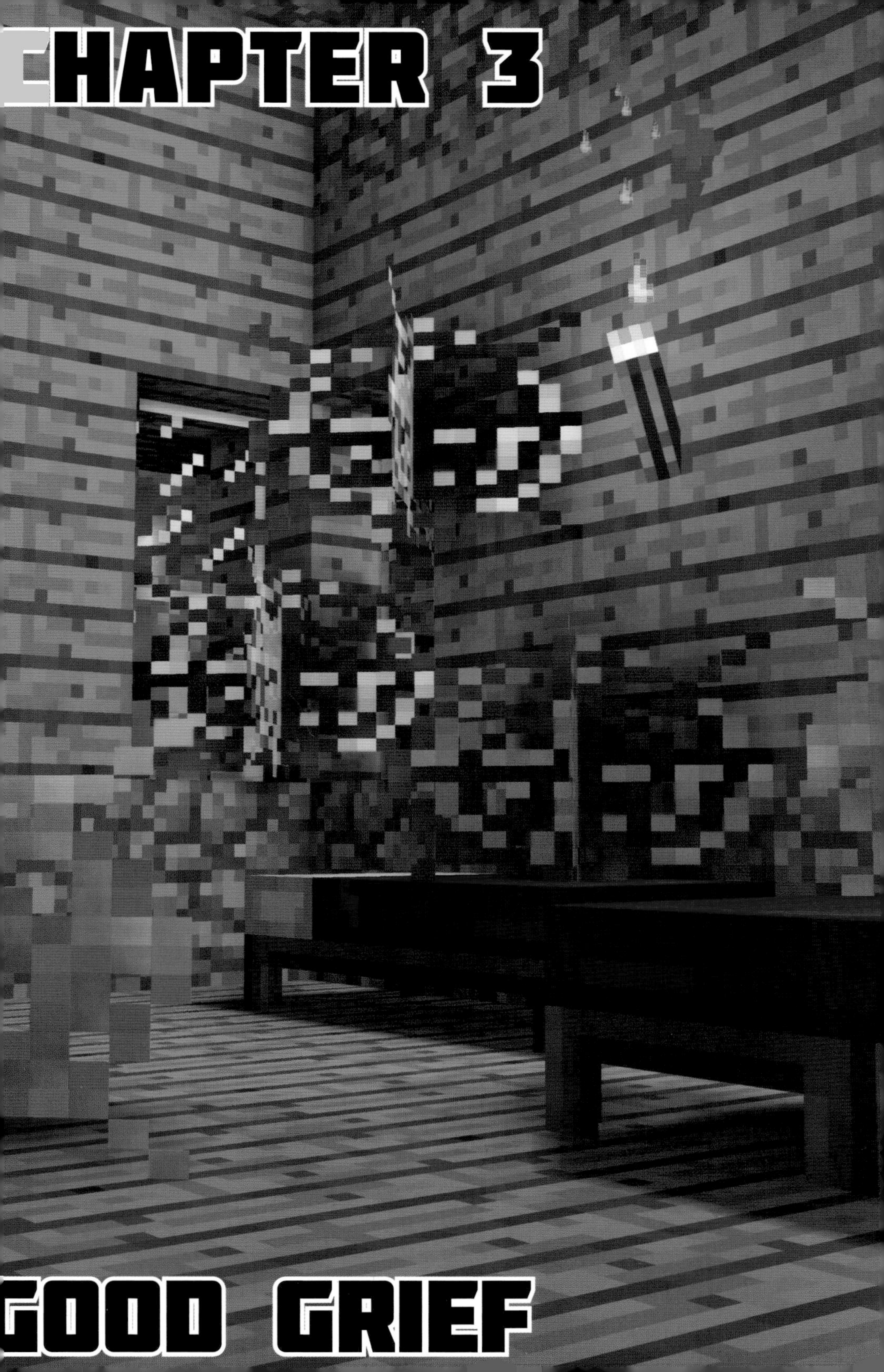

GOOD GRIEF

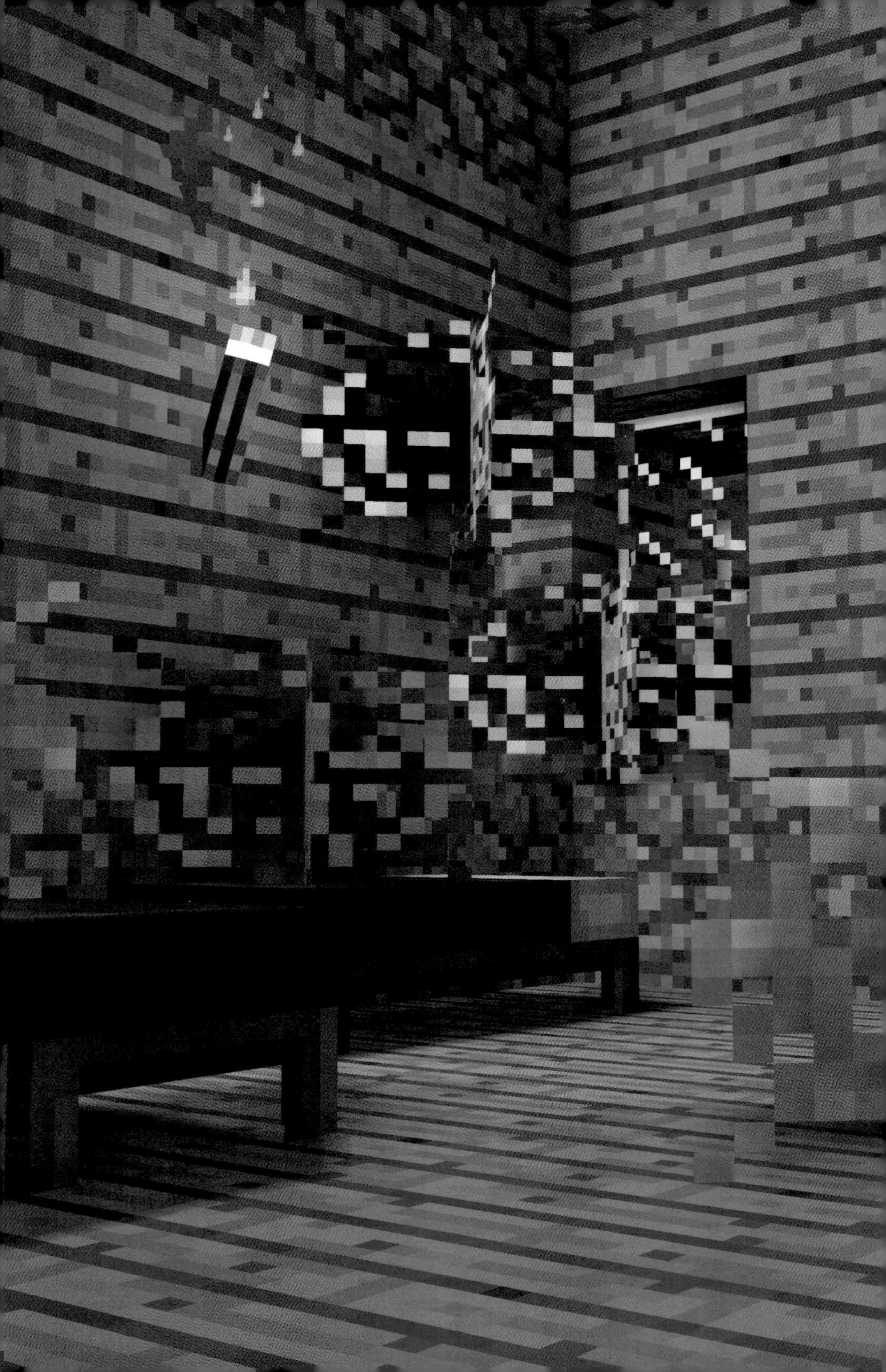

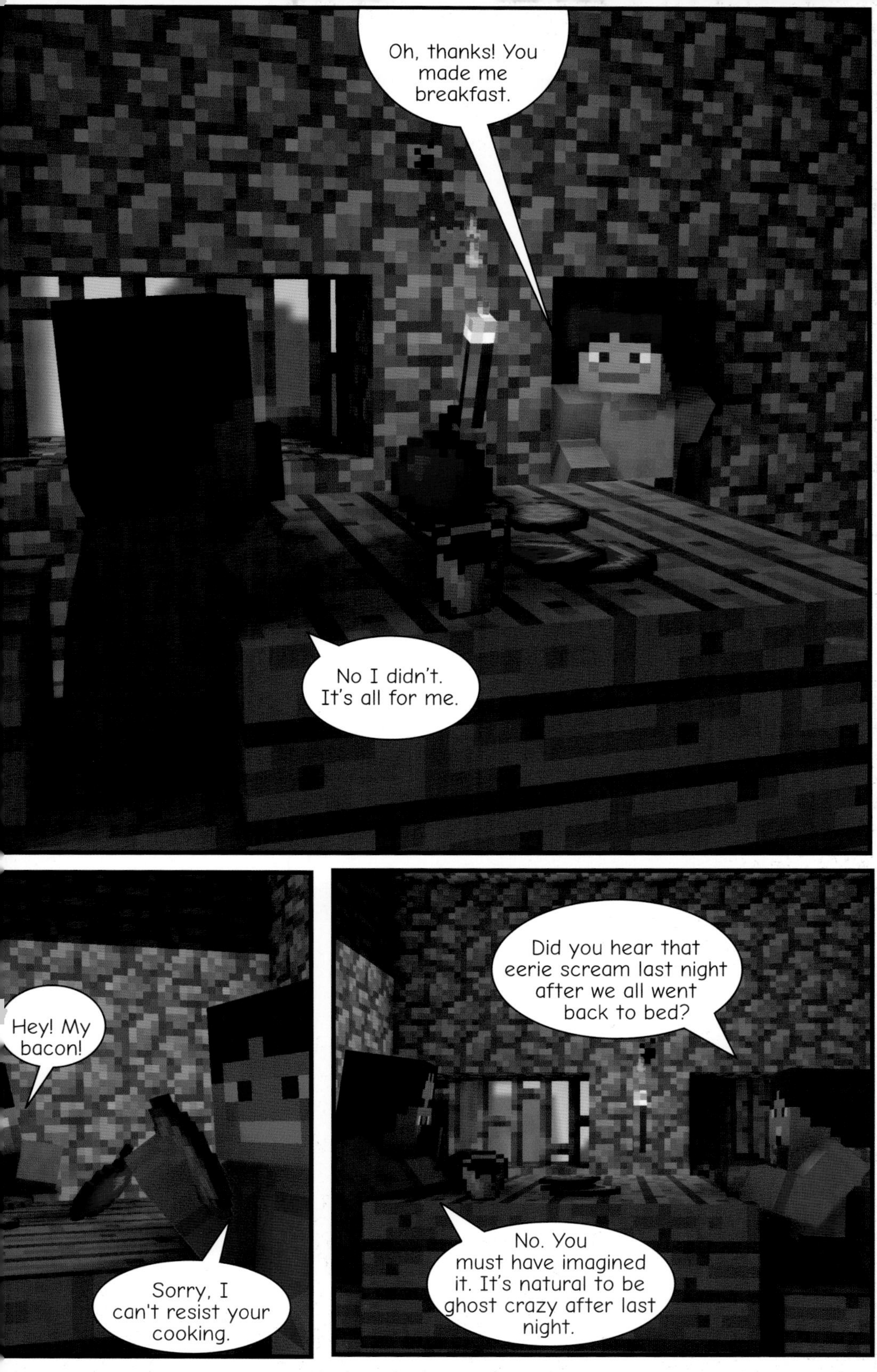
Oh, thanks! You made me breakfast.
No I didn't. It's all for me.
Hey! My bacon!
Sorry, I can't resist your cooking.
Did you hear that eerie scream last night after we all went back to bed?
No. You must have imagined it. It's natural to be ghost crazy after last night.

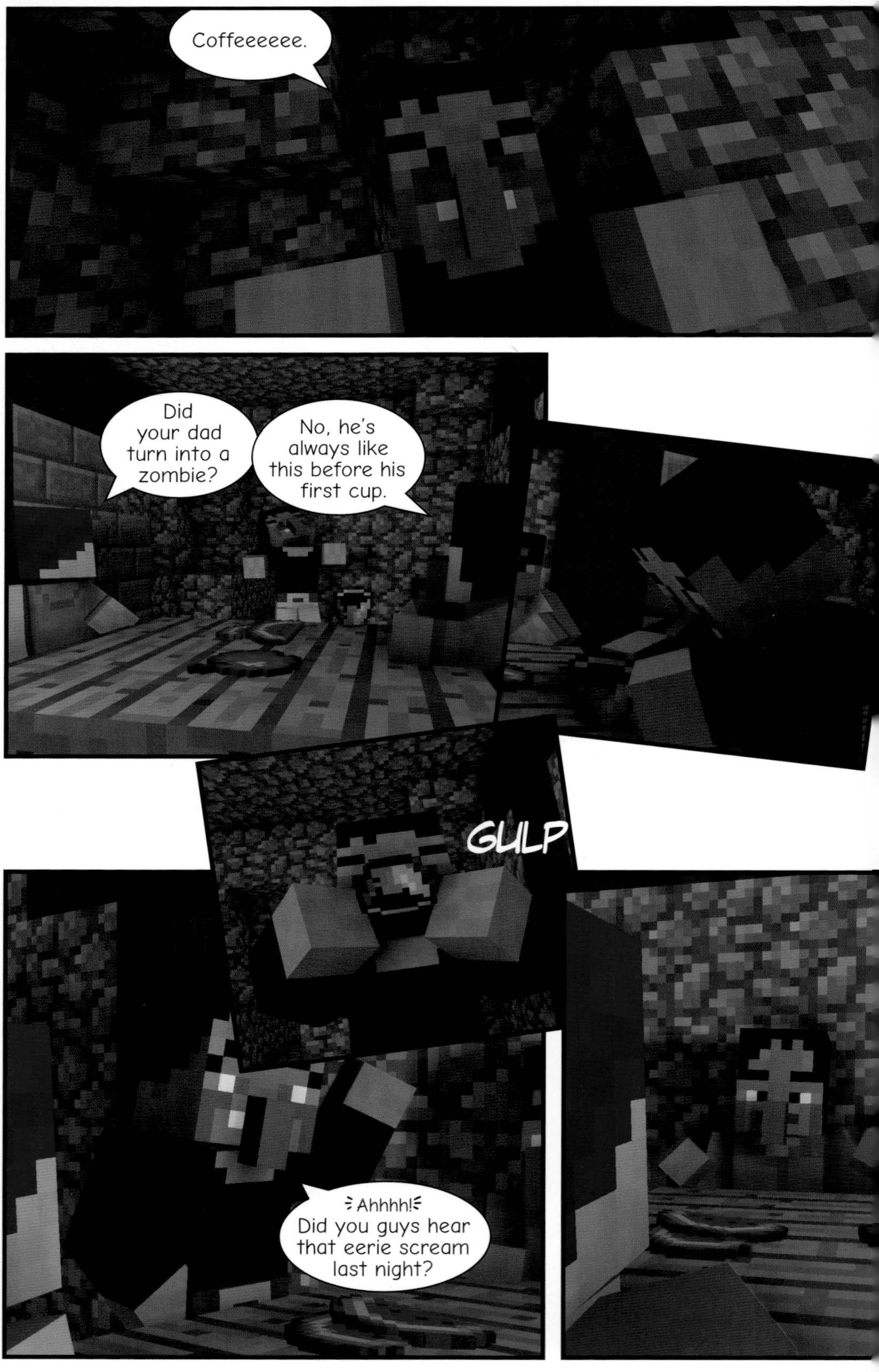
Coffeeeeee.
Did your dad turn into a zombie?
No, he's always like this before his first cup.
GULP
Ahhhh!
Did you guys hear that eerie scream last night?

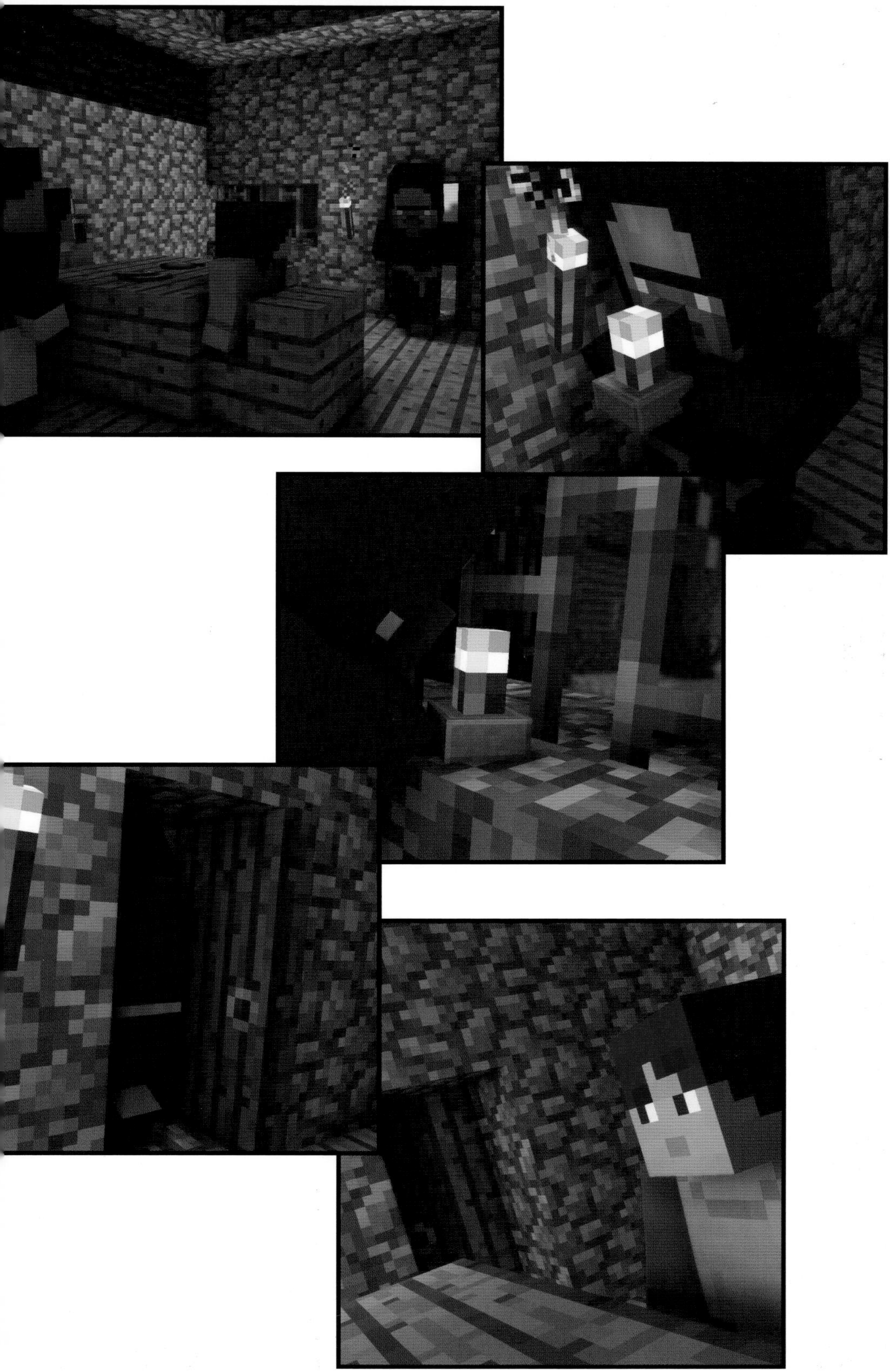

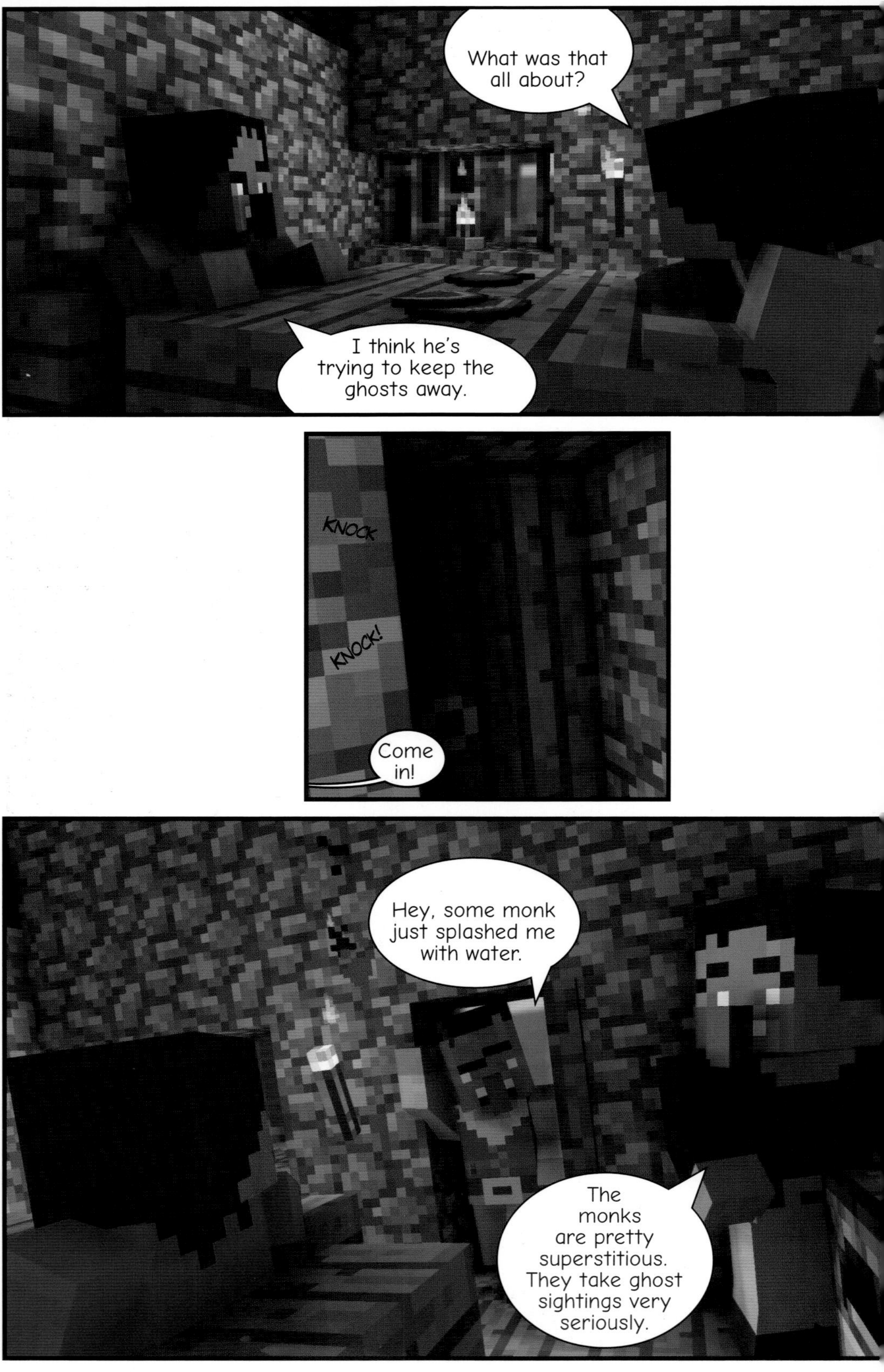
What was that all about?
I think he's trying to keep the ghosts away.
KNOCK
KNOCK!
Come in!
Hey, some monk just splashed me with water.
The monks are pretty superstitious. They take ghost sightings very seriously.

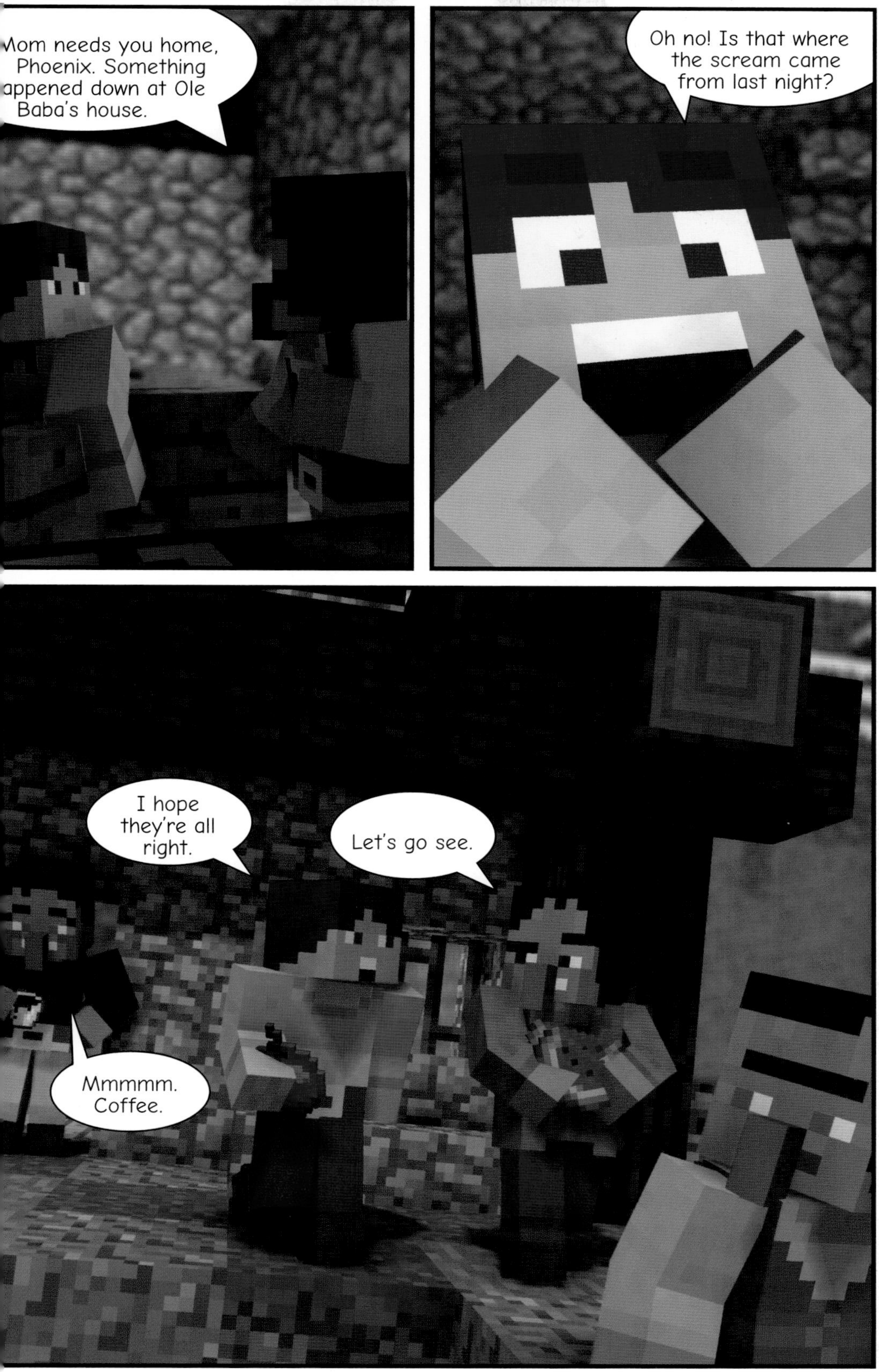
Mom needs you home, Phoenix. Something appened down at Ole Baba's house.
Oh no! Is that where the scream came from last night?
I hope they're all right.
Let's go see.
Mmmmm. Coffee.

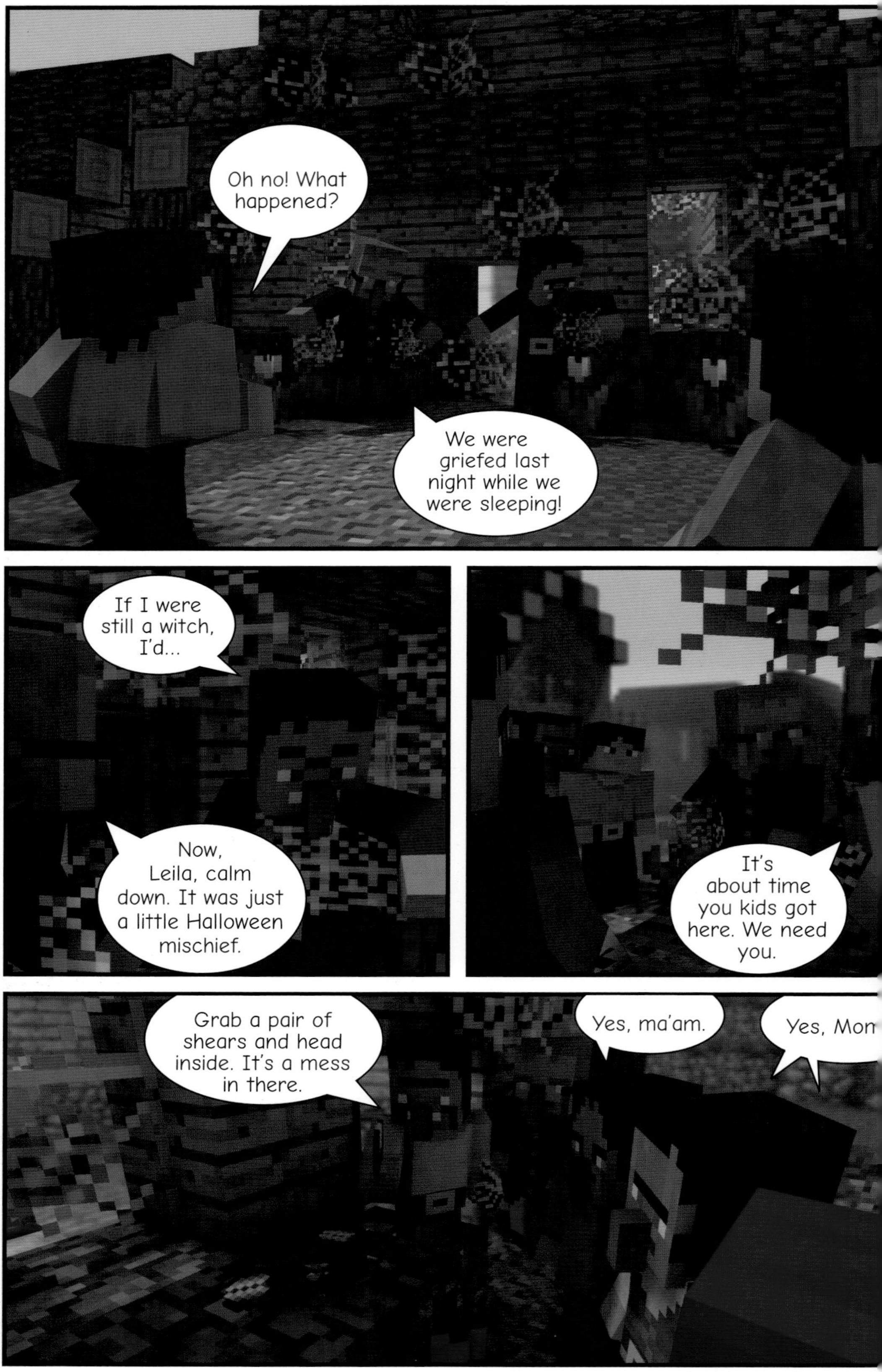
Oh no! What happened?
We were griefed last night while we were sleeping!
If I were still a witch, I'd...
Now, Leila, calm down. It was just a little Halloween mischief.
It's about time you kids got here. We need you.
Grab a pair of shears and head inside. It's a mess in there.
Yes, ma'am.

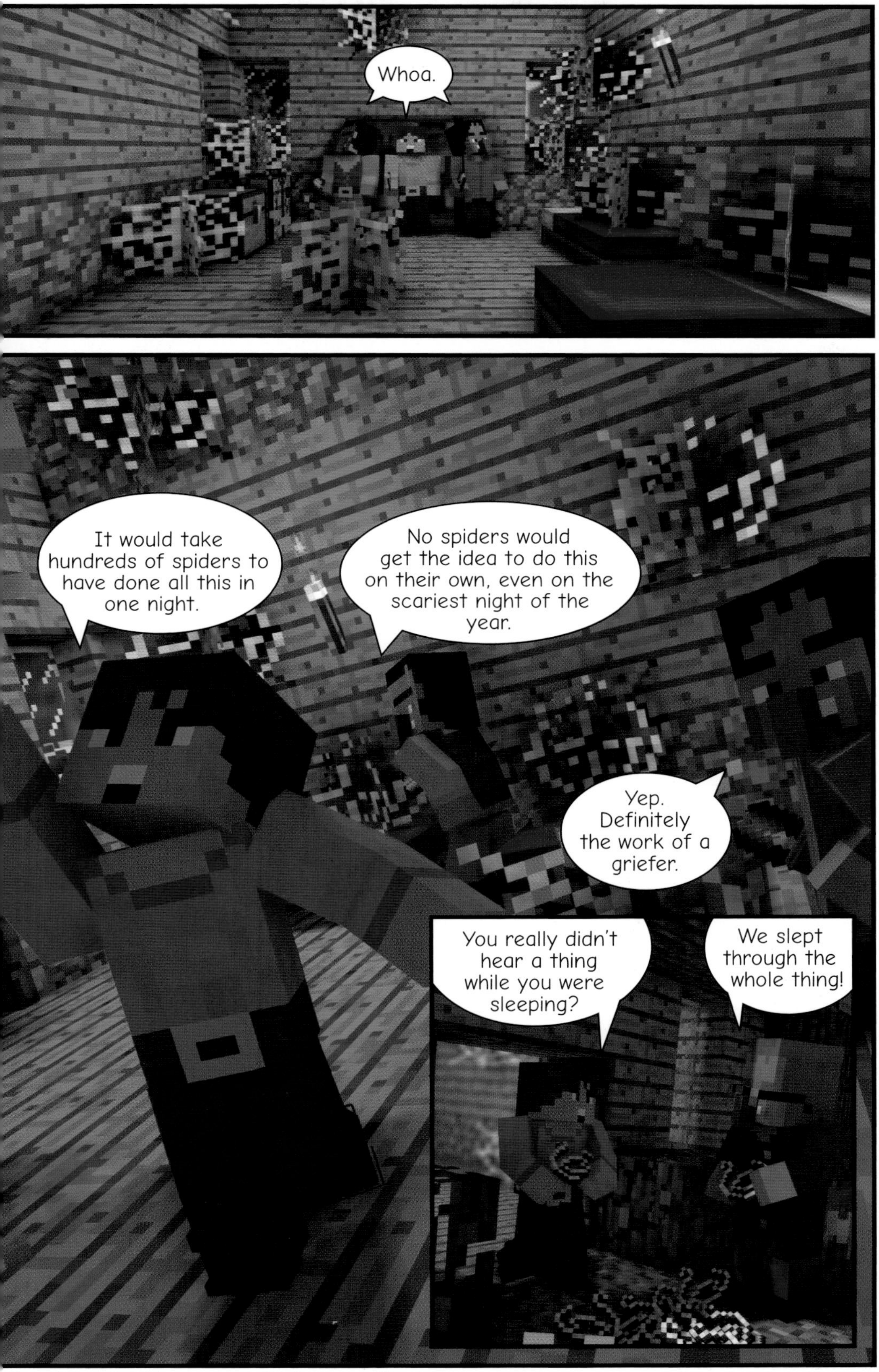
Whoa.
It would take hundreds of spiders to have done all this in one night.
No spiders would get the idea to do this on their own, even on the scariest night of the year.
Yep. Definitely the work of a griefer.
You really didn't hear a thing while you were sleeping?
We slept through the whole thing!

Ever since Leila returned home after being a witch for so long, she's been somewhat of a loud sleeper. She even keeps herself awake! We wear earplugs every night to drown out her snores.

Zzzzzzzz. Grnxxxxx.

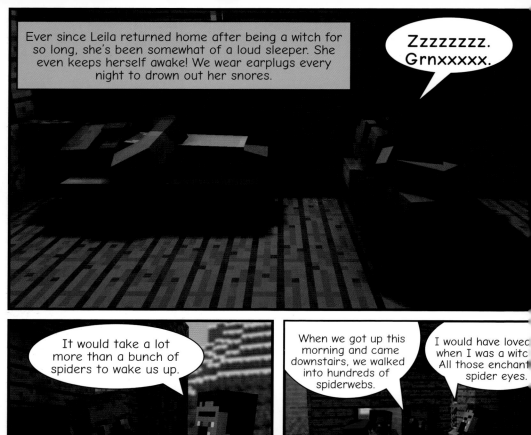

It would take a lot more than a bunch of spiders to wake us up.

When we got up this morning and came downstairs, we walked into hundreds of spiderwebs.

I would have loved when I was a witc All those enchant spider eyes.

At least you didn't get hurt. And you have all this string now!

But why did the griefer pick us?

Probably because we keep our door unlocked and can sleep through anything.

Actually, there's a chance it could be something more than just a griefer. Scrolls said...

You consulted the scrolls?!

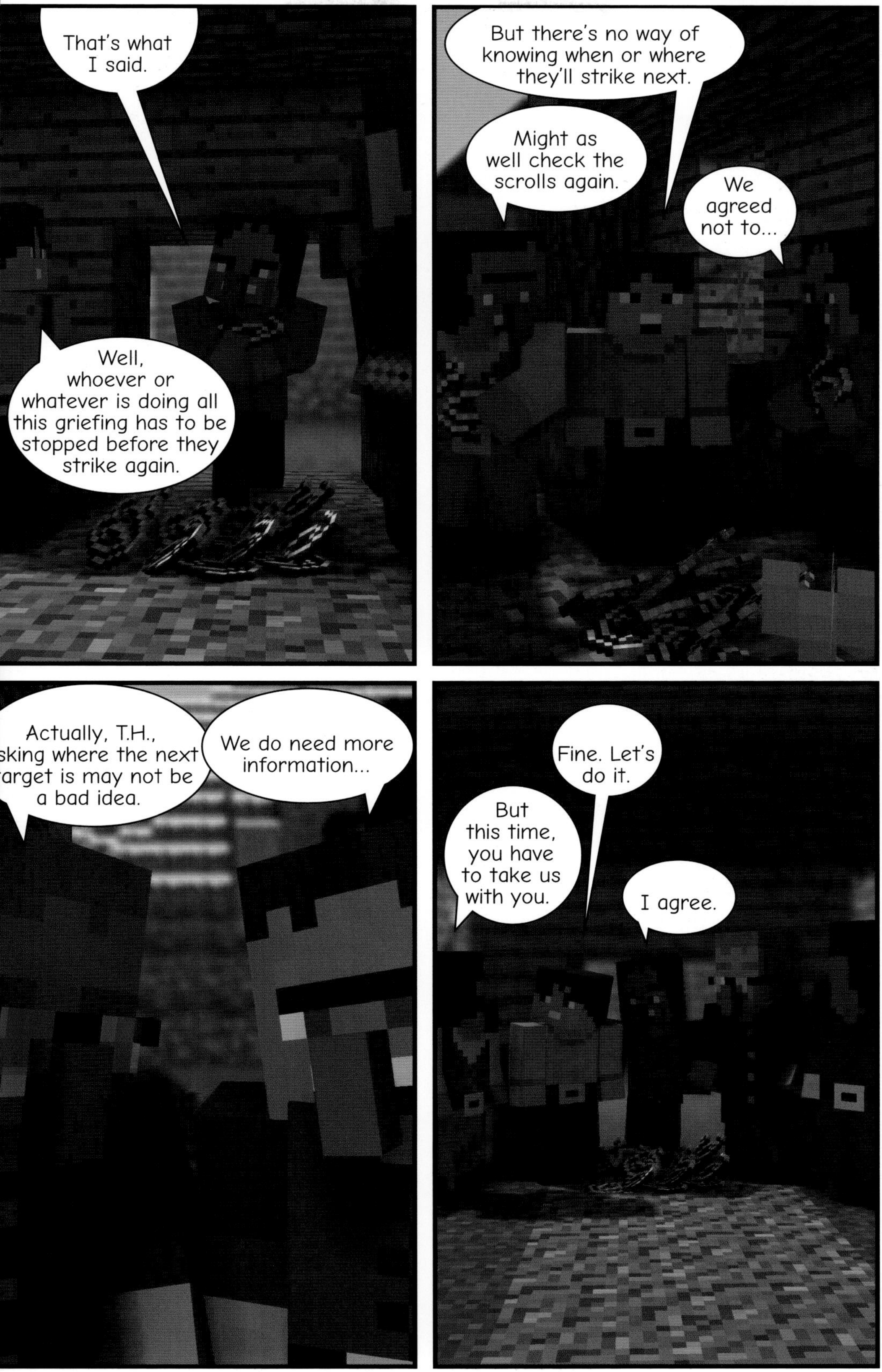
That's what I said.
Well, whoever or whatever is doing all this griefing has to be stopped before they strike again.
But there's no way of knowing when or where they'll strike next.
Might as well check the scrolls again.
We agreed not to...
Actually, T.H., sking where the next arget is may not be a bad idea.
We do need more information...
Fine. Let's do it.
But this time, you have to take us with you.
I agree.

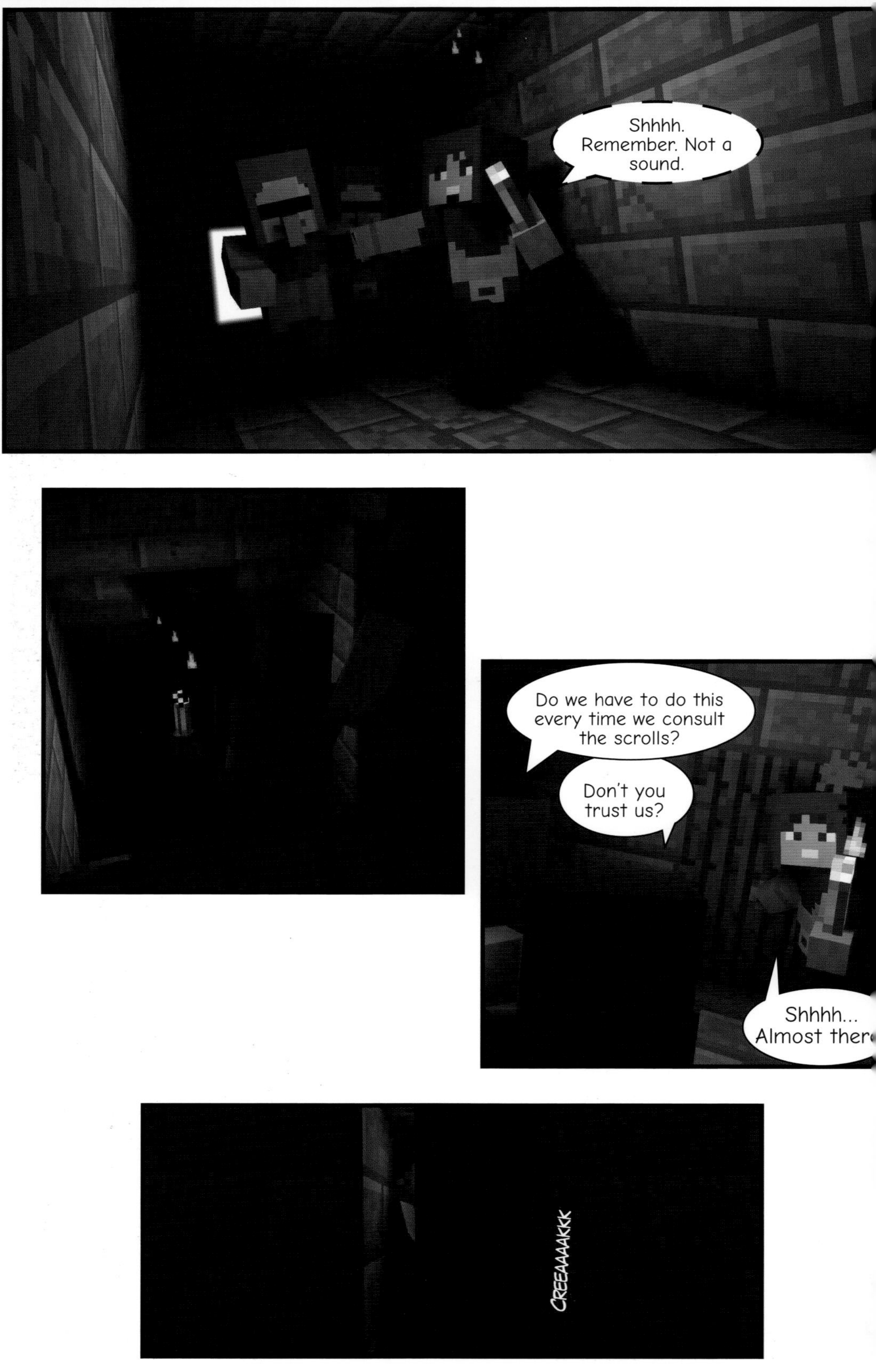
Shhhh.
Remember. Not a sound.
Do we have to do this every time we consult the scrolls?
Don't you trust us?
Shhhh...
CREEAAAAKKK

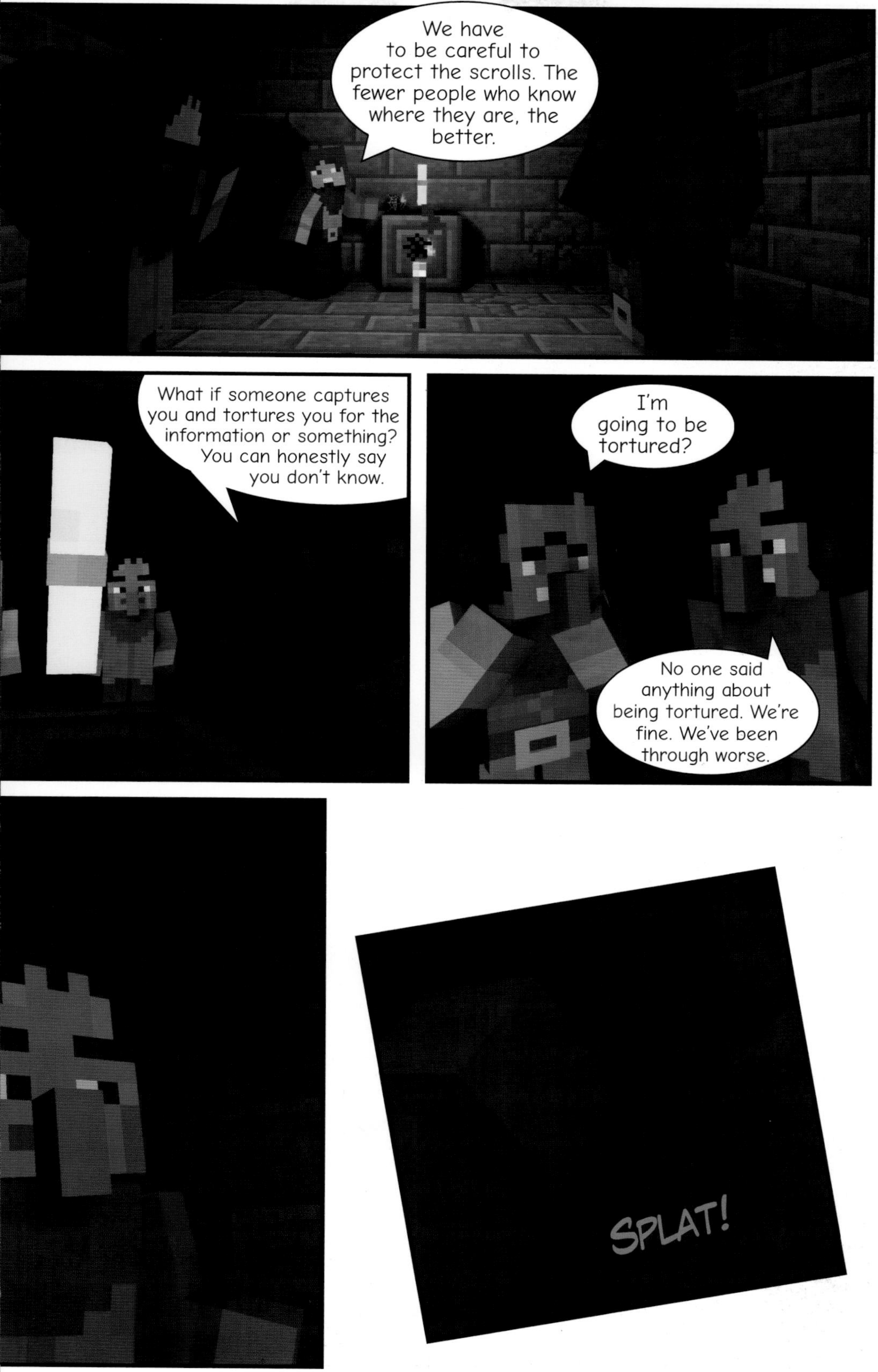
We have to be careful to protect the scrolls. The fewer people who know where they are, the better.
What if someone captures you and tortures you for the information or something? You can honestly say you don't know.
I'm going to be tortured?
No one said anything about being tortured. We're fine. We've been through worse.
SPLAT!

No matter how many times I see it, it's still really cool.

Me, too.

I have to keep the scrolls safe at all costs, you know that.

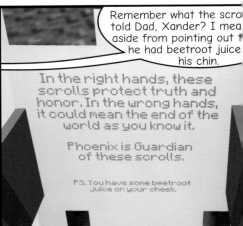

Remember what the scro told Dad, Xander? I mea aside from pointing out t he had beetroot juice his chin.

In the right hands, these scrolls protect truth and honor. In the wrong hands, it could mean the end of the world as you know it.

Phoenix is Guardian of these scrolls.

P.S. You have some beetroot juice on your cheek.

What if something happens to you? They could be lost forever.

Then the scrolls will be even safer because they'll be protected.

That's a creepy thought.

"Well, actually..."

"Who did you tell if you didn't tell us?"

"Ole Baba...I mean Bailey...knows."

"You told her and not us?"

"Let's leave this argument for another time...Ready to ask the scroll?"

"Okay, Dragon Scrolls...Please tell us where the griefer will strike next."

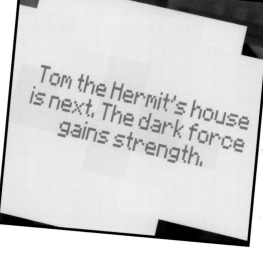

Tom the Hermit's house is next. The dark force gains strength.

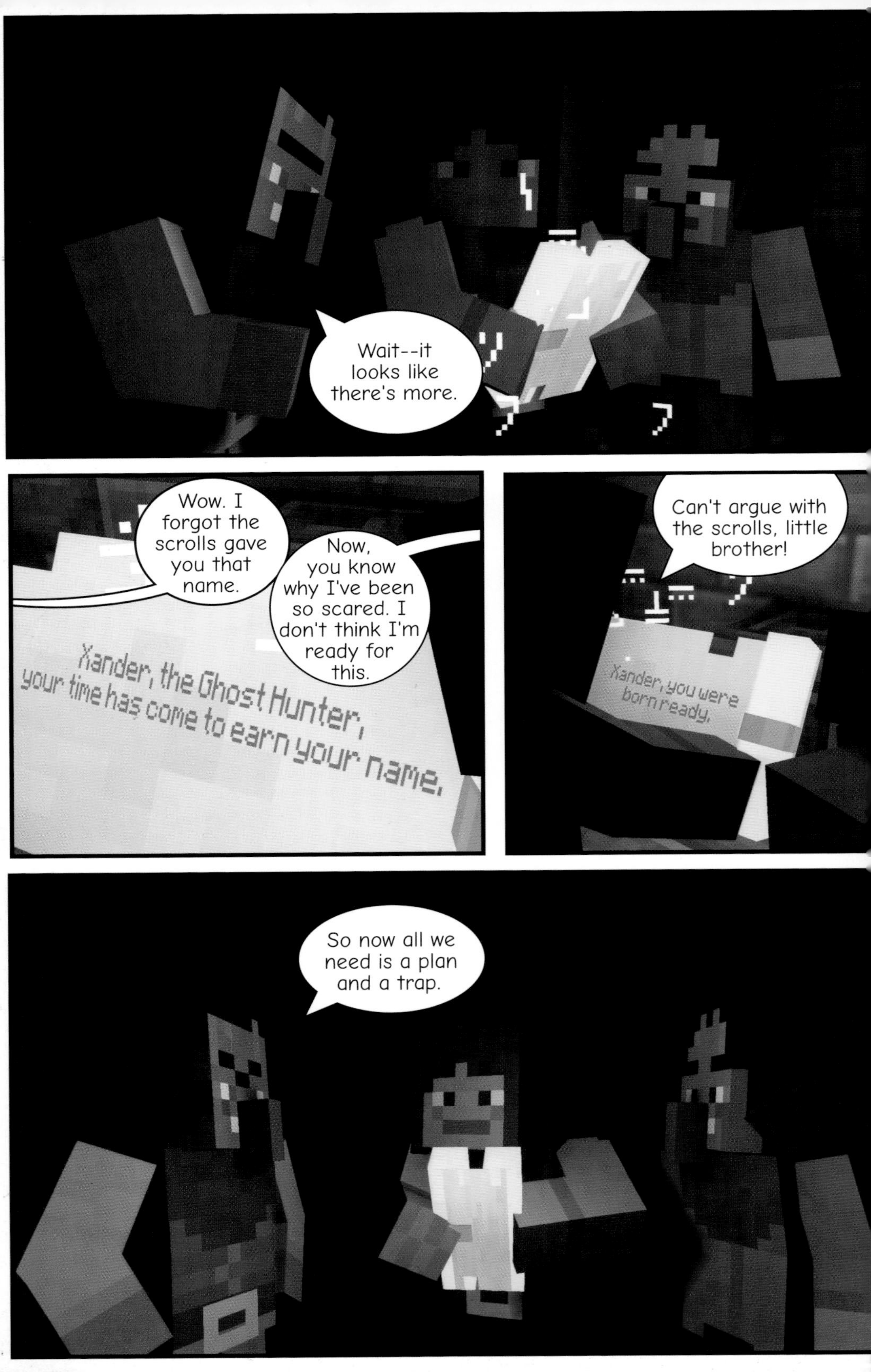

Wait--it looks like there's more.
Wow. I forgot the scrolls gave you that name.
Now, you know why I've been so scared. I don't think I'm ready for this.
Xander, the Ghost Hunter, your time has come to earn your name.
Can't argue with the scrolls, little brother!
Xander, you were born ready.
So now all we need is a plan and a trap.

CHAPTER 4

TRAPPED

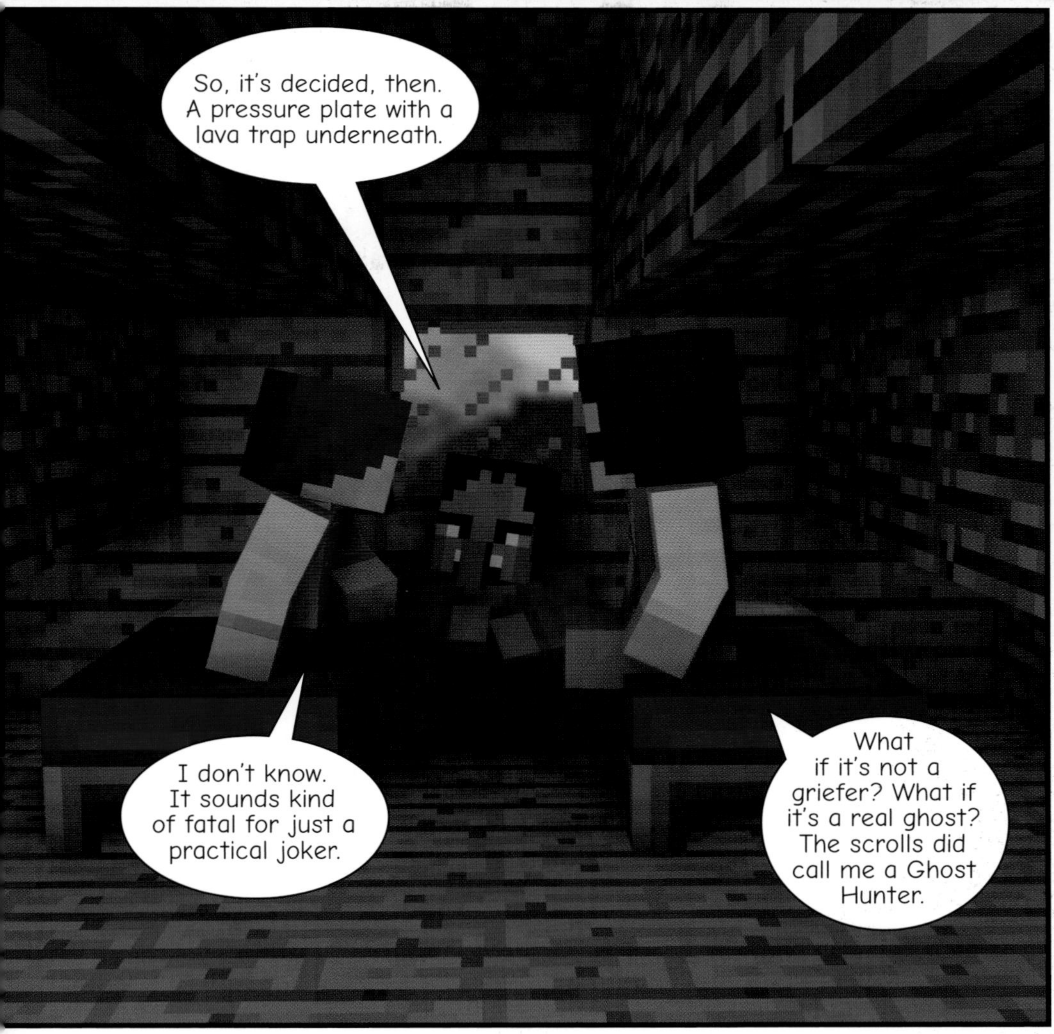
So, it's decided, then. A pressure plate with a lava trap underneath.
I don't know. It sounds kind of fatal for just a practical joker.
What if it's not a griefer? What if it's a real ghost? The scrolls did call me a Ghost Hunter.

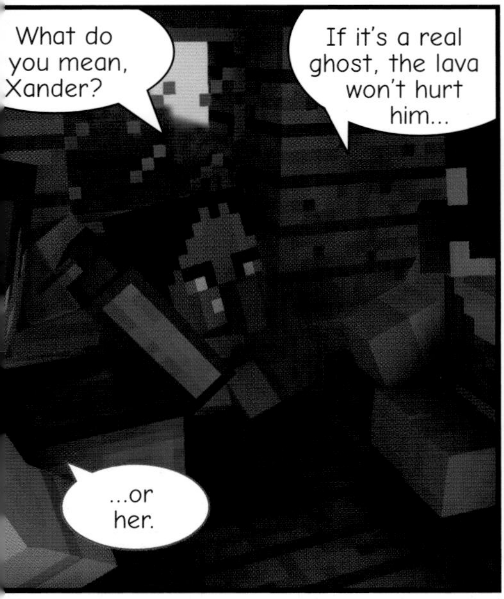
What do you mean, Xander?
If it's a real ghost, the lava won't hurt him...
...or her.

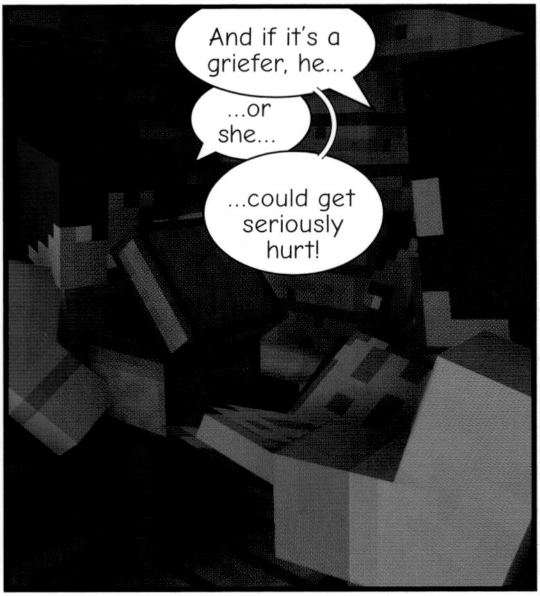
And if it's a griefer, he...
...or she...
...could get seriously hurt!

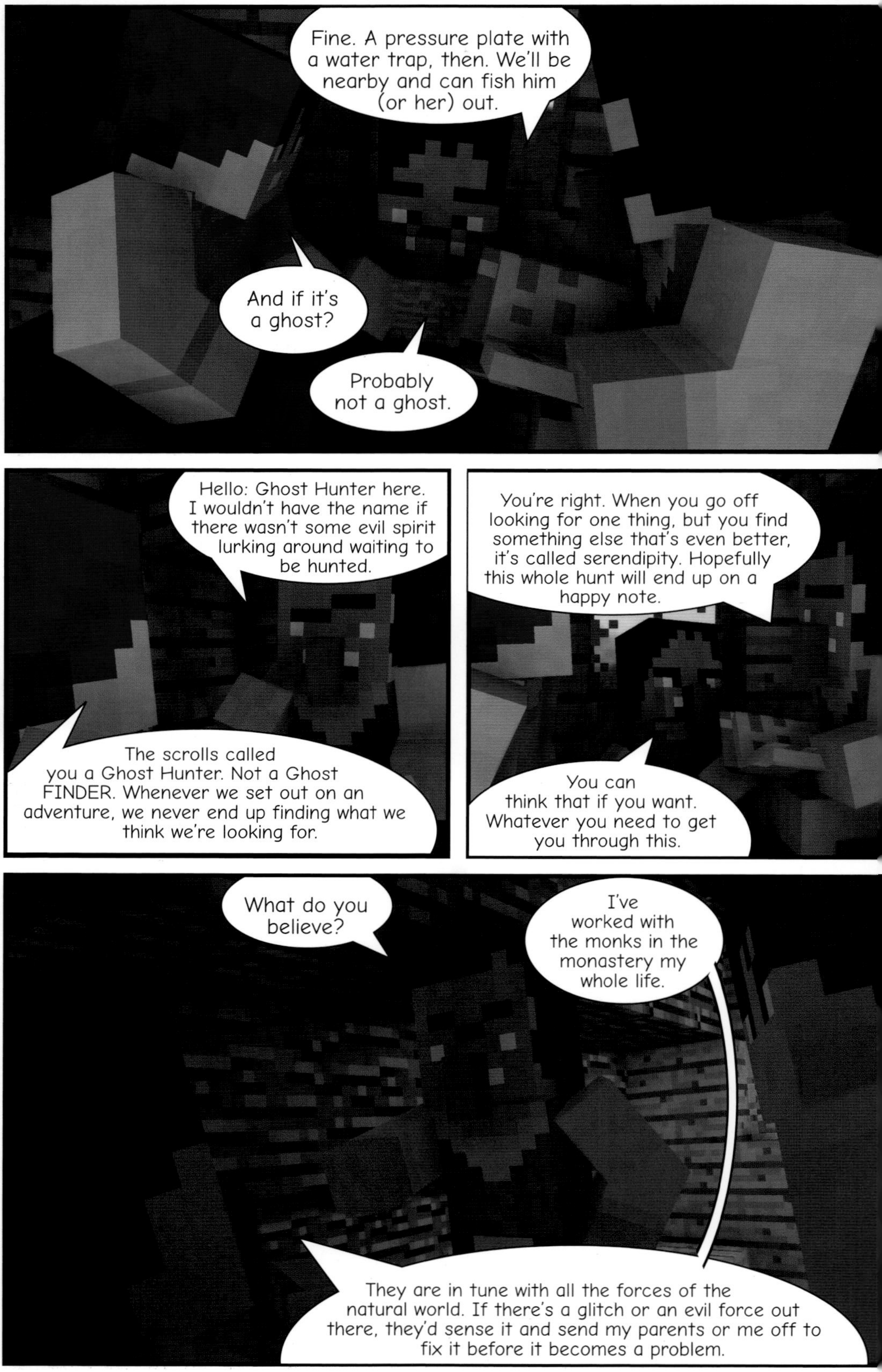
Fine. A pressure plate with a water trap, then. We'll be nearby and can fish him (or her) out.
And if it's a ghost?
Probably not a ghost.
Hello: Ghost Hunter here. I wouldn't have the name if there wasn't some evil spirit lurking around waiting to be hunted.
The scrolls called you a Ghost Hunter. Not a Ghost FINDER. Whenever we set out on an adventure, we never end up finding what we think we're looking for.
You're right. When you go off looking for one thing, but you find something else that's even better, it's called serendipity. Hopefully this whole hunt will end up on a happy note.
You can think that if you want. Whatever you need to get you through this.
What do you believe?
I've worked with the monks in the monastery my whole life.
They are in tune with all the forces of the natural world. If there's a glitch or an evil force out there, they'd sense it and send my parents or me off to fix it before it becomes a problem.

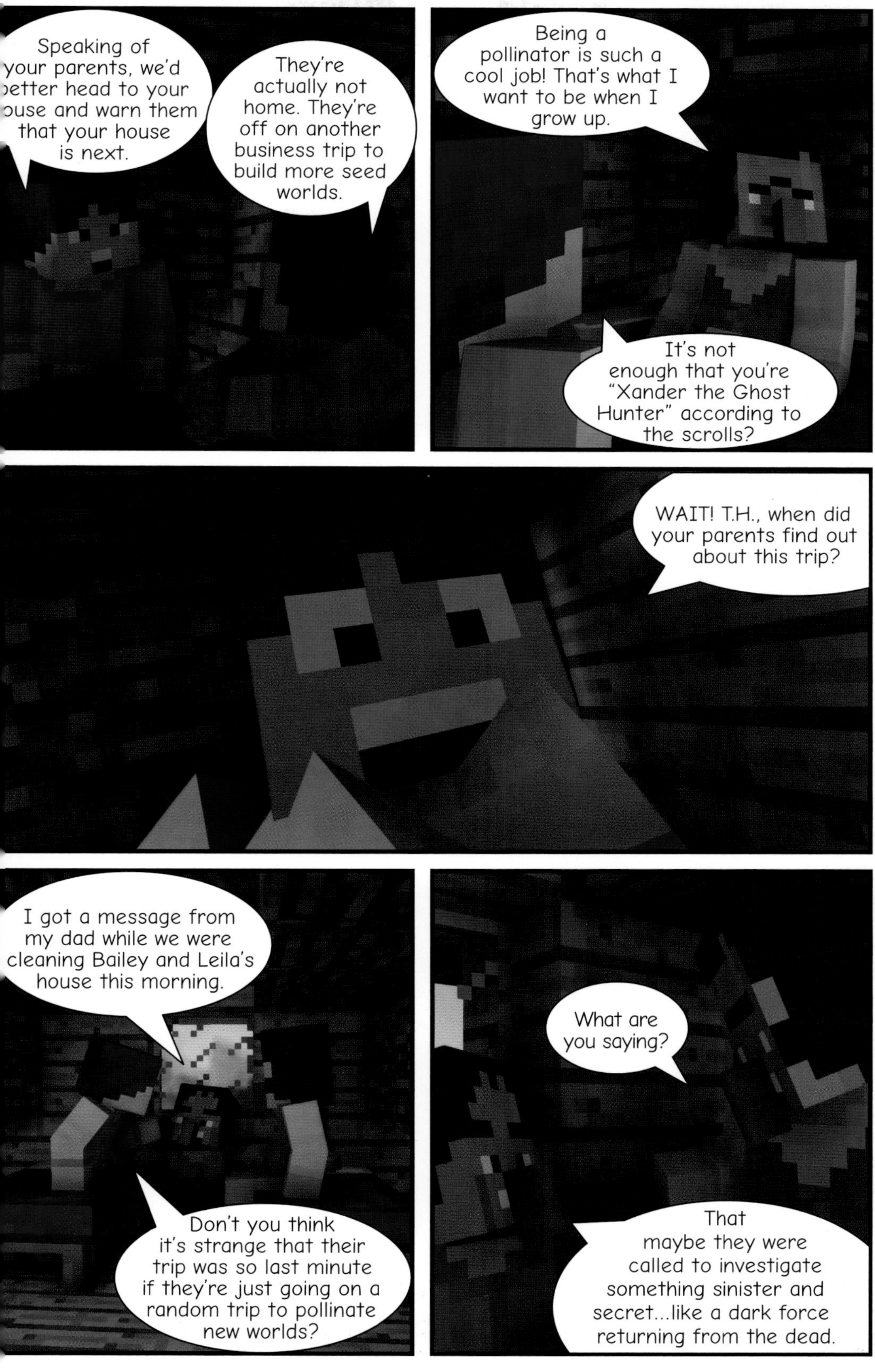
Speaking of your parents, we'd better head to your house and warn them that your house is next.
They're actually not home. They're off on another business trip to build more seed worlds.
Being a pollinator is such a cool job! That's what I want to be when I grow up.
It's not enough that you're "Xander the Ghost Hunter" according to the scrolls?
WAIT! T.H., when did your parents find out about this trip?
I got a message from my dad while we were cleaning Bailey and Leila's house this morning.
Don't you think it's strange that their trip was so last minute if they're just going on a random trip to pollinate new worlds?
What are you saying?
That maybe they were called to investigate something sinister and secret...like a dark force returning from the dead.

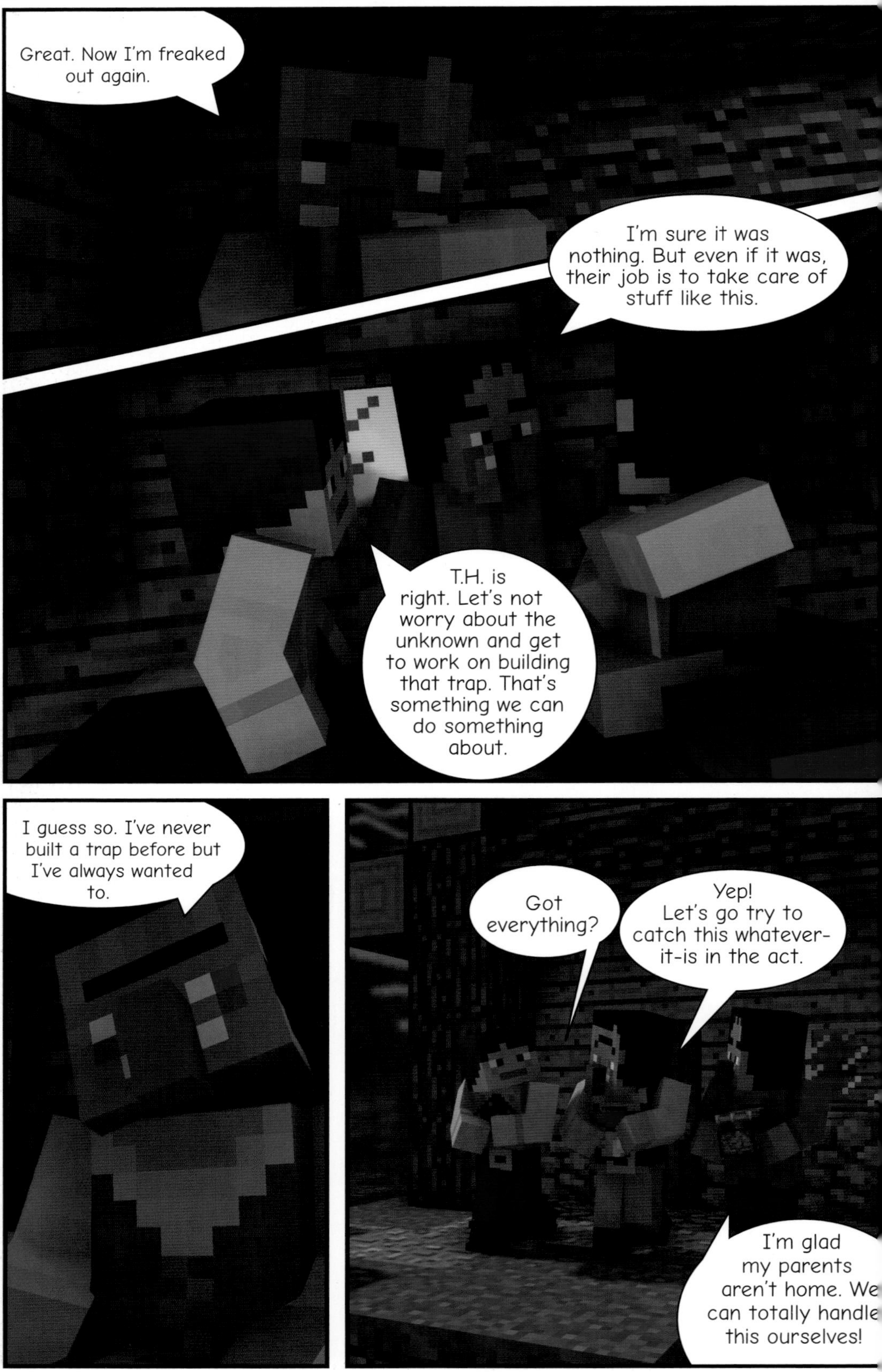
Great. Now I'm freaked out again.
I'm sure it was nothing. But even if it was, their job is to take care of stuff like this.
T.H. is right. Let's not worry about the unknown and get to work on building that trap. That's something we can do something about.
I guess so. I've never built a trap before but I've always wanted to.
Got everything?
Yep! Let's go try to catch this whatever-it-is in the act.
I'm glad my parents aren't home. We can totally handle this ourselves!

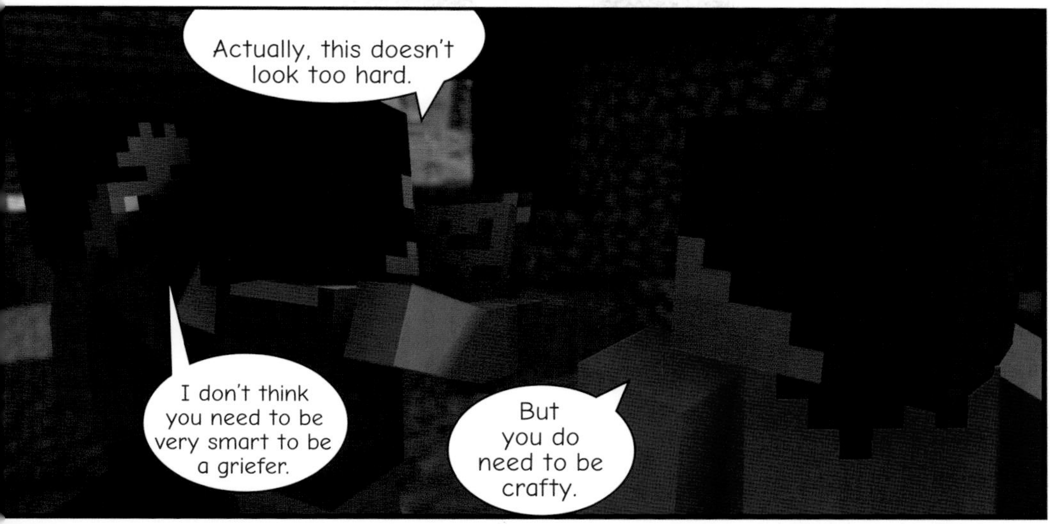
Actually, this doesn't look too hard.
I don't think you need to be very smart to be a griefer.
But you do need to be crafty.

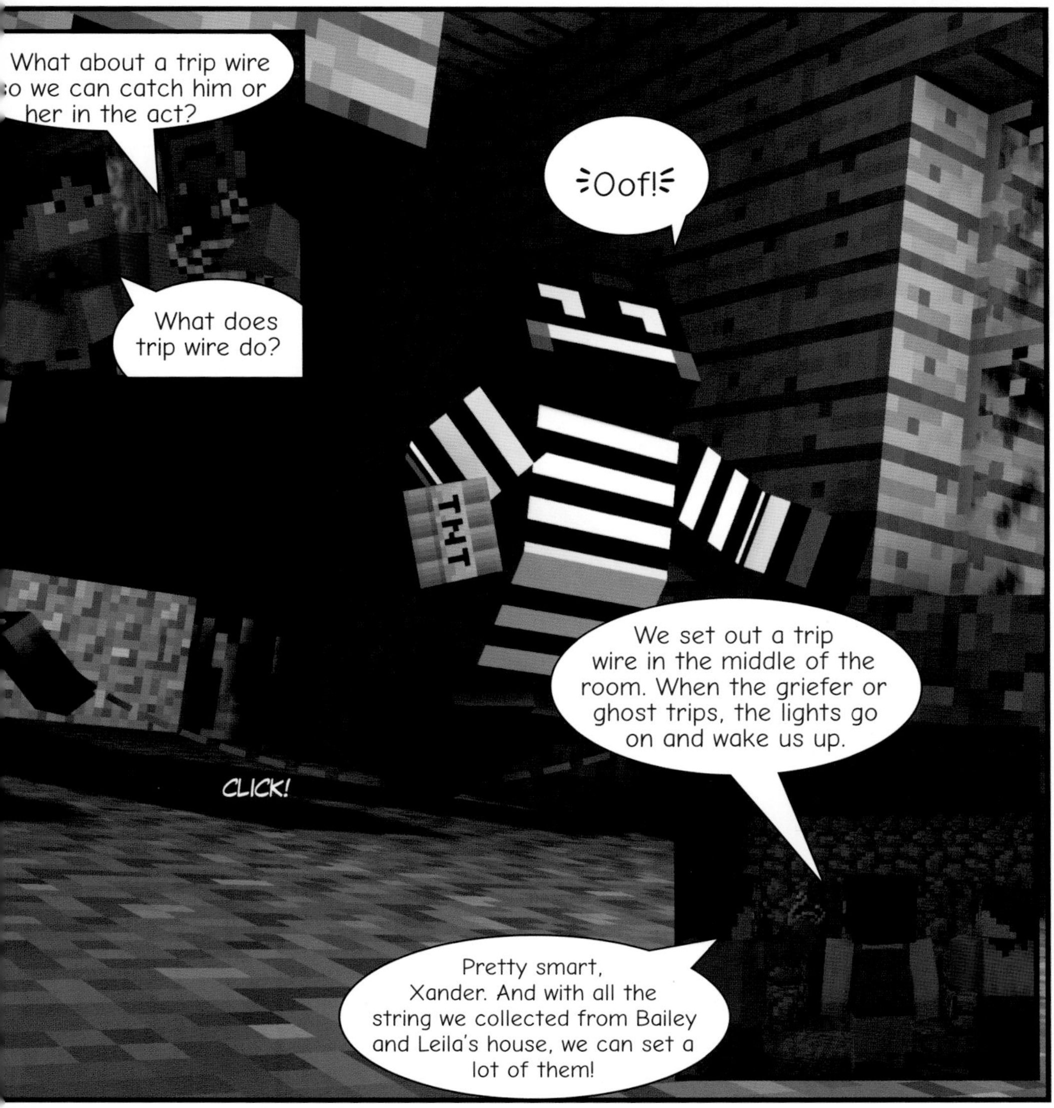
What about a trip wire so we can catch him or her in the act?
What does trip wire do?
Oof!
TNT
We set out a trip wire in the middle of the room. When the griefer or ghost trips, the lights go on and wake us up.
CLICK!
Pretty smart, Xander. And with all the string we collected from Bailey and Leila's house, we can set a lot of them!

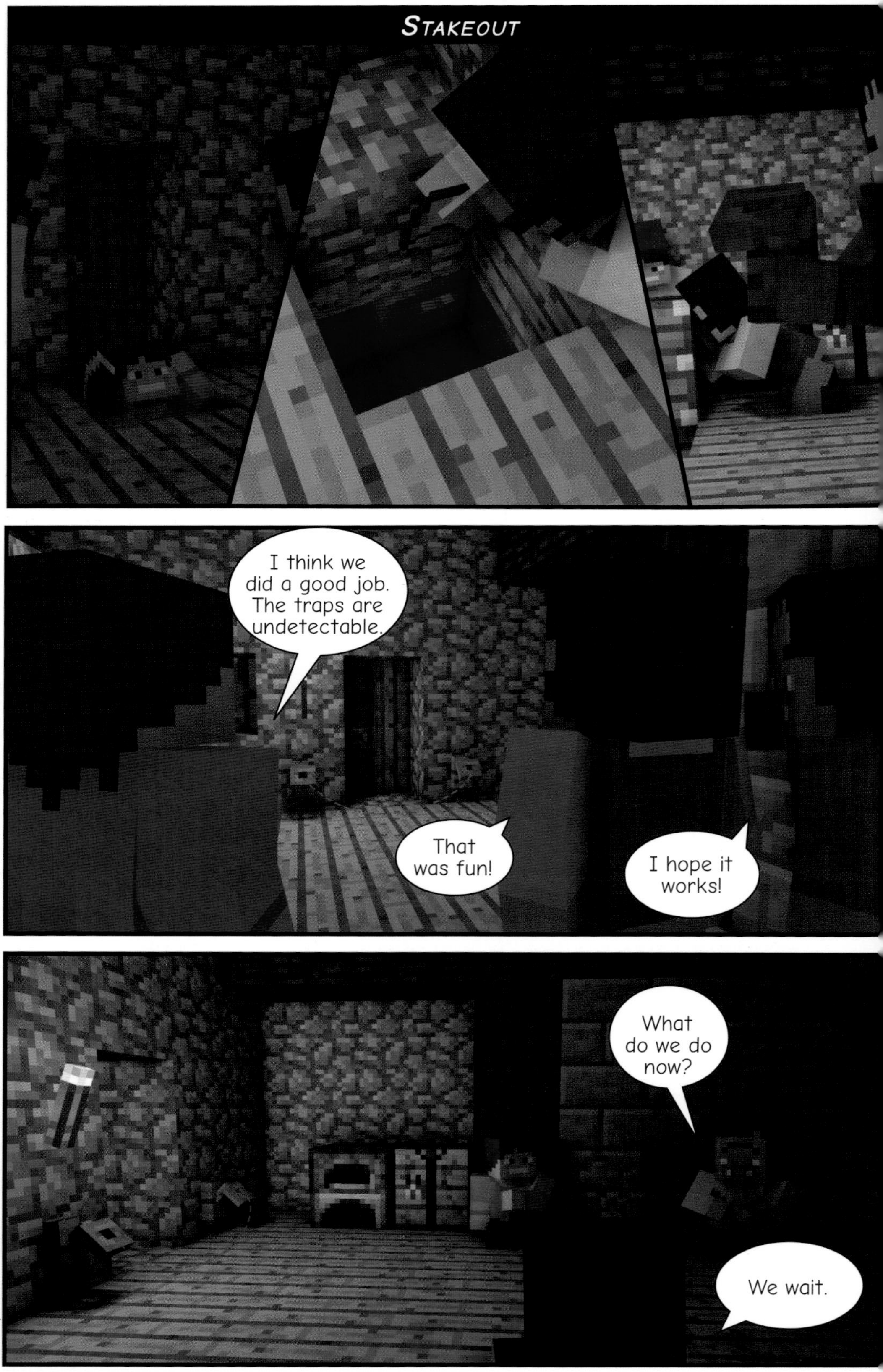
Stakeout
I think we did a good job. The traps are undetectable.
That was fun!
I hope it works!
What do we do now?
We wait.

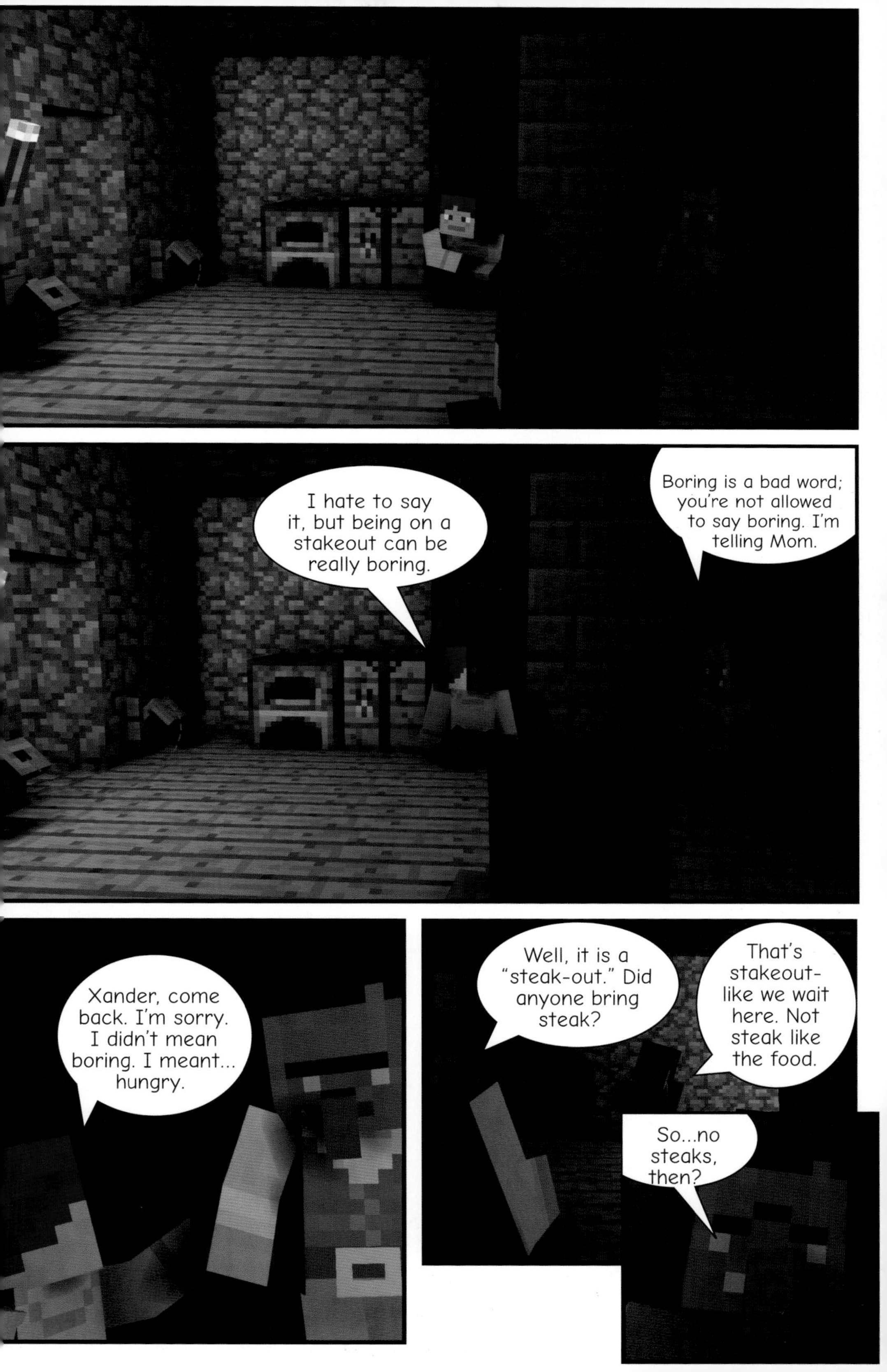
I hate to say it, but being on a stakeout can be really boring.
Boring is a bad word; you're not allowed to say boring. I'm telling Mom.
Xander, come back. I'm sorry. I didn't mean boring. I meant... hungry.
Well, it is a "steak-out." Did anyone bring steak?
That's stakeout-like we wait here. Not steak like the food.
So...no steaks, then?

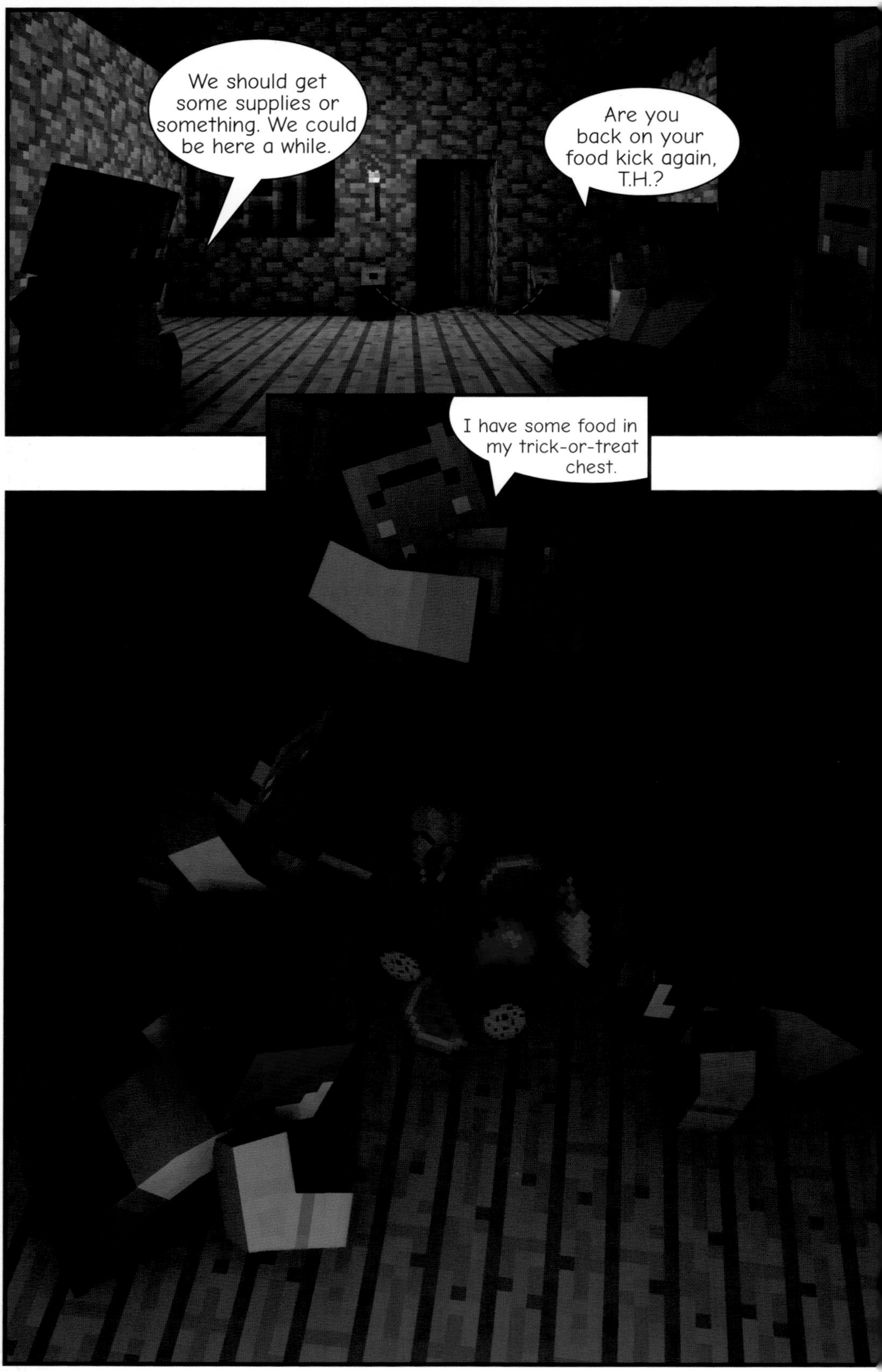
We should get some supplies or something. We could be here a while.
Are you back on your food kick again, T.H.?
I have some food in my trick-or-treat chest.

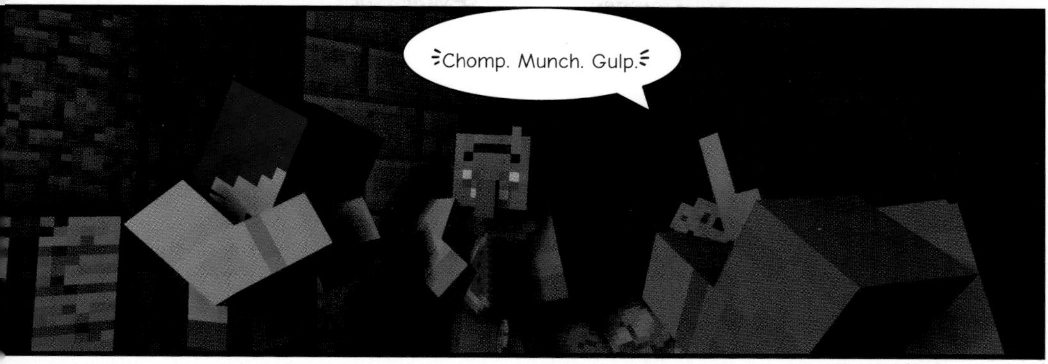
Chomp. Munch. Gulp.

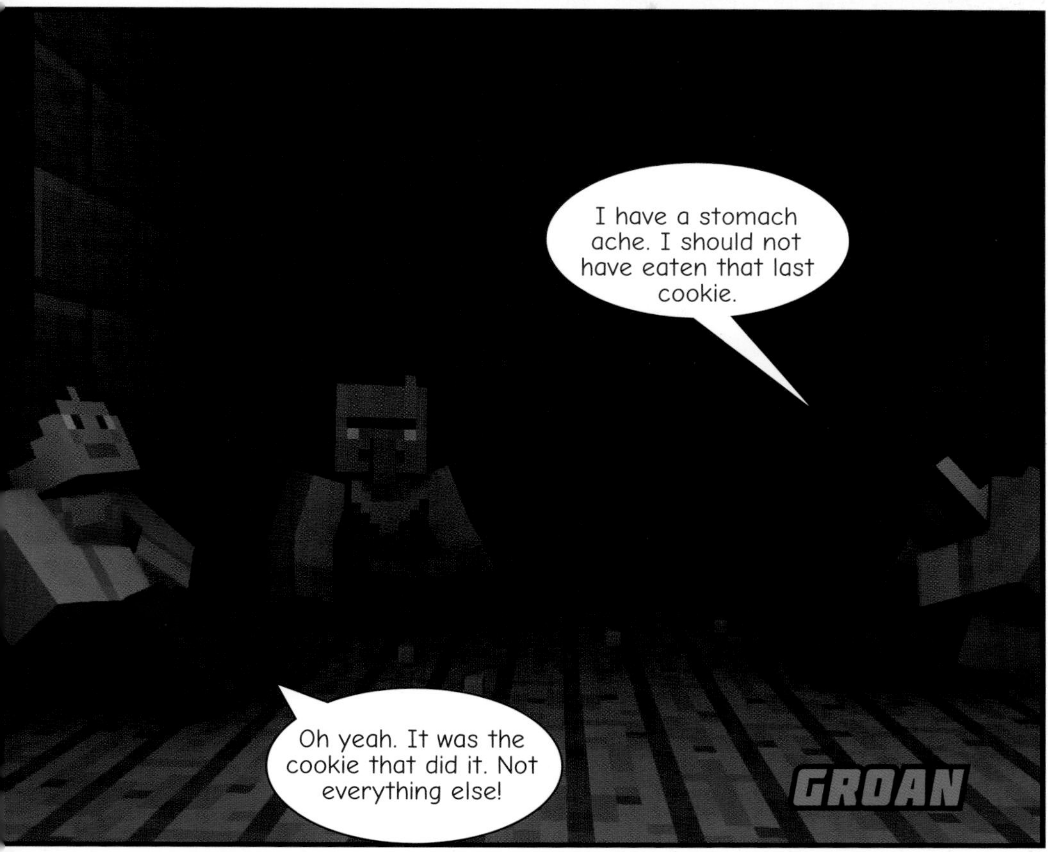
I have a stomach ache. I should not have eaten that last cookie.
Oh yeah. It was the cookie that did it. Not everything else!
GROAN

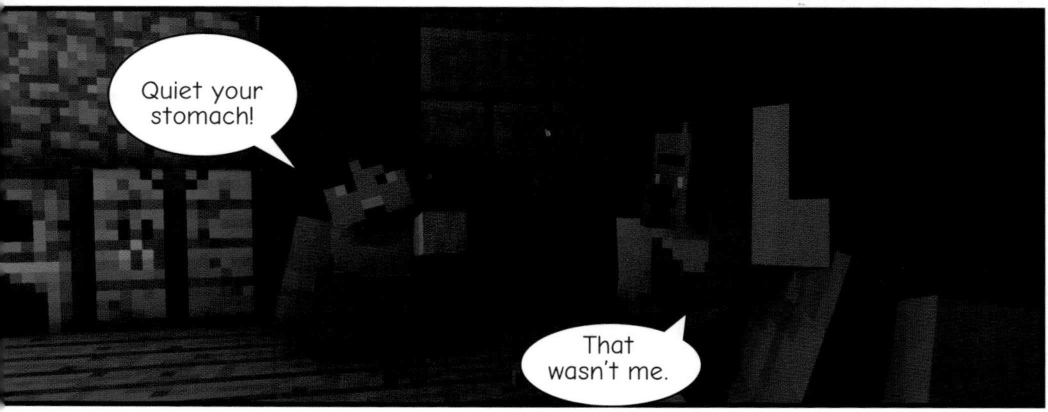
Quiet your stomach!
That wasn't me.

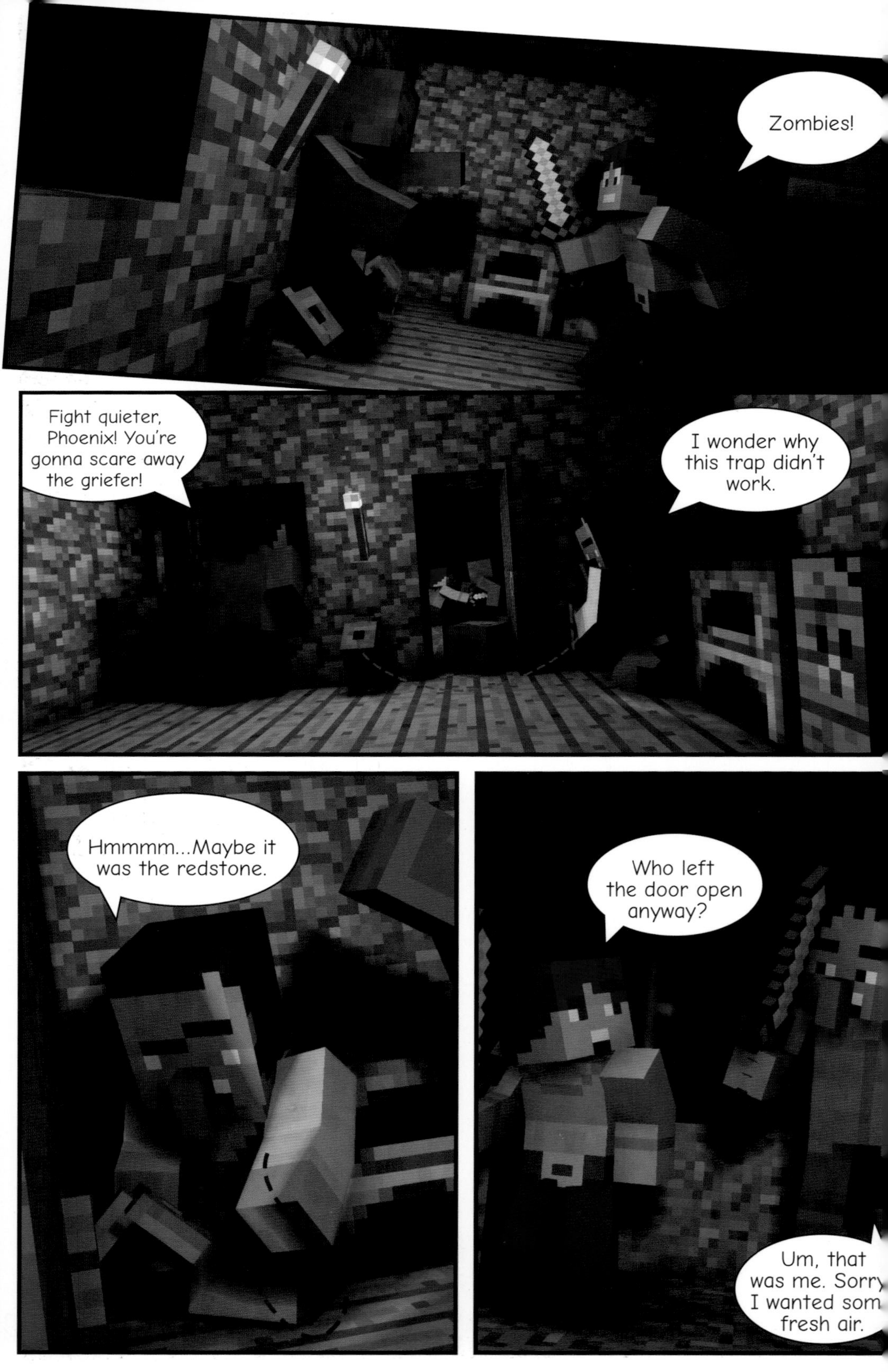
Zombies!
Fight quieter, Phoenix! You're gonna scare away the griefer!
I wonder why this trap didn't work.
Hmmmm...Maybe it was the redstone.
Who left the door open anyway?
Um, that was me. Sorry I wanted som fresh air.

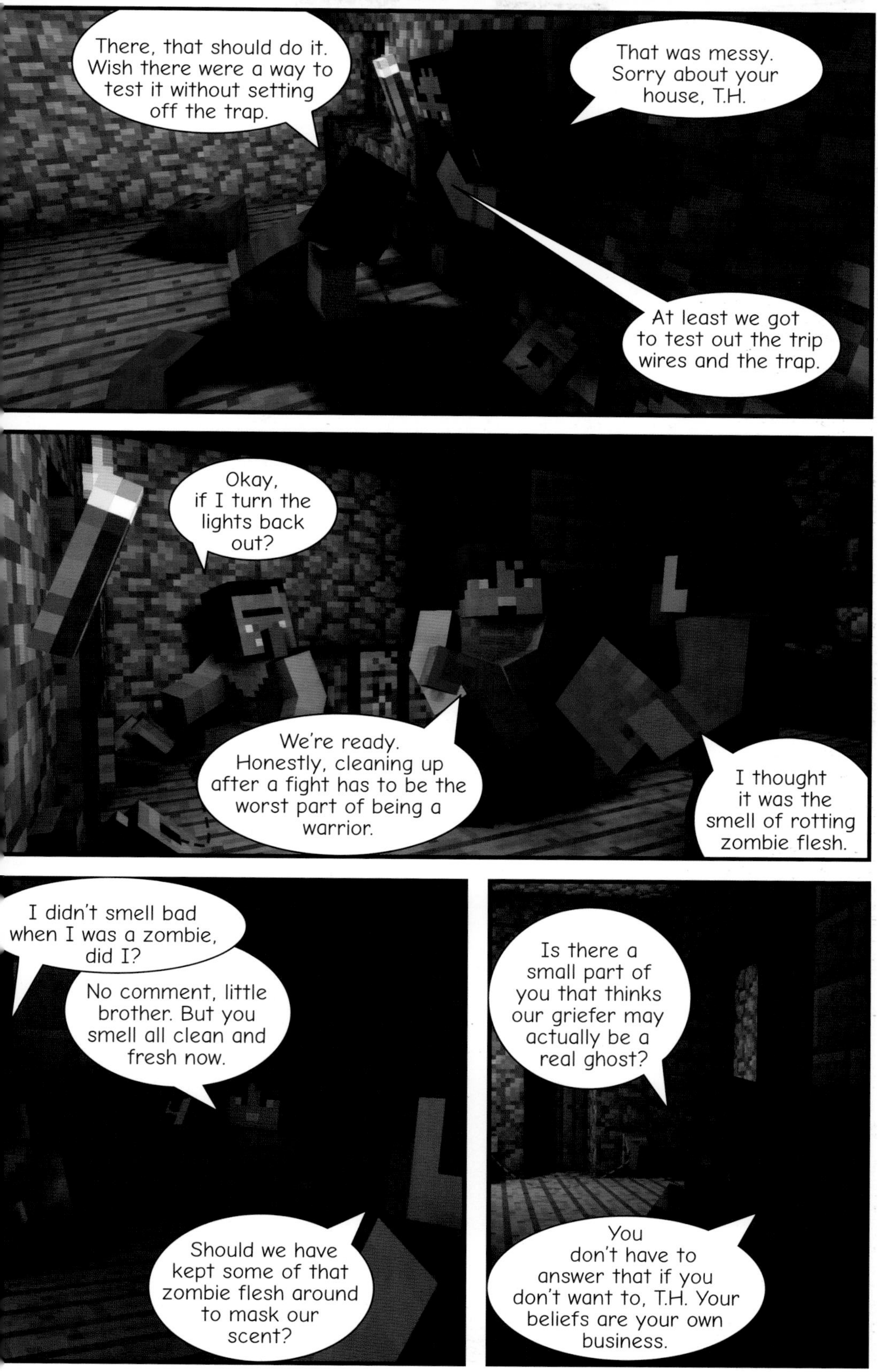
There, that should do it. Wish there were a way to test it without setting off the trap.
That was messy. Sorry about your house, T.H.
At least we got to test out the trip wires and the trap.
Okay, if I turn the lights back out?
We're ready. Honestly, cleaning up after a fight has to be the worst part of being a warrior.
I thought it was the smell of rotting zombie flesh.
I didn't smell bad when I was a zombie, did I?
No comment, little brother. But you smell all clean and fresh now.
Should we have kept some of that zombie flesh around to mask our scent?
Is there a small part of you that thinks our griefer may actually be a real ghost?
You don't have to answer that if you don't want to, T.H. Your beliefs are your own business.

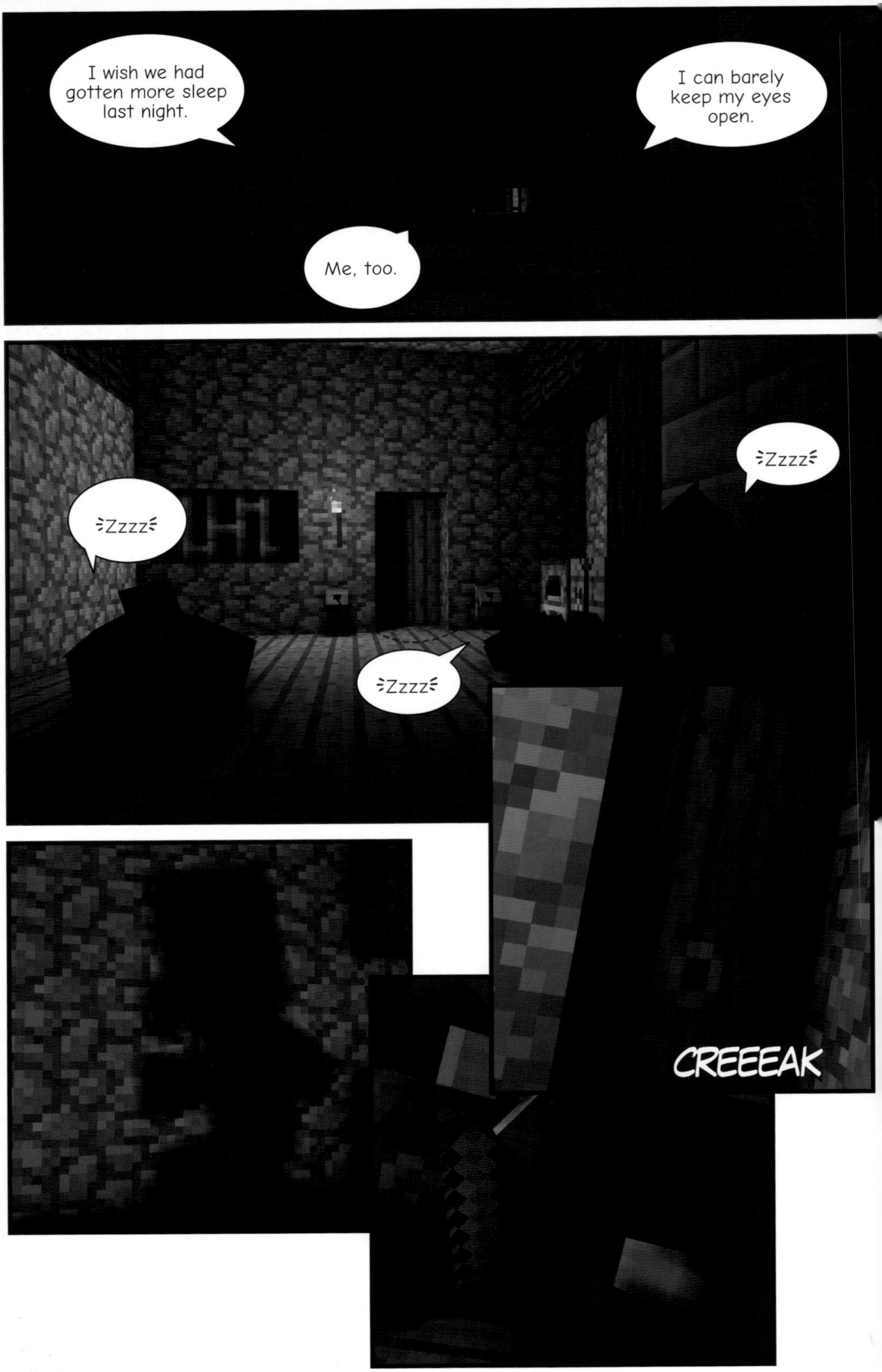
I wish we had gotten more sleep last night.
I can barely keep my eyes open.
Me, too.
Zzzz
Zzzz
Zzzz
CREEEAK

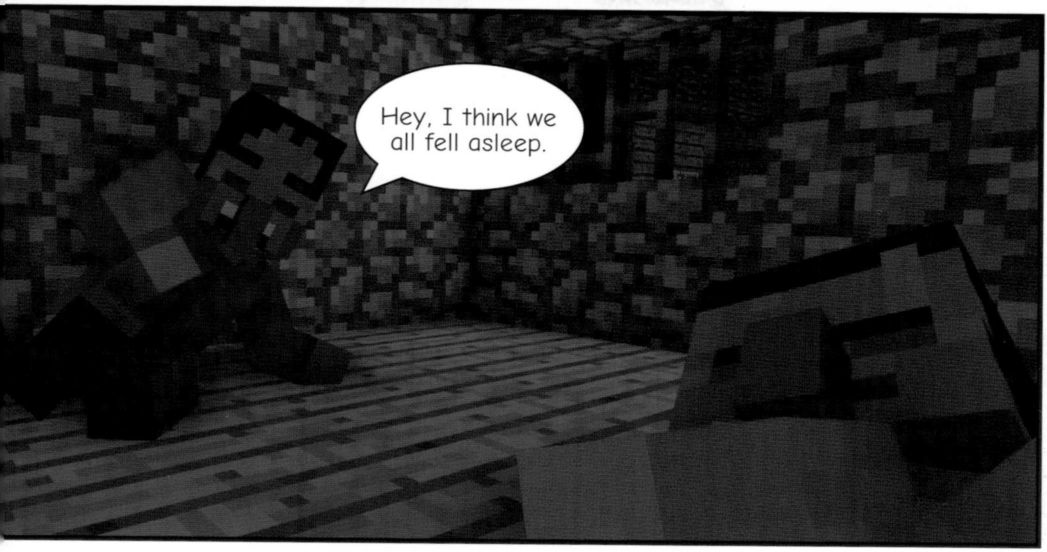
Hey, I think we all fell asleep.

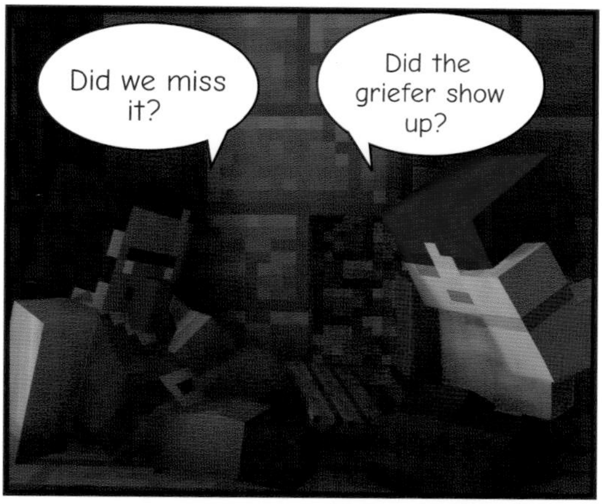
Did we miss it?
Did the griefer show up?

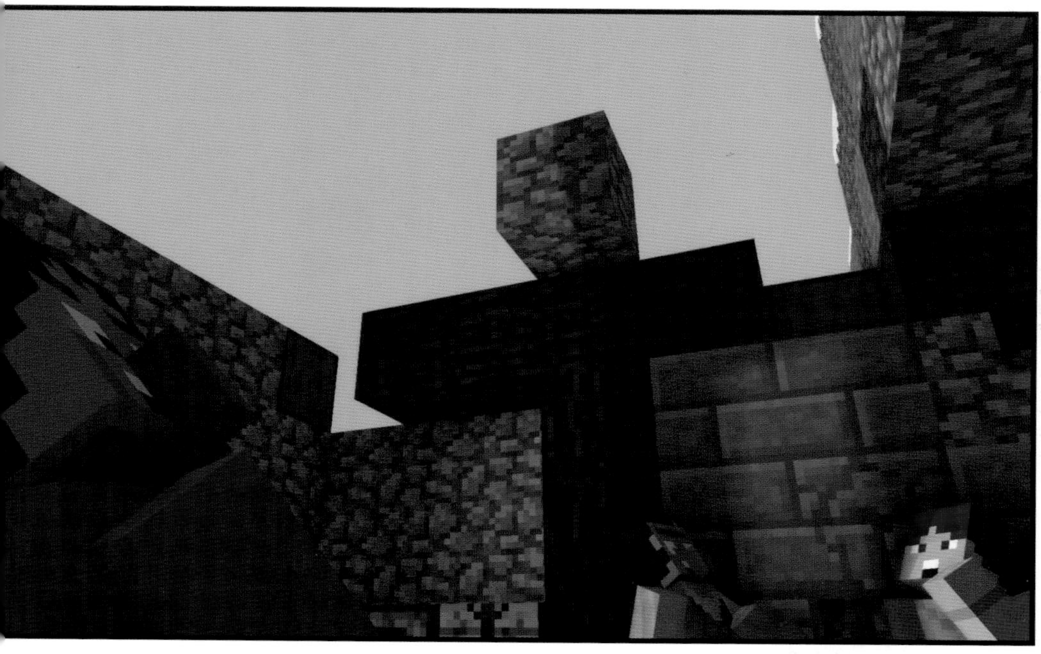

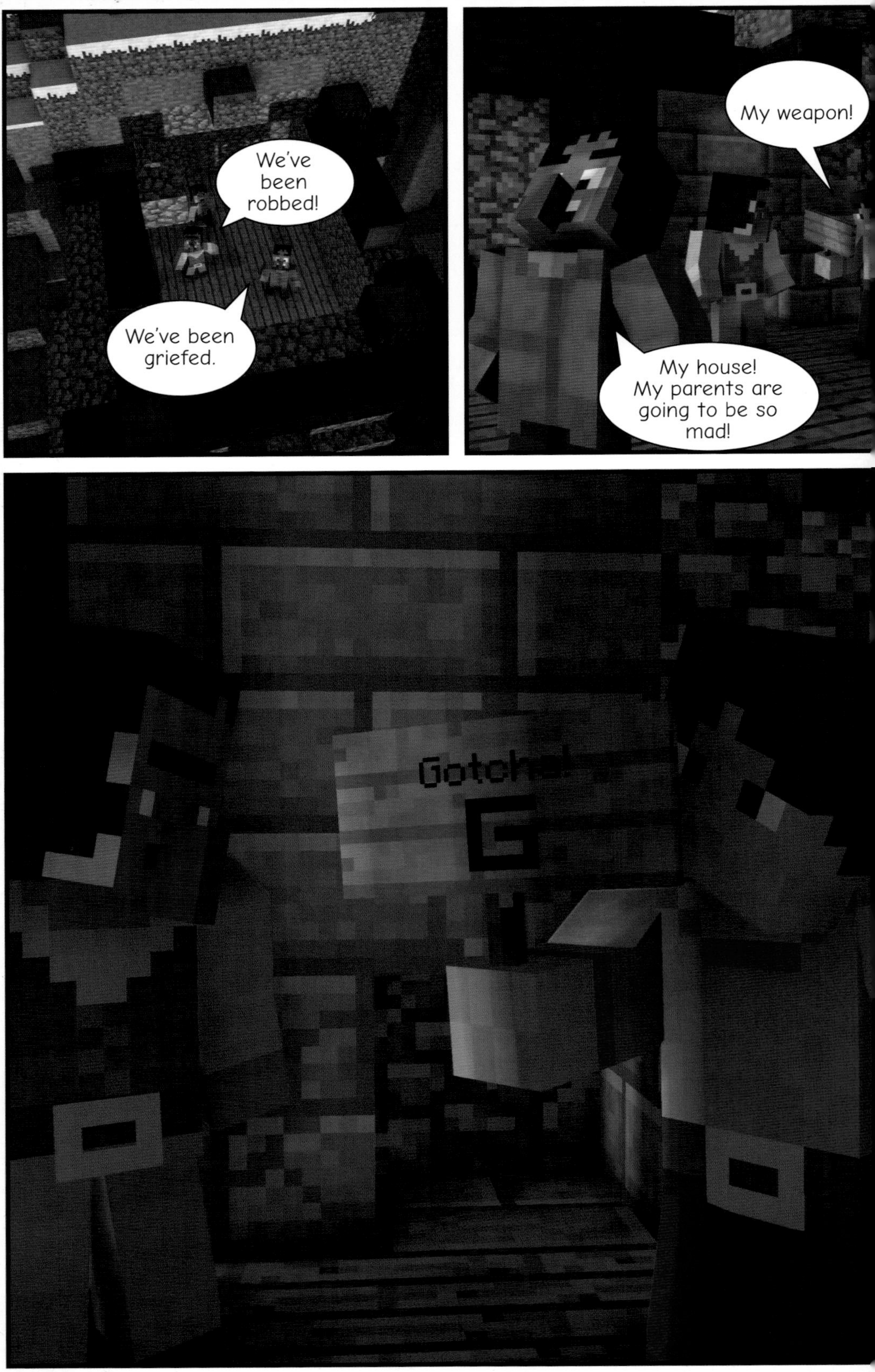
We've been robbed!
We've been griefed.
My weapon!
My house! My parents are going to be so mad!

CHAPTER 5

BAIT

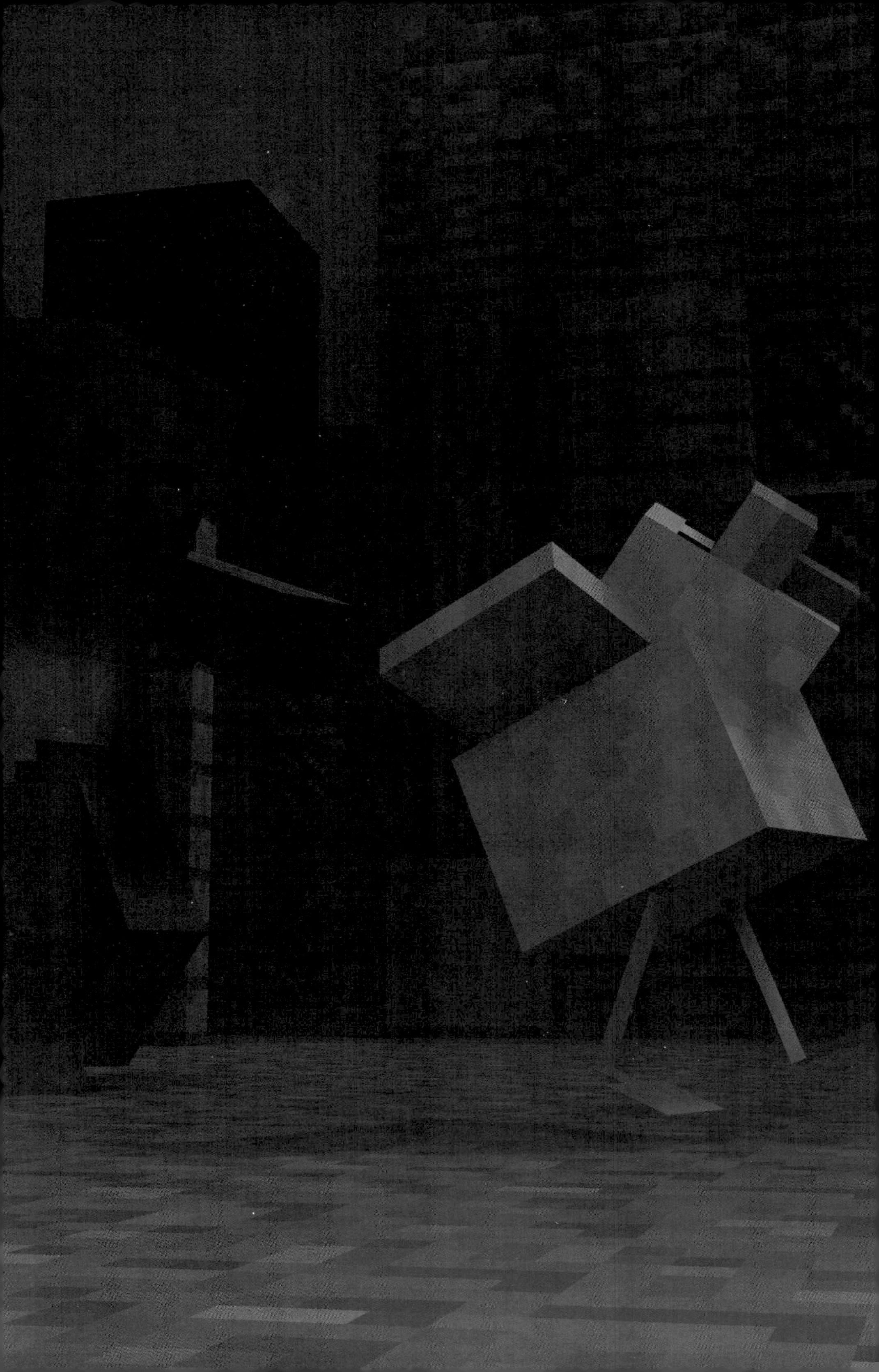

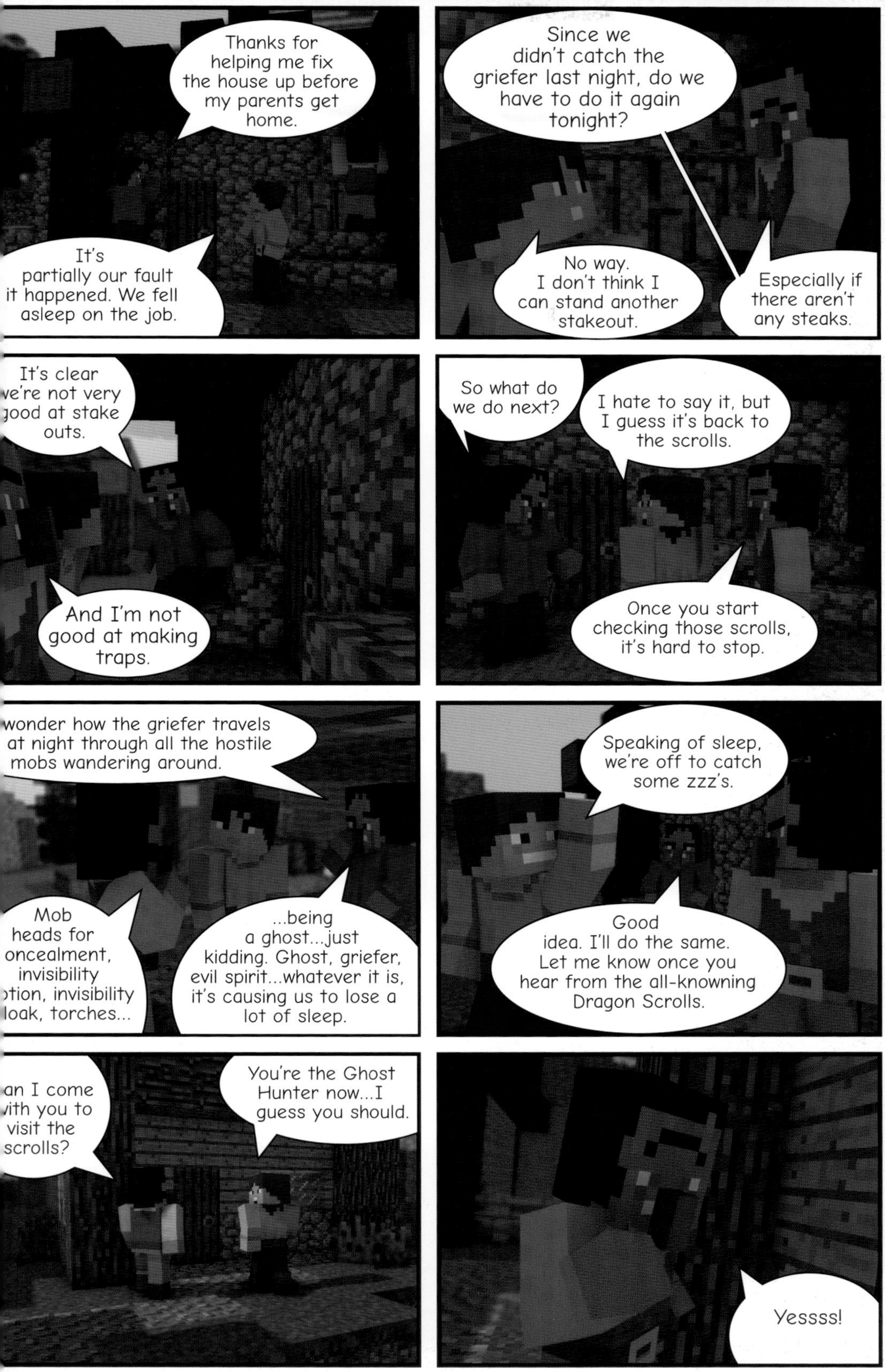

Thanks for helping me fix the house up before my parents get home.
It's partially our fault it happened. We fell asleep on the job.
Since we didn't catch the griefer last night, do we have to do it again tonight?
No way. I don't think I can stand another stakeout.
Especially if there aren't any steaks.
It's clear ve're not very jood at stake outs.
And I'm not good at making traps.
So what do we do next?
I hate to say it, but I guess it's back to the scrolls.
Once you start checking those scrolls, it's hard to stop.
wonder how the griefer travels at night through all the hostile mobs wandering around.
Mob heads for oncealment, invisibility otion, invisibility loak, torches...
...being a ghost...just kidding. Ghost, griefer, evil spirit...whatever it is, it's causing us to lose a lot of sleep.
Speaking of sleep, we're off to catch some zzz's.
Good idea. I'll do the same. Let me know once you hear from the all-knowning Dragon Scrolls.
an I come vith you to visit the scrolls?
You're the Ghost Hunter now...I guess you should.
Yessss!

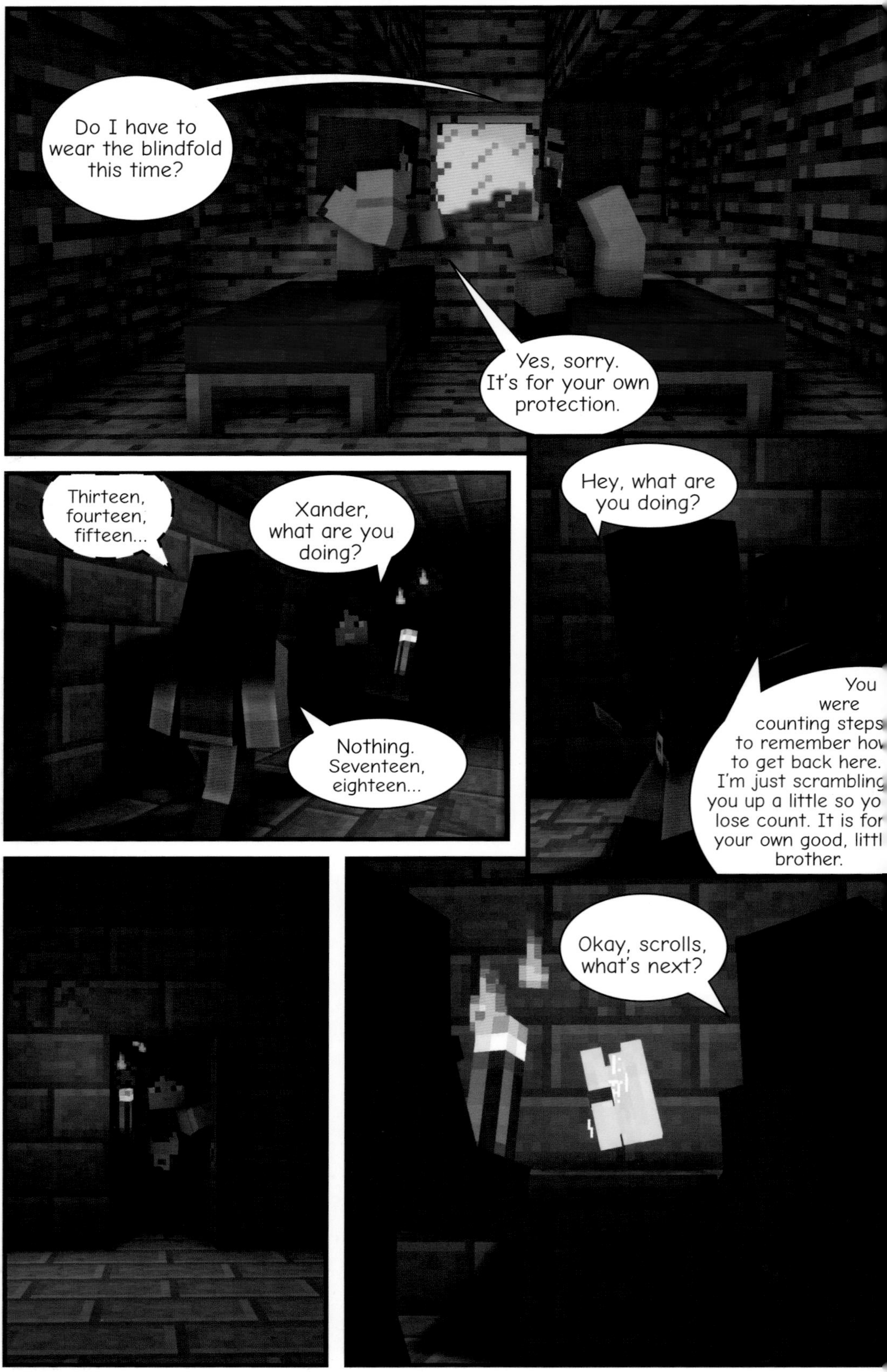

Do I have to wear the blindfold this time?
Yes, sorry. It's for your own protection.
Thirteen, fourteen, fifteen...
Xander, what are you doing?
Nothing. Seventeen, eighteen...
Hey, what are you doing?
You were counting steps to remember how to get back here. I'm just scrambling you up a little so you lose count. It is for your own good, little brother.
Okay, scrolls, what's next?

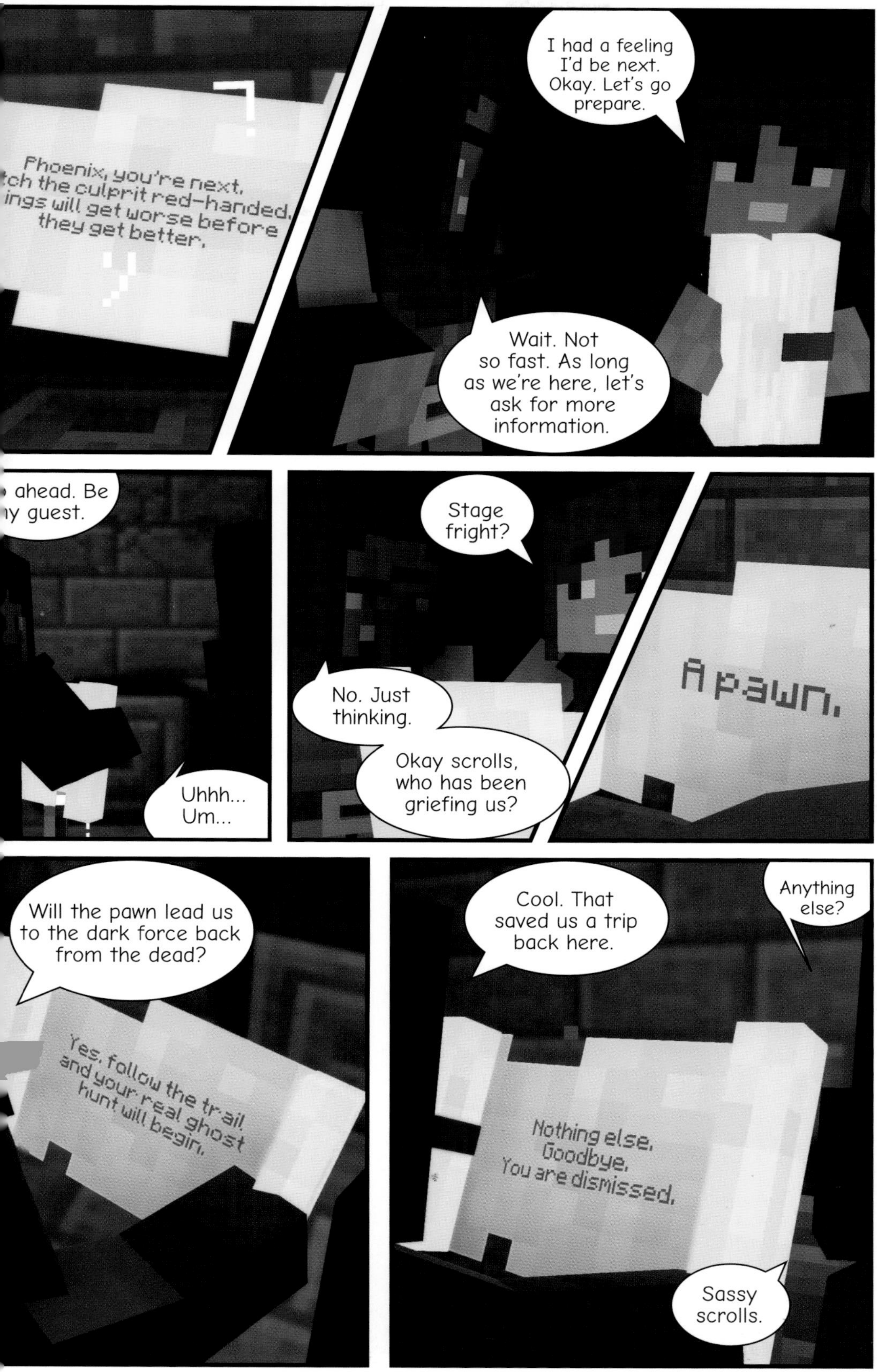

Phoenix, you're next.
tch the culprit red-handed.
ings will get worse before they get better.
I had a feeling I'd be next. Okay. Let's go prepare.
Wait. Not so fast. As long as we're here, let's ask for more information.
ahead. Be
y guest.
Uhhh... Um...
Stage fright?
No. Just thinking.
Okay scrolls, who has been griefing us?
A pawn.
Will the pawn lead us to the dark force back from the dead?
Yes, follow the trail and your real ghost hunt will begin.
Cool. That saved us a trip back here.
Anything else?
Nothing else. Goodbye. You are dismissed.
Sassy scrolls.

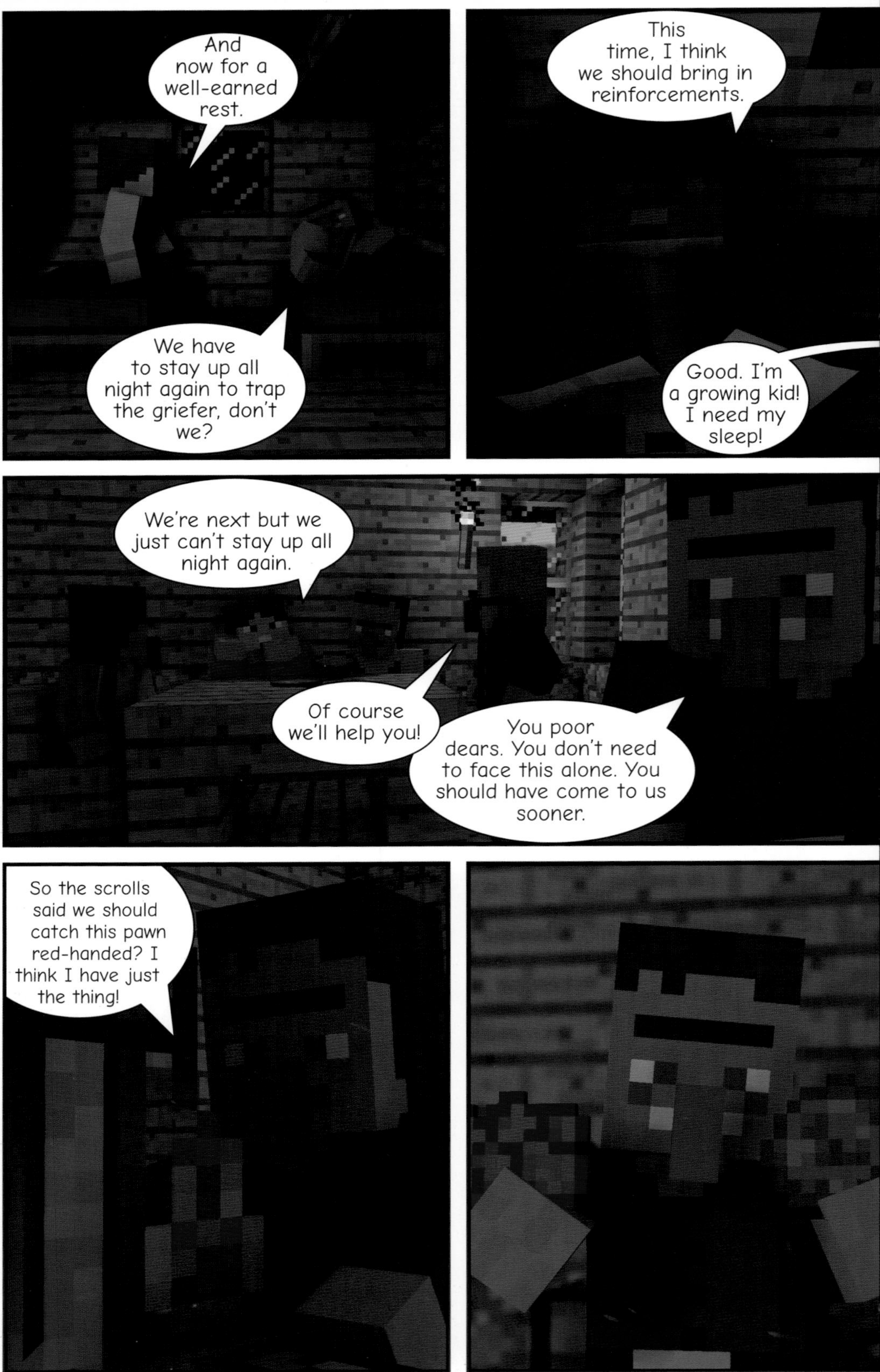
And now for a well-earned rest.
We have to stay up all night again to trap the griefer, don't we?
This time, I think we should bring in reinforcements.
Good. I'm a growing kid! I need my sleep!
We're next but we just can't stay up all night again.
Of course we'll help you!
You poor dears. You don't need to face this alone. You should have come to us sooner.
So the scrolls said we should catch this pawn red-handed? I think I have just the thing!

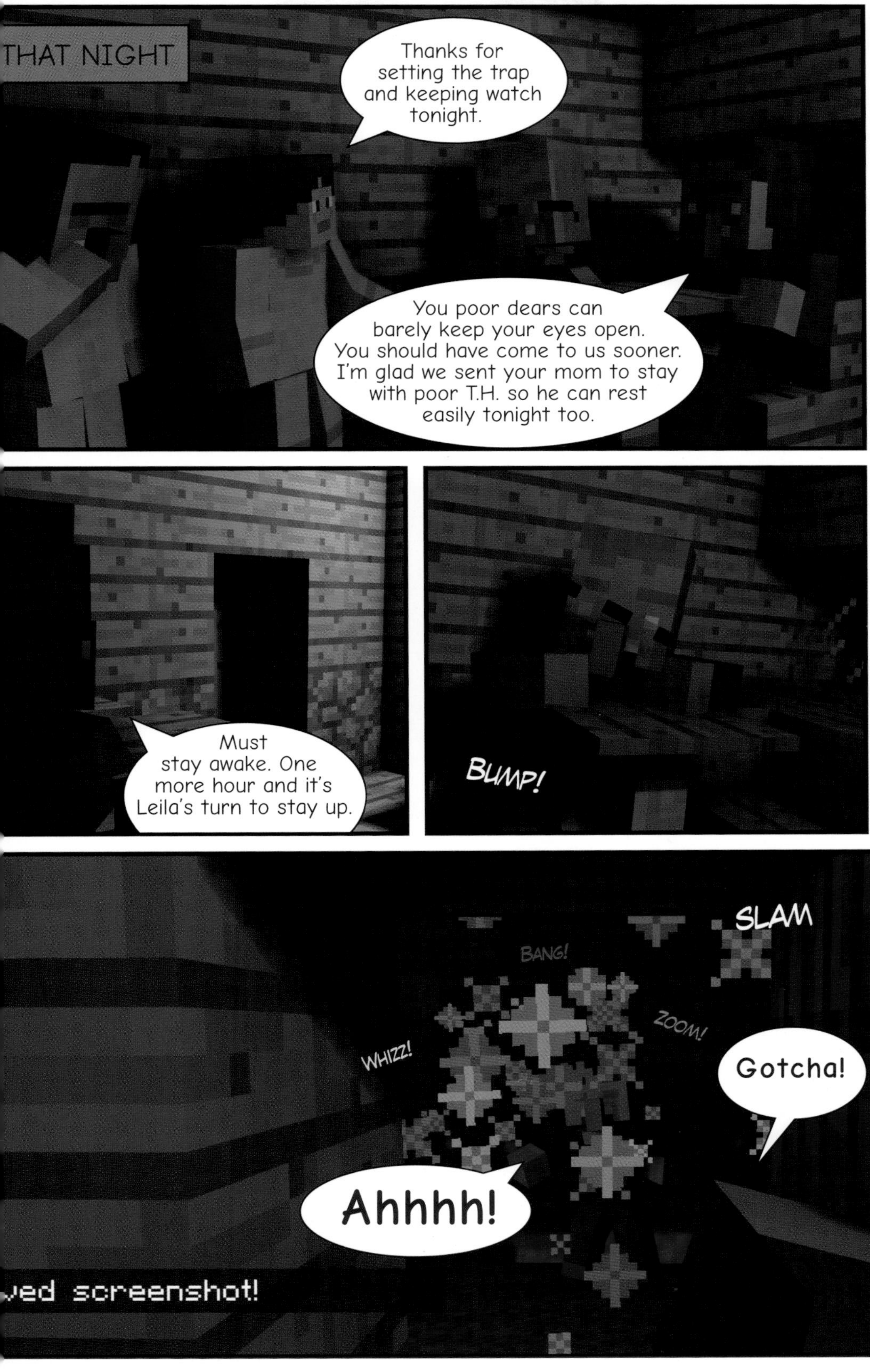

THAT NIGHT
Thanks for setting the trap and keeping watch tonight.
You poor dears can barely keep your eyes open. You should have come to us sooner. I'm glad we sent your mom to stay with poor T.H. so he can rest easily tonight too.
Must stay awake. One more hour and it's Leila's turn to stay up.
BUMP!
SLAM
BANG!
ZOOM!
WHIZZ!
Gotcha!
Ahhhh!
ved screenshot!

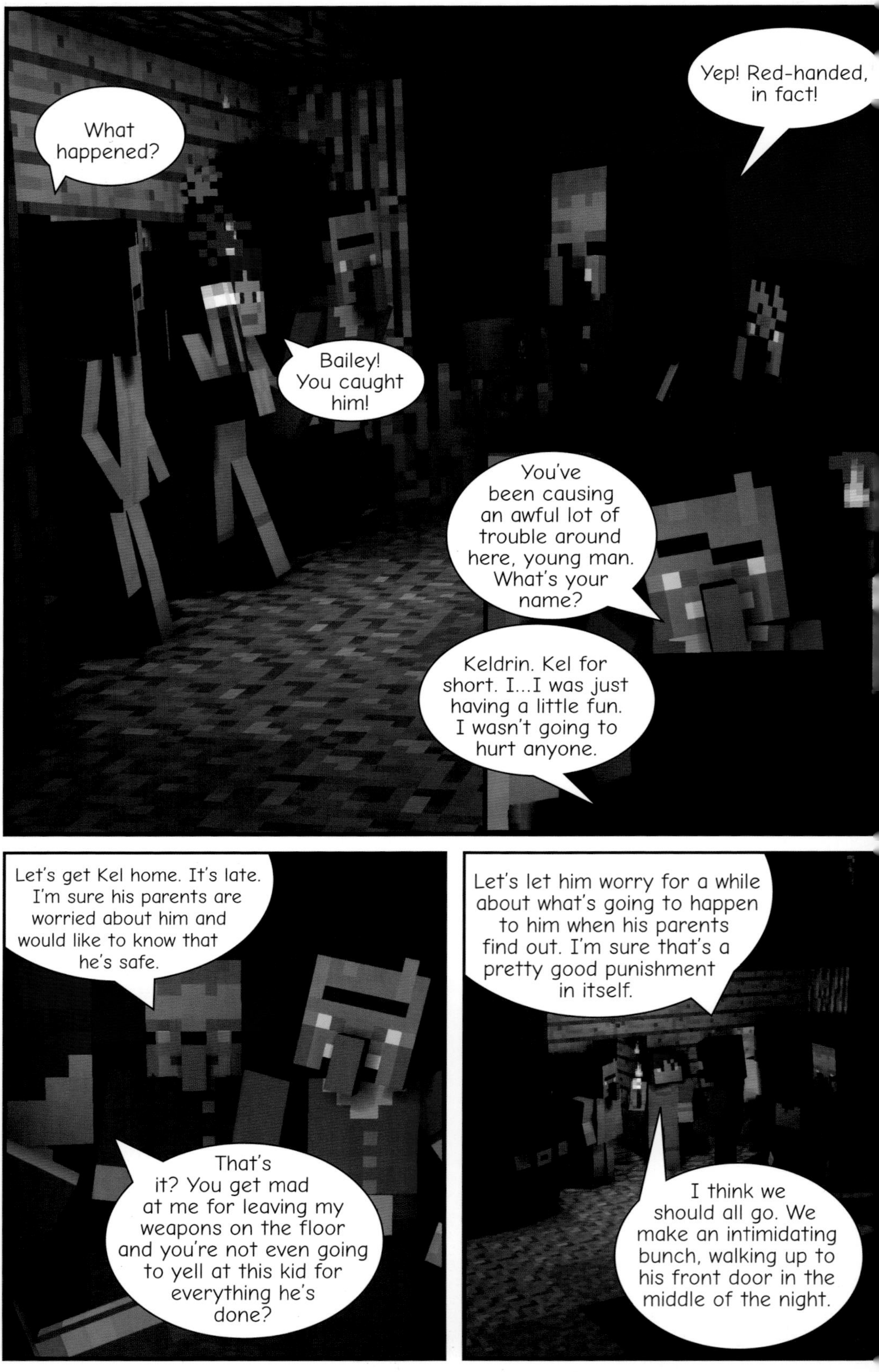
What happened?
Yep! Red-handed, in fact!
Bailey! You caught him!
You've been causing an awful lot of trouble around here, young man. What's your name?
Keldrin. Kel for short. I...I was just having a little fun. I wasn't going to hurt anyone.
Let's get Kel home. It's late. I'm sure his parents are worried about him and would like to know that he's safe.
That's it? You get mad at me for leaving my weapons on the floor and you're not even going to yell at this kid for everything he's done?
Let's let him worry for a while about what's going to happen to him when his parents find out. I'm sure that's a pretty good punishment in itself.
I think we should all go. We make an intimidating bunch, walking up to his front door in the middle of the night.

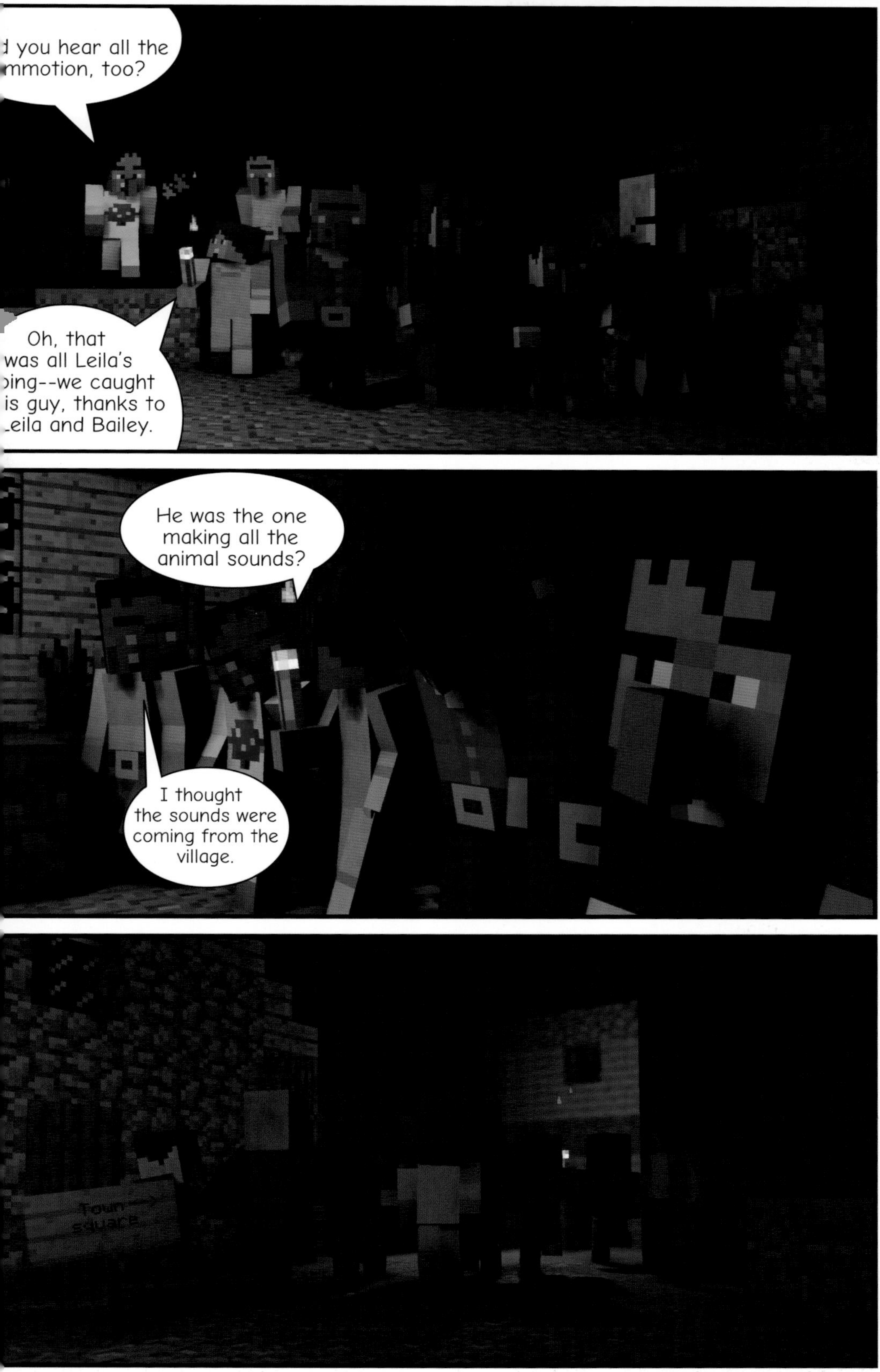
you hear all the mmotion, too?
Oh, that was all Leila's ing--we caught is guy, thanks to eila and Bailey.
He was the one making all the animal sounds?
I thought the sounds were coming from the village.
Town square

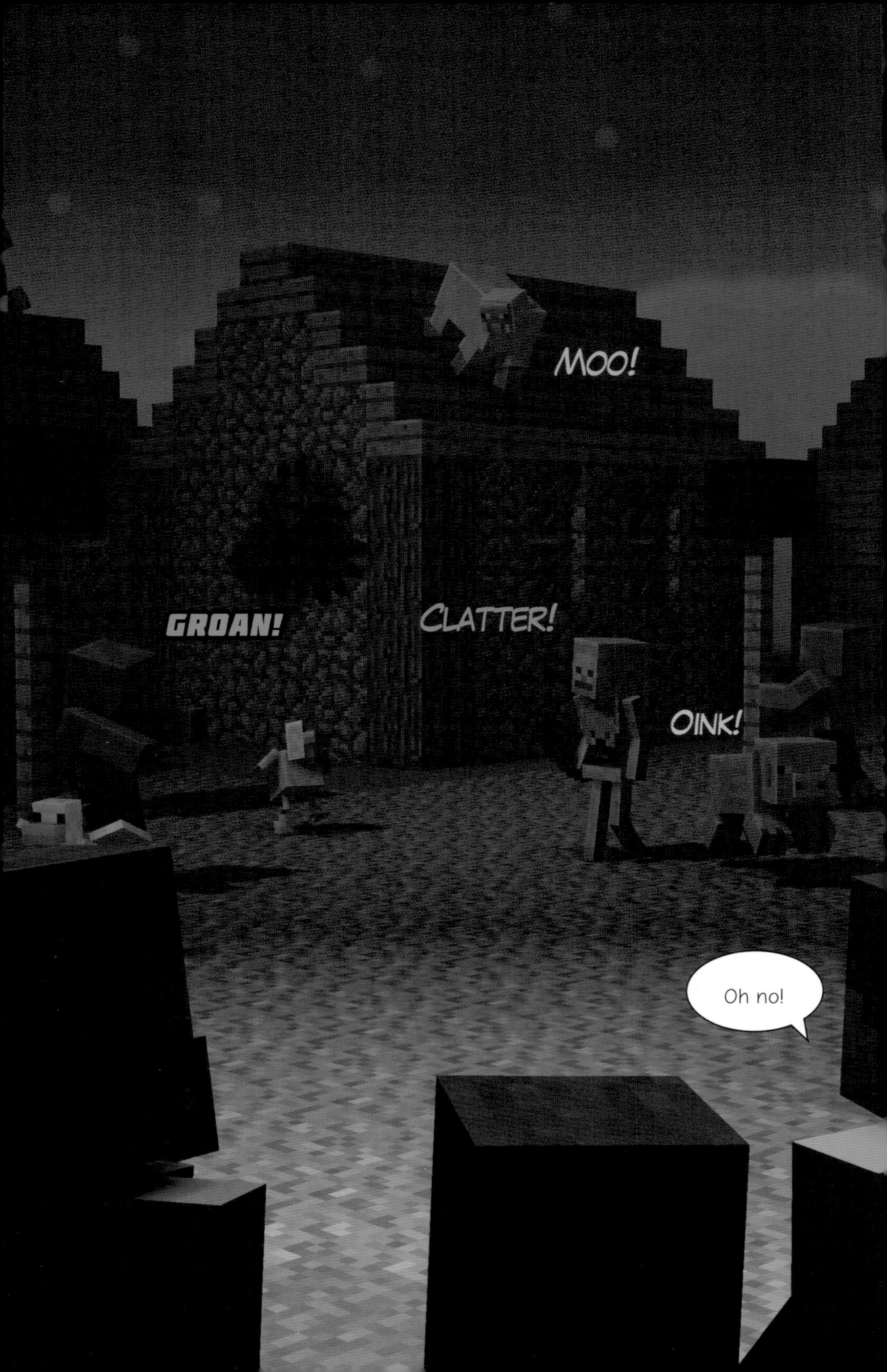
MOO!
GROAN!
CLATTER!
OINK!
Oh no!

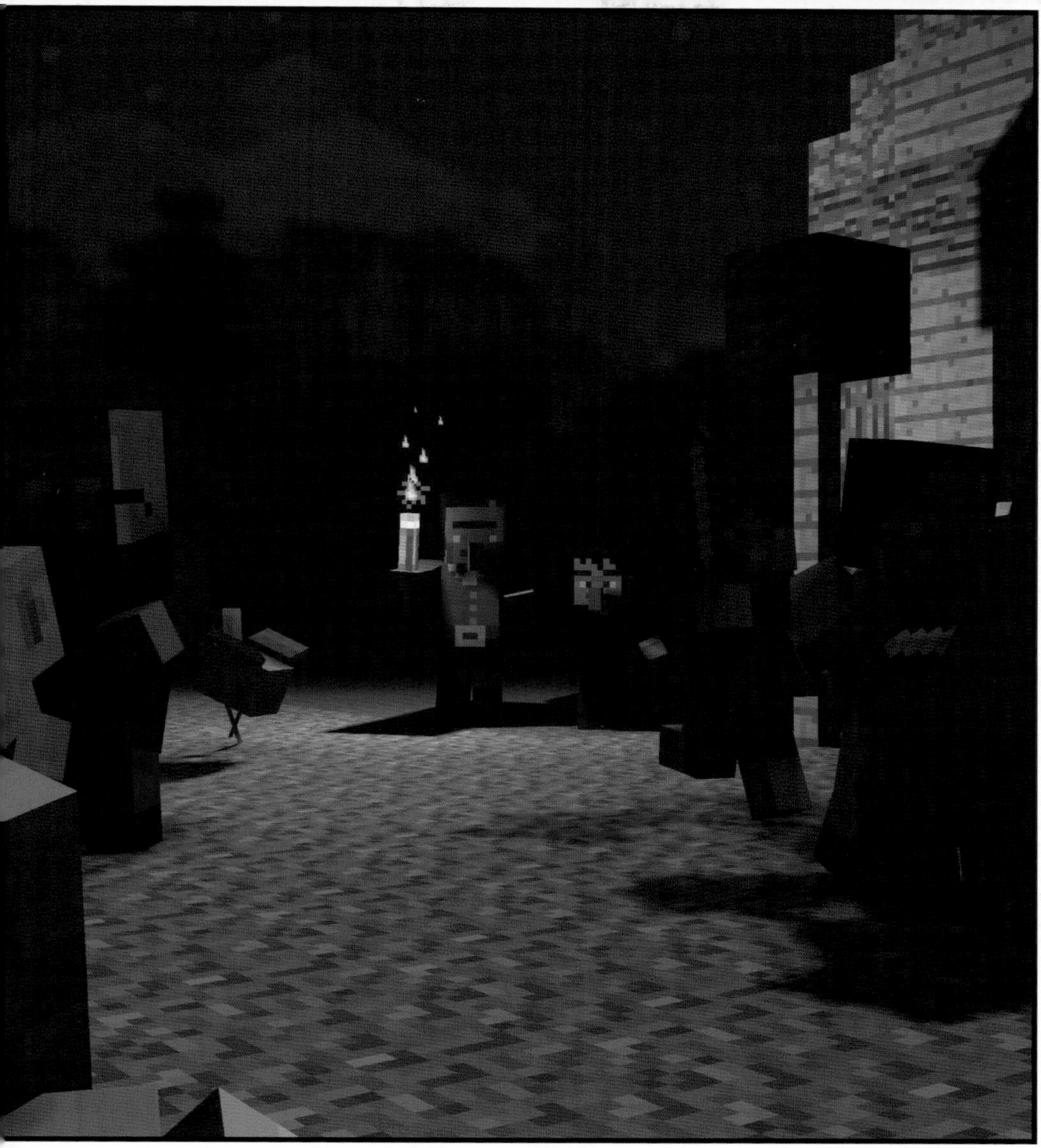

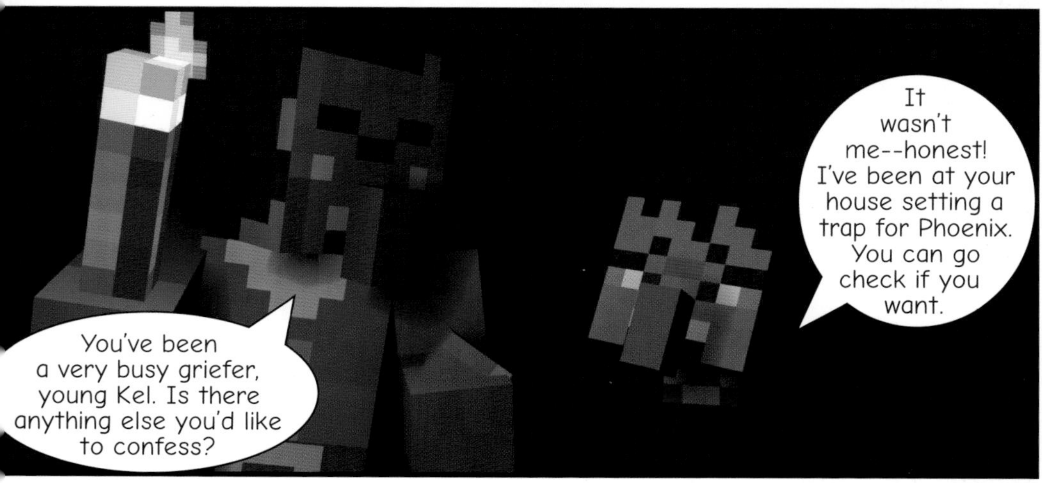
You've been a very busy griefer, young Kel. Is there anything else you'd like to confess?
It wasn't me--honest! I've been at your house setting a trap for Phoenix. You can go check if you want.

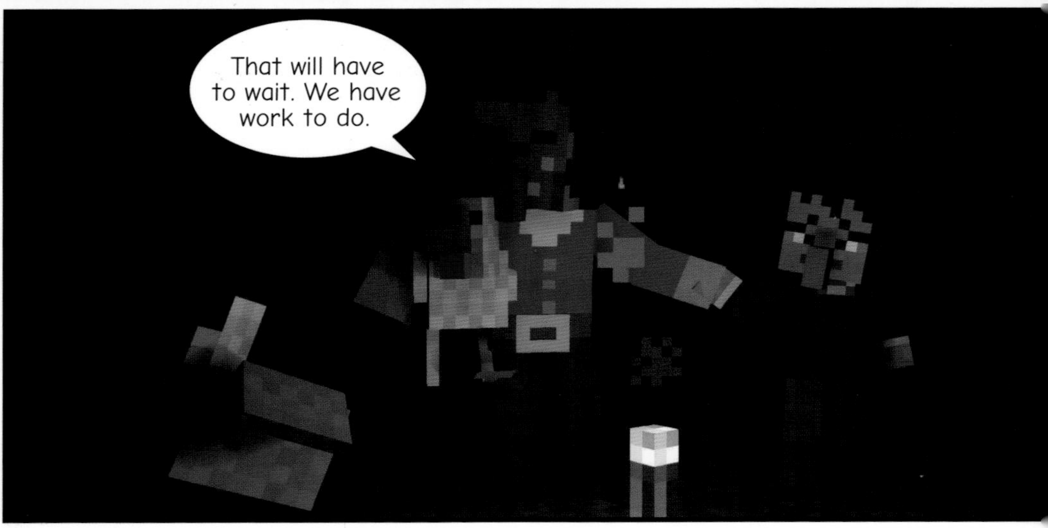
That will have to wait. We have work to do.

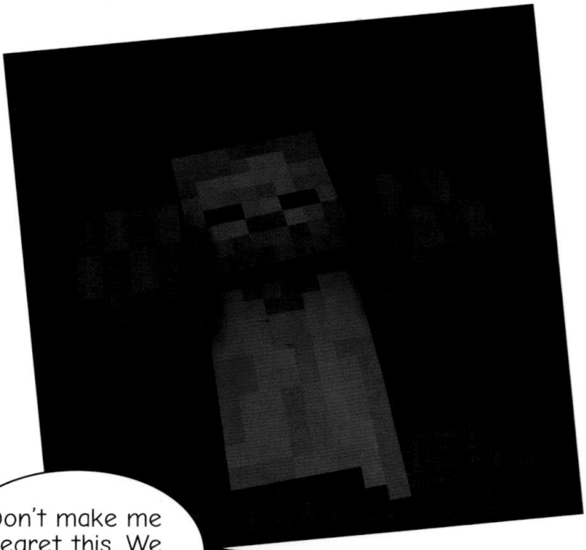

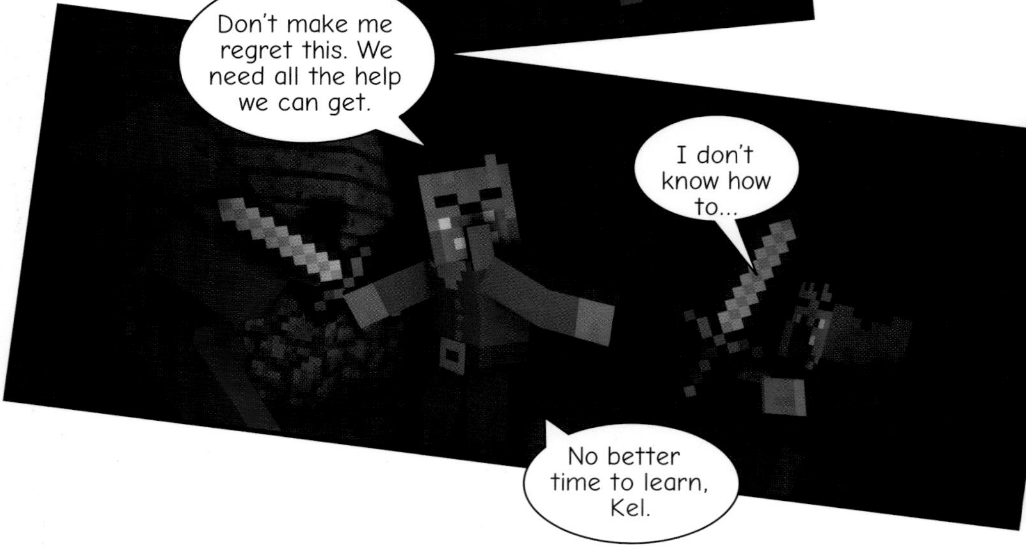
Don't make me regret this. We need all the help we can get.
I don't know how to...
No better time to learn, Kel.

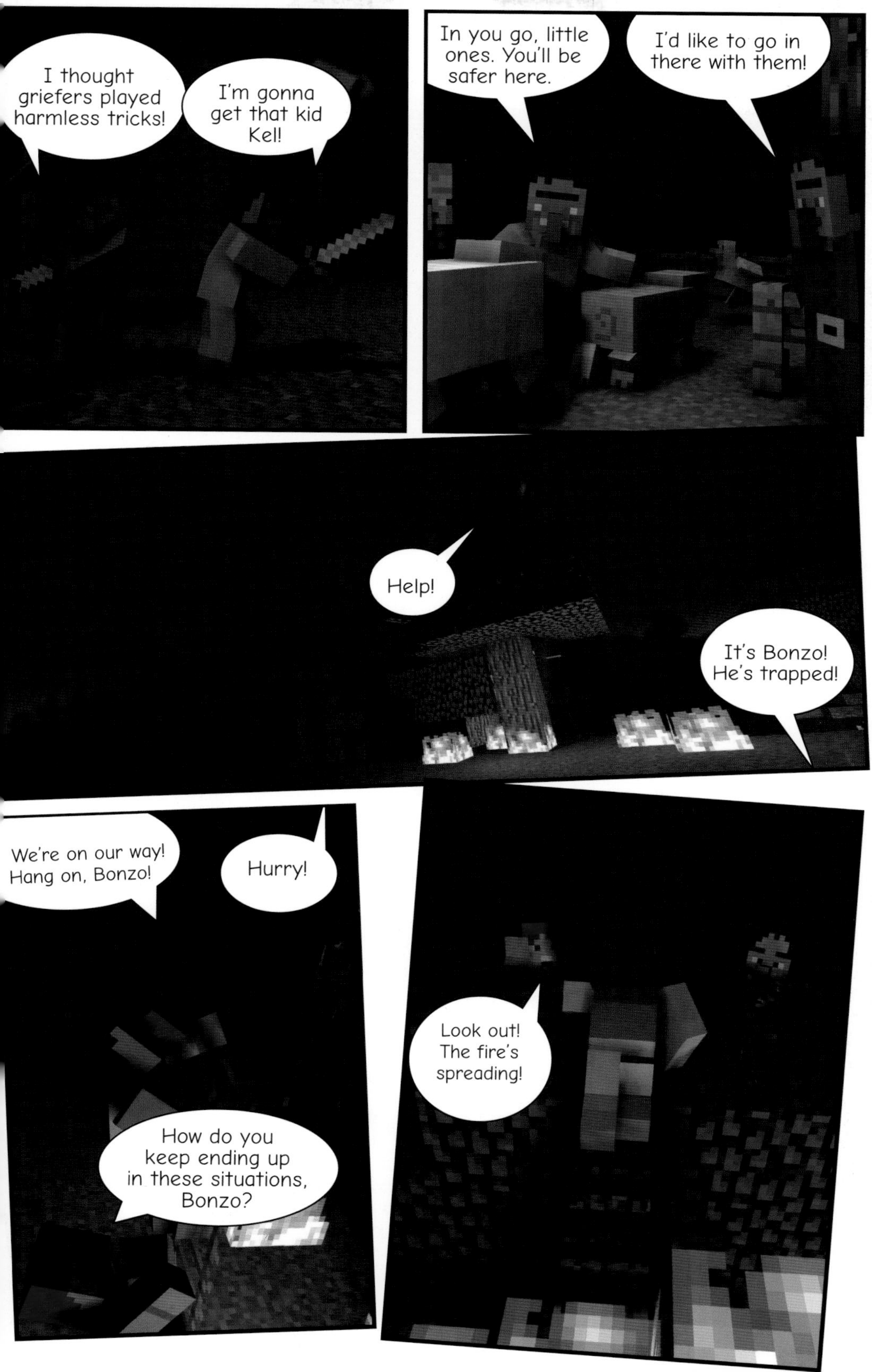
I thought griefers played harmless tricks!
I'm gonna get that kid Kel!
In you go, little ones. You'll be safer here.
I'd like to go in there with them!
Help!
It's Bonzo! He's trapped!
We're on our way! Hang on, Bonzo!
Hurry!
How do you keep ending up in these situations, Bonzo?
Look out! The fire's spreading!

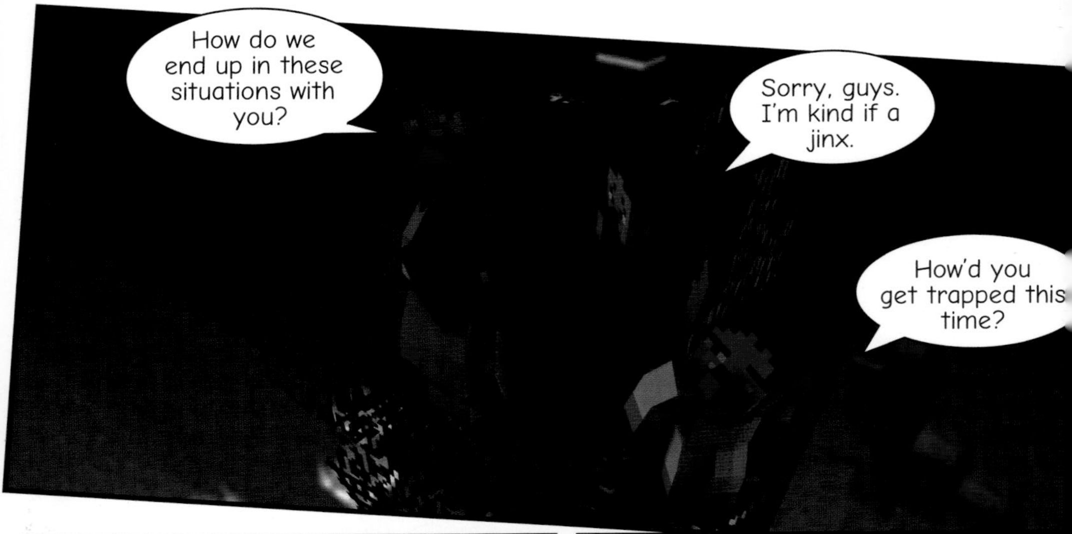
How do we end up in these situations with you?
Sorry, guys. I'm kind if a jinx.
How'd you get trapped this time?

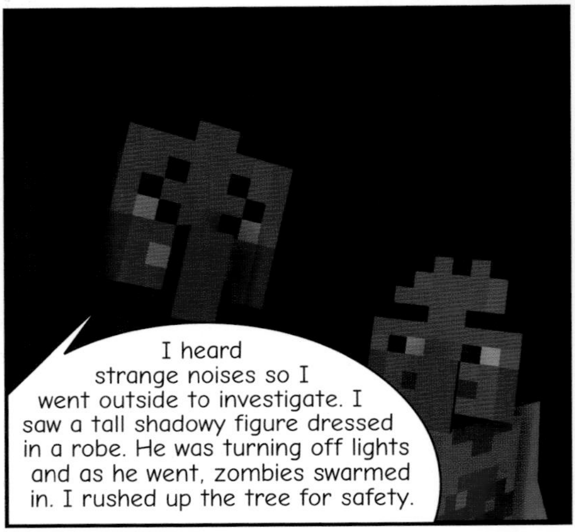
I heard strange noises so I went outside to investigate. I saw a tall shadowy figure dressed in a robe. He was turning off lights and as he went, zombies swarmed in. I rushed up the tree for safety.

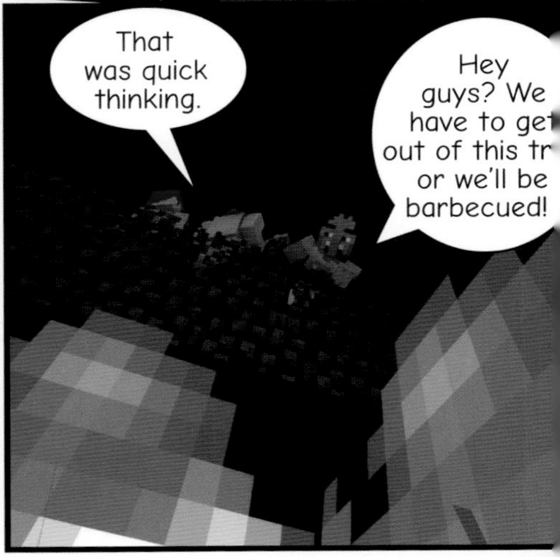
That was quick thinking.
Hey guys? We have to ge out of this tr or we'll be barbecued!

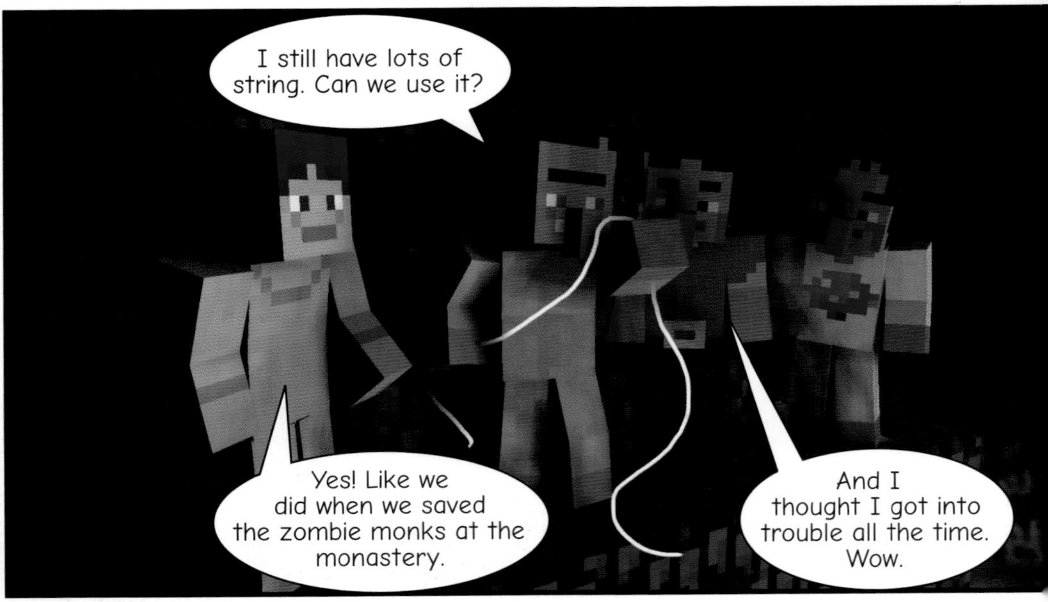
I still have lots of string. Can we use it?
Yes! Like we did when we saved the zombie monks at the monastery.
And I thought I got into trouble all the time. Wow.

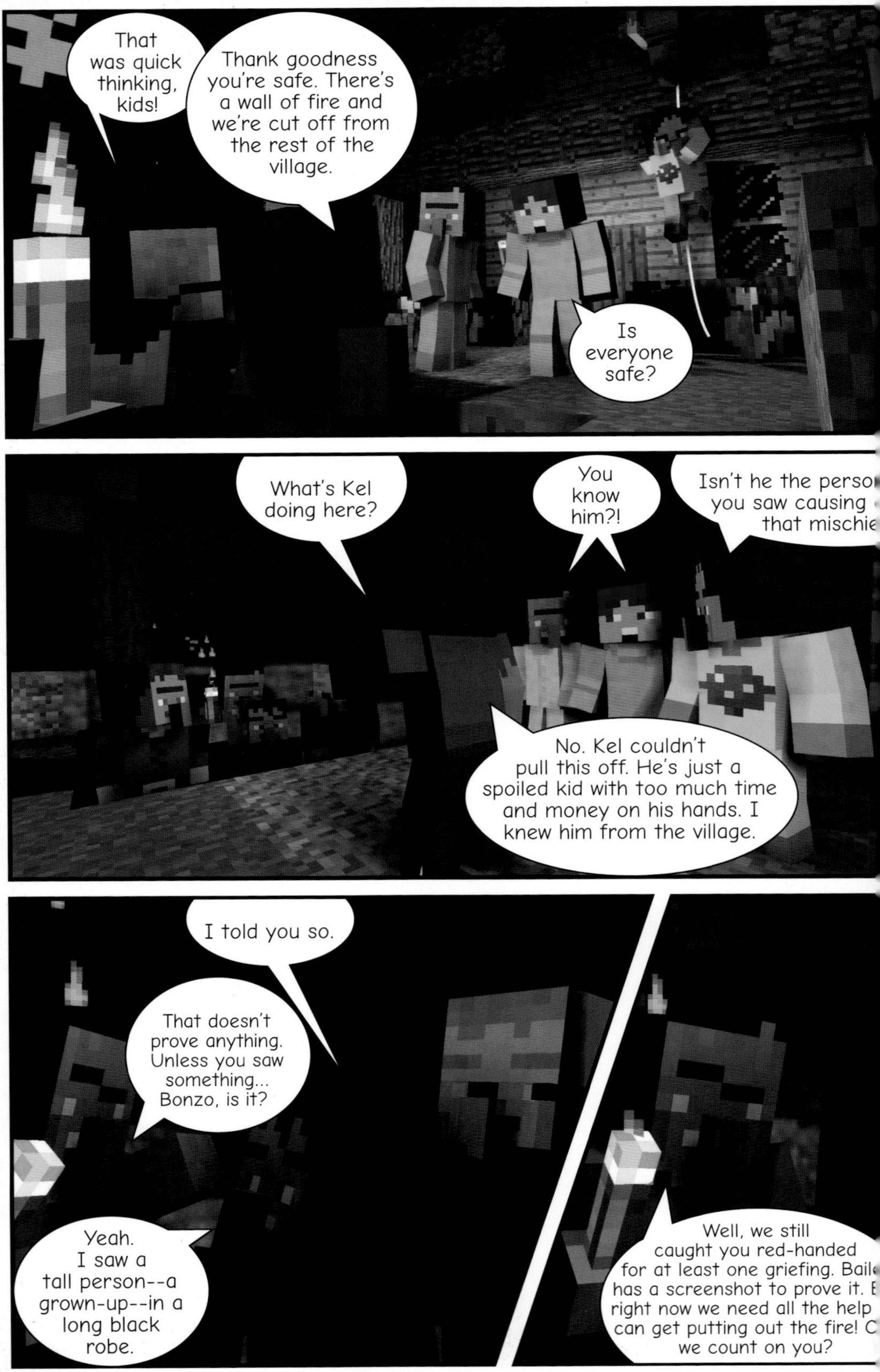
That was quick thinking, kids!
Thank goodness you're safe. There's a wall of fire and we're cut off from the rest of the village.
Is everyone safe?
What's Kel doing here?
You know him?!
Isn't he the perso
you saw causing
that mischie
No. Kel couldn't pull this off. He's just a spoiled kid with too much time and money on his hands. I knew him from the village.
I told you so.
That doesn't prove anything. Unless you saw something... Bonzo, is it?
Yeah. I saw a tall person--a grown-up--in a long black robe.
Well, we still caught you red-handed
for at least one griefing. Bail
has a screenshot to prove it.
right now we need all the help
can get putting out the fire!
we count on you?

CHAPTER 6

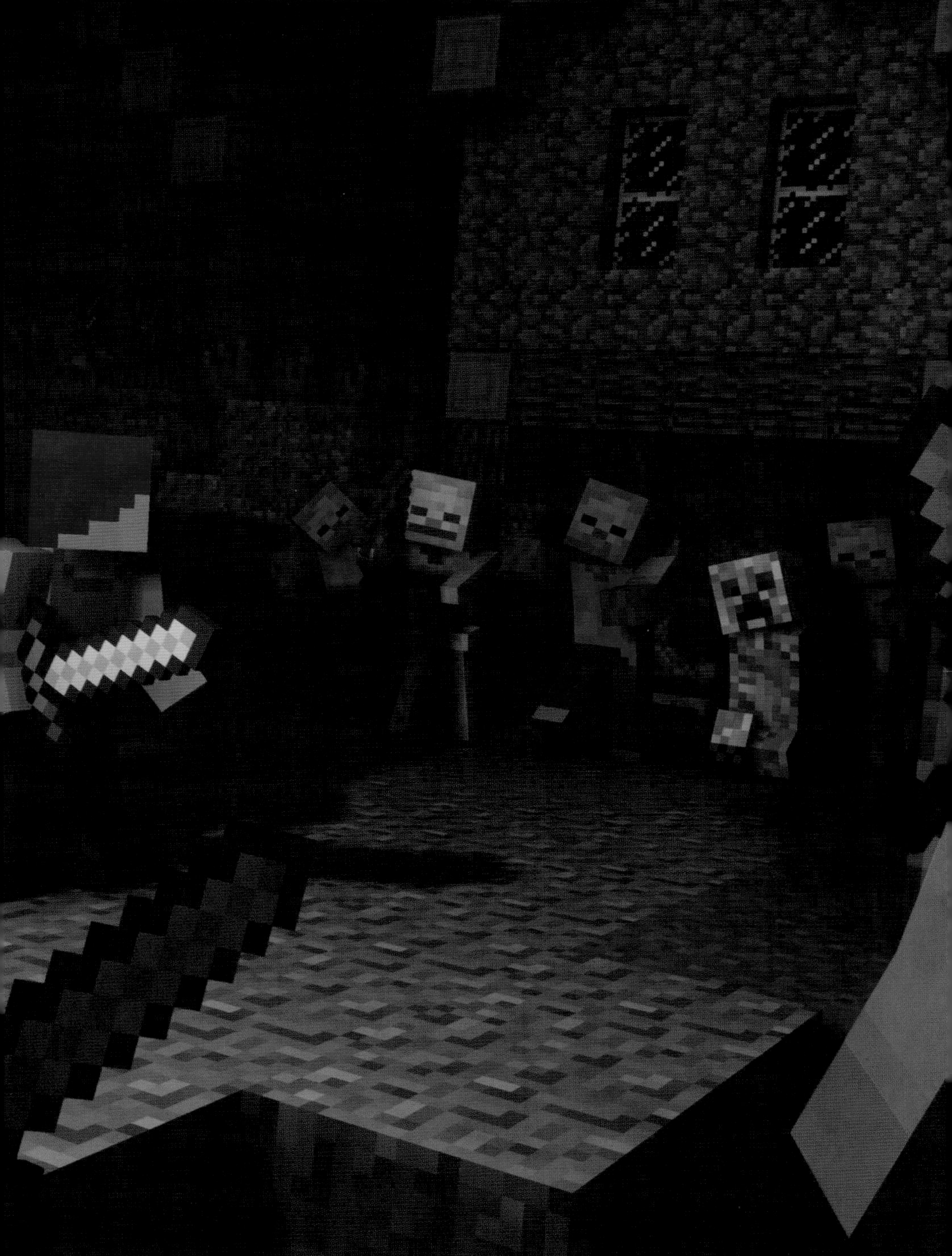

CLEANUP CREW

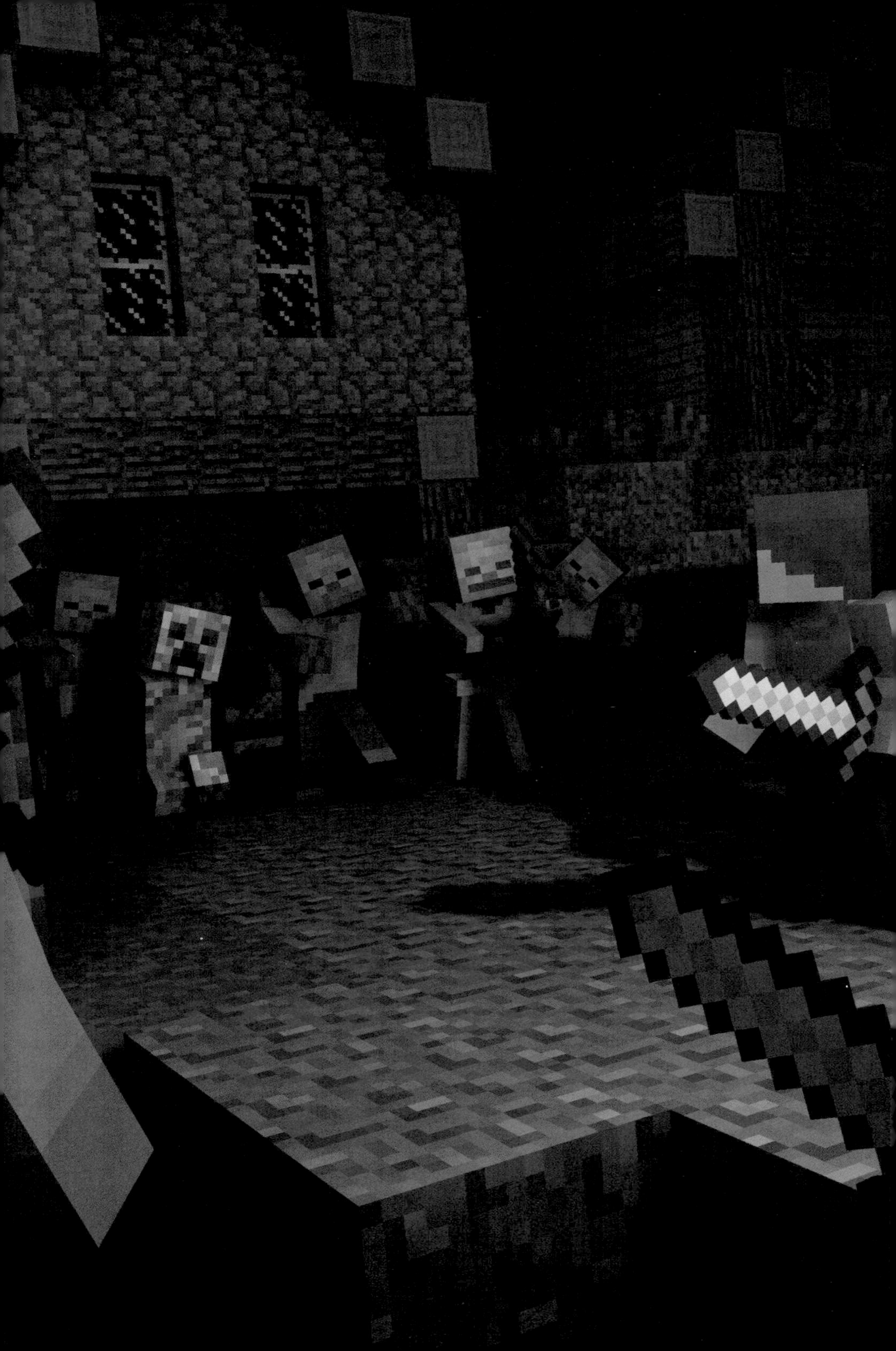

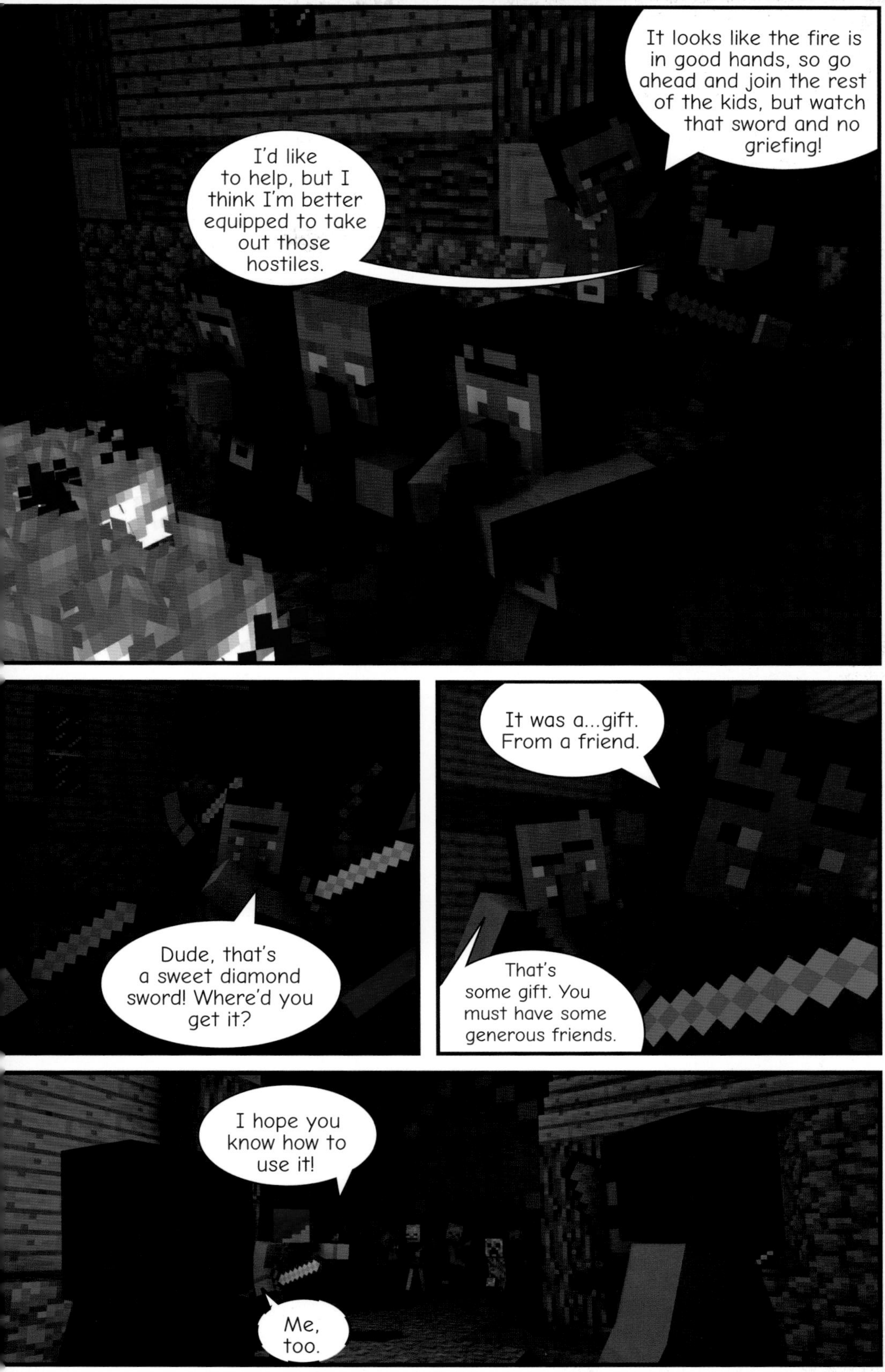
It looks like the fire is in good hands, so go ahead and join the rest of the kids, but watch that sword and no griefing!
I'd like to help, but I think I'm better equipped to take out those hostiles.
Dude, that's a sweet diamond sword! Where'd you get it?
It was a...gift. From a friend.
That's some gift. You must have some generous friends.
I hope you know how to use it!
Me, too.

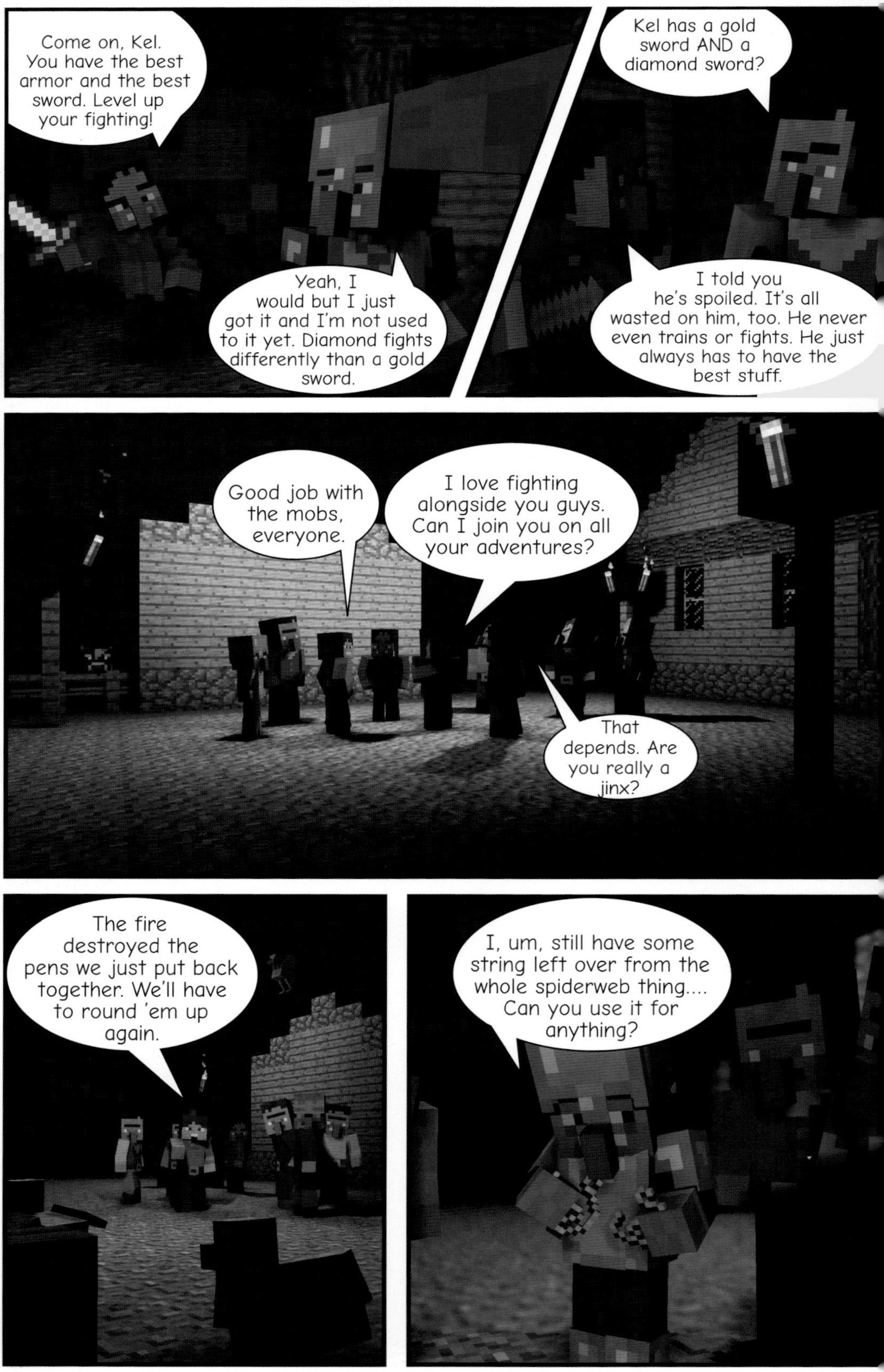
Come on, Kel. You have the best armor and the best sword. Level up your fighting!
Yeah, I would but I just got it and I'm not used to it yet. Diamond fights differently than a gold sword.
Kel has a gold sword AND a diamond sword?
I told you he's spoiled. It's all wasted on him, too. He never even trains or fights. He just always has to have the best stuff.
Good job with the mobs, everyone.
I love fighting alongside you guys. Can I join you on all your adventures?
That depends. Are you really a jinx?
The fire destroyed the pens we just put back together. We'll have to round 'em up again.
I, um, still have some string left over from the whole spiderweb thing.... Can you use it for anything?

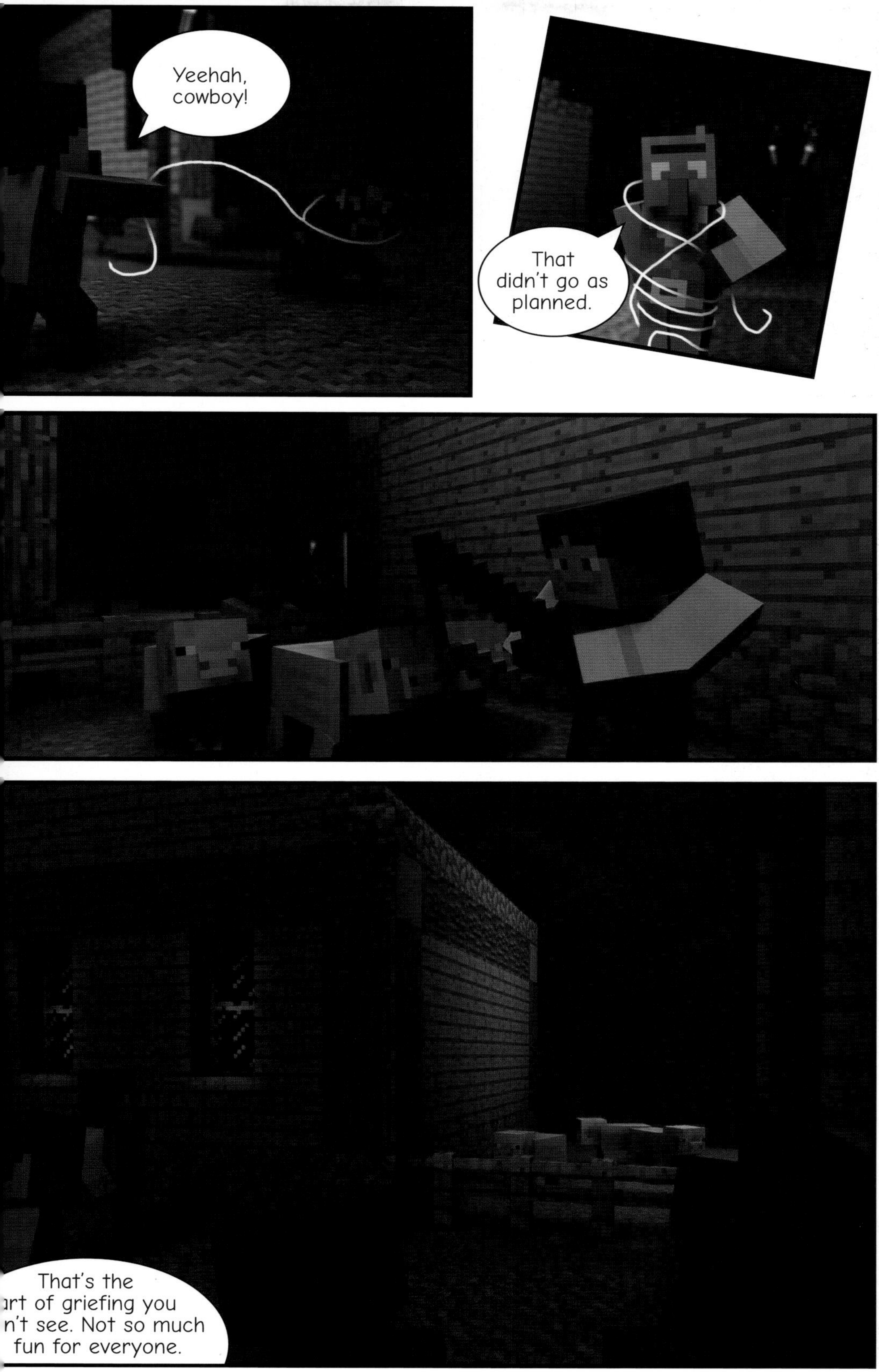
Yeehah, cowboy!
That didn't go as planned.
That's the rt of griefing you n't see. Not so much fun for everyone.

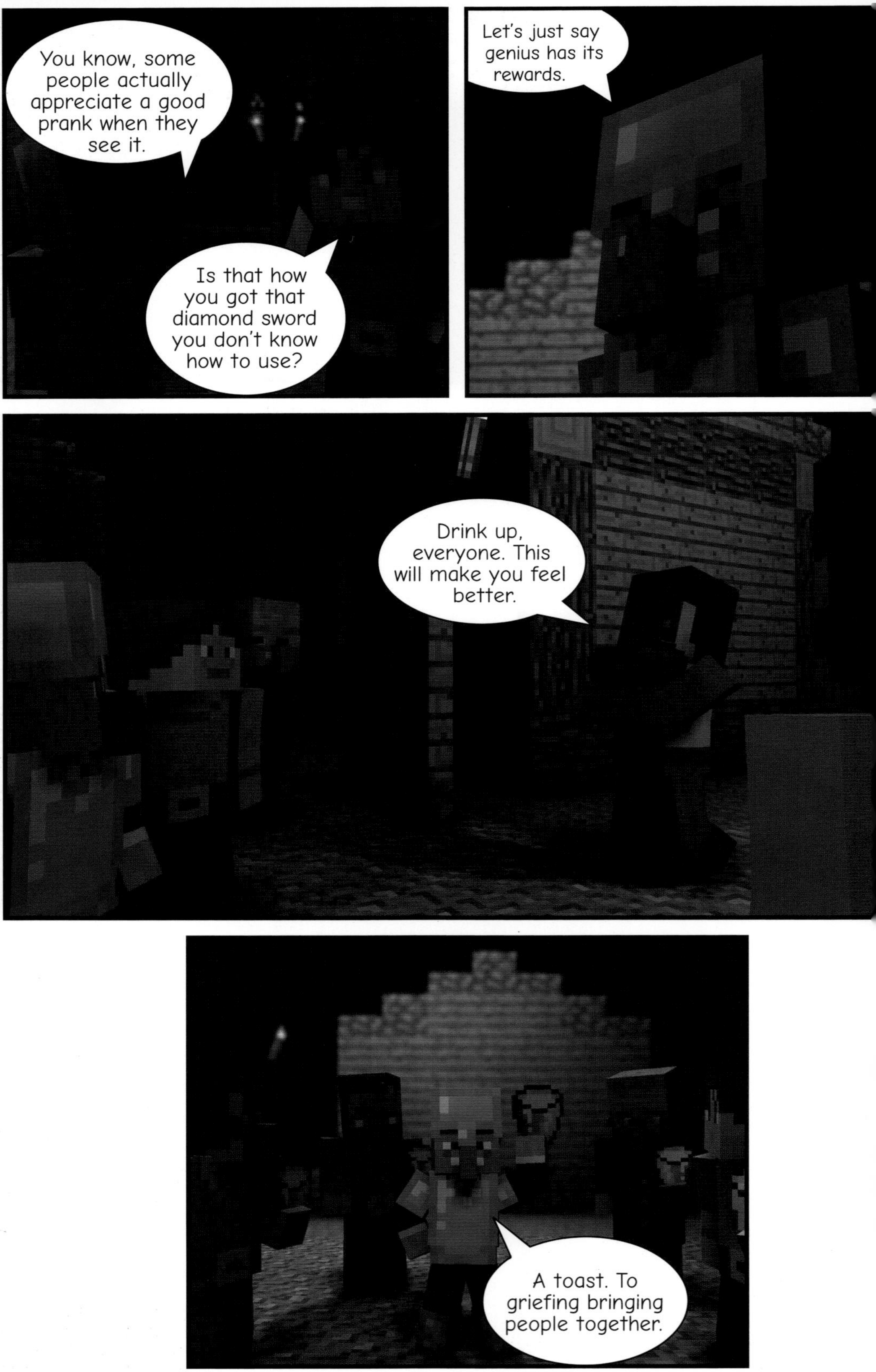

You know, some people actually appreciate a good prank when they see it.
Is that how you got that diamond sword you don't know how to use?
Let's just say genius has its rewards.
Drink up, everyone. This will make you feel better.
A toast. To griefing bringing people together.

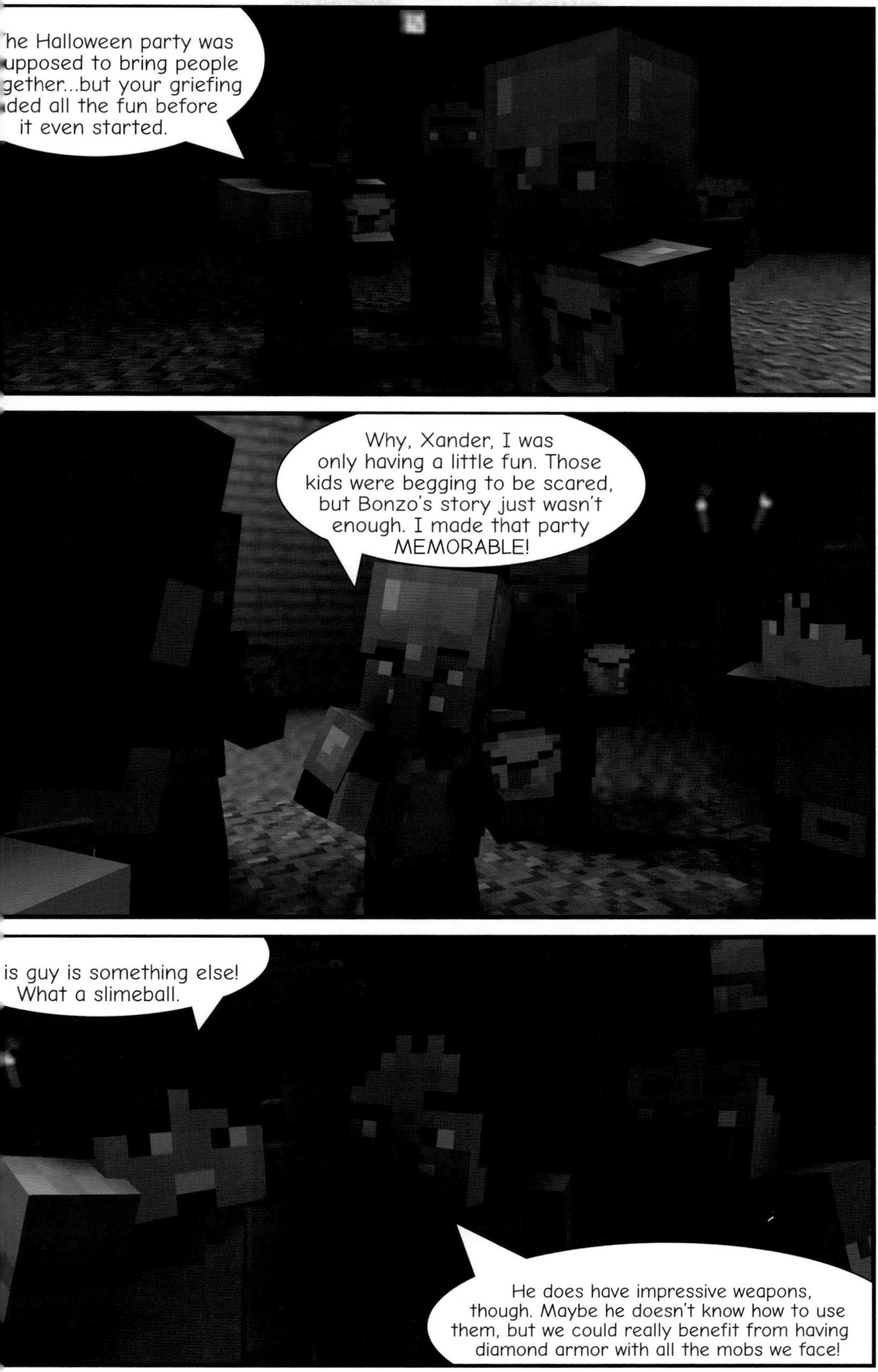
'he Halloween party was upposed to bring people gether...but your griefing ded all the fun before it even started.
Why, Xander, I was only having a little fun. Those kids were begging to be scared, but Bonzo's story just wasn't enough. I made that party MEMORABLE!
is guy is something else! What a slimeball.
He does have impressive weapons, though. Maybe he doesn't know how to use them, but we could really benefit from having diamond armor with all the mobs we face!

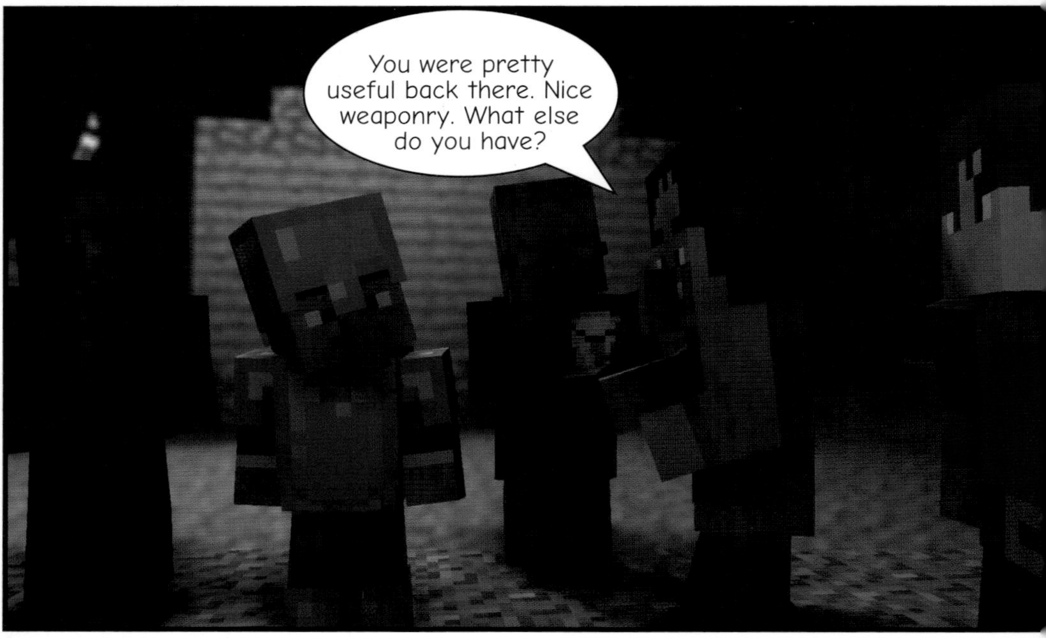
You were pretty useful back there. Nice weaponry. What else do you have?

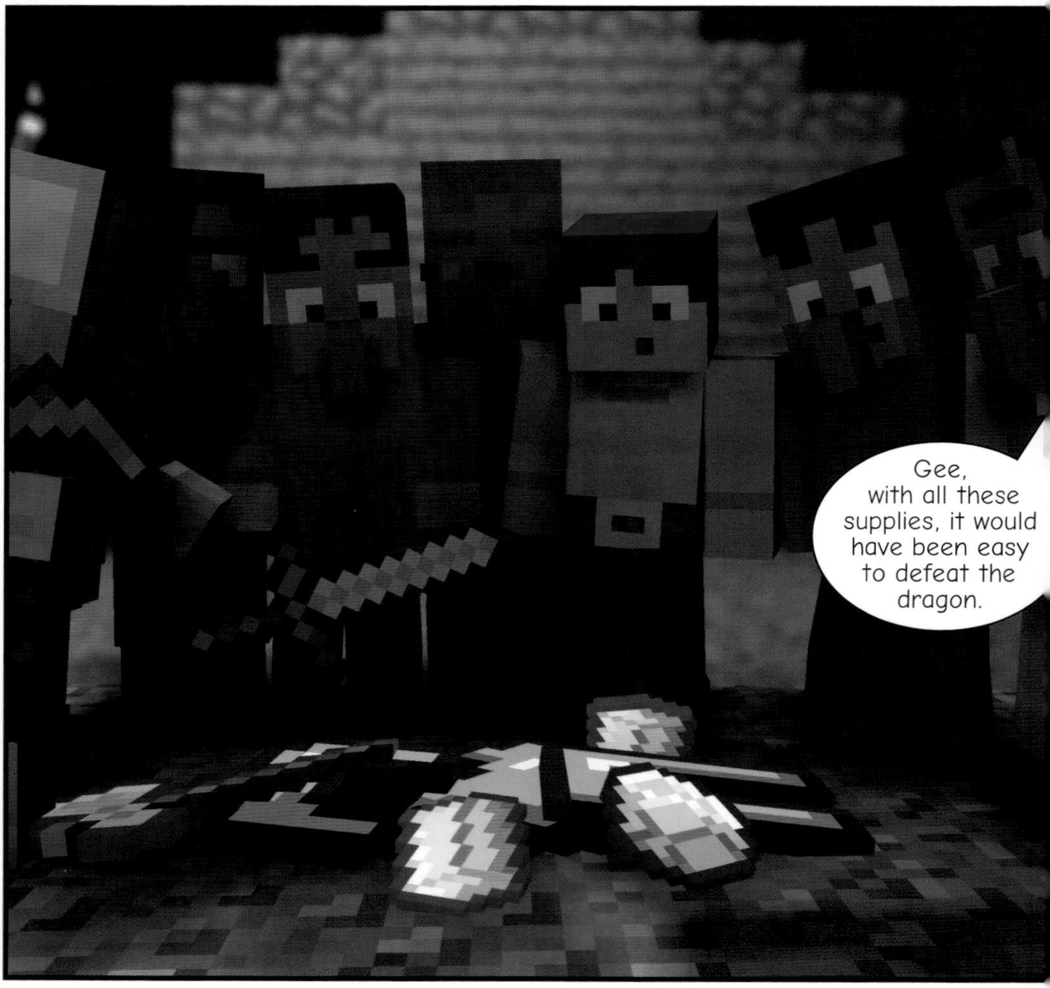
Gee, with all these supplies, it would have been easy to defeat the dragon.

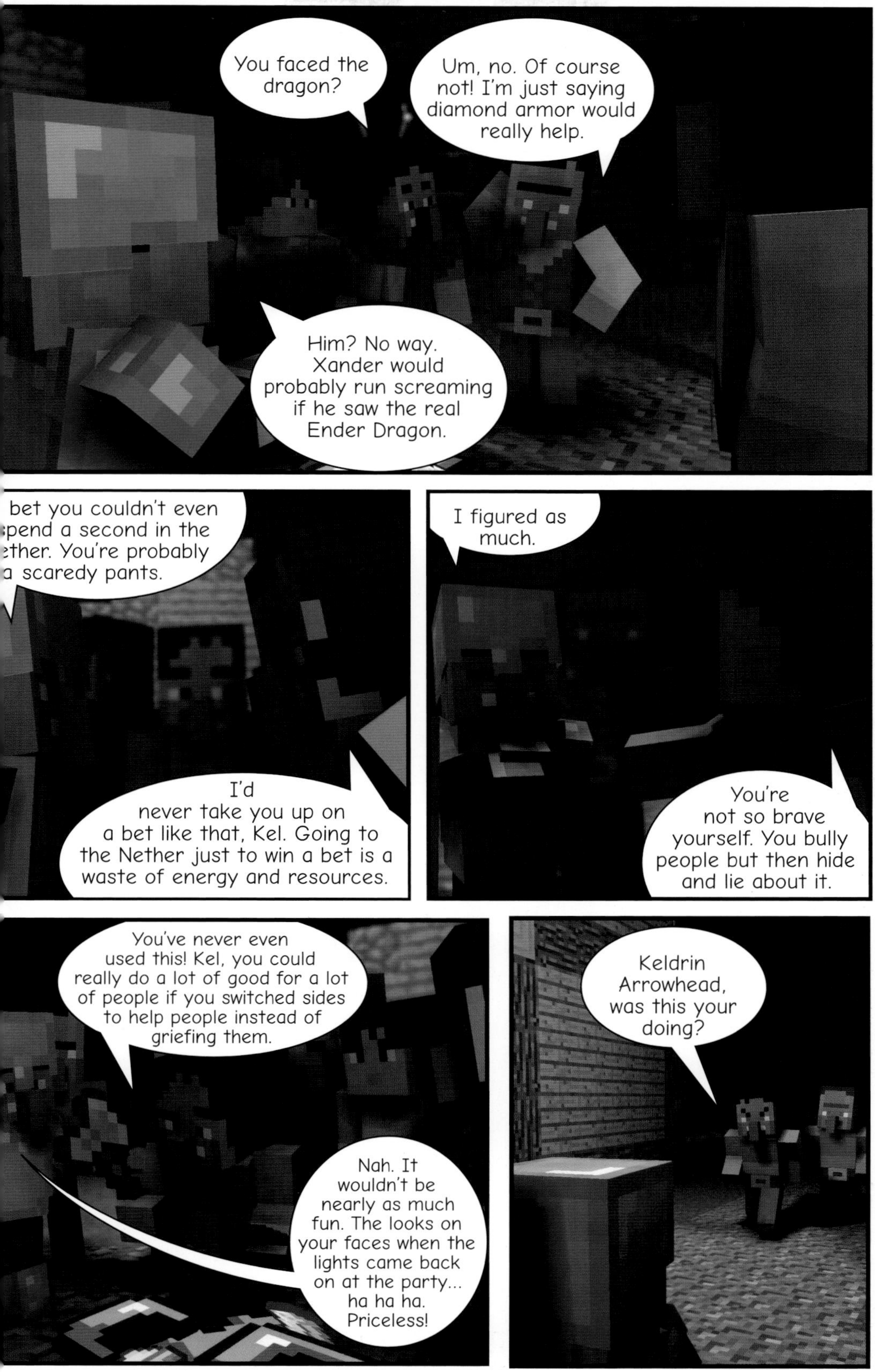
You faced the dragon?
Um, no. Of course not! I'm just saying diamond armor would really help.
Him? No way. Xander would probably run screaming if he saw the real Ender Dragon.
bet you couldn't even pend a second in the ther. You're probably a scaredy pants.
I'd never take you up on a bet like that, Kel. Going to the Nether just to win a bet is a waste of energy and resources.
I figured as much.
You're not so brave yourself. You bully people but then hide and lie about it.
You've never even used this! Kel, you could really do a lot of good for a lot of people if you switched sides to help people instead of griefing them.
Nah. It wouldn't be nearly as much fun. The looks on your faces when the lights came back on at the party... ha ha ha. Priceless!
Keldrin Arrowhead, was this your doing?

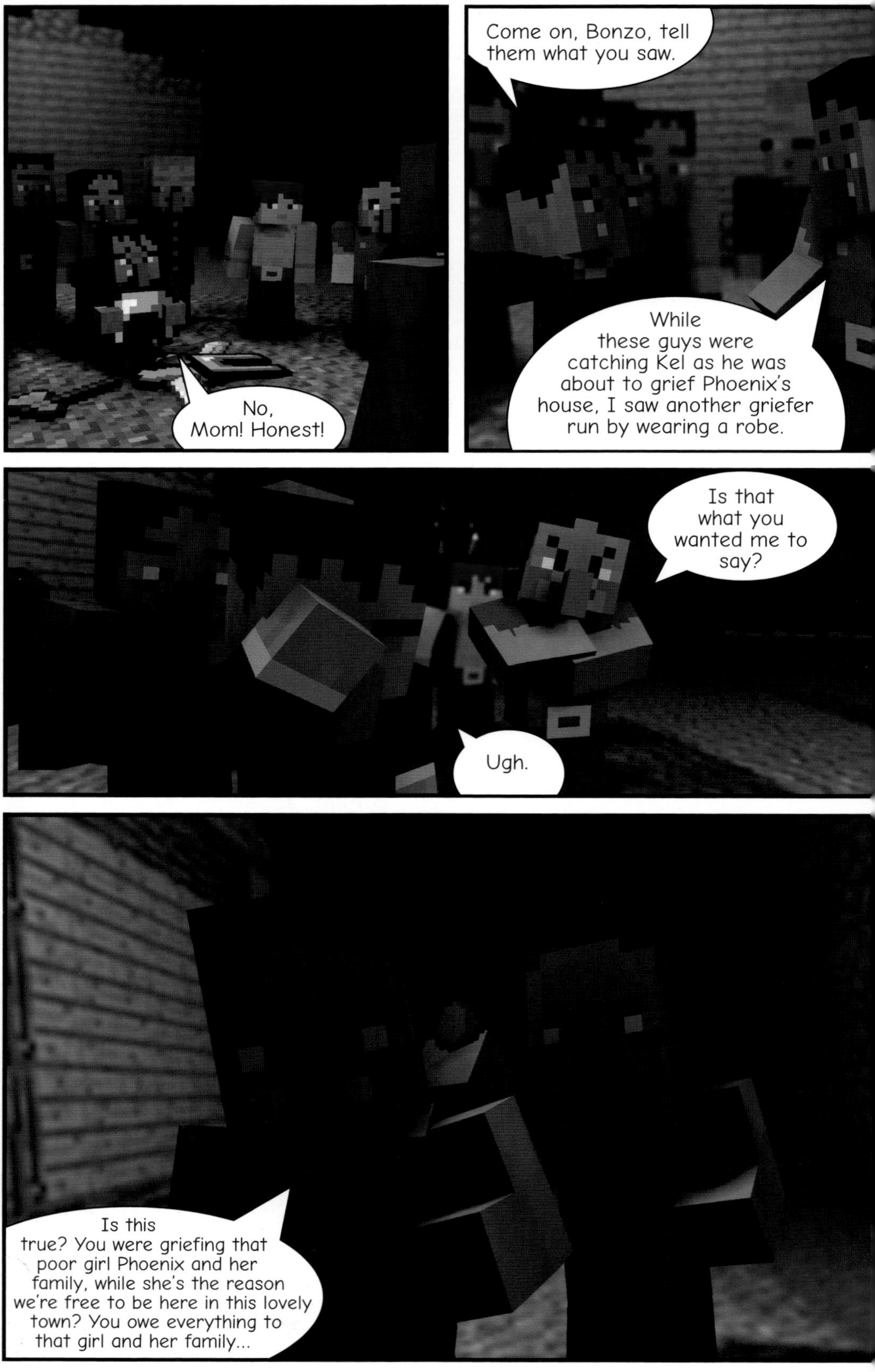

No, Mom! Honest!
Come on, Bonzo, tell them what you saw.
While these guys were catching Kel as he was about to grief Phoenix's house, I saw another griefer run by wearing a robe.
Is that what you wanted me to say?
Ugh.
Is this true? You were griefing that poor girl Phoenix and her family, while she's the reason we're free to be here in this lovely town? You owe everything to that girl and her family...

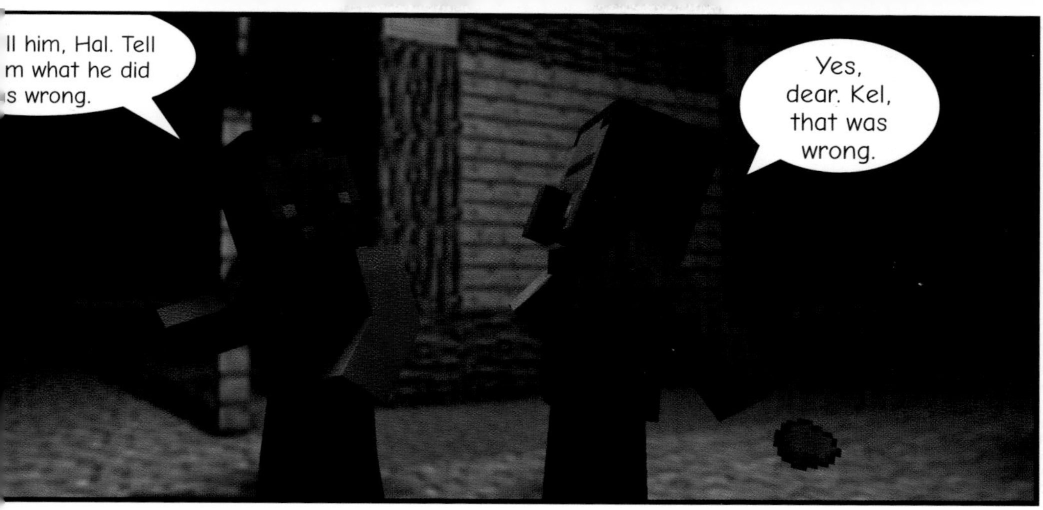
ll him, Hal. Tell
m what he did
s wrong.
Yes, dear. Kel, that was wrong.

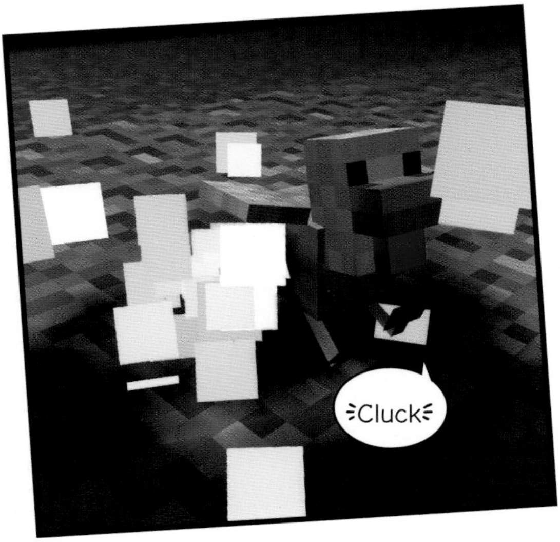
Cluck

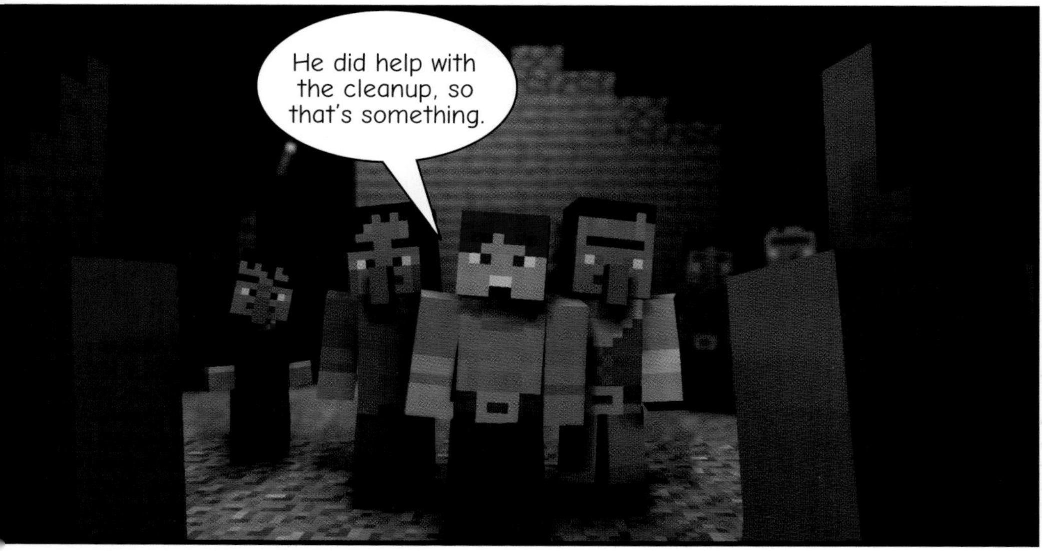
He did help with the cleanup, so that's something.

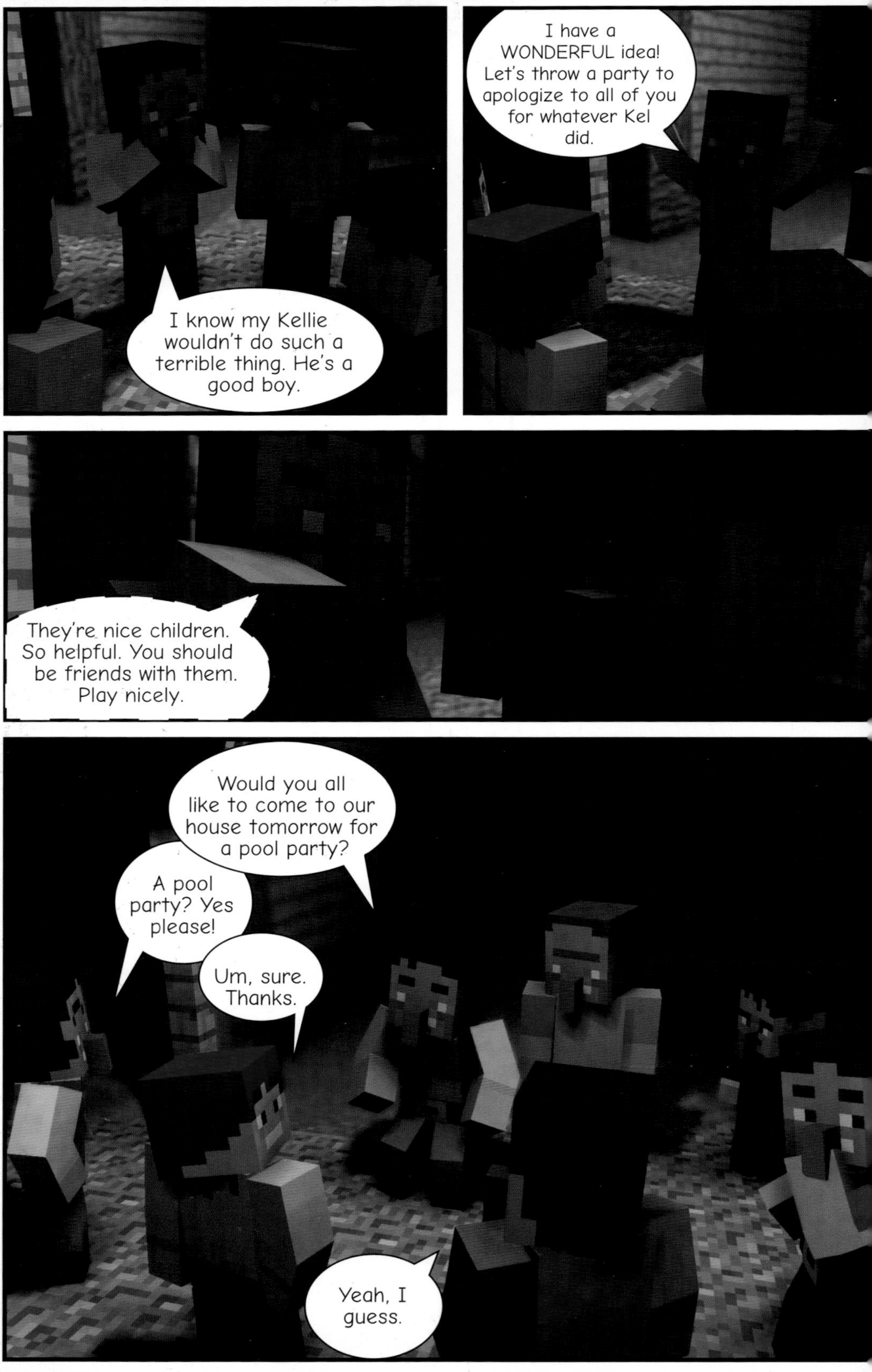
I know my Kellie wouldn't do such a terrible thing. He's a good boy.
I have a WONDERFUL idea! Let's throw a party to apologize to all of you for whatever Kel did.
They're nice children. So helpful. You should be friends with them. Play nicely.
Would you all like to come to our house tomorrow for a pool party?
A pool party? Yes please!
Um, sure. Thanks.
Yeah, I guess.

CHAPTER 7

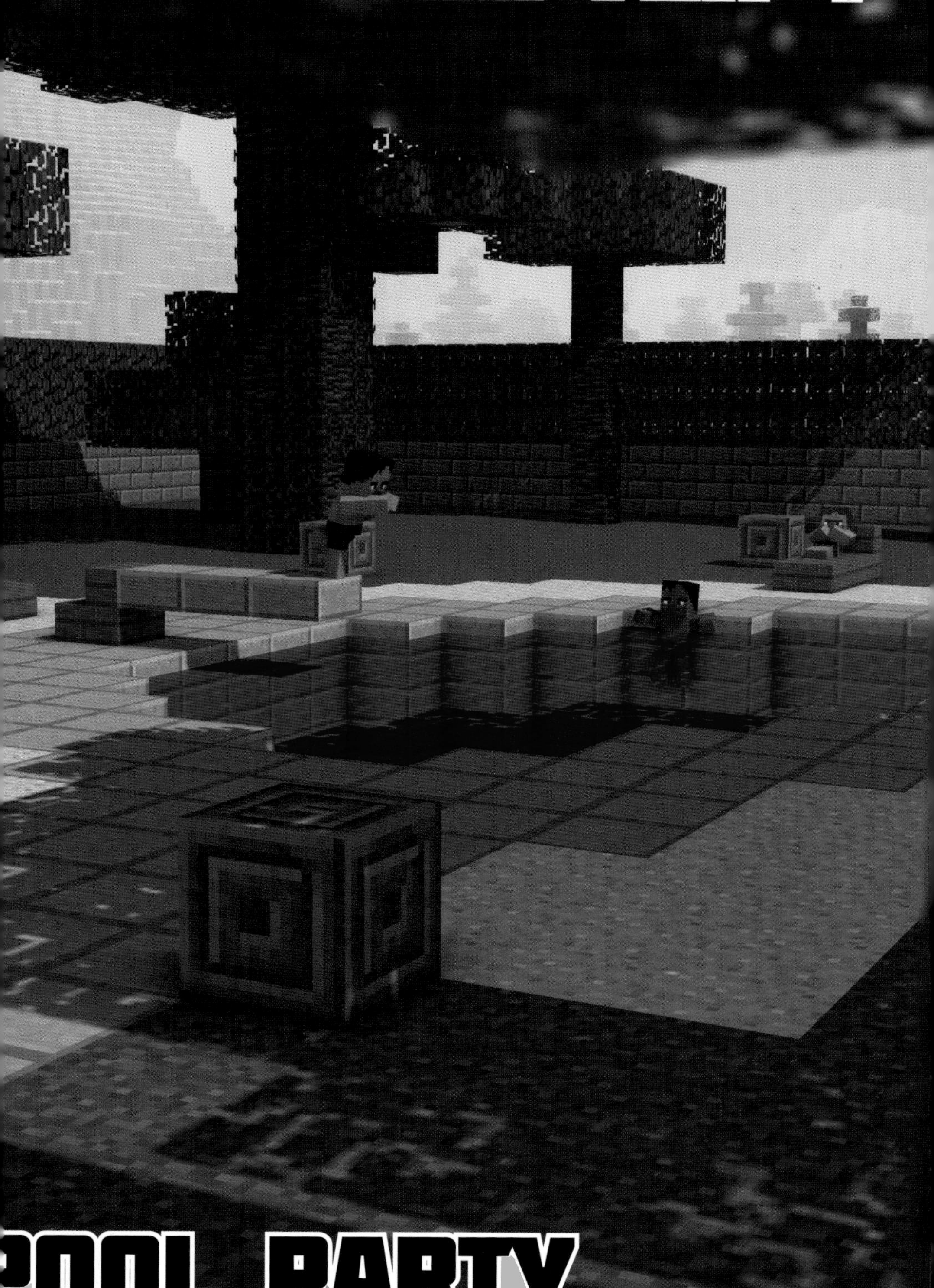

POOL PARTY

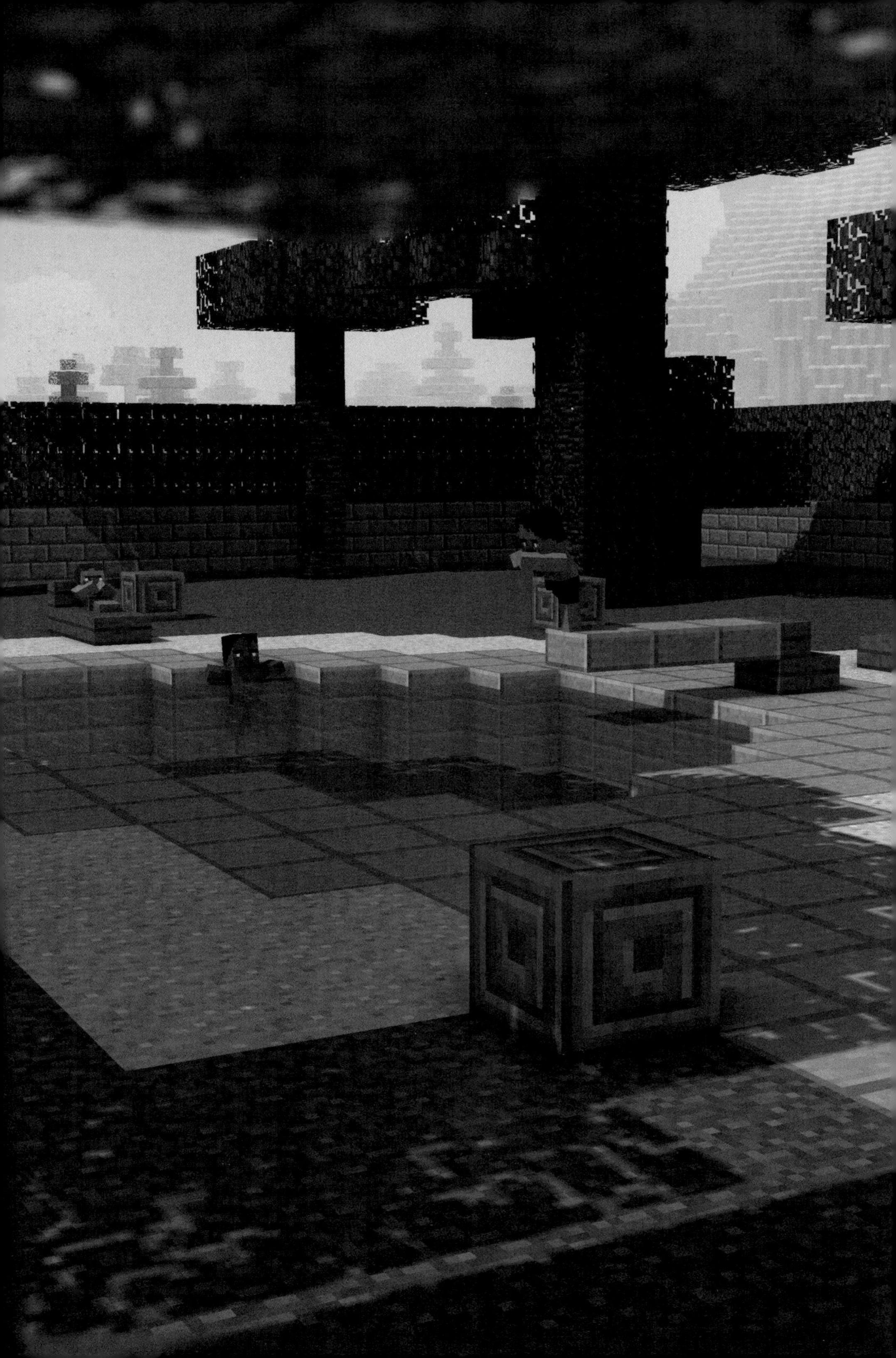

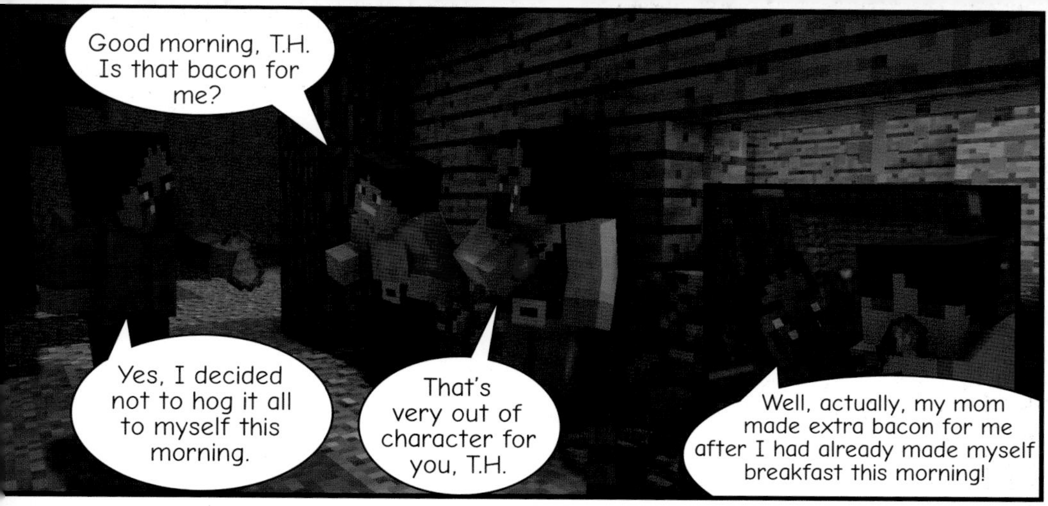
Good morning, T.H. Is that bacon for me?
Yes, I decided not to hog it all to myself this morning.
That's very out of character for you, T.H.
Well, actually, my mom made extra bacon for me after I had already made myself breakfast this morning!

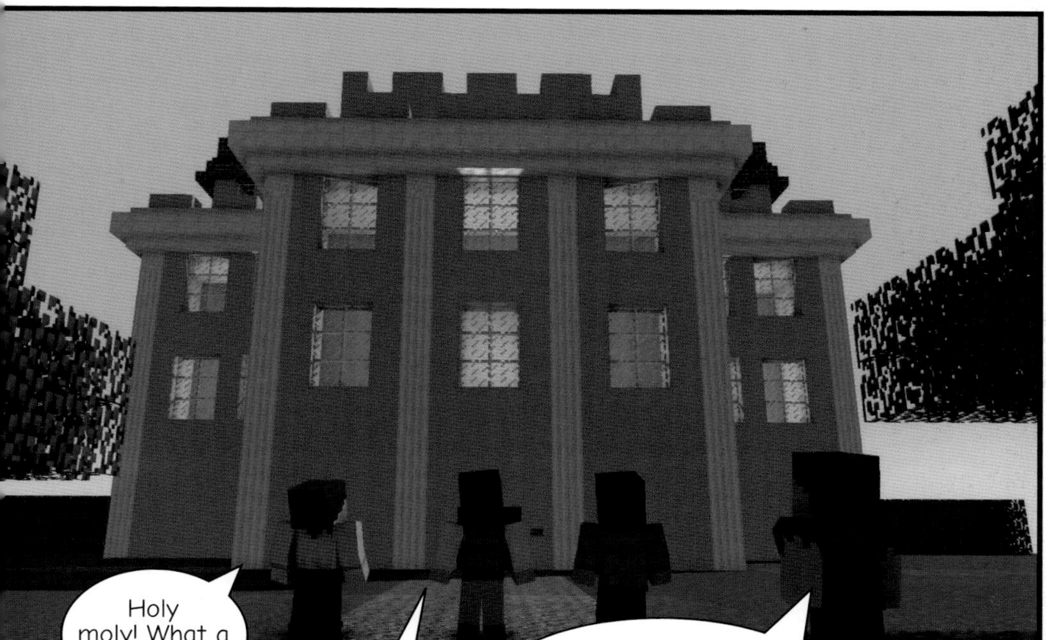
Holy moly! What a house!
How did they get all this?
Told you he was rich. Kel's dad found a gold mine. My dad was telling me about it.

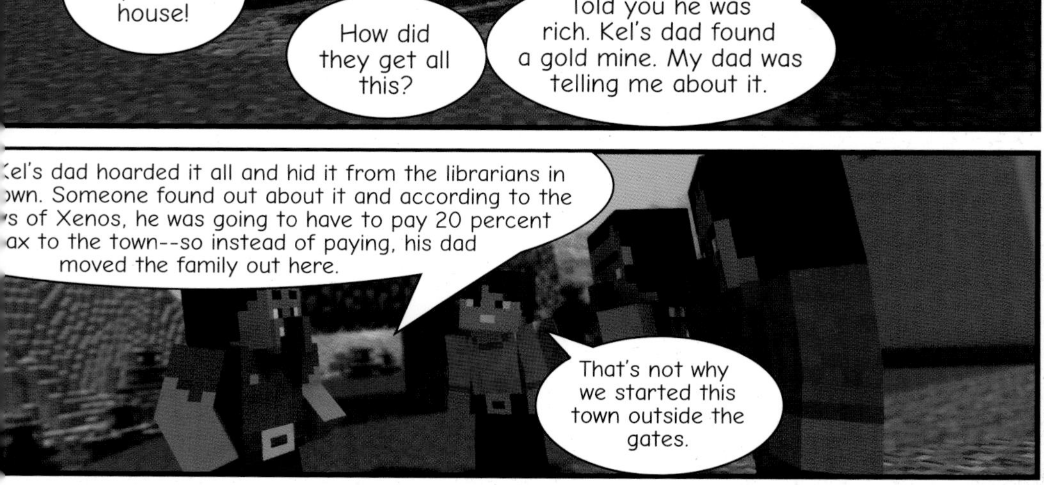
el's dad hoarded it all and hid it from the librarians in wn. Someone found out about it and according to the s of Xenos, he was going to have to pay 20 percent ax to the town--so instead of paying, his dad moved the family out here.
That's not why we started this town outside the gates.

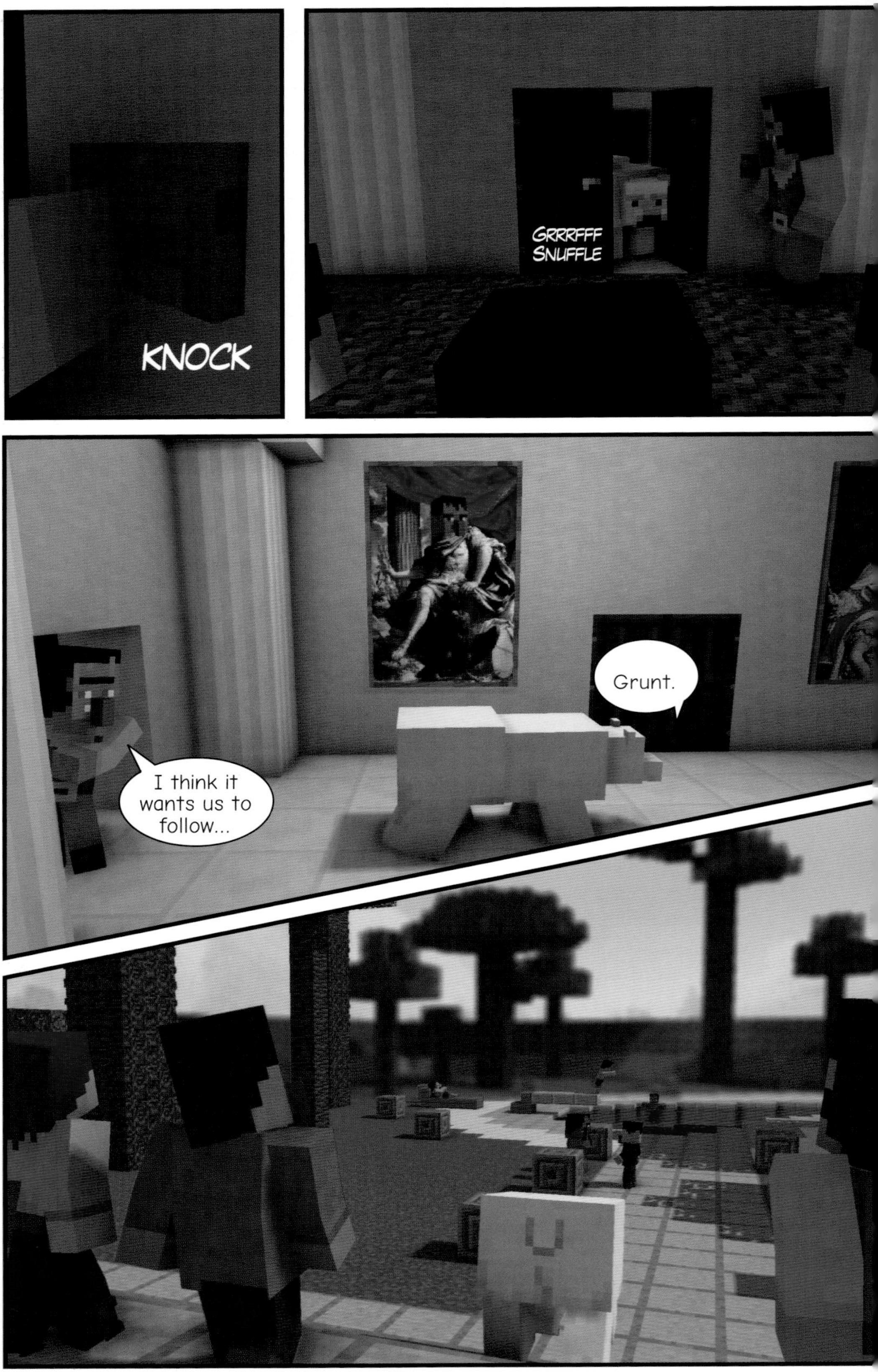
KNOCK
GRRRFFF
SNUFFLE
Grunt.
I think it wants us to follow...

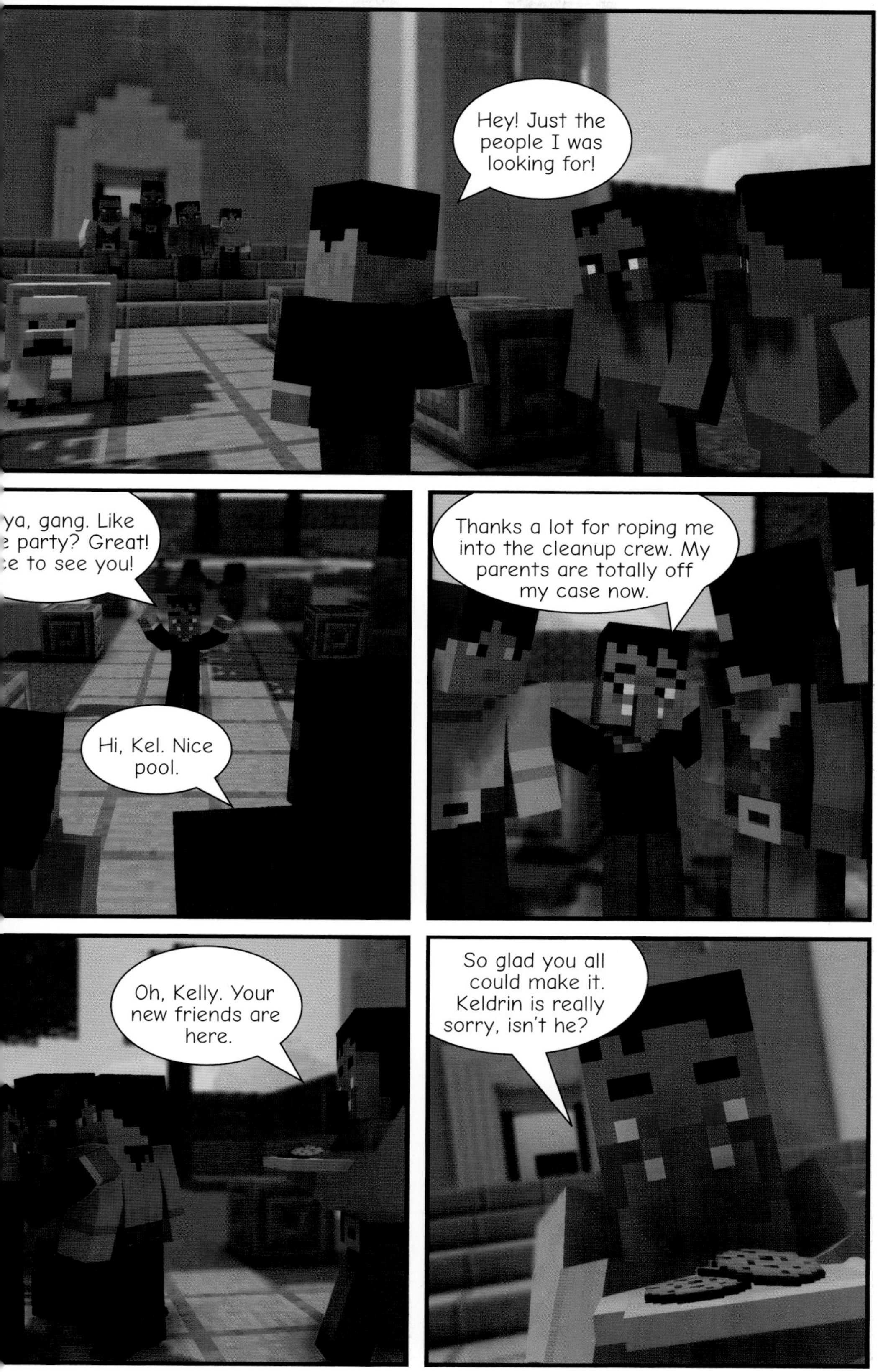
Hey! Just the people I was looking for!
ya, gang. Like e party? Great! ce to see you!
Hi, Kel. Nice pool.
Thanks a lot for roping me into the cleanup crew. My parents are totally off my case now.
Oh, Kelly. Your new friends are here.
So glad you all could make it. Keldrin is really sorry, isn't he?

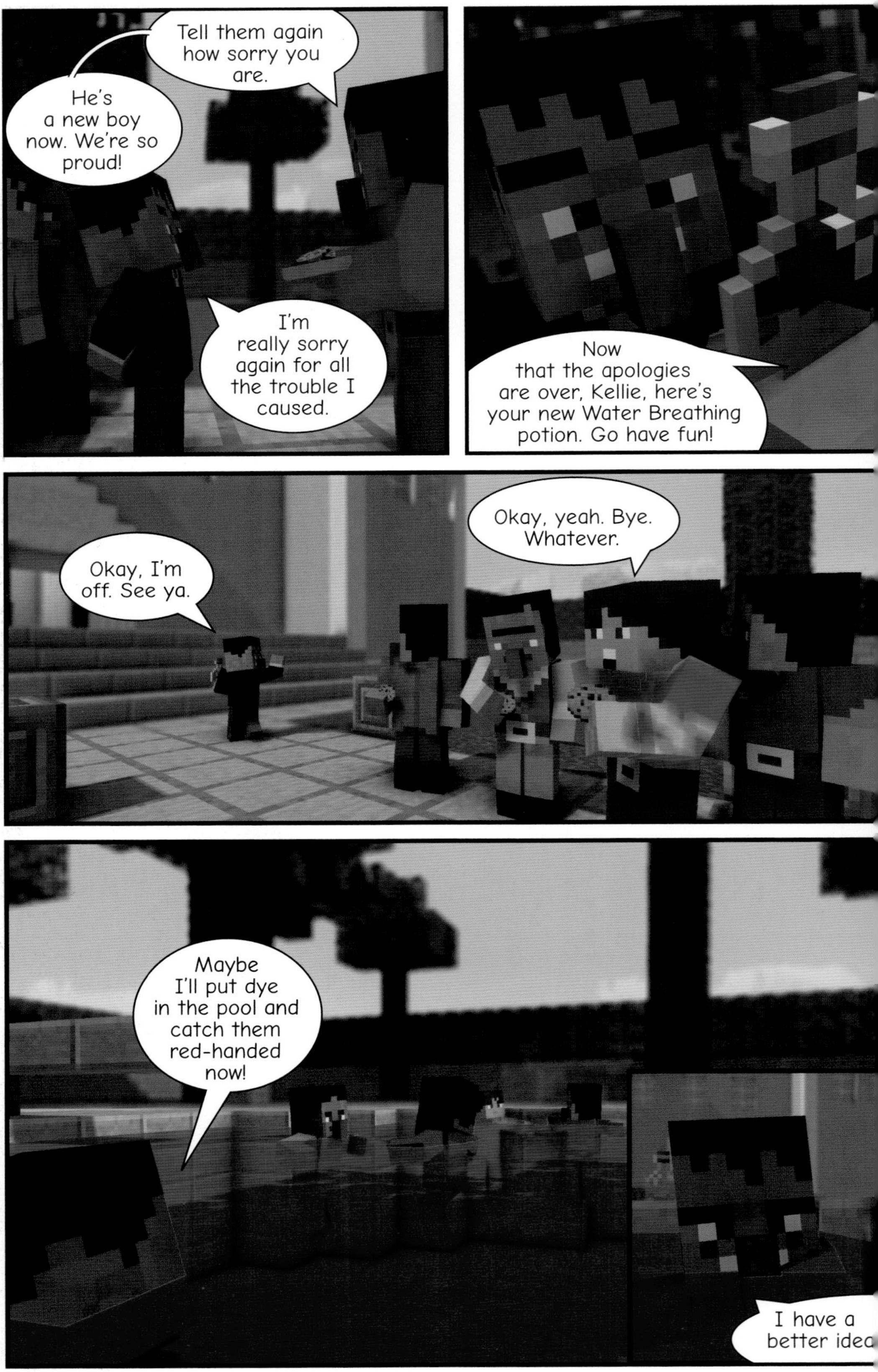
He's a new boy now. We're so proud!
Tell them again how sorry you are.
I'm really sorry again for all the trouble I caused.
Now that the apologies are over, Kellie, here's your new Water Breathing potion. Go have fun!
Okay, I'm off. See ya.
Okay, yeah. Bye. Whatever.
Maybe I'll put dye in the pool and catch them red-handed now!
I have a better idea

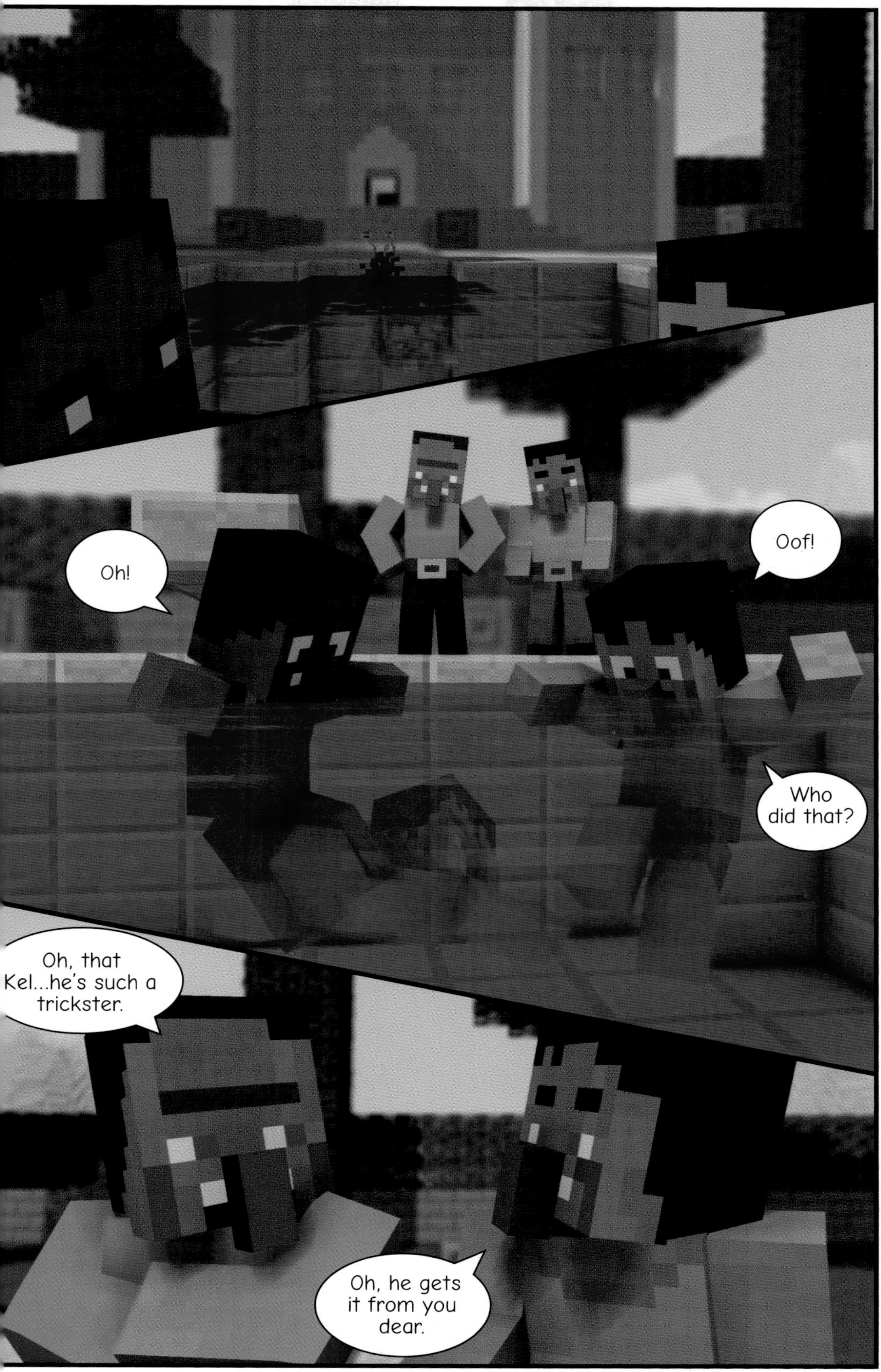
Oh!
Oof!
Who did that?
Oh, that Kel...he's such a trickster.
Oh, he gets it from you dear.

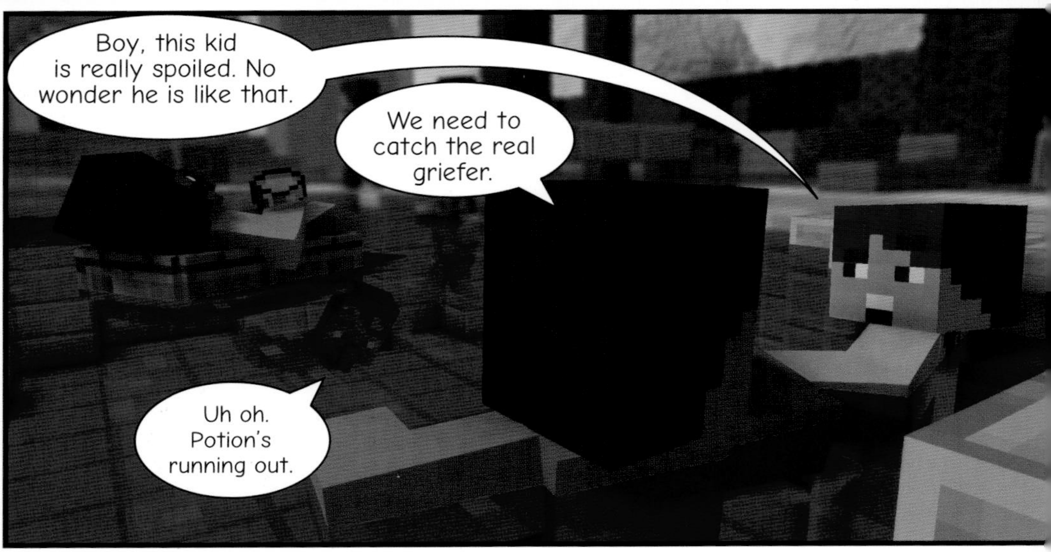
Boy, this kid is really spoiled. No wonder he is like that.
We need to catch the real griefer.
Uh oh. Potion's running out.

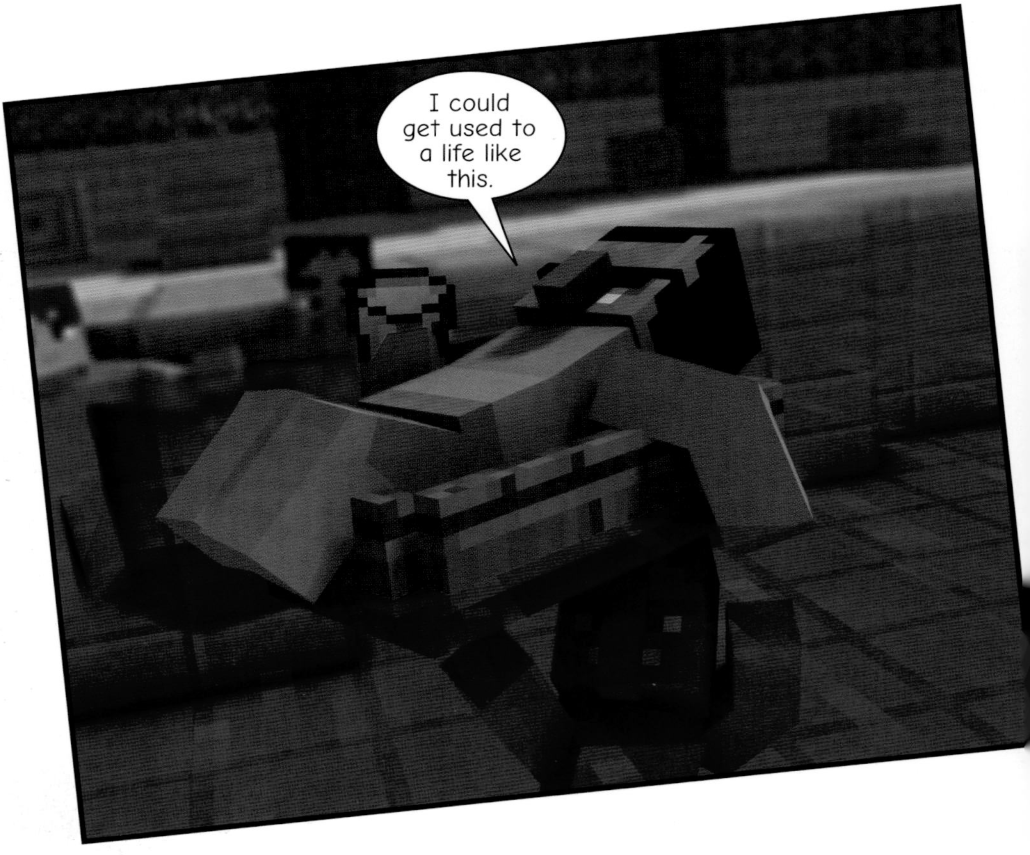
I could get used to a life like this.

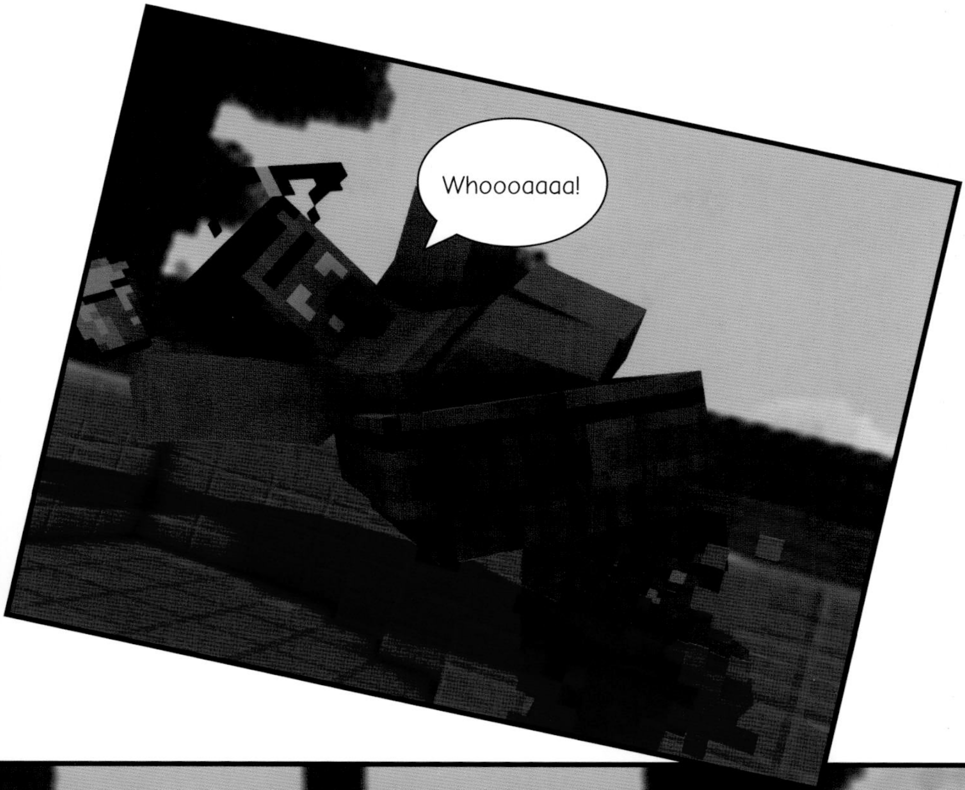
Whoooaaaa!

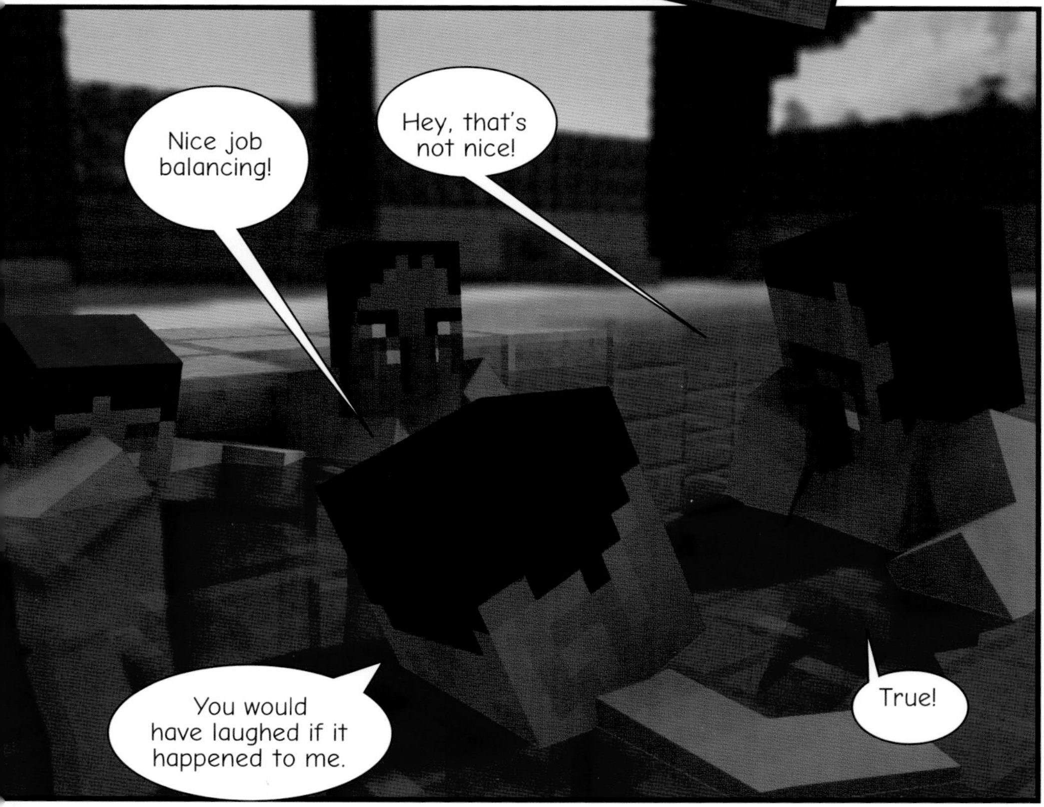
Nice job balancing!
Hey, that's not nice!
You would have laughed if it happened to me.
True!

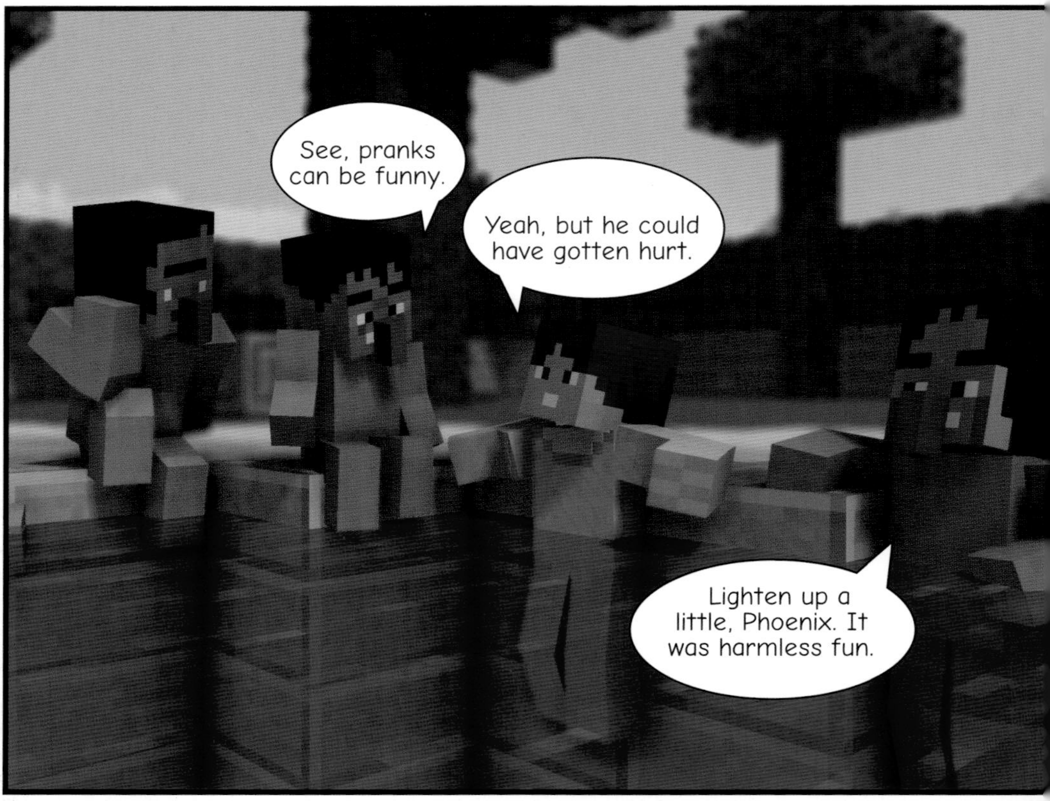
See, pranks can be funny.
Yeah, but he could have gotten hurt.
Lighten up a little, Phoenix. It was harmless fun.

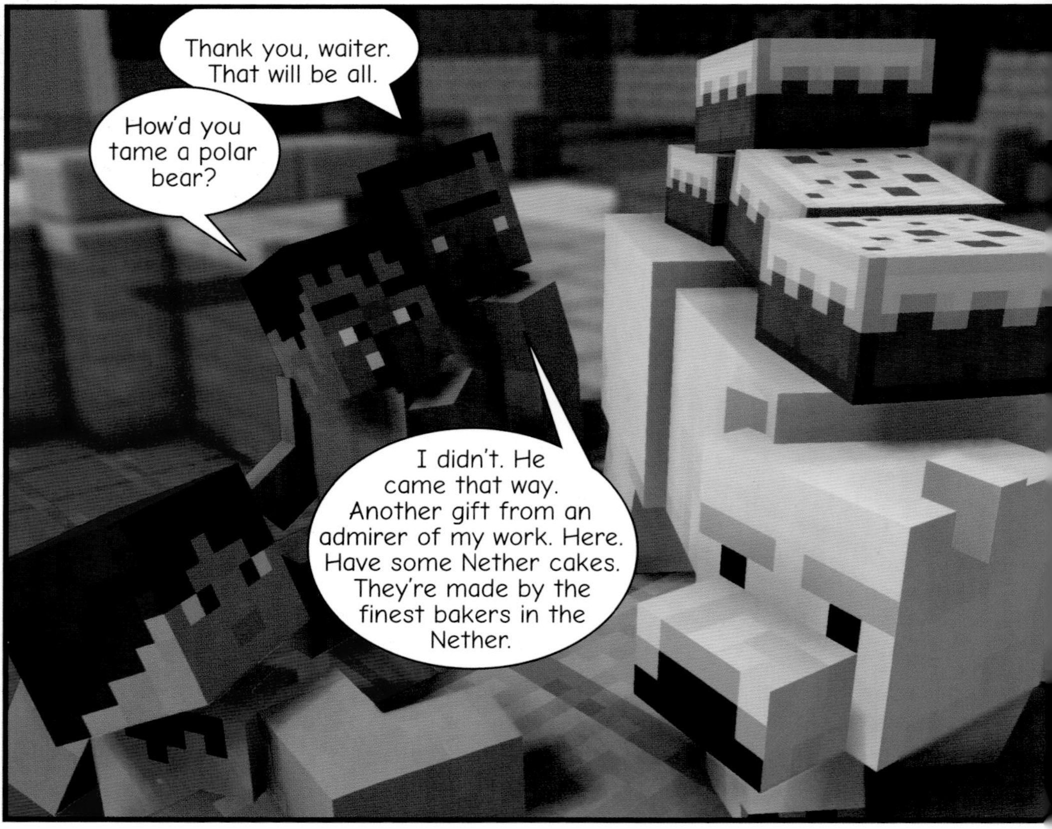
Thank you, waiter. That will be all.
How'd you tame a polar bear?
I didn't. He came that way. Another gift from an admirer of my work. Here. Have some Nether cakes. They're made by the finest bakers in the Nether.

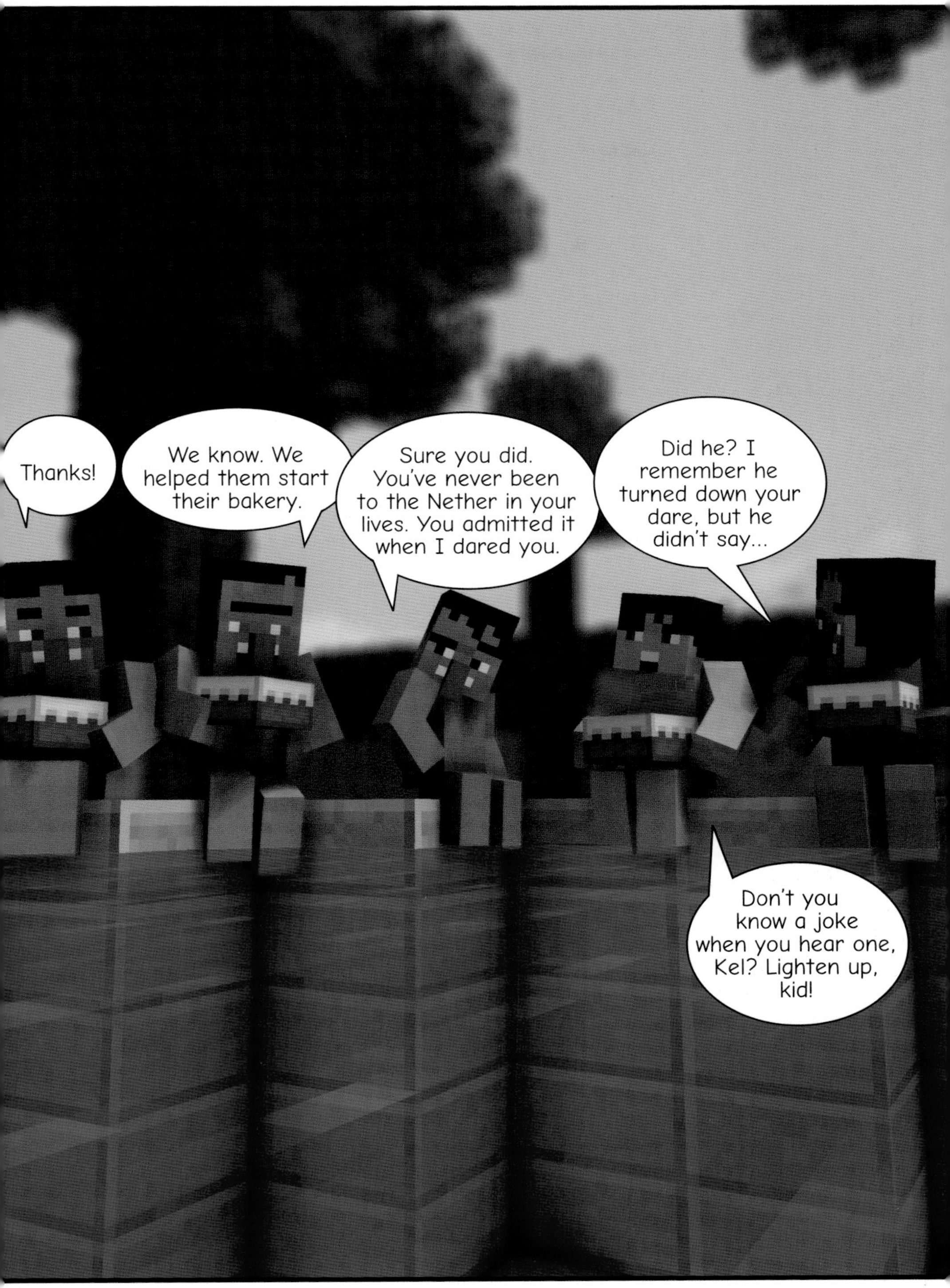
Thanks!
We know. We helped them start their bakery.
Sure you did. You've never been to the Nether in your lives. You admitted it when I dared you.
Did he? I remember he turned down your dare, but he didn't say...
Don't you know a joke when you hear one, Kel? Lighten up, kid!

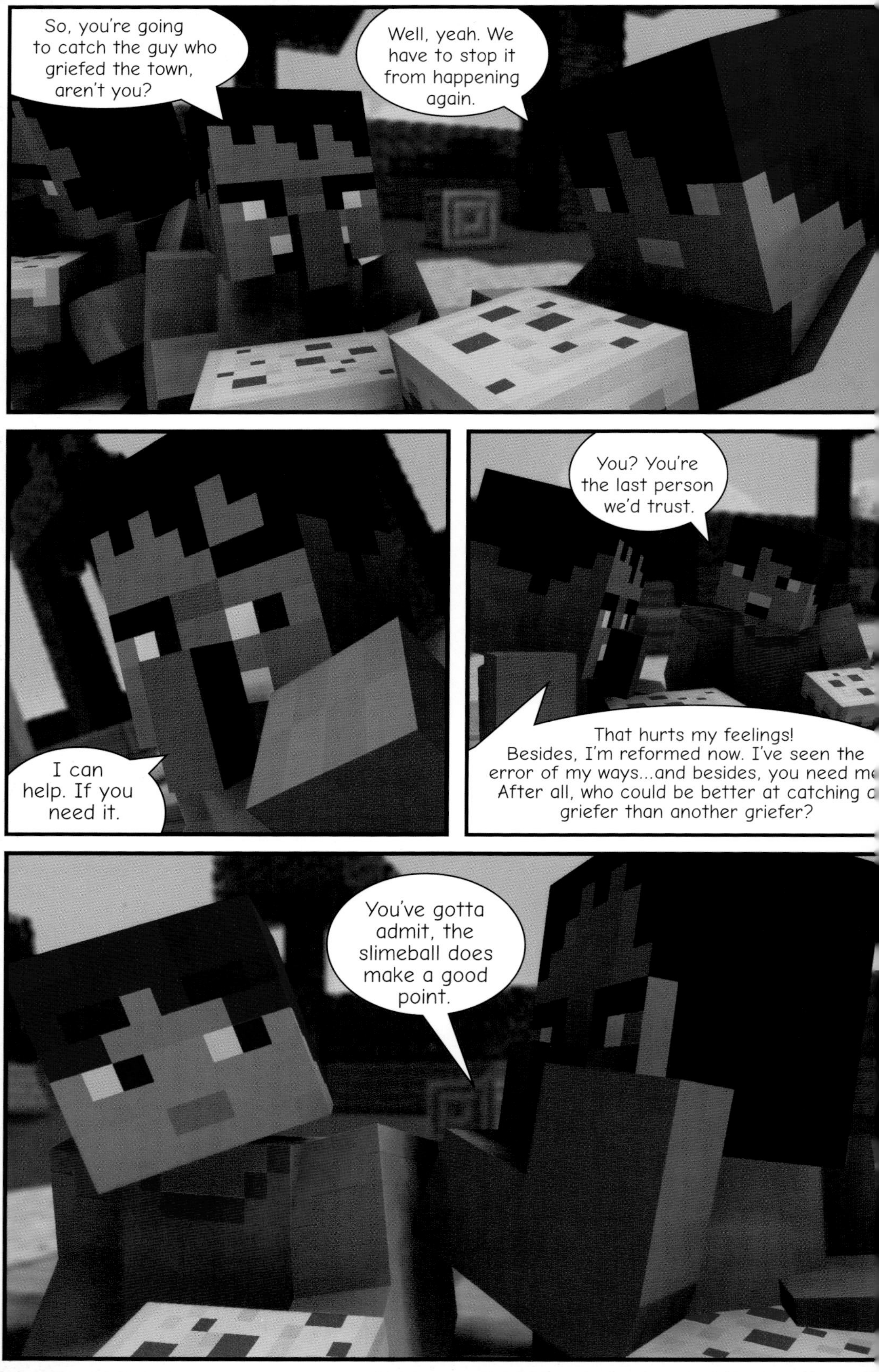
So, you're going to catch the guy who griefed the town, aren't you?
Well, yeah. We have to stop it from happening again.
I can help. If you need it.
You? You're the last person we'd trust.
That hurts my feelings! Besides, I'm reformed now. I've seen the error of my ways...and besides, you need me After all, who could be better at catching a griefer than another griefer?
You've gotta admit, the slimeball does make a good point.

CHAPTER 8

THE PLOT THICKENS

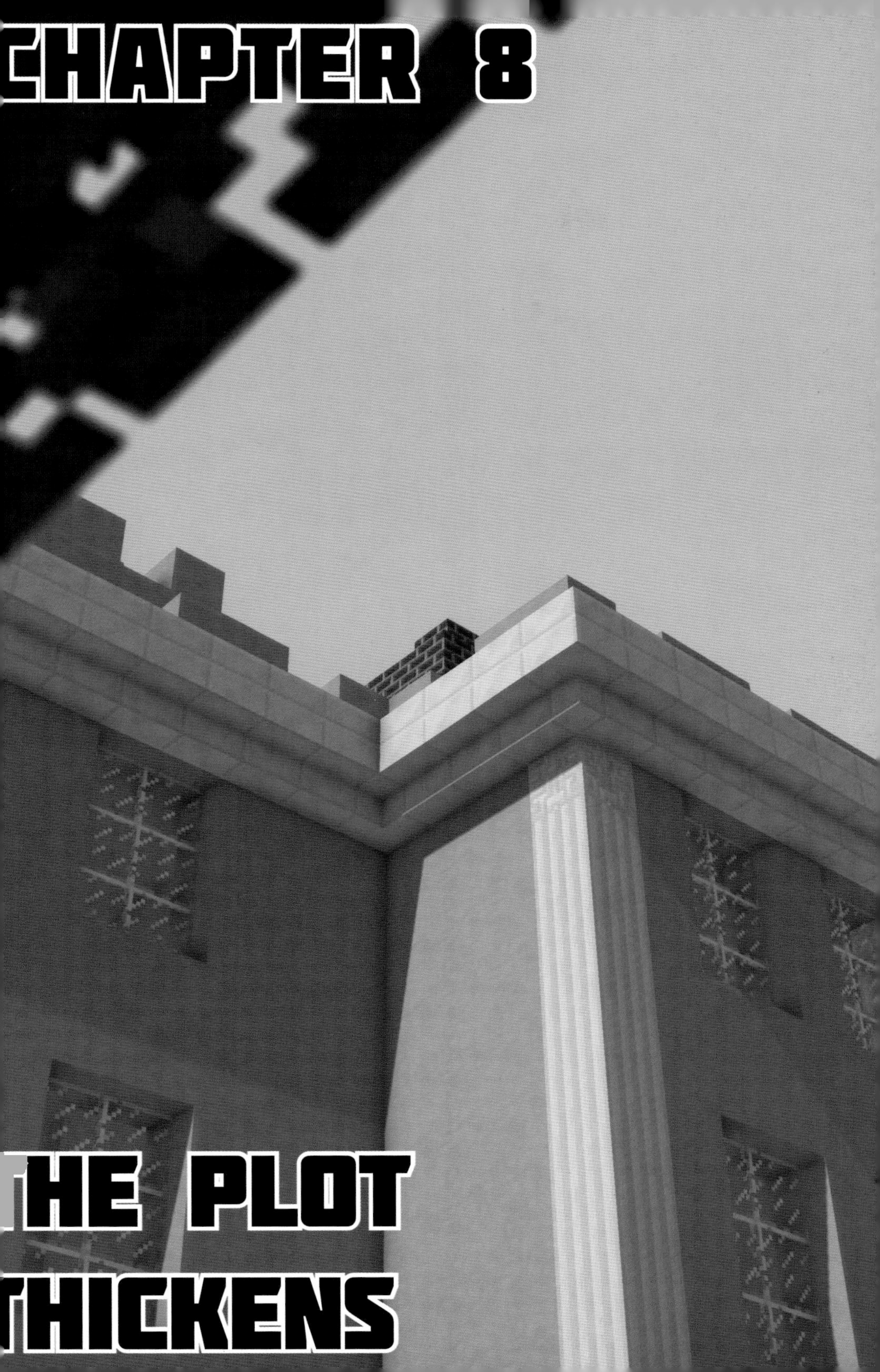

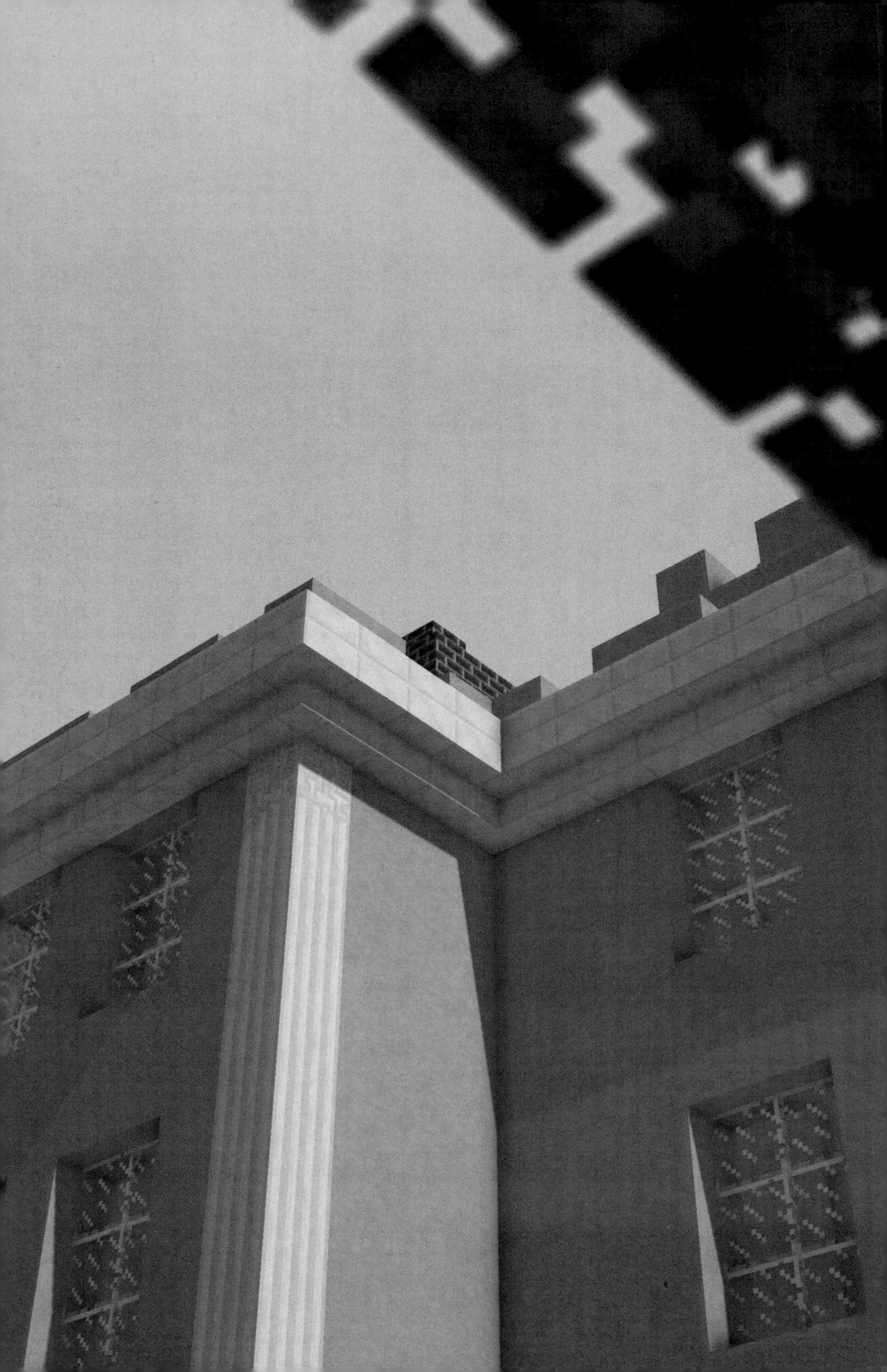

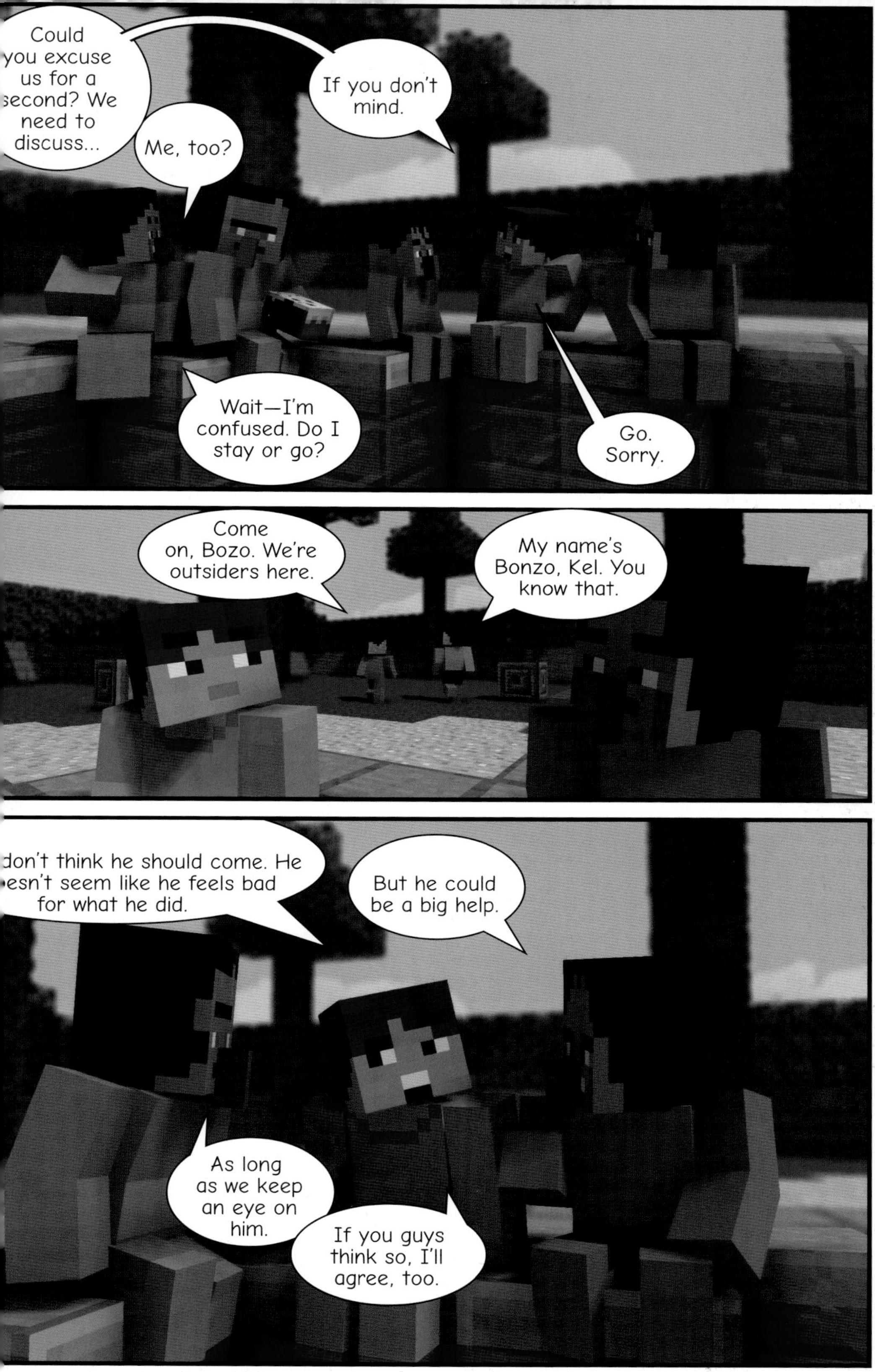
Could you excuse us for a econd? We need to discuss...
If you don't mind.
Me, too?
Wait—I'm confused. Do I stay or go?
Go. Sorry.
Come on, Bozo. We're outsiders here.
My name's Bonzo, Kel. You know that.
don't think he should come. He esn't seem like he feels bad for what he did.
But he could be a big help.
As long as we keep an eye on him.
If you guys think so, I'll agree, too.

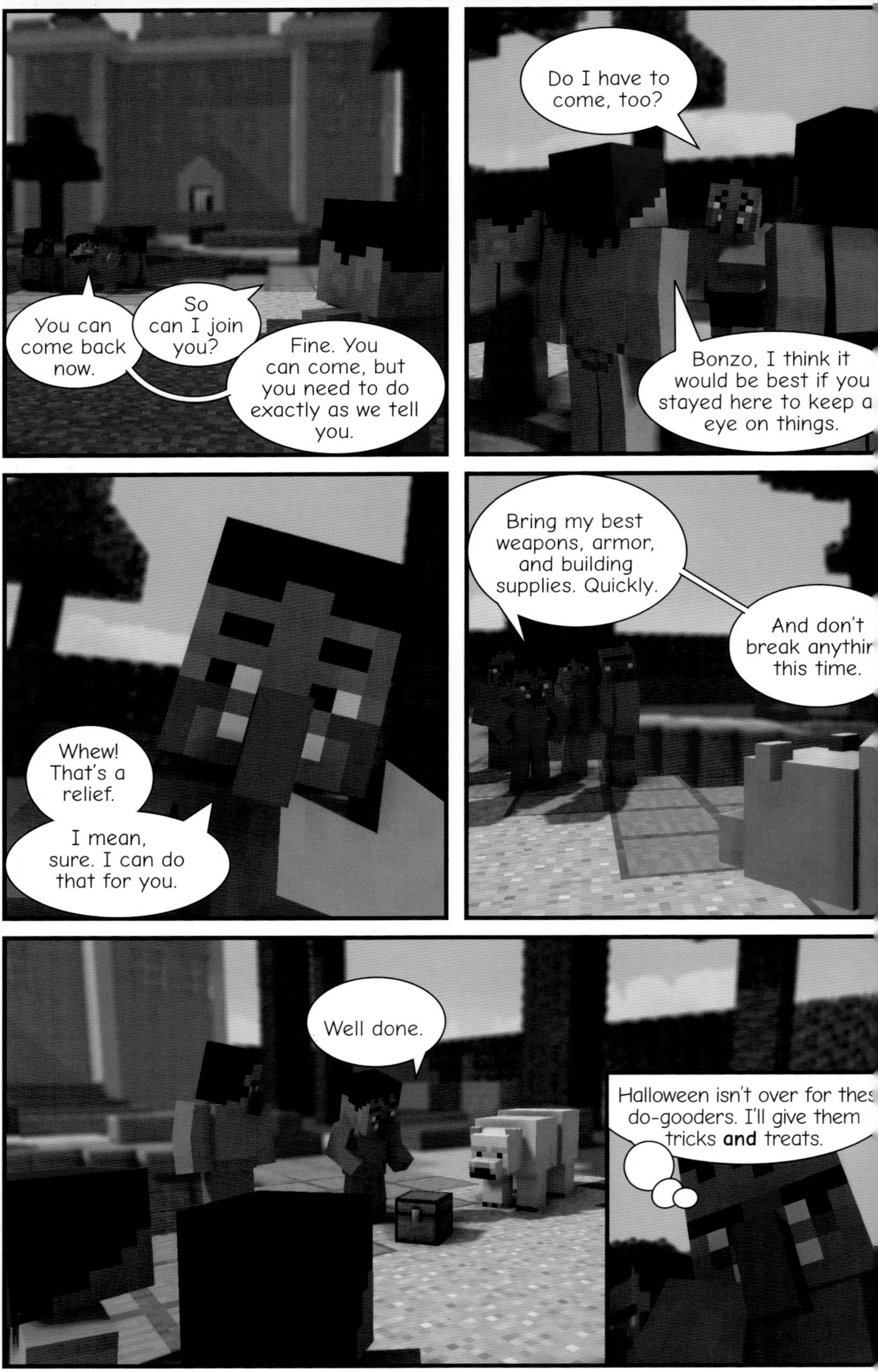
So can I join you?
You can come back now.
Fine. You can come, but you need to do exactly as we tell you.
Do I have to come, too?
Bonzo, I think it would be best if you stayed here to keep a eye on things.
Whew! That's a relief.
I mean, sure. I can do that for you.
Bring my best weapons, armor, and building supplies. Quickly.
And don't break anythi this time.
Well done.
Halloween isn't over for thes do-gooders. I'll give them tricks **and** treats.

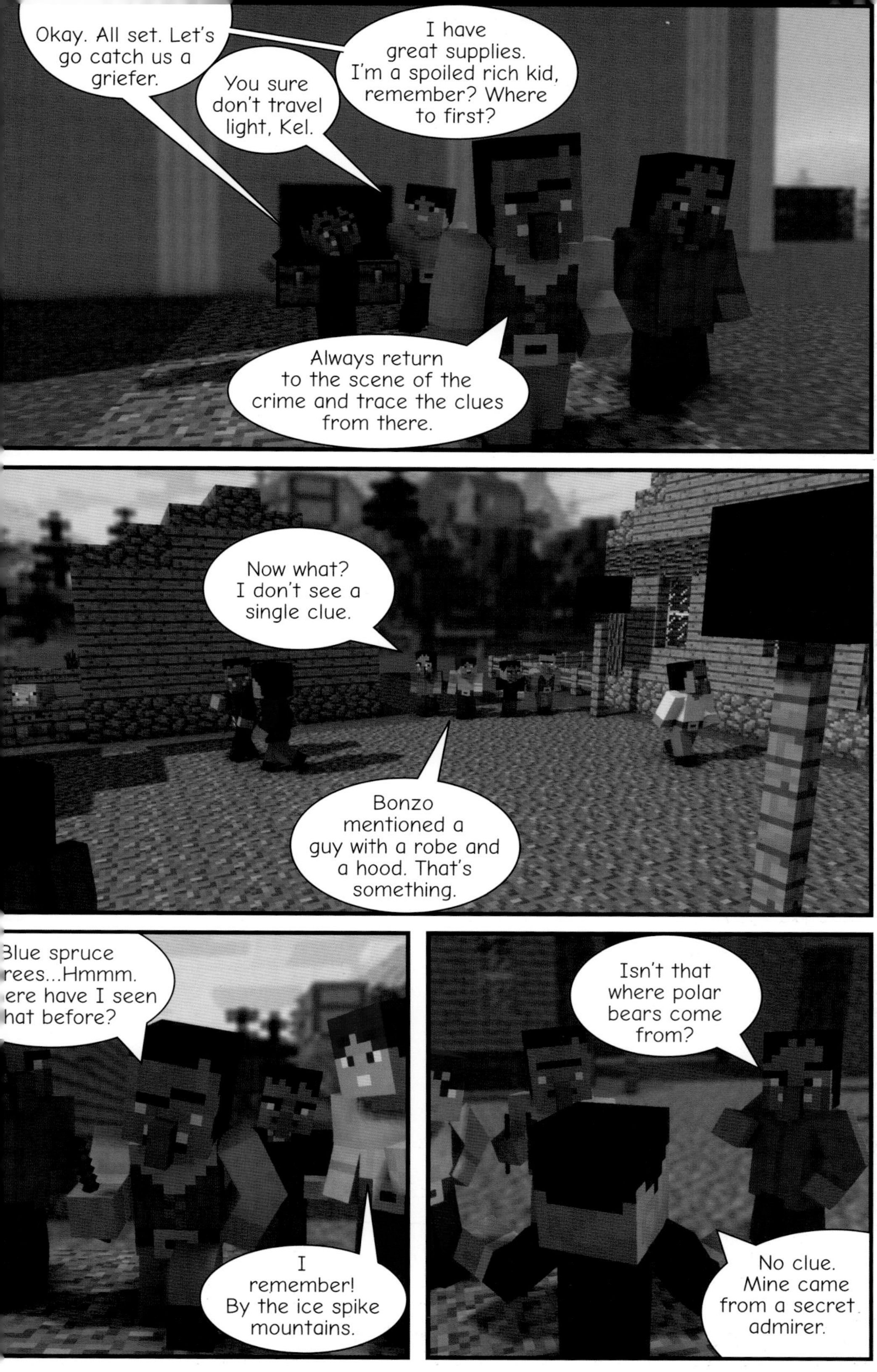
Okay. All set. Let's go catch us a griefer.
You sure don't travel light, Kel.
I have great supplies. I'm a spoiled rich kid, remember? Where to first?
Always return to the scene of the crime and trace the clues from there.
Now what? I don't see a single clue.
Bonzo mentioned a guy with a robe and a hood. That's something.
Blue spruce rees...Hmmm. ere have I seen hat before?
I remember! By the ice spike mountains.
Isn't that where polar bears come from?
No clue. Mine came from a secret admirer.

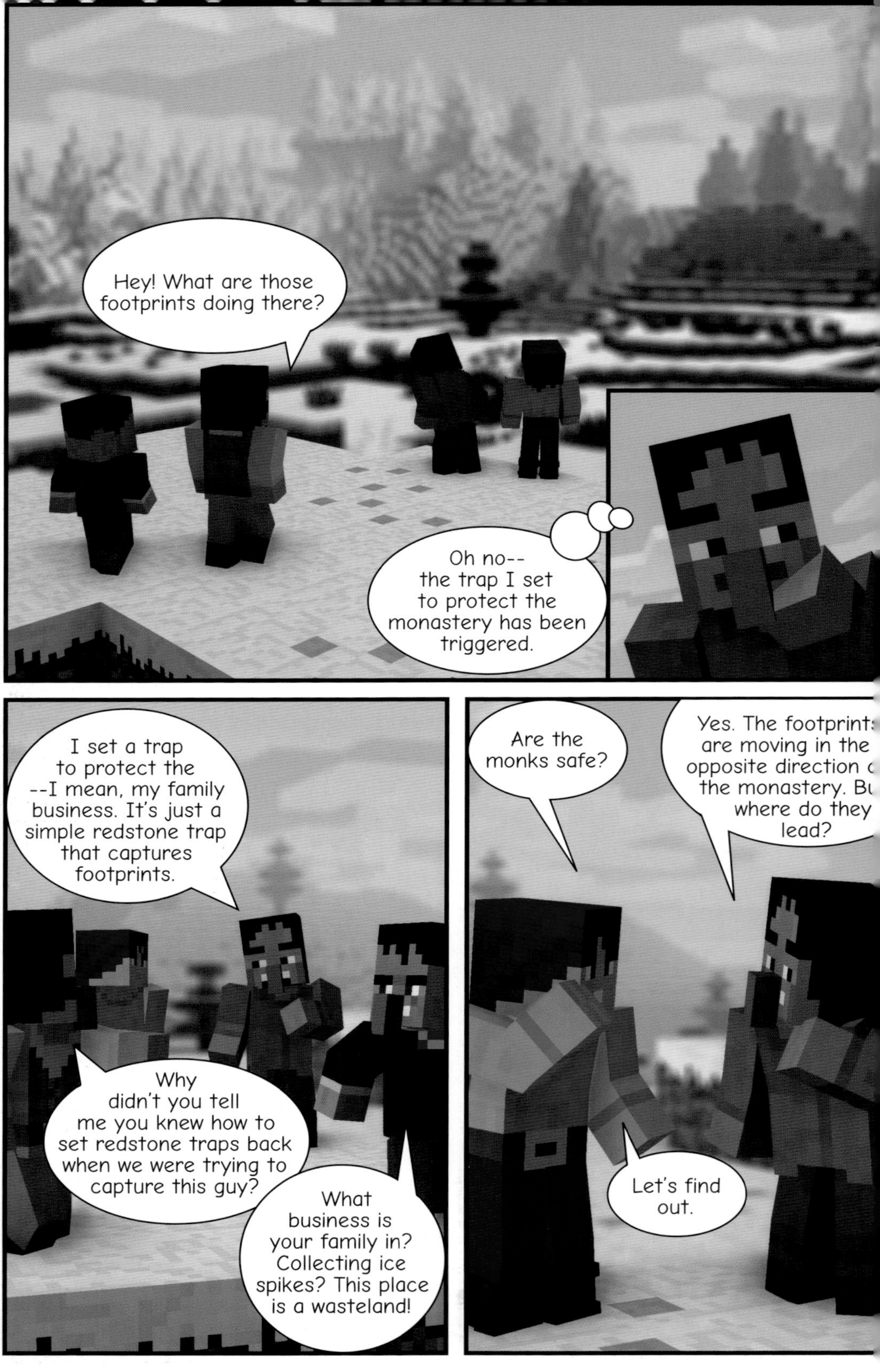
Hey! What are those footprints doing there?
Oh no-- the trap I set to protect the monastery has been triggered.
I set a trap to protect the --I mean, my family business. It's just a simple redstone trap that captures footprints.
Why didn't you tell me you knew how to set redstone traps back when we were trying to capture this guy?
What business is your family in? Collecting ice spikes? This place is a wasteland!
Are the monks safe?
Yes. The footprint are moving in the opposite direction the monastery. B where do they lead?
Let's find out.

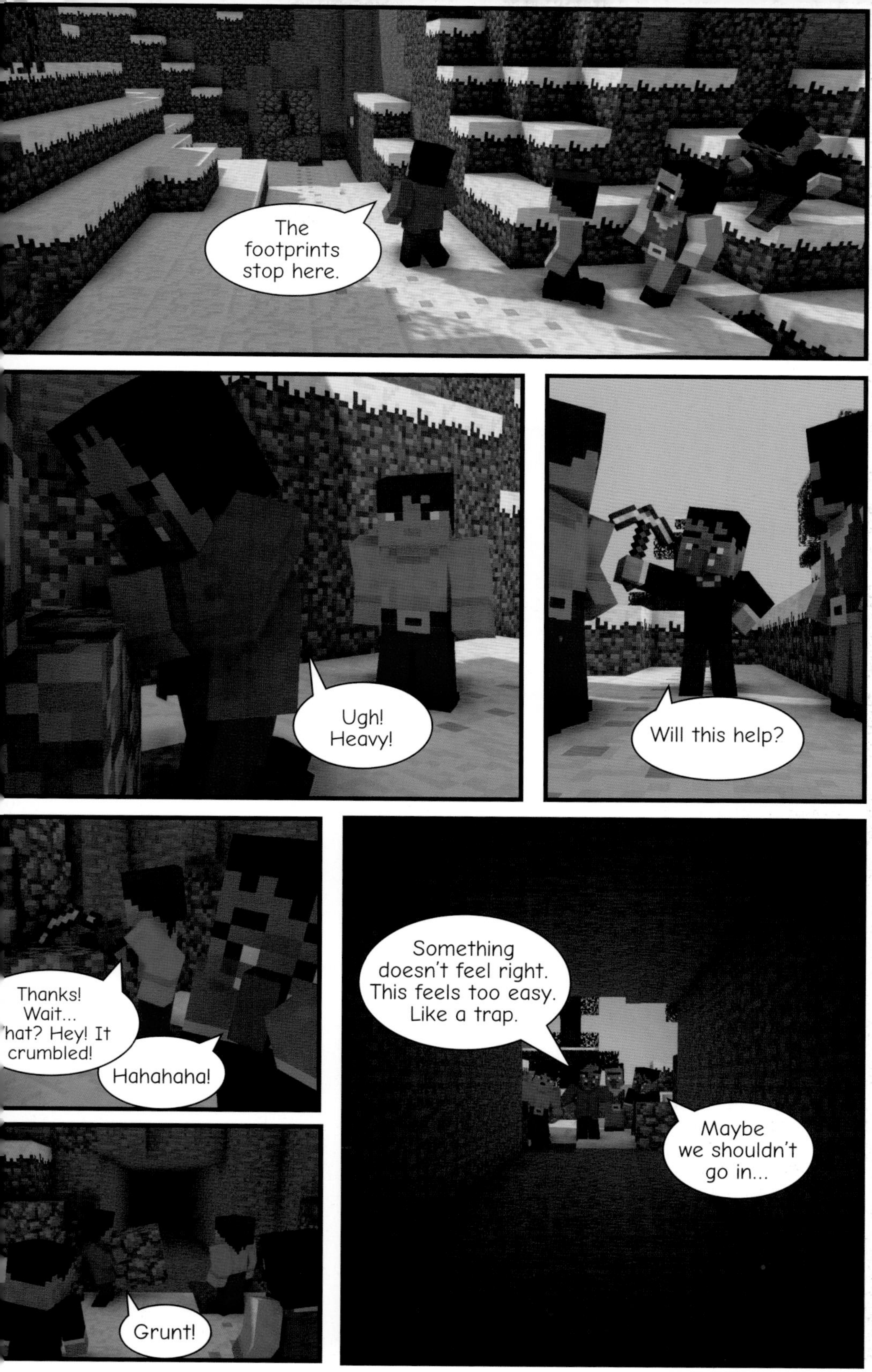
The footprints stop here.
Ugh! Heavy!
Will this help?
Thanks! Wait... 'hat? Hey! It crumbled!
Hahahaha!
Grunt!
Something doesn't feel right. This feels too easy. Like a trap.
Maybe we shouldn't go in...

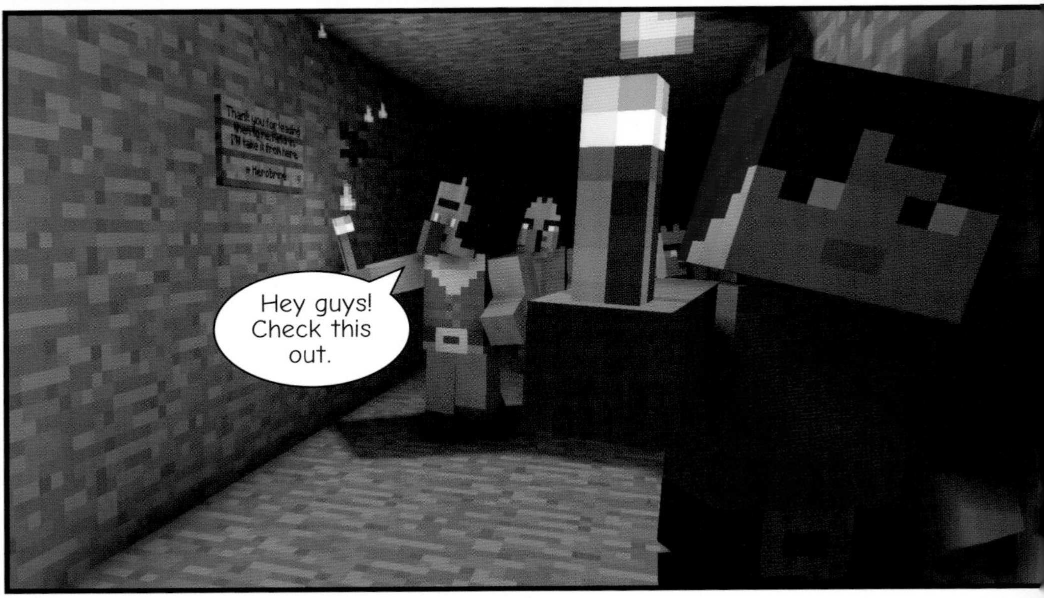
Hey guys! Check this out.

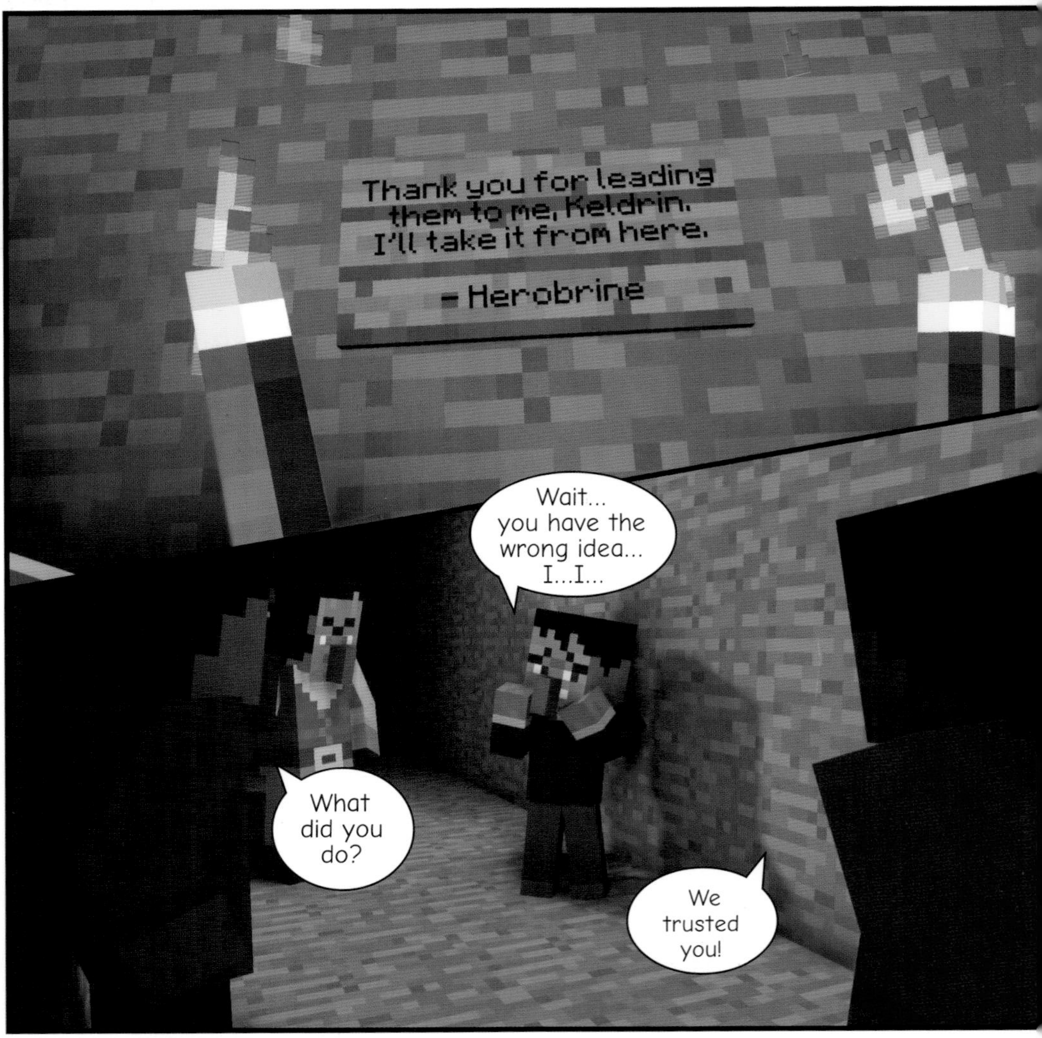
Thank you for leading them to me, Keldrin. I'll take it from here.
- Herobrine
Wait... you have the wrong idea... I...I...
What did you do?
We trusted you!

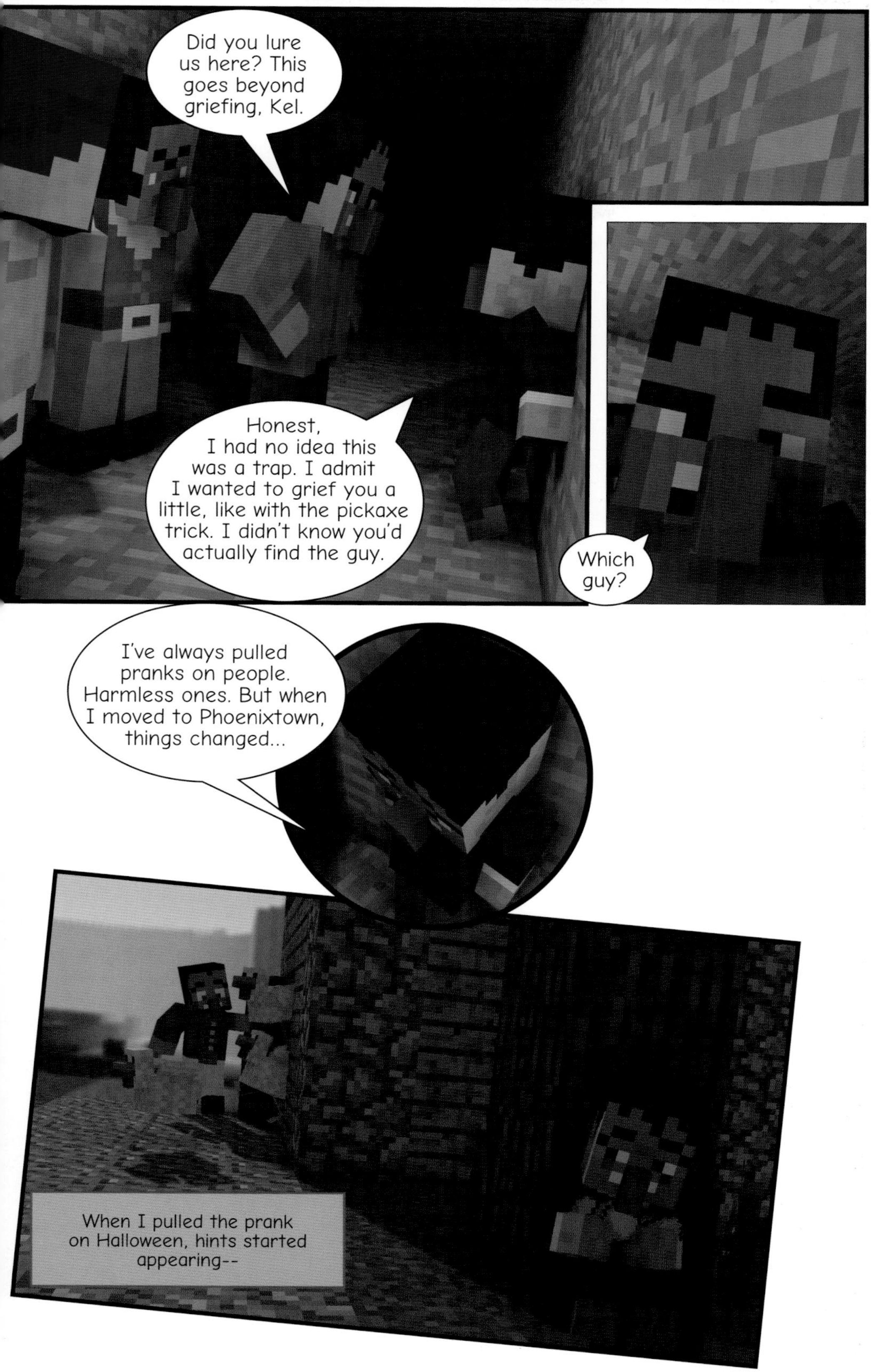
Did you lure us here? This goes beyond griefing, Kel.
Honest, I had no idea this was a trap. I admit I wanted to grief you a little, like with the pickaxe trick. I didn't know you'd actually find the guy.
Which guy?
I've always pulled pranks on people. Harmless ones. But when I moved to Phoenixtown, things changed...
When I pulled the prank on Halloween, hints started appearing--

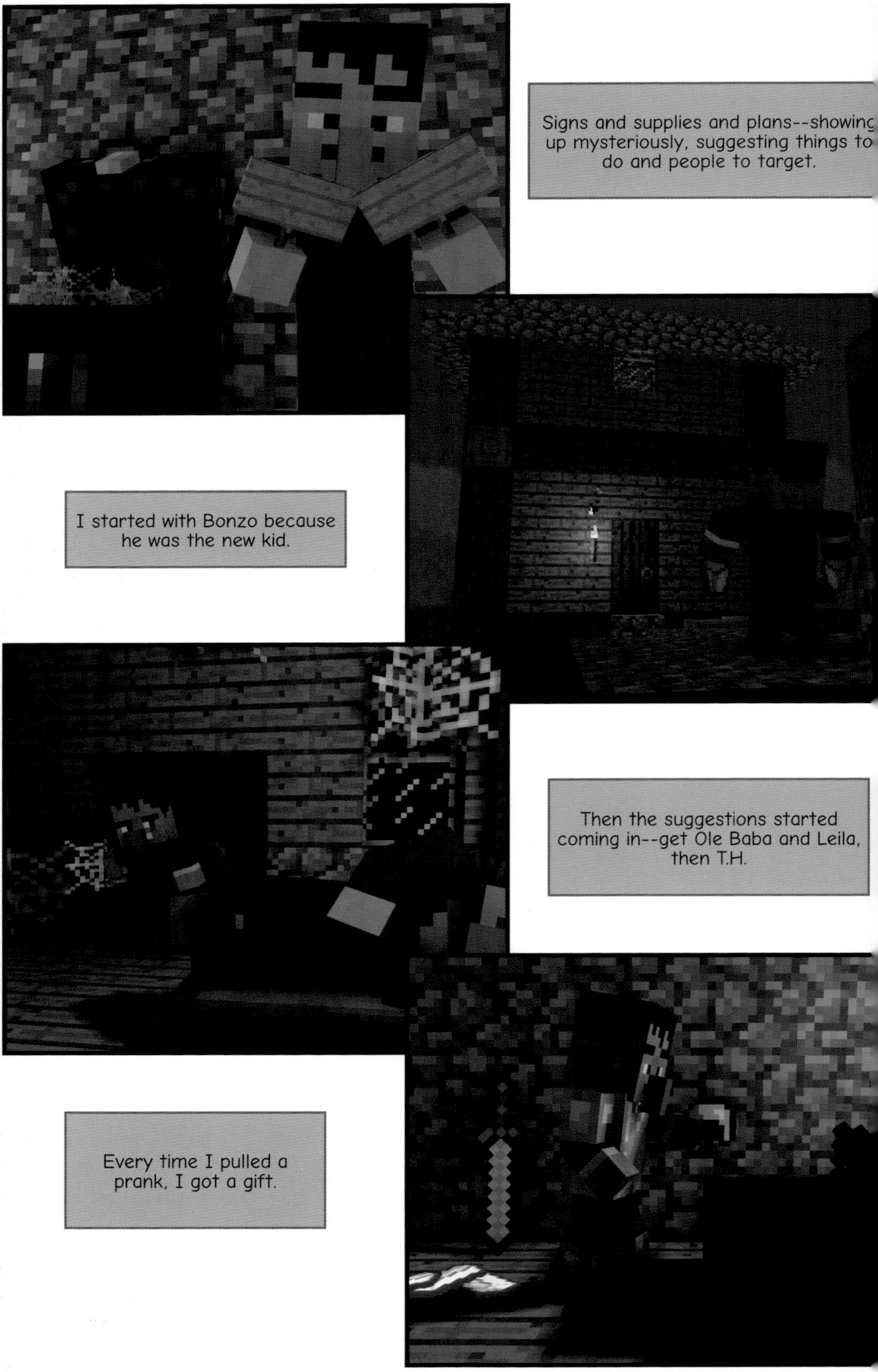
Signs and supplies and plans--showing up mysteriously, suggesting things to do and people to target.
I started with Bonzo because he was the new kid.
Then the suggestions started coming in--get Ole Baba and Leila, then T.H.
Every time I pulled a prank, I got a gift.

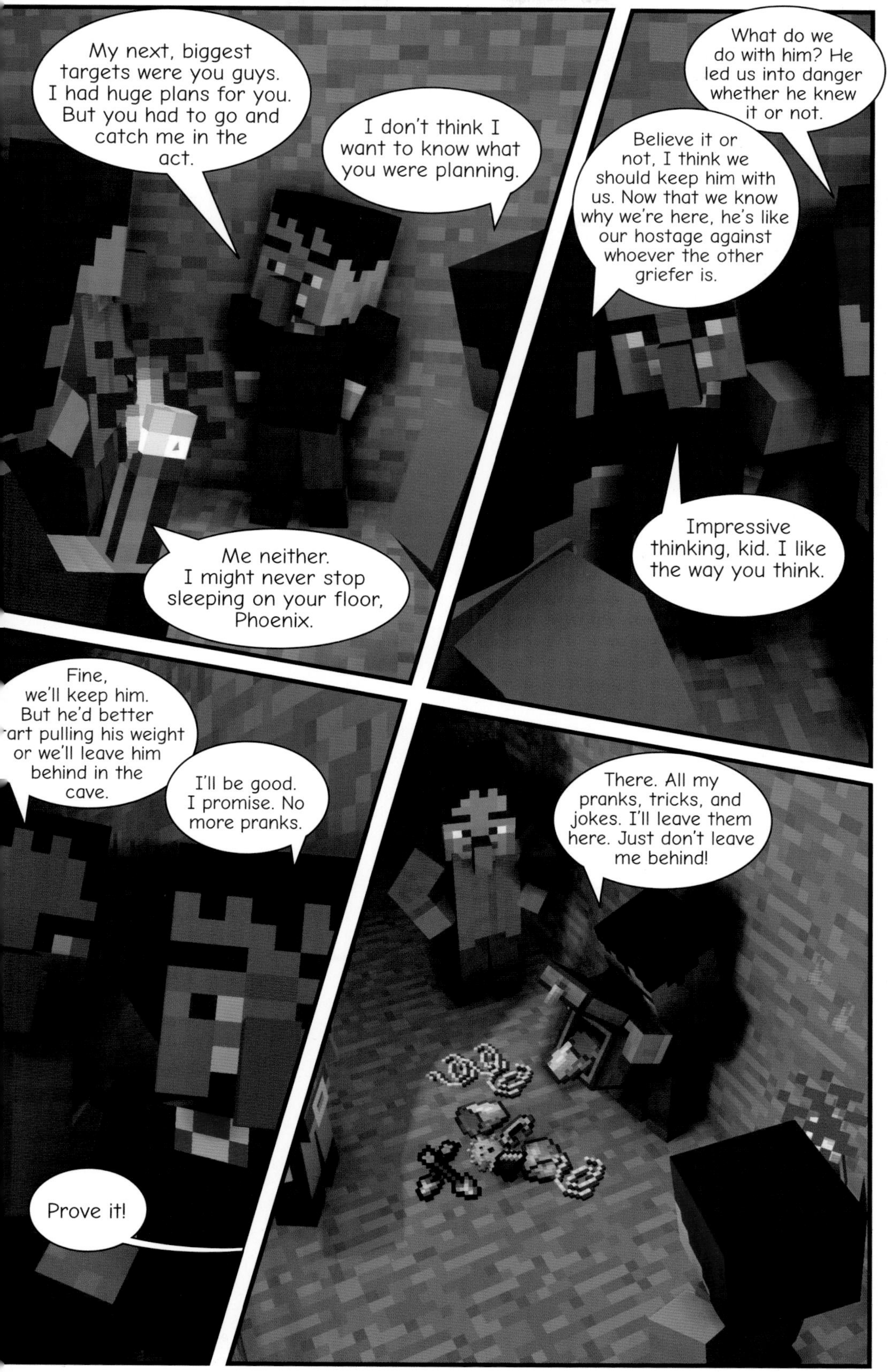

My next, biggest targets were you guys. I had huge plans for you. But you had to go and catch me in the act.
I don't think I want to know what you were planning.
Me neither. I might never stop sleeping on your floor, Phoenix.
What do we do with him? He led us into danger whether he knew it or not.
Believe it or not, I think we should keep him with us. Now that we know why we're here, he's like our hostage against whoever the other griefer is.
Impressive thinking, kid. I like the way you think.
Fine, we'll keep him. But he'd better art pulling his weight or we'll leave him behind in the cave.
I'll be good. I promise. No more pranks.
Prove it!
There. All my pranks, tricks, and jokes. I'll leave them here. Just don't leave me behind!

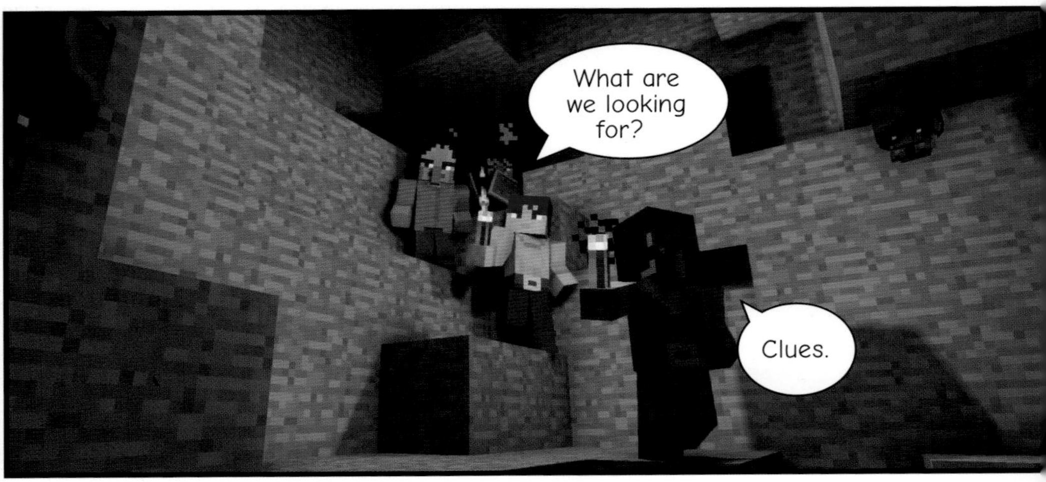
What are we looking for?
Clues.

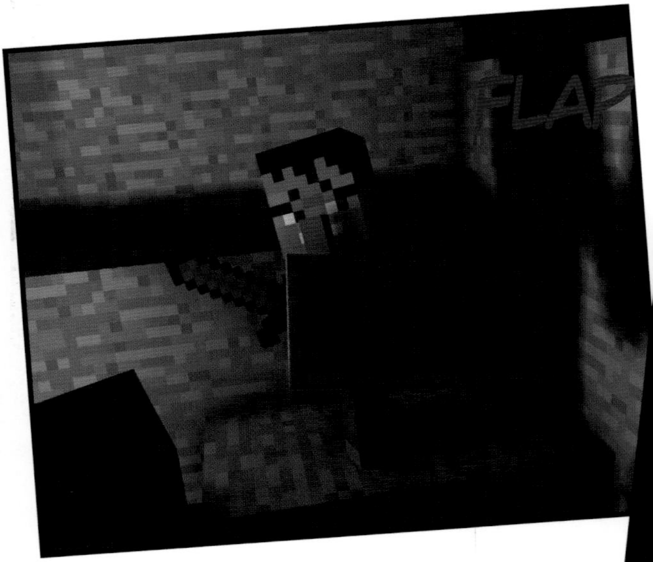
FLAP

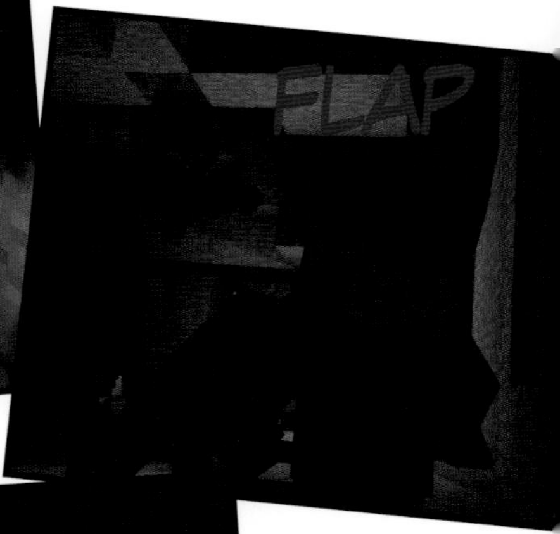
FLAP

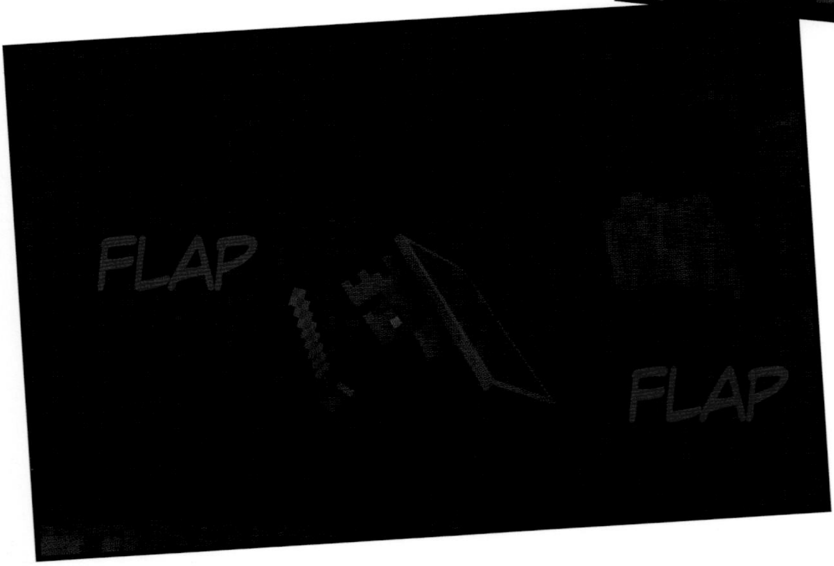
FLAP
FLAP

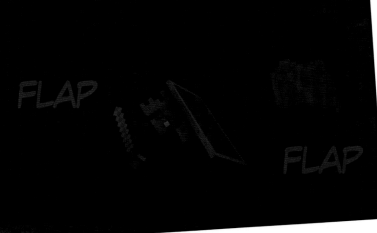

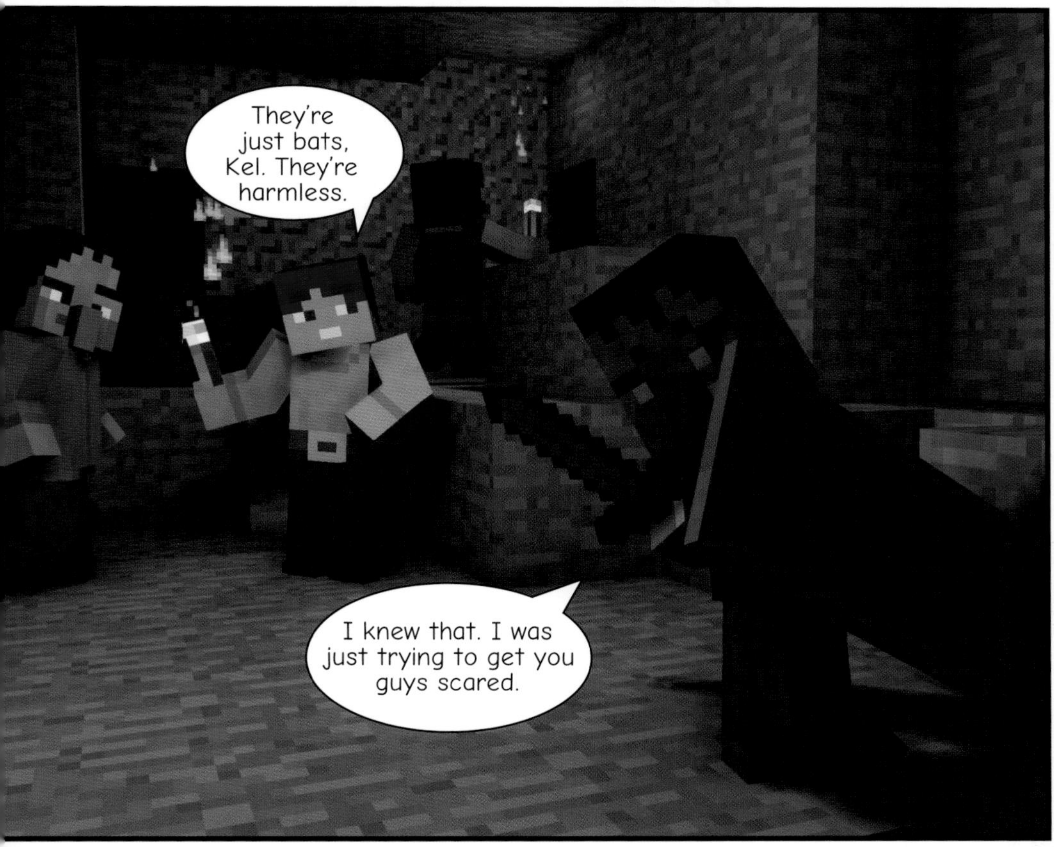
They're just bats, Kel. They're harmless.
I knew that. I was just trying to get you guys scared.

HUMMM

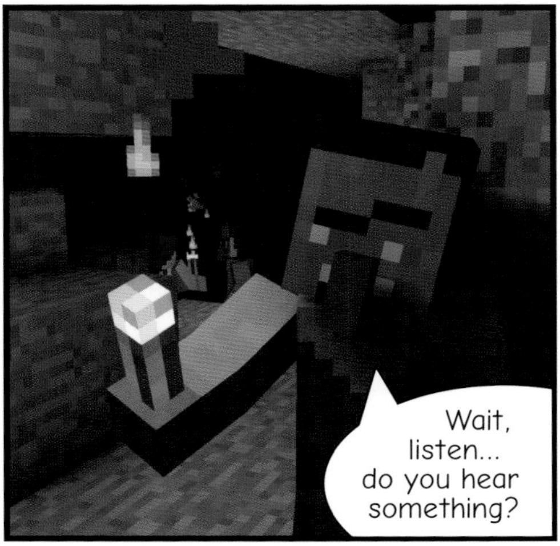
Wait, listen... do you hear something?

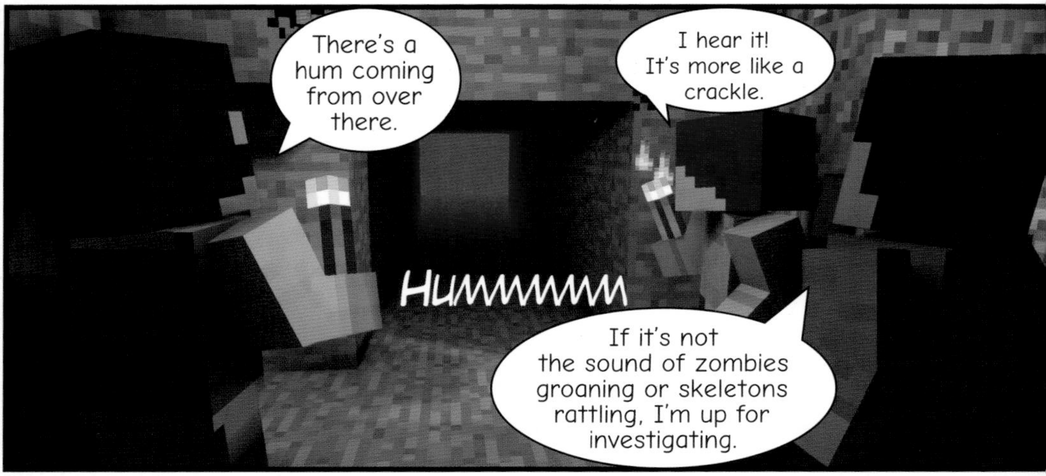
There's a hum coming from over there.
I hear it! It's more like a crackle.
HUMMMMM
If it's not the sound of zombies groaning or skeletons rattling, I'm up for investigating.

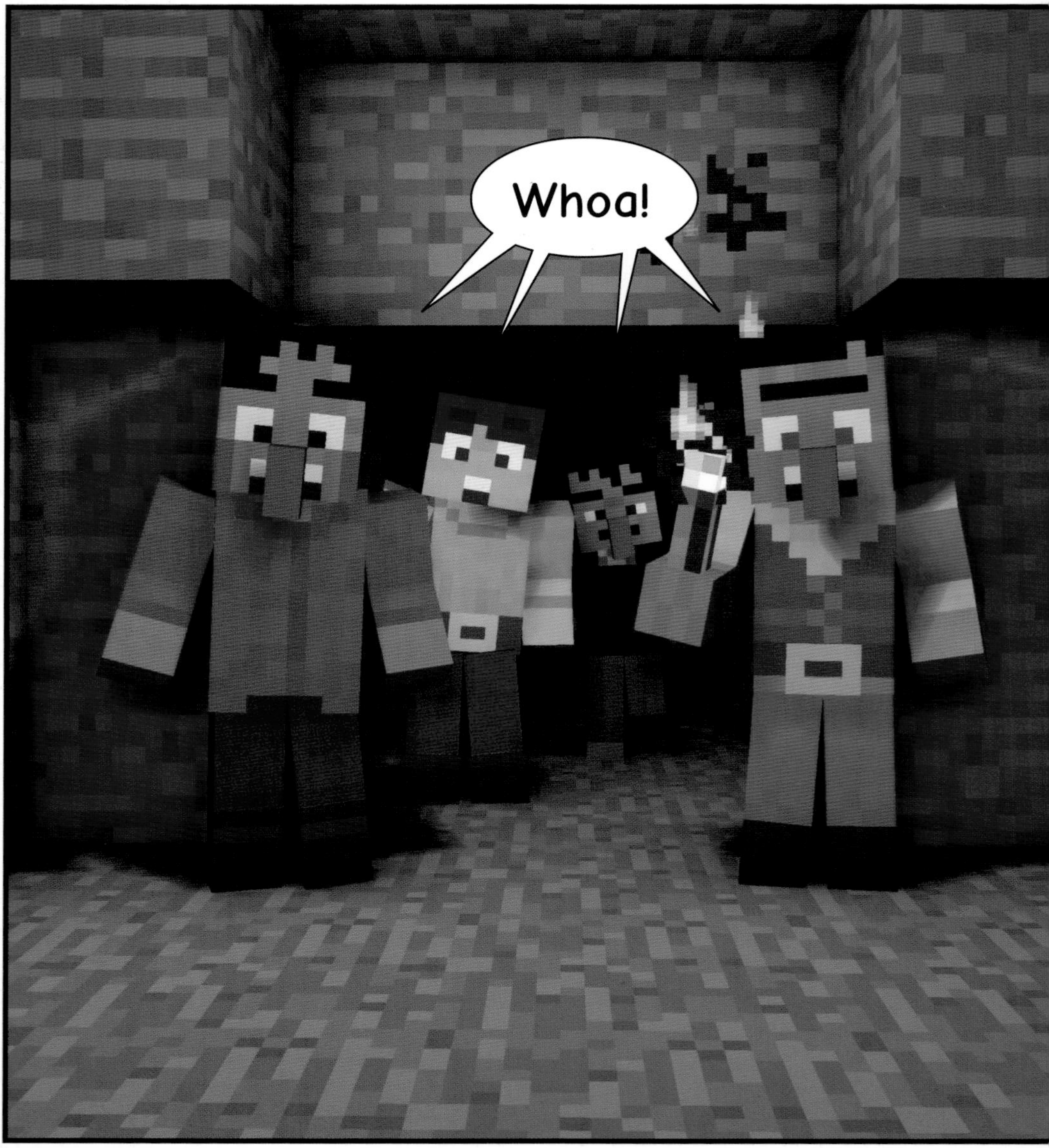
Whoa!

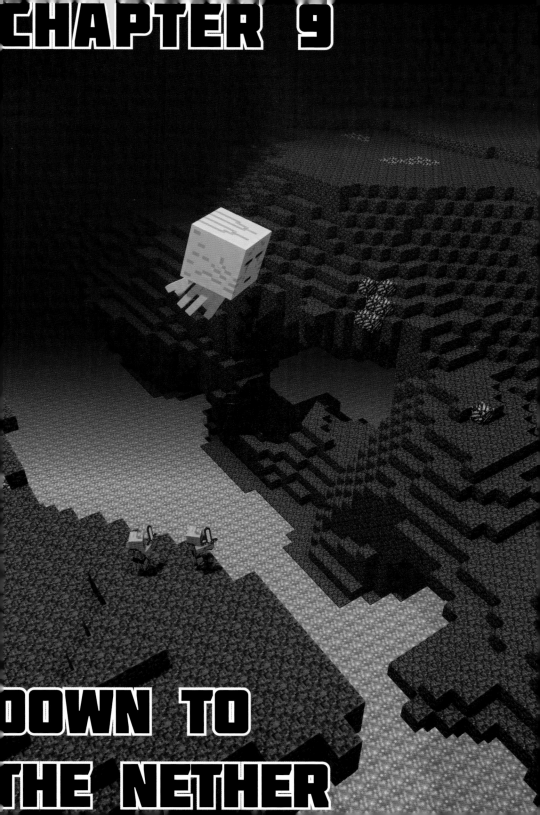

CHAPTER 9

DOWN TO THE NETHER

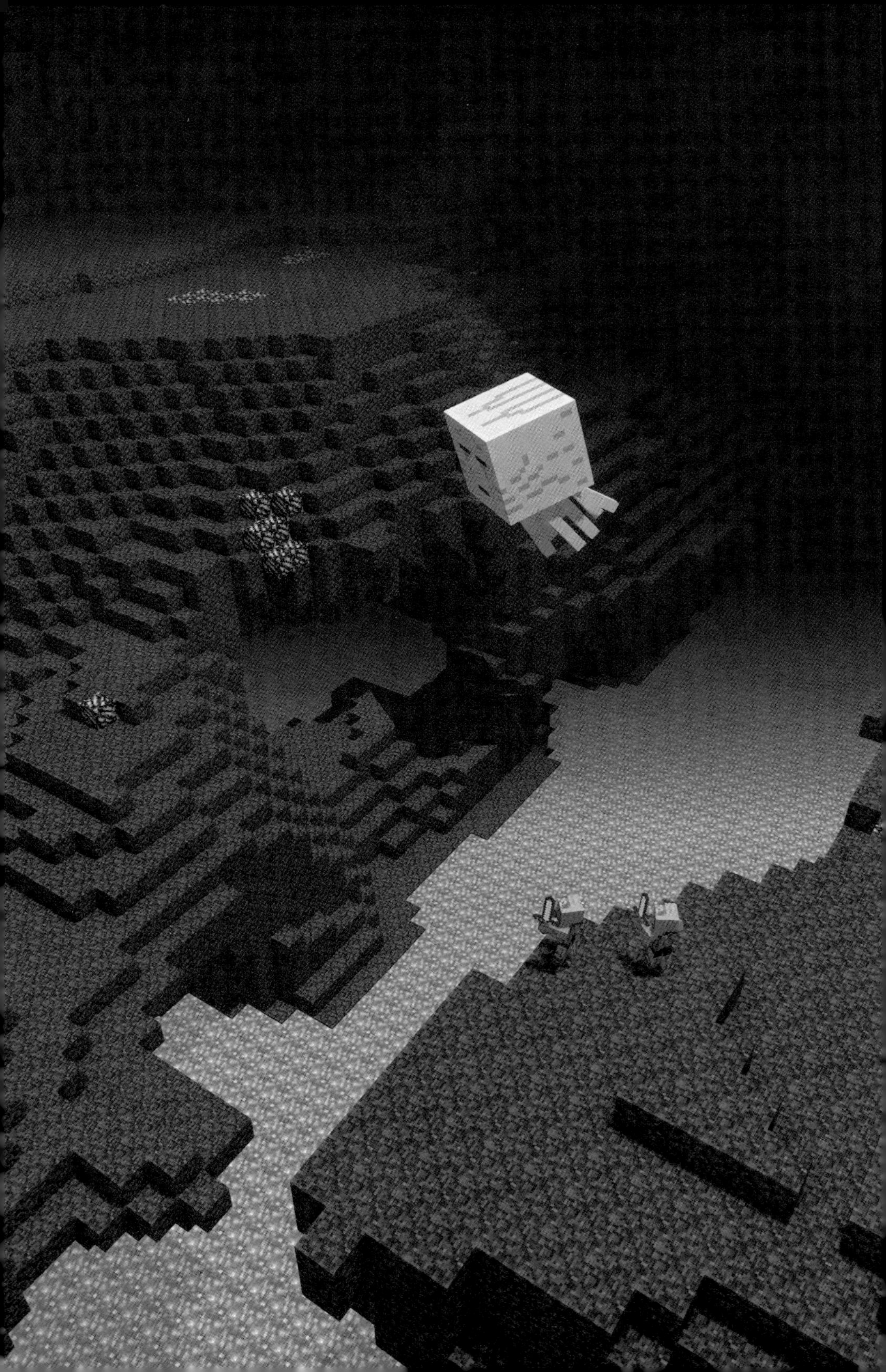

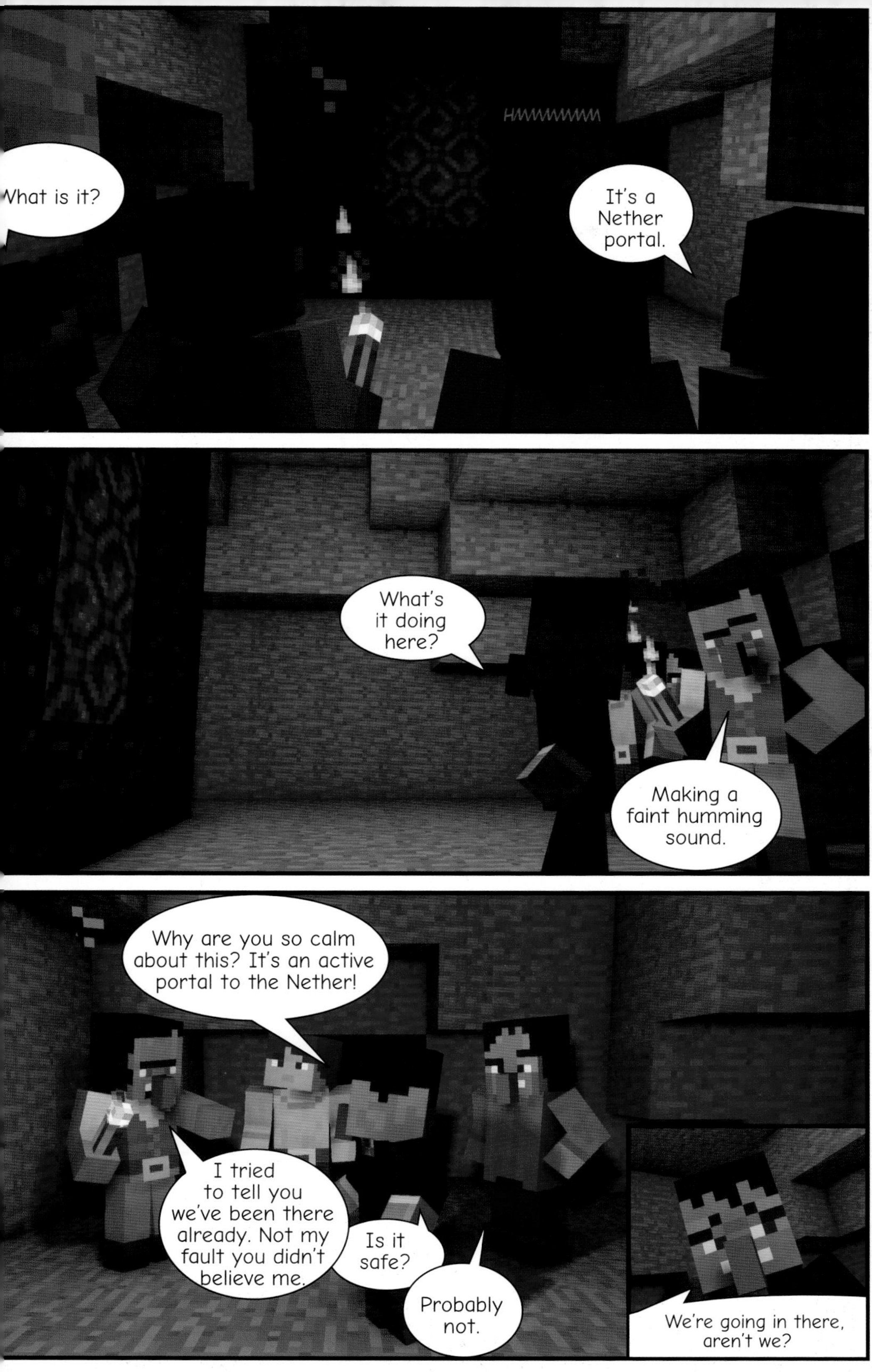
HMMMMMMM
What is it?
It's a Nether portal.
What's it doing here?
Making a faint humming sound.
Why are you so calm about this? It's an active portal to the Nether!
I tried to tell you we've been there already. Not my fault you didn't believe me.
Is it safe?
Probably not.
We're going in there, aren't we?

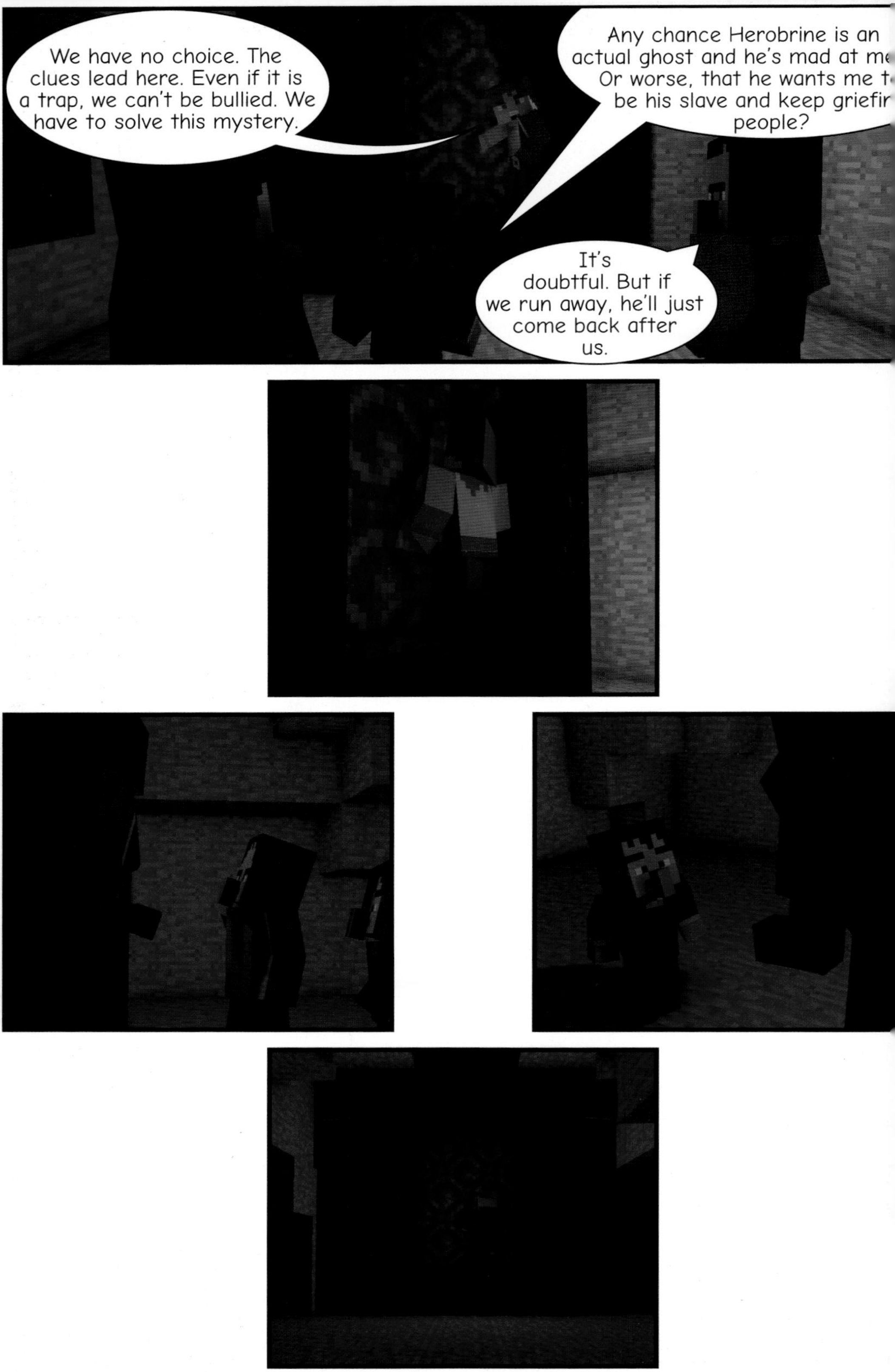
We have no choice. The clues lead here. Even if it is a trap, we can't be bullied. We have to solve this mystery.
Any chance Herobrine is an actual ghost and he's mad at m Or worse, that he wants me t be his slave and keep griefi people?
It's doubtful. But if we run away, he'll just come back after us.

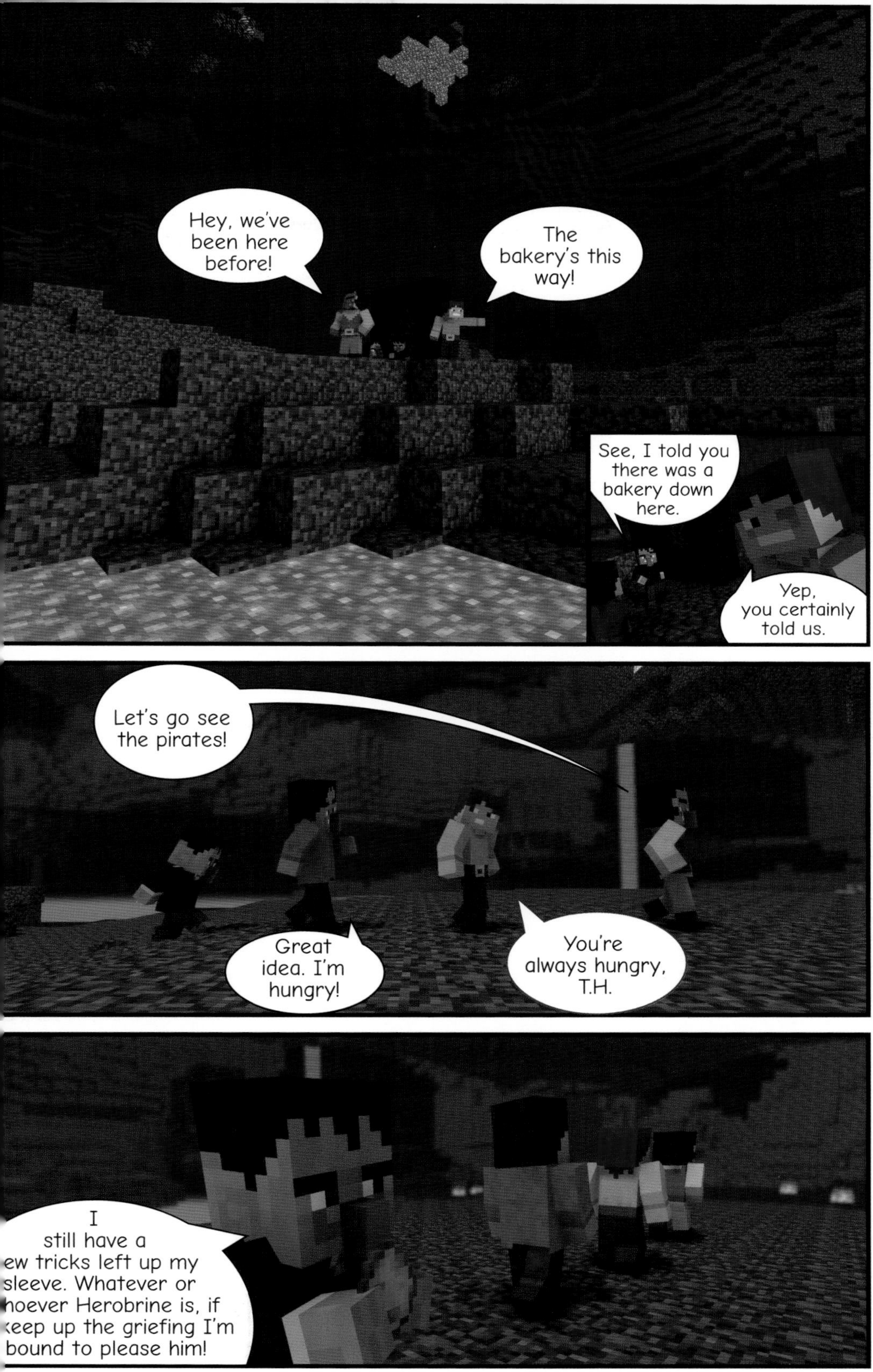
Hey, we've been here before!
The bakery's this way!
See, I told you there was a bakery down here.
Yep, you certainly told us.
Let's go see the pirates!
Great idea. I'm hungry!
You're always hungry, T.H.
I still have a
ew tricks left up my
sleeve. Whatever or
hoever Herobrine is, if
eep up the griefing I'm
bound to please him!

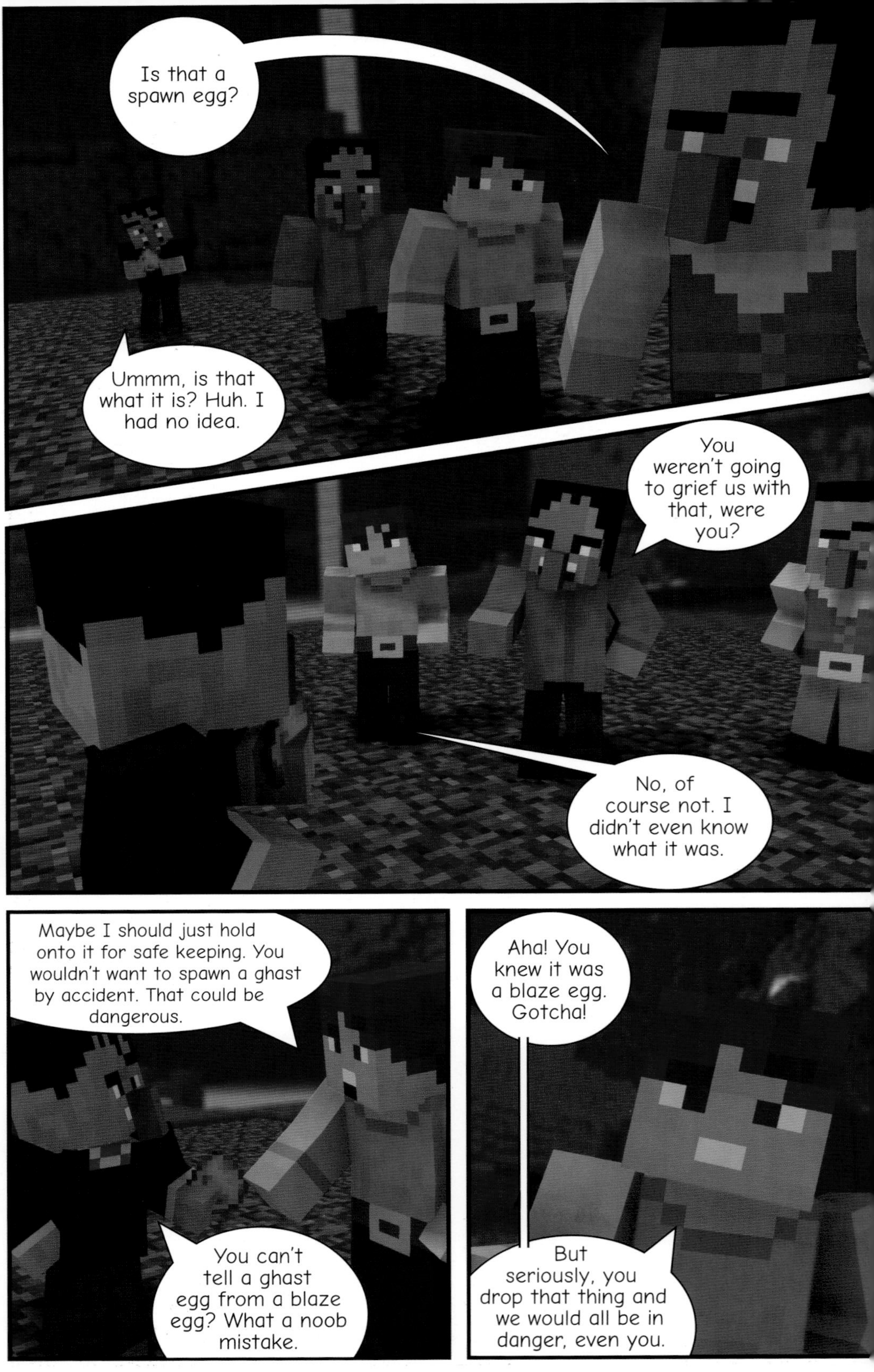
Is that a spawn egg?
Ummm, is that what it is? Huh. I had no idea.
You weren't going to grief us with that, were you?
No, of course not. I didn't even know what it was.
Maybe I should just hold onto it for safe keeping. You wouldn't want to spawn a ghast by accident. That could be dangerous.
You can't tell a ghast egg from a blaze egg? What a noob mistake.
Aha! You knew it was a blaze egg. Gotcha!
But seriously, you drop that thing and we would all be in danger, even you.

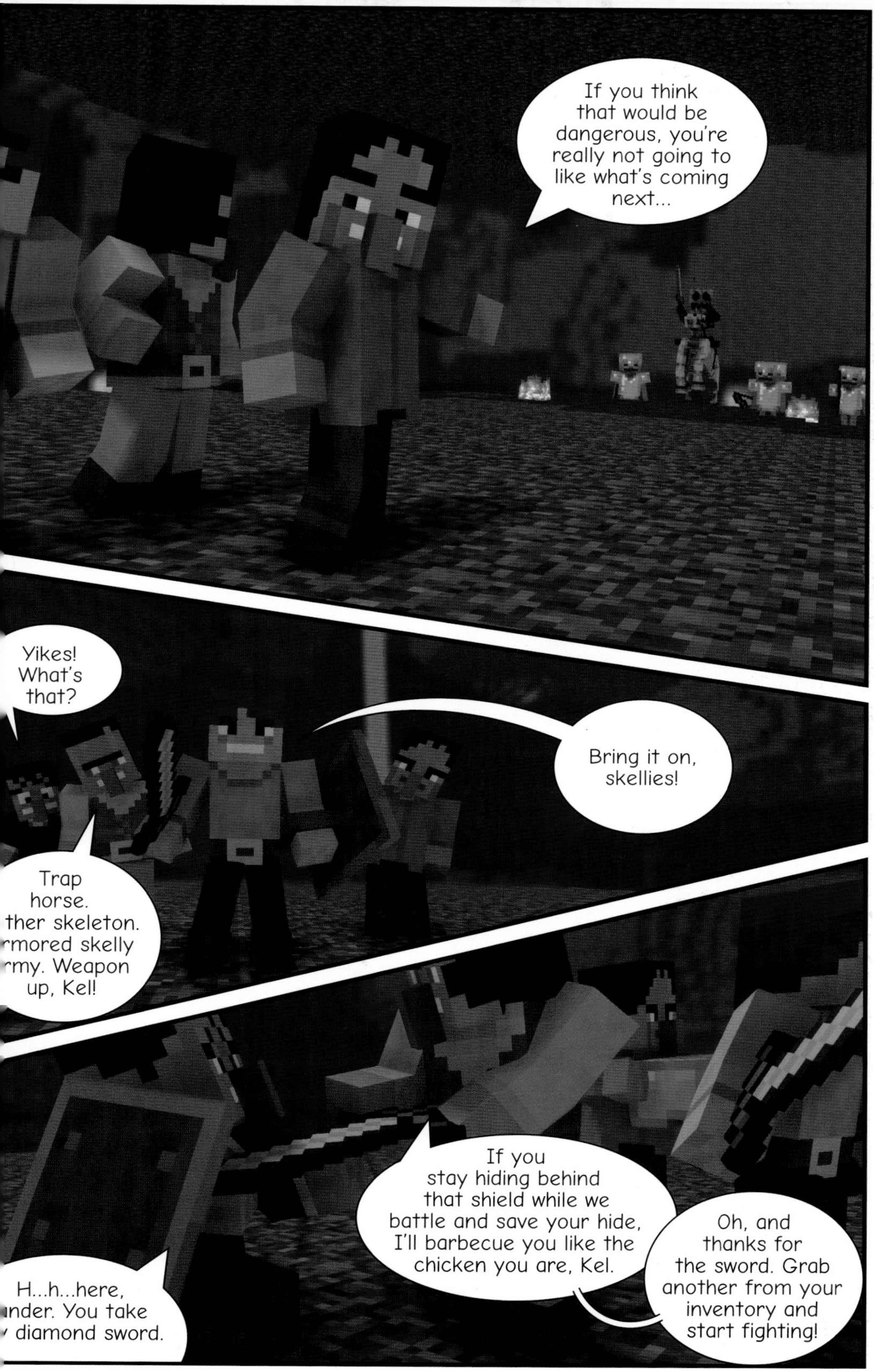

If you think that would be dangerous, you're really not going to like what's coming next...
Yikes! What's that?
Bring it on, skellies!
Trap horse. ther skeleton. rmored skelly rmy. Weapon up, Kel!
H...h...here, nder. You take diamond sword.
If you stay hiding behind that shield while we battle and save your hide, I'll barbecue you like the chicken you are, Kel.
Oh, and thanks for the sword. Grab another from your inventory and start fighting!

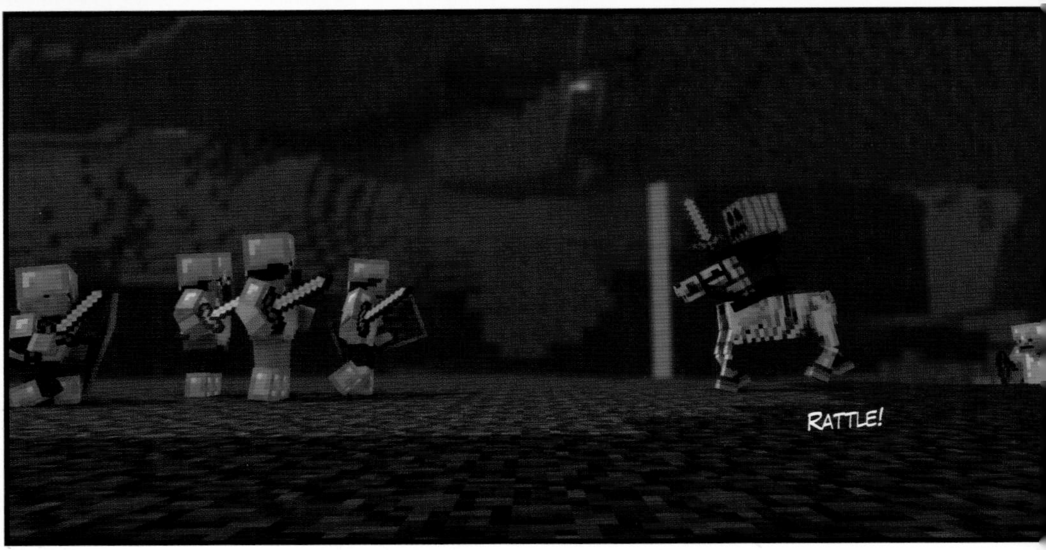
RATTLE!
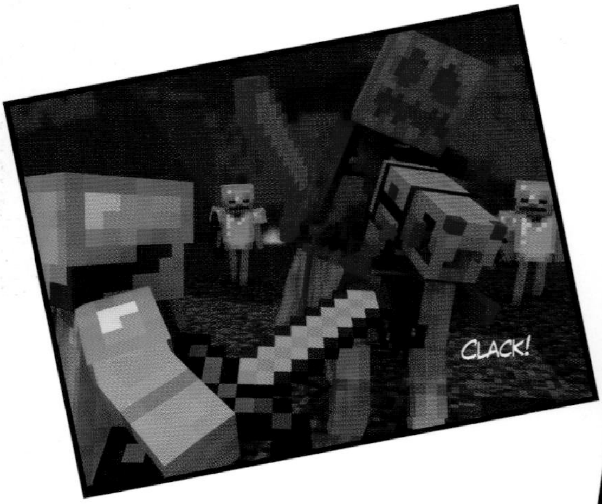
CLACK!
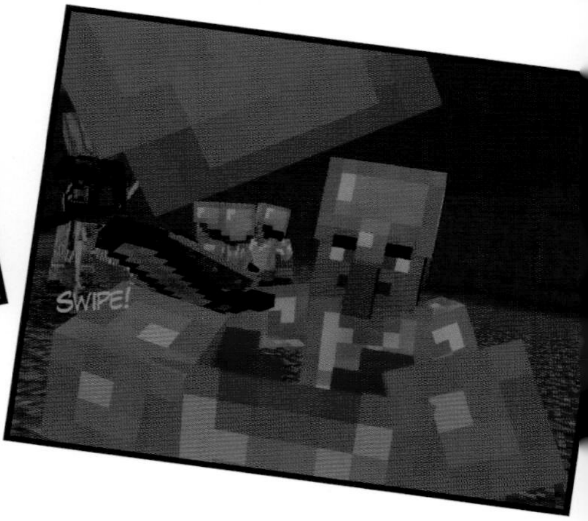
SWIPE!
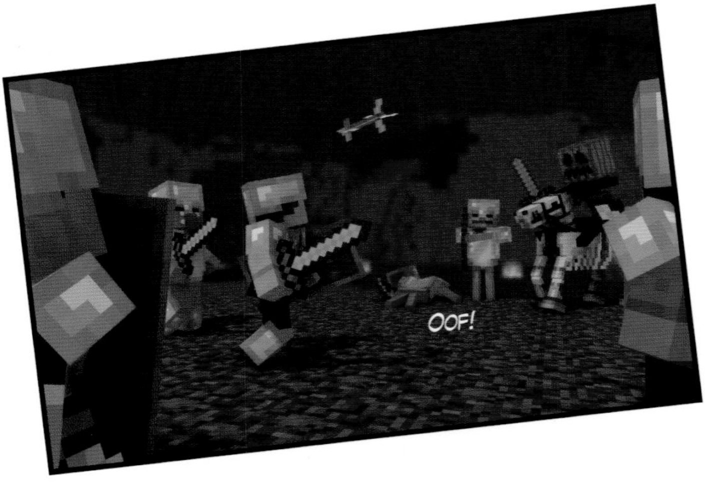
OOF!

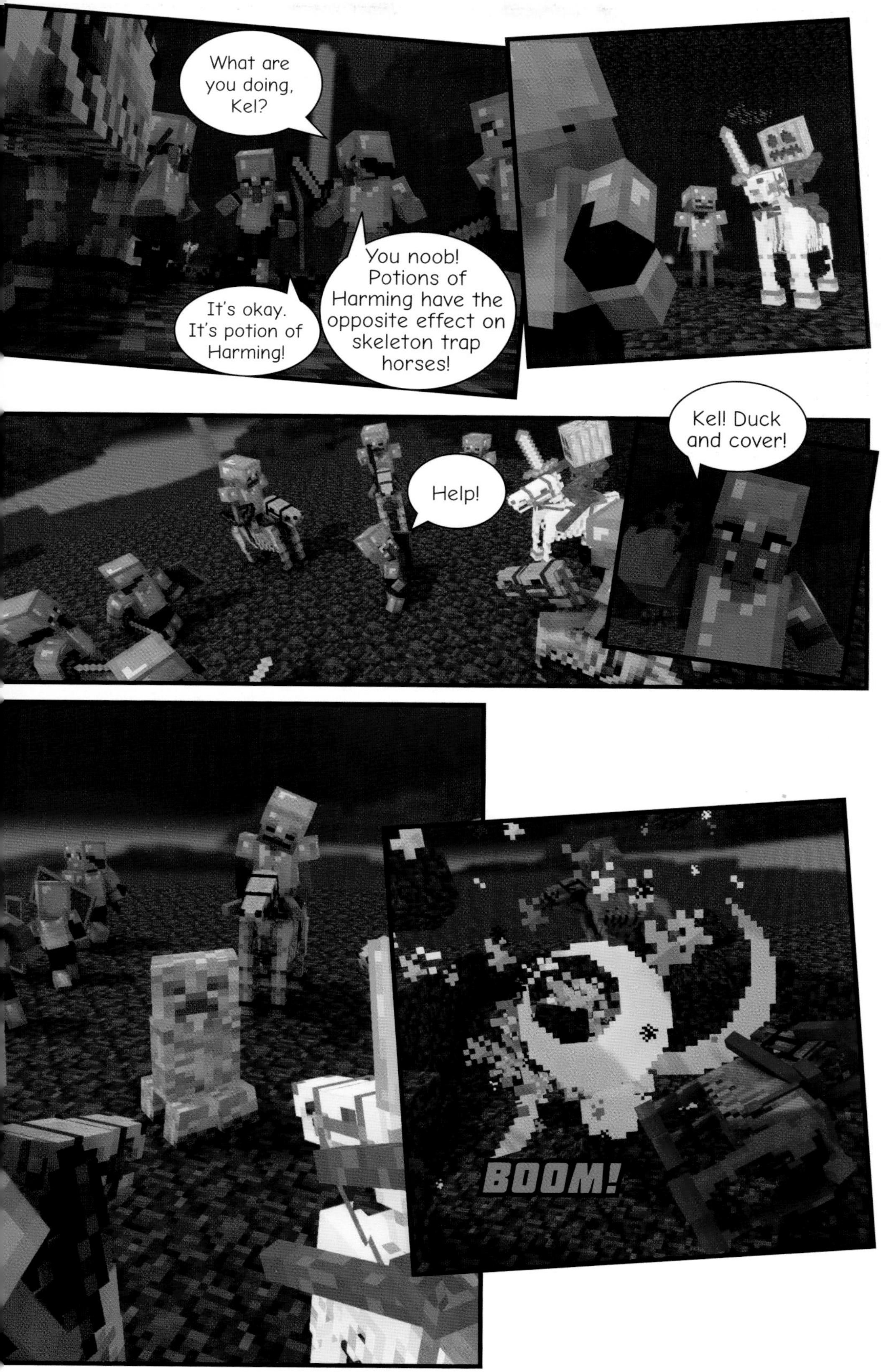

What are you doing, Kel?
It's okay. It's potion of Harming!
You noob! Potions of Harming have the opposite effect on skeleton trap horses!
Help!
Kel! Duck and cover!
BOOM!

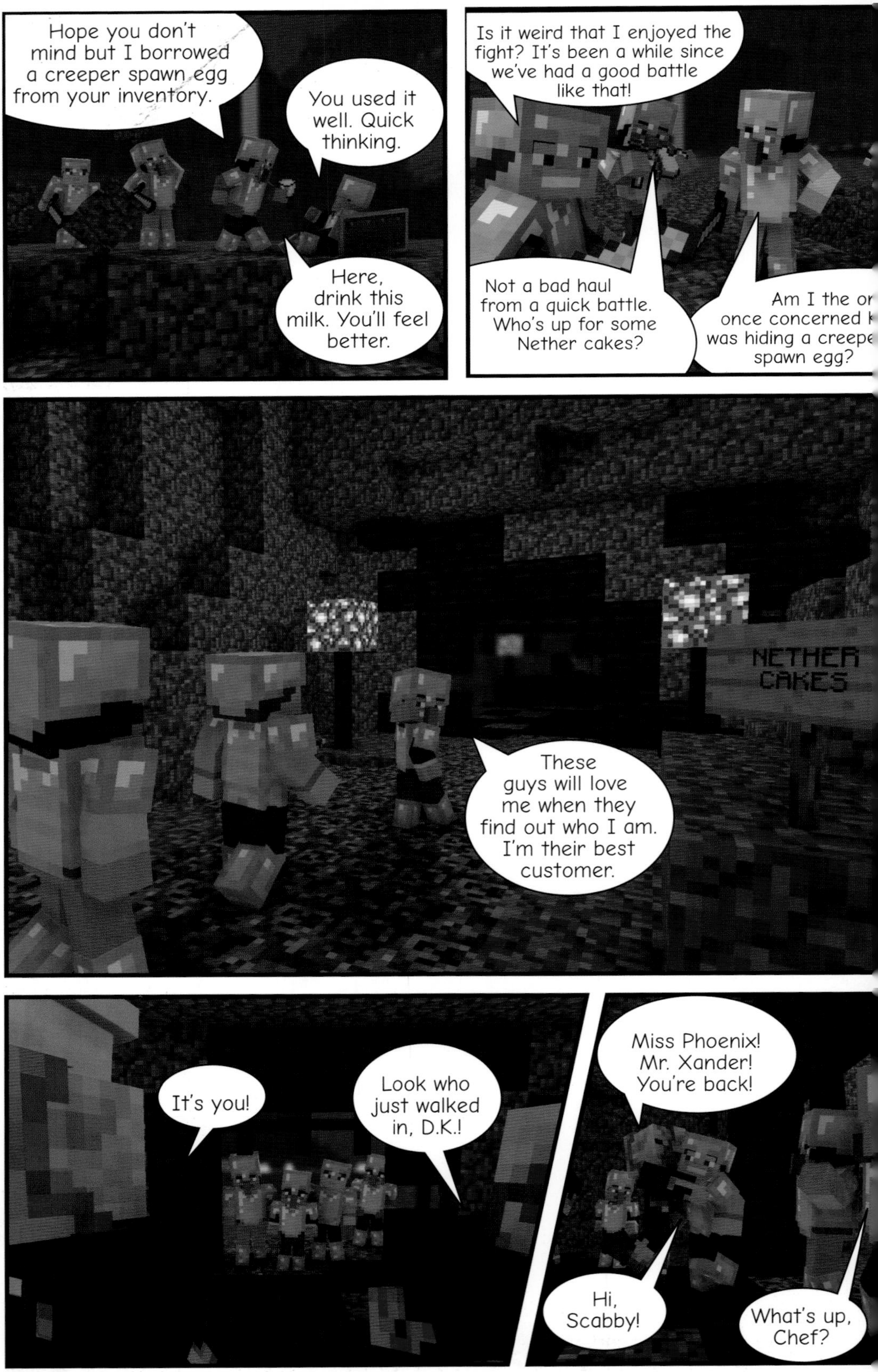
Hope you don't mind but I borrowed a creeper spawn egg from your inventory.
You used it well. Quick thinking.
Here, drink this milk. You'll feel better.
Is it weird that I enjoyed the fight? It's been a while since we've had a good battle like that!
Not a bad haul from a quick battle. Who's up for some Nether cakes?
Am I the or
once concerned k
was hiding a creepe
spawn egg?
NETHER CAKES
These guys will love me when they find out who I am. I'm their best customer.
It's you!
Look who just walked in, D.K.!
Miss Phoenix! Mr. Xander! You're back!
Hi, Scabby!
What's up, Chef?

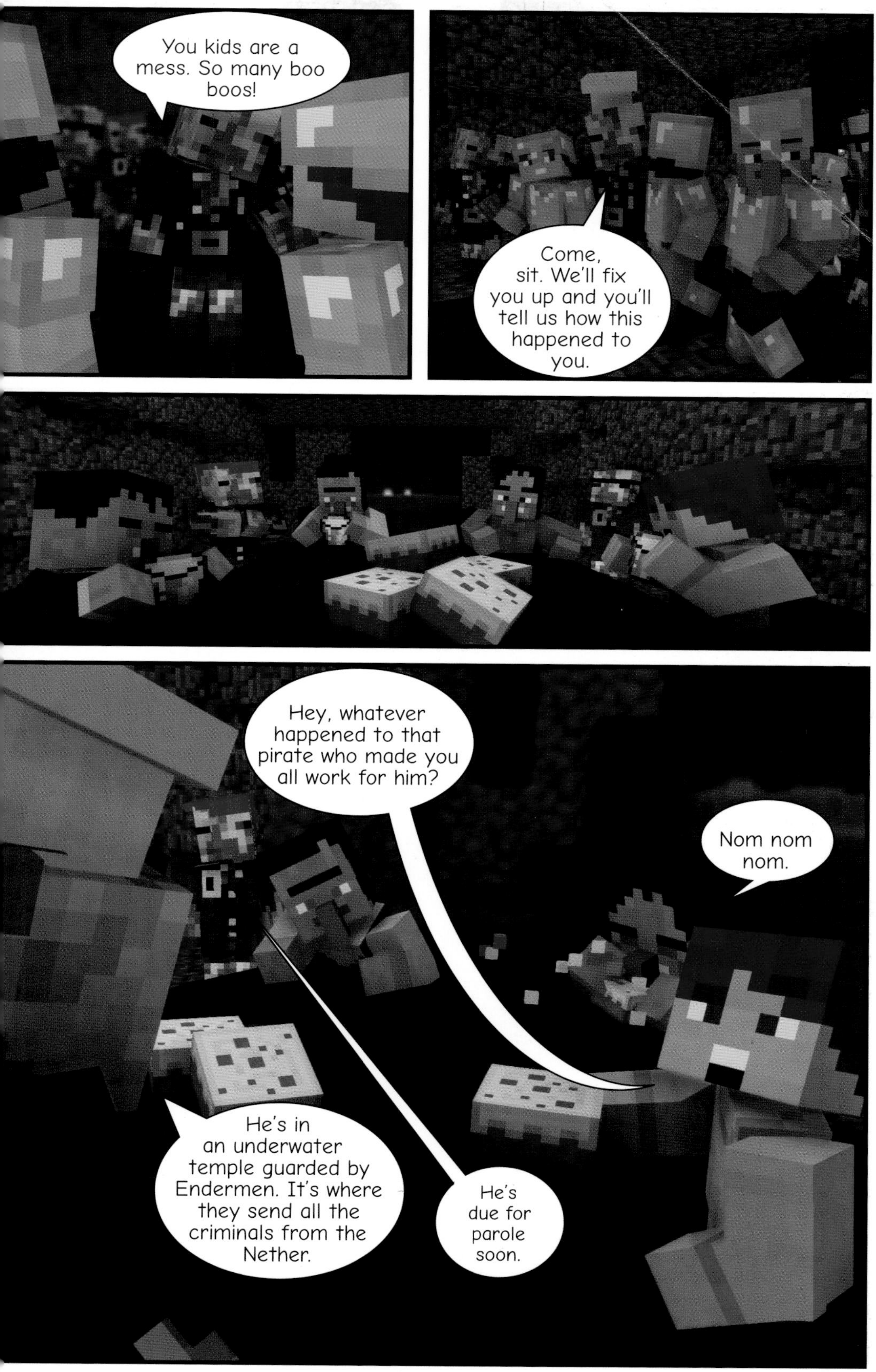
You kids are a mess. So many boo boos!
Come, sit. We'll fix you up and you'll tell us how this happened to you.
Hey, whatever happened to that pirate who made you all work for him?
Nom nom nom.
He's in an underwater temple guarded by Endermen. It's where they send all the criminals from the Nether.
He's due for parole soon.

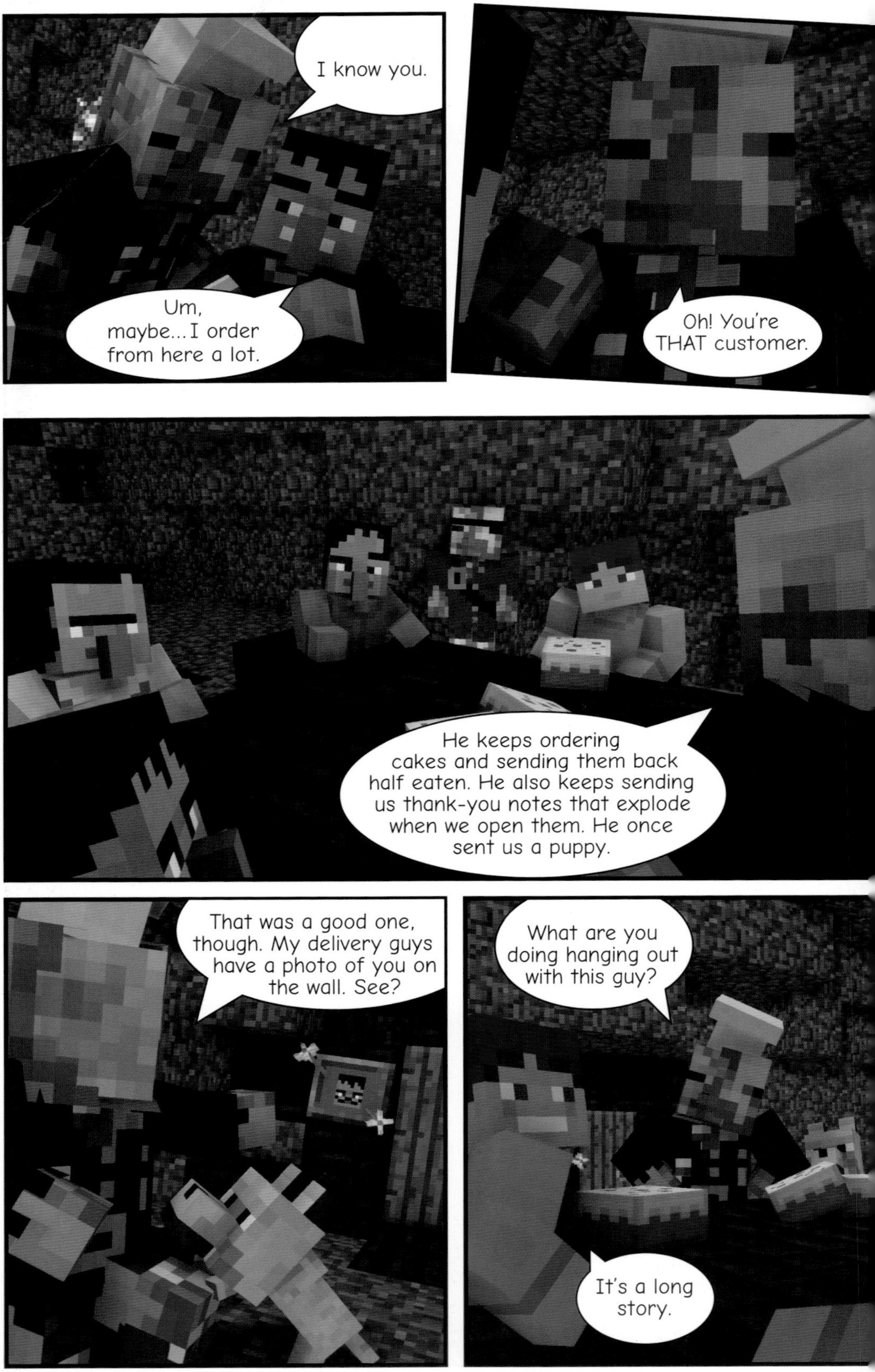
I know you.
Um, maybe... I order from here a lot.
Oh! You're THAT customer.
He keeps ordering cakes and sending them back half eaten. He also keeps sending us thank-you notes that explode when we open them. He once sent us a puppy.
That was a good one, though. My delivery guys have a photo of you on the wall. See?
What are you doing hanging out with this guy?
It's a long story.

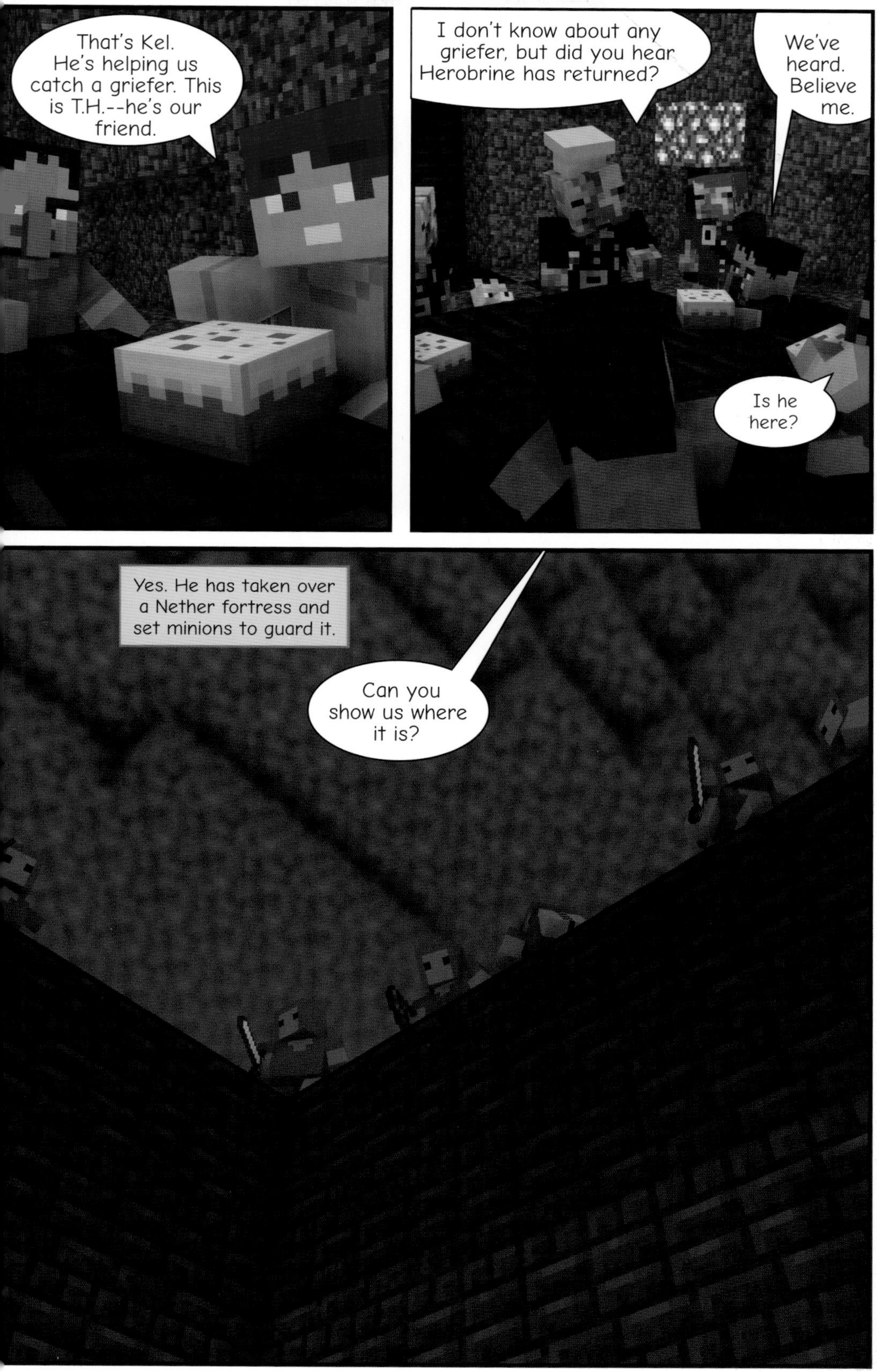
That's Kel. He's helping us catch a griefer. This is T.H.--he's our friend.
I don't know about any griefer, but did you hear Herobrine has returned?
We've heard. Believe me.
Is he here?
Yes. He has taken over a Nether fortress and set minions to guard it.
Can you show us where it is?

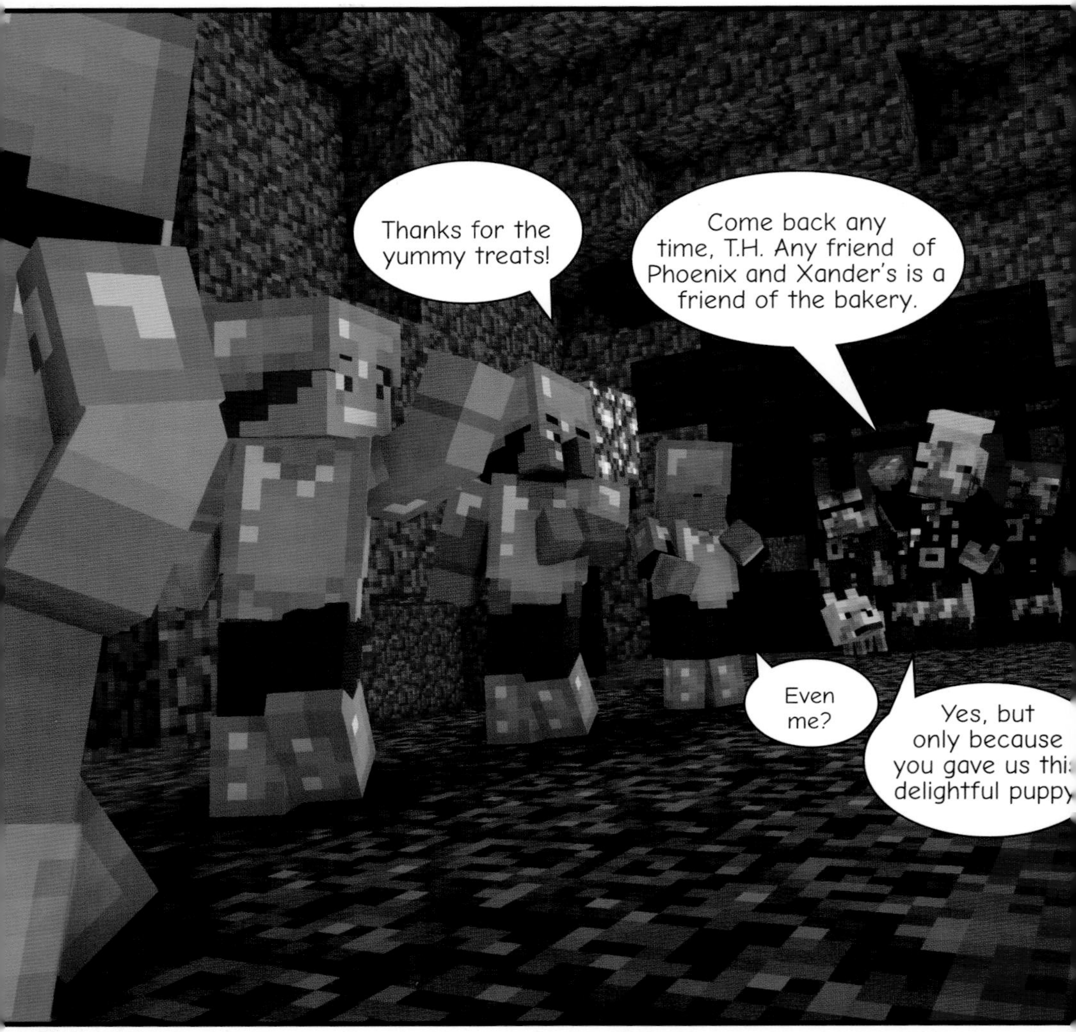
Thanks for the yummy treats!
Come back any time, T.H. Any friend of Phoenix and Xander's is a friend of the bakery.
Even me?
Yes, but only because you gave us thi
delightful pupp

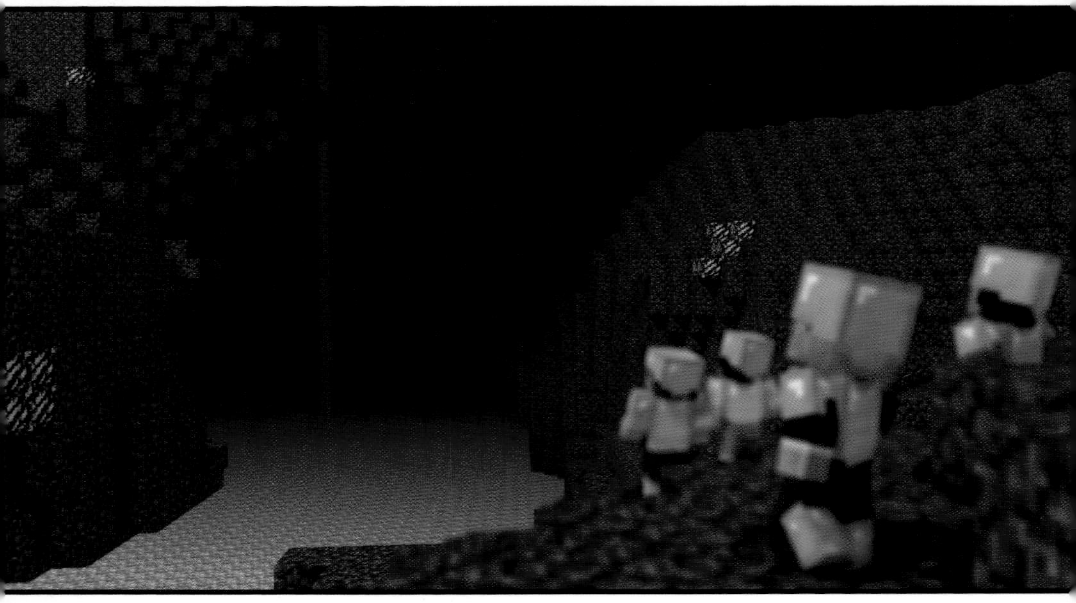

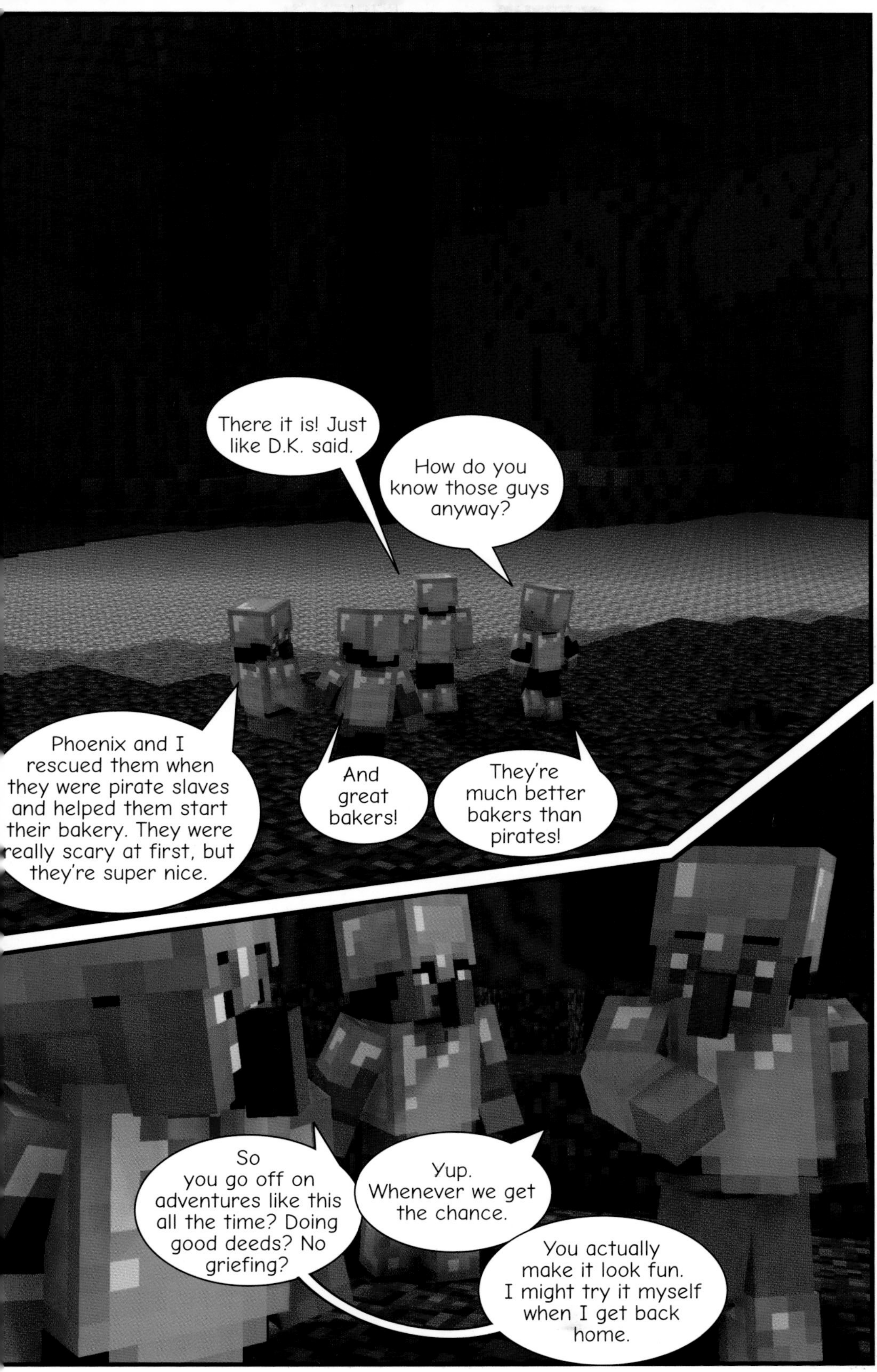
There it is! Just like D.K. said.
How do you know those guys anyway?
Phoenix and I rescued them when they were pirate slaves and helped them start their bakery. They were really scary at first, but they're super nice.
And great bakers!
They're much better bakers than pirates!
So you go off on adventures like this all the time? Doing good deeds? No griefing?
Yup. Whenever we get the chance.
You actually make it look fun. I might try it myself when I get back home.

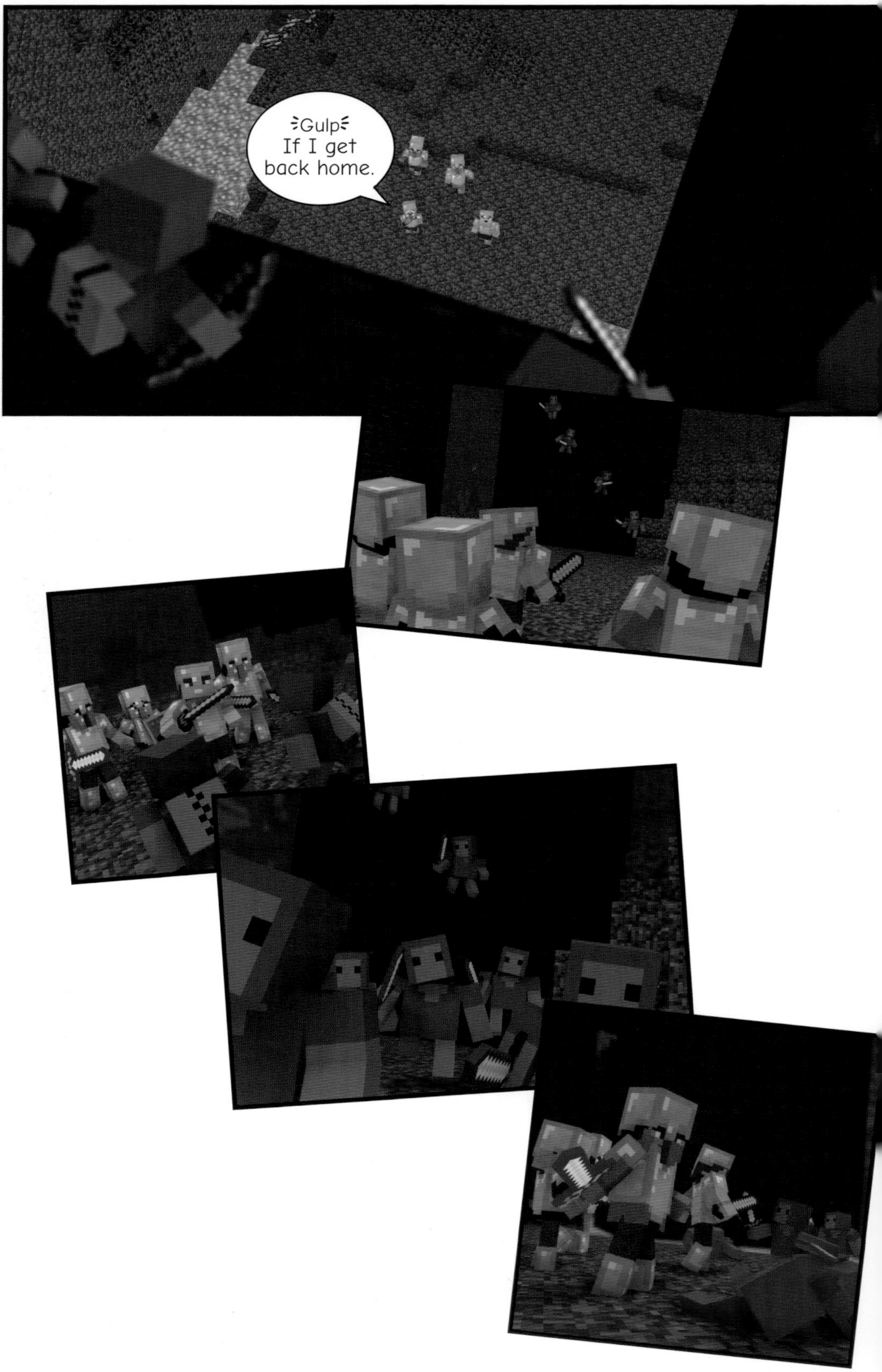
Gulp
If I get back home.

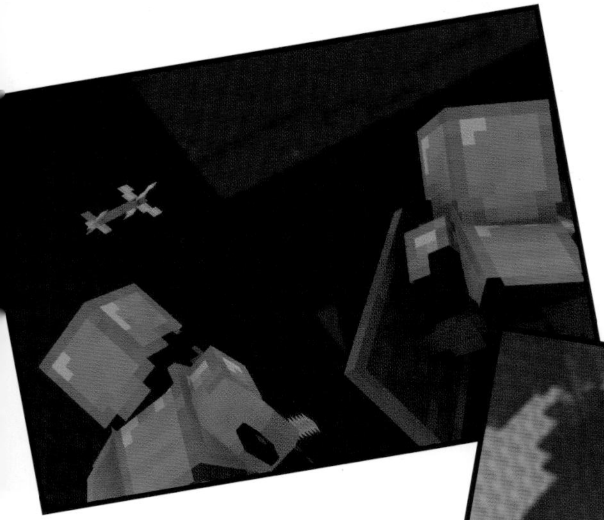
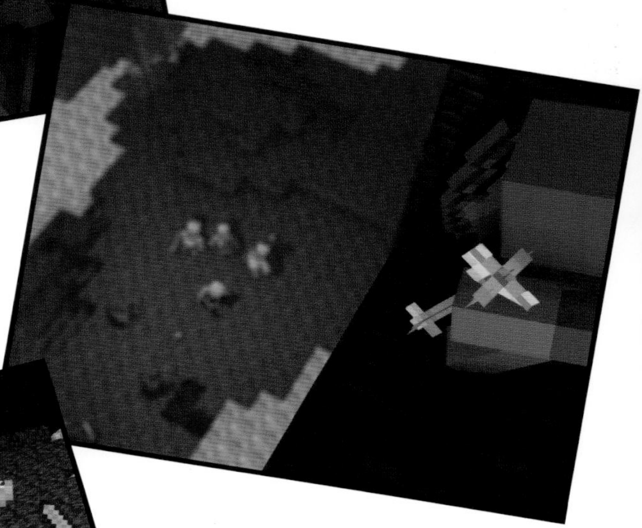
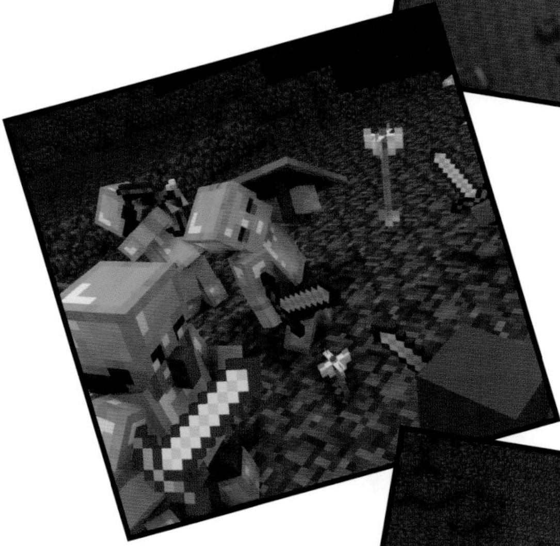
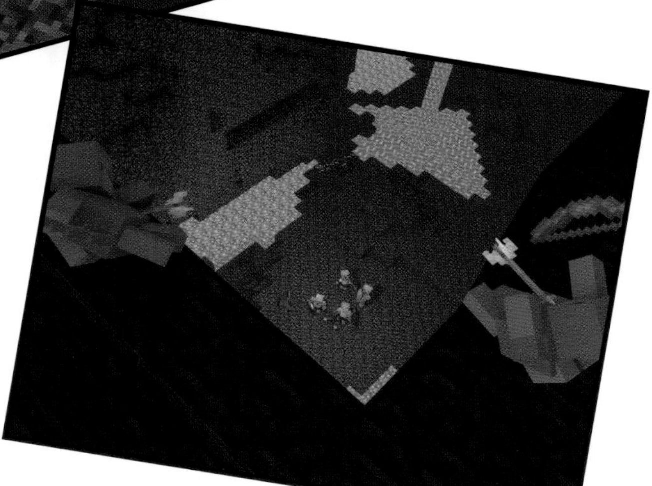

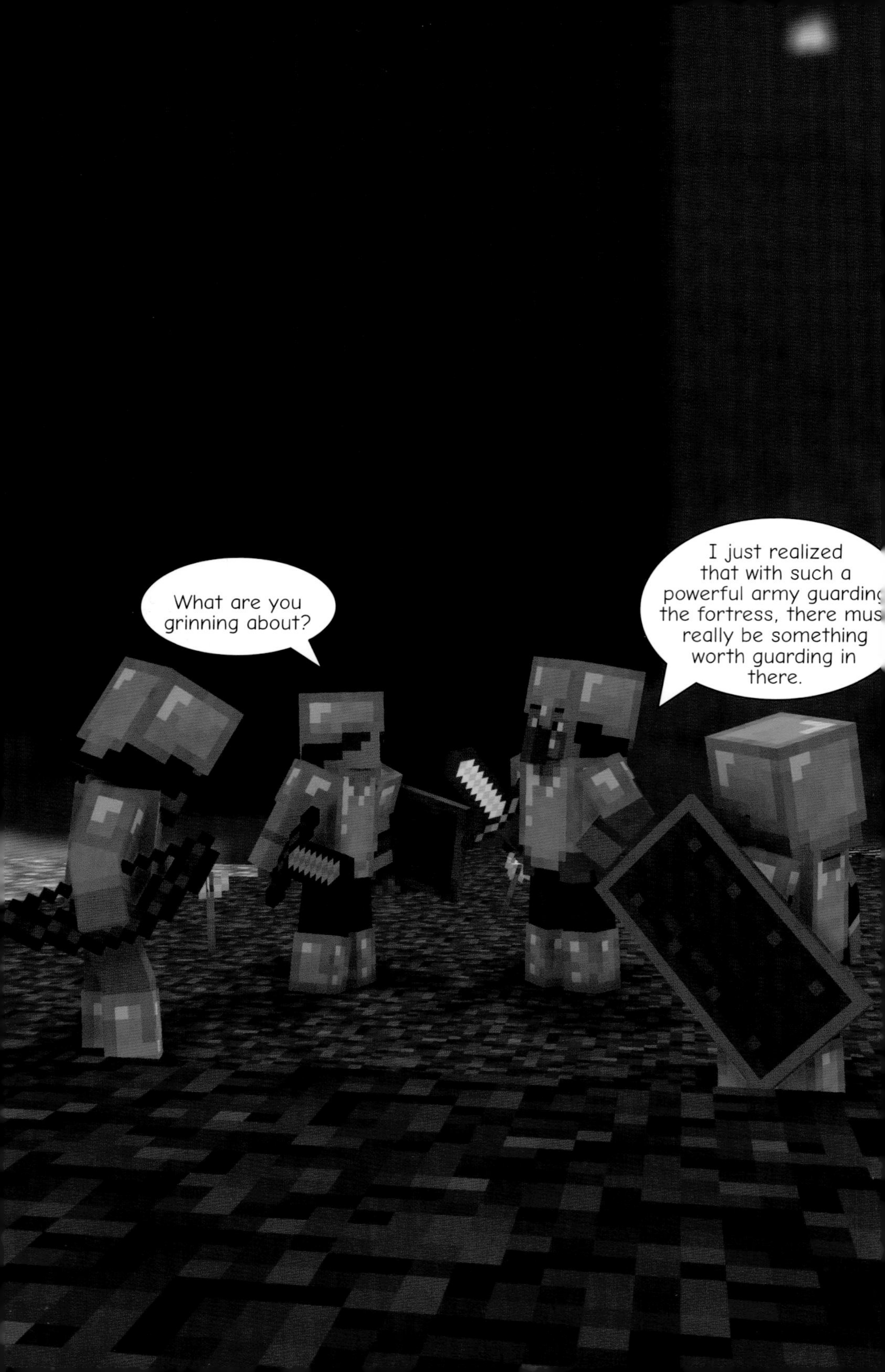
What are you grinning about?
I just realized that with such a powerful army guardin the fortress, there mus really be something worth guarding in there.

CHAPTER 10

THE FORTRESS SHADOW

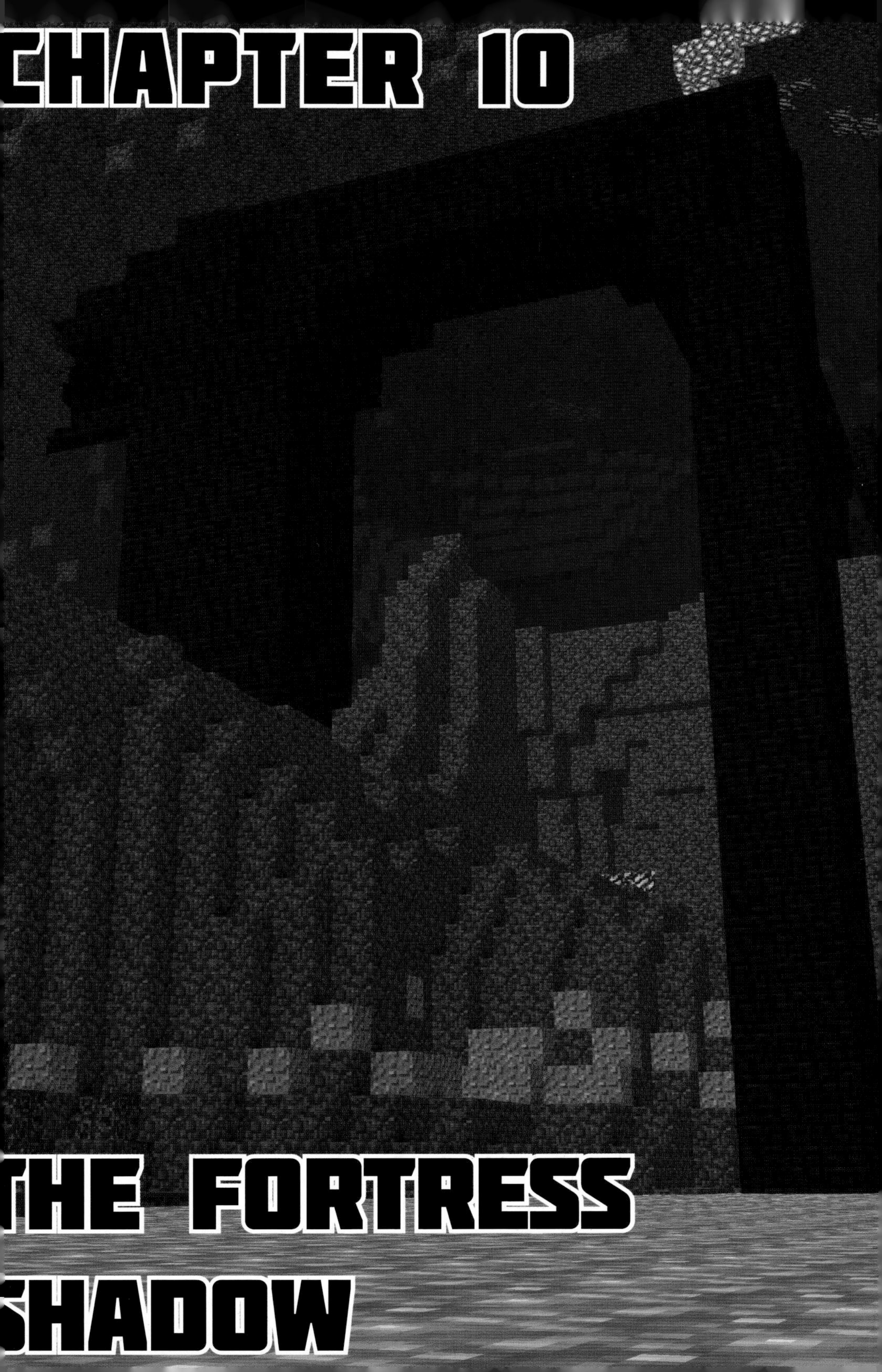

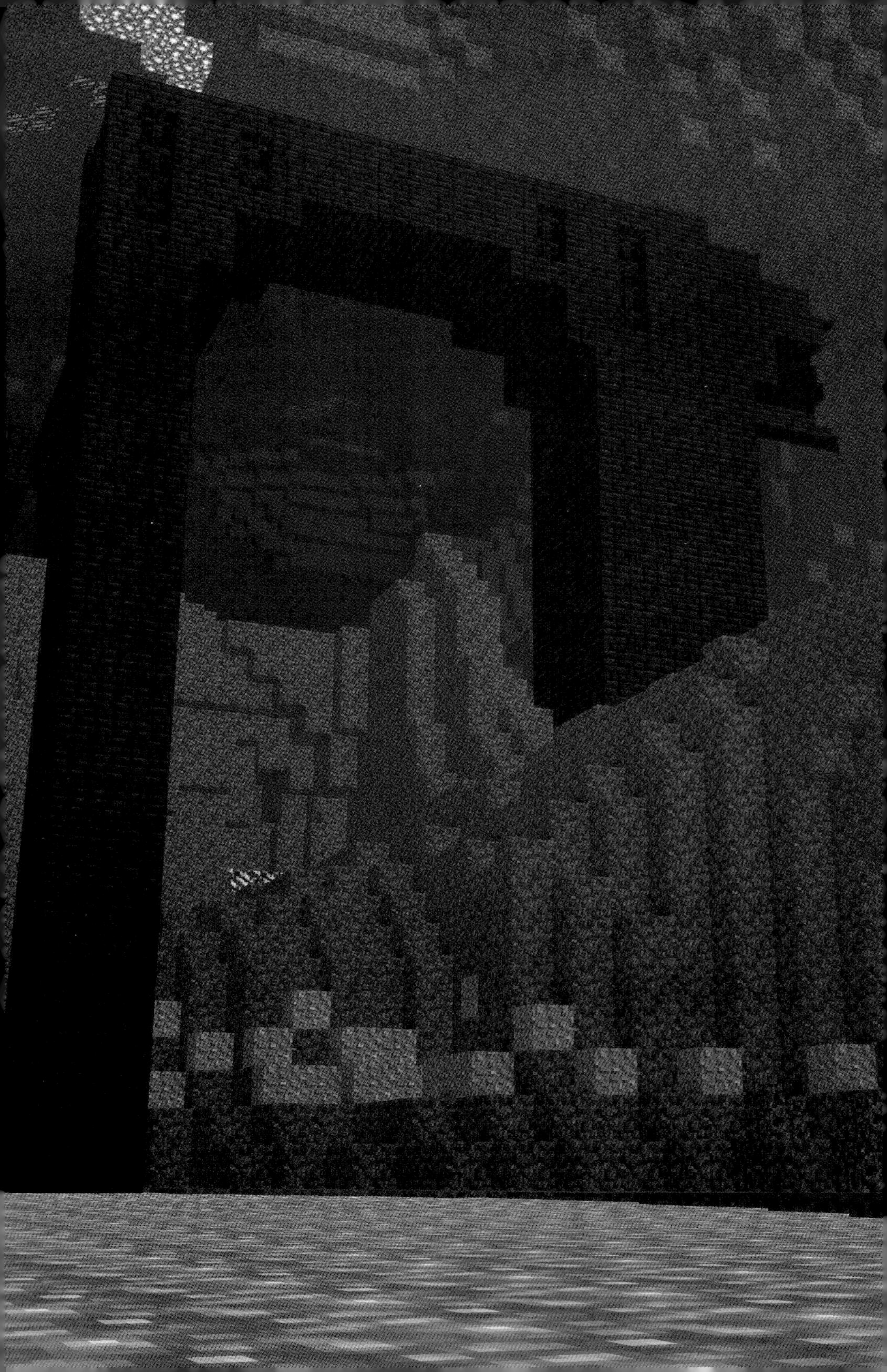

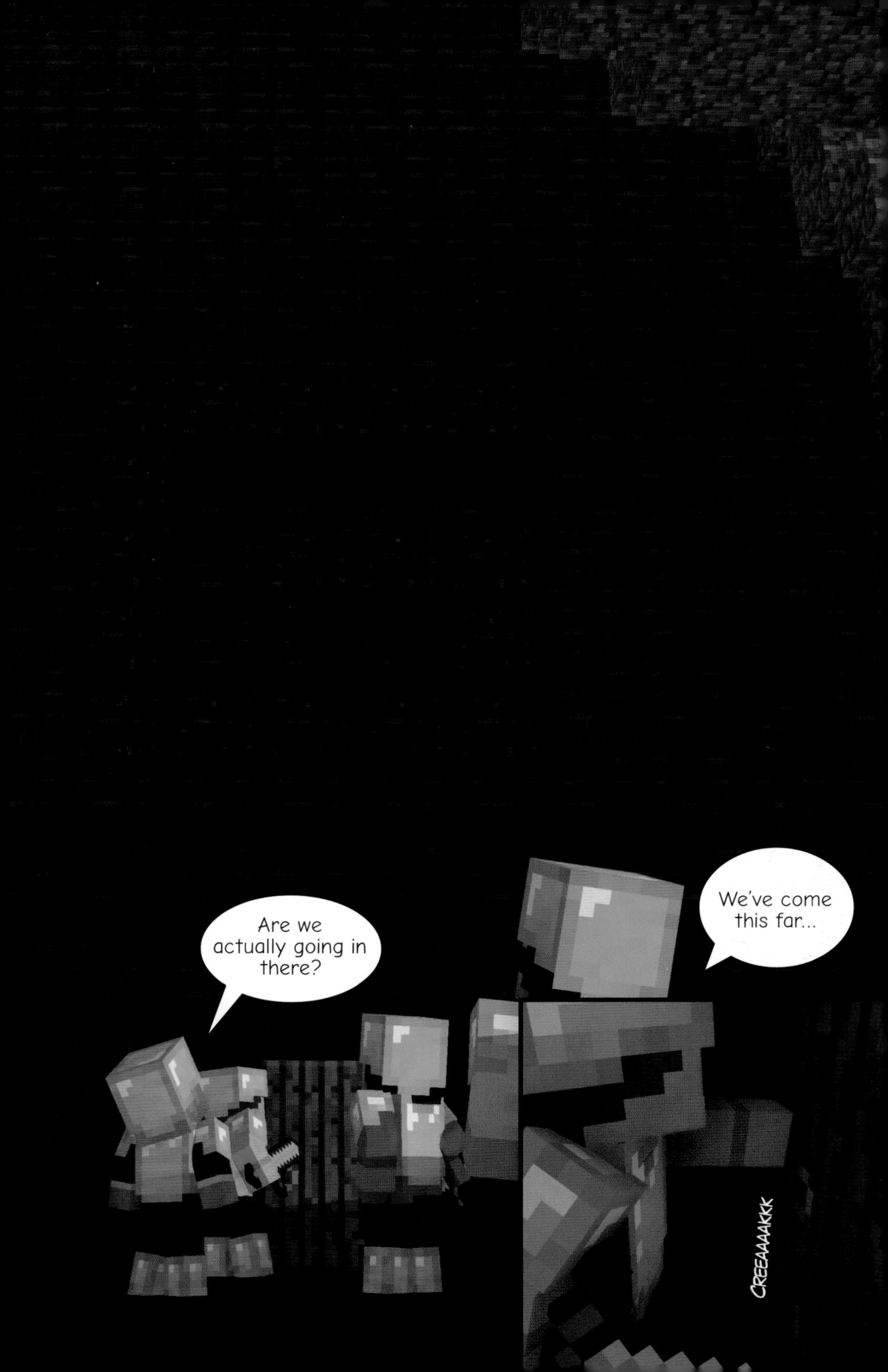
Are we actually going in there?
We've come this far...
CREEAAAAKKK

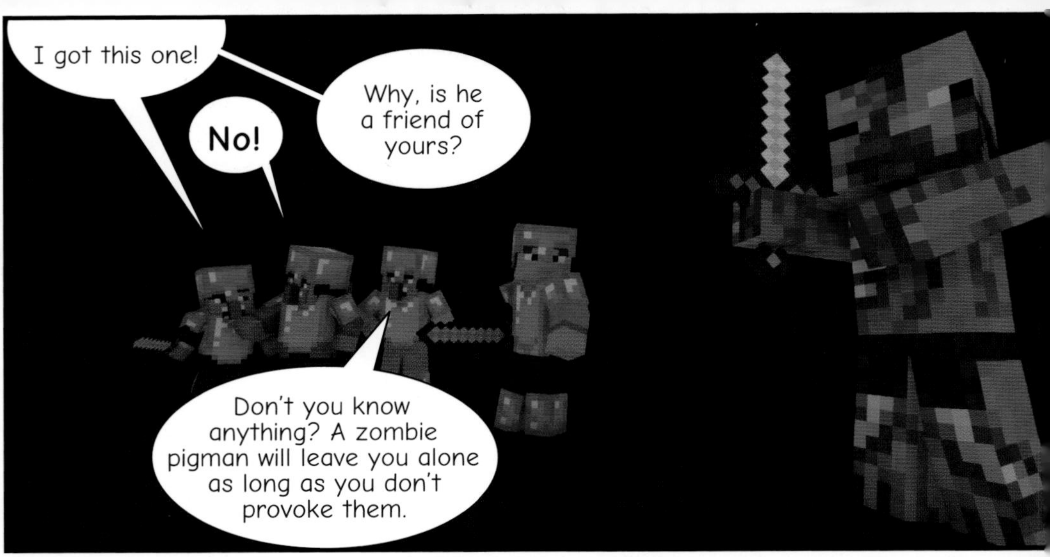
I got this one!
No!
Why, is he a friend of yours?
Don't you know anything? A zombie pigman will leave you alone as long as you don't provoke them.

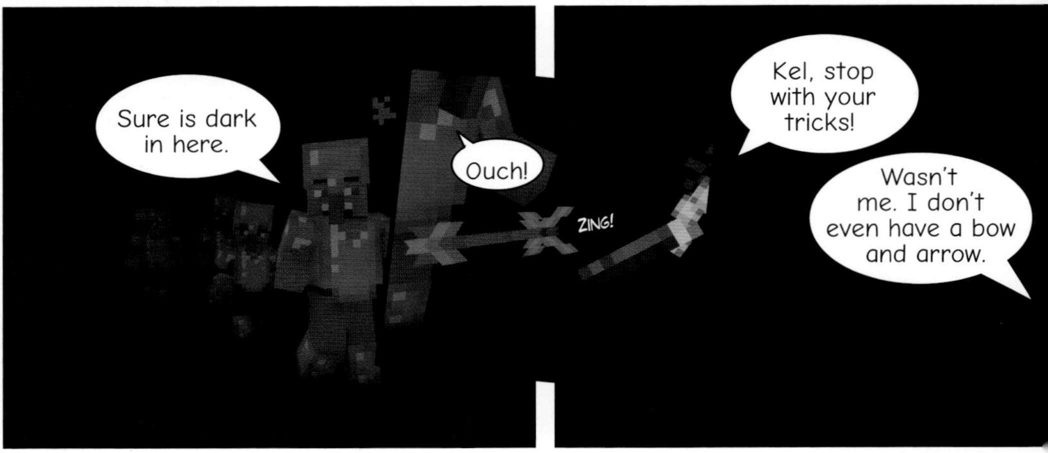
Sure is dark in here.
Ouch!
ZING!
Kel, stop with your tricks!
Wasn't me. I don't even have a bow and arrow.

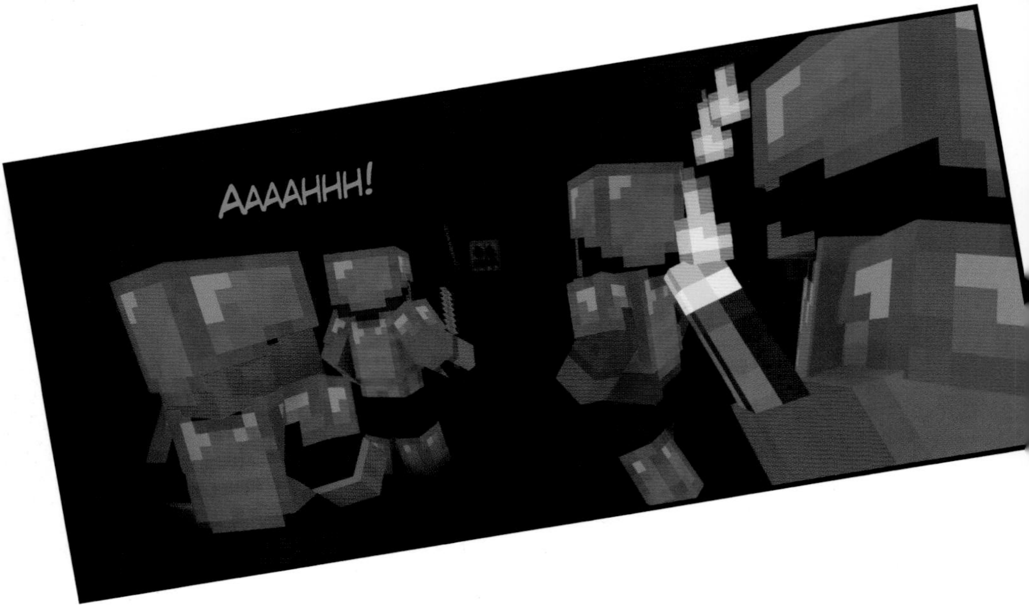
AAAAHHH!

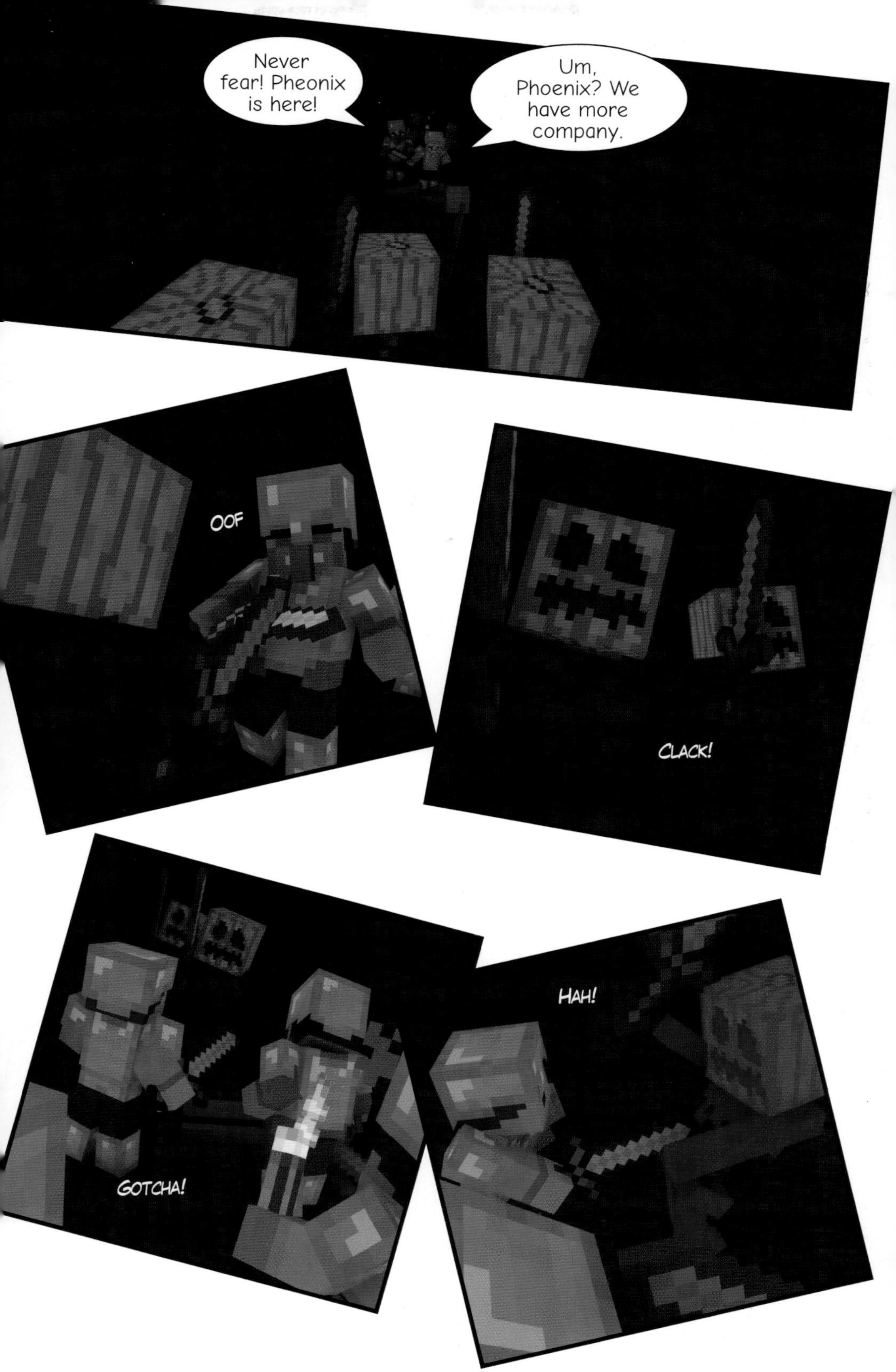
Never fear! Pheonix is here!
Um, Phoenix? We have more company.
OOF
CLACK!
GOTCHA!
HAH!

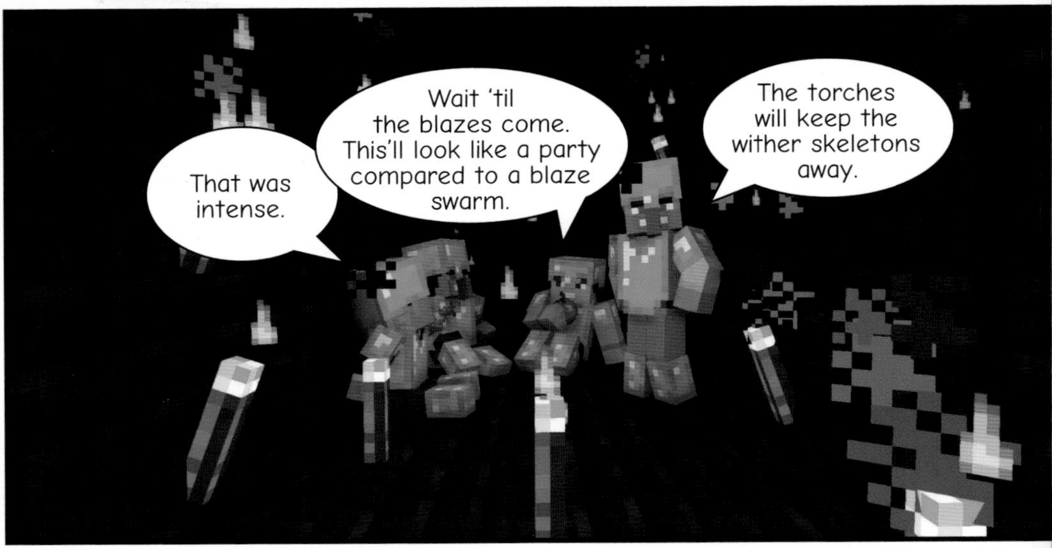
That was intense.
Wait 'til the blazes come. This'll look like a party compared to a blaze swarm.
The torches will keep the wither skeletons away.

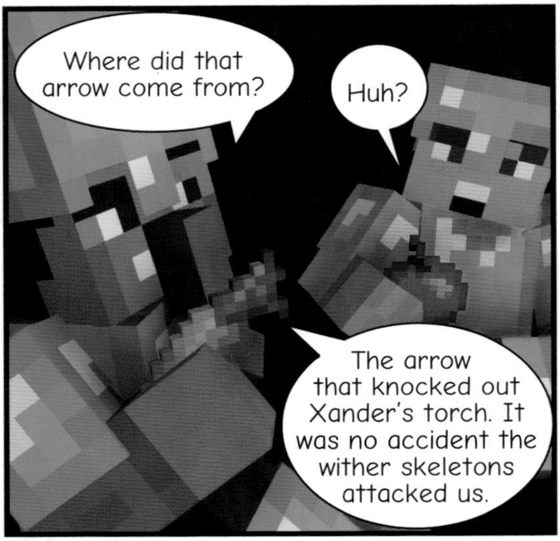
Where did that arrow come from?
Huh?
The arrow that knocked out Xander's torch. It was no accident the wither skeletons attacked us.

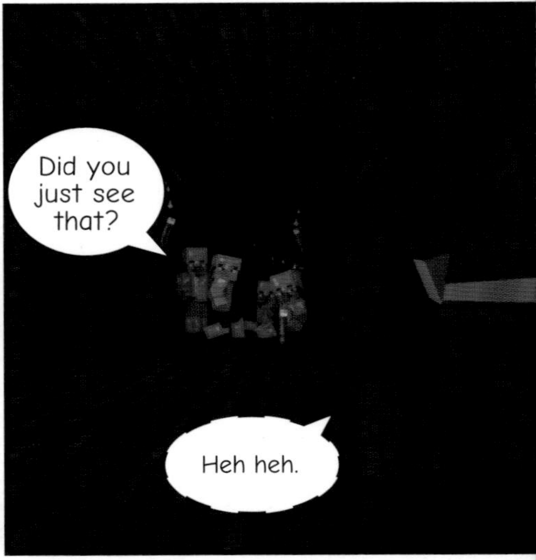
Did you just see that?
Heh heh.

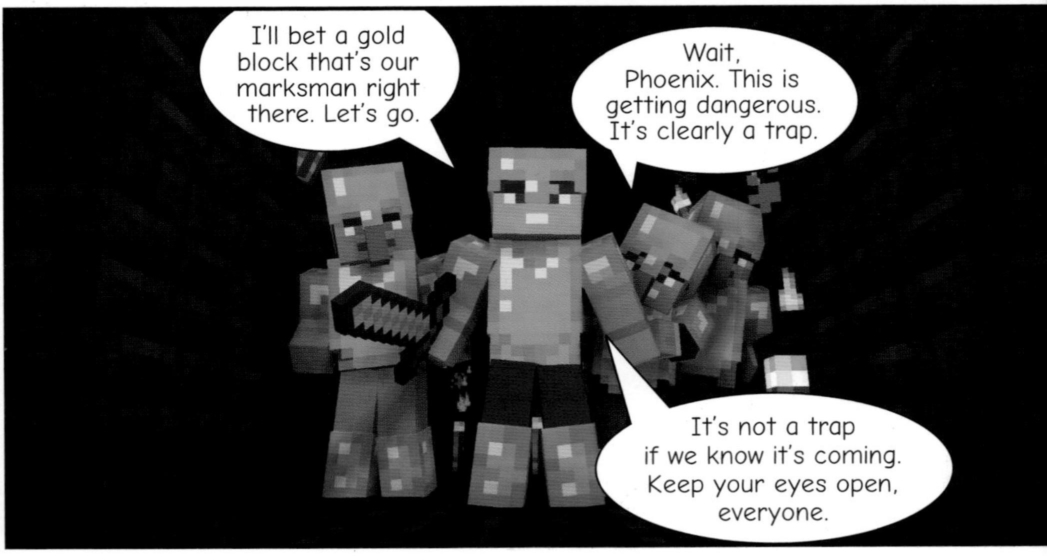
I'll bet a gold block that's our marksman right there. Let's go.
Wait, Phoenix. This is getting dangerous. It's clearly a trap.
It's not a trap if we know it's coming. Keep your eyes open, everyone.

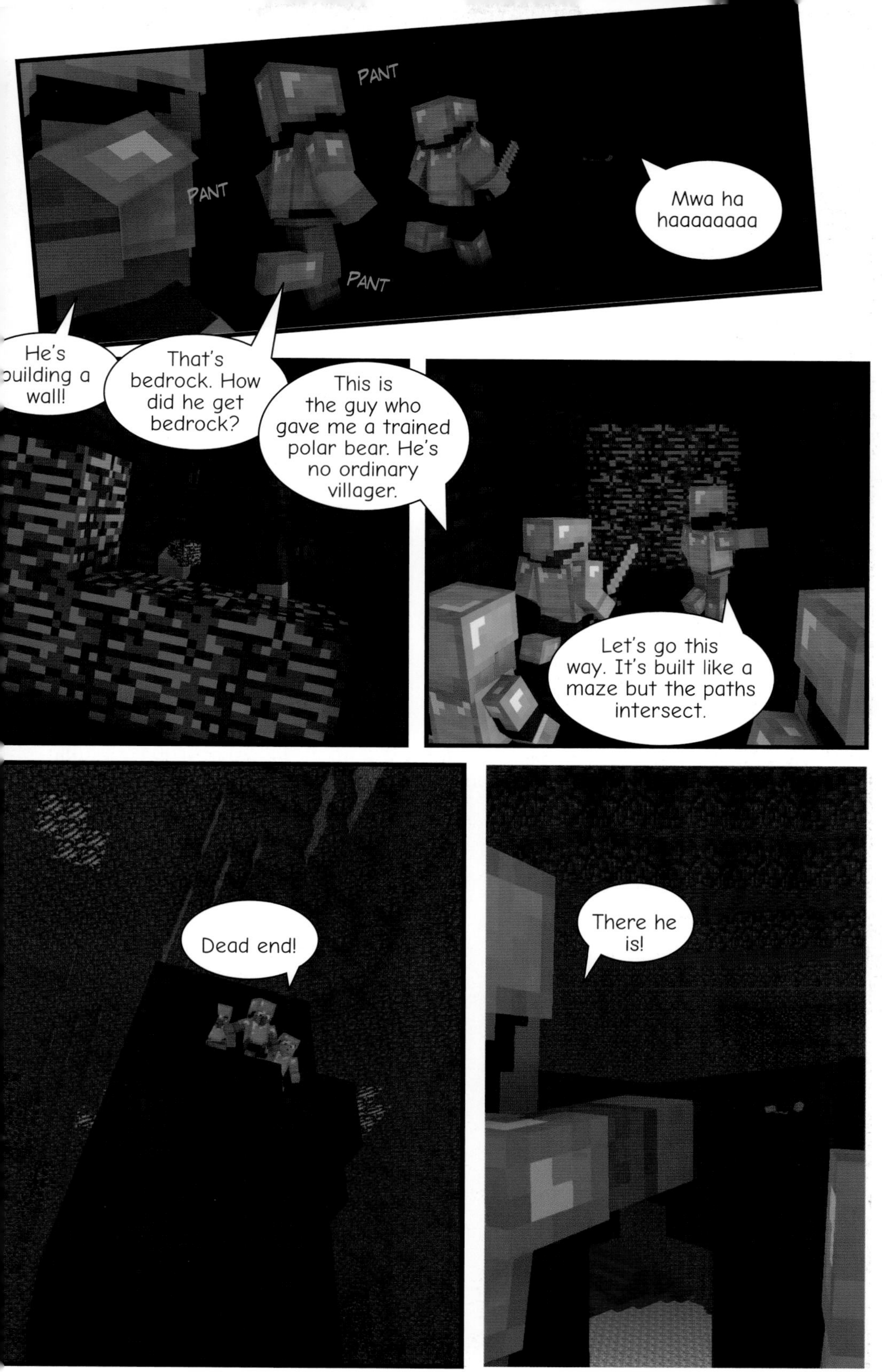
PANT
PANT
PANT
Mwa ha haaaaaaaa
He's building a wall!
That's bedrock. How did he get bedrock?
This is the guy who gave me a trained polar bear. He's no ordinary villager.
Let's go this way. It's built like a maze but the paths intersect.
Dead end!
There he is!

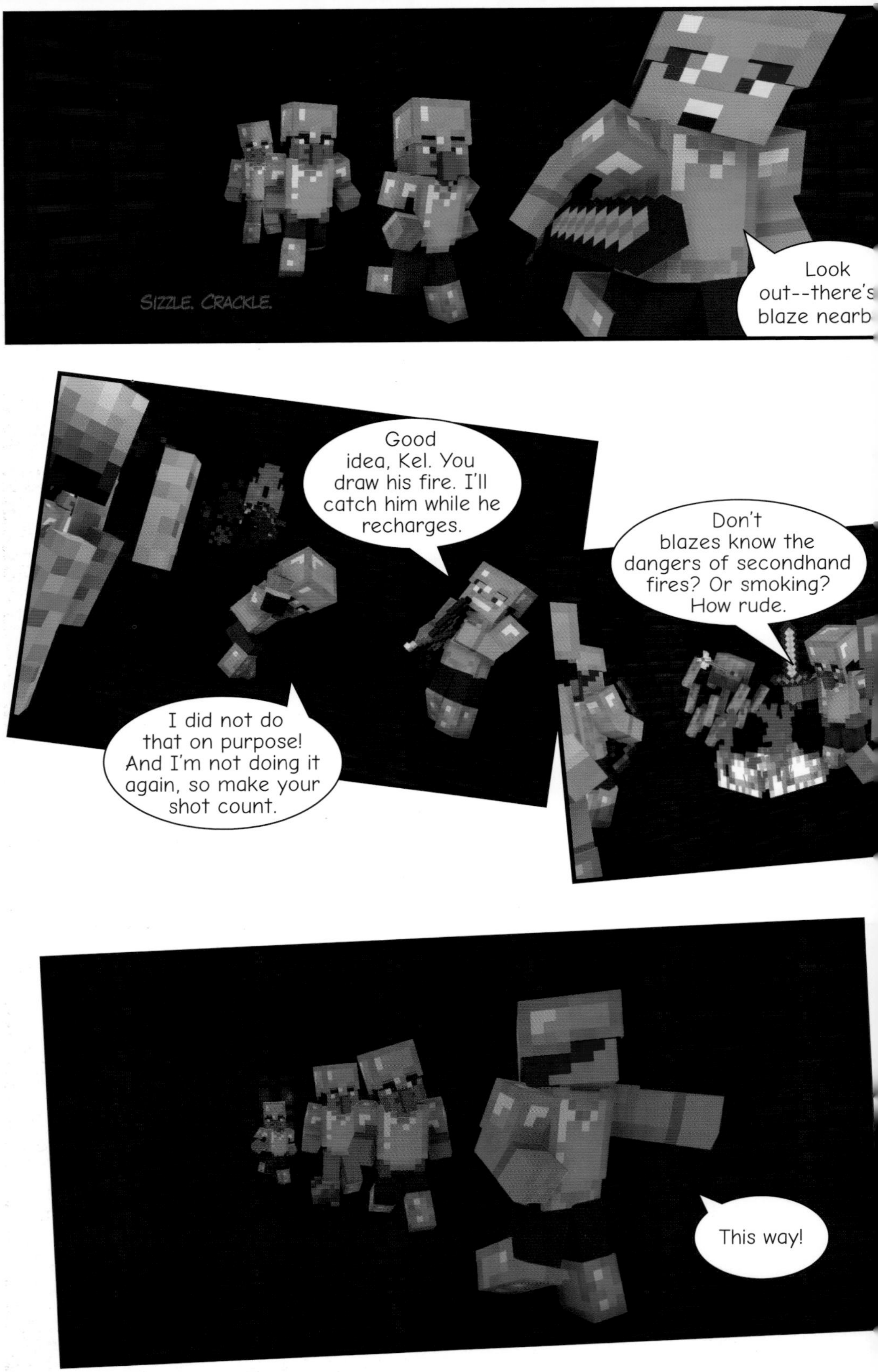
SIZZLE. CRACKLE.
Look out--there's blaze nearb
Good idea, Kel. You draw his fire. I'll catch him while he recharges.
I did not do that on purpose! And I'm not doing it again, so make your shot count.
Don't blazes know the dangers of secondhand fires? Or smoking? How rude.
This way!

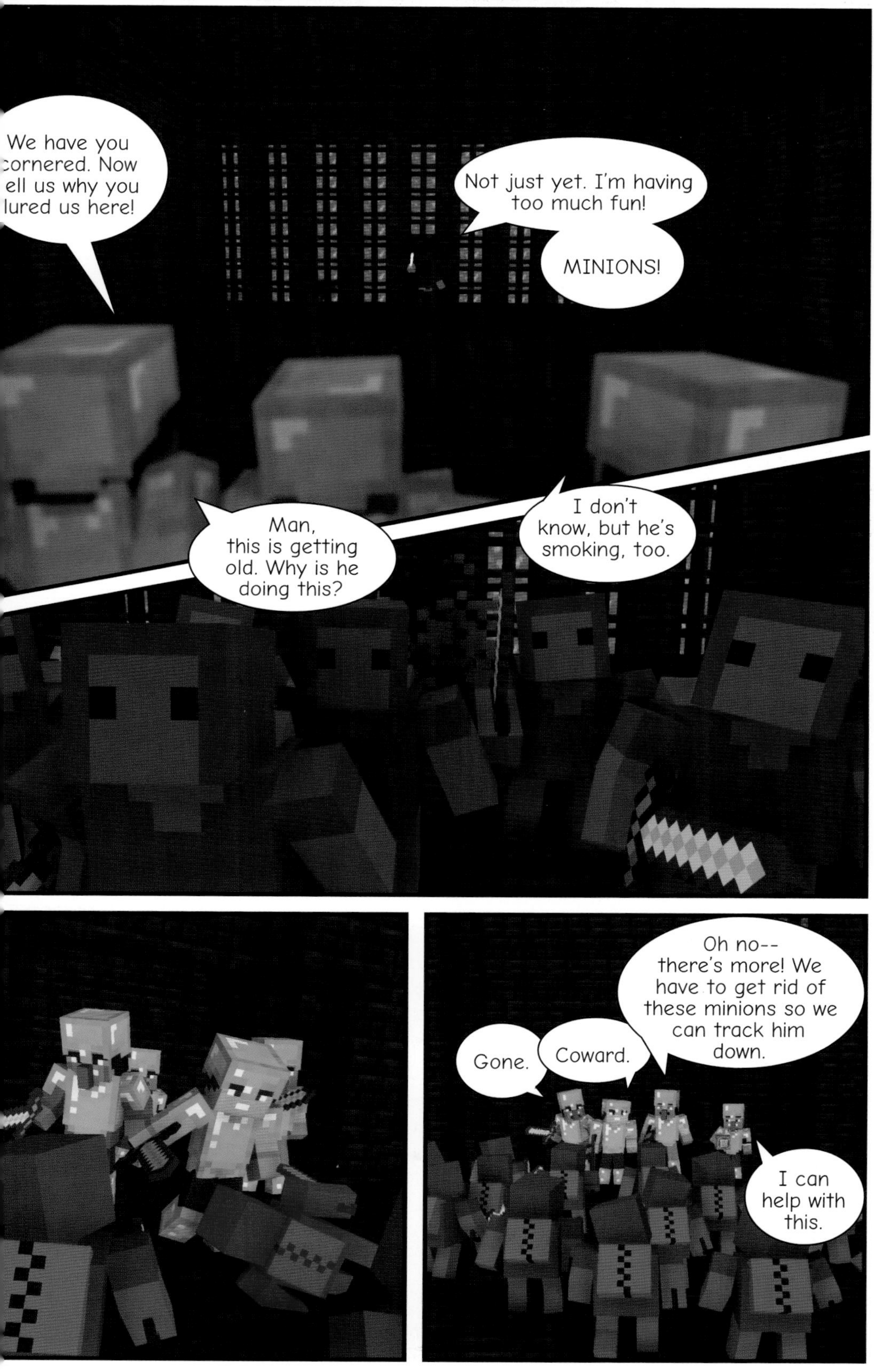

We have you cornered. Now ell us why you lured us here!
Not just yet. I'm having too much fun!
MINIONS!
Man, this is getting old. Why is he doing this?
I don't know, but he's smoking, too.
Gone.
Coward.
Oh no-- there's more! We have to get rid of these minions so we can track him down.
I can help with this.

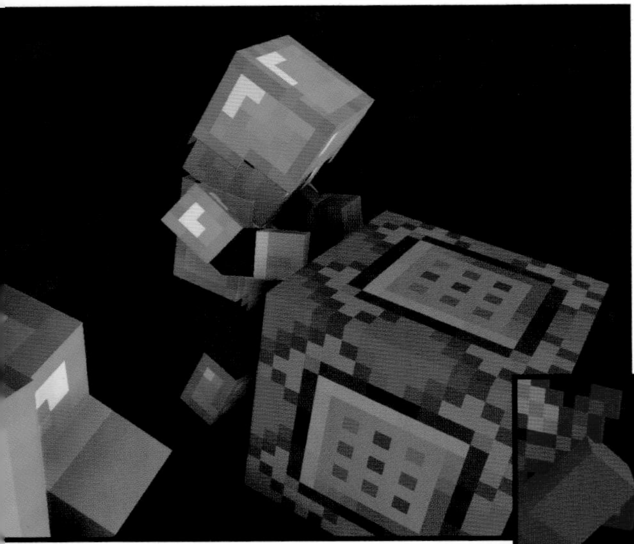

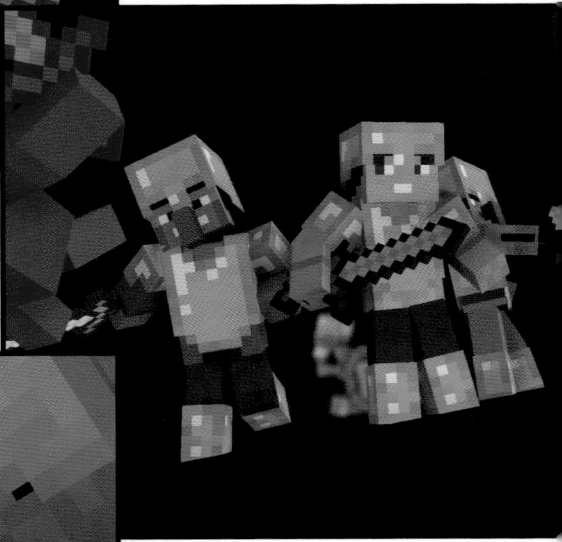

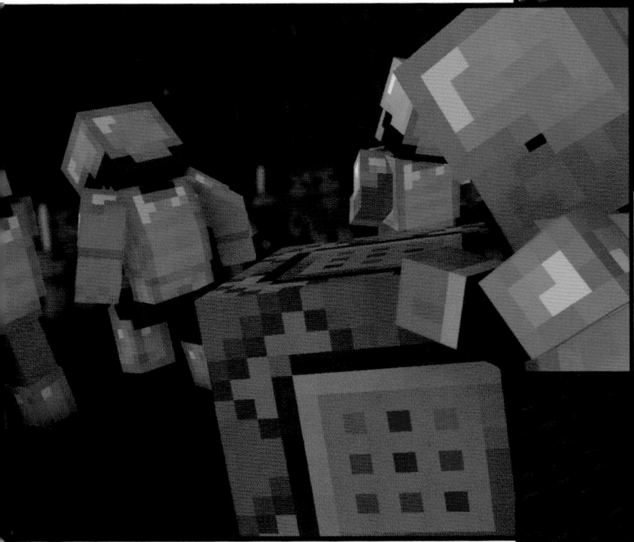

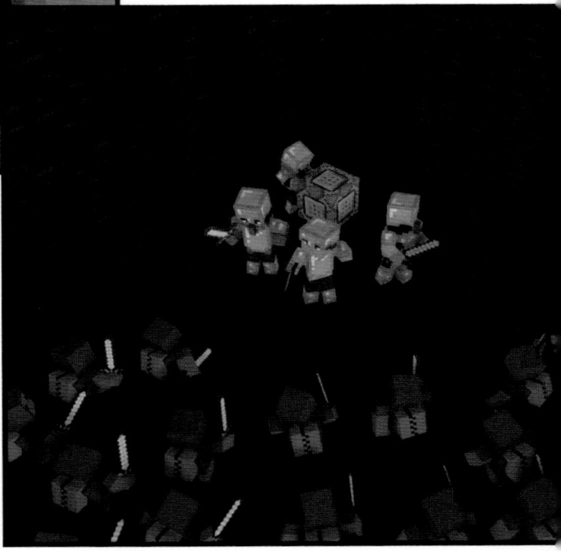

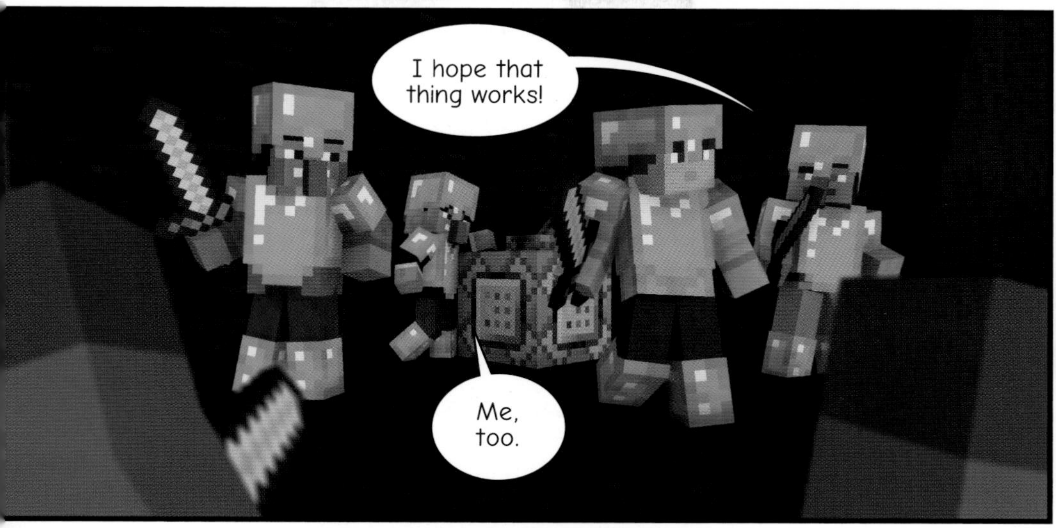
I hope that thing works!
Me, too.

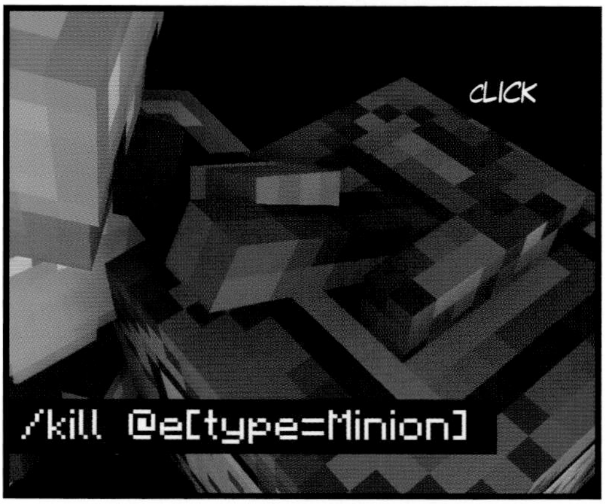
CLICK
/kill @e[type=Minion]

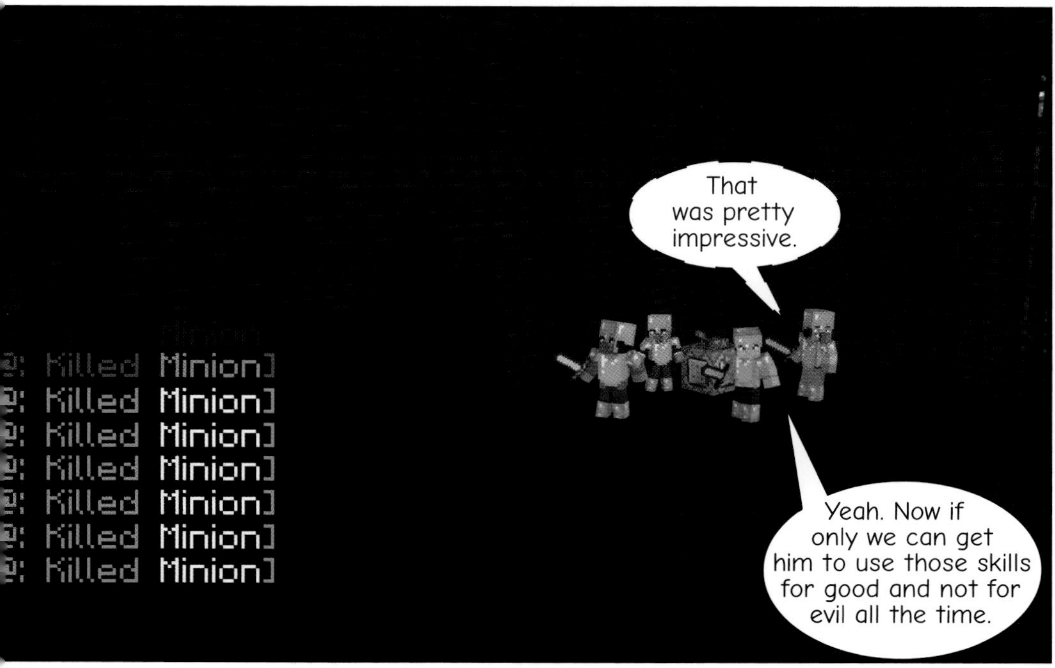
Killed Minion]
Killed Minion]
Killed Minion]
Killed Minion]
Killed Minion]
Killed Minion]
Killed Minion]
That was pretty impressive.
Yeah. Now if only we can get him to use those skills for good and not for evil all the time.

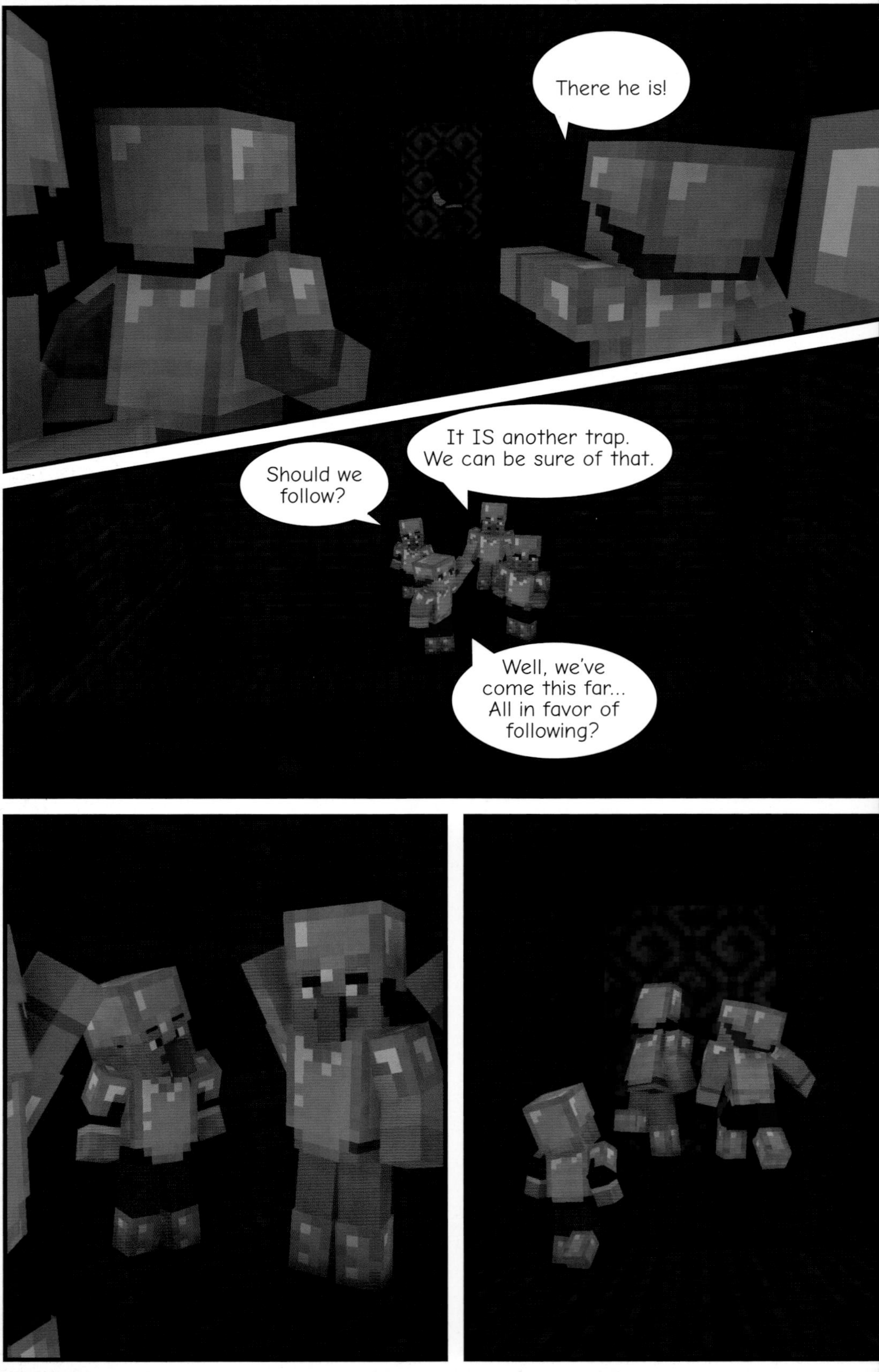
There he is!
Should we follow?
It IS another trap. We can be sure of that.
Well, we've come this far... All in favor of following?

CHAPTER 11

CORNERED

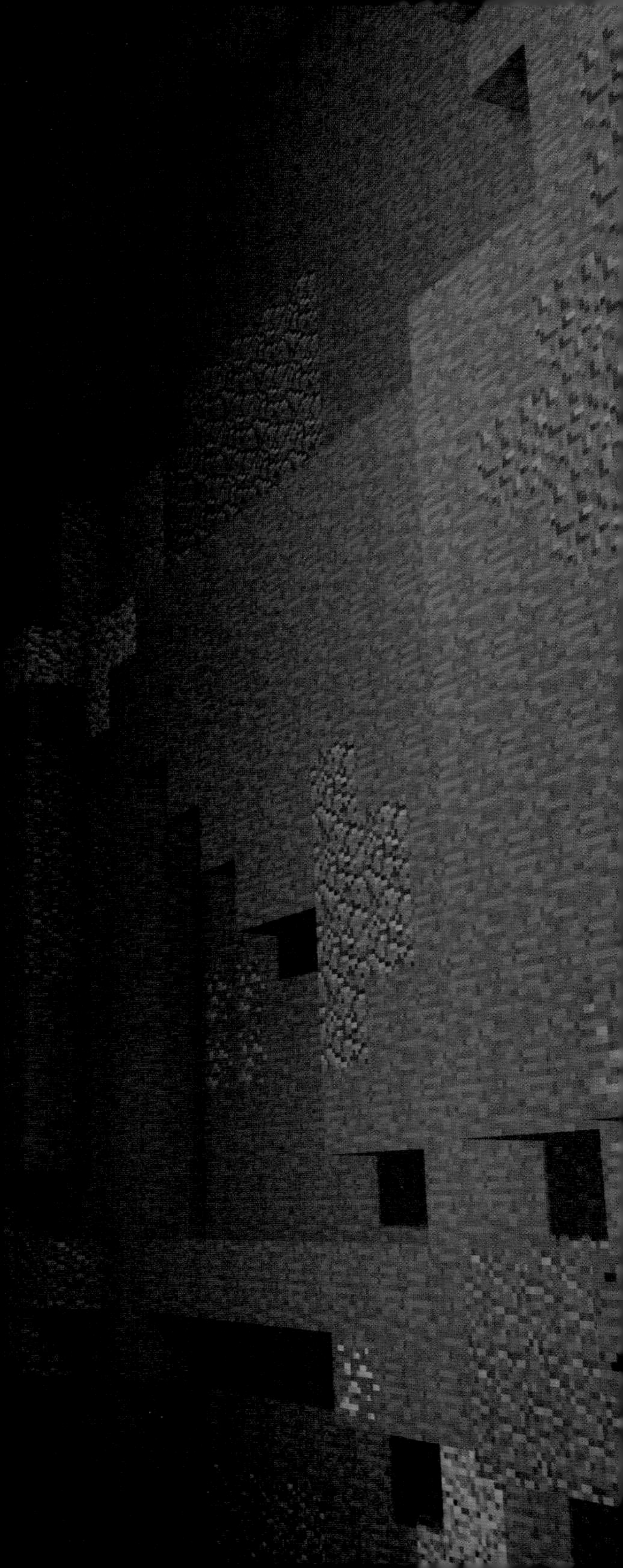

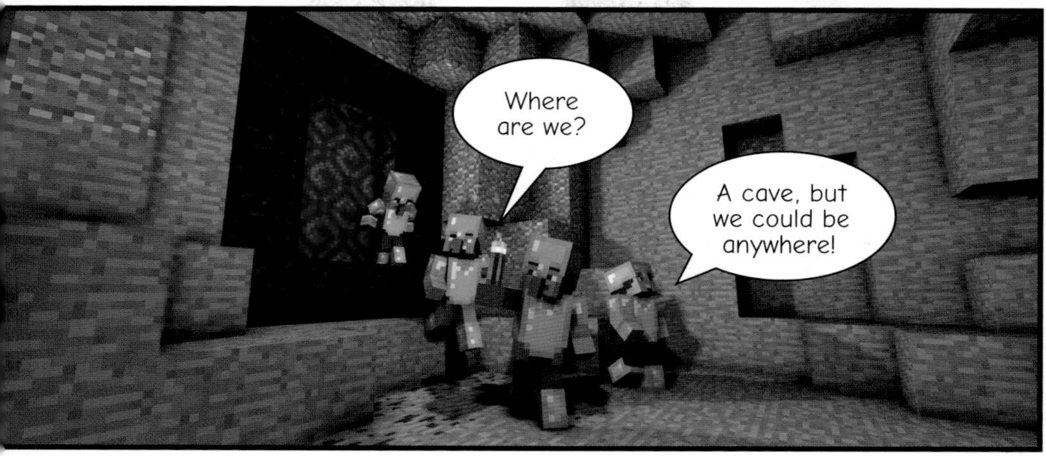

Where are we?
A cave, but we could be anywhere!

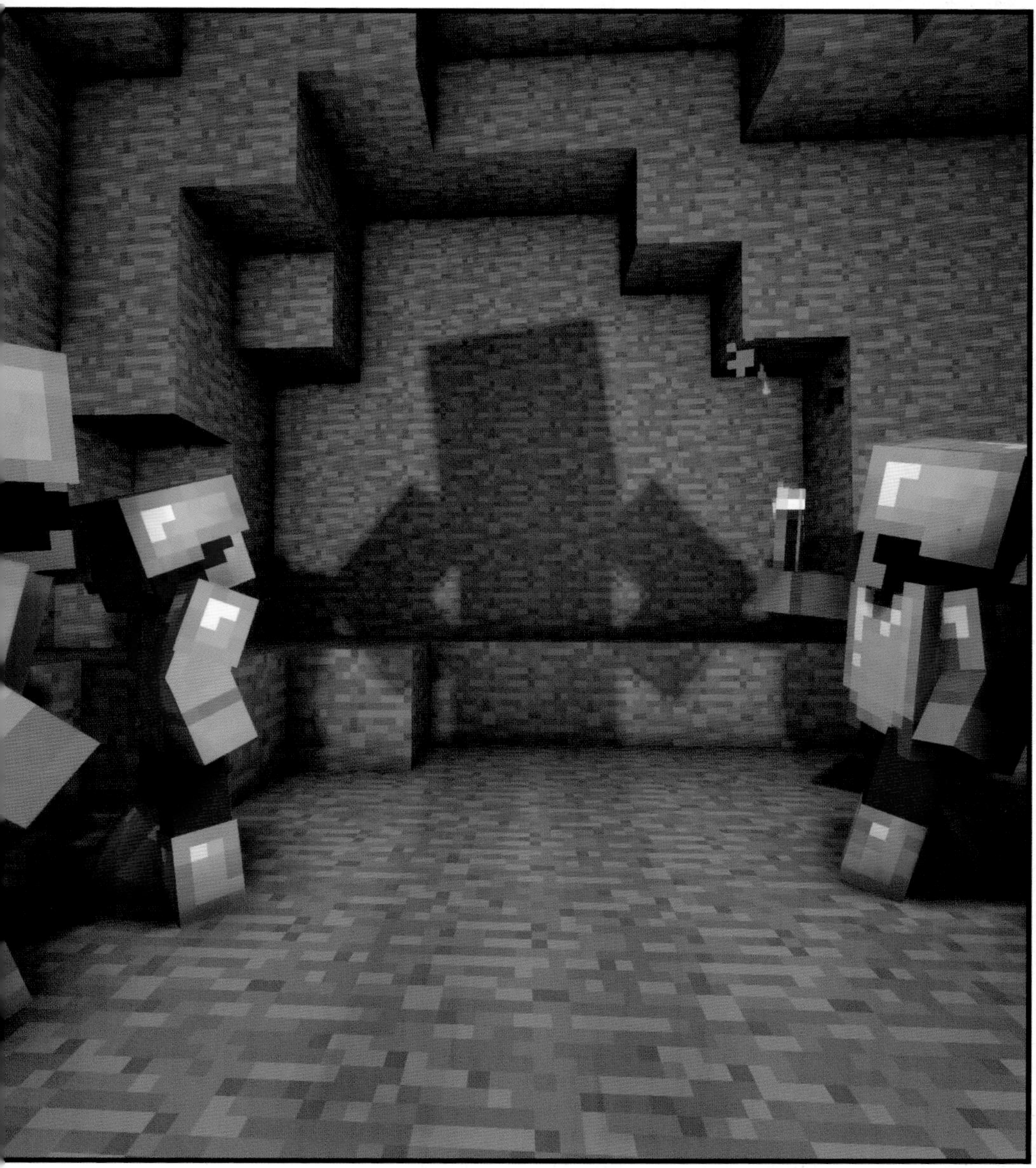

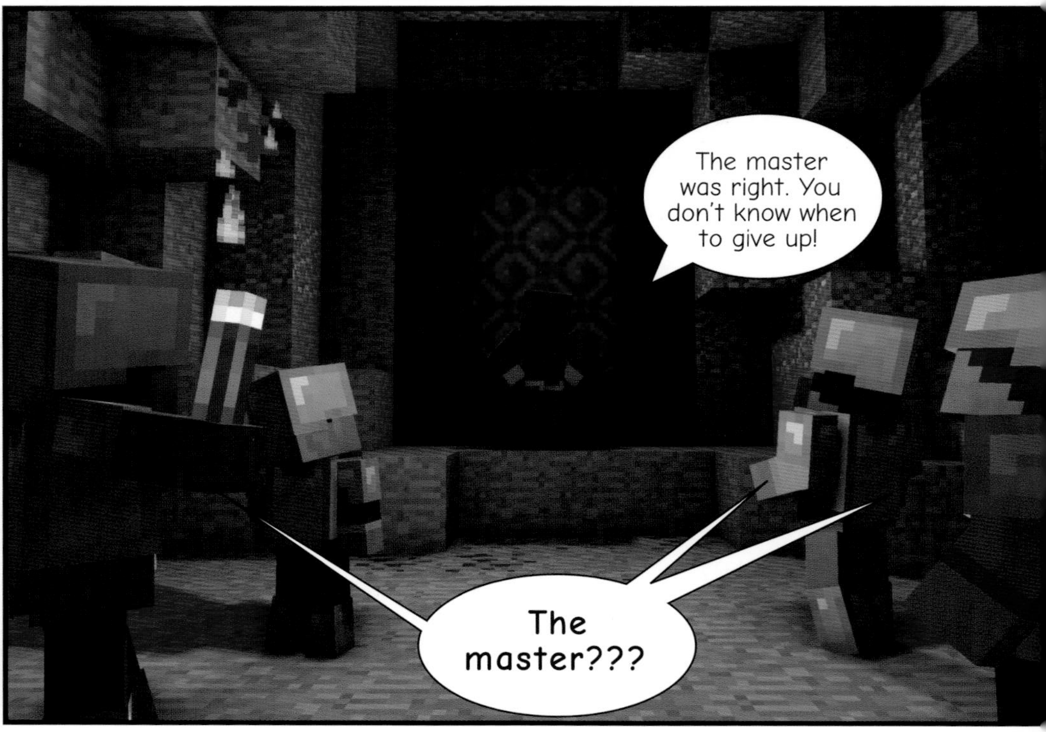
The master was right. You don't know when to give up!
The master???

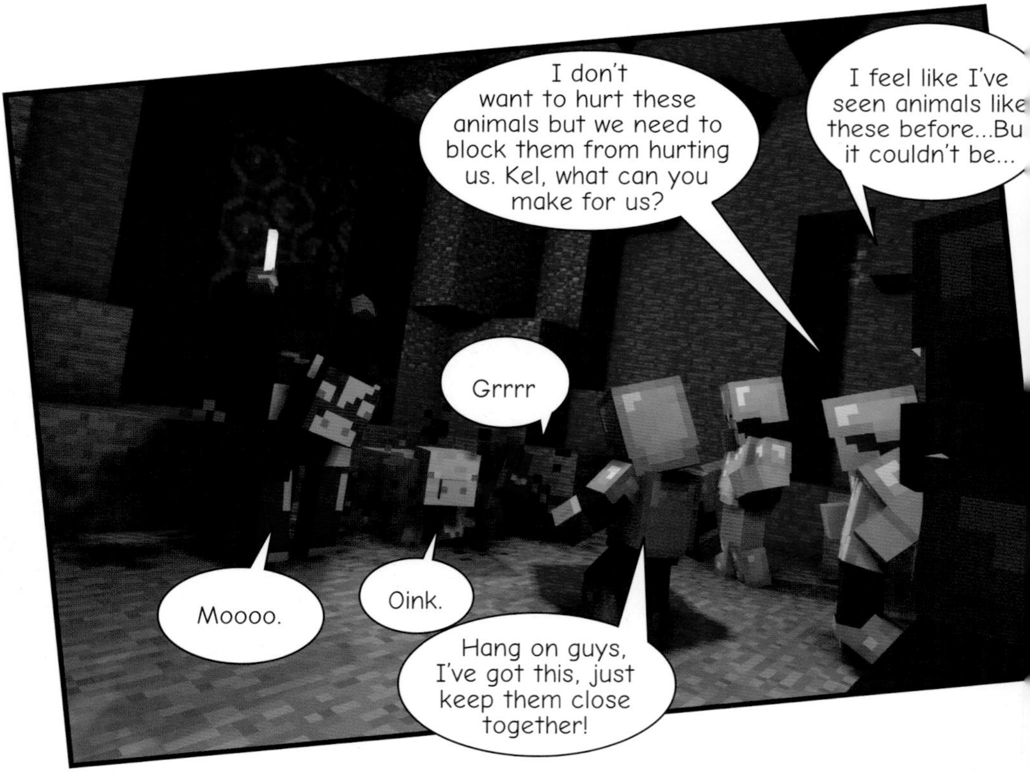
I don't want to hurt these animals but we need to block them from hurting us. Kel, what can you make for us?
I feel like I've seen animals like these before...Bu it couldn't be...
Grrrr
Moooo.
Oink.
Hang on guys, I've got this, just keep them close together!

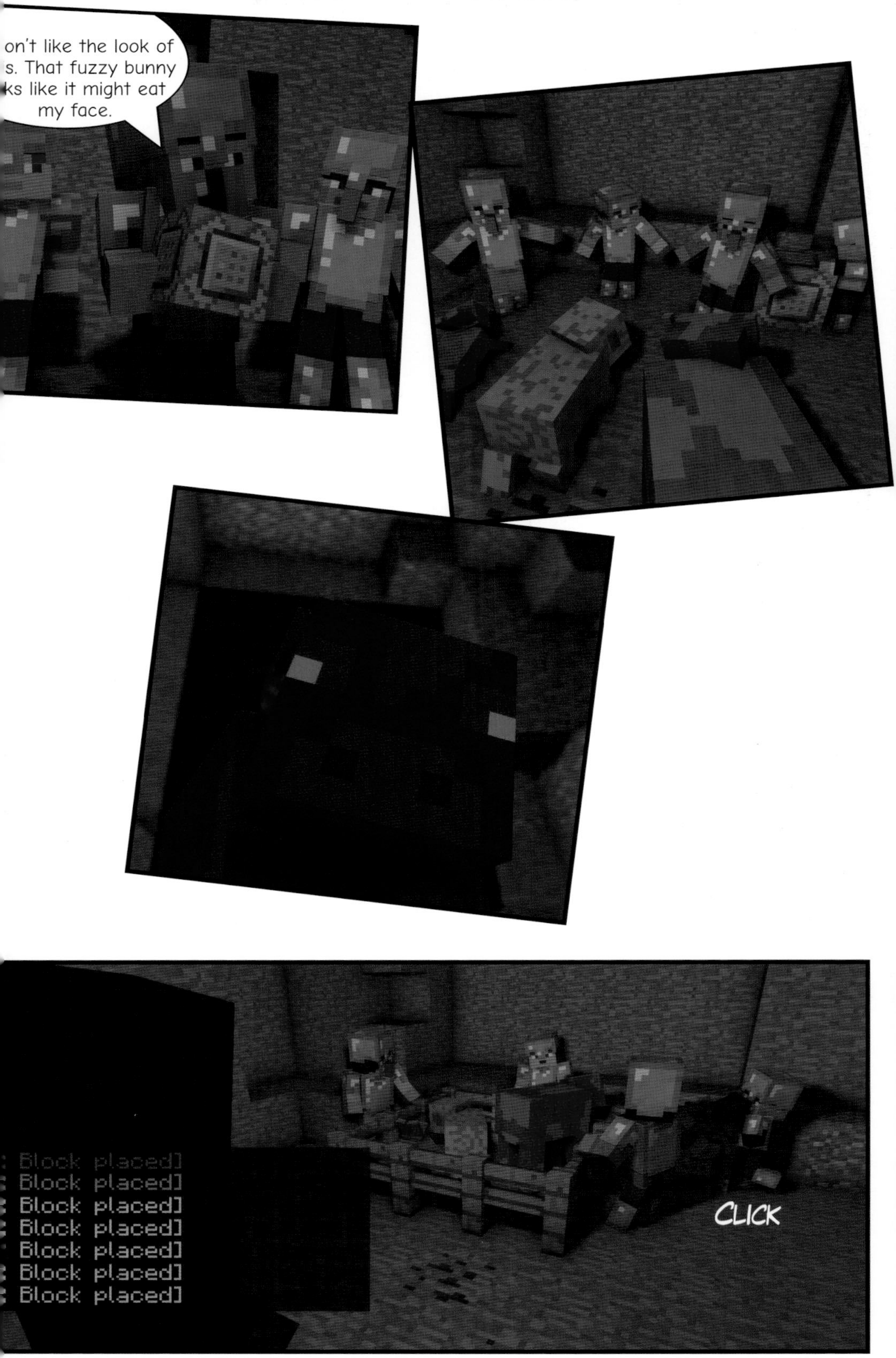
on't like the look of s. That fuzzy bunny ks like it might eat my face.
Block placed]
Block placed]
Block placed]
Block placed]
Block placed]
Block placed]
Block placed]
CLICK

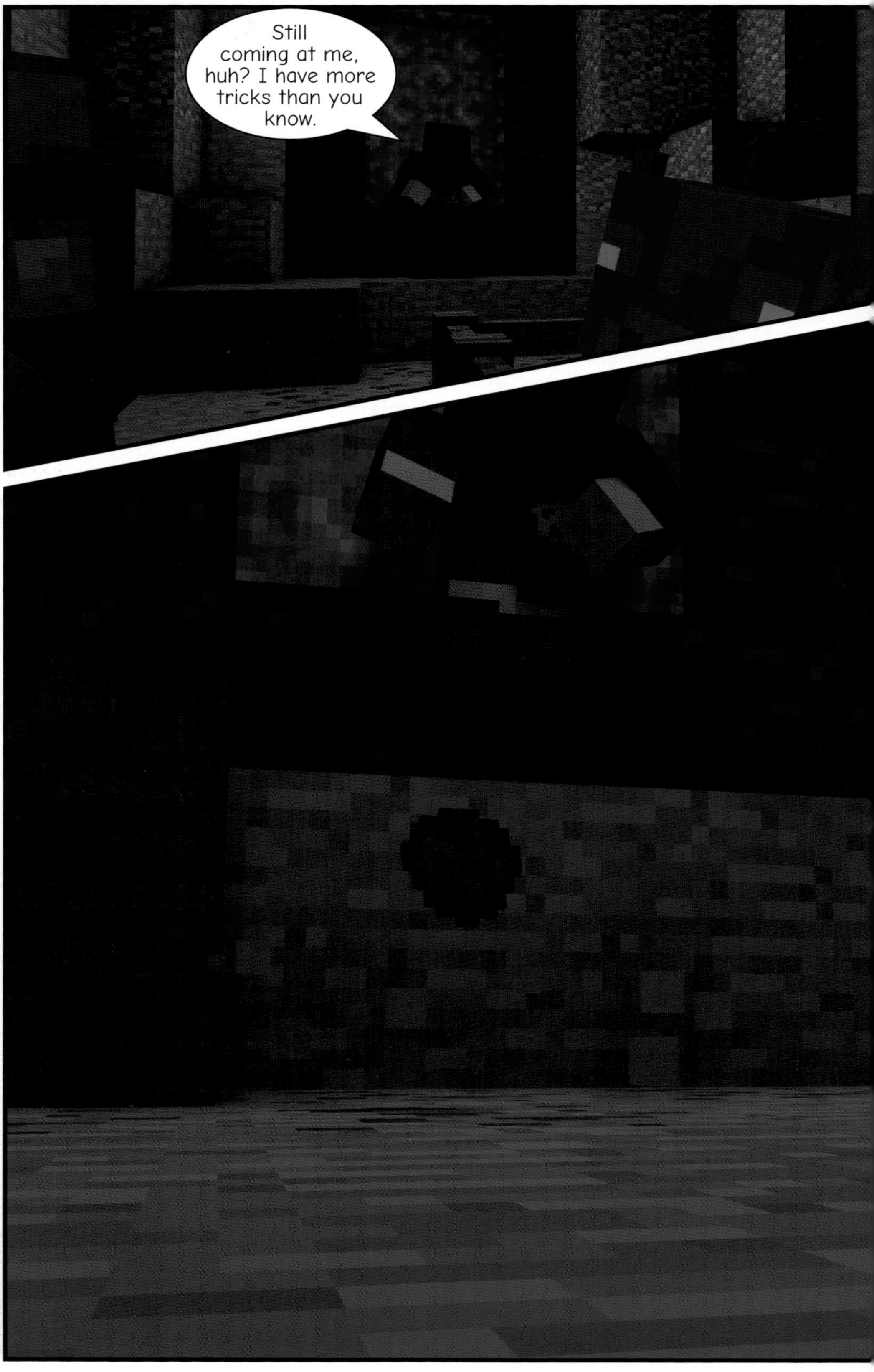
Still coming at me, huh? I have more tricks than you know.

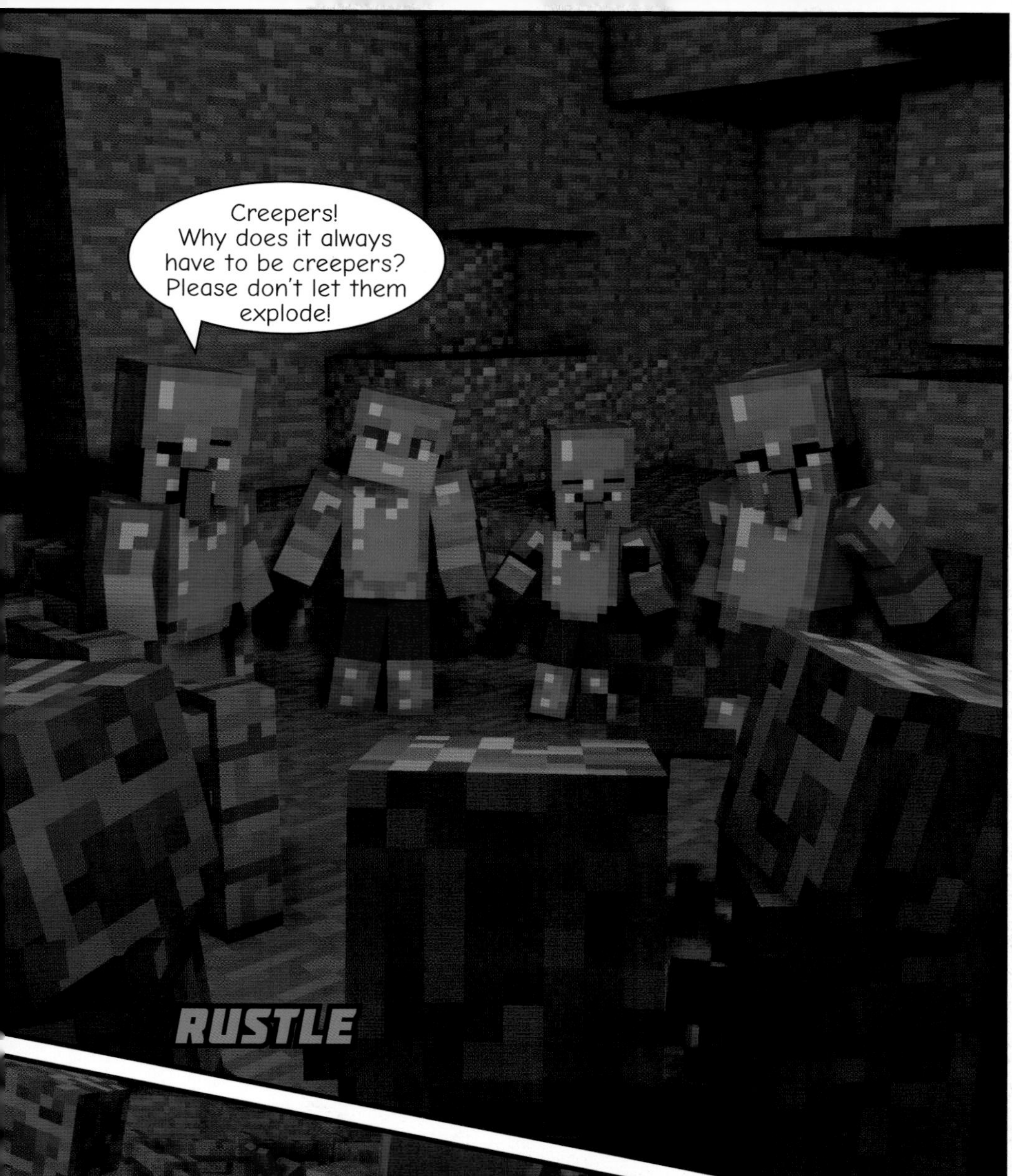
Creepers! Why does it always have to be creepers? Please don't let them explode!
RUSTLE

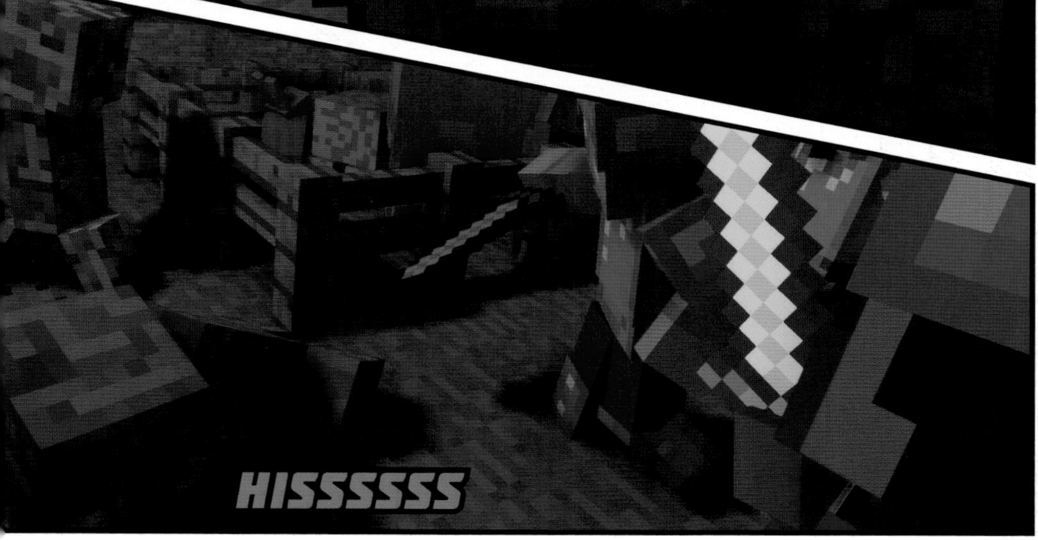
HISSSSSS

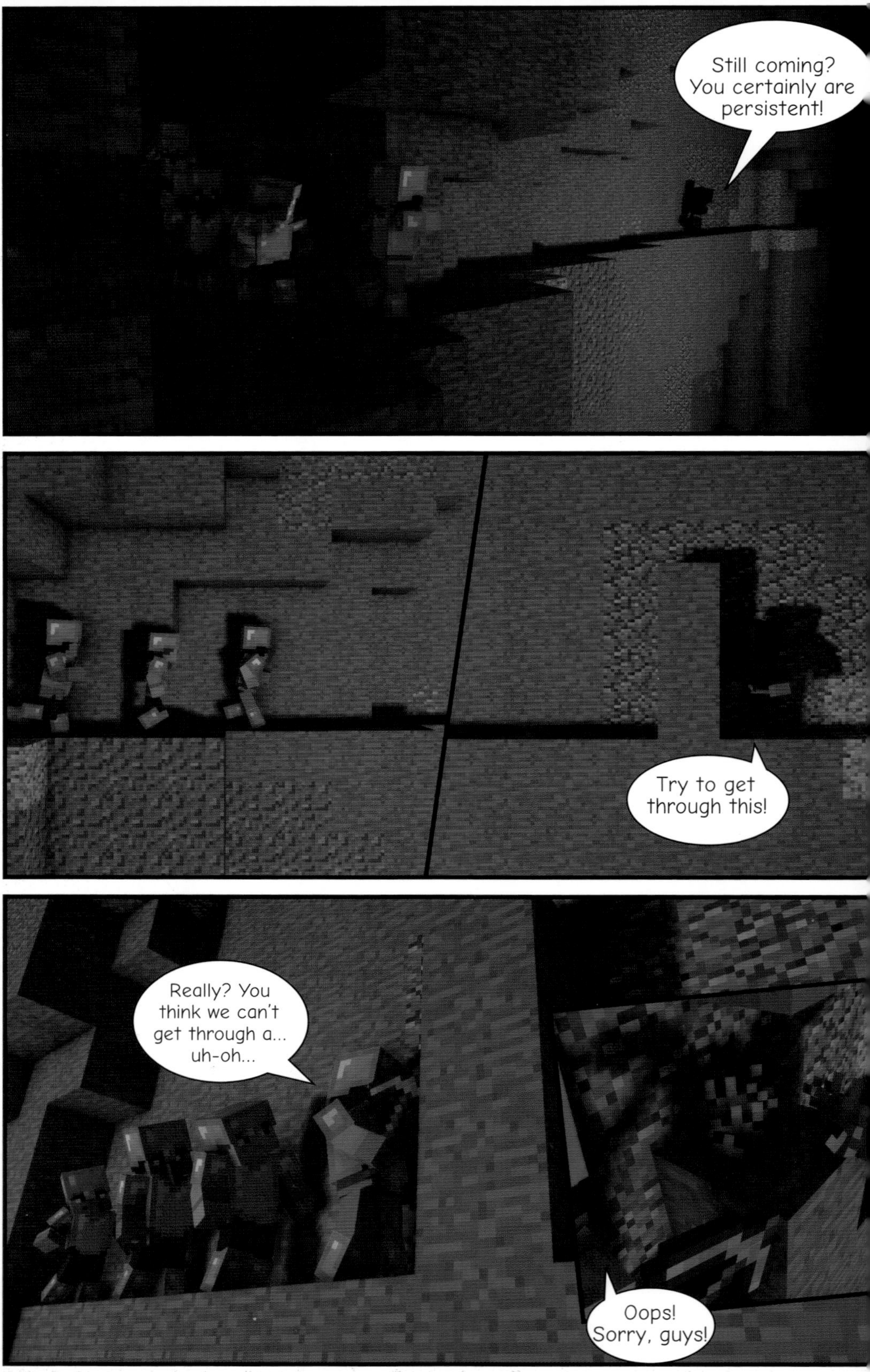
Still coming? You certainly are persistent!
Try to get through this!
Really? You think we can't get through a... uh-oh...
Oops! Sorry, guys!

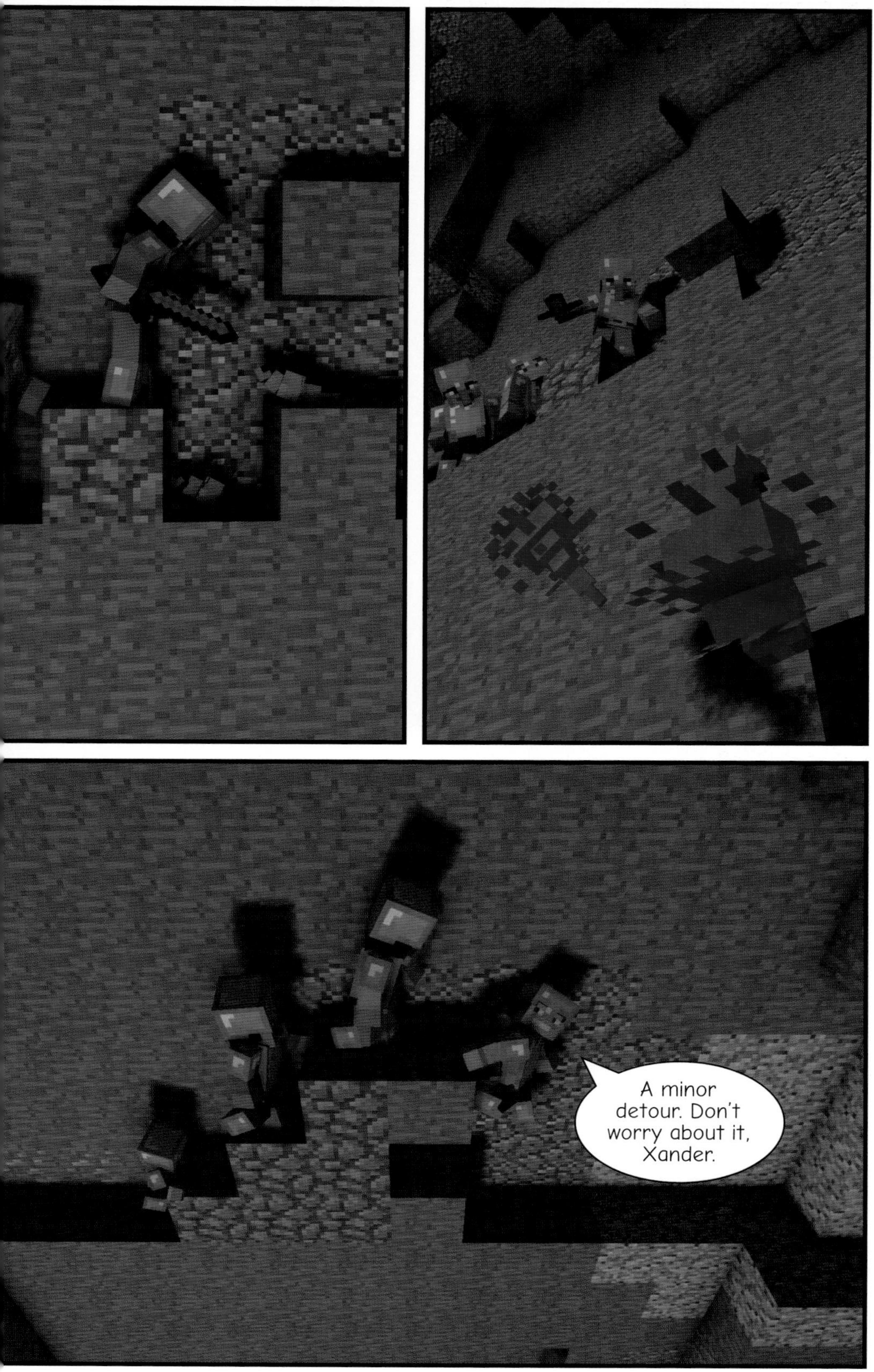
A minor detour. Don't worry about it, Xander.

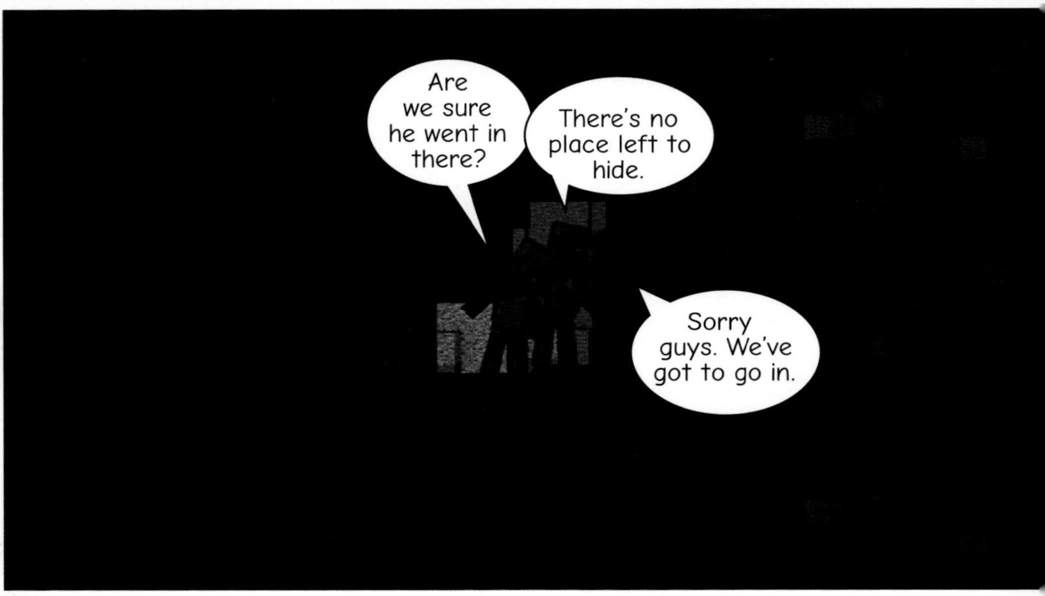
Are we sure he went in there?
There's no place left to hide.
Sorry guys. We've got to go in.

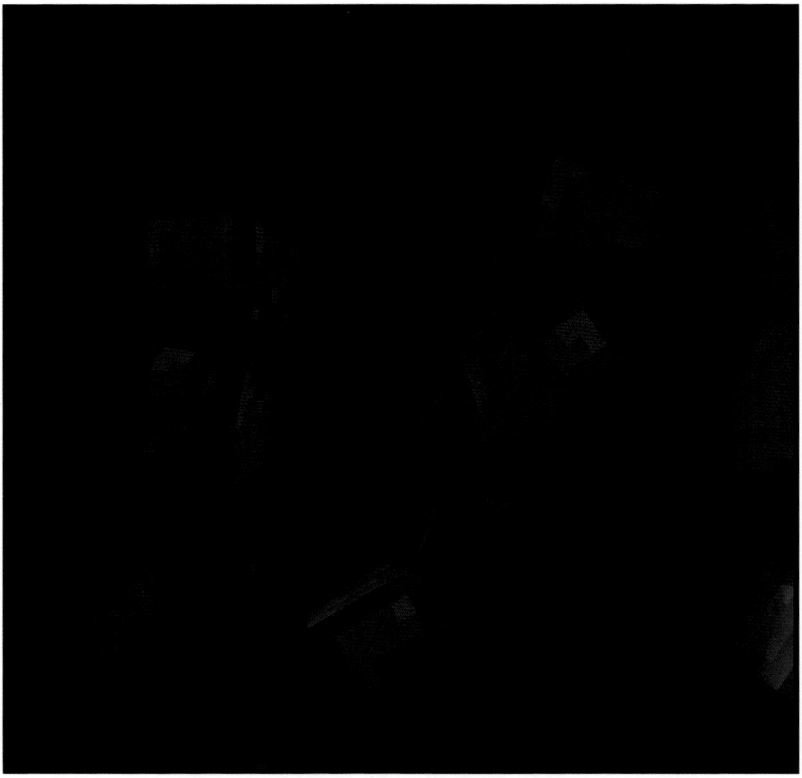

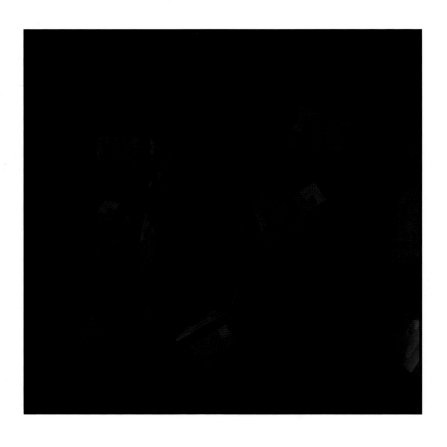

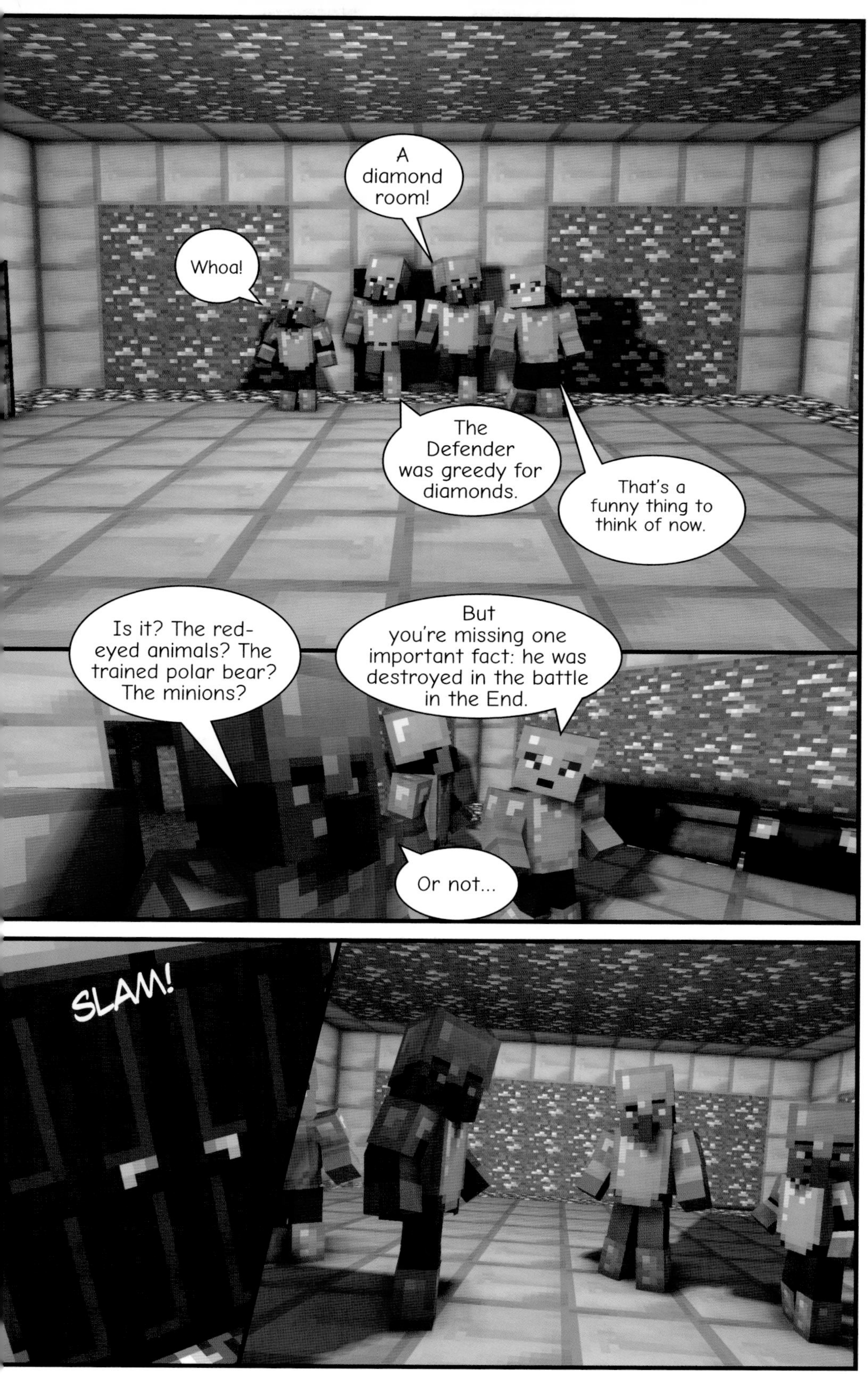
A diamond room!
Whoa!
The Defender was greedy for diamonds.
That's a funny thing to think of now.
Is it? The red-eyed animals? The trained polar bear? The minions?
But you're missing one important fact: he was destroyed in the battle in the End.
Or not...
SLAM!

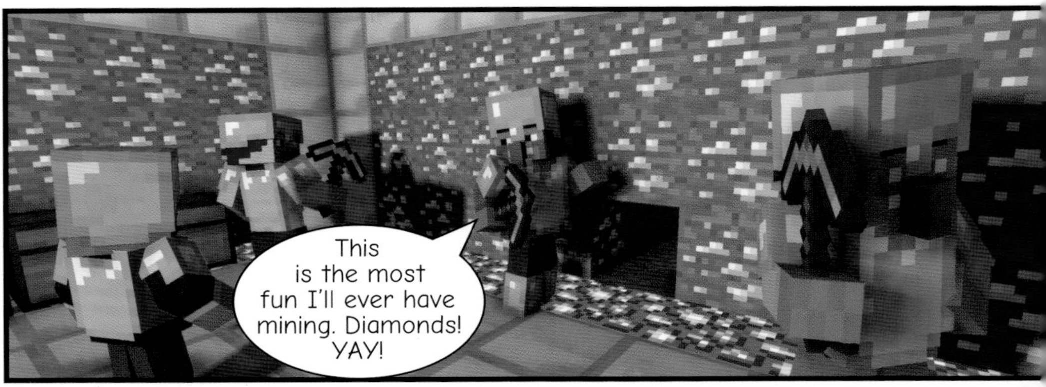
This is the most fun I'll ever have mining. Diamonds! YAY!

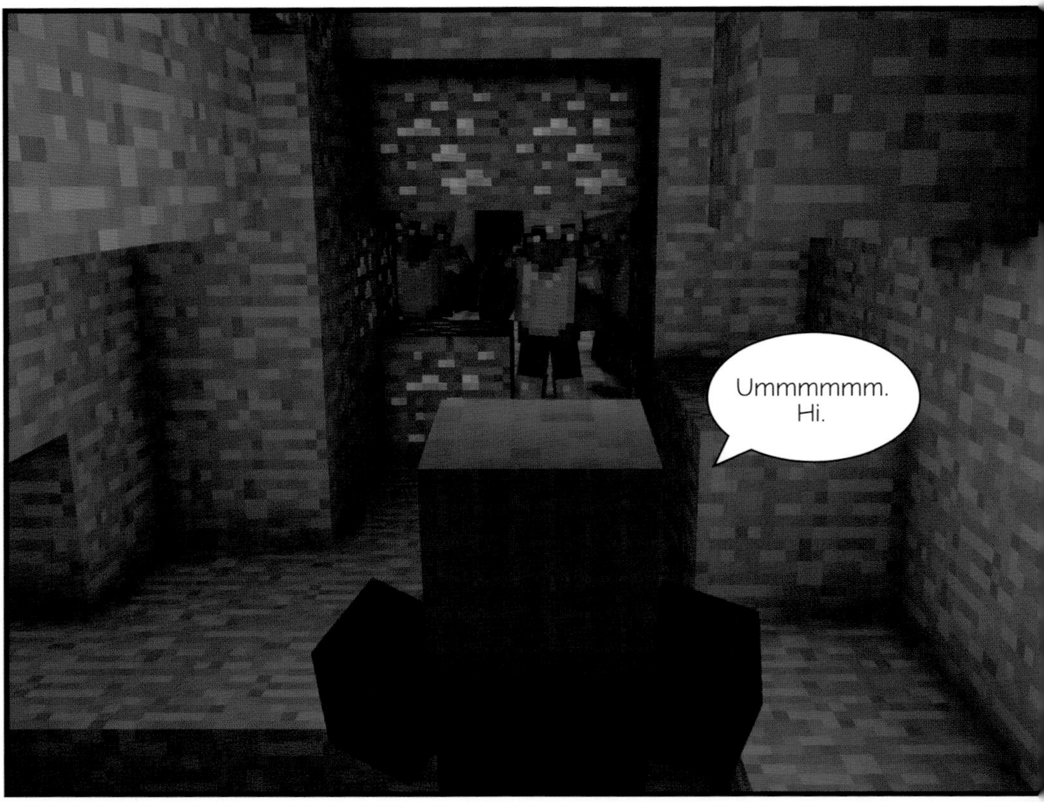
Ummmmmm. Hi.

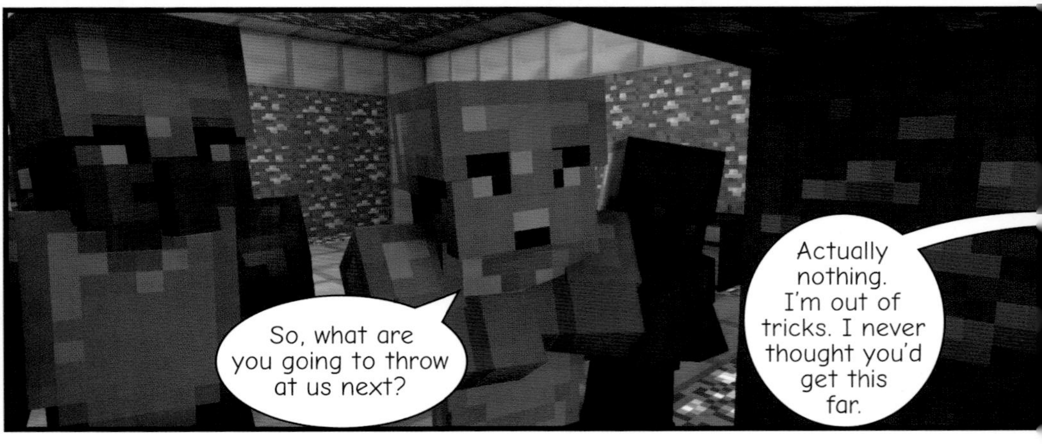
So, what are you going to throw at us next?
Actually nothing. I'm out of tricks. I never thought you'd get this far.

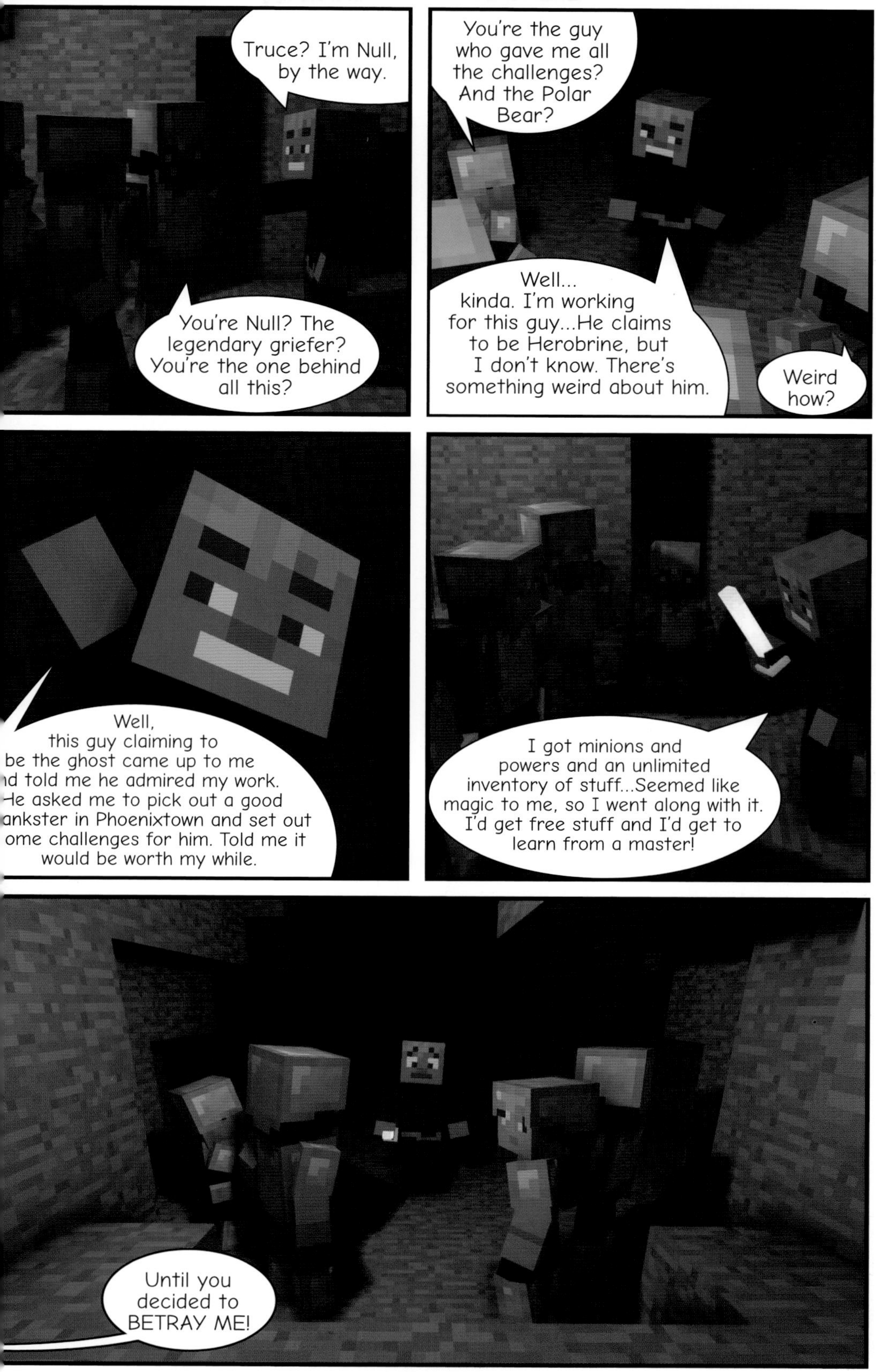

Truce? I'm Null, by the way.
You're Null? The legendary griefer? You're the one behind all this?
You're the guy who gave me all the challenges? And the Polar Bear?
Well... kinda. I'm working for this guy...He claims to be Herobrine, but I don't know. There's something weird about him.
Weird how?
Well, this guy claiming to be the ghost came up to me ıd told me he admired my work. He asked me to pick out a good ankster in Phoenixtown and set out ome challenges for him. Told me it would be worth my while.
I got minions and powers and an unlimited inventory of stuff...Seemed like magic to me, so I went along with it. I'd get free stuff and I'd get to learn from a master!
Until you decided to BETRAY ME!

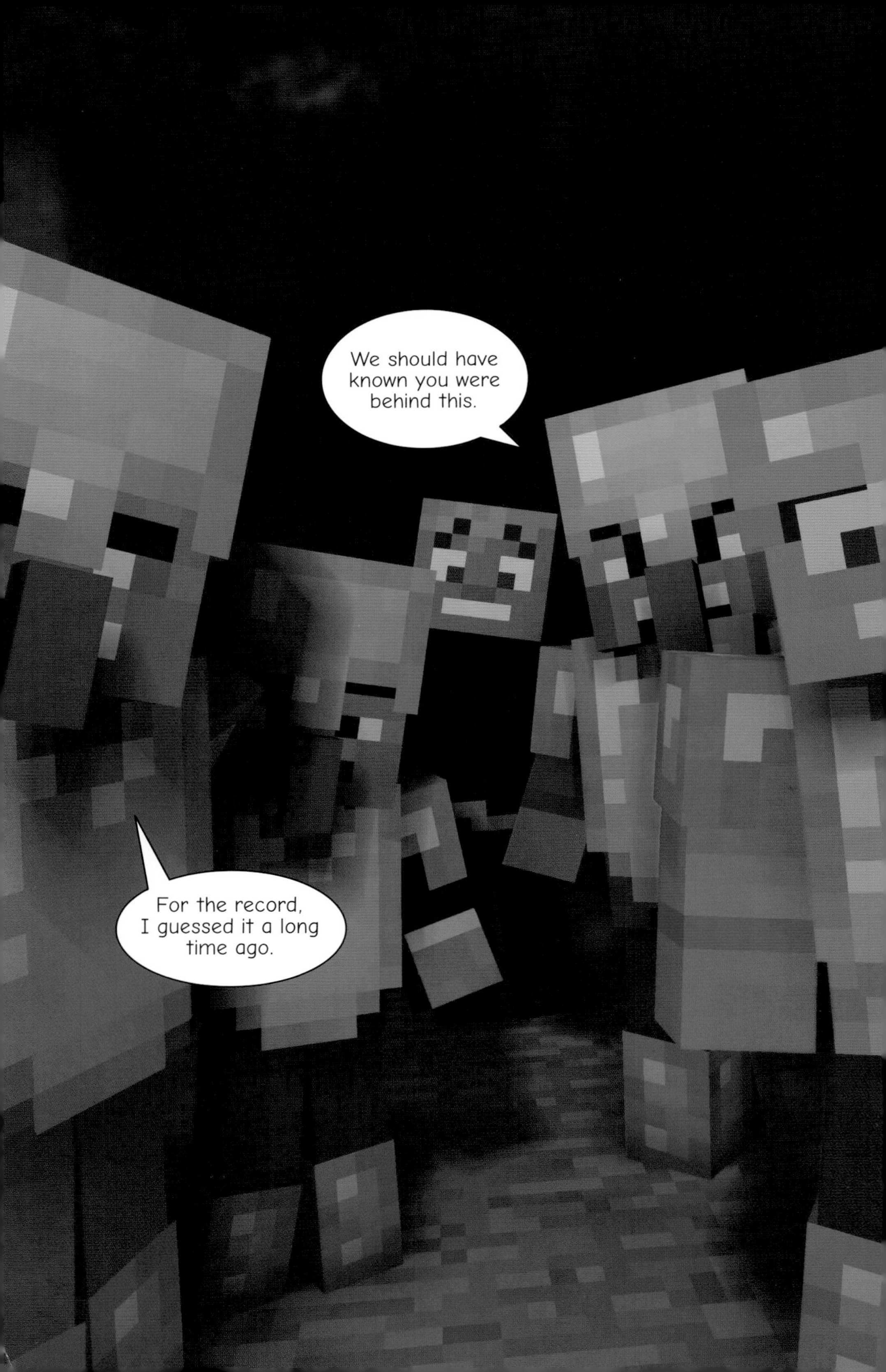
We should have known you were behind this.
For the record, I guessed it a long time ago.

CHAPTER 12

BACK FROM THE DEAD

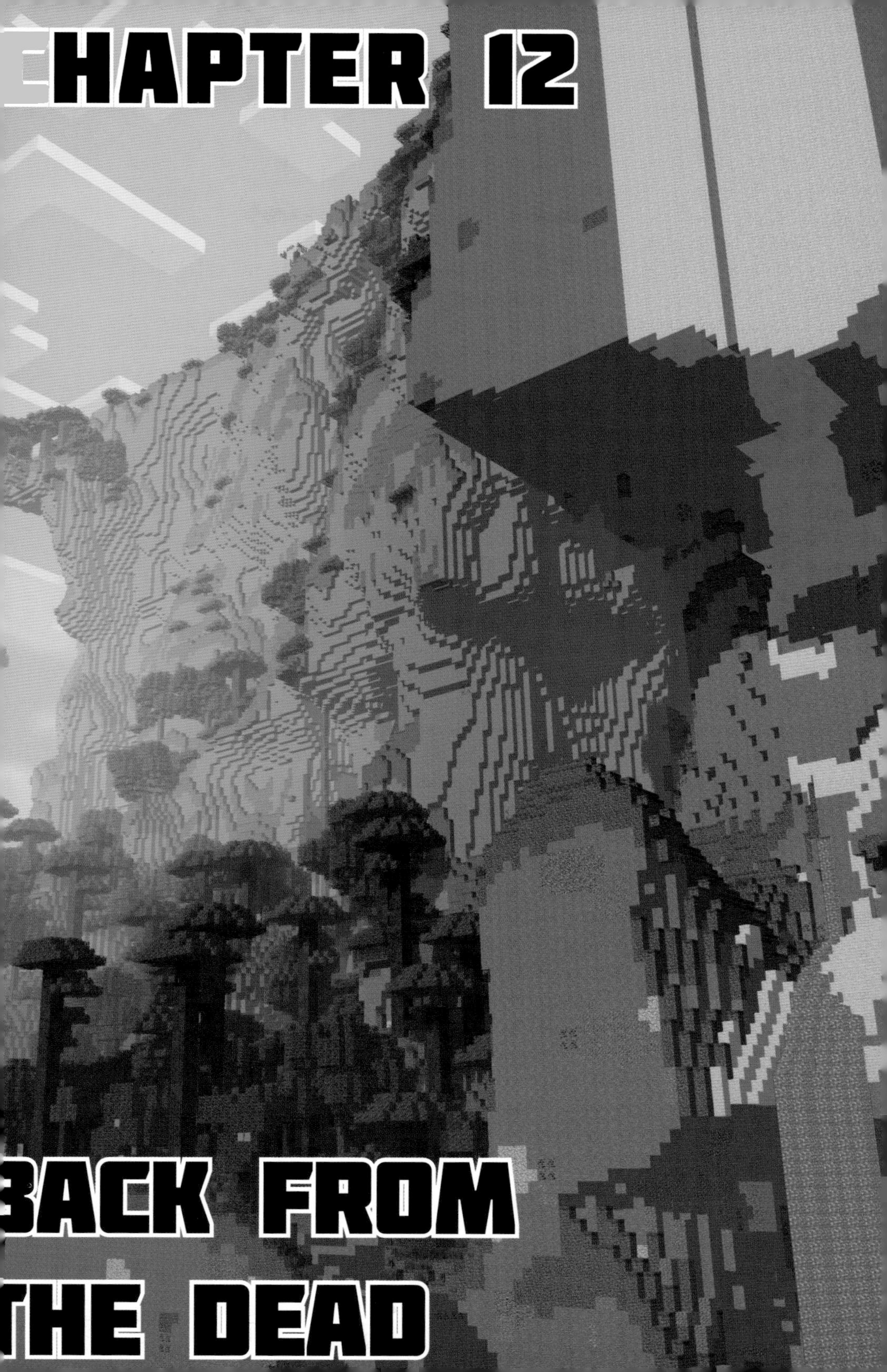

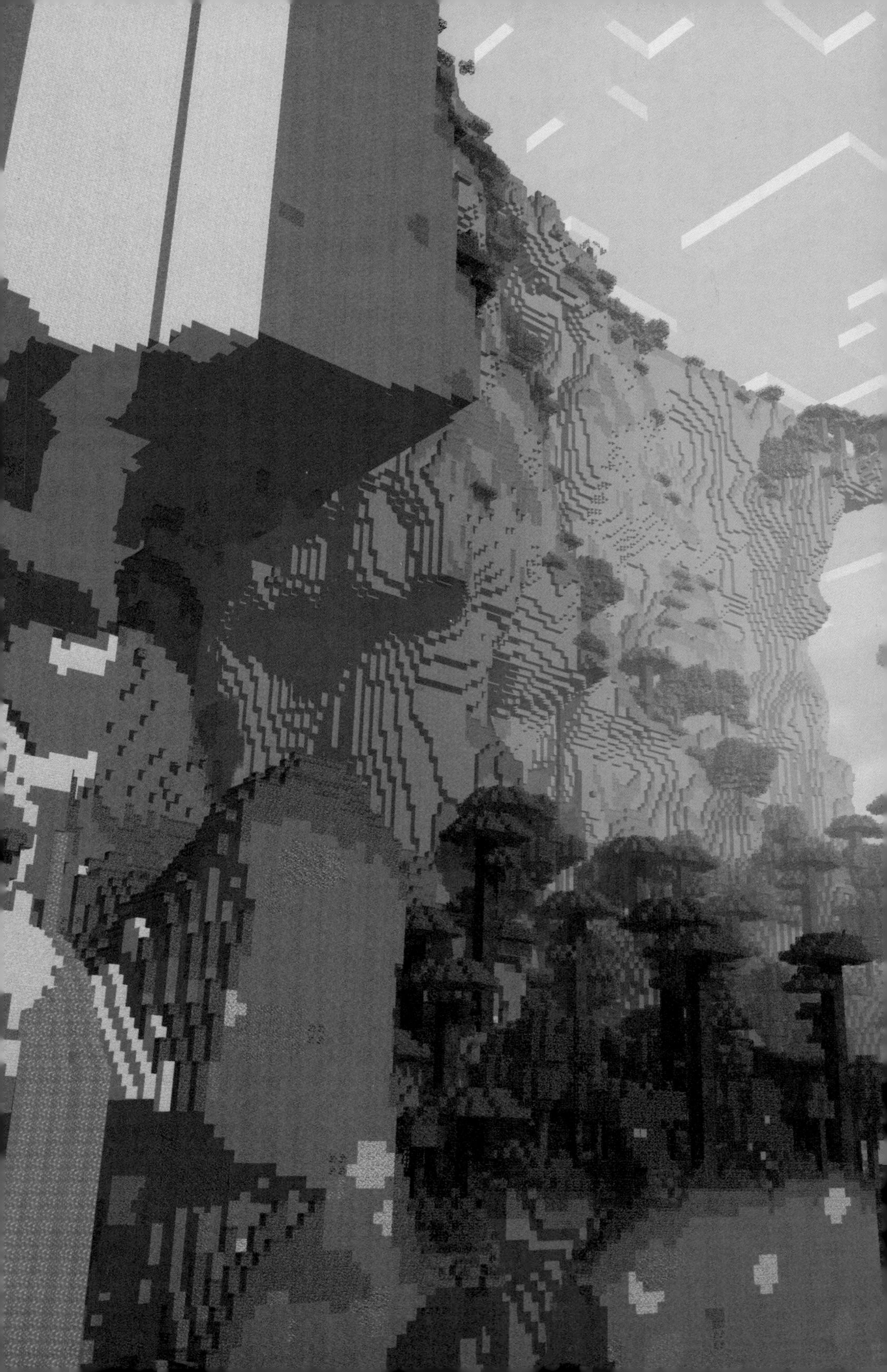

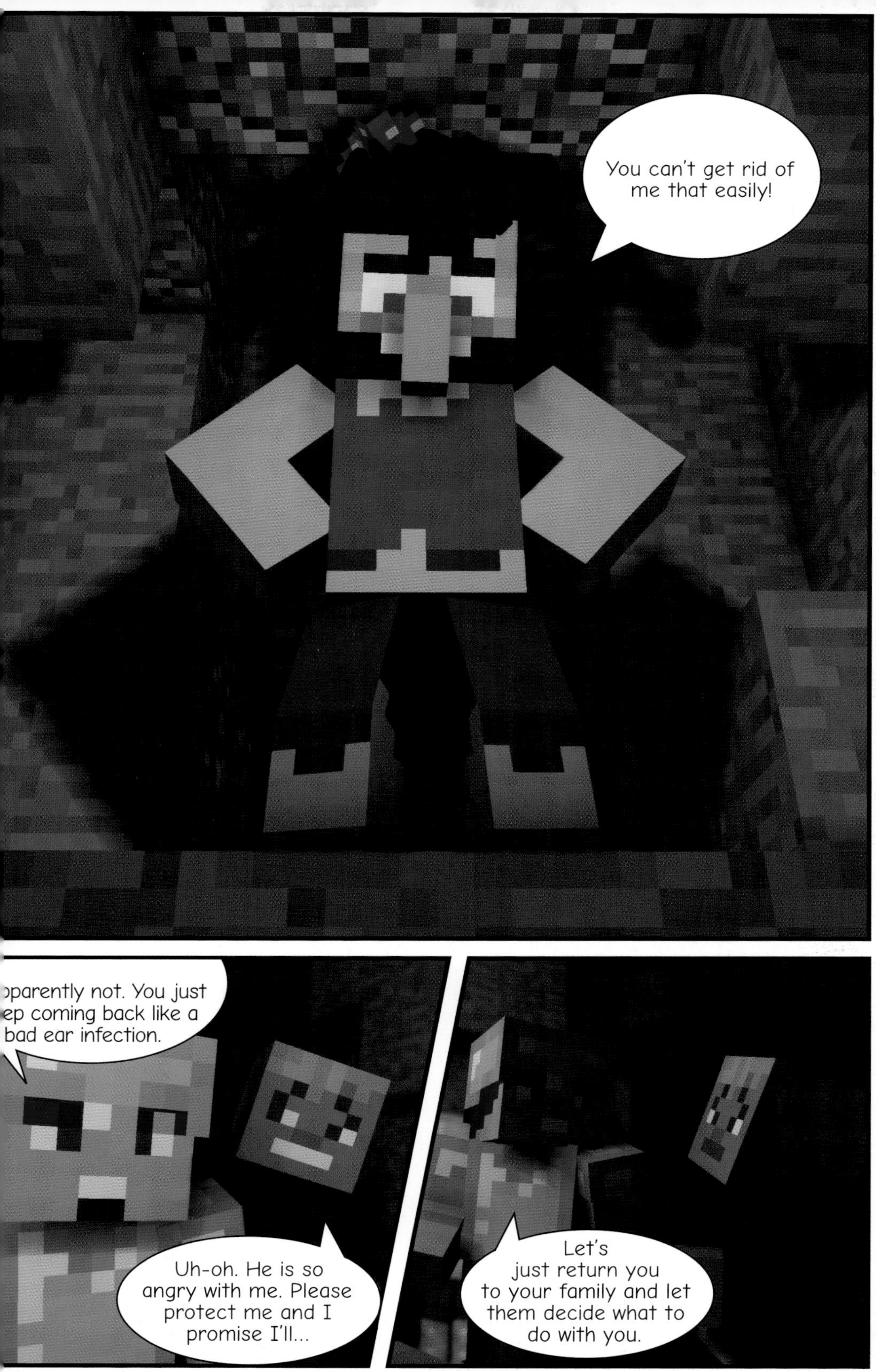
You can't get rid of me that easily!
pparently not. You just ep coming back like a bad ear infection.
Uh-oh. He is so angry with me. Please protect me and I promise I'll...
Let's just return you to your family and let them decide what to do with you.

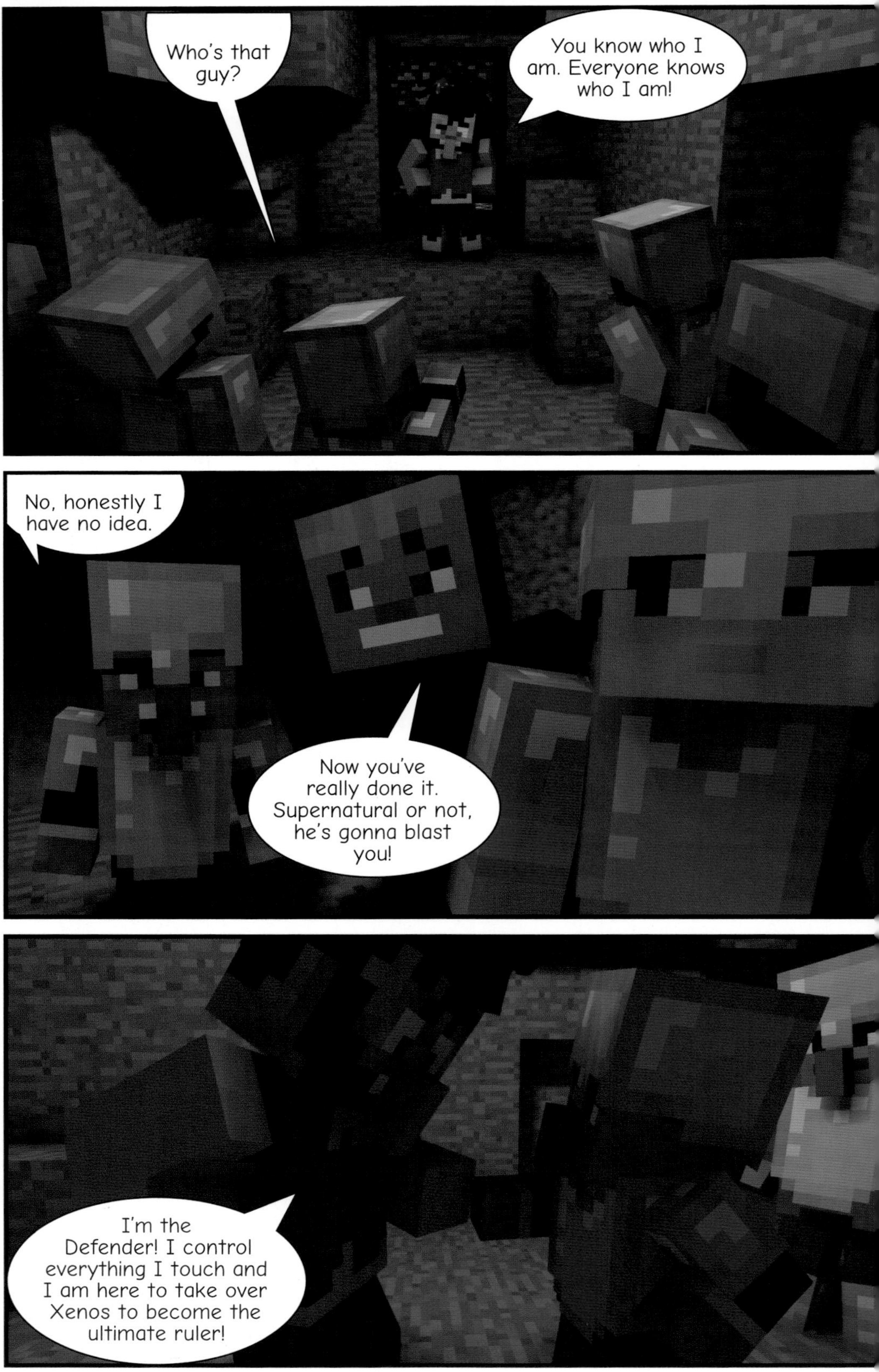
Who's that guy?
You know who I am. Everyone knows who I am!
No, honestly I have no idea.
Now you've really done it. Supernatural or not, he's gonna blast you!
I'm the Defender! I control everything I touch and I am here to take over Xenos to become the ultimate ruler!

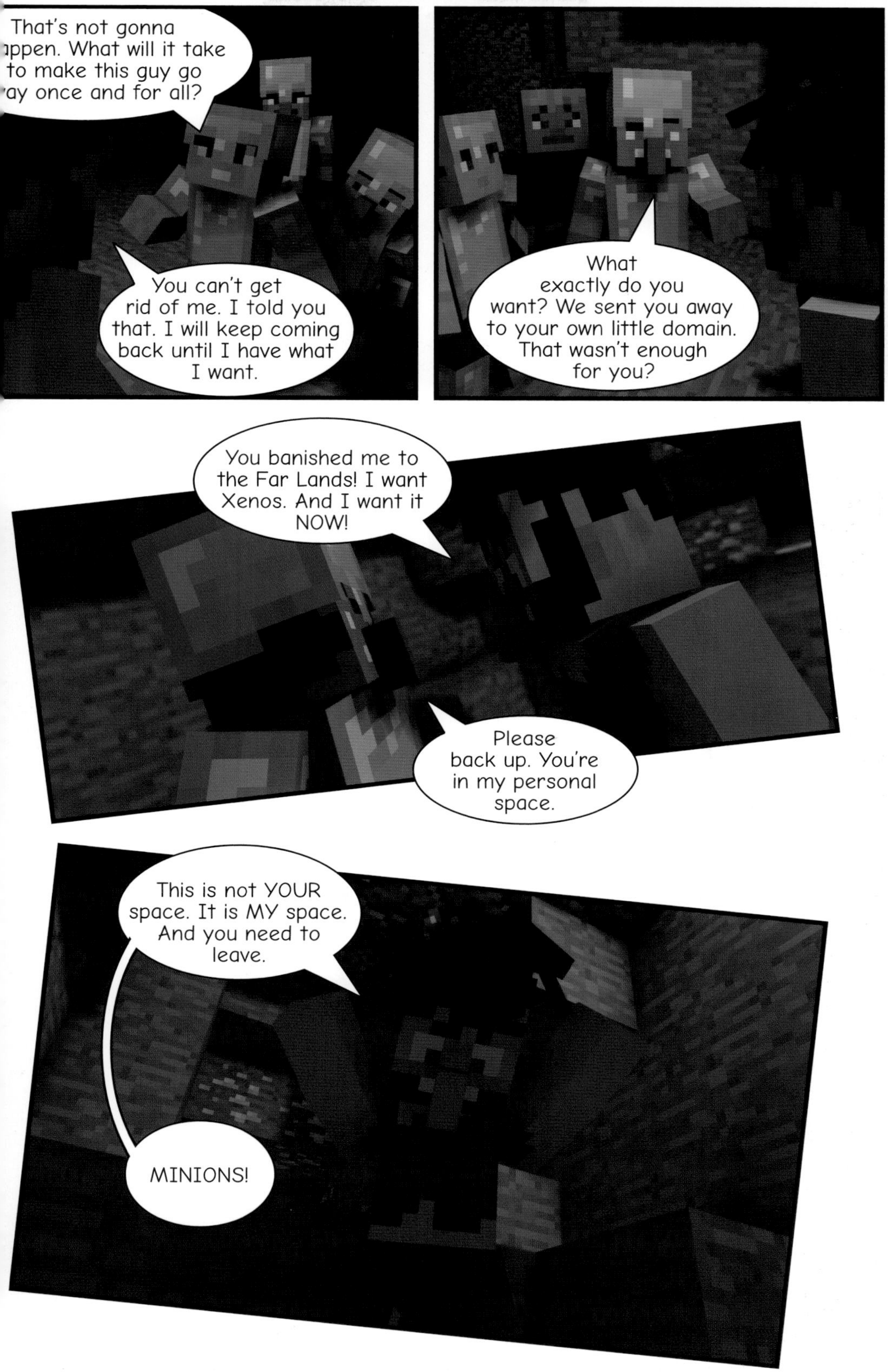
That's not gonna ppen. What will it take to make this guy go ay once and for all?
You can't get rid of me. I told you that. I will keep coming back until I have what I want.
What exactly do you want? We sent you away to your own little domain. That wasn't enough for you?
You banished me to the Far Lands! I want Xenos. And I want it NOW!
Please back up. You're in my personal space.
This is not YOUR space. It is MY space. And you need to leave.
MINIONS!

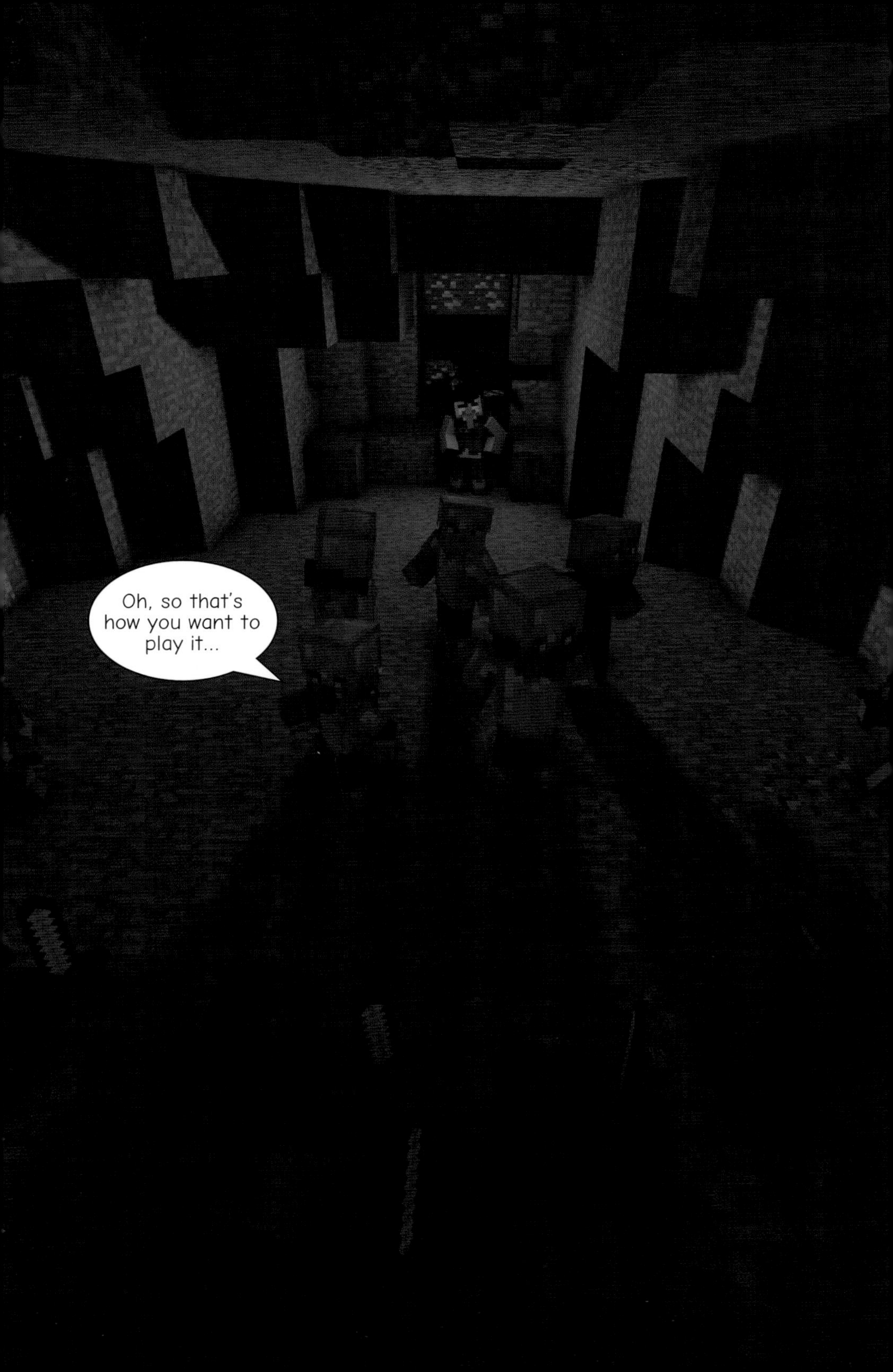
Oh, so that's how you want to play it...

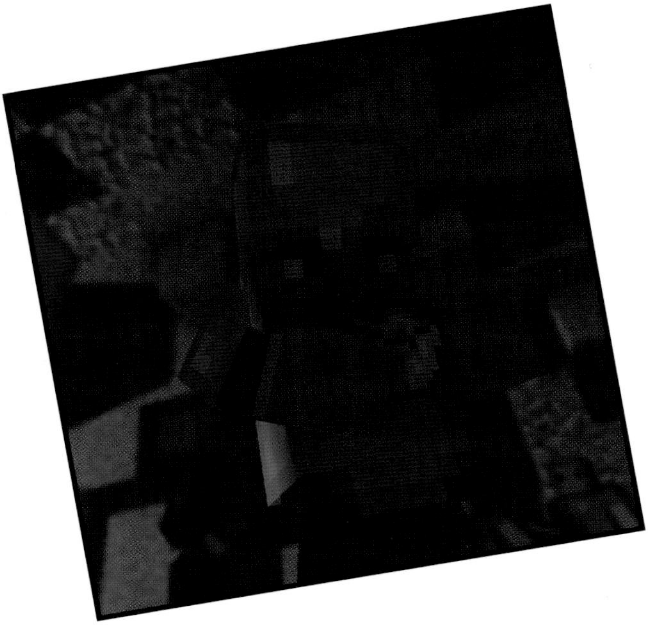

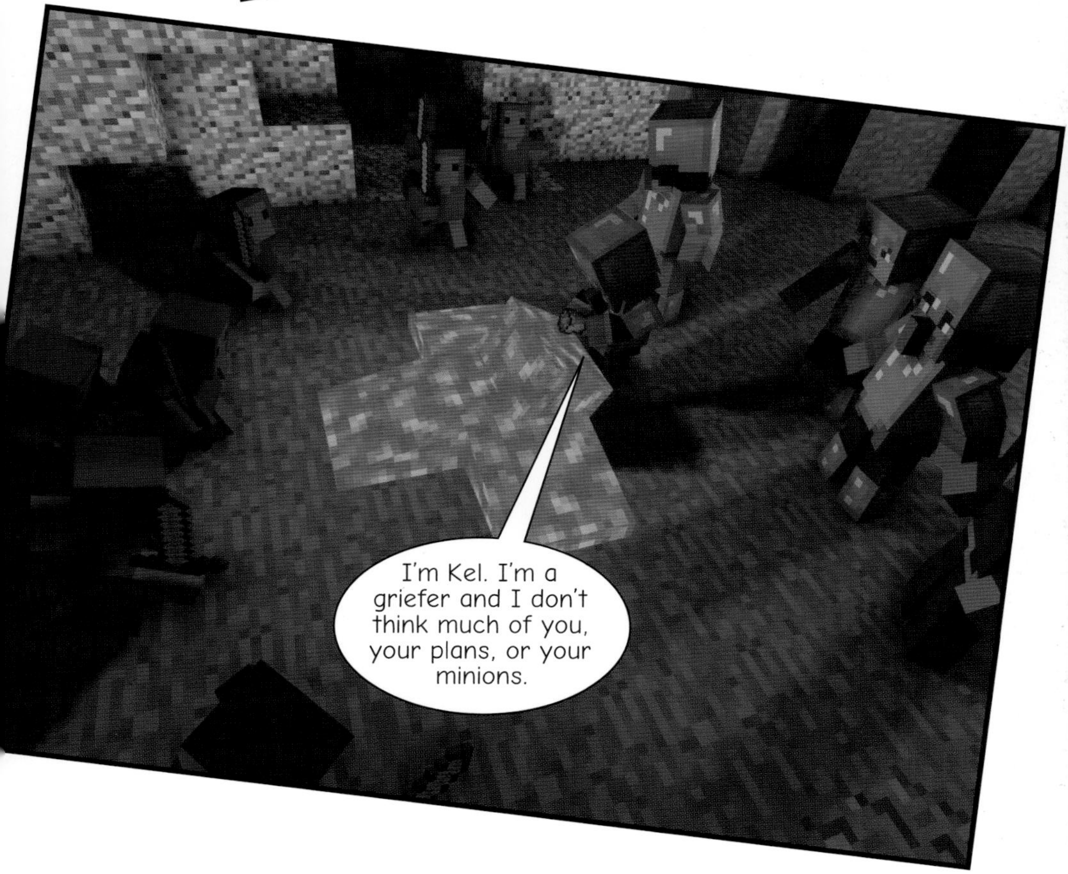
I'm Kel. I'm a griefer and I don't think much of you, your plans, or your minions.

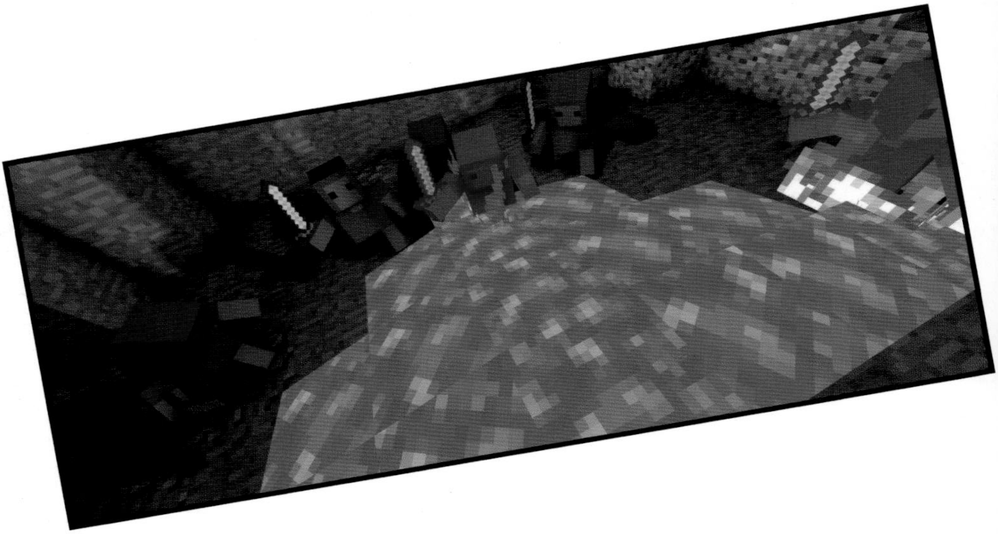

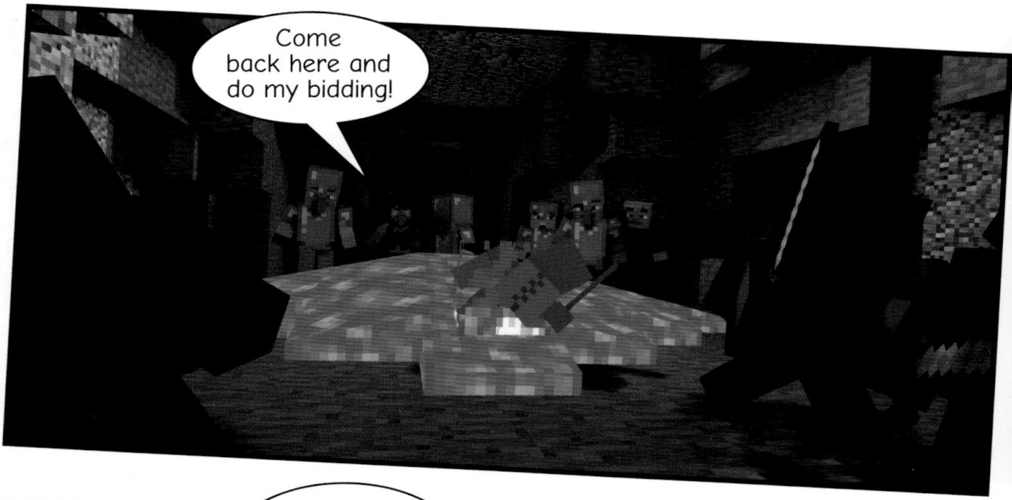
Come back here and do my bidding!

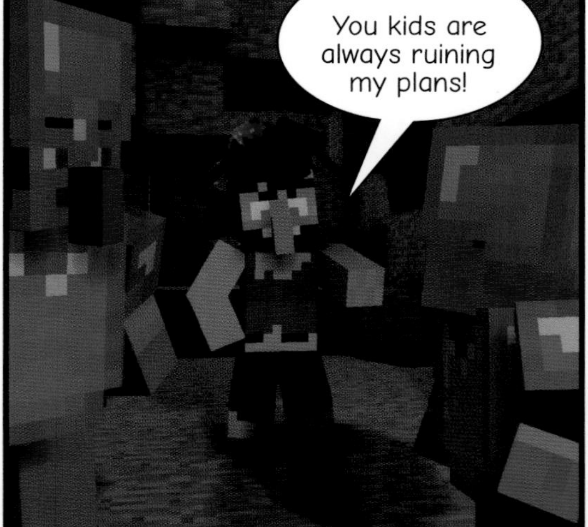
You kids are always ruining my plans!

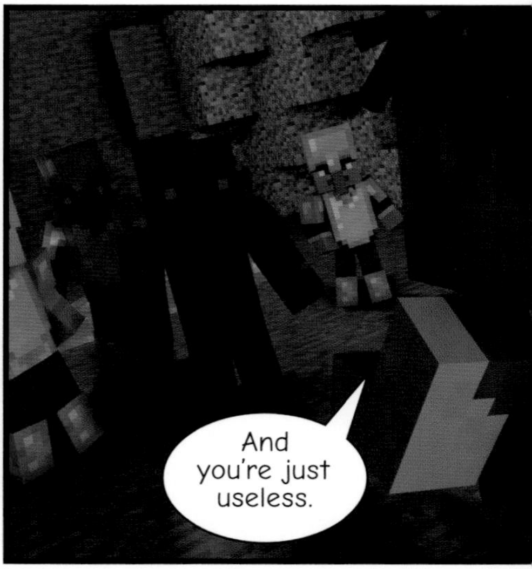
And you're just useless.

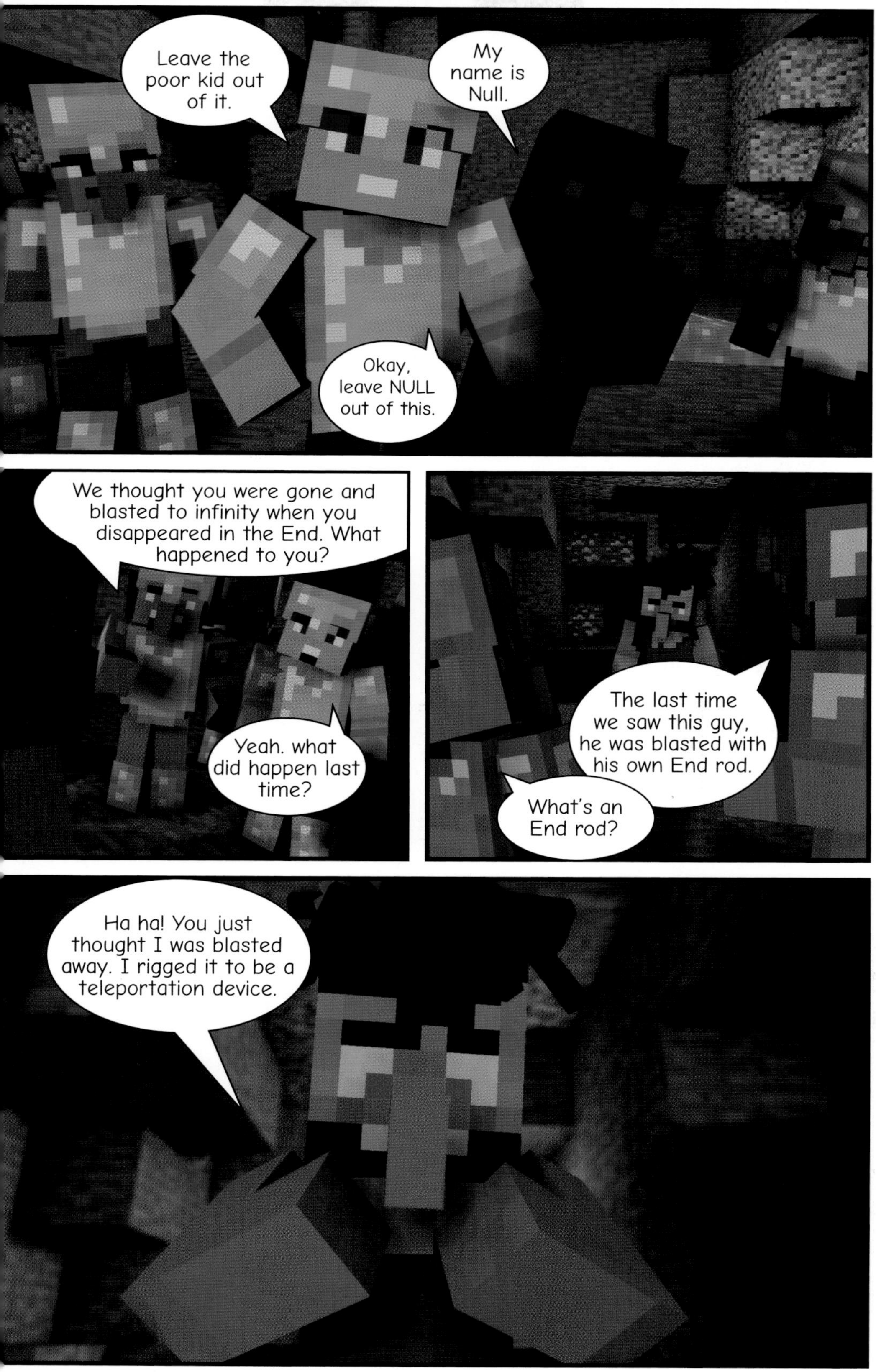
Leave the poor kid out of it.
My name is Null.
Okay, leave NULL out of this.
We thought you were gone and blasted to infinity when you disappeared in the End. What happened to you?
Yeah. what did happen last time?
The last time we saw this guy, he was blasted with his own End rod.
What's an End rod?
Ha ha! You just thought I was blasted away. I rigged it to be a teleportation device.

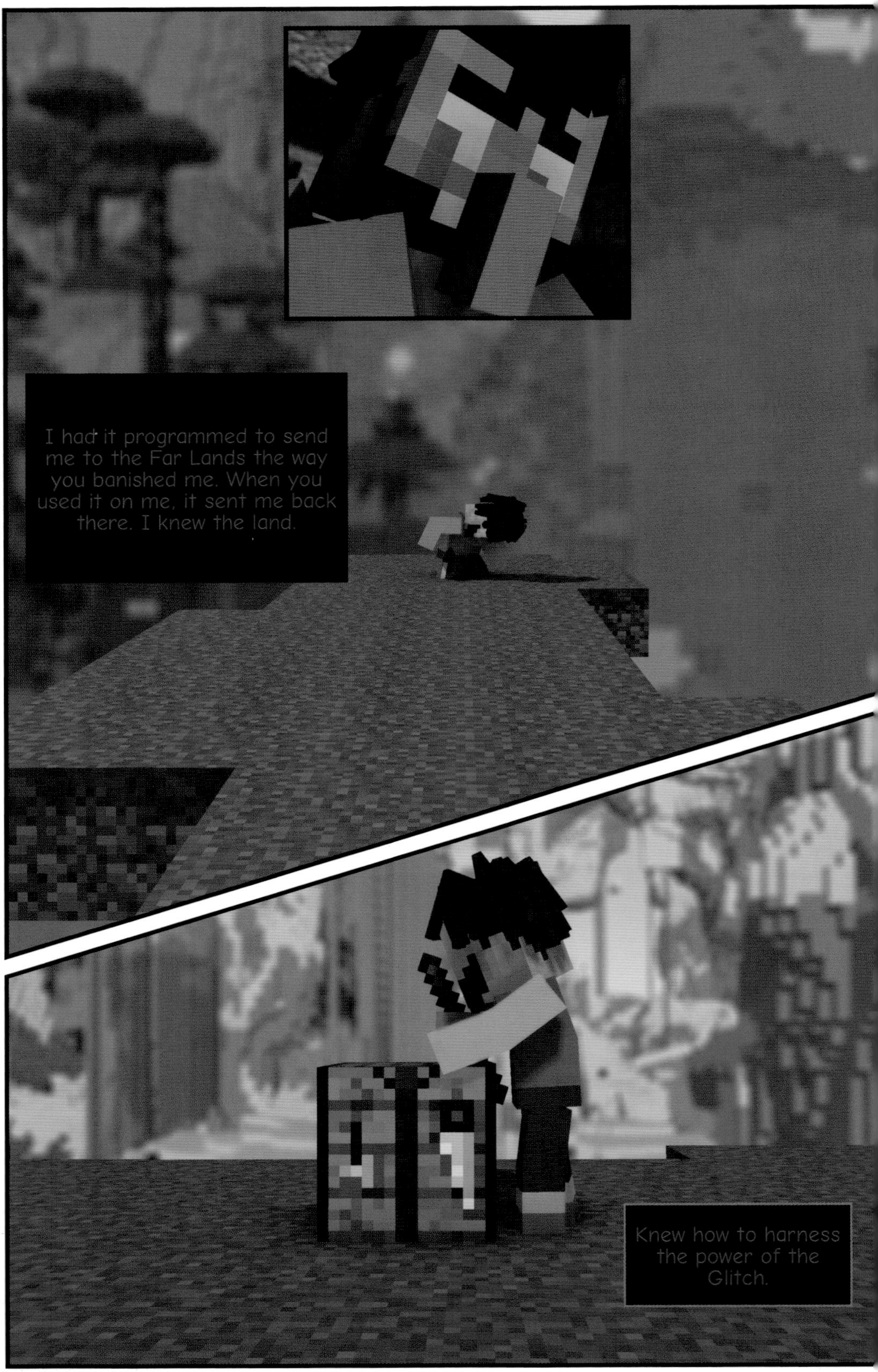
I had it programmed to send me to the Far Lands the way you banished me. When you used it on me, it sent me back there. I knew the land.
Knew how to harness the power of the Glitch.

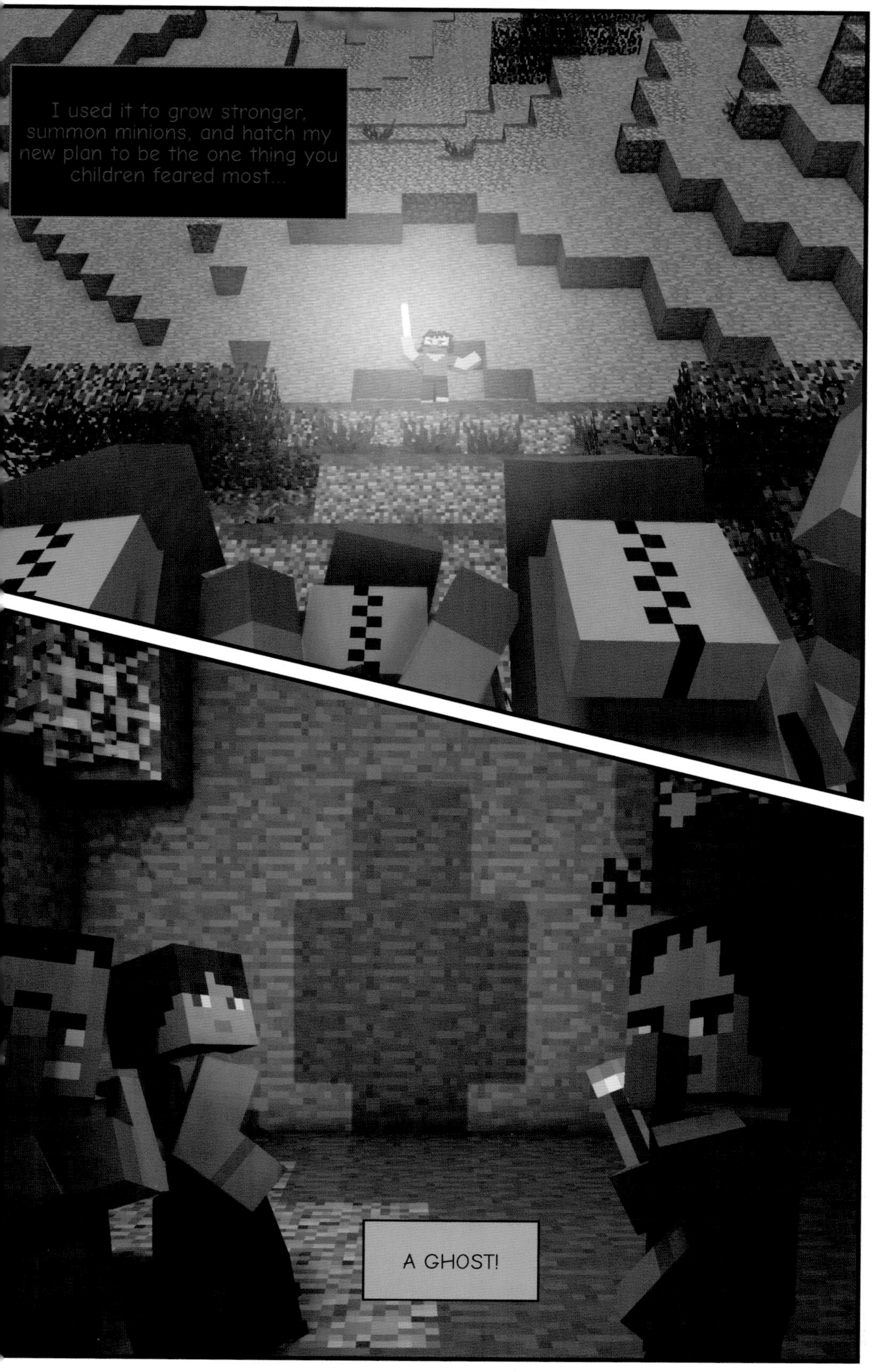
I used it to grow stronger, summon minions, and hatch my new plan to be the one thing you children feared most...
A GHOST!

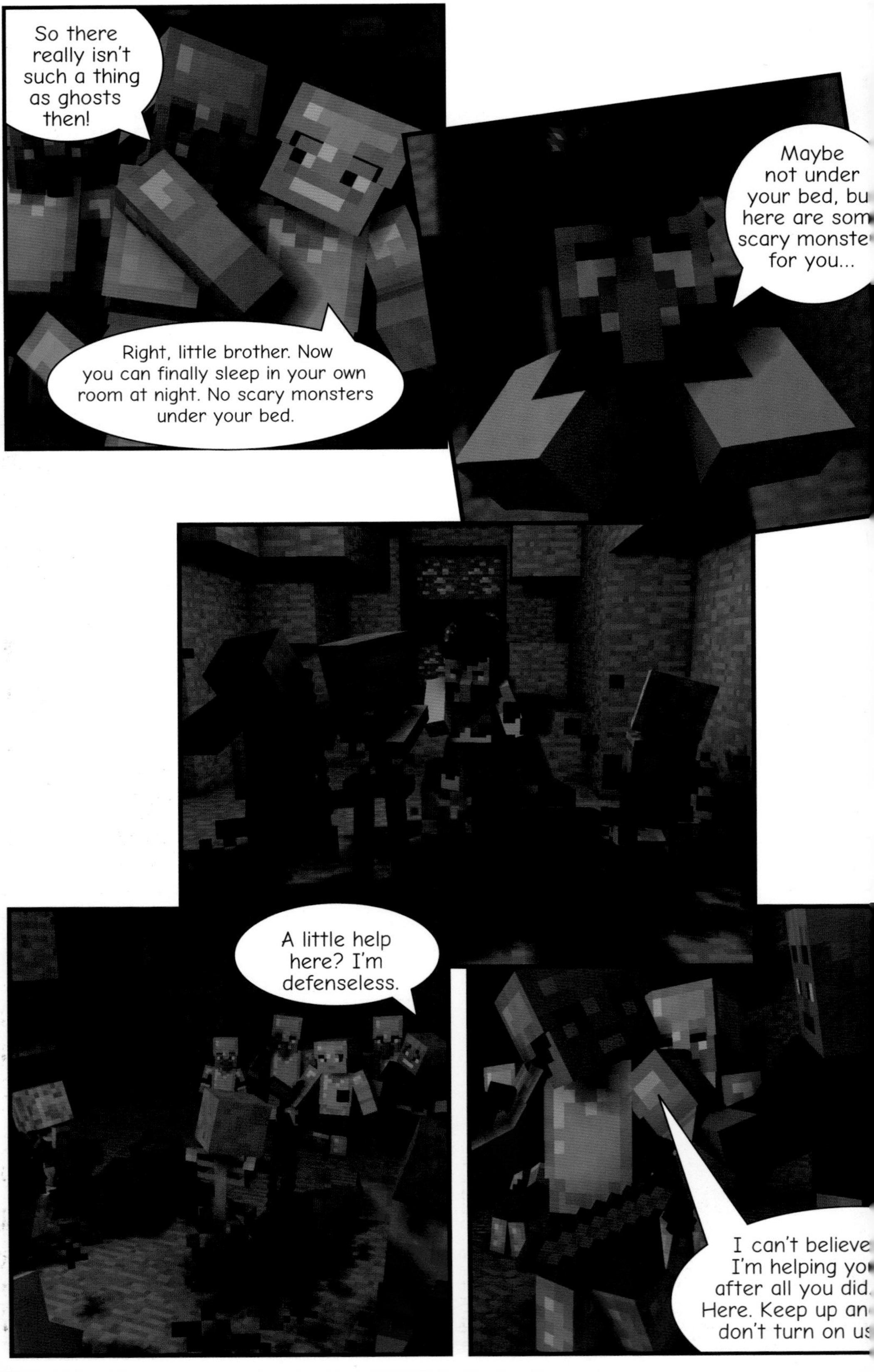
So there really isn't such a thing as ghosts then!
Right, little brother. Now you can finally sleep in your own room at night. No scary monsters under your bed.
Maybe not under your bed, bu here are som scary monste for you...
A little help here? I'm defenseless.
I can't believe I'm helping yo after all you did. Here. Keep up an don't turn on us

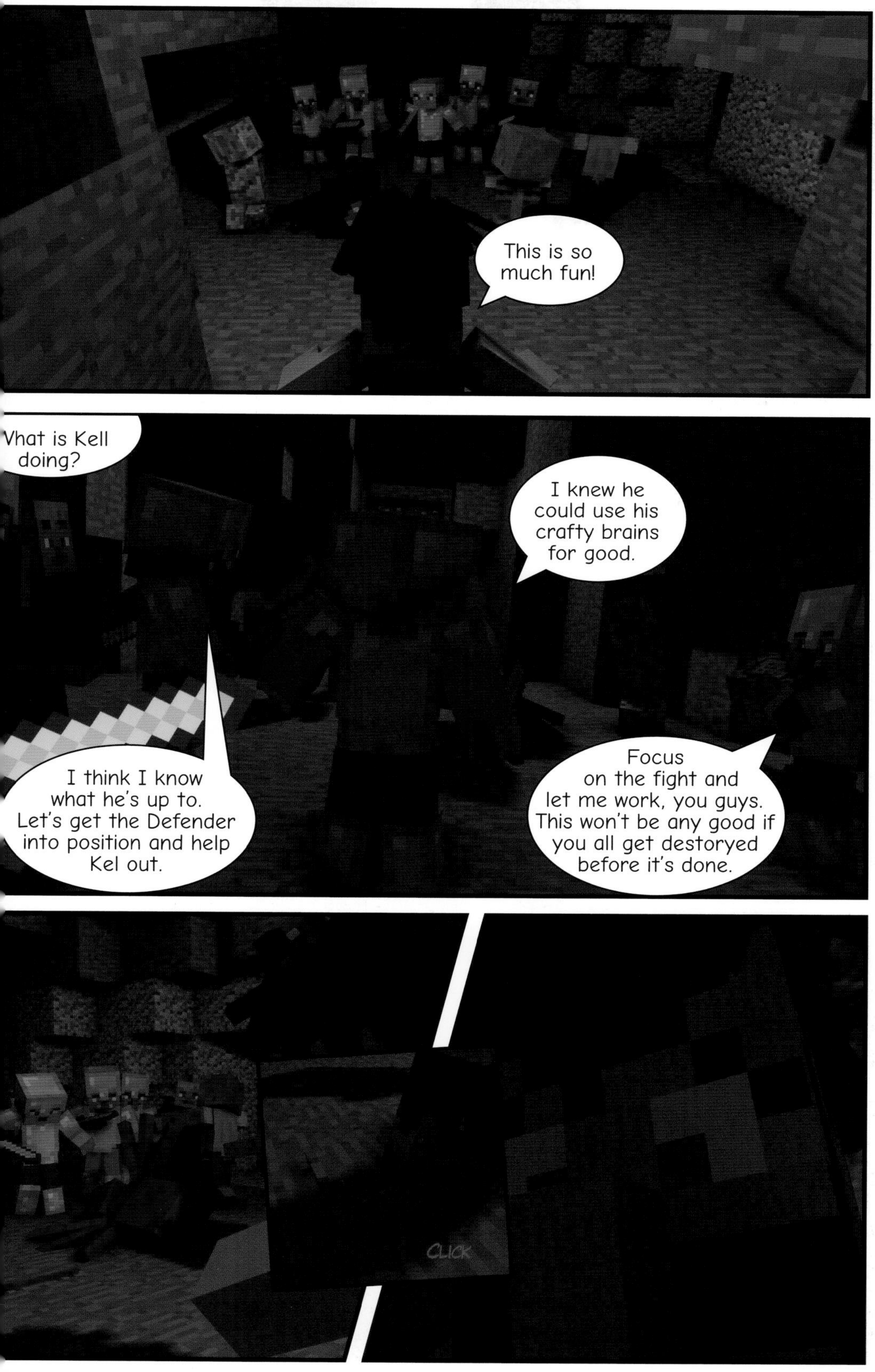
This is so much fun!
Vhat is Kell doing?
I knew he could use his crafty brains for good.
I think I know what he's up to. Let's get the Defender into position and help Kel out.
Focus on the fight and let me work, you guys. This won't be any good if you all get destoryed before it's done.
CLICK

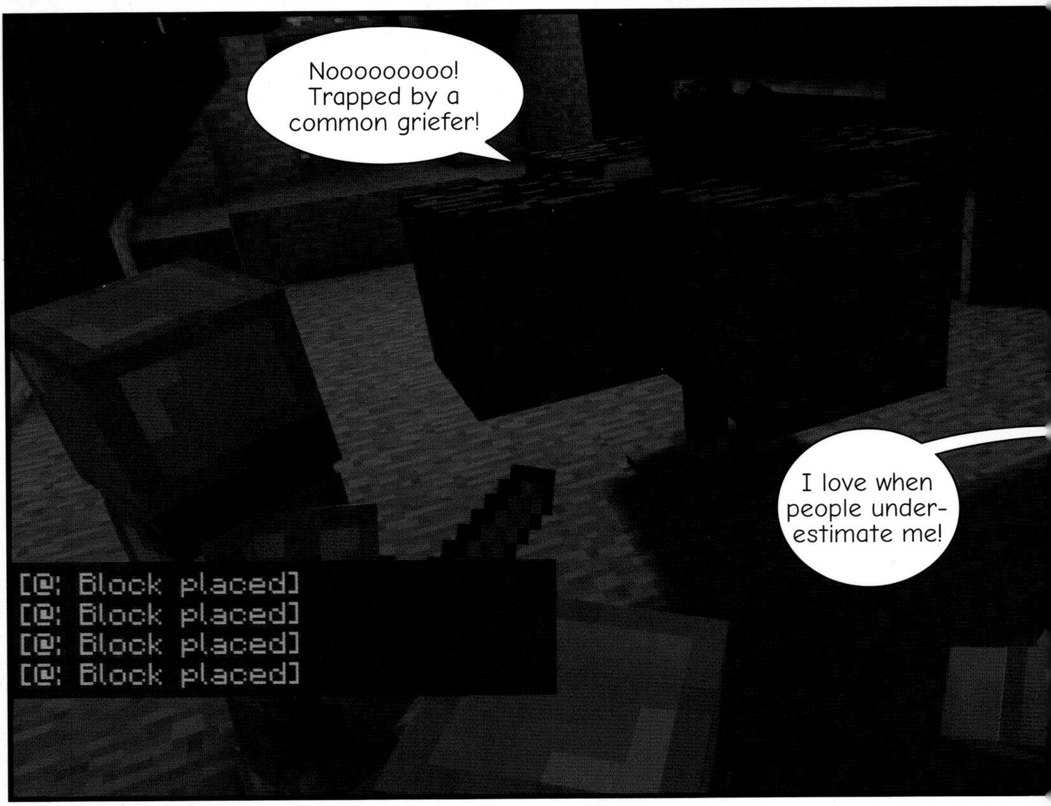
Noooooooooo! Trapped by a common griefer!
I love when people under-estimate me!
[@: Block placed]
[@: Block placed]
[@: Block placed]
[@: Block placed]

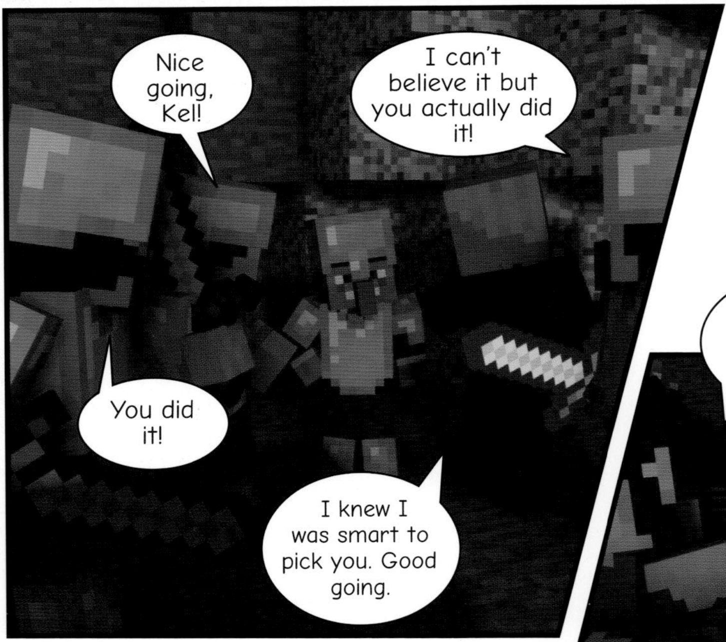
Nice going, Kel!
I can't believe it but you actually did it!
You did it!
I knew I was smart to pick you. Good going.

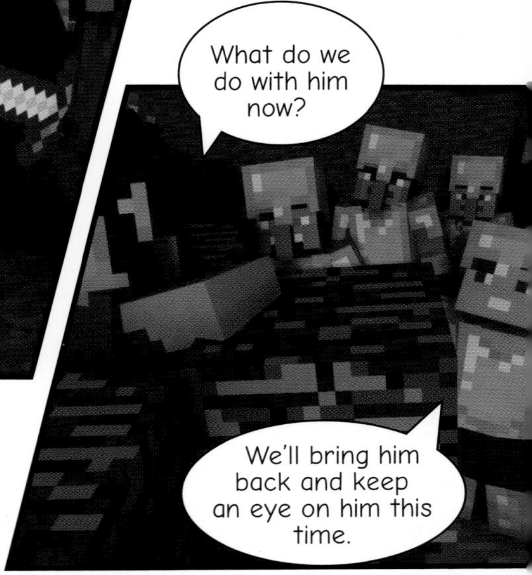
What do we do with him now?
We'll bring him back and keep an eye on him this time.

CHAPTER 13

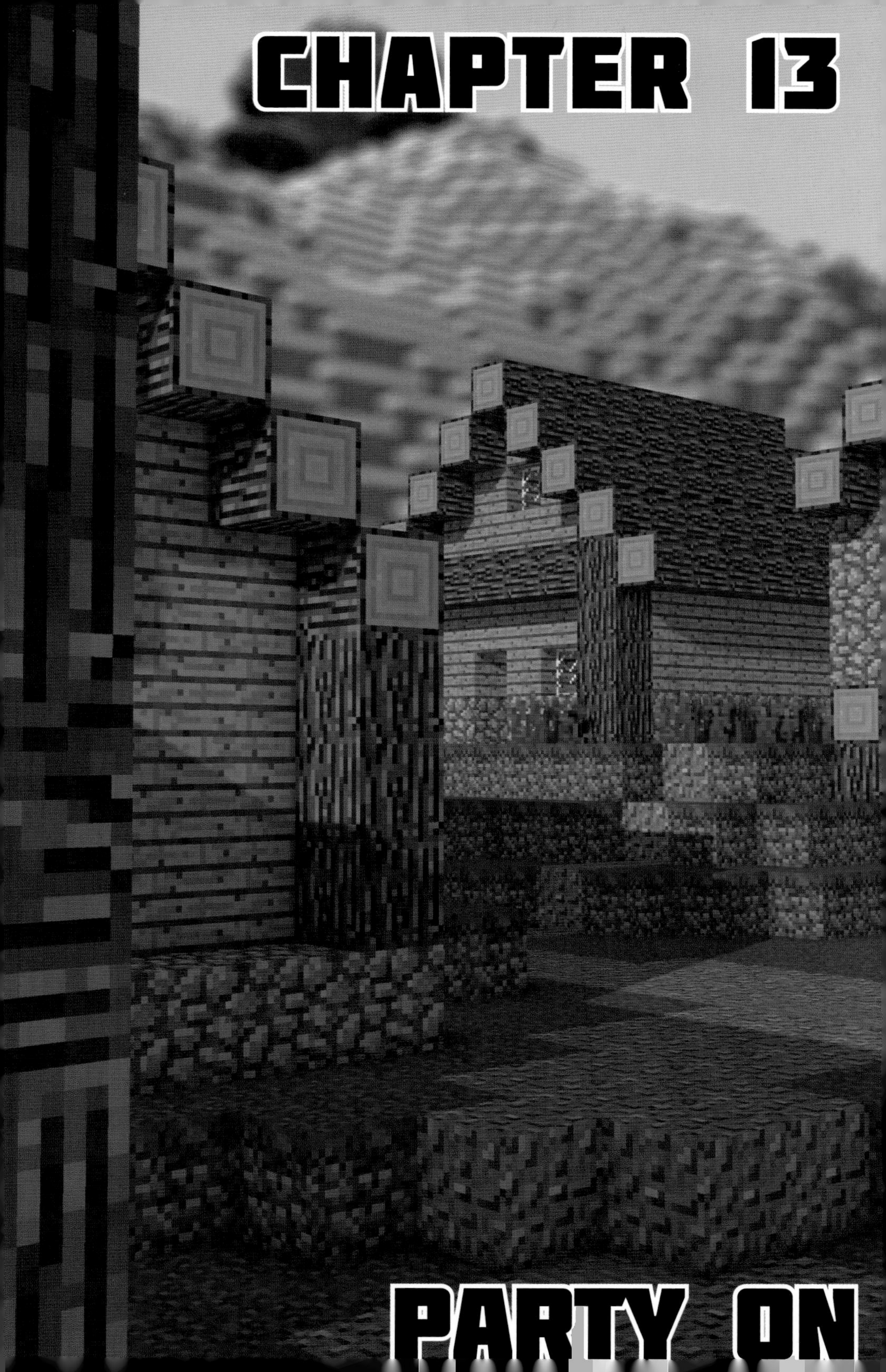

PARTY ON

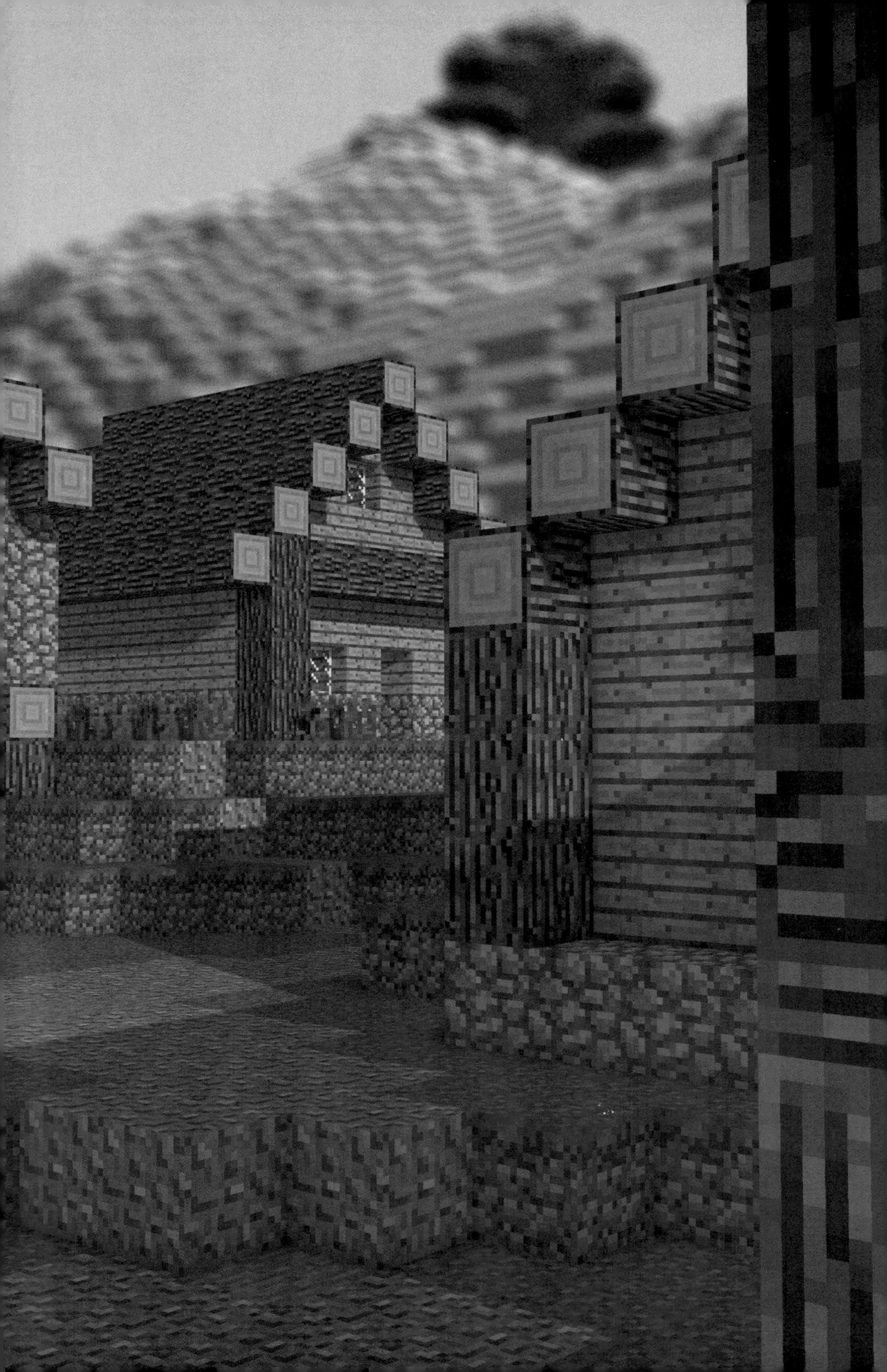

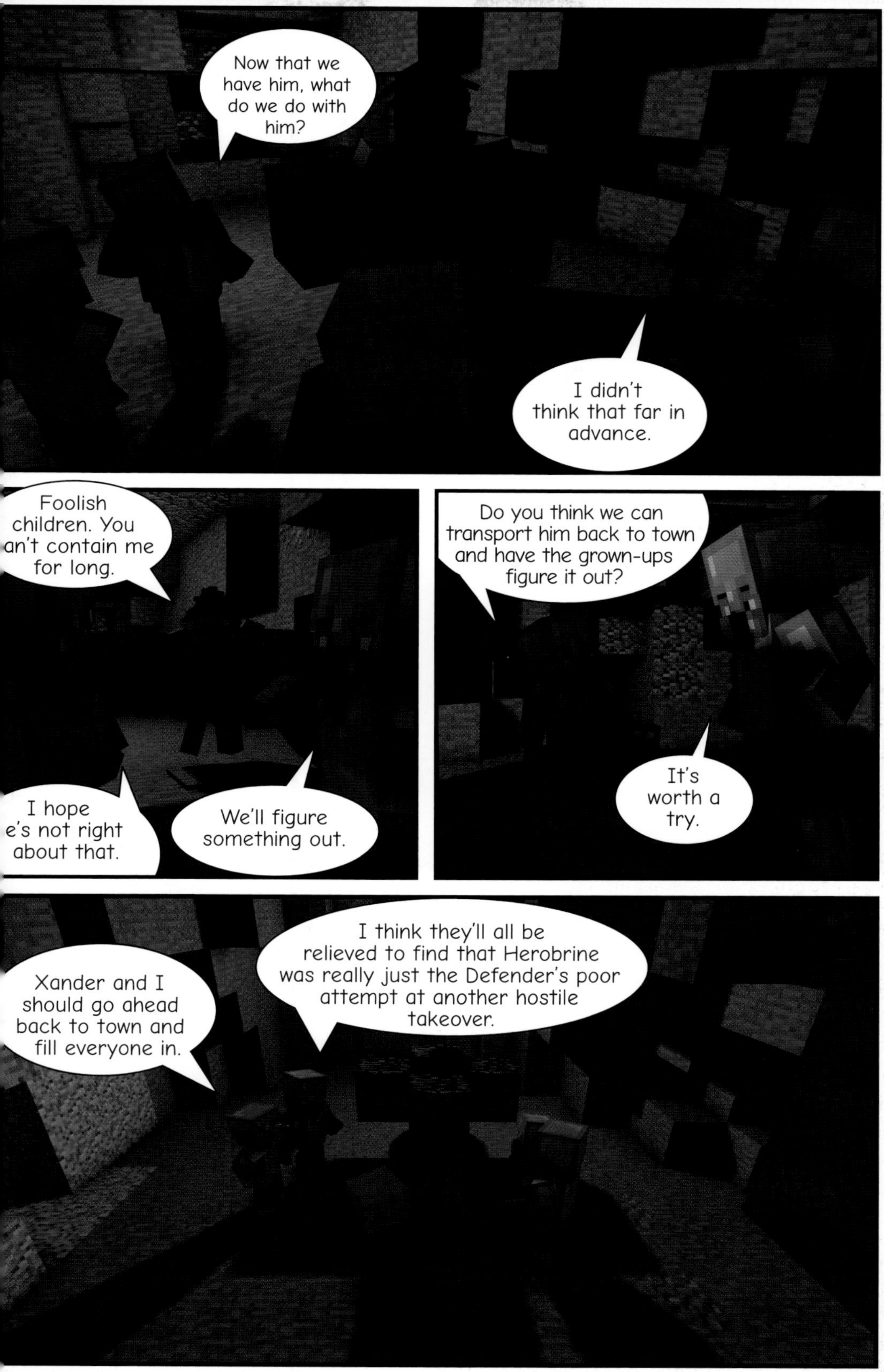
Now that we have him, what do we do with him?
I didn't think that far in advance.
Foolish children. You an't contain me for long.
I hope e's not right about that.
We'll figure something out.
Do you think we can transport him back to town and have the grown-ups figure it out?
It's worth a try.
Xander and I should go ahead back to town and fill everyone in.
I think they'll all be relieved to find that Herobrine was really just the Defender's poor attempt at another hostile takeover.

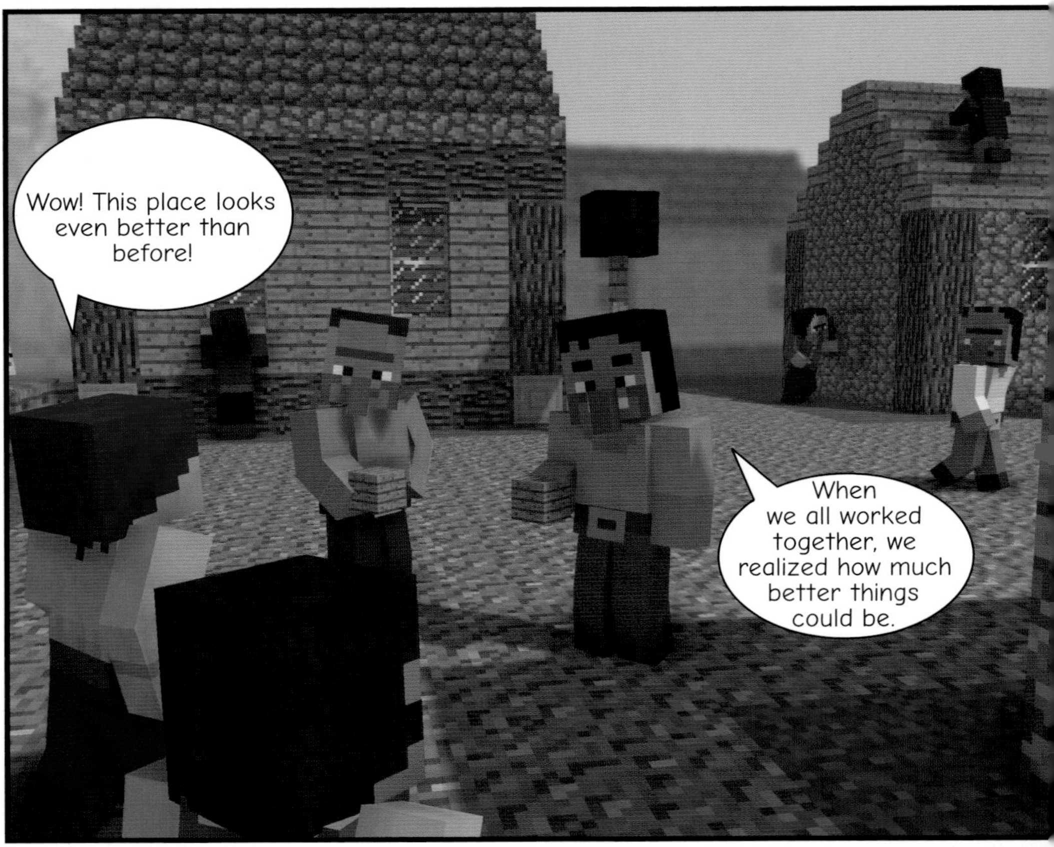
Wow! This place looks even better than before!
When we all worked together, we realized how much better things could be.

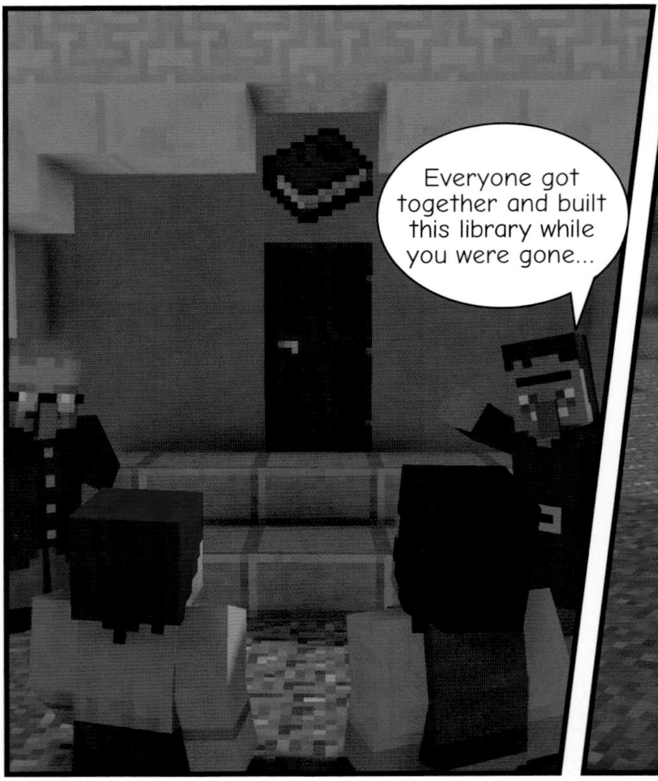
Everyone got together and built this library while you were gone...

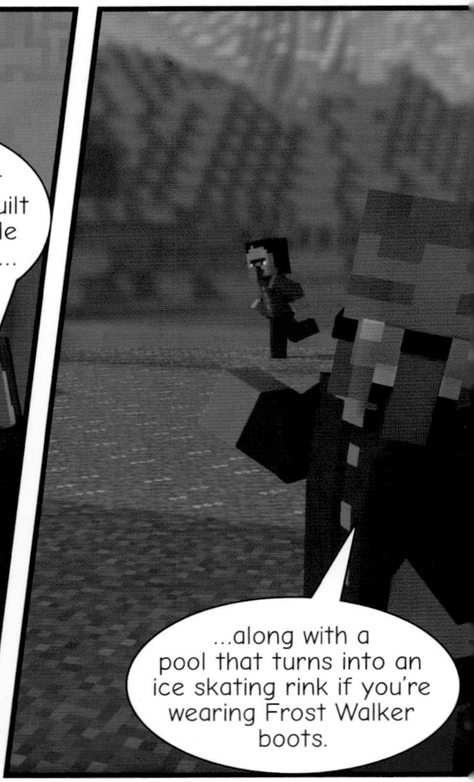
...along with a pool that turns into an ice skating rink if you're wearing Frost Walker boots.

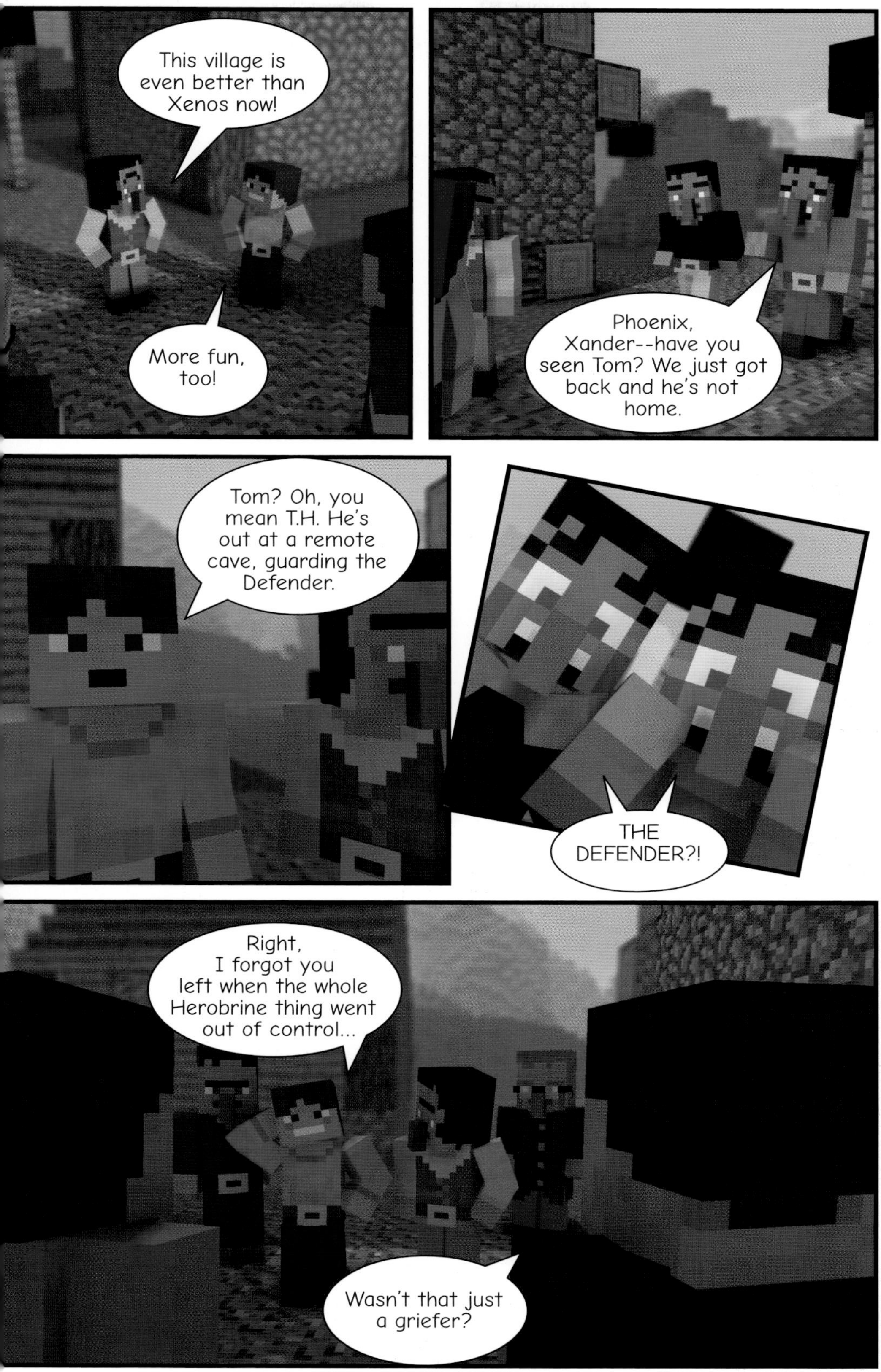
This village is even better than Xenos now!
More fun, too!
Phoenix, Xander--have you seen Tom? We just got back and he's not home.
Tom? Oh, you mean T.H. He's out at a remote cave, guarding the Defender.
THE DEFENDER?!
Right, I forgot you left when the whole Herobrine thing went out of control...
Wasn't that just a griefer?

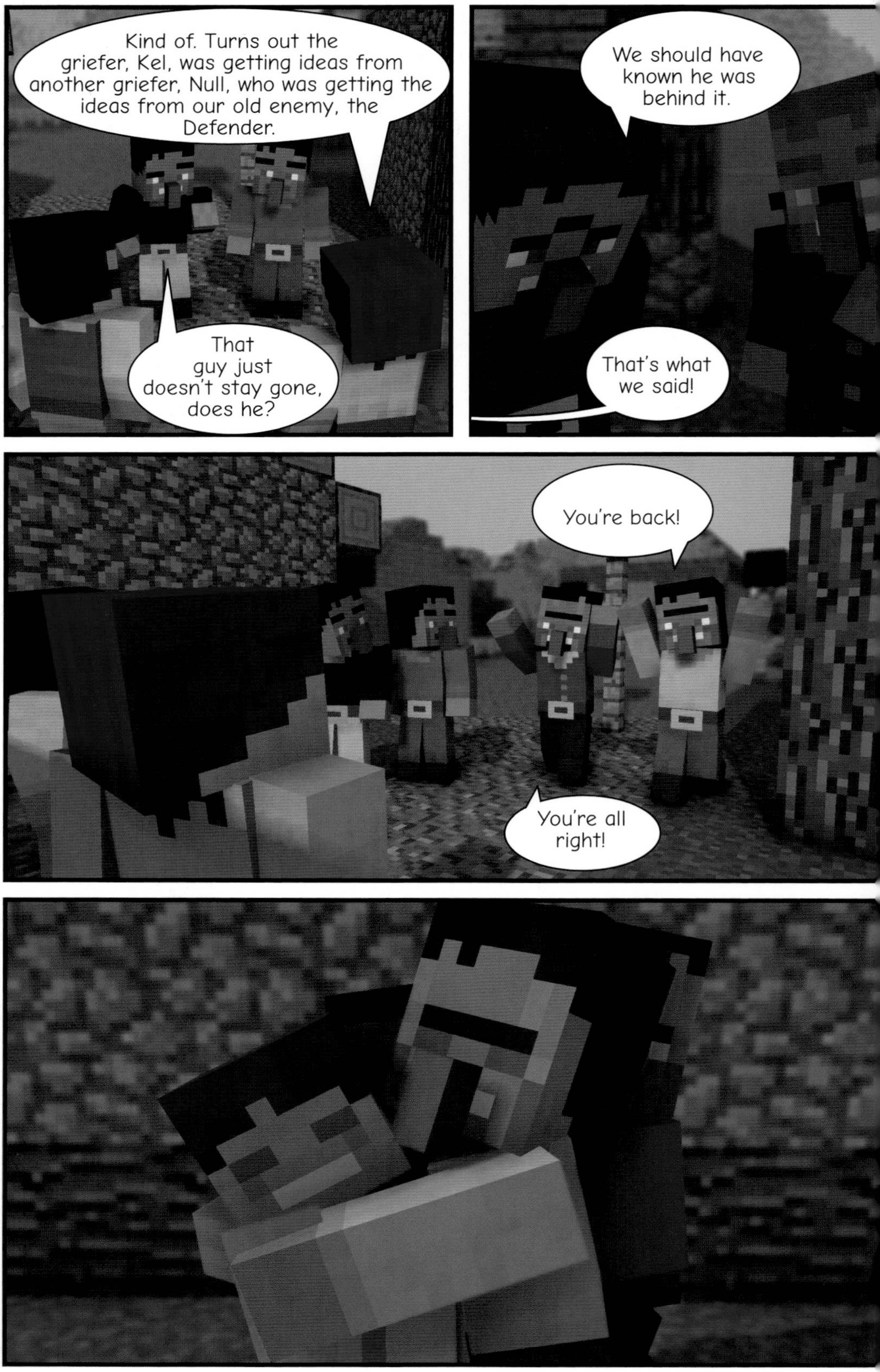
Kind of. Turns out the griefer, Kel, was getting ideas from another griefer, Null, who was getting the ideas from our old enemy, the Defender.
That guy just doesn't stay gone, does he?
We should have known he was behind it.
That's what we said!
You're back!
You're all right!

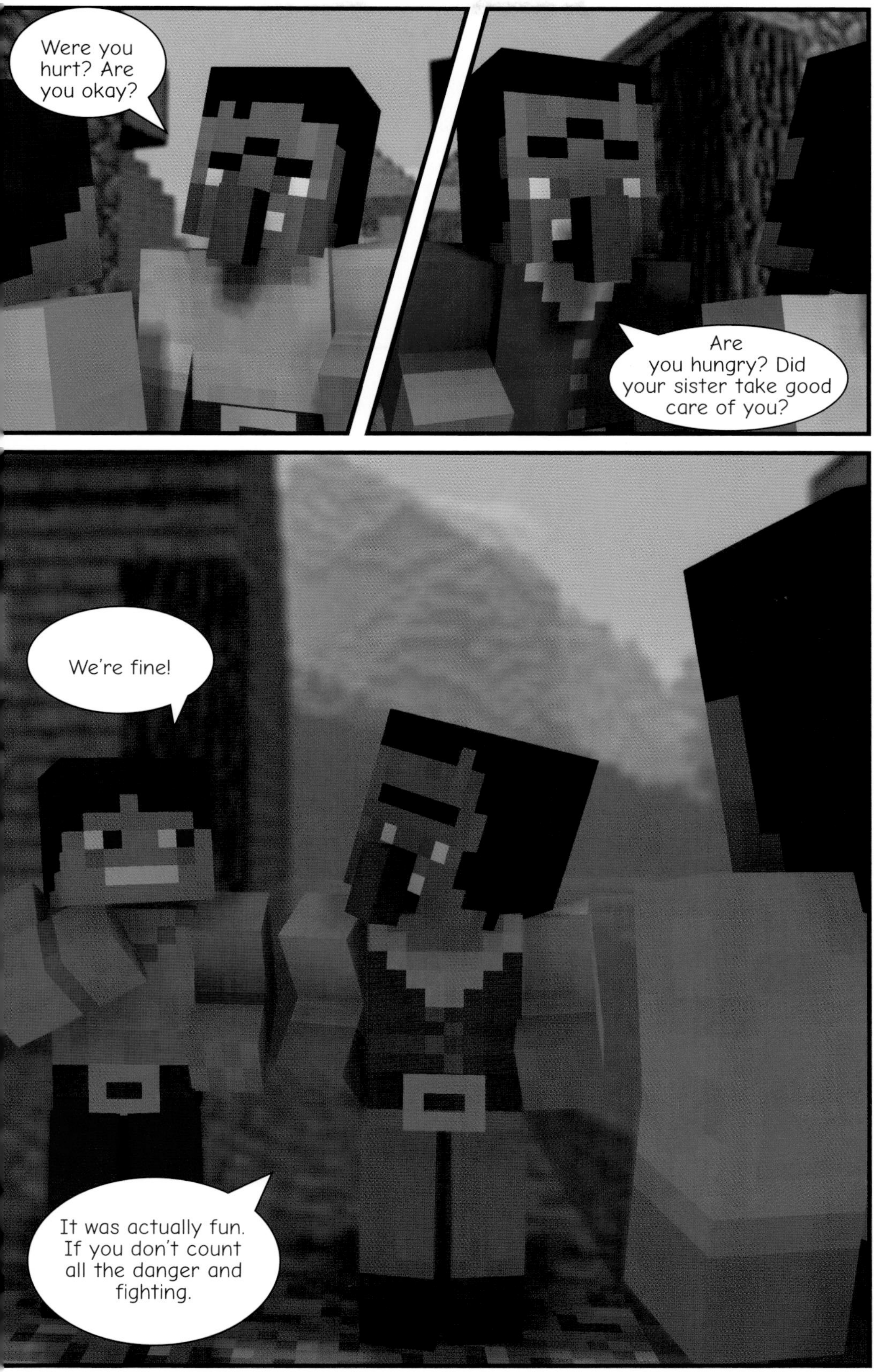
Were you hurt? Are you okay?
Are you hungry? Did your sister take good care of you?
We're fine!
It was actually fun. If you don't count all the danger and fighting.

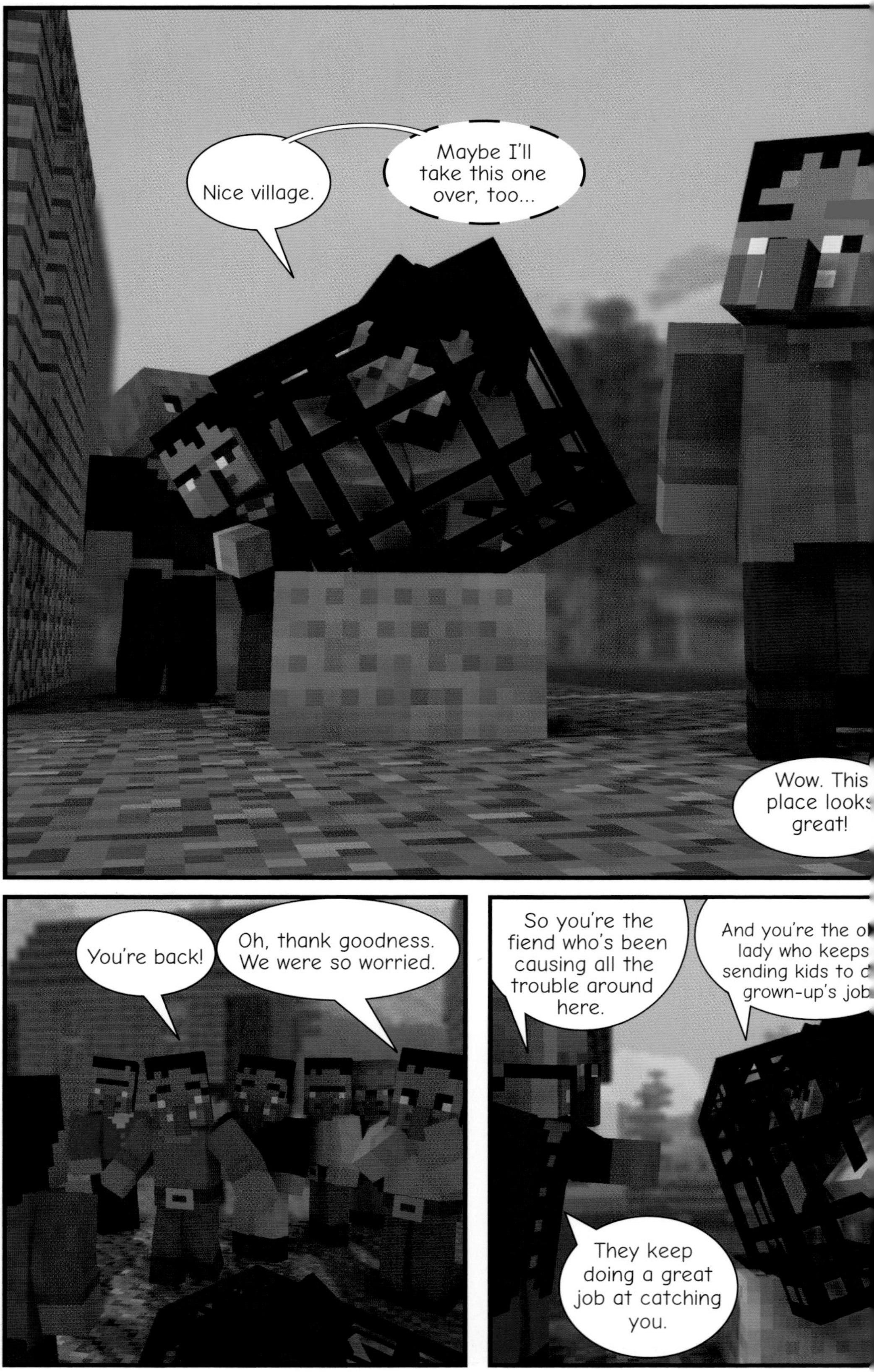

Nice village.
Maybe I'll take this one over, too...
Wow. This place looks great!
You're back!
Oh, thank goodness. We were so worried.
So you're the fiend who's been causing all the trouble around here.
And you're the o lady who keeps sending kids to d grown-up's job
They keep doing a great job at catching you.

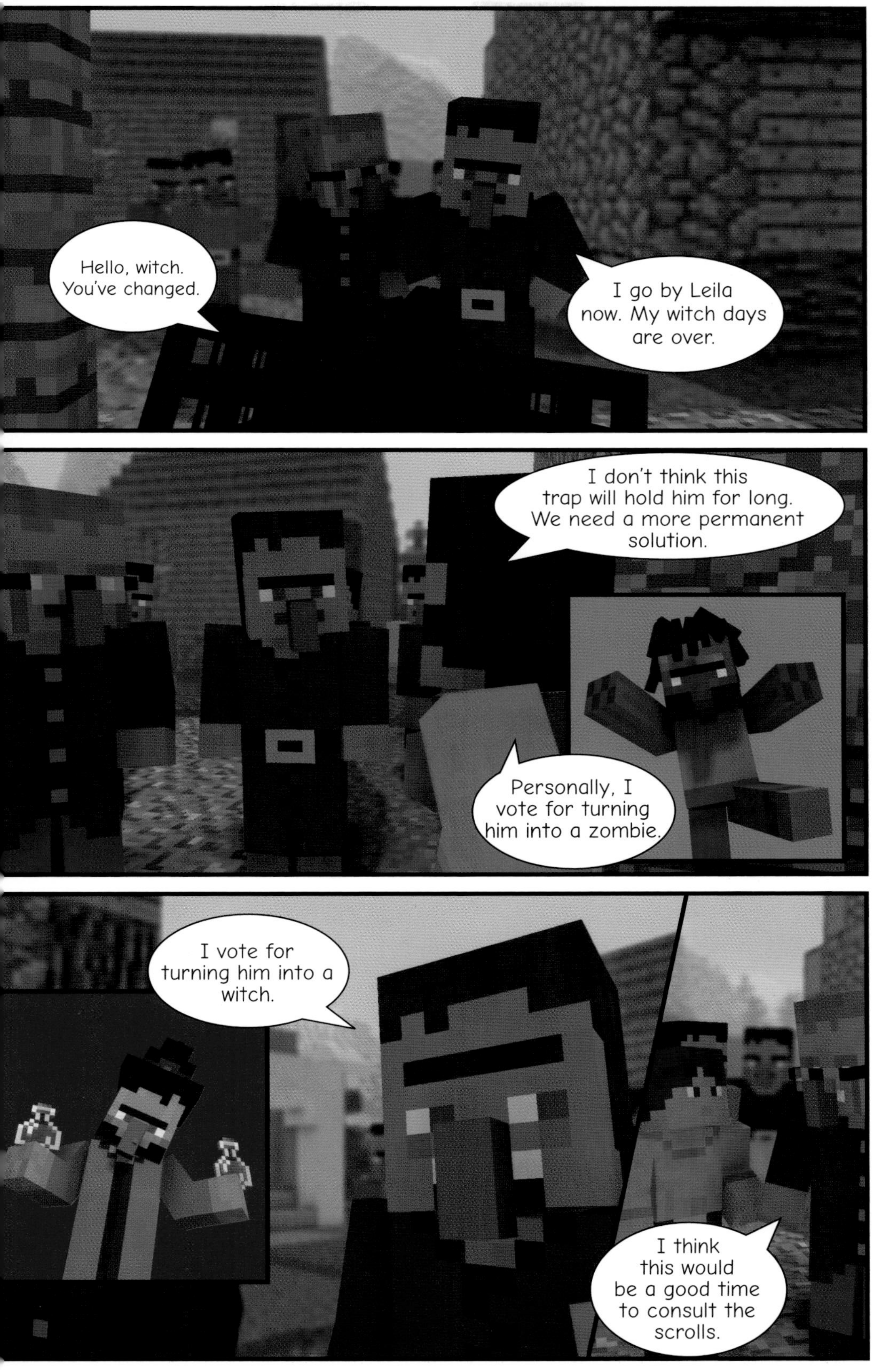
Hello, witch. You've changed.
I go by Leila now. My witch days are over.
I don't think this trap will hold him for long. We need a more permanent solution.
Personally, I vote for turning him into a zombie.
I vote for turning him into a witch.
I think this would be a good time to consult the scrolls.

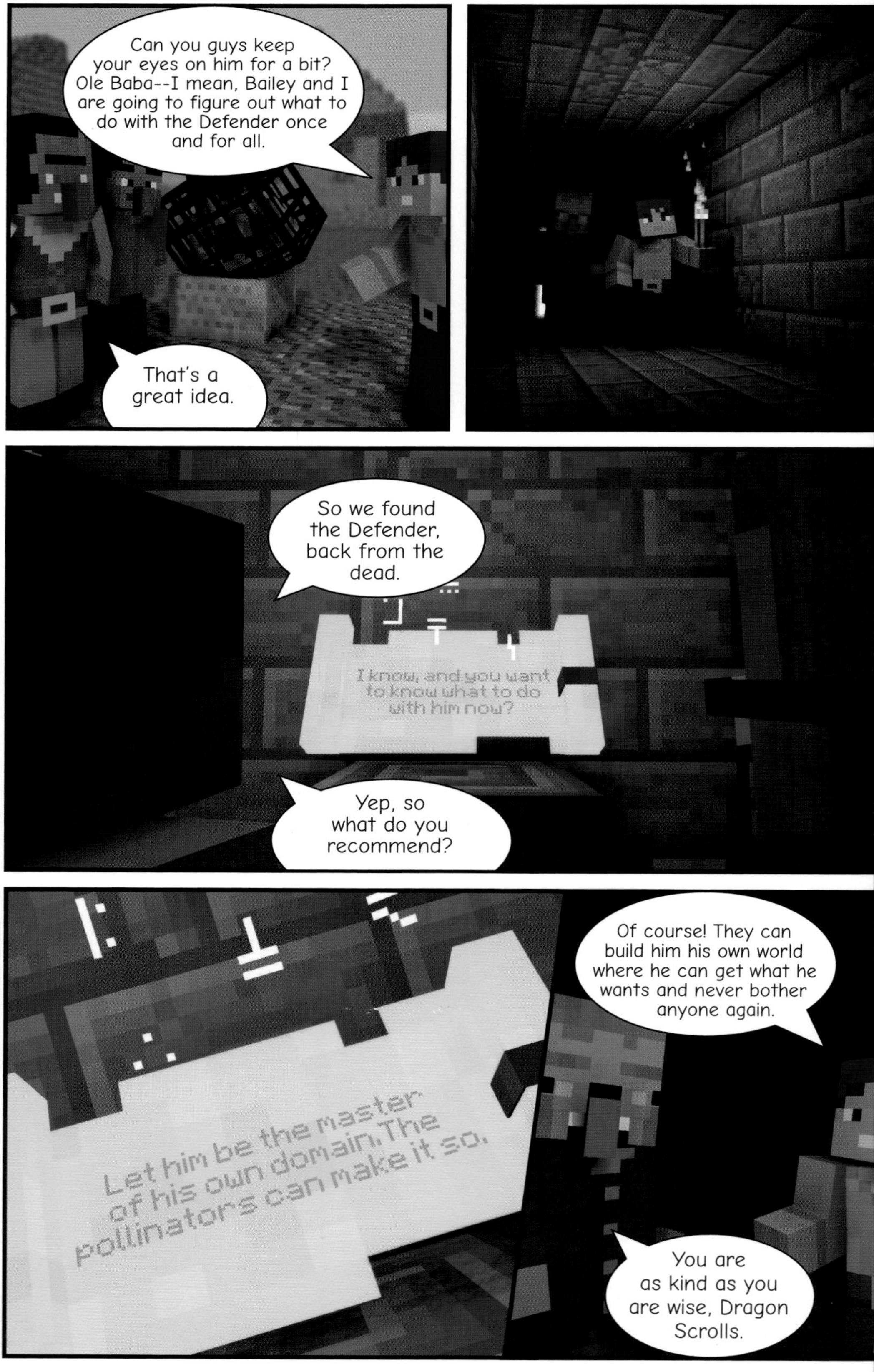
Can you guys keep your eyes on him for a bit? Ole Baba--I mean, Bailey and I are going to figure out what to do with the Defender once and for all.
That's a great idea.
So we found the Defender, back from the dead.
I know, and you want to know what to do with him now?
Yep, so what do you recommend?
Let him be the master of his own domain. The pollinators can make it so.
Of course! They can build him his own world where he can get what he wants and never bother anyone again.
You are as kind as you are wise, Dragon Scrolls.

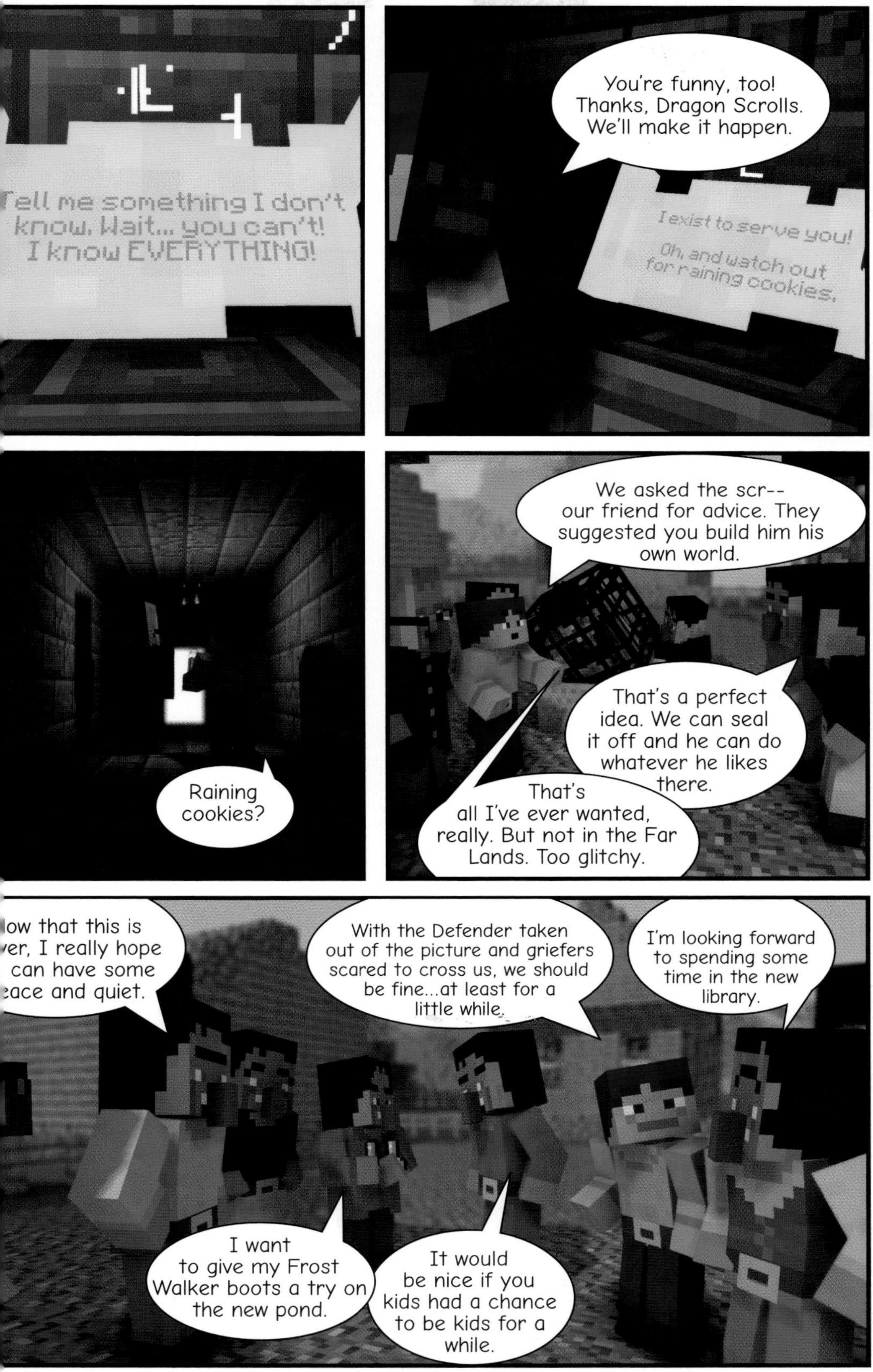
Tell me something I don't know. Wait... you can't! I know EVERYTHING!
You're funny, too! Thanks, Dragon Scrolls. We'll make it happen.
I exist to serve you!
Oh, and watch out for raining cookies.
Raining cookies?
We asked the scr-- our friend for advice. They suggested you build him his own world.
That's a perfect idea. We can seal it off and he can do whatever he likes there.
That's all I've ever wanted, really. But not in the Far Lands. Too glitchy.
ow that this is ver, I really hope can have some eace and quiet.
With the Defender taken out of the picture and griefers scared to cross us, we should be fine...at least for a little while.
I'm looking forward to spending some time in the new library.
I want to give my Frost Walker boots a try on the new pond.
It would be nice if you kids had a chance to be kids for a while.

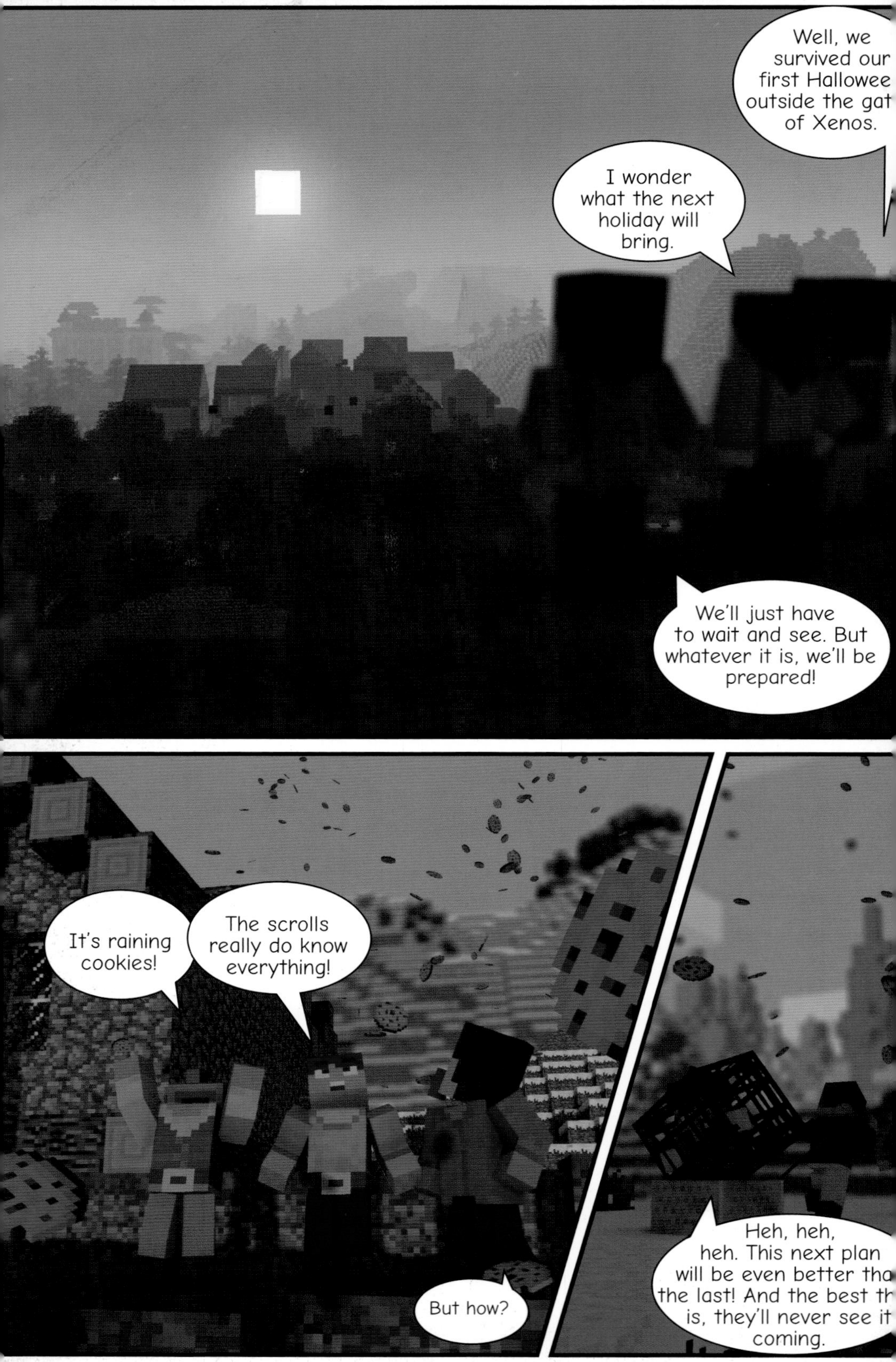
Well, we survived our first Hallowee outside the gat of Xenos.
I wonder what the next holiday will bring.
We'll just have to wait and see. But whatever it is, we'll be prepared!
It's raining cookies!
The scrolls really do know everything!
But how?
Heh, heh, heh. This next plan will be even better tha the last! And the best th is, they'll never see it coming.

AN UNOFFICIAL GRAPHIC NOVEL
FOR MINECRAFTERS

SAVING XENOS

CARA J. STEVENS
ART BY WALKER MELBY

SKY PONY PRESS
NEW YORK

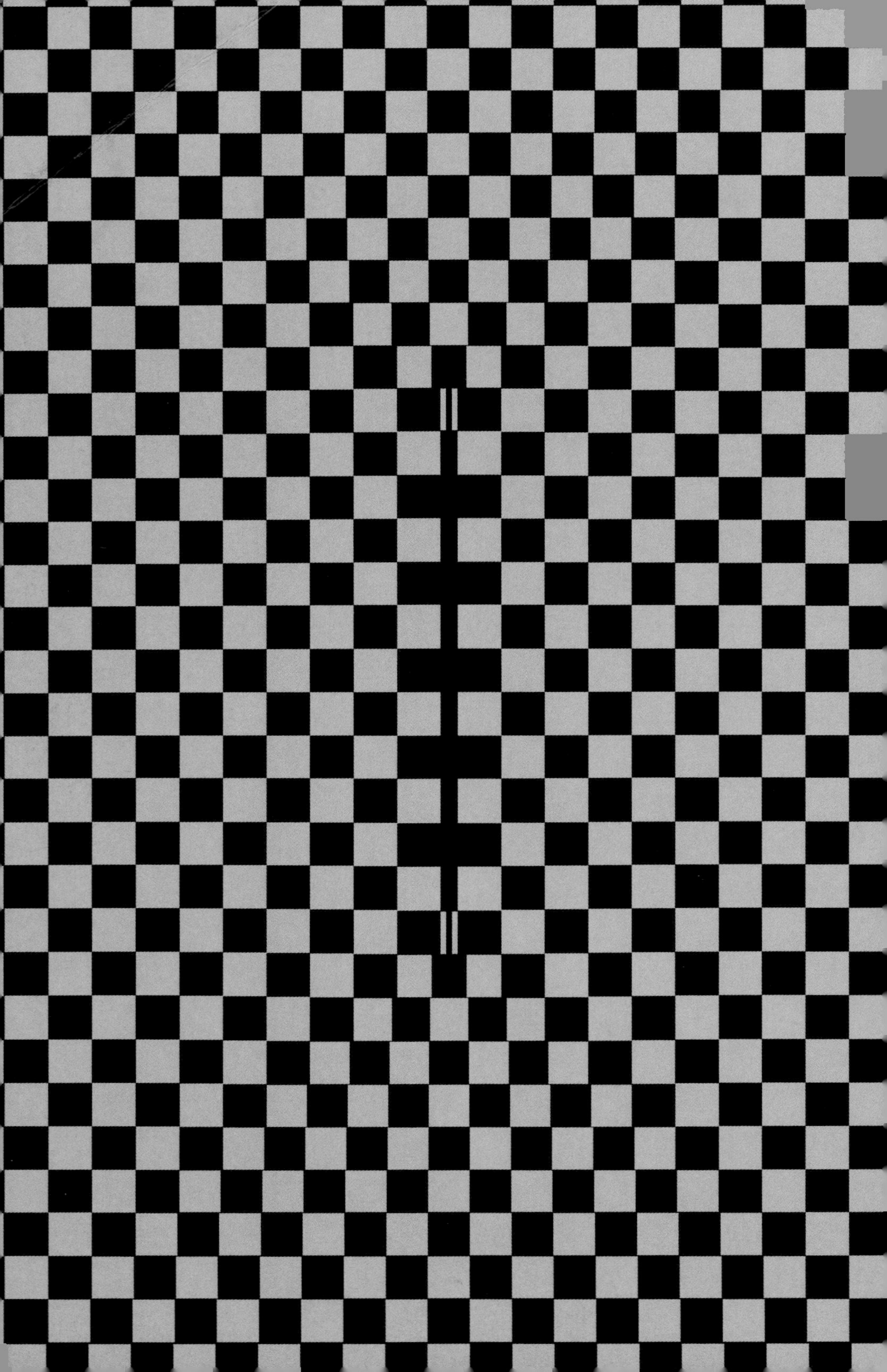

CHAPTER 1

ATCHING A PLAN

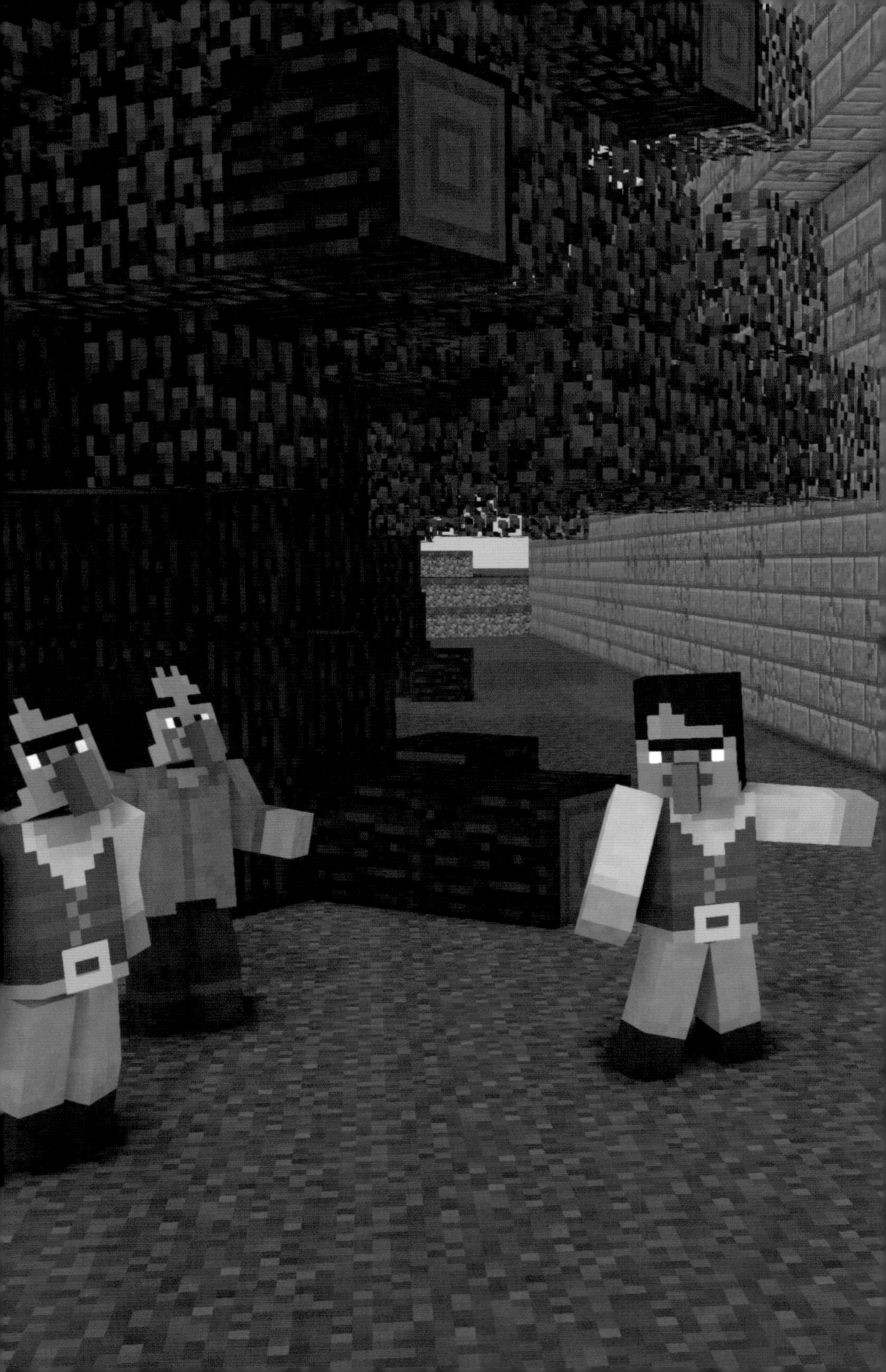

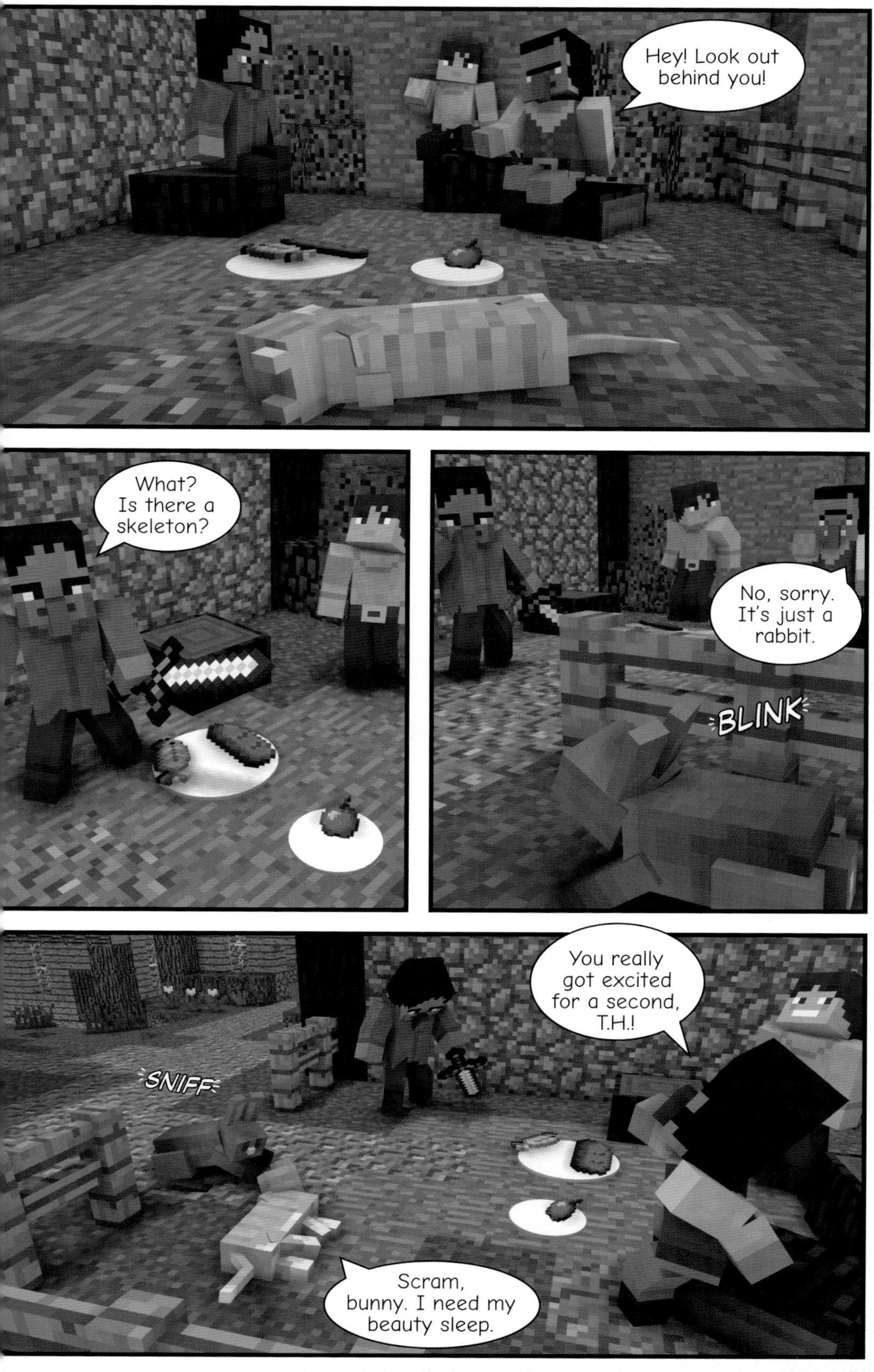
Hey! Look out behind you!
What? Is there a skeleton?
No, sorry. It's just a rabbit.
BLINK
You really got excited for a second, T.H.!
SNIFF
Scram, bunny. I need my beauty sleep.

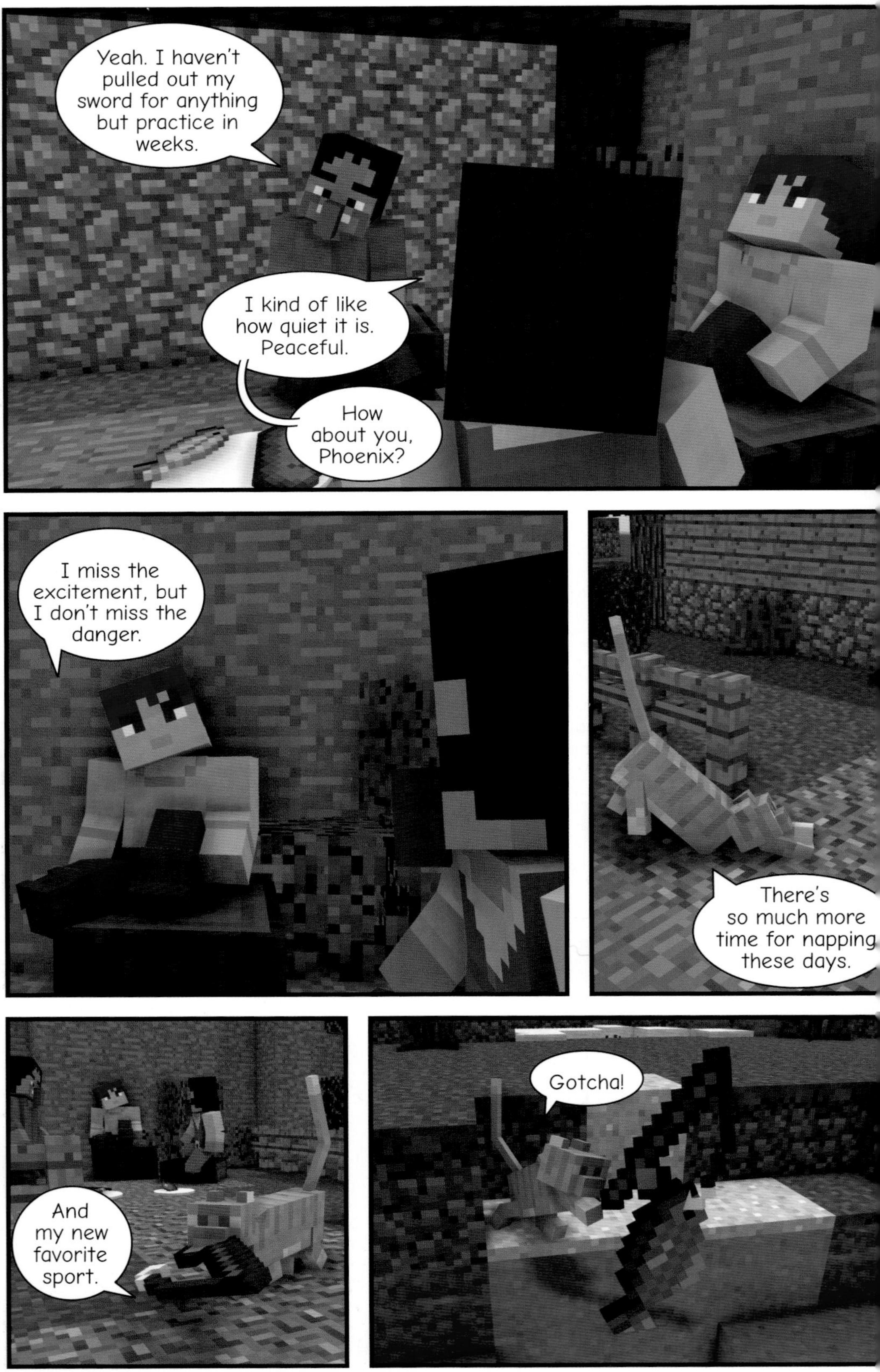
Yeah. I haven't pulled out my sword for anything but practice in weeks.
I kind of like how quiet it is. Peaceful.
How about you, Phoenix?
I miss the excitement, but I don't miss the danger.
There's so much more time for napping these days.
And my new favorite sport.
Gotcha!

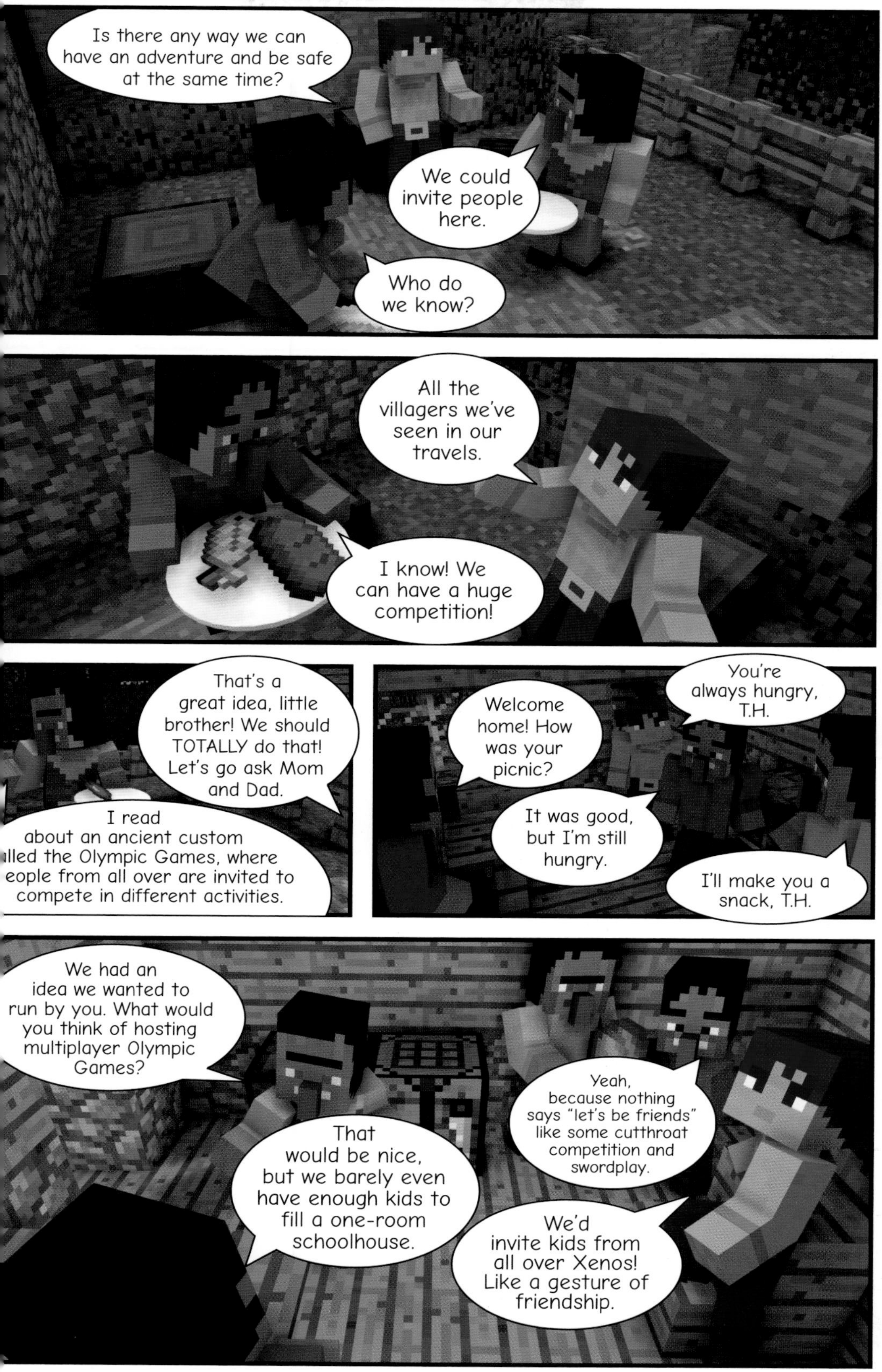
Is there any way we can have an adventure and be safe at the same time?
We could invite people here.
Who do we know?
All the villagers we've seen in our travels.
I know! We can have a huge competition!
I read about an ancient custom
lled the Olympic Games, where
eople from all over are invited to compete in different activities.
That's a great idea, little brother! We should TOTALLY do that! Let's go ask Mom and Dad.
Welcome home! How was your picnic?
You're always hungry, T.H.
It was good, but I'm still hungry.
I'll make you a snack, T.H.
We had an idea we wanted to run by you. What would you think of hosting multiplayer Olympic Games?
That would be nice, but we barely even have enough kids to fill a one-room schoolhouse.
We'd invite kids from all over Xenos! Like a gesture of friendship.
Yeah, because nothing says "let's be friends" like some cutthroat competition and swordplay.

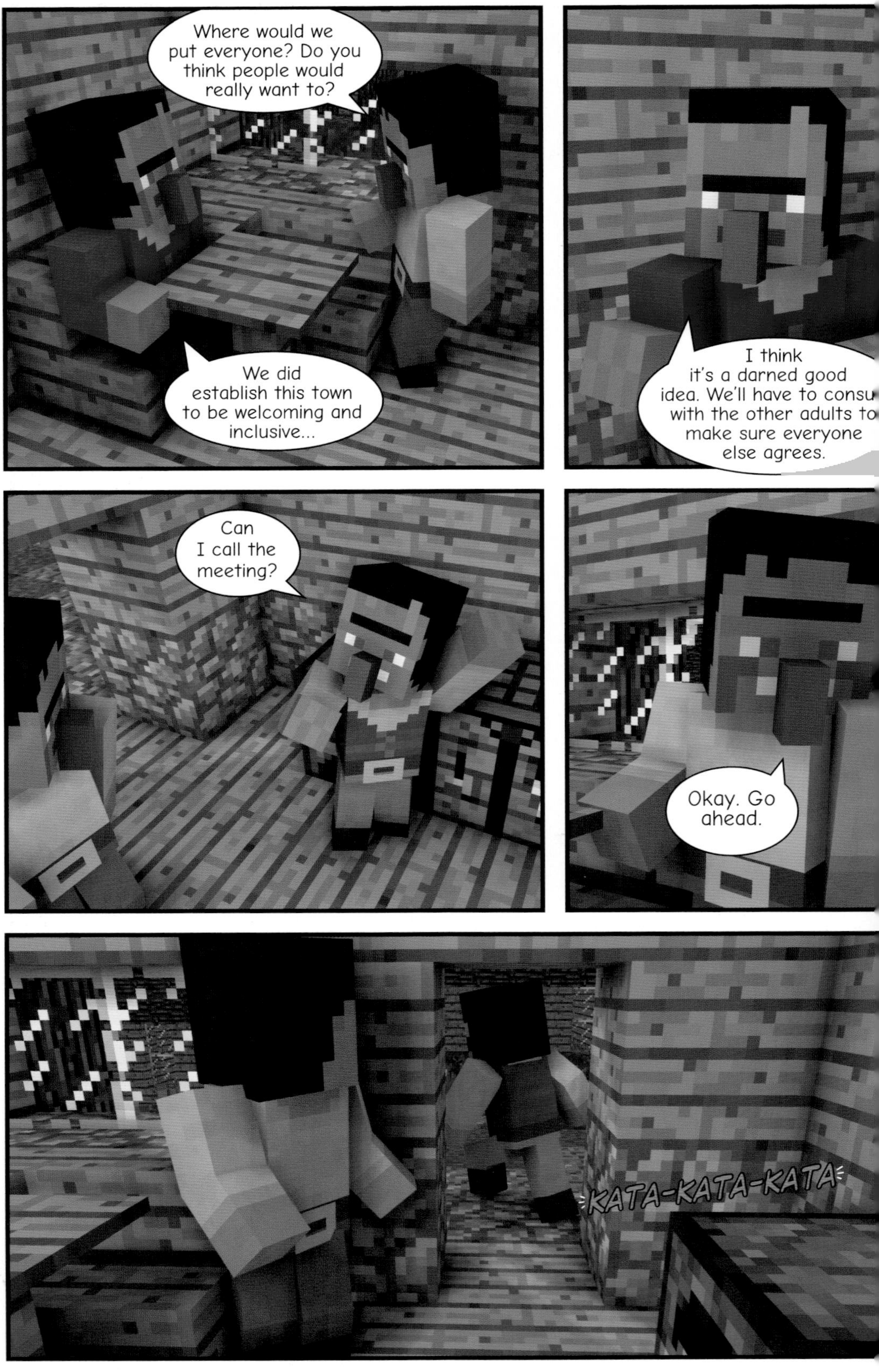
Where would we put everyone? Do you think people would really want to?
We did establish this town to be welcoming and inclusive...
I think it's a darned good idea. We'll have to consu
with the other adults to
make sure everyone else agrees.
Can I call the meeting?
Okay. Go ahead.
KATA-KATA-KATA

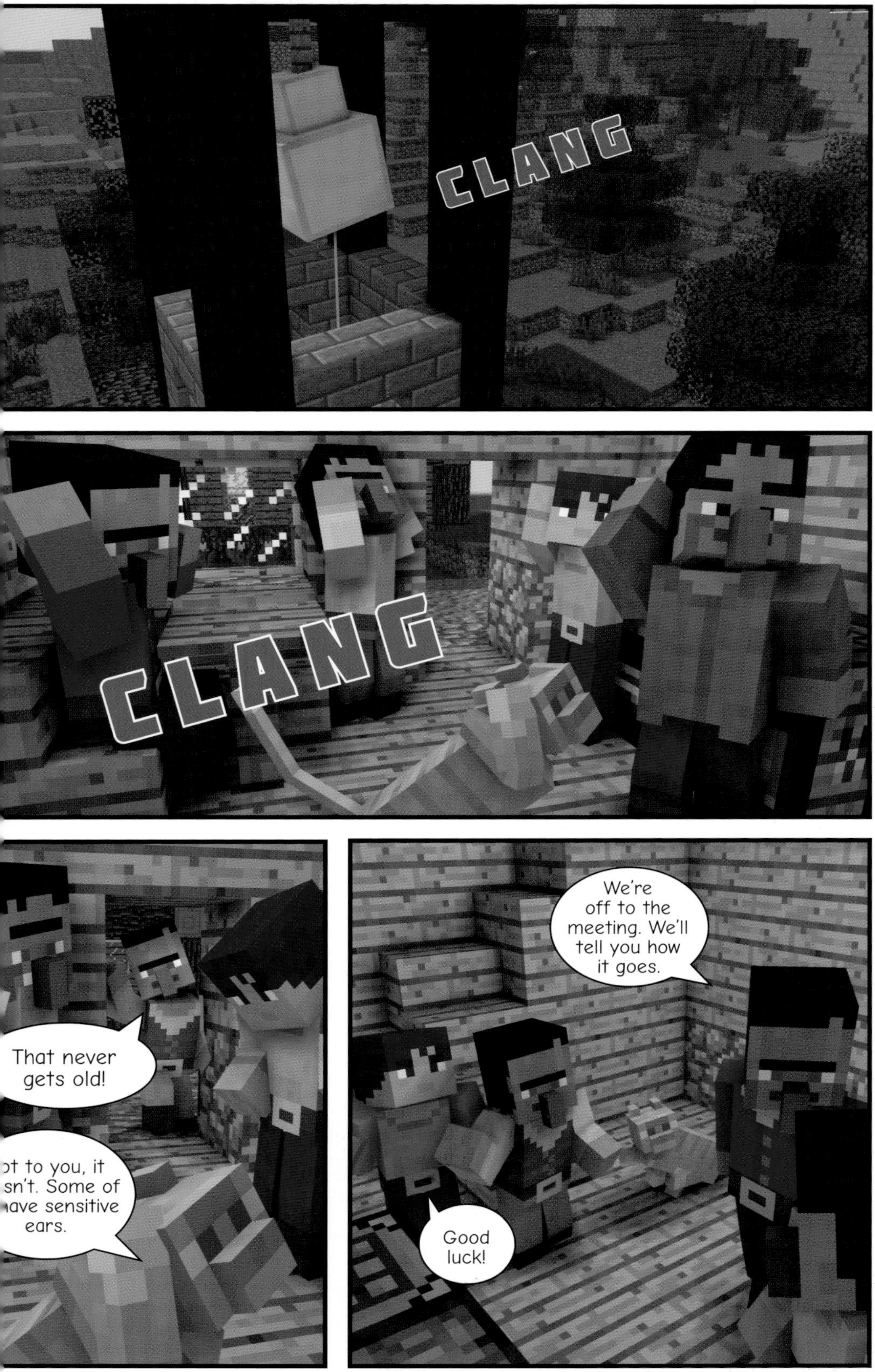
CLANG
CLANG
That never gets old!
ot to you, it sn't. Some of ave sensitive ears.
We're off to the meeting. We'll tell you how it goes.
Good luck!

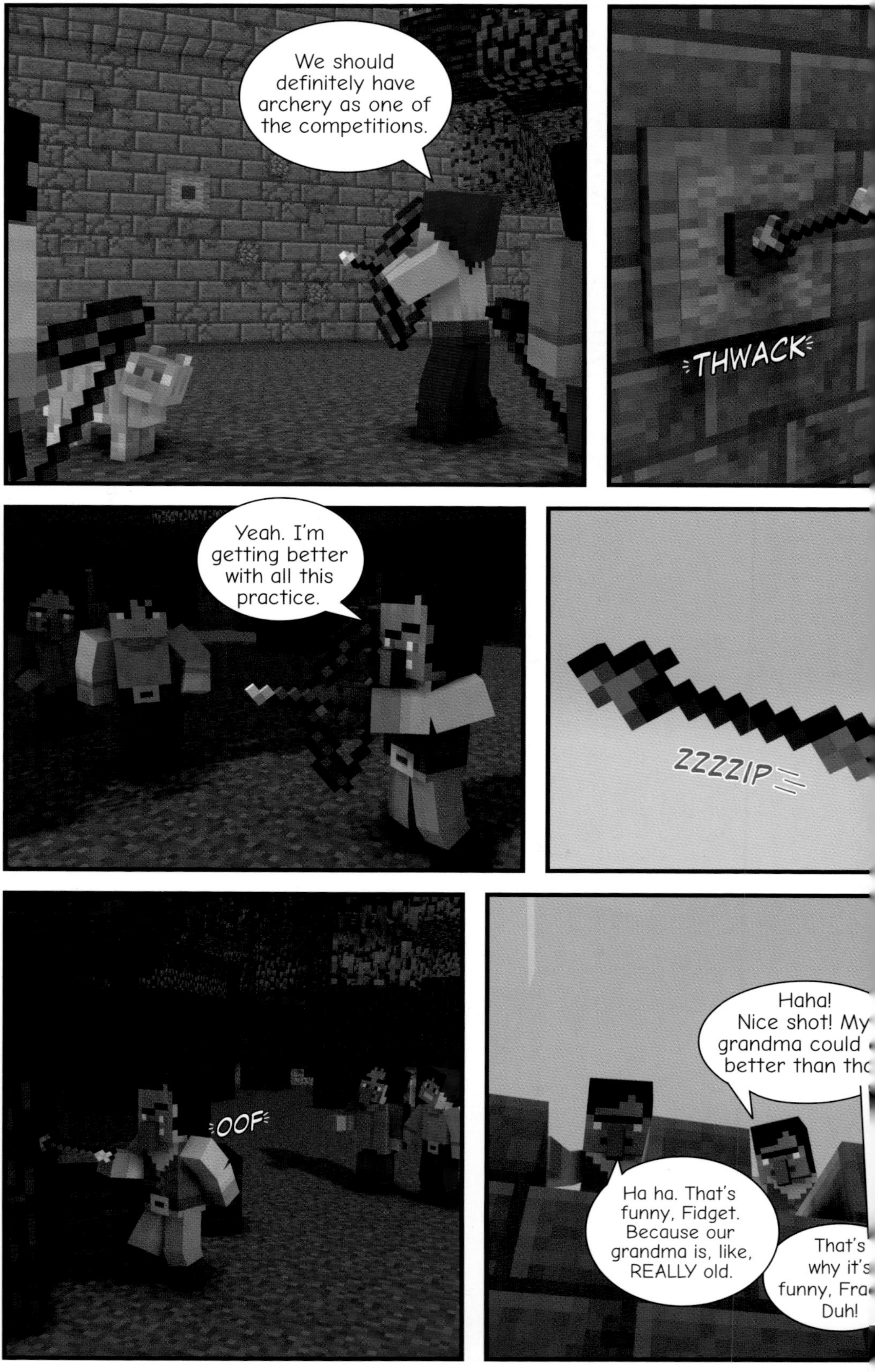
We should definitely have archery as one of the competitions.
THWACK
Yeah. I'm getting better with all this practice.
ZZZZIP
OOF
Haha! Nice shot! My grandma could better than th
Ha ha. That's funny, Fidget. Because our grandma is, like, REALLY old.
That's why it's funny, Fra Duh!

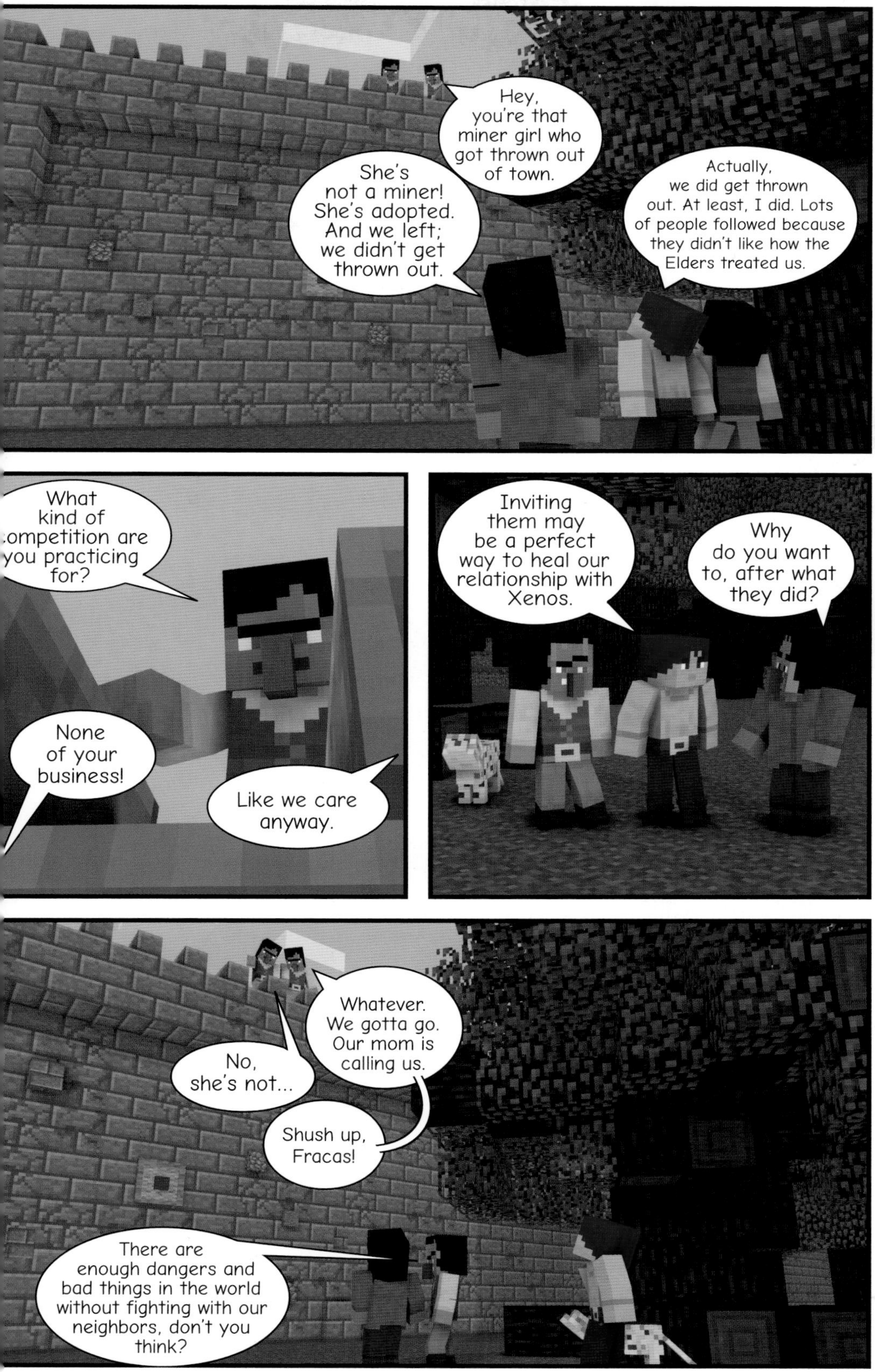
Hey, you're that miner girl who got thrown out of town.
She's not a miner! She's adopted. And we left; we didn't get thrown out.
Actually, we did get thrown out. At least, I did. Lots of people followed because they didn't like how the Elders treated us.
What kind of competition are you practicing for?
None of your business!
Like we care anyway.
Inviting them may be a perfect way to heal our relationship with Xenos.
Why do you want to, after what they did?
Whatever. We gotta go. Our mom is calling us.
No, she's not...
Shush up, Fracas!
There are enough dangers and bad things in the world without fighting with our neighbors, don't you think?

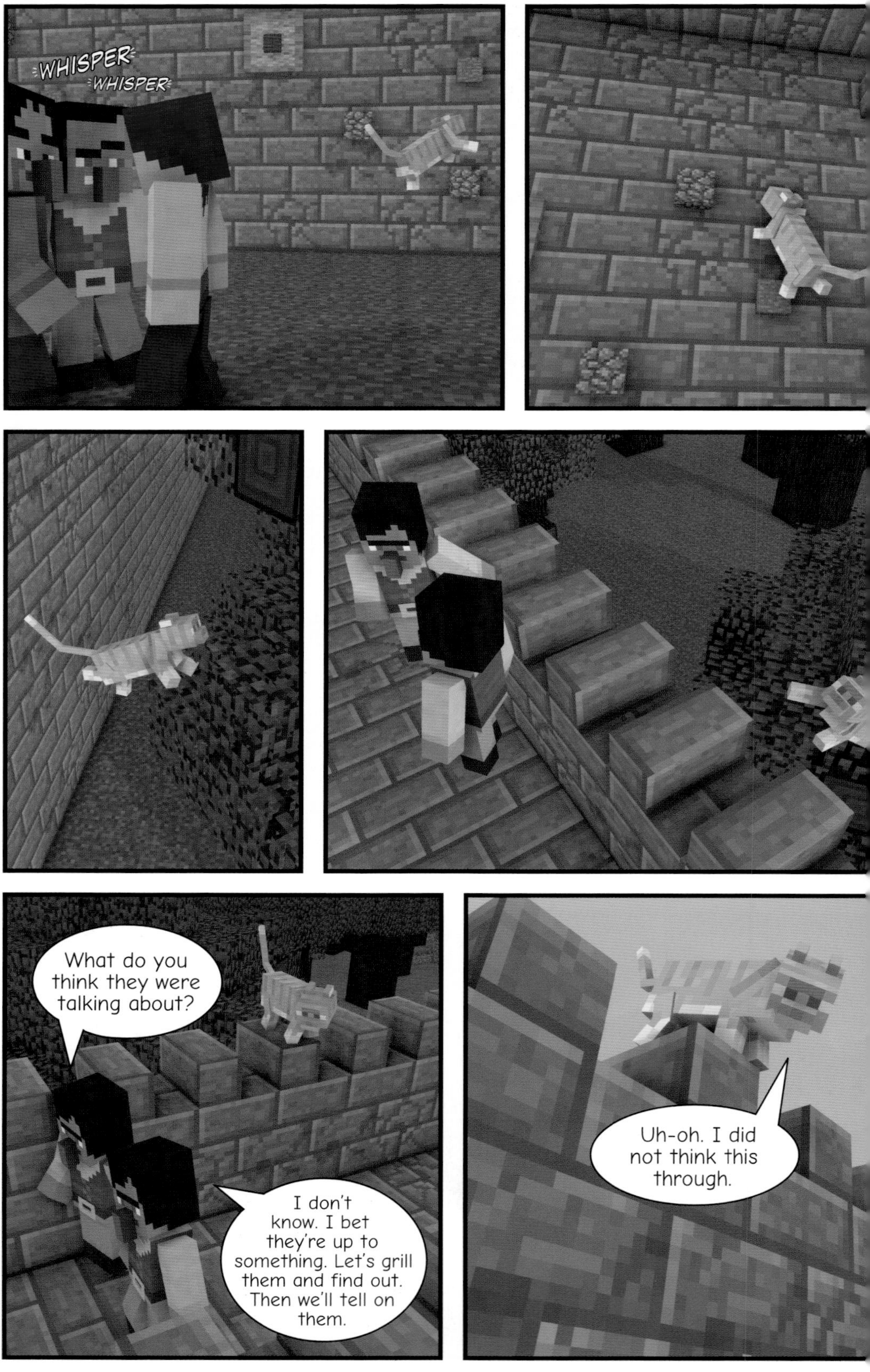
WHISPER
WHISPER
What do you think they were talking about?
I don't know. I bet they're up to something. Let's grill them and find out. Then we'll tell on them.
Uh-oh. I did not think this through.

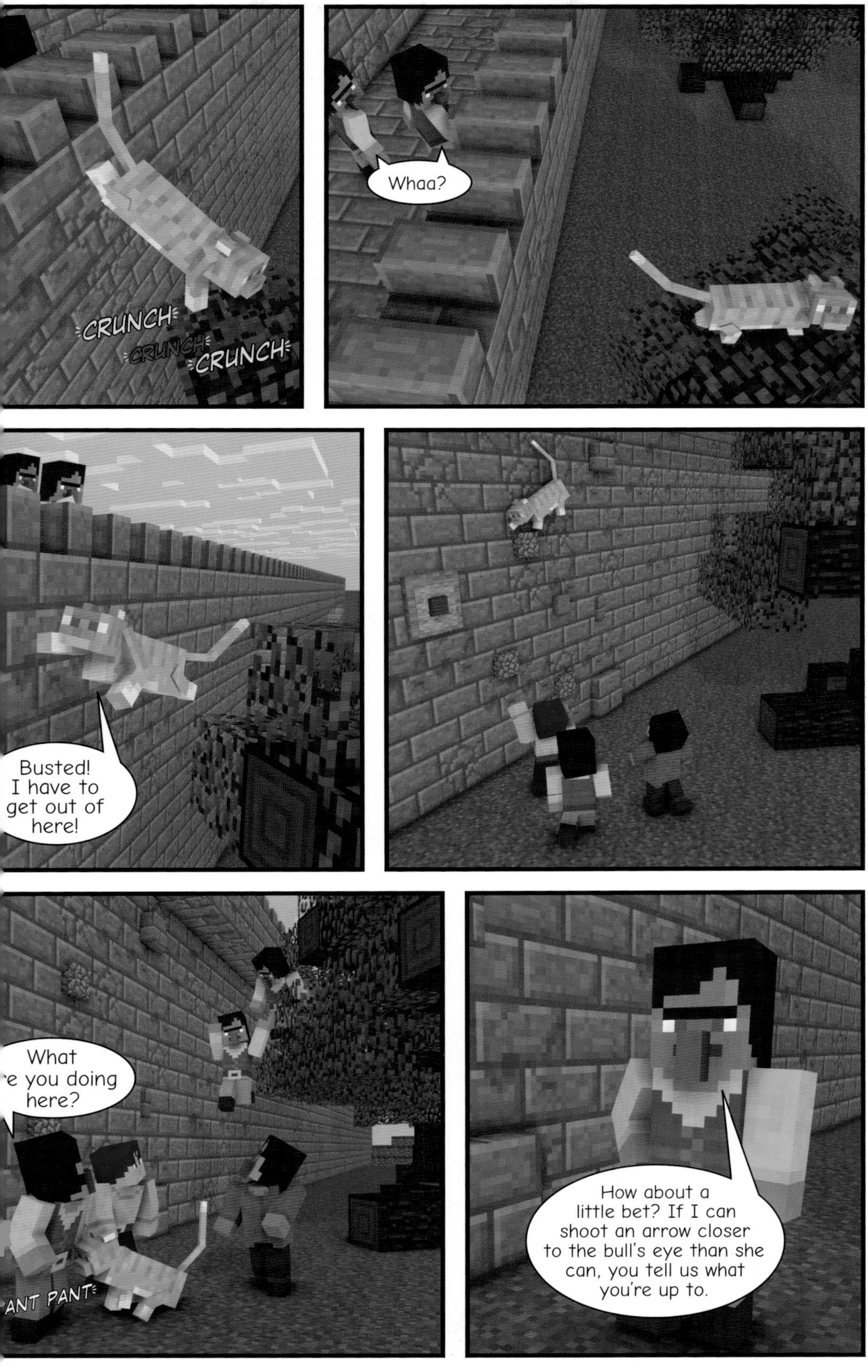
CRUNCH
CRUNCH
CRUNCH
Whaa?
Busted! I have to get out of here!
What 're you doing here?
PANT PANT
How about a little bet? If I can shoot an arrow closer to the bull's eye than she can, you tell us what you're up to.

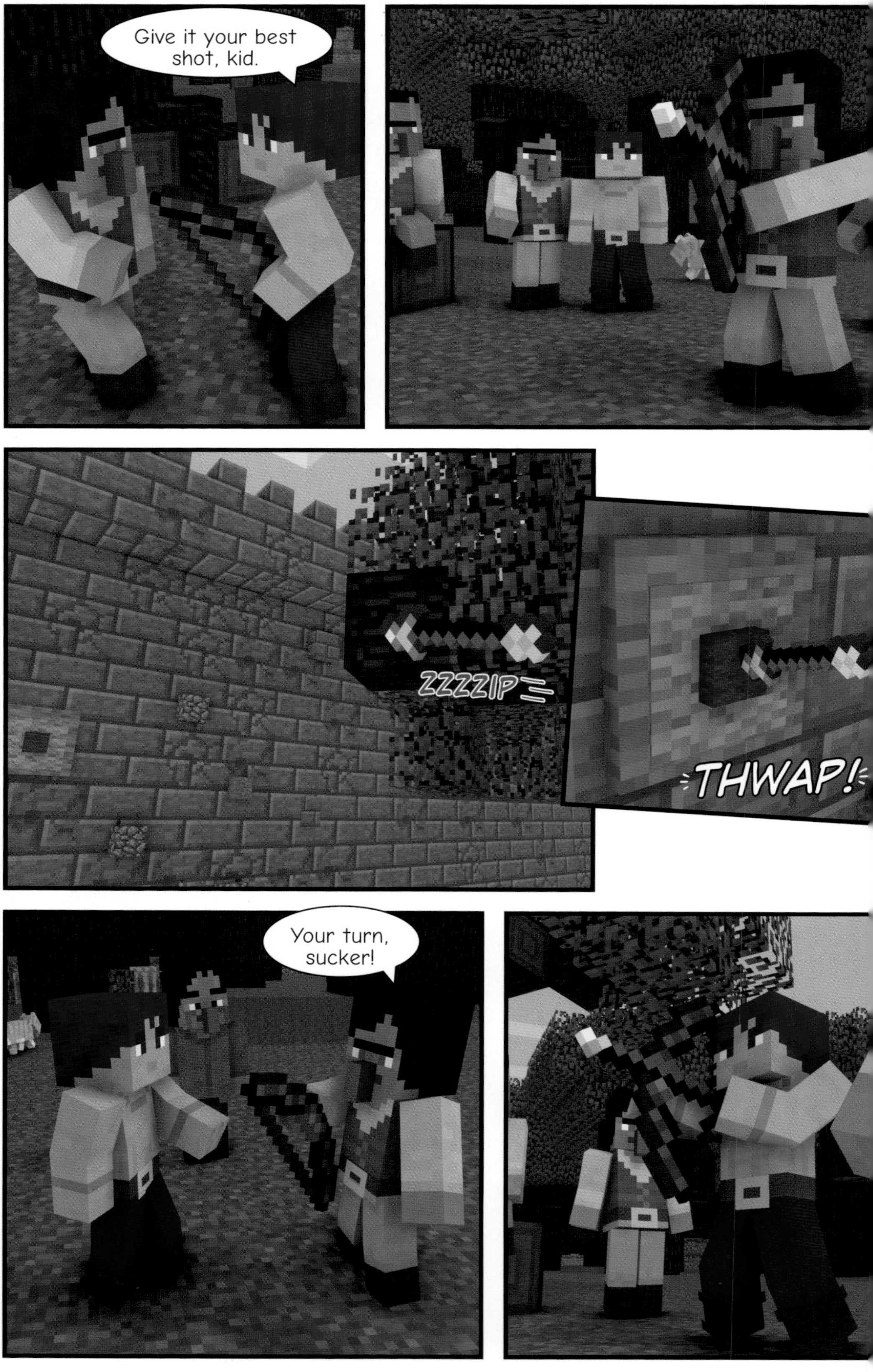
Give it your best shot, kid.
ZZZZIP
THWAP!
Your turn, sucker!

SPLIT!

Sorry, kids!

She totally schooled you, Fracas!

ur name's Fidget, ght? Why don't you ry? Just for fun.

It does look like fun...

Give it a try!

ld it just a little er than the target en you're this far ck... like this.

Thanks!

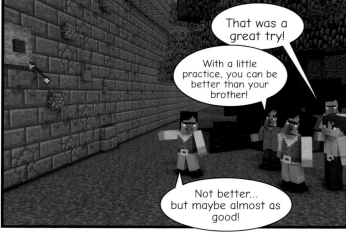

That was a great try!

With a little practice, you can be better than your brother!

Not better... but maybe almost as good!

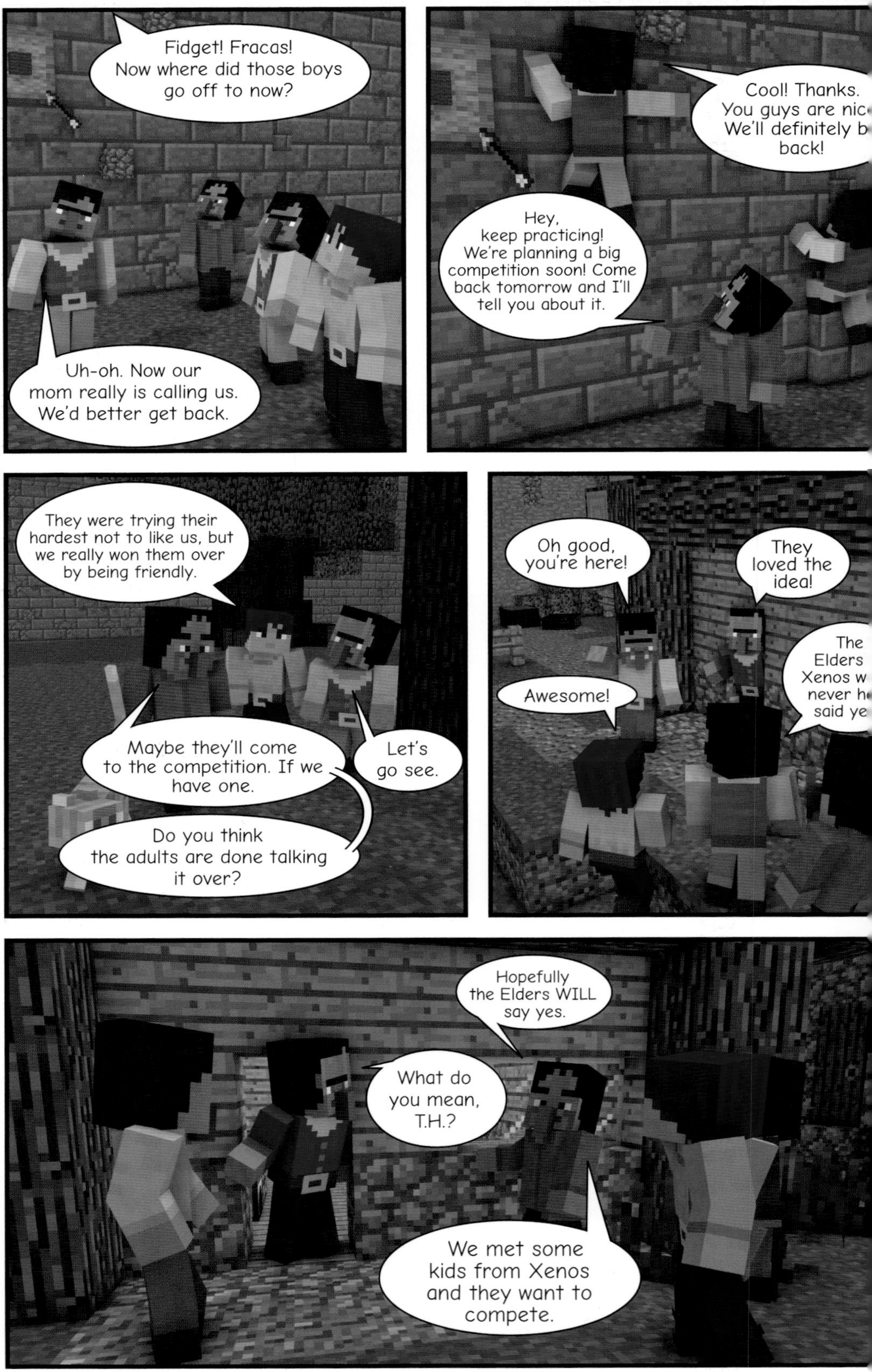
Fidget! Fracas! Now where did those boys go off to now?
Uh-oh. Now our mom really is calling us. We'd better get back.
Cool! Thanks. You guys are nic We'll definitely b back!
Hey, keep practicing! We're planning a big competition soon! Come back tomorrow and I'll tell you about it.
They were trying their hardest not to like us, but we really won them over by being friendly.
Maybe they'll come to the competition. If we have one.
Do you think the adults are done talking it over?
Let's go see.
Oh good, you're here!
They loved the idea!
Awesome!
The Elders Xenos w never h said ye
Hopefully the Elders WILL say yes.
What do you mean, T.H.?
We met some kids from Xenos and they want to compete.

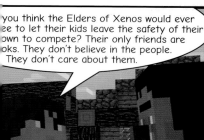

you think the Elders of Xenos would ever
ee to let their kids leave the safety of their
own to compete? Their only friends are
oks. They don't believe in the people.
They don't care about them.

YES!

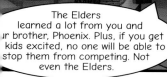

The Elders
learned a lot from you and
ur brother, Phoenix. Plus, if you get
kids excited, no one will be able to
stop them from competing. Not
even the Elders.

But
how do we get
the word out to
everyone?

Wolfie and his
family can deliver
invitations

Wolfie and Crystal
are coming tonight for the Full
Moon Festival. They're the perfect
messengers!

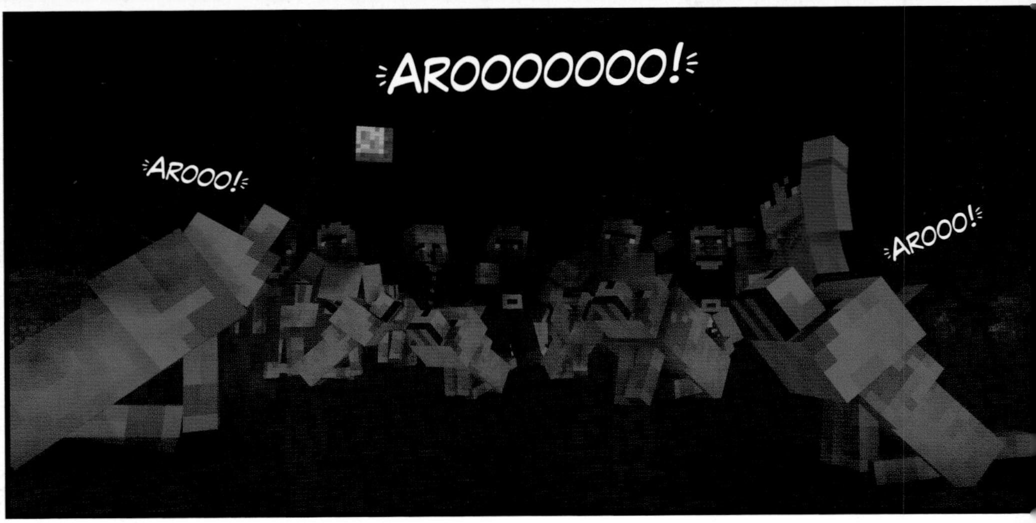
AROOOOOOO!
AROOO!
AROOO!

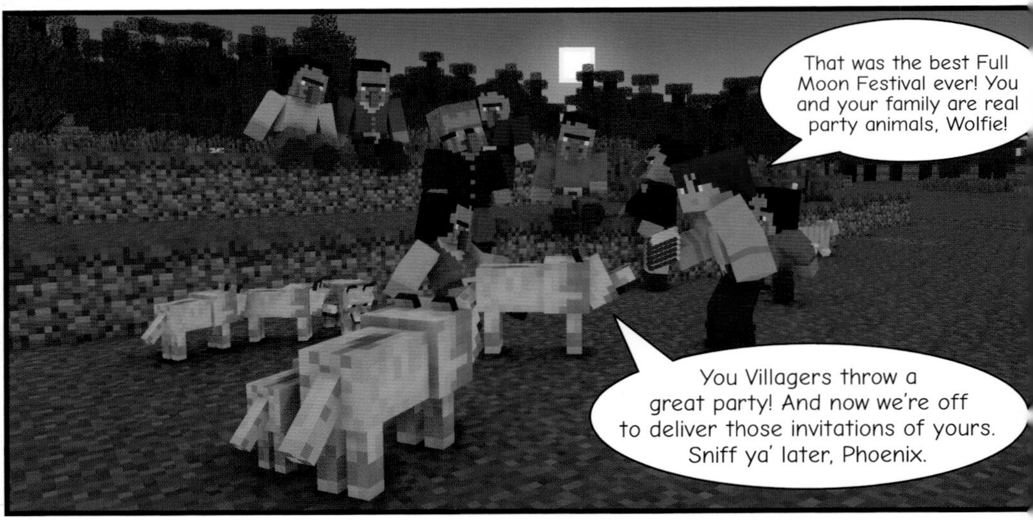
That was the best Full Moon Festival ever! You and your family are real party animals, Wolfie!
You Villagers throw a great party! And now we're off to deliver those invitations of yours. Sniff ya' later, Phoenix.

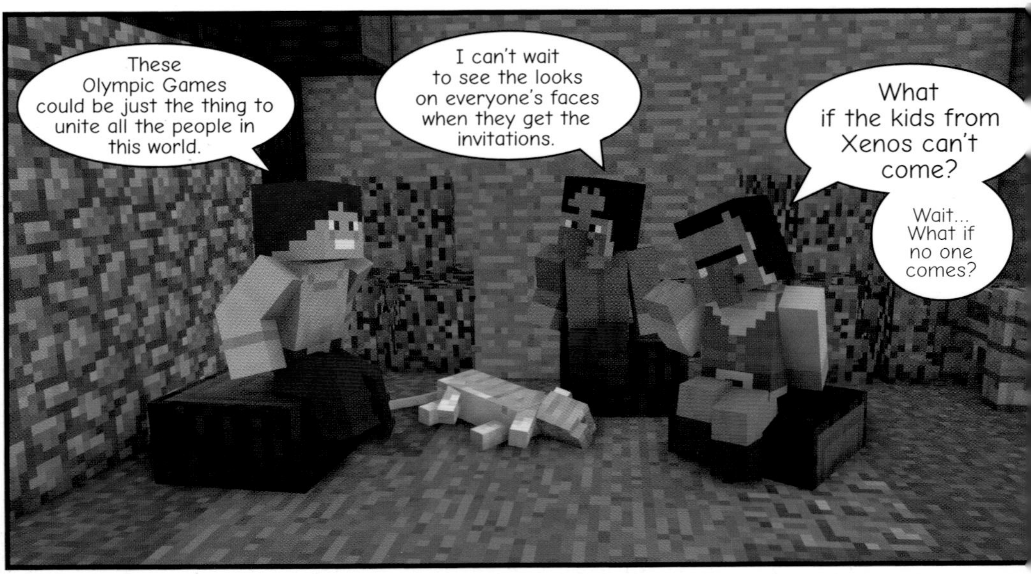
These Olympic Games could be just the thing to unite all the people in this world.
I can't wait to see the looks on everyone's faces when they get the invitations.
What if the kids from Xenos can't come?
Wait... What if no one comes?

CHAPTER 2

THE FIRST OLYMPICS

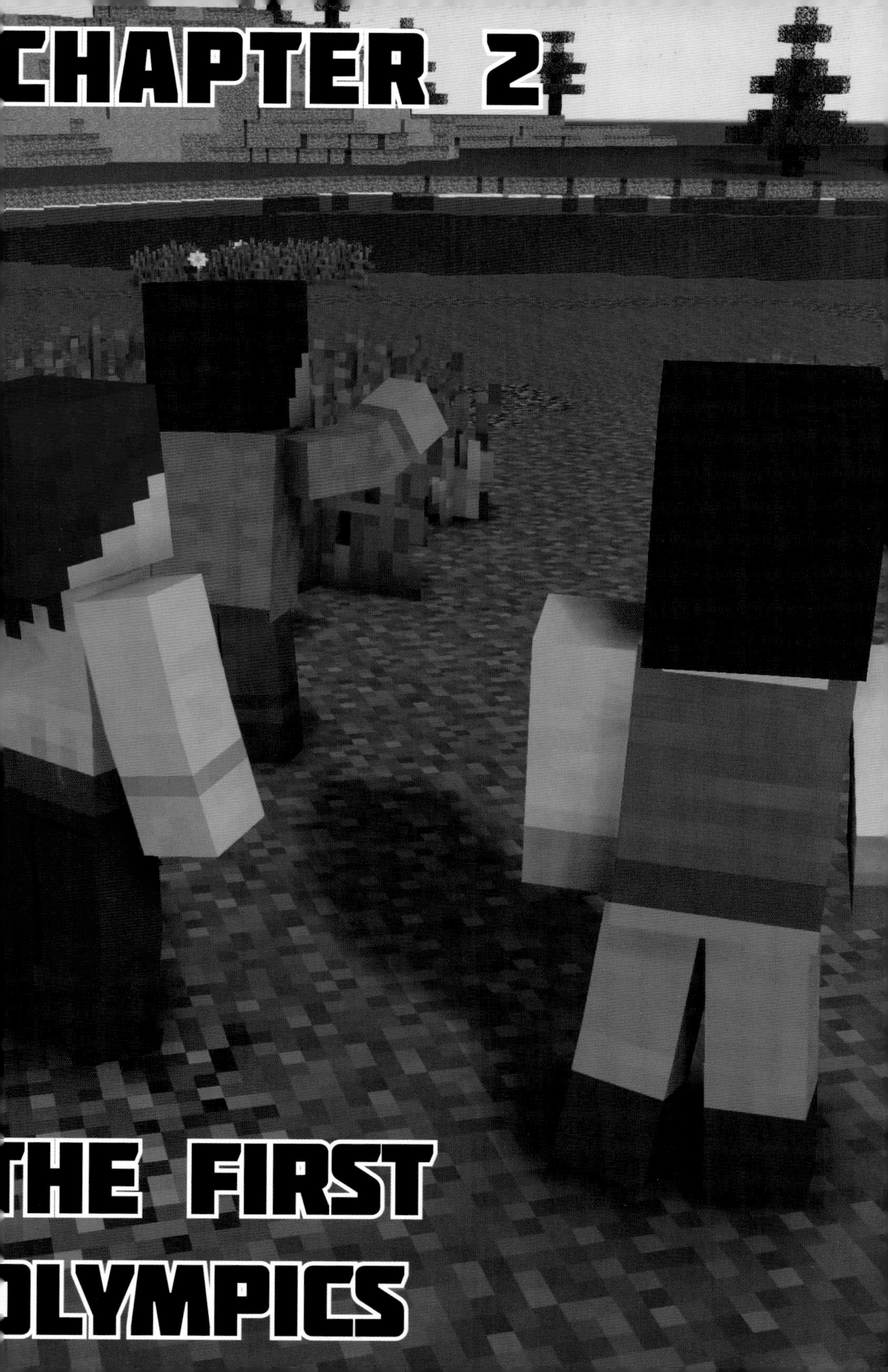

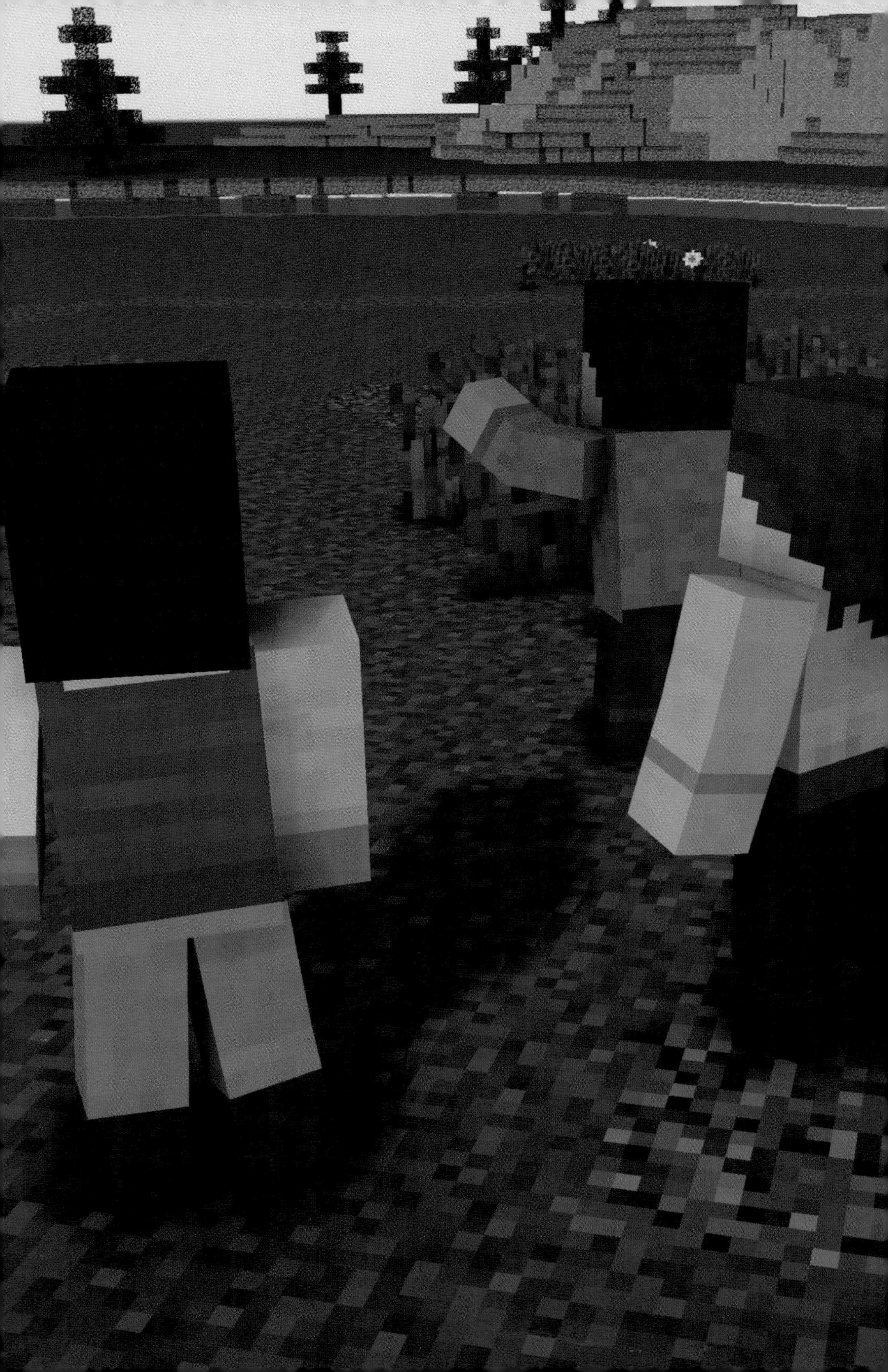

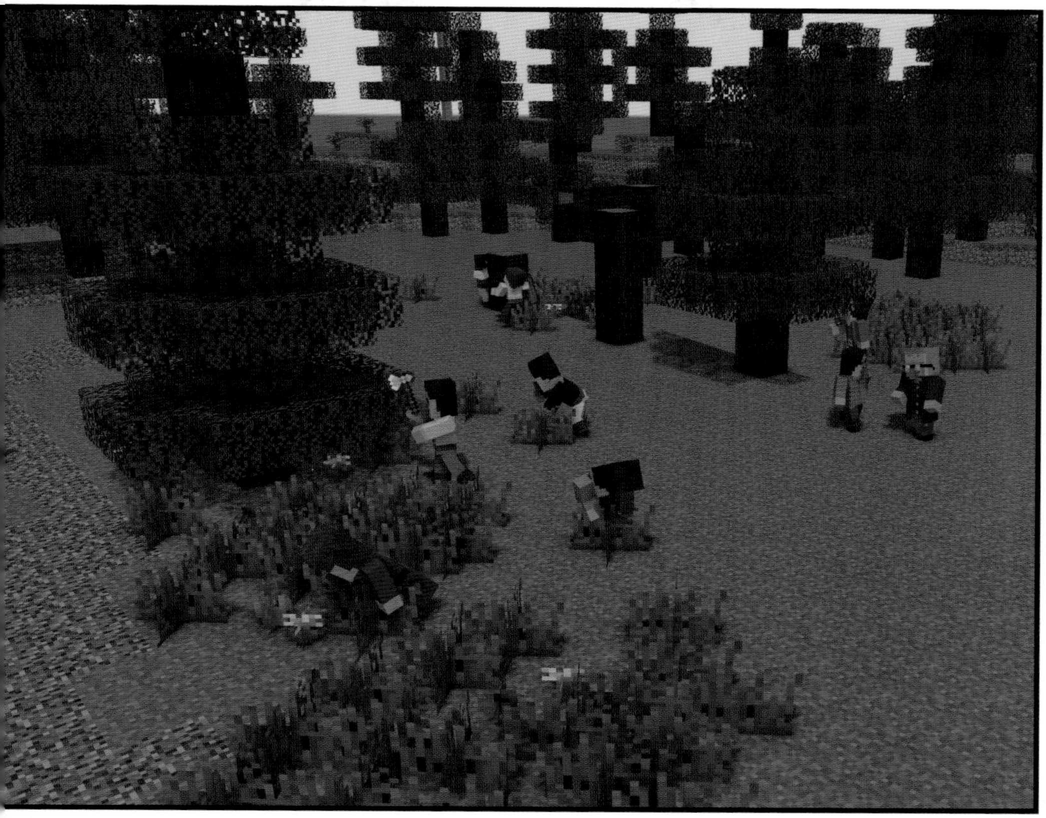

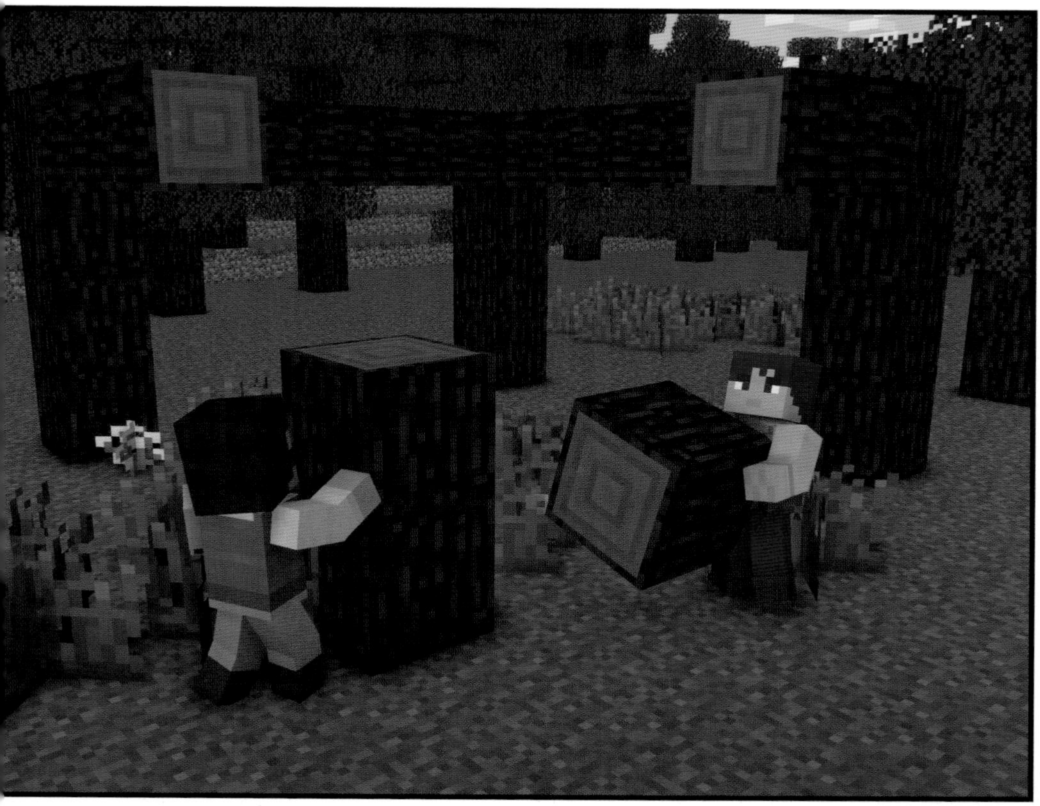

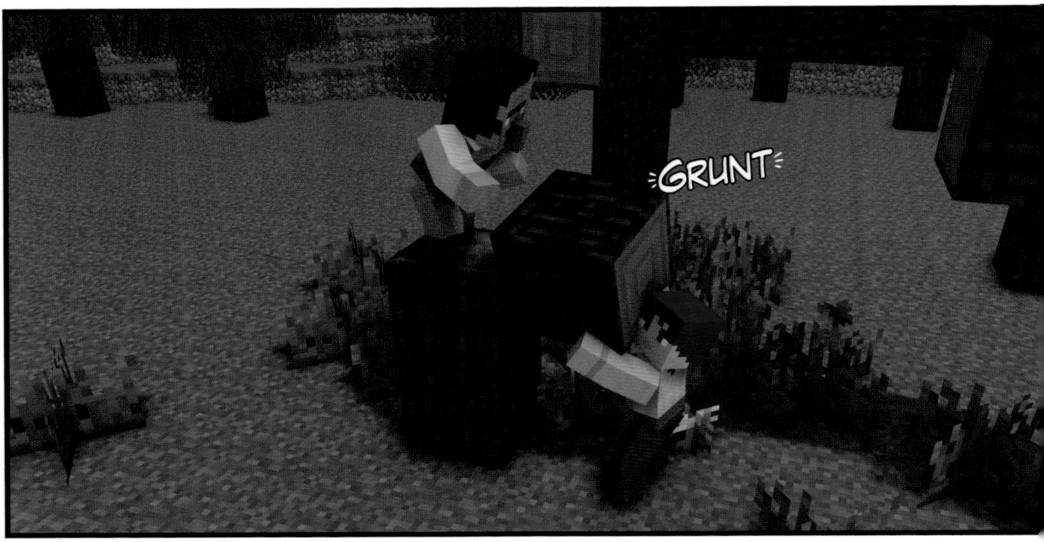
GRUNT

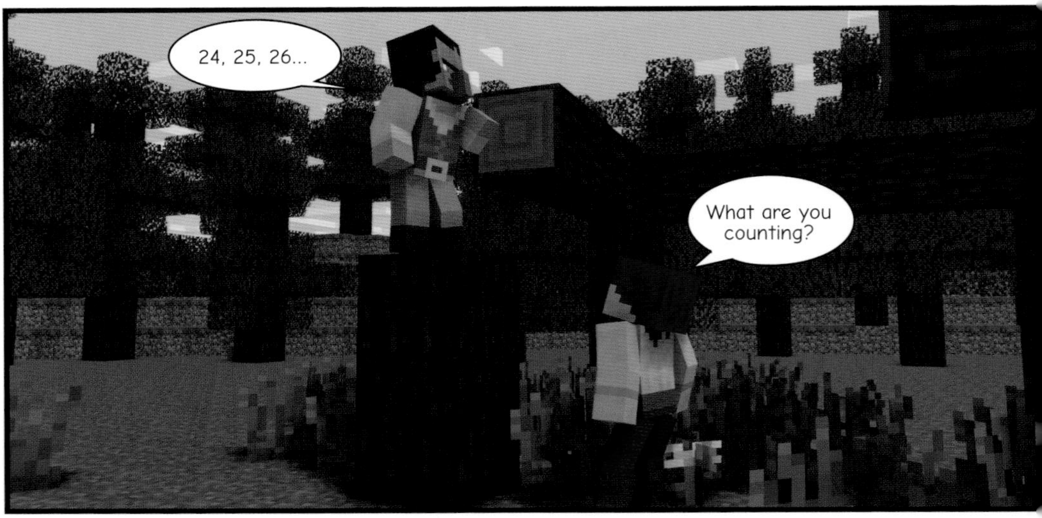
24, 25, 26...
What are you counting?

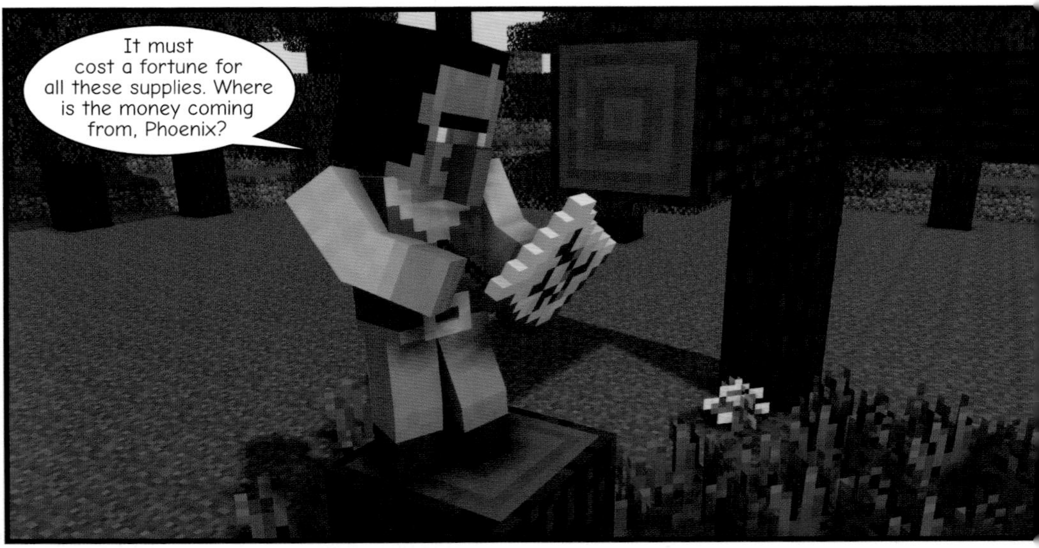
It must cost a fortune for all these supplies. Where is the money coming from, Phoenix?

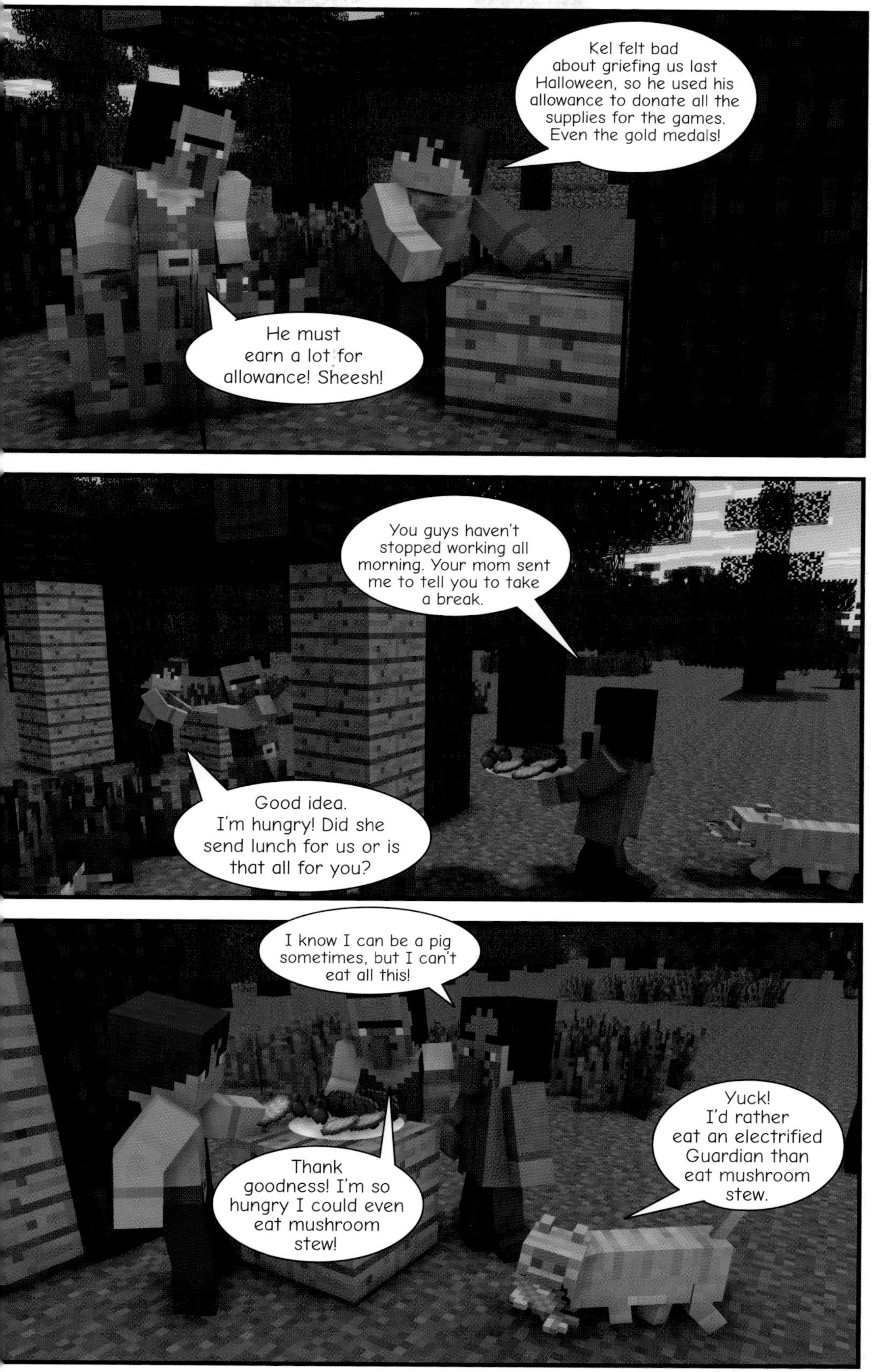
Kel felt bad about griefing us last Halloween, so he used his allowance to donate all the supplies for the games. Even the gold medals!
He must earn a lot for allowance! Sheesh!
You guys haven't stopped working all morning. Your mom sent me to tell you to take a break.
Good idea. I'm hungry! Did she send lunch for us or is that all for you?
I know I can be a pig sometimes, but I can't eat all this!
Thank goodness! I'm so hungry I could even eat mushroom stew!
Yuck! I'd rather eat an electrified Guardian than eat mushroom stew.

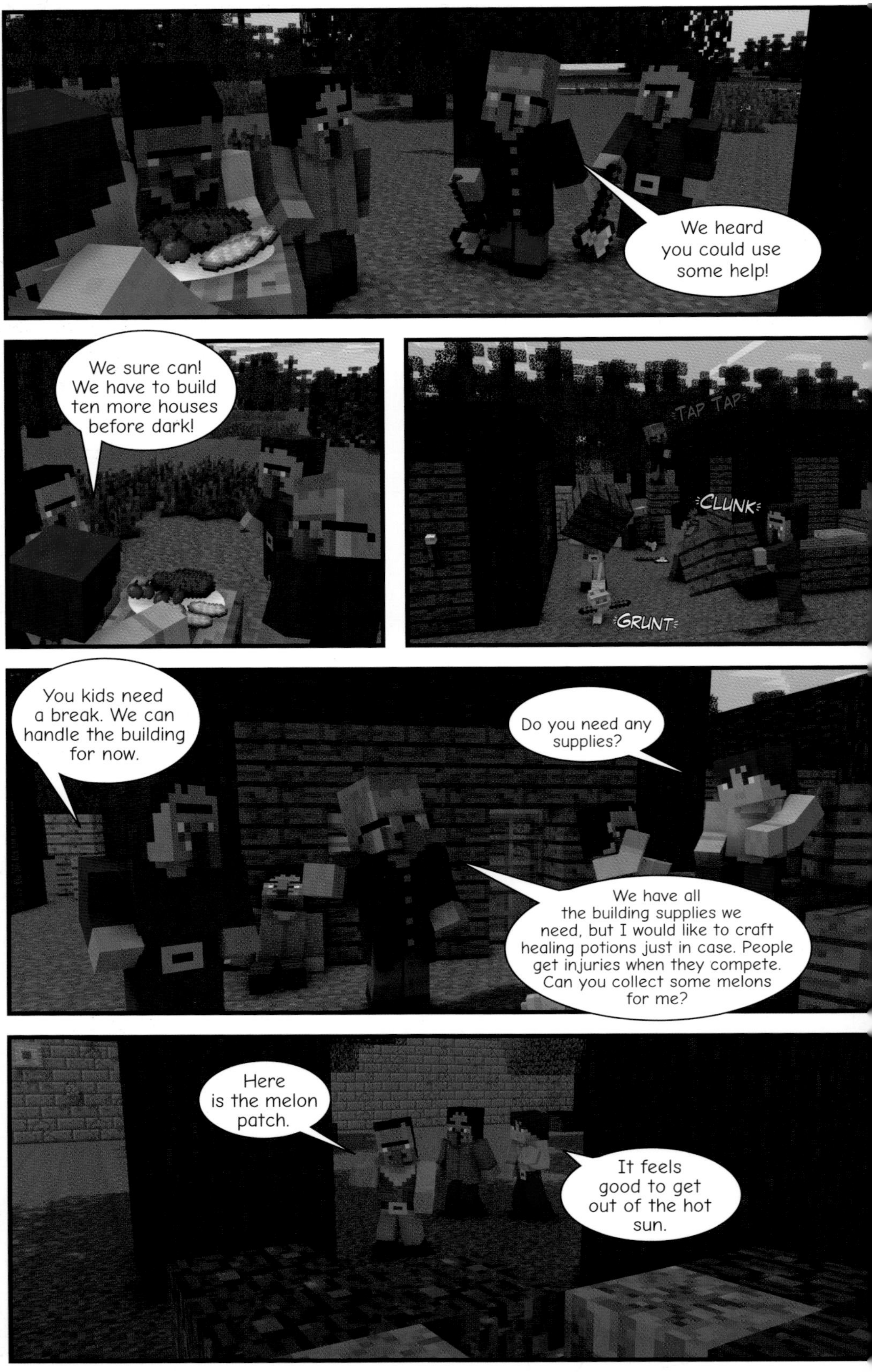
We heard you could use some help!
We sure can! We have to build ten more houses before dark!
TAP TAP
CLUNK
GRUNT
You kids need a break. We can handle the building for now.
Do you need any supplies?
We have all the building supplies we need, but I would like to craft healing potions just in case. People get injuries when they compete. Can you collect some melons for me?
Here is the melon patch.
It feels good to get out of the hot sun.

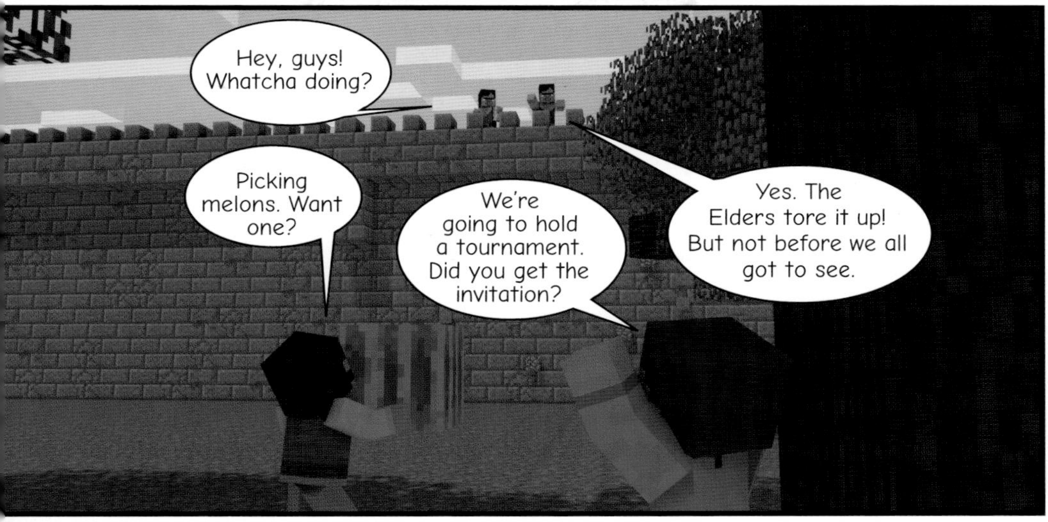
Hey, guys! Whatcha doing?
Picking melons. Want one?
We're going to hold a tournament. Did you get the invitation?
Yes. The Elders tore it up! But not before we all got to see.

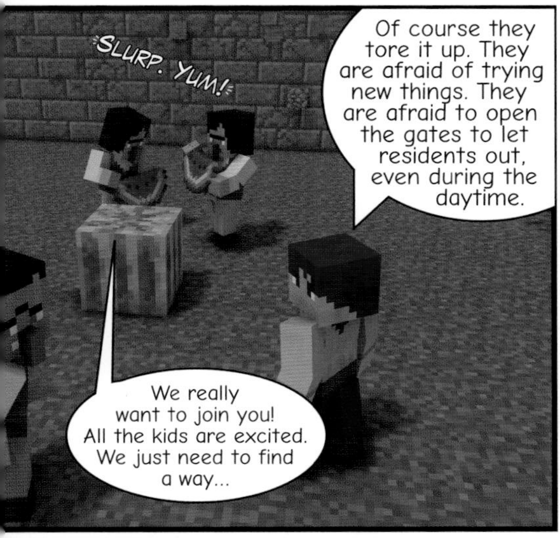
SLURP. YUM!
Of course they tore it up. They are afraid of trying new things. They are afraid to open the gates to let residents out, even during the daytime.
We really want to join you! All the kids are excited. We just need to find a way...

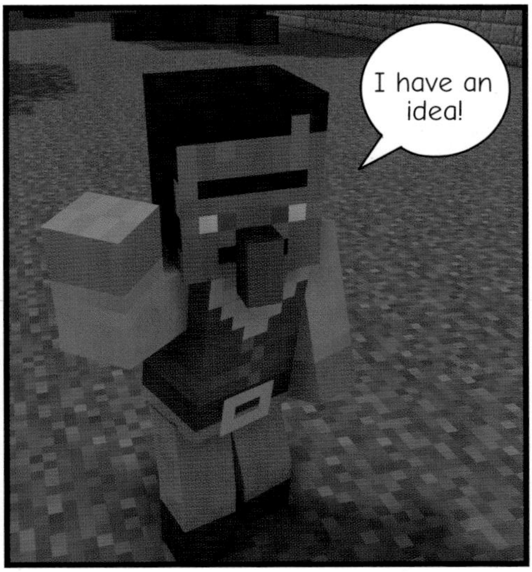
I have an idea!

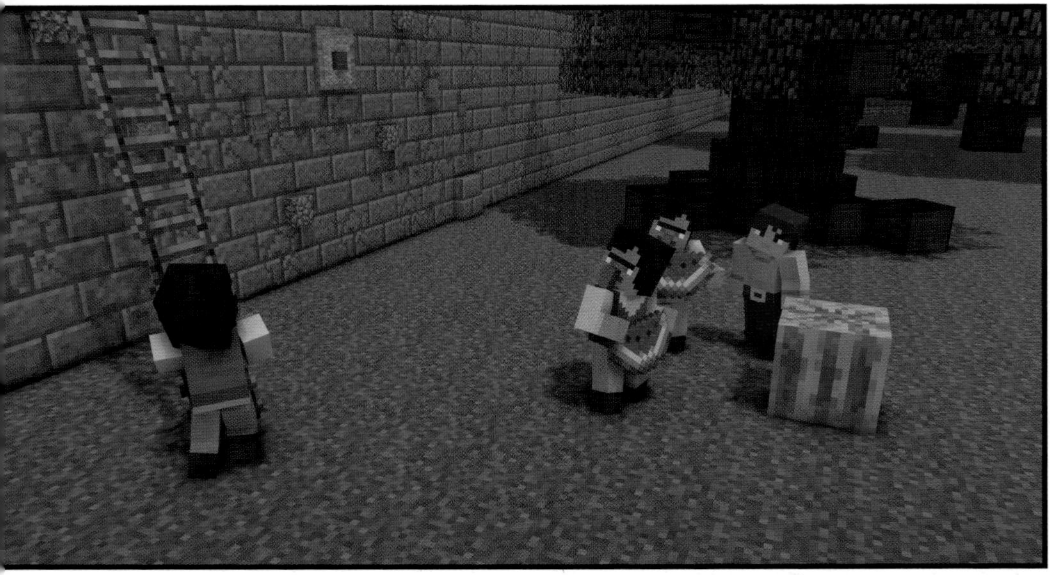

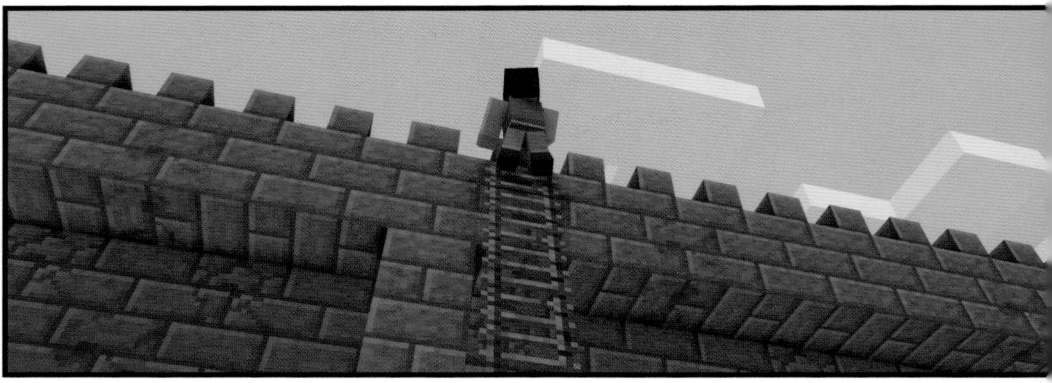

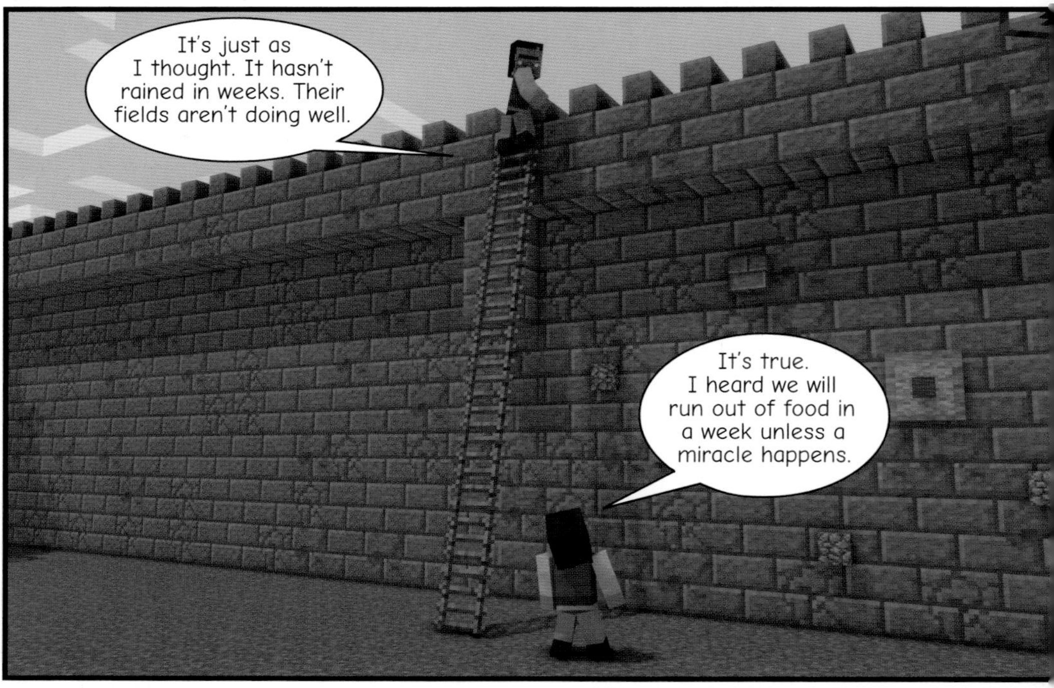
It's just as I thought. It hasn't rained in weeks. Their fields aren't doing well.
It's true. I heard we will run out of food in a week unless a miracle happens.

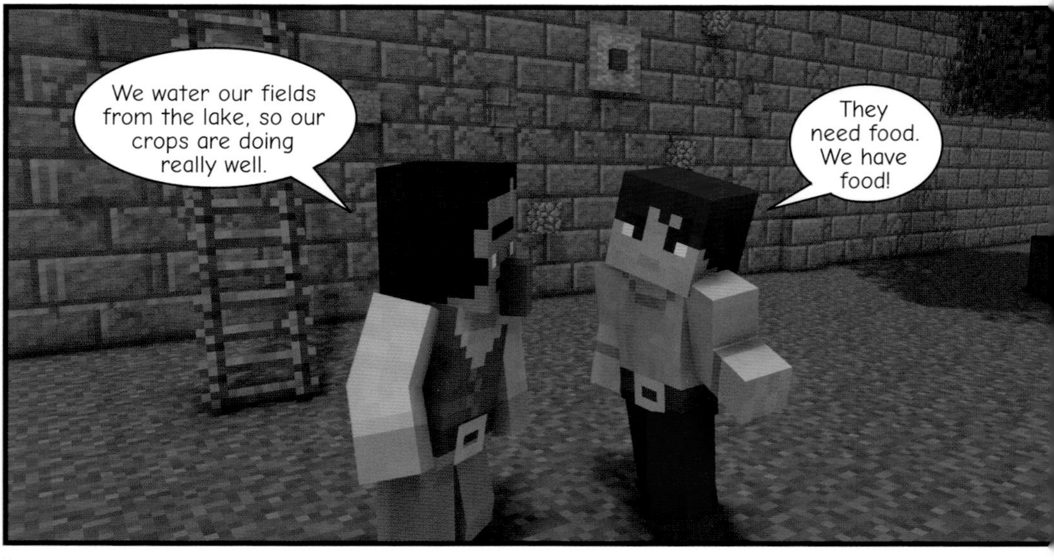
We water our fields from the lake, so our crops are doing really well.
They need food. We have food!

Here. Take this to the Village Elders. This should change their minds.
What did you say?
I offered food in exchange for letting the kids of Xenos compete in the games.
BRILLIANT!

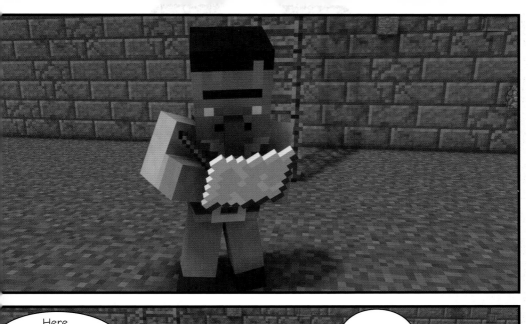

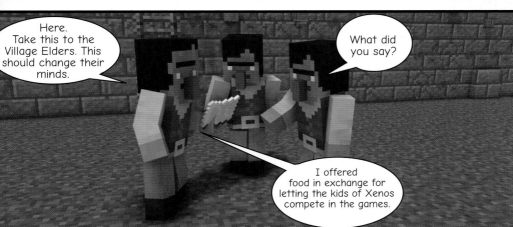

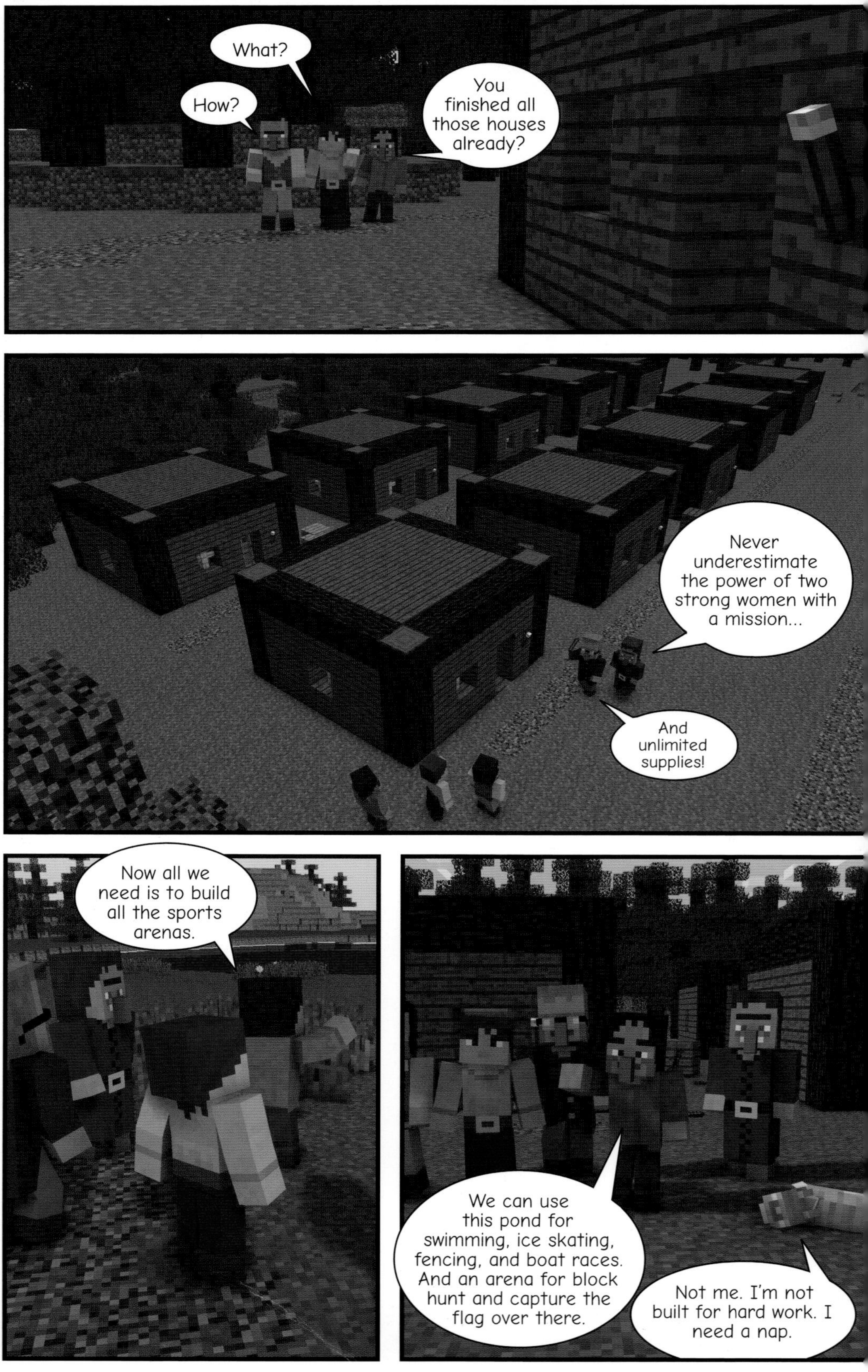
What?
How?
You finished all those houses already?
Never underestimate the power of two strong women with a mission...
And unlimited supplies!
Now all we need is to build all the sports arenas.
We can use this pond for swimming, ice skating, fencing, and boat races. And an arena for block hunt and capture the flag over there.
Not me. I'm not built for hard work. I need a nap.

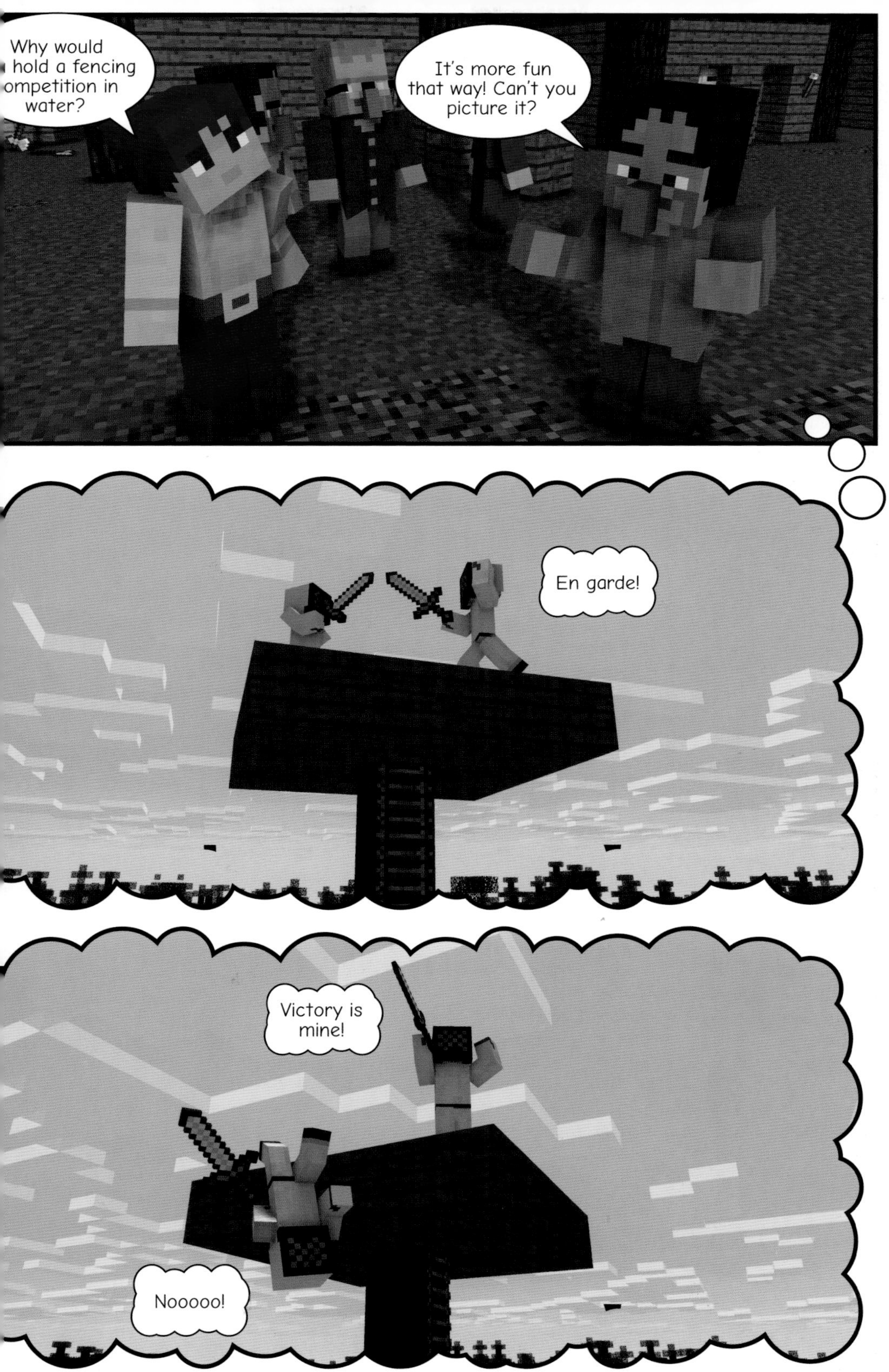
Why would
hold a fencing
ompetition in
water?
It's more fun
that way! Can't you
picture it?
En garde!
Victory is
mine!
Nooooo!

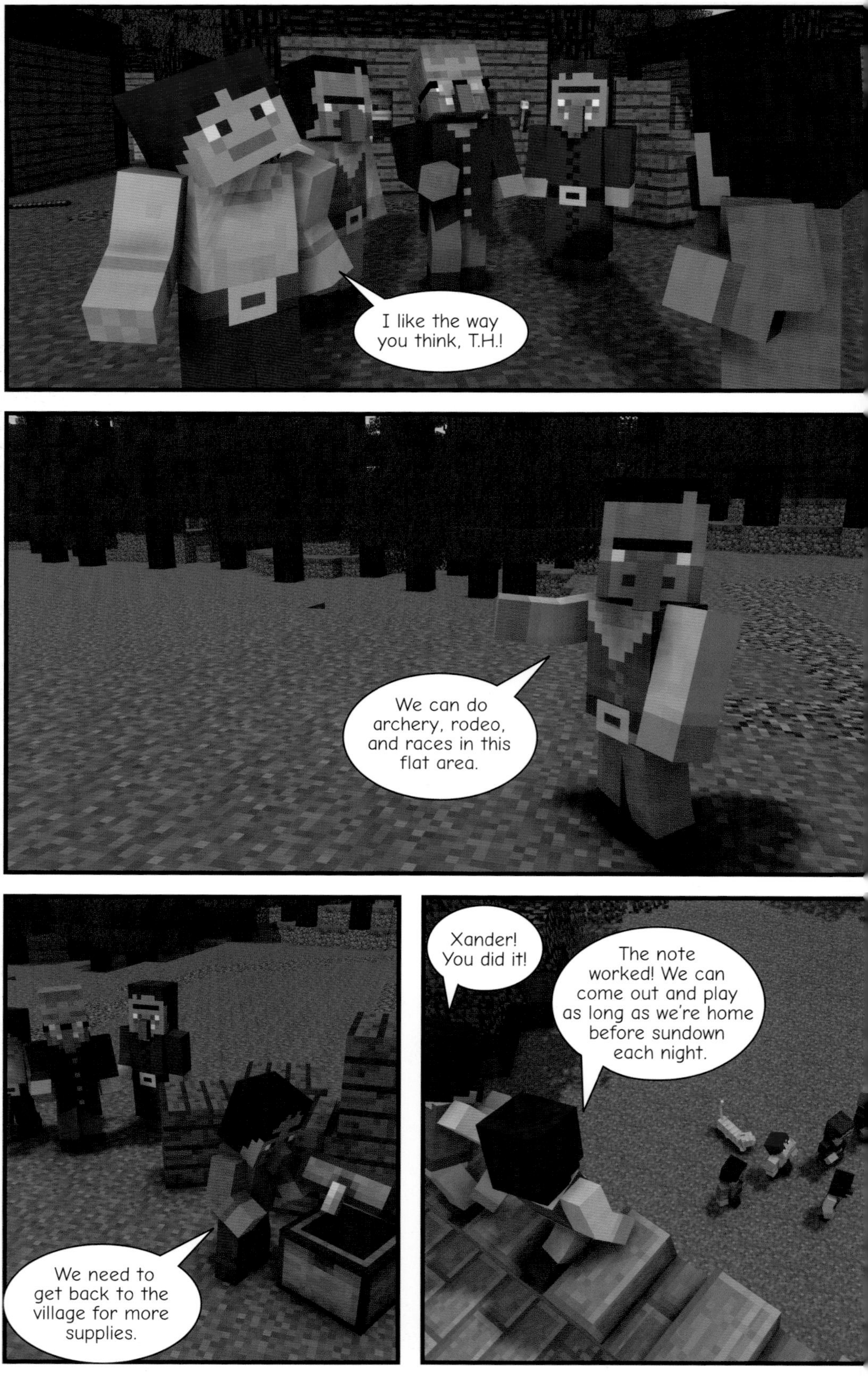
I like the way you think, T.H.!
We can do archery, rodeo, and races in this flat area.
We need to get back to the village for more supplies.
Xander! You did it!
The note worked! We can come out and play as long as we're home before sundown each night.

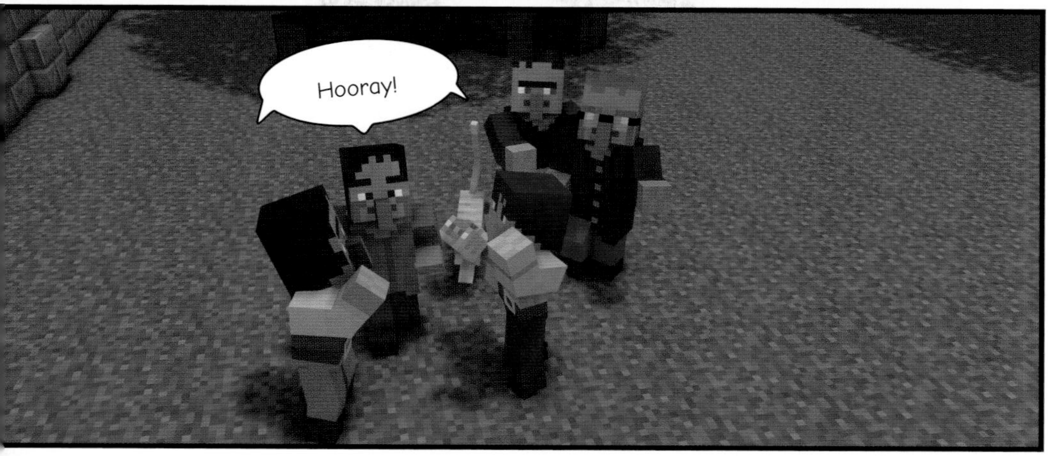
Hooray!

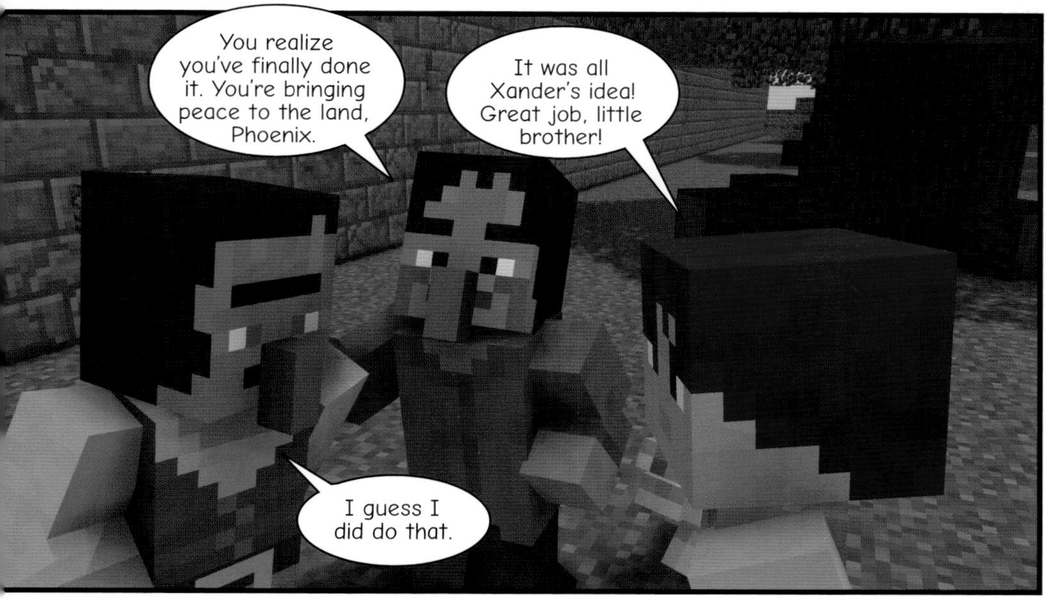
You realize you've finally done it. You're bringing peace to the land, Phoenix.
It was all Xander's idea! Great job, little brother!
I guess I did do that.

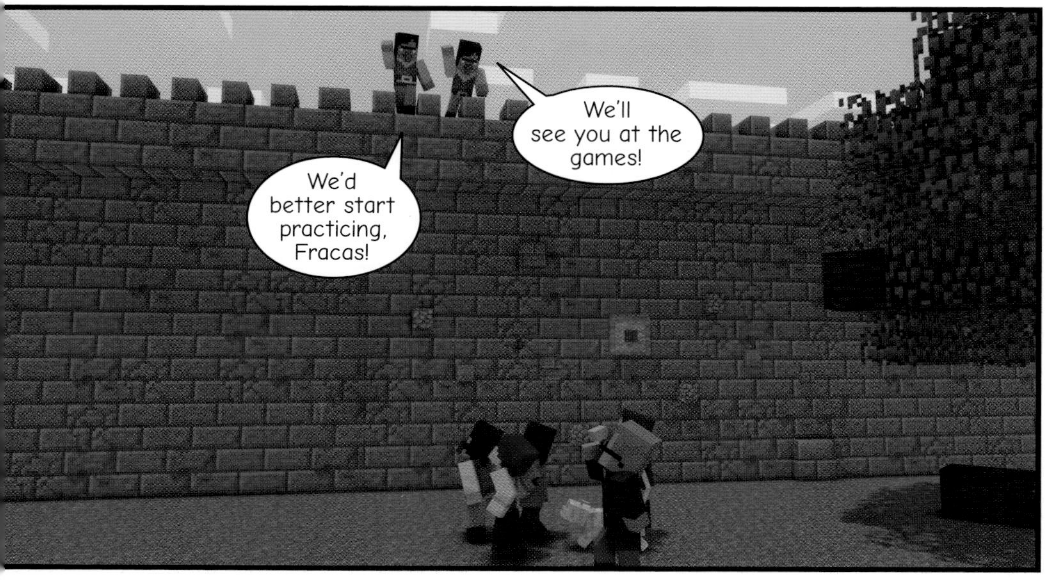
We'll see you at the games!
We'd better start practicing, Fracas!

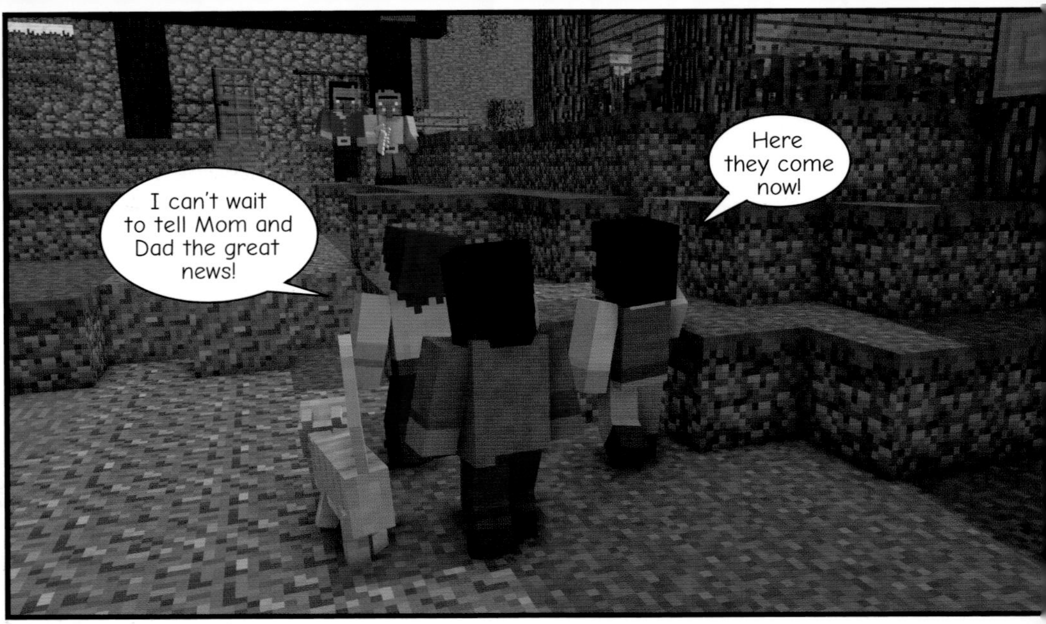
I can't wait to tell Mom and Dad the great news!
Here they come now!

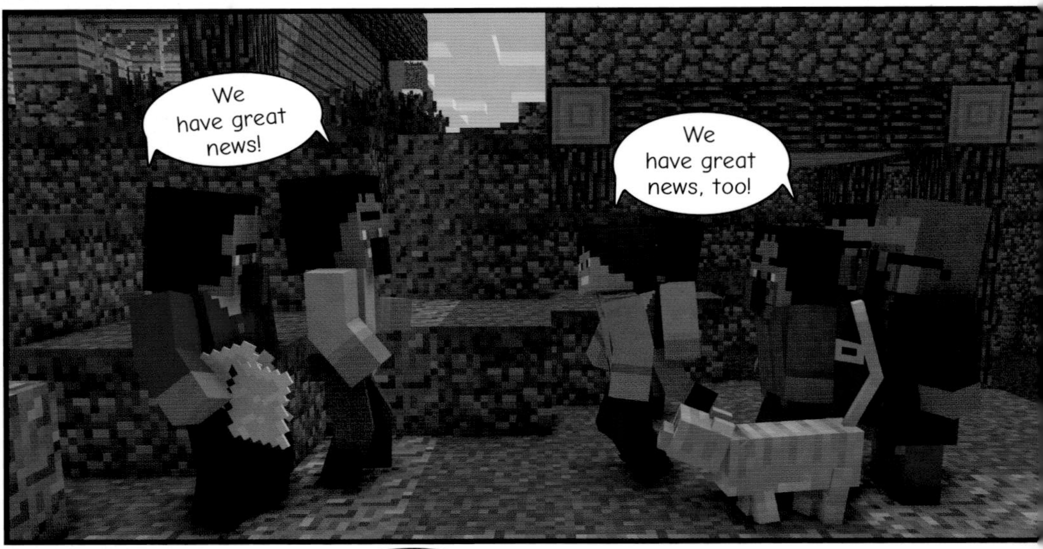
We have great news!
We have great news, too!

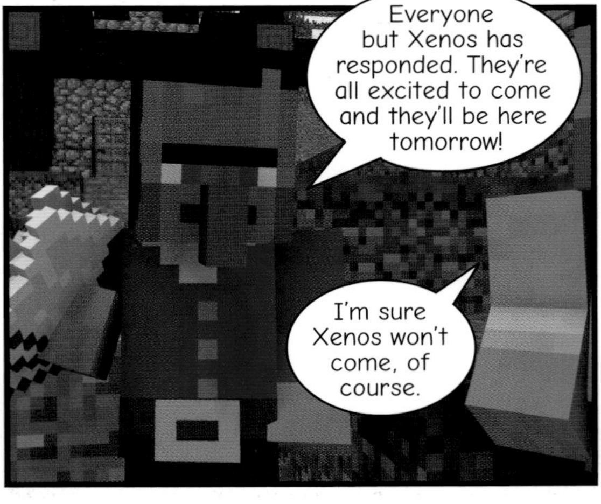
Everyone but Xenos has responded. They're all excited to come and they'll be here tomorrow!
I'm sure Xenos won't come, of course.

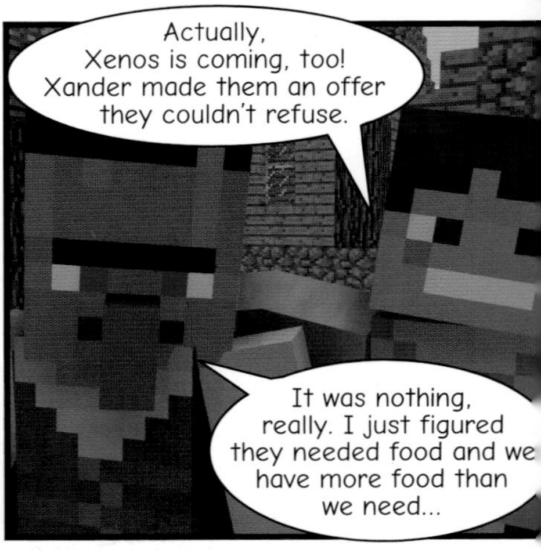
Actually, Xenos is coming, too! Xander made them an offer they couldn't refuse.
It was nothing, really. I just figured they needed food and we have more food than we need...

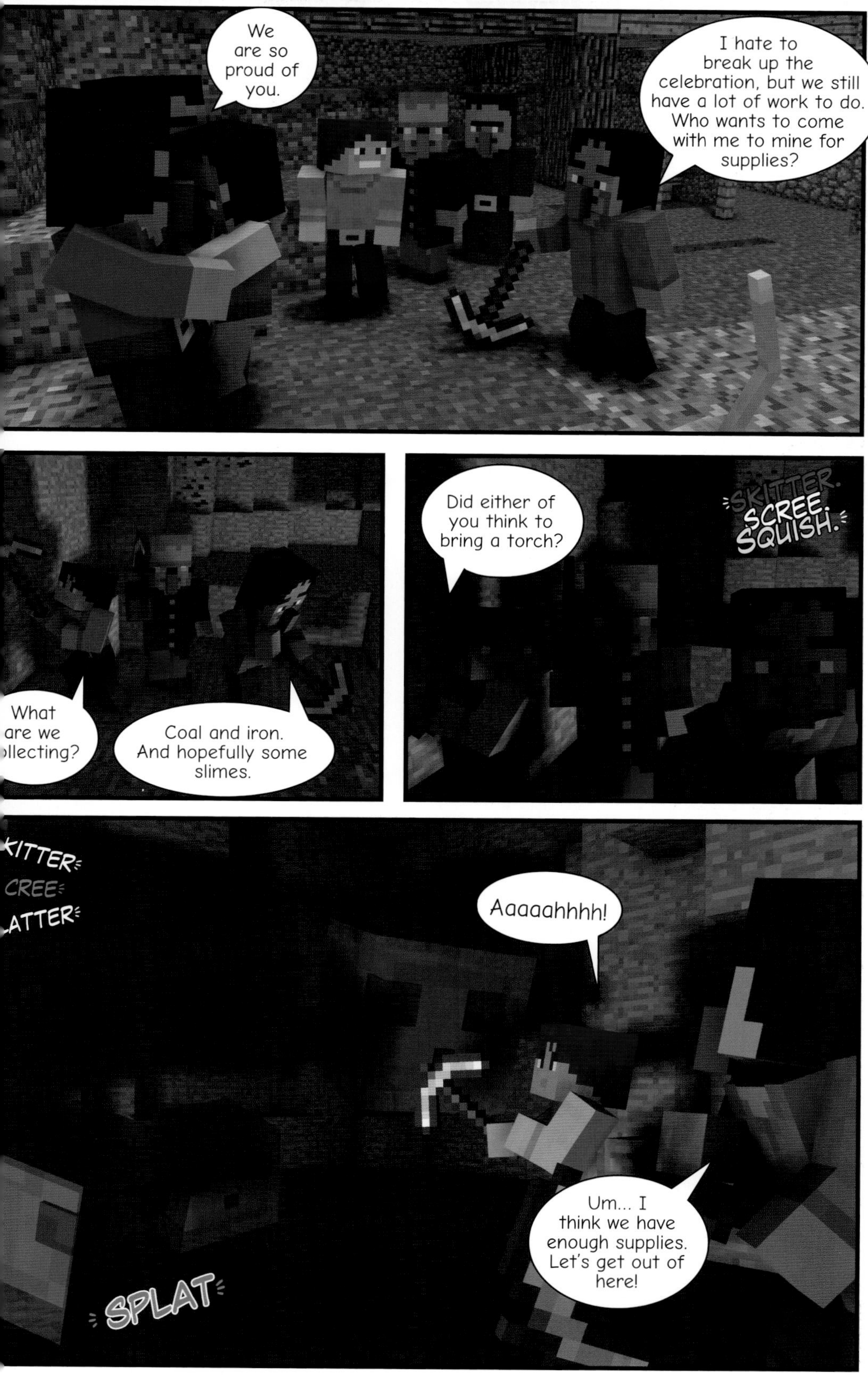

We are so proud of you.
I hate to break up the celebration, but we still have a lot of work to do. Who wants to come with me to mine for supplies?
What are we llecting?
Coal and iron. And hopefully some slimes.
Did either of you think to bring a torch?
SKITTER. SCREE. SQUISH.
KITTER
CREE
ATTER
Aaaaahhhh!
Um... I think we have enough supplies. Let's get out of here!
SPLAT

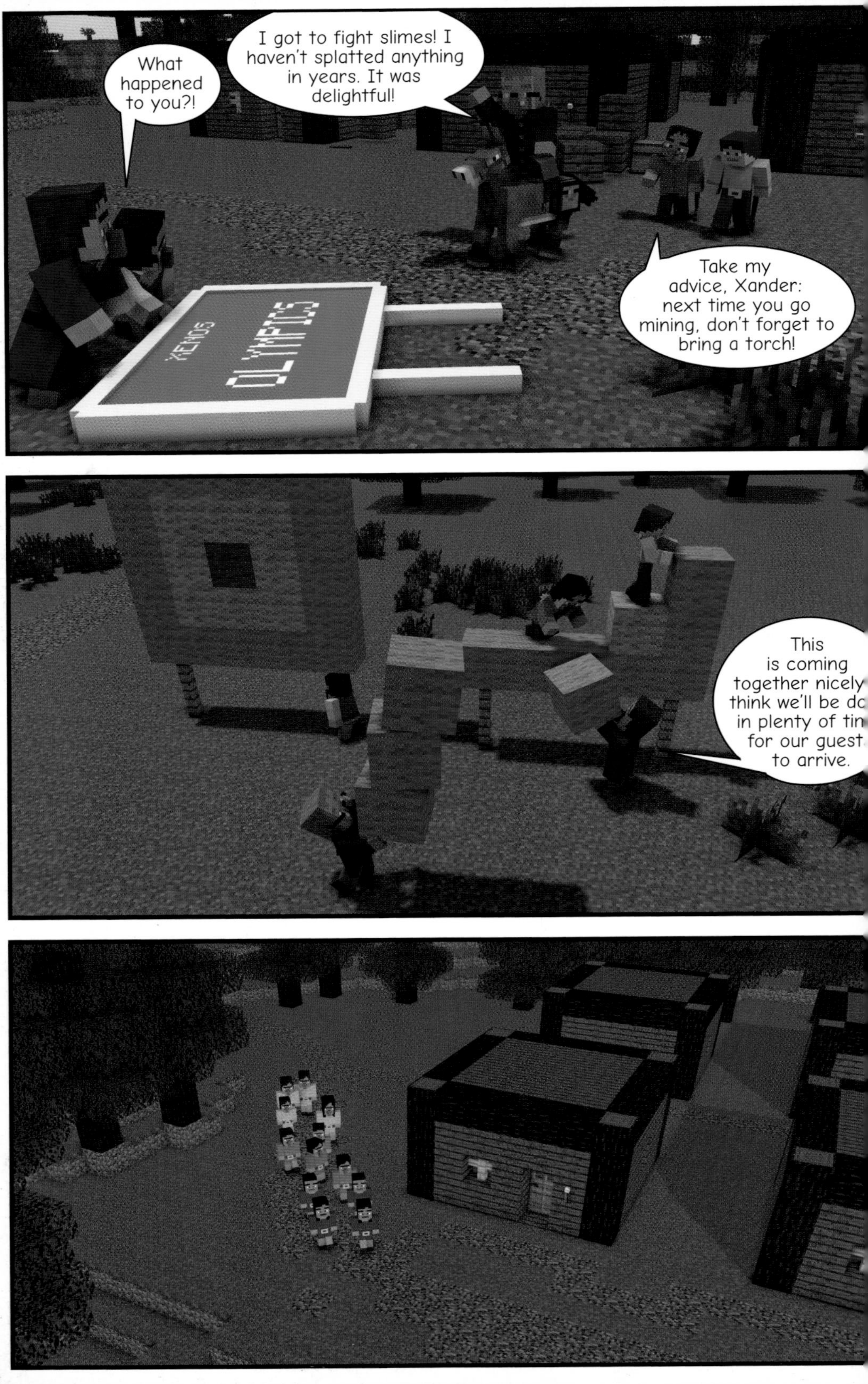
What happened to you?!
I got to fight slimes! I haven't splatted anything in years. It was delightful!
XENOS
OLYMPICS
Take my advice, Xander: next time you go mining, don't forget to bring a torch!
This is coming together nicely think we'll be do in plenty of tin for our guest to arrive.

CHAPTER 3

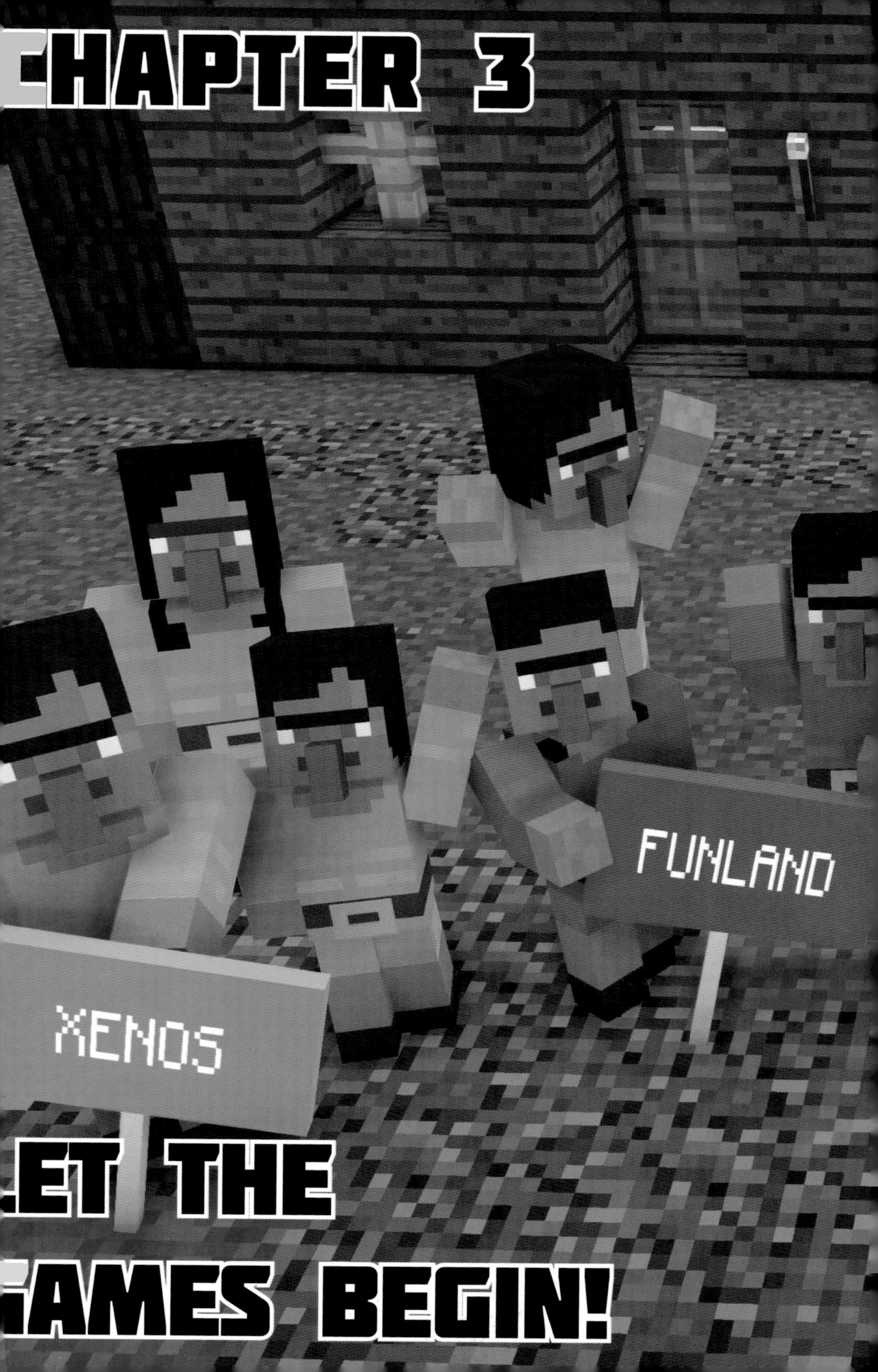
FUNLAND
XENOS

LET THE GAMES BEGIN!

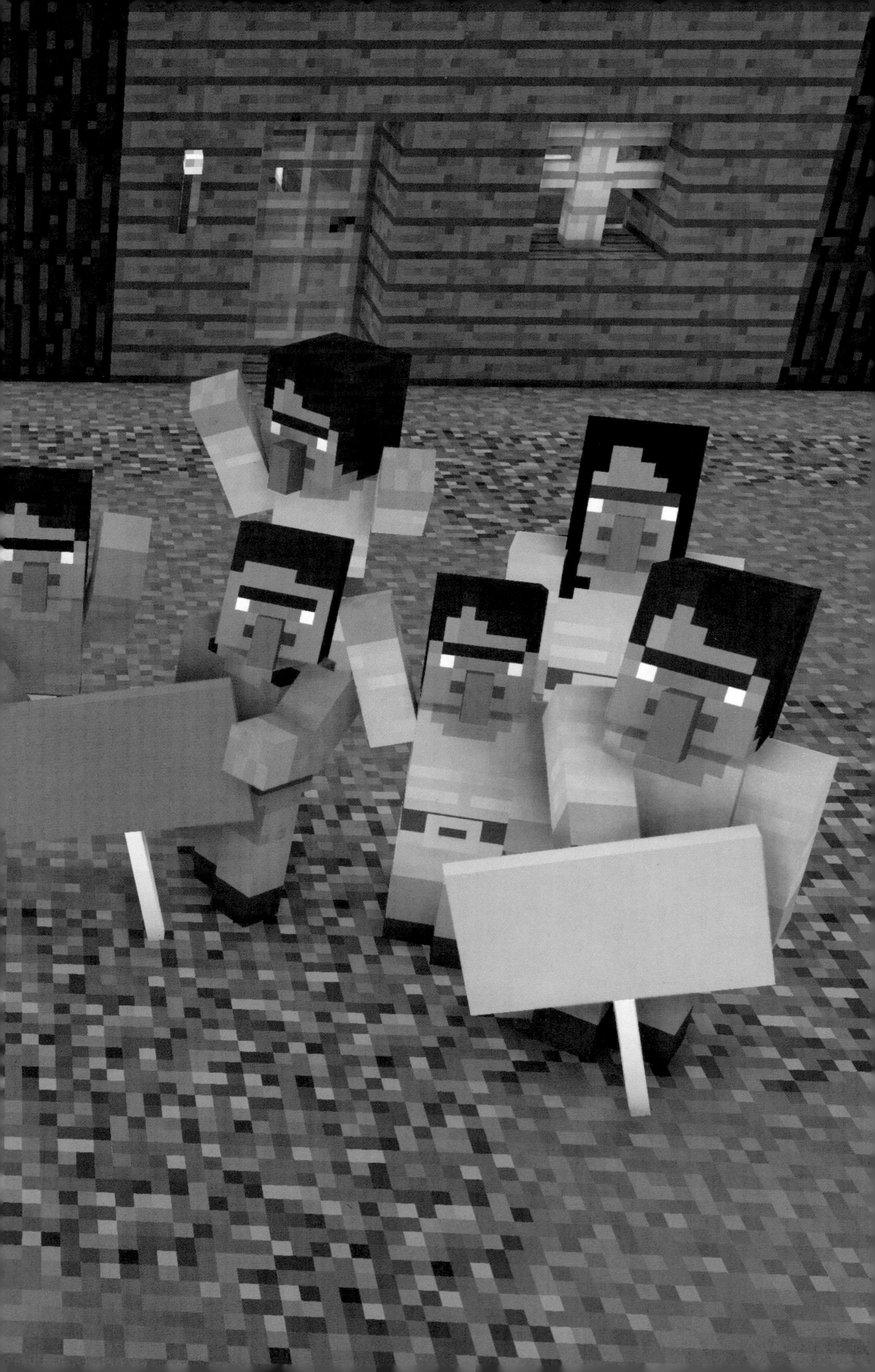

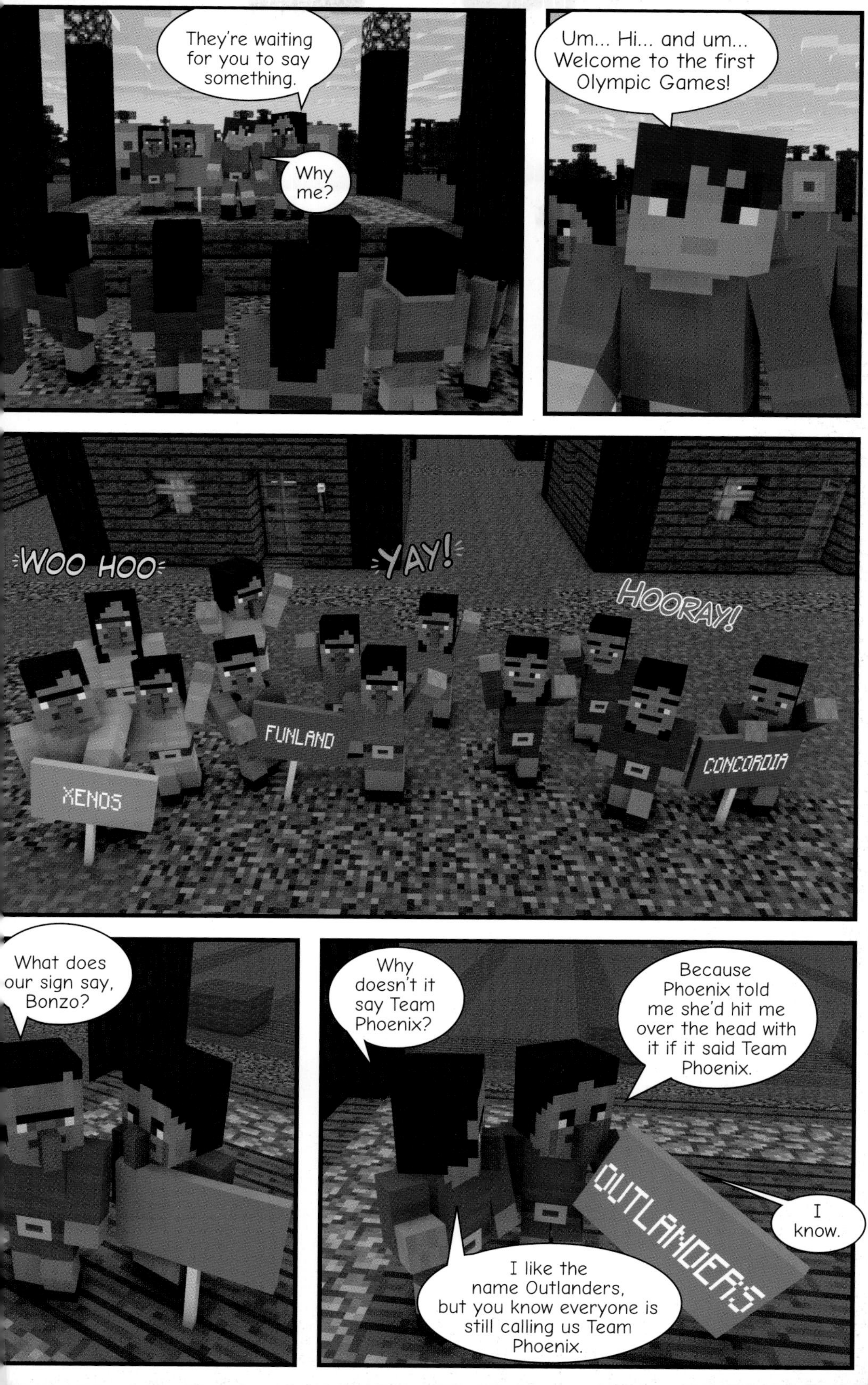

They're waiting for you to say something.
Why me?
Um... Hi... and um... Welcome to the first Olympic Games!
WOO HOO
YAY!
HOORAY!
XENOS
FUNLAND
CONCORDIA
What does our sign say, Bonzo?
Why doesn't it say Team Phoenix?
Because Phoenix told me she'd hit me over the head with it if it said Team Phoenix.
OUTLANDERS
I know.
I like the name Outlanders, but you know everyone is still calling us Team Phoenix.

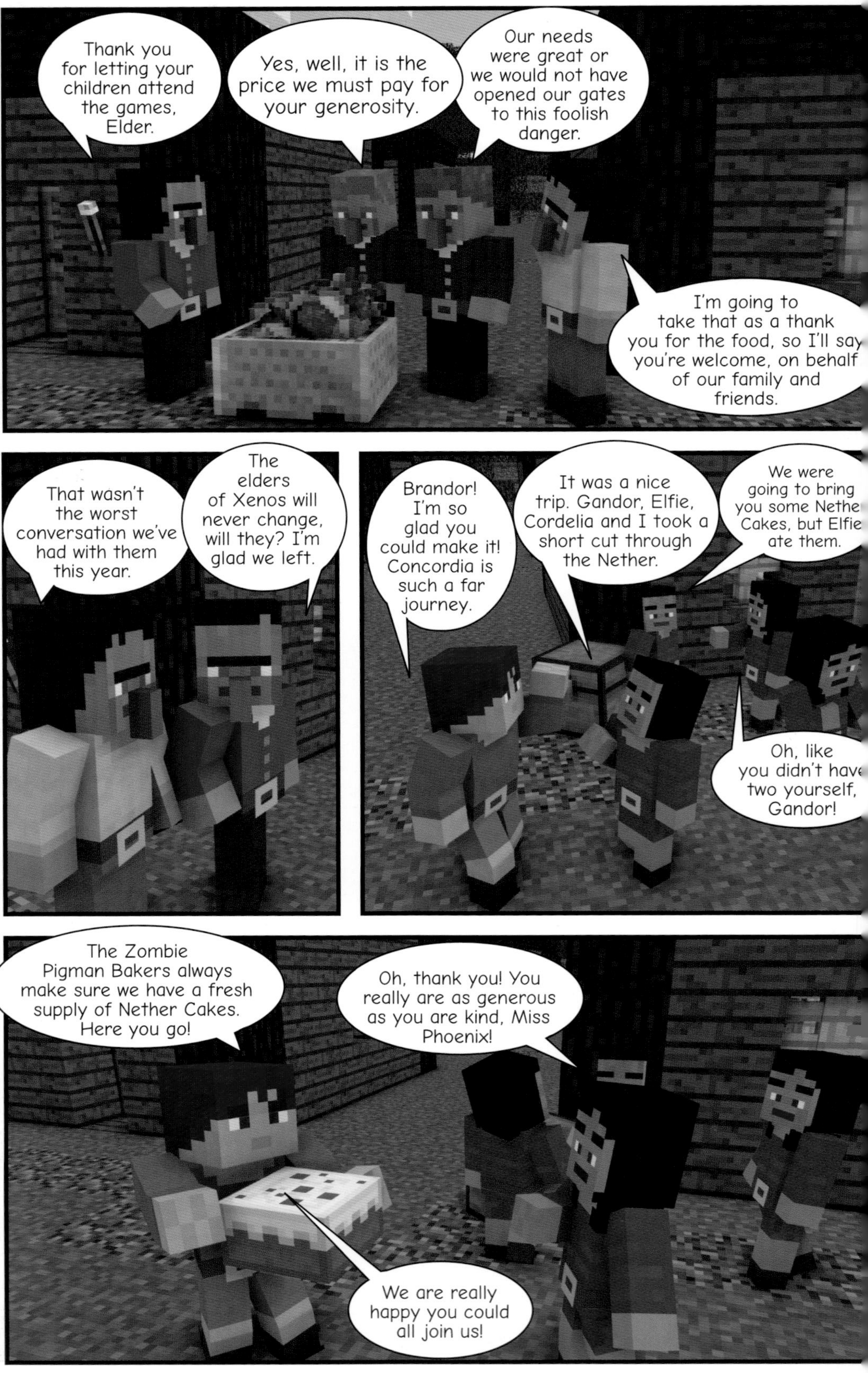
Thank you for letting your children attend the games, Elder.
Yes, well, it is the price we must pay for your generosity.
Our needs were great or we would not have opened our gates to this foolish danger.
I'm going to take that as a thank you for the food, so I'll say you're welcome, on behalf of our family and friends.
That wasn't the worst conversation we've had with them this year.
The elders of Xenos will never change, will they? I'm glad we left.
Brandor! I'm so glad you could make it! Concordia is such a far journey.
It was a nice trip. Gandor, Elfie, Cordelia and I took a short cut through the Nether.
We were going to bring you some Nethe Cakes, but Elfie ate them.
Oh, like you didn't hav two yourself, Gandor!
The Zombie Pigman Bakers always make sure we have a fresh supply of Nether Cakes. Here you go!
Oh, thank you! You really are as generous as you are kind, Miss Phoenix!
We are really happy you could all join us!

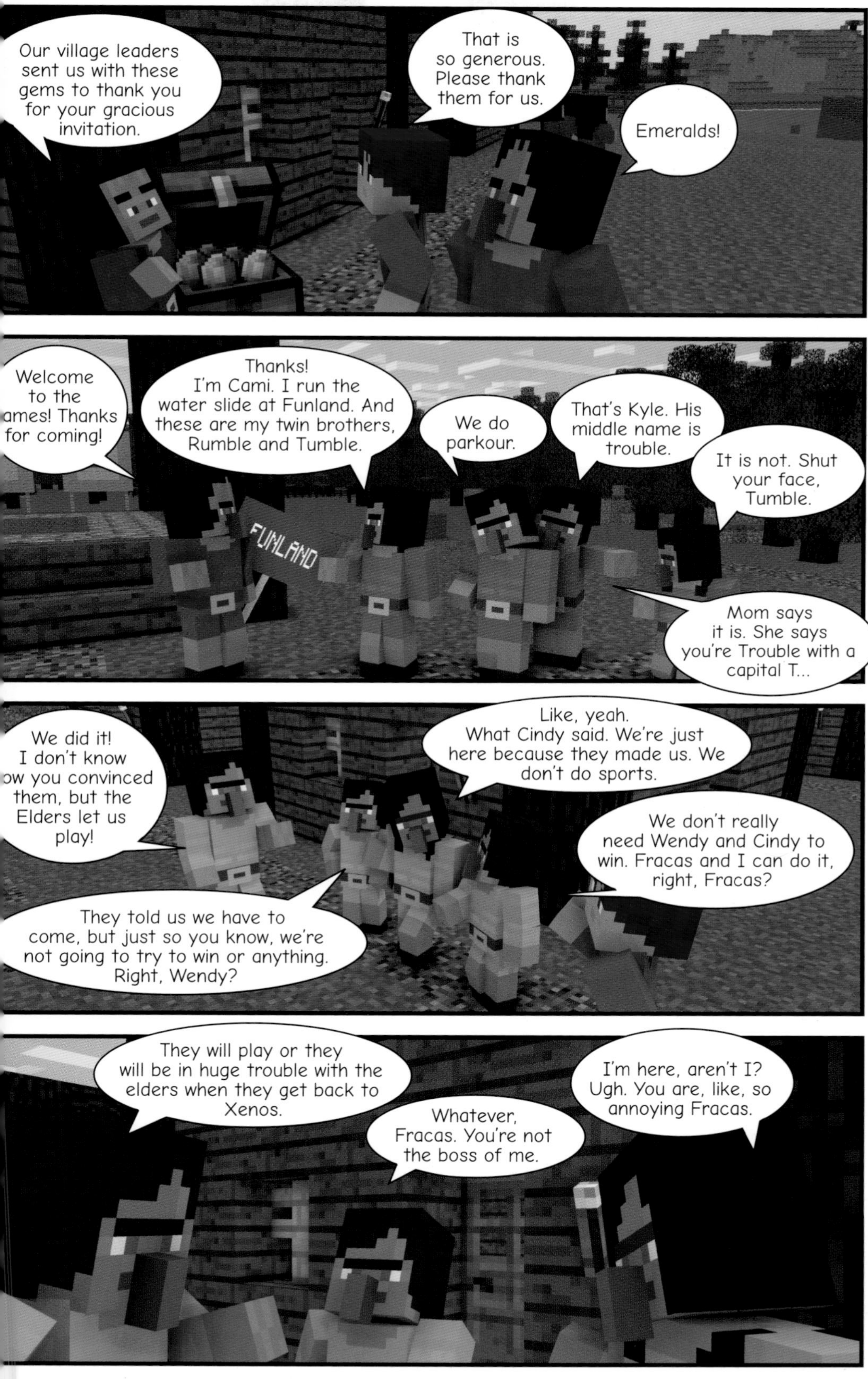
Our village leaders sent us with these gems to thank you for your gracious invitation.
That is so generous. Please thank them for us.
Emeralds!
Welcome to the ames! Thanks for coming!
Thanks! I'm Cami. I run the water slide at Funland. And these are my twin brothers, Rumble and Tumble.
FUNLAND
We do parkour.
That's Kyle. His middle name is trouble.
It is not. Shut your face, Tumble.
Mom says it is. She says you're Trouble with a capital T...
We did it! I don't know ow you convinced them, but the Elders let us play!
Like, yeah. What Cindy said. We're just here because they made us. We don't do sports.
We don't really need Wendy and Cindy to win. Fracas and I can do it, right, Fracas?
They told us we have to come, but just so you know, we're not going to try to win or anything. Right, Wendy?
They will play or they will be in huge trouble with the elders when they get back to Xenos.
Whatever, Fracas. You're not the boss of me.
I'm here, aren't I? Ugh. You are, like, so annoying Fracas.

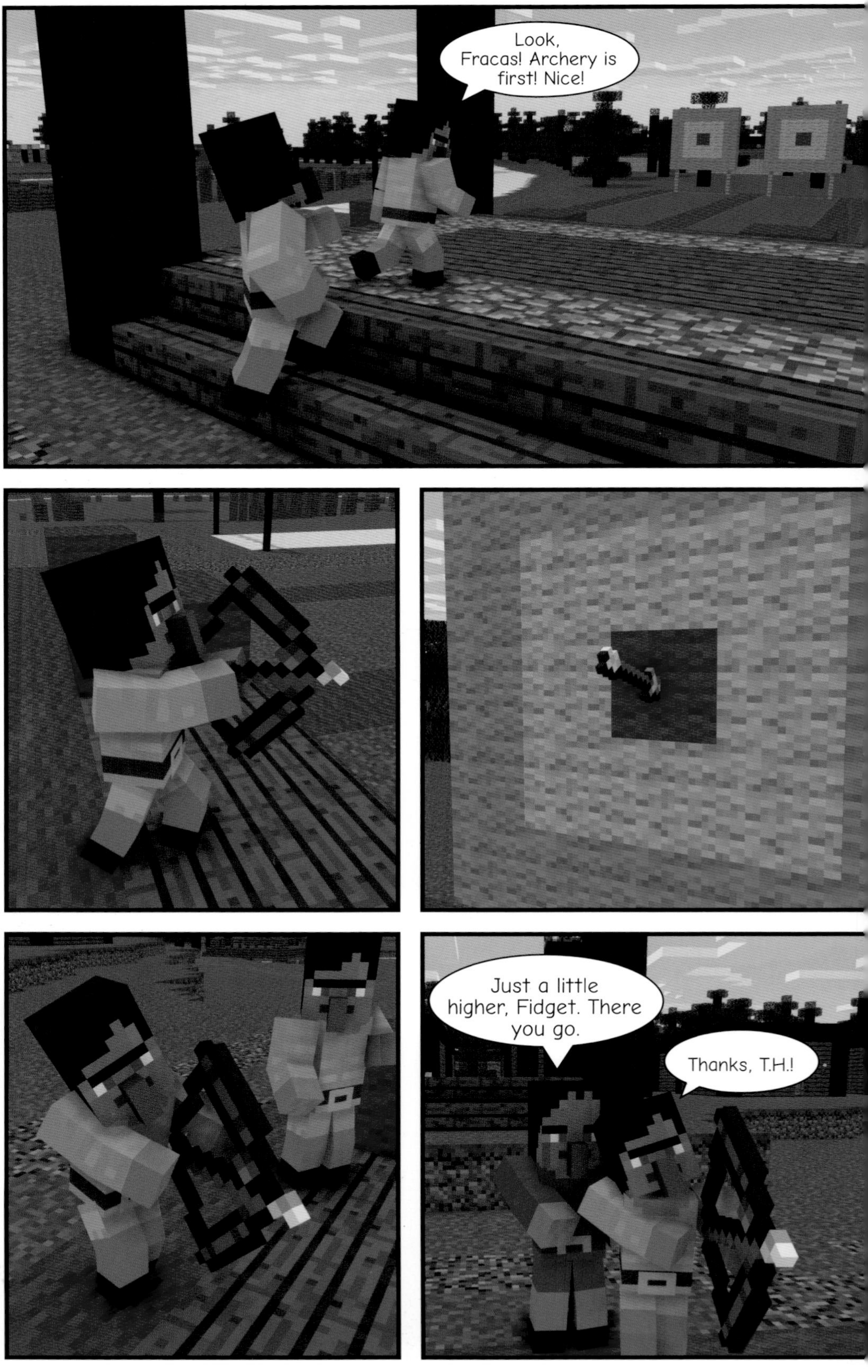
Look, Fracas! Archery is first! Nice!
Just a little higher, Fidget. There you go.
Thanks, T.H.!

Did you see that? I hit the target! Woo-hoo!
One...
CONCORDIA
Two...
Three...
Twenty points for Concordia!
Yay!
Yay!
CONCORDIA
FUNLAND
Ready, Kyle?

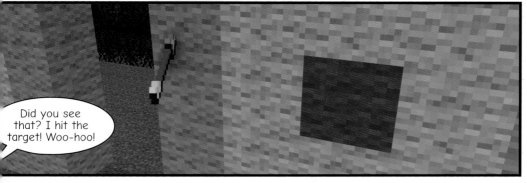

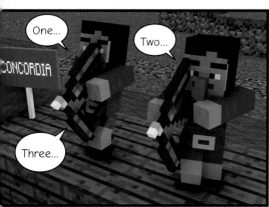

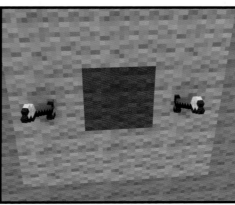

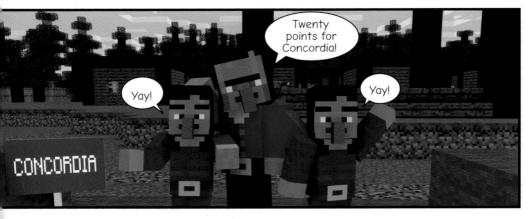

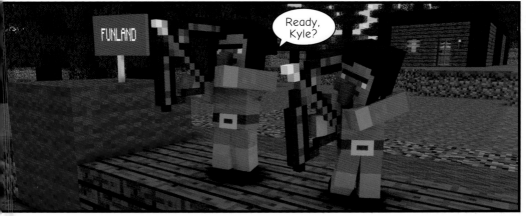

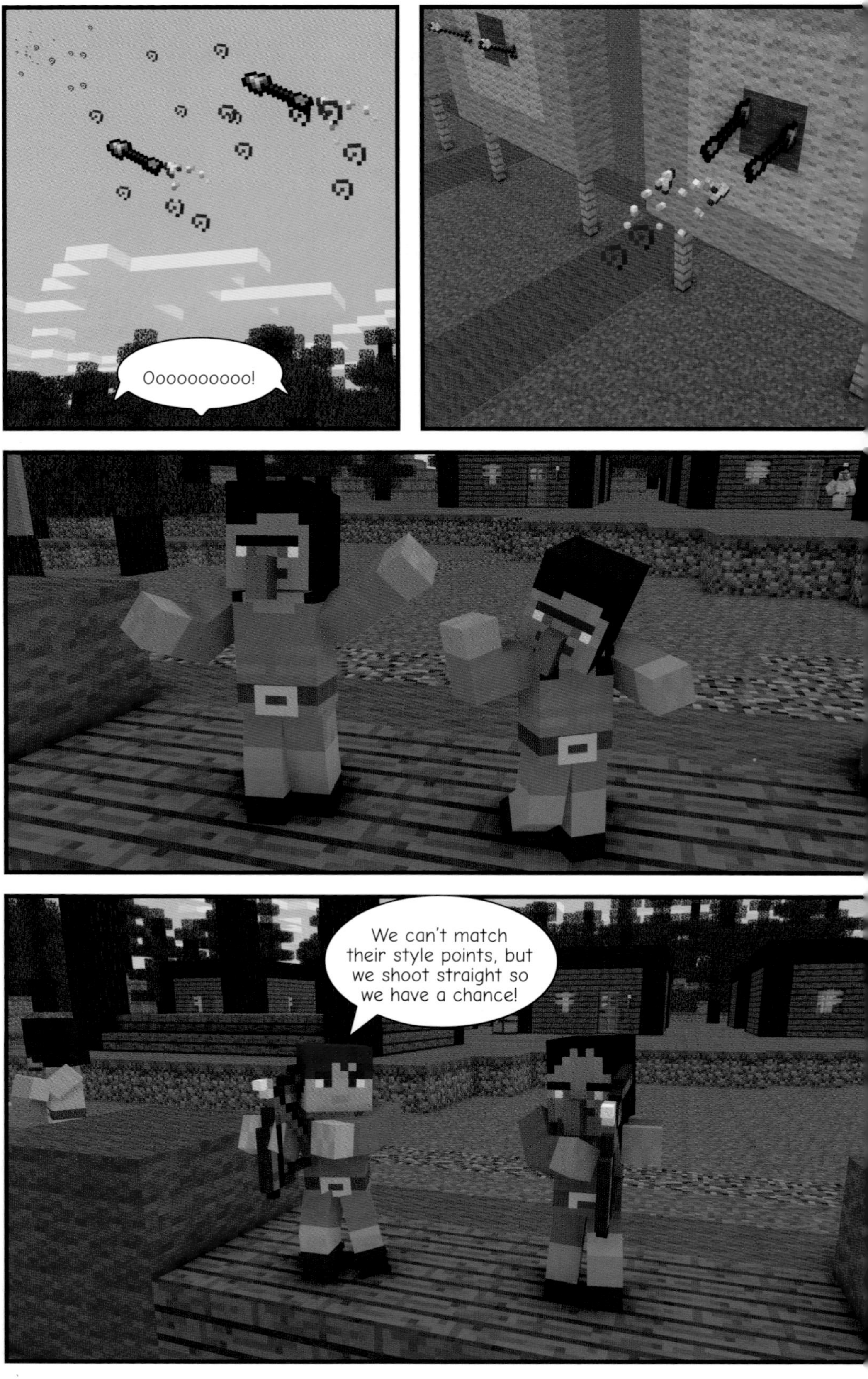
Oooooooooo!
We can't match their style points, but we shoot straight so we have a chance!

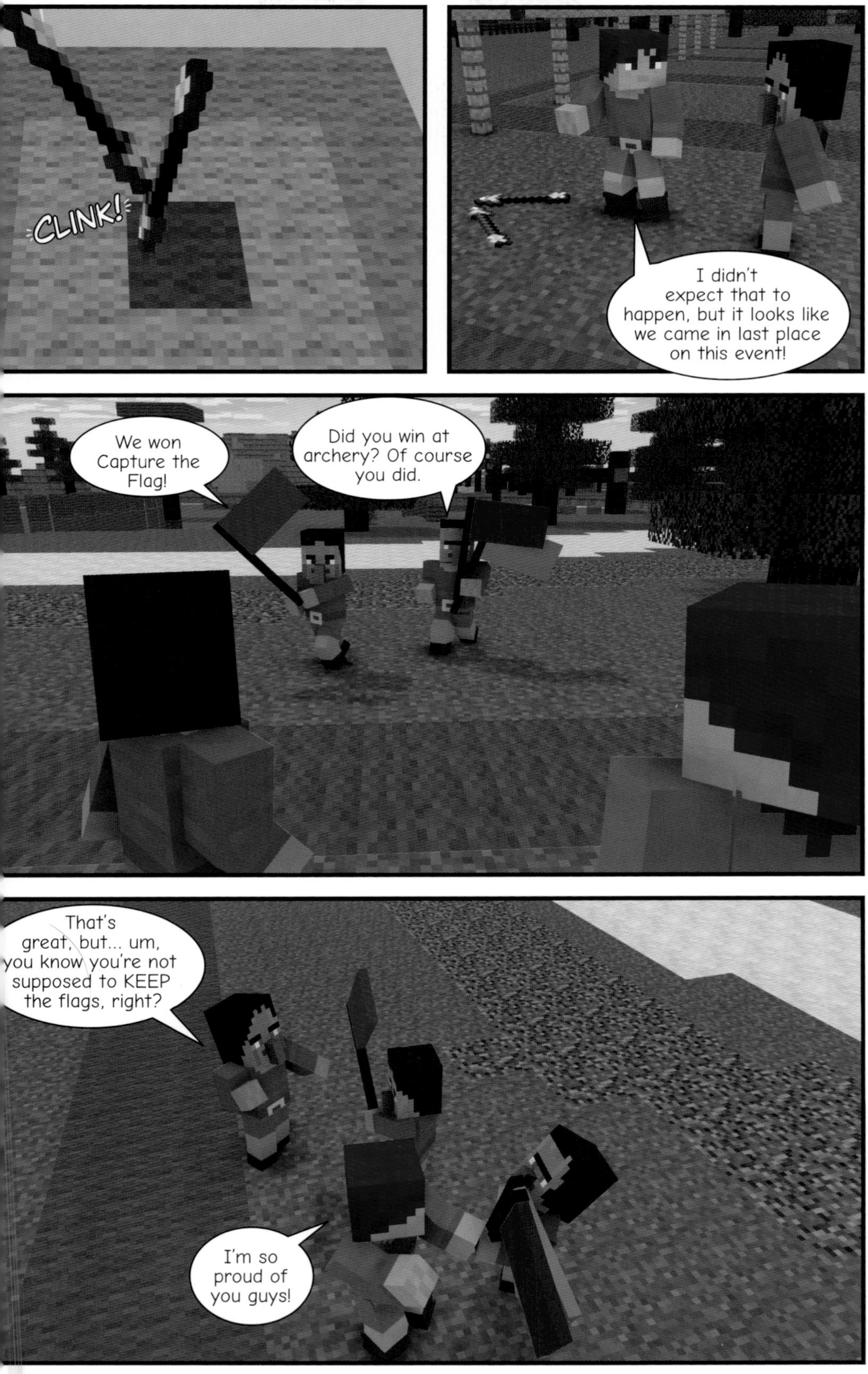
CLINK!
I didn't expect that to happen, but it looks like we came in last place on this event!
We won Capture the Flag!
Did you win at archery? Of course you did.
That's great, but... um, you know you're not supposed to KEEP the flags, right?
I'm so proud of you guys!

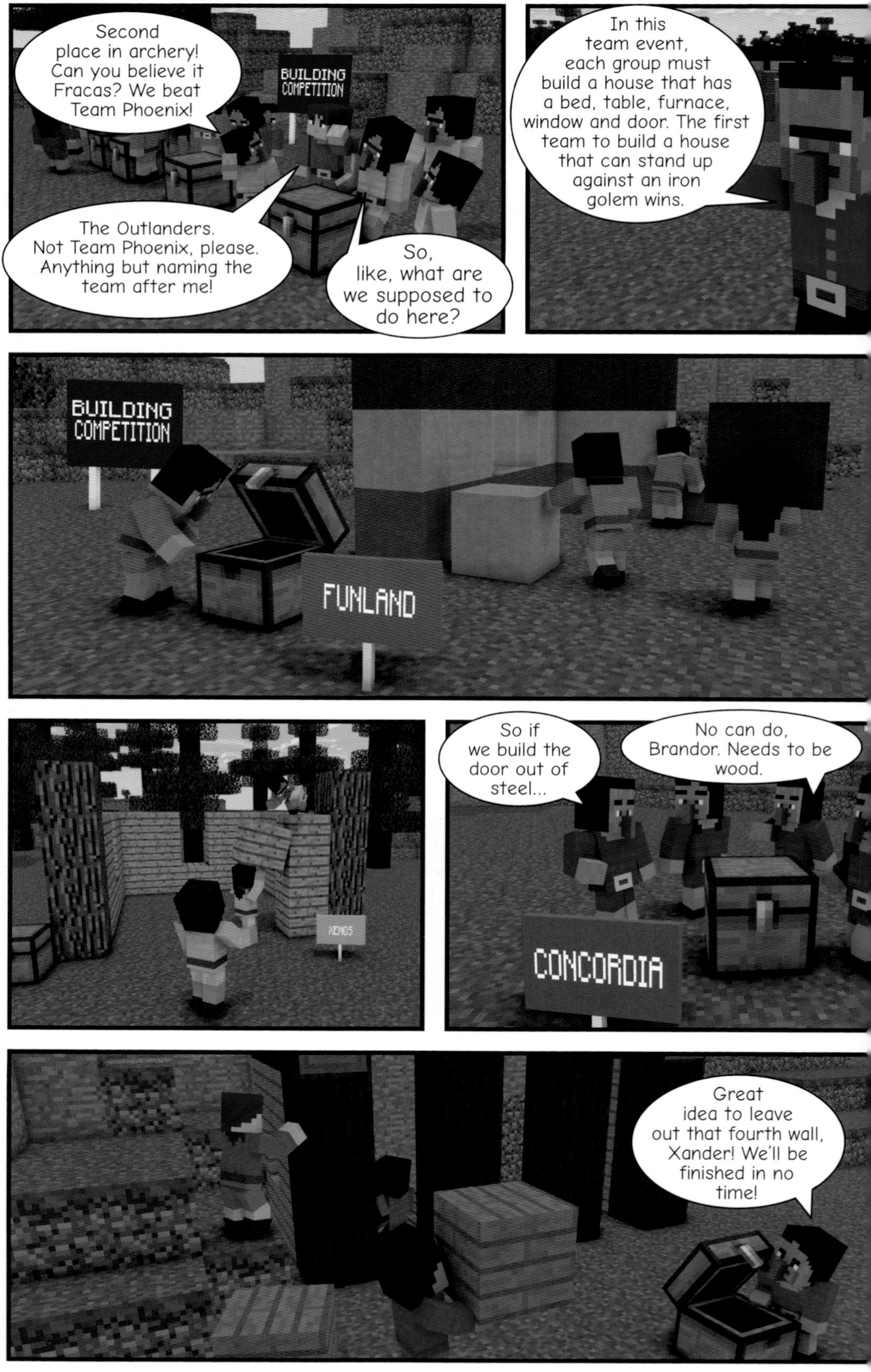

Second place in archery! Can you believe it Fracas? We beat Team Phoenix!
BUILDING COMPETITION
The Outlanders. Not Team Phoenix, please. Anything but naming the team after me!
So, like, what are we supposed to do here?
In this team event, each group must build a house that has a bed, table, furnace, window and door. The first team to build a house that can stand up against an iron golem wins.
BUILDING COMPETITION
FUNLAND
XENOS
So if we build the door out of steel...
No can do, Brandor. Needs to be wood.
CONCORDIA
Great idea to leave out that fourth wall, Xander! We'll be finished in no time!

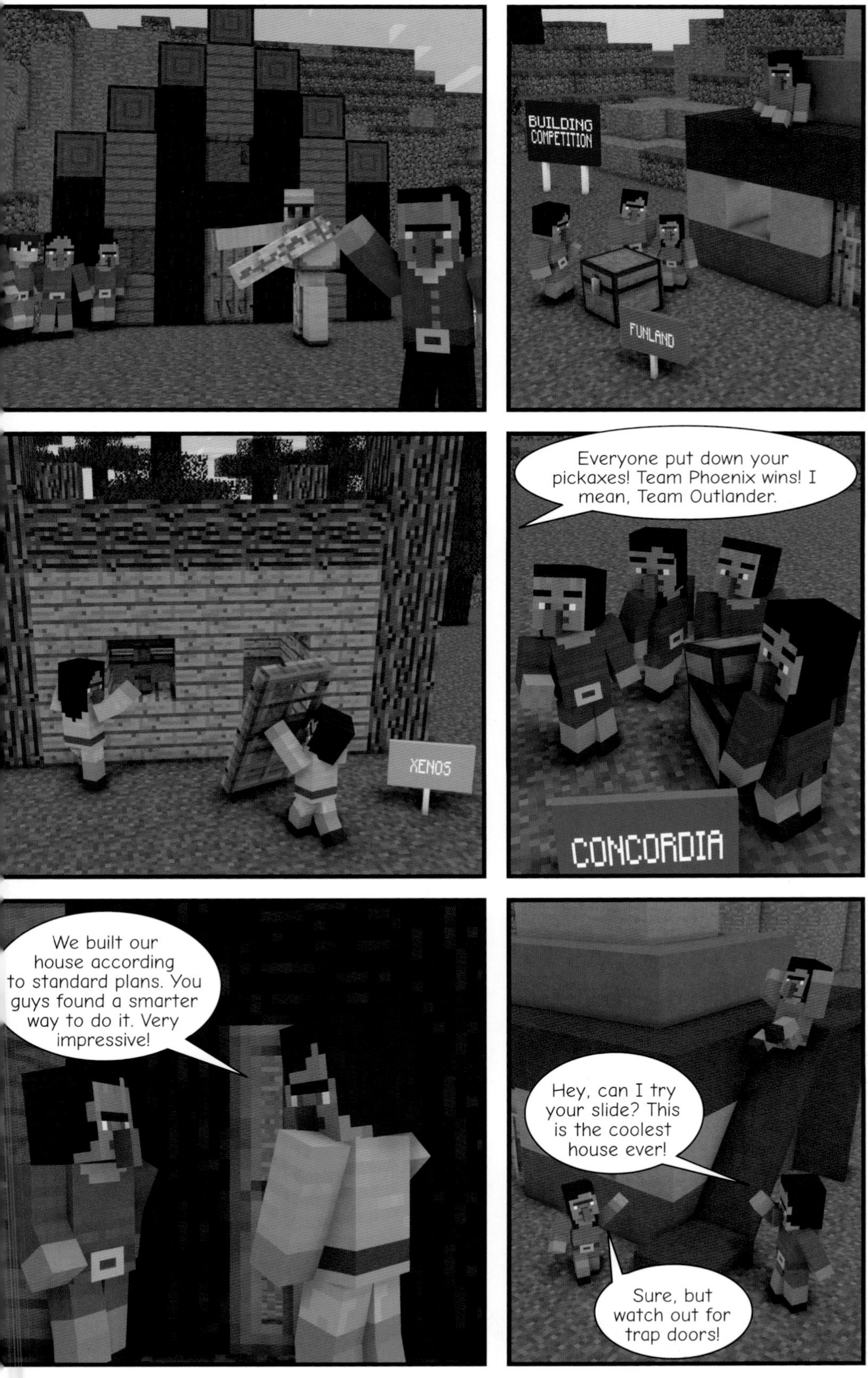
BUILDING COMPETITION
FUNLAND
XENOS
Everyone put down your pickaxes! Team Phoenix wins! I mean, Team Outlander.
CONCORDIA
We built our house according to standard plans. You guys found a smarter way to do it. Very impressive!
Hey, can I try your slide? This is the coolest house ever!
Sure, but watch out for trap doors!

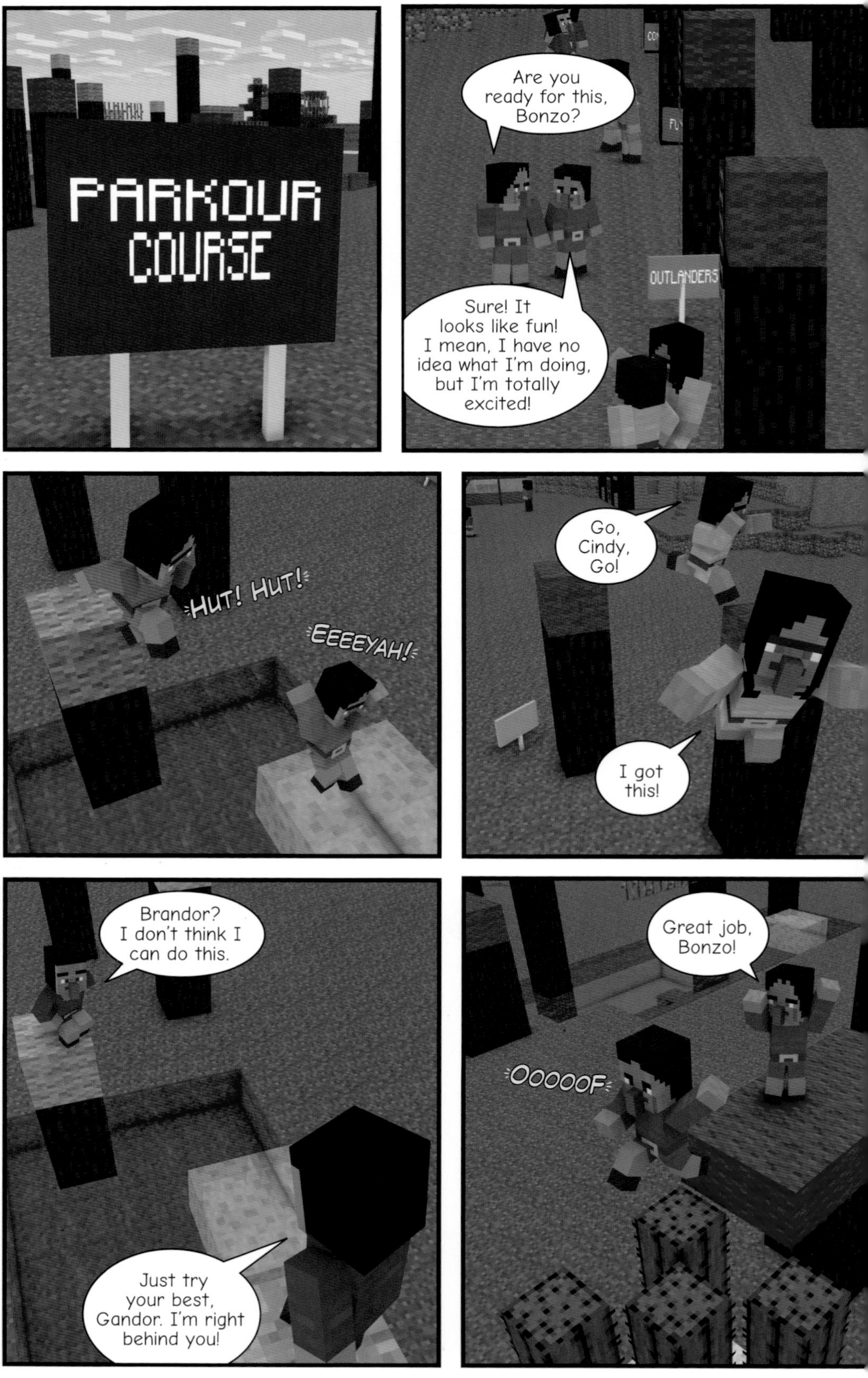
PARKOUR COURSE
Are you ready for this, Bonzo?
OUTLANDERS
Sure! It looks like fun! I mean, I have no idea what I'm doing, but I'm totally excited!
HUT! HUT!
EEEEYAH!
Go, Cindy, Go!
I got this!
Brandor? I don't think I can do this.
Just try your best, Gandor. I'm right behind you!
Great job, Bonzo!
OOOOOF

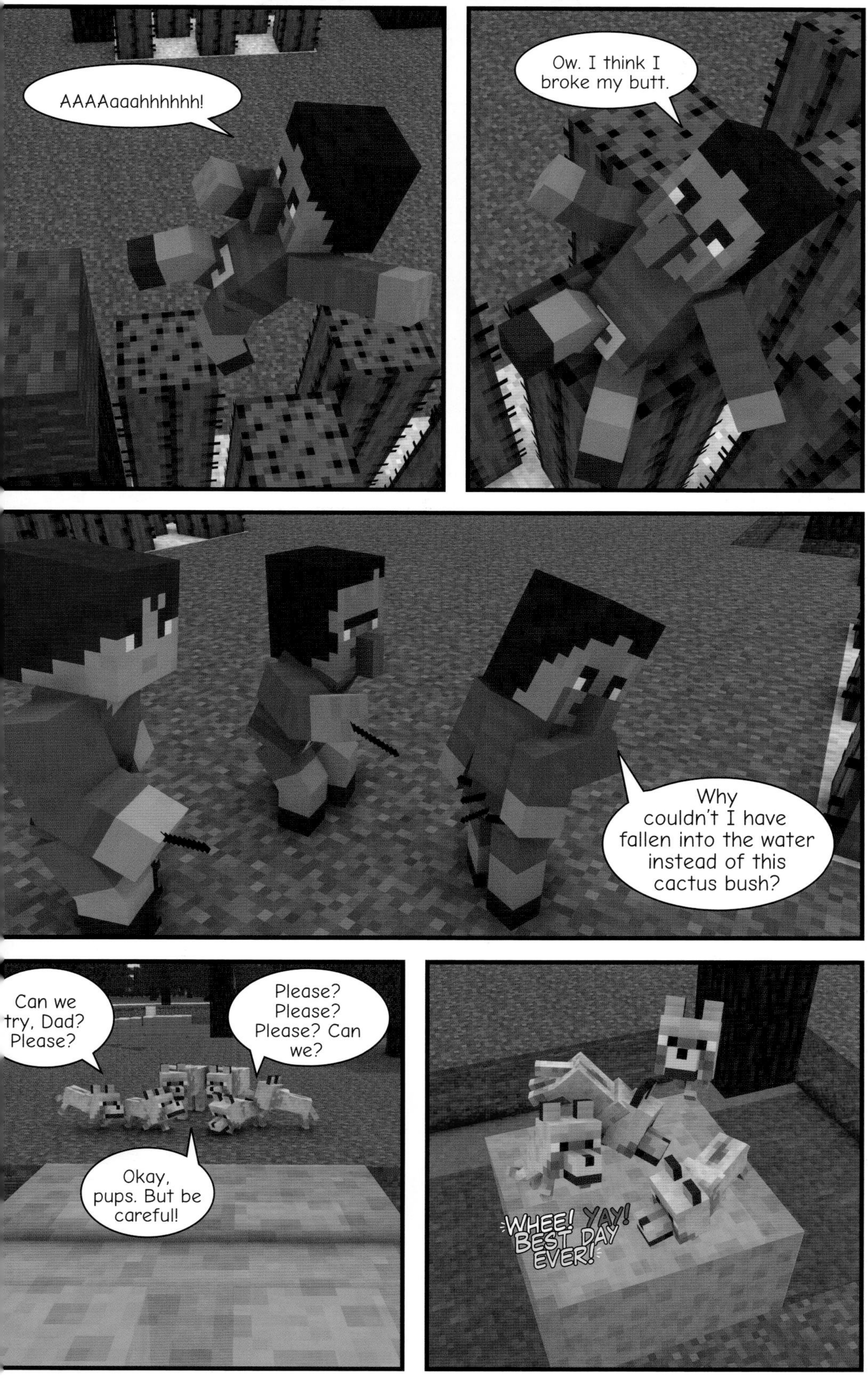
AAAAaaahhhhhh!
Ow. I think I broke my butt.
Why couldn't I have fallen into the water instead of this cactus bush?
Can we try, Dad? Please?
Please? Please? Please? Can we?
Okay, pups. But be careful!
WHEE! YAY! BEST DAY EVER!

Our next event is the mining competition! Be careful. There are real dangers down there.

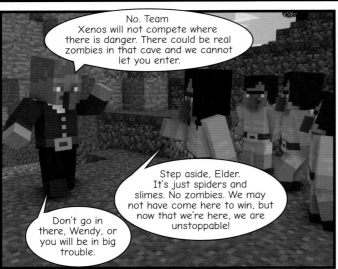

No. Team Xenos will not compete where there is danger. There could be real zombies in that cave and we cannot let you enter.

Step aside, Elder. It's just spiders and slimes. No zombies. We may not have come here to win, but now that we're here, we are unstoppable!

Don't go in there, Wendy, or you will be in big trouble.

Go on in, kids. We will deal with the consequences later. But now, LET'S MINE!

Thank you for standing up to him like that.

It wasn't for you. We need more food, and if we win, that's what we're going to ask for. I'm doing this for Xenos. Not for your silly competition.

Either way, it takes a lot to stand up to the Elders of Xenos. You are very brave.

You aren't the only one who stands up to them, Phoenix. You just make a bigger deal of it.

What's her problem?

She doesn't like me very much.

You've gotten used to people calling you a prophet and treating you like you rule this town.

Geez. Thanks a lot!

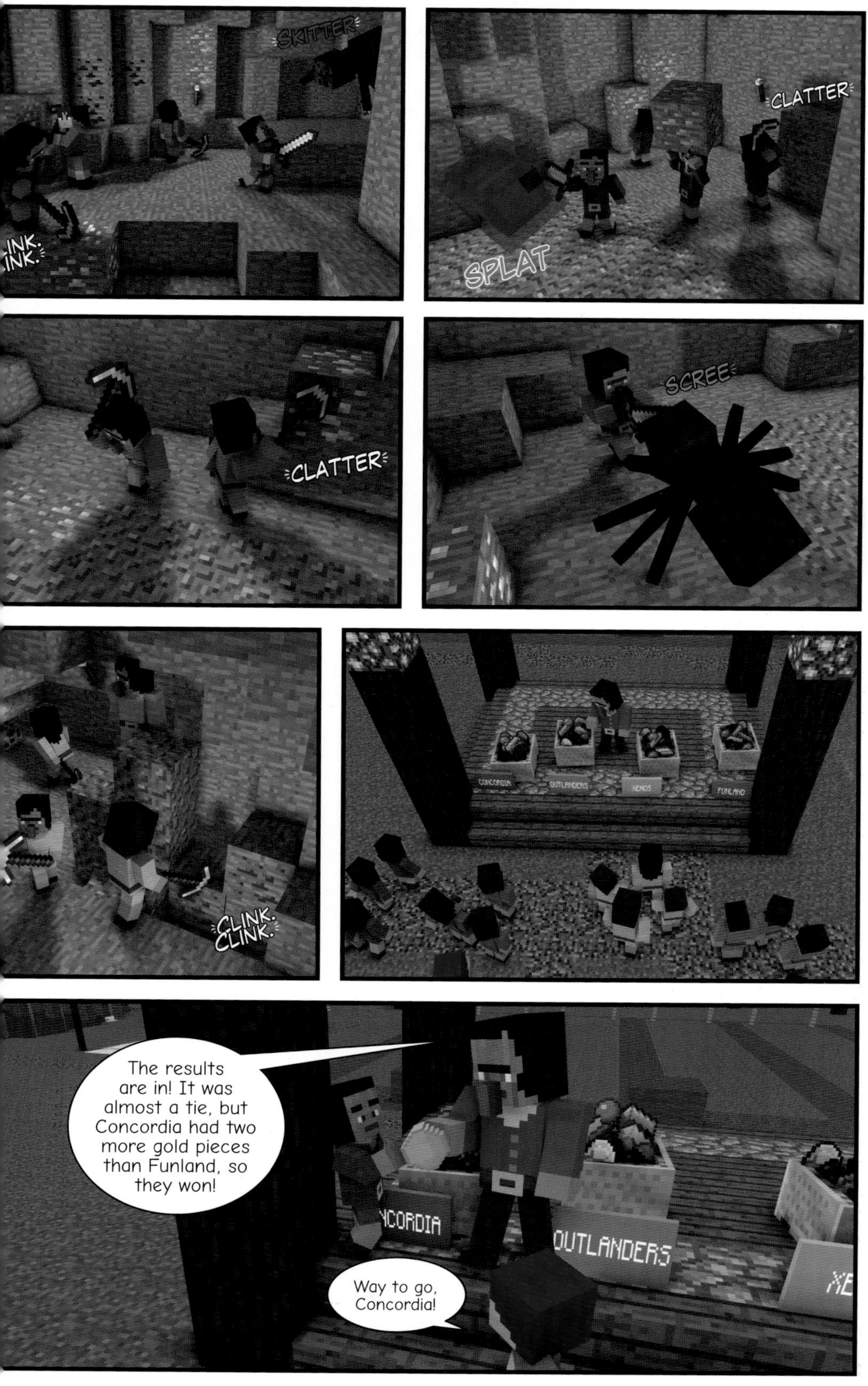
SKITTER
INK.
INK.
CLATTER
SPLAT
CLATTER
SCREE
CLINK.
CLINK.
CONCORDIA
OUTLANDERS
XENOS
FUNLAND
The results are in! It was almost a tie, but Concordia had two more gold pieces than Funland, so they won!
OUTLANDERS
Way to go, Concordia!

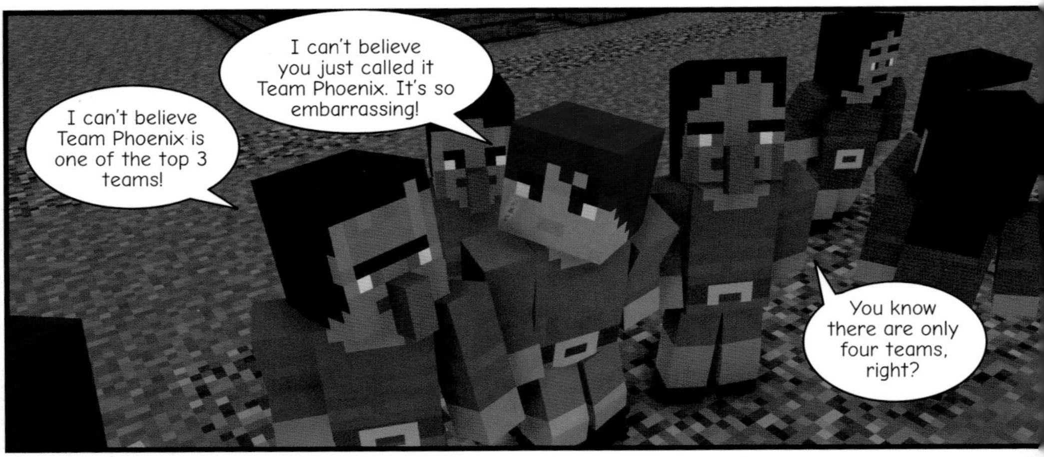
I can't believe Team Phoenix is one of the top 3 teams!
I can't believe you just called it Team Phoenix. It's so embarrassing!
You know there are only four teams, right?

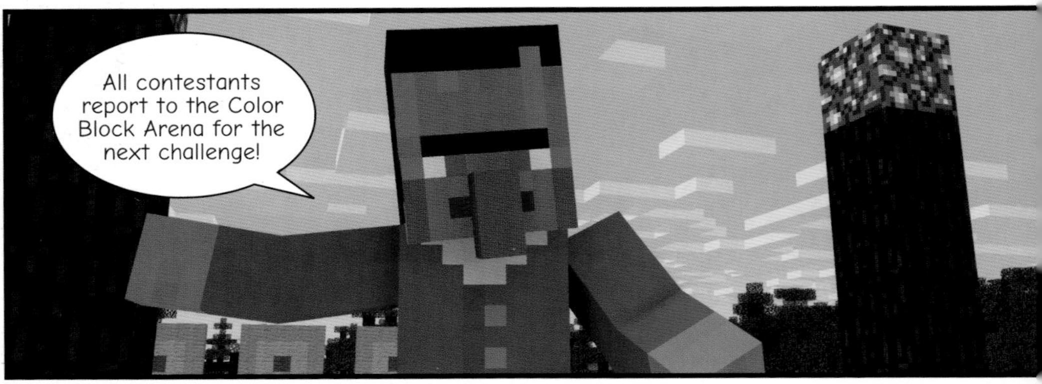
All contestants report to the Color Block Arena for the next challenge!

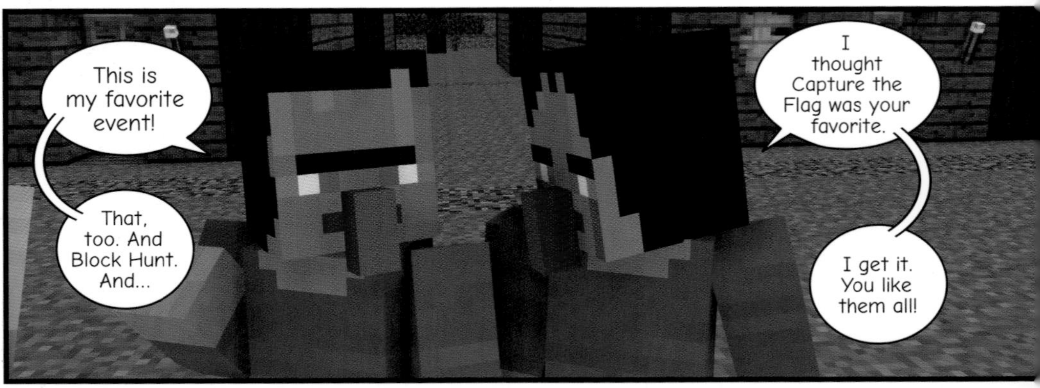
This is my favorite event!
I thought Capture the Flag was your favorite.
That, too. And Block Hunt. And...
I get it. You like them all!

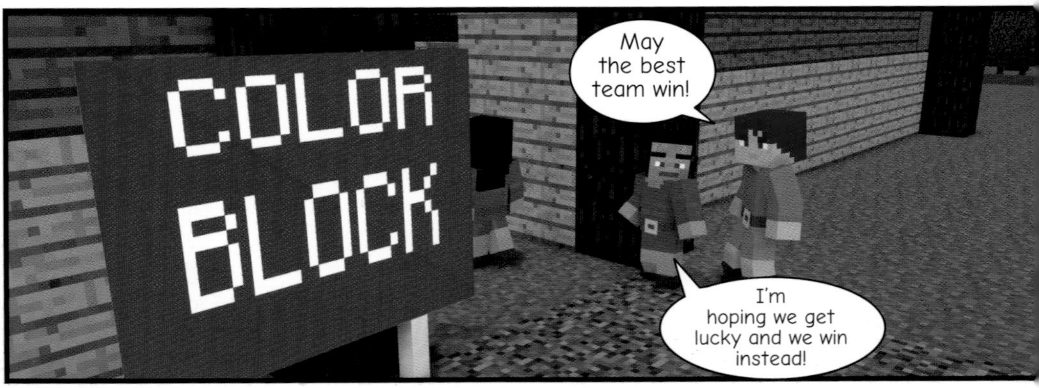
COLOR BLOCK
May the best team win!
I'm hoping we get lucky and we win instead!

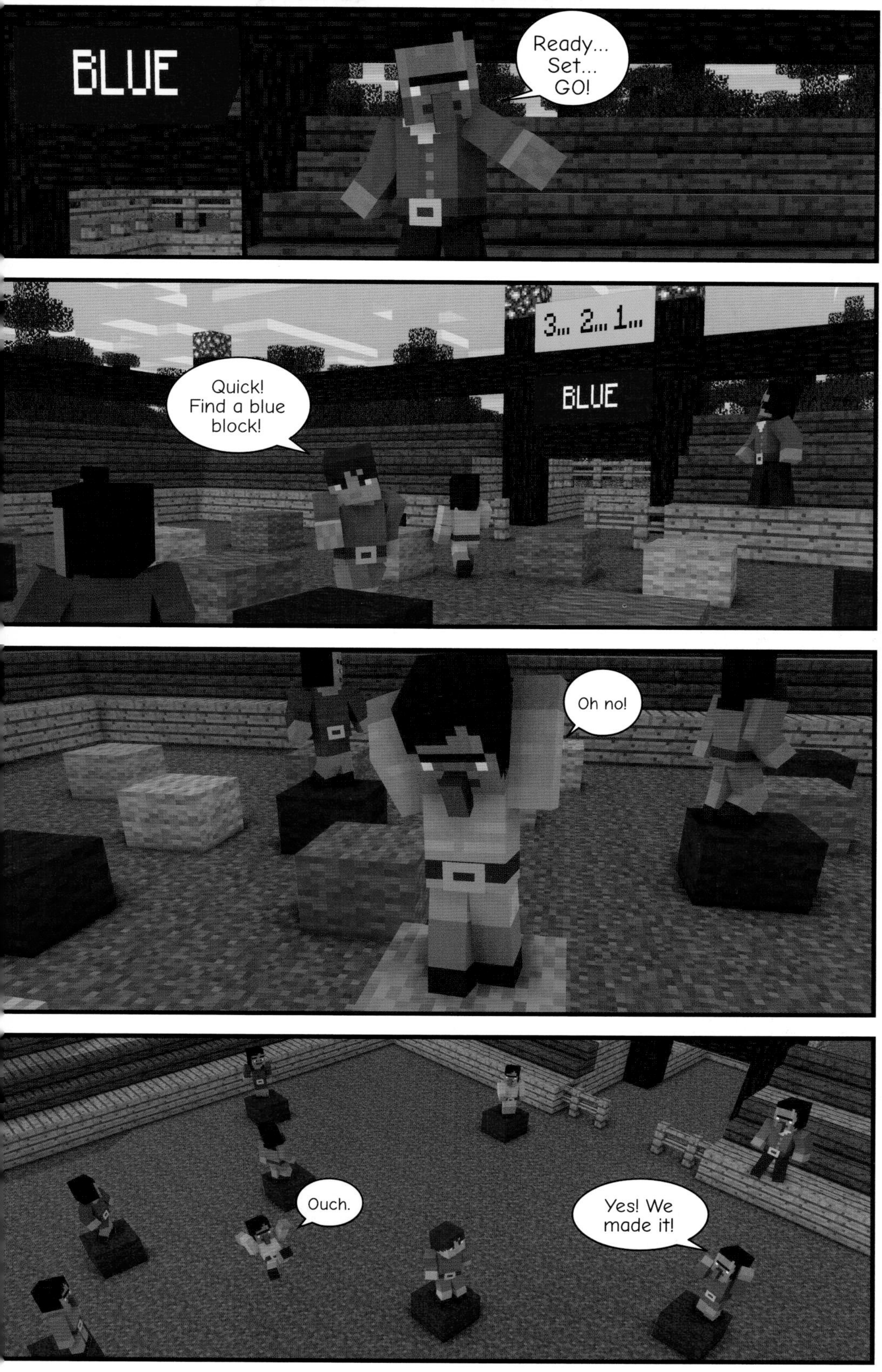
BLUE
Ready... Set... GO!
3... 2... 1...
BLUE
Quick! Find a blue block!
Oh no!
Ouch.
Yes! We made it!

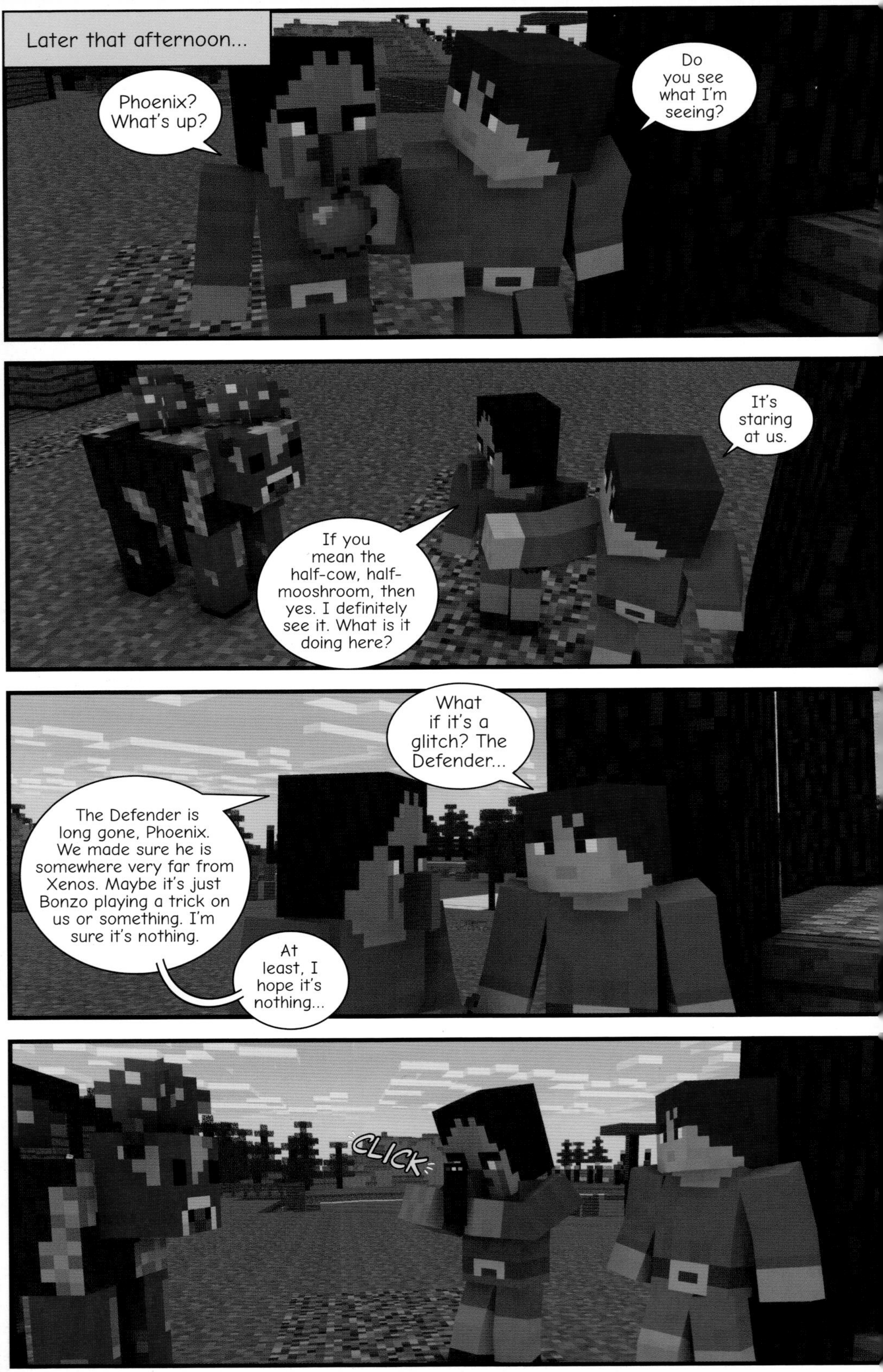
Later that afternoon...
Phoenix? What's up?
Do you see what I'm seeing?
It's staring at us.
If you mean the half-cow, half-mooshroom, then yes. I definitely see it. What is it doing here?
What if it's a glitch? The Defender...
The Defender is long gone, Phoenix. We made sure he is somewhere very far from Xenos. Maybe it's just Bonzo playing a trick on us or something. I'm sure it's nothing.
At least, I hope it's nothing...
CLICK

CHAPTER 4

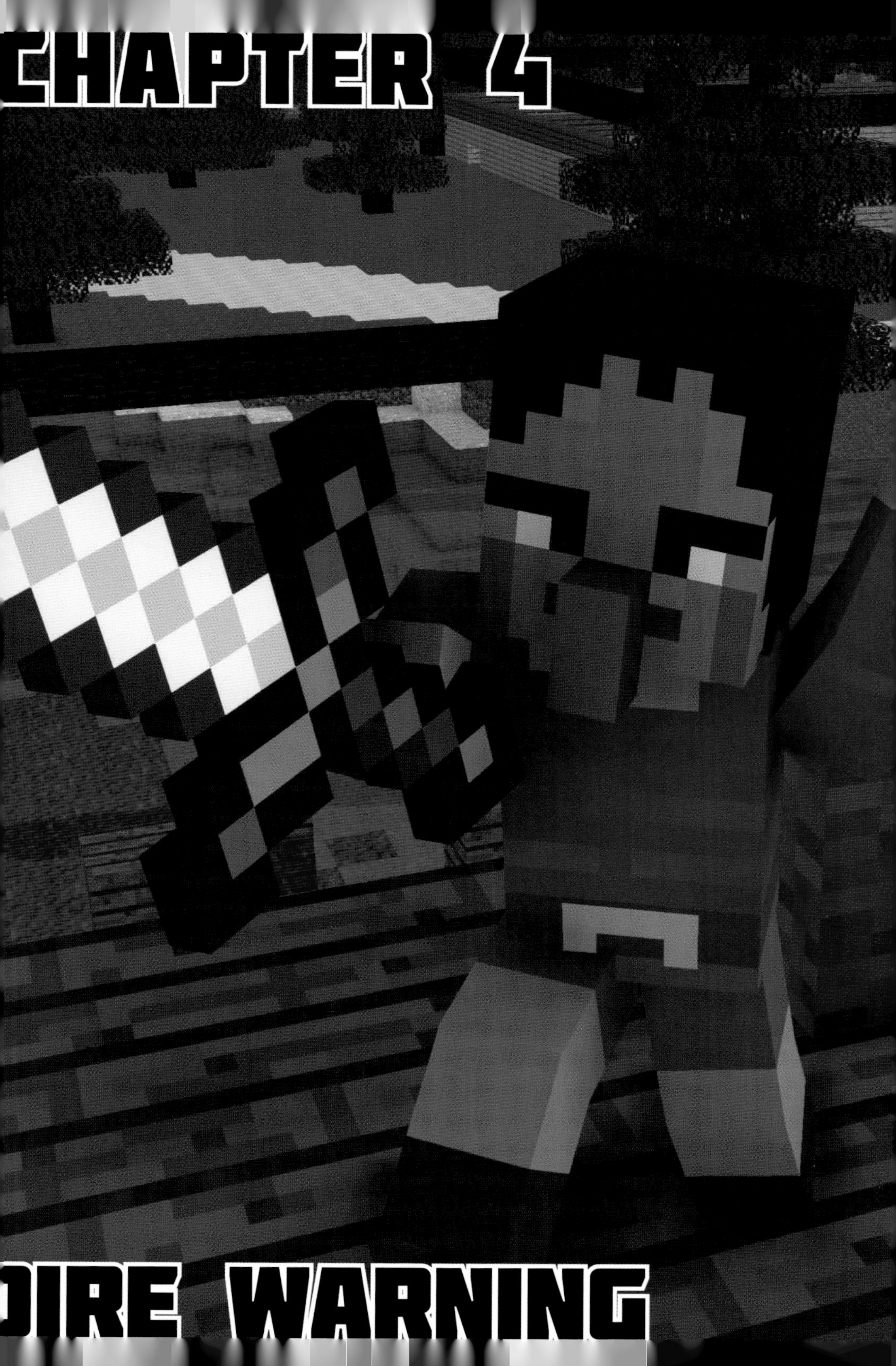

DIRE WARNING

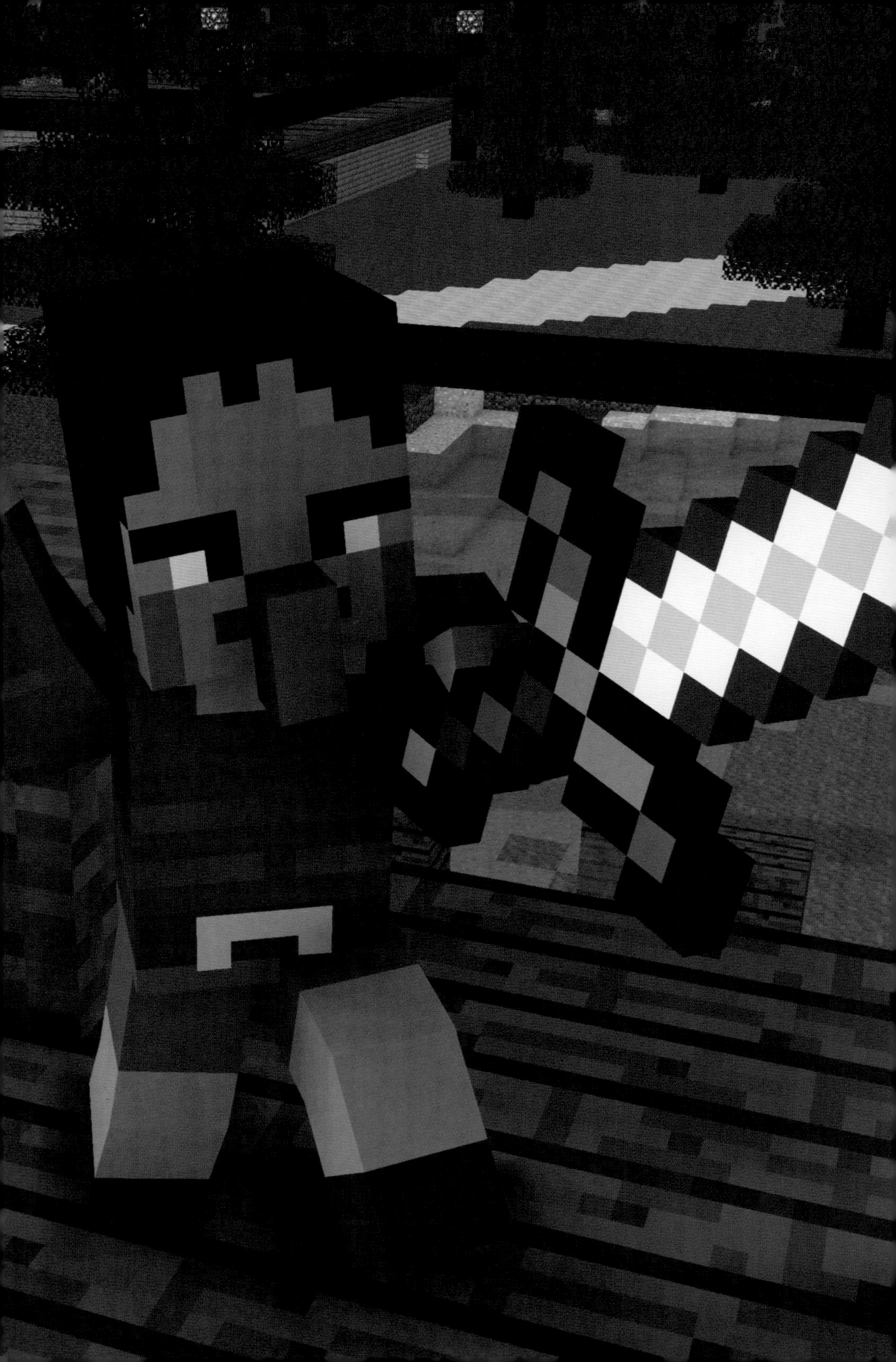

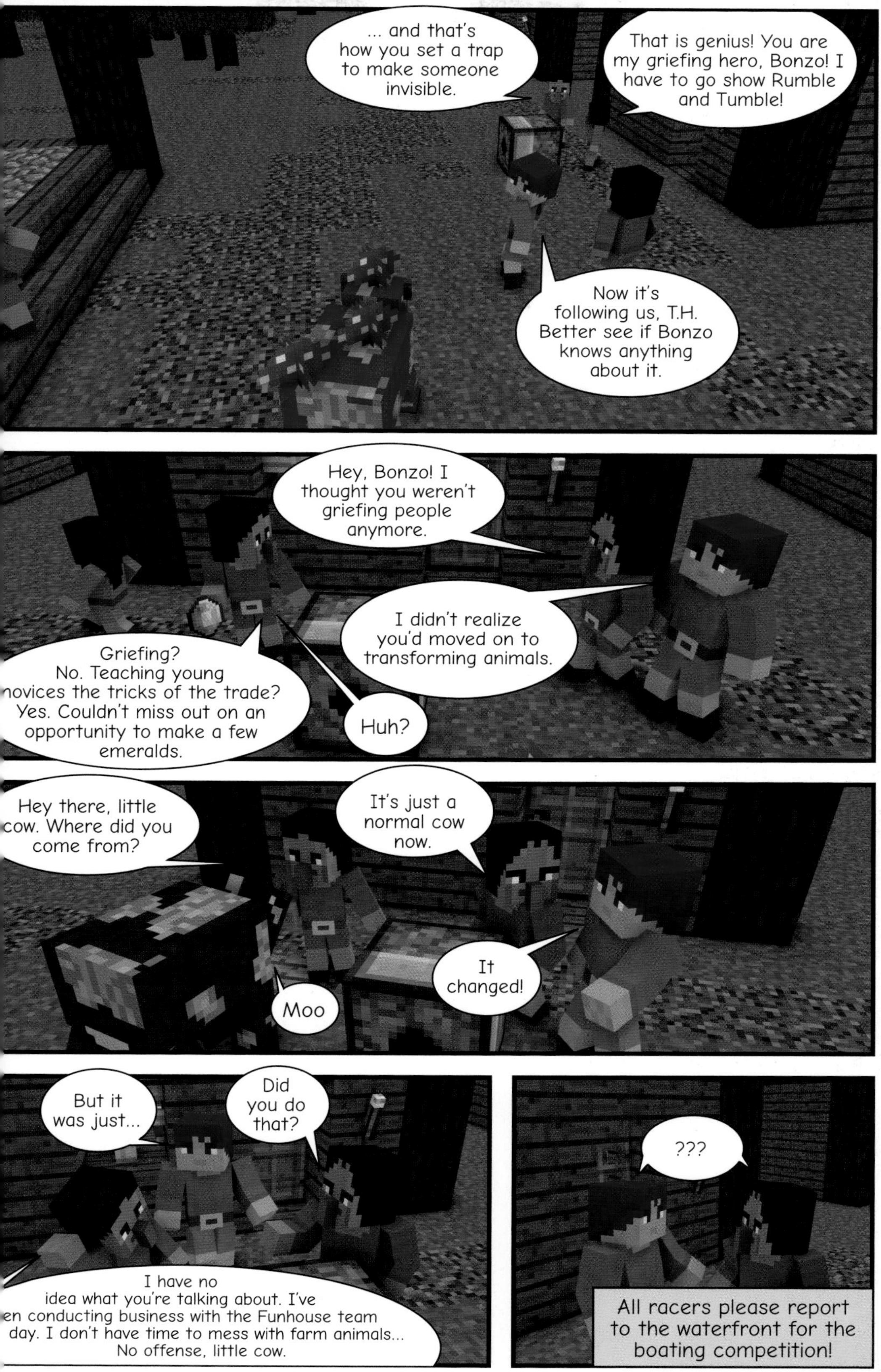
... and that's how you set a trap to make someone invisible.
That is genius! You are my griefing hero, Bonzo! I have to go show Rumble and Tumble!
Now it's following us, T.H. Better see if Bonzo knows anything about it.
Hey, Bonzo! I thought you weren't griefing people anymore.
I didn't realize you'd moved on to transforming animals.
Griefing? No. Teaching young novices the tricks of the trade? Yes. Couldn't miss out on an opportunity to make a few emeralds.
Huh?
Hey there, little cow. Where did you come from?
It's just a normal cow now.
It changed!
Moo
But it was just...
Did you do that?
I have no idea what you're talking about. I've en conducting business with the Funhouse team day. I don't have time to mess with farm animals... No offense, little cow.
???
All racers please report to the waterfront for the boating competition!

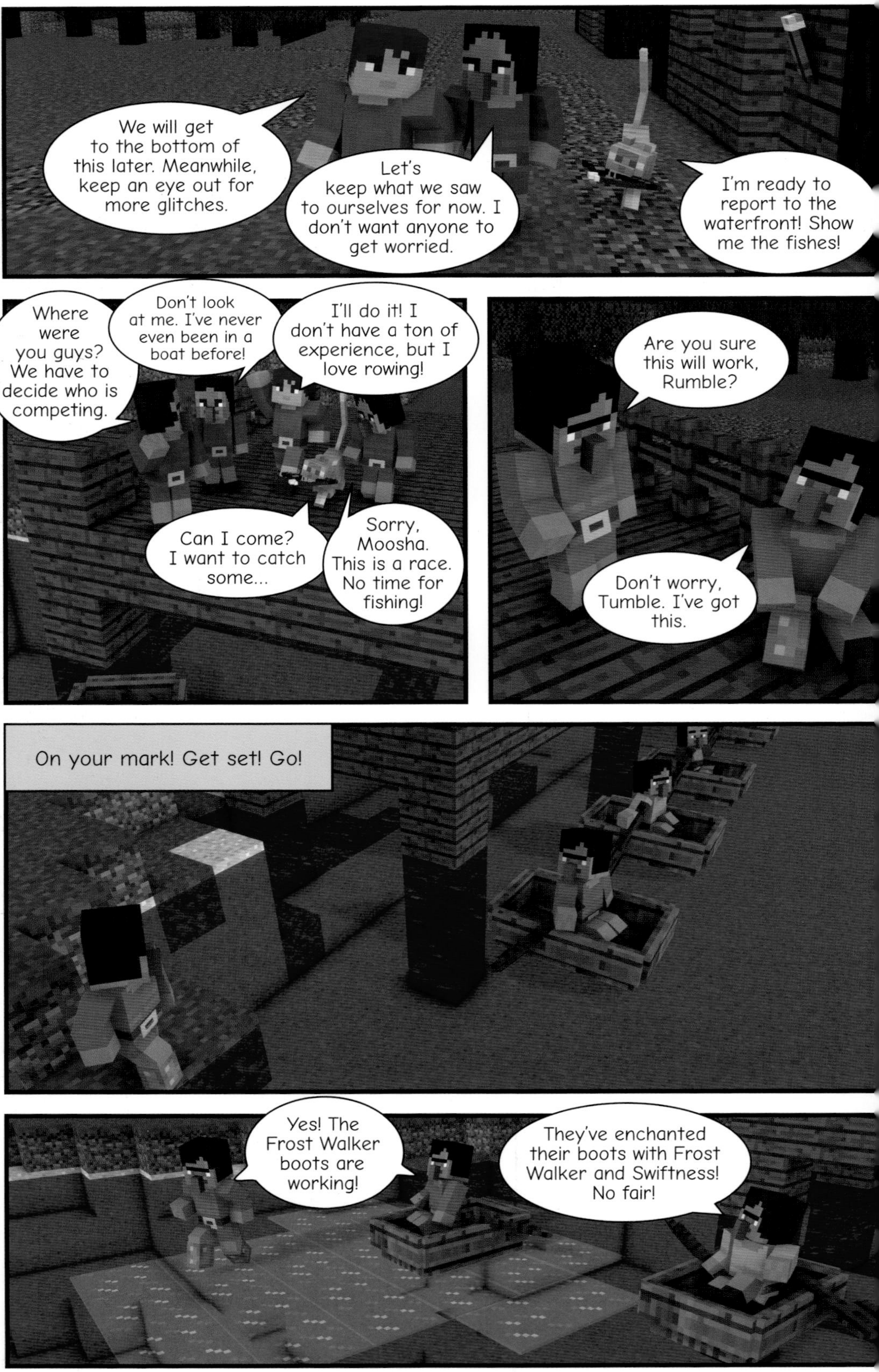
We will get to the bottom of this later. Meanwhile, keep an eye out for more glitches.
Let's keep what we saw to ourselves for now. I don't want anyone to get worried.
I'm ready to report to the waterfront! Show me the fishes!
Where were you guys? We have to decide who is competing.
Don't look at me. I've never even been in a boat before!
I'll do it! I don't have a ton of experience, but I love rowing!
Can I come? I want to catch some...
Sorry, Moosha. This is a race. No time for fishing!
Are you sure this will work, Rumble?
Don't worry, Tumble. I've got this.
On your mark! Get set! Go!
Yes! The Frost Walker boots are working!
They've enchanted their boots with Frost Walker and Swiftness! No fair!

They can't do that, can they?

Absolutely! That was a brilliant idea!

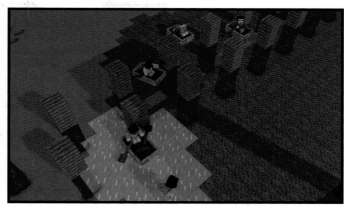

Yes!

SLAP

Well played, Rumble! That was good thinking!

Team Funland is the clear winner! Next event is fishing!

FISHING!

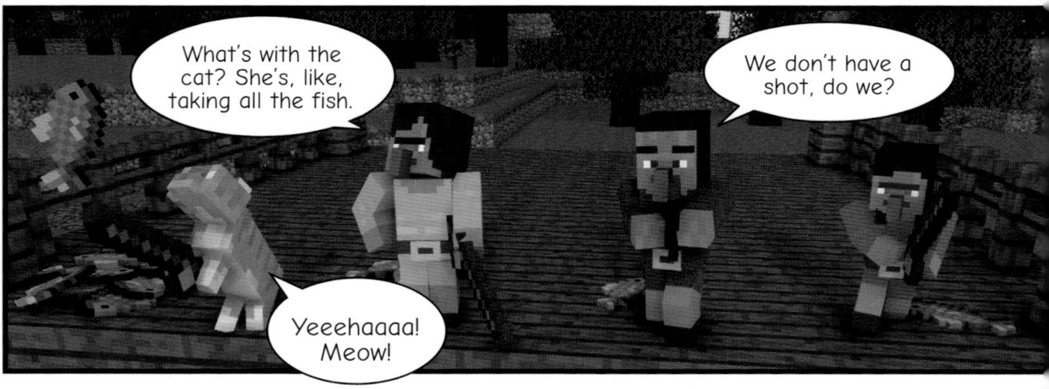
What's with the cat? She's, like, taking all the fish.
We don't have a shot, do we?
Yeeehaaaa! Meow!

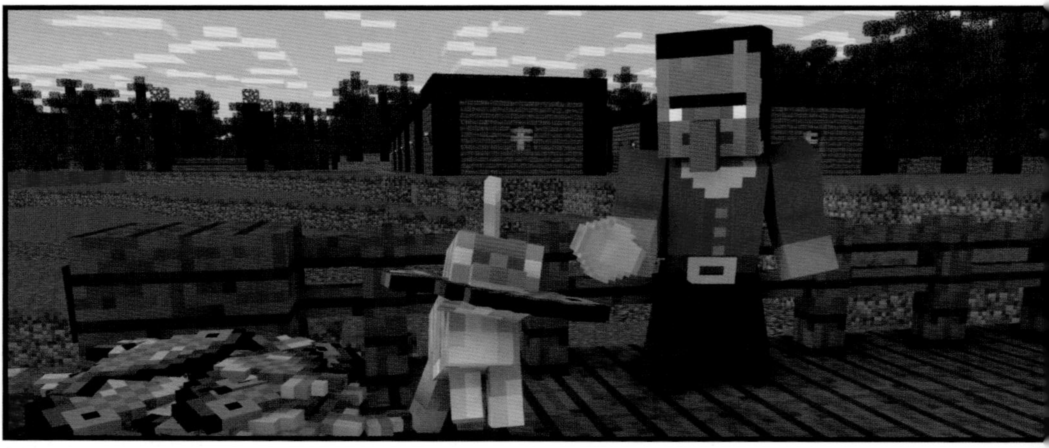

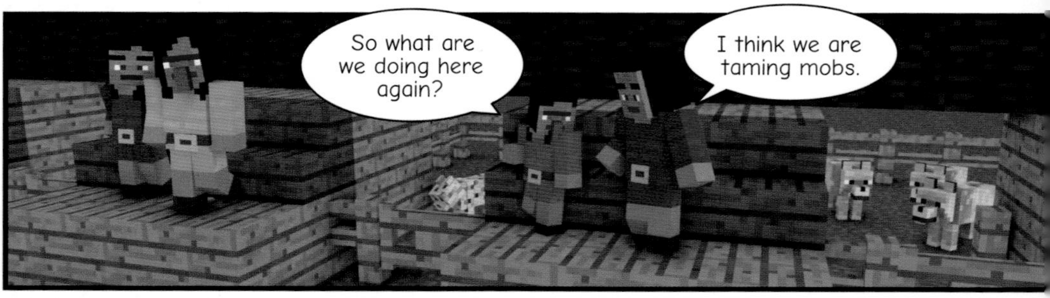
So what are we doing here again?
I think we are taming mobs.

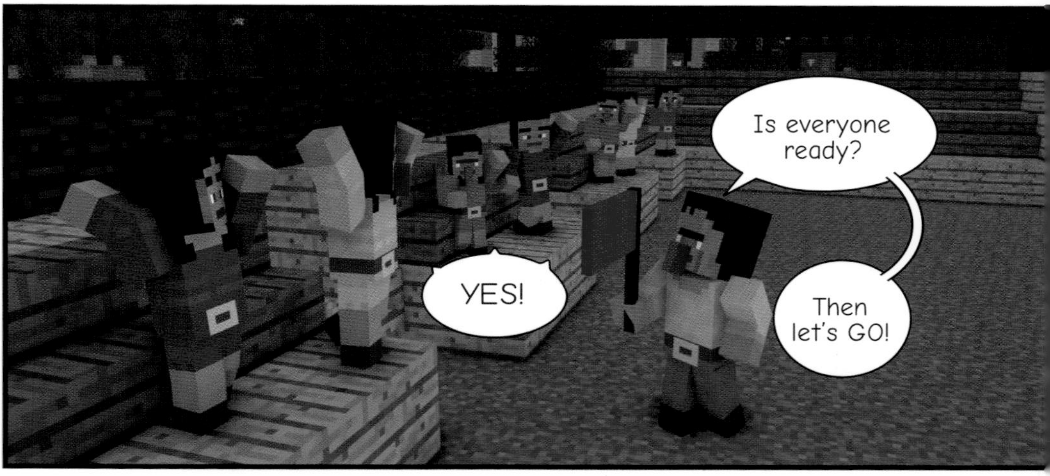
Is everyone ready?
YES!
Then let's GO!

It looks like Cordelia from Concordia is the winner!

She tamed more animals than everyone else put together!

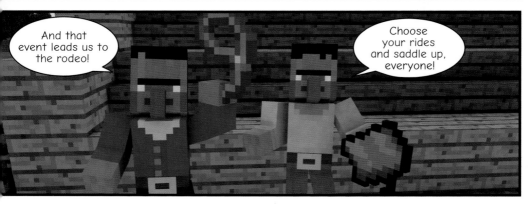

And that event leads us to the rodeo!

Choose your rides and saddle up, everyone!

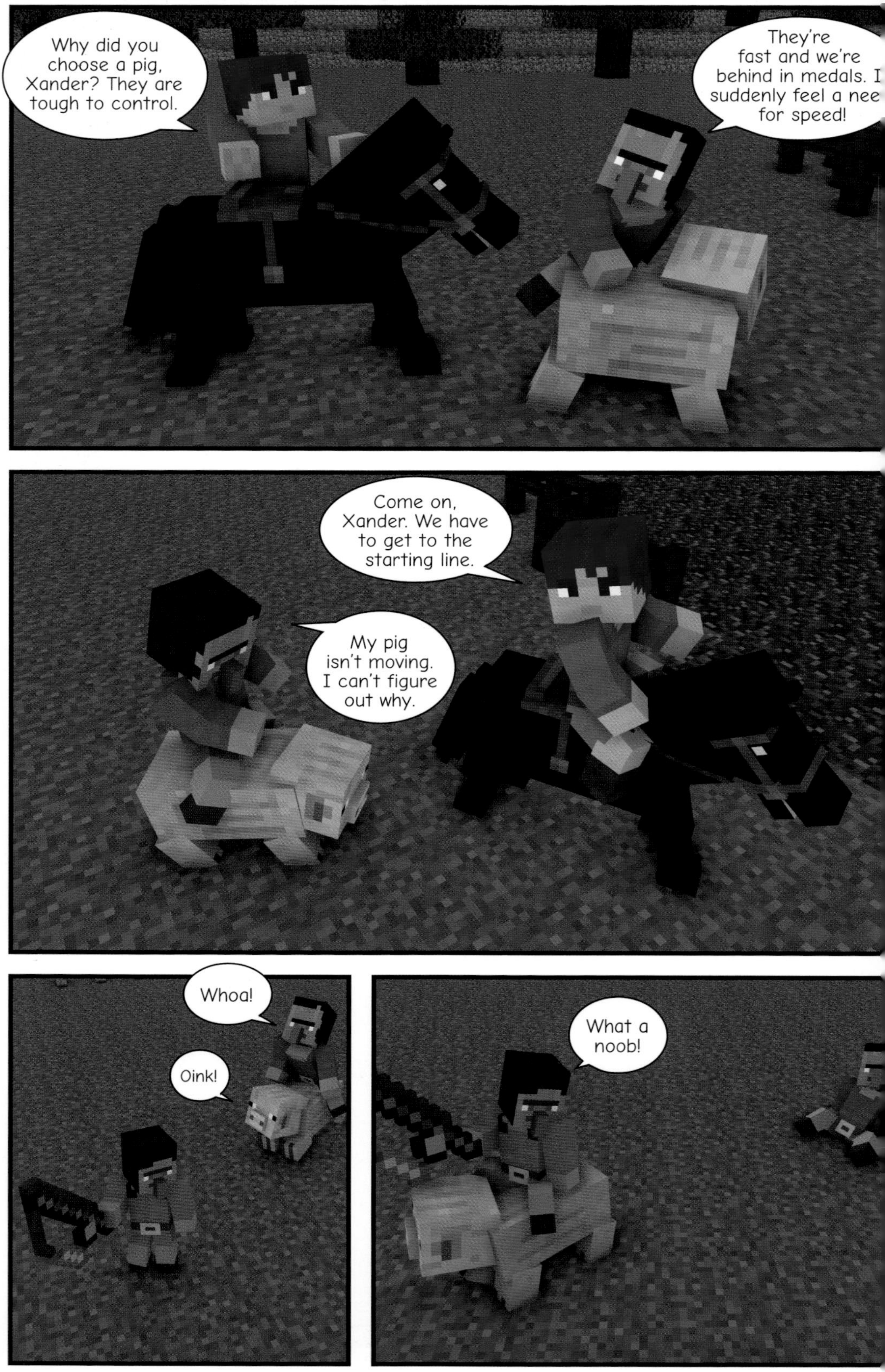
Why did you choose a pig, Xander? They are tough to control.
They're fast and we're behind in medals. I suddenly feel a nee for speed!
Come on, Xander. We have to get to the starting line.
My pig isn't moving. I can't figure out why.
Whoa!
Oink!
What a noob!

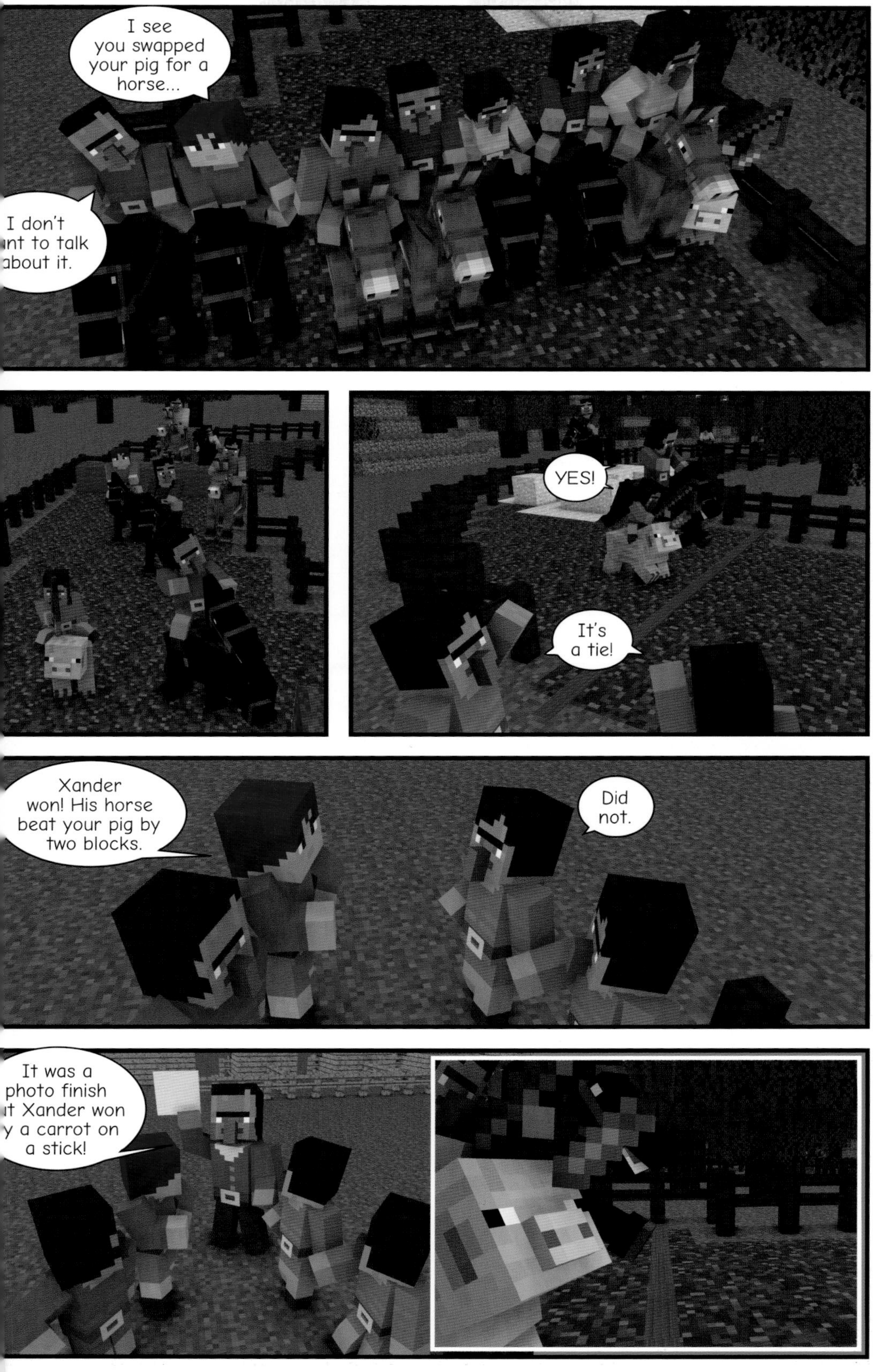
I see you swapped your pig for a horse...
I don't nt to talk about it.
YES!
It's a tie!
Xander won! His horse beat your pig by two blocks.
Did not.
It was a photo finish t Xander won y a carrot on a stick!

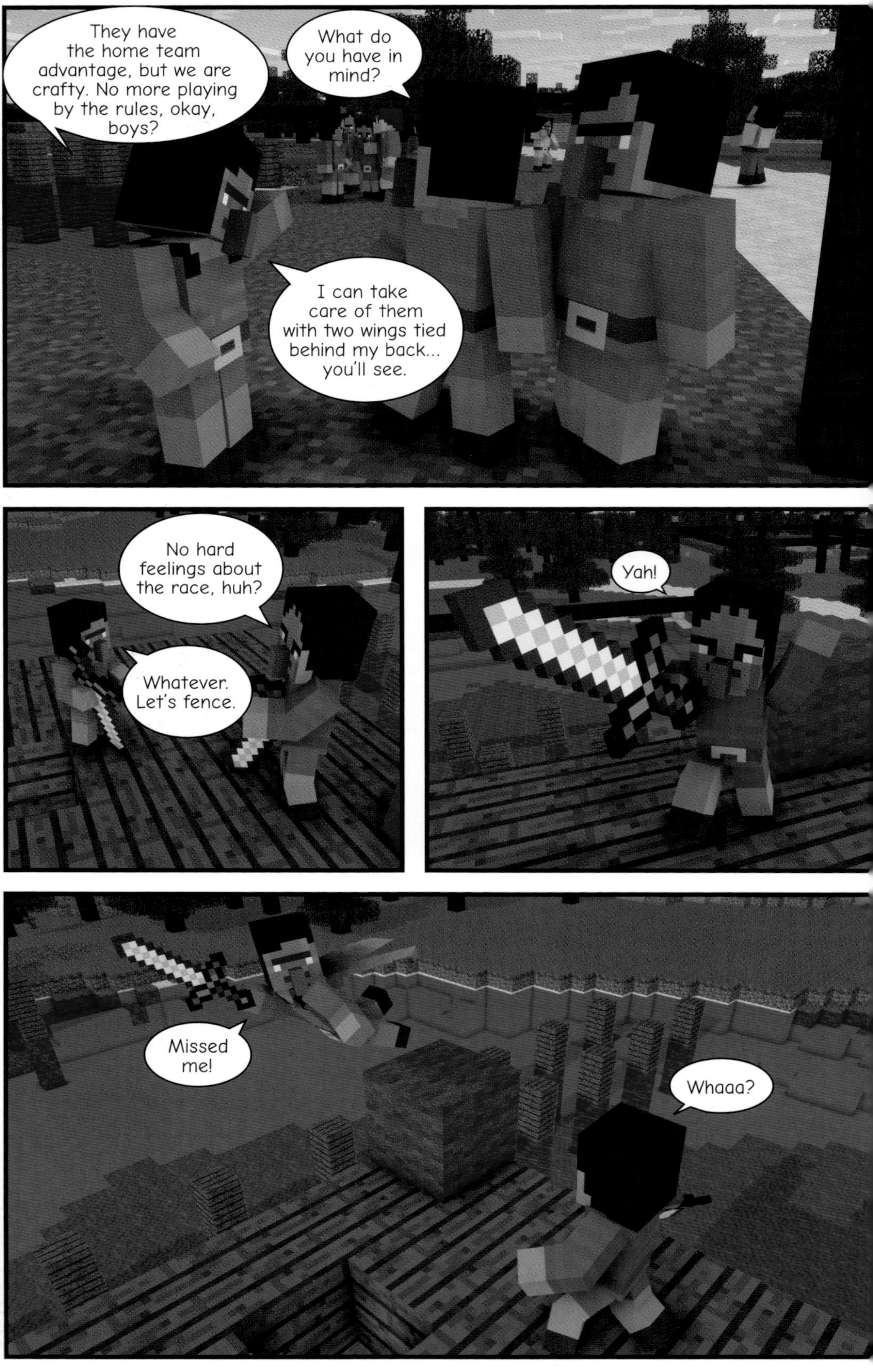
They have the home team advantage, but we are crafty. No more playing by the rules, okay, boys?
What do you have in mind?
I can take care of them with two wings tied behind my back... you'll see.
No hard feelings about the race, huh?
Whatever. Let's fence.
Yah!
Missed me!
Whaaa?

Whoooaaaa
Ha ha! You're all wet!
I should have known you'd try something like that.
Sorry, T.H. When I suggested Water Fencing as an activity, I guess I didn't think it through.
Next time we play, let's fence over a nice cushion of slime blocks!

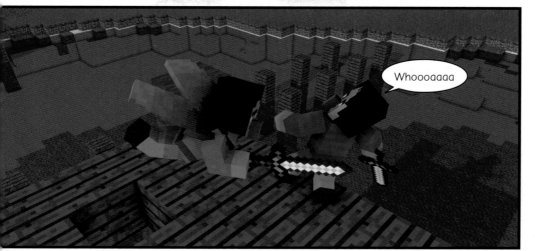

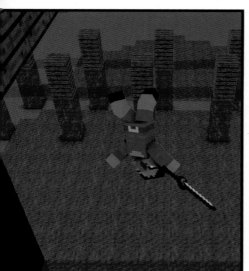

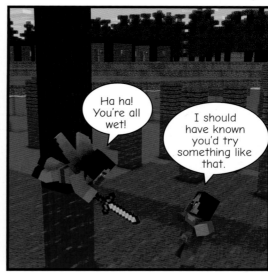

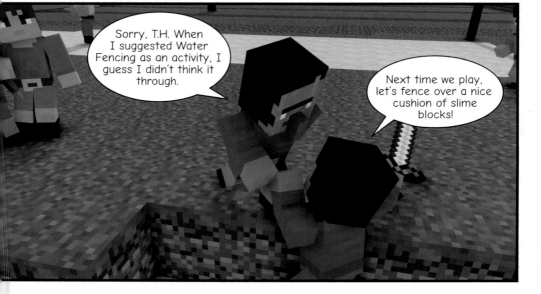

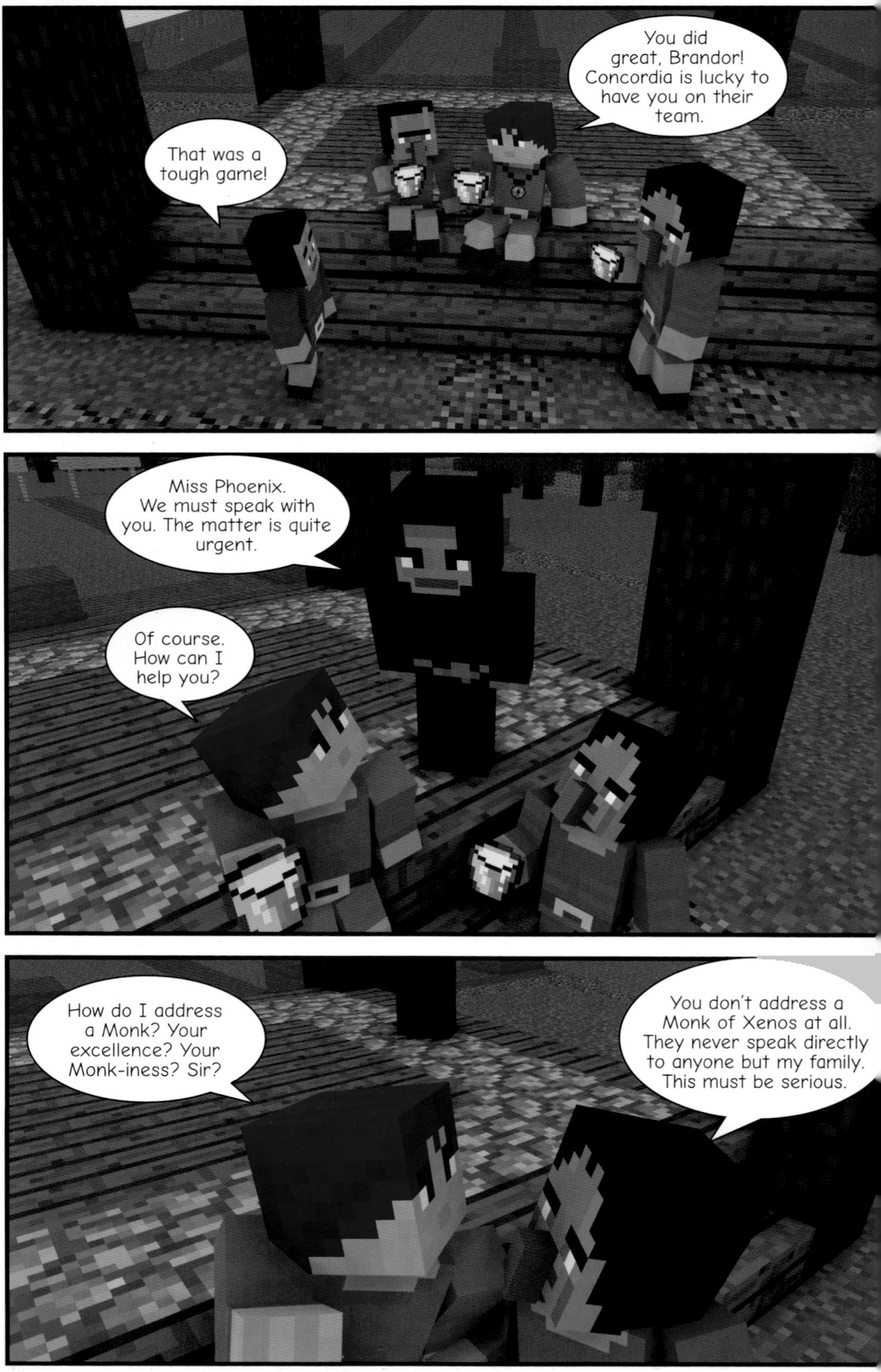
That was a tough game!
You did great, Brandor! Concordia is lucky to have you on their team.
Miss Phoenix. We must speak with you. The matter is quite urgent.
Of course. How can I help you?
How do I address a Monk? Your excellence? Your Monk-iness? Sir?
You don't address a Monk of Xenos at all. They never speak directly to anyone but my family. This must be serious.

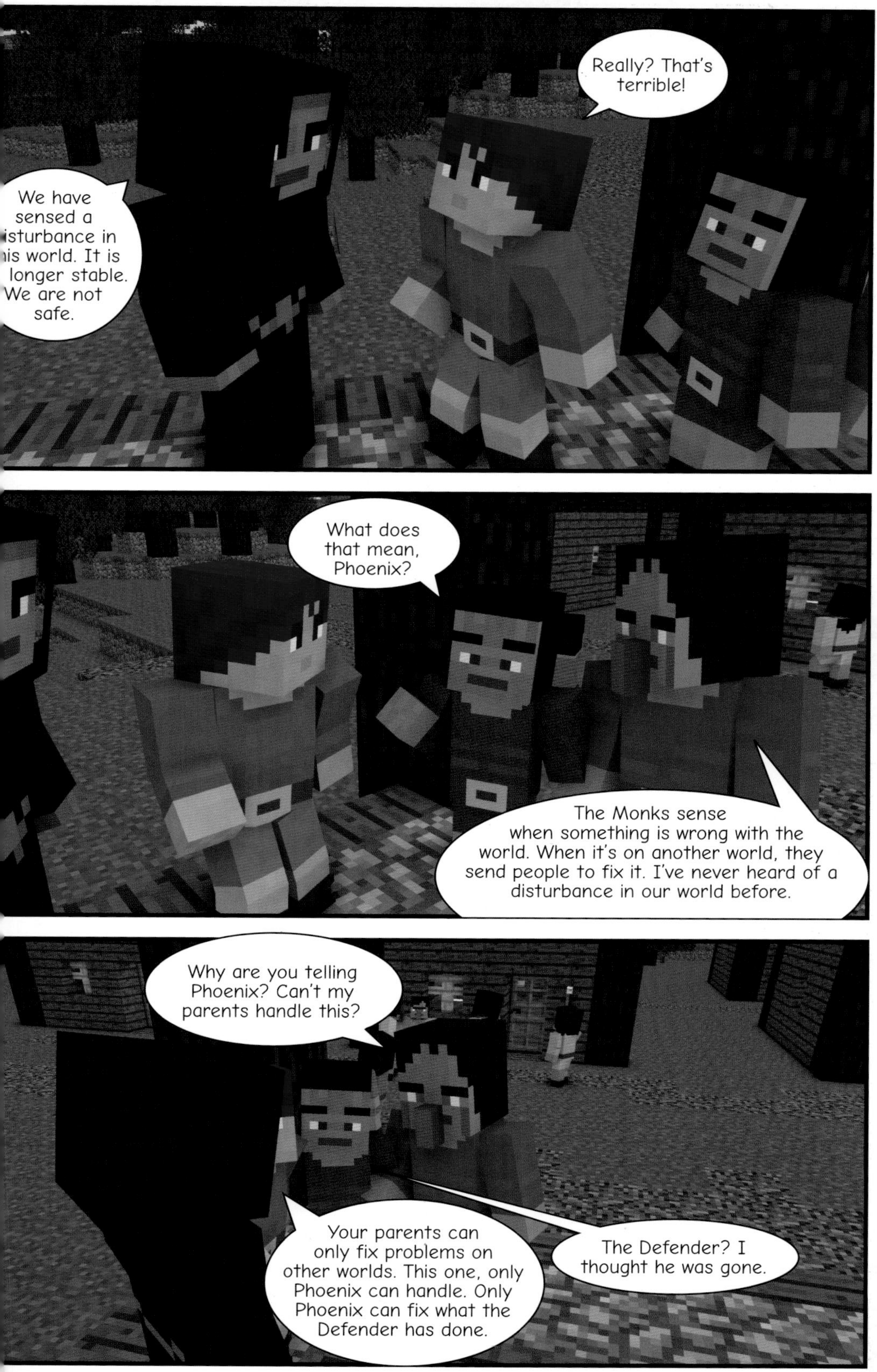
Really? That's terrible!
We have sensed a isturbance in is world. It is longer stable. We are not safe.
What does that mean, Phoenix?
The Monks sense when something is wrong with the world. When it's on another world, they send people to fix it. I've never heard of a disturbance in our world before.
Why are you telling Phoenix? Can't my parents handle this?
Your parents can only fix problems on other worlds. This one, only Phoenix can handle. Only Phoenix can fix what the Defender has done.
The Defender? I thought he was gone.

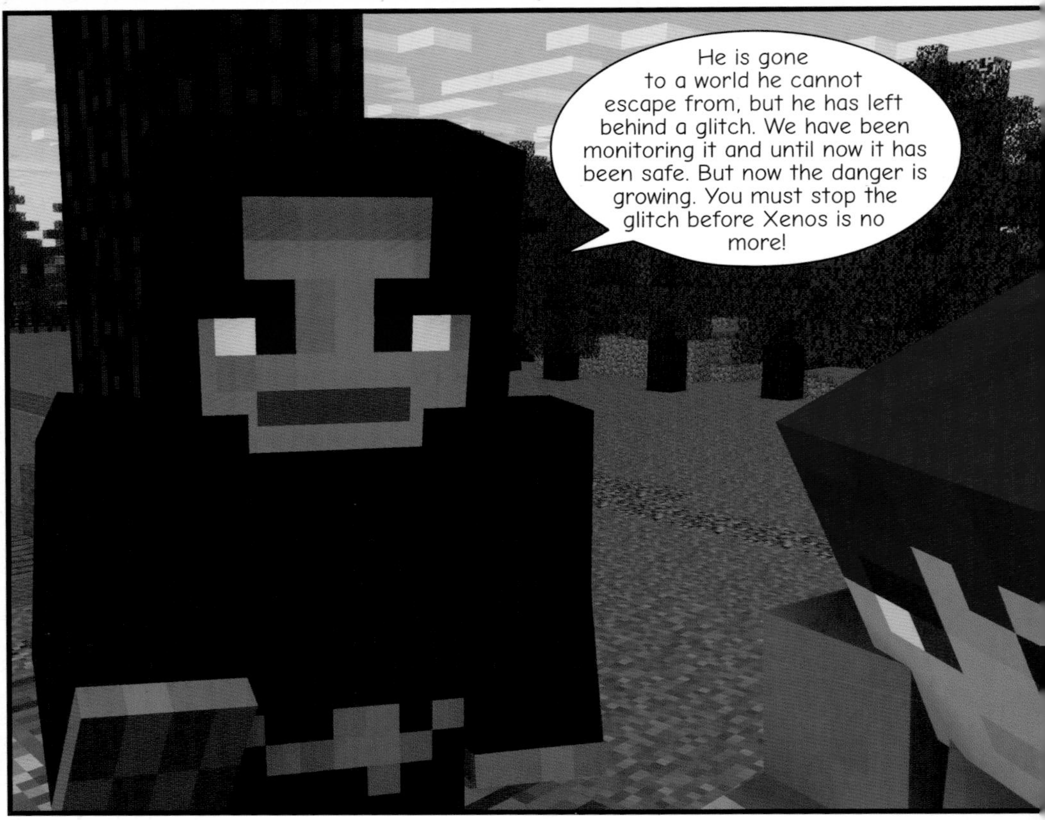
He is gone to a world he cannot escape from, but he has left behind a glitch. We have been monitoring it and until now it has been safe. But now the danger is growing. You must stop the glitch before Xenos is no more!

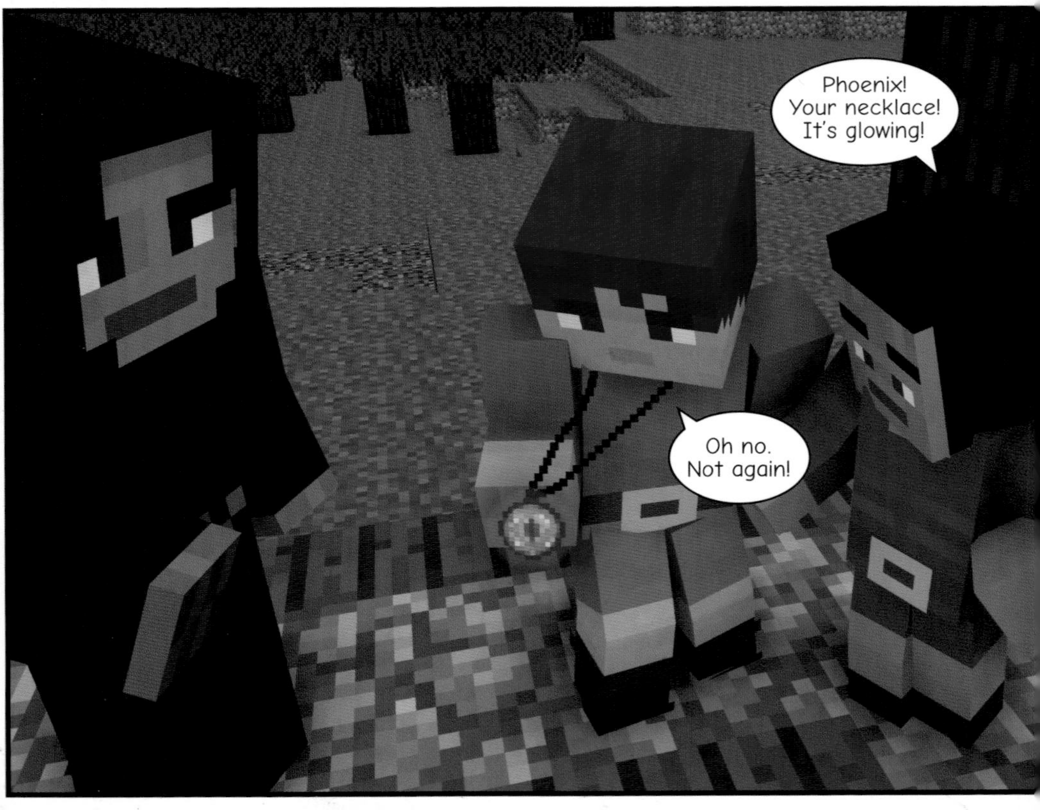
Phoenix! Your necklace! It's glowing!
Oh no. Not again!

CHAPTER 5

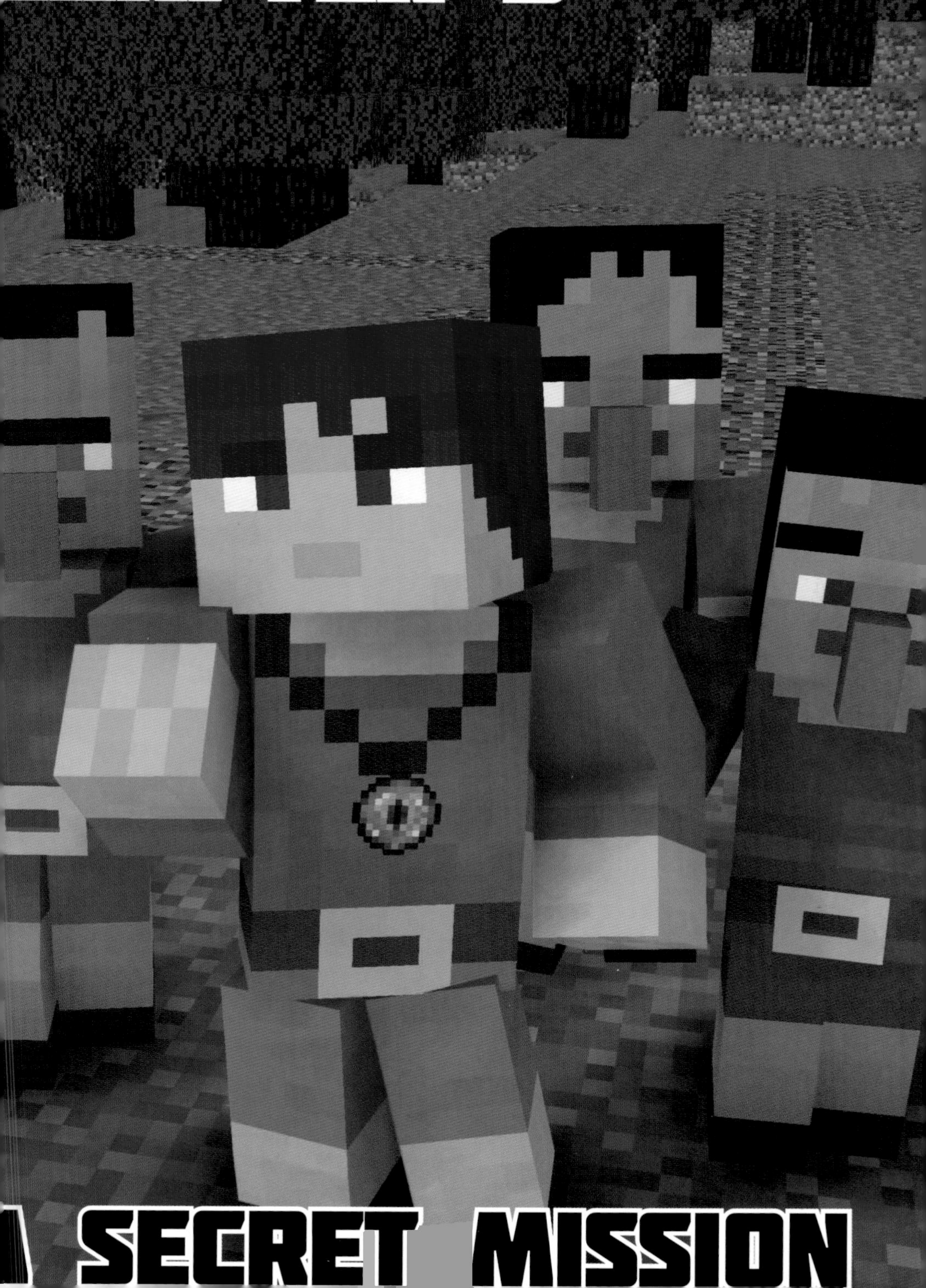

A SECRET MISSION

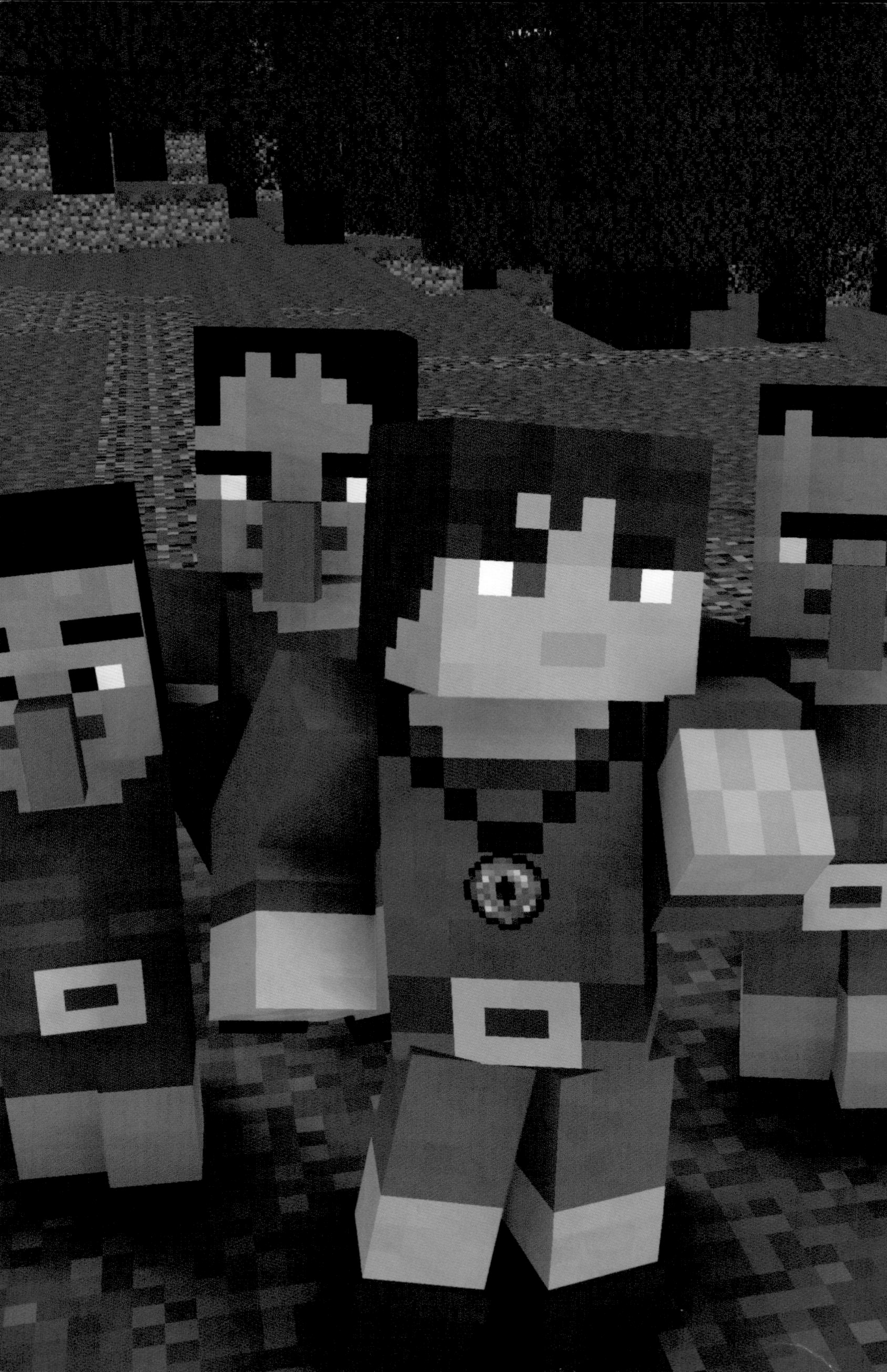

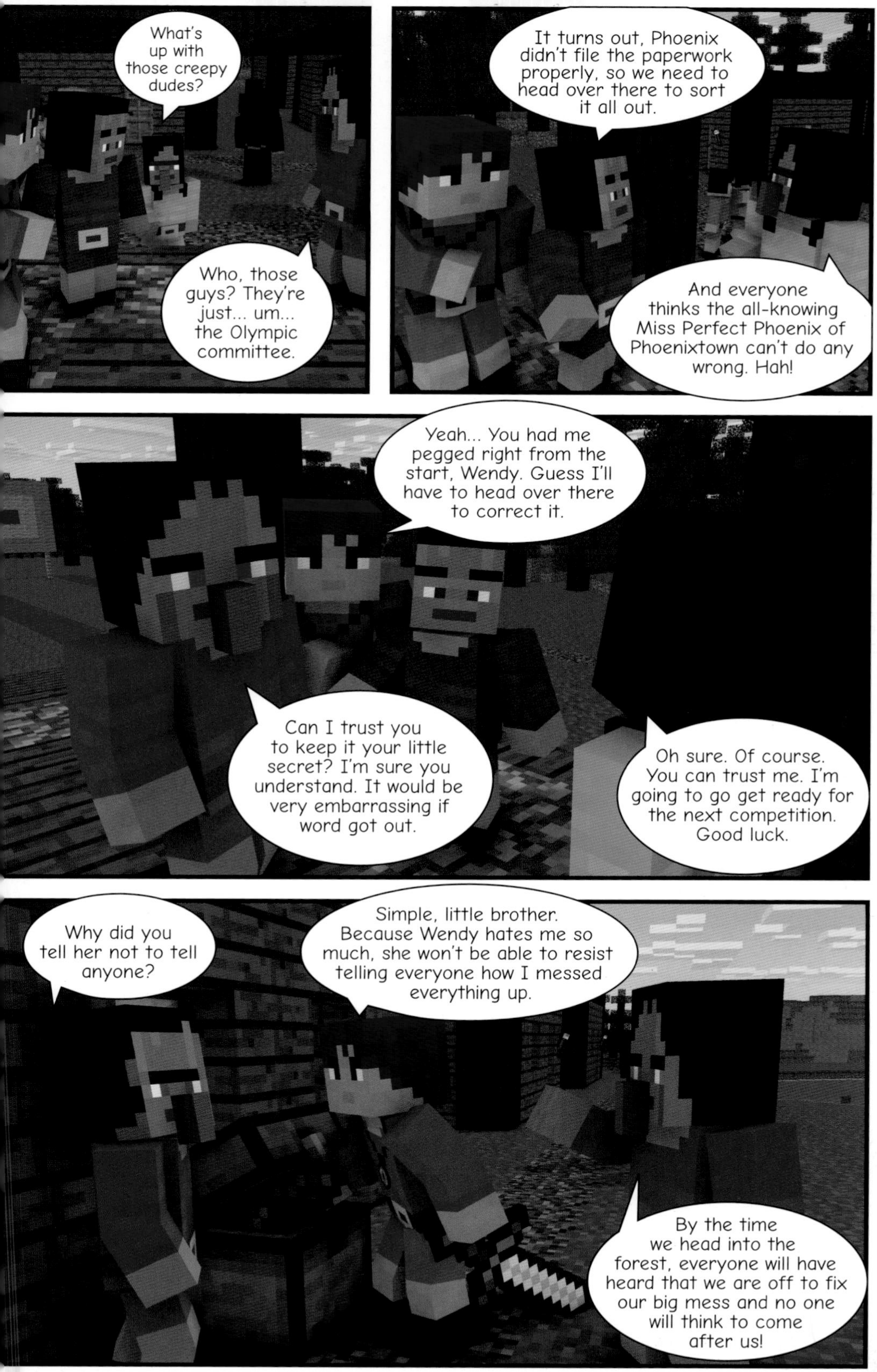
What's up with those creepy dudes?
Who, those guys? They're just... um... the Olympic committee.
It turns out, Phoenix didn't file the paperwork properly, so we need to head over there to sort it all out.
And everyone thinks the all-knowing Miss Perfect Phoenix of Phoenixtown can't do any wrong. Hah!
Yeah... You had me pegged right from the start, Wendy. Guess I'll have to head over there to correct it.
Can I trust you to keep it your little secret? I'm sure you understand. It would be very embarrassing if word got out.
Oh sure. Of course. You can trust me. I'm going to go get ready for the next competition. Good luck.
Why did you tell her not to tell anyone?
Simple, little brother. Because Wendy hates me so much, she won't be able to resist telling everyone how I messed everything up.
By the time we head into the forest, everyone will have heard that we are off to fix our big mess and no one will think to come after us!

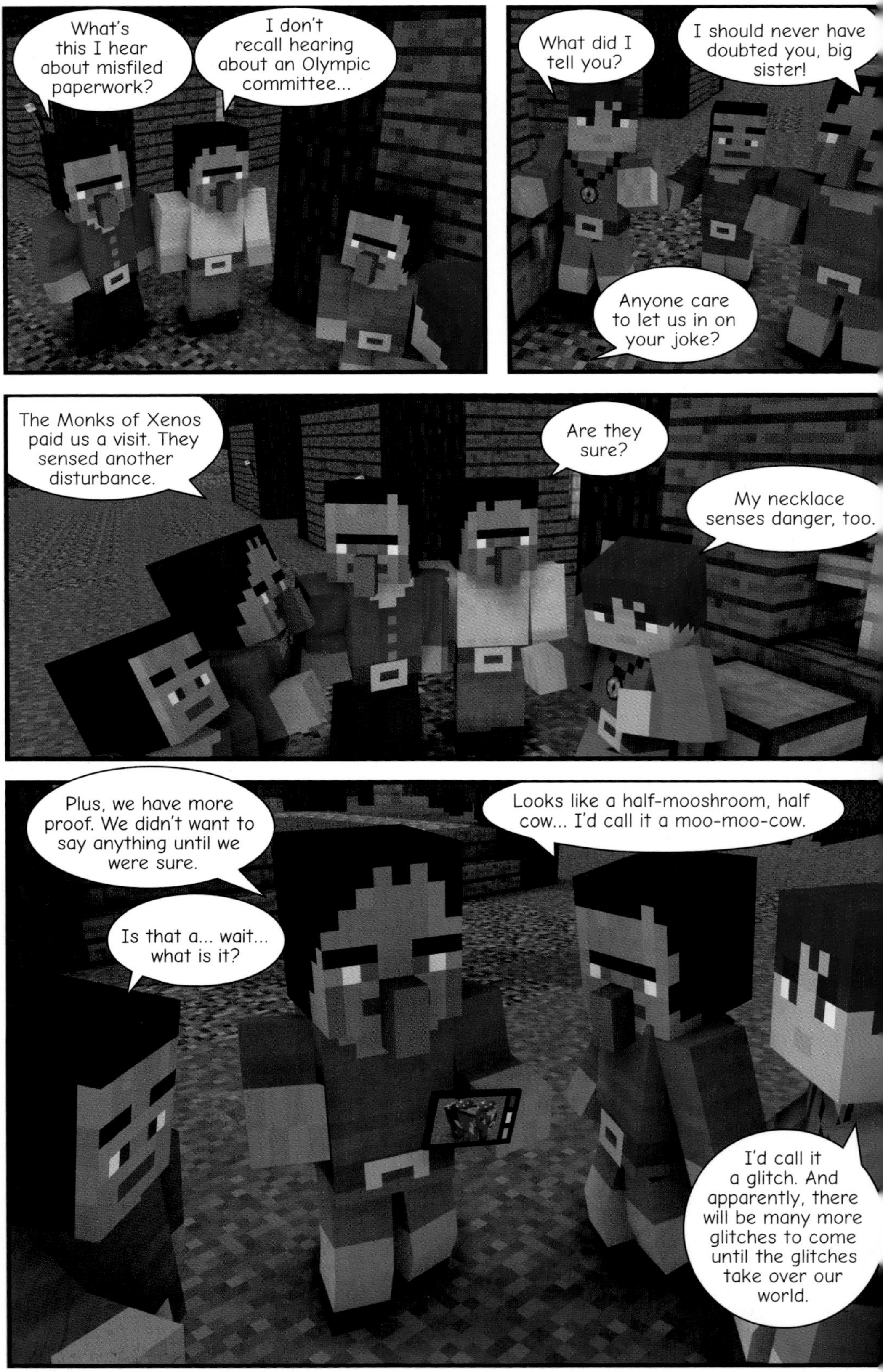
What's this I hear about misfiled paperwork?
I don't recall hearing about an Olympic committee...
What did I tell you?
I should never have doubted you, big sister!
Anyone care to let us in on your joke?
The Monks of Xenos paid us a visit. They sensed another disturbance.
Are they sure?
My necklace senses danger, too.
Plus, we have more proof. We didn't want to say anything until we were sure.
Is that a... wait... what is it?
Looks like a half-mooshroom, half cow... I'd call it a moo-moo-cow.
I'd call it a glitch. And apparently, there will be many more glitches to come until the glitches take over our world.

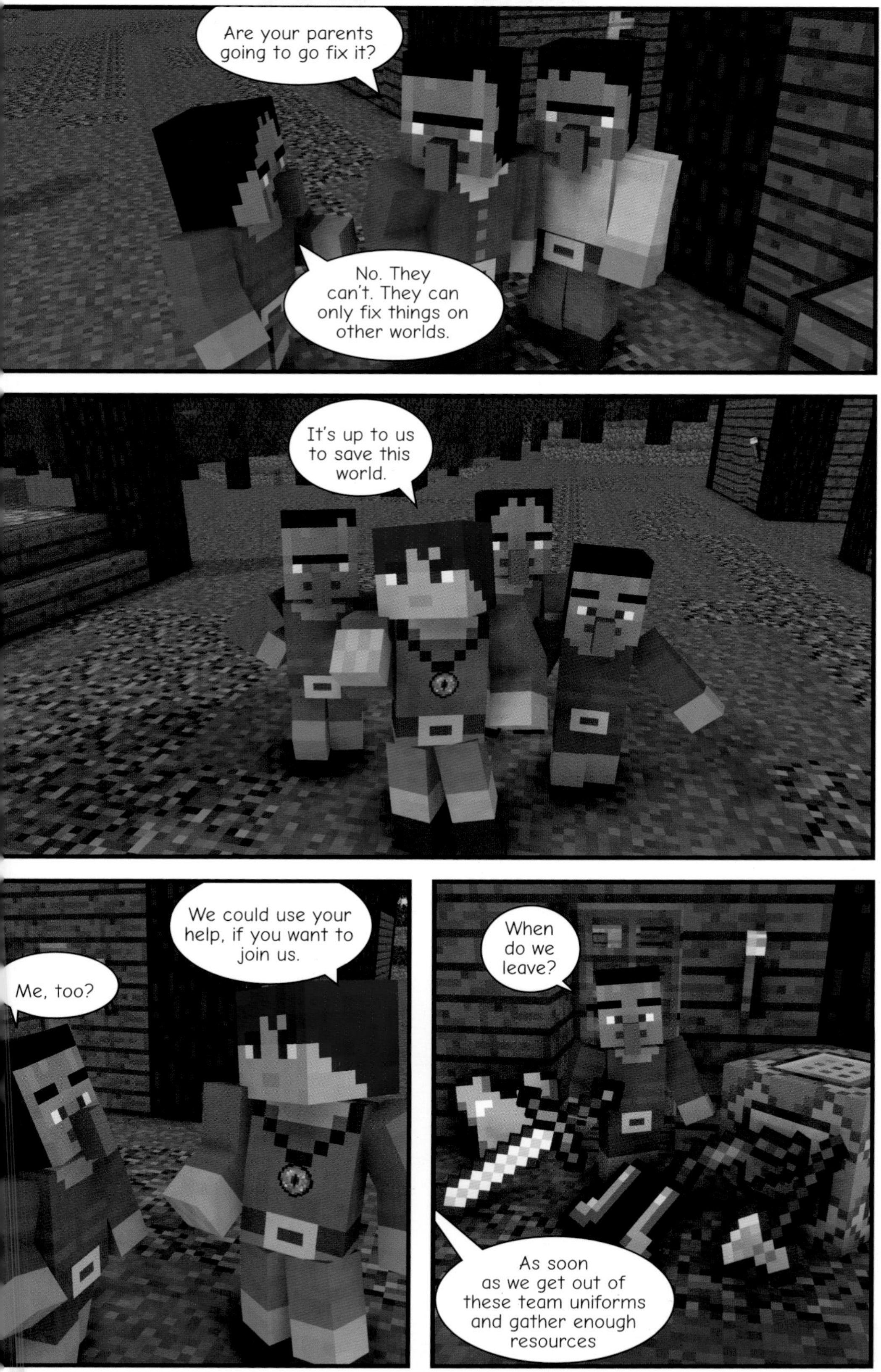
Are your parents going to go fix it?
No. They can't. They can only fix things on other worlds.
It's up to us to save this world.
We could use your help, if you want to join us.
Me, too?
When do we leave?
As soon as we get out of these team uniforms and gather enough resources

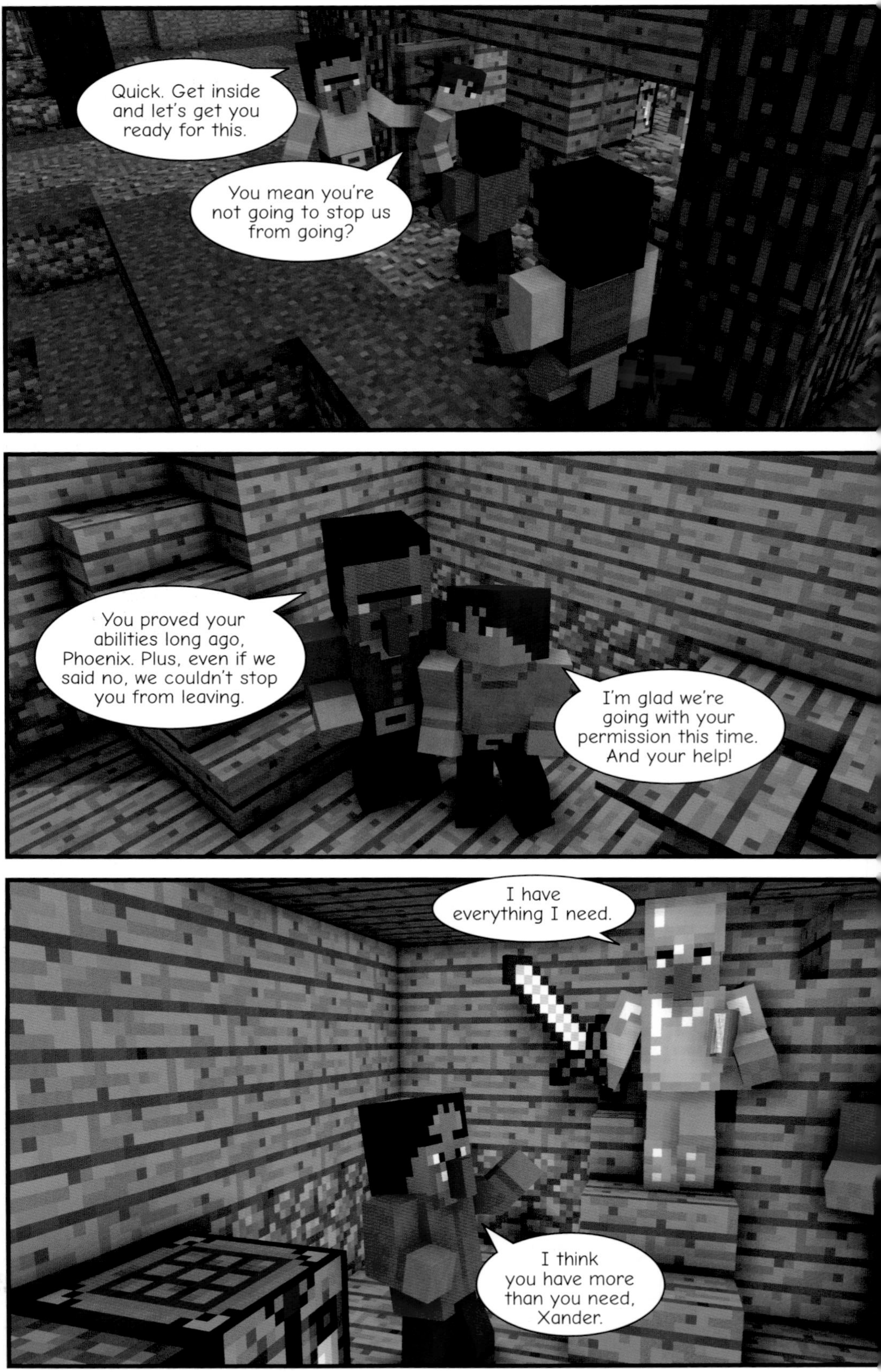
Quick. Get inside and let's get you ready for this.
You mean you're not going to stop us from going?
You proved your abilities long ago, Phoenix. Plus, even if we said no, we couldn't stop you from leaving.
I'm glad we're going with your permission this time. And your help!
I have everything I need.
I think you have more than you need, Xander.

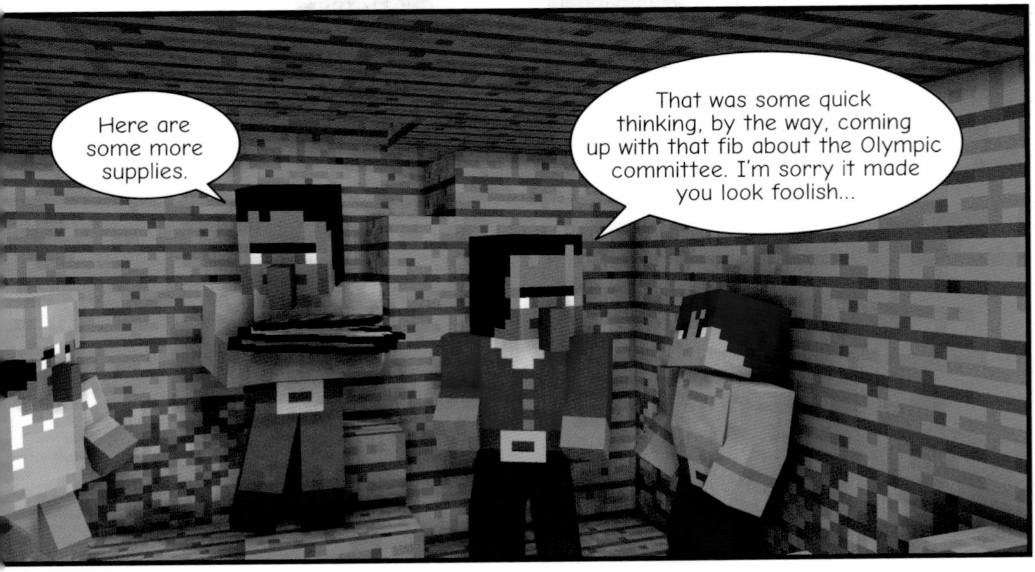
Here are some more supplies.
That was some quick thinking, by the way, coming up with that fib about the Olympic committee. I'm sorry it made you look foolish...

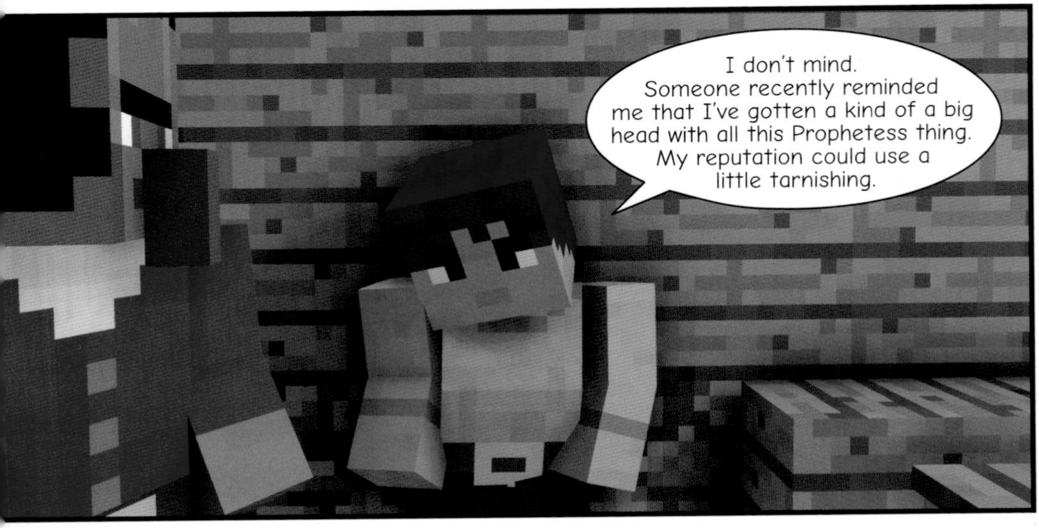
I don't mind. Someone recently reminded me that I've gotten a kind of a big head with all this Prophetess thing. My reputation could use a little tarnishing.

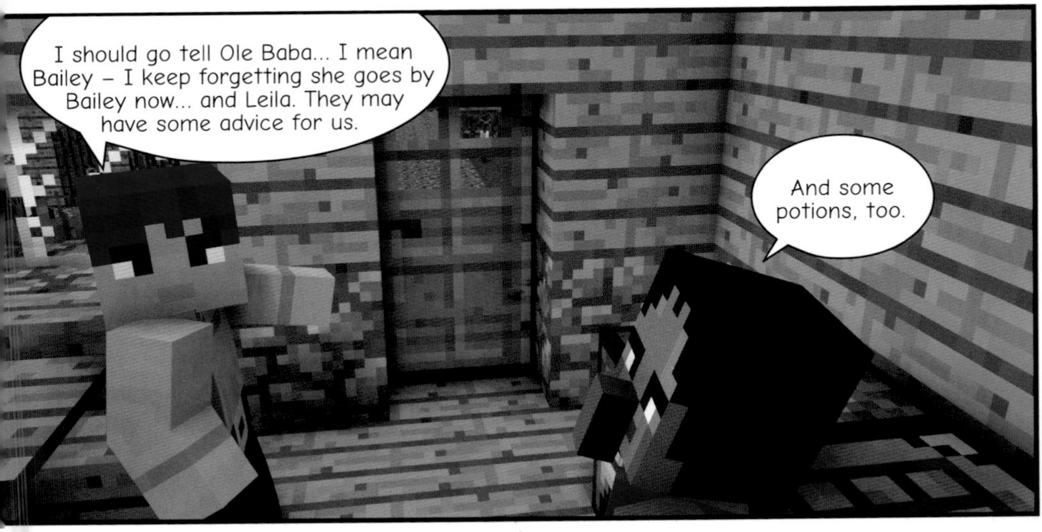
I should go tell Ole Baba... I mean Bailey – I keep forgetting she goes by Bailey now... and Leila. They may have some advice for us.
And some potions, too.

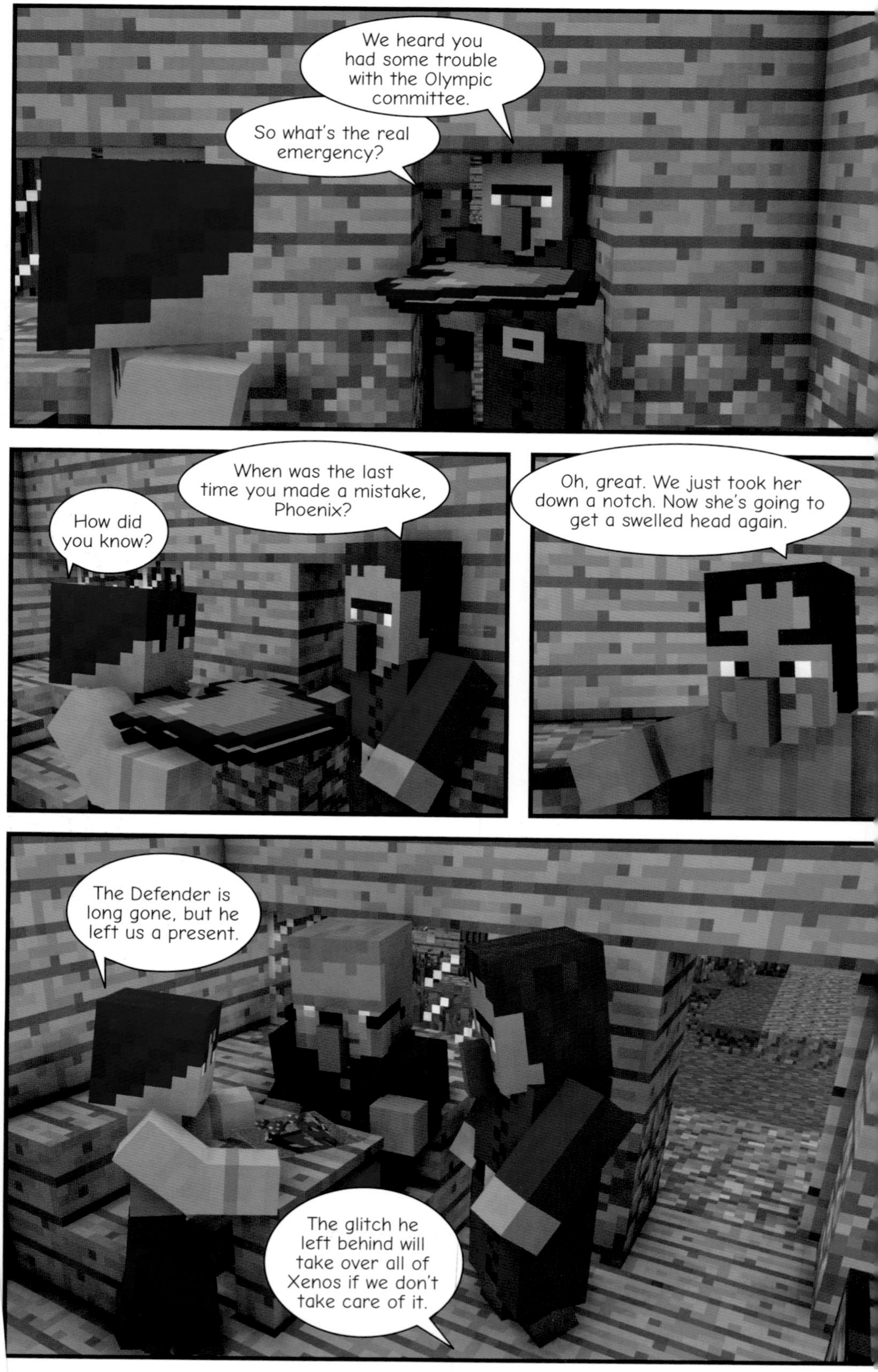
We heard you had some trouble with the Olympic committee.
So what's the real emergency?
When was the last time you made a mistake, Phoenix?
How did you know?
Oh, great. We just took her down a notch. Now she's going to get a swelled head again.
The Defender is long gone, but he left us a present.
The glitch he left behind will take over all of Xenos if we don't take care of it.

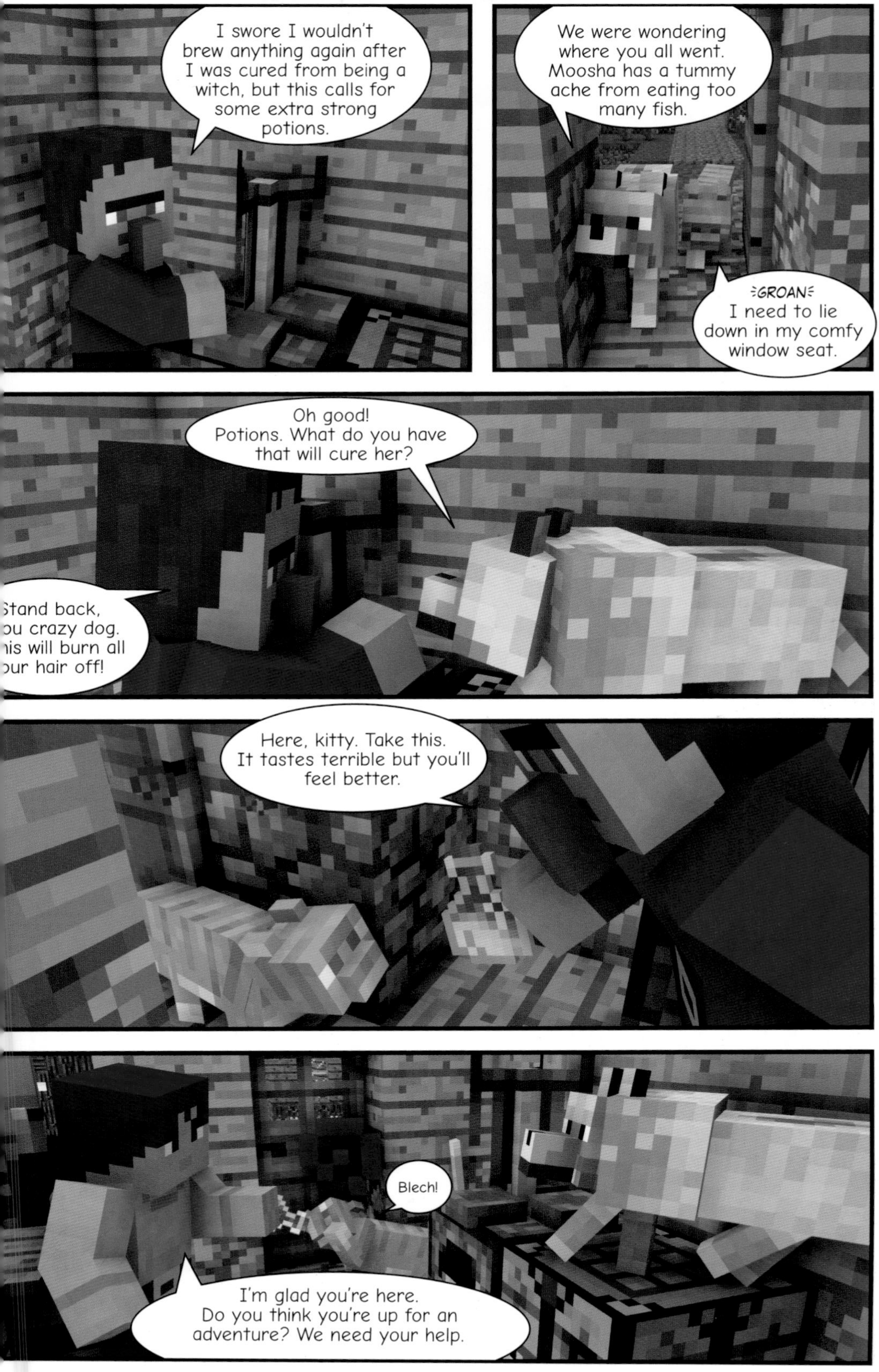
I swore I wouldn't brew anything again after I was cured from being a witch, but this calls for some extra strong potions.
We were wondering where you all went. Moosha has a tummy ache from eating too many fish.
GROAN
I need to lie down in my comfy window seat.
Oh good! Potions. What do you have that will cure her?
Stand back, ou crazy dog. nis will burn all our hair off!
Here, kitty. Take this. It tastes terrible but you'll feel better.
Blech!
I'm glad you're here. Do you think you're up for an adventure? We need your help.

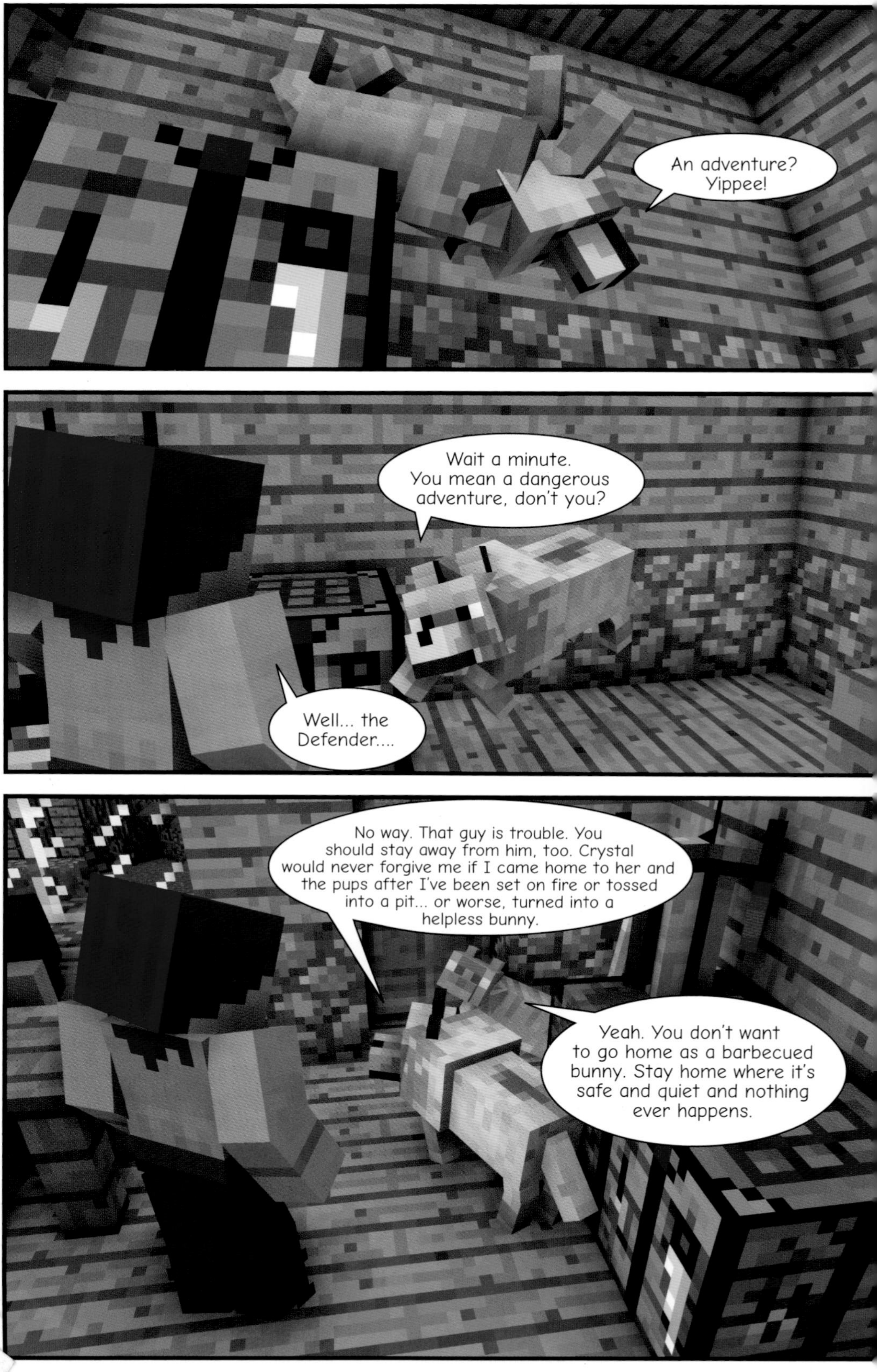
An adventure? Yippee!
Wait a minute. You mean a dangerous adventure, don't you?
Well... the Defender....
No way. That guy is trouble. You should stay away from him, too. Crystal would never forgive me if I came home to her and the pups after I've been set on fire or tossed into a pit... or worse, turned into a helpless bunny.
Yeah. You don't want to go home as a barbecued bunny. Stay home where it's safe and quiet and nothing ever happens.

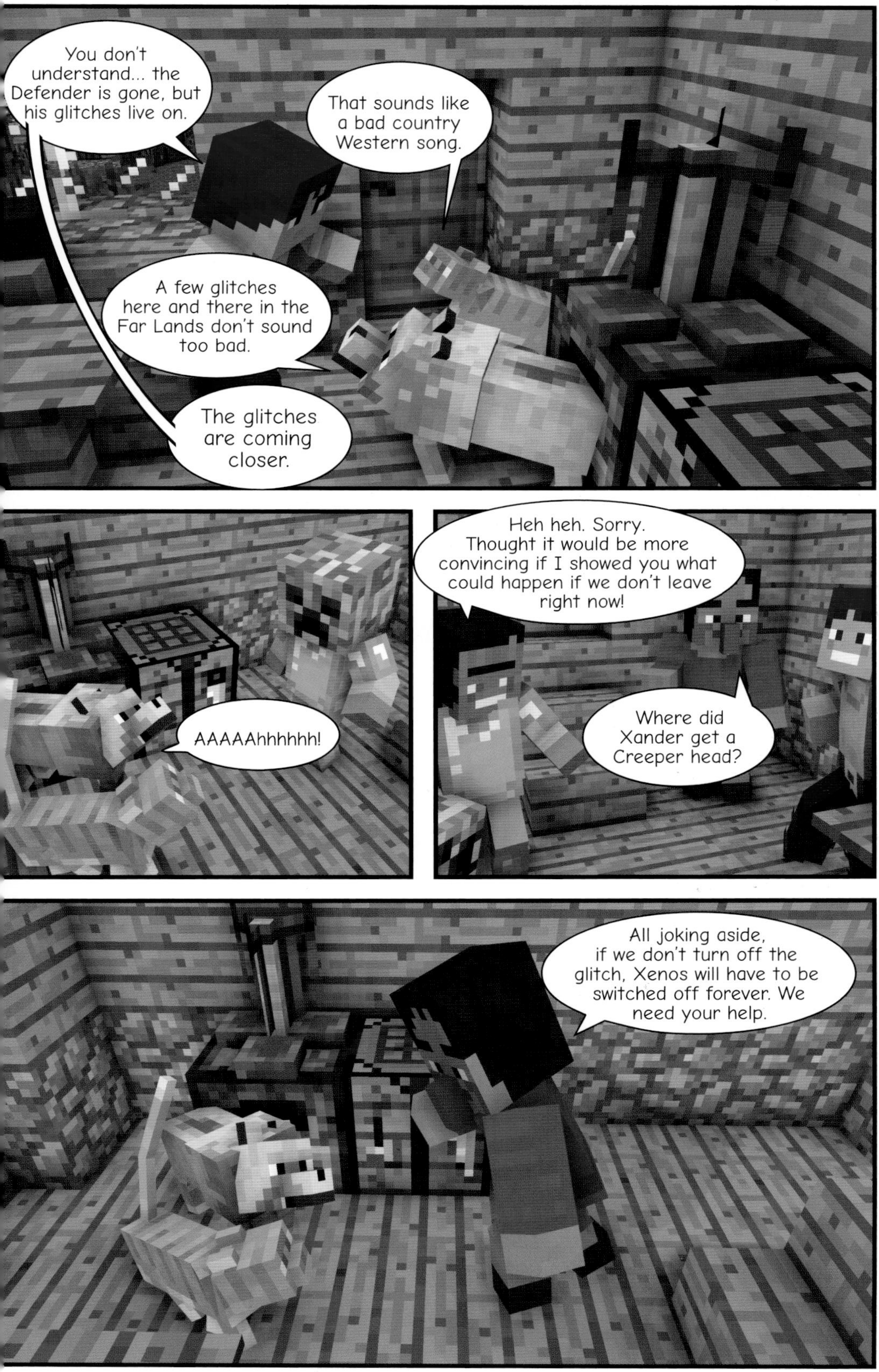
You don't understand... the Defender is gone, but his glitches live on.
That sounds like a bad country Western song.
A few glitches here and there in the Far Lands don't sound too bad.
The glitches are coming closer.
AAAAAhhhhhh!
Heh heh. Sorry. Thought it would be more convincing if I showed you what could happen if we don't leave right now!
Where did Xander get a Creeper head?
All joking aside, if we don't turn off the glitch, Xenos will have to be switched off forever. We need your help.

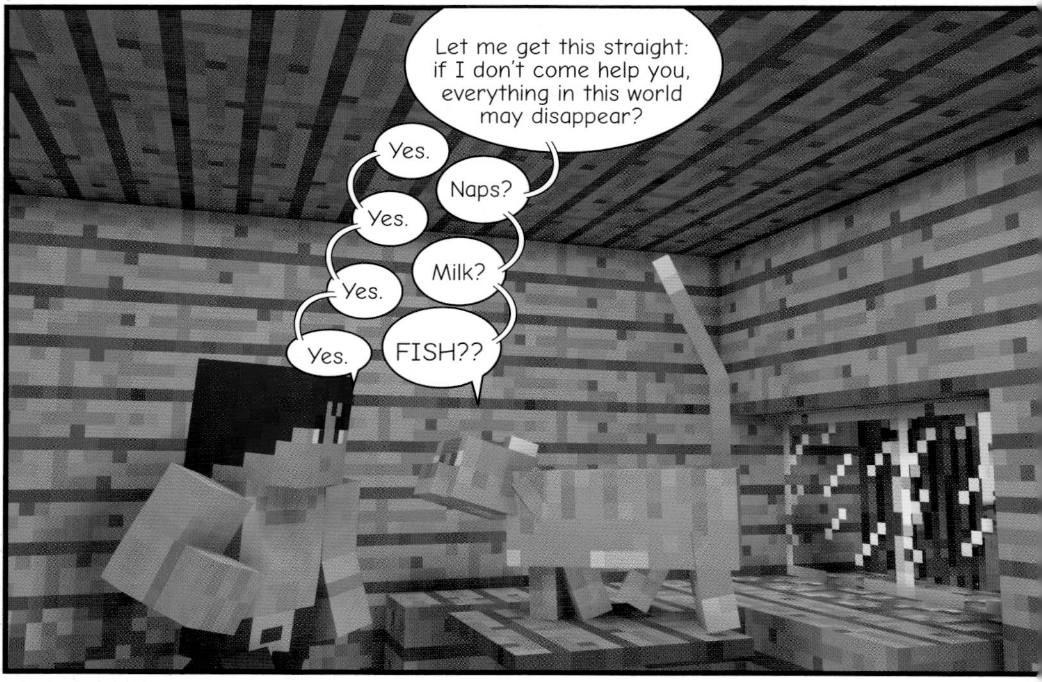
Let me get this straight: if I don't come help you, everything in this world may disappear?
Yes.
Naps?
Yes.
Milk?
Yes.
FISH??
Yes.
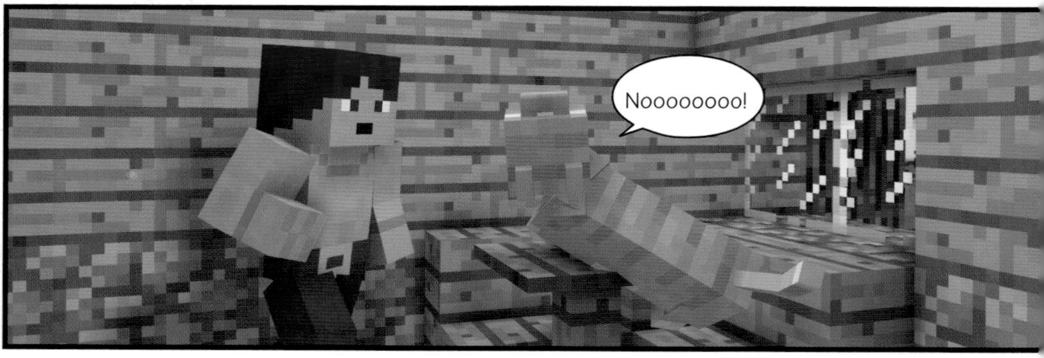
Noooooooo!
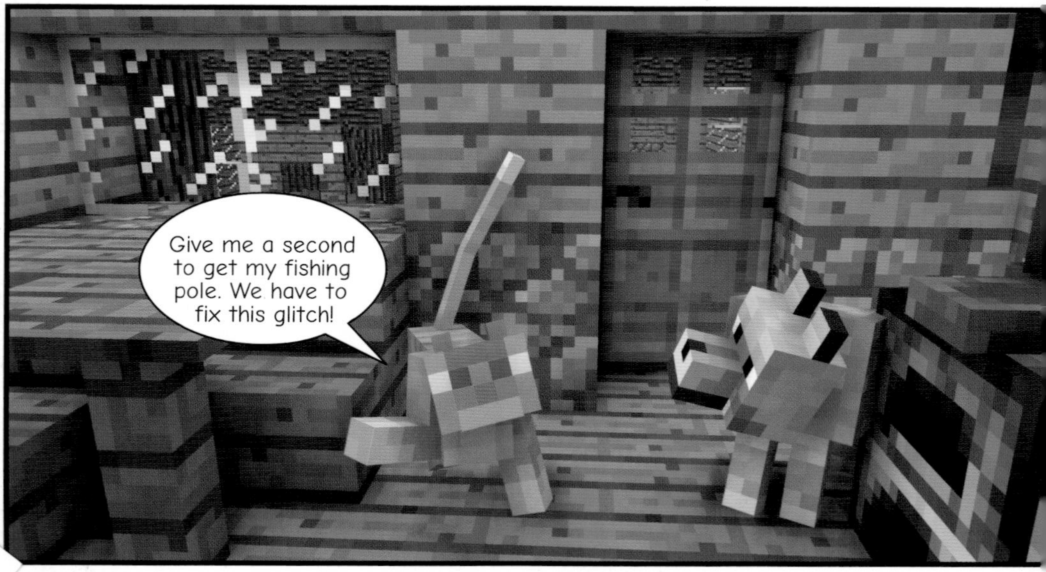
Give me a second to get my fishing pole. We have to fix this glitch!

CHAPTER 6

ZOMBIES IN THE NIGHT

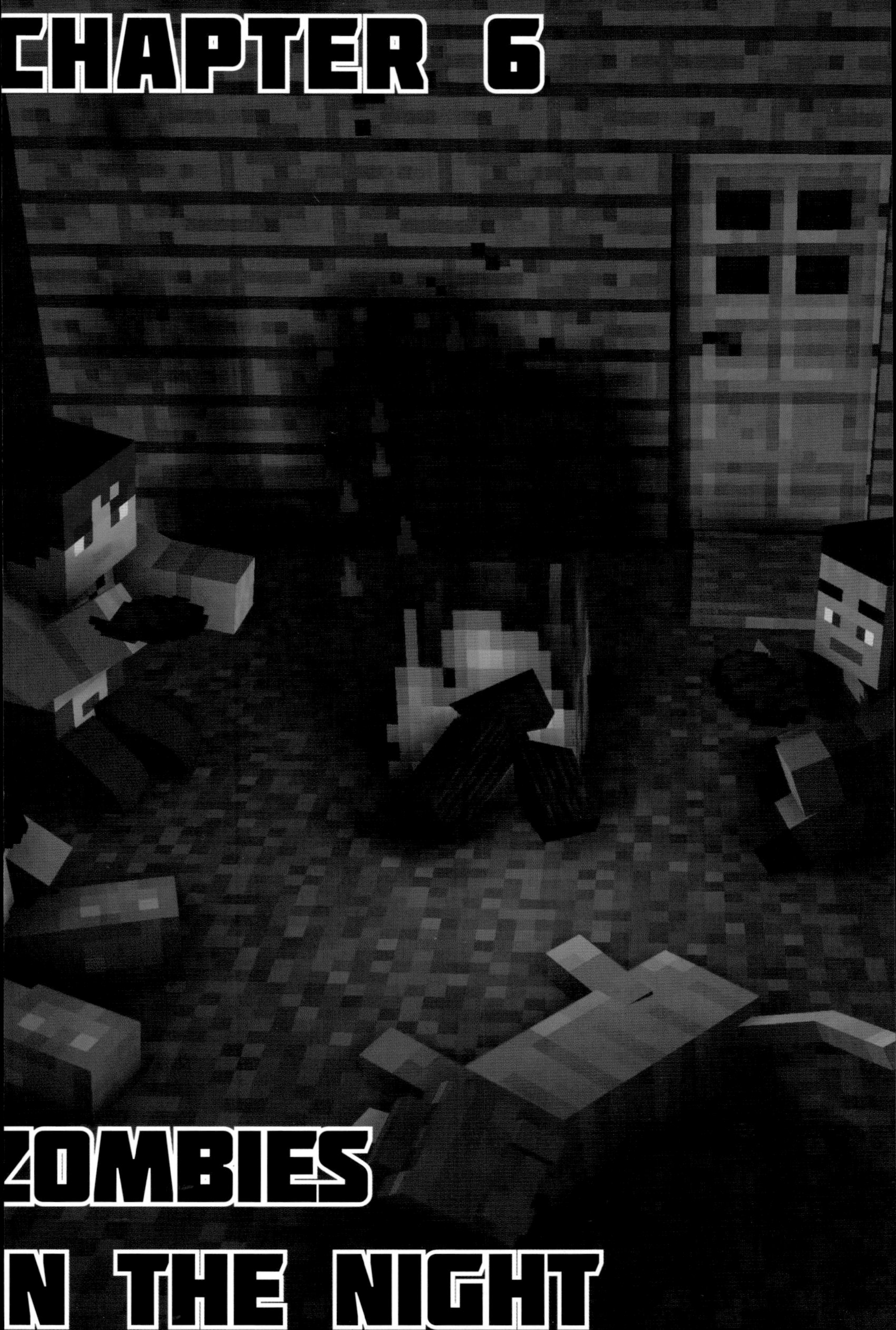

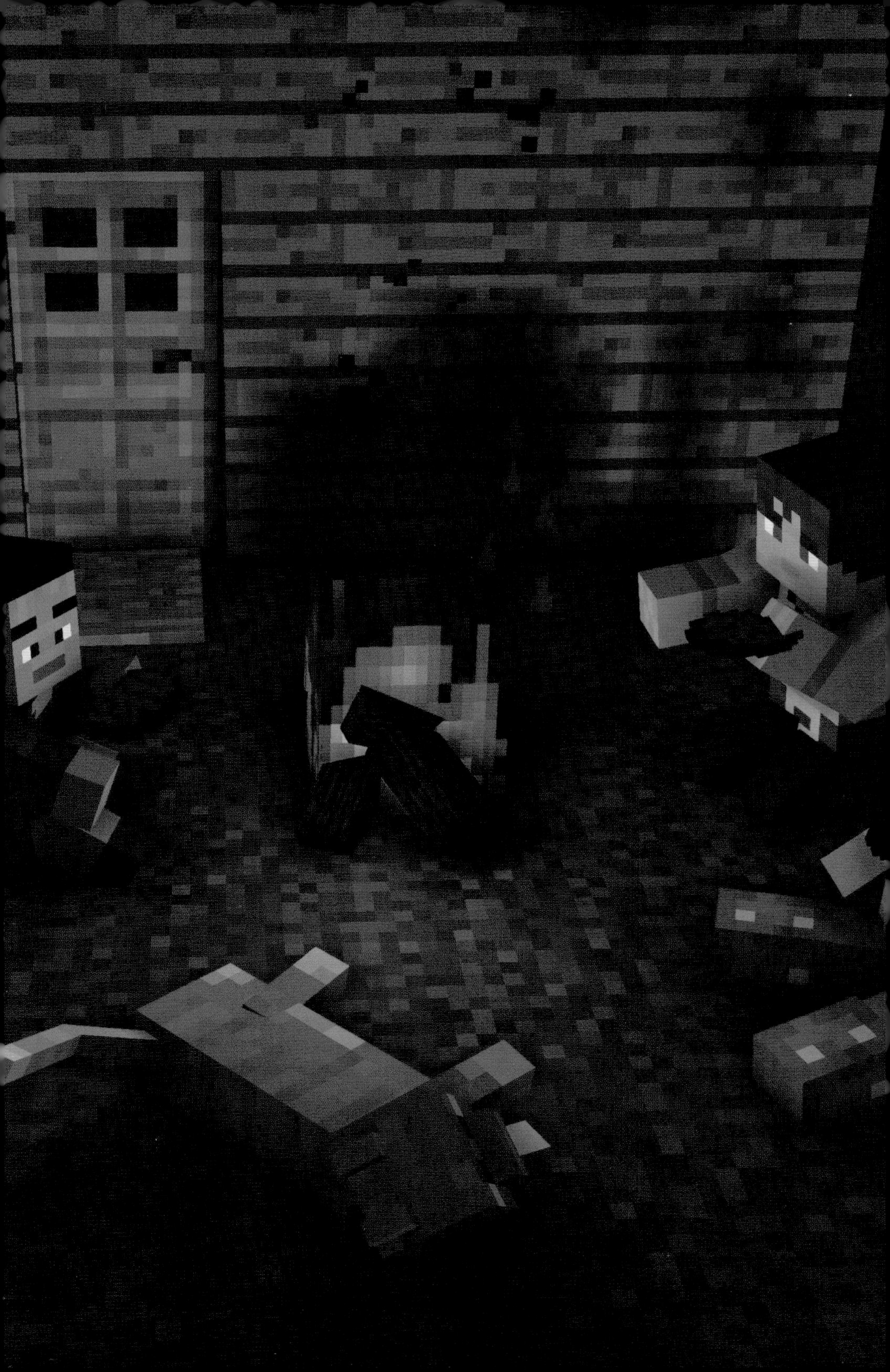

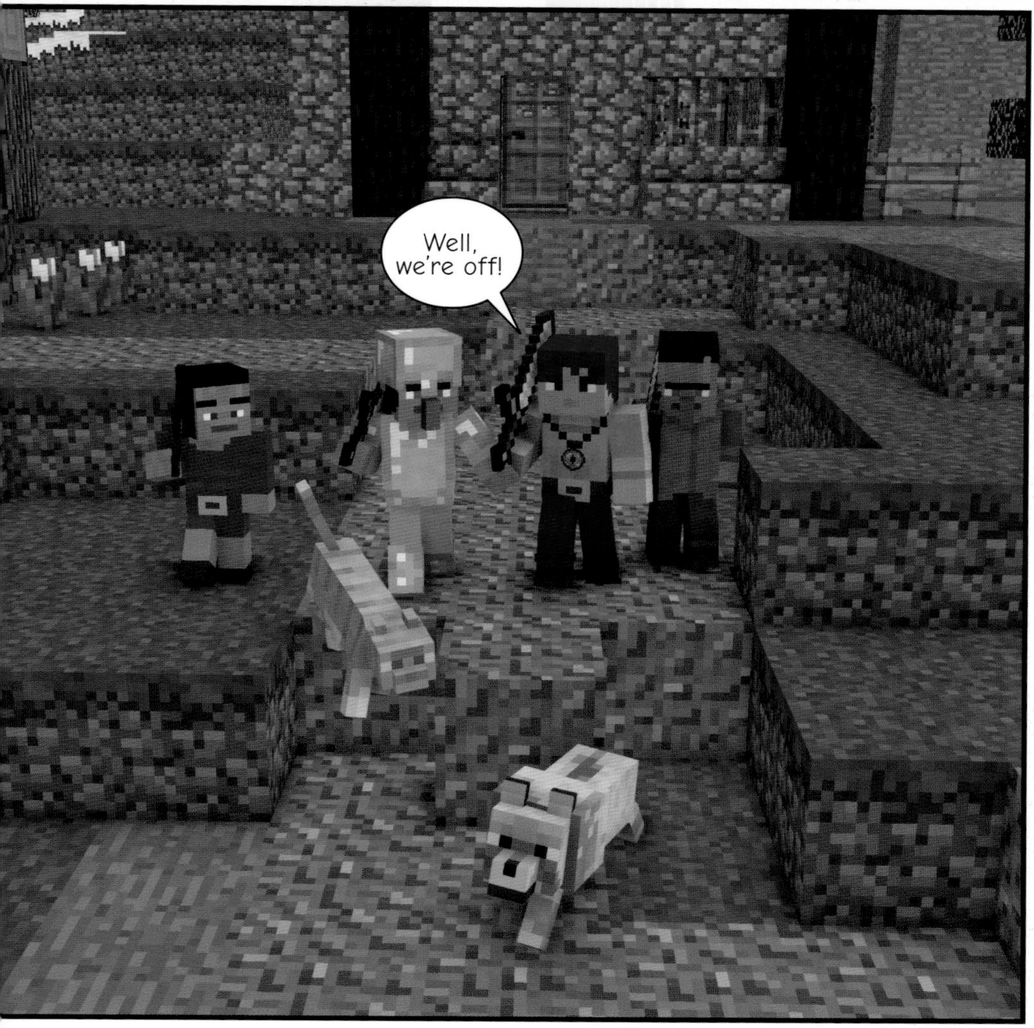
Well, we're off!

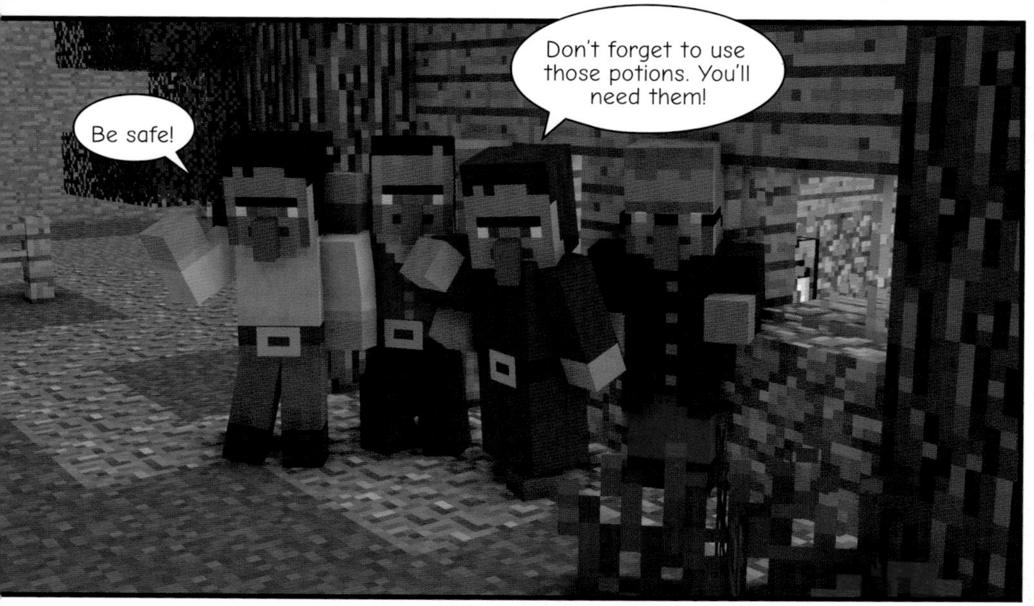
Be safe!
Don't forget to use those potions. You'll need them!

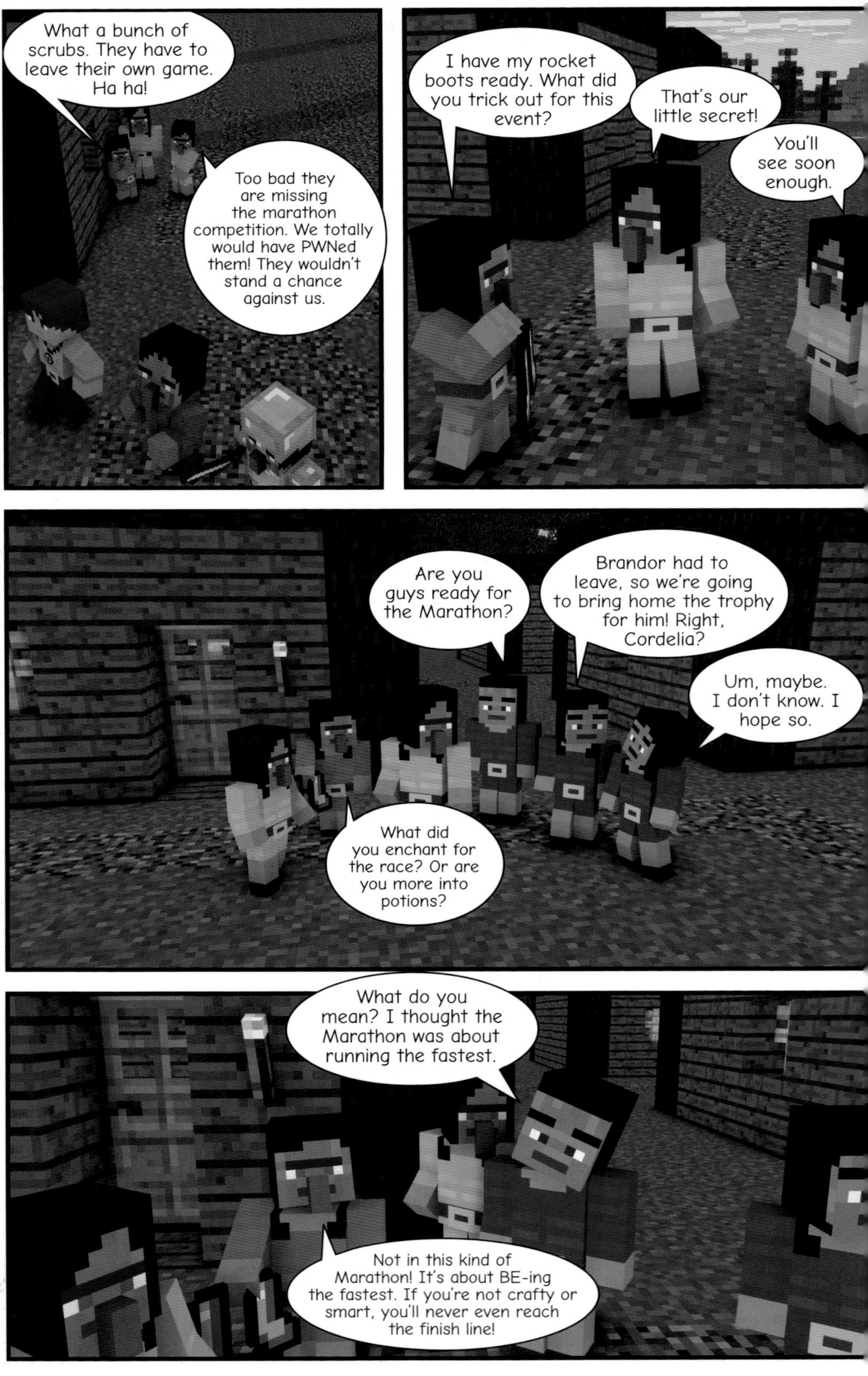
What a bunch of scrubs. They have to leave their own game. Ha ha!
Too bad they are missing the marathon competition. We totally would have PWNed them! They wouldn't stand a chance against us.
I have my rocket boots ready. What did you trick out for this event?
That's our little secret!
You'll see soon enough.
Are you guys ready for the Marathon?
Brandor had to leave, so we're going to bring home the trophy for him! Right, Cordelia?
Um, maybe. I don't know. I hope so.
What did you enchant for the race? Or are you more into potions?
What do you mean? I thought the Marathon was about running the fastest.
Not in this kind of Marathon! It's about BE-ing the fastest. If you're not crafty or smart, you'll never even reach the finish line!

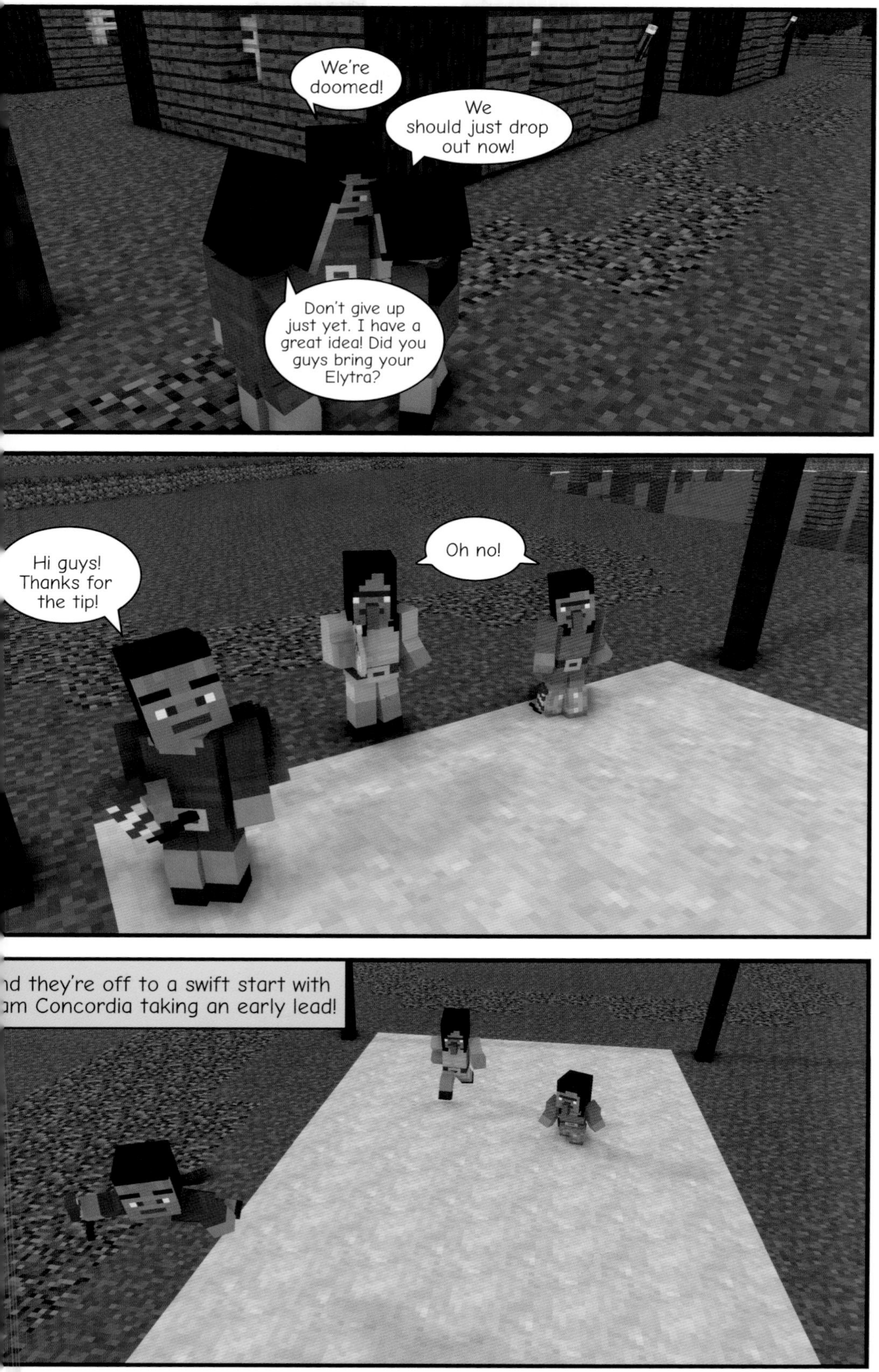
We're doomed!
We should just drop out now!
Don't give up just yet. I have a great idea! Did you guys bring your Elytra?
Hi guys! Thanks for the tip!
Oh no!
nd they're off to a swift start with
am Concordia taking an early lead!

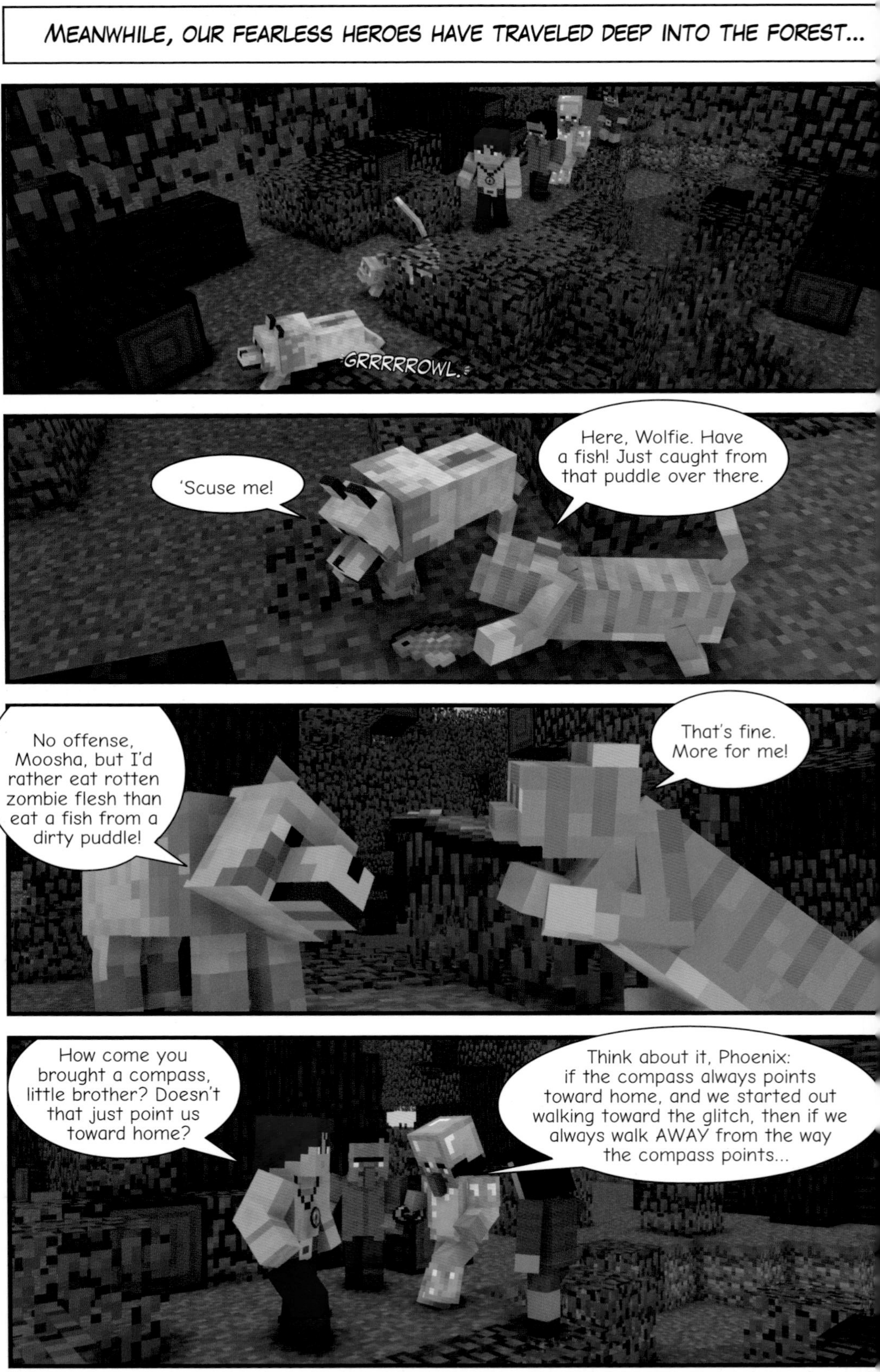
MEANWHILE, OUR FEARLESS HEROES HAVE TRAVELED DEEP INTO THE FOREST...
GRRRRROWL.
'Scuse me!
Here, Wolfie. Have a fish! Just caught from that puddle over there.
No offense, Moosha, but I'd rather eat rotten zombie flesh than eat a fish from a dirty puddle!
That's fine. More for me!
How come you brought a compass, little brother? Doesn't that just point us toward home?
Think about it, Phoenix: if the compass always points toward home, and we started out walking toward the glitch, then if we always walk AWAY from the way the compass points...

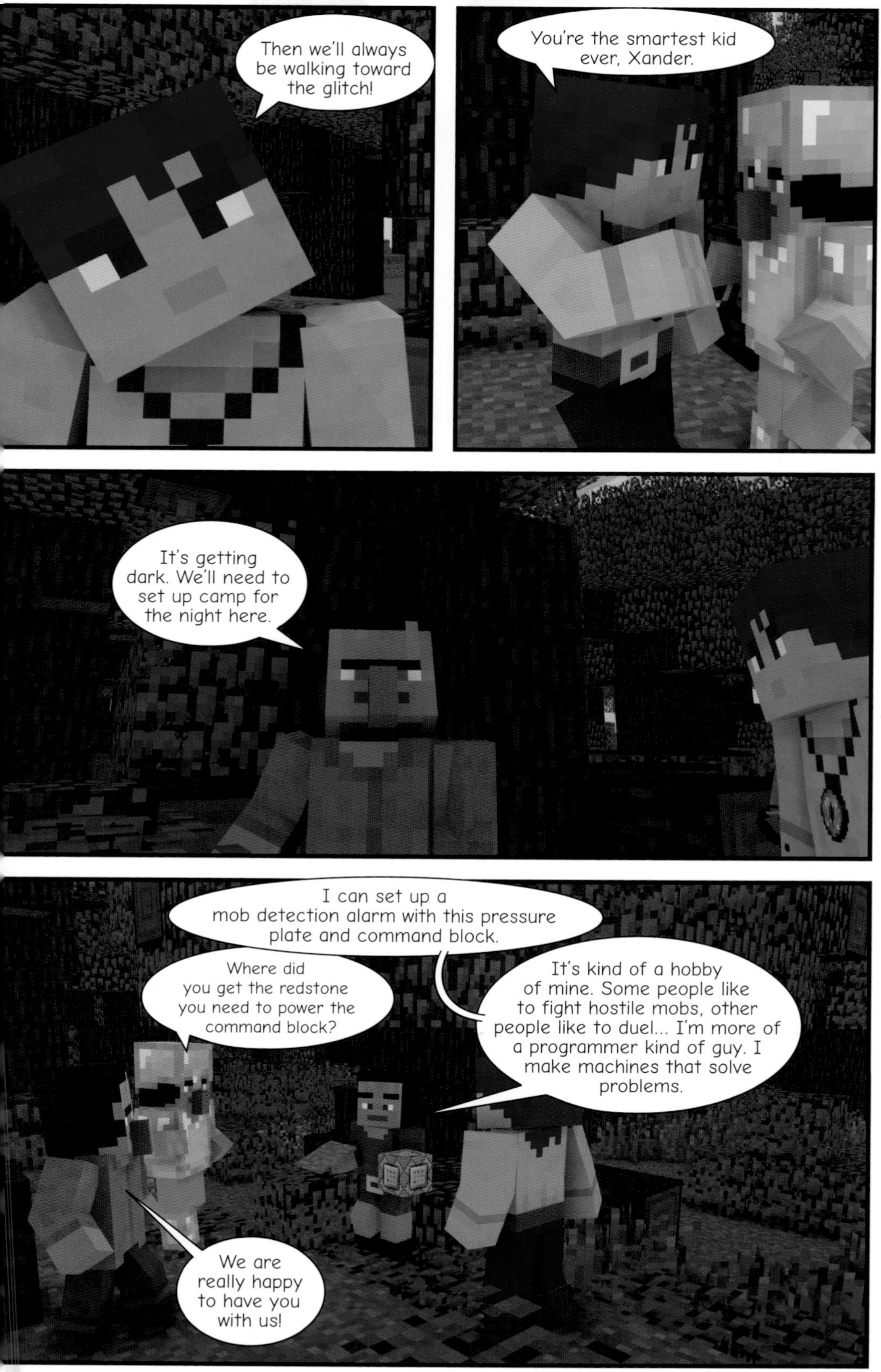
Then we'll always be walking toward the glitch!
You're the smartest kid ever, Xander.
It's getting dark. We'll need to set up camp for the night here.
I can set up a mob detection alarm with this pressure plate and command block.
Where did you get the redstone you need to power the command block?
It's kind of a hobby of mine. Some people like to fight hostile mobs, other people like to duel... I'm more of a programmer kind of guy. I make machines that solve problems.
We are really happy to have you with us!

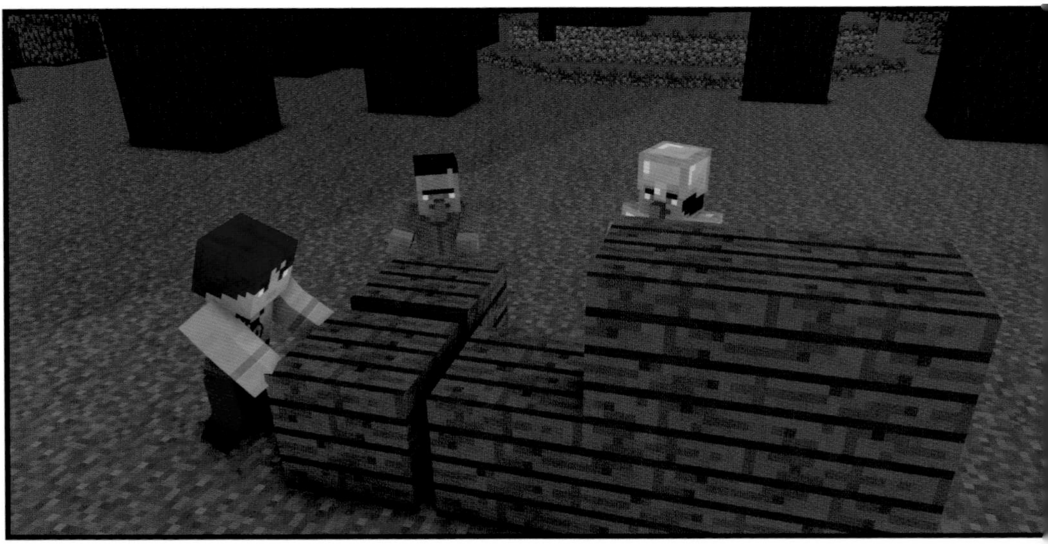

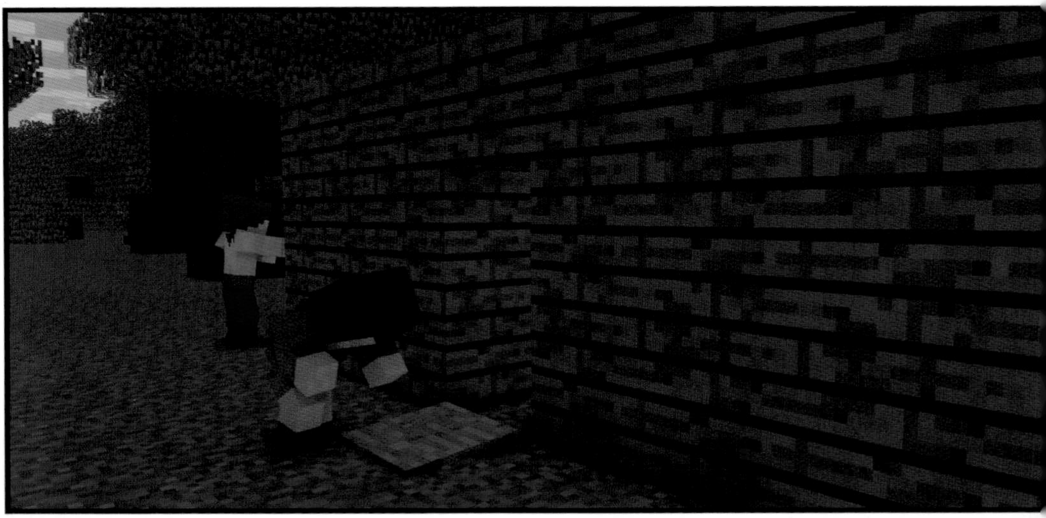

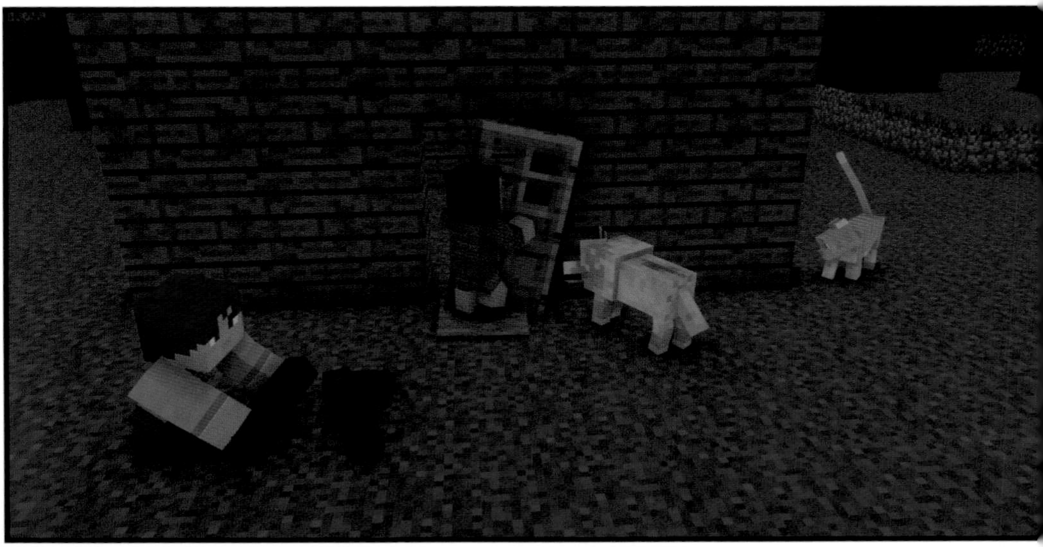

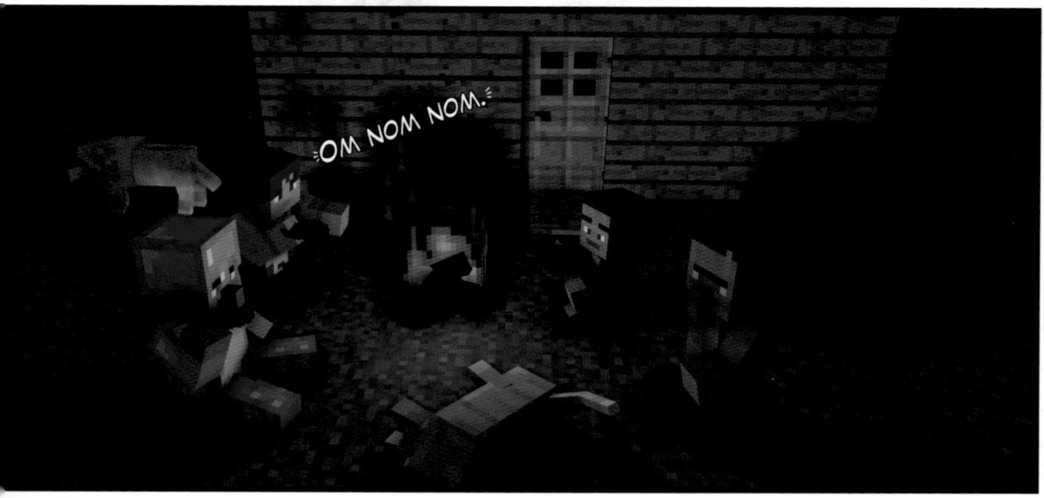
OM NOM NOM.

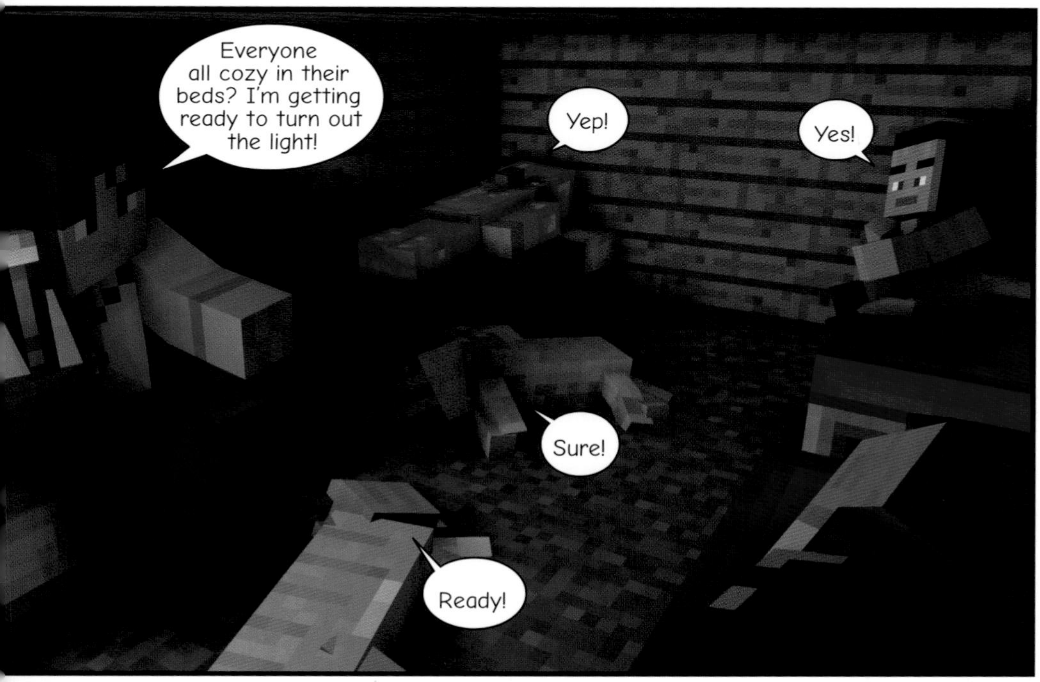
Everyone all cozy in their beds? I'm getting ready to turn out the light!
Yep!
Yes!
Sure!
Ready!

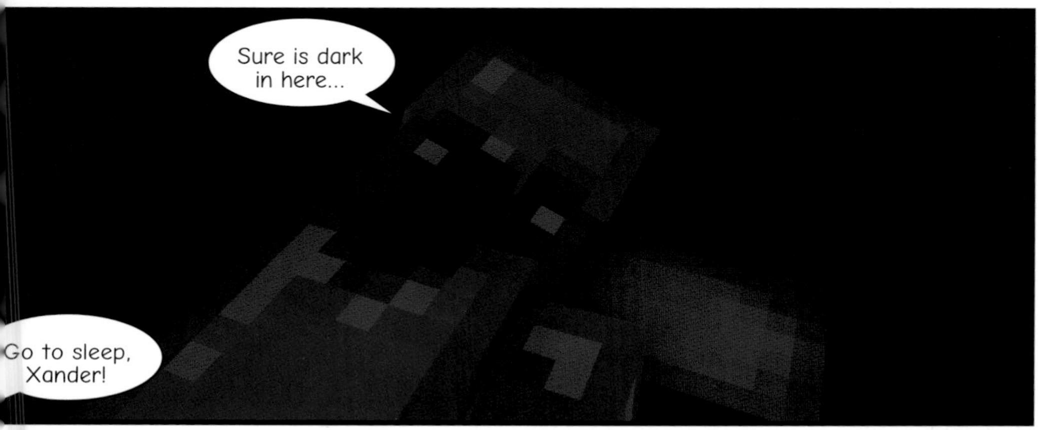
Sure is dark in here...
Go to sleep, Xander!

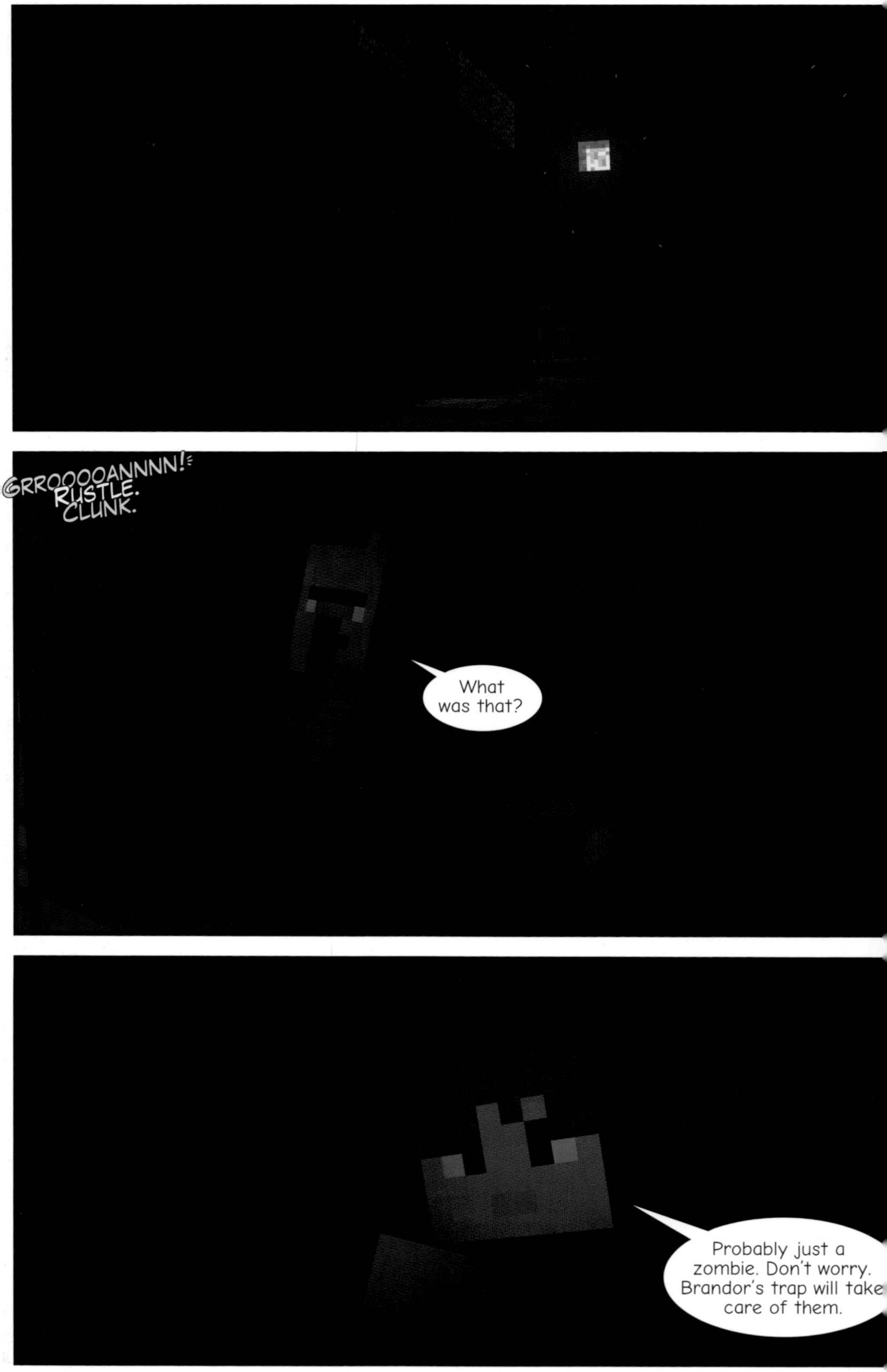
GRROOOOANNNN!
RUSTLE.
CLUNK.
What was that?
Probably just a zombie. Don't worry. Brandor's trap will take care of them.

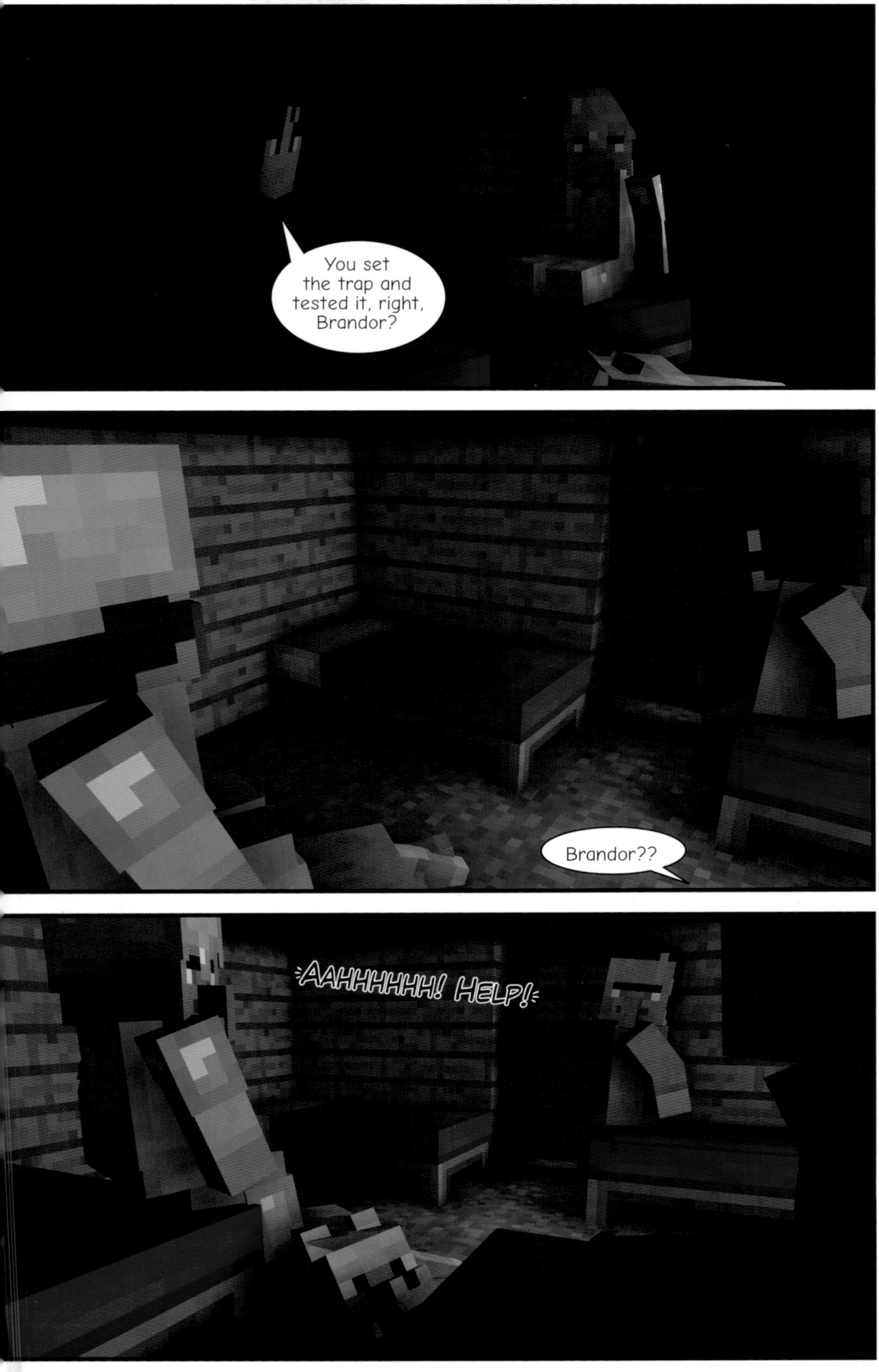
You set the trap and tested it, right, Brandor?
Brandor??
AAHHHHHH! HELP!

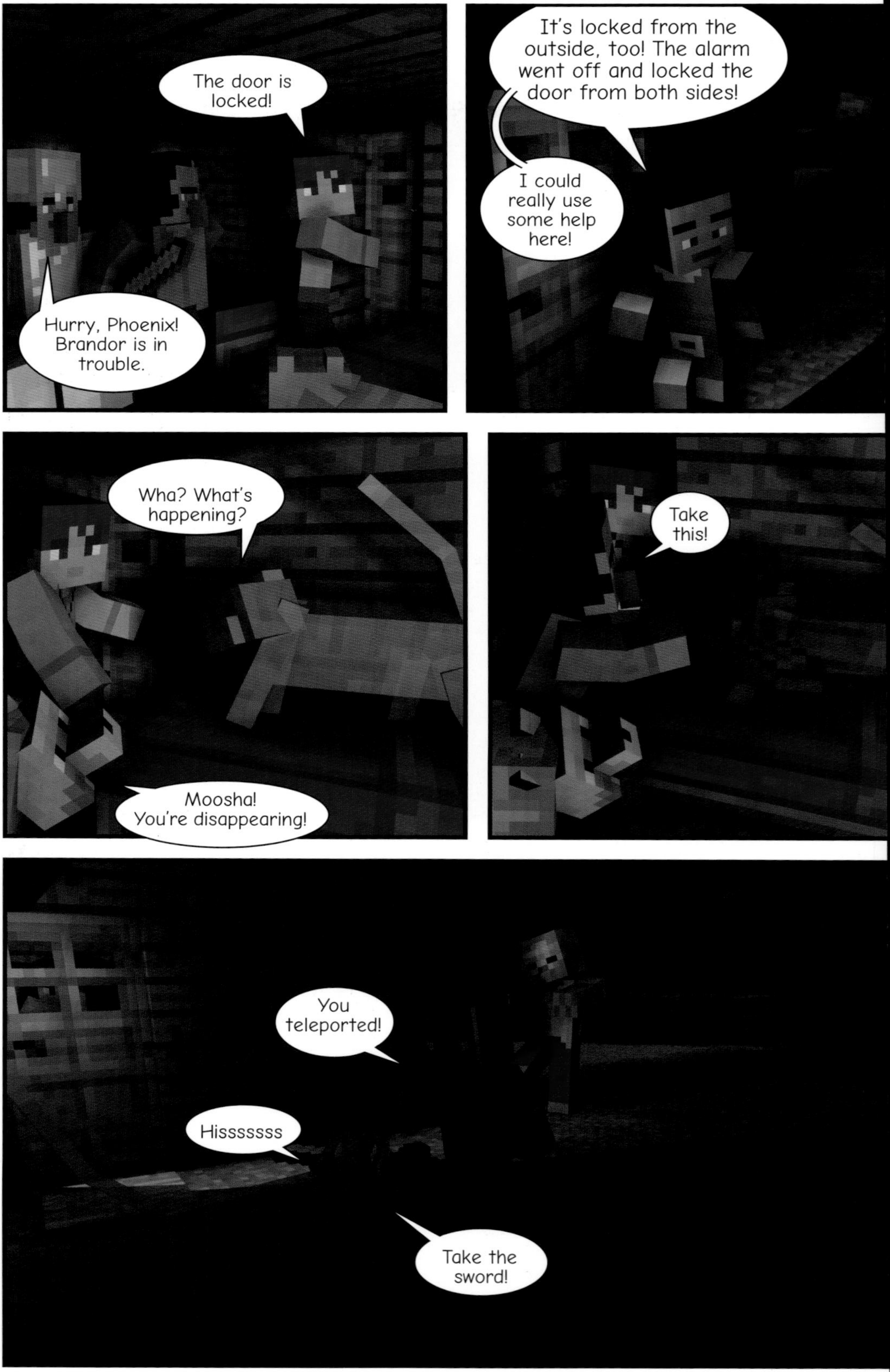
The door is locked!
Hurry, Phoenix! Brandor is in trouble.
It's locked from the outside, too! The alarm went off and locked the door from both sides!
I could really use some help here!
Wha? What's happening?
Moosha! You're disappearing!
Take this!
You teleported!
Hisssssss
Take the sword!

Aha! En garde!
OOOOF!
GRRRROOAAN!

Aaaahhhhhhh!
CLICK!

Well, at least my zombie alarm partially worked. I have to change it so the door doesn't lock on the inside, too!
I didn't know that you could teleport!
Me neither!

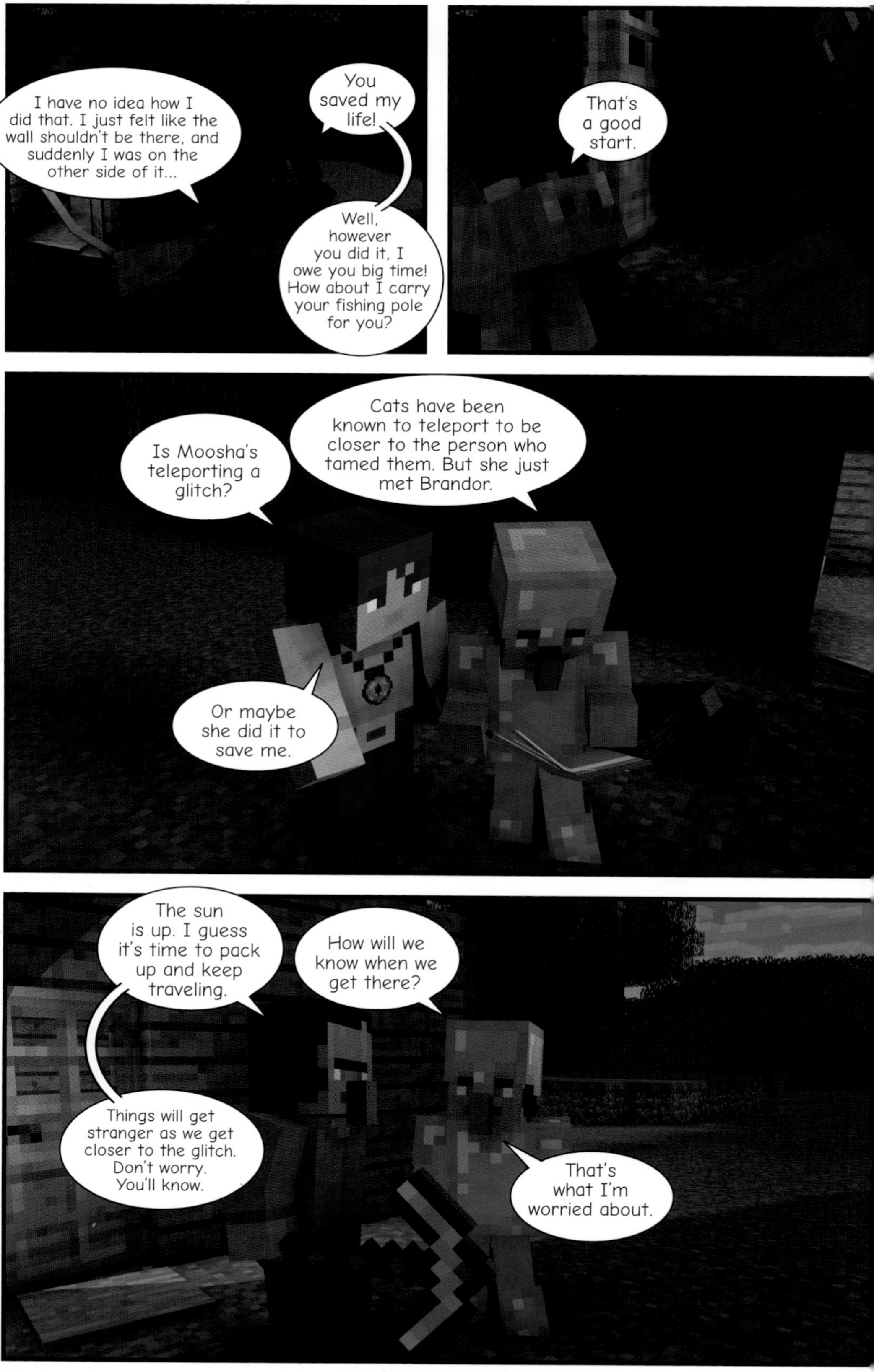
I have no idea how I did that. I just felt like the wall shouldn't be there, and suddenly I was on the other side of it...
You saved my life!
Well, however you did it, I owe you big time! How about I carry your fishing pole for you?
That's a good start.
Is Moosha's teleporting a glitch?
Cats have been known to teleport to be closer to the person who tamed them. But she just met Brandor.
Or maybe she did it to save me.
The sun is up. I guess it's time to pack up and keep traveling.
Things will get stranger as we get closer to the glitch. Don't worry. You'll know.
How will we know when we get there?
That's what I'm worried about.

CHAPTER 7

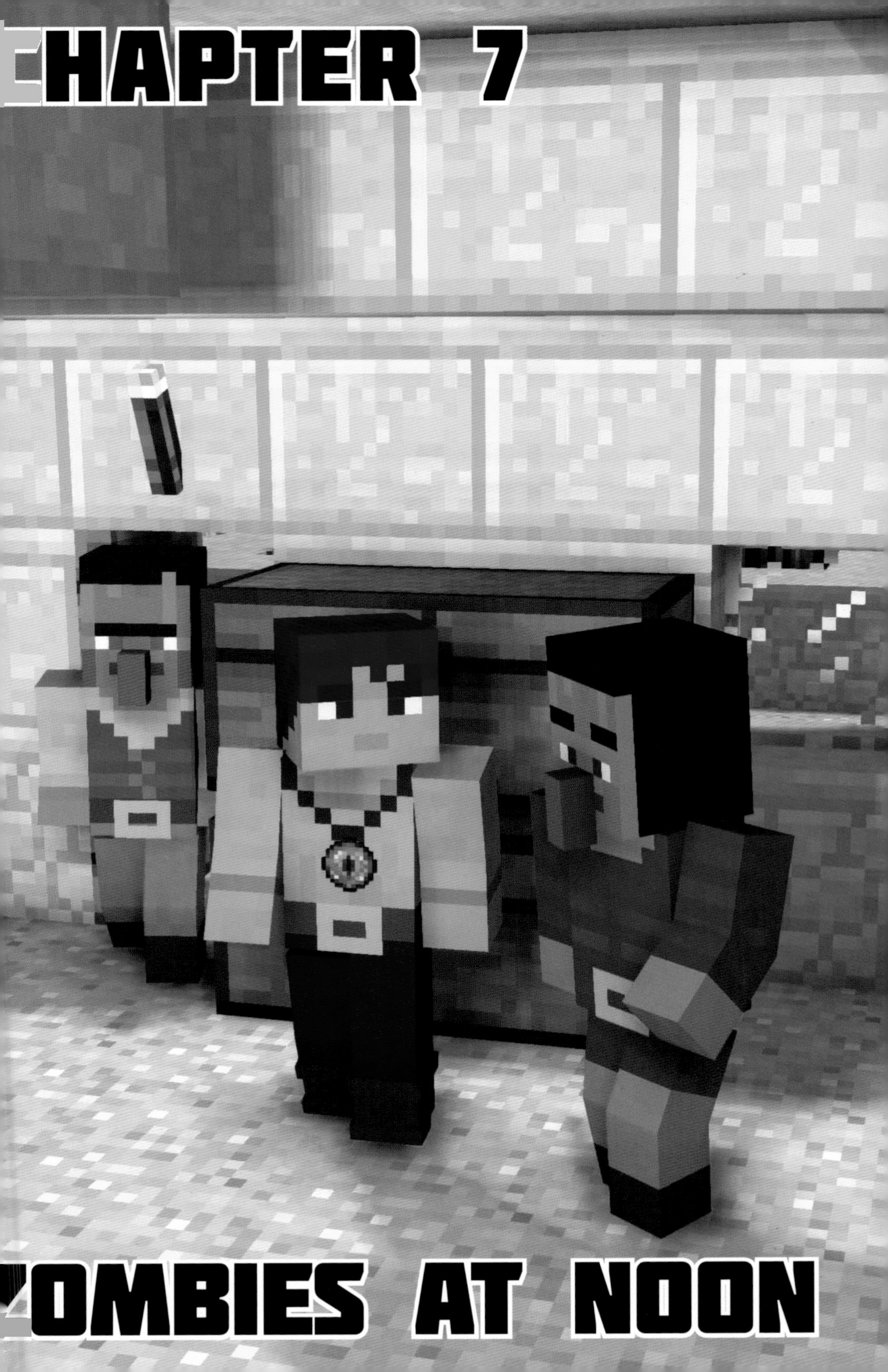

ZOMBIES AT NOON

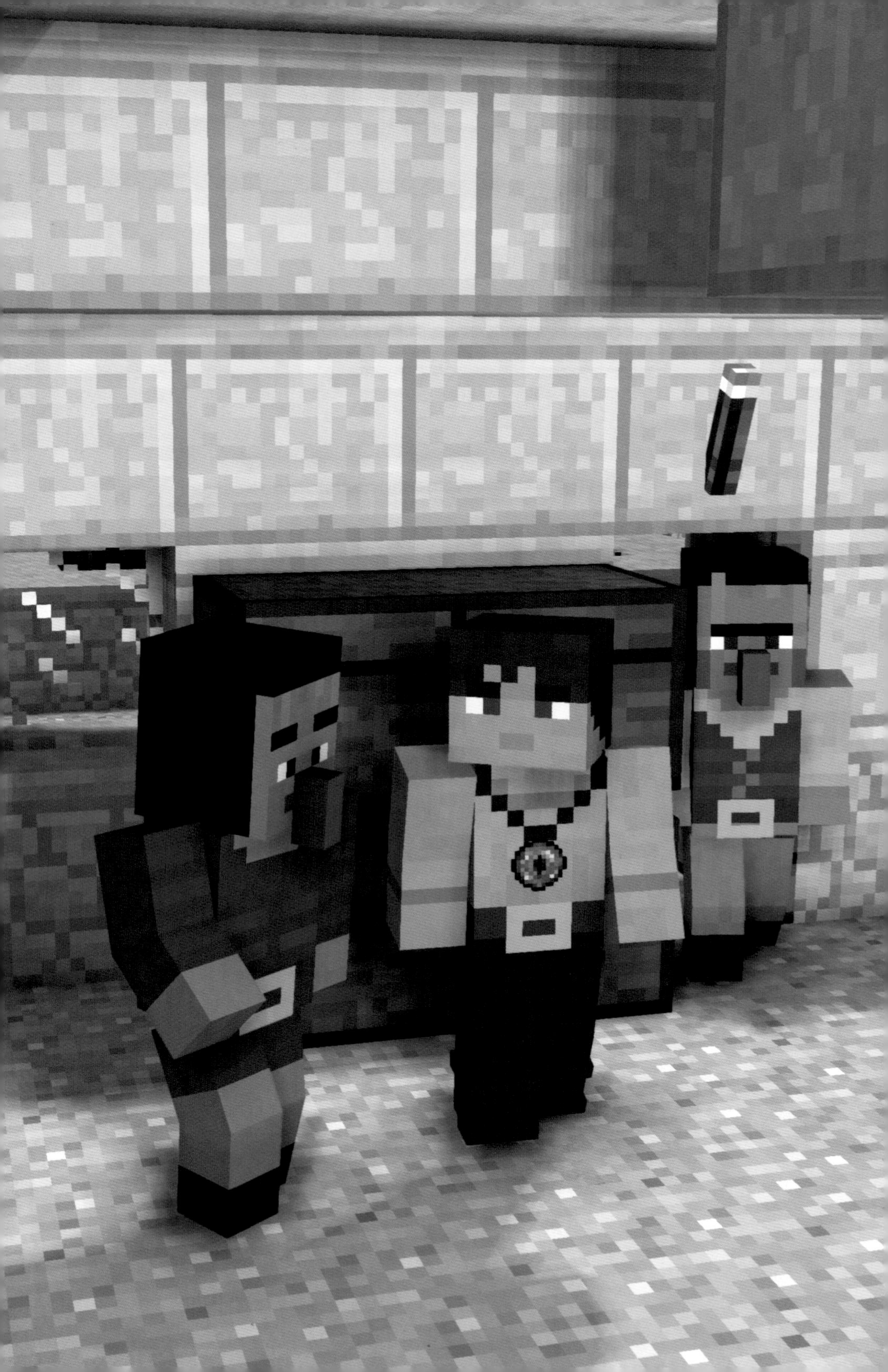

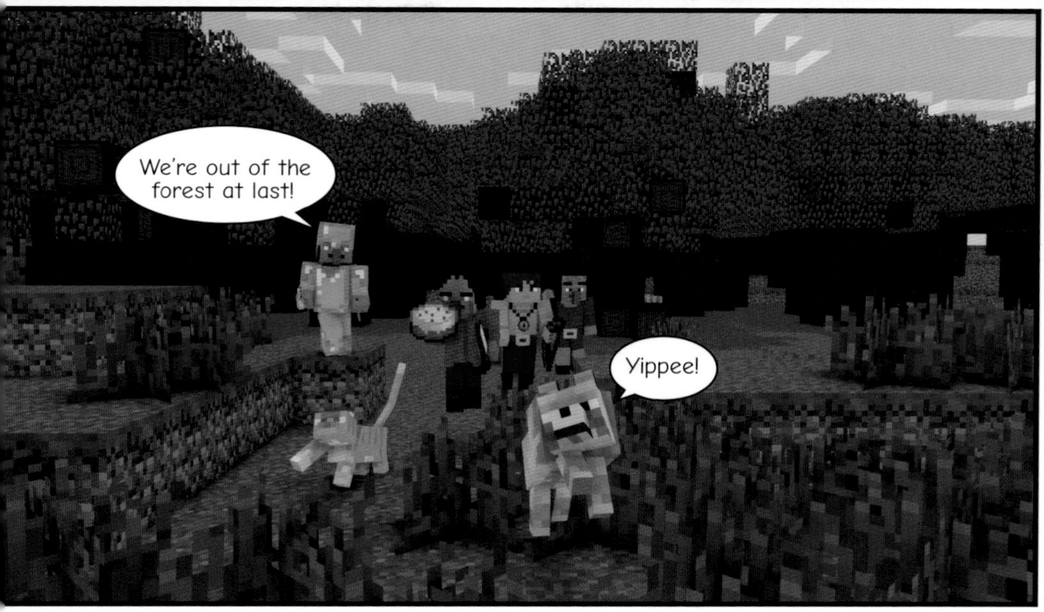
We're out of the forest at last!
Yippee!

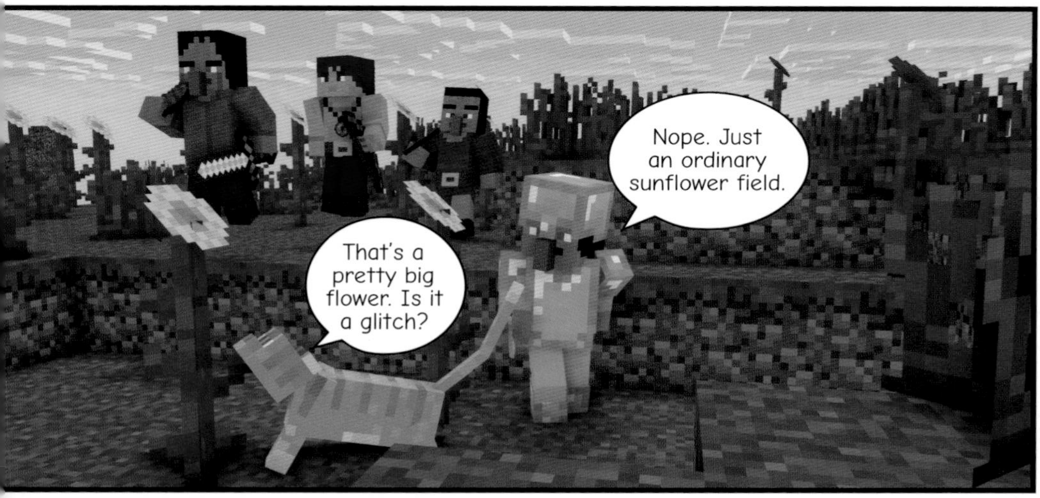
That's a pretty big flower. Is it a glitch?
Nope. Just an ordinary sunflower field.

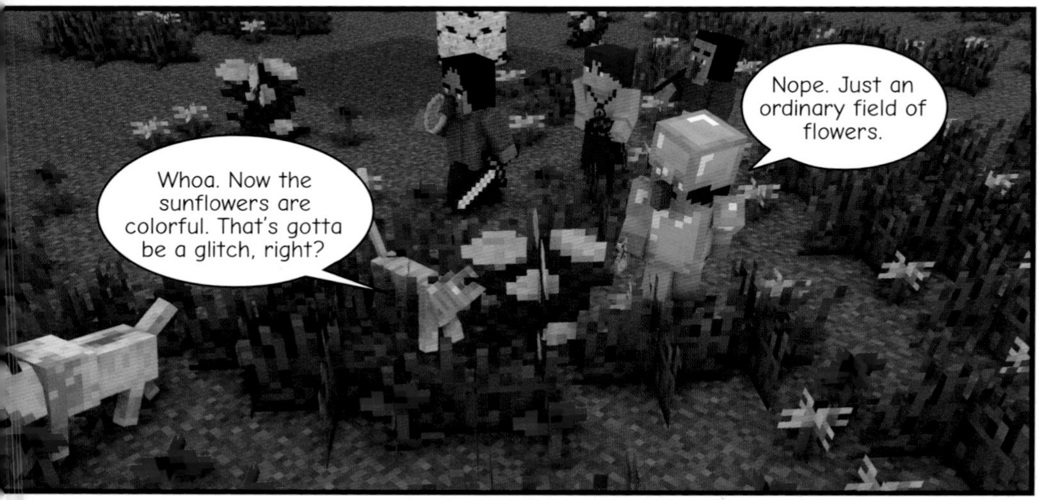
Whoa. Now the sunflowers are colorful. That's gotta be a glitch, right?
Nope. Just an ordinary field of flowers.

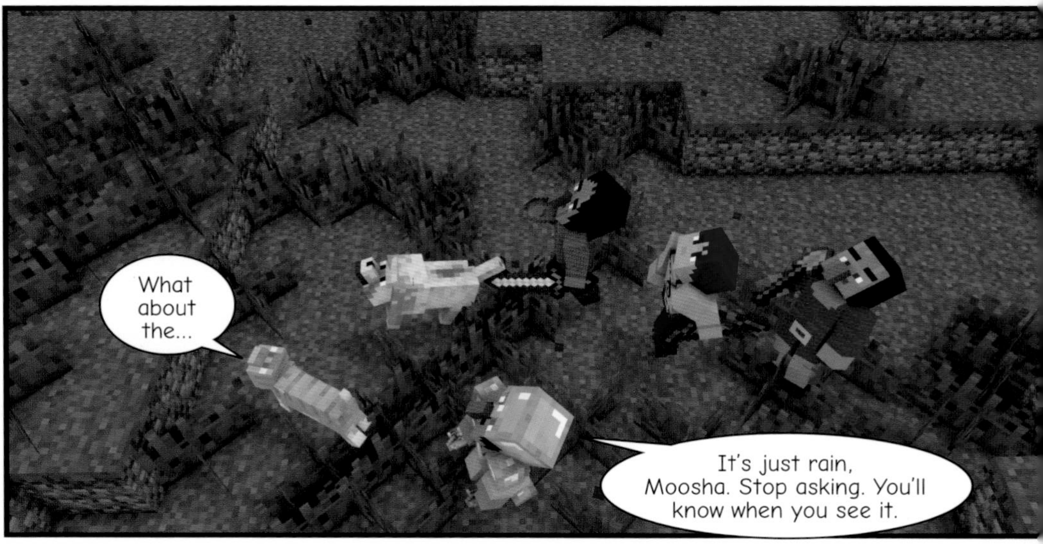
What about the...
It's just rain, Moosha. Stop asking. You'll know when you see it.
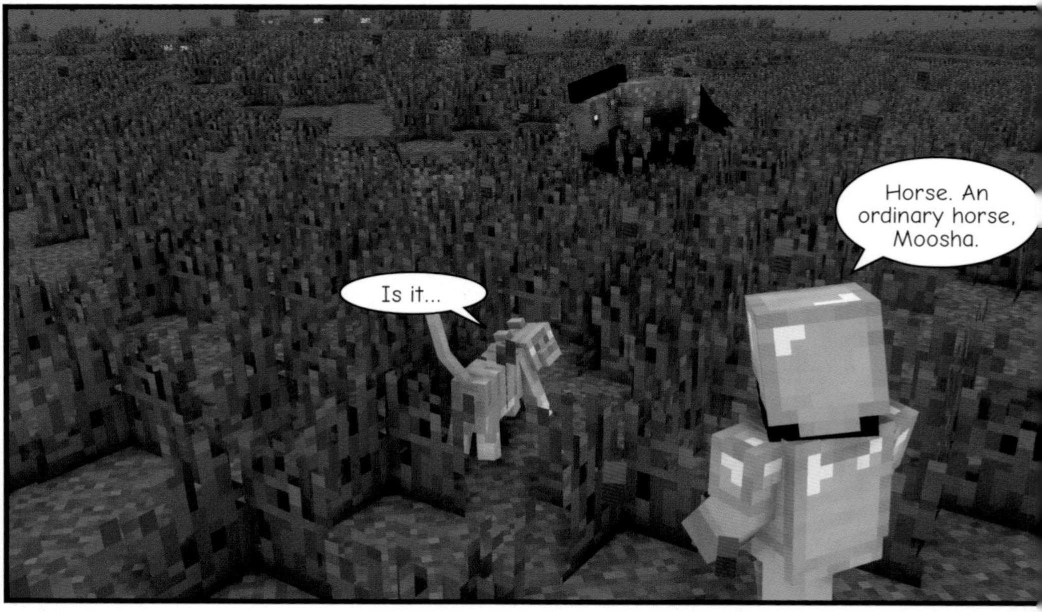
Horse. An ordinary horse, Moosha.
Is it...
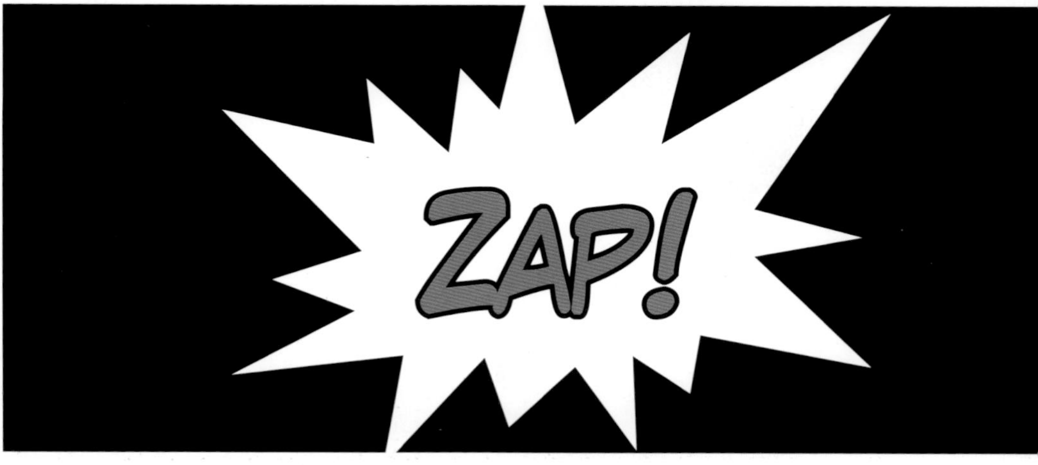
ZAP!

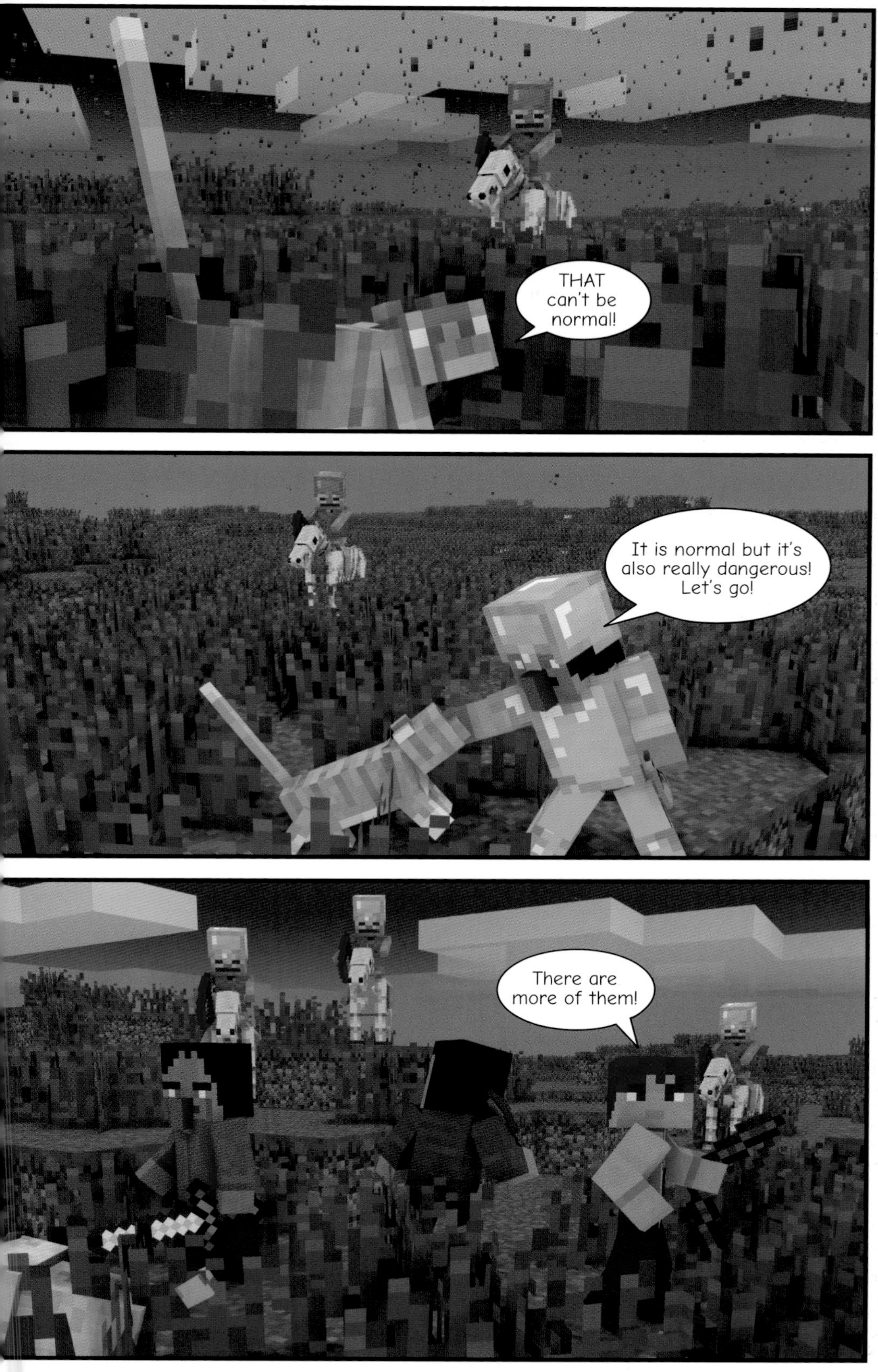
THAT can't be normal!
It is normal but it's also really dangerous! Let's go!
There are more of them!

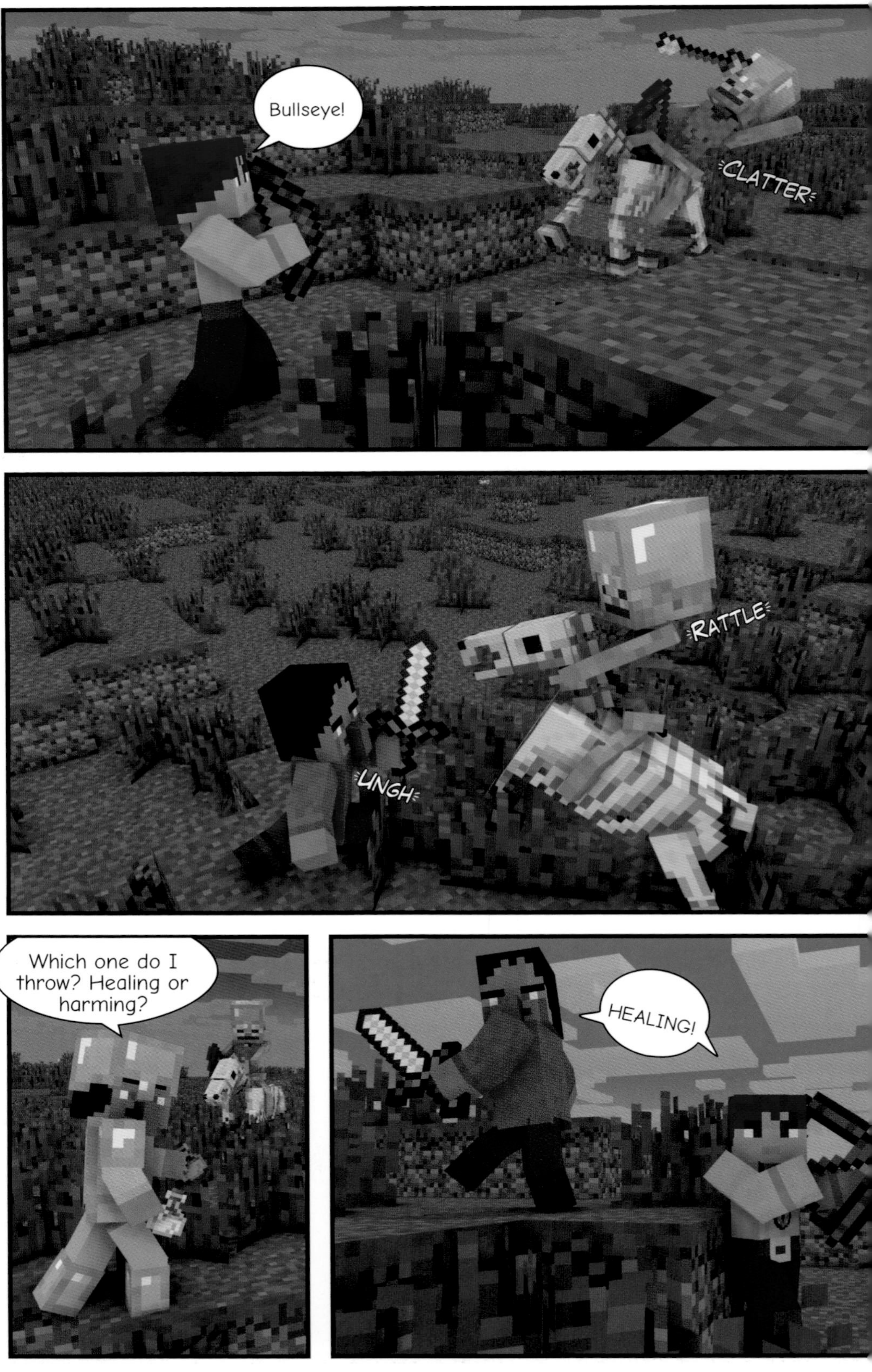
Bullseye!
CLATTER
RATTLE
UNGH
Which one do I throw? Healing or harming?
HEALING!

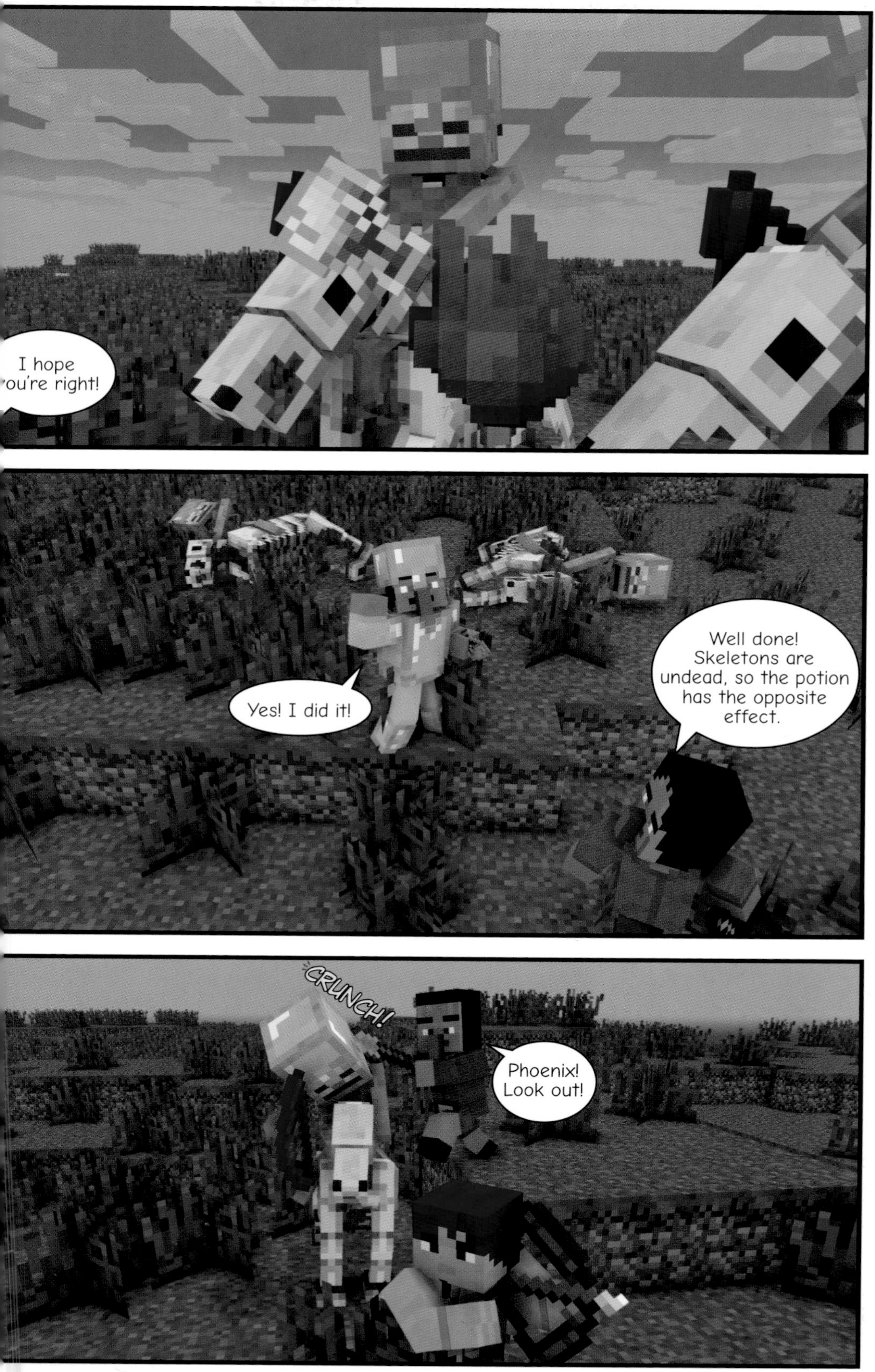
I hope
’ou’re right!
Yes! I did it!
Well done! Skeletons are undead, so the potion has the opposite effect.
CRUNCH!
Phoenix! Look out!

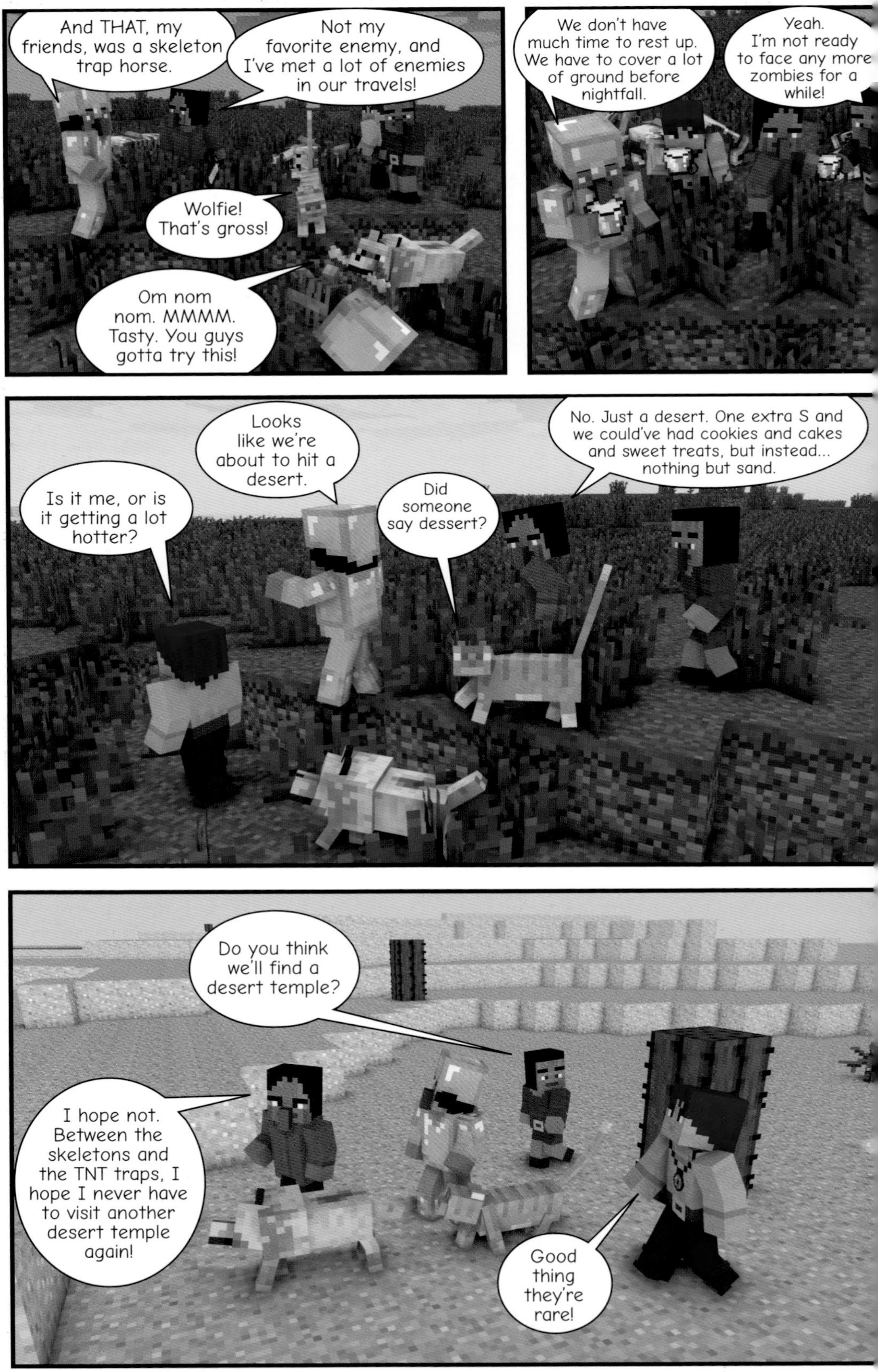

And THAT, my friends, was a skeleton trap horse.
Not my favorite enemy, and I've met a lot of enemies in our travels!
Wolfie! That's gross!
Om nom nom. MMMM. Tasty. You guys gotta try this!
We don't have much time to rest up. We have to cover a lot of ground before nightfall.
Yeah. I'm not ready to face any more zombies for a while!
Is it me, or is it getting a lot hotter?
Looks like we're about to hit a desert.
Did someone say dessert?
No. Just a desert. One extra S and we could've had cookies and cakes and sweet treats, but instead... nothing but sand.
Do you think we'll find a desert temple?
I hope not. Between the skeletons and the TNT traps, I hope I never have to visit another desert temple again!
Good thing they're rare!

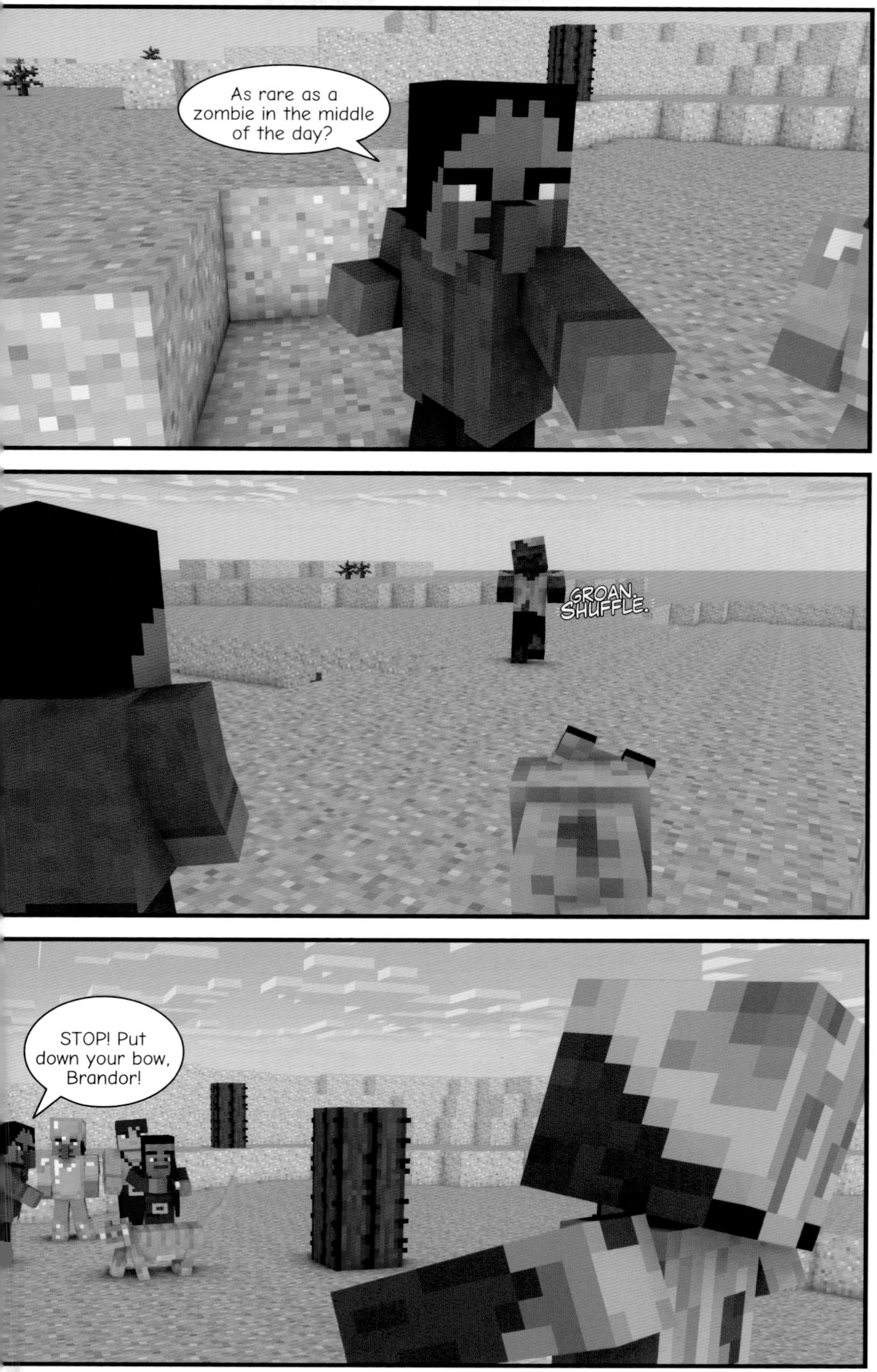
As rare as a zombie in the middle of the day?
GROAN. SHUFFLE.
STOP! Put down your bow, Brandor!

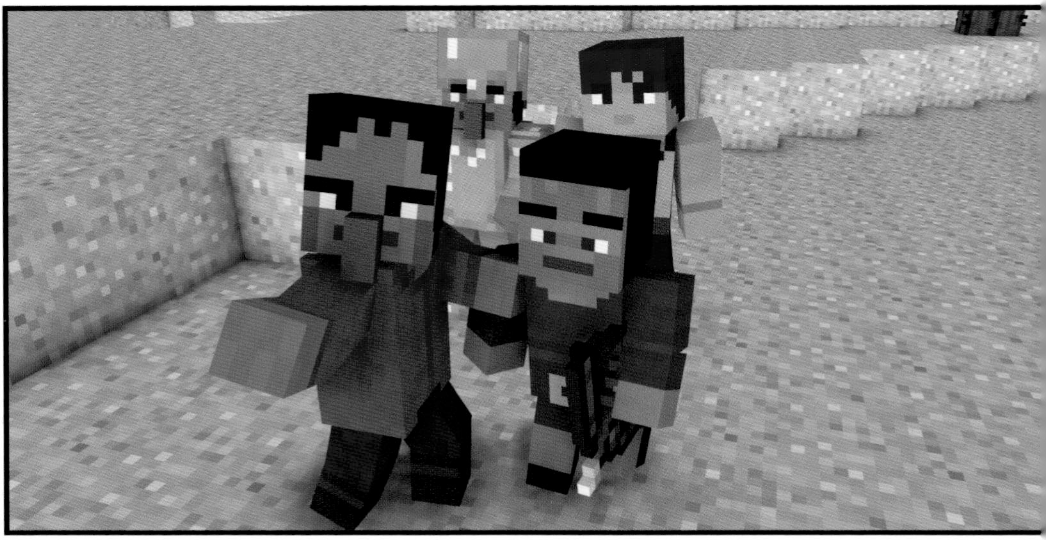

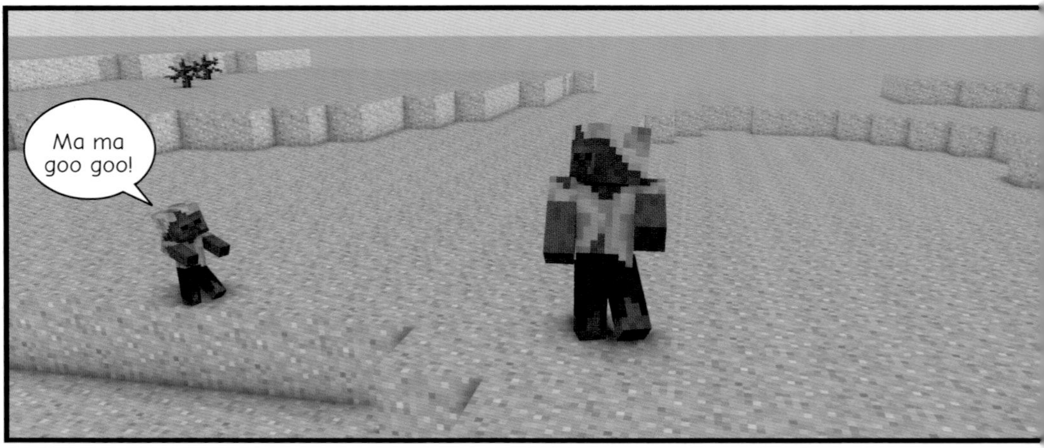
Ma ma
goo goo!

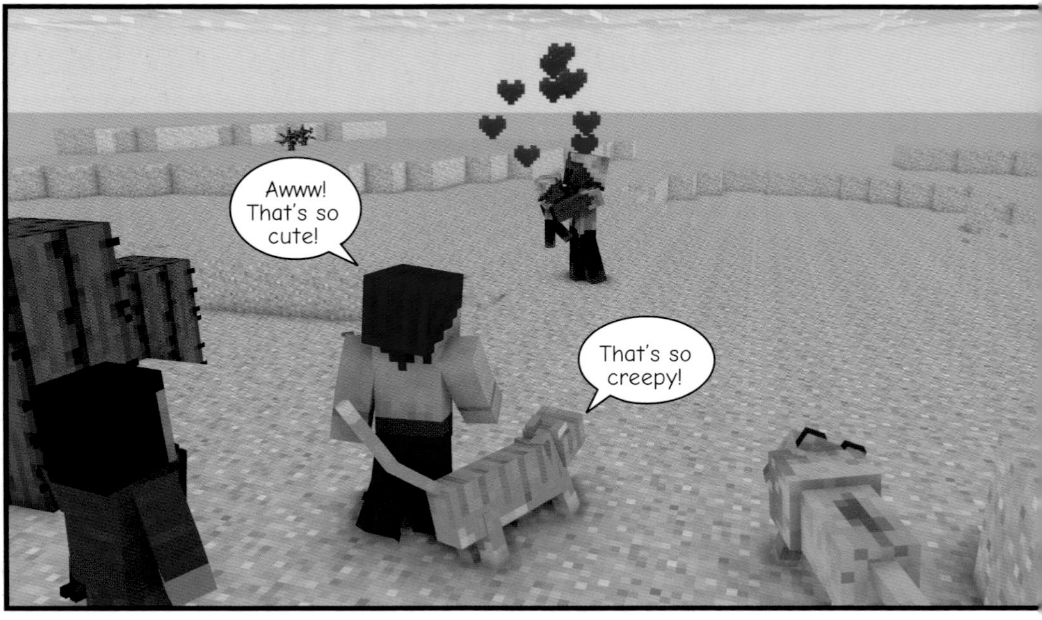
Awww!
That's so
cute!
That's so
creepy!

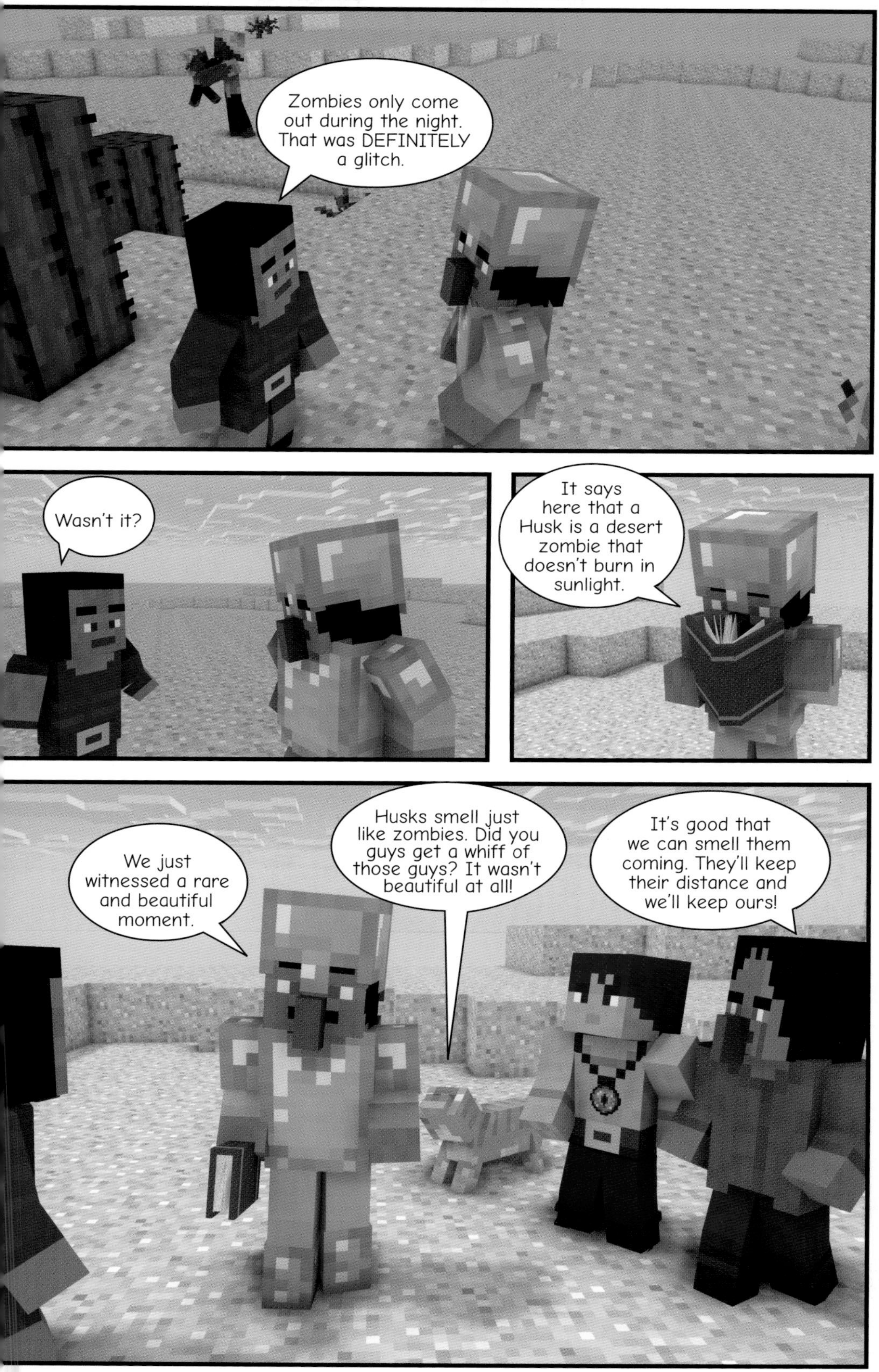
Zombies only come out during the night. That was DEFINITELY a glitch.
Wasn't it?
It says here that a Husk is a desert zombie that doesn't burn in sunlight.
We just witnessed a rare and beautiful moment.
Husks smell just like zombies. Did you guys get a whiff of those guys? It wasn't beautiful at all!
It's good that we can smell them coming. They'll keep their distance and we'll keep ours!

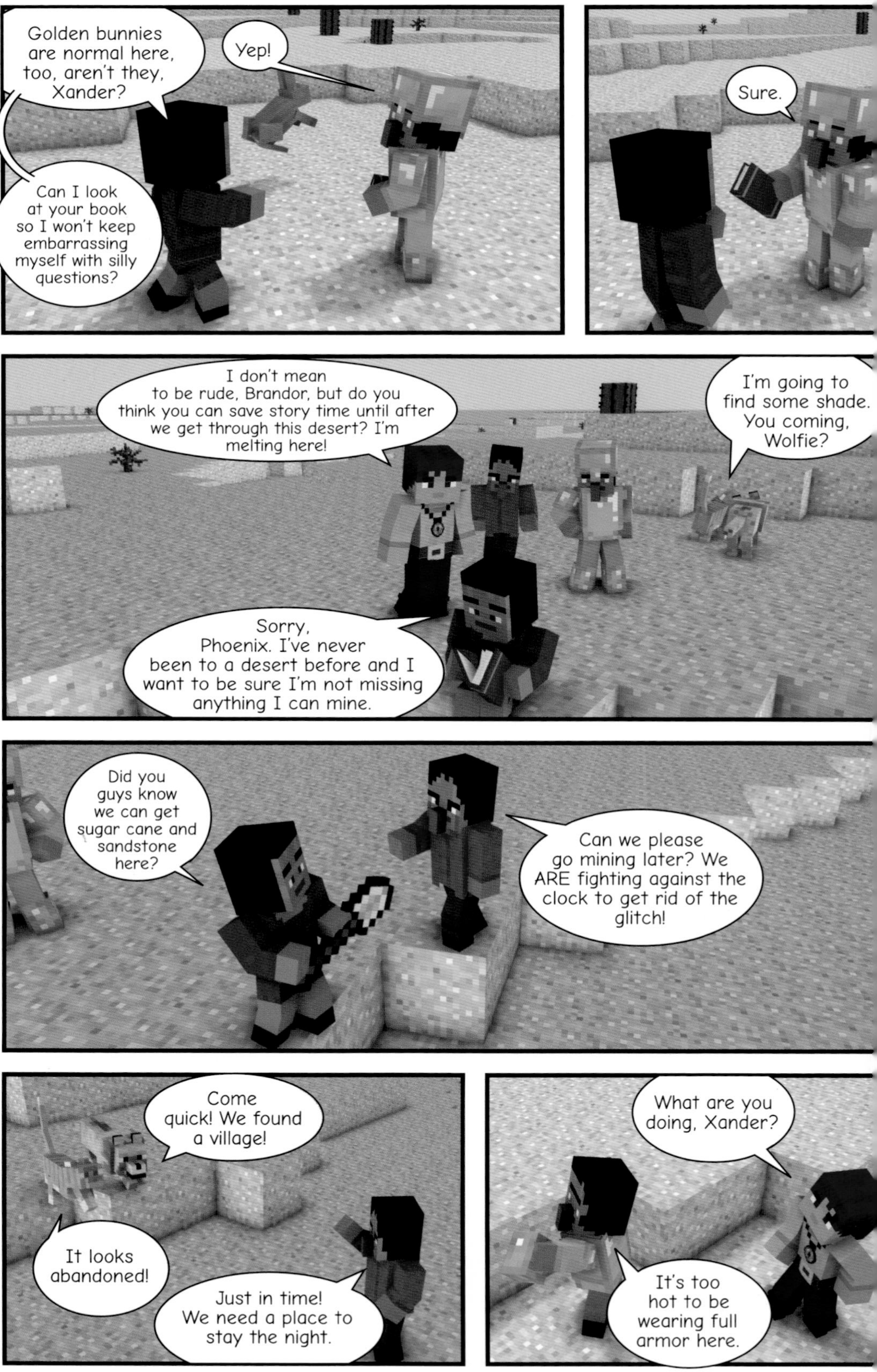
Golden bunnies are normal here, too, aren't they, Xander?
Yep!
Can I look at your book so I won't keep embarrassing myself with silly questions?
Sure.
I don't mean to be rude, Brandor, but do you think you can save story time until after we get through this desert? I'm melting here!
I'm going to find some shade. You coming, Wolfie?
Sorry, Phoenix. I've never been to a desert before and I want to be sure I'm not missing anything I can mine.
Did you guys know we can get sugar cane and sandstone here?
Can we please go mining later? We ARE fighting against the clock to get rid of the glitch!
Come quick! We found a village!
It looks abandoned!
Just in time! We need a place to stay the night.
What are you doing, Xander?
It's too hot to be wearing full armor here.

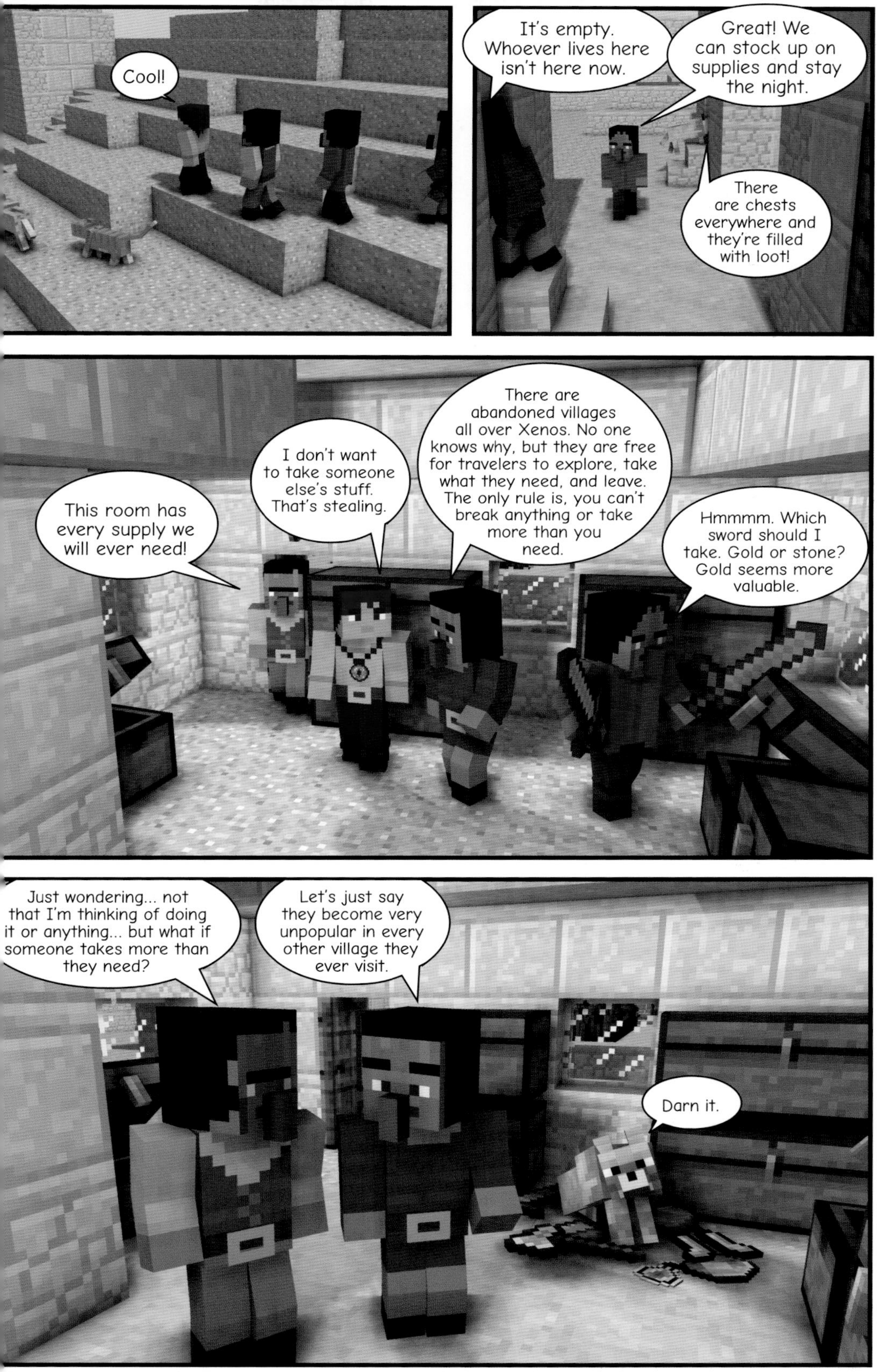
Cool!
It's empty. Whoever lives here isn't here now.
Great! We can stock up on supplies and stay the night.
There are chests everywhere and they're filled with loot!
This room has every supply we will ever need!
I don't want to take someone else's stuff. That's stealing.
There are abandoned villages all over Xenos. No one knows why, but they are free for travelers to explore, take what they need, and leave. The only rule is, you can't break anything or take more than you need.
Hmmmm. Which sword should I take. Gold or stone? Gold seems more valuable.
Just wondering... not that I'm thinking of doing it or anything... but what if someone takes more than they need?
Let's just say they become very unpopular in every other village they ever visit.
Darn it.

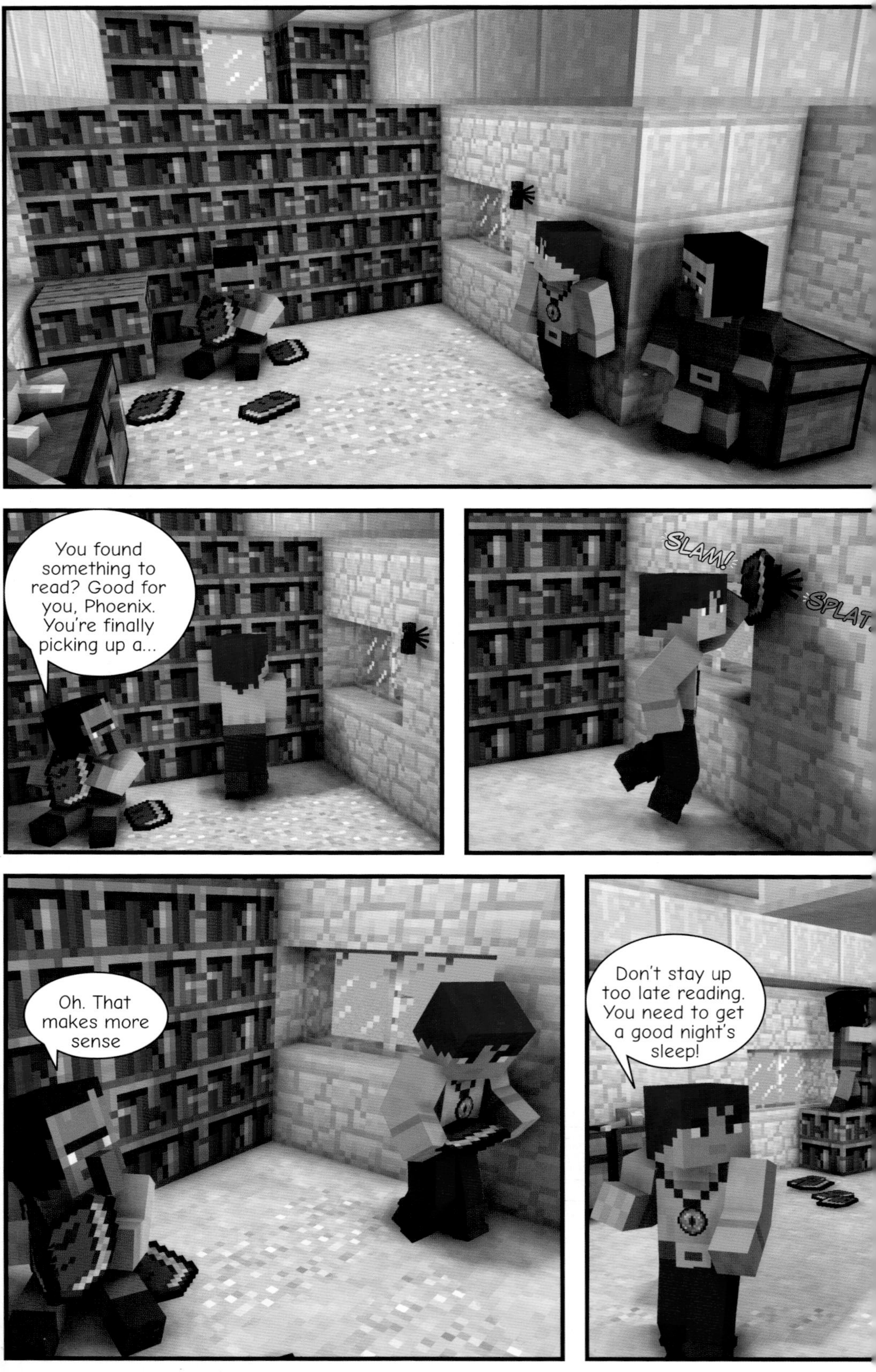

You found something to read? Good for you, Phoenix. You're finally picking up a...
SLAM!
SPLAT.
Oh. That makes more sense
Don't stay up too late reading. You need to get a good night's sleep!

CHAPTER 8

LLAGERS

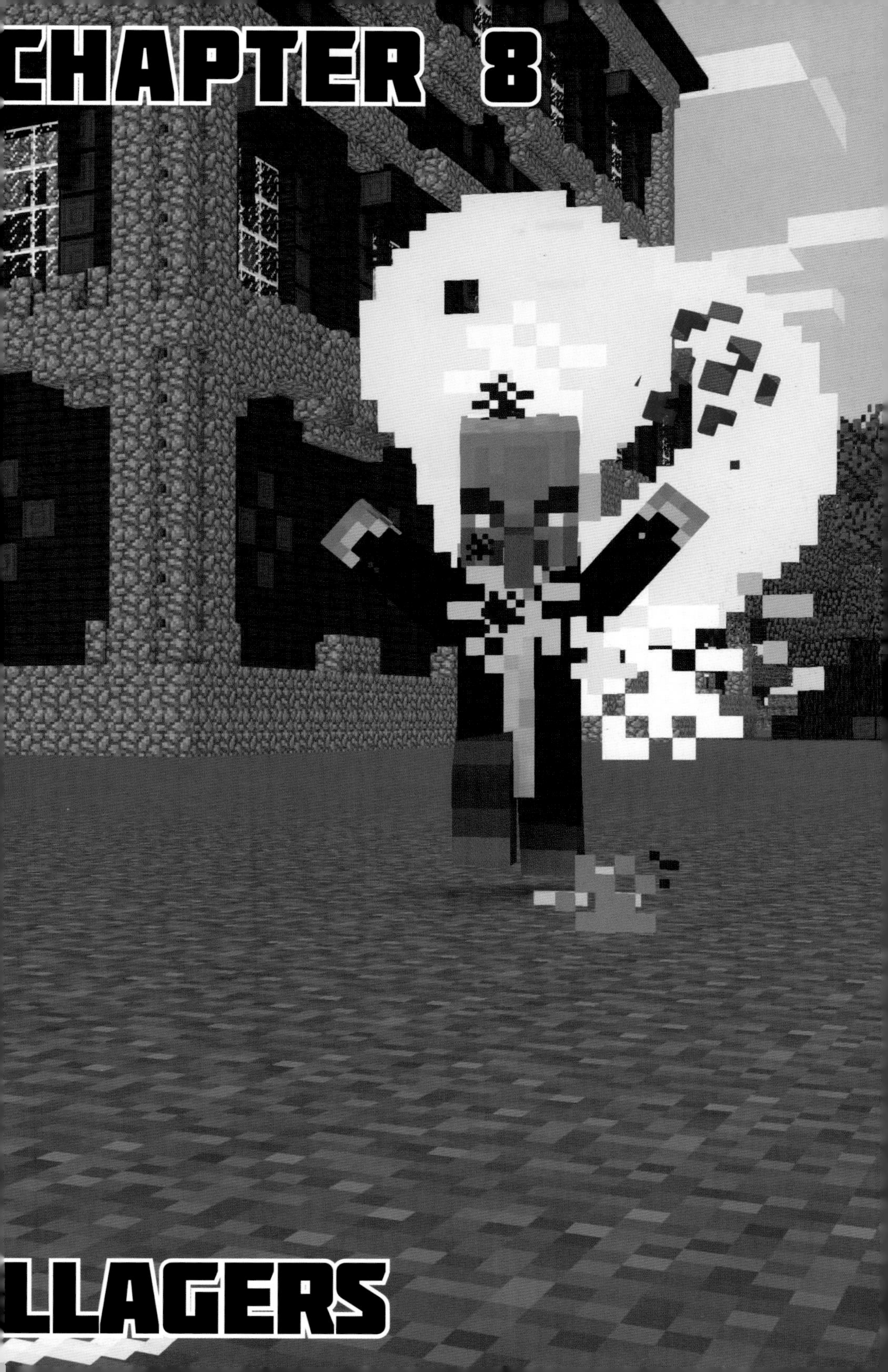

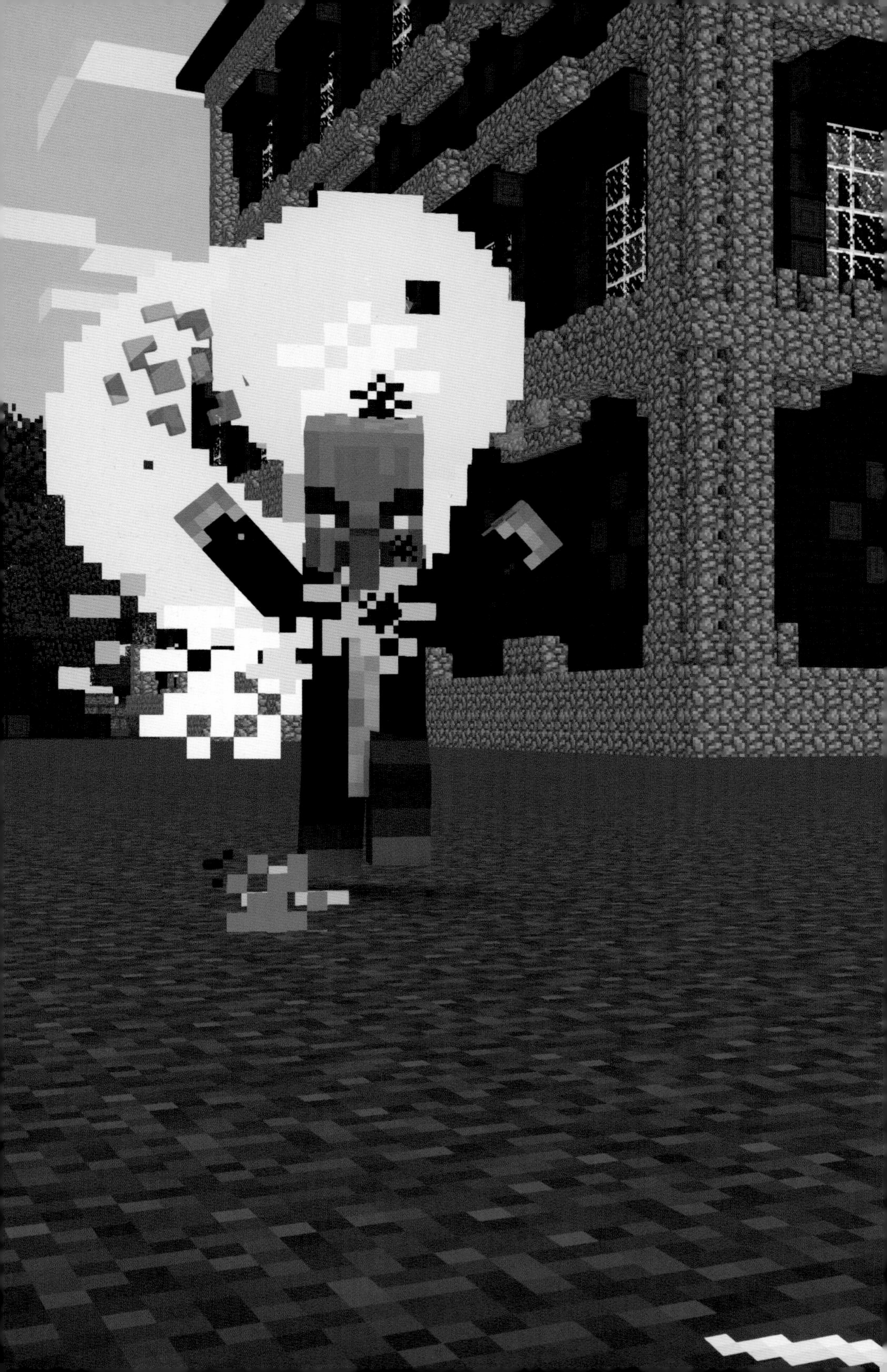

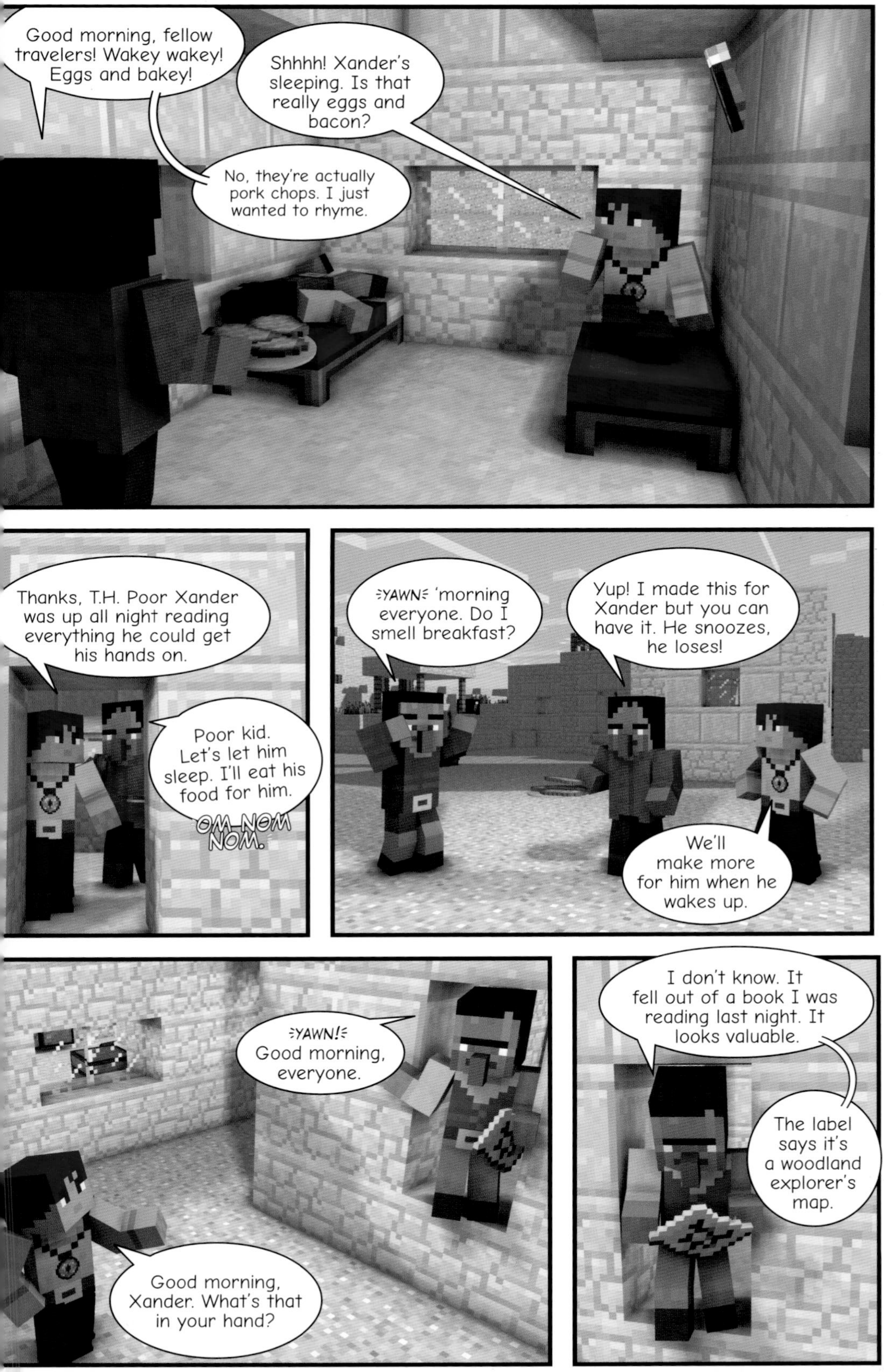
Good morning, fellow travelers! Wakey wakey! Eggs and bakey!
Shhhh! Xander's sleeping. Is that really eggs and bacon?
No, they're actually pork chops. I just wanted to rhyme.
Thanks, T.H. Poor Xander was up all night reading everything he could get his hands on.
Poor kid. Let's let him sleep. I'll eat his food for him.
OM NOM NOM.
YAWN 'morning everyone. Do I smell breakfast?
Yup! I made this for Xander but you can have it. He snoozes, he loses!
We'll make more for him when he wakes up.
YAWN! Good morning, everyone.
Good morning, Xander. What's that in your hand?
I don't know. It fell out of a book I was reading last night. It looks valuable.
The label says it's a woodland explorer's map.

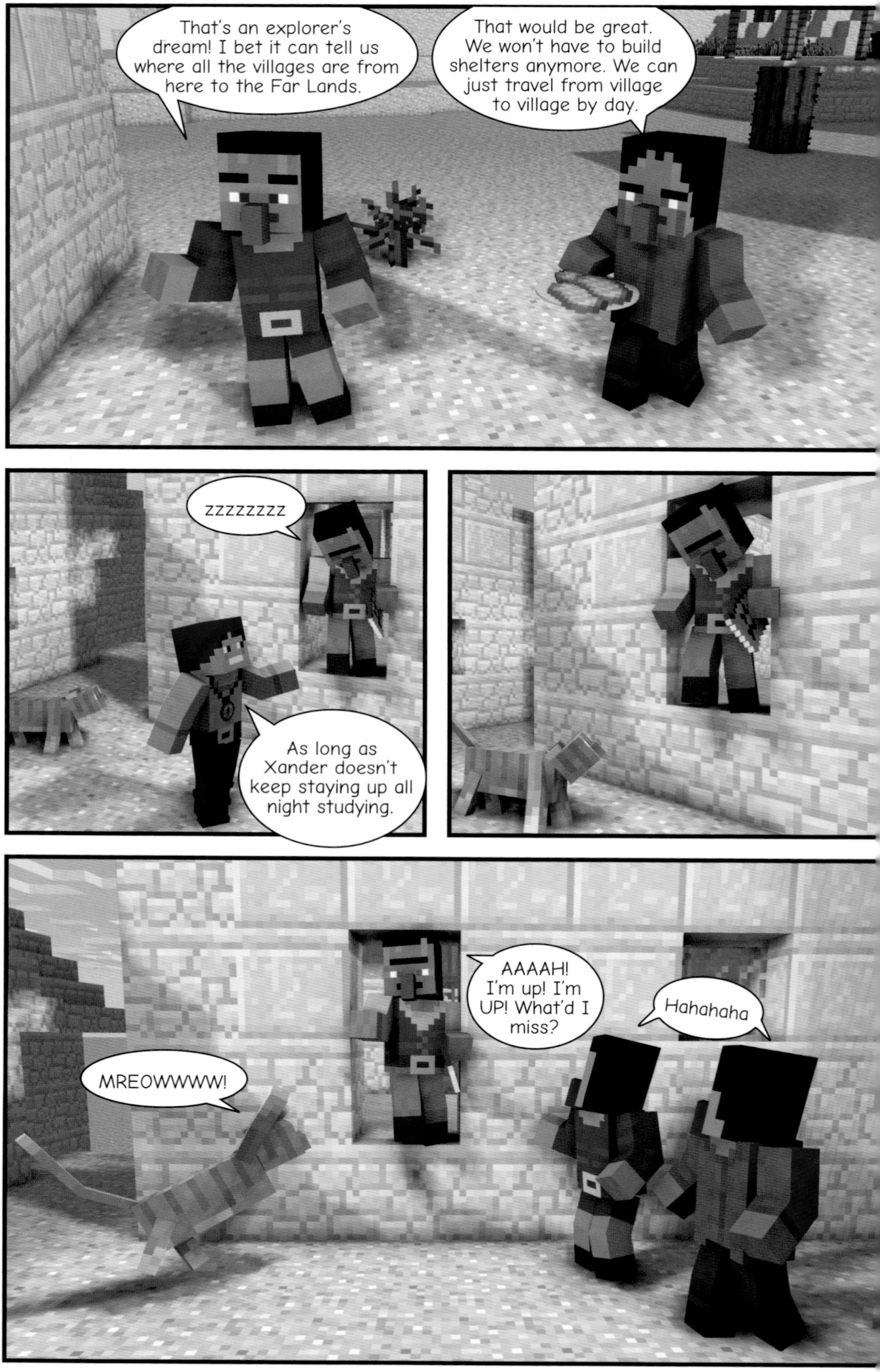
That's an explorer's dream! I bet it can tell us where all the villages are from here to the Far Lands.
That would be great. We won't have to build shelters anymore. We can just travel from village to village by day.
zzzzzzzz
As long as Xander doesn't keep staying up all night studying.
MREOWWWW!
AAAAH! I'm up! I'm UP! What'd I miss?
Hahahaha

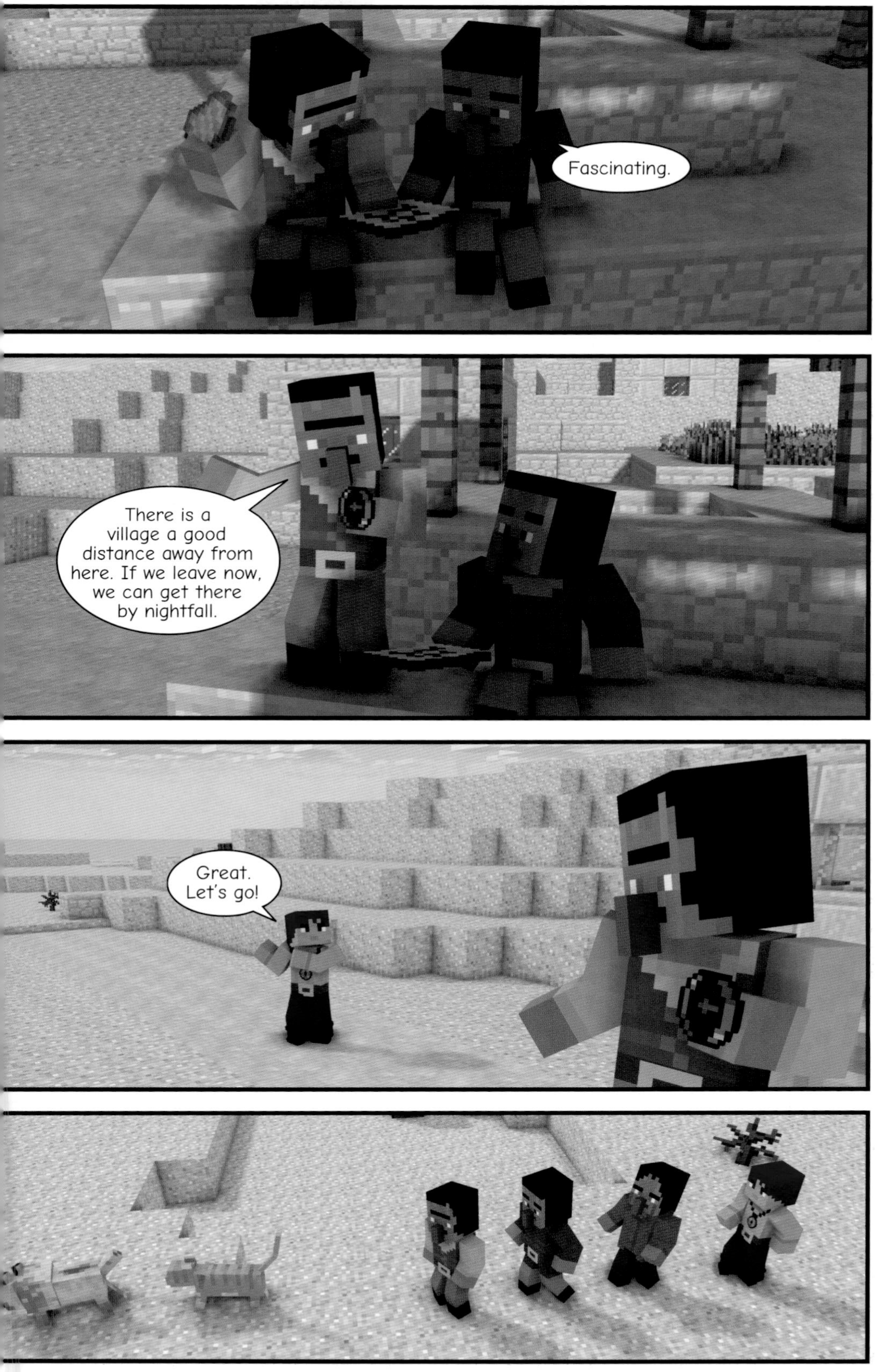

Fascinating.
There is a village a good distance away from here. If we leave now, we can get there by nightfall.
Great. Let's go!

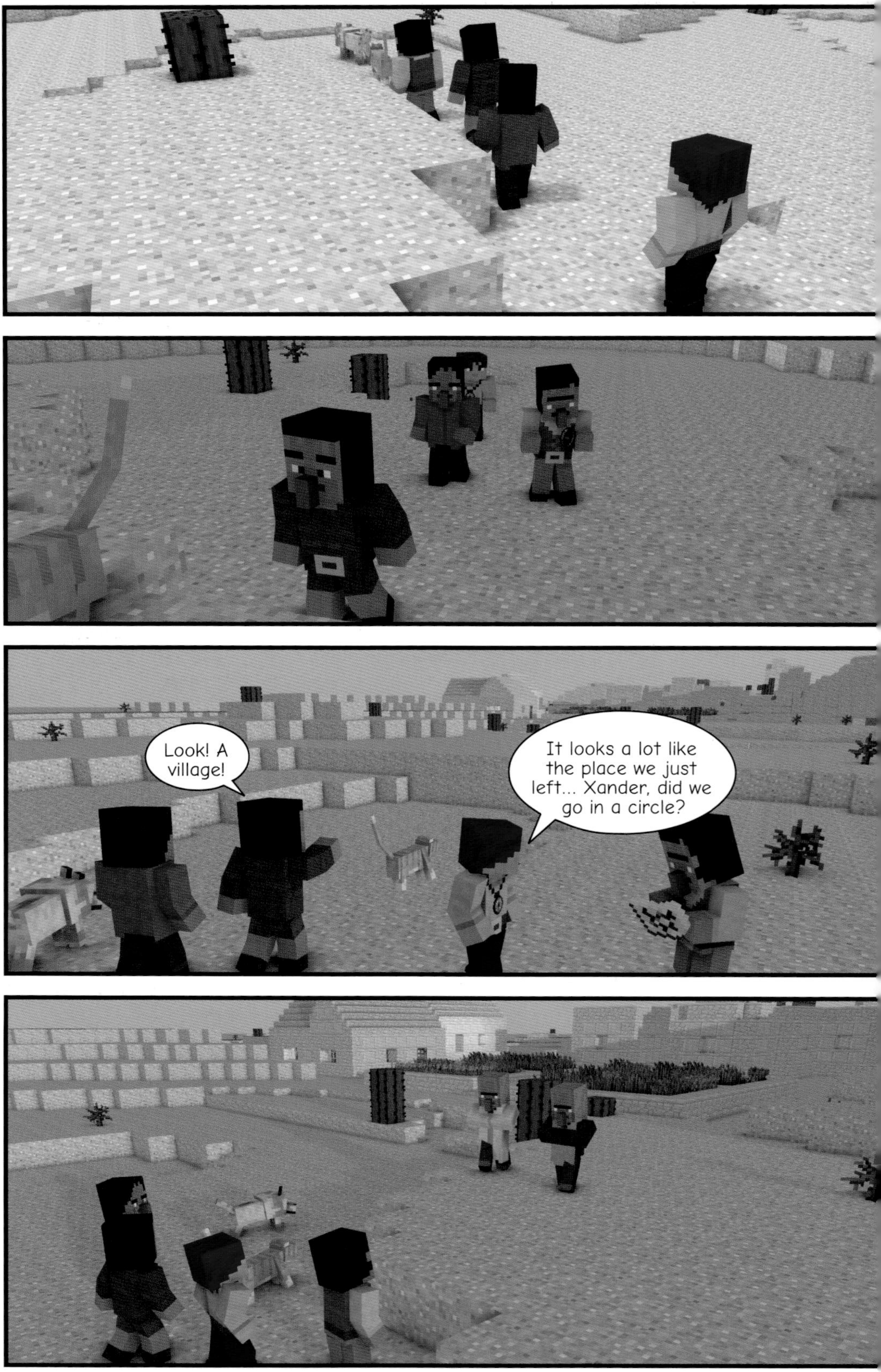
Look! A village!
It looks a lot like the place we just left... Xander, did we go in a circle?

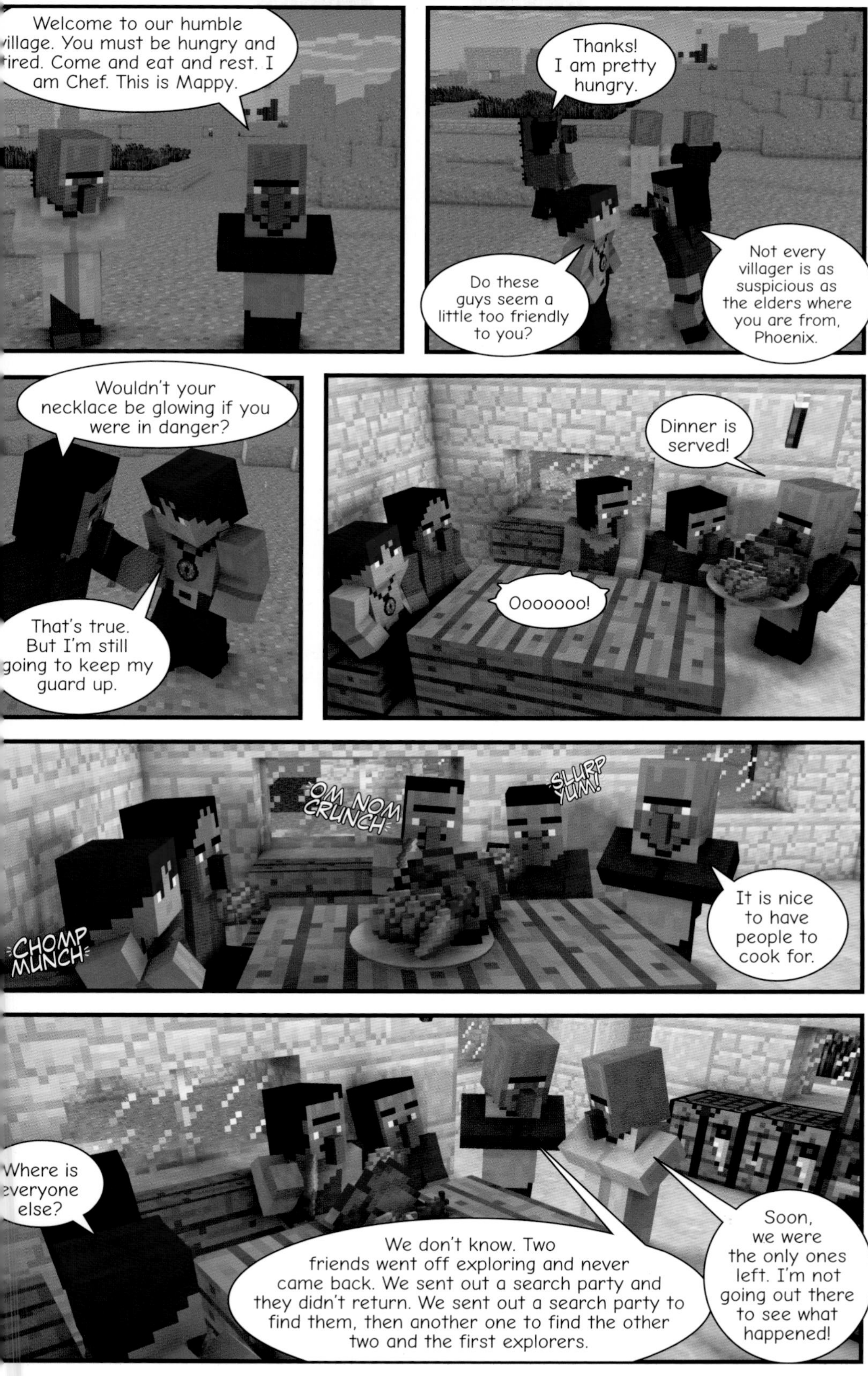

Welcome to our humble illage. You must be hungry and ired. Come and eat and rest. I am Chef. This is Mappy.
Thanks! I am pretty hungry.
Do these guys seem a little too friendly to you?
Not every villager is as suspicious as the elders where you are from, Phoenix.
Wouldn't your necklace be glowing if you were in danger?
That's true. But I'm still going to keep my guard up.
Dinner is served!
Ooooooo!
OM NOM CRUNCH
SLURP YUM!
CHOMP MUNCH
It is nice to have people to cook for.
Where is veryone else?
We don't know. Two friends went off exploring and never came back. We sent out a search party and they didn't return. We sent out a search party to find them, then another one to find the other two and the first explorers.
Soon, we were the only ones left. I'm not going out there to see what happened!

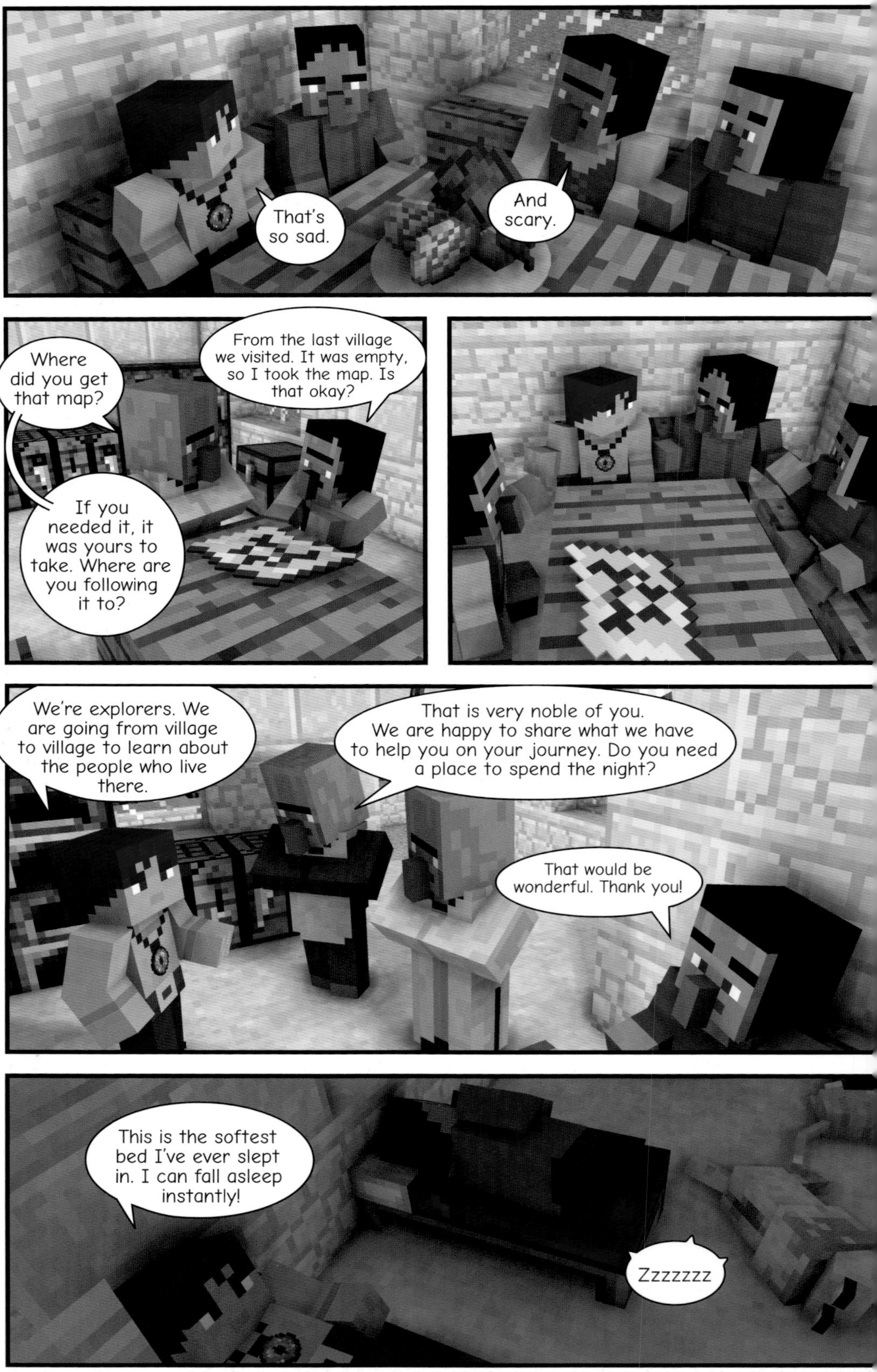
That's so sad.
And scary.
Where did you get that map?
From the last village we visited. It was empty, so I took the map. Is that okay?
If you needed it, it was yours to take. Where are you following it to?
We're explorers. We are going from village to village to learn about the people who live there.
That is very noble of you. We are happy to share what we have to help you on your journey. Do you need a place to spend the night?
That would be wonderful. Thank you!
This is the softest bed I've ever slept in. I can fall asleep instantly!
Zzzzzzz

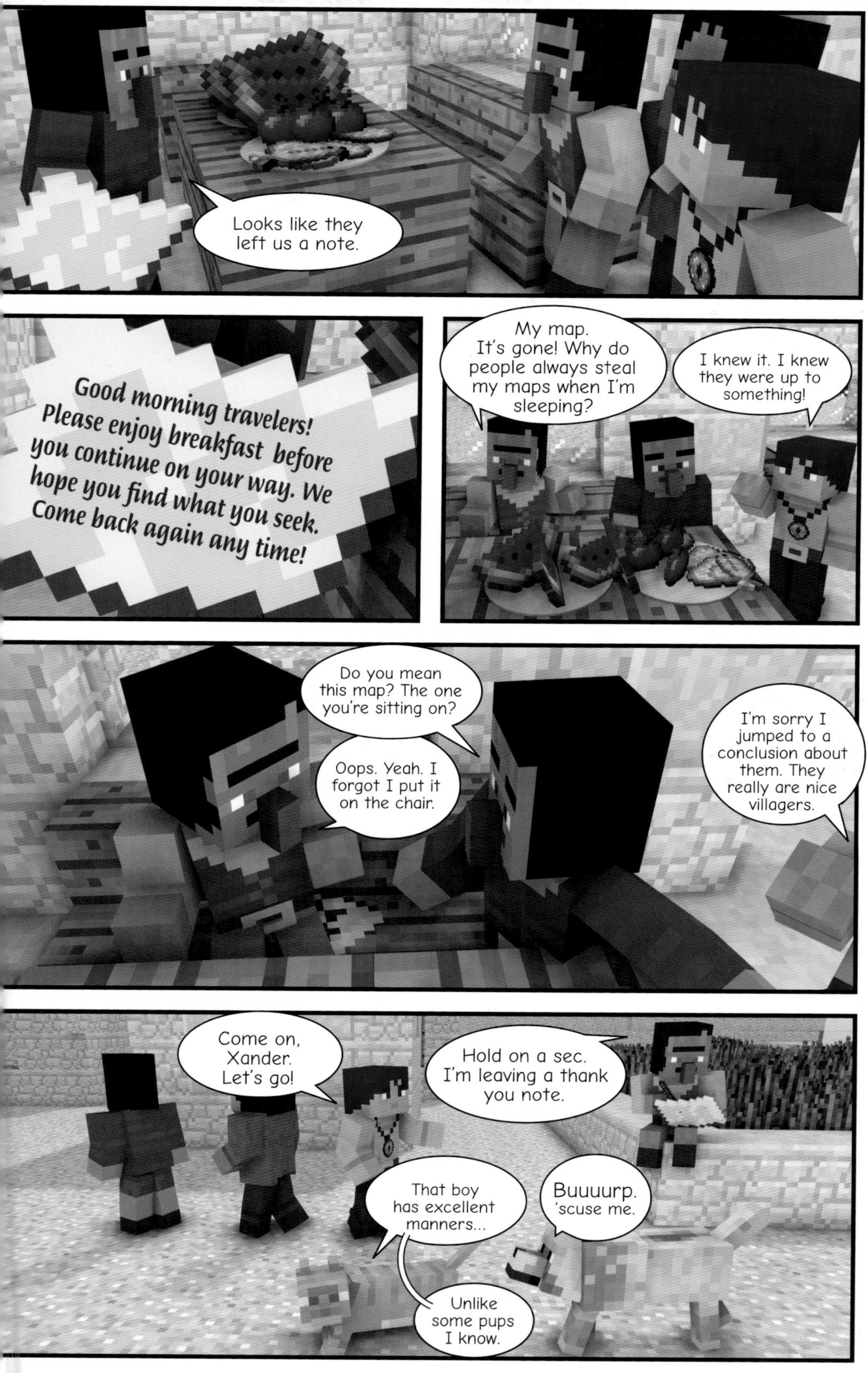
Looks like they left us a note.
Good morning travelers! Please enjoy breakfast before you continue on your way. We hope you find what you seek. Come back again any time!
My map. It's gone! Why do people always steal my maps when I'm sleeping?
I knew it. I knew they were up to something!
Do you mean this map? The one you're sitting on?
Oops. Yeah. I forgot I put it on the chair.
I'm sorry I jumped to a conclusion about them. They really are nice villagers.
Come on, Xander. Let's go!
Hold on a sec. I'm leaving a thank you note.
That boy has excellent manners...
Unlike some pups I know.
Buuuurp. 'scuse me.

I can't do it anymore. I can't go on. Too much walking and climbing and running.

Come on, lazybones. You can do it.

Thanks, partner. I owe you one.

≡GROAN≡
Yeah, you do!

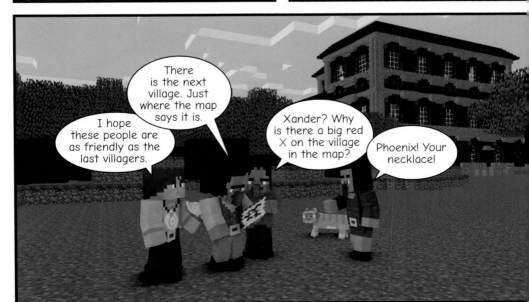

There is the next village. Just where the map says it is.

I hope these people are as friendly as the last villagers.

Xander? Why is there a big red X on the village in the map?

Phoenix! Your necklace!

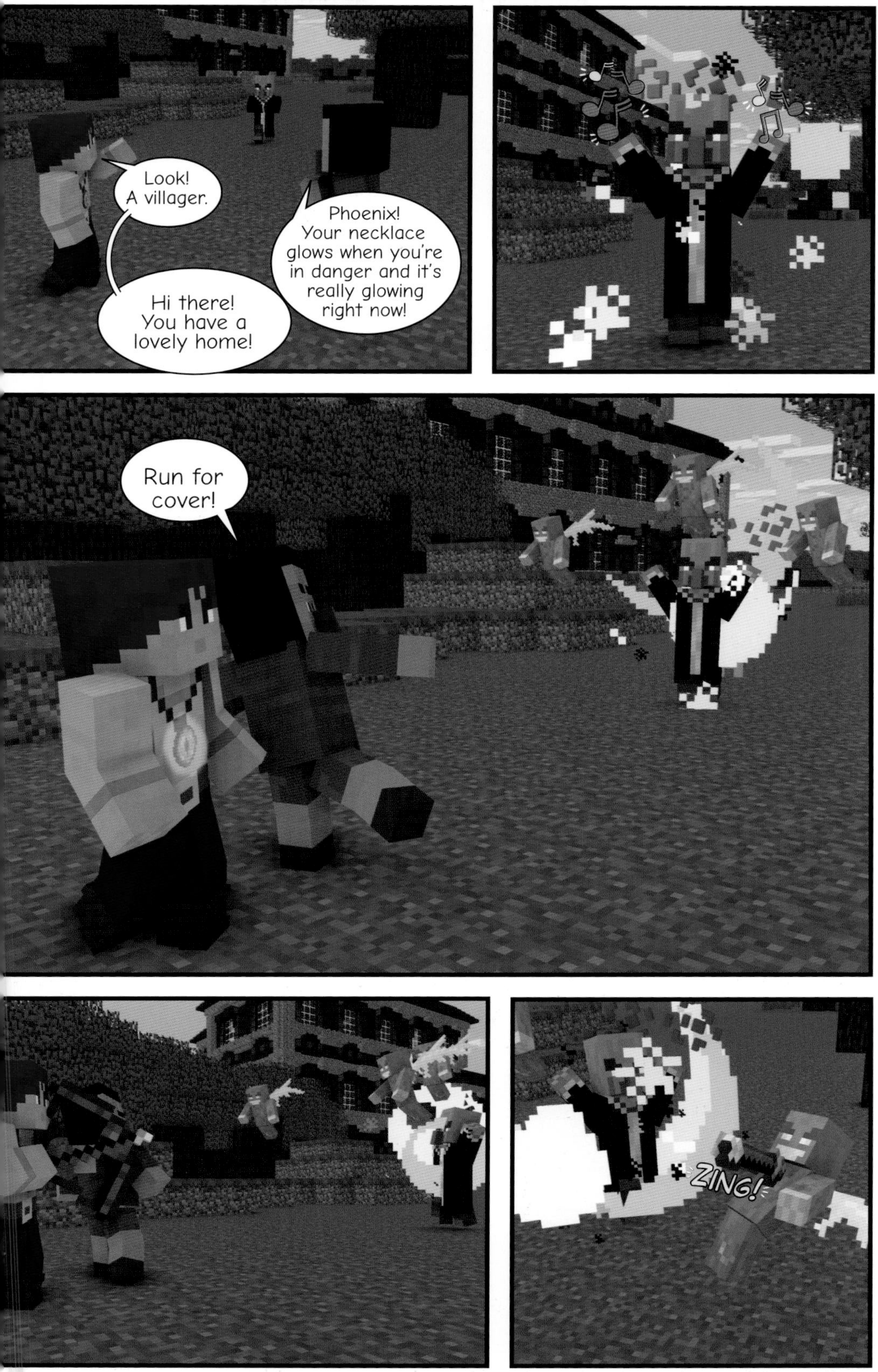
Look! A villager.
Hi there! You have a lovely home!
Phoenix! Your necklace glows when you're in danger and it's really glowing right now!
Run for cover!
ZING!

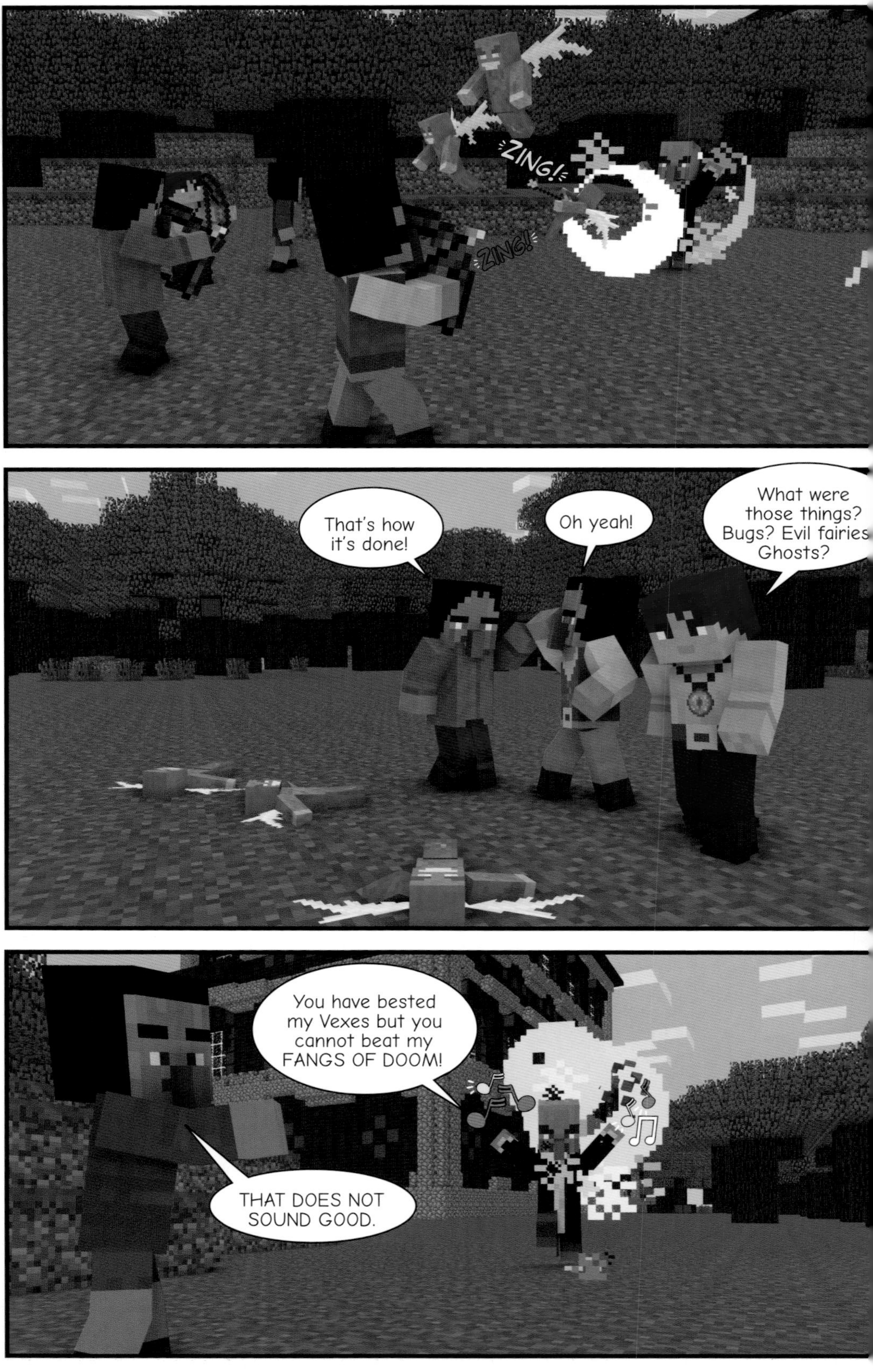
ZING!
ZING!
That's how it's done!
Oh yeah!
What were those things? Bugs? Evil fairies Ghosts?
You have bested my Vexes but you cannot beat my FANGS OF DOOM!
THAT DOES NOT SOUND GOOD.

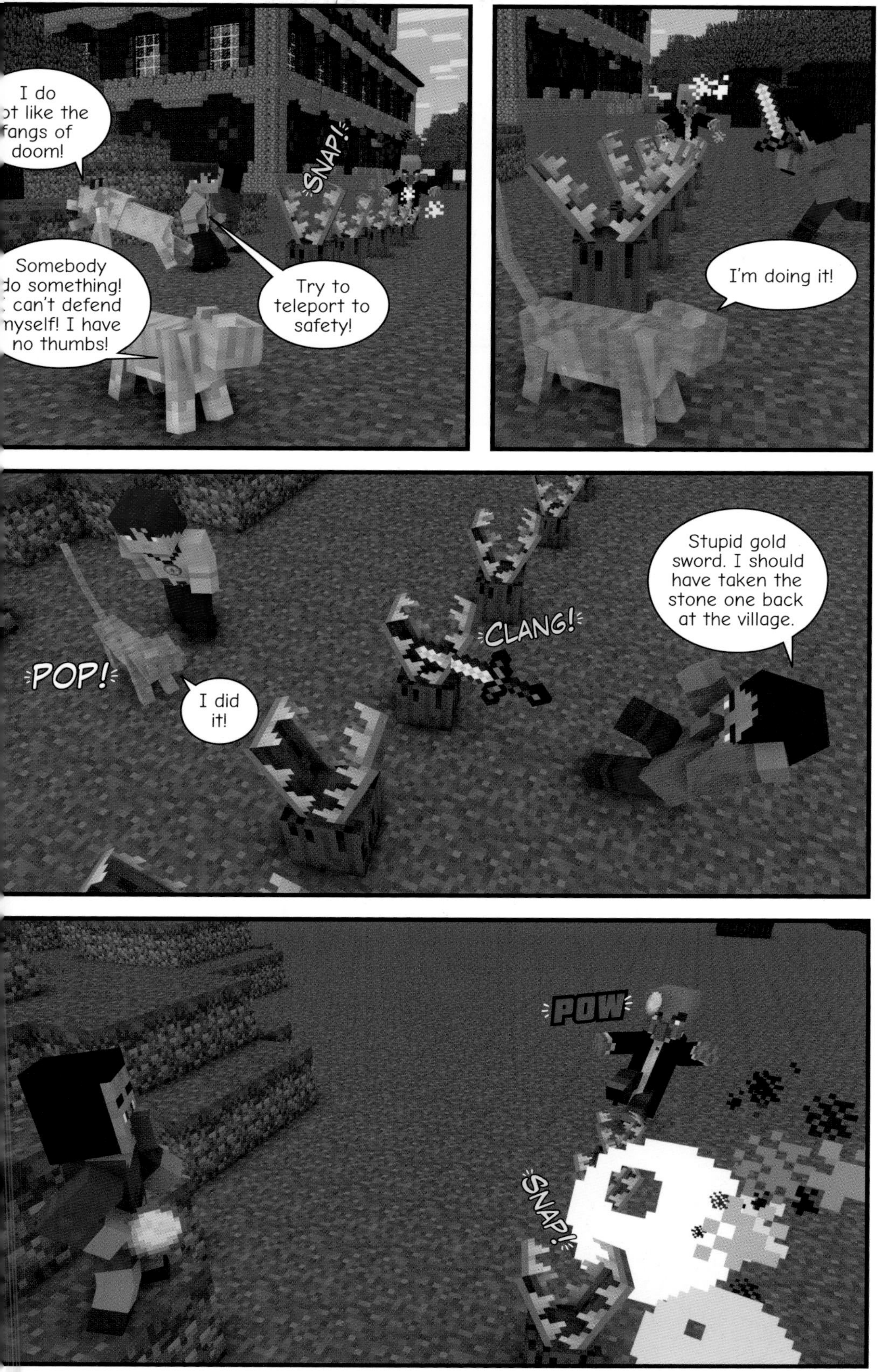

I do ot like the fangs of doom!
SNAP!
Somebody do something! can't defend myself! I have no thumbs!
Try to teleport to safety!
I'm doing it!
Stupid gold sword. I should have taken the stone one back at the village.
CLANG!
POP!
I did it!
POW
SNAP!

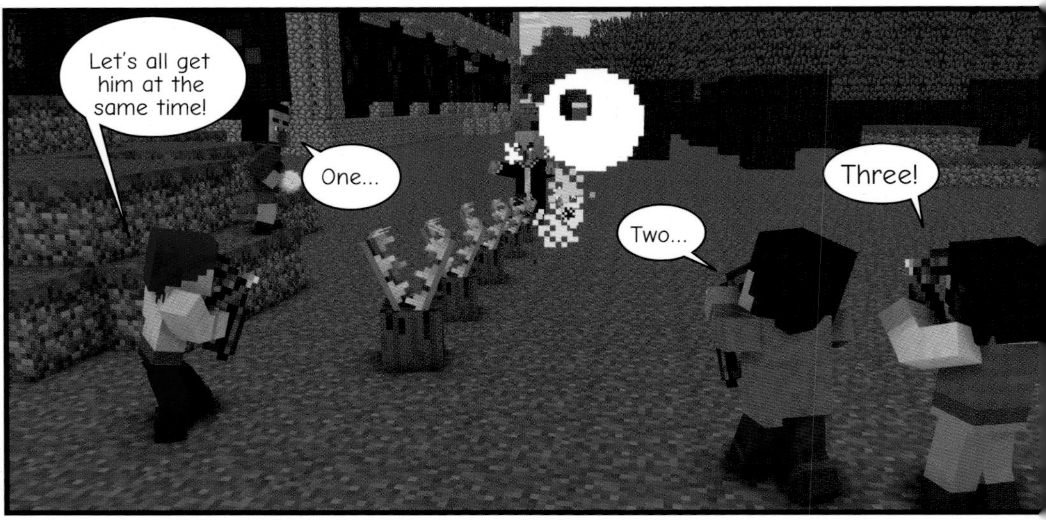
Let's all get him at the same time!
One...
Two...
Three!

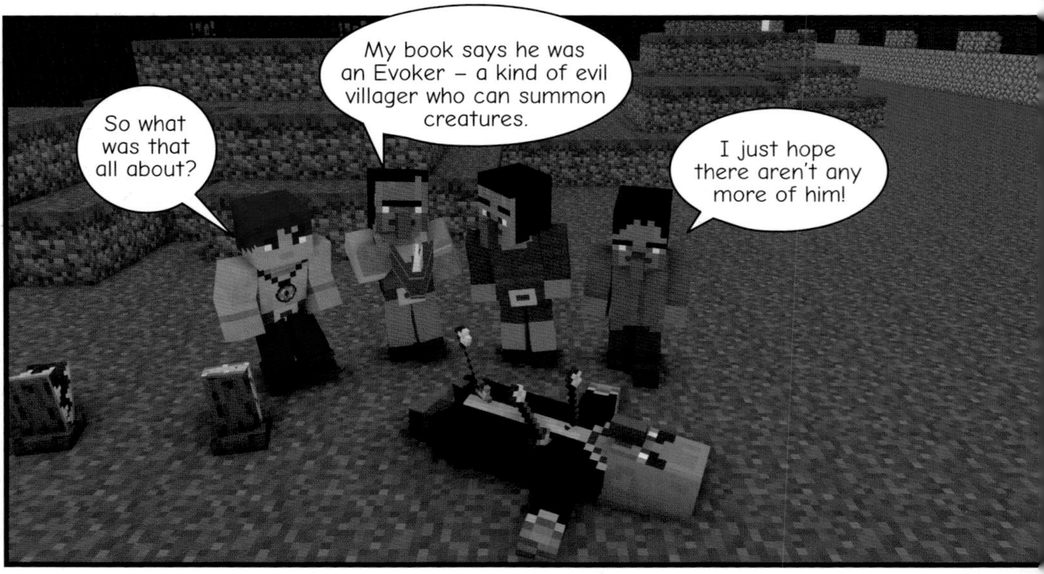
So what was that all about?
My book says he was an Evoker – a kind of evil villager who can summon creatures.
I just hope there aren't any more of him!

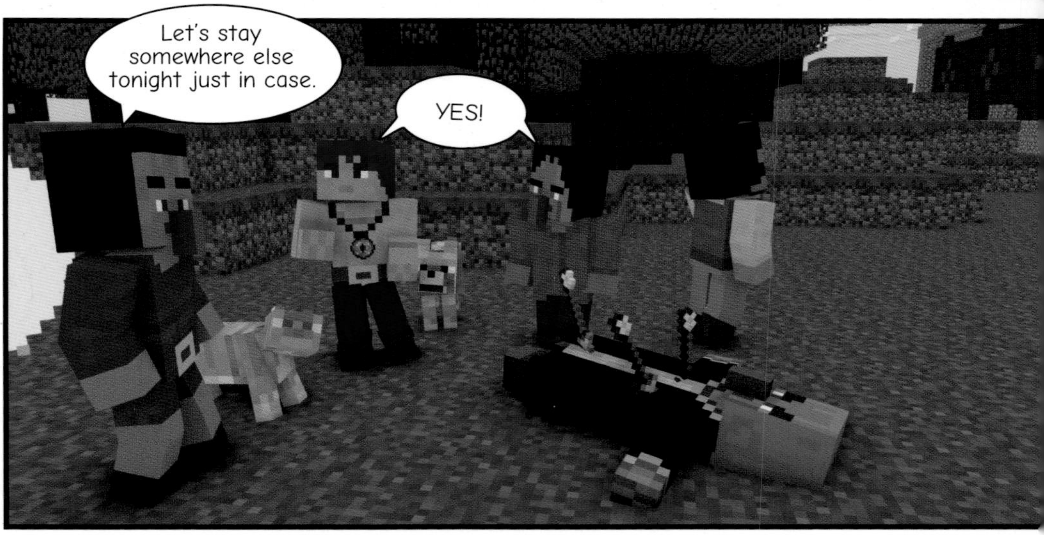
Let's stay somewhere else tonight just in case.
YES!

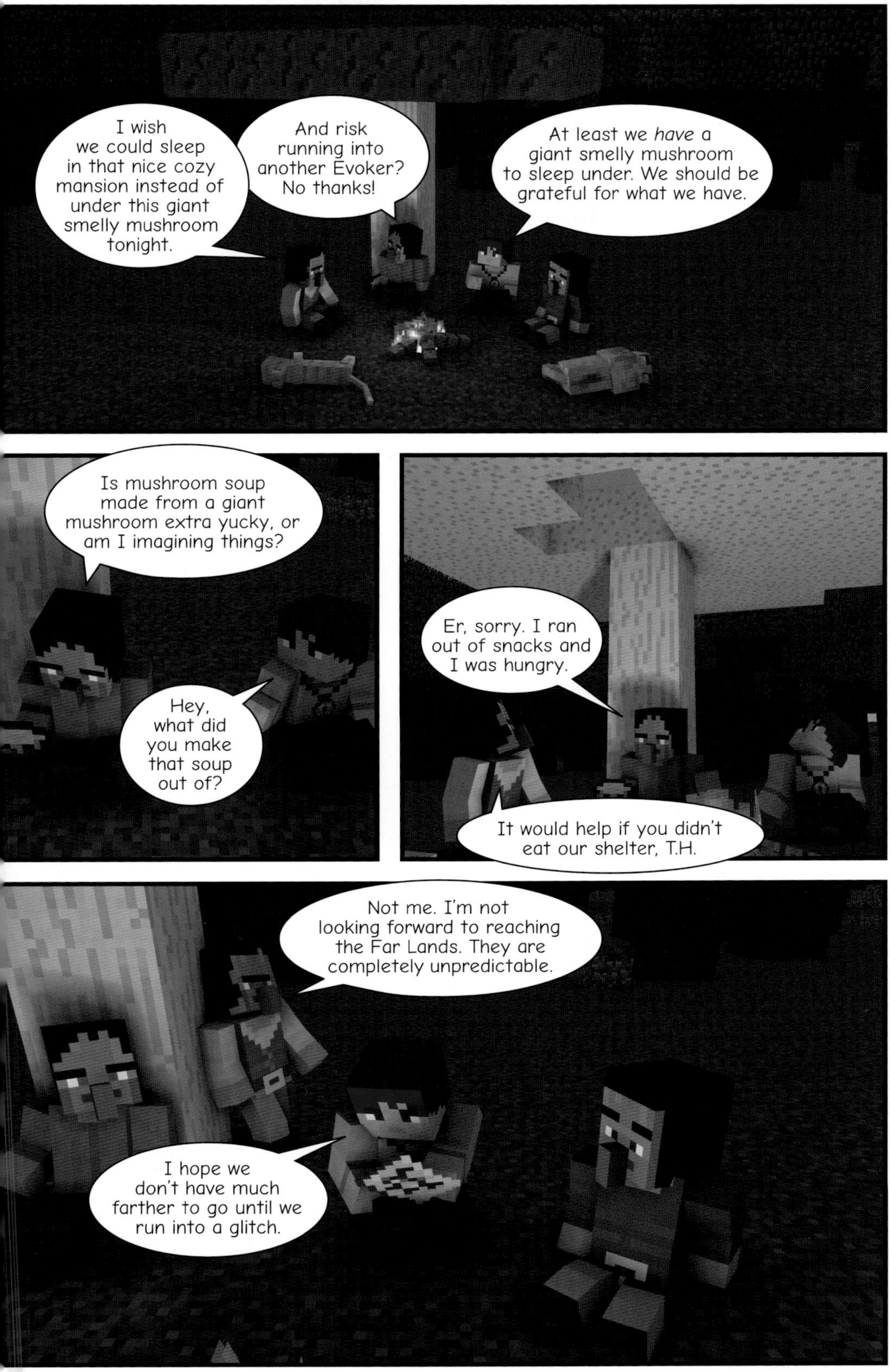
I wish we could sleep in that nice cozy mansion instead of under this giant smelly mushroom tonight.
And risk running into another Evoker? No thanks!
At least we *have* a giant smelly mushroom to sleep under. We should be grateful for what we have.
Is mushroom soup made from a giant mushroom extra yucky, or am I imagining things?
Hey, what did you make that soup out of?
Er, sorry. I ran out of snacks and I was hungry.
It would help if you didn't eat our shelter, T.H.
Not me. I'm not looking forward to reaching the Far Lands. They are completely unpredictable.
I hope we don't have much farther to go until we run into a glitch.

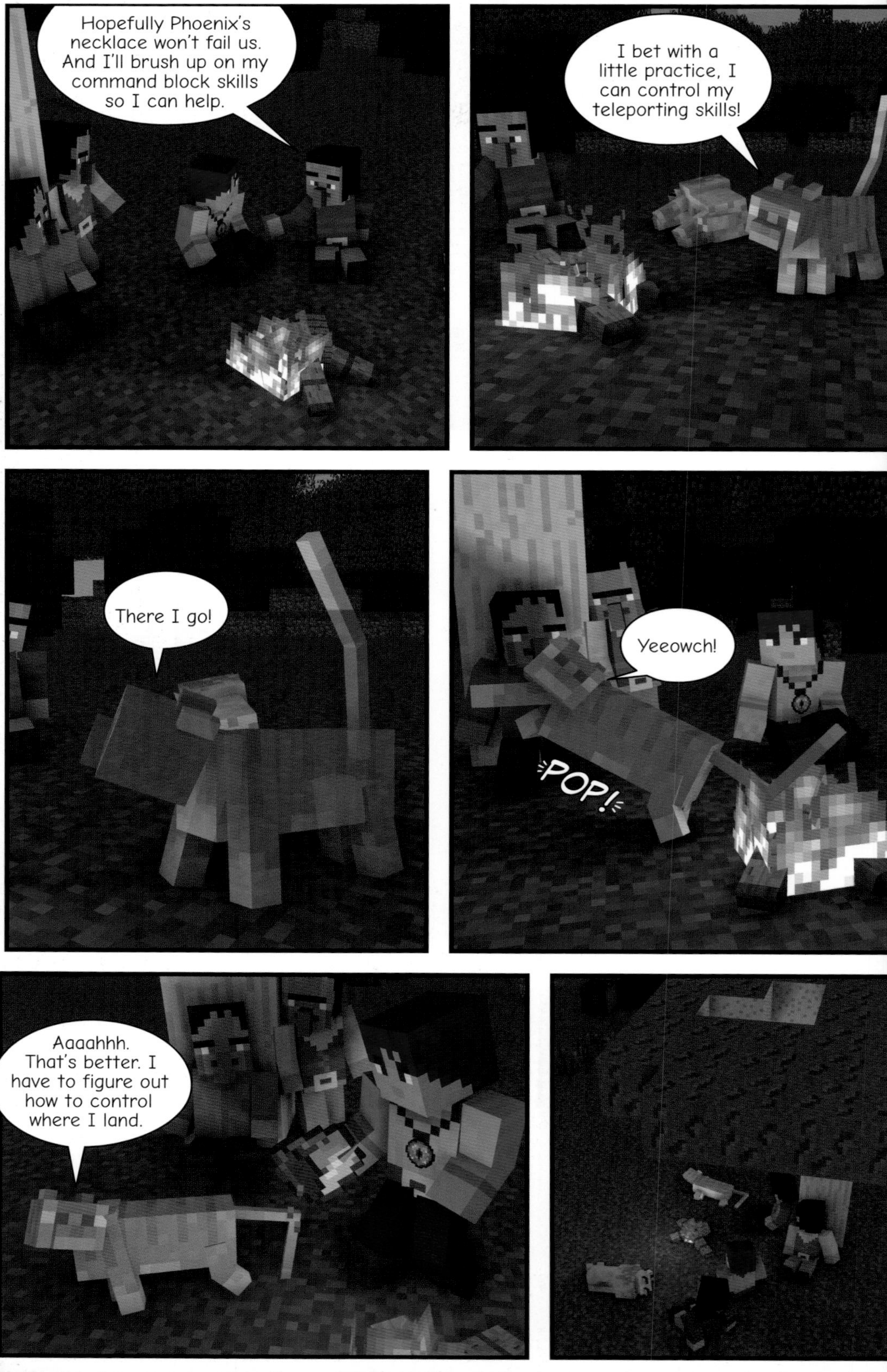
Hopefully Phoenix's necklace won't fail us. And I'll brush up on my command block skills so I can help.
I bet with a little practice, I can control my teleporting skills!
There I go!
Yeeowch!
POP!
Aaaahhh. That's better. I have to figure out how to control where I land.

CHAPTER 9

THE GLITCH

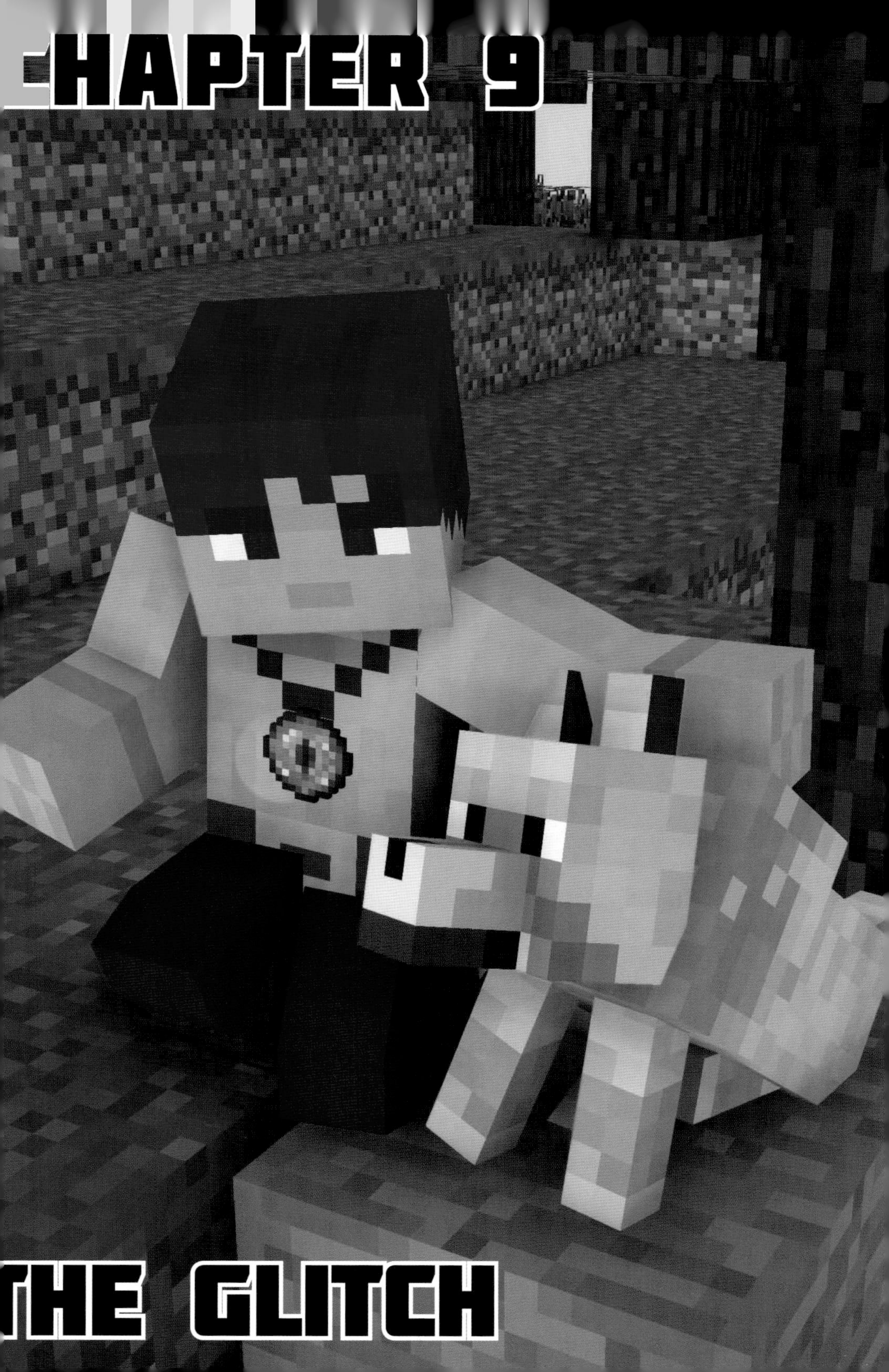

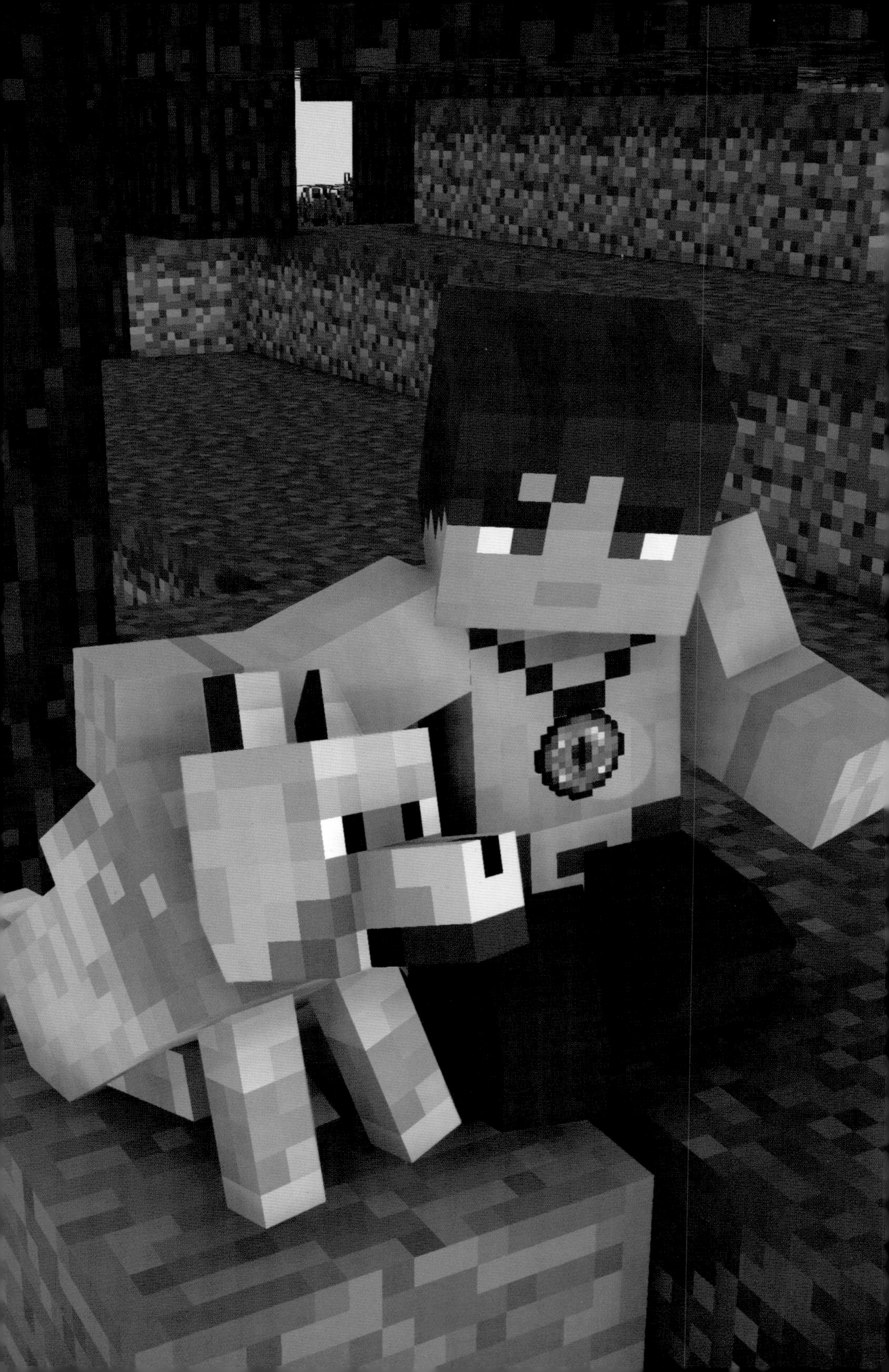

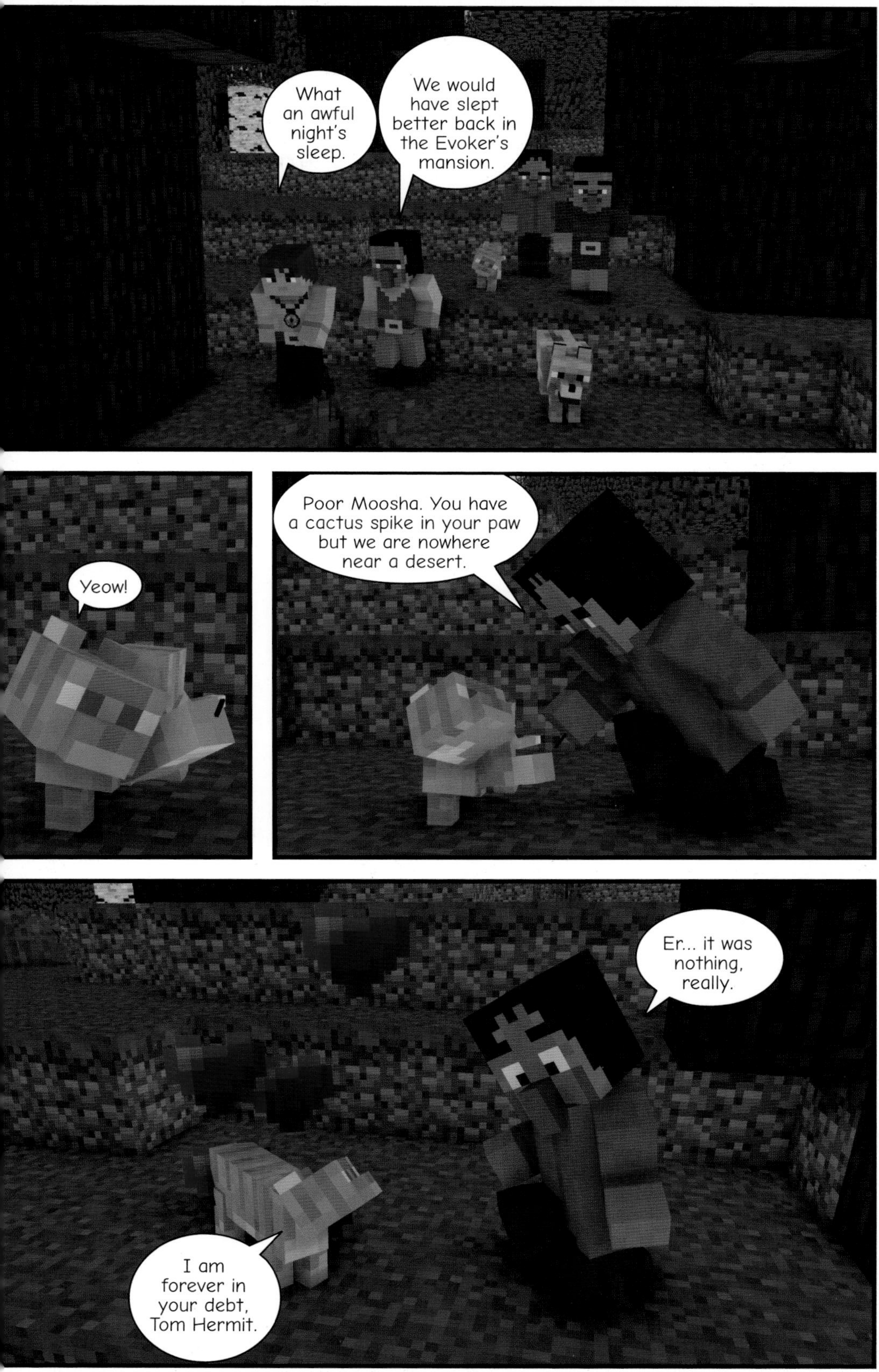
What an awful night's sleep.
We would have slept better back in the Evoker's mansion.
Yeow!
Poor Moosha. You have a cactus spike in your paw but we are nowhere near a desert.
Er... it was nothing, really.
I am forever in your debt, Tom Hermit.

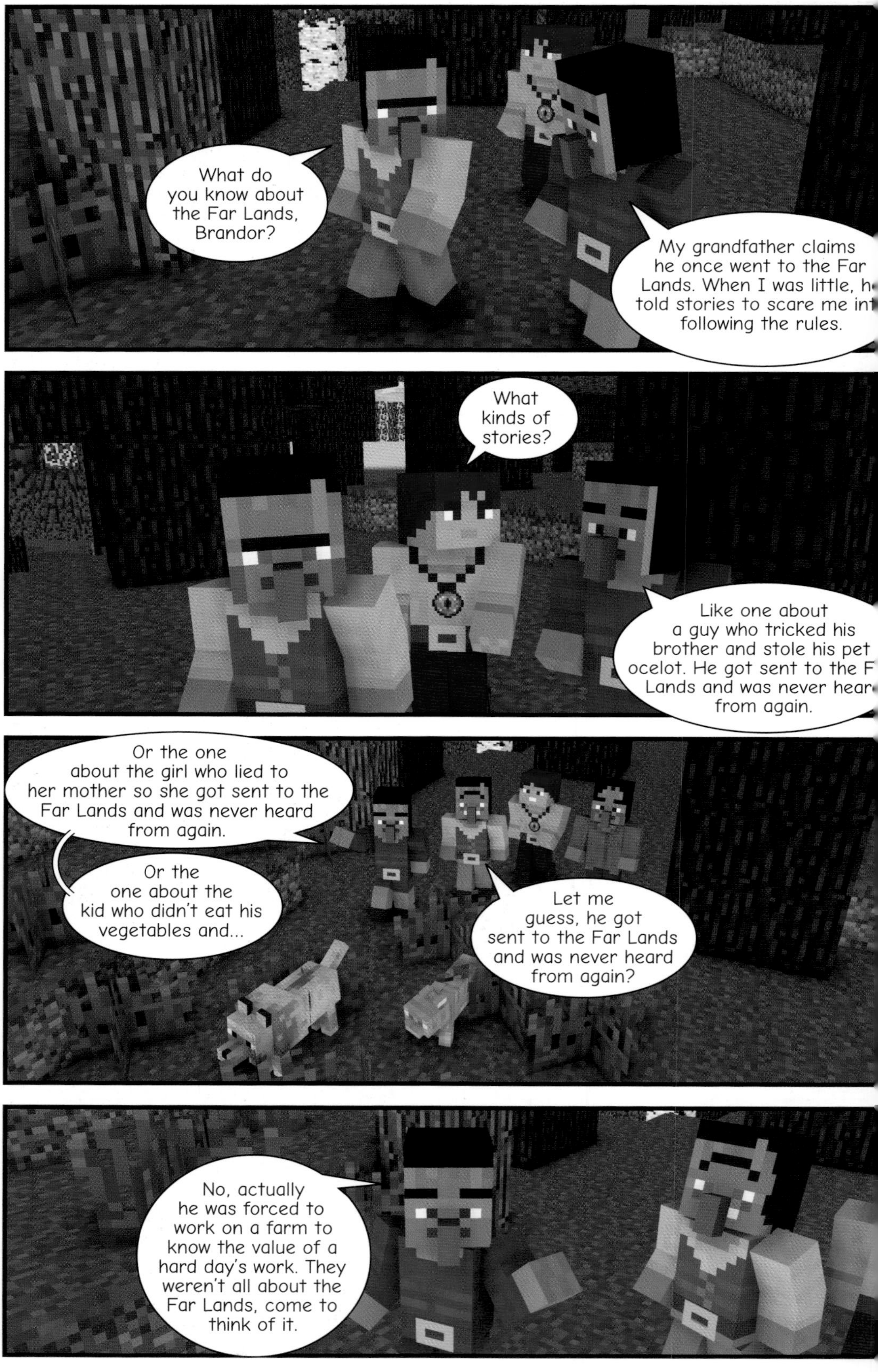
What do you know about the Far Lands, Brandor?
My grandfather claims he once went to the Far Lands. When I was little, h told stories to scare me int following the rules.
What kinds of stories?
Like one about a guy who tricked his brother and stole his pet ocelot. He got sent to the F Lands and was never hear from again.
Or the one about the girl who lied to her mother so she got sent to the Far Lands and was never heard from again.
Or the one about the kid who didn't eat his vegetables and...
Let me guess, he got sent to the Far Lands and was never heard from again?
No, actually he was forced to work on a farm to know the value of a hard day's work. They weren't all about the Far Lands, come to think of it.

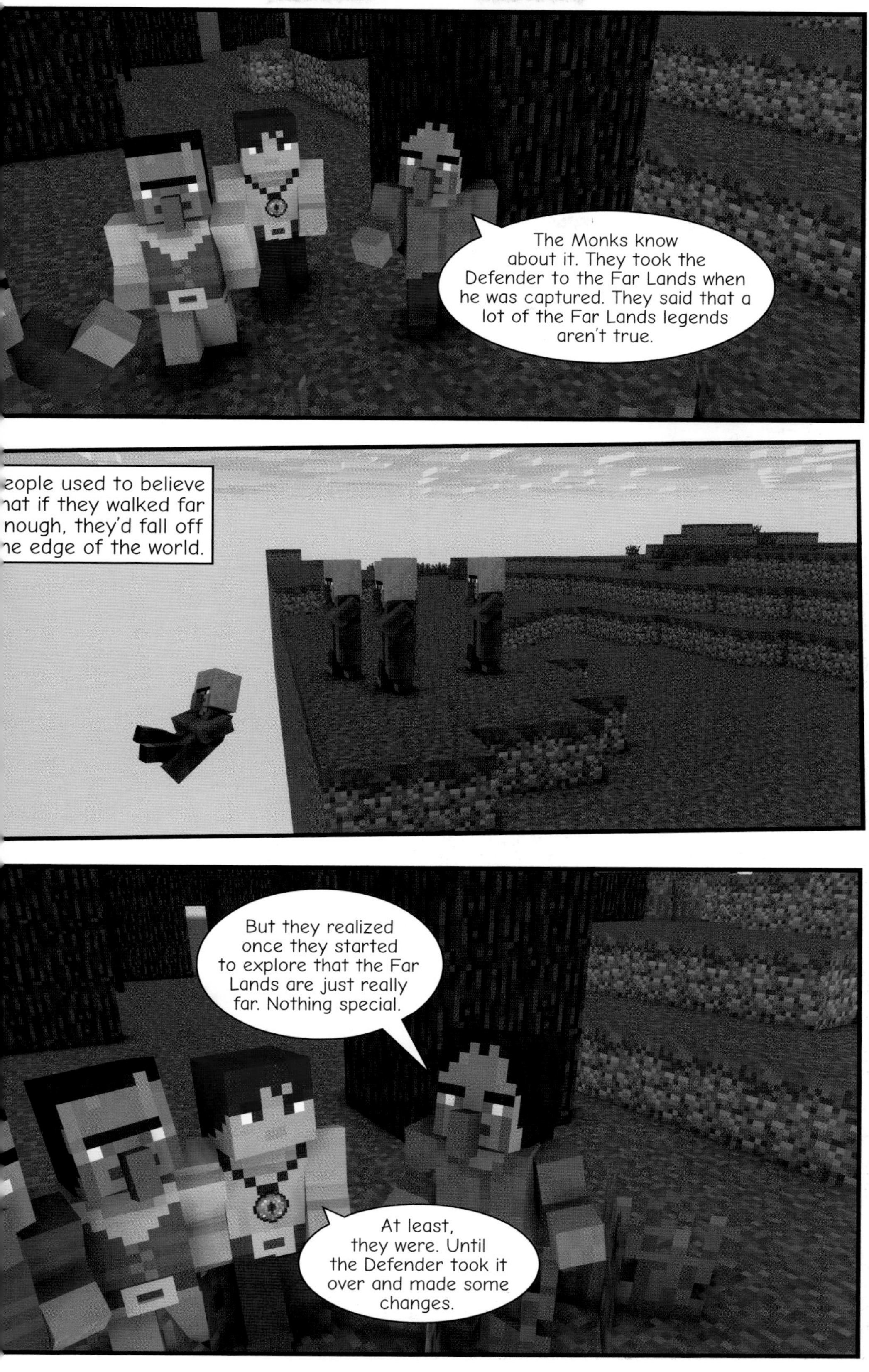
The Monks know about it. They took the Defender to the Far Lands when he was captured. They said that a lot of the Far Lands legends aren't true.
eople used to believe hat if they walked far nough, they'd fall off he edge of the world.
But they realized once they started to explore that the Far Lands are just really far. Nothing special.
At least, they were. Until the Defender took it over and made some changes.

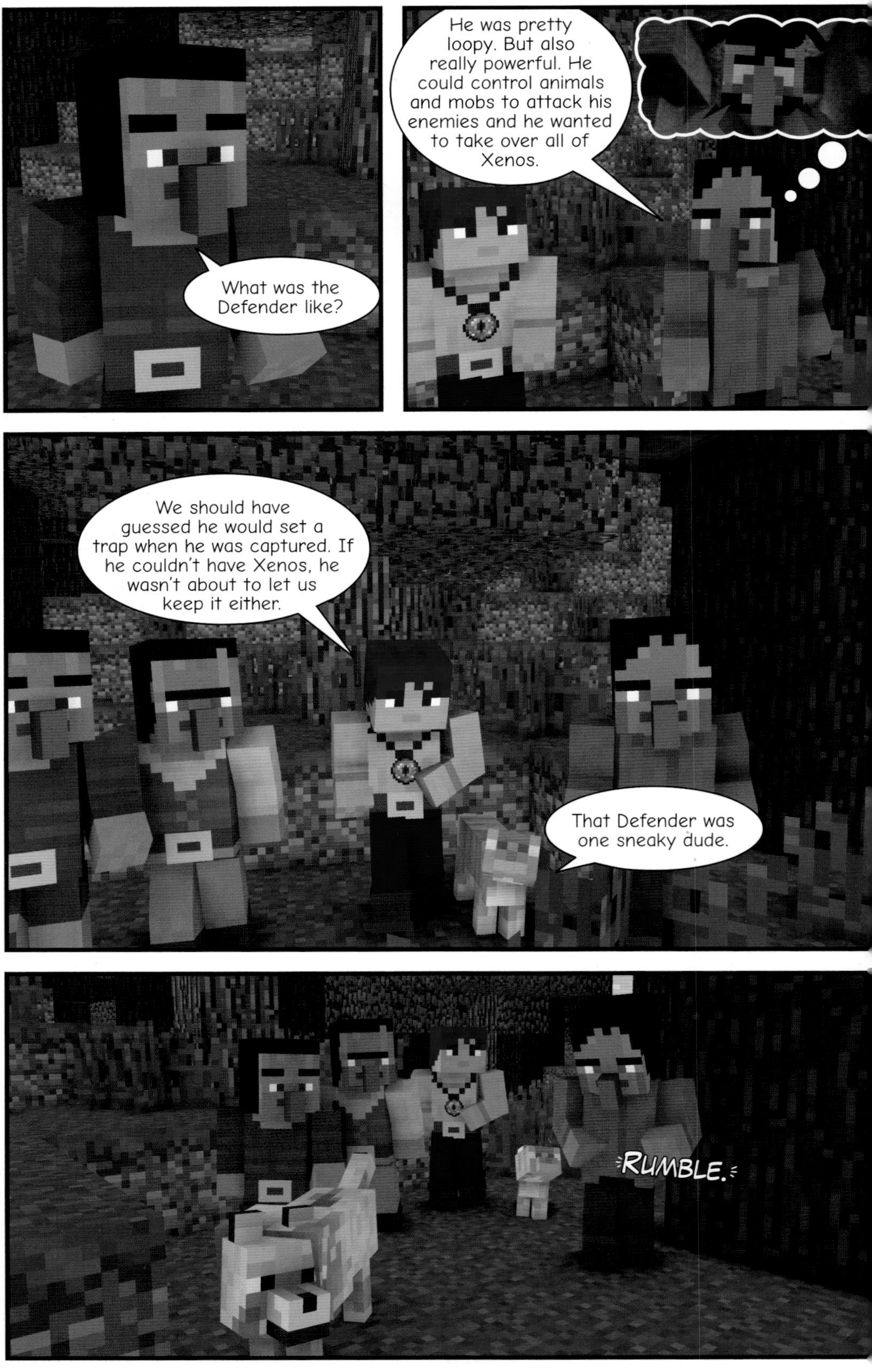
What was the Defender like?
He was pretty loopy. But also really powerful. He could control animals and mobs to attack his enemies and he wanted to take over all of Xenos.
We should have guessed he would set a trap when he was captured. If he couldn't have Xenos, he wasn't about to let us keep it either.
That Defender was one sneaky dude.
RUMBLE.

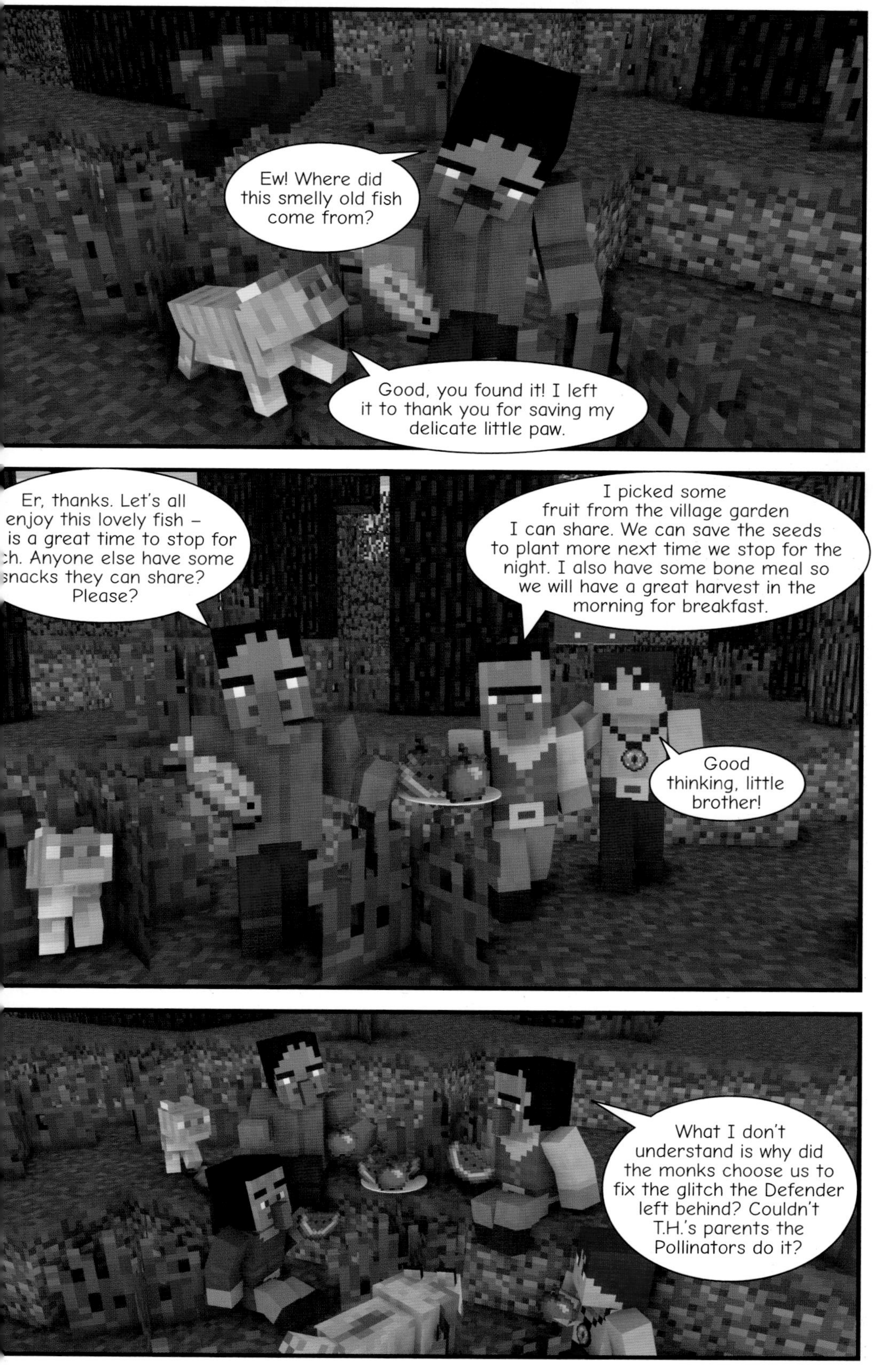
Ew! Where did this smelly old fish come from?
Good, you found it! I left it to thank you for saving my delicate little paw.
Er, thanks. Let's all enjoy this lovely fish – is a great time to stop for ch. Anyone else have some snacks they can share? Please?
I picked some fruit from the village garden I can share. We can save the seeds to plant more next time we stop for the night. I also have some bone meal so we will have a great harvest in the morning for breakfast.
Good thinking, little brother!
What I don't understand is why did the monks choose us to fix the glitch the Defender left behind? Couldn't T.H.'s parents the Pollinators do it?

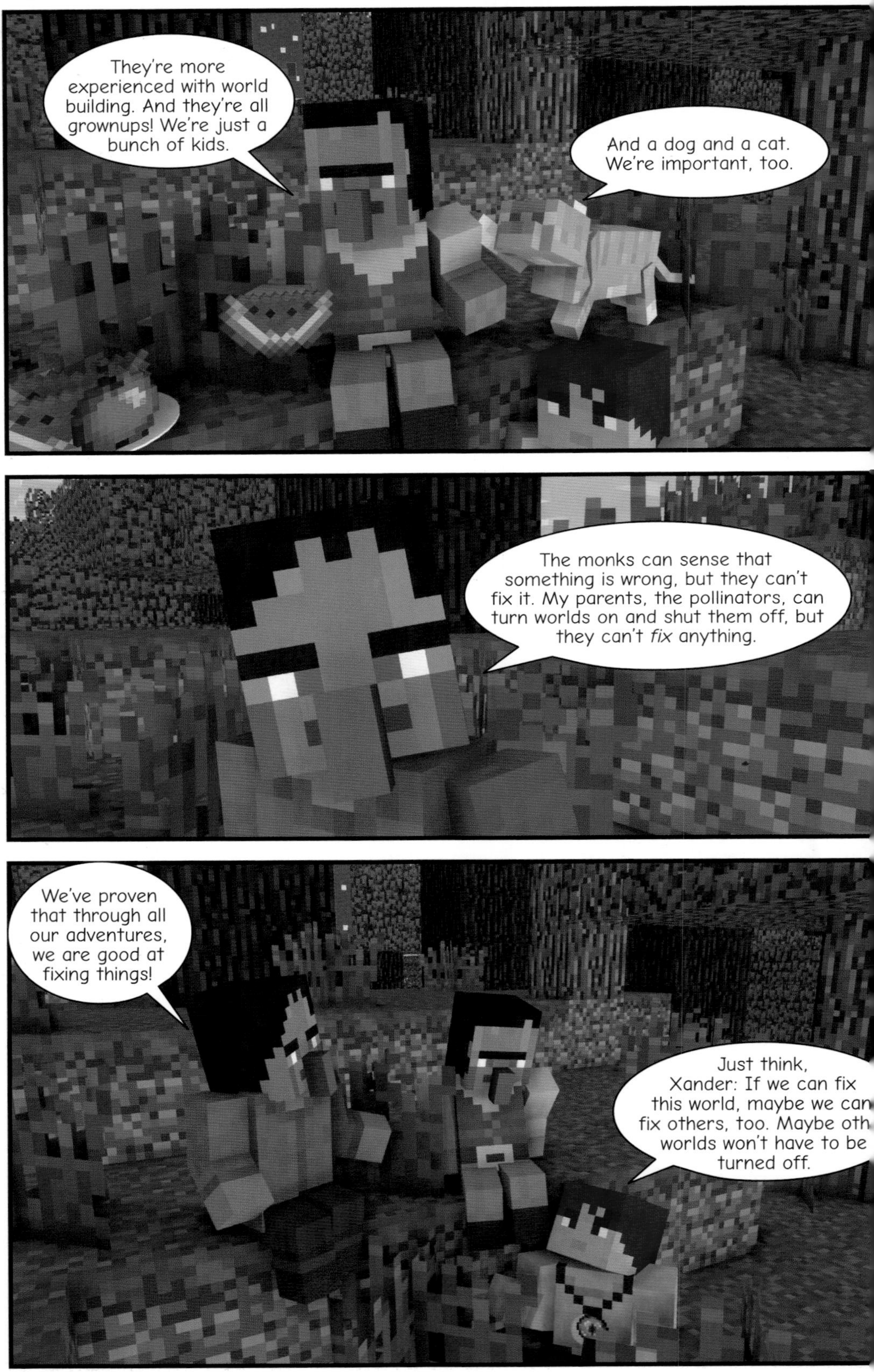

They're more experienced with world building. And they're all grownups! We're just a bunch of kids.
And a dog and a cat. We're important, too.
The monks can sense that something is wrong, but they can't fix it. My parents, the pollinators, can turn worlds on and shut them off, but they can't *fix* anything.
We've proven that through all our adventures, we are good at fixing things!
Just think, Xander: If we can fix this world, maybe we can fix others, too. Maybe oth worlds won't have to be turned off.

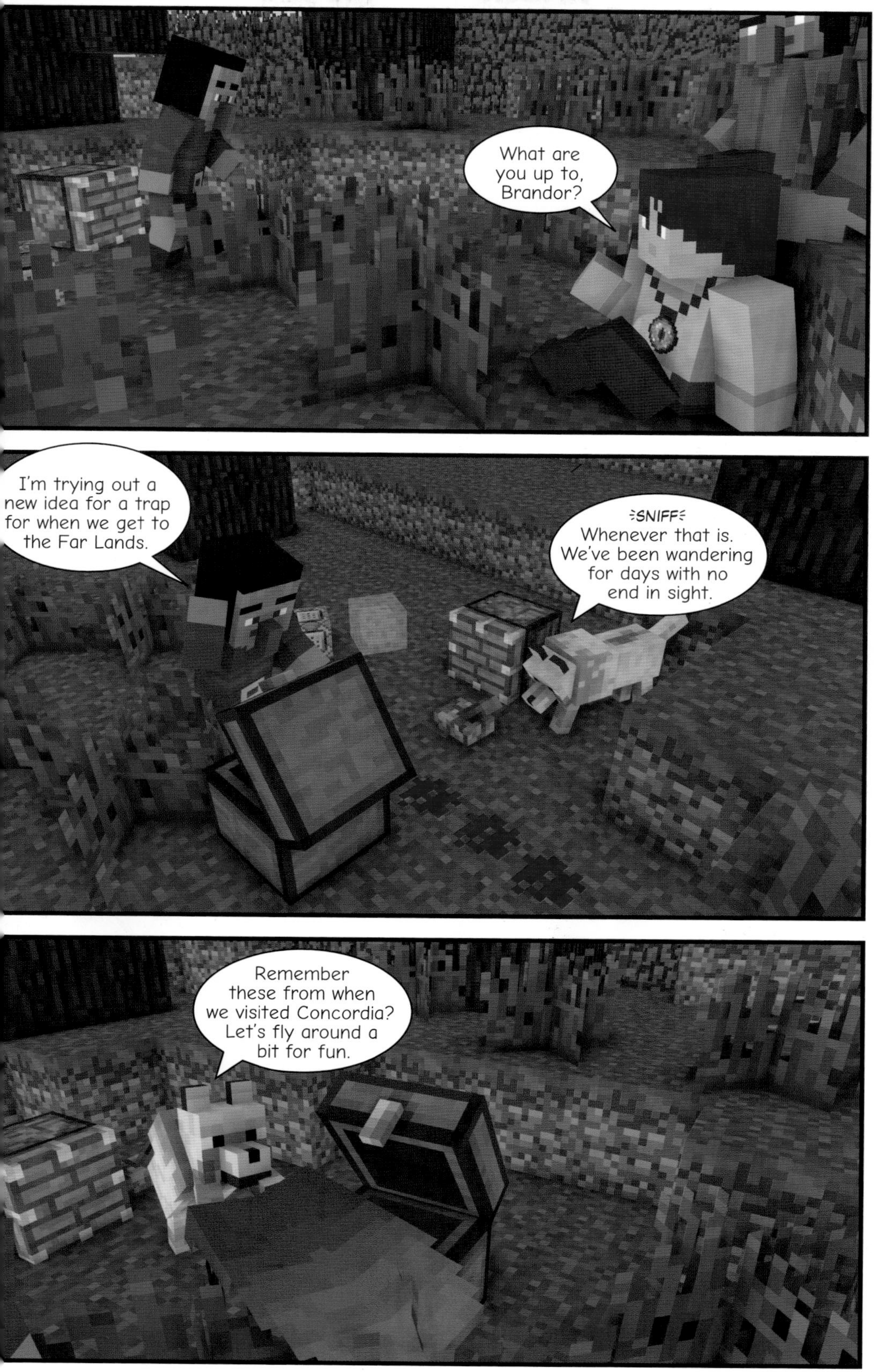
What are you up to, Brandor?
I'm trying out a new idea for a trap for when we get to the Far Lands.
SNIFF
Whenever that is. We've been wandering for days with no end in sight.
Remember these from when we visited Concordia? Let's fly around a bit for fun.

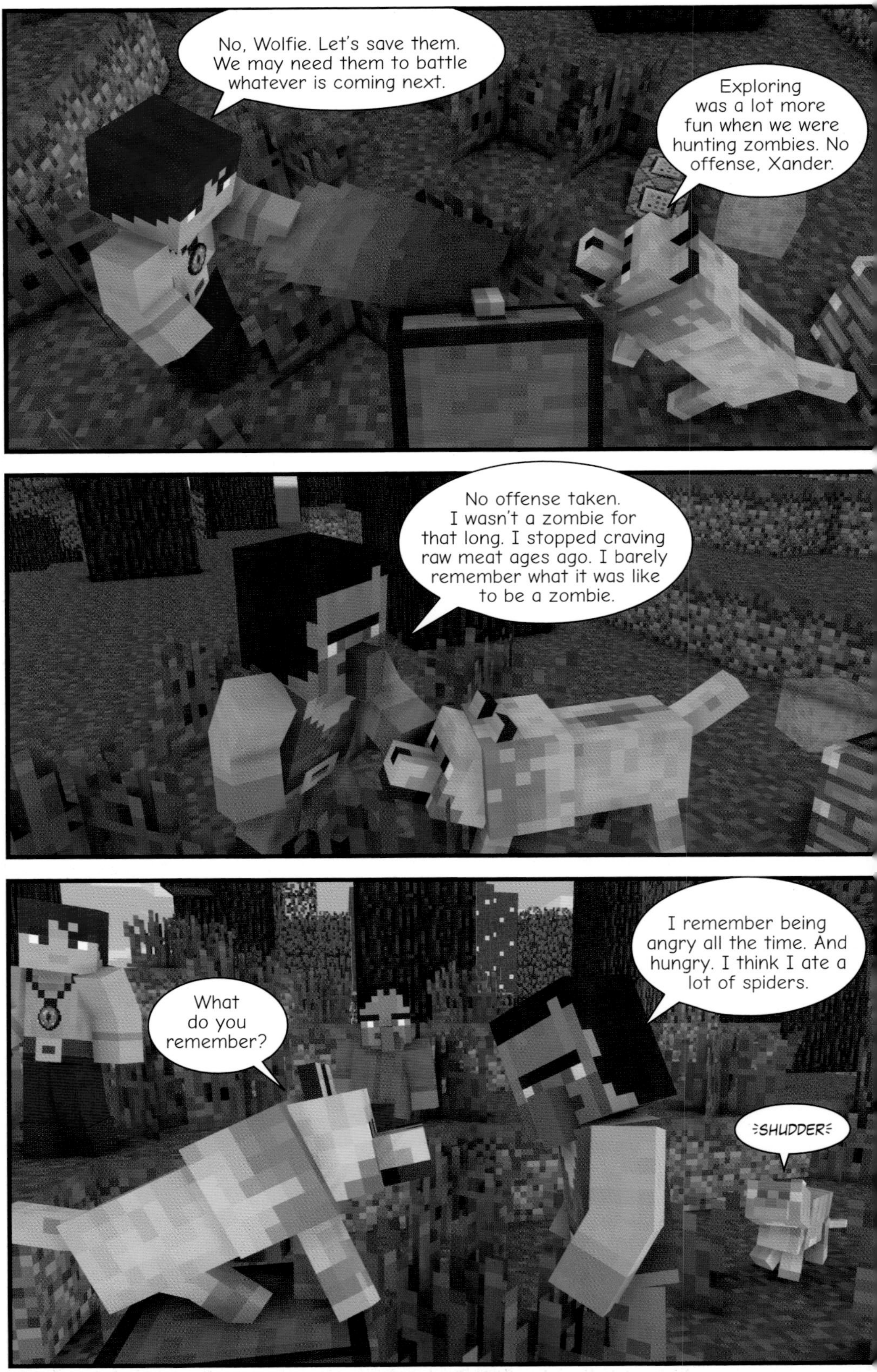
No, Wolfie. Let's save them. We may need them to battle whatever is coming next.
Exploring was a lot more fun when we were hunting zombies. No offense, Xander.
No offense taken. I wasn't a zombie for that long. I stopped craving raw meat ages ago. I barely remember what it was like to be a zombie.
What do you remember?
I remember being angry all the time. And hungry. I think I ate a lot of spiders.
SHUDDER

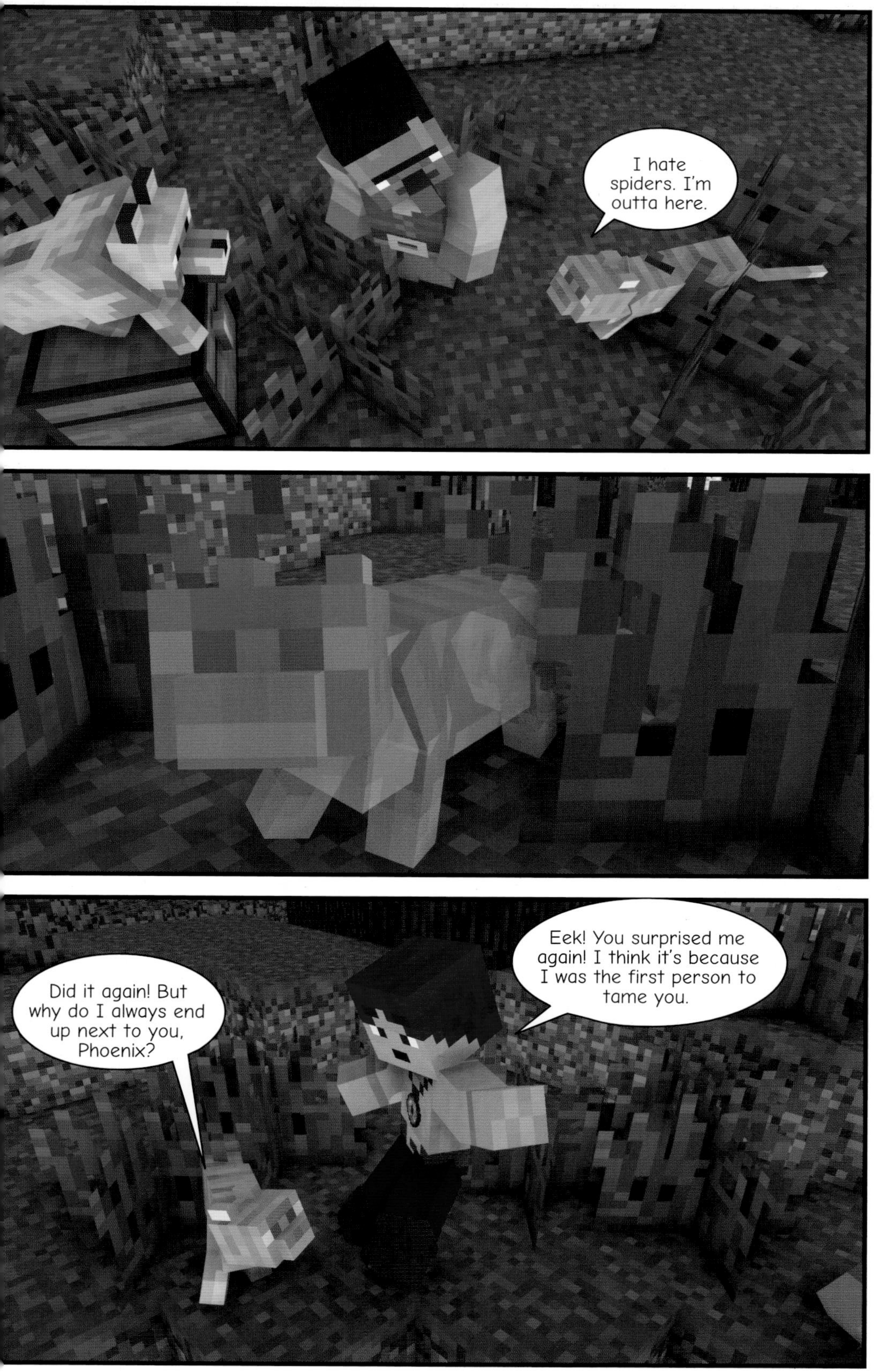
I hate spiders. I'm outta here.
Did it again! But why do I always end up next to you, Phoenix?
Eek! You surprised me again! I think it's because I was the first person to tame you.

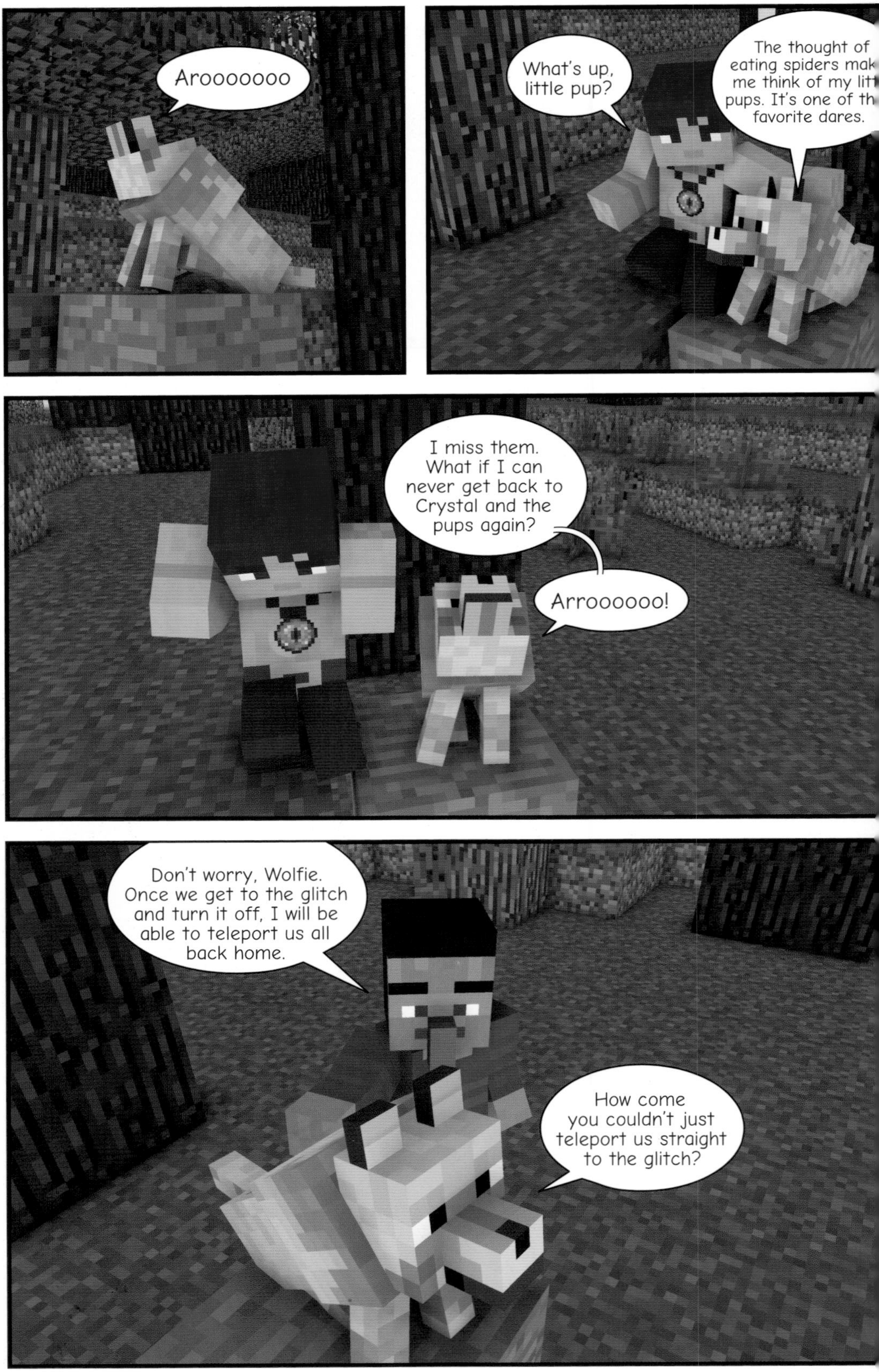
Arooooooo
What's up, little pup?
The thought of eating spiders mak me think of my litt pups. It's one of th favorite dares.
I miss them. What if I can never get back to Crystal and the pups again?
Arroooooo!
Don't worry, Wolfie. Once we get to the glitch and turn it off, I will be able to teleport us all back home.
How come you couldn't just teleport us straight to the glitch?

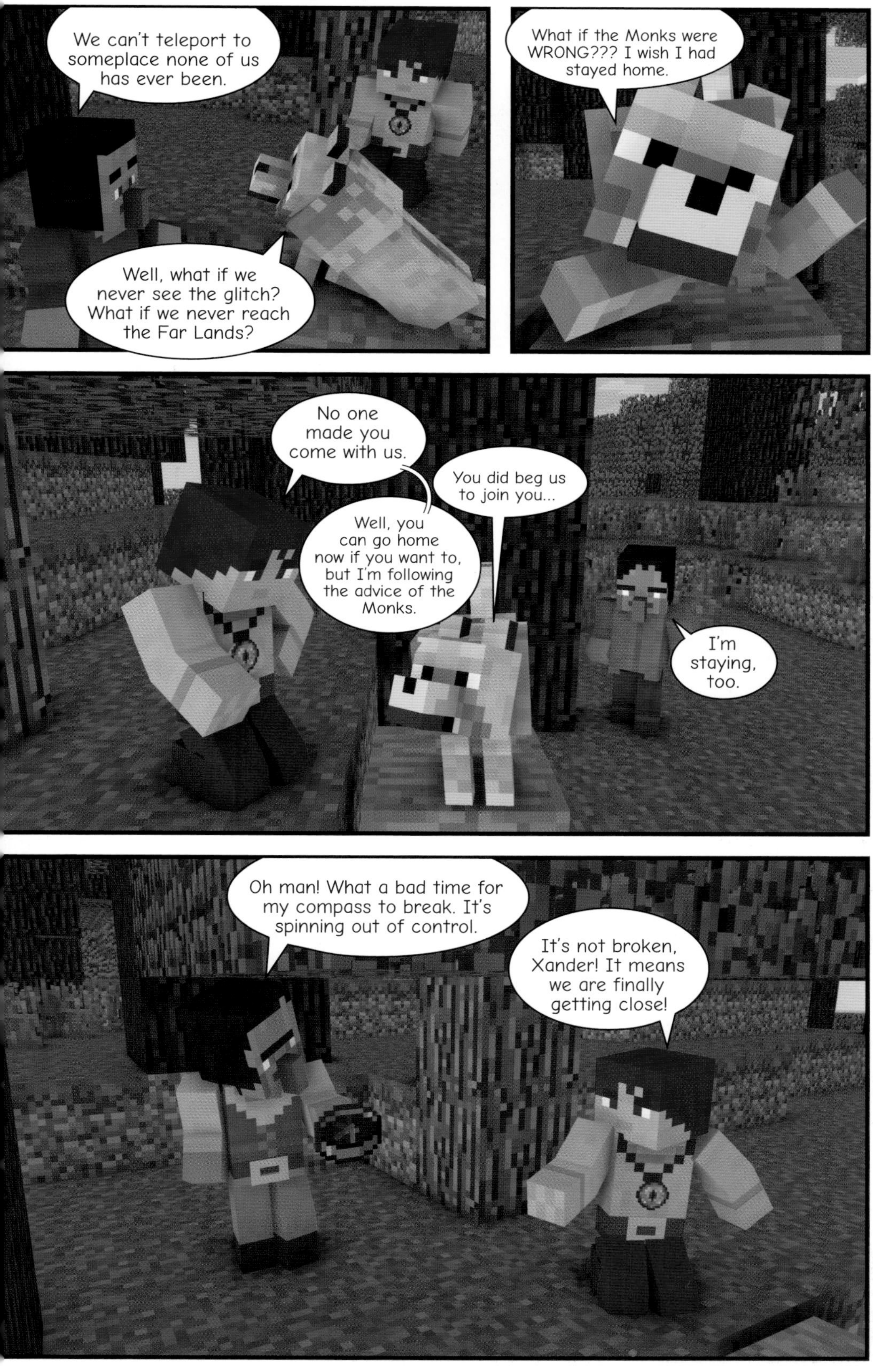
We can't teleport to someplace none of us has ever been.
Well, what if we never see the glitch? What if we never reach the Far Lands?
What if the Monks were WRONG??? I wish I had stayed home.
No one made you come with us.
Well, you can go home now if you want to, but I'm following the advice of the Monks.
You did beg us to join you...
I'm staying, too.
Oh man! What a bad time for my compass to break. It's spinning out of control.
It's not broken, Xander! It means we are finally getting close!

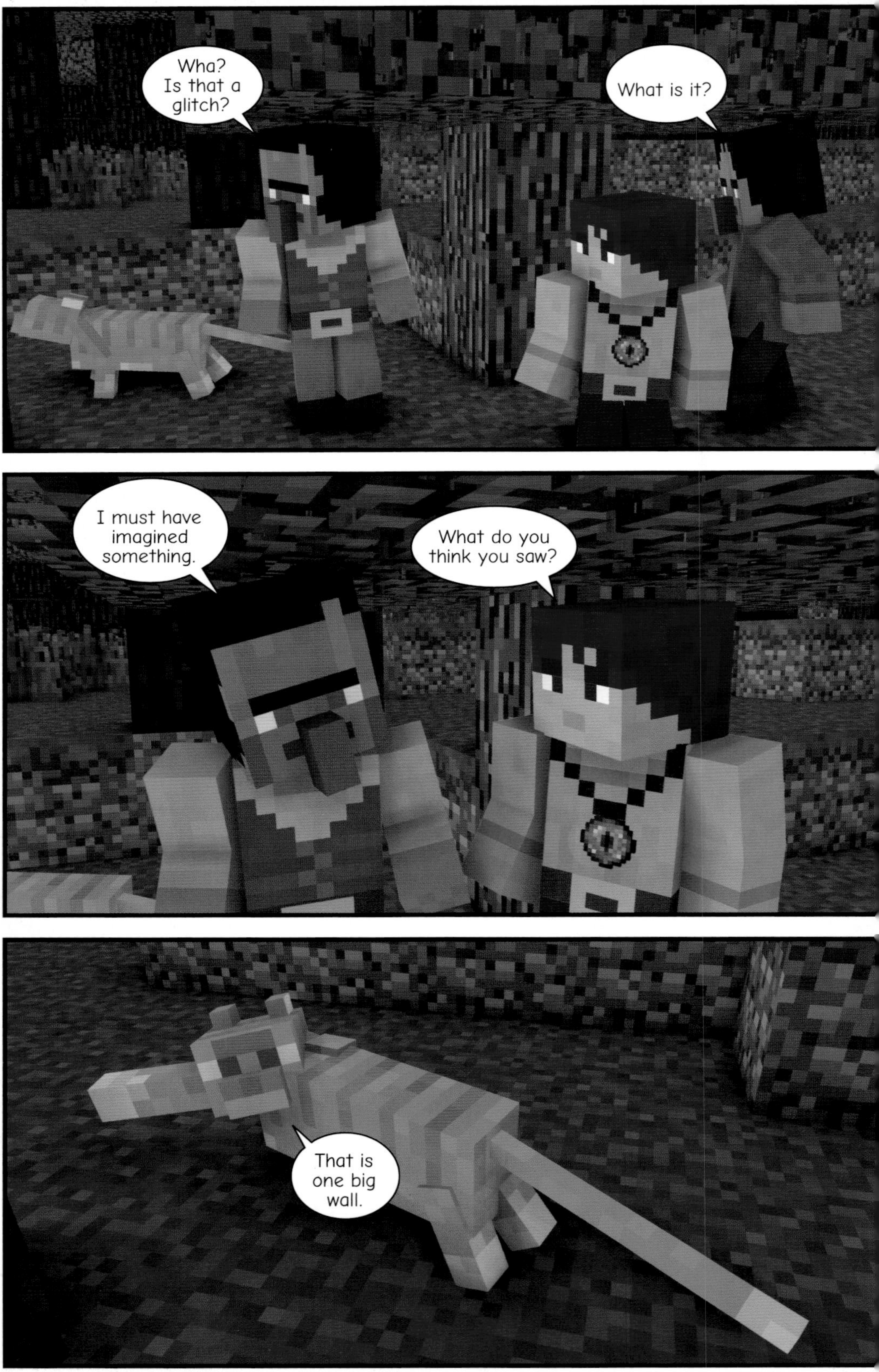
Wha?
Is that a
glitch?
What is it?
I must have
imagined
something.
What do you
think you saw?
That is
one big
wall.

CHAPTER 10

ATTACK OF THE KILLER COOKIES

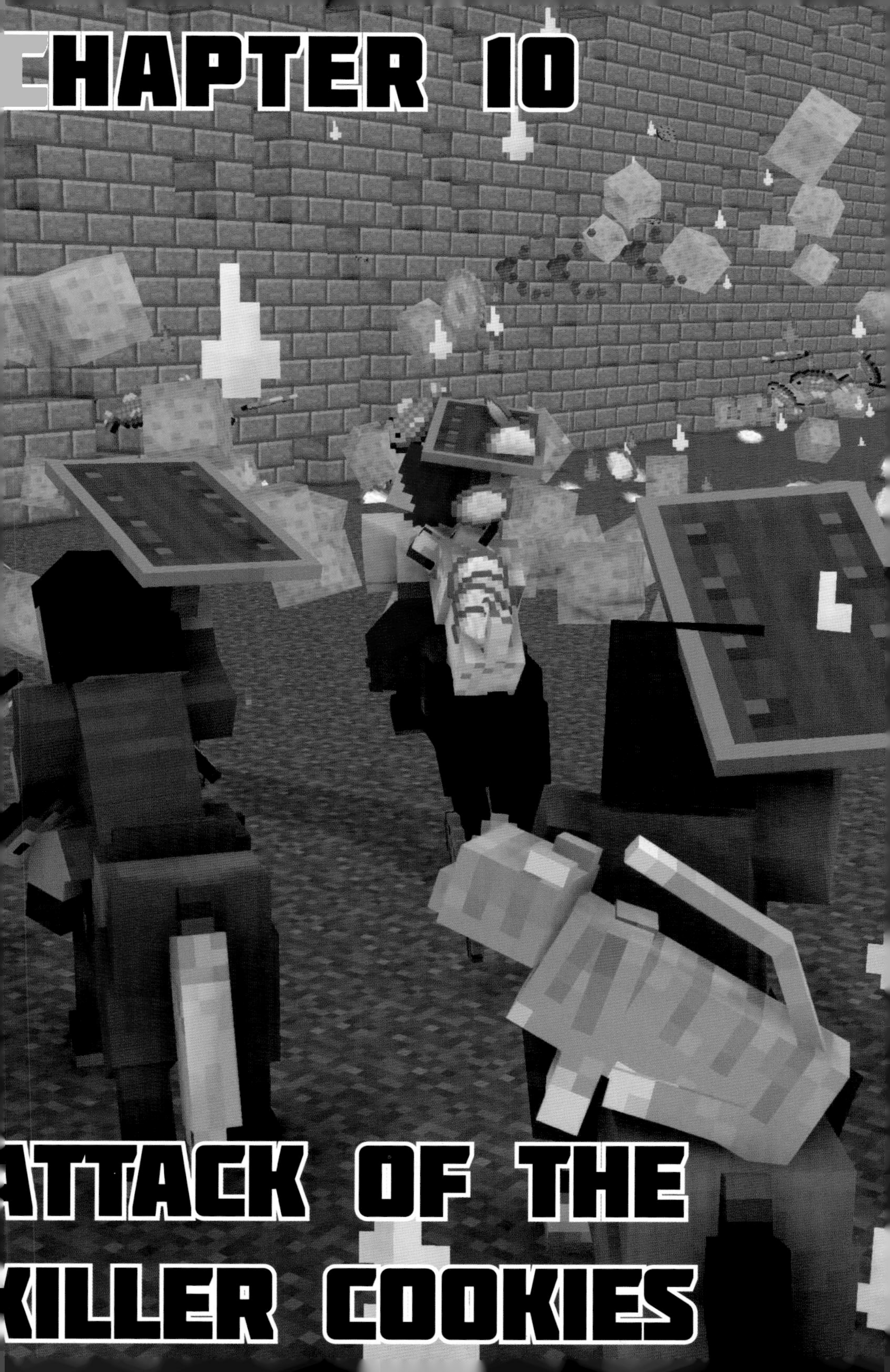

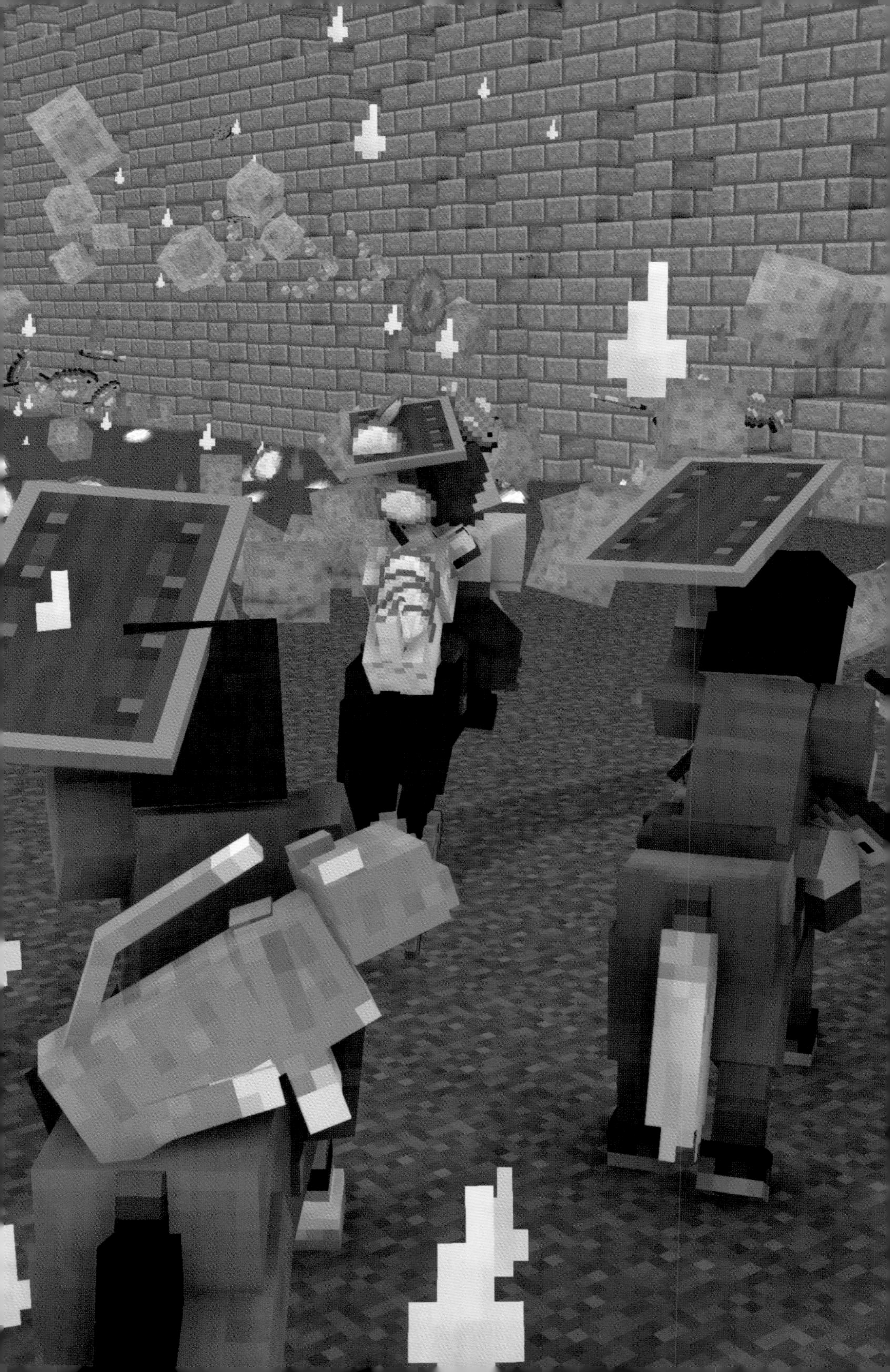

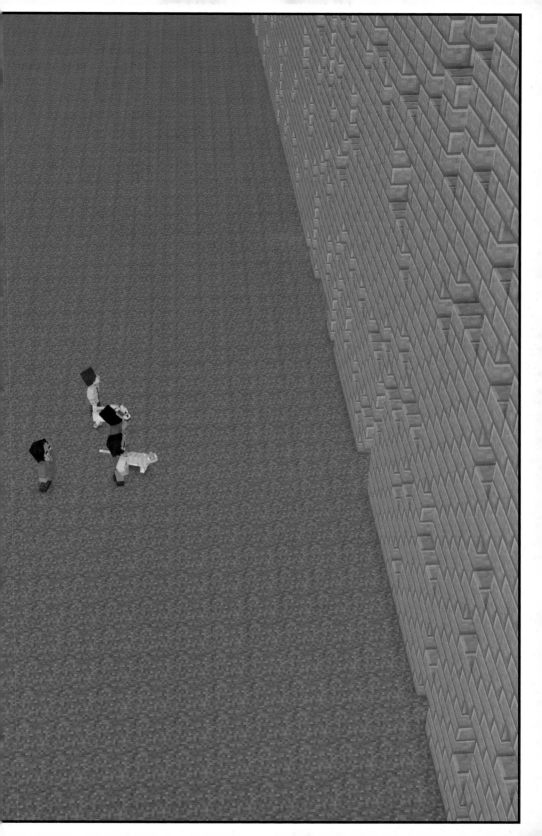

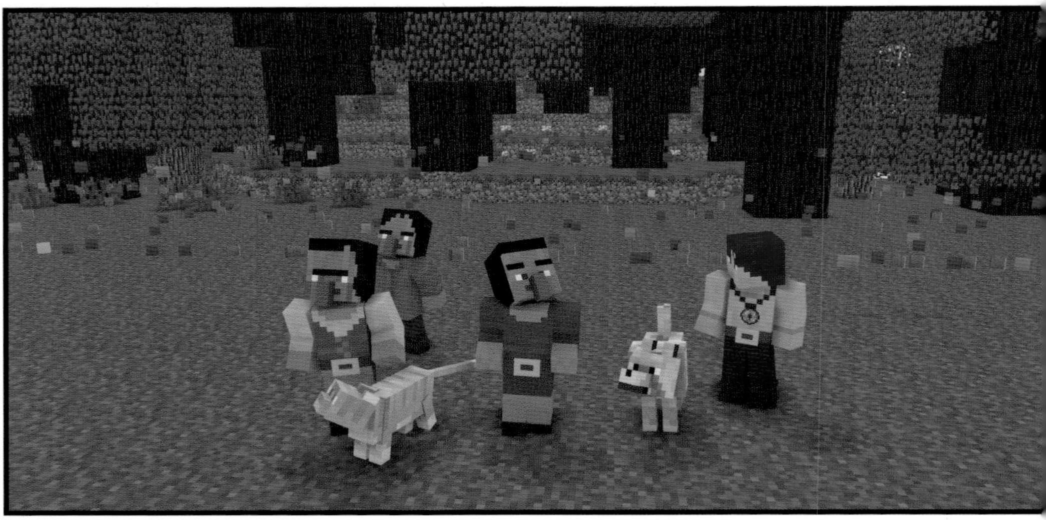

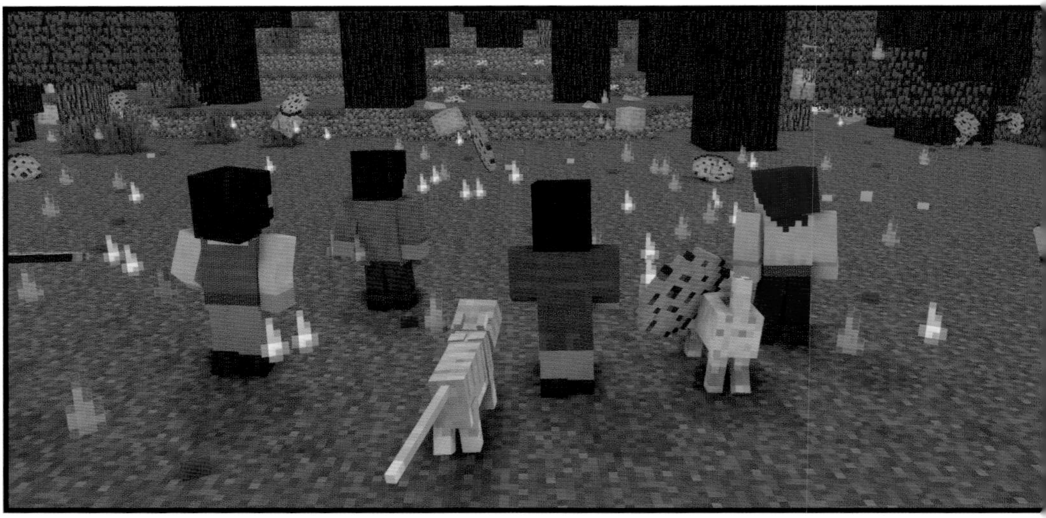

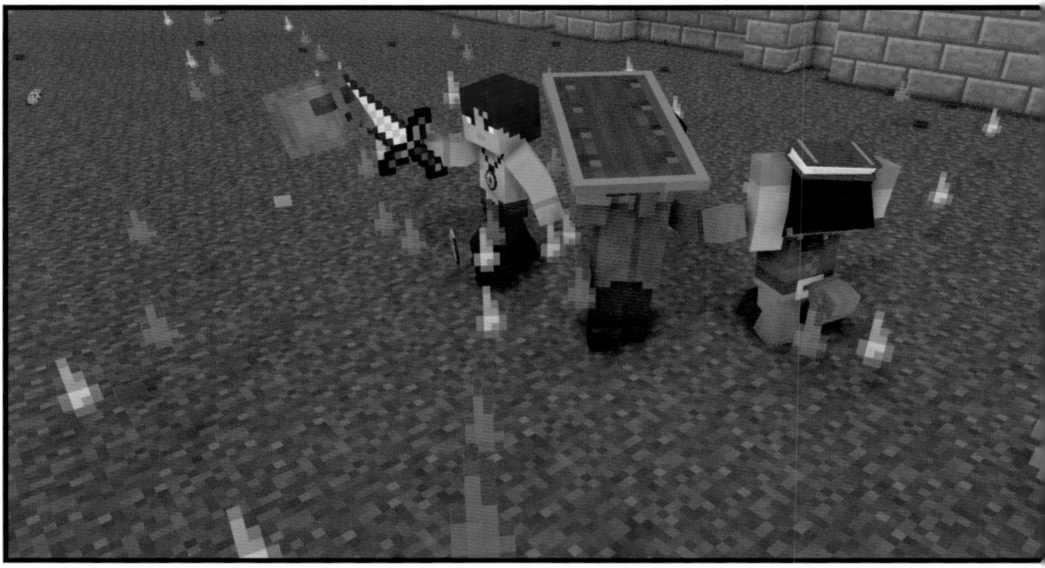

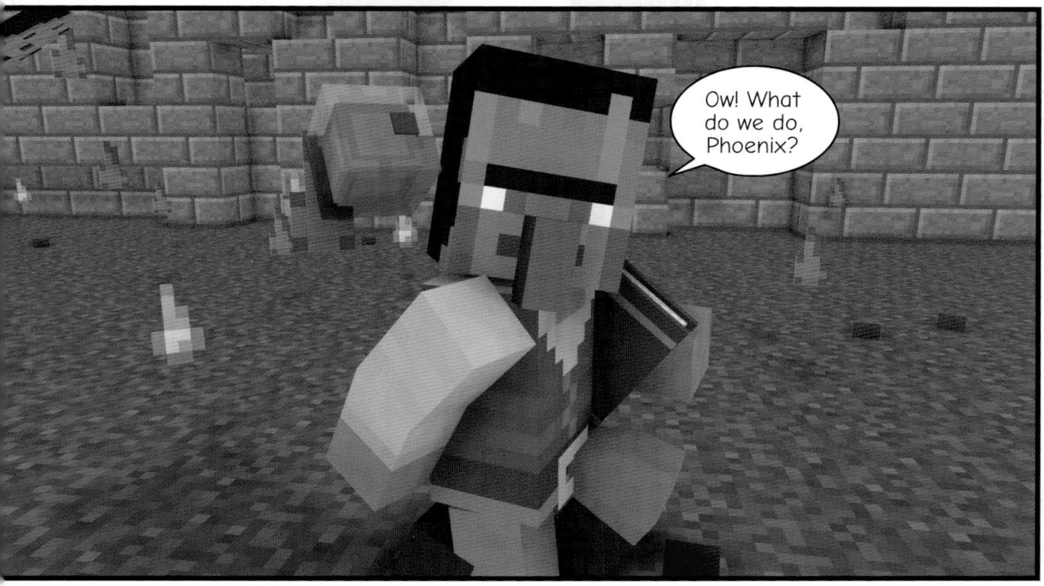
Ow! What do we do, Phoenix?

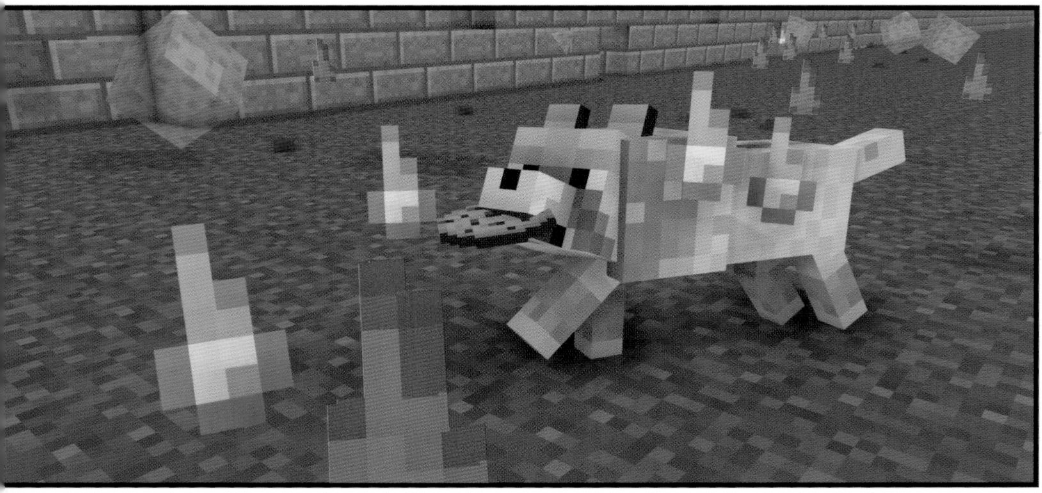

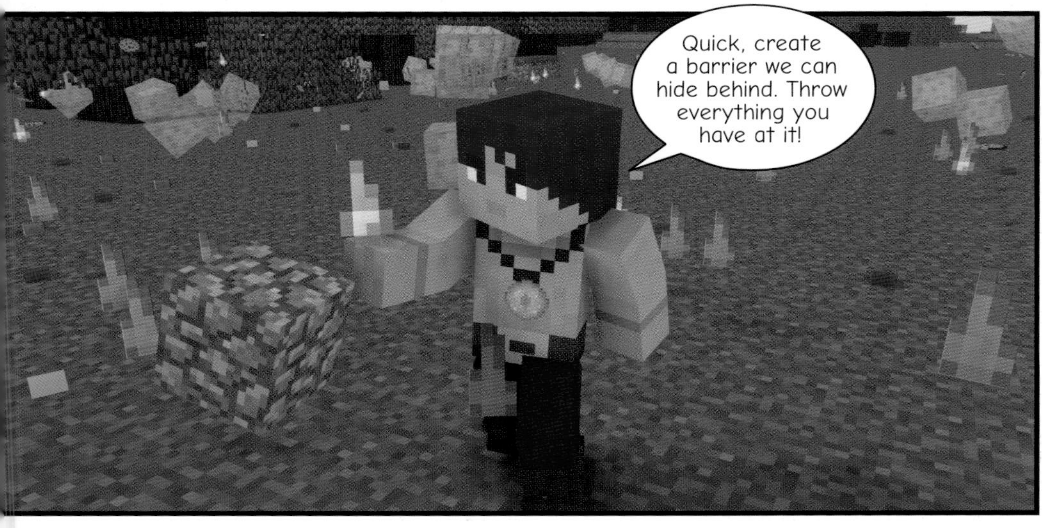
Quick, create a barrier we can hide behind. Throw everything you have at it!

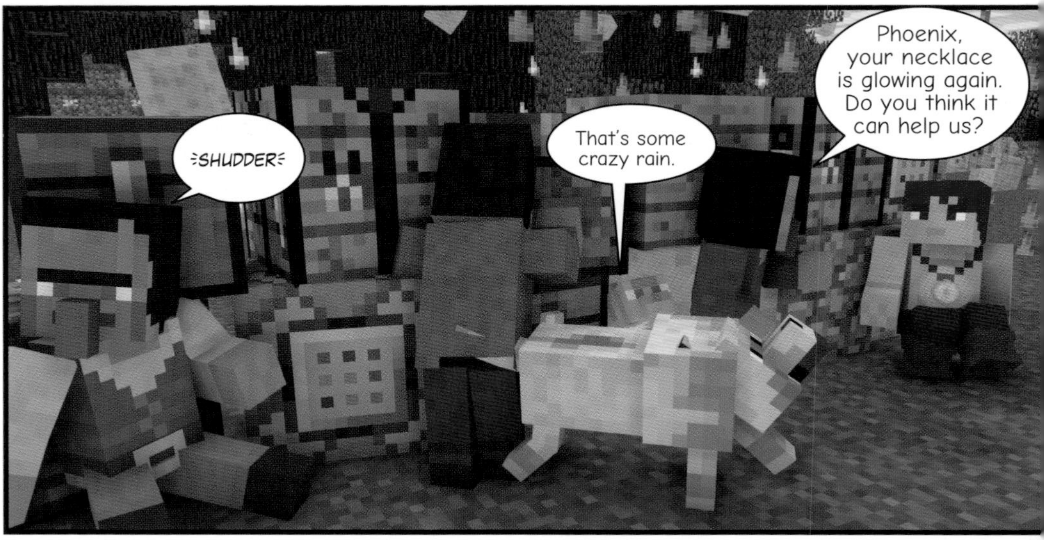

SHUDDER
That's some crazy rain.
Phoenix, your necklace is glowing again. Do you think it can help us?

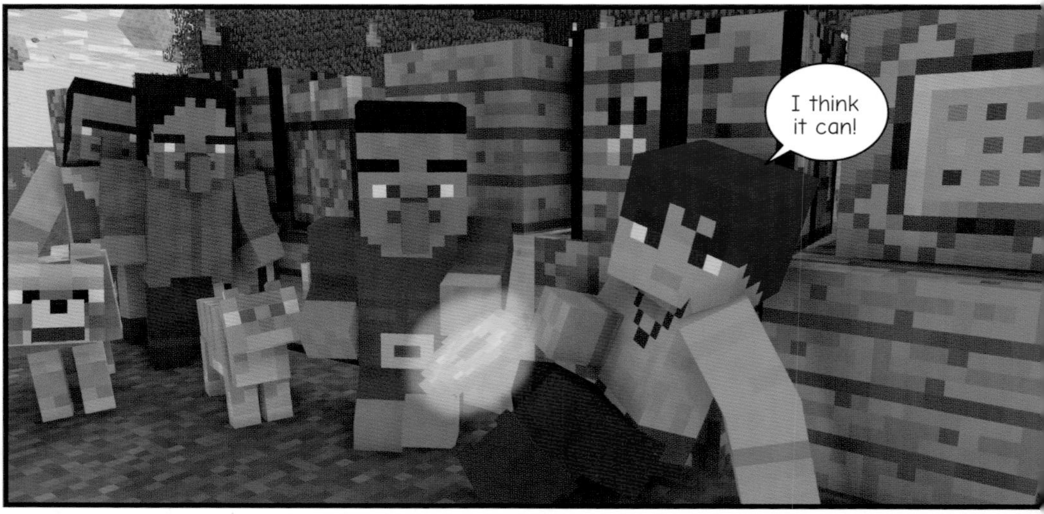

I think it can!

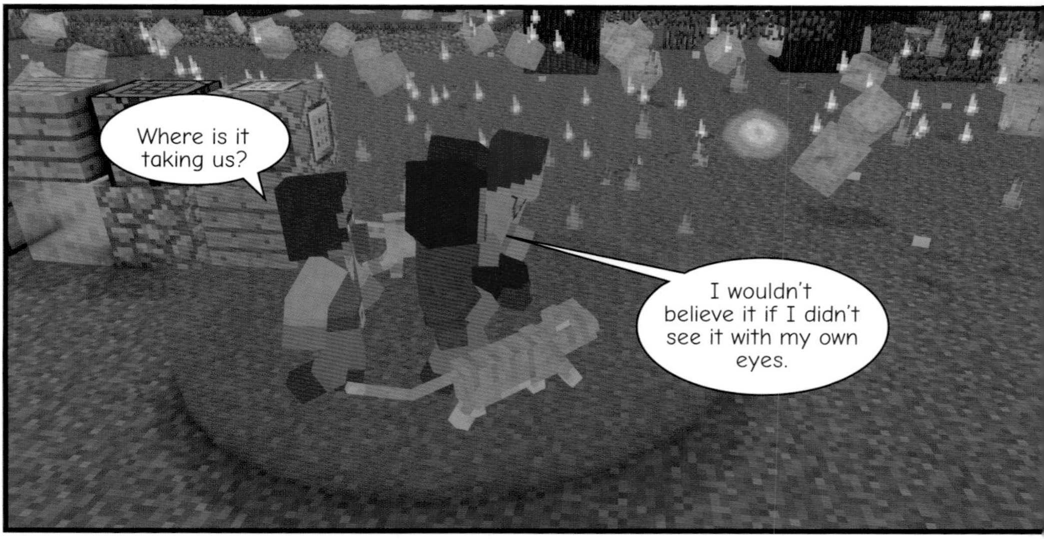

Where is it taking us?
I wouldn't believe it if I didn't see it with my own eyes.

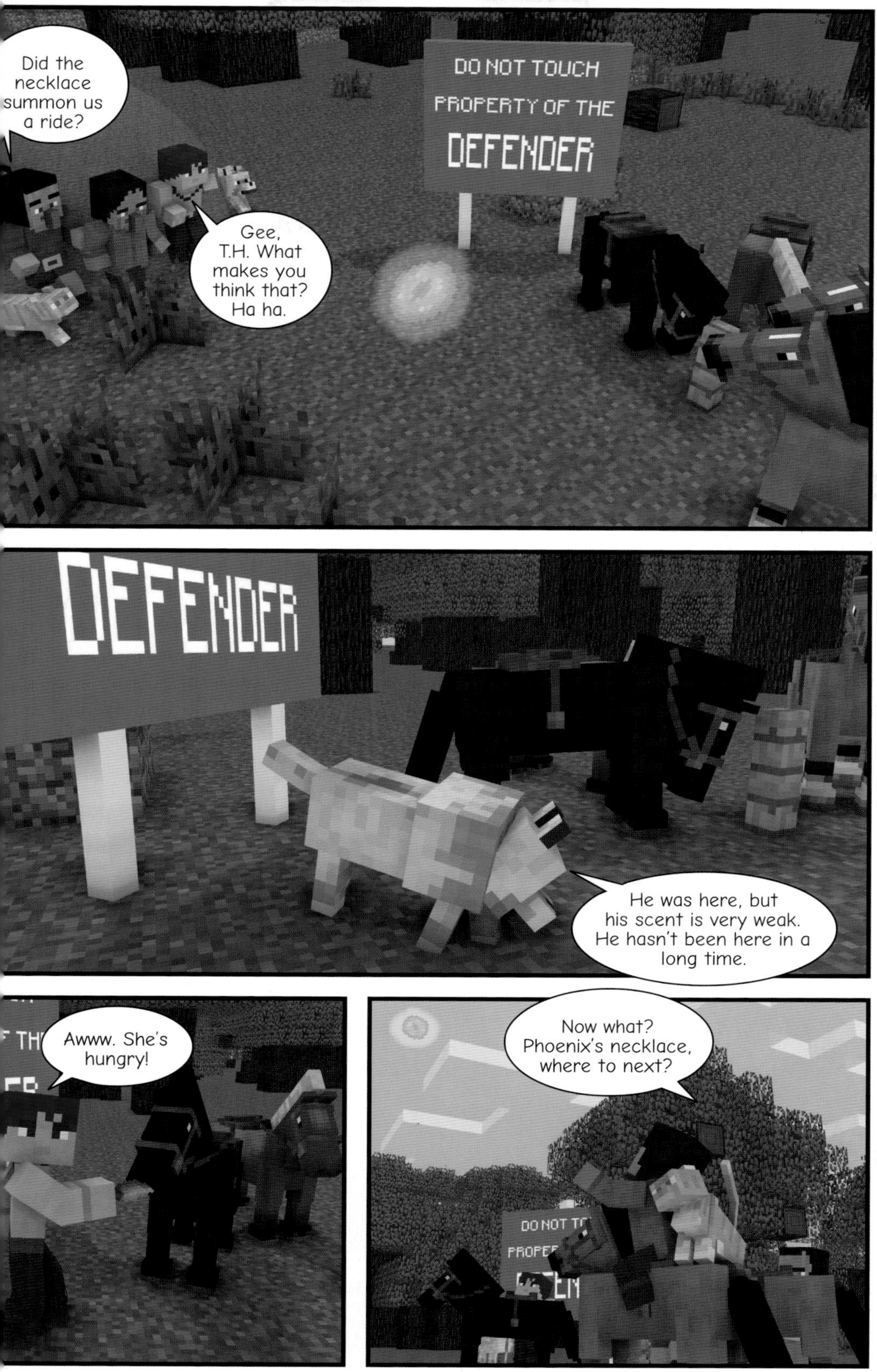
Did the necklace summon us a ride?
DO NOT TOUCH
PROPERTY OF THE
DEFENDER
Gee, T.H. What makes you think that? Ha ha.
DEFENDER
He was here, but his scent is very weak. He hasn't been here in a long time.
Awww. She's hungry!
Now what? Phoenix's necklace, where to next?

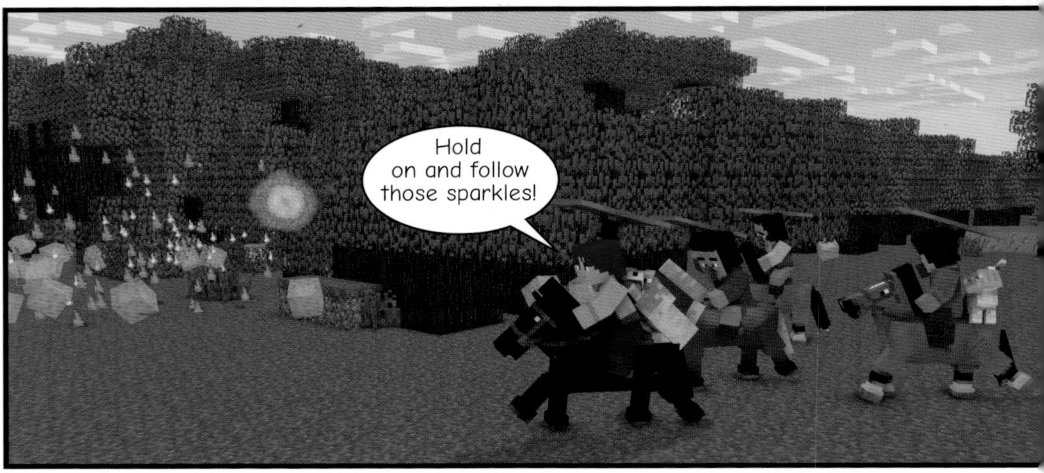
Hold on and follow those sparkles!

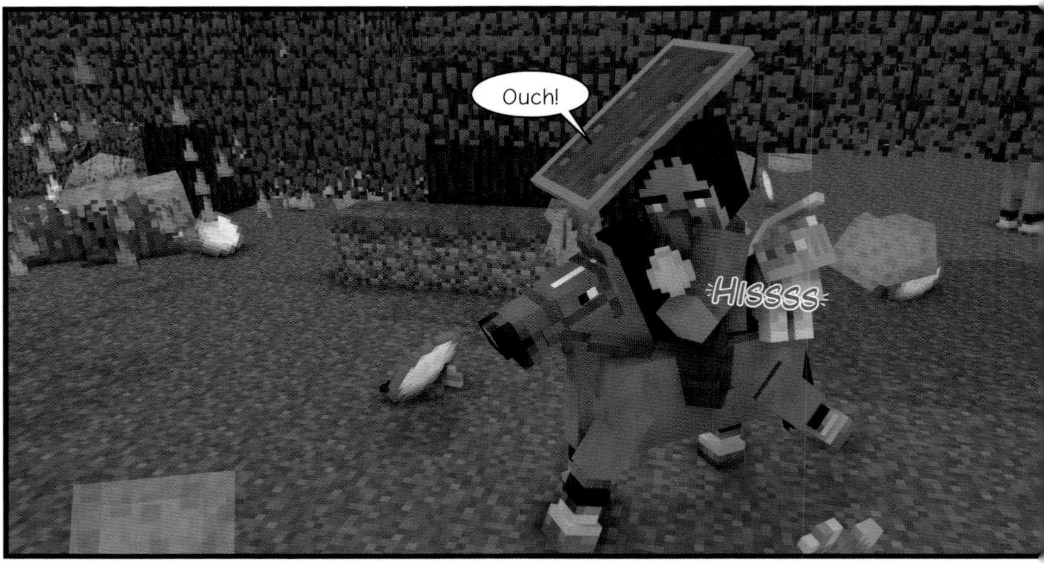
Ouch!
HISSSS

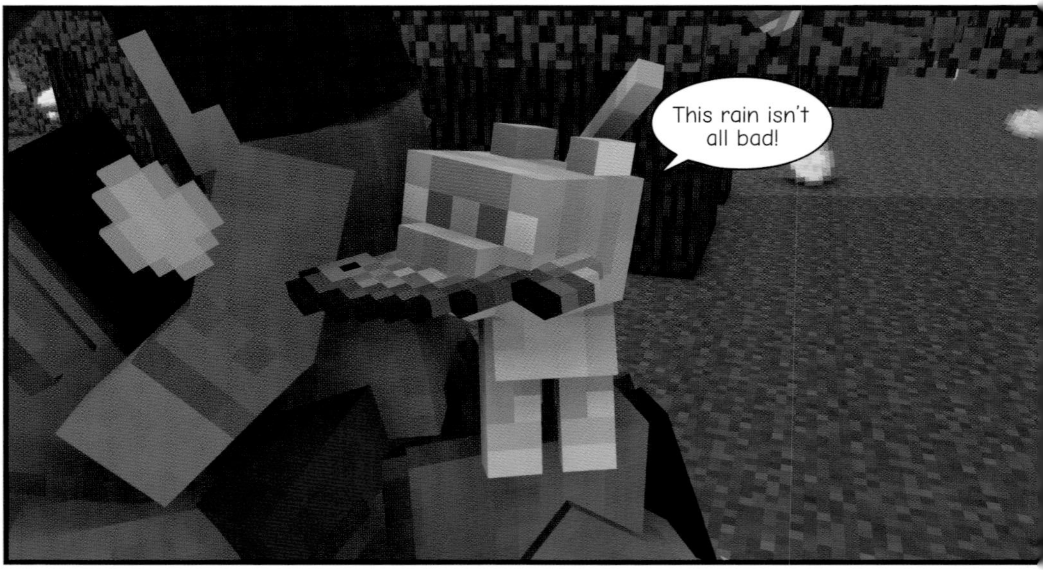
This rain isn't all bad!

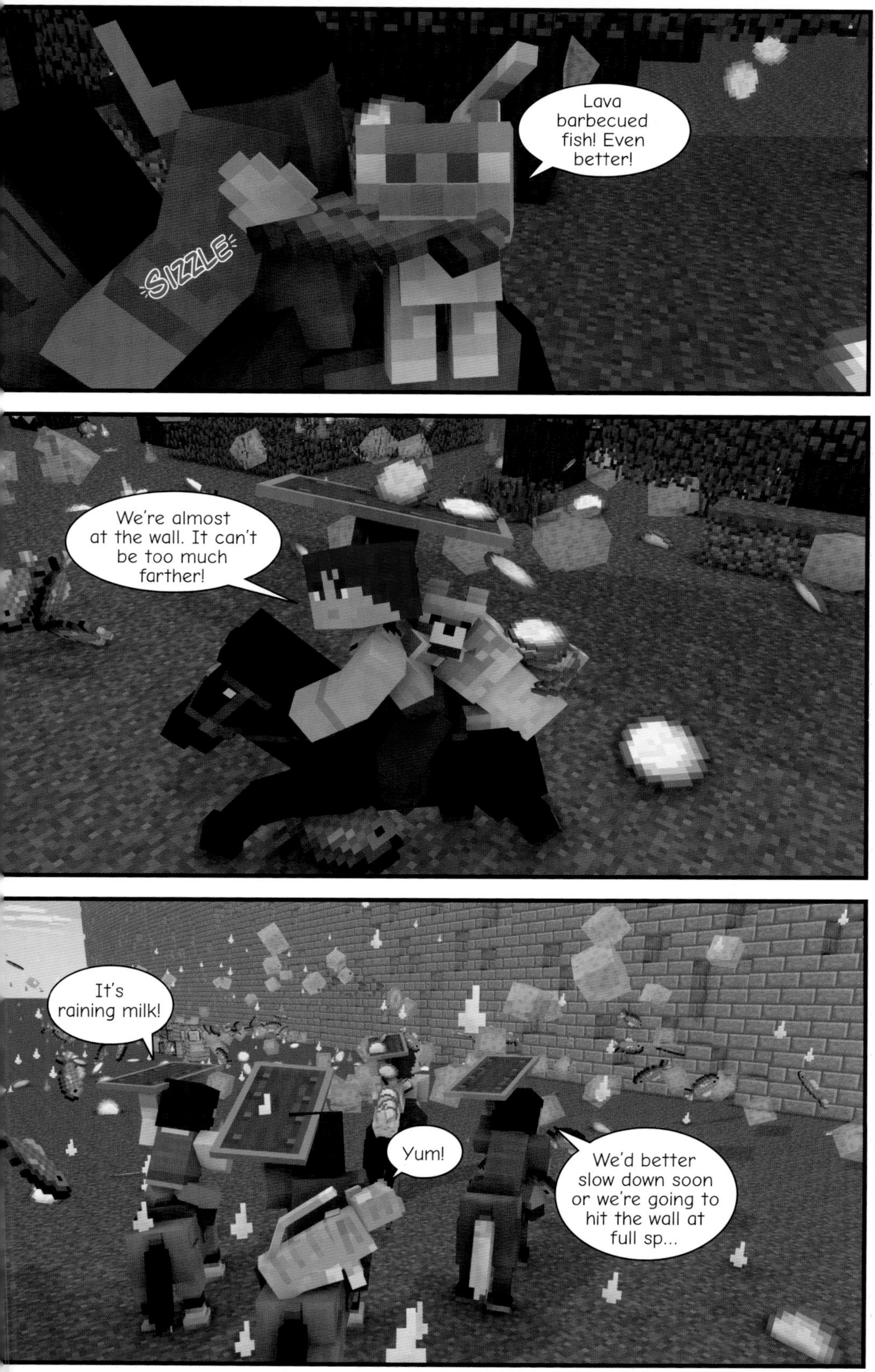
SIZZLE
Lava barbecued fish! Even better!
We're almost at the wall. It can't be too much farther!
It's raining milk!
Yum!
We'd better slow down soon or we're going to hit the wall at full sp...

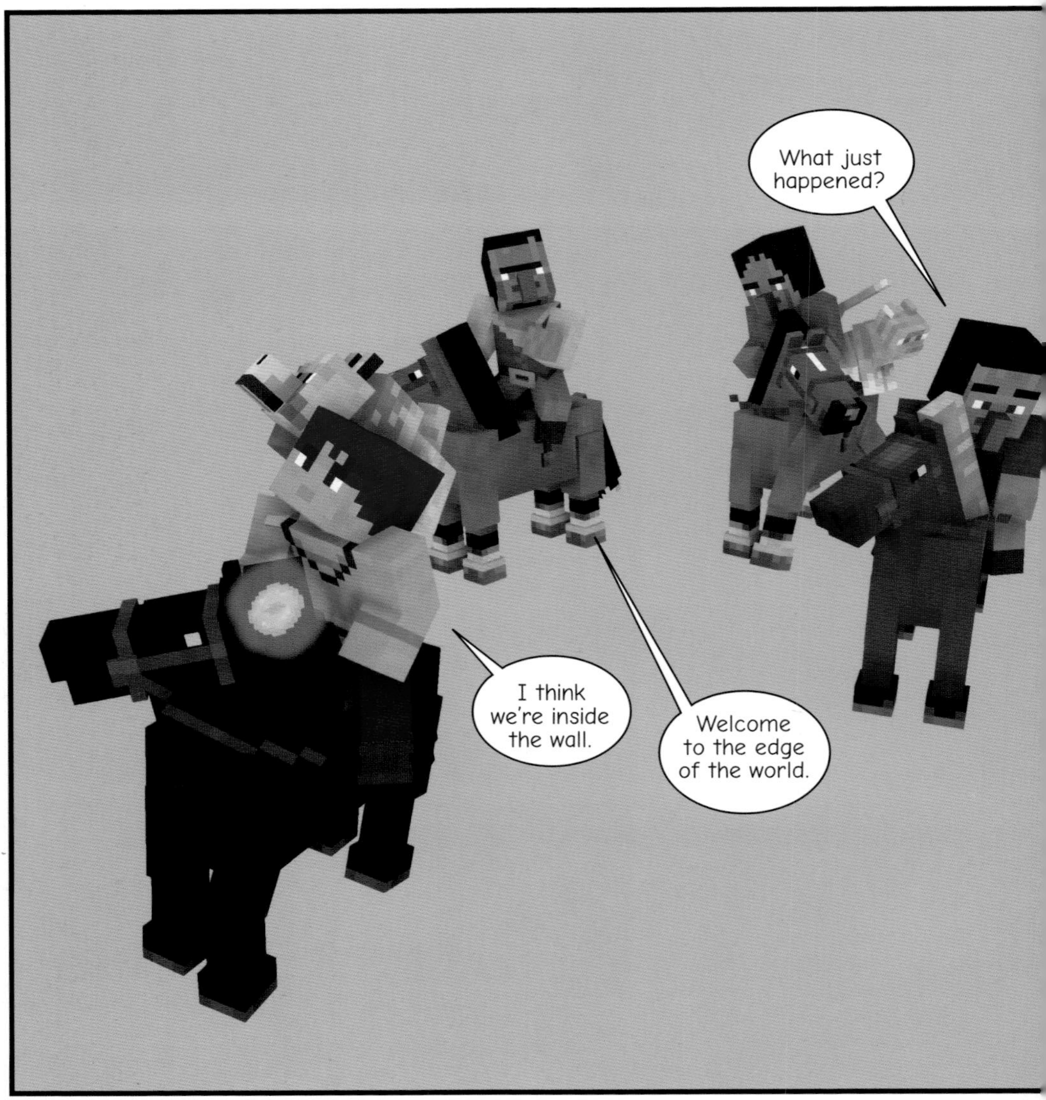
What just happened?
I think we're inside the wall.
Welcome to the edge of the world.

CHAPTER II

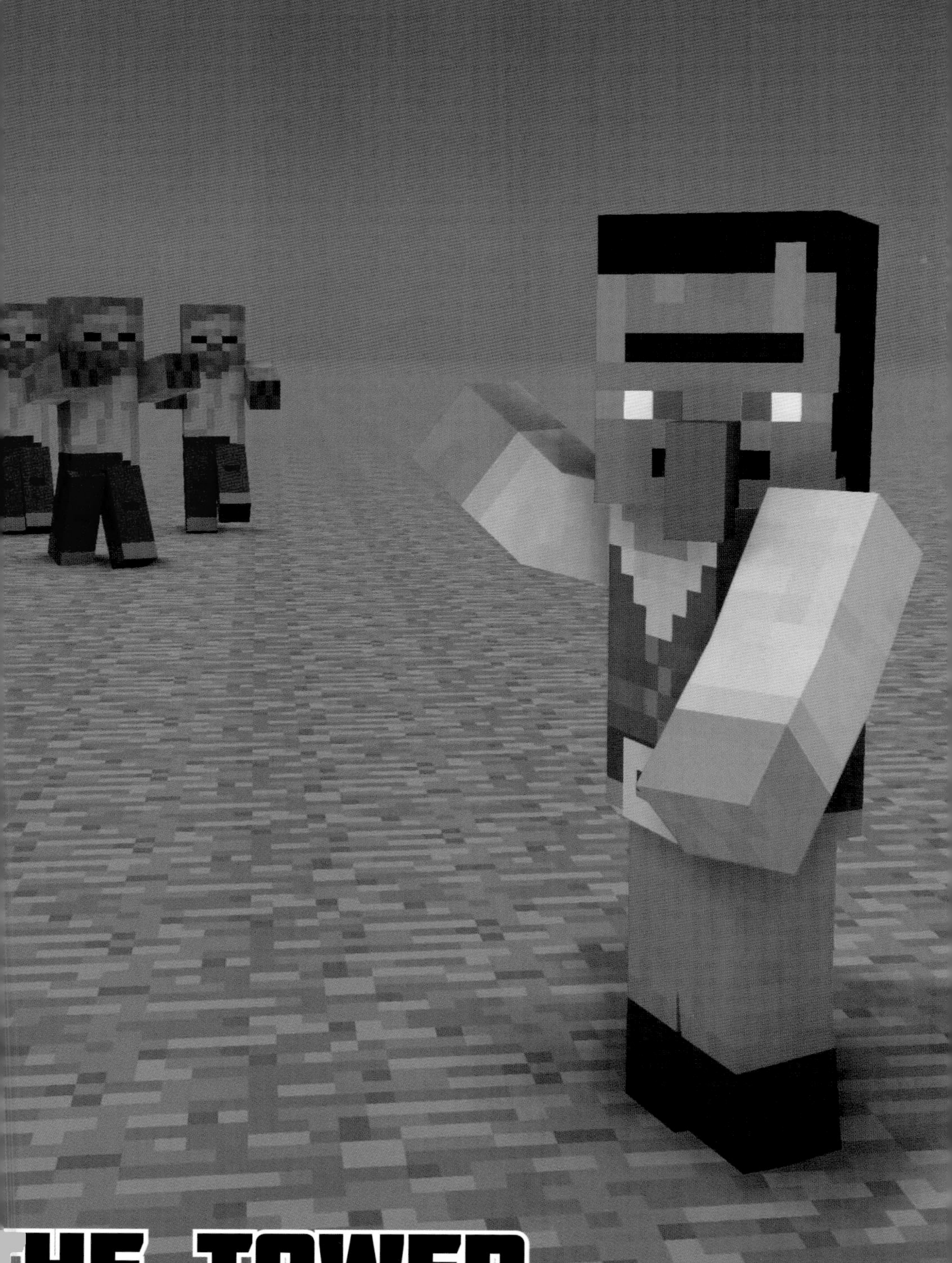

THE TOWER

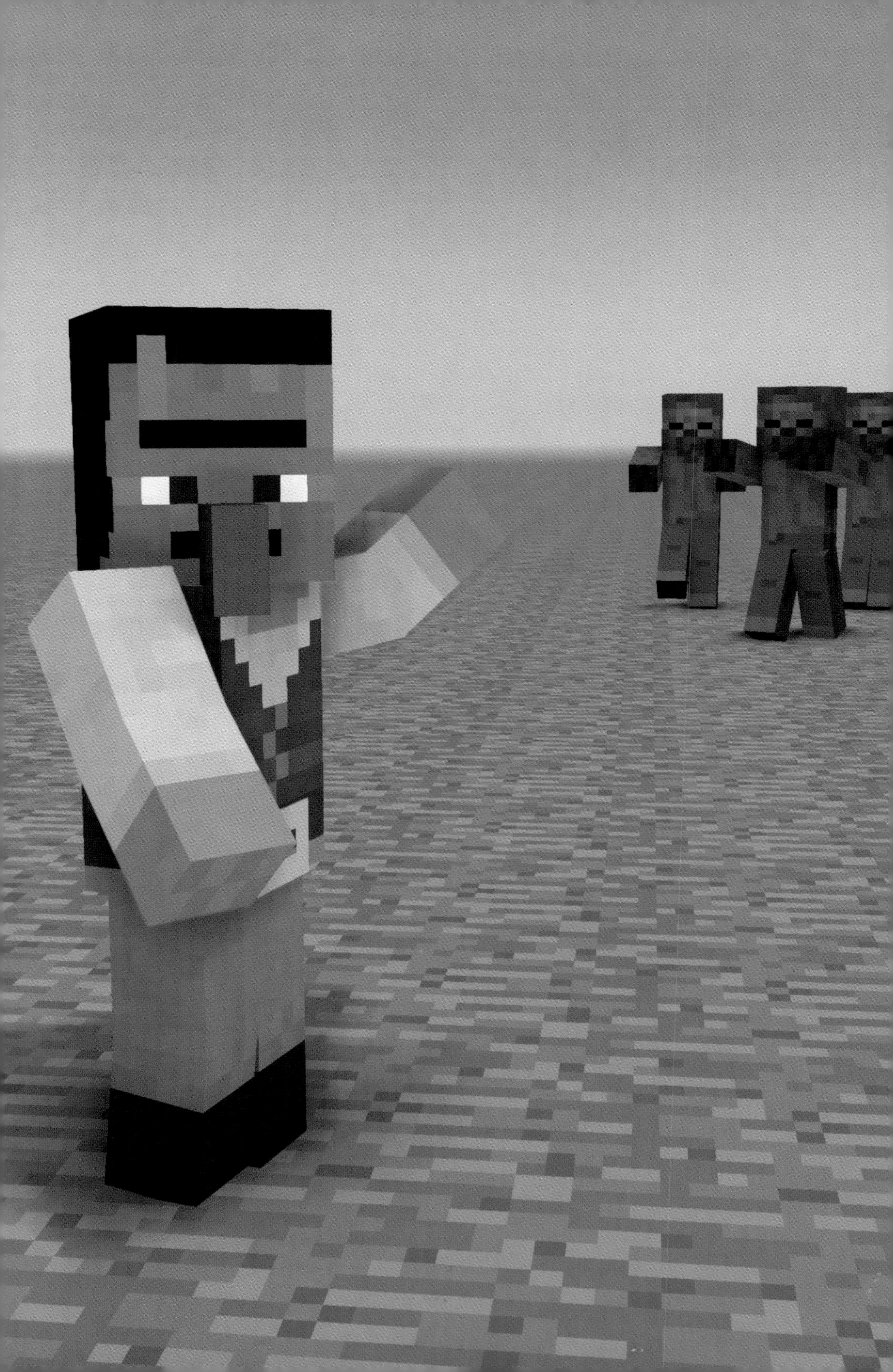

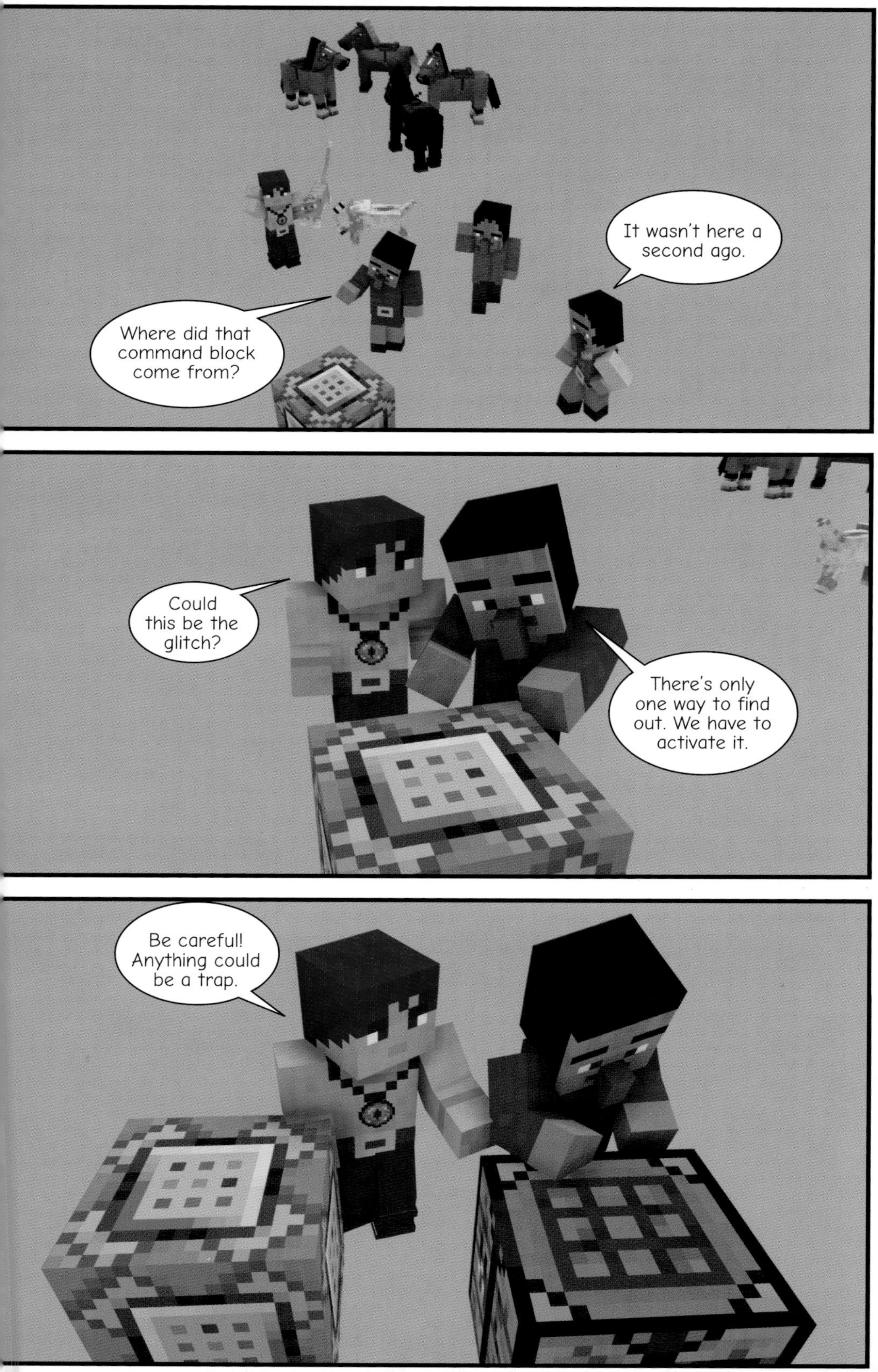
It wasn't here a second ago.
Where did that command block come from?
Could this be the glitch?
There's only one way to find out. We have to activate it.
Be careful! Anything could be a trap.

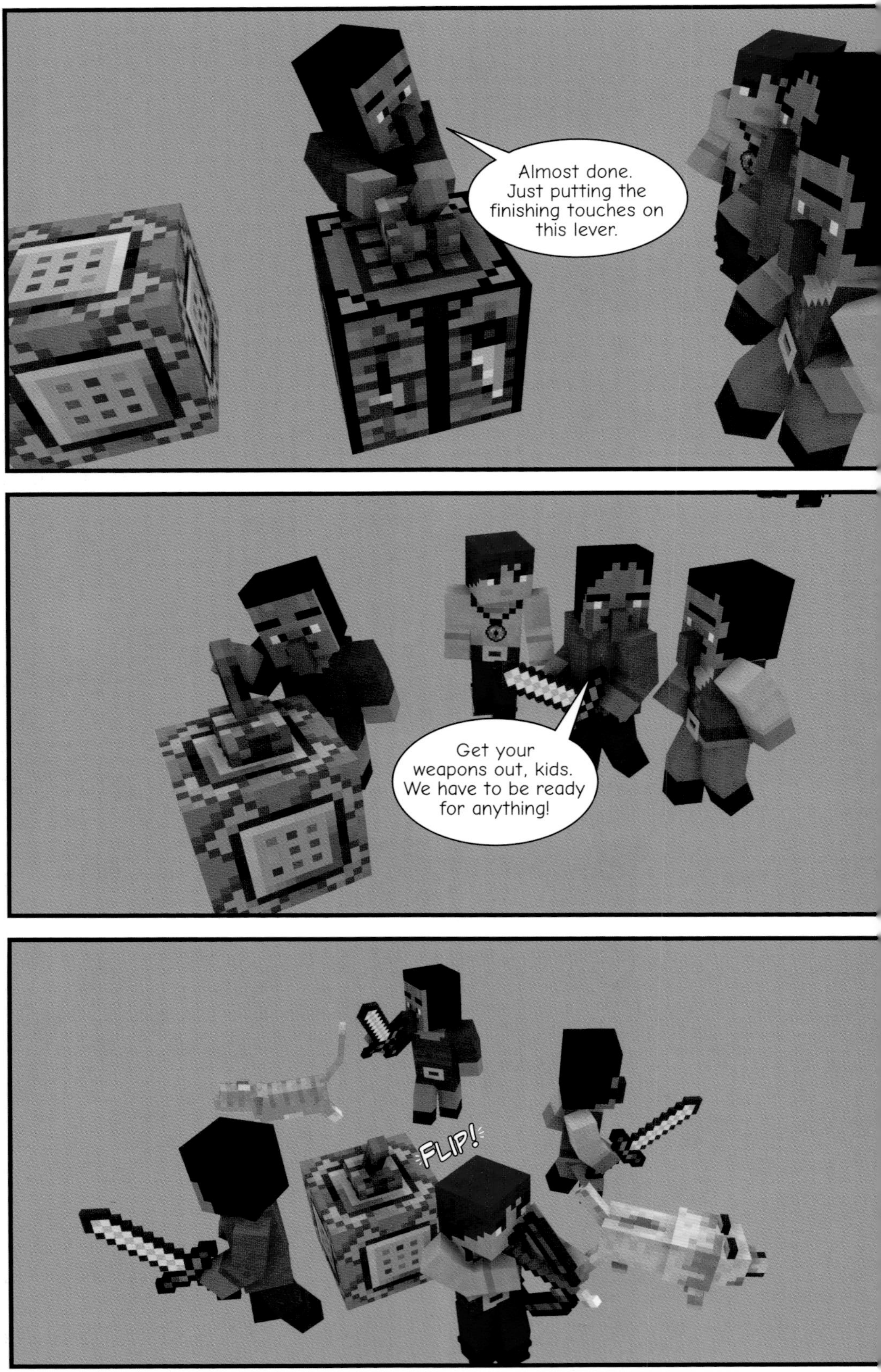
Almost done. Just putting the finishing touches on this lever.
Get your weapons out, kids. We have to be ready for anything!
FLIP!

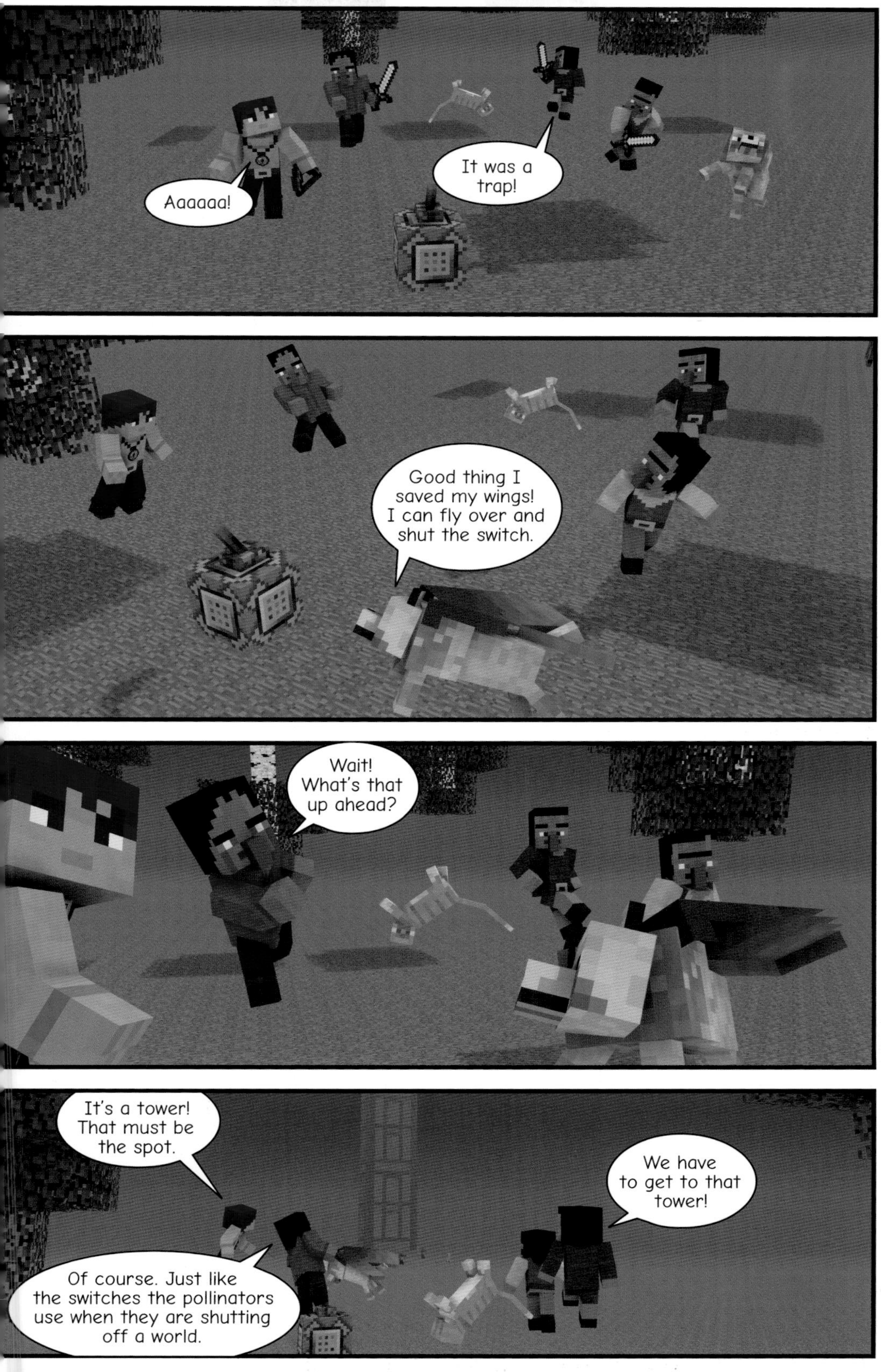
Aaaaaa!
It was a trap!
Good thing I saved my wings! I can fly over and shut the switch.
Wait! What's that up ahead?
It's a tower! That must be the spot.
We have to get to that tower!
Of course. Just like the switches the pollinators use when they are shutting off a world.

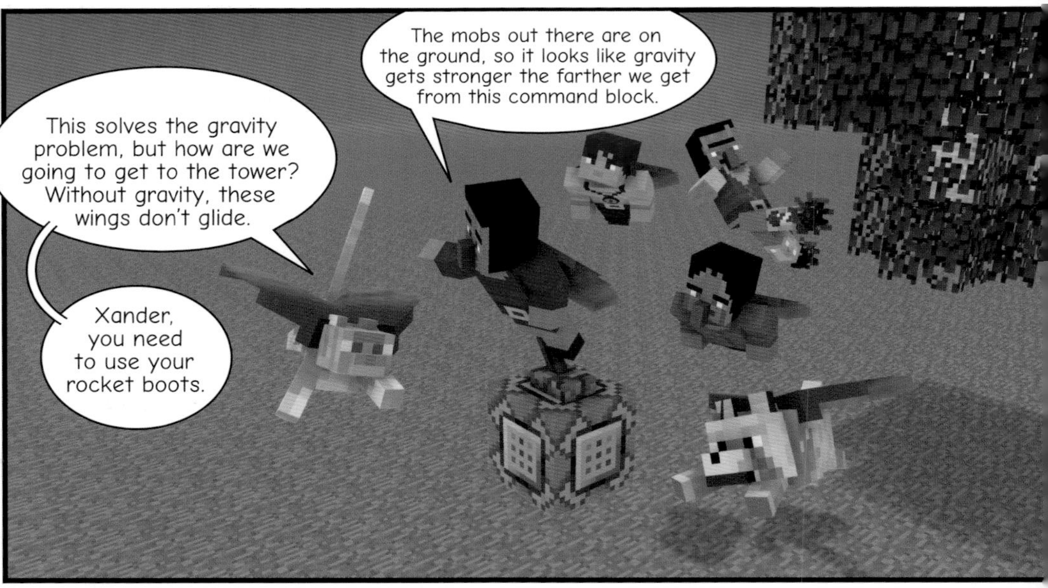
This solves the gravity problem, but how are we going to get to the tower? Without gravity, these wings don't glide.
Xander, you need to use your rocket boots.
The mobs out there are on the ground, so it looks like gravity gets stronger the farther we get from this command block.

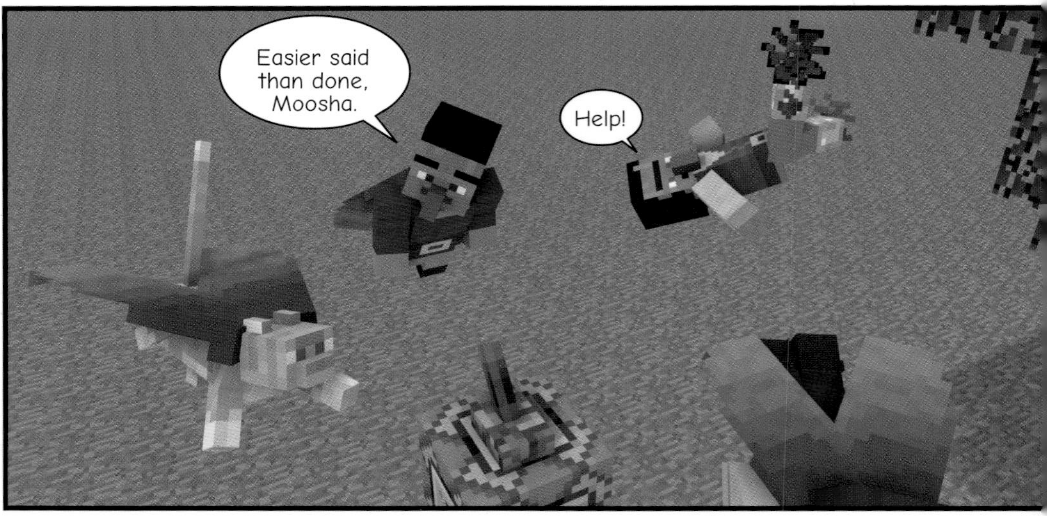
Easier said than done, Moosha.
Help!

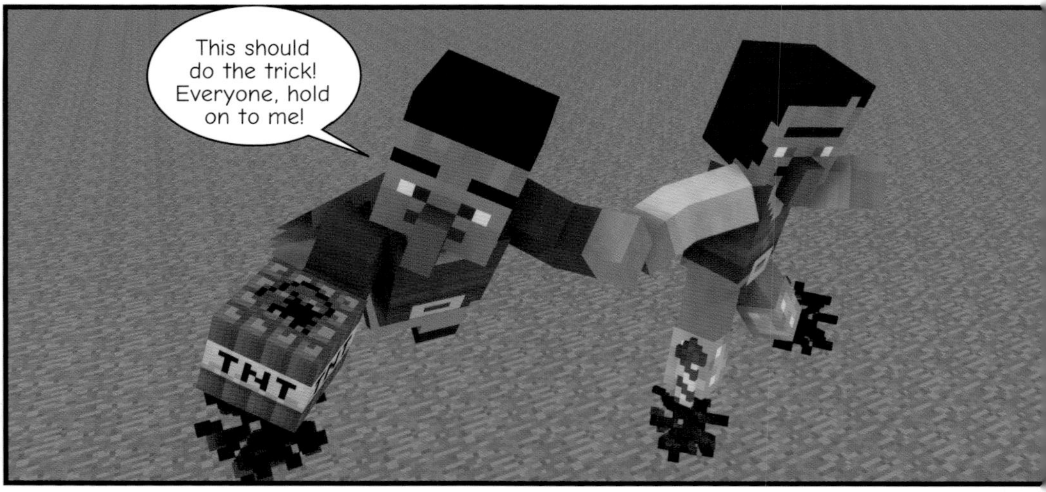
This should do the trick! Everyone, hold on to me!
TNT

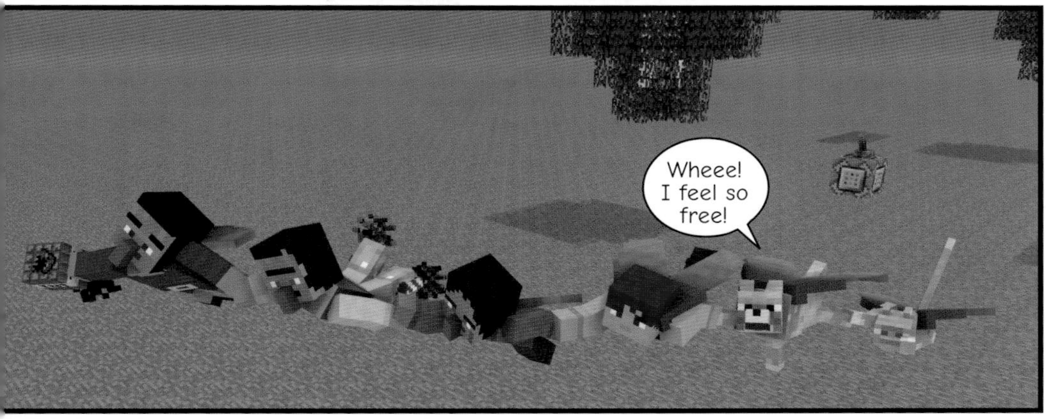
Wheee!
I feel so
free!

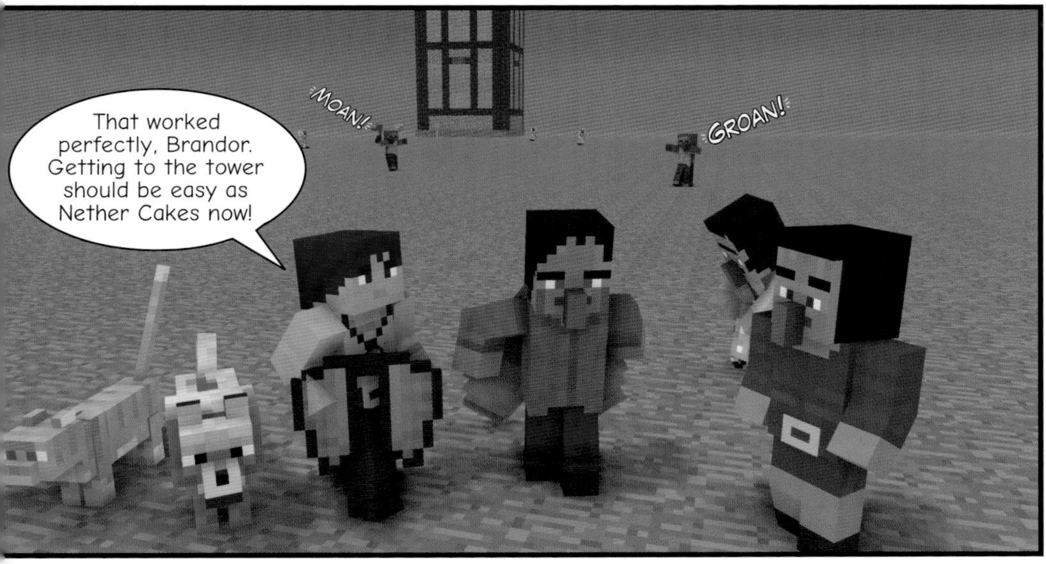
MOAN!
GROAN!
That worked
perfectly, Brandor.
Getting to the tower
should be easy as
Nether Cakes now!

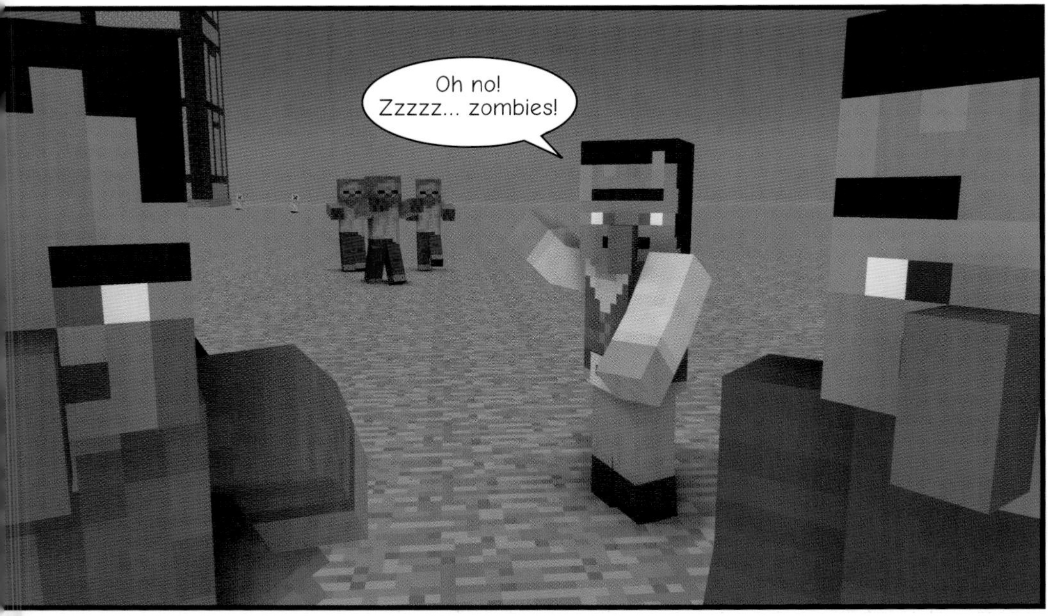
Oh no!
Zzzzz... zombies!

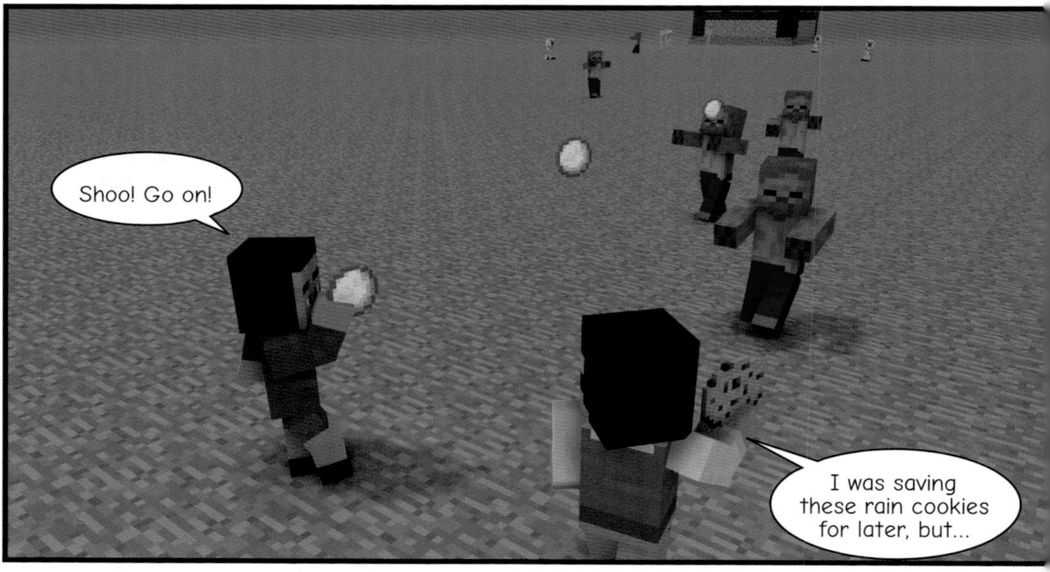
Shoo! Go on!
I was saving these rain cookies for later, but...

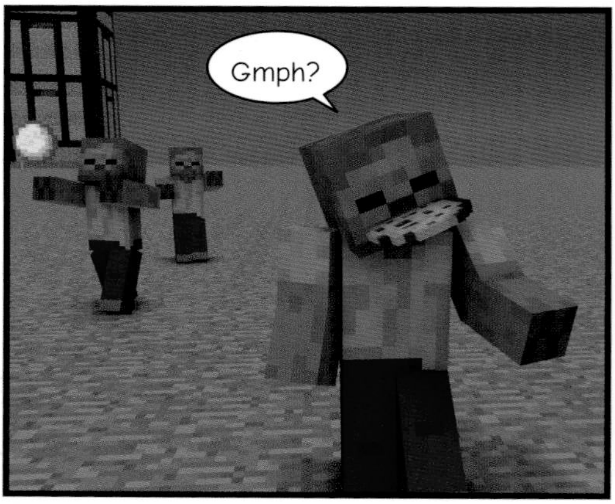
Gmph?

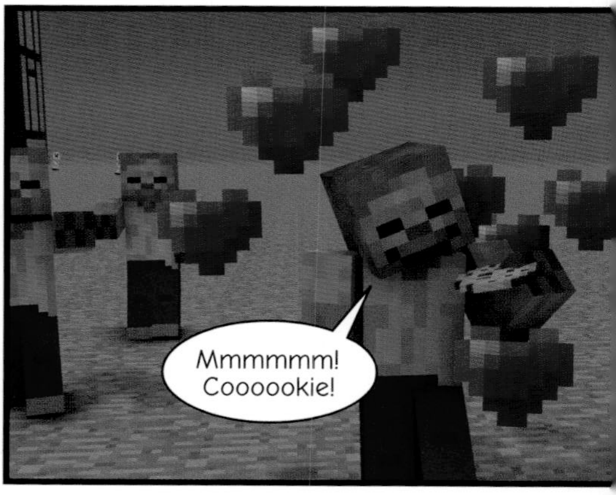
Mmmmmm! Coooookie!

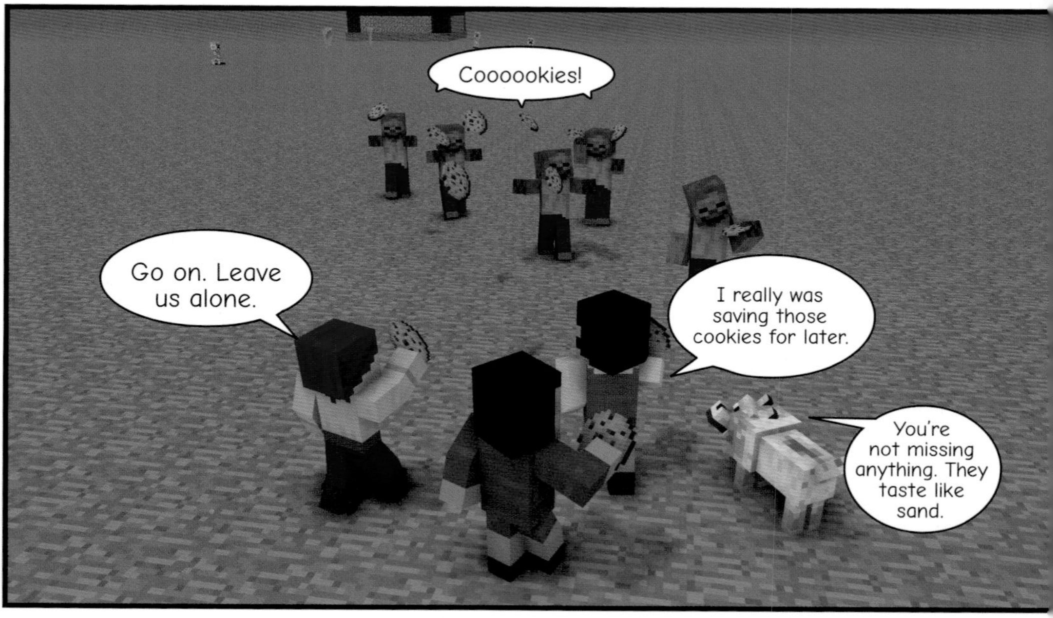
Coooookies!
Go on. Leave us alone.
I really was saving those cookies for later.
You're not missing anything. They taste like sand.

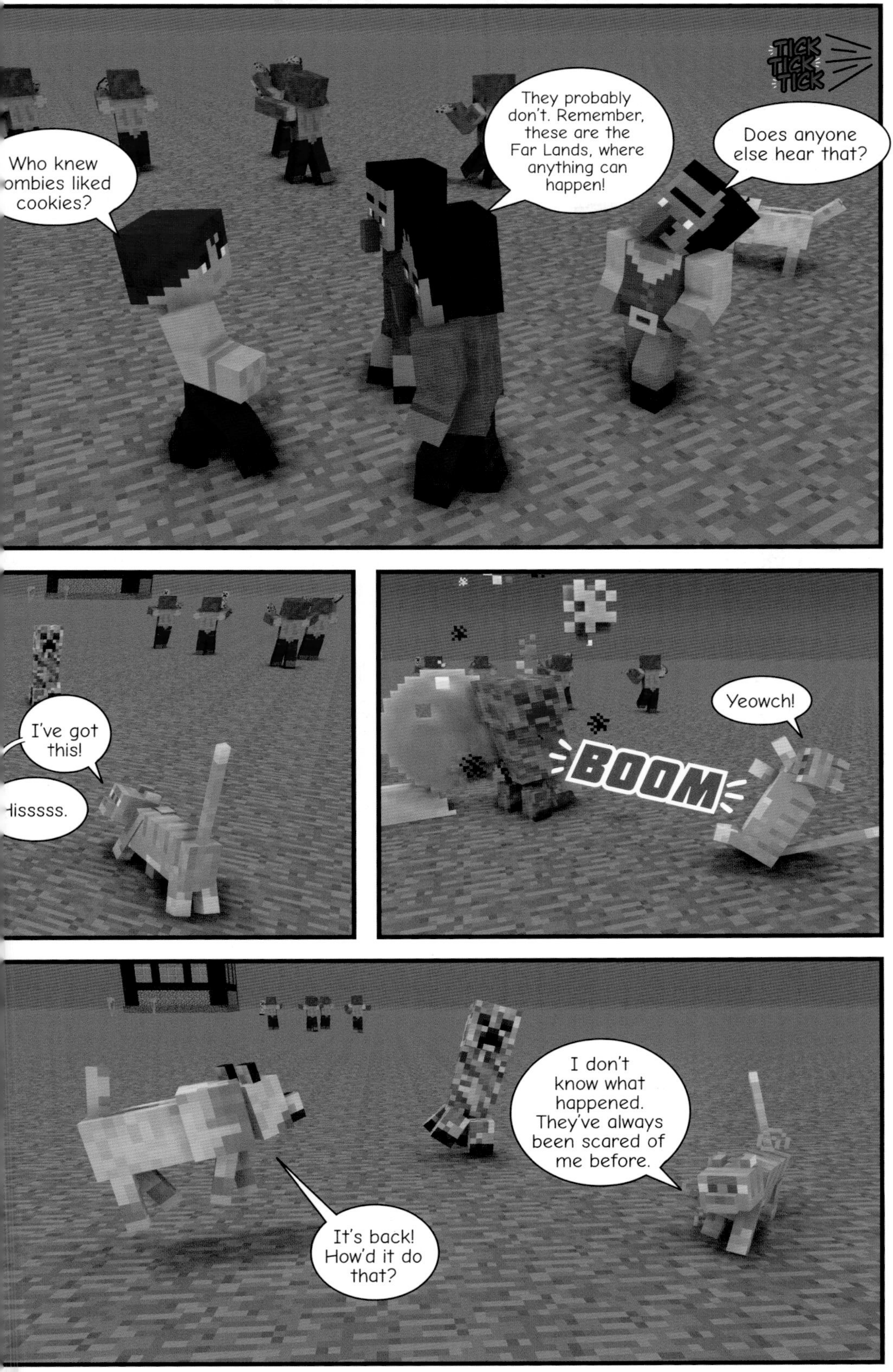
TICK TICK TICK
Who knew
ombies liked
cookies?
They probably don't. Remember, these are the Far Lands, where anything can happen!
Does anyone else hear that?
I've got this!
Hisssss.
BOOM
Yeowch!
I don't know what happened. They've always been scared of me before.
It's back! How'd it do that?

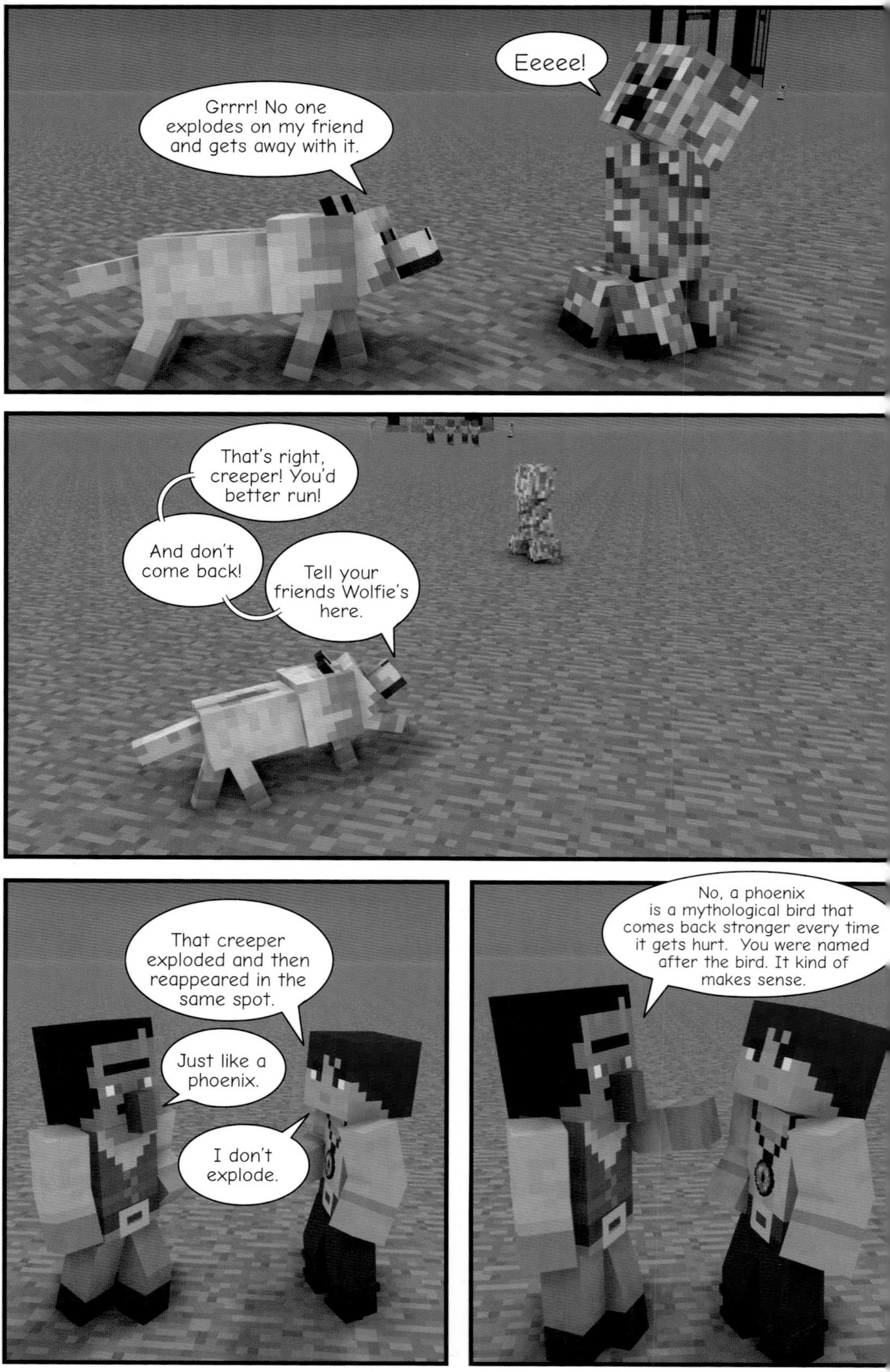
Grrrr! No one explodes on my friend and gets away with it.
Eeeee!
That's right, creeper! You'd better run!
And don't come back!
Tell your friends Wolfie's here.
That creeper exploded and then reappeared in the same spot.
Just like a phoenix.
I don't explode.
No, a phoenix is a mythological bird that comes back stronger every time it gets hurt. You were named after the bird. It kind of makes sense.

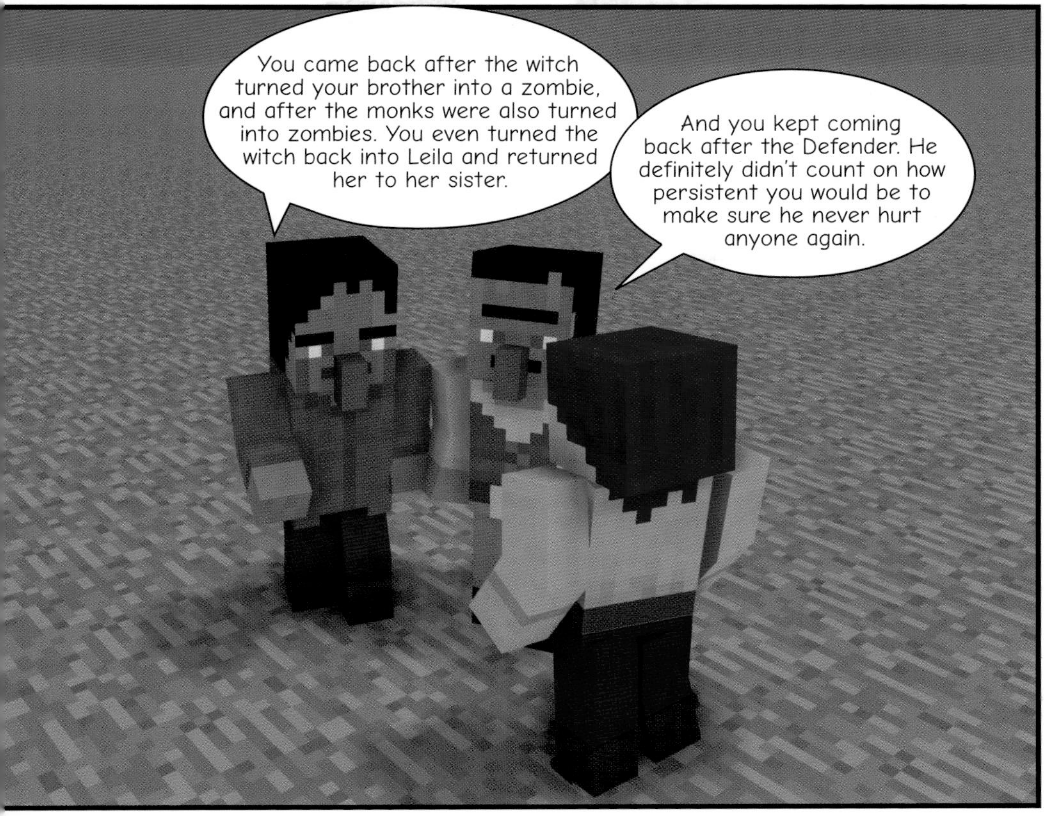
You came back after the witch turned your brother into a zombie, and after the monks were also turned into zombies. You even turned the witch back into Leila and returned her to her sister.
And you kept coming back after the Defender. He definitely didn't count on how persistent you would be to make sure he never hurt anyone again.

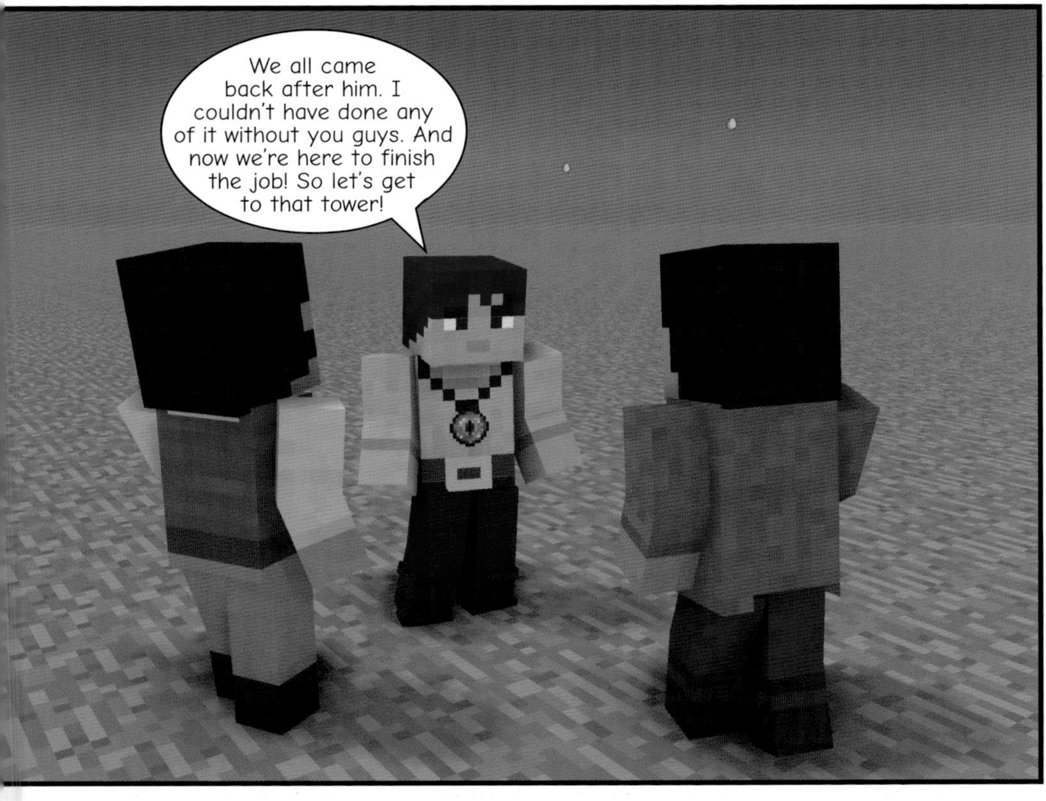
We all came back after him. I couldn't have done any of it without you guys. And now we're here to finish the job! So let's get to that tower!

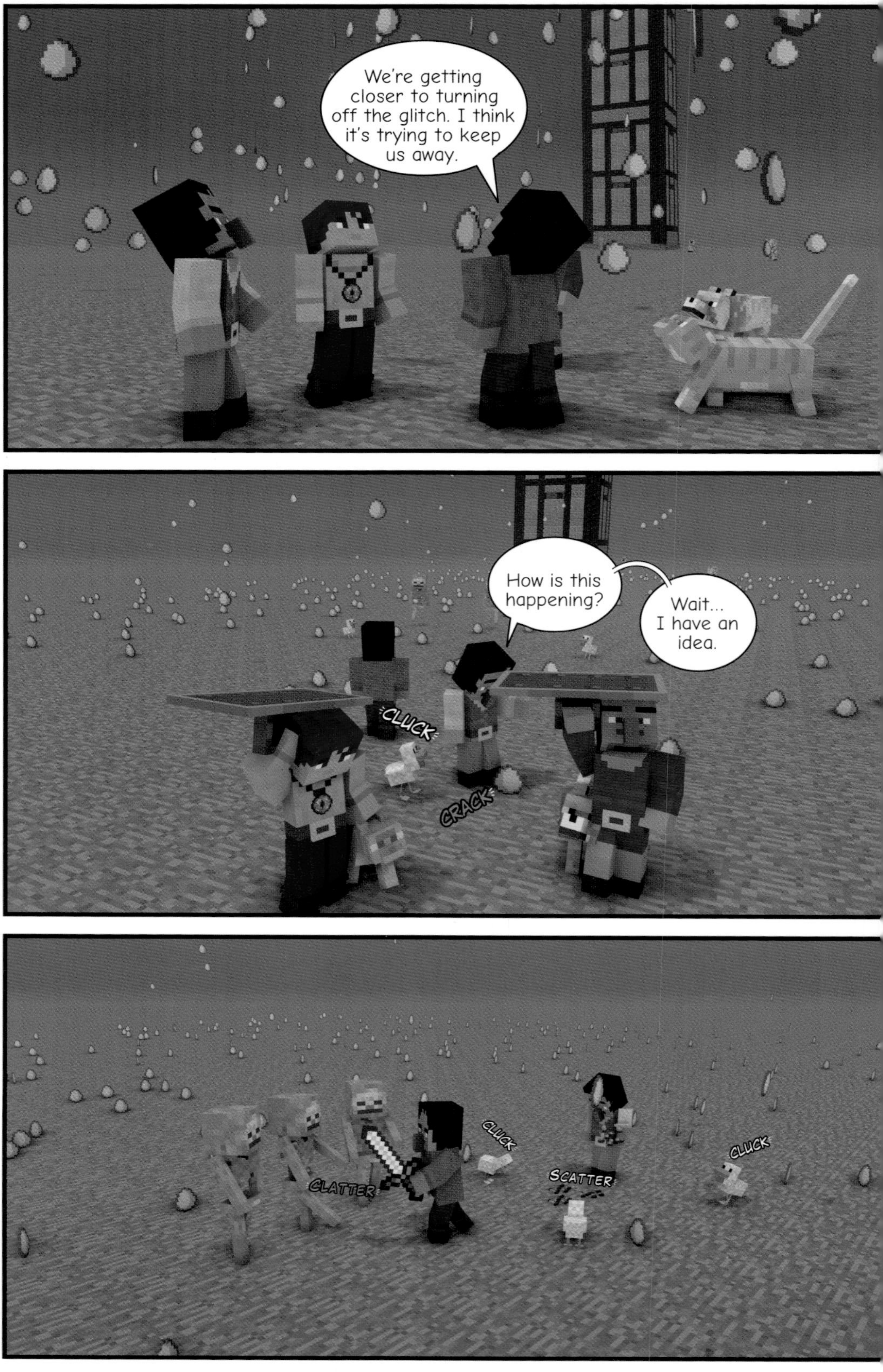
We're getting closer to turning off the glitch. I think it's trying to keep us away.
How is this happening?
Wait... I have an idea.
CLUCK
CRACK
CLATTER
CLUCK
SCATTER
CLUCK

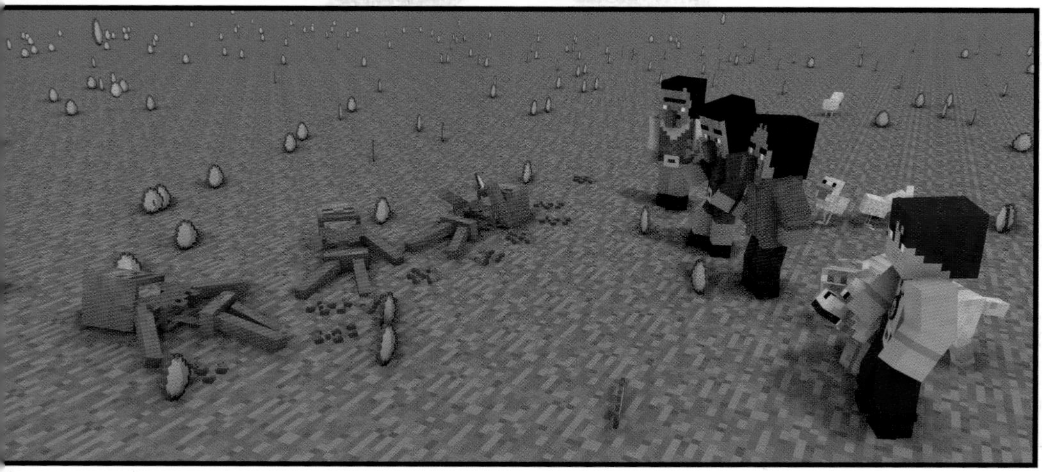

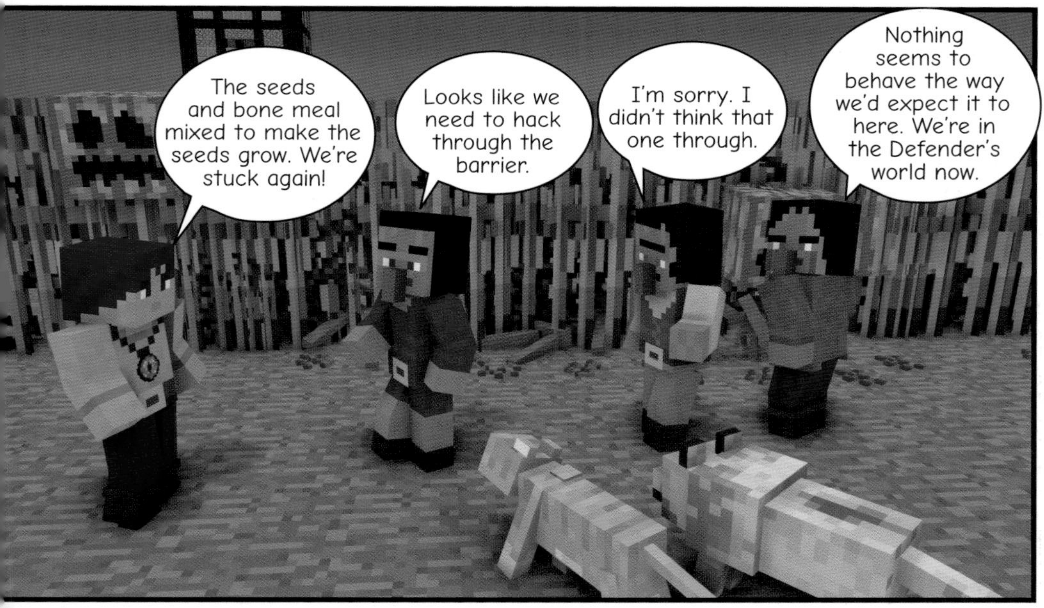
The seeds and bone meal mixed to make the seeds grow. We're stuck again!
Looks like we need to hack through the barrier.
I'm sorry. I didn't think that one through.
Nothing seems to behave the way we'd expect it to here. We're in the Defender's world now.

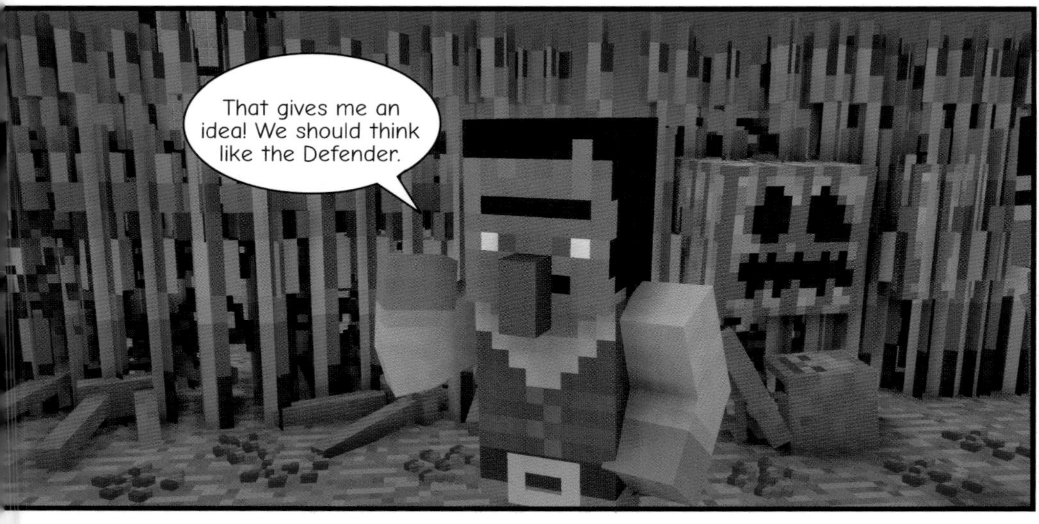
That gives me an idea! We should think like the Defender.

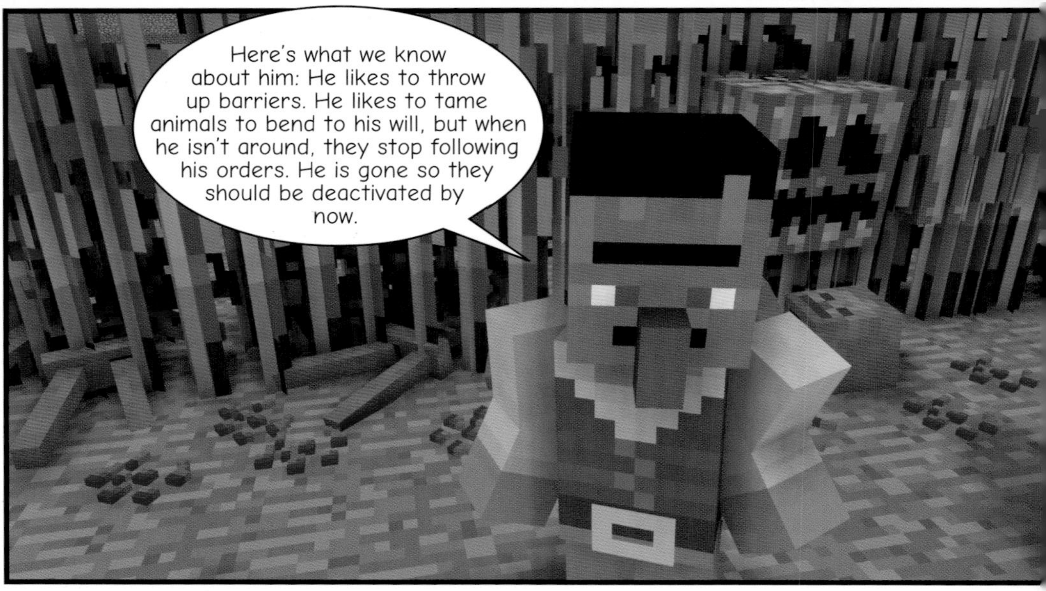
Here's what we know about him: He likes to throw up barriers. He likes to tame animals to bend to his will, but when he isn't around, they stop following his orders. He is gone so they should be deactivated by now.

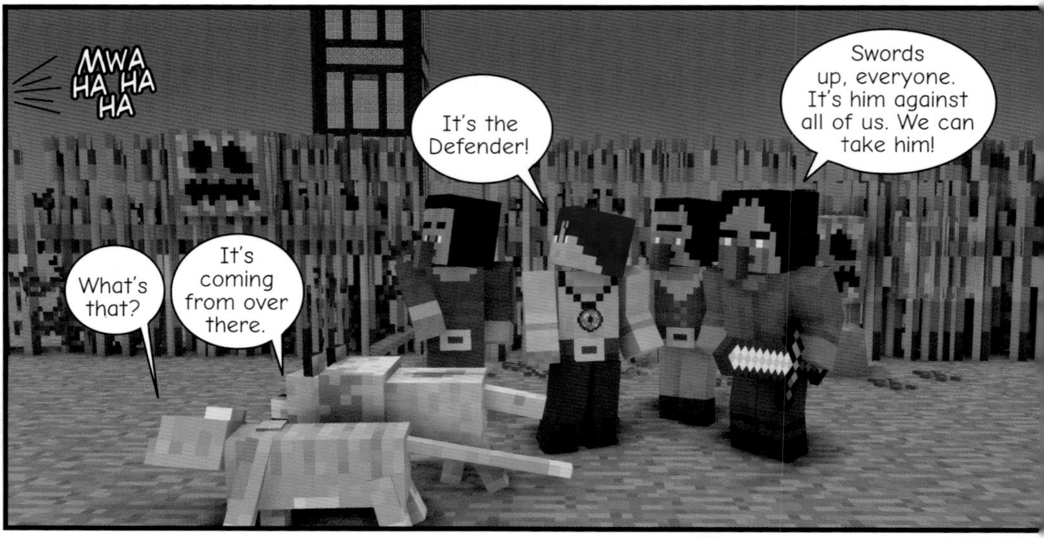
MWA HA HA HA
It's the Defender!
Swords up, everyone. It's him against all of us. We can take him!
What's that?
It's coming from over there.

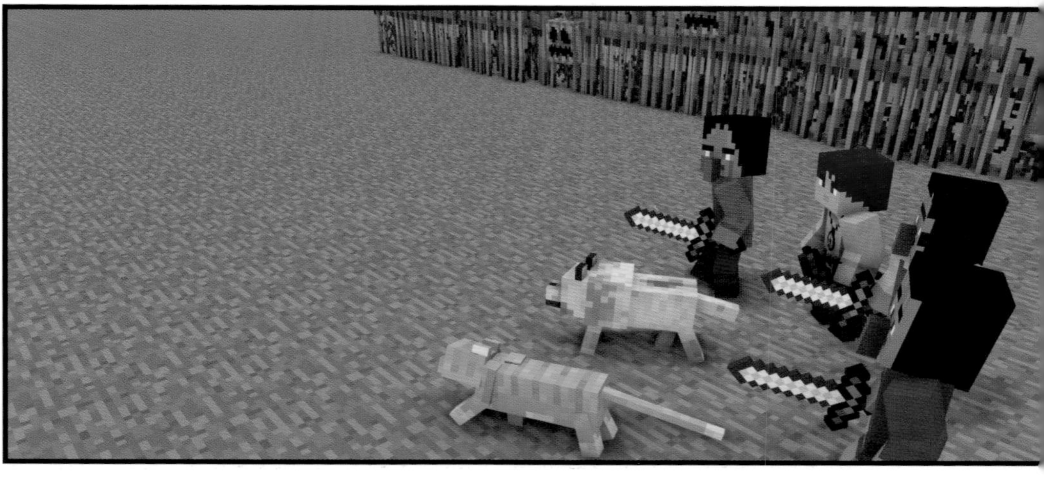

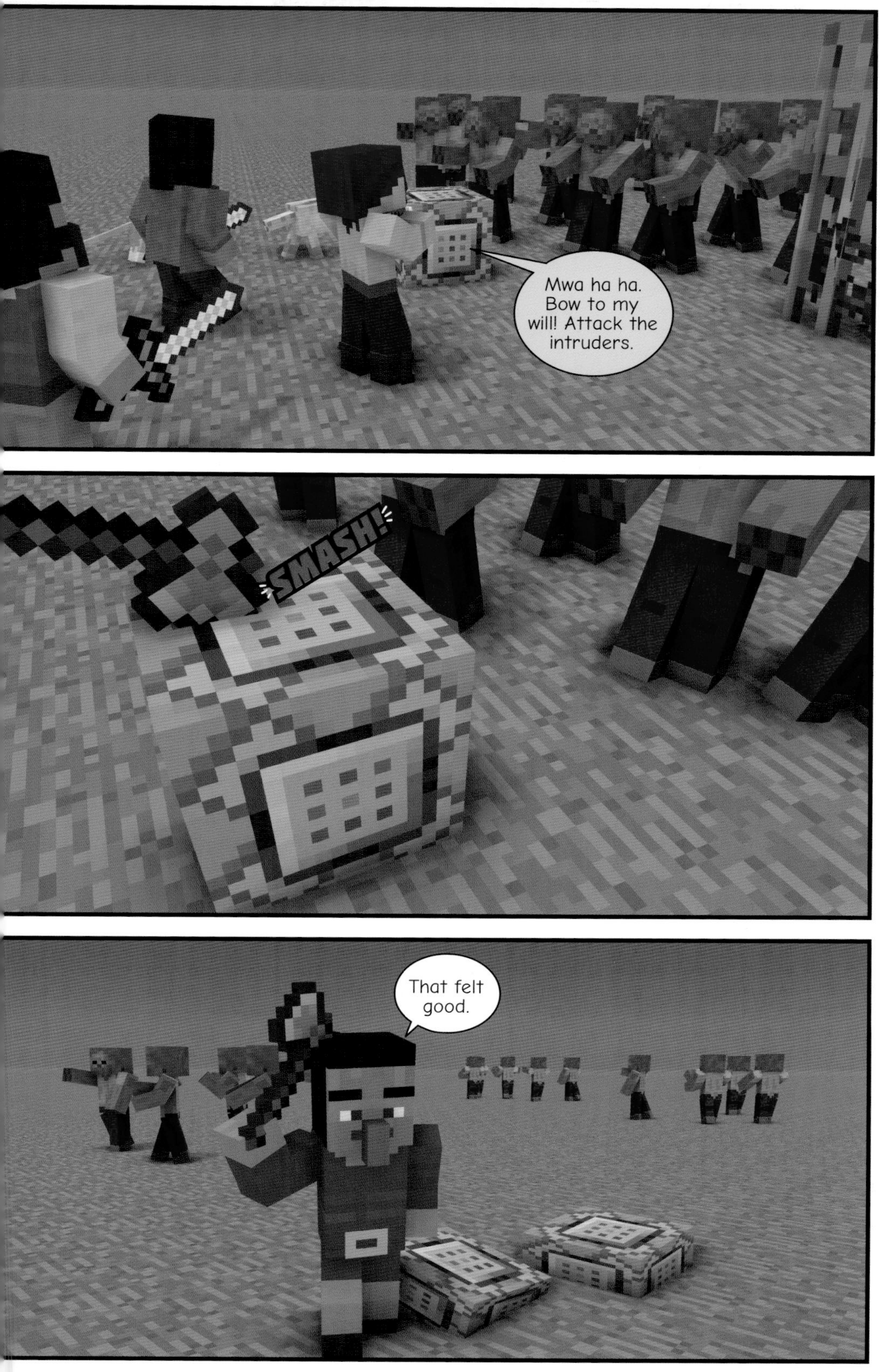
Mwa ha ha. Bow to my will! Attack the intruders.
SMASH!
That felt good.

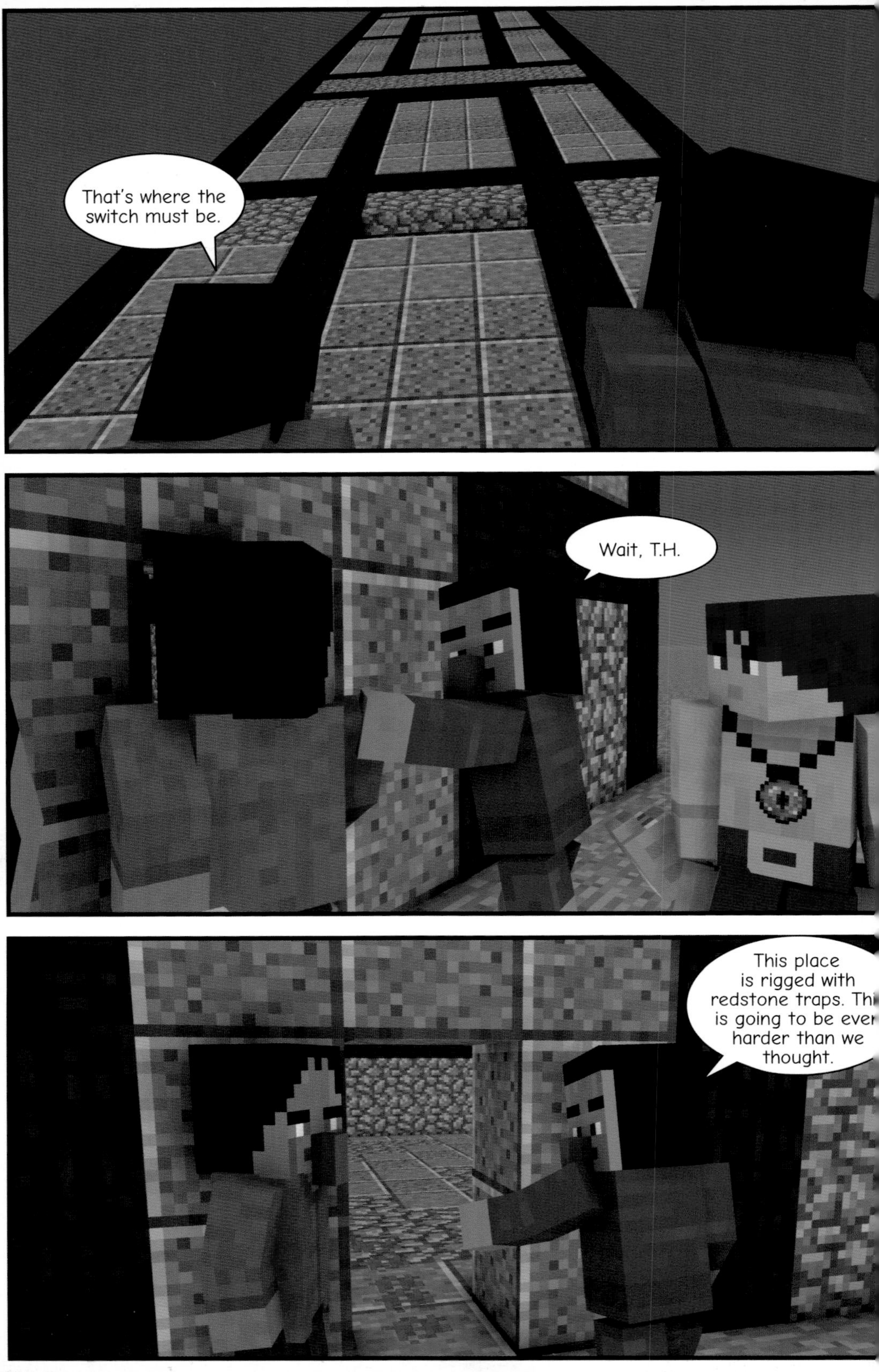
That's where the switch must be.
Wait, T.H.
This place is rigged with redstone traps. Thi is going to be eve harder than we thought.

CHAPTER 12

MAGIC MIRROR

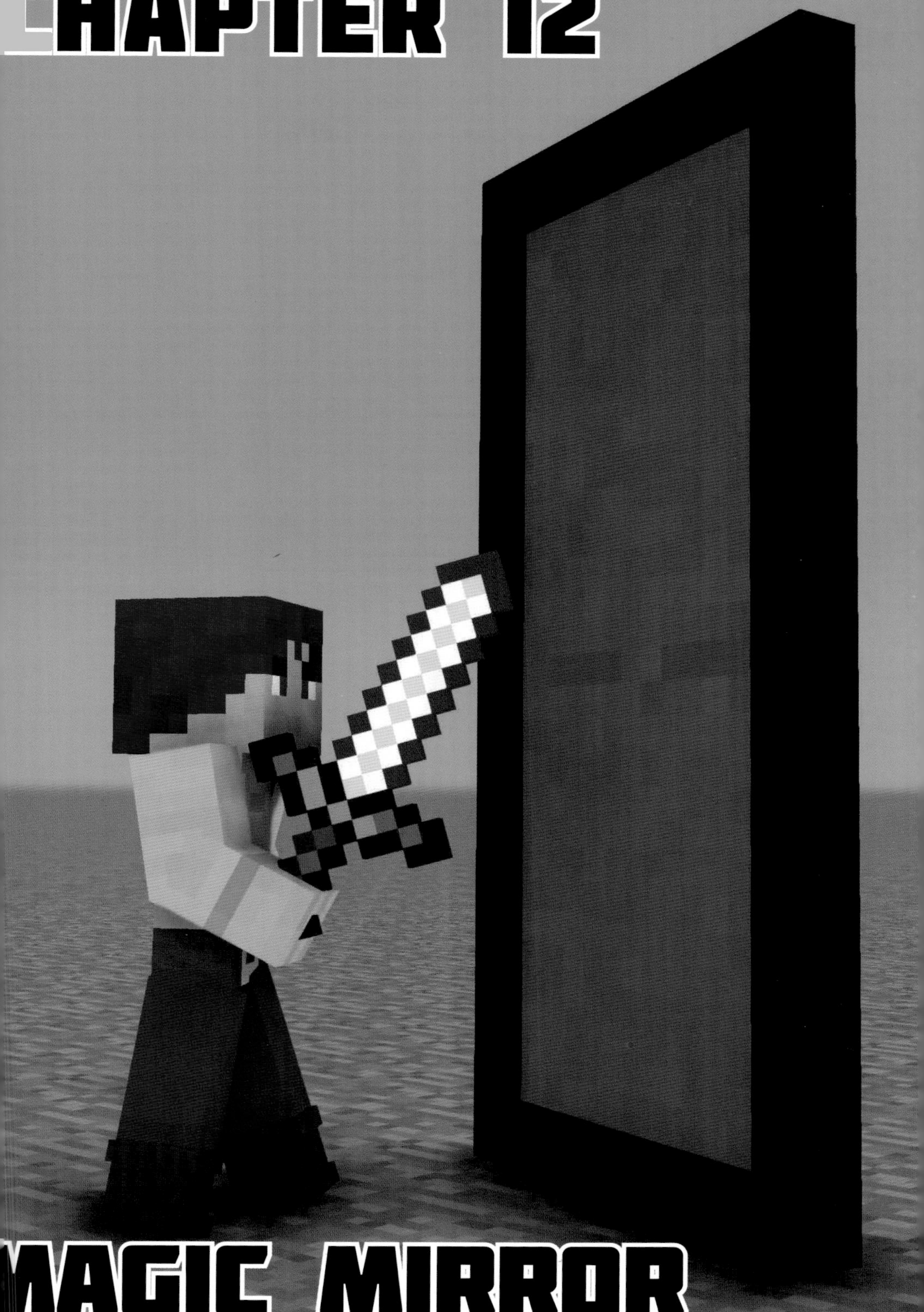

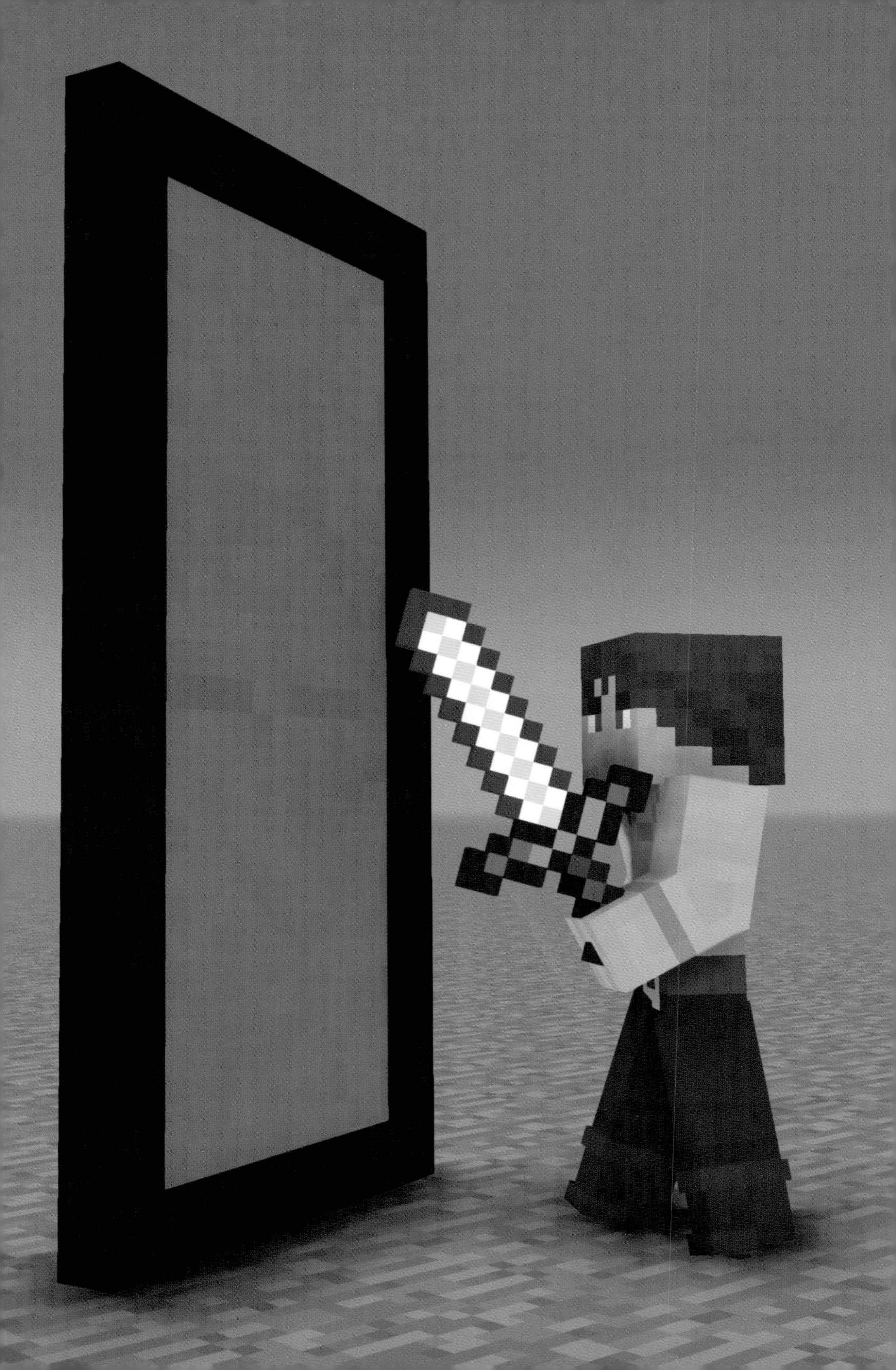

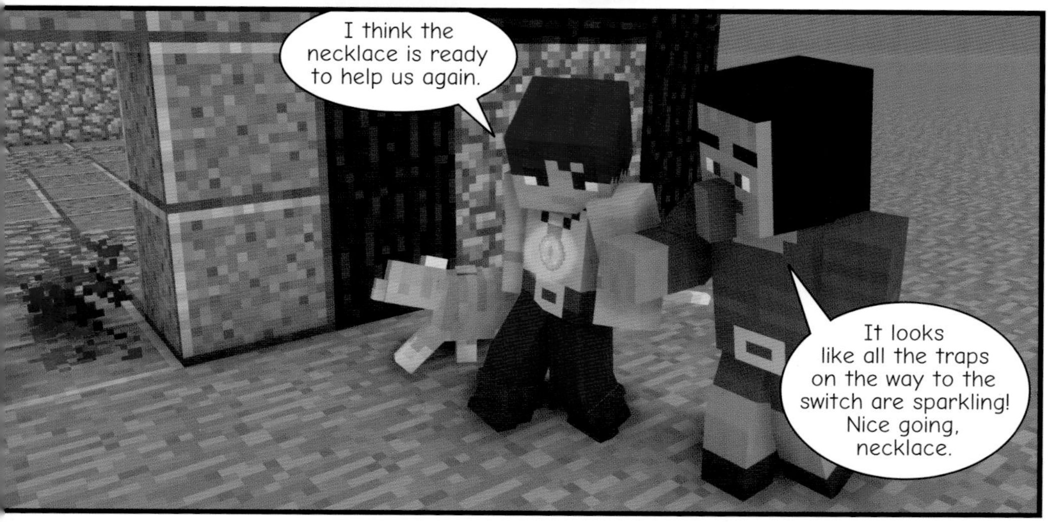
I think the necklace is ready to help us again.
It looks like all the traps on the way to the switch are sparkling! Nice going, necklace.

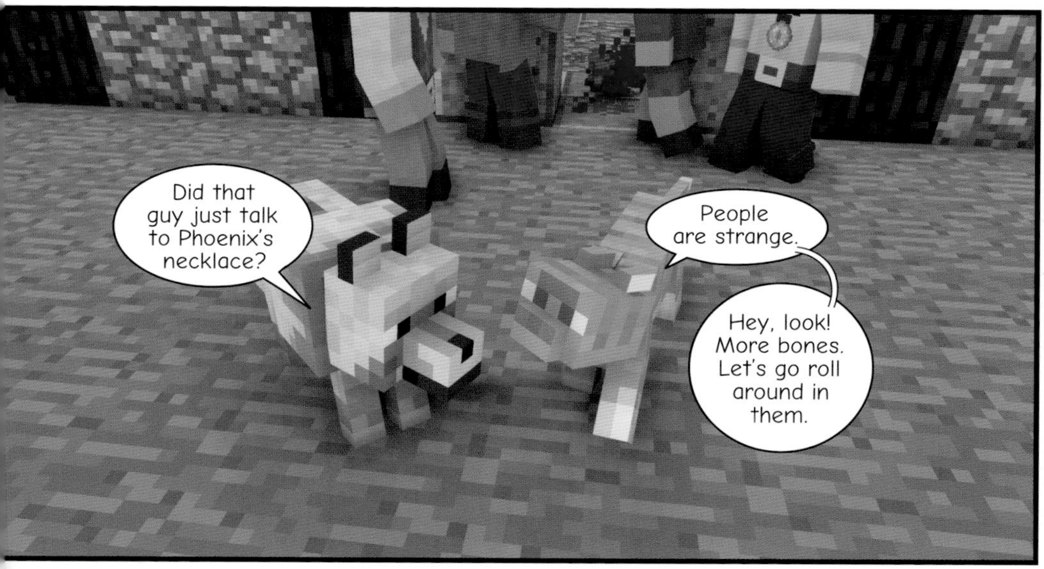
Did that guy just talk to Phoenix's necklace?
People are strange.
Hey, look! More bones. Let's go roll around in them.

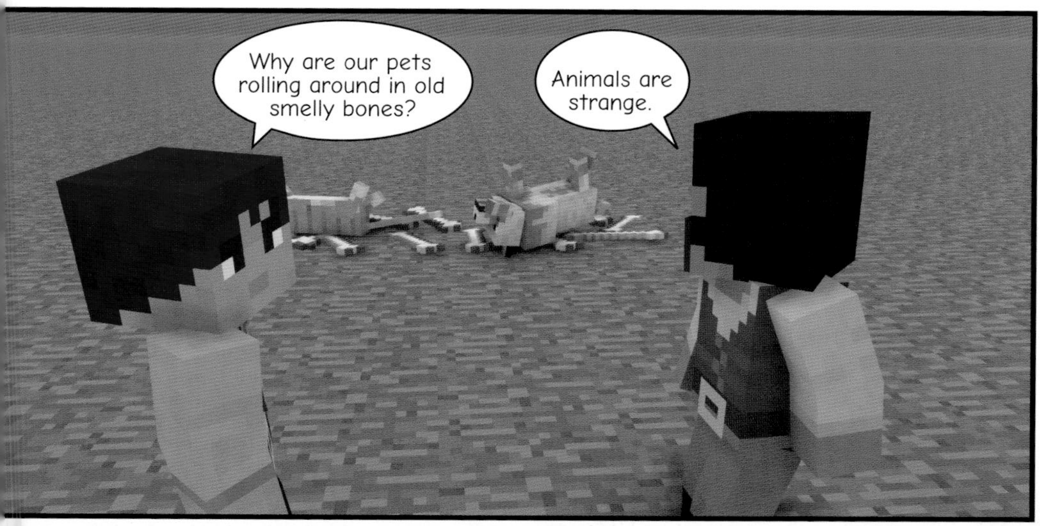
Why are our pets rolling around in old smelly bones?
Animals are strange.

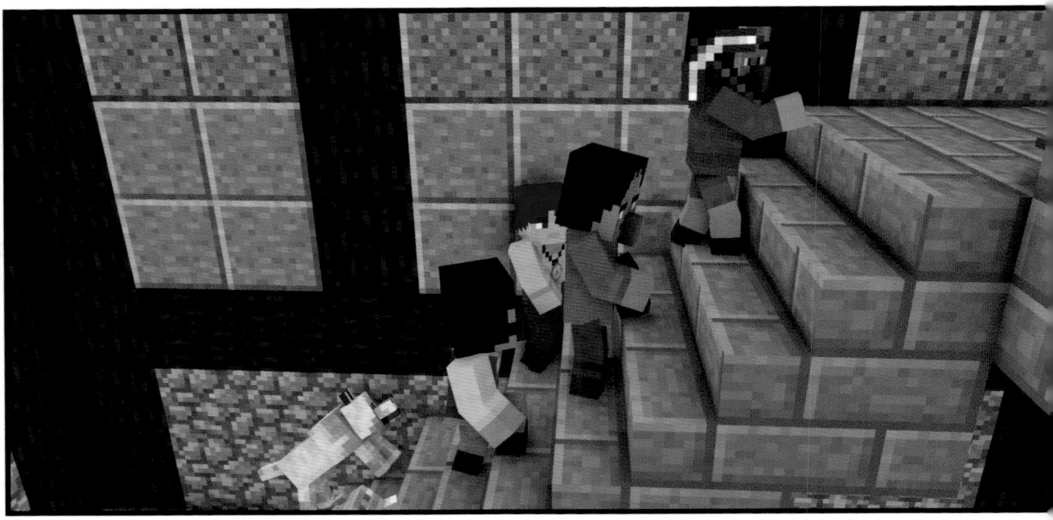

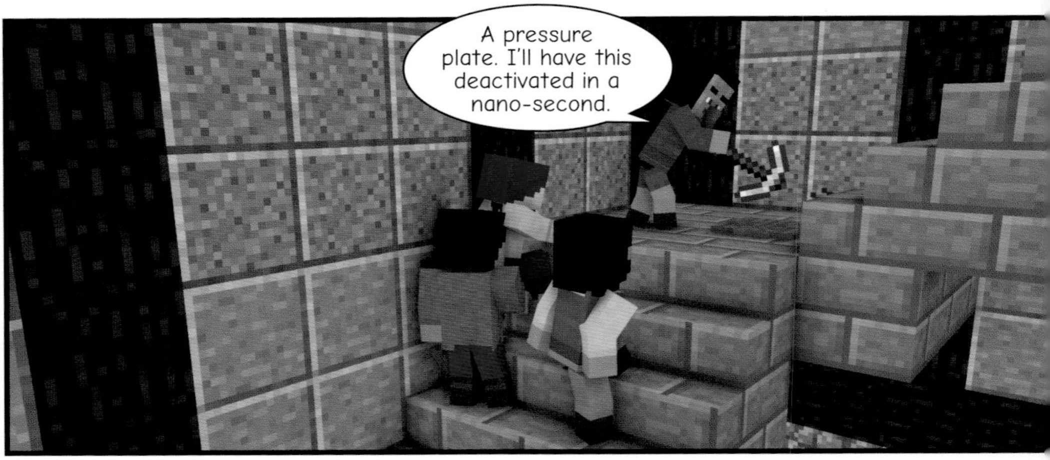
A pressure plate. I'll have this deactivated in a nano-second.

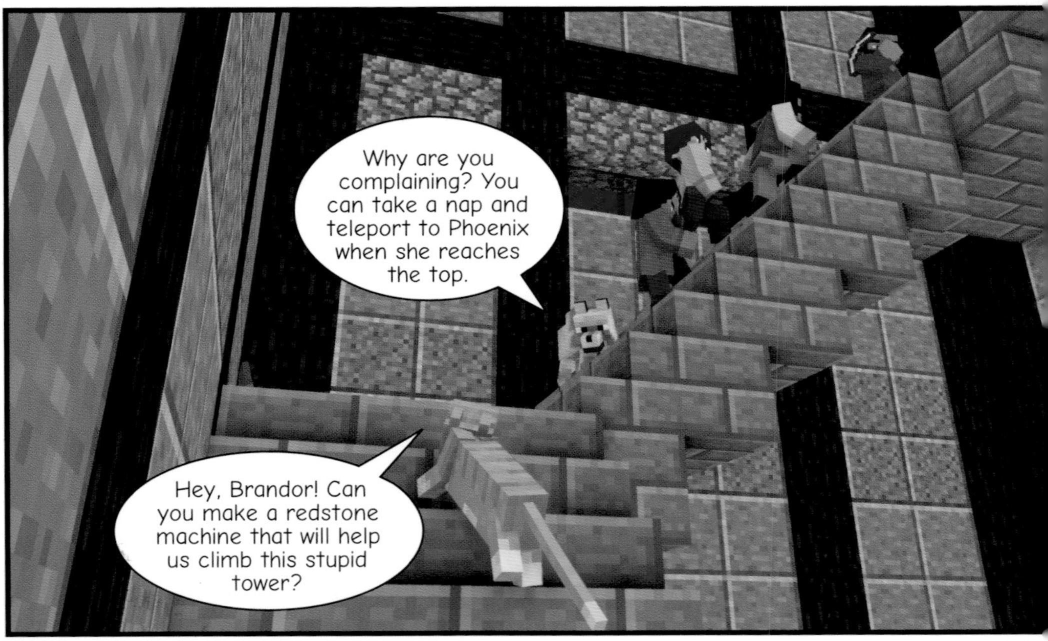
Why are you complaining? You can take a nap and teleport to Phoenix when she reaches the top.
Hey, Brandor! Can you make a redstone machine that will help us climb this stupid tower?

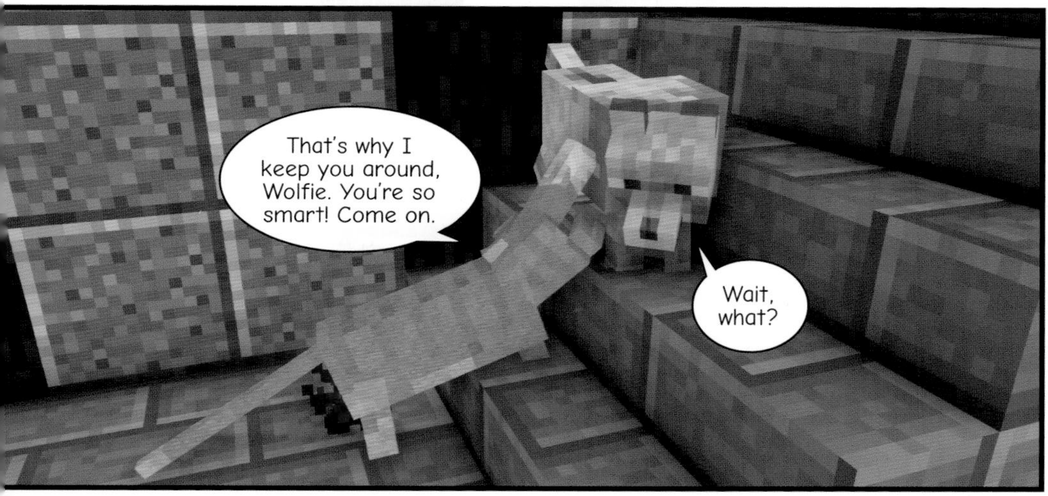
That's why I keep you around, Wolfie. You're so smart! Come on.
Wait, what?

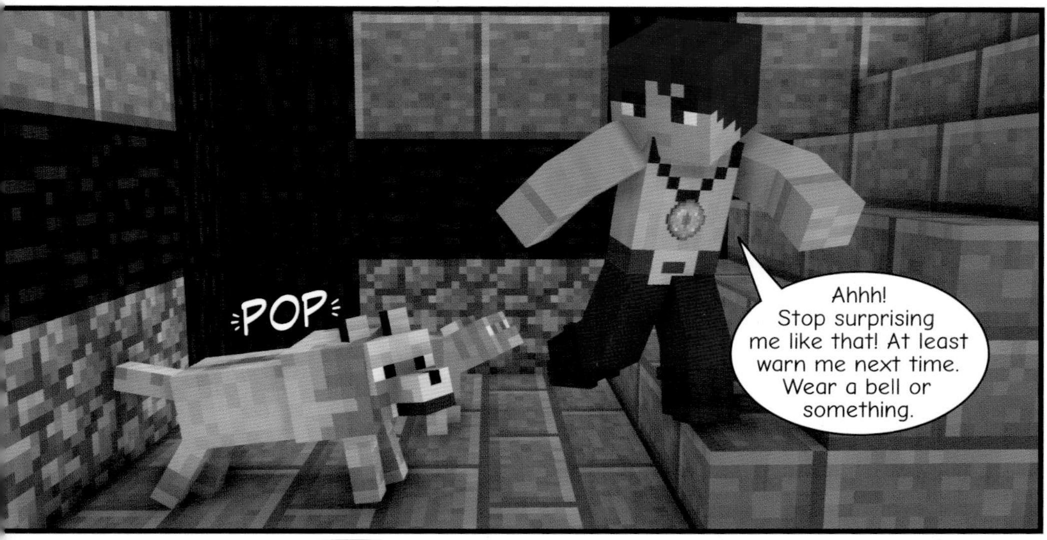
POP
Ahhh! Stop surprising me like that! At least warn me next time. Wear a bell or something.

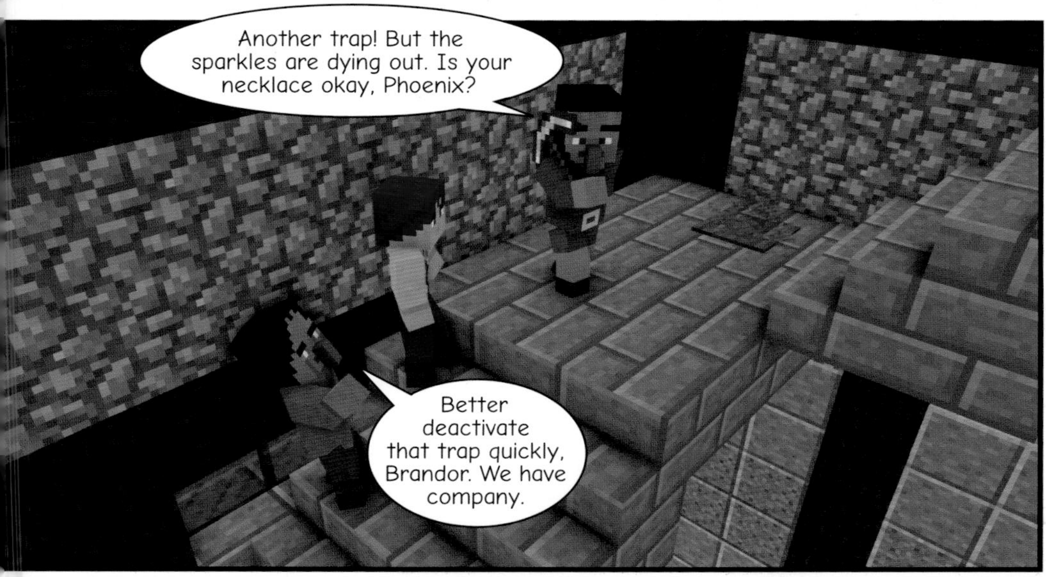
Another trap! But the sparkles are dying out. Is your necklace okay, Phoenix?
Better deactivate that trap quickly, Brandor. We have company.

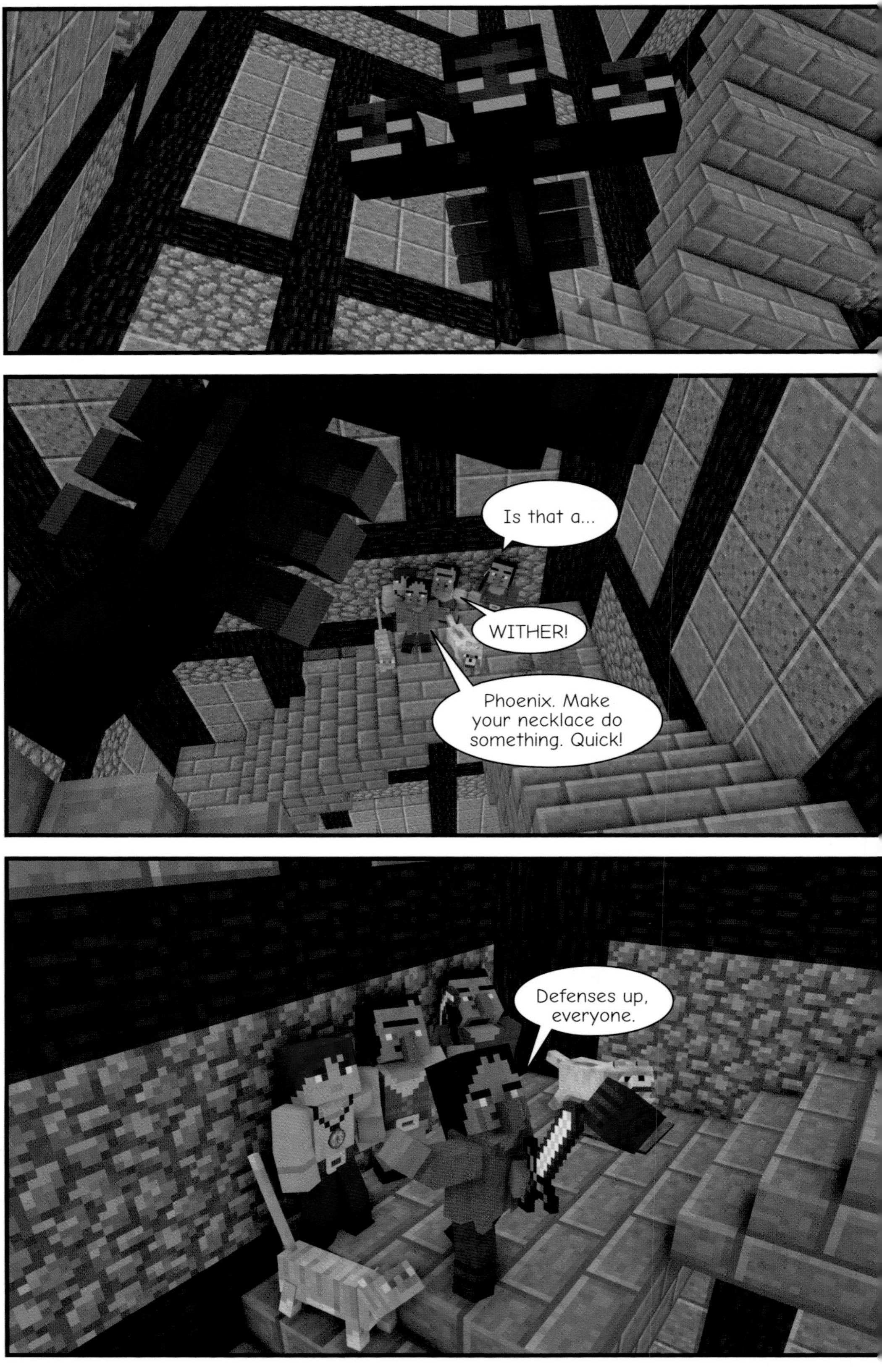
Is that a...
WITHER!
Phoenix. Make your necklace do something. Quick!
Defenses up, everyone.

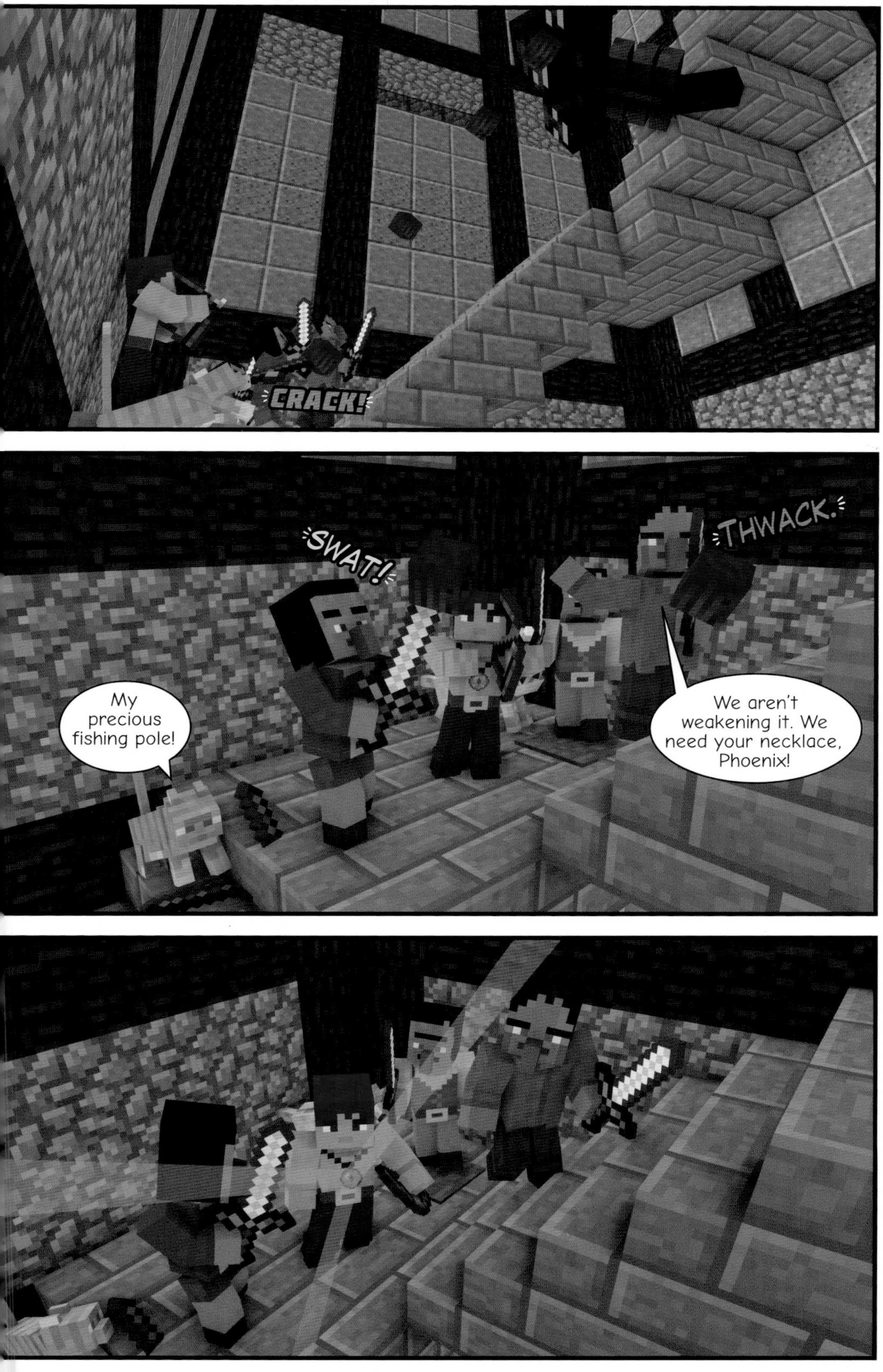
CRACK!
SWAT!
THWACK.
My precious fishing pole!
We aren't weakening it. We need your necklace, Phoenix!

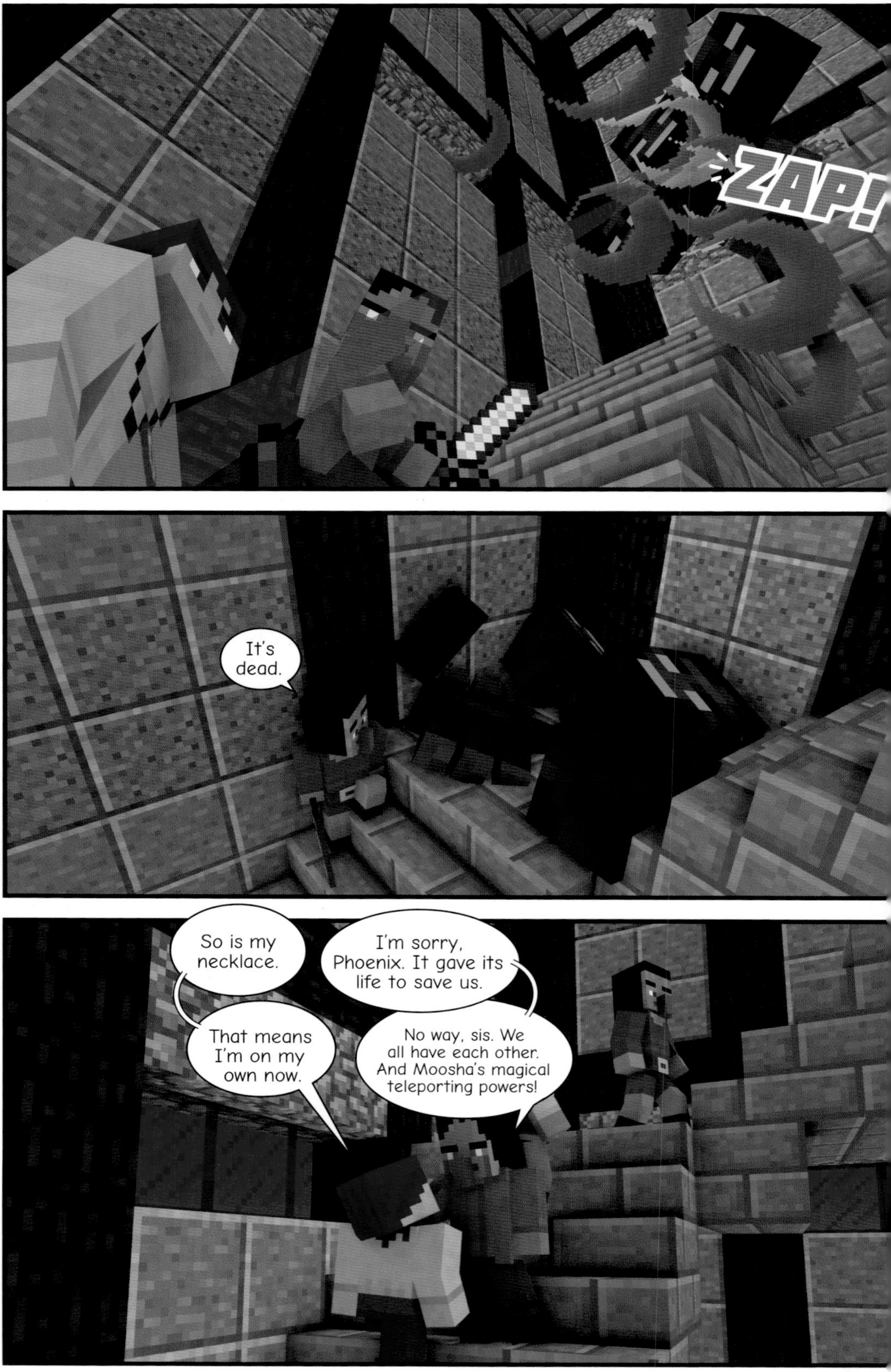
ZAP!
It's dead.
So is my necklace.
I'm sorry, Phoenix. It gave its life to save us.
That means I'm on my own now.
No way, sis. We all have each other. And Moosha's magical teleporting powers!

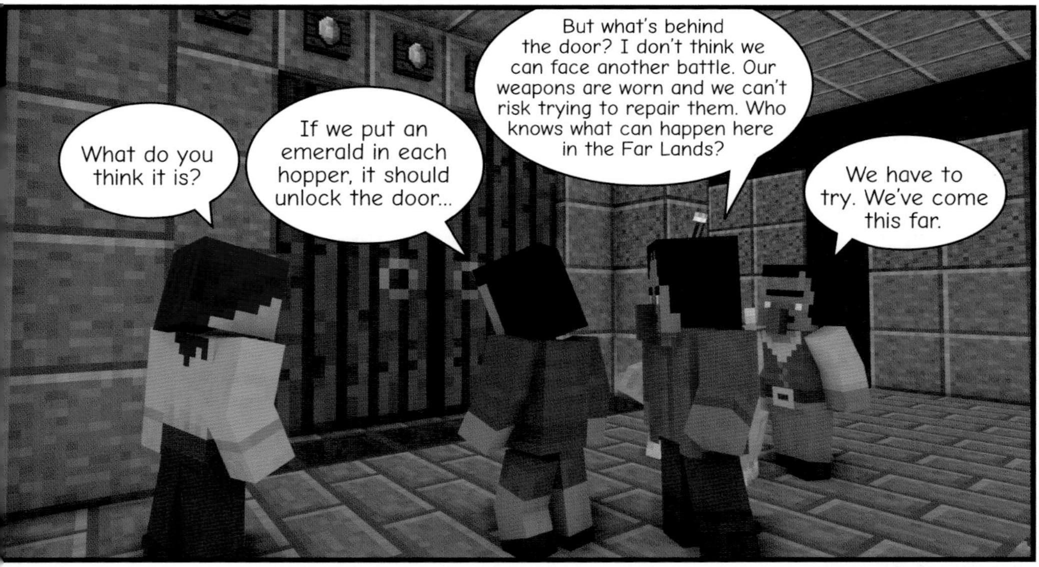
What do you think it is?
If we put an emerald in each hopper, it should unlock the door...
But what's behind the door? I don't think we can face another battle. Our weapons are worn and we can't risk trying to repair them. Who knows what can happen here in the Far Lands?
We have to try. We've come this far.

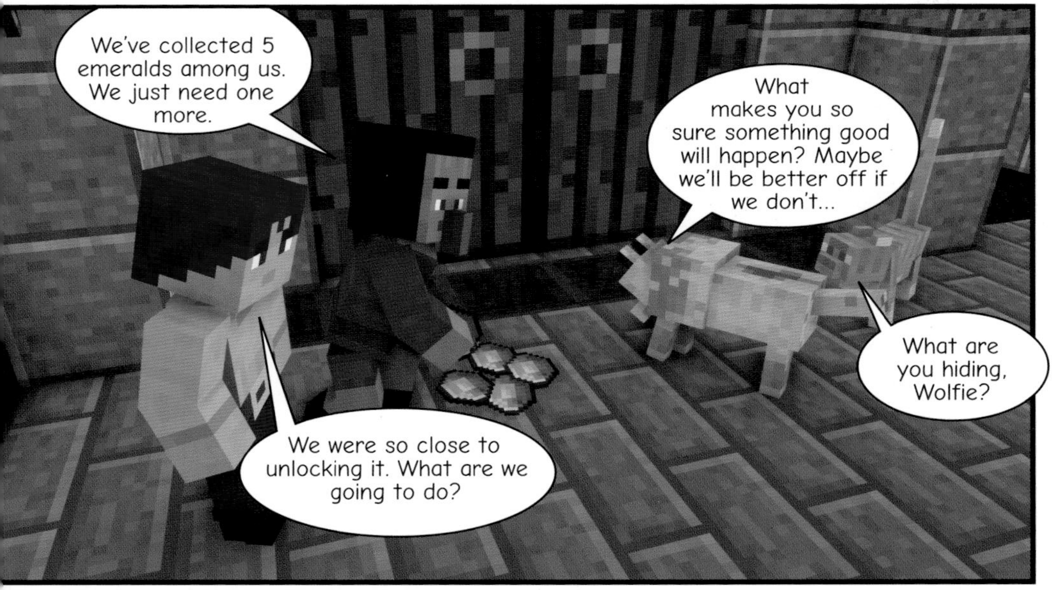
We've collected 5 emeralds among us. We just need one more.
What makes you so sure something good will happen? Maybe we'll be better off if we don't...
What are you hiding, Wolfie?
We were so close to unlocking it. What are we going to do?

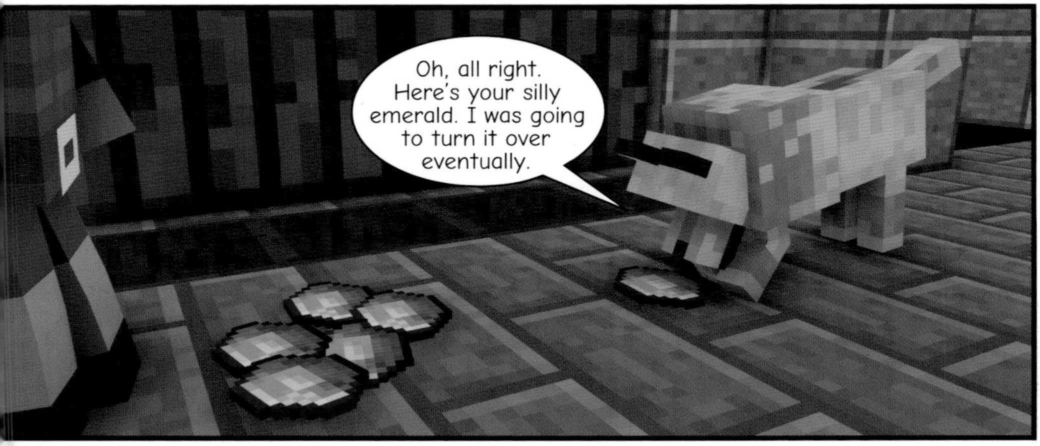
Oh, all right. Here's your silly emerald. I was going to turn it over eventually.

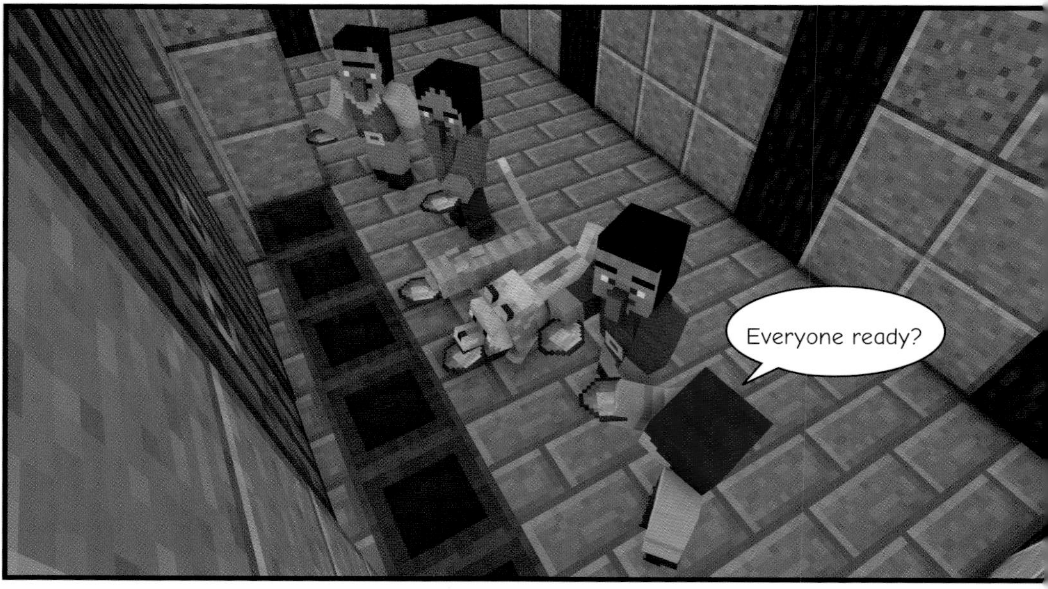
Everyone ready?
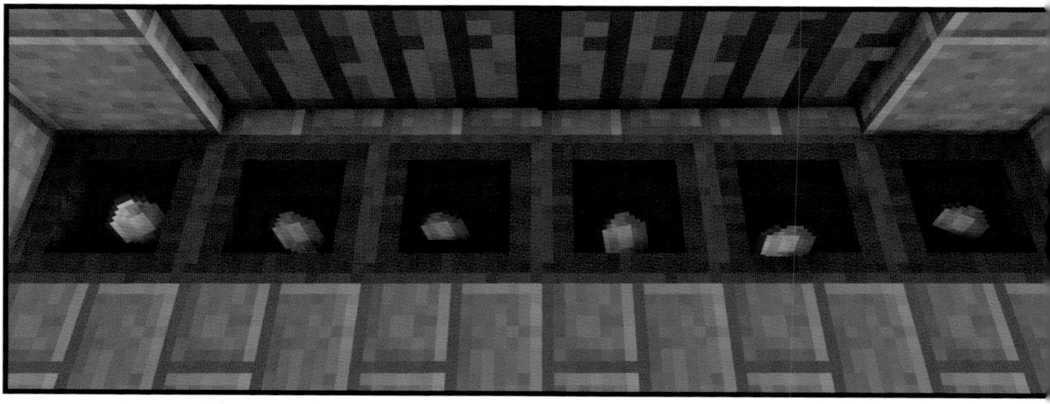
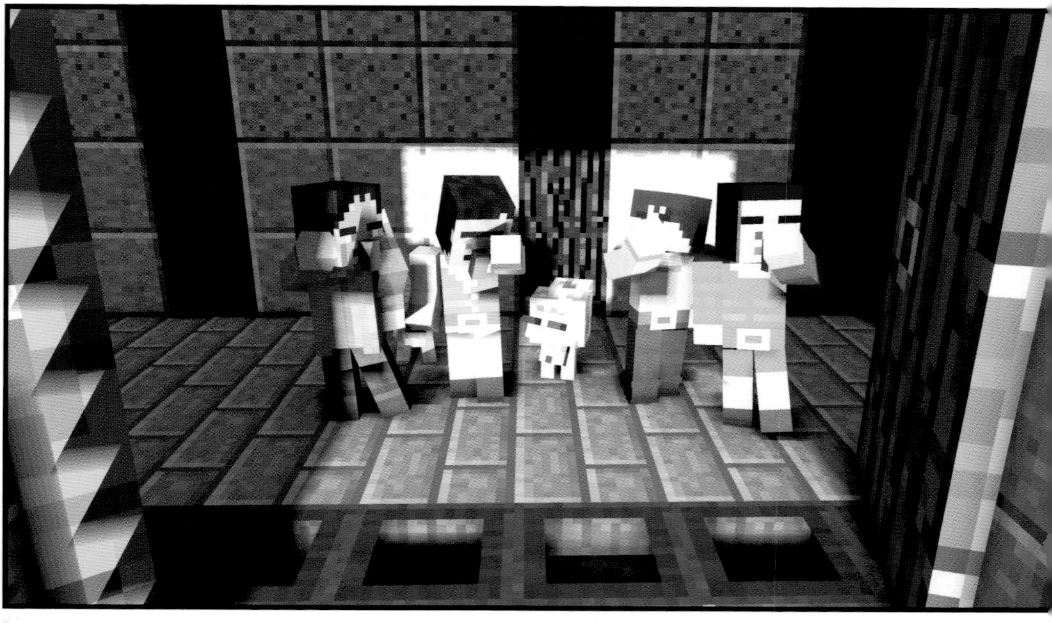

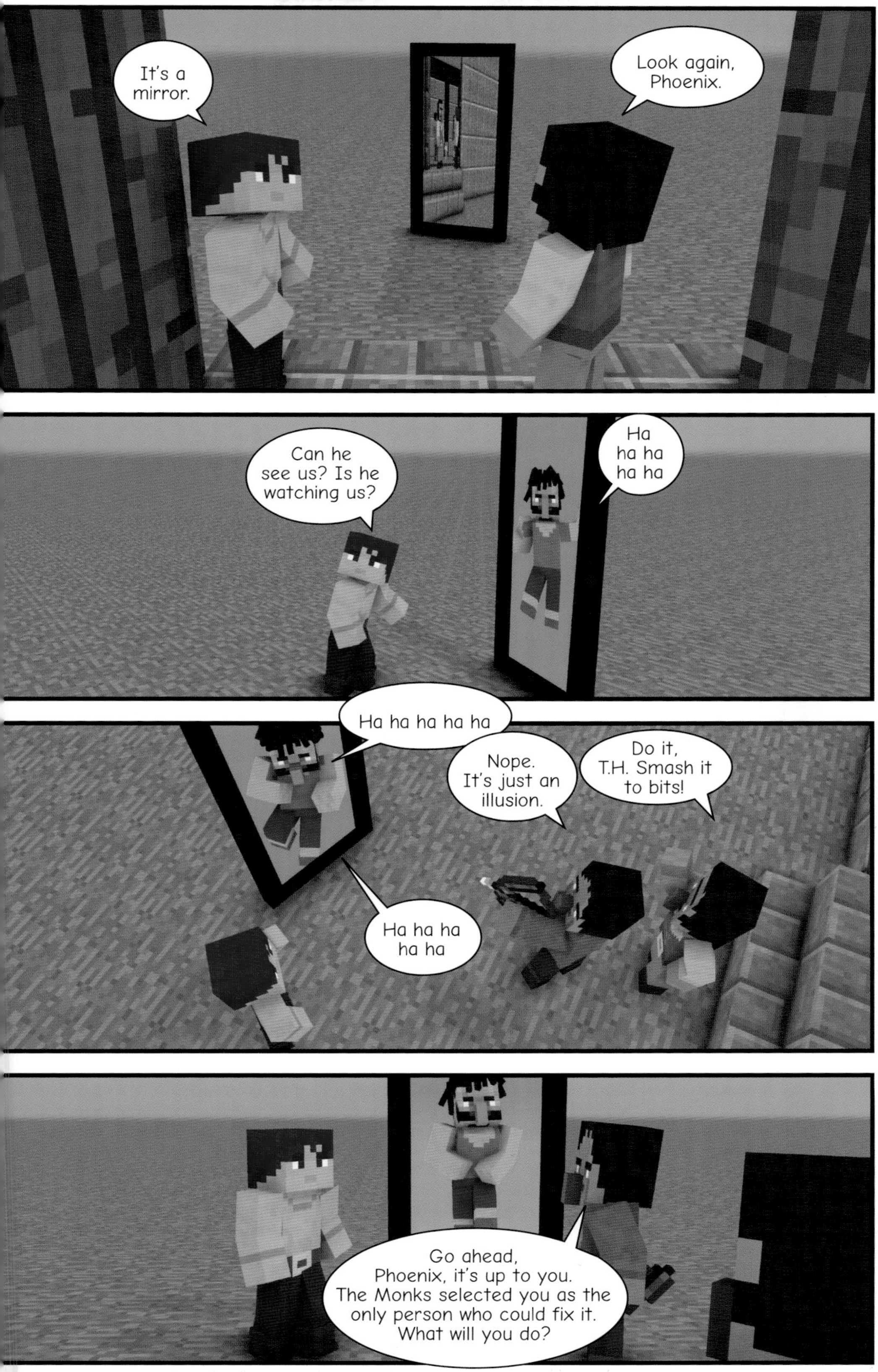
It's a mirror.
Look again, Phoenix.
Can he see us? Is he watching us?
Ha ha ha ha ha
Ha ha ha ha ha
Nope. It's just an illusion.
Do it, T.H. Smash it to bits!
Ha ha ha ha ha
Go ahead, Phoenix, it's up to you. The Monks selected you as the only person who could fix it. What will you do?

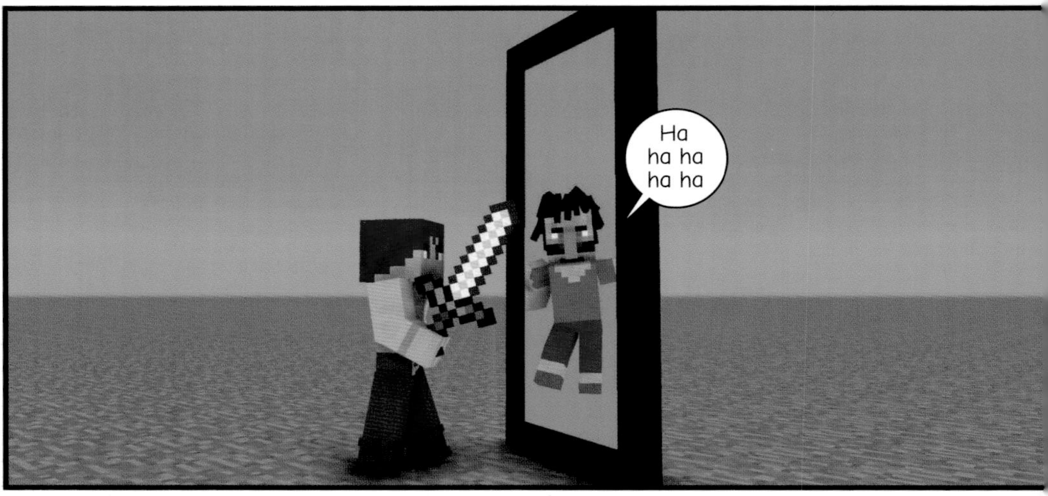
Ha
ha ha
ha ha

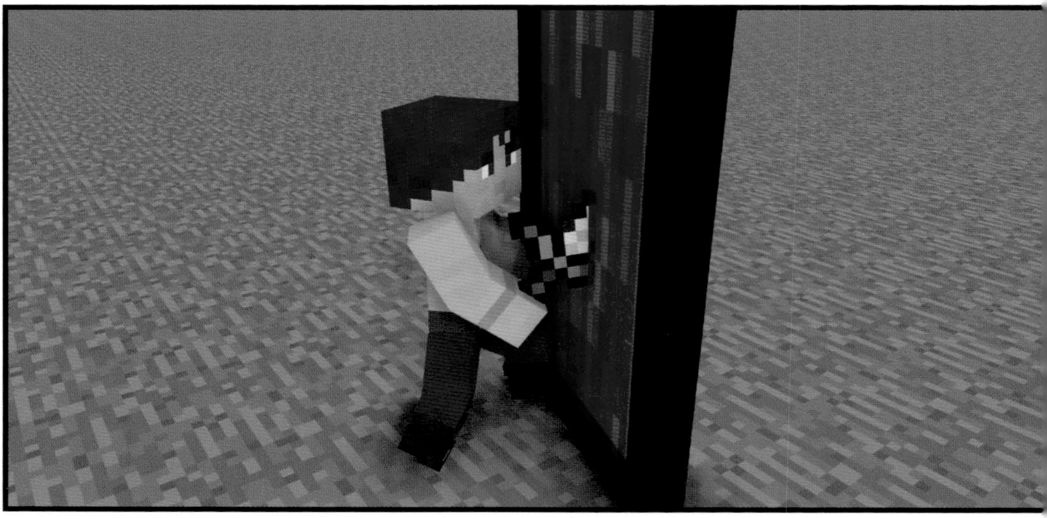

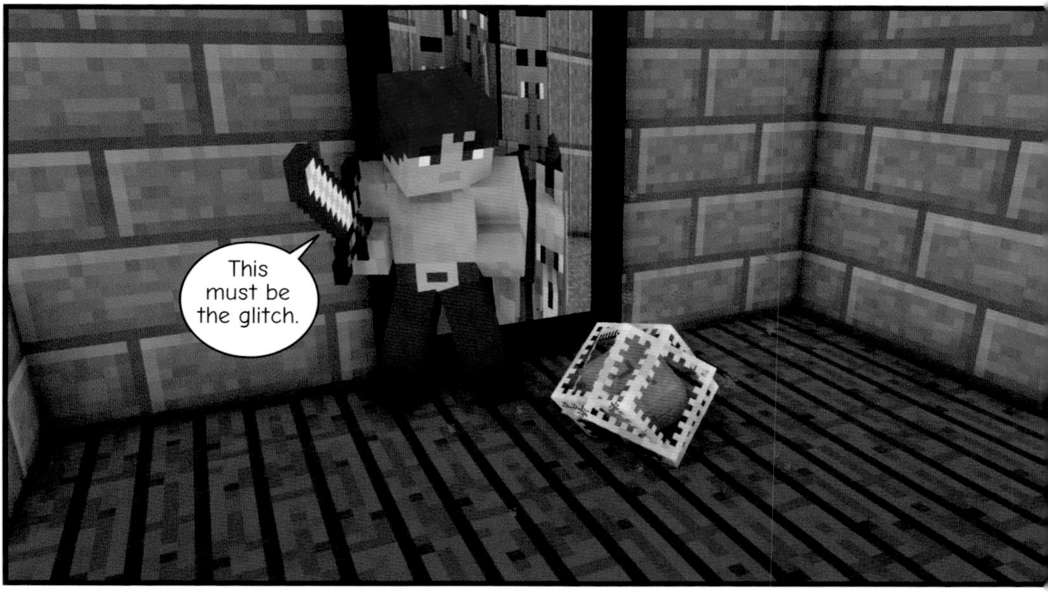
This
must be
the glitch.

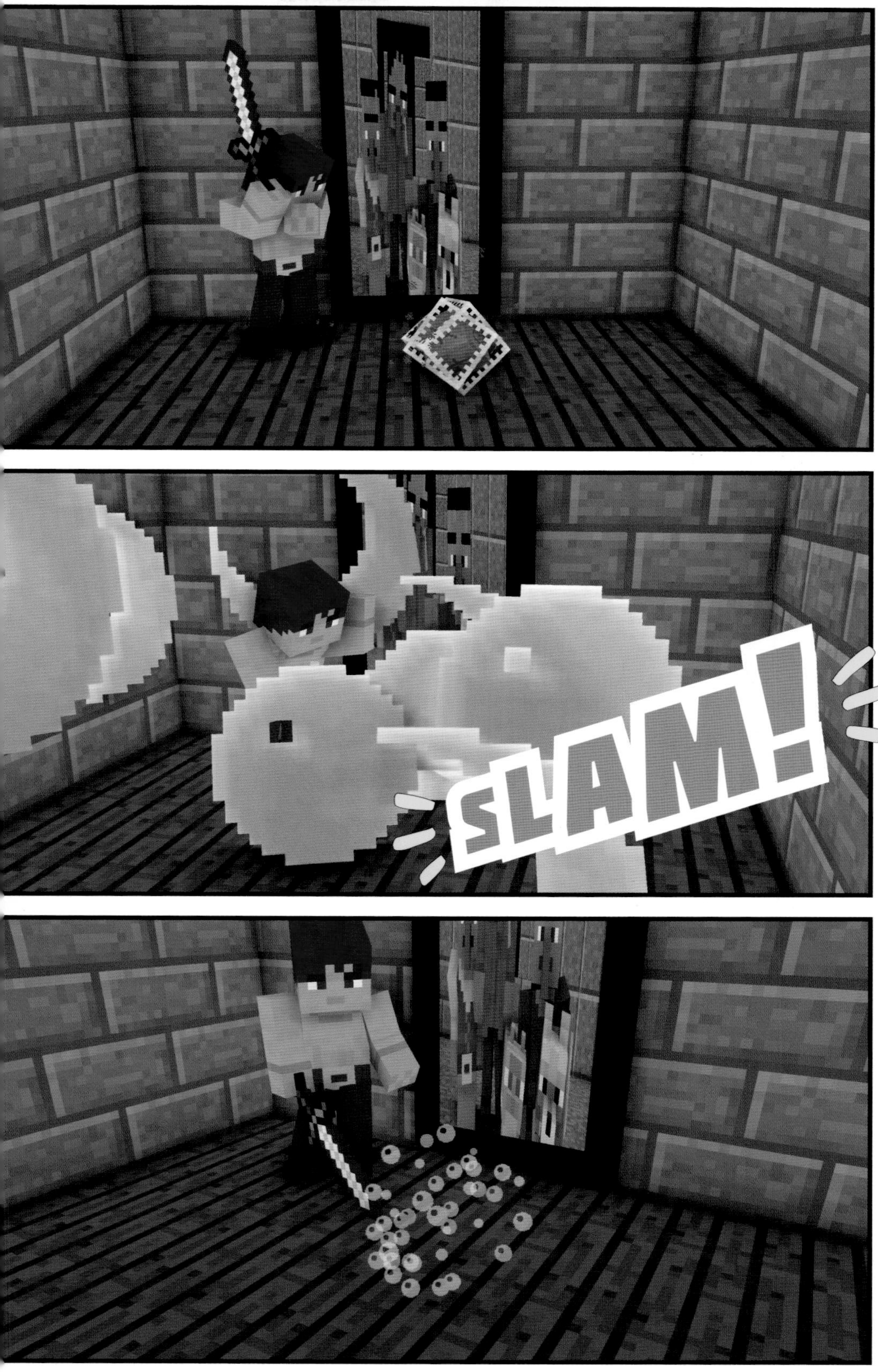
SLAM!

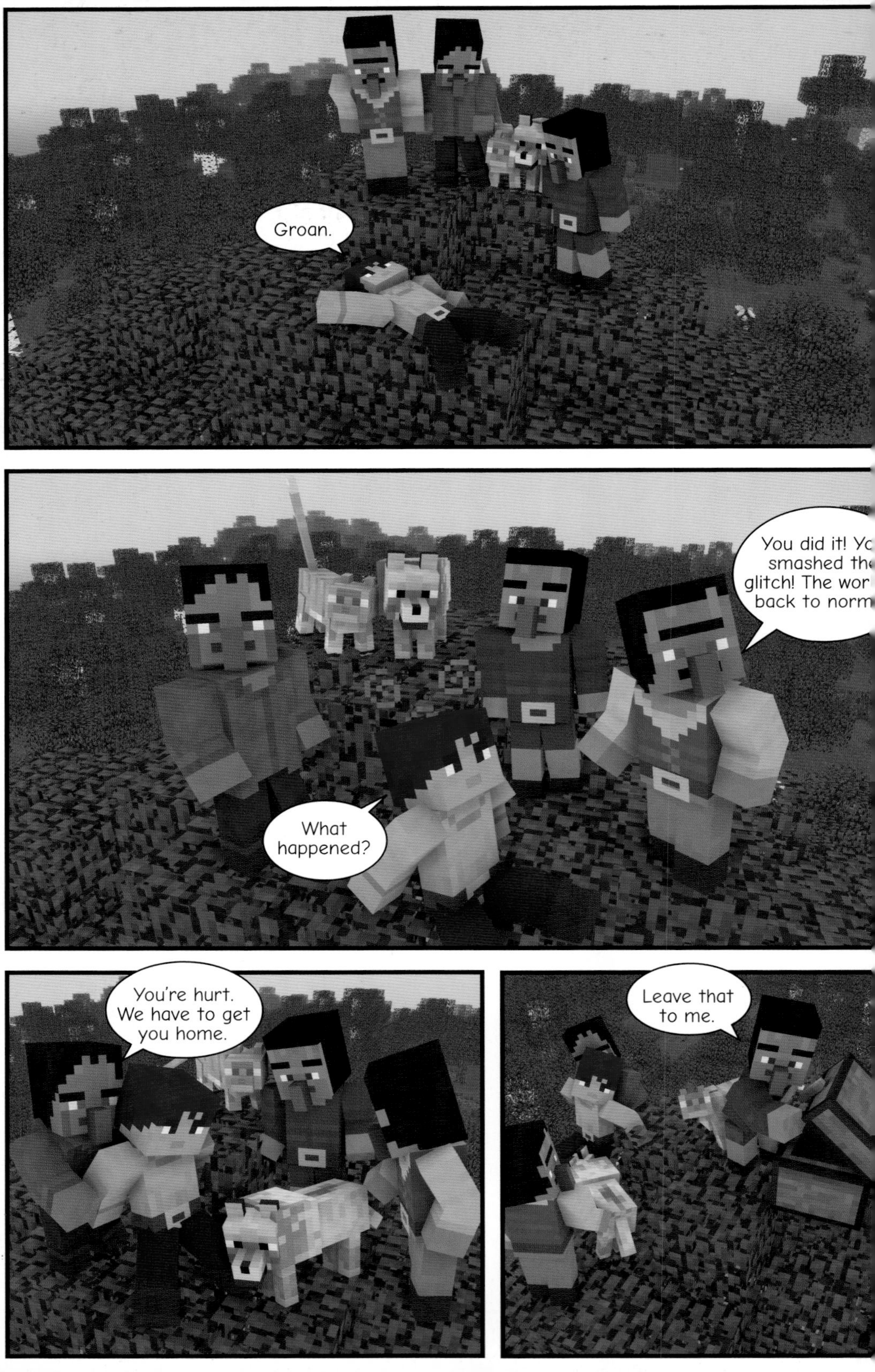
Groan.
You did it! Yo smashed th glitch! The wor back to norm
What happened?
You're hurt. We have to get you home.
Leave that to me.

CHAPTER 13

HOMECOMING

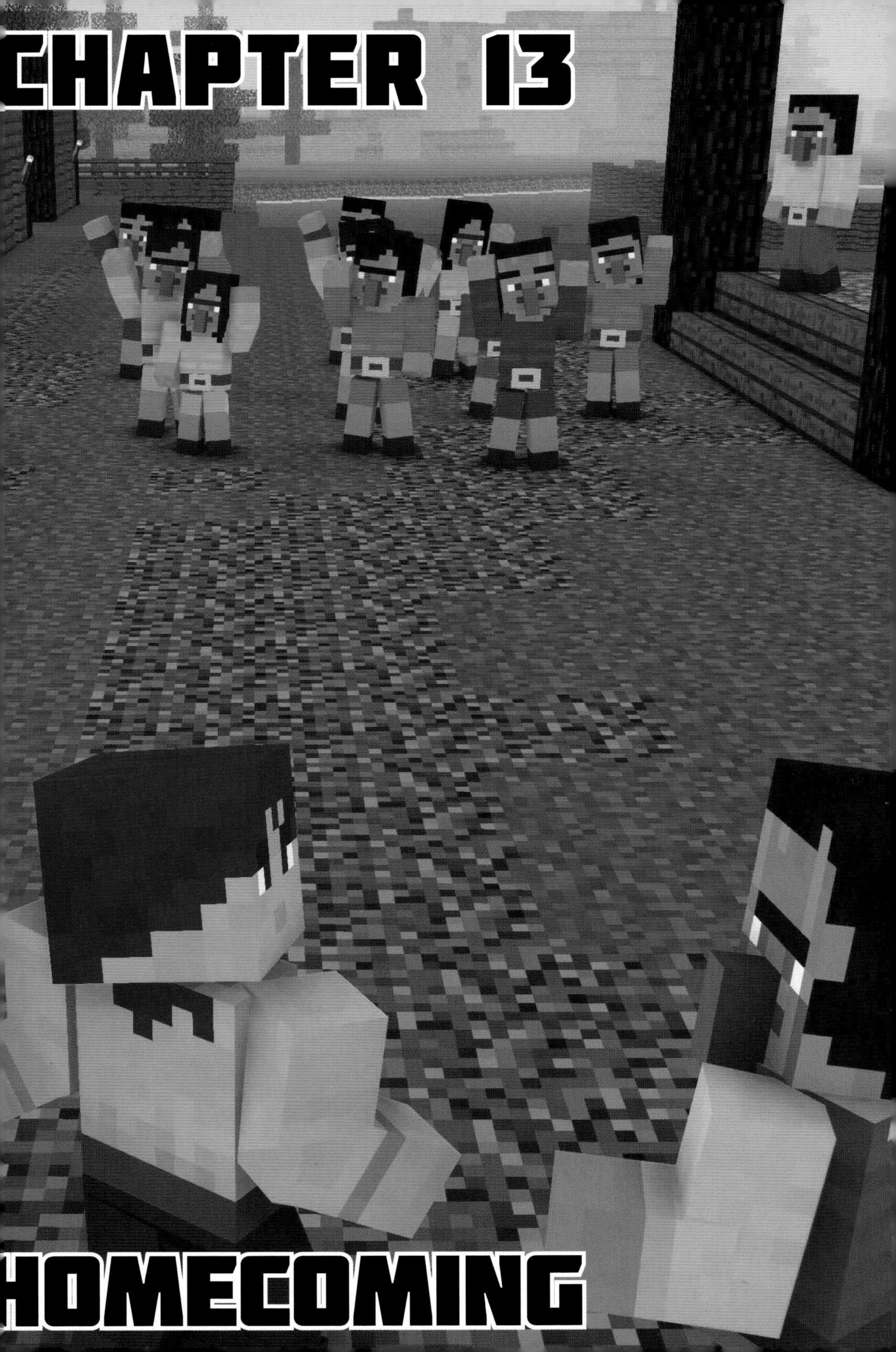

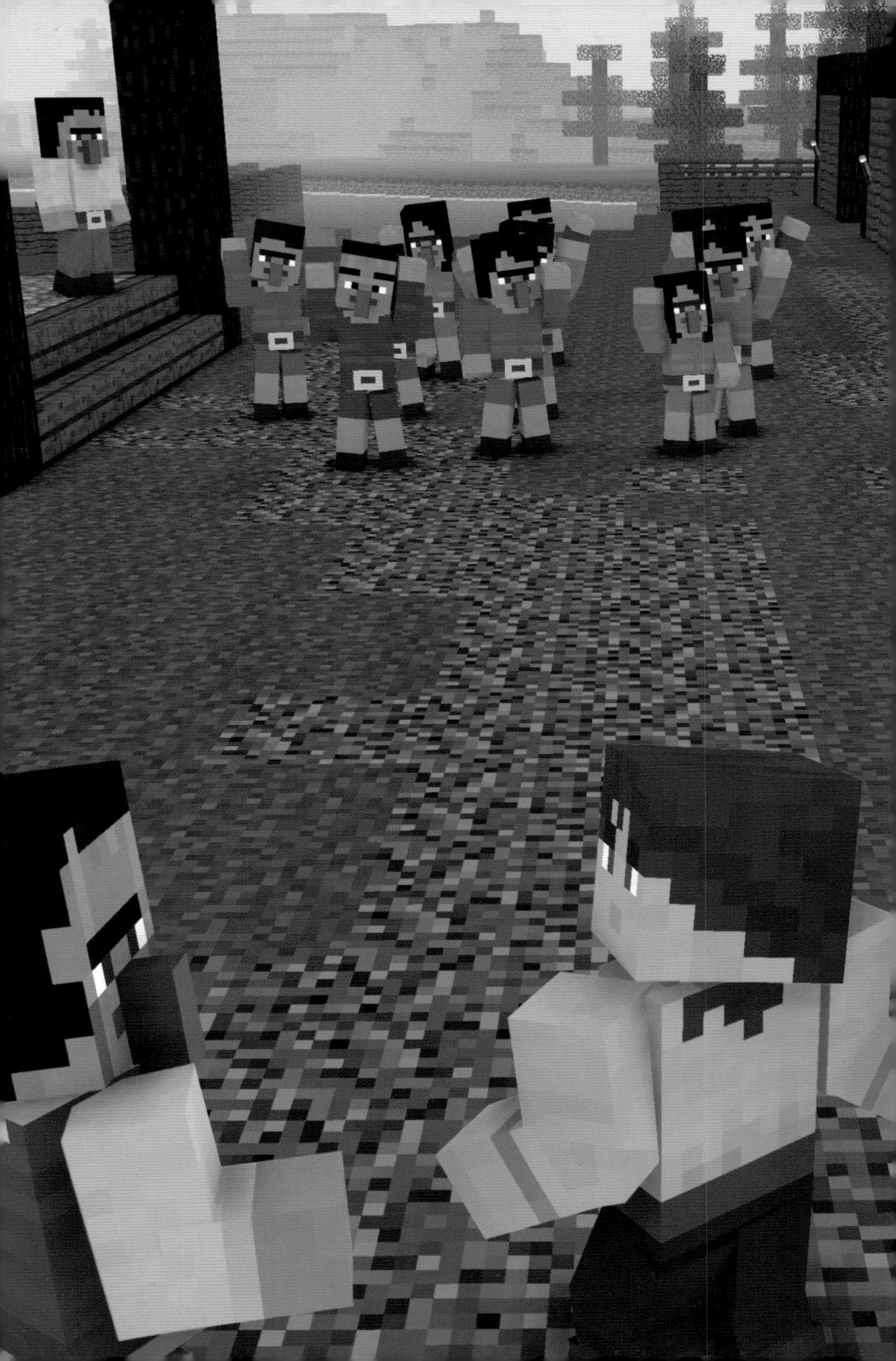

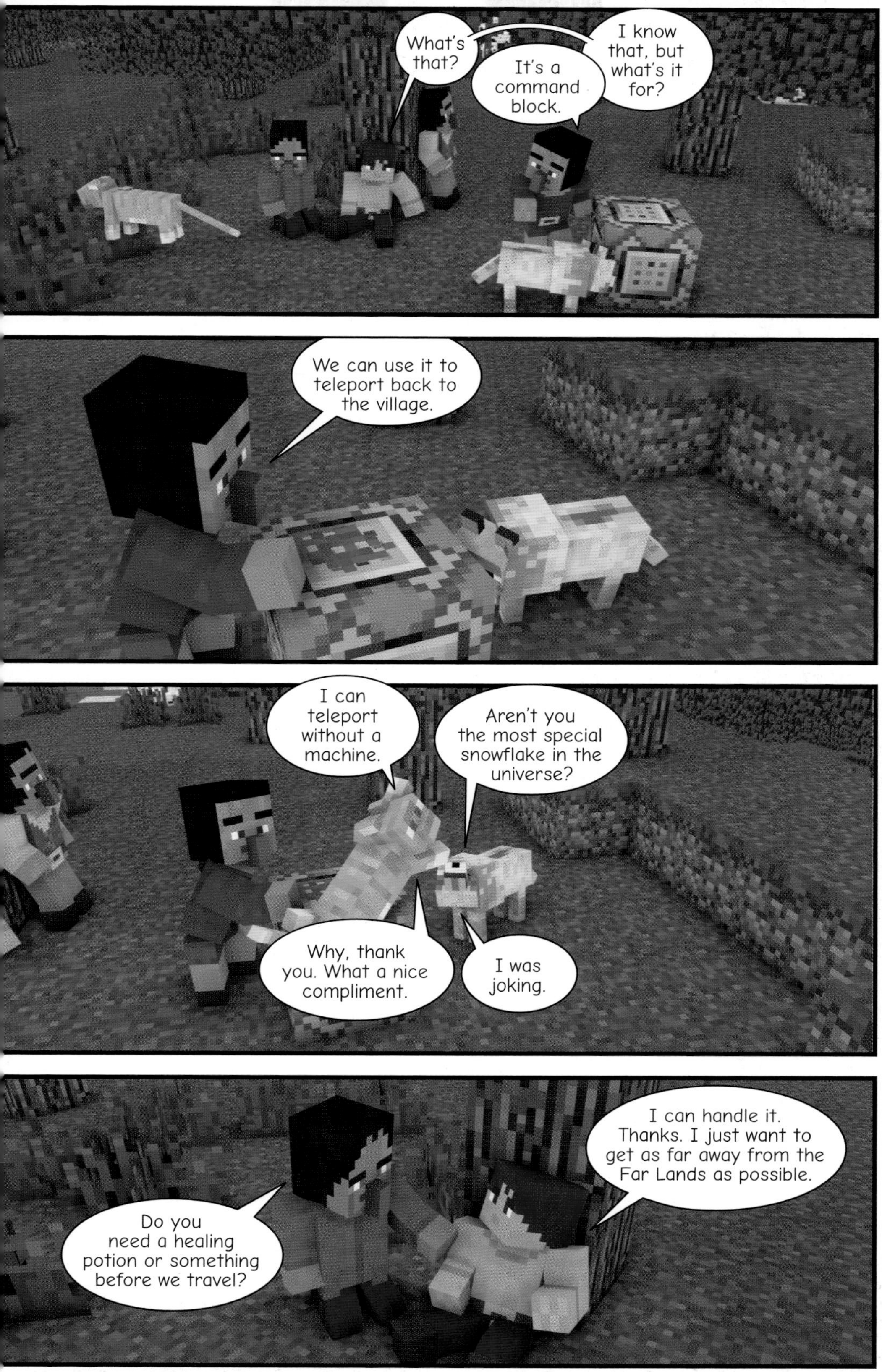
What's that?
It's a command block.
I know that, but what's it for?
We can use it to teleport back to the village.
I can teleport without a machine.
Aren't you the most special snowflake in the universe?
Why, thank you. What a nice compliment.
I was joking.
Do you need a healing potion or something before we travel?
I can handle it. Thanks. I just want to get as far away from the Far Lands as possible.

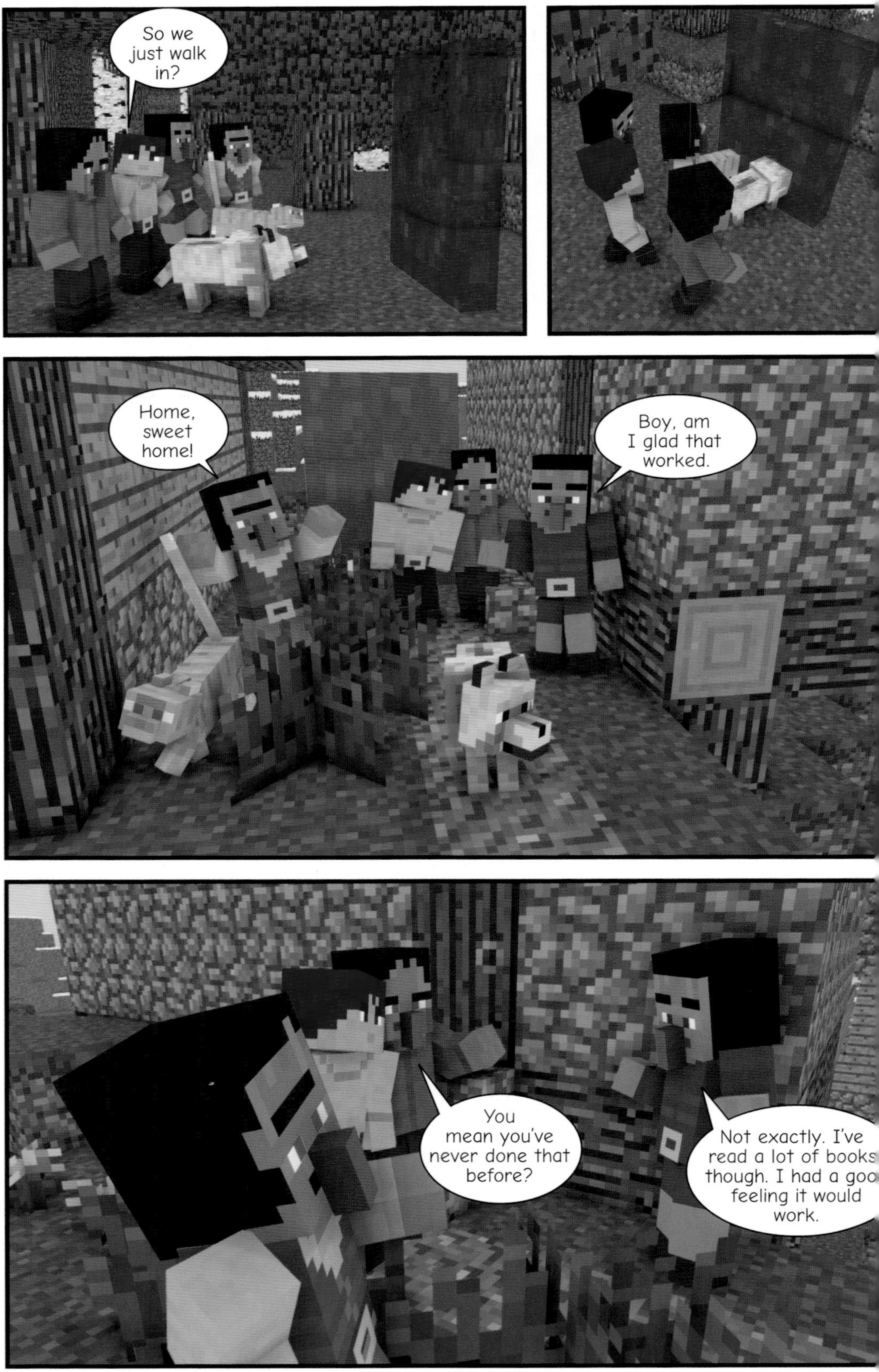
So we just walk in?
Home, sweet home!
Boy, am I glad that worked.
You mean you've never done that before?
Not exactly. I've read a lot of books though. I had a goo feeling it would work.

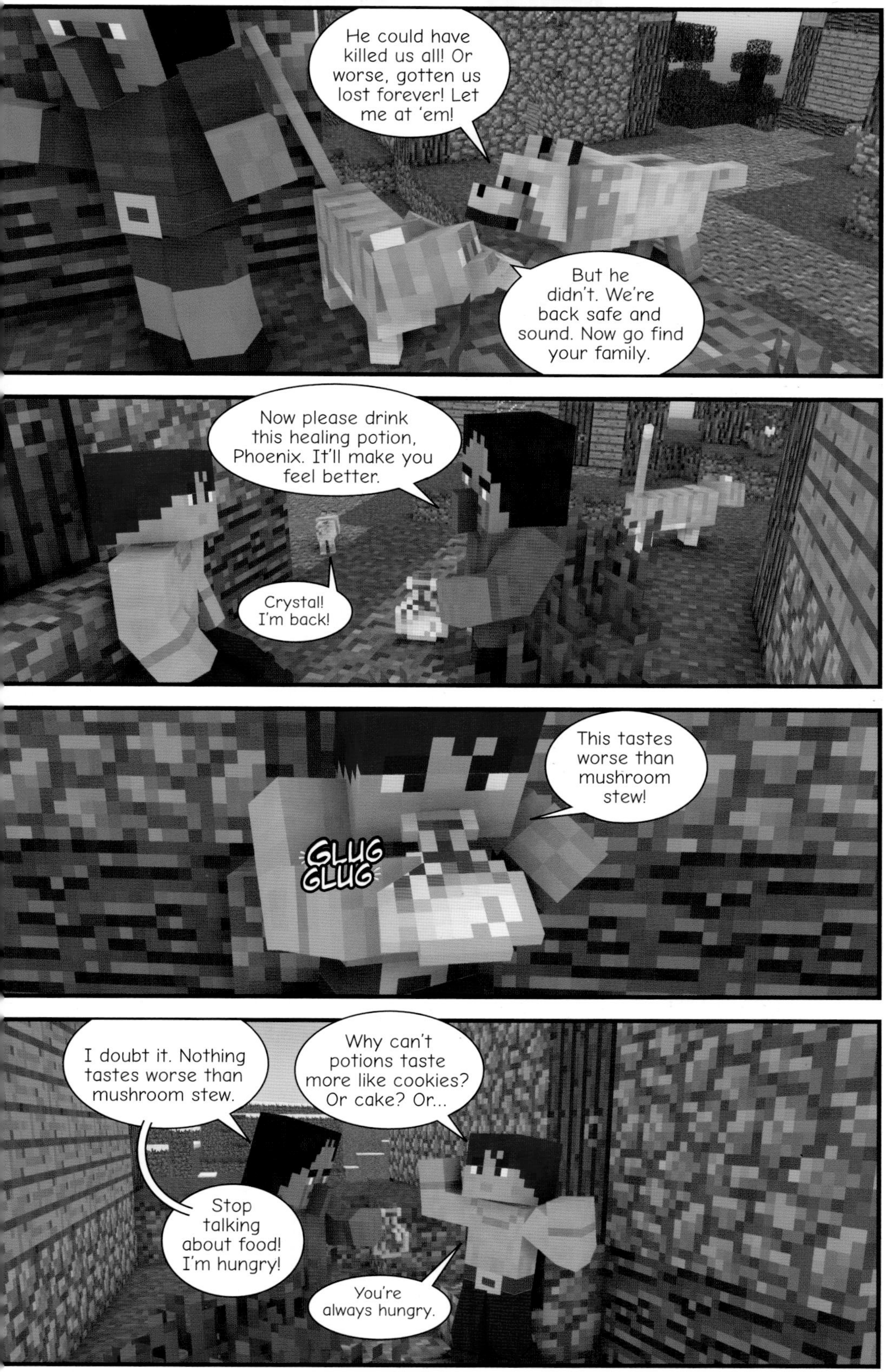
He could have killed us all! Or worse, gotten us lost forever! Let me at 'em!
But he didn't. We're back safe and sound. Now go find your family.
Now please drink this healing potion, Phoenix. It'll make you feel better.
Crystal! I'm back!
GLUG GLUG
This tastes worse than mushroom stew!
I doubt it. Nothing tastes worse than mushroom stew.
Why can't potions taste more like cookies? Or cake? Or...
Stop talking about food! I'm hungry!
You're always hungry.

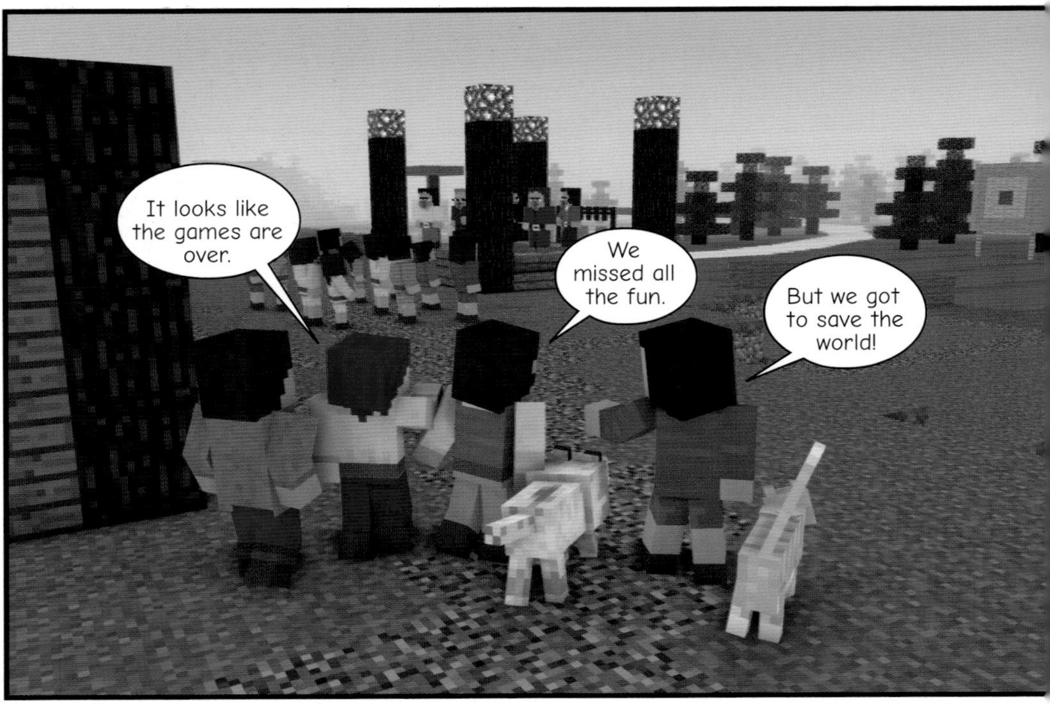
It looks like the games are over.
We missed all the fun.
But we got to save the world!

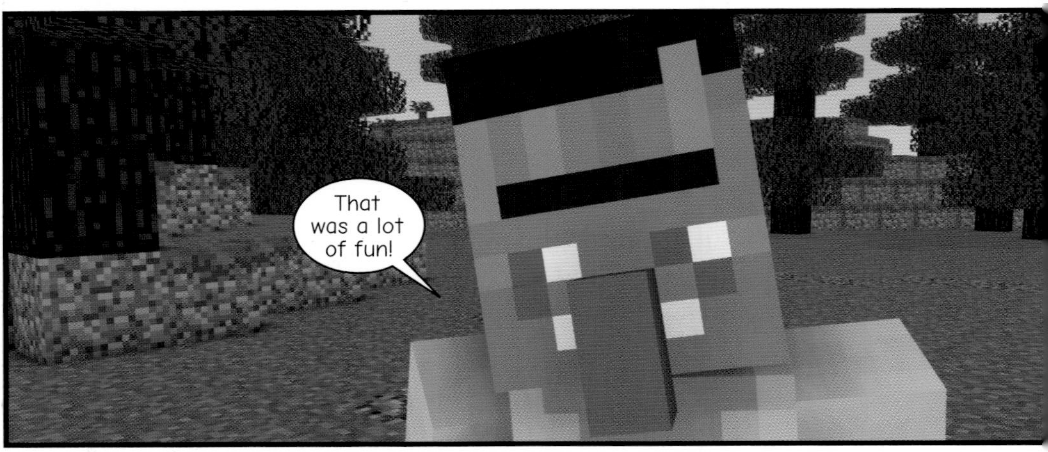
That was a lot of fun!

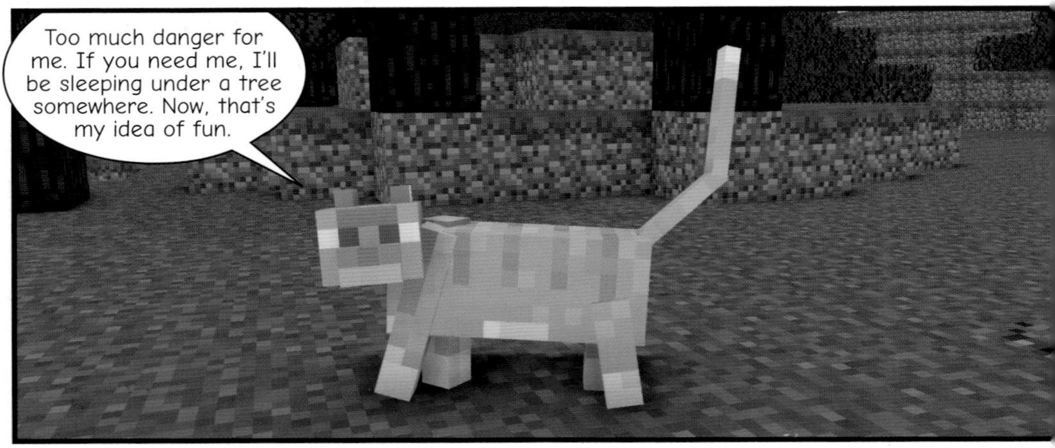
Too much danger for me. If you need me, I'll be sleeping under a tree somewhere. Now, that's my idea of fun.

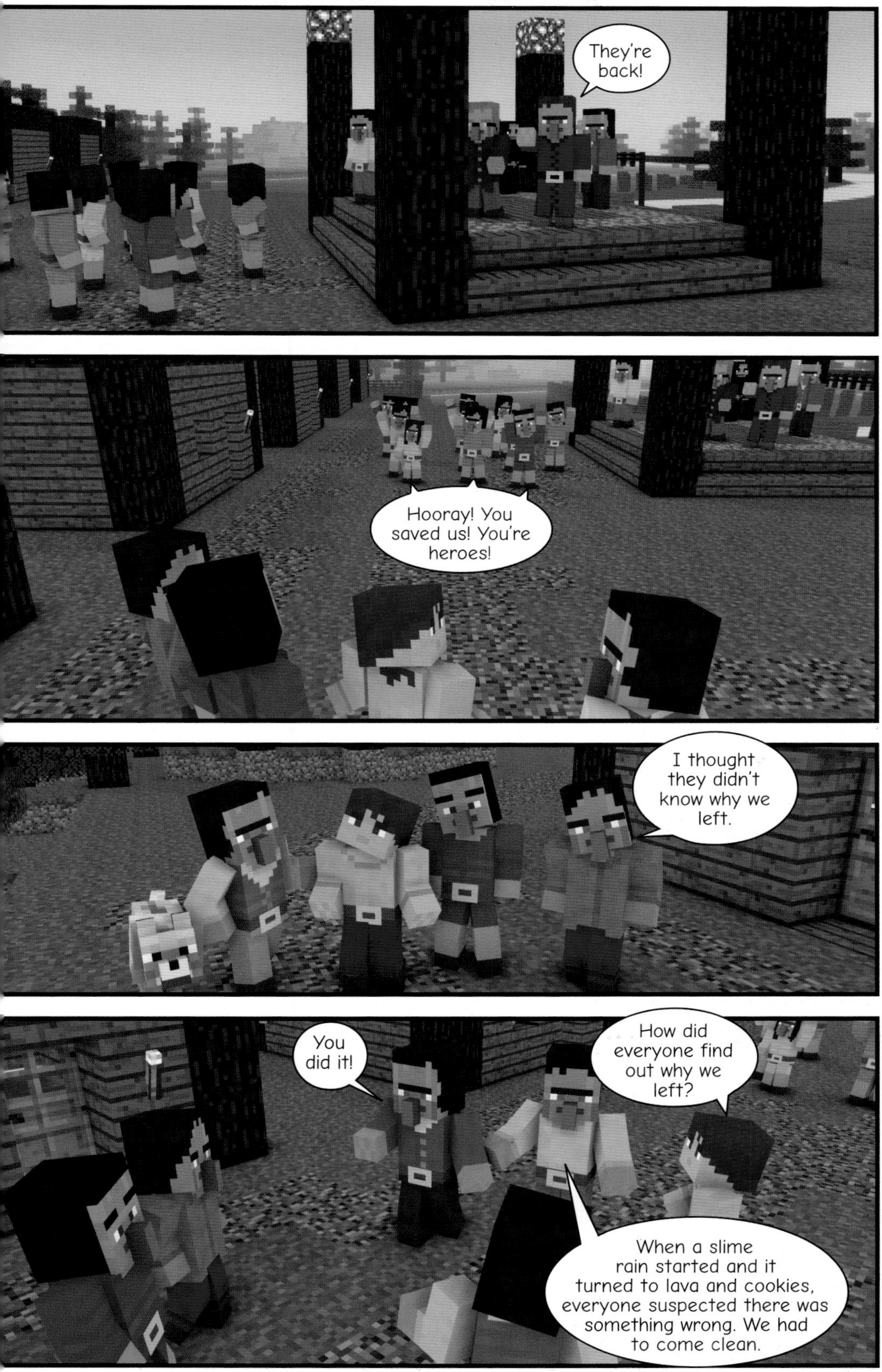
They're back!
Hooray! You saved us! You're heroes!
I thought they didn't know why we left.
You did it!
How did everyone find out why we left?
When a slime rain started and it turned to lava and cookies, everyone suspected there was something wrong. We had to come clean.

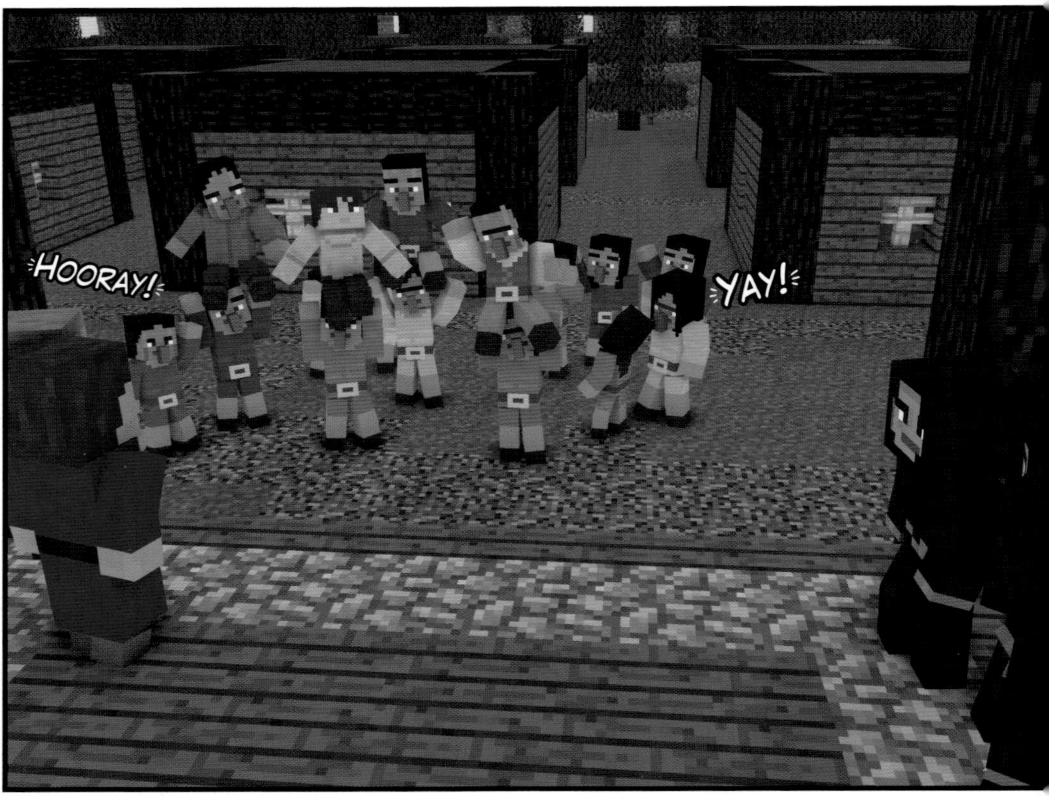
HOORAY!
YAY!

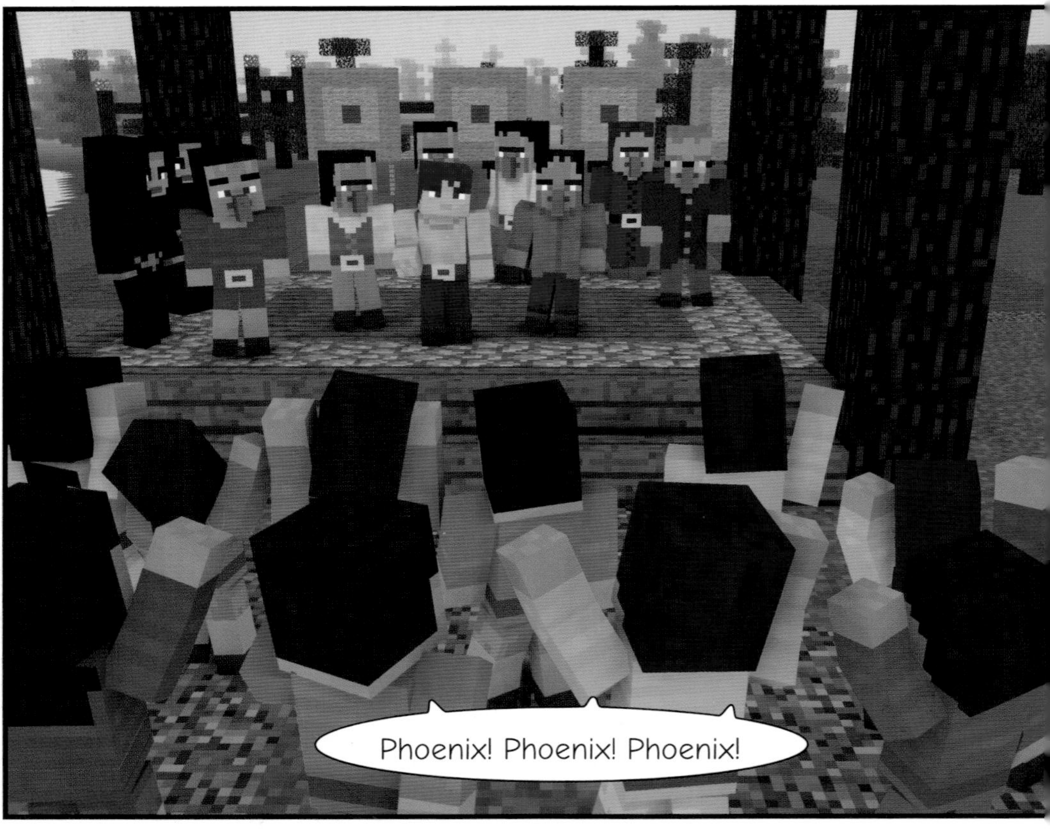
Phoenix! Phoenix! Phoenix!

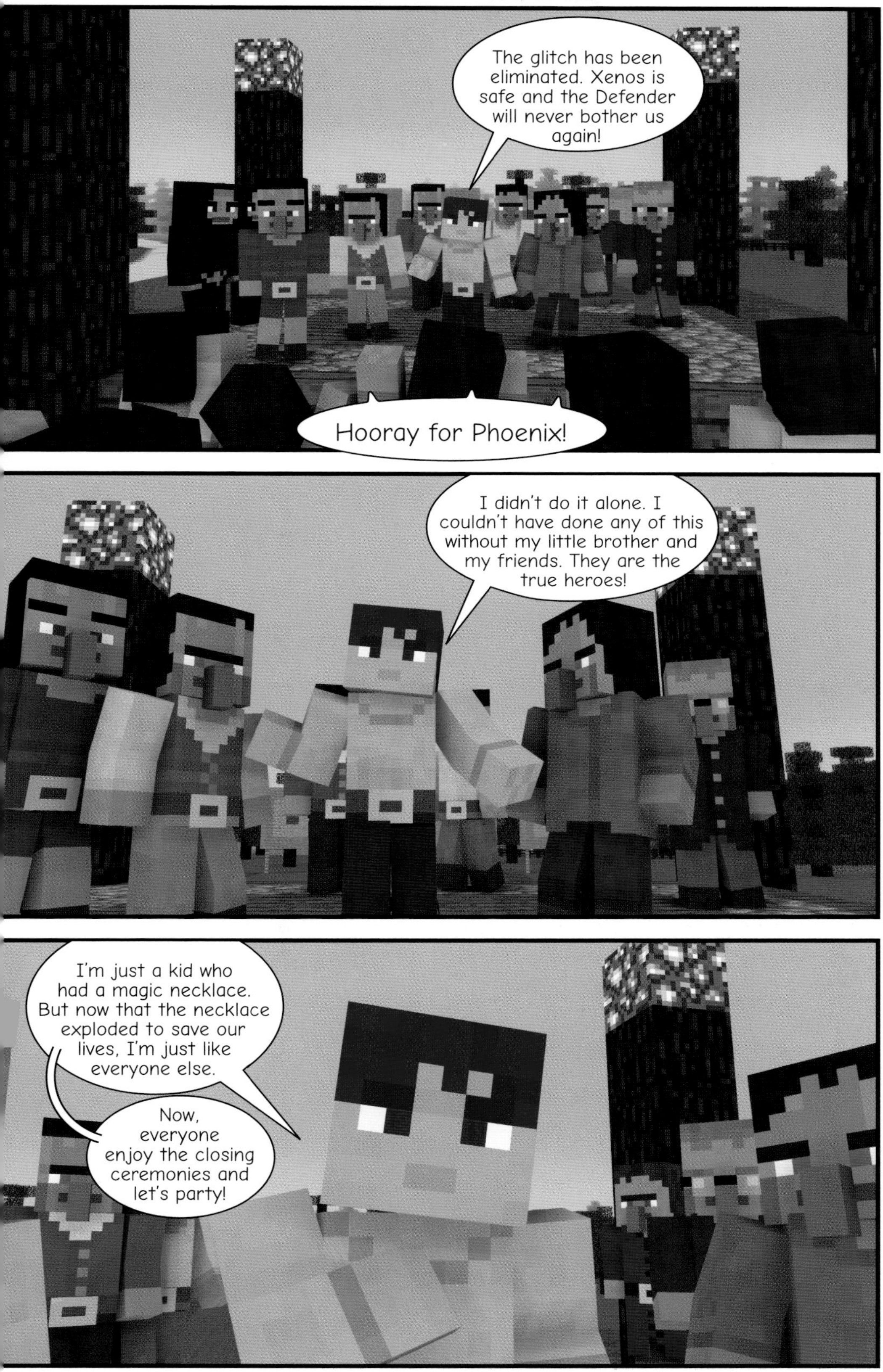
The glitch has been eliminated. Xenos is safe and the Defender will never bother us again!
Hooray for Phoenix!
I didn't do it alone. I couldn't have done any of this without my little brother and my friends. They are the true heroes!
I'm just a kid who had a magic necklace. But now that the necklace exploded to save our lives, I'm just like everyone else.
Now, everyone enjoy the closing ceremonies and let's party!

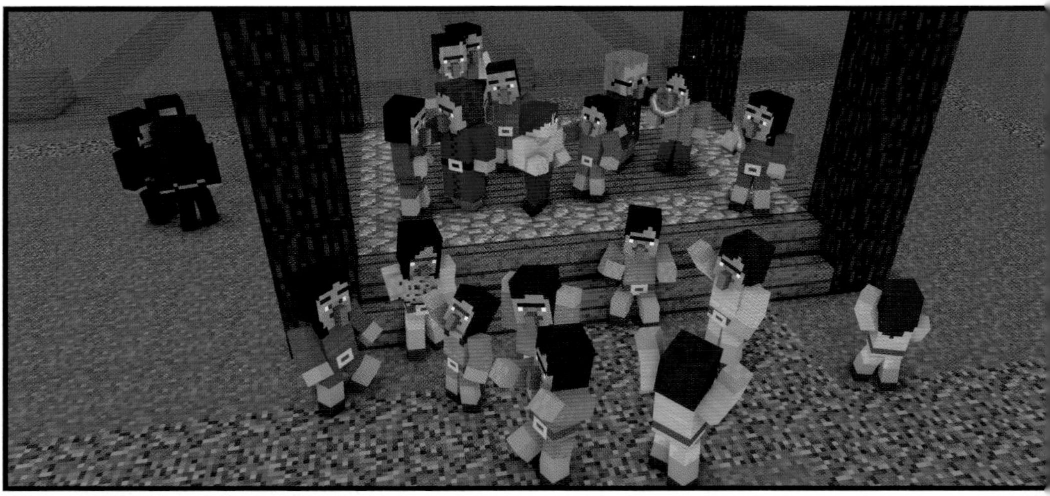

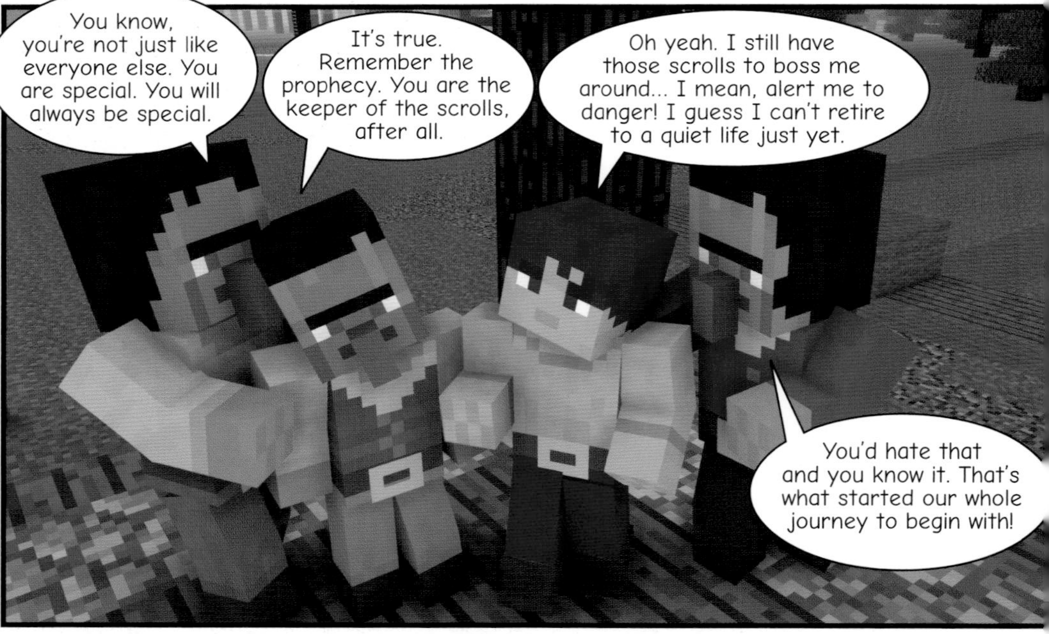

You know, you're not just like everyone else. You are special. You will always be special.
It's true. Remember the prophecy. You are the keeper of the scrolls, after all.
Oh yeah. I still have those scrolls to boss me around... I mean, alert me to danger! I guess I can't retire to a quiet life just yet.
You'd hate that and you know it. That's what started our whole journey to begin with!

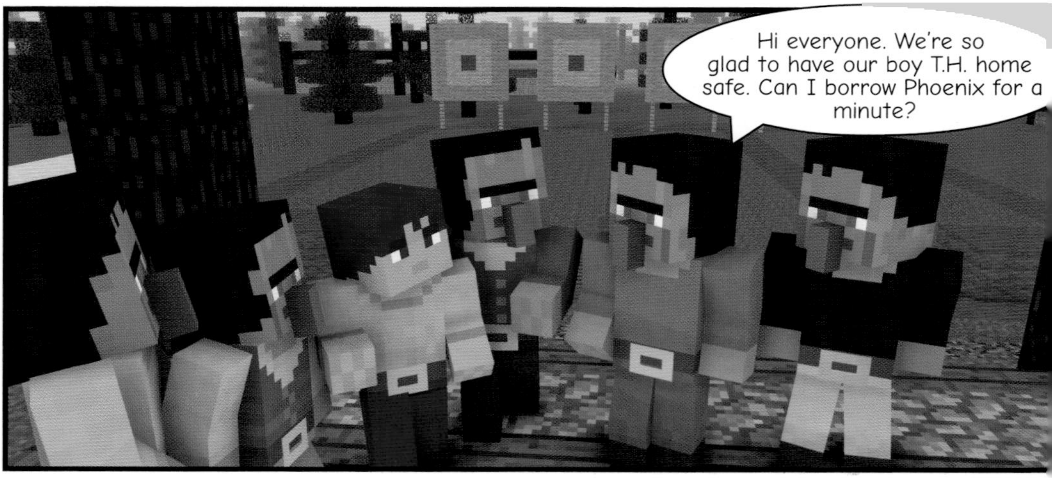

Hi everyone. We're so glad to have our boy T.H. home safe. Can I borrow Phoenix for a minute?

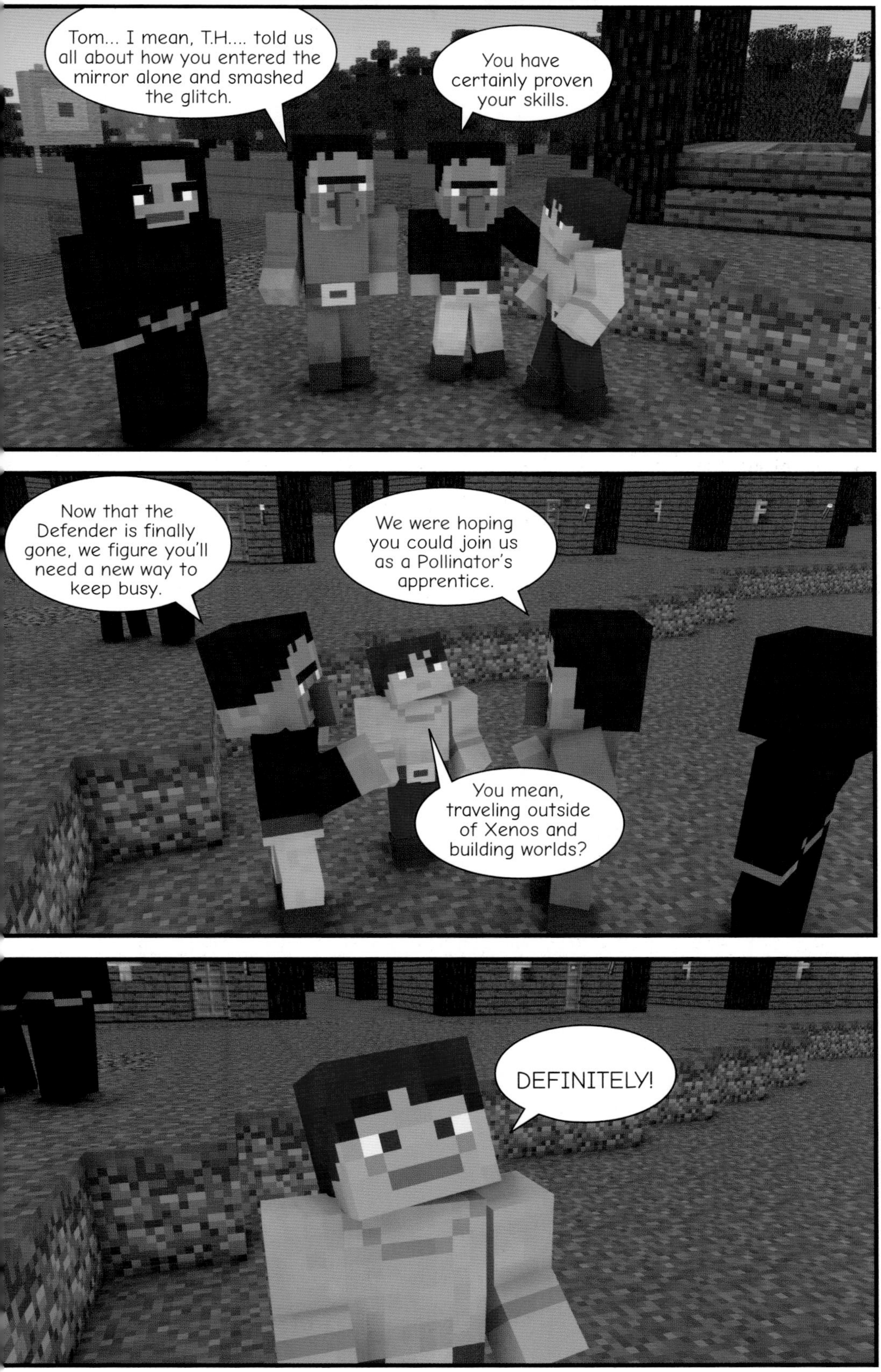
Tom... I mean, T.H.... told us all about how you entered the mirror alone and smashed the glitch.
You have certainly proven your skills.
Now that the Defender is finally gone, we figure you'll need a new way to keep busy.
We were hoping you could join us as a Pollinator's apprentice.
You mean, traveling outside of Xenos and building worlds?
DEFINITELY!

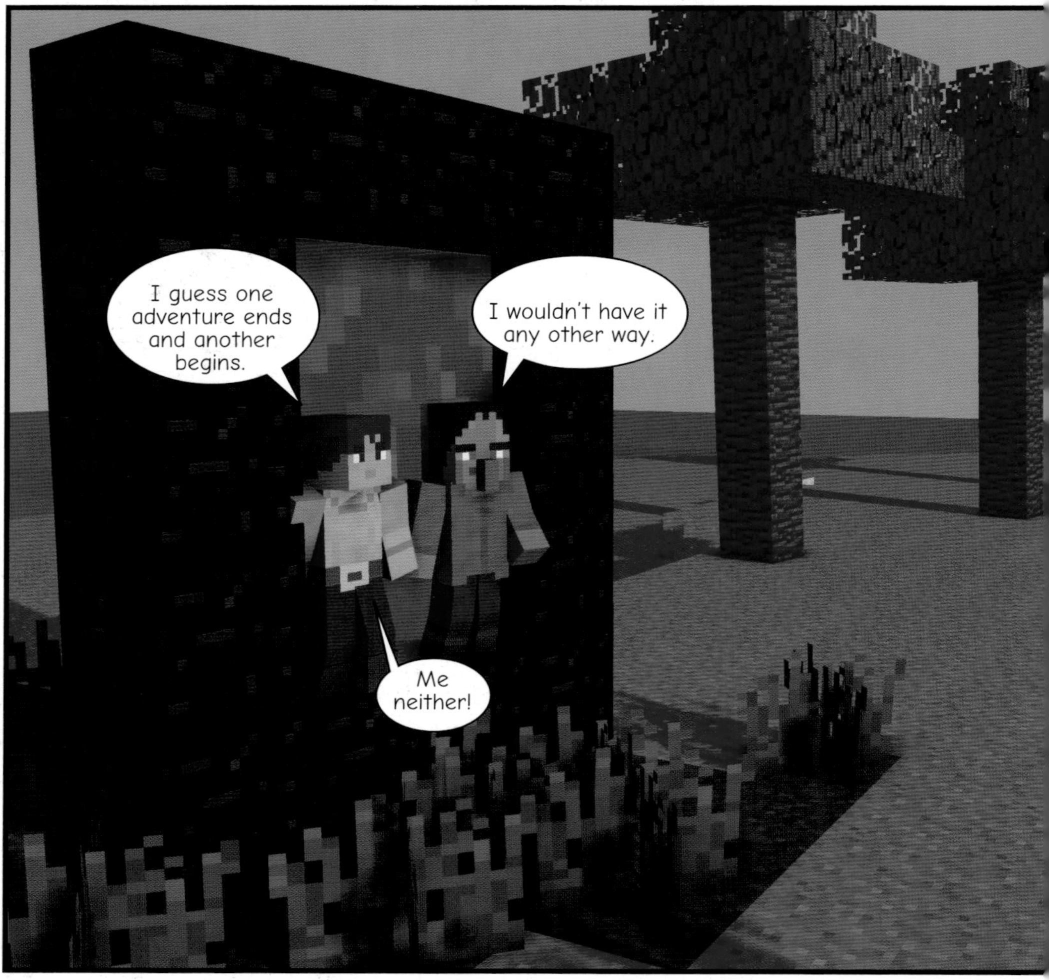
I guess one adventure ends and another begins.
I wouldn't have it any other way.
Me neither!

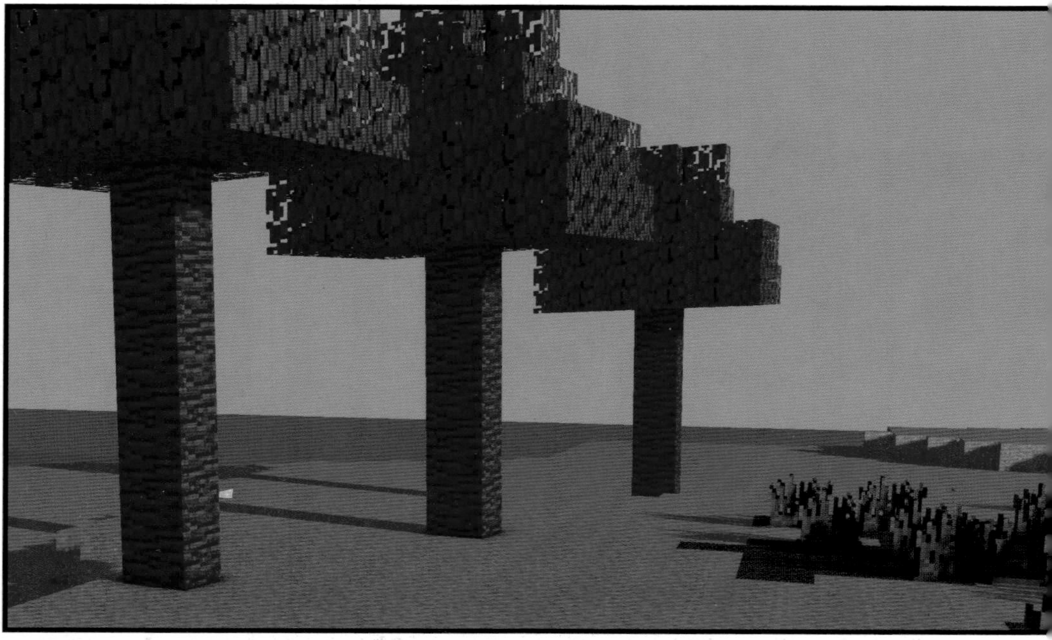

CHECK OUT THE FIRST BOOKS IN THE SERIES

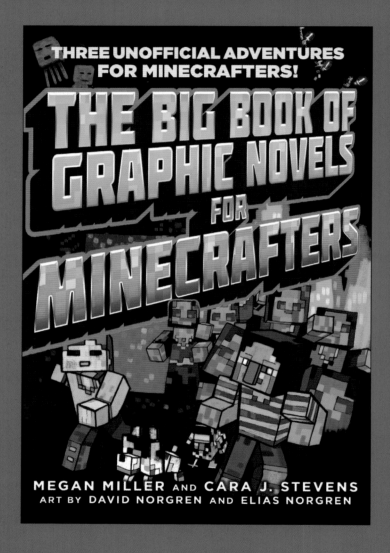

THREE UNOFFICIAL ADVENTURES FOR MINECRAFTERS!

THE BIG BOOK OF GRAPHIC NOVELS FOR MINECRAFTERS

MEGAN MILLER AND CARA J. STEVENS
ART BY DAVID NORGREN AND ELIAS NORGREN

SKY PONY PRESS
New York

ALSO, A NEW GRAPHIC NOVEL SERIES

AN UNOFFICIAL GRAPHIC NOVEL FOR MINECRAFTERS
REDSTONE JUNIOR HIGH
ZOMBIES ATE MY HOMEWORK
BOOK 1
CARA J. STEVENS
ART BY FRED BORCHERDT

AN UNOFFICIAL GRAPHIC NOVEL FOR MINECRAFTERS
REDSTONE JUNIOR HIGH
CREEPERS CRASHED MY PARTY
BOOK 2
CARA J. STEVENS
ART BY FRED BORCHERDT

AN UNOFFICIAL GRAPHIC NOVEL FOR MINECRAFTERS
REDSTONE JUNIOR HIGH
DRAGONS NEVER DIE
BOOK 3
CARA J. STEVENS
ART BY WALKER MELBY

SKY PONY PRESS
SKY PONY PRESS
NEW YORK

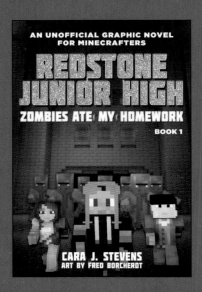

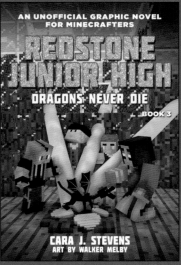